THE UNIVERSITY OF VIRGINIA EDITION OF
THE WORKS OF STEPHEN CRANE

VOLUME VIII

TALES, SKETCHES, AND REPORTS

Stephen Crane about 1895

STEPHEN CRANE

TALES, SKETCHES, AND REPORTS

EDITED BY
FREDSON BOWERS
LINDEN KENT PROFESSOR OF ENGLISH AT
THE UNIVERSITY OF VIRGINIA

WITH AN INTRODUCTION BY
EDWIN H. CADY
JAMES H. RUDY PROFESSOR OF ENGLISH AT
INDIANA UNIVERSITY

THE UNIVERSITY PRESS OF VIRGINIA

CHARLOTTESVILLE

CENTER FOR EDITIONS OF
AMERICAN AUTHORS

AN APPROVED TEXT

MODERN LANGUAGE
ASSOCIATION OF AMERICA

®

Editorial expenses for this volume have been
met in part by grants from the National
Endowment for the Humanities administered
through the Center for Editions of American
Authors of the Modern Language Association.

First published 1973

The University Press of Virginia

ISBN: 0–8139–0405–6
Library of Congress Catalog Card Number: 68–8536
Printed in the United States of America

To
Clifton Waller Barrett

FOREWORD

THIS volume brings together all of Stephen Crane's stories and sketches not printed in TALES OF ADVENTURE, TALES OF WAR, and TALES OF WHILOMVILLE, Volumes V, VI, and VII of the present edition, together with all of his journalism not printed in REPORTS OF WAR, Volume IX. This completes the publication of Crane's shorter works, established or attributed, that were not left unfinished. The unfinished manuscript material will appear, together with the poems, in Volume X, POEMS AND LITERARY REMAINS. The present collection is highly varied, and though it includes some ephemera in the journalism and offers no fictional equal to the great short stories already edited, it does present a broad view of material that is characteristic of Crane's especial talent in the shorter forms of literature, especially in the sketches which have always been deservedly popular reading.

One signed addition to the canon from London has been discovered and printed for the first time. Most of the attributions of unsigned work made by previous scholars have been accepted and various others added from Asbury Park and from London. Several dozen possible unsigned news items from Asbury Park and Avon-by-the-Sea that could be his work in the *New York Tribune* have been omitted when they were too neutral in style, subject matter, or point of view to furnish evidence that warranted their inclusion. Otherwise it is hoped that the canon of his journalism may be called substantially complete with the publication of this volume. Some of the earliest sketches and other works are printed for the first time here from previously unedited holograph manuscripts purchased from Miss Edith Crane by C. Waller Barrett for his collection housed in the University of Virginia Library. Other manuscripts have not been published before, or if so, in digested and incomplete form. A number of works have had new and more authoritative copy-texts assigned them. Many examples of unrecorded publication have been utilized.

As in earlier volumes, problems of multiple authority in radiating texts have not been wanting for pieces that were syndicated in the newspapers, and also for various magazine publications. The preservation of a few original proofs has simplified some problems; the rest have had such proofs eclectically reconstructed according to the evidence. The principles for this reconstruction have been discussed in "Multiple Authority: New Problems and Concepts of Copy-Text," *The Library*, n.s., xxvii (1972), 81–115. In all such cases the apparatus has been expanded to enable the reader to survey the total evidence of accidentals as well as substantives in the various authorities, except for unique variation in the accidentals, so that the basic documents that are of equal authority for the text may be recovered with precision.

In dealing with the newspaper articles some few conventions have necessarily been adopted. For instance, the headlines by which the reports are identified could never have originated with Crane. Many of these sketches and reports have come to be recognized by their titles quite arbitrarily from the use by an early editor of some particular newspaper as copy-text. The principle followed in this volume is to utilize the syndicate headline when this has been preserved in proof or is otherwise recoverable; failing this, the New York newspaper headlines; and failing these, the conventional titles. The subheadings that sprinkle some newspaper articles have no relation to Crane either, and since they are a distraction in a reading text they have been banished to follow the Historical Collation in separate lists. The copy-text dateline is reproduced only in reports, not sketches, and the typography has been standardized. The typography of the captions for illustrations is also normalized.

In general each item in this collection has been treated as a self-contained unit with its own styling for the accidentals, and no attempt has been made to normalize spelling or word-division and other conventions between items except when the internal evidence for variation in some authority enables an editor to restore the common forms by recorded emendation. Thus if the authoritative texts of a sketch or report invariably read *sidewalk*, that will be the form reprinted; on the other hand, if some authority for this dispatch reads *side-walk* (which holograph indicates was Crane's preferred form), normalization to the hyphenated division will be made throughout that piece in an attempt to bring the critical text a shade closer, on some concrete evidence, to the more authoritative division. The same procedure is followed when there is only one authority and it varies within itself. Otherwise, any invariable form in the copy-text will rule. For some articles printed in England, American spelling has been substituted in the copy-text by recorded emendation even if no American version of the text exists. In other matters the editing has followed the principles first laid down in "The Text of the Virginia Edition" prefixed to Volume I of the *Works*, BOWERY TALES (1969). When preserved, Crane's manuscripts have been used as copy-texts since for the accidentals they are of superior authority to the prints. In a few cases when the manuscripts have offered only a draft form of the text that was later considerably revised for publication, both versions have been printed. The arrangement of the pieces in this volume is chronologically by genres or subject matter.

The introduction by Professor Cady places these sketches and reports in the literary context of Crane's development as a writer. The editor's The Text: History and Analysis details the physical forms of the texts, their authority, transmission, and what is known of their composition and publishing history, and examines specific problems concerned with the establishment of the text in its present critical form.

The expenses of the preparation of this volume with its textual history and apparatus have been subsidized by a grant from the National Endowment for the Humanities administered through the Modern Language Association of America and its Center for Editions of American Authors, but with generous support as well from the University of Virginia.

The editor is much in debt for assistance and various courtesies to Commander Melvin H. Schoberlin USN (Ret.), who suggested various attributions and lent material from his collection; to Miss Lillian B. Gilkes, whose sharing of her parallel work on the European Letters is most gratefully acknowledged; to Professor Robert Stallman of the University of Connecticut, Professors Matthew J. Bruccoli and Joseph Katz of the University of South

Carolina, and his colleague Professor J. C. Levenson of the University of Virginia. Professor Bernice Slote of the University of Nebraska generously placed her discoveries of new material at the service of this edition and assisted in uncovering Pittsburgh and Nebraska printings. Professors Keen Butterworth and James Meriwether, who examined this volume for the seal of the Center for Editions of American Authors, made a number of suggestions. Mr. Kenneth A. Lohf, Librarian of Rare Books and Manuscripts of the Columbia University Libraries, has been of unfailing and particular assistance. The editor is grateful to the librarians of Syracuse University, Dartmouth College, and Yale University for their courtesies in making available unpublished letters in their possession. The constant assistance of the custodians of the Barrett Collection at the University of Virginia has been invaluable; Miss Helen Koiner, former head of Interlibrary Loans, and Miss Irene Norvelle have placed the editor deeply in their debt for help in the borrowing of newspapers on microfilm over an extended period. Mrs. David Yalden-Thomson began the detailed task of administering and supervising the extensive search for material in general newspaper publication and of securing reproductions of the newly discovered texts. In all, forty-two newspapers have been searched in the preparation of the present volume. The expert and scrupulous supervision of the production of this volume and the collation of its texts by the editor's Chief Research Assistant, Miss Gillian G. M. Kyles, and her assistant, Mrs. Malcolm Craig, have been essential and is gratefully acknowledged, for in these days of relatively rapid editorial publication no single scholar can hope to assume more than the ultimate responsibility for the repeated checking for accuracy of collation, reproduction, and notation enforced by the standards for CEAA editions.

The editor's personal debt to Mr. Clifton Waller Barrett and his magnificent collection at the University of Virginia remains constant and can be expressed only by the dedication of this edition to him. The editor is indebted to the Columbia University Libraries; the University of Virginia; and the Henry W. and Albert A. Berg Collection, The New York Public Library, Astor, Lenox and Tilden Foundations for permission to utilize their manuscripts and typescripts of material in this volume and to illustrate selected specimens; and to Alfred A. Knopf, Inc., which holds the Crane copyrights to unpublished material.

F. B.

Charlottesville, Virginia
June 20, 1972

CONTENTS

Tales of the Wyoming Valley: Nos. 33–35

II. SKETCHES

Sullivan County Sketches

Contents · xv

Western Sketches

Irish Sketches

Contents · xvii

III. Reports

News from Asbury Park

Possible Attributions

News, Commentary, and Descriptions

Possible Attributions

THE TEXT: HISTORY AND ANALYSIS, *by Fredson Bowers*   769

INTRODUCTION

LTHOUGH there is nothing of Stephen Crane's finest artistic quality in this volume, its publication is an event of decided importance. Crane's esthetic instinct, and eventually his conviction, favored the effect of the *auctor absconditus*. In proportion as he achieved artistic success he concealed himself. Therefore it is to his very young, his experimental but not finished, his exploratory, and his journalistic work that one must look to glimpse Crane in the habit of his own mind as it lived. We would have missed a great deal of value for the Crane student had these materials been omitted from the edition. Here lie rich veins to be mined by the biographer, the literary and intellectual historian, the psychographer, or the student of genres. It would have been fatal to the researcher in Tokyo or Delhi, in Rome or Uppsala, and painfully expensive for Americans to be left with these nuggets scattered, sometimes buried or misclassified, in the old files or even the variously incomplete collections.[1]

Aside from his masterwork, the most interesting thing about any artist has to do with his provenience, his becoming, how he got that way. And in the case of Stephen Crane there is a deeper mystery, open at last to guesswork, or perhaps faith, the substance of things hoped for, the evidence of things not seen. What would Crane have become had he lived to the ages of Melville or Clemens, or of his contemporaries Dreiser or Frost? The materials of this book shed indispensable light on Crane's provenience; but they also suggest a grounding rich with potential for the great

[1] The first and hitherto most useful collection was Olov W. Fryckstedt, *Stephen Crane: Uncollected Writings* (Uppsala, 1963); then Thomas A. Gullason, *The Complete Short Stories and Sketches of Stephen Crane* (Garden City, N.Y., 1963); and Gullason, "A Stephen Crane Find: Nine Newspaper Sketches," *Southern Humanities Review*, II (Winter 1968), 1–37; R. W. Stallman and E. R. Hagemann, *The New York City Sketches of Stephen Crane, and Related Pieces* (New York, 1966). A pioneering specialty collection is Joseph Katz, *Stephen Crane in the West and Mexico* (Kent, Ohio, 1970).

American novelist we needs must mourn, the mature artist of whom A. J. Liebling said perfectly that, had he lived, "Crane might have written long novels of an originality as hard to imagine, in retrospect, as *Maggie* and *The Red Badge* would have been to anticipate."

Recorded in these writings are seven general topics, each a constellation of characters, landscapes, behavior, emotional color, and meaning, upon which Crane developed his imagination and wrote, often masterfully; but each of them casts light forward toward what might have been, toward Stephen Crane's lost future. As I see them, these constellations are:

1. The matter of Sullivan County
2. The matter of Asbury Park
3. The matter of New York City
4. The matter of the West
5. The matter of Mexico
6. The matter of Ireland
7. The matter of England

I

In Crane's career as in this volume, the earliest block of writing that sustains serious attention appears in the "Sullivan County Sketches." Though they have an obvious base in personal experience—he went up repeatedly from Port Jervis, New York, into the mountains on camping trips with pals—it is not easy to see that this mere biography signifies much. Personally, young Crane loved baseball more than camping, and military drill or sailing at least equally; but he wrote nothing much about any of them. Like that of many an "Old American" deracinated by history, Crane's imagination returned compulsively to the memory of the Wilderness (cf. "Tales of the Wyoming Valley"). But what finally we need to know about a writer is not so much his quotidian biography as what released creative impulse in him. During 1892 hunting and camping set off Crane's impulse to literature, and one seems forced to conclude that not personal enthusiasm so much as experience shaped by literary convention accounts for that. There existed for Crane to read, notably in American literature, a long tradition of wilderness adventure writing. And from the depths of that tradition, as old as John

Smith, Governor Bradford, or William Byrd of Westover, there sprang sharply opposed literary impulses: one toward wonder and celebration, the other toward burlesque and ironic deflation.

The "Sullivan County Sketches" respond to the tradition in both modes, but mainly in the comic mode. There may be further significance to the fact that Crane began where, in a sense sound enough, American literature may be said to begin, with the sketch. As professional American literature begins with *The Sketch Book,* Crane's first ideal of sustained creative flight he imagined as "Sullivan County Sketches." He was to keep the form in view to the end, with his fatefully aborted urban studies and with that war and travel reporting which under his hand almost always turned into sketches. His looking to the atmospheres, the psychological impact, rather than "facts" dismayed editors and annoyed fellow reporters in his journalism. His long fictions became montages of sketches. The sketch became for Crane, as for Irving, his métier.

Historically the sketch had been primarily a traveler's form— Geoffrey Crayon catching hints of the shadowy grandeurs of the past, Curtis limning Syria or the Nile, Taylor drawing El Dorado or Melville Polynesia—but it had been adapted also to Thoreau traveling much at home and to Mark Twain roughing not only "it" but romantic sentiment. Hawthorne, however, was the fine genius who saw that, where Irving had moved from the atmospheric sketch to fictional exploitation of atmospheric subtleties, one might take a further step and transform atmospheric tonalities and indeterminacies into symbolic ambiguities and metaphysical ironies. Such possibilities lay at the root of Hawthorne's famous definition of the romancer as one who "may so manage his atmospherical medium as to bring out or mellow the lights and deepen or enrich the shadows of the picture."

Lacking, as we probably always shall, reliable evidence about Crane's reading, we are reduced at many crucial points to saying that either Crane (like most writers) had in fact read a lot or that he absorbed things from the climate of living tradition. Perhaps explanations are not finally so important as that one can learn to read Crane better by a little attention to literary tradition. Another way to put the issue is to notice that in looking from these writings to the generic tradition one accepts definitively the title given them by Comdr. Melvin Schoberlin in *The Sullivan County Sketches* (Syracuse, 1949).

Almost inevitably, Crane himself seems to have thought of them not as "sketches" but in part journalism and in part his "first work in fiction." [2] In a half-hearted attempt to get them published Crane remarked that, among his manuscripts, "My favorites are eight little grotesque tales of the woods which I wrote when I was clever. The trouble is that they only sum 10000 words and I can make no more." [3] It is clear enough that his inability to enlarge the proposed volume (apparently he couldn't even find the pieces when the publisher asked to see them) rested upon his declared renunciation of cleverness for reality in art. But it is too bad that we do not know which eight he thought fiction, "tales," and which he had, however unsystematically, eliminated. At any rate, Schoberlin published ten *Sketches* originally. Professors Gullason [4] and Stallman have proposed to enlarge the canon; and this edition, accepting their contribution, assembles nineteen "Sullivan County Sketches." In making the discriminations necessary at last to justify the title, one achieves perspectives which illuminate the essential Stephen Crane and the process of his growth.

To begin with, there is a quantum leap from even the best of Gullason's additions to the earliest of Schoberlin's *Sketches*. However primitively, "Four Men in a Cave" approaches fiction. Gullason's additions appear not to be sketches much more than they are tales. They report on the legendry of the folk-mind in Sullivan County with occasional side lights upon the contemporary hunting scene. They record the sort of information which still drifts out of backwoodsy areas into the media: folk-say, local history, tall tales, eccentric characters and their ways. In the light of Crane's development they are proto-*Sketches*; but, though Schoberlin was justified in leaving them out of his volume, Gullason and Stallman did well to add them to the canon. In certain intriguing respects they prepared Crane to write the *Sketches*, and through them we can watch Crane beginning to mount the rungs of his creative ladder.

[2] To John Northern Hilliard, Jan. 2, [1896], in R. W. Stallman and Lillian Gilkes, *Stephen Crane: Letters* (New York, 1960), p. 95.
[3] To Copeland and Day, [June?, 1895], *Letters*, p. 59.
[4] See *Stephen Crane Newsletter*, III, 2 (Winter 1968), p. 5.

There is precedent in *The Sketch Book*, or even in *Walden*, for a certain instability of method as the artist gropes his way toward his best effect. Like Irving or Thoreau, Crane stands upon points of view which yield perspectives compelling writer and reader to ironic reflections both on the subject matter and on the ordinary, the naïve commentator. The mind, character, and behavior of Sullivan County folk Crane steadily submits to critical reduction. But scorn to that reader thereby trapped into illusions of his own superiority!

Crane's earliest efforts to move toward the sketch proper were of course crude, as in "Hunting Wild Hogs" where he grapples with irony and atmosphere in an effort to define Sullivan County:

This county may have been formed by a very reckless and distracted giant who, observing the tract of tipped-up and impossible ground, stood off and carelessly pelted trees and boulders at it. Not admiring the results of his labors he set off several earthquakes under it and tried to wreck it. He succeeded beyond his utmost expectations, undoubtedly. In the holes and crevices, valleys and hills, caves and swamps of this uneven country, the big game of the southern part of this State have made their last stand. Isolated wanderers are sometimes chased by everybody who owns a gun, and by every dog that has legs, in thickly-populated portions of other countries, but here is where the bear tears the bark from the pines devoid of the fear of hunters until he hears the yelp of the hounds on the ridges. [202.38–203.11]

Better developed for the best of the "Sullivan County Sketches," Crane's control of atmospheric effect came to something like this (from what I still think the best) in "Killing His Bear":

In a field of snow some green pines huddled together and sang in quavers as the wind whirled among the gullies and ridges. Icicles dangled from the trees' beards, and fine dusts of snow lay upon their brows. On the ridge-top a dismal choir of hemlocks crooned over one that had fallen. The dying sun created a dim purple and flame-colored tumult on the horizon's edge and then sank until level crimson beams struck the trees. As the red rays retreated, armies of shadows stole forward. A gray, ponderous stillness came heavily in the steps of the sun. . . .

Off over the ridges, through the tangled sounds of night, came the yell of a hound on the trail. . . . The cry of the hound grew louder and louder, then passed away to a faint yelp, then still louder. At first it had a strange vindictiveness and bloodthirstiness in it. Then it grew mournful as the wailing of a lost thing, as, perhaps, the dog gained on a fleeing bear. A hound, as he nears large game, has the griefs of the world on his shoulders and his baying tells of the approach of death. He is sorry he came. [249.7–250.2]

The control here at once of tonalities and of structural effects is worthy of the master who would powerfully control the atmospheric media, all radically different, of constituent sketches within *The Red Badge of Courage,* "The Open Boat," or "The Blue Hotel." The sketch largely quoted from "Killing His Bear" is more complex than the quotation shows (the story's protagonist and register having been left out), and it is daring. There is Crane's temperamental boldness in the coloration of the sunset and the voicing of the dog. But he wins his bet by a superb feat of equilibrium, balancing the purple prose against the sudden bathos, homely but accurate and as revealing as it is deliberate, which achieves his ironic aim: "He is sorry he came."

The feat is the more impressive because it is not, to use Crane's apologetic word, merely "clever." The drop from "purple and flame-colored tumult" to the sorrow of the ambivalent dog predicts and foreshadows the movement, the progress of the work in its totality, as I have elsewhere explained.[5] Nothing large or greatly significant, of course, "Killing His Bear" is a bold artistic success, as striking in atmospheric effect as in its ironies. Though students of genres might find it instructive to argue whether it is at last a "sketch" or a "grotesque little tale," the distinction is less important than the difference between "Killing His Bear" and, for instance, "Sullivan County Bears."

When one looks to the most interesting of the proto-*Sketches,* however, he catches a glimpse of a different but an important Stephen Crane. "The Way in Sullivan County" is rather surprisingly subtitled "A Study in the Evolution of the Hunting Yarn." It is almost unique among Crane's writings because it admits to his self-conscious command, his thorough understanding of the depth and the cultural ground of a major folk and literary genre, the tall tale.

Crane wrote so little confessed and serious criticism (the

[5] *Stephen Crane* (New York, 1962), pp. 99–100.

nonseriousness of "The Way in Sullivan County" is of course expressive) that this is worth recording at some length:

A country famous for its hunting and its hunters is naturally prolific of liars. . . . Every man cultivates what taste he has for prevarication lest his neighbors may look down on him. One can buy sawlogs from a native and take his word that the bargain is square, but ask the same man how many deer he has killed in his lifetime and he will stop working, take a seat on the snake-fence and paralyze the questioner with a figure that would look better than most of the totals to the subscription lists for monuments to national heroes. The inhabitants grow up to regard each other with painful suspicion. So there is very little field for the expert liars among their fellows. They must keep to a certain percentage or they will lose caste, but there is little pleasure in it for them because everybody knows everybody else. The only real enjoyment is when the unoffending city man appears. They welcome him with joyful cries. After he recovers from a paroxysm of awe and astonishment he seizes his pen and with flashing eye and trembling, eager fingers, writes those brief but lurid sketches which fascinate and charm the reading public while the virtuous bushwhacker, whittling a stick near by, smiles in his own calm and sweet fashion. . . .

It is inevitable that this should be the state of society in Sullivan County as well as in Pike County, and the vicinity of Scranton, Penn. In a shooting country, no man should tell just exactly what he did. He should tell what he would have liked to do or what he expected to do, just as if he accomplished it. And they all take the proper course, bringing the bump of creative genius up to a high point of development and adding little legends to the hunting lore of the region, which will undoubtedly go down the ages and impress coming generations with the fact that the Sullivan County bushwhackers were very great men indeed. [220.15–221.25]

To move directly from "The Way in Sullivan County" (published May 8, 1892) to "Four Men in a Cave" (published July 3, 1892) is to be faced at once with the inevitability of understanding what was always one of Stephen Crane's natural stances and always one of his natural modes of irony. One could call it "frontier" or "Western," "Old South-West" or "picaresque," perhaps "adolescent," certainly "masculine" and probably "precivilized"; but at any rate Crane's personality, like his imagination, lived vitally in one of the major modes of American humor. The

"Sullivan County Sketches" are not merely shot through and through with that humor, they are founded upon it.

As in *Moby-Dick*, there are really no women in the "Sullivan County Sketches," only the furious "brown giantess" of "An Explosion of Seven Babies." There is thus one of the sorts of irony Crane expected out of life in the fact that, as Schoberlin saw long ago, it was to a woman, Lily Brandon Munroe, that, in renouncing them, Crane explained the "Sketches." He had, he confided, given up "the clever school in literature" and "developed all alone" a "creed . . . identical with the one of Howells and Garland"—realism, of course. It is evident that he thought of the "Sketches" as done in a repudiated "clever, Rudyard-Kipling style." [6]

Though it is futile to categorize by school any writer who died so young as Stephen Crane, among his ambivalences was the tension between his love for the neoromantic and the realistic,[7] the magnetism of polar loadstones, Kipling and Howells. In Crane's sensibility and imagination the tension stood constant; he finally repudiated neither, and both affected his work fatefully. For what the observation is worth, the effect on Crane might someday be worth studying of the fact that, while Howells steadily hated war, aristocratic and plutocratic conspicuous consumption, and athletics, Kipling felt ambivalent toward them. The "Sullivan County Sketches," through their irony, are almost always ambivalent.

"Sir Walter Scottism," as Mark Twain damningly called it, or "the *beau ideal,*" as Cooper apologetically termed it, aside, a comic ambivalence, an often guffawing irony, lay deep in the tradition. Kipling recognized that single men in barracks "ain't a bunch o' plaster saints," but it is not easy to see how realizingly he knew that such men think romantic elevation funny. Crane, athlete, outdoorsman, rebellious son of a preacher, bohemian, knew what he knew exactly. The apparently universal modes of masculine humor (as in soldiers, athletes, and men who work in the open air) run to coarse, ego-deflating horseplay, to practical jokes, put-downs, and put-ons.

---

[6] *Letters*, pp. 31–32.

[7] For efforts at definition, see Cady, *The Light of Common Day: Realism in American Fiction* (Bloomington, Ind., 1971).

Hunting humor had always run in these grooves. Ironic laughter, the tenderfoot put-on, the boaster "sold," must have antedated Noah. On the frontier, in the American wilderness, there had been an absolute psychological necessity ("The Big Bear of Arkansas," Davy Crockett in fact and fiction) to deflate the bragging Nimrod. But it was also true that after the wilderness was gone, after pot-hunting, bounty hunting, and hide- or fur-hunting had lost economic meaning, precisely in the circumstances of cut-over, second-growth Sullivan County, the hunter had become an anachronism. However deep his preconscious urge, the hunter was himself become altogether fair game for the ironist.

Hence Crane's owlishness about Sullivan County bushwhackers in general and, treating of legend, historical particular. Much more importantly, hence the grotesquerie of the "tales" among the "Sullivan County Sketches." When there are "tales" their formula is rudimentary but fairly well designed for one effect: the exaggerated egotism of "a little man" is tested by his companions or by circumstances, or both; the little one wins or loses; but in either case the end is bathetic, and the bathos illustrates the folly of mankind. Atmospheric manipulation, more or less subtle, and circumstances traditional to the humor of the strenuous life supply the grotesquerie. The patterns are really too pervasive to need or bear illustration.

If the "Sullivan County Sketches" appear strikingly uneven as art, there is probably nothing to say about that fact except that it illustrates, as from the beginning, the mystery of Stephen Crane. The enigma rests not in the fact that his earliest work was sometimes crude but in the fact that some of it became surprisingly good—and, of course, that we know in retrospect that it served as preparation for the brilliance to come. Some criticism records the perception in this writing of patterns of symbolism. Perhaps in these cases perception depends upon faith; but I think it is fair to notice that there is scant agreement among the critics as to the symbols they see.

There has appeared, on the other hand, an opportunity to watch young Crane in his workshop. Contrary to an opinion prevalent before Crane manuscripts were available to scrutiny, Crane revised diligently, repeatedly, sometimes radically, as successive states of *The Red Badge of Courage* manuscripts reveal. There can be no doubt that Crane's thorough reworking of these early pieces helped teach him to write because we have had the luck to discover a version of an early draft.

Allowing for lag between composition and publication, time for Crane to place his pieces with Willis Fletcher Johnson, and Johnson to arrange for their appearance in the *Tribune* on summer Sundays when readers' minds might be turned to the out-of-doors, it is reasonable to suppose that Crane had been writing them during the winter, maybe the spring, of the year when he would have been a twenty-year-old sophomore if he had returned to college. Somewhere in that period he drafted an untitled piece now called "The Fishermen" which after revision would be published on July 10, 1892, as "The Octopush," the second of Schoberlin's *Sketches*. The difference between "The Fishermen," which survives as a typescript possibly transcribed by Cora Crane, and "The Octopush" registers more than a hundred revisions in a piece which contains only about 1,300 words.

Differences between these revisions and those of later works are impressive at a glance. Though in the many reworkings of *The Red Badge of Courage* (1893–95) almost every imaginable revision occurred, by 1897, when Crane was writing "The Five White Mice," his pen seems mainly to have revised as it ran and in the manuscript only one sentence has been radically altered. In "The Fishermen," Crane bore down on the surfaces, not the structure. He knew his intention and realized it in the final bathos. He ground upon polishing up the textures of diction and syntax, and he smoothed the run of his tale's progression.

He was unmistakably Stephen Crane. In "The Fishermen," perhaps for the first time, "The little man sat down and swore crimson oaths"—and of course Crane let it stand. But in revision he worked to sharpen eye and ear and make himself more Cranean, as the following parallel shows:

"The Fishermen"	"The Octopush"
About noontime he corraled the entire outfit on one huge stump where they lunched. Later he distributed them about, each to his personal stump. They fished. He	At noon, the individual corraled the entire outfit upon a stump, where they lunched while he entertained them with anecdote. Afterward, he redistributed them,

contemplated the scene and made occasional observations which rang across the waters to them, in bass solos.

Towards the close of the day, he grew silent and, evidently, thoughtful. When the sun had slid down until it only threw a red flare among the trees, one of the four men stood up and shouted to the individual:

"You had better take us ashore now."

The other three repeated: "Yes, take us ashore now."

The individual raised himself on his stump suddenly and waving a black bottle around his head, roared: : You fellersh —hic—kin all go—hic—ter blazerish."

There were a few moments of intense silence. Then the man who had sttod up, drew a long, deep breath and sat down heavily. The rest were frozen in silence.

The night came creeping over the tree-tops. The stillness of evening rested upon the waters. The individual began to curse in

each to his personal stump. They fished. He contemplated the scene and made observations which rang across the water to the four men in bass solos. Toward the close of the day, he grew evidently thoughtful, indulging in no more spasmodic philosophy. The four men fished intently until the sun had sunk down to some tree-tops and was peering at them like the face of an angry man over a hedge.[8] Then one of the four stood up and shouted across to where the individual sat enthroned upon the stump.

"You had better take us ashore, now." The other three repeated. "Yes, come take us ashore."

Whereupon the individual carefully took an erect position. Then, waving a great yellow-brown bottle and tottering, he gave vent to a sepulchral roar.

"You fellersh—hic—kin all go —hic—ter blazersh."

The sun slid down and threw a flare upon the silence, coloring it red. The man who had stood up drew a long, deep breath and sat down heavily. Stupefaction rested upon the four men.

Dusk came and fought a battle with the flare before their eyes. Tossing shadows and red beams mingled in combat. Then the

[8] Moved from the previous paragraph of "The Fishermen," where it read: "They fished until the sun slunk down behind some tree-tops and peered at them like the face of an angry man over a hedge." [235.1–3]

deep maudlin tones. "Dern fools," he said, "dern fools! Why don'tcher g'home?" [235.12–30]

stillness of evening lay upon the waters.

The individual began to curse in deep maudlin tones. "Dern fools," he said, "Dern fools! Why don't'cher g'home?" [231.26–232.11]

(Both texts in unedited form)

Variations in accidentals and paragraphing between "The Fishermen" and "The Octopush" may have been originated at the *Tribune's* copydesk, but there can be no doubt that Crane himself revised to good effect. Not every change improved "The Octopush," but most of them did; and the business with the metaphor of *the flare* exemplifies authorial revision at its best. Rethinking, it seems safe to argue, Crane saw that he had mistaken his muse when he wrote of the sunset, "When the sun had slid down until it only threw a red flare among the trees, . . ." For one thing, the image was mistimed: developmentally its drama more properly associated itself with the drunken rebellion of the guide, the onset of absurd conflict. More importantly, the latent combat implications of *the flare* cried out in Crane's imagination both for elaboration toward synesthetic shock and for close reworking of the image as an objective correlative for the psychological moment. When he deleted the earlier notation, moved down the page, and wrote, "The sun slid down and threw a flare upon the silence, coloring it red. . . . Dusk came and fought a battle with the flare before their eyes. Tossing shadows and red beams mingled in combat," he was discovering and realizing himself as Stephen Crane. That way lay his greatness.

II

The classic vacation puzzle for inhabitants of the world Stephen Crane inherited was the choice between the mountains or the shore. With his brother and family in Port Jervis but his mother active in the Methodist work of Ocean Grove, youthful Crane got the advantages of both. The matter of Asbury Park, whence he filed stories as a stringer for the *New York Tribune,* served him immediately less well than that of Sullivan County. Yet one of Crane's potentialities, even one of his links to Joseph Conrad, was the sense of the sea he learned on the Jersey Coast.

For book

		words
Lines - "war is kind" published a. s.		
Lines - never yet published		1210
Little French play not		3280
The Reluctant Voyagers " northern news syndicate England		
A self made man		2000
Manacled " N.Y. Truth		1500
A Dark Brown Dog " Editions - u.s.		2500
Moonlight on the Snow " England or u.s.		4000
The wisdom of the Present		650
An Eloquence of Grief		875
An Explosion of Seven Babies		1425
The man from Duluth		3065
The crowds from New York Theatres		2075
The Silver Pageant		770
1 - Uncle Clarence - The Camel -		695
2 - " "		
3 - " "		
Mining		2350
1 - Wyoming Tales		1800
2 - " "		2690
3 - " "		2540
Article N.Y.		650
Croydon Tragedy		595
A man by the name of Mud		1015
Poker Game		1080
Article N.Y.		950

Inventory list (Columbia University)

			words
✶ ✗	How the donkey lifted the hills ✓	Bacheller.	1000
	From our Scranton correspondent ✓		1470
	The Mesmeric Mountain ✓		1195
	Interesting Notes (3) ✓		1600
✓ 1-	Irish Notes	Westminster Gazette ✓	1400
✓ 2-	" "	" "	
✓ 3-	" "	" "	
✓ 4-	" "	" "	
✓ 1-	London Notes	Saturday Review	
✓ 2-	" "	" " ✓	
✓ 3-	" "	" " ✓	
✓	And if He wills, we must die ✓ ✓		2235
	Twelve O'clock ✓	Pall Mall magazine ✓	3000
⊤ ✓	An Illusion in Red and White. Bacheron U.S. ✓		2000
	Mad as a Hatter ✓		
✗	The Snake ✓	Bacheller Syndicate	1250
✗	The pursuit of the Piles ✓	" "	1250
	Battle Hymn ✓	Pall Mall Magazine ?)	
	Spitzbergen Stories ✓		
✗	The Victory of the moon ✓	Bacheller Syndicate U.S.	1500
	The Voice of the Mountain ✓		1250
P	When man falls ✓	N.Y. Press	1500
P	The Owl ✓	" "	2000
P	The Fire ✓	" "	2000
P	Binks Day in the Country ✓	" "	2000
✶	Christmas Dinner won in Battle. Plumbers trade Journal N.Y.		2000
✶ ✗ P	Sketches of Nebraska Life ✓	Bacheller.	1000
P	The Pursuit of the Butter & Egg man ✓	the Press	500

Inventory list (Columbia University)

a Tent in agony ✓   Cosmopolitan
the Octopush ✓   the Tribune
the Hermit ✓   " "
a Ghoul's Accountant ✓ " "
the Black Dog ✓   " "
the Bear Hunt ✓   " "
P an Experiment in Luxury ✓ the Press ✓
P Billie Atkins Journey ✓ " "
X a Tale of mere chance ✓ Bacheller Syn.
a Texas Legend ✓
Duel Between Alarm-Clock etc. ✓
Diamonds and Diamonds ✓
Mexican Notes ✓   23 65
Journey on Engine from London to Scotland ✓ McClure
a Desertion ✓   15 20
Six years afloat ✓   Published through McClure
a Knowing Canine ✓   "
Filibustering industry ✓   "
Greek war correspondent ✓   "
The White hat in Greece ✓   "
Suda Bay ✓   "
Bowlders —   "
Velestino —   "
Crane, writes of Texas ✓   "

Inventory list (Columbia University)

As Walt Whitman demonstrated, there used to be an amphibious quality to the inhabitants of that endless strand which stretches from Cape May up the Hudson River to Stony Point and from Peekskill back down, around and through all the isles to Narragansett Bay (after that it becomes purely Yankee territory, and Yankees may be depended upon to speak well for it). Obviously no blue-water sailor, Crane knew the coasts and their shipping, the shores and their often terrible surf. His ironic eye was easily attracted to studies in comparative culture between the shore people and vacationers—to the advantage of neither ("The Captain," "The Reluctant Voyagers"). But ultimately his artistic development was served by what his imagination gained from studies like "The Wreck of the *New Era*" and "Ghosts on the Jersey Coast." One of the insufficiencies of *The Red Badge of Courage* lies in the absence from its combat scenes of any sense of the real presence of the bullet. But part of the greatness of "The Open Boat" arises from its realizing sense of the real presence, in the beginning, of the comber and, at the end, of the murderous surf.

For the rest, what is now interesting in Crane's Asbury Park dispatches is not so much (*pace* Professor Elconin) what might have transpired after Crane made fun of the Junior Order of United American Mechanics as it is the bitterness of his extended attacks on "the Founder" of Ocean Grove, the "millionaire" James A. Bradley. It echoes Garland and his gospel according to Henry George, the attack on the "unearned increment." It echoes Howells, whose offensive against capitalism in "The Editor's Study" of *Harper's Monthly* had been a *cause célèbre* and thus an intellectual fact of life since before Crane's fifteenth birthday and whose novels had become increasingly intransigent from *Annie Kilburn*, 1888, through *A Hazard of New Fortunes*, 1889, and *The Quality of Mercy*, 1891–92, into *The World of Chance*, which was running serially when Crane wrote "On the Boardwalk" early in August 1892.

The previous August, Crane had reported Hamlin Garland as having said in a lecture at Avon-by-the-Sea that Howells "is a many-sided man, a humorist of astonishing delicacy and imagination . . . by all odds the most American and vital of our literary men to-day. He stands for all that is progressive and humanitarian" ("Howells Discussed . . ."). At New Year's 1892

Garland had reported on Howells' new editorship of *The Cosmo-politan*: "Unquestionably Mr. Howells will be a greater power than ever in the radical wing of American literature." [9] Now Crane grasped his chance to be a " 'terrible young radical' " and lambasted "the Founder":

James A. Bradley . . . is a millionaire, who bought the land upon which this resort is situated years ago for a nominal price. He still has great possessions here. A part of them is the ocean front. Everybody knows him and everybody calls him "Founder Bradley." He is a familiar figure at any hour of the day. He wears a white sun-umbrella with a green lining and has very fierce and passionate whiskers, whose rigidity is relieved by an occasional twinkle in his bright Irish eye. He walks habitually with bended back and thoughtful brow, continually in the depths of some great question of finance, involving, mayhap, a change in the lumber market or the price of nails. He is noted for his wealth, his whiskers and his eccentricities. . . .

"Founder" Bradley has lots of sport with his ocean front and boardwalk. It amuses him and he likes it. It warms his heart to see the thousands of people tramping over his boards, helter-skeltering in his sand and diving into that ocean of the Lord's which is adjacent to the beach of James A. Bradley. He likes to edit signs and have them tacked up around. There is probably no man in the world that can beat "Founder" Bradley in writing signs. . . . He is no mere bungler nor trivial paint-slinger. He has those powers of condensation which are so much admired at this day. For instance: "Modesty of apparel is as becoming to a lady in a bathing suit as to a lady dressed in silks and satins." There are some very sweet thoughts in that declaration. It is really a beautiful expression of sentiment. It is modest and delicate. Its author merely insinuates. There is nothing to shake vibratory senses in such gentle phraseology. Supposing he had said: "Don't go in the water attired merely in a tranquil smile," or "Do not appear on the beach when only enwrapped in reverie." A thoughtless man might have been guilty of some such unnecessary uncouthness. But to "Founder" Bradley it would be impossible. He is not merely a man. He is an artist. ["On the Boardwalk" (518.14–519.34)]

III

Where one can see quite a bit and quite early into Crane's becoming in the "Sullivan County Sketches," there is less satisfac-

[9] "Mr. Howells's Plans," *Boston Evening Transcript*, Jan. 1, 1892, p. 1.

tion in his sketches of New York. A major frustration now springs from the fact that he simply did not live to become the great, deep-visioned novelist of New York he might have been, whom we shall never have because Crane's New York is forever gone. *Maggie* is a masterpiece of its sort: but the sort is youthful, of course. The history of our literature can only go on mourning Crane and Norris for the might-have-beens in the novel of Robert Frost's generation.

Meanwhile we have a wealth of the studies of New York left unresolved by Crane. There are *Maggie* studies, some little gems like "An Ominous Baby" or "A Dark-Brown Dog." There are New York "tough" sketches of the ilk which so fascinated Howells when Crane explained that the secret of the tough was that he felt that "everything was 'on' him." Crane made street studies, amusement studies, slum studies, bohemian studies, the extraordinary (for Crane) "Mr. Binks' Day Off," night-life sketches —were there ever, really, intended to be any "Midnight Sketches"?

One of Crane's most intriguing studies was the piece—really one in two matched parts—"An Experiment in Misery," "An Experiment in Luxury." Among many things they demonstrate is that Crane could both think and write rings around Theodore Dreiser and that Dreiser would have been substantially helped if he had known how to borrow understandingly from his predecessor and model. One glimpses, extrapolating hence as from "The Monster," what a forty-year-old Crane might have become. But as they stand the paired "Experiments" may be seen to be strikingly revelatory of Crane's mind. The shock, and the candle power, of revelation come from the unmistakable fact that Crane felt no respect for either misery or luxury as such. The flophouse experiment, like "The Men in the Storm," illustrated Crane's exterior generalization that the trouble with the poor was finally cowardice. "An Experiment in Luxury," however, Crane built discursively. What "the youth" perceived in the brownstone house of opulence was calculated to offer no comfort to Herbert Spencer or Mark Hanna. The ironies, often explicit, are murderous, the perceptions probing, the comprehension of social realities rich and searching. It is the product of a first-rate intellect; and what it says is that, though of course the rich are freer, prouder, more comfortable, all the reasons for esteeming them, especially their esteeming themselves, all the apologies, are whited sepulchers.

The ideas thus expressed tell us a great deal about Stephen Crane's perceptions, beliefs, and sensibility. Perhaps the *locus classicus* from which to argue that Stephen, the much prayed-for and prayed-over preacher's kid turned tough, had become intellectually a very radicalized, demythologized Christian is "An Experiment in Luxury." But after one has recognized the stance and after one has noticed the marvellous range from "A Desertion" to "The Devil's Acre," from "A Great Mistake" to "A Lovely Jag in a Crowded Car," what is there to say? Only, again, that the potential was wonderful and that, so far as he actually went, Crane himself covered the New York situation as he saw it pretty well in his justly famous letter to Catherine Harris as quoted by Thomas Beer: "perhaps you have been informed that I am not very friendly to Christianity as seen around town. I do not think that much can be done with the Bowery as long as the [poor?] are in their present state of conceit. . . . The missions for children are another thing and if you will have Mr. Rockefeller give me a hundred street cars and some money I will load all the babes off to some pink world where cows can lick their noses and they will never see their families any more." [10]

Ironies more real than casuistical or literary lay behind Crane's once obscure "In the Depths of a Coal Mine," however, and perhaps that was why comparison between the early manuscript and what *McClure's Magazine* printed reveals some of Crane's bitterest handling of social inequity. A first irony resides in the fact that Stephen had financed the first "publication" of *Maggie* by the sale of coal-mining stock inherited from his mother. [11] He had tried to capture fame by financing a plea for the poor with proceeds from the atrocities he and C. K. Linson recorded in Scranton. Linson [12] says that *McClure's* made Crane tone down his account of Dunmore mine Number Five. No doubt Linson was in general right, and some editing down took place. But there are ample objective reasons to doubt the reliability of Linson's

---

[10] See *Letters*, p. 133.

[11] See Joseph Katz, "Stephen Crane: Muckraker," *Columbia Library Columns*, xvii (Feb., 1968), 2–7.

[12] *My Stephen Crane* (Syracuse, 1958), pp. 65–70.

memory, evidence that he was not above faking things a little; and I am inclined to Professor Bowers' observation that Crane revised radically before he submitted any text to *McClure's.*

To begin with, "In the Depths" as printed is by no means "innocuous"; it hits hard, especially in its accounts of the exploitation of children—the breaker boys:

before them always is the hope of one day getting to be door-boys down in the mines and, later, mule-boys. And yet later laborers and helpers. Finally when they have grown to be great big men they may become miners, real miners, and go down and get "squeezed," or perhaps escape to a shattered old man's estate with a mere "miner's asthma." They are very ambitious. [592.26–32]

Both Crane and *McClure's* let that stand; and, with much else which stands, it is far from innocuous; and Crane's integrity had not been compromised by any nervous Nellie at the office.

What came out of the text (I think largely if not entirely before submission) is peculiarly interesting for three reasons. It provides a rare case of Crane's editorializing—all for the men against the bosses. But because it editorialized it violated Crane's esthetic ethic, which meant to *present*, not explain or argue. And perhaps much more for reasons of artistic integrity than for fear of the commercial ethic of the office, Crane deleted all or most of the external comment and replaced it with the moving symbolic drama of the mule who once restored to sunlight and the relative heaven of the surface could not by any means be forced back down the mine: "No cudgellings could induce him."

What went out was commentary: "When I had studied mines and the miner's life underground and above ground, I wondered at many things but I could not induce myself to wonder why the miners strike and otherwise object to their lot." Surviving all the dangers of his war in the bowels of nature, the miner, stifling in middle age slowly from what we now call "black lung," will have "the joy of looking back upon a life spent principally for other men's benefit until the disease racks and wheezes him into the grave. . . . One cannot go down in the mines often before he finds himself wondering why it is that coal-barons get so much and these miners, swallowed by the grim black mouths of the earth day after day get proportionately so little."

Crane, whose sense of life was war, instinctively held with the men against the generals. One of his deletions told the anecdote of "about twenty coal-brokers and other men who make neat livings by fiddling with the market" who got trapped by equipment failure down a mine and had to climb a thousand feet of ladders to get shakenly out—and created a newspaper sensation:

I hasten to express my regards for these altogether estimable coal-brokers . . . but I must confess to a delight at for once finding the coal-broker associated in hardship and danger with the coal-miner. I confess to a dark and sinful glee at the descriptions of their pangs and their agonies. It seemed to me a partial and obscure vengeance. And yet this is not to say that they were not all completely virtuous and immaculate coal-brokers.

If all men who stand uselessly and for their own extraordinary profit between the miner and the consumer were annually doomed to a certain period of danger and darkness in the mines, they might at last comprehend the misery and bitterness of men who toil for existence at these hopelessly grim tasks. They would begin to understand then the value of the miner, perhaps. Then maybe they would allow him a wage according to his part. [606.40–607.13]

The difference between the miner on one side and the bum or Bowery stiff on the other was, clearly, that the miner suffered from no cowardice. In dealing with such an industrial soldier Crane felt at one with "the radical wing of American literature." What might he not have written in 1920?

IV

McClure sent Crane down the mines, and the Bacheller syndicate fulfilled one of his dreams and provided two new sets of experience for him by sending him out to accumulate the matter of the West and the matter of Mexico between late January and the middle of May 1895. As Owen Wister could have told Crane, it was growing too late to see anything of the Old West in its prime, and Crane registered his own sense of that in "The Blue Hotel"; but he saw enough to enrich his imagination permanently. Mexico, of course, was at that date a frontier for the North American mind.

At last the real thing Crane had to say about the West he said artistically in two of his best short stories. In its own way, "The

Blue Hotel" and "The Bride Comes to Yellow Sky" each testifies to the reductive sensibility of a realist (which Crane often but of course not always possessed) contemplating the absurdities and indecencies of that neoromantic sensibility which was then busily incubating what would eventually burgeon as Horse-Opera in all its glories. Crane also had fun with that in various lesser pieces; but his finest, most typical mood spoke from the dialogue he recorded with a farmer blasted by blizzards in "Nebraska's Bitter Fight for Life." Destitute, near starving, the horses dying in the fields, even the spring seed consumed, the farmers got too little or sometimes none of the Eastern aid eagerly given but callously diverted:

"I hain't had no aid!"
"How did you get along?"
"Don't git along, stranger. Who the hell told you I did get along?"
[418.4–7]

An obvious part of the unspoken *donnée* for "The Blue Hotel," that dialogue provides ironic counterpoint to the activities of every character in this short story. But Crane in the West proved not to be much of a travel writer. Bacheller's investment in him was not inspired. And, while he picked up some momentum south of the border, his reporting struck a vein not equal to his best. Part of the trouble sprang from Crane's concept of his role as traveler. Far from the passionate pilgrim, he imagined himself a New York "Kid," retailing in sporting language the sensations of "the youthful stranger, with the blonde and innocent hair" in the presence of foreign scenes and folk but associated with North Americans—business or professional men who were rather sporting types. The character Crane assumed might later have been invented by Fitzgerald or Hemingway. Crane was eventually to make a promising go of him in "The Five White Mice"; and his aborted "A Man by the Name of Mud" shows that he continued to muse about "the Kid." Could he have created his own prototype for *The Sun Also Rises*?

At any rate, his mind was also quickened by other things. The landscape of mighty peaks stayed with him, as may be seen in the poem from *War Is Kind* which begins and ends with the lines:

> In the night
> Grey heavy clouds muffled the valleys,
> And the peaks looked toward God, alone.

He stayed in Mexico long enough to discover in himself a feeling for cultural relativity and to express, in "The Mexican Lower Classes," a piece Bacheller did not print, a new depth to his radical sentiment. The Indians of Mexico shook him: why should they "insist upon existence at all"? And then he saw what the wise traveler always sees—that the use of the foreign is to comprehend life at home.

The striking fact about those Indians, he recognized, was that "you cannot ascertain that they feel at all the modern desperate rage at the accident of birth." And insofar as this might be true, the Indians contrasted absolutely with the folk Crane had studied in the lower depths of New York:

> The people of the slums of our own cities fill a man with awe. That vast army with its countless faces immovably cynical, that vast army that silently confronts eternal defeat, it makes one afraid. One listens for the first thunder of the rebellion, the moment when this silence shall be broken by a roar of war. Meanwhile one fears this class, their numbers, their wickedness, their might—even their laughter. There is a vast national respect for them. They have it in their power to become terrible. And their silence suggests everything. [436.25–33]

We do not, of course, have any such American novelist as that implied here.

V

What came of Crane's Irish and his English sketches was mainly that long joke (finished by a hack who did not quite see the point) *The O'Ruddy.* As travel writing Crane's "Irish Sketches" are substantially superior to anything of the sort he had attempted before. He always wrote best from the realist's "dramatic" or pictorial point of view. But his difference from Henry James as travel writer now appears clearly. Crane never took the high-toned or "distinguished" point of view: like Lincoln, Crane the artist had an eye avid to see common people—those whom God must have loved because He made so many of them.

Still, there was then just an intriguing chance that Crane in

England, guided by Frederic, befriended by Conrad and by James himself, might after his fashion have become an heir, infinitely different from Edith Wharton, of James. In his "New Invasion of Britain," Crane waxed wonderfully funny, wonderfully perceptive, about certain Home Counties types: "London is simply alive with bounders. At the clubs the topic is solely bounders. . . . The bounders have taken London's attention by assault." Having heard "Jones" so classified, might the foreigner dare ask the victim "What is a bounder?" It was a puzzle: "Perhaps bounders can fight. If bounders came in sizes and Jones was a small one and enfeebled from much bounding, the question might be practicable."

But, as it was and must remain, Stephen Crane had too little time to live much deeper into British life than the level reached by his well-done and well-named "London Impressions." At last the best of his studies in comparative culture, the best of his English sketches, "The Scotch Express," became also one of his most modernist writings. Like "The Monster" it looks over the heads of his more typical works toward that future which was not to be. Now the great value in "The Scotch Express" is Crane's having defined there, rather casually, that concept of a courage beyond irony upon which his life and the best of his art were founded:

It should be a well-known fact that, all over the world, the engine-driver is the finest type of man that is grown. He is the pick of the earth. He is altogether more worthy than the soldier and better than the men who move on the sea in ships. He is not paid too much, nor do his glories weight his brow, but for outright performance carried on constantly, coolly, and without elation by a temperate, honest, clear-minded man he is the further point. And so the lone human at his station in a cab, guarding money, lives and the honor of the road, is a beautiful sight. The whole thing is aesthetic. [746.24–33]

Like every account of Stephen Crane this one ends, then, in anticlimax. There is no escape.

E. H. C.

I Tales and Sketches

No. 1   UNCLE JAKE AND THE BELL-HANDLE

UNCLE JAKE was a good, old soul. In fact, there was not a better, kinder man in the whole county than old Uncle Jake and when he was going to the city to sell his turnips and buy any amount of sugar, molasses, starch and such things, he promised his twenty-eight year old niece that she should go down to the city with him and he would "take her round," he said, in a lordly way. This, considering that he had only been to the city once before himself, was a very generous offer and Sarah was very glad to have an uncle who was so worldly minded and knew all about the big cities and all that.

So the next day at sunrise Uncle Jake dressed himself in his best suit of black clothes and Sarah arrayed her angular form in her best calico gown, and put on her cotton mitts and the lilac sun-bonnet with the sun-flowers on it. After surveying his niece with a good deal of pride and some misgivings about the city men, whom he thought might be likely to steal such a lovely creature, he kissed his wife good-bye as if he were going to Europe for ten years, clambered upon the high seat, pulled Sarah up beside him as if she had been a bundle of straw, flourished his whip, smiled blandly and confidently upon his wife, the two hired men and a neighbor's-boy, and drove away.

The two large fat horses walked up hill and trotted down dale and Uncle Jake's white beard blew about in the wind, first over on one cheek and then over on another, as he sat up on the high seat with his legs braced, pulling the fat horses' heads this way and that. As the sun commenced to get warm, Sarah put up the big cotton umbrella over the lilac sun-bonnet with the sun-flowers, the dusty wheels rattled, the turnips in the wagon bobbed and rolled about as if each one was possessed of a restless devil, and Uncle Jake, and Sarah, and the turnips and the sun-bonnet, rode gaily toward the city.

Soon the houses began to appear closer together, there were more tin-cans and other relics strewn about the road-side, they began to get views of multitudes of back-yards, with washes on lines; grimy, smoky factories; stock yards filled with discordant mobs of beasts; whole trains of freight cars, standing on side tracks; dirty children, homeless dogs and wandering pigs. To Uncle Jake's experienced eye, this denoted that they were entering the city.

Beer saloons commenced to loom up occasionally with gentlemen standing in front of them who wore their hats over their right eyes, or their left eyes, or their ears, or whichever member they deemed it proper, as gentlemen of leisure and of sporting proclivities. Old Uncle Jake nodded benignly at these gentlemen, who he doubtless thought had heard he was coming to town and had "knocked off" work to see him go past, while the gentlemen nearly swallowed their tobacco in their amazement at the white-haired old "duck" but recovering themselves winked bleared eyes and bowed red noses at the lilac bonnet with the sun-flowers but that was immediately focussed on some body's wash line in the back-yard opposite, where, it seemed half of the men of the family were given over to wearing red nether garments and the other half were partial to white, thereby imparting a picturesque and lurid appearance to the line of clothes, dangling in the breeze. They reached the Main Street of the town and Uncle Jake sold his turnips to a dealer who beat the old man down considerably by lying to him about "market prices." They spent the morning in going about to the different stores buying their supplies. Uncle Jake would take his niece by the hand and enter a store, calling the first clerk he saw "Mr. Jones and Co." or whatever name he saw on the sign board. After cordially shaking him by the hand, he would introduce his little niece, Miss Sarah Bottomley Perkins, and announce that she was only twenty-eight years, seven months and—how many days, Saree? Don't know? Well, never mind. Well, sir, crops was never better than this year, by George, sir. Had Mr. Jones and Co. noticed the amazin' manner in which cucumber pickles grew this year or the astounding manner in which early pumpkins came up? No? Well, well, he hoped he would see Mr. Jones and Co. in a year or two. But he couldn't say. His wife, poor critir, had the most astonishing case of plumbago that had been in Green County since '58 when old Bill William's wife's second-cousin took down with it. Well, he supposed he must be going. The best of friends must part. If Mr. Jones and Co. ever kim out in Green County he knew he had a place at old Jake Perkinses board. "Good-bye, my boy. Heaven bless you."

Then the old gentleman would buy three yards of calico or seven pounds of brown sugar maybe, and bidding an affectionate good-bye to the clerk, take his niece by the hand and leave, waving his hand back at the store, while in sight, to the imminent danger of a collision between the fat horses and the street cars.

Uncle Jake spent the morning this way. Some of the clerks, understanding the old man and being gentlemen, listened politely and deferentially to his ramblings, while others who were not troubled that way, snickered behind his back at the other clerks, and pointed their fingers at him, while the old man beamed a world of peace and good will toward all men from the glasses of his spectacles.

At noon, they put up the fat horses at a livery stable whose proprietor charged Uncle Jake fifty-cents more than he did anyone else, merely on principle. They went to a hotel and were ushered into the parlor to await the summons of the dinner gong.

Uncle Jake and his niece walked about the spare hotel parlor and were both filled with amazement at what they deemed its magnificence. Uncle Jake's curiosity was immense. He wandered about the room, running his hands over the picture frames and feeling of the upholstery of the chairs.

In an evil hour, he came upon the bell-handle.

It was an old fashioned affair arranged in a sort of brass scoop or cup from which projected the long handle. He looked at it for some time and wondered what it was for. He pressed on it and no tap commenced to flow ginger-pop. Finally he pulled it.

Now it came to pass, that, at precisely that moment, a waiter of the hotel made a terrific onslaught on a gong that was sure to make any horses in the vicinity run away and awaken all the late sleepers for blocks around.

Uncle Jake's pull on the bell-handle and the sound of the gong were identical.

"Good Lord! what have I did! Holy Mackerel! I have gone and done it!"

With these words, Uncle Jake sank, pale-faced, back on a chair like a man who has been stricken down with a stuffed club.

The old man's hair stood on end. He was "done up," as he expressed it. His manner conveyed a sense of terror to his niece who seemed inclined to fill the air with her lamentations but suppressed herself enough to cry "Oh! uncle! uncle! what have you done," asking him the same momentous question he had asked himself a moment before.

"Done, Sarah? Done? Oh, sufferin' Susan, that I should live to see this day! Done? I've called out the fire department, or the police force or the ambulance corps or something else that's awful! Oh! miserable man! maybe it's the insurance agents or the Board of Health and this poor old carcass will never get home alive."

His violent agitation made the innocent maiden still more bent on howling but her uncle stopped her as before.

"S-s-s-h! Sar-ee! S-s-s-h! My pore girl, you now see your old uncle a fergitive from justice, a critir hounded by the dogs of the law! S-s-s-h! Make no sound er they'll be down on us like a passel of wolves!"

Impressed by her uncle's manner, Sarah kept quiet while the old man went about the room on his tip toes, peering out the window in momentary expectation of seeing the police force, the ambulance corps, and the fire department come up the street.

"Thank goodness, Sar-ee, that the militia can't be called out on such short notice and they'll have time to find out that it is a mistake. To see this innocent country plunged into er civil war by the hand of an ignorant old man, would be terr'ble."

The old man peeped out the door and said "Come Sar-ee! S-s-s-h! The minions of the law may be on our track any minute."

Out they went into the street, hand in hand, giving cautious glances about and starting at any sudden sound. Every eye seemed to them to be full of suspicion. When they would see a policeman, they would turn up an alley or a side street. The city was very quiet and the blue buttons were out in full force, so the "fergitive from justice" and his companion went around a good many corners. When they arrived at the livery stable, their route from the hotel if it could be mapped would look like a brain-twisting Chinese puzzle. They hurried the hostlers and Uncle Jake's hand shook the reins up and down as if he were knocking flies off the fat horses.

They drove down by-ways until they reached their road home where the fat horses were surprised into making the exertion of their lives.

Uncle Jake and Sarah cast many fearful glances behind them until they were safe in the shelter of the old barn-yard.

There with fat horses breathing heavily beside him, the cows looking solemnly over the fence and all the delights of his old heart about him, he made a vow never again to touch "no bell-handles nor pull out no plugs agin, as long as I live, bein's as how my grey hairs were like to be lowered in sorrer this blessed day."

No. 2 GREED RAMPANT

SCENE—Paradise, N.J.
Time—The end of it.

Dramatis Personae.

Mr. John P. St. Peter.
Crowd of Gentiles.
Mob of Jews.

Mr. St. Peter is discovered, seated comfortably upon a small box near the turnstile at the Twoforty Gate, the main entrance to Paradise, N.J.

He is slumbering peacefully and the dull rattle of his snore mingles harmoniously with the sounds of low sweet music from within. The lights burn dim, and throw soft, rose hues over the

dreaming Mr. St. Peter. All is quietness and infinite rest.*****
***************Suddenly, discordant sounds can be heard
from without. There is a hollow roar as of an approaching
tempest, in the air. The lights of Paradise swing and flicker as
if a wind had intruded. The guardian of the gates arouses
himself and places his hand behind his ear in a listening attitude. Signs of perturbation appear upon his countenance. The
roar comes gradually louder.*********It develops into the
sound of loud voices raised in wrath, discussions, dissensions,
quarrels, bickerings, and the noise of wildly scrambling feet.
Mr. St. Peter rushes to the turnstile.***** Enter, without, a
disheveled mob of Jews. They make a furious rush for the
turnstile. Thirteen clothes-dealers try to squeeze through the
turnstile at one time. Two-score pawn-brokers attempt to climb
over the iron-railing. Mr. St. Peter makes a gallant resistance.
He bats the invaders over the head with his huge key and
pushes them back. There ensues a dreadful melee. They fight
among themselves. There is a shrill chorus of angry voices.
One Jew attempts to go legitimately through the turnstile. His
companions drag him back by his coat-tails. All then try to go
through first. Mr. St. Peter is in immense consternation. The
Jews engage in a fierce battle at the gate. There is a repetition
of the shrill chorus of angry voices. Mr. St. Peter frenziedly
tears a handful from the little grey fringe of hair that encircles
his venerable head. Wildest uproar! Greatest confusion! Finally,
a wise Jew, after pondering a moment, takes a valuable dollar-
and-a-half ring from his finger and, then in full view of the
palpitating throng, he hurls it down the stairs behind them.
Instantly every eye is fixed upon the flight of the ring. A single
impulse animates the entire body. The mob forgetting all else,
turns and plunges, dives headlong, in pursuit. They tumble
over each other in their anxiety to grasp the precious trinket.
The wise Jew now has a clear field. He flies unmolested through
the turnstile and is three quarters of the way down the centre
aisle before he is discovered by his comrades. They set up a
howl and charge on the turnstile. Mr. St. Peter's eyes start
from his head. With his hair on end, he climbs upon his little
box and draws his gown carefully about his legs. The Jews
pour through in a torrent. The turnstile clicks like a crazy

stem-winding watch. The metal grows hot from the friction. It seethes and throws off steam. Mr. St. Peter is compelled to dash a pail of water upon it. The Jews pour in like a run-away flood. The turnstile rocks like a tree in a storm.***** The Jews swarm down the centre aisle. They all attempt to sit down in the front seats. In consequence, there is another frightful row. They bleed from wounds; their clothing is in tatters; yet they madly hurl themselves upon each other like wild animals.***** ******** Many have fainted. The rest fight for programmes.** *********Mr. St. Peter mops his brow and sinks down upon his box with the eyes of a bewildered hunted thing.*********Low murmuring sounds heard from without. Mr. St. Peter starts up, listens, wrings his hands and then tears out half the little fringe of hair about his head.***********Mutterings seem to be coming gradually nearer. Mr. St. Peter tears out the other half of the little fringe.*********Enter crowd of Gentiles. They pass in. The turnstile clicks. Mr. St. Peter beams. The Gentiles march in an orderly and modest manner, down the centre aisle. Suddenly they stop and gaze in amazement. Every good seat in the house is occupied by a Jew. The entire front is a wriggling mass of big noses and diamonds. They rise in a tremendous wall. The Gentiles are compelled to take the rear seats. The Gentiles grieve. No view for them at all. They can't see anything. The Jews look back in scorn and sneer at the unfortunate Gentiles. The air is full of the reflected rays of seventy-three diamonds.***********The leading Gentiles confer and a thoughtful Gentile thinks. Finally the thoughtful Gentile proposes a plan. After listening to his whispered proposal they pat him on the back and evidently tell him that he has a great head. The thoughtful Gentile gets a piece of white cloth from the floor, which probably some Jew had brought with him, hoping to do a little business with the inhabitants of Paradise, N.J., but had inadvertently lost it in the melee. The thoughtful Gentile takes a fountain pen from his pocket and carefully prints a sign upon the cloth. Then raising it upon a walking stick, he exhibits it after the manner of a transparency. He marches slowly along in front of the Jews. The Jews observe him and read the sign. They start, quiver, and rise out of their seats, their eyes bulging. An electric spasm sweeps over the throng of money-lenders and clothing dealers, for upon the sign they read:

> ## JOB LOTS. JOB LOTS.
>
> DOWN IN SHEOL, CAPE MAY COUNTY, NEW JERSEY.
>
> Selling out at 2 per cent of cost.

With a convulsive movement they vacate the front seats. Down the centre aisle, they again tumble over each other. They squirm, they buffet, they pant, they fly headlong. The Gentiles facetiously cheer them on. Mr. St. Peter hurriedly opens the fire-exits, and then climbs up on the top fresco of the central archway, where he tangles his legs and arms around a beam and hangs on for dear life. The floor swirls and trembles beneath the mighty, tempestuous rush of the mad Jews. They hurl themselves down the stairway. It is an avalanche of bargain hunters. A row of twenty-three Jews are telescoped at the first landing. The terrific thunder of their footfalls grows fainter and fainter—it dies away in hollow rumble. Mr. St. Peter climbs down and swoons on the floor.

In the meantime, the Gentiles had moved up to the front seats.

No. 3   THE CAPTAIN

HE IS the skipper of a catboat and a member of the village fire department. He always wears two uniforms, to be prepared for an emergency. When he goes to a fire he wears his yachting dress; when he is in command of his gallant ship, the *Anna*, he still wears his fire department uniform. The uniform which marks him as the skipper of the *Anna* is a straw hat—a most wonderful straw hat, of sun-burned yellow, with a rusty ribbon around it and a piece of twine, a peak-halyard, so to speak, running from it to a button-hole of his coat. That is all there is to the uniform of the commander. But as for the uniform of the fireman that is a different thing. He wears it on his left breast; it is shield-shaped, it is of tin, and on it are red letters designating the name of his engine company. That is all there is of it, but it is quite enough. He is a thin man with a mustache that may be gray from salt encrustation, or "wind-burn," or age. At any rate it is gray and if it is not handsome it is at least a mustache. As for the rest of his face his cheek, if you speak of him as the commander of a vessel, is weather-beaten; if as the member of a fire department, burned—you might almost say scorched. His name—perhaps it is Maltravers; perhaps it is De Courcey; perhaps it is only Smith, or Jones, but whatever it is he is first, last and all the time "the Captain."

The Captain is a wit. His wit does not cut or even sparkle. It isn't that kind of wit. It's too dignified. It comes on slowly, to preserve the nautical connection of this sketch, with a full spread of canvas, but making little headway. It does not come about, or tack or reef, or do anything else that a racing yacht in command of a young and ambitious captain might be expected to do. His wit just runs slowly before the wind, comes into collision with you in a dull, heavy fashion, swings clear and drifts away until the sails fill again.

It is a most remarkable and mysterious wit, expressed at regular intervals and in a long drawl. You have to take in sail generally to meet it, for if you are bowling along you will cross the bows; there will not be any collision; you will not feel the bump of its square bows and—you will not know that you have been cruising in the same waters with the Captain's wit.

The wind is blowing freshly up the Sound. The sky is as clear as the hollow of a bluebell. The water has that dark sparkle, which is neither green nor blue nor black—the flash of a darkly tinted jewel. The breeze throws thin wafers off the crests of the waves and tosses them lightly against your cheek, cool and damp and refreshing, like the spray of violet water. There is not a mark in the sweep of the sky. There is not a shadow on the swinging water of the Sound, save the dancing reflection of the *Anna's* sail. There is only clearness in the air, and the wind comes up between the green shores with freshening force.

"Captain," says the young woman from Baltimore, the young

woman with a soft voice and the slightest Southern accent, "is a squall coming?"

The Captain, without the quiver of a muscle, with no gleam in his watery eye, with no play around the corner of his mouth, looks up at his peak, glances down the Sound, off to the east, up to the peak again, and then takes a tighter hold on his tiller. For a moment he is thoughtful, and then he breaks the trying silence.

"Yes, Miss," he says, in his fearfully long drawl, "there is."

"Oh!" cries the Baltimore girl, "I'm so glad. From which direction is it coming?"

The Captain looks up and studies the top of his mast.

"It's coming," he says, with agonizing deliberation, "from my house. My baby ain't missed a chance to squall in three months!"

Then the Baltimore girl gives a little laugh, a pretty enough laugh to win any man's approval, and says: "Captain, what a fine sailor you are, to be sure!"

"I was raised on the water," says the Captain solemnly.

"That is a handsome badge you have, Captain," says the young woman from Philadelphia. "May I look at it?"

The Captain gives a startled glance, unpins the clasp slowly, hands over his fire department uniform in a pained, doubtful way, and anxiously watches her turn it over in her hand.

"It's handsome," she says.

"It's pretty likely," he answers, with pardonable pride.

"And do you go to fires?"

"Always when I'm ashore."

"Captain," with the most marked admiration for his greatness, "did you ever put out a fire?"

"No-o-o," with his magnificent drawl.

"Why?"

"Always git there too late."

Then comes a long pause, in which the uniform is returned to the member of the fire department.

"And I never started a fire either," says the Captain after a silence on his part for five minutes.

"How is that, Captain?"

"I mean never since I was married," he replies. "She—my wife—does that," and a faint smile cracks his dry cheeks.

The wind is strong enough now to make the boat leap like a racehorse. She occasionally takes a dive and throws a bucketful of water on the deck. Every one is getting wet. The young woman from New-York gets fairly drenched over the shoulders and head. Perhaps it is because she has pretty hair; perhaps it is because no woman likes to have her hair soaked in salt water; but, however that may be, she unfastens her hair and it tumbles about her shoulders, a mass of dark brown, with threads of it blown across her cheek and throat and drops glistening where the water in the dark curls is struck by the slanting sun.

"How do I look, Captain," she asks, putting her elbows on her knees and laying a hand on each cheek so that she can lean forward and look into his face with dark, flashing and tantalizing eyes.

"Look like the gypsies that camps in the woods back of our house," he says, carefully measuring his words.

"They're pretty, aren't they?" asks the "smart young man" from nowhere.

"Well," answers the captain-fireman cautiously, "they're wild, you know."

Then the young woman thinks that her hair is dry and puts it up again.

"What do you think of it now, Captain?" she asks.

No answer.

"What do you think of my hair now, Captain?" she repeats.

The Captain looks up and glances at his host.

"You done pretty well," he says.

"You like it then?"

"Oh, ye-e-s, I like it. I ain't h-a-a-rd to please."

The Baltimore girl thinks she would like to fish and asks the Captain with her most fascinating accent just touched with her Southern softness, if she may.

"Yes," says the son of the sea, "take that boat-hook and that piece of string. Then put a bent pin on the string and fish."

"What do you think I'll catch?" she says, flashing a bewildering smile on him.

"Well," he answers in a low voice, but with ineffable scorn, "you might catch some of those young men. Ain't any of 'em heavy enough to break your line."

The *Anna* is in the harbor now and every one is getting ready to go ashore in the small boats.

"Good-by, Captain," says the Philadelphia girl, "I hope we can go out again to-morrow."

The party is in the small boats and half way to shore, so that in the twilight on his craft, as he moves about the deck, the Captain looks like a phantom sailor. Then he places his hand to his mouth and halloos with his comfortable drawl.

"Oh, Miss," he cries out. His voice coming across the now still air as the oars strike the smooth waters of the harbor is pleasing in its tones and fulness. "Oh, Miss, there'll be two squalls to-morrow, one up to the house, one out on the Sound," and his chuckle, which comes floating after the echo of his words, smacks of the sea and its freshness.

No. 4   THE RELUCTANT VOYAGERS

CHAPTER I

Two men sat by the sea waves.

"Well, I know I'm not handsome," said one, gloomily. He was poking holes in the sand with a discontented cane.

The companion was watching the waves play. He seemed over-come with perspiring discomfort as a man who is resolved to set another man right.

Suddenly, his mouth turned into a straight line. "To be sure you are not," he cried vehemently. "You look like thunder. I do not desire to be unpleasant, but I must assure you that your freckled skin continually reminds spectators of white wall paper with gilt roses on it! The top of your head looks like a little wooden plate! And your figure—heavens!"

For a time they were silent. They stared at the waves that purred near their feet like sleepy sea-kittens.

Finally the first man spoke.

"Well," said he, defiantly, "what of it?"

"What of it," exploded the other. "Why, it means that you'd look like blazes in a bathing-suit."

They were again silent. The freckled man seemed ashamed. His tall companion glowered at the scenery.

"I am decided," said the freckled man suddenly. He got boldly up from the sand and strode away. The tall man followed, walking sarcastically and glaring down at the round, resolute figure before him.

A bath-clerk was looking at the world with superior eyes through a hole in a board. To him the freckled man made application, waving his hands over his person in illustration of a snug fit. The bath-clerk thought profoundly. Eventually, he handed out a blue bundle with an air of having phenomenally solved the freckled man's dimensions.

The latter resumed his resolute stride.

"See here," said the tall man, following him, "I bet you've got a regular toga, you know. That fellow couldn't tell——"

"Yes, he could," interrupted the freckled man, "I saw correct mathematics in his eyes."

"Well, supposin' he has missed your size. Supposin'——"

"Tom," again interrupted the other, "produce your proud clothes and we'll go in."

The tall man swore bitterly. He went to one of a row of little wooden boxes and shut himself in it. His companion repaired to a similar box.

At first he felt like an opulent monk in a too-small cell and he turned round two or three times to see if he could. He arrived, finally, into his bathing-dress. Immediately he dropped gasping upon a three-cornered bench. The suit fell in folds about his reclining form. There was silence, save for the caressing calls of the waves without.

Then he heard two shoes drop on the floor in one of the little coops. He began to clamor at the boards like a penitent at an unforgiving door.

"Tom," called he, "Tom——"

A voice of wrath, muffled by cloth, came through the walls. "You go t' blazes."

The freckled man began to groan, taking the occupants of the entire row of coops into his confidence.

"Stop your noise," angrily cried the tall man from his hidden den. "You rented the bathing-suit, didn't you? Then——"

"It ain't a bathing-suit," shouted the freckled man at the boards. "It's an auditorium, a ballroom or something. It ain't a bathing-suit."

The tall man came out of his box. His suit looked like blue skin. He walked with grandeur down the alley between the rows of coops. Stopping in front of his friend's door, he rapped on it with passionate knuckles.

"Come out of there, y' ol' fool," said he, in an enraged whisper. "It's only your accursed vanity. Wear it anyhow. What difference does it make? I never saw such a vain ol' idiot!"

As he was storming the door opened and his friend confronted him. The tall man's legs gave way and he fell against the opposite door.

The freckled man regarded him sternly.

"You're an ass," he said.

His back curved in scorn. He walked majestically down the alley. There was pride in the way his chubby bare feet patted the boards. The tall man followed, weakly, his eyes riveted upon the figure ahead.

As a disguise the freckled man had adopted the stomach of importance. He moved with an air of some sort of procession, across a board walk, down some steps and out upon the sand.

There was a pug dog and three old women on a bench, a man and a maid with a book and a parasol, a sea-gull drifting high in the wind, and a distant, tremendous meeting of sea and sky. Down on the wet sand stood a girl being wooed by the breakers.

The freckled man moved with stately tread along the beach. The tall man, numb with amazement, came in the rear. They neared the girl.

Suddenly the tall man was seized with convulsions. He laughed, and the girl turned her head.

She perceived the freckled man in the bathing-suit. An expression of wonderment overspread her charming face. It changed in a moment to a pearly smile.

This smile seemed to smite the freckled man. He obviously tried to swell and fit his suit. Then he turned a shriveling glance upon his companion and fled up the beach. The tall man ran after him, pursuing with mocking cries that tingled his flesh like stings of insects. He seemed to be trying to lead the way out of the world. But at last he stopped and faced about.

"Tom Sharp," said he between his clenched teeth, "you are an unutterable wretch! I could grind your bones under my heel."

The tall man was in a trance with glazed eyes fixed on the bathing-dress. He seemed to be murmuring: "Oh, good Lord! Oh, good Lord! I never saw such a suit! I never saw such a suit!"

The freckled man made the gesture of an assassin.

"Tom Sharp, you——"

The other was still murmuring. "Oh, good Lord! I never saw such a suit! I never——"

The freckled man ran down into the sea.

Chapter II

The cool swirling waters took his temper from him, and it became a thing that is lost in the ocean. The tall man floundered in and the two forgot and rollicked in the waves.

The freckled man, in endeavoring to escape from mankind, had left all save a solitary fisherman under a large hat, and three boys in bathing-dress, laughing and splashing upon a raft made of old spars.

The two men swam softly over the ground swells.

The three boys dived from their raft and turned their jolly faces shoreward. It twisted slowly around and around and began to move seaward on some unknown voyage. The freckled man laid his face to the water and swam toward the raft with a practiced stroke. The tall man followed, his bended arm appearing and disappearing with the precision of machinery.

The craft crept away, slowly and warily, as if luring. The little wooden plate on the freckled man's head looked at the shore like a round, brown eye, but his gaze was fixed on the raft that slyly appeared to be waiting. The tall man used the little wooden plate as a beacon.

At length the freckled man reached the raft and climbed

aboard. He lay down on his back and puffed. His bathing-dress spread about him like a dead balloon. The tall man came, snorted, shook his tangled locks and lay down by the side of his companion.

They were over-come with a delicious drowsiness. The planks of the raft seemed to fit their tired limbs. They gazed dreamily up into the vast sky of summer.

"This is great," said the tall man. His companion grunted blissfully.

Gentle hands from the sea rocked their craft and lulled them to peace. Lapping waves sang little rippling sea-songs about them. The two men issued contented groans.

"Tom," said the freckled man.

"What?" said the other.

"This is great."

They lay and thought.

A fish-hawk, soaring, suddenly turned and darted at the waves. The tall man indolently twisted his head and watched the bird plunge its claws into the water. It heavily arose with a silver gleaming fish.

"That bird has got his feet wet again. It's a shame," murmured the tall man sleepily. "He must suffer from an endless cold in the head. He should wear rubber boots. They'd look great, too. If I was him, I'd—Great Scott!"

He had partly arisen and was looking at the shore.

He began to scream. "Ted! Ted! Ted! Look!"

"What's matter?" dreamily spoke the freckled man. "You remind me of when I put the birdshot in your leg." He giggled softly.

The agitated tall man made a gesture of supreme eloquence. His companion up-reared and turned a startled gaze shoreward.

"Lord," he roared, as if stabbed.

The land was a long, brown streak with a rim of green, in which sparkled the tin roofs of huge hotels. The hands from the sea had pushed them away. The two men sprang erect and did a little dance of perturbation.

"What shall we do? What shall we do?" moaned the freckled man, wriggling fantastically in his dead balloon.

The changing shore seemed to fascinate the tall man and for a time he did not speak.

Suddenly he concluded his minuet of horror. He wheeled about and faced the freckled man. He elaborately folded his arms.

"So," he said, in slow, formidable tones. "So! This all comes from your accursed vanity, your bathing-suit, your idiocy! You have murdered your best friend."

He turned away. His companion reeled as if stricken by an unexpected arm.

He stretched out his hands. "Tom, Tom," wailed he, beseeching, "don't be such a fool."

The broad back of his friend was occupied by a contemptuous sneer.

Three ships fell off the horizon. Landward, the hues were blending. The whistle of a locomotive sounded from an infinite distance as if tooting in heaven.

"Tom! Tom! My dear boy," quavered the freckled man, "don't speak that way to me."

"Oh, no, of course not," said the other, still facing away and throwing the words fiercely over his shoulder. "You suppose I am going to accept all this calmly, don't you? Not make the slightest objection? Make no protest at all, hey?"

"Well, I—I——" began the freckled man.

The tall man's wrath suddenly exploded. "You've abducted me! That's the whole amount of it! You've abducted me!"

"I ain't," protested the freckled man. "You must think I'm a fool."

The tall man swore, and sitting down, dangled his legs angrily in the water. Natural law compelled his companion to occupy the other end of the raft.

Over the waters, little shoals of fish spluttered, raising tiny tempests. Languid jelly-fish floated near, tremulously waving a thousand legs. A row of porpoises trundled along like a procession of cogwheels. The sky became greyed save where over the land, sunset colors were assembling.

The two voyagers, back to back and at either end of the raft, quarreled at length.

"What did you want to foller me for?" demanded the freckled man in a voice of indignation.

"If your figure hadn't been so like a bottle, we wouldn't be here," replied the tall man.

Chapter III

The fires in the west blazed away and solemnity spread over the sea. Electric lights began to blink like eyes. Night menaced the voyagers with a dangerous darkness, and fear came to bind their souls together. They huddled fraternally in the middle of the raft.

"I feel like a molecule," said the freckled man in subdued tones.

"I'd give two dollars for a cigar," muttered the tall man.

A V-shaped flock of ducks flew toward Barnegat, between the voyagers and a remnant of yellow sky. Shadows and winds came from the vanished eastern horizon.

"I think I hear voices," said the freckled man.

"That Dollie Ramsdell was an awfully nice girl," said the tall man.

When the coldness of the sea night came to them, the freckled man found he could by a peculiar movement of his legs and arms encase himself in his bathing-dress. The tall man was compelled to whistle and shiver. As night settled finally over the sea, red and green lights began to dot the blackness. There were mysterious shadows between the waves.

"I see things comin'," murmured the freckled man.

"I wish I hadn't ordered that new dress suit for the hop to-morrow night," said the tall man reflectively.

The sea became uneasy and heaved painfully, like a lost bosom, when little forgotten heart-bells try to chime with a pure sound. The voyagers cringed at magnified foam on distant wave crests. A moon came and looked at them.

"Somebody's here," whispered the freckled man.

"I wish I had an almanac," remarked the tall man, regarding the moon.

Presently they fell to staring at the red and green lights that twinkled about them.

"Providence will not leave us," asserted the freckled man.

"Oh, we'll be picked up shortly. I owe money," said the tall man.

He began to thrum on an imaginary banjo.

"I have heard," said he, suddenly, "that captains with healthy ships beneath their feet will never turn back after having once started on a voyage. In that case we will be rescued by some ship bound for the golden seas of the south. Then, you'll be up to some of your confounded devilment and we'll get put off. They'll maroon us! That's what they'll do! They'll maroon us! On an island with palm trees and sun-kissed maidens and all that. Sun-kissed maidens, eh? Great! They'd——"

He suddenly ceased and turned to stone. At a distance a great, green eye was contemplating the sea-wanderers.

They stood up and did another dance. As they watched the eye grew larger.

Directly the form of a phantom-like ship came into view. About the great, green eye there bobbed small yellow dots. The wanderers could hear a far-away creaking of unseen tackle and flapping of shadowy sails. There came the melody of the waters as the ship's prow thrusted its way.

The tall man delivered an oration.

"Ha!" he exclaimed, "here come our rescuers! The brave fellows! How I long to take the manly captain by the hand! You will soon see a white boat with a star on its bow drop from the side of yon ship. Kind sailors in blue and white will help us into the boat and conduct our wasted frames to the quarter-deck, where the handsome, bearded captain with gold bands all around, will welcome us. Then in the hard-oak cabin, while the wine gurgles and the Havanas glow, we'll tell our tale of peril and privation."

The ship came on like a black hurrying animal with froth-filled maw. The two wanderers stood up and clasped hands. Then they howled out a wild duet that rang over the wastes of sea.

The cries seemed to strike the ship.

Men with boots on yelled and ran about the deck. They picked up heavy articles and threw them down. They yelled more. After hideous creakings and flappings, the vessel stood still.

In the meantime the wanderers had been chanting their song for help. Out in the blackness they beckoned to the ship and coaxed.

A voice came to them.

"Hello," it said.

They puffed out their cheeks and began to shout. "Hello! Hello! Hello!"

"Wot do yeh want?" said the voice.

The two wanderers gazed at each other, and sat suddenly down on the raft. Some pall came sweeping over the sky and quenched their stars.

But almost immediately the tall man got up and bawled miscellaneous information. He stamped his foot, and, frowning into the night, swore threateningly.

The vessel seemed fearful of these moaning voices that called from a hidden cavern of the water. And now one voice was filled with a menace. A number of men with enormous limbs that threw vast shadows over the sea as the lanterns flickered, held a debate and made gestures.

Off in the darkness the tall man began to clamor like a mob. The freckled man sat in astounded silence, with his legs weak.

After a time one of the men of enormous limbs seized a rope that was tugging at the stern and drew a small boat from the shadows. Three giants clambered in and rowed cautiously toward the raft. Silver water flashed in the gloom as the oars dipped.

About fifty feet from the raft the boat stopped. "Who er you?" asked a voice.

The tall man braced himself and explained. He drew vivid pictures, his twirling fingers illustrating like live brushes.

"Oh," said the three giants.

The voyagers deserted the raft. They looked back, feeling in their hearts a mite of tenderness for the wet planks. Later,

they wriggled up the side of the vessel and climbed over a railing.

On deck they met a man.

He held a lantern to their faces. "Got any chewin' tew-
bacca?" he inquired.

"No," said the tall man, "we ain't."

The man had a bronzed face and a solitary whisker. Peculiar
lines about his mouth were shaped into an eternal smile of
derision. His feet were bare and clung handily to crevices.
Fearful trousers were supported by a piece of suspender that
went up the wrong side of his chest and came down the right
side of his back, dividing him into triangles.

"Ezekiel P. Sanford, capt'in schooner *Mary Jones*, of
Nyack, N.Y., boun' from Little Egg Harbor, N.J., to Athens,
N.Y., genelmen," he said.

"Ah," said the tall man, "delighted, I'm sure."

There were a few moments of silence. The giants were
hovering in the gloom and staring.

Suddenly, astonishment exploded the captain.

"Wot th' devil——" he shouted, "wot th' devil yeh got on?"

"Bathing-suits," said the tall man. He made another statement.

CHAPTER IV

The schooner went on. The two voyagers sat down and
watched. After a time they began to shiver. The soft blackness of the summer night passed away, and grey mists writhed
over the sea. Soon lights of early dawn went charging across
the sky and the twin beacons on the Highlands grew dim and
sparkled faintly, as if a monster were dying. The dawn penetrated the marrow of the two men in bathing-dress.

The captain used to pause opposite them, hitch one hand in
his suspender and laugh.

"Well, I be dog-hanged," he frequently said.

The tall man grew furious. He snarled in a mad undertone
to his companion. "This rescue ain't right. If I had known——"

He suddenly paused, transfixed by the captain's suspender.
"It's goin' to break," cried he, in an ecstatic whisper. His eyes

grew large with excitement as he watched the captain laugh. "It'll break in a minute, sure."

But the commander of the schooner recovered and invited them to drink and eat. They followed him along the deck, and fell down a square, black hole into the cabin.

It was a little den, with walls of a vanished whiteness. A lamp shed an orange light. In a sort of recess two little beds were hiding. A wooden table, immovable, as if the craft had been builded around it, sat in the middle of the floor. Overhead the square hole was studded with a dozen stars. A footworn ladder led to the heavens.

The captain produced ponderous crackers and some cold broiled ham. Then he vanished in the firmament like a fantastic comet.

The freckled man sat quite contentedly like a stout squaw in a blanket. The tall man walked about the cabin and sniffed. He was angered at the crudeness of the rescue, and his shrinking clothes made him feel too large. He contemplated his unhappy state.

Suddenly he broke out. "I won't stand this, I tell you! Heavens and earth, look at the—say, what in blazes did you want to get me in this thing for, anyhow? You're a fine old duffer, you are! Look at that ham!"

The freckled man grunted. He seemed somewhat blissful. He was seated upon the bench, comfortably enwrapped in his bathing-dress.

The tall man stormed about the cabin.

"This is an outrage! I'll see the captain! I'll tell him what I think of——"

He was interrupted by a pair of legs that appeared among the stars. The captain came down the ladder. He brought a coffee pot from the sky.

The tall man bristled forward. He was going to denounce everything.

The captain was intent upon the coffee pot, balancing it carefully and leaving his unguided feet to find the steps of the ladder.

But the wrath of the tall man faded. He twirled his fingers in excitement and renewed his ecstatic whisperings to the freckled man.

"It's goin' to break! Look, quick, look! It'll break in a minute!"

He was transfixed with interest, forgetting his wrongs in staring at the perilous passage.

But the captain arrived on the floor with triumphant suspender.

"Well," said he, "after yeh have et, maybe ye'd like t' sleep some! If so, yeh can sleep on them beds."

The tall man made no reply, save in a strained undertone. "It'll break in about a minute! Look, Ted, look, quick!"

The freckled man glanced in at the little beds on which were heaped boots and oilskins. He made a courteous gesture.

"My dear sir, we could not think of depriving you of your beds. No, indeed. Just a couple of blankets, if you have them, and we'll sleep very comfortably on these benches."

The captain protested, politely twisting his back and bobbing his head. The suspender tugged and creaked. The tall man partially suppressed a cry and took a step forward.

The freckled man was sleepily insistent, and shortly the captain gave over his deprecatory contortions. He fetched a pink quilt with yellow dots on it to the freckled man, and a black one with red roses on it to the tall man.

Again he vanished in the firmament. The tall man gazed until the last remnant of trousers disappeared from the sky. Then he wrapped himself up in his quilt and lay down. The freckled man was puffing contentedly, swathed like an infant. The yellow polka dots rose and fell on the vast pink of his chest.

The wanderers slept. In the quiet could be heard the groanings of timbers as the sea seemed to crunch them together. The lapping of water along the vessel's side sounded like gaspings. A hundred spirits of the wind had got their wings entangled in the rigging and in soft voices were pleading to be loosened.

The freckled man was awakened by a foreign noise. He opened his eyes and saw his companion standing by his couch.

His comrade's face was wan with suffering. His eyes glowed in the darkness. He raised his arms, spreading them out like a clergyman at a grave. He groaned deep in his chest.

"Good Lord!" yelled the freckled man, starting up. "Tom, Tom, what is th' matter?"

The tall man spoke in a fearful voice. "To New York," he said, "to New York in our bathing-suits."

The freckled man sank back. The shadows of the cabin threw mysteries about the figure of the tall man, arrayed like some ancient and potent astrologer in the black quilt with the red roses on it.

Chapter V

Directly the tall man went and lay down and began to groan.

The freckled man felt the miseries of the world upon him. He grew angry at the tall man for awakening him. They quarreled.

"Well," said the tall man, finally, "we're in a fix."

"I know that," said the other, sharply.

They regarded the ceiling in silence.

"What in thunder are we going to do?" demanded the tall man, after a time. His companion was still silent. "Say," repeated he, angrily, "what in thunder are we going to do?"

"I'm sure I don't know," said the freckled man, in a dismal voice.

"Well, think of something," roared the other. "Think of something, you old fool. You don't want to make any more idiots of yourself, do you?"

"I ain't made an idiot of myself."

"Well, think. Know anybody in the city?"

"I know a fellow up in Harlem," said the freckled man.

"You know a fellow up in Harlem," howled the tall man. "Up in Harlem! How the dickens are we to—say, you're crazy!"

"Well, we can take a cab," cried the other, waxing indignant.

The tall man grew suddenly calm. "Do you know any one else?" he asked, measuredly.

"I know another fellow somewhere on Park Place."

"Somewhere on Park Place," repeated the tall man in an unnatural manner. "Somewhere on Park Place." With an air of sublime resignation he turned his face to the wall.

The freckled man sat erect and frowned in the direction of his companion. "Well, now, I suppose you are going to sulk.

You make me ill! It's the best we can do, ain't it? Hire a cab and go look that fellow up on Park—— What's that? What's that? You can't afford it? What nonsense! You are getting—— Oh! Well, maybe we can beg some clothes of the captain. Eh? Did I see 'im? Certainly, I saw 'im. Yes, it is improbable that a man who wears trousers like that can have clothes to lend. No, I won't wear oilskins and a sou'wester. To Athens? Of course not! I don't know where it is. Do you? I thought not! With all your grumbling about other people, you never know anything important yourself. What? Broadway? I'll be hanged first. We can't get off at Harlem, man alive. There are no cabs in Harlem. I don't think we can bribe a sailor to take us ashore and bring a cab to the dock, for the very simple reason that we have nothing to bribe him with. What? No, of course not. See here, Tom Sharp, don't you swear at me like that. I won't have it. What's that? I ain't, either. I ain't! What? I am not! It's no such thing! I ain't! I've got more than you have, anyway. Well, you ain't doing anything so very brilliant yourself—just lyin' there and cussin'." At length the tall man feigned to prodigiously snore. The freckled man thought with such vigor that he fell asleep.

After a time he dreamed that he was in a forest where bass drums grew on the trees. There came a strong wind that banged the fruit about like empty pods. A frightful din was in his ears.

He awoke to find the captain of the schooner standing over him.

"We're at New York, now," said the captain, raising his voice above the thumping and banging that was being done on deck, "an' I s'pose you fellers wanta go ashore."

He chuckled in an exasperating manner. "Jes' sing out when yeh wanta go," he added, leering at the freckled man.

The tall man awoke, came over and grasped the captain by the throat.

"If you laugh again I'll kill you," he said.

The captain gurgled and waved his legs and arms.

"In the first place," the tall man continued, "you rescued us in a deucedly shabby manner. It makes me ill to think of it. I've a mind to mop you 'round just for that. In the second place, your vessel is bound for Athens, N.Y., and there's no sense in it. Now, will you or will you not turn this ship about and take us back where our clothes are? or to Philadelphia, where we belong?"

He furiously shook the captain. Then he eased his grip and awaited a reply.

"I can't," yelled the captain, "I can't. This here vessel don't belong to me. I've got to——"

"Well, then," interrupted the tall man, "can you lend us some clothes?"

"Hain't got 'em." The captain backed away. His face was red and his eyes were glaring.

"Well, then," said the tall man, advancing, "can you lend us some money?"

"Hain't got none," replied the captain, promptly. Something over-came him and he laughed.

"Thunderation," roared the tall man. He seized the captain, who began to have wriggling contortions. The tall man kneaded him as if he were biscuits. "You infernal scoundrel," he bellowed, "this whole affair is some wretched plot. And you are in it. I am about to kill you."

The solitary whisker of the captain did acrobatics like a strange demon upon his chin. His eyes stood perilously from his head. The suspender wheezed and tugged like the tackle of a sail.

Suddenly the tall man released his hold. Great expectancy sat upon his features. "It's going to break," he cried, rubbing his hands.

But the captain howled and vanished in the sky.

The freckled man then came forward. He appeared filled with sarcasm.

"So!" said he. "So! You've settled the matter. The captain is the only man in the world who can help us, and I daresay he'll do anything he can now."

"That's all right," said the tall man. "If you don't like the way I run things, you shouldn't have come on this trip at all."

They had another quarrel.

At the end of it they went on deck. The captain stood at the stern addressing the bow with opprobrious language. When he perceived the voyagers he began to fling his fists about in the air.

"I'm goin' to put yeh off," he yelled. The wanderers stared at each other.

"Hum," said the tall man.

The freckled man looked at his companion. "He's going to put us off, you see," he said complacently.

The tall man began to walk about and move his shoulders. "I'd like to see you do it," he said defiantly.

The captain tugged at a rope. A boat came at his bidding. "I'd like to see you do it," the tall man repeated continually. An imperturbable man in rubber boots climbed down into the boat and seized the oars. The captain motioned downward. His whisker had a triumphant appearance.

The two wanderers looked at the boat. "I guess we'll have to get in," murmured the freckled man.

The tall man was standing like a granite column. "I won't!" said he. "I won't! I don't care what you do, but I won't."

"Well, but——" expostulated the other. They held a furious debate.

In the meantime the captain was darting about making sinister gestures, but the back of the tall man held him at bay. The crew, much depleted by the departure of the imperturbable man into the boat, looked on from the bow.

"You're a fool," the freckled man concluded his argument.

"So?" inquired the tall man, highly exasperated.

"So? Well, if you think you're so bright, we'll go in the boat and then you'll see."

He climbed down into the craft and seated himself in an ominous manner at the stern.

"You'll see," he said to his companion, as the latter floundered heavily down. "You'll see!"

The man in rubber boots calmly rowed the boat toward the dock. As they went the captain leaned over a railing and laughed. The freckled man was seated very victoriously.

"Well, wasn't this the right thing after all?" he inquired in a pleasant voice. The tall man made no reply.

Chapter VI

As they neared the dock something seemed suddenly to occur to the freckled man.

"Great heavens," he murmured. He stared at the approaching shore.

"My, what a plight, Tommie," he quavered.

"Do you think so?" spoke up the tall man. "Why, I really thought you liked it." He laughed in a hard voice. "Lord, what a figure you'll cut."

This laugh jarred the freckled man's soul. He became mad.

"Thunderation, turn the boat around," he roared. "Turn 'er round, quick. Man alive, we can't—turn 'er round, d'ye hear."

The tall man in the stern gazed at his companion with glowing eyes.

"Certainly not," he said. "We're going on. You insisted upon it." He began to prod his companion with words.

The freckled man stood up and waved his arms.

"Sit down," said the tall man. "You'll tip the boat over."

The other began to shout.

"Sit down," said the tall man again.

Words bubbled from the freckled man's mouth. There was a little torrent of sentences that almost choked him. And he protested passionately with his hands.

But the boat went on to the shadow of the docks. The tall man was intent upon balancing it as it rocked dangerously during his comrade's oration.

"Sit down," he continually repeated.

"I won't," raged the freckled man. "I won't do anything." The boat wabbled with these words.

"Say," he continued, addressing the oarsman, "just turn this boat round, will you. Where in thunder are you taking us to, anyhow?"

The oarsman looked at the sky and thought. Finally he spoke. "I'm doin' what th' cap'n sed."

"Well, what the blazes do I care what th' cap'n sed?" demanded the freckled man. He took a violent step. "You just turn this boat round or——"

The small craft reeled. Over one side water came flashing in. The freckled man cried out in fear and gave a great jump to the other side. The tall man roared orders, and the oarsman made efforts. The boat acted for a moment like an animal on a slackened wire. Then it upset.

"Sit down," said the tall man in a final roar as he was plunged into the water. The oarsman dropped his oars to grapple with the gunwale. He went down saying unknown words. The freckled man's explanation or apology was strangled by the water.

Two or three tugs let off whistles of astonishment and continued on their paths. A man dozing on a dock aroused and began to caper. The passengers of a ferryboat all ran to the near railing.

A miraculous person in a small boat was bobbing on the waves near the piers. He sculled hastily toward the scene. It was a swirl of waters in the midst of which the dark bottom of the boat appeared, whale-like.

Two heads suddenly came up.

"839," said the freckled man, chokingly. "That's it! 839."

"What is?" said the tall man.

"That's the number of that feller on Park Place. I just remembered."

"You're the bloomingest——" the tall man said.

"It wasn't my fault," interrupted his companion. "If you hadn't——" He tried to gesticulate, but one hand held to the keel of the boat and the other was supporting the form of their oarsman. The latter had fought a battle with his immense rubber boots and had been conquered.

The rescuer in the other small boat came fiercely. As his craft glided up he reached out and grasped the tall man by the collar and dragged him into the boat, interrupting what was, under the circumstances, a very brilliant flow of rhetoric directed at the freckled man. The oarsman of the wrecked craft was taken tenderly over the gunwale and laid in the bottom of the boat. Puffing and blowing, the freckled man climbed in.

"You'll upset this one before we can get ashore," the other voyager remarked.

As they turned toward the land they saw that the nearest

dock was lined with people. The freckled man gave a little moan.

But the staring eyes of the crowd were fixed on the limp form of the man in rubber boots. A hundred hands reached down to help lift the body up. On the dock some men grabbed it and began to beat it and roll it. A policeman tossed the spectators about. Each individual in the heaving crowd sought to fasten his eyes on the blue-tinted face of the man in rubber boots. They surged to and fro while the policeman beat them indiscriminately.

The wanderers came modestly up the dock and gazed shrinkingly at the throng. They stood for a moment, holding their breath to see the first finger of amazement leveled at them.

But the crowd bended and surged in absorbing anxiety to view the man in rubber boots, whose face fascinated them. The sea-wanderers were as though they were not there.

They stood without the jam and whispered hurriedly.

"839," said the freckled man.

"All right," said the tall man.

Under the pummeling hands the oarsman showed signs of life. The voyagers watched him make a protesting kick at the legs of the crowd, the while uttering angry groans.

"He's better," said the tall man, softly; "let's make off."

Together, they stole noiselessly up the dock. Directly in front of it they found a row of six cabs.

The drivers, on top, were filled with a mighty curiosity. They had driven hurriedly from the adjacent ferry-house when they had seen the first running sign of an accident. They were straining on their toes and gazing at the tossing backs of the men in the crowd.

The wanderers made a little detour and then went rapidly toward a cab. They stopped in front of it and looked up.

"Driver," called the tall man, softly.

The man was intent.

"Driver," breathed the freckled man. They stood for a moment and gazed imploringly.

The cabman suddenly moved his feet. "By Jimmy, I bet he's a goner," he said in an ecstacy, and he again relapsed into a statue.

The freckled man groaned and wrung his hands. The tall man climbed into the cab.

"Come in here," he said to his companion. The freckled man climbed in and the tall man reached over and pulled the door shut. Then he put his head out of the window.

"Driver," he roared sternly, "839 Park Place—and quick."

The cabman looked down and met the eye of the tall man. "Eh?—Oh—839? Park Place? Yessir." He reluctantly gave his horse a clump on the back. As the conveyance rattled off the wanderers huddled back among the dingy cushions and heaved great breaths of relief.

"Well, it's all over," said the freckled man, finally. "We're about out of it. And quicker than I expected. Much quicker. It looked to me sometimes that we were doomed. I am thankful to find it not so. I am rejoiced. And I hope and trust that you—well, I don't wish to—perhaps it is not the proper time to—that is, I don't wish to intrude a moral at an inopportune moment, but, my dear, dear fellow, I think the time is ripe to point out to you that your obstinacy, your selfishness, your villainous temper and your various other faults can make it just as unpleasant for your own self, my dear boy, as they frequently do for other people. You can see what you brought us to, and I most sincerely hope, my dear, dear fellow, that I shall soon see those signs in you which shall lead me to believe that you have become a wiser man."

No. 5 WHY DID THE YOUNG CLERK SWEAR? OR, THE UNSATISFACTORY FRENCH

ALL was silent in the little gents' furnishing store. A lonely clerk with a blond mustache and a red necktie raised a languid hand to his brow and brushed back a dangling lock. He yawned and gazed gloomily at the blurred panes of the windows.

Without, the wind and rain came swirling round the brick buildings and went sweeping over the streets. A horse-car rumbled stolidly by. In the mud on the pavements, a few pedestrians struggled with excited umbrellas.

"The deuce!" remarked the clerk. "I'd give ten dollars if somebody would come in and buy something, if 'twere only cotton socks."

He awaited amid the shadows of the gray afternoon. No customers came. He heaved a long sigh and sat down on a high stool. From beneath a stack of unlaundried shirts he drew a French novel with a picture on the cover. He yawned again, glanced lazily toward the street, and settled himself as comfortably as the gods would let him upon the high stool.

He opened the book and began to read. Soon it could have been noticed that his blond mustache took on a curl of enthusiasm, and the refractory locks on his brow showed symptoms of soft agitation.

"Silvere did not see the young girl for some days," read the clerk. "He was miserable. He seemed always to inhale that subtle perfume from her hair. At night he saw her eyes in the stars.

"His dreams were troubled. He watched the house. Eloise did not appear. One day he met Vibert. Vibert wore a black frock-coat. There were wine stains on the right breast. His collar was soiled. He had not shaved.

"Silvere burst into tears. 'I love her! I love her! I shall die!' Vibert laughed scornfully. His necktie was second-hand. Idiotic, this boy in love. Fool! Simpleton! But at last he pitied him. 'She goes to the music teacher's every morning, silly.' Silvere embraced him.

"The next day Silvere waited on the street corner. A vendor was selling chestnuts. Two gamins were fighting in an alley. A woman was scrubbing some steps. This great Paris throbbed with life.

"Eloise came. She did not perceive Silvere. She passed with a happy smile on her face. She looked fresh, fair, innocent. Silvere felt himself swooning. 'Ah, my God!'

"She crossed the street. The young man received a shock that sent the warm blood to his brain. It had been raining. There was mud. With one slender hand Eloise lifted her skirts. Silvere, leaning forward, saw her——"

A young man in a wet mackintosh came into the little gents' furnishing store.

"Ah, beg pardon," said he to the clerk, "but, do you have an agency for a steam laundry here? I have been patronizing a Chinaman down th' avenue for some time, but he—what? No? You have none here? Well, why don't you start one, anyhow? It'd be a good thing in this neighborhood. I live just 'round the corner, and it'd be a great thing for me. I know lots of people who would—what? Oh, you don't? Oh!"

As the young man in the wet mackintosh retreated, the clerk with a blond mustache made a hungry grab at the novel. He continued to read: "handkerchief fall in a puddle. Silvere sprang forward. He picked up the handkerchief. Their eyes met. As he returned the handkerchief, their hands touched. The young girl smiled. Silvere was in ecstasies. 'Ah, my God!'

"A baker opposite was quarreling over two sous with an old woman. A gray-haired veteran with a medal upon his breast and a butcher's boy were watching a dog-fight. The smell of dead animals came from adjacent slaughter-houses. The letters on the sign over the tinsmith's shop on the corner shone redly like great clots of blood. It was hell on roller-skates."

Here the clerk skipped some seventeen chapters descriptive of a number of intricate money transactions, the moles on the neck of a Parisian dressmaker, the process of making brandy, the milk-leg of Silvere's aunt, life in the coal-pits and scenes in the Chamber of Deputies. In these chapters the reputation of the architect of Charlemagne's palace was vindicated, and it was explained why Eloise's grandmother didn't keep her stockings pulled up.

Then he proceeded: "Eloise went to the country. The next day Silvere followed. They met in the fields. The young girl had donned the garb of the peasants. She blushed. She looked fresh, fair, innocent. Silvere felt faint with rapture. 'Ah, my God!'

"She had been running. Out of breath, she sank down in the hay. She held out her hand. 'I am glad to see you.' Silvere was enchanted at this vision. He bended toward her. Suddenly, he burst into tears. 'I love you! I love you! I love you!' he stammered.

"A row of red and white shirts hung on a line some distance away. The third shirt from the left had a button off the neck. A cat on the rear steps of a cottage near the shirts was drinking milk from a platter. The northeast portion of the platter had a crack in it.

" 'Eloise!' Silvere was murmuring, hoarsely. He leaned toward her until his warm breath moved the curls on her neck. 'Eloise!' murmured Jean."

"Young man," said an elderly gentleman with a dripping umbrella to the clerk with a blond mustache, "have you any night-shirts open front and back? Eh? Night-shirts open front and back, I said. D'you hear, eh? *Night-shirts open front and back!* Well, then, why didn't you say so? It would pay you to be a trifle more polite, young man. When you get as old as I am, you will find out that it pays to—what? I didn't see you adding any column of figures. In that case I'm sorry. You have no night-shirts open front and back, eh? Well, good-day."

As the elderly gentleman vanished, the clerk with a blond mustache grasped the novel like some famished animal. He read on: "A peasant stood before the two children. He wrung his hands. 'Have you seen a stray cow?' 'No,' cried the children in the same breath. The peasant wept. He wrung his hands. It was a supreme moment.

" 'She loves me!' cried Silvere to himself, as he changed his clothes for dinner.

"It was evening. The children sat by the fireplace. Eloise wore a gown of clinging white. She looked fresh, fair, innocent. Silvere was in raptures. 'Ah, my God!'

"Old Jean the peasant saw nothing. He was mending harness. The fire crackled in the fireplace. The children loved each other. Through the open door to the kitchen came the sound of old Marie shrilly cursing the geese who wished to enter. In front of the window, two pigs were quarreling over a vegetable. Cattle were lowing in a distant field. A hay-wagon creaked slowly past. Thirty-two chickens were asleep in the branches of a tree. This subtle atmosphere had a mighty effect upon Eloise. It was beating down her self-control. She felt herself going. She was choking.

"The young girl made an effort. She stood up. 'Good-night. I must go.' Silvere took her hand. 'Eloise!' he murmured. Outside, the two pigs were fighting.

"A warm blush overspread the young girl's face. She turned

wet eyes toward her lover. She looked fresh, fair, innocent. Silvere was maddened. 'Ah, my God!'

"Suddenly, the young girl began to tremble. She tried vainly to withdraw her hand. But her knee——"

"I wish to get my husband some shirts," said a shopping-woman with six bundles. The clerk with a blond mustache made a private gesture of despair and rapidly spread a score of differently patterned shirts upon the counter. "He's very particular about his shirts," said the shopping-woman. "Oh, I don't think any of these will do. Don't you keep the Invincible brand? He always wears that kind. He says they fit him better. And he's very particular about his shirts. What? You don't keep them? No? Well, how much do you think they would come at? Haven't the slightest idea? Well, I suppose I must go somewhere else, then. Um—good-day."

The clerk with the blond mustache was about to make further private gestures of despair, when the shopping-woman with six bundles turned and went out. His fingers instantly closed nervously over the book. He drew it from its hiding-place and opened it at the place where he had ceased. His hungry eyes seemed to eat the words upon the page. He continued: "struck cruelly against a chair. It seemed to awaken her. She started. She burst from the young man's arms. Outside, the two pigs were grunting amiably.

"Silvere took his candle. He went toward his room. He was in despair. 'Ah, my God!'

"He met the young girl on the stairs. He took her hand. Tears were raining down his face. 'Eloise!' he murmured.

"The young girl shivered. As Silvere put his arms about her, she faintly resisted. This embrace seemed to sap her life. She wished to die. Her thoughts flew back to the old well and the broken hayrakes at Plassans.

"The young girl looked fresh, fair, innocent. 'Eloise!' murmured Silvere. The children exchanged a long, clinging kiss. It seemed to unite their souls.

"The young girl was swooning. Her head sank on the young man's shoulder. There was nothing in space except these warm kisses on her neck. Silvere enfolded her. 'Ah, my God!'"

"Say, young feller," said a youth with a tilted cigar to the clerk with a blond mustache, "where th'ell is Billie Carcart's joint round here? Know?"

"Next corner," said the clerk, fiercely.

"Oh, th'ell," said the youth, "yehs needn't git gay. See? When a feller asts a civil question yehs needn't git gay. See? Th'ell."

The youth stood and looked aggressive for a moment. Then he went away.

The clerk seemed almost to leap upon the book. His feverish fingers twirled the pages. When he found the place he glued his eyes to it. He read:

"Then, a great flash of lightning illumined the hallway. It threw livid hues over a row of flower-pots in the window-seat. Thunder shook the house to its foundation. From the kitchen arose the voice of old Marie in prayer.

"Eloise screamed. She wrenched herself from the young man's arms. She sprang inside her room. She locked the door. She flung herself face downward on the bed. She burst into tears. She looked fresh, fair, innocent.

"The rain, pattering upon the thatched roof, sounded, in the stillness, like the footsteps of spirits. In the sky toward Paris there shone a crimson light.

"The chickens had all fallen from the tree. They stood, sadly, in a puddle. The two pigs were asleep under the porch.

"Upstairs, in the hallway, Silvere was furious."

The clerk with a blond mustache gave, here, a wild scream of disappointment. He madly hurled the novel with the picture on the cover from him. He stood up and said "Damn!"

No. 6 AT CLANCY'S WAKE

SCENE: *Room in the house of the lamented* CLANCY. *The curtains are pulled down. A perfume of old roses and whiskey hangs in the air. A weeping woman in black is seated at a table in the centre. A group of wide-eyed children are sobbing in a corner. Down the side of the room is a row of mourning friends*

of the family. Through an open door can be seen, half-hid-
den in shadows, the silver and black of a coffin.

WIDOW—Oh, wirra, wirra, wirra!

CHILDREN—B-b boo-hoo-hoo!

FRIENDS (*conversing in low tones*)—Yis, Moike Clancy was a foine mahn.—Sure!—None betther!—No, I don't t'ink so!—Did he?— Sure, in all th' elictions!—He was th' bist in the warrud!—He licked 'im widin an inch of his loife, aisy, an' th' other wan a big shtrappin' buck of a mahn, an' him jest free of th' pneumonia!—Yis, he did!—They carried th' warrud by six hunder!—Yis, he was a foine mahn!—None betther, Gawd sav' 'im.

(*Enter* MR. SLICK, *of the "Daily Blanket," shown in by a maid-servant whose hair has become disarranged through much tear-shedding. He is attired in a suit of gray check, and wears a red rose in his buttonhole.*)

MR. SLICK—Good-afternoon, Mrs. Clancy. This is a sad misfortune for you, isn't it?

WIDOW—Oh, indade, indade, young mahn, me poor heart is bruk!

MR. SLICK—Very sad, Mrs. Clancy. A great misfortune, I'm sure. Now, Mrs. Clancy, I've called to——

WIDOW—Little did I t'ink, young mahn, win they brought poor Moike in, that it was th' lasht.

MR. SLICK (*with conviction*)—True! True! Very true, in-deed! It was a great grief to you, Mrs. Clancy. I've called this morning, Mrs. Clancy, to see if I could get from you a short obituary notice for the *Blanket* if you could——

WIDOW—An' his hid was done up in a rag, an' he was cursin' frightful. A domned Oytalian lit fall th' hod as Moike was walkin' pasht as dacint as you plaze. Win they carried 'im in, him all bloody, an' ravin' tur'ble 'bout Oytalians, me heart was near bruk, but I niver tawt—I niver tawt—I—I niver—— (*Breaks forth into a long, forlorn cry. The children join in, and the chorus echoes wailfully through the rooms.*)

MR. SLICK (*as the yell, in a measure, ceases*)—Yes, indeed, a sad, sad affair. A terrible misfortune! Now, Mrs. Clancy——

WIDOW (*turning suddenly*)—Mary Ann! Where's thot lazy divil of a Mary Ann? (*As the servant appears.*) Mary Ann, bring th' bottle. Give th' gintlemin a dhrink. * * * Here's to Hiven savin' yez, young mahn! (*Drinks.*)

MR. SLICK (*drinks*)—A noble whiskey, Mrs. Clancy. Many thanks. Now, Mrs. Clancy——

WIDOW—Take anodder wan! Take anodder wan! (*Fills his glass.*)

MR. SLICK (*impatiently*)—Yes, certainly, Mrs. Clancy, certainly. (*He drinks.*) Now, could you tell me, Mrs. Clancy, where your late husband was——

WIDOW—Who—Moike? Oh, young mahn, yez can just say thot he was th' foinest mahn livin' an' breathin', an' niver a wan in th' warrud was betther. Oh, but he had th' tindther heart for 'is fambly, he did! Don't I remimber win he clipped little Patsey wid th' bottle, an' didn't he buy th' big rockin'-horse th' minit he got sober? Sure he did. Pass th' bottle, Mary Ann. (*Pours a beer glass about half-full for her guest.*)

MR. SLICK (*taking a seat*)—True, Mr. Clancy was a fine man, Mrs. Clancy—a *very* fine man. Now, I——

WIDOW (*plaintively*)—An' don't yez loike th' rum? Dhrink th' rum, mahn. It was me own Moike's fav'rite bran'. Well I remimber win he fotched it home, an' half th' demijohn gone a'ready, an' him a-cursin' up th' stairs as dhrunk as Gawd plazed. It was a—— Dhrink th' rum, young mahn, dhrink th' rum. If he cud see yez now, Moike Clancy wud git up from 'is——

MR SLICK (*desperately*)—Very well, very well, Mrs. Clancy! Here's your good health! Now, can you tell me, Mrs. Clancy, when was Mr. Clancy born?

WIDOW—Win was he borrun? Sure, divil a bit do I care win he was borrun. He was th' good mahn to me an' his childher, an' Gawd knows I don't care win he was borrun. Mary Ann, pass th' bottle. Wud yez kape th' gintlemin shtarvin' for a dhrink here in Moike Clancy's own house? Gawd save yez!

(*When the bottle appears she pours a huge quantity out for her guest.*)

MR. SLICK—Well, then, Mrs. Clancy, *where* was he born?

WIDOW (*staring*)—In Oirland, mahn, in Oirland! Where

did yez t'ink? (*Then, in sudden wheedling tones*) An' ain't yez goin' to dhrink th' rum? Are yez goin' to shirk th' good whiskey what was th' pride of Moike's loife, an' him gettin' full on it an' breakin' th' furniter t'ree nights a week hand-runnin'? Shame an yez, an' Gawd save yer sowl! Dhrink it oop now, there's a dear, dhrink it oop now, an' say: "Moike Clancy, be all th' powers in th' shky Hiven sind yez rist!"

MR. SLICK (*to himself*)—Holy smoke! (*He drinks, then regards the glass for a long time.*) * * * Well, now, Mrs. Clancy, give me your attention for a moment, please. When did——

WIDOW—An' oh, but he was a power in th' warrud! Divil a mahn cud vote right widout Moike Clancy at 'is elbow. An' in the calkus, sure didn't Mulrooney git th' nominashun jes' by raison of Moike's atthackin' th' opposashun wid th' shtove-poker. Mulrooney got it as aisy as dhirt, wid Moike rowlin' under th' tayble wid th' other candeedate. He was a good cit'zen, was Moike—divil a wan betther.

(MR. SLICK *spends some minutes in collecting his faculties.*)

MR. SLICK (*after he decides that he has them collected*) —Yes, yes, Mrs. Clancy, your husband's h-highly successful pol-pol-political career was w-well known to the public; but what I want to know is—what I want to know is—what I want to know——(*Pauses to consider.*)

WIDOW (*finally*)—Pass th' glasses, Mary Ann, yez lazy divil; give th' gintlemin a dhrink. Here (*tendering him a glass*), take anodder wan to Moike Clancy, an' Gawd save yez for yer koindness to a poor widee woman!

MR. SLICK (*after solemnly regarding the glass*)—Certainly, I-I'll take a drink. Certainly, M-Mish Clanshy. Yes, certainly, Mish Clanshy. Now, Mish Clanshy, w-w-wash was Mr. Clanshy's n-name before he married you, Mish Clanshy?

WIDOW (*astonished*)—Why, divil a bit else but Clancy!

MR. SLICK (*after reflection*)—Well, but I mean—I mean, Mish Clanshy, I mean—what was date of birth? Did marry you 'fore then, or d-did marry you when 'e was born in N' York, Mish Clanshy?

WIDOW—Phwat th' divil——

MR. SLICK (*with dignity*)—Ansher my queshuns, pleash,

Mish Clanshy. Did 'e bring chil'en withum f'm Irelan', or was you, after married in N' York, mother those chil'en 'e brought f'm Irelan'?

Widow—Be th' powers above, I——

Mr. Slick (*with gentle patience*)—I don't shink y' unnerstan' m' queshuns, Mish Clanshy. What I wanna fin' out is, what was 'e born in N' York for when he, before zat, came f'm Irelan'? Dash what puzzles me. I-I'm completely puzzled. An' alsho, I wanna fin' out—I wanna fin' out, if poshble—zat is, if it's poshble shing, I wanna fin' out—I wanna fin' out—if poshble—I wanna—shay, who the blazesh is dead here, anyhow?

No. 7   SOME HINTS FOR PLAY-MAKERS

We present herewith a few valuable receipts for popular dramas. It is needless to say that we have followed models which have received the sanction of tradition, and are upheld at the present day by a large and important portion of the public. We do not hesitate to claim a great excellence for our receipts, and if they withstand the ravages of time and the assaults of the press with the same fortitude that characterized their predecessors along the same lines, we have no doubt that our posterity far over the horizon of the future will turn their delighted eyes upon theatrical attractions identical with those which will here charm the senses of the enlightened public.

The plans given below are short, concise and direct; the literary essentials only are given. Play-makers using the receipts should fill in well with unimportant characters and specialty people. The dramas can be lengthened or shortened to suit the temper of the audience.

I.

An Irish melodrama. This play can be called "Acushla Mavourneen" or "Mavourneen Acushla," according to which title is preferred by the star.

Cast: Hero; Heroine; Villain.

Scene: *The Lakes of Killarney, or, perchance, the Glen of Kildare. Mountains and lake. Foreground, canvas rocks and waterfall, grass mats; also rustic bridge, upon which is dis-covered the* HEROINE, *leaning against the railing and gazing down into the mirrored depths below.*

HEROINE (*reflectively*)—Ah me!

(*Enter the* VILLIAN. *He glides forward and grabs the* HEROINE *carefully.*)

VILLAIN—Ha, ha, Mary Merryweather, my pretty gazelle! At last—at last! Seek not to flee! You cannot escape me!

HEROINE—Help!

VILLAIN—At last you are in my power!

HEROINE—Help!

(*Enter* HERO.)

HERO—Not while a true son of Erin remains alive!

(*He seizes the* VILLAIN, *and, with the* VILLAIN'S *assistance, drops the* VILLAIN *over the railing of the rustic bridge into the mirrored depths below. Splash made in pan of water by club in hands of supe.*)

Curtain.

II.

A society play. Entitle this anything you please, so long as the one you hit upon does not refer particularly to anything connected with the drama.

CAST: THE DUCHESS; HER NIECE; A NICE MAN; and Intriguing, Spiteful, Contemptible, Malicious, Well-bred and Devilish Men and Women.

ACT I.

SCENE: *Drawing-room in town house of* THE DUCHESS, *who, with* HER NIECE, *is discovered seated.*

THE DUCHESS—My dear Lucy, all men are odious pigs.

HER NIECE—But, dear ahnt——

(*Enter the Intriguing, Spiteful, Contemptible, Malicious, Well-bred and Devilish Men and Women, one at a time and in pairs. They retail sundry scandals about* A NICE MAN. *When they retire,* HER NIECE *sheds tears on the back of a chair. There is a great and bitter woe in her eyes.*)

THE DUCHESS—My dear Lucy, all men are odious pigs.

Mournful curtain.

ACT II.

SCENE: *Drawing-room in the town house of* THE DUCHESS. HER NIECE *discovered reading note.*

HER NIECE (*with sudden joy*)—Oh! then, he is really the pink of perfection, and not an odious pig, as I thought. Dottie Hightights, at the Tinsel Theatre, is his own grandmamma, and not a bad, wicked woman, as I thought.

(*Enter* A NICE MAN.)

HE—Lucy!

SHE—Albert!

Quick curtain.

III.

This is an affair with much life and go to it. It should be called "Mr. Williams, of Williamsburg," or, perhaps, "Mr. Washington, of Washington Market."

CAST: HERO; HEROINE; SISTER TO THE HERO; BROTHER TO THE HEROINE; and Various Foreign Villains.

SCENE: *The exterior of the office of the Transatlantic Cable Co., Paris. Enter* Various Foreign Villains.

A MINOR VILLAIN—Oh, but these Americans are devils—sacré bleu!

CHIEF VILLAIN (*rapidly*)—But at last we have the accursed Gringo in our clutches. This telegram, sent to the office of Bank, Note & Co., Wall street, New York, will cause them to pay over the eight million dollars of the girl's fortune to our confederates. Then the accursed Gringo will be in our clutches.

(*Dark, tan-colored rejoicing by the Villains. Then enter the* HERO, *tranquilly, with a Colt's revolver, 44 calibre.*)

HERO—Well, you are a beautiful collection of portraits. Move, and I blow you full of holes!

CHIEF VILLAIN (*exultantly*)—Little good is your Arizona plaything now, accursed Gringo! I have but to send this despatch and——

HERO (*calmly*)—Pray don't excite yourself, my dear baron. *I know that you have not the price of a cablegram.*

(*Consternation among the Villains.*)

CHIEF VILLAIN—Curses on this cool American! Sapristi, he has outwitted us at every turn. He foiled us on the brick-red plains of Arizona, and he has foiled us here. We are but children in the hands of this devilish American. But for him——

(*Exit Villains biting their nails. The* HERO *returns his weapon to a handy pocket and lights a cigar. Marriage of the* HERO *to the* HEROINE, *and of the* SISTER TO THE HERO *to the* BROTHER TO THE HEROINE.)

Curtain.

IV.

Concerning this play, we, with our large knowledge of the public pulse, declare that if you use the material given with any intelligence at all, you should score the success of your life. Use an English idiom for a title.

CAST: A STERN MAN with white whiskers; HIS NEPHEW, a meek-appearing youth from whom valorous words come strangely; DAUGHTER TO STERN MAN; Maid-servant, Dancer, Guests, Musicians, Singers, Acrobats, Jugglers, etc.

ACT I.

SCENE: *The exterior of Brickmansion-on-the-Hudson. Picket-fence, grass mats, flowers.* STERN MAN *and* NEPHEW *discovered. Guests reclining at short distance.*

NEPHEW—Sir, your cruel and unjust treatment is driving me an exile from my home and native land. I admit that you may perhaps think yourself in the right, but as sure as my name is Percy Armistead, you will one day live to regret this hour.

STERN MAN (*in an asphalt voice*)—No more of this idle talk, sir! Get you gone, and never more darken my doors! Sooner than marry my daughter to you, I would see her, in her youth and beauty, laid in the grave. Your luggage will presently be at the door. In the meantime, that my guests may not lack entertainment, I have procured Lestelle Twofete, the celebrated and lovely dancer from the Palacio di Blaze, who will now render us her new and beautiful dance, entitled "Butterflies in the Dark."

(*Dance; stage lights lowered; rainbow effects.*)

STERN MAN—Bravo, my dear Lestelle, bravo! What, sir (*turning fiercely upon Nephew*)—are you not yet gone?

NEPHEW (*gulping back evidence of strong emotion*)— I go in one moment, cruel uncle; but before leaving my native shore forever, I cannot refrain from singing that original ballad entitled, "In the Wrong Room, or, When She Turned Up the Gas, He Jumped from an Eighth-story Window."

(*Song by* NEPHEW.)

ONE OF THE GUESTS—How sad to see the departure of this young man! It makes me quite doleful.

ANOTHER GUEST—Yes, indeed. Pray let us have some merriment to dispel the mournfulness of this occasion.

(*They produce musical instruments from various convenient places, and line up across the stage.*)

(*Grand chorus; obbligato solo on valise, checked for Paterson, N.J., by* NEPHEW.)

Curtain.

ACT II.

SCENE: *Drawing-room.* DAUGHTER TO STERN MAN *discovered musing. Maid-servant dusting chairs.*

DAUGHTER—Ah me! how long it seems since Percy left us! The hours drag by on leaden wings. Well (*sighs*), I must try to make the time, until his return, go as quickly as possible.

(*Song and dance by* DAUGHTER.)

MAID-SERVANT—Sure it's the light feet yez have got, Miss Amy! That dance reminds me of the song I just heard four men singing out in the front yard.

DAUGHTER—Pray call them in, dear Jane. (*Aside to audience.*) Anything to keep my mind from dwelling upon poor Percy's absence.

(*Exit Maid-servant. Enter Quartet. They sing.*)

(*Later the Maid-servant re-enters with Musicians, Jugglers,*

Tumblers, etc., whom she has found in the front yard, and brings in to make her young mistress forget her grief. Grand entertainment. Enter STERN MAN.)

STERN MAN—Ah, my dear Amy! having a little amusement? (*Shows telegram.*) Here's a despatch from Percy saying that he has forgiven me, and will return in eighteen months.

DAUGHTER—Oh, how glad that makes me! Come, we will sing our old duet that we have not sung since dear Percy left.

(*Duet; involuntary chorus by Jugglers, Acrobats, etc.*)

STERN MAN—And, now, cannot our friends here afford us some entertainment to while away the time until Percy's return?

(*A man comes to the front and sings a topical song. At its conclusion enter* NEPHEW.)

DAUGHTER—Dear Percy, how I have longed for this moment!

NEPHEW—Dearest Amy, in honor of this occasion I will give a recitation—my own composition.

(*Recitation—"The Escape from Paterson." Red lights; rolling-mill thunder.*)

STERN MAN—And now let us sing that good old song entitled, "O'Shaughnessy Fanned Him with an Axe"; your old favorite, my dear boy.

(*Song, with grand chorus by Acrobats, Jugglers, etc.*)

Curtain.

No. 8 AN OMINOUS BABY

A BABY was wandering in a strange country. He was a tattered child with a frowsled wealth of yellow hair. His dress, of a checked stuff, was soiled and showed the marks of many conflicts like the chain-shirt of a warrior. His sun-tanned knees shone above wrinkled stockings which he pulled up occasionally with an impatient movement when they entangled his feet. From a gaping shoe there appeared an array of tiny toes.

He was toddling along an avenue between rows of stolid, brown houses. He went slowly, with a look of absorbed interest on his small, flushed face. His blue eyes stared curiously.

Carriages went with a musical rumble over the smooth asphalt. A man with a chrysanthemum was going up steps. Two nursery maids chatted as they walked slowly, while their charges hobnobbed amiably between perambulators. A truck wagon roared thunderously in the distance.

The child from the poor district made way along the brown street filled with dull gray shadows. High up, near the roofs, glancing sun-rays changed cornices to blazing gold and silvered the fronts of windows. The wandering baby stopped and stared at the two children laughing and playing in their carriages among the heaps of rugs and cushions. He braced his legs apart in an attitude of earnest attention. His lower jaw fell and disclosed his small, even teeth. As they moved on, he followed the carriages with awe in his face as if contemplating a pageant. Once one of the babies, with twittering laughter, shook a gorgeous rattle at him. He smiled jovially in return.

Finally a nursery maid ceased conversation and, turning, made a gesture of annoyance.

"Go 'way, little boy," she said to him. "Go 'way. You're all dirty."

He gazed at her with infant tranquillity for a moment and then went slowly off, dragging behind him a bit of rope he had acquired in another street. He continued to investigate the new scenes. The people and houses struck him with interest as would flowers and trees. Passengers had to avoid the small, absorbed figure in the middle of the sidewalk. They glanced at the intent baby face covered with scratches and dust as with scars and powder smoke.

After a time, the wanderer discovered upon the pavement, a pretty child in fine clothes playing with a toy. It was a tiny fire engine painted brilliantly in crimson and gold. The wheels rattled as its small owner dragged it uproariously about by means of a string. The babe with his bit of rope trailing behind him paused and regarded the child and the toy. For a long while he remained motionless, save for his eyes, which followed all movements of the glittering thing.

The owner paid no attention to the spectator but continued his joyous imitations of phases of the career of a fire engine. His gleeful baby laugh rang against the calm fronts of the houses. After a little, the wandering baby began quietly to sidle nearer. His bit of rope, now forgotten, dropped at his feet. He removed his eyes from the toy and glanced expectantly at the other child.

"Say," he breathed, softly.

The owner of the toy was running down the walk at top speed. His tongue was clanging like a bell and his legs were galloping. An iron post on the corner was all ablaze. He did not look around at the coaxing call from the small, tattered figure on the curb.

The wandering baby approached still nearer and, presently, spoke again. "Say," he murmured, "le' me play wif it?"

The other child interrupted some shrill tootings. He bended his head and spoke disdainfully over his shoulder.

"No," he said.

The wanderer retreated to the curb. He failed to notice the bit of rope, once treasured. His eyes followed as before the winding course of the engine, and his tender mouth twitched.

"Say," he ventured at last, "is dat yours?"

"Yes," said the other, tilting his round chin. He drew his property suddenly behind him as if it were menaced. "Yes," he repeated, "it's mine."

"Well, le' me play wif it?" said the wandering baby, with a trembling note of desire in his voice.

"No," cried the pretty child with determined lips. "It's mine! My ma-ma buyed it."

"Well, tan't I play wif it?" His voice was a sob. He stretched forth little, covetous hands.

"No," the pretty child continued to repeat. "No, it's mine."

"Well, I want to play wif it," wailed the other. A sudden, fierce frown mantled his baby face. He clenched his thin hands and advanced with a formidable gesture. He looked some wee battler in a war.

"It's mine! It's mine!" cried the pretty child, his voice in the treble of outraged rights.

"I want it," roared the wanderer.

"It's mine! It's mine!"

"I want it!"

"It's mine!"

The pretty child retreated to the fence, and there paused at bay. He protected his property with outstretched arms. The small vandal made a charge. There was a short scuffle at the fence. Each grasped the string to the toy and tugged. Their faces were wrinkled with baby rage, the verge of tears.

Finally, the child in tatters gave a supreme tug and wrenched the string from the other's hands. He set off rapidly down the street, bearing the toy in his arms. He was weeping with the air of a wronged one who has at last succeeded in achieving his rights. The other baby was squalling lustily. He seemed quite helpless. He wrung his chubby hands and railed.

After the small barbarian had got some distance away, he paused and regarded his booty. His little form curved with pride. A soft, gleeful smile loomed through the storm of tears. With great care, he prepared the toy for travelling. He stopped a moment on a corner and gazed at the pretty child whose small figure was quivering with sobs. As the latter began to show signs of beginning pursuit, the little vandal turned and vanished down a dark side street as into a swallowing cavern.

No. 9   A GREAT MISTAKE

AN ITALIAN kept a fruit stand on a corner where he had good aim at the people who came down from the elevated station and at those who went along two thronged streets. He sat most of the day in a backless chair that was placed strategically.

There was a babe living hard by, up five flights of stairs, who regarded this Italian as a tremendous being. The babe had investigated this fruit stand. It had thrilled him as few things he had met with in his travels had thrilled him. The sweets of the world laid there in dazzling rows, tumbled in luxurious heaps. When he gazed at this Italian seated amid such splendid treasure, his lower lip hung low and his eyes raised to the vendor's face were filled with deep respect, worship, as if he saw omnipotence.

The babe came often to this corner. He hovered about the stand and watched each detail of the business. He was fasci-

nated by the tranquility of the vendor, the majesty of power
and possession. At times, he was so engrossed in his contemplation that people, hurrying, had to use care to avoid
bumping him down.

He had never ventured very near to the stand. It was his
habit to hang warily about the curb. Even there he resembled
a babe who looks unbidden at a feast of gods.

One day, however, as the baby was thus staring, the vendor
arose and going along the front of the stand, began to polish
oranges with a red pocket-handkerchief. The breathless spectator moved across the sidewalk until his small face almost
touched the vendor's sleeve. His fingers were gripped in a fold
of his dress.

At last, the Italian finished with the oranges and returned
to his chair. He drew a newspaper printed in his language from
behind a bunch of bananas. He settled himself in a comfortable
position and began to glare savagely at the print. The babe was
left face to face with the massed joys of the world.

For a time he was a simple worshipper at this golden shrine.
Then tumultuous desires began to shake him. His dreams were
of conquest. His lips moved. Presently into his head there came
a little plan.

He sidled nearer, throwing swift and cunning glances at the
Italian. He strove to maintain his conventional manner, but the
whole plot was written upon his countenance.

At last he had come near enough to touch the fruit. From
the tattered skirt came slowly his small dirty hand. His eyes
were still fixed upon the vendor. His features were set, save for
the under lip, which had a faint fluttering movement. The
hand went forward.

Elevated trains thundered to the station and the stairway
poured people upon the sidewalks. There was a deep sea roar
from feet and wheels going ceaselessly. None seemed to perceive the babe engaged in the great venture.

The Italian turned his paper. Sudden panic smote the babe.
His hand dropped and he gave vent to a cry of dismay. He
remained for a moment staring at the vendor. There was evidently a great debate in his mind. His infant intellect had defined the Italian. The latter was undoubtedly a man who would

eat babes that provoked him. And the alarm in him when the vendor had turned his newspaper brought vividly before him the consequences if he were detected.

But at this moment, the vendor gave a blissful grunt and tilting his chair against a wall, closed his eyes. His paper dropped unheeded.

The babe ceased his scrutiny and again raised his hand. It was moved with supreme caution toward the fruit. The fingers were bent, claw-like, in the manner of great heart-shaking greed.

Once he stopped and chattered convulsively because the vendor moved in his sleep. The babe with his eyes still upon the Italian again put forth his hand and the rapacious fingers closed over a round bulb.

And it was written that the Italian should at this moment open his eyes. He glared at the babe a fierce question. Thereupon the babe thrust the round bulb behind him and with a face expressive of the deepest guilt, began a wild but elaborate series of gestures declaring his innocence.

The Italian howled. He sprang to his feet, and with three steps overtook the babe. He whirled him fiercely and took from the little fingers a lemon.

No. 10   A DARK-BROWN DOG

A CHILD was standing on a street-corner. He leaned with one shoulder against a high board-fence and swayed the other to and fro, the while kicking carelessly at the gravel.

Sunshine beat upon the cobbles, and a lazy summer wind raised yellow dust which trailed in clouds down the avenue. Clattering trucks moved with indistinctness through it. The child stood dreamily gazing.

After a time, a little dark-brown dog came trotting with an intent air down the sidewalk. A short rope was dragging from his neck. Occasionally he trod upon the end of it and stumbled.

He stopped opposite the child, and the two regarded each other. The dog hesitated for a moment, but presently he made some little advances with his tail. The child put out his hand and called him. In an apologetic manner the dog came close, and the two had an interchange of friendly pattings and waggles. The dog became more enthusiastic with each moment of the interview, until with his gleeful caperings he threatened to overturn the child. Whereupon the child lifted his hand and struck the dog a blow upon the head.

This thing seemed to overpower and astonish the little dark-brown dog, and wounded him to the heart. He sank down in despair at the child's feet. When the blow was repeated, together with an admonition in childish sentences, he turned over upon his back, and held his paws in a peculiar manner. At the same time with his ears and his eyes he offered a small prayer to the child.

He looked so comical on his back, and holding his paws peculiarly, that the child was greatly amused and gave him little taps repeatedly, to keep him so. But the little dark-brown dog took this chastisement in the most serious way, and no doubt considered that he had committed some grave crime, for he wriggled contritely and showed his repentance in every way that was in his power. He pleaded with the child and petitioned him, and offered more prayers.

At last the child grew weary of this amusement and turned toward home. The dog was praying at the time. He lay on his back and turned his eyes upon the retreating form.

Presently he struggled to his feet and started after the child. The latter wandered in a perfunctory way toward his home, stopping at times to investigate various matters. During one of these pauses he discovered the little dark-brown dog who was following him with the air of a footpad.

The child beat his pursuer with a small stick he had found. The dog lay down and prayed until the child had finished, and resumed his journey. Then he scrambled erect and took up the pursuit again.

On the way to his home the child turned many times and beat the dog, proclaiming with childish gestures that he held him in contempt as an unimportant dog, with no value save for a moment. For being this quality of animal the dog apologized and eloquently expressed regret, but he continued stealthily to follow the child. His manner grew so very guilty that he slunk like an assassin.

When the child reached his door-step, the dog was industriously ambling a few yards in the rear. He became so agitated with shame when he again confronted the child that he forgot the dragging rope. He tripped upon it and fell forward.

The child sat down on the step and the two had another interview. During it the dog greatly exerted himself to please the child. He performed a few gambols with such abandon that the child suddenly saw him to be a valuable thing. He made a swift, avaricious charge and seized the rope.

He dragged his captive into a hall and up many long stairways in a dark tenement. The dog made willing efforts, but he could not hobble very skilfully up the stairs because he was very small and soft, and at last the pace of the engrossed child grew so energetic that the dog became panic-stricken. In his mind he was being dragged toward a grim unknown. His eyes grew wild with the terror of it. He began to wiggle his head frantically and to brace his legs.

The child redoubled his exertions. They had a battle on the stairs. The child was victorious because he was completely absorbed in his purpose, and because the dog was very small. He dragged his acquirement to the door of his home, and finally with triumph across the threshold.

No one was in. The child sat down on the floor and made overtures to the dog. These the dog instantly accepted. He beamed with affection upon his new friend. In a short time they were firm and abiding comrades.

When the child's family appeared, they made a great row. The dog was examined and commented upon and called names. Scorn was leveled at him from all eyes, so that he became much embarrassed and drooped like a scorched plant. But the child went sturdily to the center of the floor, and, at the top of his voice, championed the dog. It happened that he was roaring protestations, with his arms clasped about the dog's neck, when the father of the family came in from work.

The parent demanded to know what the blazes they were making the kid howl for. It was explained in many words that the infernal kid wanted to introduce a disreputable dog into the family.

A family council was held. On this depended the dog's fate, but he in no way heeded, being busily engaged in chewing the end of the child's dress.

The affair was quickly ended. The father of the family, it appears, was in a particularly savage temper that evening, and when he perceived that it would amaze and anger everybody if such a dog were allowed to remain, he decided that it should be so. The child, crying softly, took his friend off to a retired part of the room to hobnob with him, while the father quelled a fierce rebellion of his wife. So it came to pass that the dog was a member of the household.

He and the child were associated together at all times save when the child slept. The child became a guardian and a friend. If the large folk kicked the dog and threw things at him, the child made loud and violent objections. Once when the child had run, protesting loudly, with tears raining down his face and his arms outstretched, to protect his friend, he had been struck in the head with a very large saucepan from the hand of his father, enraged at some seeming lack of courtesy in the dog. Ever after, the family were careful how they threw things at the dog. Moreover, the latter grew very skilful in avoiding missiles and feet. In a small room containing a stove, a table, a bureau and some chairs, he would display strategic ability of a high order, dodging, feinting and scuttling about among the furniture. He could force three or four people armed with brooms, sticks and handfuls of coal, to use all their ingenuity to get in a blow. And even when they did, it was seldom that they could do him a serious injury or leave any imprint.

But when the child was present, these scenes did not occur. It came to be recognized that if the dog was molested, the child would burst into sobs, and as the child, when started, was very riotous and practically unquenchable, the dog had therein a safeguard.

However, the child could not always be near. At night, when he was asleep, his dark-brown friend would raise from some black corner a wild, wailful cry, a song of infinite lowliness and despair, that would go shuddering and sobbing among the buildings of the block and cause people to swear. At these times the singer would often be chased all over the kitchen and hit with a great variety of articles.

Sometimes, too, the child himself used to beat the dog, although it is not known that he ever had what could be truly called a just cause. The dog always accepted these thrashings with an air of admitted guilt. He was too much of a dog to try to look to be a martyr or to plot revenge. He received the blows with deep humility, and furthermore he forgave his friend the moment the child had finished, and was ready to caress the child's hand with his little red tongue.

When misfortune came upon the child, and his troubles overwhelmed him, he would often crawl under the table and lay his small distressed head on the dog's back. The dog was ever sympathetic. It is not to be supposed that at such times he took occasion to refer to the unjust beatings his friend, when provoked, had administered to him.

He did not achieve any notable degree of intimacy with the other members of the family. He had no confidence in them, and the fear that he would express at their casual approach often exasperated them exceedingly. They used to gain a certain satisfaction in underfeeding him, but finally his friend the child grew to watch the matter with some care, and when he forgot it, the dog was often successful in secret for himself.

So the dog prospered. He developed a large bark, which came wondrously from such a small rug of a dog. He ceased to howl persistently at night. Sometimes, indeed, in his sleep, he would utter little yells, as from pain, but that occurred, no doubt, when in his dreams he encountered huge flaming dogs who threatened him direfully.

His devotion to the child grew until it was a sublime thing. He wagged at his approach; he sank down in despair at his departure. He could detect the sound of the child's step among all the noises of the neighborhood. It was like a calling voice to him.

The scene of their companionship was a kingdom governed by this terrible potentate, the child; but neither criticism nor rebellion ever lived for an instant in the heart of the one subject. Down in the mystic, hidden fields of his little dog-soul bloomed flowers of love and fidelity and perfect faith.

The child was in the habit of going on many expeditions to observe strange things in the vicinity. On these occasions his friend usually jogged aimfully along behind. Perhaps, though, he went ahead. This necessitated his turning around every quarter-minute to make sure the child was coming. He was filled with a large idea of the importance of these journeys. He would carry himself with such an air! He was proud to be the retainer of so great a monarch.

One day, however, the father of the family got quite exceptionally drunk. He came home and held carnival with the cooking utensils, the furniture and his wife. He was in the midst of this recreation when the child, followed by the dark-brown dog, entered the room. They were returning from their voyages.

The child's practised eye instantly noted his father's state. He dived under the table, where experience had taught him was a rather safe place. The dog, lacking skill in such matters, was, of course, unaware of the true condition of affairs. He looked with interested eyes at his friend's sudden dive. He interpreted it to mean: Joyous gambol. He started to patter across the floor to join him. He was the picture of a little dark-brown dog en route to a friend.

The head of the family saw him at this moment. He gave a huge howl of joy, and knocked the dog down with a heavy coffee-pot. The dog, yelling in supreme astonishment and fear, writhed to his feet and ran for cover. The man kicked out with a ponderous foot. It caused the dog to swerve as if caught in a tide. A second blow of the coffee-pot laid him upon the floor.

Here the child, uttering loud cries, came valiantly forth like a knight. The father of the family paid no attention to these calls of the child, but advanced with glee upon the dog. Upon being knocked down twice in swift succession, the latter apparently gave up all hope of escape. He rolled over on his back and held his paws in a peculiar manner. At the same time with his eyes and his ears he offered up a small prayer.

But the father was in a mood for having fun, and it occurred to him that it would be a fine thing to throw the dog out of the window. So he reached down and grabbing the animal by a leg, lifted him, squirming, up. He swung him two or three times hilariously about his head, and then flung him with great accuracy through the window.

The soaring dog created a surprise in the block. A woman watering plants in an opposite window gave an involuntary shout and dropped a flower-pot. A man in another window leaned perilously out to watch the flight of the dog. A woman, who had been hanging out clothes in a yard, began to caper wildly. Her mouth was filled with clothes-pins, but her arms gave vent to a sort of exclamation. In appearance she was like a gagged prisoner. Children ran whooping.

The dark-brown body crashed in a heap on the roof of a shed five stories below. From thence it rolled to the pavement of an alleyway.

The child in the room far above burst into a long, dirgelike cry, and toddled hastily out of the room. It took him a long time to reach the alley, because his size compelled him to go downstairs backward, one step at a time, and holding with both hands to the step above.

When they came for him later, they found him seated by the body of his dark-brown friend.

No. 11   AN EXCURSION TICKET

BILLIE ATKINS is a traveler. He has seen the cold blue gleam of the Northern lakes, the tangled green thickets of Florida and the white peaks of the Rockies. All this has he seen and much more, for he has been a tramp for sixteen years.

One winter evening when the "sitting room" of a lodging house just off the Bowery was thronged with loungers Billie came in, mellow with drink and in the eloquent stage. He chose to charm them with a description of a journey from Denver to Omaha. They all listened with appreciation, for when Billie is quite drunk he tells a tale with indescribable gestures and humorous emotions that makes one feel that, after all, the buffets of fate are rather more comic than otherwise.

It seems that when Billie was in Denver last winter it sudenly occurred to him that he wished to be in Omaha. He did not deem it necessary to explain this fancy: he merely announced that he happened to be in Denver last winter and that then it occurred to him that he wished to be in Omaha. Apparently these ideas come to his class like bolts of compelling lightning. After that swift thought, it was impossible for Denver to contain him; he must away to Omaha. When the night express on the Union Pacific pulled out Billie "made a great sneak" behind some freight cars and climbed onto the "blind" end of the baggage car.

It was a very dark night and Billie congratulated himself that he had not been discovered. He huddled to a little heap on the car platform and thought, with a woman's longing, of Omaha.

However, it was not long before an icy stream of water struck Billie a startling blow in the face, and as he raised his eyes he saw in the red glare from the engine a very jocular fireman crouching on the coal and holding the nozzle of a small hose in his hand. And at frequent intervals during the night this jocular fireman would climb up on the coal and play the hose on Billie. The drenched tramp changed his position and curled himself up into a little ball and swore graphically, all to no purpose. The fireman persisted with his hose and when he thought that Billie was getting too comfortable he came back to the rear of the tender and doused him with a pailful of very cold water.

But Billie stuck to his position. For one reason, the express went too fast for him to get safely off, and for another reason he wished to go to Omaha.

The train rushed into the cold gray of dawn on the prairies. The biting chill of the morning made Billie shake in his wet clothes. He adjusted himself on the edge of the rocking car platform where he could catch the first rays of the sun. And it was this change of position that got him into certain difficulties. At about eight o'clock the express went roaring through a little village. Billie, sunning himself on the edge of the steps, espied three old farmers seated on the porch of the village store. They grinned at him and waved their arms.

"I taut they was jest givin' me er jolly," said Billie, "so I waved me hand at 'em an' gives 'em er laugh, an' th' train went on. But it turned out they wasn't motionin' t' me at all, but was all th' while givin' er tip t' th' brakey that I was on th' blind. An' 'fore I knew it th' brakey came over th' top, or aroun' th' side, or somehow, an' I was a-gittin' kicked in th' neck.

"'Gitoffahere! gitoffahere!'

"I was dead escared b'cause th' train was goin' hell bentin'.

"'Gitoffahere! gitoffahere!'

"'Oh, please, mister,' I sez, 'I can't git off—th' train's goin' too fast.'

"But he kept on kickin' me fer a while til finally he got tired an' stopped th' train b'cause I could a-never got off th' way she was runnin'. By this time th' passengers in all th' cars got onto it that they was puttin' er bum off th' blind, an' when I got down off th' step, I see every winder in th' train was fuller heads, an' they gimme er great laugh until I had t' turn me back an' walk off."

As it happened, the nearest station to where Billie then found himself was eighteen miles distant. He dried his clothes as best he could and then swore along the tracks for a mile or two. But it was weary business—tramping along in the vast vacancy of the plains. Billie got tired and lay down to wait for a freight train. After a time one came and as the long string of boxcars thundered past him, he made another "great sneak" and a carefully calculated run and grab. He got safely on the little step and then he began to do what he called "ridin' th' ladder." That is to say, he clung to the little iron ladder that is fastened to the end of each car. He remained hanging there while the long train crept slowly over the plains.

He did not dare to show himself above the top of the car for fear of the brakeman. He considered himself safe down between the ends of the jolting cars, but once, as he chanced to look toward the sky, he saw a burly brakeman leaning on the brakewheel and regarding him.

"Come up here," said the brakeman.

Billie climbed painfully to the top of the car.

"Got any money?" said the brakeman.

"No," replied Billie.

"Well, then, gitoffahere," said the brakeman, and Billie received another installment of kicks. He went down the ladder and puckered his mouth and drew in his breath, preparatory to getting off the car, but the train had arrived at a small grade and Billie became frightened. The little wheels were all a-humming and the cars lurched like boats on the sea.

"Oh, please, mister," said Billie, "I can't git off. It's a-goin' too fast."

The brakeman swore and began the interesting operation of treading, with his brass toed boots, on Billie's fingers. Billie hung hard. He cast glances of despair at the rapid fleeting ground and shifted his grip often. But presently the brakeman's heels came down with extraordinary force and Billie involuntarily released his hold.

He fell in a heap and rolled over and over. His face and body were scratched and bruised, and on the top of his head there was a contusion that fitted like a new derby. His clothes had been rags, but they were now exaggerated out of all semblance of clothes. He sat up and looked at the departing train. "Gawd-dernit," he said, "I'll never git t' Omaha at this rate."

Presently Billie developed a most superhuman hunger. He saw the houses of a village some distance away, and he made for them, resolved to have something to eat if it cost a life. But still he knew he would be arrested if he appeared on the streets of any well organized, respectable town in the trousers he was then obliged to wear. He was in a quandary until by good fortune he perceived a pair of brown overalls hanging on a line in the rear of an isolated house.

He "made a great sneak on 'em." This sort of thing requires patience, but not more than an hour later, he bore off a large square of cloth which he had torn from one leg of the overalls. At another house he knocked at the door and when a woman came he stood very carefully facing her and requested a needle and thread. She gave them to him, and he waited until she had shut the door before he turned and went away.

He retired then into a thick growing patch of sunflowers on the outskirts of the town and started in to sew the piece of overall to his trousers. He had not been engaged long at his task before "two hundred kids" accumulated in front of the sunflower patch and began to throw stones at him. For some time the sky was darkened by a shower of missiles of all sizes. Occasionally Billie, without his trousers, would make little forays, yelling savage threats. These would compel the boys to retire some distance, but they always returned again with renewed ardor. Billie thought he would never get his trousers mended.

But this adventure was the cause of his again meeting Black John Randolph, who Billie said was "th' whitest pardner" he ever had. While he was engaged in conflict with the horde of boys a negro came running down the road and began to belabor them with a boot blacking kit. The boys ran off, and Billie saw with delight that his rescuer was Black John Randolph, whom he had known in Memphis.

Billie, unmolested, sewed his trousers. Then he told Black John that he was hungry, and the two swooped down on the town. Black John shined shoes until dark. He shined for all the available citizens of the place. Billie stood around and watched. The earnings were sixty cents. They spent it all for gingerbread, for it seems that Billie had developed a sudden marvelous longing for gingerbread.

Having feasted, Billie decided to make another attempt for Omaha. He and Black John went to the railroad yard and there they discovered an east-bound freight car that was empty save for one tramp and seven cans of peaches. They parleyed with the tramp and induced him to give up his claim on two-thirds of the car. They settled very comfortably, and that night Billie was again on his way to Omaha. The three of them lived for twenty-four hours on canned peaches, and would have been happy ever after no doubt if it had not happened that their freight car was presently switched off to a side line, and sent careering off in the wrong direction.

When Billie discovered this he gave a whoop and fell out of the car, for he was very particular about walking, and he did not wish to be dragged far from the main line. He trudged back to it, and there discovered a lumber car that contained about forty tramps.

This force managed to overawe the trainmen for a time and compel a free ride for a few miles, but presently the engine was stopped, and the trainmen formed in war array and advanced with clubs.

Billie had had experience in such matters. He "made a sneak." He repaired to a coal car and cuddled among the coal. He buried his body completely, and of his head only his nose and his eyes could have been seen.

The trainmen spread the tramps out over the prairie in a wide fleeing circle, as when a stone is hurled into a placid creek. They remained cursing in their beards, and the train went on.

Billie, snug in his bed, smiled without disarranging the coal that covered his mouth, and thought of Omaha.

But in an hour or two he got impatient, and upreared his head to look at the scenery. An eagle eyed brakeman espied him.

"Got any money?"

"No."

"Well, then, gitoffahere."

Billie got off. The brakeman continued to throw coal at him until the train had hauled him beyond range.

"Hully mack'rel," said Billie, "I'll never git t' Omaha."

He was quite discouraged. He lay down on a bank beside the track to think, and while there he went to sleep. When he awoke a freight train was thundering past him. Still half asleep, he made a dash and a grab. He was up the ladder and on top of the car before he had recovered all of his faculties. A brakeman charged on him.

"Got any money?"

"No, but, please, mister, won't yeh please let me stay on yer train fer a little ways? I'm awful tired, an' I wanta git t' Omaha."

The brakeman reflected. Then he searched Billie's pockets, and finding half a plug of tobacco, took possession of it. He decided to let Billie ride for a time.

Billie perched on top of the car and admired the changing scenery while the train went twenty miles. Then the brakeman induced him to get off, considering no doubt that a twenty mile ride was sufficient in exchange for a half plug of tobacco.

The rest of the trip is incoherent, like the detailed accounts of great battles. Billie boarded trains and got thrown off on his head, on his left shoulder, on his right shoulder, on his hands and knees. He struck the ground slanting, straight from above and full sideways. His clothes were shredded and torn like the sails of a gale blown brig. His skin was tattooed with bloody lines, crosses, triangles, and all the devices known to geometry. But he wouldn't walk, and he was bound to reach Omaha. So he let the trainmen use him as a projectile with which to bombard the picturesque Western landscape.

And eventually he reached Omaha. One night, when it was snowing and cold winds whistled among the city's chimneys, he arrived in a coal car. He was filled with glee that he had reached the place of his endeavor. He could not repress his pride when he thought of the conquered miles. He went forth from the coal car with a blithe step.

The police would not let him stand on a corner nor sit down anywhere. They drove him about for two or three hours, until he happened to think of the railroad station. He went there, and was just getting into a nice doze by the warm red stove in the waiting room, when an official of some kind took him by the collar, and leading him calmly to the door, kicked him out into the snow. After that he was ejected from four saloons in rapid succession.

"Hully mack'rel!" he said, as he stood in the snow and quavered and trembled.

Until three o'clock in the morning various industrious policemen kept him moving from place to place as if he were pawn in a game of chess, until finally Billie became desperate and approached an officer in this fashion:

"Say, mister, won't yeh please arrest me? I wanta go t' jail so's I kin sleep."

"What?"

"I say, won't yer please arrest me? I wanta go to t' jail so's I kin sleep."

The policeman studied Billie for a moment. Then he made an impatient gesture.

"Oh, can't yeh arrest yerself? The jail's a long ways from here, an' I don't wanta take yeh way up there."

"Sure—I kin," said Billie. "Where is it?"

The policeman gave him directions, and Billie started for the jail.

He had considerable difficulty in finding it. He was often obliged to accost people in the street.

"Please, mister, can yeh tell me where the jail is?"

At last he found it, and after a short parley, they admitted him. They gave him permission to sleep on a sort of an iron slab swung by four chains from the ceiling. Billie sank down upon this couch and arrayed his meager rags about his form. Before he was completely in the arms of the slumber god, however, he made a remark expressive of a new desire, a sudden born longing. "Hully mack'rel. I mus' start back fer Denver in th' mornin'."

No. 12   THE SNAKE

WHERE the path wended across the ridge, the bushes of huckleberry and sweet fern swarmed at it in two curling waves until it was a mere winding line traced through the tangle. There was no interference by clouds and as the rays of the sun fell full upon the ridge they called into voice innumerable insects which chanted the heat of the summer day in steady throbbing unending chorus.

A man and a dog came from the laurel thickets of the valley where the white brook brawled with the rocks. They followed the deep line of the path across the ridge. The dog—a large lemon and white setter—walked, tranquilly meditative, at his master's heels.

Suddenly from some unknown and yet near place in advance there came a dry shrill whistling rattle that smote motion instantly from the limbs of the man and the dog. Like the fingers of a sudden death, this sound seemed to touch the man at the nape of the neck, at the top of the spine, and change him, as swift as thought, to a statue of listening horror, surprise, rage. The dog, too—the same icy hand was laid upon him and he stood crouched and quivering, his jaw drooping, the froth of terror upon his lips, the light of hatred in his eyes.

Slowly the man moved his hands toward the bushes but his

glance did not turn from the place made sinister by the warning rattle. His fingers unguided sought for a stick of weight and strength. Presently they closed about one that seemed adequate and holding this weapon poised before him, the man moved slowly forward, glaring. The dog with his nervous nostrils fairly fluttering moved warily, one foot at a time, after his master.

But when the man came upon the snake, his body underwent a shock as from a revelation, as if after all he had been ambushed. With a blanched face, he sprang backward and his breath came in strained gasps, his chest heaving as if he were in the performance of an extraordinary muscular trial. His arm with the stick made a spasmodic defensive gesture.

The snake had apparently been crossing the path in some mystic travel when to his sense there came the knowledge of the coming of his foes. The dull vibration perhaps informed him and he flung his body to face the danger. He had no knowledge of paths; he had no wit to tell him to slink noiselessly into the bushes. He knew that his implacable enemies were approaching; no doubt they were seeking him, hunting him. And so he cried his cry, an incredibly-swift jangle of tiny bells, as burdened with pathos as the hammering upon quaint cymbals by the Chinese at war—for, indeed, it was usually his death-music.

"Beware! Beware! Beware!"

The man and the snake confronted each other. In the man's eyes was hatred and fear. In the snake's eyes was hatred and fear. These enemies maneuvered, each preparing to kill. It was to be battle without mercy. Neither knew of mercy for such a situation. In the man was all the wild strength of the terror of his ancestors, of his race, of his kind. A deadly repulsion had been handed from man to man through long dim centuries. This was another detail of a war that had begun evidently when first there were men and snakes. Individuals who do not participate in this strife incur the investigations of scientists. Once there was a man and a snake who were friends, and at the end, the man lay dead with the marks of the snake's caress just over his East Indian heart. In the formation of devices hideous and horrible, nature reached her supreme point in the making of the snake, so that priests who really paint hell well, fill it with snakes instead of fire. These curving forms, these scintillant colorings create at once, upon sight, more relentless animosities than do shake barbaric tribes. To be born a snake is to be thrust into a place a-swarm with formidable foes. To gain an appreciation of it, view hell as pictured by priests who are really skilful.

As for this snake in the pathway, there was a double curve some inches back of its head which merely by the potency of its lines made the man feel with tenfold eloquence the touch of the death-fingers at the nape of his neck. The reptile's head was waving slowly from side to side and its hot eyes flashed like little murder-lights. Always in the air was the dry shrill whistling of the rattles.

"Beware! Beware! Beware!"

The man made a preliminary feint with his stick. Instantly the snake's heavy head and neck was bended back on the double curve and instantly the snake's body shot forward in a low straight hard spring. The man jumped backward with a convulsive chatter and swung his stick. The blind, sweeping blow fell upon the snake's head and hurled him so that steel-colored plates were for a moment uppermost. But he rallied swiftly, agilely, and again the head and neck bended back to the double curve and the steaming wide-open mouth made its desperate effort to reach its enemy. This attack, it could be seen, was despairing but it was nevertheless impetuous, gallant, ferocious, of the same quality as the charge of the lone chief when the walls of white faces close upon him in the mountains. The stick swung unerringly again and the snake, mutilated, torn, whirled himself into the last coil.

And now the man went sheer raving mad from the emotions of his fore-fathers and from his own. He came to close quarters. He gripped the stick with his two hands and made it speed like a flail. The snake, tumbling in the anguish of final despair, fought, bit, flung itself upon this stick which was taking its life.

At the end, the man clutched his stick and stood watching in silence. The dog came slowly and with infinite caution stretched his nose forward, sniffing. The hair upon his neck and back moved and ruffled as if a sharp wind was blowing. The last muscular quivers of the snake were causing the rattles to still sound their treble cry, the shrill, ringing war-chant and hymn of the grave of the thing that faces foes at once countless, implacable and superior.

"Well, Rover," said the man, turning to the dog with a grin of victory, "we'll carry Mr. Snake home to show the girls."

His hands still trembled from the strain of the encounter but he pried with his stick under the body of the snake and hoisted the limp thing upon it. He resumed his march along the path and the dog walked, tranquilly meditative, at his master's heels.

No. 13   STORIES TOLD BY AN ARTIST

A Tale About How "Great Grief" Got His Holiday Dinner

WRINKLES had been peering into the little drygoods box that acted as a cupboard. "There is only two eggs and a half of a loaf of bread left," he announced brutally.

"Heavens!" said Warwickson from where he lay smoking on the bed. He spoke in his usual dismal voice. By it he had earned his popular name of Great Grief.

Wrinkles was a thrifty soul. A sight of an almost bare cupboard maddened him. Even when he was not hungry, the ghosts of his careful ancestors caused him to rebel against it. He sat down with a virtuous air. "Well, what are we going to do?" he demanded of the others. It is good to be the thrifty man in a crowd of unsuccessful artists, for then you can keep the others from starving peacefully. "What are we going to do?"

"Oh, shut up, Wrinkles," said Grief from the bed. "You make me think."

Little Pennoyer, with head bended afar down, had been busily scratching away at a pen and ink drawing. He looked up from his board to utter his plaintive optimism.

"The *Monthly Amazement* may pay me to-morrow. They ought to. I've waited over three months now. I'm going down there to-morrow, and perhaps I'll get it."

His friends listened to him tolerantly, but at last Wrinkles could not omit a scornful giggle. He was such an old man, almost twenty-eight, and he had seen so many little boys be brave. "Oh, no doubt, Penny, old man." Over on the bed, Grief croaked deep down in his throat. Nothing was said for a long time thereafter.

The crash of the New York streets came faintly. Occasionally one could hear the tramp of feet in the intricate corridors of this begrimed building that squatted, slumbering and aged between two exalted commercial structures that would have had to bend afar down to perceive it. The light snow beat pattering into the window corners and made vague and grey the vista of chimneys and roofs. Often, the wind scurried swiftly and raised a long cry.

Great Grief leaned upon his elbow. "See to the fire, will you, Wrinkles?"

Wrinkles pulled the coal box out from under the bed and threw open the stove door preparatory to shoveling some fuel. A red glare plunged at the first faint shadows of dusk. Little Pennoyer threw down his pen and tossed his drawing over on the wonderful heap of stuff that hid the table. "It's too dark to work." He lit his pipe and walked about, stretching his shoulders like a man whose labor was valuable.

When the dusk came it saddened these youths. The solemnity of darkness always caused them to ponder. "Light the gas, Wrinkles," said Grief.

The flood of orange light showed clearly the dull walls lined with sketches, the tousled bed in one corner, the mass of boxes and trunks in another, the little fierce stove and the wonderful table. Moreover, there were some wine colored draperies flung in some places, and on a shelf, high up, there was a plaster cast dark with dust in the creases. A long stovepipe wandered off in the wrong direction and then twined impulsively toward a hole in the wall. There were some extensive cobwebs on the ceiling.

"Well, let's eat," said Grief.

Later there came a sad knock at the door. Wrinkles, arranging a tin pail on the stove, little Pennoyer busy at slicing the bread, and Great Grief, affixing the rubber tube to the gas stove, yelled: "Come in!"

The door opened and Corinson entered dejectedly. His overcoat was very new. Wrinkles flashed an envious glance at it, but almost immediately he cried: "Hello, Corrie, old boy!"

Corinson sat down and felt around among the pipes until he found a good one. Great Grief had fixed the coffee to boil on the gas stove, but he had to watch it closely, for the rubber tube was short, and a chair was balanced on a trunk and then the gas stove was balanced on the chair. Coffee making was a feat.

"Well," said Grief, with his back turned, "how goes it, Corrie? How's Art, hey?" He fastened a terrible emphasis upon the word.

"Crayon portraits," said Corinson.

"What?" They turned toward him with one movement, as if from a lever connection. Little Pennoyer dropped his knife.

"Crayon portraits," repeated Corinson. He smoked away in profound cynicism. "Fifteen dollars a week, or more, this time of year, you know." He smiled at them calmly like a man of courage.

Little Pennoyer picked up his knife again. "Well, I'll be blowed," said Wrinkles. Feeling it incumbent upon him to think, he dropped into a chair and began to play serenades on his guitar and watch to see when the water for the eggs would boil. It was a habitual pose.

Great Grief, however, seemed to observe something bitter in the affair. "When did you discover that you couldn't draw?" he said, stiffly.

"I haven't discovered it yet," replied Corinson, with a serene air. "I merely discovered that I would rather eat."

"Oh!" said Grief.

"Hand me the eggs, Grief," said Wrinkles. "The water's boiling."

Little Pennoyer burst into the conversation. "We'd ask you to dinner, Corrie, but there's only three of us and there's two eggs. I dropped a piece of bread on the floor, too. I'm shy one."

"That's all right, Penny," said the other, "don't trouble yourself. You artists should never be hospitable. I'm going, anyway. I've got to make a call. Well, good night, boys. I've got to make a call. Drop in and see me."

When the door closed upon him, Grief said: "The coffee's

done. I hate that fellow. That overcoat cost thirty dollars, if it cost a red. His egotism is so tranquil. It isn't like yours, Wrinkles. He——"

The door opened again and Corinson thrust in his head. "Say, you fellows, you know it's Thanksgiving to-morrow."

"Well, what of it?" demanded Grief.

Little Pennoyer said: "Yes, I know it is, Corrie, I thought of it this morning."

"Well, come out and have a table d'hote with me to-morrow night. I'll blow you off in good style."

While Wrinkles played an exuberant air on his guitar, little Pennoyer did part of a ballet. They cried ecstatically: "Will we? Well, I guess yes!"

When they were alone again Grief said: "I'm not going, anyhow. I hate that fellow."

"Oh, fiddle," said Wrinkles. "You're an infernal crank. And, besides, where's your dinner coming from to-morrow night if you don't go? Tell me that."

Little Pennoyer said: "Yes, that's so, Grief. Where's your dinner coming from if you don't go?"

Grief said: "Well, I hate him, anyhow."

As To Payment of the Rent

Little Pennoyer's four dollars could not last forever. When he received it he and Wrinkles and Great Grief went to a table d'hote. Afterward little Pennoyer discovered that only two dollars and a half remained. A small magazine away down town had accepted one out of the six drawings that he had taken them, and later had given him four dollars for it. Penny was so disheartened when he saw that his money was not going to last forever that, even with two dollars and a half in his pockets, he felt much worse then he had when he was penniless, for at that time he anticipated twenty-four. Wrinkles lectured upon "Finance."

Great Grief said nothing, for it was established that when he received six dollar checks from comic weeklies he dreamed of renting studios at seventy-five dollars per month, and was likely to go out and buy five dollars' worth of second hand curtains and plaster casts.

When he had money Penny always hated the cluttered den in the old building. He desired then to go out and breathe boastfully like a man. But he obeyed Wrinkles, the elder and the wise, and if you had visited that room about ten o'clock of a morning or about seven of an evening you would have thought that rye bread, frankfurters and potato salad from Second avenue were the only foods in the world.

Purple Sanderson lived there, too, but then he really ate. He had learned parts of the gasfitter's trade before he came to be such a great artist, and when his opinions disagreed with that of every art manager in New York he went to see a plumber, a friend of his, for whose opinion he had a great deal of respect. In consequence he frequented a very neat restaurant on Twenty-third street and sometimes on Saturday nights he openly scorned his companions.

Purple was a good fellow, Grief said, but one of his singularly bad traits was that he always remembered everything. One night, not long after little Pennoyer's great discovery, Purple came in and as he was neatly hanging up his coat, said: "Well, the rent will be due in four days."

"Will it?" demanded Penny, astounded. Penny was always astounded when the rent came due. It seemed to him the most extraordinary occurrence.

"Certainly it will," said Purple with the irritated air of a superior financial man.

"My soul!" said Wrinkles.

Great Grief lay on the bed smoking a pipe and waiting for fame. "Oh, go home, Purple. You resent something. It wasn't me—it was the calendar."

"Try and be serious a moment, Grief."

"You're a fool, Purple."

Penny spoke from where he was at work. "Well, if those *Amazement* people pay me when they said they would I'll have money then."

"So you will, dear," said Grief, satirically. "You'll have money to burn. Did the *Amazement* people ever pay you when they said they would? You're wonderfully important all of a sudden, it seems to me. You talk like an artist."

Wrinkles, too, smiled at little Pennoyer. "The *Established Magazine* people wanted Penny to hire models and make a try for them, too. It will only cost him a big blue chip. By the time he has invested all the money he hasn't got and the rent is two weeks overdue he will be able to tell the landlord to wait seven months until the Monday morning after the day of publication. Go ahead, Penny."

It was the habit to make game of little Pennoyer. He was always having gorgeous opportunities, with no opportunity to take advantage of his opportunities.

Penny smiled at them, his tiny, tiny smile of courage.

"You're a confident little cuss," observed Grief, irrelevantly.

"Well, the world has no objection to your being confident, also, Grief," said Purple.

"Hasn't it?" said Grief. "Well, I want to know!"

Wrinkles could not be light spirited long. He was obliged to despair when occasion offered. At last he sank down in a chair and seized his guitar. "Well, what's to be done?" he said. He began to play mournfully.

"Throw Purple out," mumbled Grief from the bed.

"Are you fairly certain that you will have money then, Penny?" asked Purple.

Little Pennoyer looked apprehensive. "Well, I don't know," he said.

And then began that memorable discussion, great in four minds. The tobacco was of the "Long John" brand. It smelled like burning mummies.

How Pennoyer Disposed of His Sunday Dinner

Once Purple Sanderson went to his home in St. Lawrence county to enjoy some country air, and, incidentally, to explain his life failure to his people. Previously, Great Grief had given him odds that he would return sooner than he then planned, and everybody said that Grief had a good bet. It is not a glorious pastime, this explaining of life failures.

Later, Great Grief and Wrinkles went to Haverstraw to visit Grief's cousin and sketch. Little Pennoyer was disheartened, for it is bad to be imprisoned in brick and dust and cobbles when your ear can hear in the distance the harmony of the summer sunlight upon leaf and blade of green. Besides, he did not hear Wrinkles and Grief discoursing and quarreling in the den and Purple coming in at six o'clock with contempt.

On Friday afternoon he discovered that he only had fifty cents to last until Saturday morning, when he was to get his check from the *Gamin*. He was an artful little man by this time, however, and it is as true as the sky that when he walked toward the *Gamin* office on Saturday he had twenty cents remaining.

The cashier nodded his regrets. "Very sorry, Mr.—er—Pennoyer, but our pay day, you know, is on Monday. Come around any time after ten."

"Oh, it don't matter," said Penny. As he walked along on his return he reflected deeply how he could invest his twenty cents in food to last until Monday morning any time after ten. He bought two coffee cakes in a Third avenue bakery. They were very beautiful. Each had a hole in the center and a handsome scallop all around the edges.

Penny took great care of those cakes. At odd times he would rise from his work and go to see that no escape had been made. On Sunday he got up at noon and compressed breakfast and noon into one meal. Afterward he had almost three-quarters of a cake still left to him. He congratulated himself that with strategy he could make it endure until Monday morning, any time after ten.

At three in the afternoon there came a faint-hearted knock. "Come in," said Penny. The door opened and old Tim Connegan, who was trying to be a model, looked in apprehensively. "I beg pardon, sir," he said, at once.

"Come in, Tim, you old thief," said Penny. Tim entered, slowly and bashfully. "Sit down," said Penny. Tim sat down and began to rub his knees, for rheumatism had a mighty hold upon him.

Penny lit his pipe and crossed his legs. "Well, how goes it?"

Tim moved his square jaw upward and flashed Penny a little glance.

"Bad?" said Penny.

The old man raised his hand impressively. "I've been to every studio in the hull city and I never see such absences in my life. What with the seashore and the mountains, and this and that resort, I think all the models will be starved by fall. I found one man in up on Fifty-seventh street. He ses to me: 'Come around Tuesday—I may want yez and I may not.' That was last week. You know, I live down on the Bowery, Mr. Pennoyer, and when I got up there on Tuesday, he ses: 'Confound you, are you here again?' ses he. I went and sat down in the park, for I was too tired for the walk back. And there you are, Mr. Pennoyer. What with tramping around to look for men that are a thousand miles away, I'm near dead."

"It's hard," said Penny.

"It is, sir. I hope they'll come back soon. The summer is the death of us all, sir, it is. Sure, I never know where my next meal is coming until I get it. That's true."

"Had anything to-day?"

"Yes, sir—a little."

"How much?"

"Well, sir, a lady give me a cup of coffee this morning. It was good, too, I'm telling you."

Penny went to his cupboard. When he returned, he said: "Here's some cake."

Tim thrust forward his hands, palms erect. "Oh, now, Mr. Pennoyer, I couldn't. You——"

"Go ahead. What's the odds?"

"Oh, now——"

"Go ahead, you old bat."

Penny smoked.

When Tim was going out, he turned to grow eloquent again. "Well, I can't tell you how much I'm obliged to you, Mr. Pennoyer. You——"

"Don't mention it, old man."

Penny smoked.

No. 14   THE SILVER PAGEANT

"IT's rotten," said Grief.

"Oh, it's fair, old man. Still, I would not call it a Great Contribution to American Art," said Wrinkles.

"You've got a good thing, Gaunt, if you go at it right," said little Pennoyer.

These were all volunteer orations. The boys had come in one by one and spoken their opinions. Gaunt listened to them no more than if they had been so many match-peddlers. He never heard anything, close at hand, and he never saw anything excepting that which transpired across a mystic wide sea. The shadow of his thoughts was in his eyes, a little grey mist, and, when what you said to him had passed out of your mind, he asked: "Wha–a–at?" It was understood that Gaunt was very good to tolerate the presence of the universe, which was noisy and interested in itself. All the younger men, moved by an instinct of faith, declared that he would one day be a great artist if he would only move faster than a pyramid. In the meantime, he did not hear their voices. Occasionally when he saw a man take vivid pleasure in life, he faintly evinced an admiration. It seemed to strike him as a feat. As for him, he was watching that silver pageant across a sea.

When he came from Paris to New York somebody told him that he must make his living. He went to see some book-publishers and talked to them in his manner—as if he had just been stunned. At last, one of them gave him drawings to do and it did not surprise him. It was merely as if rain had come down.

Great Grief went to see him in his studio and returned to the den to say: "Gaunt is working in his sleep. Somebody ought to set fire to him."

It was then that the others went over and smoked and gave their opinions of a drawing. Wrinkles said: "Are you really looking at it, Gaunt? I don't think you've seen it yet. Gaunt?"

"What?"

"Why don't you look at it?"

When Wrinkles departed, the model, who was resting at that time, followed him into the hall and waved his arms in rage.

"That feller's crazy. Yeh ought t' see——" and he recited lists of all the wrongs that can come to models.

It was a superstitious little band over in the den. They talked often of Gaunt. "He's got pictures in his eyes," said Wrinkles. They had expected genius to blindly stumble at the preface and ceremonies of the world and each new flounder by Gaunt made a stir in the den. It awed them and they waited.

At last, one morning, Gaunt burst into the room. They were all as dead men.

"I'm going to paint a picture." The mist in his eyes was pierced by a feverish gleam. His gestures were wild and extravagant. Grief stretched out smoking on the bed—Wrinkles and little Pennoyer working at their drawing-boards tilted against the table—were suddenly frozen. If bronze statues had come and danced heavily before them, they could not have been thrilled further.

Gaunt tried to tell them of something but it became knotted in his throat and then suddenly he dashed out again.

Later they went earnestly over to Gaunt's studio. Perhaps he would tell them of what he saw across the sea.

He lay dead upon the floor. There was a little grey mist before his eyes.

When they finally arrived home that night they took a long time to undress for bed and then came the moment when they waited for some one to put out the gas. Grief said at last with the air of a man whose brain is desperately driven: "I wonder—I—what do you suppose he was going to paint?"

Wrinkles reached and turned out the gas and from the sudden profound darkness, he said: "There is a mistake. He couldn't have had pictures in his eyes."

No. 15 A DESERTION

THE gaslight that came with an effect of difficulty through the dust-stained windows on either side of the door, gave strange hues to the faces and forms of the three women who stood gabbling in the hall-way of the tenement. They made rapid gestures and in the back-ground, their enormous shadows mingled in terrific conflict.

"Aye, she ain't so good as he thinks she is, I'll bet. He can watch over 'er an' take care of 'er all he pleases but when she wants t' fool 'im, she'll fool 'im. An' how does he know she ain't foolin' 'im now?"

"Oh, he thinks he's keepin' 'er from goin' t' th' bad, he does. Oh, yes. He ses she's too purty t' let run 'round alone. Too purty! Huh! My Sadie——"

"Well, he keeps a clost watch on 'er, you bet. On'y las' week, she met my boy Tim on th' stairs an' Tim hadn't said two words to 'er b'fore th' ol' man begin t' holler. 'Dorter, dorter, come here, come here!'"

At this moment, a young girl entered from the street and it was evident from the injured expressions suddenly assumed by the three gossipers that she had been the object of their discussion. She passed them with a slight nod and they swung about into a row to stare after her.

On her way up the long flights, the girl unfastened her veil. One could then clearly see the beauty of her eyes but there was in them a certain furtiveness that came near to marring the effects. It was a peculiar fixture of gaze, brought from the street, as of one who there saw a succession of passing dangers with menaces aligned at every corner.

On the top floor, she pushed open a door and then paused on the threshold, confronting an interior that appeared black and flat like a curtain. Perhaps, some girlish ideas of hobgoblins assailed her then, for she called in a little breathless voice: "Daddie!"

There was no reply. The fire in the cooking-stove in the room crackled at spasmodic intervals. One lid was misplaced and the girl could now see that this fact created a little flushed crescent upon the ceiling. Also, a series of tiny windows in the stove caused patches of red upon the floor. Otherwise, the room was heavily draped with shadows.

The girl called again. "Daddie!"

Yet there was no reply.

"Oh, daddie!"

Presently she laughed as one familiar with the humors of an

old man. "Oh, I guess yer cussin'-mad about yer supper, dad," she said and she almost entered the room but suddenly faltered, overcome by a feminine instinct to fly from this black interior, peopled with imagined dangers.

Again she called. "Daddie!" Her voice had an accent of appeal. It was as if she knew she was foolish but yet felt obliged to insist upon being re-assured. "Oh, daddie!"

Of a sudden, a cry of relief, a feminine announcement that the stars still hung, burst from her. For, according to some mystic process, the smouldering coals of the fire went a-flame with sudden, fierce brilliance, splashing parts of the walls, the floor, the crude furniture, with a hue of blood-red. And in this dramatic out-burst of light, the girl saw her father seated at a table with his back turned toward her.

She entered the room, then, with an aggrieved air, her logic evidently concluding that somebody was to blame for her nervous fright. "Oh, yer on'y sulkin' 'bout yer supper! I thought mebbe ye'd gone somewheres."

Her father made no reply. She went over to a shelf in the corner, and taking a little lamp, she lit it and put it where it would give her light as she took off her hat and jacket in front of the tiny mirror. Presently, she began to bustle among the cooking utensils that were crowded into the sink and as she worked she rattled talk at her father, apparently disdaining his mood.

"I'd 'a come home earlier t' night dad, on'y that fly foreman, he kep' me in th' shop 'til half-past-six. What a fool. He came t' me, yeh know, an' he ses: 'Nell, I wanta give yeh some brotherly advice'—Oh, I know him an' his brotherly advice—'I wanta give yeh some brotherly advice. Yer too purty, Nell,' he ses, 't' be workin' in this shop an' paradin' th' streets alone, without somebody t' give yeh good brotherly advice an' I wanta warn yeh, Nell, I'm a bad man but I ain't as bad as some an' I wanta warn yeh!' 'Oh, g'long 'bout yer business,' I ses. I know 'im. He's like all of 'em, on'y he's a little slyer, I know 'im. 'You g'long 'bout yer business,' I ses. Well, he sed after a while that he guessed some evenin' he'd come up an' see me. 'Oh, yeh will,' I ses, 'yeh will? Well, you jest let my ol' man ketch yeh comin' foolin' 'round our place. Yeh'll wish yeh went t' some other girl t' give brotherly advice.' 'What th'ell do I care fer yer father?' he ses. 'What's he t' me?' 'If he throws yeh down stairs, yeh'll care for 'im,' I ses. 'Well,' he ses, 'I'll come when 'e ain't in, b'Gawd, I'll come when 'e ain't in.' 'Oh, he's allus in when it means takin' care 'a me,' I ses. 'Don't yeh fergit it, either. When it comes t' takin' care 'a his dorter, he's right on deck every single possible time.'"

After a time, she turned and addressed cheery words to the old man. "Hurry up th' fire, daddie! We'll have supper pretty soon."

But still her father was silent and his form in its sullen posture was motionless.

At this, the girl seemed to see the need of the inauguration of a feminine war against a man out of temper. She approached him breathing soft, coaxing syllables.

"Daddie! Oh, daddie! O-o-oh, daddie!" It was apparent from a subtle quality of valor in her tones that this manner of onslaught upon his moods had usually been successful but to-night it had no quick effect. The words, coming from her lips, were like the refrain of an old ballad but the man remained stolid.

"Daddie! My daddie! Oh, daddie, are yeh *mad* at me, really-truly *mad* at me!"

She touched him lightly upon the arm. Should he have turned then he would have seen the fresh, laughing face, with dew-sparkling eyes, close to his own.

"Oh, daddie! My daddie! Pretty daddie!"

She stole her arm about his neck and then slowly bended her face toward his. It was the action of a queen who knows that she reigns notwithstanding irritations, trials, tempests.

But suddenly, from this position, she leaped backward with the mad energy of a frightened colt. Her face was in this instant turned to a grey, featureless thing of horror. A yell, wild and hoarse as a brute-cry, burst from her. "Daddie!" She flung herself to a place near the door where she remained, crouching, her eyes staring at the motionless figure, splattered by the quivering flashes from the fire. Her arms extended, and her frantic fingers at once besought and repelled. There was in them an expression of eagerness to caress and an expression of the most intense loathing. And the girl's hair that had been a splendor was in these moments changed to a disordered mass that hung and swayed in witch-like fashion.

Again, a terrible cry burst from her. It was more than the shriek of agony—it was directed, personal, addressed to him in the chair, the first word of a tragic conversation with the dead.

It seemed that when she had put her arm about its neck, she had jostled the corpse in such a way, that now she and it were face to face. The attitude expressed an intention of arising from the table. The eyes, fixed upon hers, were filled with an unspeakable hatred.

The cries of the girl aroused thunders in the tenement. There was a loud slamming of doors and presently there was a roar of feet upon the boards of the stairway. Voices rang out sharply.

"What is it?"

"What's th' matter?"

"He's killin' her!"

"Slug 'im with anythin' yeh kin lay hold of, Jack."

But over all this came the shrill shrewish tones of a woman. "Ah, th' damned ol' fool, he's drivin' 'er inteh th' street—that's what he's doin'. He's drivin' 'er inteh th' street."

No. 15a NOTEBOOK DRAFT

IN THE dark hall-way of the tenement three women were quarreling animatedly. Their gestures made enormous shadows that, further back, mingled in terrific combat.

A young girl came from the street and brushed past them on her way up-stairs.

They wheeled then instantly to watch her and ceased quarreling temporarily that they might criticise her face, her clothes, her manners. It was apparent that they thought she was superior to them in many ways. They were extremely vindictive.

The girl entered a room on the top floor of the house, bursting in with a joyous air, as one who was assured of a warm welcome. However, the room seemed empty and she hesitated near the threshold suddenly, giving vent to a little feminine cry. "Oh!"

There was before her a sombre gloom save where, from the front of the kitchen stove, there shone forth four little squares of crimson light.

The girl turned and looked down the stairs again. "I wonder where dad's gone," she said to herself. Then she turned and looked at the room again as if this silent interior could answer her question.

Presently she discerned a familiar shape seated at the table with its back turned to her. She had not discerned it in the shrouding shadows.

She entered then with a repetition of her joyous cry. "Oh, daddie," she said, pouting "I thought you had gone out."

No. 16   A CHRISTMAS DINNER WON IN BATTLE

Tom had set up a plumbing shop in the prairie town of Levelville as soon as the people learned to care more about sanitary conditions than they did about the brand of tobacco smoked by the inhabitants of Mars. Nevertheless he was a wise young man for he was only one week ahead of the surveyors. A railroad, like a magic wand, was going to touch Levelville and change it to a great city. In an incredibly short time, the town had a hotel, a mayor, a board of aldermen and more than a hundred real estate agents, besides a blue print of the plans for a street railway three miles long. When the cow boys rode in with their customary noise to celebrate the fact that they had been paid, their efforts were discouraged by new policemen in uniform. Levelville had become a dignified city.

As the town expanded in marvelous circles out over the prairies, Tom bestrode the froth of the wave of progress. He was soon one of the first citizens. These waves carry men to fortune with sudden sweeping movements, and Tom had the courage, the temerity and the assurance to hold his seat like a knight errant.

In the democratic and genial atmosphere of this primary boom, he became an intimate acquaintance of Colonel Fortman, the president of the railroad, and with more courage, temerity and assurance, had already fallen violently in love with his daughter, the incomparable Mildred. He carried his intimacy with the colonel so far as to once save his life from the flying might of the 5.30 express. It seems that the colonel had ordered the engineer of the 5.30 to make his time under all circumstances; to make his time if he had to run through fire, blood and earthquake. The engineer decided that the usual rule relating to the speed of trains when passing through freight yards could not concern an express that was ordered to slow down for nothing but the wrath of heaven and in consequence, at the time of this incident, the 5.30 was shrieking through the Levelville freight yard at fifty miles an hour, roaring over the switches and screaming along the lines of box cars. The colonel and Tom were coming from the shops. They had just rounded the corner of a car and stepped out upon the main track when this whirring, boiling, howling demon of an express came down upon them. Tom had an instant in which to drag his companion off the rails; the train whistled past them like an enormous projectile. "Damn that fellow—he's making his time," panted the old colonel gazing after the long speeding shadow with its two green lights. Later he said very soberly: "I'm much obliged to you for that Tom, old boy."

When Tom went to him a year later, however, to ask for the hand of Mildred, the colonel replied: "My dear man, I think you are insane. Mildred will have over a million dollars at my death, and while I don't mean to push the money part of it too far forward, yet Mildred with her beauty, her family name and her wealth, can marry the finest in the land. There isn't anyone too great for her. So you see, my dear man, it is impossible that she could consider you for a moment."

Whereupon Tom lost his temper. He had the indignation of a good, sound-minded, fearless-eyed young fellow who is assured of his love and assured almost of the love of the girl. Moreover, it filled him with unspeakable rage to be called "My dear man."

They then accused each other of motives of which neither were guilty, and Tom went away. It was a serious quarrel. The colonel told Tom never to dare to cross his threshold. They passed each other on the street without a wink of an eye to disclose the fact that one knew that the other existed. As time went on the colonel became more massively aristocratic and more impenetrably stern. Levelville had developed about five grades of society, and the Fortmans mingled warily with the dozen families that formed the highest and iciest grades. Once when the colonel and Mildred were driving through town, the girl bowed to a young man who passed them.

"Who the deuce was that?" said the colonel airily. "Seems to me I ought to know that fellow."

"That's the man that saved your life from the 5.30," replied Mildred.

"See here, young lady," cried the colonel angrily, "don't you take his part against me."

About a year later came the great railway strike. The papers of the city foreshadowed it vaguely from time to time, but no one apparently took the matter in a serious way. There had been threats and rumors of threats but the general public had seemed to view them as idle bombast. At last, however, the true situation displayed itself suddenly and vividly. Almost the entire force of the great P. C. C. and W. U. system went on strike. The people of the city awoke one morning to find the grey sky of dawn splashed with a bright crimson color. The strikers had set ablaze one of the company's shops in the suburbs and the light from it flashed out a red ominous signal of warning foretelling the woe and despair of the struggle that was to ensue. Rumors came that the men usually so sober, industrious and imperturbable were running in a wild mob, raving and destroying. Whereupon, the people who had laughed to scorn any idea of being prepared for this upheaval began to assiduously abuse the authorities for not being ready to meet it.

That morning Tom, in his shirt sleeves, went into the back part of his shop to direct some of his workmen about a certain job, and when he came out he was well covered by as honest a coating of grime and soot as was ever worn by journeyman. He went to the sink to dispose of this adornment and while there he heard his men talking of the strike. One was saying: "Yes, sir; sure as th' dickens! They say they're goin' t' burn th' president's house an' everybody in it." Tom's body stiffened at these words. He felt himself turn cold. A moment later he left the shop forgetting his coat, forgetting his covering of soot and grime.

In the main streets of the city there was no evident change. The horses of the jangling street cars still slipped and strained in the deep mud into which the snow had been churned. The store windows were gay with the color of Christmas. Innumerable turkeys hung before each butcher's shop. Upon the walks the business men had formed into little eager groups discussing the domestic calamity. Against the leaden-hued sky, over the tops of the buildings, arose a great leaning pillar of smoke marking the spot upon which stood the burning shop.

Tom hurried on through that part of town which was composed of little narrow streets with tiny grey houses on either side. There he saw a concourse of Slavs, Polacs, Italians and Hungarians, laborers of the company, floundering about in the mud and raving, conducting a riot in their own inimitable way. They seemed as blood-thirsty, pitiless, mad, as starved wolves. And Tom presented a figure no less grim as he ran through the crowd, coatless and now indeed hatless, with pale skin showing through the grime. He went until he came to a stretch of commons across which he could see the Fortman's house standing serenely with no evidences of riot about it. He moderated his pace then.

When he had gone about half way across this little snow-covered common, he looked back, for he heard cries. Across the white fields, winding along the muddy road, there came a strange procession. It resembled a parade of Parisians at the time of the first revolution. Fists were wildly waving and at times hoarse voices rang out. It was as if this crowd was delirious from drink. As it came nearer Tom could see women— gaunt and ragged creatures with inflamed visages and rolling eyes. There were men with dark sinister faces whom Tom had never before seen. They had emerged from the earth, so to speak, to engage in this carousal of violence. And from this procession there came continual threatening ejaculations, shrill cries for revenge, and querulous voices of hate, that made a sort of barbaric hymn, a pagan chant of savage battle and death.

Tom waited for them. Those in the lead evidently considered him to be one of their number since his face was grimed and his garments dishevelled. One gigantic man with bare and brawny arms and throat, gave him invitation with a fierce smile. "Come ahn, Swipsey, while we go roast 'em."

A raving grey-haired woman, struggling in the mud, sang a song which consisted of one endless line:

"We'll burn th' foxes out,
We'll burn th' foxes out,
We'll burn th' foxes out."

As for the others, they babbled and screamed in a vast variety of foreign tongues. Tom walked along with them listening to the cries that came from the terrible little army, marching with clenched fists and with gleaming eyes fastened upon the mansion that upreared so calmly before them.

When they arrived, they hesitated a moment, as if awed by the impassive silence of the structure with closed shutters and barred doors, which stolidly and indifferently confronted them.

Then from the centre of the crowd came the voice of the grey-headed old woman: "Break in th' door! Break in th' door!" And then it was that Tom displayed the desperation born of his devotion to the girl within the house. Although he was perhaps braver than most men, he had none of that magnificent fortitude, that gorgeous tranquility amid upheavals and perils which is the attribute of people in plays; but he stepped up on the porch and faced the throng. His face was wondrously pallid and his hands trembled but he said: "You fellows can't come in here."

There came a great sarcastic howl from the crowd. "Can't we?" They broke into laughter at this wildly ridiculous thing. The brawny, bare-armed giant seized Tom by the arm. "Get outa th' way, you yap," he said between his teeth. In an instant Tom was punched and pulled and knocked this way and that way, and amid the pain of these moments he was conscious that members of the mob were delivering thunderous blows upon the huge doors. Directly indeed they crashed down and he felt the crowd sweep past him and into the house. He clung to a railing; he had no more sense of balance than a feather. A blow in the head had made him feel that the ground swirled and heaved around him. He had no further interest in rioting, and such scenes of excitement. Gazing out over the common he saw two patrol wagons, loaded with policemen, and the lashed horses galloping in the mud. He wondered dimly why they were in such a hurry.

But at that moment a scream rang from the house out through the open doors. He knew the voice and, like an electric shock it aroused him from his semi-stupor. Once more alive, he turned and charged into the house as valiant and as full of rage as a Roman. Pandemonium reigned within. There came yells and roars, splinterings, cracklings, crashes. The scream of Mildred again rang out; this time he knew it came from the dining-room before whose closed door, four men were as busy as miners with improvised pick and drill.

Tom grasped a heavy oaken chair that stood ornamentally in the hall and, elevating it above his head, ran madly at the four men. When he was almost upon them, he let the chair fly. It seemed to strike all of them. A heavy oak chair of the old English type is one of the most destructive of weapons. Still, there seemed to be enough of the men left for they flew at him from all sides like dragons. In the dark of the hallway, Tom put down his head and half-closed his eyes and plied his fists. He knew he had but a moment in which to stand up, but there was a sort of grim joy in knowing that the most terrific din of this affray was going straight through the dining-room door, and into the heart of Mildred and when she knew that her deliverer was—— He saw a stretch of blood-red sky flame under his lids and then sank to the floor, blind, deaf, and nerveless.

When the old colonel arrived in one of the patrol wagons, he did not wait to see the police attack in front but ran around to the rear. As he passed the dining-room windows he saw his wife's face. He shouted, and when they opened a window he clambered with great agility into the room. For a minute they deluged each other with shouts of joy and tears. Then finally the old colonel said: "But they did not get in here. How was that?"

"Oh, papa," said Mildred, "they were trying to break in when somebody came and fought dreadfully with them and made them stop."

"Heavens, who could it have been?" said the colonel. He went to the door and opened it. A group of police became visible hurrying about the wide hall but near the colonel's feet lay a body with a white still face.

"Why, it's—it's——" ejaculated the colonel in great agitation.

"It's Tom," cried Mildred.

When Tom came to his senses he found that his fingers were

clasped tightly by a soft white hand which by some occult power of lovers he knew at once.

"Tom," said Mildred.

And the old colonel from further away said: "Tom, my boy!"

But Tom was something of an obstinate young man. So as soon as he felt himself recovered sufficiently, he arose and went unsteadily toward the door.

"Tom, where are you going?" cried Mildred.

"Where are you going, Tom?" called the colonel.

"I'm going home," said Tom doggedly. "I didn't intend to cross this threshold—I——" He swayed unsteadily and seemed almost about to fall. Mildred screamed and ran toward him. She made a prisoner of him. "You shall not go home," she told him.

"Well," began Tom weakly yet persistently, "I——"

"No, no, Tom," said the colonel, "you are to eat a Christmas dinner with us to-morrow and then I wish to talk with you about—about——"

"About what?" said Tom.

"About—about—damnitall, about marrying my daughter," cried the colonel.

No. 17   THE VOICE OF THE MOUNTAIN

THE old man Popocatepetl was seated on a high rock with his white mantle about his shoulders. He looked at the sky, he looked at the sea, he looked at the land—nowhere could he see any food. And he was very hungry, too.

Who can understand the agony of a creature whose stomach is as large as a thousand churches, when this same stomach is as empty as a broken water jar?

He looked longingly at some islands in the sea. "Ah, those flat cakes! If I had them." He stared at storm-clouds in the sky. "Ah what a drink is there." But the King of Everything, you know, had forbidden the old man Popocatepetl to move at all because he feared that every footprint would make a great hole in the land. So the old fellow was obliged to sit still and wait for his food to come within reach. Anyone who has tried this plan knows what intervals lie between meals.

Once his friend, the little eagle, flew near and Popocatepetl called to him. "Ho, tiny bird, come and consider with me as to how I shall be fed."

The little eagle came and spread his legs apart and considered manfully, but he could do nothing with the situation. "You see," he said, "this is no ordinary hunger which one goat will suffice——"

Popocatepetl groaned an assent.

"—but it is an enormous affair," continued the little eagle, "which requires something like a dozen stars. I don't see what can be done unless we get that little creature of the earth—that little animal with two arms, two legs, one head and a very brave air, to invent something. He is said to be very wise."

"Who claims it for him?" asked Popocatepetl.

"He claims it for himself," responded the eagle.

"Well, summon him! Let us see! He is doubtless a kind little animal and when he sees my distress he will invent something."

"Good!" The eagle flew until he discovered one of these small creatures. "Oh, tiny animal, the great chief Popocatepetl summons you!"

"Does he indeed?"

"Popocatepetl, the great chief," said the eagle again, thinking that the little animal had not heard rightly.

"Well, and why does he summon me?"

"Because he is in distress and he needs your assistance."

The little animal reflected for a time and then said: "I will go!"

When Popocatepetl perceived the little animal and the eagle he stretched forth his great solemn arms. "Oh, blessed little animal with two arms, two legs, a head, and a very brave air, help me in my agony. Behold, I, Popocatepetl, who saw the King of Everything fashioning the stars, I, who knew the sun in his childhood, I, Popocatepetl, appeal to you, little animal. I am hungry."

After a while the little animal asked: "How much will you pay?"

"Pay?" said Popocatepetl.

"Pay?" said the eagle.

"Assuredly," quoth the little animal. " 'Pay'!"

"But," demanded Popocatepetl, "were you never hungry? I tell you I am hungry and is your first word then 'pay'?"

The little animal turned coldly away. "Oh, Popocatepetl, how much wisdom has flown past you since you saw the King of Everything fashioning the stars and since you knew the sun in his childhood? I said 'pay' and moreover your distress measures my price. It is our law. Yet it is true that we did not see the King of Everything fashioning the stars. Nor did we know the sun in his childhood."

Then did Popocatepetl roar and shake in his rage. "Oh, louse —louse—louse! Let us bargain then! How much for your blood?" Over the head of the little animal hung death.

But he instantly bowed himself and prayed: "Popocatepetl, the great, you who saw the King of Everything fashioning the stars and who knew the sun in his childhood, forgive this poor little animal. Your sacred hunger shall be my care. I am your servant."

"It is well," said Popocatepetl at once, for his spirit was ever kindly. "And now what will you do?"

The little animal put his hand upon his chin and reflected. "Well, it seems you are hungry and the King of Everything has forbidden you to go for food in fear that your monstrous feet will riddle the earth with holes. What you need is a pair of wings."

"A pair of wings!" cried Popocatepetl delightedly.

"A pair of wings," screamed the eagle in joy.

"How very simple, after all!"

"And yet how wise!"

"But," said Popocatepetl, after the first outburst, "who can make me these wings?"

The little animal replied: "I and my kind are great, because at times we can make one mind control a hundred thousand bodies. This is the secret of our performances. It will be nothing for us to make wings for even you, great Popocatepetl. I and my kind will come"—continued the crafty little animal— "we will come and dwell on this beautiful plain that stretches from the sea to the sea and we will make wings for you."

Popocatepetl wished to embrace the little animal. "Oh, glorious! Oh, best of little brutes! Run! run! run! Summon your kind, dwell in the plain and make me wings. Ah, when once Popocatepetl can soar on his wings from star to star, then indeed——"

Poor old stupid Popocatepetl! The little animal summoned his kind, they dwelt on the plains, they made this and they made that, but they made no wings for Popocatepetl.

And sometimes when the thunderous voice of the old peak rolls and rolls, if you know that tongue, you can hear him say: "Oh, traitor! Traitor! Traitor! Where are my wings? My wings, traitor! I am hungry! Where are my wings?"

But this little animal merely places his finger beside his nose and winks.

"Your wings, indeed, fool! Sit still and howl for them! Old idiot!"

No. 18   HOW THE DONKEY LIFTED THE HILLS

MANY people suppose that the donkey is lazy. This is a great mistake. It is his pride.

Years ago, there was nobody quite so fine as the donkey. He was a great swell in those times. No one could express an opinion of anything without the donkey showing him where he was wrong in it. No one could mention the name of an important personage without the donkey declaring how well he knew him.

The donkey was above all things a proud and aristocratic beast.

One day a party of animals were discussing one thing and another, until finally the conversation drifted around to mythology.

"I have always admired that giant, Atlas," observed the ox in the course of the conversation. "It was amazing how he could carry things."

"Oh, yes, Atlas," said the donkey. "I knew him very well. I

once met a man and we got talking of Atlas. I expressed my admiration for the giant and my desire to meet him some day, if possible. Whereupon the man said that there was nothing quite so easy. He was sure that his dear friend, Atlas, would be happy to meet so charming a donkey. Was I at leisure next Monday? Well, then, could I dine with him upon that date? So, you see, it was all arranged. I found Atlas to be a very pleasant fellow."

"It has always been a wonder to me how he could have carried the earth on his back," said the horse.

"Oh, my dear sir, nothing is more simple," cried the donkey. "One has only to make up one's mind to it and then—do it. That is all. I am quite sure that if I wished I could carry a range of mountains upon my back."

All the others said, "Oh, my!"

"Yes I could," asserted the donkey, stoutly. "It is merely a question of making up one's mind. I will bet."

"I will wager also," said the horse. "I will wager my ears that you can't carry a range of mountains upon your back."

"Done," cried the donkey.

Forthwith the party of animals set out for the mountains. Suddenly, however, the donkey paused and said: "Oh, but look here! Who will place this range of mountains upon my back? Surely I cannot be expected to do the loading also."

Here was a great question. The party consulted. At length the ox said: "We will have to ask some men to shovel the mountains upon the donkey's back."

Most of the others clapped their hoofs or their paws and cried: "Ah, that is the thing."

The horse, however, shook his head doubtfully. "I don't know about these men. They are very sly. They will introduce some deviltry into the affair."

"Why, how silly," said the donkey. "Apparently you do not understand men. They are the most gentle, guileless creatures."

"Well," retorted the horse, "I will doubtless be able to escape since I am not to be encumbered with any mountains. Proceed."

The donkey smiled in derision at these observations by the horse.

Presently they came upon some men who were laboring away

like mad, digging ditches, felling trees, gathering fruits, carrying water, building huts.

"Look at these men, would you," said the horse. "Can you trust them after this exhibition of their depravity? See how each one selfishly——"

The donkey interrupted with a loud laugh.

"What nonsense!"

And then he cried out to the men: "Ho, my friends, will you please come and shovel a range of mountains upon my back?"

"What?"

"Will you please come and shovel a range of mountains upon my back?"

The men were silent for a time. Then they went apart and debated. They gesticulated a great deal.

Some apparently said one thing and some another. At last they paused and one of their number came forward.

"Why do you wish a range of mountains shovelled upon your back?"

"It is a wager," cried the donkey.

The men consulted again. And, as the discussion became older, their heads went closer and closer together, until they merely whispered, and did not gesticulate at all. Ultimately they cried: "Yes, certainly we will shovel a range of mountains upon your back for you."

"Ah, thanks," said the donkey.

"Here is surely some deviltry," said the horse behind his hoof to the ox.

The entire party proceeded then to the mountains. The donkey drew a long breath and braced his legs.

"Are you ready?" asked the men.

"All ready," cried the donkey.

The men began to shovel.

The dirt and the stones flew over the donkey's back in showers. It was not long before his legs were hidden. Presently only his neck and head remained in view. Then at last this wise donkey vanished. There had been made no great effect upon the range of mountains. They still towered toward the sky.

The watching crowd saw the heap of dirt and stones make

a little movement and then was heard a muffled cry. "Enough! Enough! It was not two ranges of mountains. The wager was for one range of mountains. It is not fair! It is not fair!"

But the new men only laughed as they shovelled on.

"Enough! Enough! Oh, woe is me—thirty snow-capped peaks upon my little back. Ah, these false, false men. Oh, virtuous, wise and holy men, desist."

The men again laughed. They were as busy as fiends with their shovels.

"Ah, brutal, cowardly, accursed men, ah, good, gentle and holy men, please remove some of those damnable peaks. I will adore your beautiful shovels forever. I will be a slave to the beckoning of your little fingers. I will no longer be my own donkey—I will be your donkey."

The men burst into a triumphant shout and ceased shovelling.

"Swear it, mountain-carrier!"

"I swear! I swear! I swear!"

The other animals scampered away then, for these men in their plots and plans were very terrible. "Poor old foolish fellow," cried the horse; "he may keep his ears. He will need them to hear and count the blows that are now to fall upon him."

The men unearthed the donkey. They beat him with their shovels. "Ho, come on, slave." Encrusted with earth, yellow-eyed from fright, the donkey limped towards his prison. His ears hung down like the leaves of the plantain during the great rain.

So now, when you see a donkey with a church, a palace, and three villages upon his back, and he goes with infinite slowness, moving but one leg at a time, do not think him lazy. It is his pride.

No. 19 THE VICTORY OF THE MOON

THE Strong Man of the Hills lost his wife. Immediately he went abroad calling aloud. The people all crouched afar in the dark of their huts and cried to him when he was yet a long distance away. "No, no; Great Chief, we have not even seen the imprint of your wife's sandal in the sand. If we had seen it, you would have found us bowed down in worship before the marks of her ten glorious brown toes for we are but poor devils of Indians and the grandeur of the sun's rays on her hair would have turned our eyes to dust."

"Her toes are not brown. They are pink," said the Strong Man from the Hills. "Therefore do I believe that you speak truth when you say you have not seen her, good little men of the valley. In this matter of her great loveliness, however, you speak a little too strongly. As she is no longer among my possessions, I have no mind to hear her praised. Whereabouts is the best man of you?"

None of them had stomach for this honor at the time. They surmised that the Strong Man of the Hills had some plan for combat, and they knew that the best man of them would have in this encounter only the strength of the meat in the grip of the fire. "Great King," they said in one voice, "there is no best man here."

"How is this?" roared the Strong Man. "There must be one who excels. It is a law. Let him step forward then."

But they solemnly shook their heads. "There is no best man here."

The Strong Man turned upon them so furiously that many fell to the ground. "There must be one. Let him step forward." Shivering, they huddled together and tried, in their fear, to thrust each other toward the Strong Man.

At this time a young philosopher approached the throng slowly. The philosophers of that age were all young men in the full heat of life. The old greybeards were, for the most part, very stupid, and were so accounted.

"Strong Man from the Hills," said the young philosopher, "go to yonder brook and bathe. Then come and eat of this fruit. Then gaze for a time at the blue sky and the green earth. Afterwards I have something to say to you."

"You are not so wise that I am obliged to bathe before listening to you?" demanded the Strong Man, insolently.

"No," said the young philosopher. All the people thought this reply very strange.

"Why, then, must I bathe and eat of fruit and gaze at the earth and the sky?"

"Because they are pleasant things to do."

"Have I, do you think, any thirst at this time for pleasant things?"

"Bathe, eat, gaze," said the young philosopher with a gesture.

The Strong Man did indeed whirl his bronzed and terrible limbs in the silver water. Then he lay in the shadow of a tree and ate the cool fruit and gazed at the sky and the earth. "This is a fine comfort," he said. After a time he suddenly struck his forehead with his finger. "By the way, did I tell you that my wife had fled from me?"

"I knew it," said the young philosopher.

Later the Strong Man slept peacefully. The young philosopher smiled.

But in the night the little men of the valley came clamoring: "Oh, Strong Man of the Hills, the moon derides you!"

The philosopher went to them in the darkness. "Be still, little people. It is nothing. The derision of the moon is nothing."

But the little men of the valley would not cease their uproar. "Oh, Strong Man! Strong Man, awake! Awake! The moon derides you!"

Then the Strong Man aroused and shook his locks away from his eyes. "What is it, good little men of the valley?"

"Oh, Strong Man, the moon derides you! Oh, Strong Man!"

The Strong Man looked and there indeed was the moon laughing down at him. He sprang to his feet and roared: "Ah, old fat lump of a moon, you laugh? Have you then my wife?"

The moon said no word, but merely smiled in a way that was like a flash of silver bars.

"Well, then, moon, take this home to her," thundered the Strong Man, and he hurled his spear.

The moon clapped both hands to its eye and cried, "Oh! Oh!"

The little people of the valley cried: "Oh, this is terrible, Strong Man! He has smitten our sacred moon in the eye!"

The young philosopher cried nothing at all.

The Strong Man threw his coat of crimson feathers upon the ground. He took his knife and felt its edge. "Look you, philosopher," he said. "I have lost my wife, and yet the bath, the meal of fruit in the shade, the sight of sky and earth are still good to me, but when this false moon derides me there must be a killing."

"I understand you," said the young philosopher. The Strong Man ran off into the night. The little men of the valley clapped their hands in ecstasy and terror. "Ah, ah! What a battle there will be!"

The Strong Man went into his own hills and gathered there many great rocks and trunks of trees. It was strange to see him erect upon a peak of the mountains and hurling these things at the moon. He kept the air full of them.

"Fat moon, come closer!" he shouted. "Come closer, and let it be my knife against your knife. Oh, to think we are obliged to tolerate such an old, fat, stupid, lazy, good-for-nothing moon! You are ugly as death, while I—— Oh, moon, you stole my beloved, and it was nothing, but when you stole my beloved and laughed at me, it became another matter. And yet you are so ugly, so fat, so stupid, so lazy, so good-for-nothing. Ah, I shall go mad! Come closer, moon, and let me examine your round, grey skull with this club."

And he always kept the air full of great missiles.

The moon merely laughed, and said: "Why should I come closer?"

Wildly did the Strong Man pile rock upon rock. He builded him a tower that was the father of all towers. It made the mountains appear to be babes. Upon the summit of it he swung his great club and flourished his knife.

The little men in the valley far below beheld a great storm and at the end of it they said: "Look, the moon is dead!" The cry went to and fro on the earth: "The moon is dead!"

The Strong Man went to the home of the moon. She, the sought one, lay upon a cloud and her little foot dangled over the side of it. The Strong Man took this little foot in his two hands and kissed it. "Ah, beloved!" he moaned, "I would rather this little foot was upon my dead neck than that moon should ever have the privilege of seeing it."

She leaned over the edge of the cloud and gazed at him. "How dusty you are! Why do you puff so? Veritably, you are an ordinary person. Why did I ever find you interesting?"

The Strong Man flung his knife into the air and turned back toward the earth. "If the young philosopher had been at my elbow," he reflected bitterly, "I would doubtless have gone at the matter in another way. What does my strength avail me in this contest?"

The battered moon, limping homeward, replied to the Strong Man from the Hills: "Aye, surely! My weakness is in this thing as strong as your strength. I am victor with my ugliness, my age, my stoutness, my stupidity, my laziness, my good-for-nothingness. Woman is woman. Men are equal in everything save good fortune. I envy you not."

No. 20 THE JUDGMENT OF THE SAGE

A BEGGAR crept wailing through the streets of a city. A certain man came to him there and gave him bread, saying: "I give you this loaf, because of God's word." Another came to the beggar and gave him bread, saying: "Take this loaf; I give it because you are hungry."

Now there was a continual rivalry among the citizens of this town as to who should appear to be the most pious man, and the event of the gifts to the beggar made discussion. People gathered in knots and argued furiously to no particular purpose. They appealed to the beggar, but he bowed humbly to the ground, as befitted one of his condition, and answered: "It is a singular circumstance that the loaves were of one size and of the same quality. How, then, can I decide which of these men gave bread more piously?"

The people heard of a philosopher who travelled through their country, and one said: "Behold, we who give not bread to beggars are not capable of judging those who have given bread to beggars. Let us, then, consult this wise man."

"But," said some, "mayhap this philosopher, according to your rule that one must have given bread before judging they who give bread, will not be capable."

"That is an indifferent matter to all truly great philosophers." So they made search for the wise man, and in time they came upon him, strolling along at his ease in the manner of philosophers.

"Oh, most illustrious sage," they cried.

"Yes," said the philosopher promptly.

"Oh, most illustrious sage, there are two men in our city, and one gave bread to a beggar, saying: 'Because of God's word.' And the other gave bread to the beggar, saying: 'Because you are hungry.' Now, which of these, oh, most illustrious sage, is the more pious man?"

"Eh?" said the philosopher.

"Which of these, oh, most illustrious sage, is the more pious man?"

"My friends," said the philosopher suavely addressing the concourse, "I see that you mistake me for an illustrious sage. I am not he whom you seek. However, I saw a man answering my description pass here some time ago. With speed you may overtake him. Adieu."

No. 21   ART IN KANSAS CITY

"WHEN I was in Kansas City," said my Uncle Clarence, "I met a cow who interested me very much which somewhat surprised me as during my travels in the West I had met vast herds of cattle in the ordinary social way without being particularly edified either by their deportment or their speech. But this Kansas City cow was a superior creature quite different from others of her species. Some of her water-colour sketches were remarkable productions for an amateur and I believe she might have carved out a career in that line if her ambitions had not been ruthlessly smothered by her nominal owner who gave as his reason that people were beginning to complain that her milk was thin. He would, he said, allow her to paint in oils but for this she had no fancy. This man was a singularly evil person and I believe his sole object in prohibiting his cow to sketch in water-colours was to deliver a stunning blow to the progress of art in Kansas City. If she had begun to paint in oils I have no doubt that he would have stopped her on the ground that people were complaining her milk was too thick. The poor cow considered her life quite blighted and indeed when I first saw her she was in bitter tears. I called across the fence to her to enquire the cause of her woe and she replied giving me her version of the water-colour incident as I have told it. Afterward I found it to be quite correct. I so pitied her that I made a personal appeal to her owner and told him that he was senselessly depriving the community of the light of an artistic star but he rejoined with candor that he did not give a damn. He was, he said, in the milk business and to this argument I of course did not make a spirited reply."

No. 22 A TALE OF MERE CHANCE

Being an Account of the Pursuit of the Tiles, the Statement of the Clock, and the Grip of a Coat of Orange Spots, together with some Criticism of a Detective said to be Carved from an Old Table-leg.

YES, my friend, I killed the man, but I would not have been detected in it were it not for some very extraordinary circumstances. I had long considered this deed, but I am a delicate and sensitive person, you understand, and I hesitated over it as the diver hesitates on the brink of a dark and icy mountain pool. A thought of the shock of contact holds one back.

As I was passing his house one morning, I said to myself: "Well, at any rate if she loves him, it will not be for long." And after that decision I was not myself, but a sort of a machine.

I rang the bell and the servants admitted me to the drawing room. I waited there while the tall old clock placidly ticked its speech of time. The rigid and austere chairs remained in possession of their singular imperturbability, although of course they were aware of my purpose, but the little white tiles of the floor whispered one to another and looked at me.

Presently he entered the room, and I, drawing my revolver, shot him. He screamed—you know that scream—mostly amazement—and as he fell forward his blood was upon the little white tiles. They huddled and covered their eyes from this rain. It seemed to me that the old clock stopped ticking as a man may gasp in the middle of a sentence, and a chair threw itself in my way as I sprang toward the door.

A moment later I was walking down the street—tranquil, you understand—and I said to myself: "It is done. Long years from this day I will say to her that it was I who killed him. After time has eaten the conscience of the thing she will admire my courage."

I was elated that the affair had gone off so smoothly, and I felt like returning home and taking a long, full sleep, like a tired workingman. When people passed me, I contemplated their stupidity with a sense of satisfaction.

But those accursed little white tiles!

I heard a shrill crying and chattering behind me and, looking back, I saw them, blood-stained and impassioned, raising their little hands and screaming: "Murder! It was he!" I have said that they had little hands. I am not so sure of it, but they had some means of indicating me as unerringly as pointing fingers. As for their movement, they swept along as easily as dry, light leaves are carried by the wind. Always they were shrilly piping their song of my guilt.

My friend, may it never be your fortune to be pursued by a crowd of little blood-stained tiles. I used a thousand means to be free from the clash-clash of those tiny feet. I ran through the world at my best speed, but it was no better than that of an ox, while they, my pursuers, were always fresh, eager, relentless.

I am an ingenious person, and I used every trick that a desperately fertile man can invent. Hundreds of times I had almost evaded them, when some smoldering, neglected spark would blaze up and discover me.

I felt that the eye of conviction would have no terrors for me, but the eyes of suspicion which I saw in city after city, on road after road, drove me to the verge of going forward and saying: "Yes, I have murdered."

People would see the following, clamorous troop of blood-stained tiles and give me piercing glances, so that these swords played continually at my heart. But we are a decorous race, thank God. It is very vulgar to apprehend murderers on the public streets. We have learned correct manners from the English. Besides, who can be sure of the meaning of clamoring tiles? It might be merely a trick in politics.

Detectives? What are detectives? Oh, yes, I have read of them and their deeds, when I come to think of it. The prehistoric races must have been remarkable. I have never been able to understand how the detectives navigated in stone boats. Still, specimens of their pottery excavated in Tamaulipas show a remarkable knowledge of mechanics. I remember the little hydraulic—what's that? Well, what you say may be true, my friend, but I think you dream.

The little stained tiles. My friend, I stopped in an inn at the ends of the earth, and in the morning they were there flying like birds and pecking at my window.

I should have escaped. Heavens, I should have escaped! What was more simple? I murdered and then walked into the world, which is wide and intricate.

Do you know that my own clock assisted in the hunt of me? They asked what time I left my home that morning and it replied at once: "Half-after eight." The watch of a man I had chanced to pass near the house of the crime told the people: "Seven minutes after nine." And of course the tall old clock in the drawing room went about day after day repeating: "Eighteen minutes after nine."

Do you say that the man who caught me was very clever? My friend, I have lived long, and he was the most incredible blockhead of my experience. An enslaved, dust-eating Mexican vaquero wouldn't hitch his pony to such a man. Do you think he deserves credit for my capture? If he had been as pervading as the atmosphere, he would never have caught me. If he was a detective, as you say, I could carve a better one from an old table-leg. But the tiles! That is another matter. At night I think they flew in a long high flock like pigeons. In the day, little mad things, they murmured on my trail like frothymouthed weazels.

I see that you note these great, round, vividly orange spots on my coat. Of course, even if the detective was really carved from an old table-leg, he could hardly fail to apprehend a man thus badged. As sores come upon one in the plague, so came these spots upon my coat. When I discovered them I made effort to free myself of this coat. I tore, tugged, wrenched at it, but around my shoulders it was like the grip of a dead man's arms. Do you know that I have plunged in a thousand lakes? I have smeared this coat with a thousand paints. But day and night the spots burn like lights. I might walk from this jail to-day if I could rid myself of this coat, but it clings—clings—clings.

At any rate the person you call a detective was not so clever to discover a man in a coat of spotted orange, followed by shrieking blood-stained tiles.

Yes, that noise from the corridor is most peculiar. But they are always there, muttering and watching, clashing and jostling. It sounds as if the dishes of hades were being washed. Yet I have become used to it. Once, indeed, in the night, I cried out to them: "In God's name, go away, little blood-stained tiles." But they doggedly answered: "It is the law."

No. 23 THE CAMEL

"No MAN," observed my Uncle Clarence musingly, "likes to find grass in his whiskey and this is why, during all that journey, I did not allow the camel to eat anything. When I first made up my mind to travel in the State of Maine I set about contriving some scheme to provide myself with proper nourishment during the trip without shocking the delicate nerves of the people of Maine who, one and all, men, women and children, bitterly loathe even a furtive suggestion of whiskey. As far as the frontier of Maine the camel carried on his back three cases of soda and one dozen bottles of the best Scotch. I had thought of bringing lemons, sugar and cloves for use in cold weather but I was told these articles could be purchased in Maine if the intention of the purchaser was concealed from the grocer. At the frontier, I with the aid of a wonderful mechanism injected the whiskey into one of the camel's stomachs and into the other stomach I injected the soda-water, afterward hiding the mechanism in my boots since, as the mechanism had injected the nourishment into the camel it was also to be employed in getting it out again. Then seizing the camel by its halter I walked boldly into Maine.

"There was a town at no great distance and I went at once to the principal hotel for luncheon. Placing my camel in the care of the hostler somewhat to his surprise. The town was rather enlivened and upon asking the cause of the gala aspect, I was told that the corner-stone of a new church was to be laid in the afternoon and it had been made the occasion for no inconsiderable celebration. The clergy of the whole county were to be in attendance with all the prominent laymen. After luncheon I strolled out to witness this interesting ceremony. There was a great concourse of people and a band ready to play in the proper intervals and under the trees long tables heavy with refreshments. On a decorated stand were gathered the flower of the county's clergy.

"Now I had been careless about one thing. I esteem myself as a thoughtful person but in contriving my receptacle for whiskey and soda, I had taken no thought of a possible effect upon the camel. The chief orator of the day was bestowing his ringing eloquence upon us and the vast crowd was breathlessly intent upon each word when I heard shouts of alarm and amazement from the crowd and upon turning my eyes toward the middle of the uproar I perceived my camel making his way toward the speaker's stand. He was smiling with an expression of foolish good-nature and his legs were spraddling out in his drunken attempt to keep himself erect. The chief orator of the day cut a burning sentence in the middle, gave a shriek whoop and fell backwards, disappearing amid the crash of lumber and the tearing of bunting.

"As near as I remember now it was the first time I had seen a clergyman climb a tree. I was astonished at their agility. It seemed but a moment before the trees were black with clergymen. The band fled in a body leaving a broad wake of musical instruments. My agitation had been so extreme that I was not capable of following events with my usual clearness but presently I seemed to be alone with the camel and the corner-stone. When I indignantly approached the brute I found him munching the bass-drum which a thoughtless bandsman had failed to take with him. From the trees above me resounded cries and moans. The committee of well-known citizens who escorted me and the camel over the frontier on the evening of that same day courteously informed me that they only carried their shot-guns as a protection against the cold night-air."

No. 24 A FREIGHT CAR INCIDENT

"REMEMBER that time, Major?" said the railroad man.

"You bet I do," rejoined the major.

"Go ahead and tell it," said the others.

The major lifted his glass and carefully scrutinized the bright liquid. "Well, Tom's line you see, was just being put through the interior of the State at that time, and one day he asked me to go out with him to some little town which he was going to open with an auction sale of lots and free beer and sandwiches for the people, and all that, you know. Well, I went along, and there was a big freight car loaded down with kegs and provisions. Everybody was having a great time. Tom got ill during the sale, so he went into a little shanty to lie down, while I went over to the freight car to get some ice to put on his head. I was in the car scouting around after ice when, all of a sudden, some one slammed the door to, and made the inside of the car as dark as pitch. Then somebody in the darkness began to swear like a pirate, and I heard him swing his revolver loose. I began to see the game then. It seems that there was a fellow around there that a good many people wanted to kill, and they said they were going to kill him that day at the sale, too. Somebody had pointed him out to me during the morning, and I had heard him brag, so I recognized this voice in the darkness. I think he decided that they had slammed the door on him so that when he opened it to come out they could get a good fair chance to make a sieve of him. The way that man swore was positively frightful.

"He wasn't very good company, either. I stood still so long that I felt the bones in my legs creak like old timbers, and I didn't breathe any harder than a canary bird. He went on swearing at a great rate.

"I began to think of Tom and his pain, wishing he had died rather than I had come for that ice.

"At last I found that I had got to move. There was no help
for it. My legs refused to support me in this position any longer.
My head was growing dizzy, and if I didn't change my attitude
I would fall down. I hadn't remained motionless for so very
long either, but in a darkness where a man can't tell whether
he is standing on his feet or his ears, the faculty of balance
isn't much to be counted on. My heart stopped short when I
felt myself sway, but I shifted one foot quickly, and there I
was again. But that accursed foot had made a squeak.

"The fellow listened for a moment, and then he yelled: 'Who
th' hell is in here?'

"I didn't say a word, but just dropped down to the floor as
easy as a sack of oats.

"He listened for a time, and then bellowed out again: 'Who's
in here?' I supposed he figured that it wasn't one of his enemies,
or they would have got him while he was swearing to himself
over in the corner.

" 'Who's in here, by Gawd! Come along now, galoot, an' speak
up er I'll begin t' bore leetle holes in yeh! Who er yeh, anyhow!
Whistle some now, by Gawd, er I'll fair eat ye!'

"He was beginning to get mad as a wildcat. I could fairly hear
that fellow lashing himself into a rage, and getting more crazy
every minute. All the kegs were up in his corner, and when I
felt around with one hand I couldn't find a thing to get behind.
Every second I expected to hear him begin to work his gun, and
if you have ever lain in the darkness and wondered at what
precise spot the impending bullet would strike, you know how
I felt. So when he yelled out again, 'Who er you?' I spoke
up and said, 'It's only me.'

" 'Thunder,' cried he, in a roar like a bull. 'Who's me! Give
yer hull damn name an' pedigree, mister, if yeh ain't fond of
reg'lar howling, helling row!'

" 'I'm from Houston,' said I.

" 'Houston,' said he, with a snort. 'An' what er yeh doin' here,
stranger?'

" 'I came out to the sale,' I told him.

" 'Hum,' said he; and then he remained still for some time
over in his end of the car.

"I was congratulating myself that I ran no more chance of

trouble with this fiend, and that the whole thing was now a mere matter of waiting for some merciful fate to let me out, when suddenly the fellow said: 'Mister!'

" 'Sir?' said I.

" 'Open that there door!'

" 'Er—what?'

" 'Open that there door!'

" 'Er—the door to the car?'

"He began to froth at the mouth, I think. 'Sure,' he roared. 'Th' door t' th' car! There hain't fifty doors here, be ther! Slid 'er open or else, mister, you be a goner sure!' And then he cursed my ancestors for fifteen generations.

" 'Well—but—look here,' said I. 'Ain't—look here—ain't they going to shoot as soon as anybody opens that door. It——'

" 'None 'a yer damned business, stranger,' the fellow howled. 'Open that there door, er I'll everlastin'ly make er ventilator of yeh. Come on, now! Step up!' He began to prowl over in my direction. 'Where are yeh? Come on now, galoot! Where are yeh? Oh, just lemme lay my ol' gun ag'in yeh an' I'll fin' out! Step up!'

"This cat-like approach in the darkness was too much for me. 'Hold on,' said I, 'I'll open the door.'

"He gave a grunt and paused. I got up and went over to the door.

" 'Now, stranger,' the fellow said, 'es soon as yeh open th' door, jest step erside an' watch Luke Burnham peel th' skin off er them skunks.'

" 'But, look here——' said I.

" 'Stranger, this hain't no time t' arger! Open th' door!'

"I put my hand on the door and prepared to slide my body along with it. I had hoped to find it locked, but unfortunately it was not. When I gave it a preliminary shake, it rattled easily, and I could see that there was going to be no trouble in opening the door.

"I turned toward the interior of the car for one last remonstrance. 'Say, I haven't got anything to do with this thing. I'm just up here from Houston to go to the sale——'

"But the fellow howled again: 'Stranger, er you makin' a damn' fool 'a me? By the——'

" 'Hold on,' said I. 'I'll open the door.'

"I got all prepared, and then turned my head. 'Are you ready?'

" 'Let 'er go!'

"He was standing back in the car. I could see the dull glint of the revolvers in each hand.

" 'Let 'er go!' he said again.

"I braced myself, and put one hand out to reach the end of the door, then with a groan, I pulled. The door slid open, and I fell on my hands and knees in the end of the car.

" 'Hell,' said the fellow. I turned my head. There was nothing to be seen but blue sky and green prairie, and the little group of yellow board shanties with a red auction flag and a crowd of people in front of one of them.

"The fellow swore and flung himself out of the car. He went prowling off toward the crowd with his guns held barrels down and with his nervous fingers on the triggers. I followed him at a respectful distance.

"As he came near to them he began to walk like a cat on wet pavements, lifting each leg away up. 'Where is he? Where is th' white-livered skunk what slammed thet door on me? Where is he? Where is he? Let 'im show hisself! He dassent! Where is he? Where is he?'

"He went among them, bellowing in his bull fashion, and not a man moved. 'Where's all these galoots what was goin' t' shoot at me? Where be they? Let 'em come! Let 'em show theirselves! Let 'em come at me! Oh, there's them here as has got guns hangin' to 'em, but let 'em pull 'em! Let 'em pull 'em onct! Jest let 'em tap 'em with their fingers, an' I'll drive a stove-hole through every last one 'a their low-down hides! Lessee a man pull a gun! Lessee! An' lessee th' man what slammed th' door on me. Let 'im projuce hisself, th' ——,' and he cursed this unknown individual in language that was like black smoke.

"But the men with guns remained silent and grave. The crowd for the most part gave him room enough to pitch a circus tent. When the train left he was still roaring around after the man who had slammed the door."

"And so they didn't kill him after all," said some one at the end of the narrative.

"Oh, yes, they got him that night," said the major. "In a saloon somewhere. They got him all right."

No. 25 A PROLOGUE

A GLOOMY STAGE. SLENDER CURTAINS AT A WINDOW, CENTRE. BEFORE THE WINDOW, A TABLE, AND UPON THE TABLE, A LARGE BOOK, OPENED. A MOONBEAM, NO WIDER THAN A SWORD-BLADE, PIERCES THE CURTAINS AND FALLS UPON THE BOOK.

A MOMENT OF SILENCE.

FROM WITHOUT, THEN—AN ADJACENT ROOM IN INTENTION—COME SOUNDS OF CELEBRATION, OF RIOTOUS DRINKING AND LAUGHTER. FINALLY, A SWIFT QUARREL. THE DIN AND CRASH OF A FIGHT. A LITTLE STILLNESS. THEN A WOMAN'S SCREAM. "AH, MY SON, MY SON."

A MOMENT OF SILENCE.

CURTAIN.

No. 26 A YELLOW UNDER-SIZED DOG

HARLEM has always been famed for its geographical oblivion, being second only to Brooklyn in this branch, but lately it has become celebrated for a dog. The dog belongs to one of a gang of laborers who are engaged in blasting out the mountainous abodes of the goats to make room for gigantic apartment hotels.

"Mulligan," said the foreman, "yez bether sind yer dawg to remain at home or some day he'll be going high wid th' rocks whin th' blhastin' goes off."

But the blasting had some particular fascination for the dog. He was of an observing and imaginative mind and the mystery of this process took great hold upon him. Perched at a safe distance, he gave each detail his serious attention. He was yellow and under-sized; not very intellectual in appearance; but he certainly mastered the science of throwing rocks into the air.

For a long time one point baffled the dog. Previous to every thunderous report a certain man in a red shirt walked out into the lot and made strong signs and whooped. Then innumerable people appeared, closing the windows of all the houses in the vicinity. Now this yellow, under-sized dog puzzled for hours as to why the gesticulations and whoops of this man in the red shirt should create such energy in the arms of all the servant girls of the neighborhood. The man in the red shirt was possessed of peculiar power. This made him very impressive to the dog. The man never even ate his dinner but what the little dog squatted in front of him and watched with large, inquiring eyes.

Finally the dog's interest got so keen that when the man went on his trips of gesticulation and whoop he went too and contemplated the effect. Of course a knowledge of the meaning of gestures was always denied him, but he knew the significance of a whoop and very soon he took to whooping with the man in the red shirt. He got to know when a blast was ready, and when the man was to go whooping, and invariably he accompanied him. The dog became a part of the force. He assumed responsibility and with it dignity. He exhibits great contempt now for even the swellest dogs of the locality. The presence of another dog on the lot makes him furious. The workmen think it is because he is afraid they will learn blasting and so become his rivals.

The dog is able to concentrate more thought upon his task than an average man, or even a man who is above the average. He has only a little brain, perhaps, but at any rate he devotes it entirely to his business.

When the blast is preparing the little dog stands around in illy-concealed impatience. The moment it is in readiness he is off, wildly excited. He howls at all the windows that should be closed and at others that are not important. He leaps frantically into the air, uttering at all times the most extraordinary cries. If you did not know the little dog was engaged in blasting you would think he was throwing fits.

All the servant girls know him and promptly close the windows. He will endure no carelessness; he is there to see that the windows are closed, and he will submit to no quibble. The task of the man in the red shirt is now an easy one. He merely goes along and superintends the dog. But the dog does his work so thoroughly that even the office of superintendent is mainly an honorary position.

A peculiar result of the dog's occupation is the fact that his voice is developing in a marvelous way. He can now make more noise than eight ordinary dogs and when he is working it could easily be supposed that a general dog fight was in progress.

When the dog walks home at night with the workingmen many people take note of him. He is yellow, under-sized; more than ordinarily insignificant in appearance, but his manner has undergone such a change that he could hardly fail to attract attention. He has none of that careless doggishness which may be said to stamp almost the entire canine race. He has, on the contrary, a demeanor of such sobriety and dignity that few people fail to gaze after him, as he paces thoughtfully along. Many of them say, as did a man who stood on the corner the other evening: "There goes a dog with a good deal of business responsibility upon his shoulders."

No. 27 A DETAIL

THE tiny old lady in the black dress and curious little black bonnet had at first seemed alarmed at the sound made by her feet upon the stone pavements. But later she forgot about it, for she suddenly came into the tempest of the Sixth Avenue shopping district, where from the streams of people and vehicles went up a roar like that from headlong mountain torrents.

She seemed then like a chip that catches, recoils, turns and wheels, a reluctant thing in the clutch of the impetuous river. She hesitated, faltered, debated with herself. Frequently she seemed about to address people; then of a sudden she would evidently lose her courage. Meanwhile the torrent jostled her, swung her this and that way.

At last, however, she saw two young women gazing in at a shop window. They were well-dressed girls; they wore gowns with enormous sleeves that made them look like full-rigged ships with all sails set. They seemed to have plenty of time; they leisurely scanned the goods in the window. Other people had made the tiny old woman much afraid because, obviously, they were speeding to keep such tremendously important engagements. She went close to them and peered in at the same window. She watched them furtively for a time; then finally she said: "Excuse me!" The girls looked down at this old face with its two large eyes turned toward them. "Excuse me but can you tell me where I can get any work?"

For an instant the two girls stared. Then they seemed about to exchange a smile but at the last moment they checked it. The tiny old lady's eyes were upon them. She was quaintly serious, silently expectant. She made one marvel that in that face the wrinkles showed no trace of experience, knowledge; they were simply little soft innocent creases. As for her glance it had the trustfulness of ignorance and the candor of babyhood.

"I want to get something to do, because I need the money," she continued, since in their astonishment they had not replied to her first question. "Of course I'm not strong and I couldn't do very much but I can sew well and in a house where there was a good many men folks, I could do all the mending. Do you know any place where they would like me to come?"

The young women did then exchange a smile but it was a subtly tender smile, the verge of personal grief.

"Well, no, madame," hesitatingly said one of them at last, "I don't think I know anyone."

A shade passed over the tiny old lady's face, a shadow of the wing of disappointment. "Don't you?" she said with a little struggle to be brave in her voice.

Then the girl hastily continued: "But if you will give me your address, I may find some one and if I do, I will surely let you know of it."

The tiny old lady dictated her address, bending over to watch the girl write on a visiting card with a little silver pencil. Then she said: "I thank you very much." She bowed to them, smiling, and went on down the avenue.

As for the two girls they went to the curb and watched this aged figure, small and frail, in its black gown and curious black bonnet. At last, the crowd, the innumerable wagons, intermingling and changing with uproar and riot, suddenly engulfed it.

No. 27a EARLY DRAFT

THE old lady had at first seemed alarmed at the sound made by her feet upon the stone pavements. Later, she forgot them when she came upon the turmoil of the Sixth Avenue shopping district. She looked in respect and awe at these people who were so pressed for time, at these trucks that roared like dragons, at complexity.

Sometimes she seemed to doubt her own wisdom; she hesitated, faltered, debated with herself.

Frequently she seemed about to address people; then suddenly she would lose courage and pass on.

At last, however, she saw two young women gazing in at a shop window. They seemed to have plenty of time; they proceeded leisurely. Other people had made her afraid because, obviously, they were speeding to keep such important engagements.

She went close to the two young women and peered in at the same window. She watched them furtively for a time; then finally she said:

"Excuse me!" The young women looked down at this old face with its two large eyes turned toward them. "Excuse me but can you tell me where I can get any work?"

For an instant the two young women seemed about to exchange a smile but at the last moment they intercepted this significant look because the old lady's eyes were upon their faces and she was quaintly serious and innocent. She seemed like a flower carried by the winds of destiny through a world of lies and she made one marvel that in that face the wrinkles showed no trace of experience, knowledge; they were simply little soft creases. As for her glance it had the trustfulness of ignorance and the candor of babyhood.

"I want to get something to do, because I need the money," she continued, since in their astonishment they had not replied to her first question. "Of course I am not very strong and I couldn't do very much but I can sew well and in a house where there was a good many men folks, I could do all the mending. Do you know any place where they would like me to come?"

Then the two young women did exchange a smile but it was a subtly tender smile, the verge of personal grief.

"Well, no, madame," said one of them at last, "I don't think I know anyone."

A shade passed over the old lady's face, the shadow of the wing of first disappointment. "Don't you?" she said with an attempt at courage.

Then the young woman hastily continued: "But if you will give me your address, I may find some one and if I do, I will surely let you know of it."

The old lady dictated her address, bending over to watch the other write it on a visiting card with a little silver pencil. Then she said: "I thank you very much." She bowed to them, smiling, and went on down the avenue.

The two girls went to the edge of the side-walk and watched this aged figure, tiny and frail, in its black dress and curious black bonnet. At last, the crowd, the innumerable wagons, intermingling and changing with uproar and riot, swallowed it, as if the mouth of a monster had opened. The girls stood wondering.

No. 28   DIAMONDS AND DIAMONDS

JIMMIE the Mole derived his name from a certain way he would look at you when you lied to him. Lie to Jimmie in those days and he would shrug down his shoulders and squint at you most horribly and steadfastly until you grew nervous, probably, and went away. But when he was lying to you, he was a polished and courtly gentleman with no shadow of facial deformity about him.

Once Jimmie was smitten with a financial famine. He was about to take a trip to Boston, too, where some confiding man had offered him work in a concert hall as a sweet singer of ballads. Jimmie had a Tenderloin voice. This means a tenor well-suited to the air: "She has fallen by the way-side." Sometimes he went forth into the great wide-world and made money with this voice.

Jimmie being penniless and anxious to go to Boston, went to see the Flasher. "You better go over to Nellie Doyer's and borrow enough money for my ticket to Boston and then let me take your ring along with me. I'll see if I can't cop out a small bundle." The obedient Flasher borrowed money for the ticket and the obedient Flasher gave her ring to Jimmie.

Jimmie went to Boston and for two weeks made glad the rafters with his Tenderloin voice.

While standing in a corner saloon one morning, he espied a large fat personage in black clothing and with a large diamond stuck in a shirt emphatically soiled. This man seemed to strike Jimmie with considerable interest. He hung near and furtively watched this fat person drink whiskey.

Once he found himself at the bar elbow to elbow with this man. As has been said, Jimmie was often a courtly and polished gentleman. "I beg your pardon," he said, "but would you like to buy a ring?"

The fat person had not been a Boston alderman for nothing. He turned sharply and said: "No."

"I'm in hard luck just now and I need a hundred bad or I wouldn't think of selling it. If you happen to know of anybody who might like a nice diamond, I hope you won't mind telling me."

The fat person relented at this point because Jimmie's voice was obviously that of a courtly and polished gentleman. "Well, no, I don't remember anybody just now. Let's look at the ring."

Jimmie held forth a graceful hand.

"Fine stone," said the ex-alderman.

"Yes," replied Jimmie. "A present from my girl in Chicago. She'll be crazy when she finds out that I've blown it in. Can't help it though. Hard luck is hard luck. I came here looking for a theatrical job—that's my business—but I don't get a thing but a frost from every manager I strike. Hard luck is hard luck."

"Sure," said the fat person. "How much do you want for the ring?"

"Well, I'll take a hundred," answered Jimmie candidly, "and the ring is worth that to anybody. It'll stand me a hundred in any pawn-shop but I don't want to get up against the pawn-shops anymore and when I've got anything to sell I'd rather have it go outright to some good fellow."

The fat person again gazed down at the ring. "Let me see it off your finger, will you?"

"Sure," said Jimmie.

The other looked at the ring close and for inside and outside. "Looks like a good ring."

"It is a good ring. I'd like to see a man prove there was anything fake about that ring."

"Dan," called the fat person to the bartender. "How's that for a gig-lamp?" He pushed the trinket over the bar.

"Gee," cried the bartender, holding it high. "Say, that's a peach."

The fat person said to Jimmie: "Young feller, I'm almost coming around to giving up a hundred for it myself."

Jimmie shrugged his shoulders. "A hundred and it's yours."

The other again examined the ring. Finally he said: "Well—you bring it around to a jeweler's with me and if he says it's worth the money you say it is, why, I'll throw down a hundred for it." Whereupon he cast a keen eye at Jimmie.

But Jimmie promptly cried: "Certainly. Come ahead."

When they walked into the street, the fat person rather shied away from Jimmie and with singular intentness he kept his eyes straight to the front. "You say—" he observed. "You say your girl in Chicago gave you this ring?"

"Oh, that's on the level all right," answered the Mole. "But—" he added and he looked squarely at the fat person, "I've heard people say that they saw it on the finger of a ranchman from Montana just a little while before he came to Chicago on a skate."

"Um," said the fat person with a quick sidelong glance. He whistled indifferently.

When they had entered the jeweler's shop, the fat person crowded his great form against the show-case and said: "My friend, would you mind telling us what this ring is worth?"

When the jeweler appeared he seemed bored. Evidently he was bored because he thought somebody was going to be swindled but why this should bore him more than it should enrage him or make him weep, none can tell.

"Let's see it." Jimmie gave him the ring and he went away. When he returned, he drummed on the counter and stared at the ceiling. "It's worth about two hundred dollars."

"It is, is it?" said the fat person.

"Yes."

"Would you give two hundred for it?"

"If I was buying diamonds for myself I might. But as a dealer, I might give a hundred. Or maybe a hundred and fifty."

"You would, would you?" said the fat person. Jimmie took the ring again and the two marched away.

The fat person led swiftly some distance down the sidewalk. When he stopped he said: "Well, I'll take the ring at a hundred."

"All right," said the Mole. "I'll keep to my bargain although it seems as if I might have struck higher."

"A hundred dollars is a good deal of money," said the fat person. "The Montana——"

"Take the ring," said Jimmie.

The other counted out the hundred in bills. "Here's your money—gimme the ring." At this point they eyed each other warily but the transfer was made in safety. This ornament of politics had the ring and the polished and courtly gentleman had the bills.

"Well, good-bye, old boy," cried the fat person.

"Good luck to you," rejoined Jimmie. "I'd come and break a cold bottle with you only I must light out for Chicago to see my girl. Say," he said facing around again, "I almost wish I hadn't——"

But the fat person waved his hand gaily and walked rapidly away. "Ta-ta, old boy," he cried. Jimmie the Mole gazed after him wistfully.

The next morning Jimmie was in New York. When he arrived at Flasher's flat she was at breakfast. He took from his pocket one hundred dollars in bills and from his finger he took her ring. He laid them on the table before her.

"There," he said with a tired sigh.

"Same old game, Jimmie?"

"Same old game."

"You always were so smooth, Jimmie," murmured Flasher.

This money would have endured some time if the Mole had not fallen in love with his luck and gone to the races. In consequence he was again obliged to borrow the two hundred dollar diamond from Flasher.

The next day he appeared in a jewelry shop in a remote

East-side street. "Fred," he said to the proprietor, "I want you to make me a ringer for this again." He handed the man the diamond ring. "And, look here, I won't pay more than three dollars either. A guy in Boston the other day charged me four dollars and a half for the same fake you make."

If you are a politician and you allow a man to substitute a ring of paste and gold-plate for a two-hundred-dollar diamond ring and sell it to you for a hundred dollars merely because you have had a jeweler appraise the real diamond—if you are this kind of an ass and dwell in a live ward, let your idiocy be known. It will make you friends. People will laugh and vote for you out of a sense of humor. If you don't believe it, look at the returns and see who was elected last year to the board of aldermen from the 204th ward of the city of Boston.

No. 29   THE AUCTION

SOME said that Ferguson gave up sailoring because he was tired of the sea. Some said that it was because he loved a woman. In truth it was because he was tired of the sea and because he loved a woman.

He saw the woman once, and immediately she became for him the symbol of all things unconnected with the sea. He did not trouble to look again at the grey old goddess, the muttering slave of the moon. Her splendors, her treacheries, her smiles, her rages, her vanities, were no longer on his mind. He took heels after a little human being, and the woman made his thought spin at all times like a top; whereas the ocean had only made him think when he was on watch.

He developed a grin for the power of the sea, and, in derision, he wanted to sell the red and green parrot which had sailed four voyages with him. The woman, however, had a sentiment concerning the bird's plumage, and she commanded Ferguson to keep it in order, as it happened, that she might forget to put food in its cage.

The parrot did not attend the wedding. It stayed at home and blasphemed at a stock of furniture, bought on the instalment plan, and arrayed for the reception of the bride and groom.

As a sailor, Ferguson had suffered the acute hankering for port; and being now always in port, he tried to force life to become an endless picnic. He was not an example of diligent and peaceful citizenship. Ablution became difficult in the little apartment, because Ferguson kept the wash-basin filled with ice and bottles of beer: and so, finally, the dealer in second-hand furniture agreed to auction the household goods on commission. Owing to an exceedingly liberal definition of a term, the parrot and cage were included. "On the level?" cried the parrot, "On the level? On the level? On the level?"

On the way to the sale, Ferguson's wife spoke hopefully. "You can't tell, Jim," she said. "Perhaps some of 'em will get to biddin', and we might get almost as much as we paid for the things."

The auction room was in a cellar. It was crowded with people and with house furniture; so that as the auctioneer's assistant moved from one piece to another he caused a great shuffling. There was an astounding number of old women in curious bonnets. The rickety stairway was thronged with men who wished to smoke and be free from the old women. Two lamps made all the faces appear yellow as parchment. Incidentally they could impart a lustre of value to very poor furniture.

The auctioneer was a fat, shrewd-looking individual, who seemed also to be a great bully. The assistant was the most imperturbable of beings, moving with the dignity of an image on rollers. As the Fergusons forced their way down the stairway, the assistant roared: "Number twenty-one!"

"Number twenty-one!" cried the auctioneer. "Number twenty-one! A fine new handsome bureau! Two dollars? Two dollars is bid! Two and a half! Two and a half! Three? Three is bid. Four! Four dollars! A fine new handsome bureau at four dollars! Four dollars! Four dollars! F-o-u-r d-o-l-l-a-r-s! Sold at four dollars."

"On the level?" cried the parrot, muffled somewhere among furniture and carpets. "On the level? On the level?" Every one tittered.

Mrs. Ferguson had turned pale, and gripped her husband's arm. "Jim! Did you hear? The bureau—four dollars——"

Ferguson glowered at her with the swift brutality of a man afraid of a scene. "Shut up, can't you!"

Mrs. Ferguson took a seat upon the steps; and hidden there by the thick ranks of men, she began to softly sob. Through her tears appeared the yellowish mist of the lamplight, streaming about the monstrous shadows of the spectators. From time to time these latter whispered eagerly: "See, that went cheap!" In fact when anything was bought at a particularly low price, a murmur of admiration arose for the successful bidder.

The bedstead was sold for two dollars, the mattresses and springs for one dollar and sixty cents. This figure seemed to go through the woman's heart. There was derision in the sound of it. She bowed her head in her hands. "Oh, God, a dollar-sixty! Oh, God, a dollar-sixty!"

The parrot was evidently under heaps of carpet, but the dauntless bird still raised the cry, "On the level?"

Some of the men near Mrs. Ferguson moved timidly away upon hearing her low sobs. They perfectly understood that a woman in tears is formidable.

The shrill voice went like a hammer, beat and beat, upon the woman's heart. An odor of varnish, of the dust of old carpets, assailed her and seemed to possess a sinister meaning. The golden haze from the two lamps was an atmosphere of shame, sorrow, greed. But it was when the parrot called that a terror of the place and of the eyes of the people arose in her so strongly that she could not have lifted her head any more than if her neck had been of iron.

At last came the parrot's turn. The assistant fumbled until he found the ring of the cage, and the bird was drawn into view. It adjusted its feathers calmly and cast a rolling wicked eye over the crowd.

> "Oh, the good ship Sarah sailed the seas,
> And the wind it blew all day——"

This was the part of a ballad which Ferguson had tried to teach it. With a singular audacity and scorn, the parrot bawled these lines at the auctioneer as if it considered them to bear some particular insult.

The throng in the cellar burst into laughter. The auctioneer attempted to start the bidding, and the parrot interrupted with a repetition of the lines. It swaggered to and fro on its perch, and gazed at the faces of the crowd, with so much rowdy understanding and derision that even the auctioneer could not confront it. The auction was brought to a halt; a wild hilarity developed, and every one gave jeering advice.

Ferguson looked down at his wife and groaned. She had cowered against the wall, hiding her face. He touched her shoulder and she arose. They sneaked softly up the stairs with heads bowed.

Out in the street, Ferguson gripped his fists and said: "Oh, but wouldn't I like to strangle it!"

His wife cried in a voice of wild grief: "It—it m—made us a laughing-stock in—in front of all that crowd!"

For the auctioning of their household goods, the sale of their home—this financial calamity lost its power in the presence of the social shame contained in a crowd's laughter.

No. 30 A MAN BY THE NAME OF MUD

DEEP in a leather chair, the Kid sat looking out at where the rain slanted before the dull brown houses and hammered swiftly upon an occasional lonely cab. The happy crackle from the great and glittering fire-place behind him had evidently no meaning of content for him. He appeared morose and unapproachable and when a man appears morose and unapproachable it is a fine chance for his intimate friends. Three or four of them discovered his mood and so hastened to be obnoxious.

"What's wrong, Kid? Lost your thirst?"

"He can never be happy again. He has lost his thirst."

"That's right, Kid. When you quarrel with a man who can whip you, resort to sarcastic reflection and distance."

They cackled away persistently, but the Kid was mute and continued to stare gloomily at the street.

Once a man who had been writing letters looked up and said: "I saw your friend at the Comique the other night." He waited a moment and then added, "In back."

The Kid wheeled about in his chair at this information and all the others saw then that it was important. One man said with deep intelligence: "Ho, ho, a woman, hey? A woman's come between the two Kids. A woman! Great—eh?" The Kid launched a glare of scorn across the room and then turned again to a contemplation of the rain. His friends continued to do all in their power to worry him but they fell, ultimately, before his impregnable silence.

As it happened, he had not been brooding upon his friend's mysterious absence at all. He had been concerned with himself. Once in a while he seemed to perceive certain futilities and lapsed then immediately into a state of voiceless dejection. These moods were not frequent.

An unexplained thing in his mind however was greatly enlightened by the words of the gossip. He turned then from his harrowing scrutiny of the amount of pleasure he achieved from living and settled into a comfortable reflection upon the state of his comrade, the other Kid.

Perhaps it could be indicated in this fashion: "Went to Comique, I suppose. Saw girl. Secondary part, probably. Thought her rather natural. Went to Comique again. Went again. One time happened to meet omnipotent and good-natured friend. Broached subject to him with great caution. Friend said: 'Why certainly, my boy, come round to-night and I'll take you in back. Remember, it's against all rules but I think that in your case, etc.,' Kid went. Chorus girls winked same old wink. 'Here's another dude on the prowl.' Kid, aware of this, swearing under his breath and looking very stiff. Meets girl. Knew beforehand that the foot-lights might have sold him but finds her very charming. Does not say single thing to her which she naturally expected to hear. Makes no reference to her beauty nor her voice—if she has any. Perhaps takes it for granted that she knows. Girl don't exactly love this attitude but then feels admiration because after all she can't tell whether he thinks her nice or whether he don't. New scheme, this. Worked by occasional guys in Rome and Egypt but still, new scheme. Kid goes away. Girl thinks. Later, nails omnipotent and good-natured friend. 'Who was that you brought back?' 'Oh, him? Why, he——' Describes the Kid's wealth, feats and virtues—virtues of disposition. Girl propounds clever question: 'Why did he wish to meet me?' Omnipotent person says: 'Damned if I know.'

"Later, Kid asks girl to supper. Not wildly anxious but very evident that he asks her because he likes her. Girl accepts—goes to supper. Kid very good comrade and kind. Girl begins to think that here at last is a man who understands her. Details ambitions—long, wonderful ambitions. Explains her points of superiority over the other girls of stage. Says their lives disgust her. She wants to work and study and make something of herself. Kid smokes vast number of cigarettes. Displays, and feels, deep sympathy. Recalls but faintly that he has heard it on previous occasions. They have an awfully good time. Part at last in front of apartment house. 'Good-night, old chap.' 'Good-night.' Squeeze hands hard. Kid has no information at all about kissing her good-night but don't even try. Noble youth. Wise youth. Kid goes home and smokes. Feels strong desire to kill people who say intolerable things of the girl in rows. 'Narrow, mean, stupid, ignorant, damnable people.' Contemplates the broad fine liberality of his own experienced mind.

"Kid and girl become very chummy. Kid like a brother. Listens to her troubles. Takes her out to supper regularly and regularly. Chorus girls now tacitly recognize him as the main guy. Sometimes, maybe, girl's mother sick. Can't go to supper. Kid always very noble. Understands perfectly the probabilities of there being others. Lays for 'em but makes no discoveries. Begins to wonder whether he is a winner or whether she is a girl of marvelous cleverness. Can't tell. Maintains himself with dignity however. Only occasionally inveighs against the men who prey upon the girls of the stage. Still noble.

"Time goes on. Kid grows less noble. Perhaps decides not to be noble at all, or as little as he can. Still inveighs against the men who prey upon the girls of the stage. Thinks the girl stunning. Wants to be dead sure there are no others. Once, suspects it and immediately makes the colossal mistake of his life—takes the girl to task. Girl won't stand it for a minute. Harangues him. Kid surrenders and pleads with her—pleads with her. Kid's name is mud."

No. 31   A SELF-MADE MAN

An Example of Success that Anyone Can Follow

Tom had a hole in his shoe. It was very round and very uncomfortable, particularly when he went on wet pavements. Rainy days made him feel that he was walking on frozen dollars although he had only to think for a moment to discover he was not.

He used up almost two packs of playing cards by means of putting four cards at a time inside his shoe as a sort of temporary sole which usually lasted about half a day. Once he put in four aces for luck. He went down town that morning and got refused work. He thought it wasn't a very extraordinary performance for a young man of ability and he was not sorry that night to find his packs were entirely out of aces.

One day, Tom was strolling down Broadway. He was in pursuit of work, although his pace was slow. He had found that he must take the matter coolly. So he puffed tenderly at a cigarette and walked as if he owned stock. He imitated success so successfully that if it wasn't for the constant reminder (king, queen, deuce and tray) in his shoe, he would have gone into a store and bought something.

He had borrowed five cents that morning of his land-lady, for his mouth craved tobacco. Although he owed her much for board, she had unlimited confidence in him because his stock of self-assurance was very large indeed. And as it increased in a proper ratio with the amount of his bills, his relations with her seemed on a firm basis. So he strolled along and smoked with his confidence in fortune in nowise impaired by his financial condition.

Of a sudden he perceived an old man seated upon a railing and smoking a clay pipe.

He stopped to look because he wasn't in a hurry and because it was an unusual thing on Broadway to see old men seated upon railings and smoking clay pipes.

And to his surprise the old man regarded him very intently in return. He stared, with a wistful expression, into Tom's face and he clasped his hands in trembling excitement.

Tom was filled with astonishment at the old man's strange demeanor. He stood puffing at his cigarette, and tried to understand matters. Failing, he threw his cigarette away, took a fresh one from his pocket and approached the old man.

"Got a match?" he enquired, pleasantly. The old man, much agitated, nearly fell from the railing as he leaned dangerously forward.

"Sonny, can you read?" he demanded in a quavering voice.

"Certainly, I can," said Tom, encouragingly. He waived the affair of the match.

The old man fumbled in his pocket. "You look honest, sonny. I've been lookin' fur an honest feller fur a'most a week. I've set on this railing fur six days," he cried, plaintively.

He drew forth a letter and handed it to Tom. "Read it fur me, sonny, read it," he said, coaxingly.

Tom took the letter and leaned back against the railing. As he opened it and prepared to read, the old man wriggled like a child at a forbidden feast.

Thundering trucks made frequent interruptions and seven men in a hurry jogged Tom's elbow but he succeeded in reading what follows:

> Office of Ketchum R. Jones, attorney at law
> Tin Can, Nevada, July 19, 18—

Rufus Wilkins, Esq.
Dear sir:

I have as yet received no acknowledgement of the draft from the sale of the north section lots, which I forwarded to you on June 25th. I would request an immediate reply concerning it.

Since my last I have sold the three corner lots at five thousand each. The city grew so rapidly in that direction that they were surrounded by brick stores almost before you would know it. I have also sold for four thousand dollars the ten acres of out-lying sage-brush which you once foolishly tried to give away. Mr. Simpson of Boston bought the tract. He is very shrewd no doubt but he hasn't been in the West long. Still, I think if he holds it for about a thousand years, he may come out all right.

I worked him with the projected-horse-car-line gag.

Inform me of the address of your New York attorneys and I will send on the papers. Pray do not neglect to write me concerning the draft sent on June 25th.

In conclusion I might say that if you have any Eastern friends who are after good Western investments inform them of the glorious future of Tin Can. We now have three railroads, a bank, an electric light plant, a projected horse-car line, and an art society. Also, a saw manufactory, a patent car-wheel mill, and a Methodist church. Tin Can is marching forward to take her proud stand as the metropolis of the West. The rose-hued future holds no glories to which Tin Can does not——

Tom stopped abruptly. "I guess the important part of the letter came first," he said.

"Yes," cried the old man, "I've heard enough. It is just as I thought. George has robbed his dad."

The old man's frail body quivered with grief. Two tears trickled slowly down the furrows of his face.

"Come, come, now," said Tom, patting him tenderly on the back. "Brace up, old feller. What you want to do is to get a lawyer and go put the screws on George."

"Is it really?" asked the old man, eagerly.

"Certainly, it is," said Tom.

"All right," cried the old man, with enthusiasm. "Tell me where to get one." He slid down from the railing and prepared to start off.

Tom reflected. "Well," he said, finally, "I might do for one myself."

"What," shouted the old man in a voice of admiration, "are you a lawyer as well as a reader?"

"Well," said Tom again, "I might appear to advantage as one. All you need is a big front," he added, slowly. He was a profane young man.

The old man seized him by the arm. "Come on, then," he cried, "and we'll go put the screws on George."

Tom permitted himself to be dragged by the weak arms of his companion around a corner and along a side street. As they proceeded, he was internally bracing himself for a struggle, and putting large bales of self-assurance around where they would be likely to obstruct the advance of discovery and defeat.

By the time they reached a brown-stone house hidden away in a street of shops and ware-houses, his mental balance was so admirable that he seemed to be in possession of enough information and brains to ruin half of the city, and he was no more concerned about the king, queen, deuce and tray than if they had been discards that didn't fit his draw. Too, he infused so much confidence and courage into his companion, that the old man went along the street, breathing war, like a decrepit hound on the scent of new blood.

He ambled up the steps of the brown-stone house as if he were charging earth-works. He unlocked the door and they passed along a dark hall-way. In a rear room they found a man seated at table engaged with a very late breakfast. He had a diamond in his shirt front and a bit of egg on his cuff.

"George," said the old man in a fierce voice that came from his aged throat with a sound like the crackle of burning twigs, "here's my lawyer Mr.—er—ah—Smith and we want to know what you did with the draft that was sent on June 25th."

The old man delivered the words as if each one was a musket shot. George's coffee spilled softly upon the table-cover and his fingers worked convulsively upon a slice of bread. He turned a white, astonished face toward the old man and the intrepid Thomas.

The latter, straight and tall, with a highly legal air, stood at the old man's side. His glowing eyes were fixed upon the face of the man at the table. They seemed like two little detective cameras taking pictures of the other man's thoughts.

"Father, what d—do you mean," faltered George totally unable to withstand the two cameras and the highly legal air.

"What do I mean?" said the old man with a feeble roar as from an ancient lion. "I mean that draft—that's what I mean.

Give it up or we'll–we'll——" he paused to gain courage by a glance at the formidable figure at his side—"we'll put the screws on you."

"Well, I was—I was only borrowin' it for 'bout a month," said George.

"Ah," said Tom.

George started, glared at Tom and then began to shiver like an animal with a broken back. There were a few moments of silence. The old man was fumbling about in his mind for more imprecations. George was wilting and turning limp before the glittering orbs of the valiant attorney. The latter, content with the exalted advantage he had gained by the use of the expression, "Ah," spoke no more but continued to stare.

"Well," said George, finally, in a weak voice, "I s'pose I can give you a check for it, 'though I was only borrowin' it for 'bout a month. I don't think you have treated me fairly, father, with your lawyers and your threats and all that. But I'll give you the check."

The old man turned to his attorney. "Well?" he asked.

Tom looked at the son and held an impressive debate with himself. "I think we may accept the check," he said coldly after a time.

George arose and tottered across the room. He drew a check that made the attorney's heart come privately into his mouth. As he and his client passed triumphantly out, he turned a last highly legal glare upon George that reduced that individual to a mere paste.

On the side-walk, the old man went into a spasm of delight and called his attorney all the admiring and endearing names there were to be had.

"Lord, how you settled him," he cried ecstatically.

They walked slowly back toward Broadway. "The scoundrel," murmured the old man. "I'll never see 'im again. I'll dersert 'im. I'll find a nice quiet boarding-place and——"

"That's all right," said Tom. "I know one. I'll take you right up," which he did.

He came near being happy ever after. The old man lived, at advanced rates, in the front room at Tom's boarding-house. And the latter basked in the proprietress' smiles which had a commercial value and were a great improvement on many we see.

The old man, with his quantities of sage-brush, thought Thomas owned all the virtues mentioned in high-class literature, and his opinion, too, was of commercial value. Also, he knew a man who knew another man who received an impetus which made him engage Thomas on terms that were highly satisfactory. Then it was that the latter learned he had not succeeded sooner because he did not know a man who knew another man.

So it came to pass that Tom grew to be Thomas G. Somebody. He achieved that position in life from which he could hold out for good wines when he went to poor restaurants. His name became entangled with the name of Wilkins in the ownership of vast and valuable tracts of sage-brush in Tin Can, Nevada.

At the present day he is so great that he lunches frugally at high prices. His fame has spread through the land as a man who carved his way to fortune with no help but his undaunted pluck, his tireless energy, and his sterling integrity.

Newspapers apply to him now, and he writes long signed articles to struggling young men, in which he gives the best possible advice as to how to become wealthy. In these articles, he, in a burst of glorification, cites the king, queen, deuce, and tray, the four aces, and all that. He alludes tenderly to the nickel he borrowed and spent for cigarettes as the foundation of his fortune.

"To succeed in life," he writes, "the youth of America have only to see an old man seated upon a railing and smoking a clay pipe. Then go up and ask him for a match."

No. 32   AT THE PIT DOOR

THE long file of people, two abreast, waiting resignedly for the hour of 7:30 P.M., look round sharply at the open space beside them when the girl with the guitar gives a preliminary strum. They are prepared to welcome anything calculated to chase monotony, for even half-penny comic papers after a time cease

to amuse, and those reminiscent of past performances develop,
when they pass a certain class, into first-class bores. This is why
the guitar girl comes opportunely, and when she lifts up her
chin and sings in a raucous voice to a tum-tum accompaniment, the two-abreast crowd listens with all its ears. E 243, at
the end of the queue, looks on tolerantly, being a man with
musical tastes and consequently of a genial disposition. Here
singeth one:

When you meet a nice young person and you feel you've seen a worse
    one,
  And you seek a interduction, don't you know,
You are puzzled how to greet her, tho no lady could be neater,
  So very shy and strickly comilfo.
You puzzle all your mind and brains, you take a deuced lot of pains,
  You ponder and consider, and you think
It's a foolish, silly waste of time, take this advice, dear boys of mine,
  For all you've got to do is—give a wink.
Give a wink, boys——

The long line that reaches to the pit doors finds itself forced
to hum the enticing chorus, either in shrill soprano or growling
bass, and one young lady by herself, with a pince-nez and opera
glasses, screws up her lips to whistle it. The guitar girl gives a
second song—a sentimental one this time, with good-byes forever and weeping sweethearts and departing emigrants, and a
waltz refrain, and nearly everybody dead and done for in the
last verse. Then the guitar girl brings a scarlet plush bag that
suggests the offertory, and going down the line, gleans as much
as eightpence-halfpenny.

A stout man in a tweed cap and loose tweed suit, that cries
aloud at elbows and knees for the darning-needle; he has a
Windsor chair with him, and a slip of carpet, and these he
places on the ground with much care and particularity. Throws
then his tweed cap on the ground, slips his jacket off, thumps
himself on his broad chest, and bows to his audience.

"Lydies and Gentlemen: I prepose this evenin' to clime your
kind indulgence whilst I submit to your notice a few feats of
strength. I don't prefess to do anything that's not done perfectly
striteforward, and I invite your attention to watch whether I do
anything that can be called trickery. If any one can bowl me out

at pretendin' to do something I don't do, why I'll forfeit"—here the stout man slaps an apparently empty pocket—"I will forfeit five golding sovereigns."

The long line has been a little unconcerned at the acrobat's lecture; but the mention of as much as five pounds seems to quicken its interests. The heads turn round and watch the stout man acutely.

"I first take up the chair between my teeth—thus." The Windsor chair is swung to and fro in the air. "I then place the foot of one of its legs on my chin—thus." The Windsor chair turns lazily round on its perilous axis. "I now place my head between my knees, and I 'old the chair in my mouth—thus."

The stout man contorts himself into a preposterous position and does a kind of flag-signaling with the Windsor chair. "I now puts the chair one side, and I ventures to trespass on your valuable time for a few minutes whilst I show you some feats equal to those"—(the stout man for the first time speaks with acerbity)—"equal to those that so-called acribats at the music 'alls are getting their thirty pun a week for."

The stout man holds one foot high and dances round on the other foot in the manner of the ladies at the Moulin Rouge; he performs the unattractive "splits," he stands on his head for a few moments; he walks about on his hands; he does nearly everything that nobody else wants to do. After each achievement he blows a quick kiss to the patient crowd. "Thanking you one and all, lydies and gentlemen, for assisting me by your kind attention, I now ast you to remember that a man's got his livin' to make, altho p'raps we may 'ave different ways of doing it. Can you oblige, miss, by starting the subscription list with a copper? If I can only get a good-looking—— Thank you kindly, miss. And you, sir."

A melancholy staring boy on the pavement opposite. It is quite clear that he is about to do something; it is by no means clear what that something is to be. When that stout man has put on his coat and shouldered his Windsor chair and lifted his tweed cap to the crowd politely, the melancholy boy moistens his lips and grasps the lamp-post with one hand. Then he whistles. He whistles, truth to say, extremely well, and he goes stolidly thru the overture to "Zampa" and a frivolous polka, closing with

"Rule Britannia" in such a spirit as to make every youth in the waiting line feel that unless he gives the melancholy youth at least a penny he is nothing better than a traitor to his country.

A rattling of bones! A banging of tambourines! A ping-pong of banjos! Six men in straw hats and white canvas suits with scarlet stripes and perspiring blackened faces are in a semi-circle exchanging noisy repartee and—when they can think of no repartee—shouting loudly "Ooray!"

"D' you 'member that lil song of yours, Bones, that used to make people cry?"

"Do I 'member?" inquires Bones (in the Ollendorfian manner) "that lil song of mine that used to make people cry? Yes, sir; I do 'member that lil song of mine that used to make people cry."

"Will you 'blige me by singing of it now?"

Bones is a short boy with a stubbled sandy mustache showing thru the lamp-black on his face. He steps out of the semi-circle, makes a bow that is almost obsequious, whilst the others clatter and twang thru the symphony. Then Bones looks up at the side of the theatre, and with a sort of ferocious pathos sings:—

> Little Nellie's joined the ingels,
> She has flown to realms above:
> Never more shall we 'ere see her;
> Gorn's the little soul we love.
>
> But the mem'ry of her features,
> Always wif us will remine,
> And the sound of tiny voices,
> Lingers in our ears agine.

The semi-circle joins in, taking its several parts in a strenuous way.

> Gorn, gorn is she, gorn from all earthly strife,
> Free from all sorrer . . . .

The lugubrious purple song has three verses, and the number is enough. The line of pit patrons becomes quite depressed and sniffs a good deal, and one lady, borrowing her husband's handkerchief, weeps openly and without restraint.

"Song and dence!" shouts Tambourine, "entitled, 'Hev you seen a colored coon called Pete!' "

Again a noisy prelude. It is Tambourine himself who steps out this time, and he dances a few steps on the graveled space as earnest of what is to come, and to a red-faced white-capped servant who is gazing intently out of the side window of a neighboring hotel he waves affectionate greetings and hugs his left side as tho the sight of the red-faced domestic had affected his heart.

I'm a sassy nigger gal, and me front name it is Sal,

Soft chorus from the semi-circle:—

Hev ye seen a colored coon called Pete?

Tambourine continues:—

And the games we darkies play, in the night and in the day,

Soft chorus as before:—

Hev ye seen a colored coon called Pete?

"But I want to ask you suthin' and——"

The long straight crowd is beginning to look at its watches. The hour is 7:30 precisely, and what the crowd asks with much impatience is, that if they don't mean to open the doors at 7:30, what on earth makes them put 7:30 in the paper for? The worst of theatres is that you can never—— A sound of moving bolts. A closing up in the ranks of the long line. A warning word from E 243. The song stops and the minstrels hurry forward to the moving crowd with their straw hats outstretched. It is too late. The crowd is so much engaged in feeling for its half-crowns and in keeping a steady eye on the gaping open doorway that it cannot trouble about any more gifts to entertainers.

" 'Pon me bloomin' oath," says Tambourine with much annoyance, "if this ain't jest like me nawsty luck!"

Tales of the Wyoming Valley
Nos. 33–35

No. 33   THE BATTLE OF FORTY FORT

THE Congress, sitting at Philadelphia, had voted our Wyoming country two companies of infantry for its protection against the Indians with the single provision that we raise the men and arm them ourselves. This was not too brave a gift but no one could blame the poor Congress and indeed one could wonder that they found occasion to think of us at all since at the time every gentleman of them had his coat-tails gathered high in his hands in readiness for flight to Baltimore. But our two companies of foot were no sooner drilled, equipped and in readiness to defend the colony when they were ordered off down to the Jerseys to join General Washington. So it can be seen what service Congress did us in the way of protection. Thus the Wyoming Valley, sixty miles deep in the wilderness, held its log-houses full of little beside mothers, maids and children. To the clamor against this situation, the badgered Congress could only reply by the issue of another generous order directing that one full company of foot be raised in the town of Westmoreland for the defense of said town and that the said company find their own arms, ammunition and blankets. Even people with our sense of humor could not laugh at this joke.

When the first two companies were forming, I had thought to join one but my father forbade me, saying that I was too young although I was full sixteen, tall and very strong. So it turned out that I was not off fighting with Washington's army when Butler with his rangers and Indians raided Wyoming. Perhaps I was in the better place to do my duty, if I could.

When wandering Indians visited the settlements, their drunkenness and insolence were extreme but the few white men remained calm and often enough pretended oblivion to insults which because of their wives and families they dared not attempt to avenge. In my own family, my father's imperturbability was scarce superior to my mother's coolness and such was our faith in them that we twelve children also seemed to be fearless. Neighbor after neighbor came to my father in despair of the defenceless condition of the valley and declaring that they were about to leave everything and flee over the mountains to Stroudsburg. My father always wished them Godspeed and said no more. If they urged him to fly also, he usually walked away from them.

Finally there came a time when all the Indians vanished. We rather would have had them tipsy and impudent in the settlements; we knew what their disappearance portended. It was the serious sign. Too soon the news came that "Indian Butler" was on his way.

The valley was vastly excited. People with their smaller possessions flocked into the block-houses and militia officers rode everywhere to rally every man. A small force of Continentals—regulars of the line—had joined our people and the little army was now under the command of a Continental officer, Major Zebulon Butler.

I had thought that with all this hub-bub of an impending life and death struggle in the valley that my father would allow the work on our farm to slacken. But in this I was notably mistaken. The milking and the feeding and the work in the fields went on as if there never had been an Indian south of the Canadas. My mother and my sisters continued to cook, to wash, to churn, to spin, to dye, to mend, to make soap, to make maple sugar. Just before the break of each day, my younger brother Andrew and myself tumbled out for some eighteen hours' work and woe to us if we departed the length of a dog's tail from the laws which our father had laid down. It was a life with which I was familiar but it did seem to me that with the Indians almost upon us, he might have allowed me at least to go to the Fort and see our men drilling.

But one morning we aroused as usual at his call from the foot of the ladder and dressing more quickly than Andrew I climbed down from the loft to find my father seated by a blazing fire reading by its light in his bible.

"Son," said he.

"Yes, father?"

"Go and fight."

Without a word more, I made hasty preparation. It was the first time in my life that I had a feeling that my father could change his mind. So strong was this fear that I did not even risk a good-bye to my mother and sisters. At the end of the clearing I looked back. The door of the house was open and in the blazing light of the fire I saw my father seated as I had left him.

At Forty Fort, I found between three and four hundred under arms while the stockade itself was crowded with old people and women and children. Many of my acquaintances welcomed me; indeed I seemed to know everybody save a number of the Continental officers. Colonel Zebulon Butler was in chief command while directly under him was Colonel Denison, a man of the valley and much respected. Colonel Denison asked news of my father whose temper he well knew. He said to me: "If God spares Nathan Denison I shall tell that obstinate old fool my true opinion of him. He will get himself and all his family butchered and scalped."

I joined Captain Bidlack's company for the reason that a number of my friends were in it. Every morning we were paraded and drilled in the open ground before the Fort and I learnt to present arms and to keep my heels together although to this day I have never been able to see any point to these accomplishments and there was very little of the presenting of arms or of the keeping together of heels in the battle which followed these drills. I may say truly that I would now be much more grateful to Captain Bidlack if he had taught me to run like a wild horse.

There was considerable friction between the officers of our militia and the Continental officers. I believe the Continental officers had stated themselves as being in favor of a cautious policy whereas the men of the valley were almost unanimous in their desire to meet Indian Butler more than half way. They knew the country they said and they knew the Indians and they deduced that the proper plan was to march forth and attack the British force near the head of the valley. Some of the more hot-headed ones rather openly taunted the Continentals but these veterans of Washington's army remained silent and composed amid more or less wildness of talk. My own concealed opinions were that although our people were brave and determined, they had much better allow the Continental officers to manage the valley's affairs.

At the end of June, we heard the news that Colonel John Butler with some four hundred British and Colonial troops which he called the Rangers and with about five hundred Indians had entered the valley at its head and taken Fort Wintermoot after an opposition of a perfunctory character. I could present arms very well but I do not think I could yet keep my heels together. But Indian Butler was marching upon us and even Captain Bidlack refrained from being annoyed at my refractory heels.

The officers held councils of war but in truth both Fort and Camp rang with a discussion in which everybody joined with great vigor and endurance. I may except the Continental officers who told us what they thought we should do and then declaring that there was no more to be said remained in a silence which I thought was rather grim. The result was that on the 3rd of July, our force of about 300 men marched away, amid the roll of drums and the proud career of flags to meet Indian Butler and his two kinds of savages. There yet remains with me a vivid recollection of the close row of faces above the stockade of old Forty Fort which viewed our departure with that profound anxiety which only an imminent danger of murder and scalping can produce. I myself was never particularly afraid of the Indians for to my mind the great and almost the only military virtue of the Indians was that they were silent men in the woods. If they were met squarely on terms approaching equality, they could always be whipped. But it was another matter to a fort filled with women and children and cripples to whom the coming of Indians spelled pillage, arson and massacre. The British sent against us in those days some curious upholders of the honor of the King and although Indian Butler who usually led them afterward contended that everything was performed with decency and care for the rules, we always found that such of our dead whose bodies we recovered invariably lacked hair on the tops of their heads and if worse wasn't done to them we wouldn't even use the word mutilate.

Colonel Zebulon Butler rode along the column when we halted once for water. I looked at him eagerly, hoping to read in his face some sign of his opinions. But on that soldierly mask I could read nothing although I am certain now that he felt that the fools among us were going to get us well beaten. But there was no vacillation in the direction of our march. We went straight until we could hear through the woods the infrequent shots of our leading party at retreating Indian scouts.

Our Colonel Butler then sent forward four of his best officers who reconnoitred the ground in the enemy's front like so many engineers marking the place for a bastion. Then each of the six companies were told their place in the line. We of Captain Bidlack's company were on the extreme right. Then we formed in line and marched into battle with me burning with the high resolve to kill Indian Butler and bear his sword into Forty Fort while at the same time I was much shaken that one of Indian Butler's Indians might interfere with the noble plan. We moved stealthily among the pine trees and I could not forbear looking constantly to right and left to make certain that everybody was of the same mind about this advance. With our Captain Bidlack was Captain Durkee of the Regulars. He was also a valley man and it seemed that every time I looked behind me I met the calm eye of this officer and I came to refrain from looking behind me.

Still, I was very anxious to shoot Indians and if I had doubted my ability in this direction I would have done myself a great injustice for I could drive a nail to the head with a rifle-ball at respectable range. I contend that I was not at all afraid of the enemy but I much feared that certain of my comrades would change their minds about the expediency of battle on the 3rd July 1778.

But our company was as steady and straight as a fence. I do not know who first saw dodging figures in the shadows of the trees in our front. The first fire we received however was from our flank where some hidden Indians were yelling and firing, firing and yelling. We did not mind the war-whoops. We had heard too many drunken Indians in the settlements before the war. They wounded the lieutenant of the company next to ours and a moment later they killed Captain Durkee. But we were steadily advancing and firing regular volleys into the shifting frieze of figures before us. The Indians gave their cries as if the imps of Hades had given tongue to their emotions. They fell back before us so rapidly and so cleverly that one had to watch his chance as the Indians sped from tree to tree. I had a sudden burst of rapture that they were beaten and this was accentuated when I stepped over the body of an Indian whose forehead had a hole in it as squarely in the middle as if the location had been previously surveyed. In short we were doing extremely well.

Soon we began to see the slower figures of white men through the trees and it is only honest to say that they were easier to shoot. I myself caught sight of a fine officer in a uniform that seemed of green and buff. His sword-belt was fastened by a great shining brass plate and, no longer feeling the elegancies of marksmanship, I fired at the brass plate. Such was the conformation of the ground between us that he disappeared as if he had sunk in the sea. We, all of us, were loading behind the trees and then charging ahead with fullest confidence.

But suddenly from our own left came wild cries from our men while at the same time the yells of Indians redoubled in that direction. Our rush checked itself instinctively. The cries rolled toward us. Once I heard a word which sounded like "Quarter." Then to be truthful our line wavered. I heard Captain Bidlack give an angry and despairing shout and I think he was killed before he finished it.

In a word, our left wing had gone to pieces. It was in complete rout. I know not the truth of the matter but it seems that Colonel Denison had given an order which was misinterpreted for the order to retreat. At any rate there can be no doubt of how fast the left wing ran away.

We ran away too. The company on our immediate left was the company of regulars and I remember some red-faced and powder-stained men bellowing at me contemptuously. That company stayed and, for the most part, died. I don't know what they mustered when we left the Fort but from the battle eleven worn and ragged men emerged.

In my running was wisdom. The country was suddenly full of fleet Indians, upon us with the tomahawk. Behind me as I ran I could hear the screams of men cleaved to the earth. I think the first things that most of us discarded were our rifles. Afterward upon serious reflection I could not recall where I gave my rifle to the grass.

I ran for the river. I saw some of our own men running ahead of me and I envied them. My point of contact with the river was the top of a high bank. But I did not hesitate to leap for the water with all my ounces of muscle. I struck out strongly for the other shore. I expected to be shot in the water. Up stream and down stream, I could hear the crack of rifles but none of the enemy seemed to be paying direct heed to me. I swam so well that I was soon able to put my feet on the slippery round stones and wade. When I reached a certain sandy beach, I lay down and puffed and blew my exhaustion. I watched the scene on the river. Indians appeared in groups on the opposite bank firing at various heads of my comrades who like me had chosen the Susquehanna as their refuge. I saw more than one hand fling up and the head turn sideways and sink.

I set out for home. I set out for home in that perfect spirit of dependence which I had always felt toward my father and my mother. When I arrived I found nobody in the living room but my father seated in his great chair and reading his bible, even as I had left him.

The whole shame of the business came upon me suddenly. "Father," I choked out, "we have been beaten."

"Aye," said he, "I expected it."

No. 34   THE SURRENDER OF FORTY FORT

IMMEDIATELY after the battle of July 3rd, my mother said: "We had best take the children and go into the Fort."

But my father replied: "I will not go. I will not leave my property. All that I have in the world is here and if the savages destroy it they may as well destroy me also."

My mother said no other word. Our household was ever given

to stern silence and such was my training that it did not occur to me to reflect that if my father cared for his property, it was not my property and I was entitled to care somewhat for my life.

Colonel Denison was true to the word which he had passed to me at the Fort before the battle. He sent a messenger to my father, and this messenger stood in the middle of our living-room and spake with a clear indifferent voice. "Colonel Denison bids me come here and say that John Bennet is a wicked man and the blood of his own children will be upon his head." As usual my father said nothing. After the messenger had gone, he remained silent for hours in his chair by the fire and this stillness was so impressive to his family that even my mother walked on tip-toe as she went about her work. After this long time my father said: "Mary."

Mother halted and looked at him. Father spoke slowly and as if every word was wrested from him with violent pangs. "Mary, you take the girls and go to the Fort. I and Solomon and Andrew will go over the mountain to Stroudsburg."

Immediately my mother called us all to set about packing such things as could be taken to the Fort. And by night-fall we had seen them within its pallisade and my father, myself and my little brother Andrew who was only eleven years old were off over the hills on a long march to the Delaware settlements. Father and I had our rifles but we seldom dared to fire them because of the roving bands of Indians. We lived as well as we could on blackberries and raspberries. For the most part, poor little Andrew rode first on the back of my father and then on my back. He was a good little man and only cried when he would wake in the dead of night very cold and very hungry. Then my father would wrap him in an old grey coat that was so famous in the Wyoming country that there was not even an Indian who did not know of it. But this act he did without any direct display of tenderness for the fear I suppose that he would weaken little Andrew's growing manhood. Now in these days of safety and even luxury, I often marvel at the iron spirit of the people of my young days. My father without his coat and no doubt very cold, would then sometimes begin to pray to his God in the wilderness but in low voice because of the Indians.

It was July but even July nights are cold in the pine-mountains, breathing a chill which goes straight to the bones.

But it is not my intention to give in this section the ordinary adventures of the masculine part of my family. As a matter of fact my mother and the girls were undergoing in Forty Fort trials which made as nothing the happenings on our journey which ended in safety.

My mother and her small flock were no sooner established in the crude quarters within the pallisade than negotiations were opened between Colonel Denison and Colonel Zebulon Butler on the American side and "Indian Butler" on the British side for the capitulation of the Fort with such arms and military stores as it contained, the lives of the settlers to be strictly preserved. But, "Indian Butler" did not seem to feel free to promise safety for the lives of the Continental Butler and the pathetic little fragment of the regular troops. These men always fought so well against the Indians that whenever the Indians could get them at their mercy there was small chances of anything but a massacre. So every regular left before the surrender and I fancy that Colonel Zebulon Butler considered himself a much abused man for if we had left ourselves entirely under his direction there is no doubt but what we could have saved the valley. He had taken us out on July 3rd because our militia officers had almost threatened him. In the end he had said: "Very well, I can go as far as any of you." I was always on Butler's side of the argument but, owing to a singular arrangement of circumstances, my opinion at the age of sixteen counted upon neither the one side nor the other.

The Fort was left in charge of Colonel Denison. He had stipulated before the surrender that no Indians should be allowed to enter the stockade and molest these poor families of women whose fathers and brothers were either dead or fled over the mountains unless their physical debility had been such that they were able neither to get killed in the battle nor to take the long trail to the Delaware. Of course this excepts those men who were with Washington.

For several days, the Indians obedient to the British officers, kept out of the Fort but soon they began to enter in small bands and went sniffing and poking in every corner to find plunder. Our people had hidden everything as well as they were able and for a period little was stolen. My mother told me that the first thing of importance to go was Colonel Denison's hunting-shirt made of "fine forty" linen. It had a double cape and was fringed about the cape and about the wristbands. Colonel Denison at the time was in my mother's cabin. An Indian entered and rolling a thieving eye about the place sighted first of all the remarkable shirt which Colonel Denison was wearing. He seized the shirt and began to tug while the Colonel backed away tugging and protesting at the same time. The women folk saw at once that the Colonel would be tomahawked if he did not give up his shirt and they begged him to do it. He finally elected not to be tomahawked and came out of his shirt. While my mother unbuttoned the wristbands the Colonel cleverly dropped into the lap of a certain Polly Thornton a large packet of Continental bills and his money was thus saved for the settlers.

Colonel Denison had several stormy interviews with Indian Butler and the British commander finally ended in frankly declaring that he could do nothing with the Indians at all. They were beyond control and the defenceless people in the Fort would have to take the consequence. I do not mean that Colonel Denison was trying to recover his shirt; I mean that he was objecting to a situation which was now almost unendurable. I wish to record also that the Colonel lost a large beaver hat. In both cases he willed to be tomahawked and killed rather than suffer the indignity but mother prevailed over him. I must confess to this discreet age that my mother engaged in fisticuffs with a squaw. This squaw came into the cabin and without preliminary discussion attempted to drag from my mother the petticoat she was wearing. My mother forgot the fine advice she had given to Colonel Denison. She proceeded to beat the squaw out of the cabin and although the squaw appealed to some warriors who were standing without the warriors only laughed and my mother kept her petticoat.

The Indians took the feather beds of the people and ripping them open, flung the feathers broadcast. Then they stuffed these sacks full of plunder and flung them across the backs of such of the settlers' horses as they had been able to find. In the old days my mother had had a side saddle of which she was very proud when she rode to meeting on it. She had also a brilliant scarlet cloak which every lady had in those days and which I can remember as one of the admirations of my childhood. One day my mother had the satisfaction of seeing a squaw ride off from the Fort with this prize saddle reversed on a small nag and with the proud squaw thus mounted wearing the scarlet cloak also reversed. My sister Martha told me afterward that they laughed even in their misfortunes. A little later they had the satisfaction of seeing the smoke from our house and barn arising over the tops of the trees.

When the Indians first began their pillaging, an old Mr. Sutton who occupied a cabin near my mother's cabin anticipated them by donning all his best clothes. He had had a theory that the Americans would be free to retain the clothes that they wore. And his best happened to be a suit of Quaker grey from beaver to boots in which he had been married. Not long afterward my mother and my sisters saw passing the door an Indian arrayed in Quaker grey from beaver to boots. The only odd thing which impressed them was that the Indian had appended to the dress a long string of Yankee scalps. Sutton was a good Quaker and if he had been wearing the suit there would have been no string of scalps.

They were in fact badgered, insulted, robbed by the Indians so openly that the British officers would not come into the Fort at all. They stayed in their camp affecting to be ignorant of what was transpiring. It was about all they could do. The Indians had only one idea of war and it was impossible to reason with them when they were flushed with victory and stolen rum.

The hand of fate fell heavily upon one rogue whose ambition it was to drink everything that the Fort contained. One day he inadvertently came upon a bottle of spirits of camphor and in a few hours he was dead.

But it was known that General Washington contemplated sending a strong expedition into the valley to clear it of the invaders and thrash them. Soon there were no enemies in the country save small roving parties of Indians who prevented work in the fields and burned whatever cabins that earlier torches had missed.

The first large party to come into the valley was composed mainly of Captain Spaulding's company of regulars and at its head rode Colonel Zebulon Butler. My father, myself and little Andrew returned with this party to set to work immediately to build out of nothing a prosperity similar to that which had vanished in the smoke.

No. 35 "OL' BENNET" AND THE INDIANS

MY FATHER was so well-known of the Indians that as I was saying his old grey coat was a sign throughout the Northern country. I know of no reason for this save that he was honest and obstreperously minded his own affairs and could fling a tomahawk better than the best Indian. I will not declare upon how hard it is for a man to be honest and to mind his own affairs but I fully know that it is hard to throw a tomahawk as my father threw it, straighter than a bullet from a duelling pistol. He had always dealt fairly with the Indians and I cannot tell why they hated him so bitterly unless it was that when an Indian went foolishly drunk, my father would deplore it with his foot if it so happened that the drunkenness was done in our cabin. It is true to say that when the war came, a singular large number of kicked Indians journeyed from the Canadas to revisit with torch and knife the scenes of the kickings.

If people had thoroughly known my father, he would have had no enemies. He was the best of men. He had a code of behaviour for himself and for the whole world as well. If people wished his good opinion they only had to do exactly as he did and to have his views. I remember that once my sister Martha made me a waistcoat of rabbits' skins and generally it was considered a great ornament. But one day my father espied me in it and commanded me to remove it forever. Its appearance was indecent, he said, and such a garment tainted the soul of him who wore it. In the ensuing fortnight, a poor peddler arrived from the Delaware who had suffered great misfortunes in the snows. My father fed him and warmed him and when he gratefully departed, gave him the rabbits' skin waistcoat and the poor man went off clothed indecently in a garment that would taint his soul. Afterward, in a daring mood, I asked my father why he had so cursed this peddler and he recommended that I should study my bible more closely and there read that my own devious ways should be mended before I sought to judge the enlightened acts of my elders. He set me to plough-ing the upper twelve acres and I was hardly allowed to loose my grip of the plough handles until every furrow was drawn.

The Indians called my father "ol' Bennet" and he was known broadcast as a man whose doom was sealed when the red-skins caught him. As I have said, the feeling is inexplicable to me. But Indians who had been abused and maltreated by outright ruffians, against whom revenge could with a kind of propriety be directed—many of these Indians avowedly gave up a sense of genuine wrong in order to direct a fuller attention to the getting of my father's scalp. This most unfair disposition of the Indians was a great deep anxiety to all of us up to the time when General Sullivan and his avenging army marched through the valley and swept our tormentors afar.

And yet great calamities could happen in our valley even after the coming and passing of General Sullivan. We were partly mistaken in our gladness. The British force of Loyalists and Indians met Sullivan in one battle and finding themselves over-matched and beaten, they scattered in all directions. The Loyalists for the most part went home but the Indians cleverly broke up into small bands and General Sullivan's army had no sooner marched beyond the Wyoming valley than some of these small bands were back into the valley, plundering outlying cabins and shooting people from the thickets and woods that bordered the fields.

General Sullivan had left a garrison at Wilkesbarre and at this time we lived in its strong shadow. It was too formidable for the Indians to attack and it could protect all who valued protection enough to remain under its wings but it could do little against the flying small bands. My father chafed in the shelter of the garrison. His best lands lay beyond Forty Fort and he wanted to be at his ploughing. He made several brief references to his ploughing which led us to believe that his ploughing was the fundamental principle of life. None of us saw any means of contending him. My sister Martha began to weep but it no more mattered than if she had begun to laugh. My mother said nothing. Aye, my wonderful mother said nothing. My father said that he would go plough some of the land above Forty Fort. Immediately, this was with us some sort of a law. It was like a rain or a wind or a drought.

He went, of course. My young brother Andrew went with him and he took the new span of oxen and a horse. They began to plough a meadow which lay in a bend of the river above Forty Fort. Andrew rode the horse hitched ahead of the oxen. At a certain thicket the horse shied so that little Andrew was almost thrown down. My father seemed to have begun a period of apprehension at this time but it was of no service. Four Indians suddenly appeared out of the thicket. Swiftly and in silence, they pounced with tomahawk, rifle and knife upon my father and my brother and in a moment they were captives of the red-skins—that fate whose very phrasing was a thrill to the heart of every colonist. It spelled death or that horrible simple absence, vacancy, mystery which is harder than death.

As for us, he had told my mother that if he and Andrew were not returned at sun-down, she might construe a calamity. So at sun-down we gave the news to the fort and directly we heard the alarm-gun, booming out across the dusk like a salute to the death of my father, a solemn final declaration. At the sound of this gun, my sisters all began newly to weep. It simply defined our misfortune. In the morning, a party was sent out which came upon the deserted plough, the oxen calmly munching and the horse still excited and affrighted. The soldiers found the trail of four Indians. They followed this trail some distance over the mountain but the red-skins with their captives had a long start and pursuit was all but useless. The result of this expedition was that we knew at least that father and Andrew had not been massacred immediately. But in those days this was a most meagre consolation. It was better to wish them well dead.

My father and Andrew were hurried over the hills at a

terrible pace by the four Indians. Andrew told me afterward that he could think sometimes that he was dreaming of being carried off by goblins. The red-skins said no word and their mocassined feet made no sound. They were like evil spirits. But it was as he caught glimpses of father's pale face, every wrinkle in it deepened and hardened, that Andrew saw everything in its light. And Andrew was but thirteen years old. It is a tender age at which to be burned at the stake.

In time the party came upon two more Indians who had as a prisoner, a man named Lebbeus Hammond. He had left Wilkesbarre in search of a strayed horse. He was riding the animal back to the fort when the Indians caught him. He and my father knew each other well and their greeting was like them.

"What, Hammond! You here?"

"Yes; I'm here."

As the march was resumed, the principal Indian bestrode Hammond's horse but the horse was very high-nerved and scared and the bridle was only a temporary one made from hickory withes. There was no saddle. And so finally the principal Indian came off with a crash, alighting with exceeding severity upon his head. When he got upon his feet he was in such a rage that the three captives thought to see him dash his tomahawk into the skull of the trembling horse and indeed his arm was raised for the blow but suddenly he thought better of it. He had been touched by a real point of Indian inspiration. The party was passing a swamp at the time so he mired the horse almost up to its eyes and left it to the long death.

I had said that my father was well-known of the Indians and yet I have to announce that none of his six captors knew him. To them, he was a complete stranger for upon camping the first night they left my father unbound. If they had had any idea that he was "ol' Bennet" they would never have left him unbound. He suggested to Hammond that they try to escape that night but Hammond seemed not to care to try it yet.

In time, they met a party of over forty Indians commanded by a Loyalist. In this band there were many who knew my father. They cried out with rejoicing when they perceived him.

"Ha!" they shouted. "Ol' Bennet!" They danced about him, making gestures expressive of the torture. Later in the day my father accidentally pulled a button from his coat and an Indian took it from him. My father asked to be allowed to have it again for he was a very careful man and in those days all good husbands were trained to bring home the loose buttons. The Indian laughed and explained that a man who was to die at Wyallusing—one day's march—need not be particular about a button.

The three prisoners were now sent off in care of seven Indians while the Loyalist took the remainder of his men down the valley to further harass the settlers. The seven Indians were now very careful of my father, allowing him scarce a wink. Their tomahawks came up at the slightest sign. At the encampment that night, they bade the prisoners lie down and then placed poles across them. An Indian lay upon either end of these poles. My father managed however to let Hammond know that he was determined to make an attempt to escape. There was only one night between him and the stake and he was resolved to make what use he could of it. Hammond seems to have been dubious from the start but the men of that time were not daunted by broad risks. In his opinion the rising would be a failure but this did not prevent him from agreeing to rise with his friend. My brother Andrew was not considered at all. No one asked him if he wanted to rise against the Indians. He was only a boy and supposed to obey his elders. So, as none asked his views, he kept them to himself but I wager you he listened, all ears, to the furtive consultations, consultations which were mere casual phrases at times and at other times swift brief sentences shot out in a whisper.

The band of seven Indians relaxed in vigilance as they approached their own country and on the last night from Wyallusing the Indian part of the camp seemed much inclined to take deep slumber after the long and rapid journey. The prisoners were held to the ground by poles as on the previous night and then the Indians pulled their blankets over their heads and passed into heavy sleep. One old warrior sat by the fire as guard but he seems to have been a singularly inefficient man for he was continuously drowsing and if the captives could have got rid of the poles across their chests and legs, they would have made their fight sooner.

The camp was on a mountain-side amid a forest of lofty pines. The night was very cold and the blasts of wind swept down upon the crackling, resinous fire. A few stars peeped through the feathery pine branches. Deep in some gulch could be heard the roar of a mountain-stream.

At one o'clock in the morning, some of the Indians arose and releasing the prisoners commanded them to mend the fire. The prisoners brought dead pine branches; the ancient warrior on watch sleepily picked away with his knife at a deer's head which he had roasted; the other Indians retired again to their blankets, perhaps each depending upon the others for the exercise of precautions. It was a tremendously slack business; the Indians were feeling security because they knew that the prisoners were too wise to try to run away.

The warrior on watch mumbled placidly to himself as he picked at the deer's head. Then he drowsed again; just a short nap of a man who had been up too long. My father stepped quickly to a spear and backed away from the Indian; then he drove it straight through his chest. The Indian raised himself spasmodically and then collapsed into that camp-fire which the captives had made burn so brilliantly and as he fell he screamed. Instantly, his blanket, his hair, he himself, began to burn and over him was my father tugging frantically to get the spear out again.

My father did not recover the spear. It had so gone through the old warrior that it could not readily be withdrawn and my father left it.

The scream of the watchman instantly aroused the other warriors who as they scrambled in their blankets found over them a terrible white-lipped creature with an axe—an axe, the most appallingly brutal of weapons. Hammond buried his weapon in the head of the leader of the Indians even as the man gave out his first great cry. The second blow missed an agile warrior's head but caught him in the nape of the neck and he swung to bury his face in the red-hot ashes at the edge of the fire.

Meanwhile, my brother Andrew had been gallantly snapping

empty guns. In fact he snapped three empty guns at the Indians who were in the purest panic. He did not snap the fourth gun but took it by the barrel and, seeing a warrior rush past him, he cracked his skull with the clubbed weapon. He told me however that his snapping of the empty guns was very effective because it made the Indians jump and dodge.

Well, this slaughter in the red glare of the fire on the lonely mountain-side endured until two shrieking creatures ran off through the trees but even then my father hurled a tomahawk with all his strength. It struck one of the fleeing Indians in the shoulder. His blanket dropped from him and he ran on practically naked.

The three whites looked at each other, breathing deeply. Their work was plain to them in the five dead and dying Indians underfoot. They hastily gathered weapons and mocassins and in six minutes from the time when my father had hurled the spear through the Indian sentinel, they had started to make their way back to the settlements, leaving the camp-fire to burn out its short career alone amid the dead.

No. 36 AN ILLUSION IN RED AND WHITE

Nights on the Cuban blockade were long, at times exciting, often dull. The men on the small leaping despatch boats became as intimate as if they had all been buried in the same coffin. Correspondents who in New York had passed as fairly good fellows sometimes turned out to be perfect rogues of vanity and selfishness, but still more often the conceited chumps of Park Row became the kindly and thoughtful men of the Cuban blockade. Also each correspondent told all he knew and sometimes more. For this gentle tale I am indebted to one of the brightening stars of New York journalism.

"Now this is how I imagine it happened. I don't say it happened this way, but this is how I imagine it happened. And it always struck me as being a very interesting story. I hadn't been on the paper very long, but just about long enough to get a good show, when the city editor suddenly gave me this sparkling murder assignment.

"It seems that up in one of the back counties of New York State a farmer had taken a dislike to his wife, and so he went into the kitchen with an axe, and in the presence of their four little children he had just casually rapped his wife on the nape of the neck with the head of this axe. It was early in the morning, but he told the children they had better go to bed. Then he took his wife's body out in the woods and buried it.

"This farmer's name was Jones. The widower's eldest child was named Freddy. A week after the murder one of the long-distance neighbors was rattling past the house in his buckboard when he saw Freddy playing in the road. He pulled up and asked the boy about the welfare of the Jones family.

" 'Oh, we're all right,' said Freddy, 'only ma—she ain't—she's dead.'

" 'Why, when did she die?' cried the startled farmer. 'What did she die of?'

" 'Oh,' answered Freddy, 'last week a man with red hair and big white teeth and real white hands came into the kitchen and killed ma with an axe.'

"The farmer was indignant with the boy for telling him this strange childish nonsense and drove off, much disgruntled. But he recited the incident at a tavern that evening, and when people began to miss the familiar figure of Mrs. Jones at the Methodist Church on Sunday mornings they ended by having an investigation. The calm Jones was arrested for murder, and his wife's body was lifted from its grave in the woods and buried by her own family.

"The chief interest now centred upon the children. All four declared that they were in the kitchen at the time of the crime, and that the murderer had red hair. The hair of the virtuous Jones was grey. They said that the murderer's hands were white. Jones's hands were the color of black walnut. They said that the murderer's teeth were large and white. Jones only had about eight teeth, and these were small and brown. They lifted their dazed, innocent faces, and, crying simply because the mysterious excitement and their new quarters frightened them, they repeated this heroic legend without important deviation, and without the parroty sameness which excited suspicion.

"Women came to the jail and wept over them and made little frocks for the girls and little breeches for the boys, and idiotic detectives questioned them at length. Always they upheld the theory of the murderer with the red hair, big white teeth and white hands. Jones sat in his cell, his chin sullenly on his first vest button. He knew nothing about any murder, he said. He thought his wife had gone on a visit to some relatives. He had had a quarrel with her, and she had said that she was going to leave him for a time, so that he might have proper opportunities for cooling down. Had he seen the blood on the floor? Yes, he had seen the blood on the floor. But he had been cleaning and skinning a rabbit at that spot on the day of his wife's disappearance. He had thought nothing of it. What had his children said when he returned from the fields? They had told him that their mother had been killed by an axe in the hands of a man with red hair, big white teeth and white hands. To questions as to why he had not informed the police of the county, he answered that he had not thought it a matter of sufficient importance. He had cordially hated his wife, anyhow, and he was glad to be rid of her. He decided afterward that she had run off, and he had never credited the fantastic tale of the children.

"Of course, there was very little doubt in the minds of the majority that Jones was guilty, but there was a fairly strong following who insisted that Jones was a coarse and brutal man, and perhaps weak in his head—yes—but not a murderer. They pointed to the children and declared that children could never lie on a system, and these kids when asked said that the murder had been committed by a man with red hair, large white teeth and white hands. I myself had a number of interviews with the children, and I was amazed at the convincing power of their little story. Shining in the depths of the limpid upturned eyes one could fairly see tiny mirrored images of men with red hair, big white teeth and white hands.

"Now I'll tell you how it happened—how I imagine it was done. Some time after burying his wife in the woods Jones strolled back to the house. Seeing nobody, he called out in the familiar fashion, 'Mother!' Then the kids came out whimpering. 'Where is your mother?' said Jones. The children looked at him blankly. 'Why, pa,' said Freddy, 'you came in here and hit ma with the axe and then you sent us to bed.' 'Me?' cried Jones. 'I haven't been near the house since breakfast time.'

"The children did not know how to reply. Their meagre little senses informed them that their father had been the man with the axe, but he denied it, and to their minds everything was a mere great puzzle with no meaning whatever, save that it was mysteriously sad and made them cry.

" 'What kind of a looking man was it?' said Jones. Freddy hesitated. 'Now—he looked a good deal like you, pa.'

" 'Like me?' said Jones. 'Why I thought you said he had red hair?'

" 'No, I didn't,' replied Freddy. 'I thought he had grey hair like yours.'

" 'Well,' said Jones, 'I saw a man with kind of red hair going along the road up yonder, and I thought maybe that might have been him.'

"Little Lucy, the second child, here piped up with intense conviction: 'His hair was a little teeny bit red. I saw it.'

" 'No,' said Jones, 'the man I saw had very red hair. And what did his teeth look like? Were they big and white?'

" 'Yes,' answered Lucy, 'they were.'

"Even Freddy seemed to incline to think it. 'His teeth may have been big and white.'

"Jones said little more at that time. Later he intimated to the children that their mother had gone off on a visit, and although they were full of wonder and sometimes wept because of the oppression of an incomprehensible feeling in the air, they said nothing. Jones did his chores and housework. Everything was smooth.

"The morning after the day of the murder Jones and his children had a breakfast of hominy and milk. 'Well, this man with red hair and big white teeth, Lucy?' said Jones. 'Did you notice anything else about him?'

"Lucy straightened in her chair and showed the childish desire to come out with brilliant information which would gain her father's approval.

" 'He had white hands—hands all white——'

" 'How about you, Freddy?'

" 'I didn't look at them much, but I think they were white,' answered the boy.

" 'And what did little Martha notice?' cried the tender parent. 'Did she see the big, bad man?'

"Martha, aged four, replied solemnly: 'His hair was all yed and his hands was white—all white.'

" 'That's the man I saw up the road,' said Jones to Freddy.

" 'Yes, sir; it seems like it must have been him,' said the boy, his brain now in complete confusion.

"Again Jones allowed the subject of his wife's murder to lapse. The children did not know that it was a murder, of course. Adults were always performing in a way to make children's heads swim. For instance, what could be more incomprehensible than that a man with two horses dragging a queer thing should walk all day, making the grass turn down and the earth turn up? And why did they cut the long grass and put it in a barn? And what was a cow for? Did the water in the well like to be there? All these actions and things were grand because they were associated with the high estate of grown-up people, but they were deeply mysterious. If, then, a man with red hair, big white teeth and white hands should hit their mother on the nape of the neck with an axe, it was merely a phenomenon of grown-up life. Little Henry, the baby, when he had a want, howled and pounded the table with his spoon. That was all of life to him. He was not concerned with the fact that his mother had been murdered.

"One day Jones said to the children, suddenly: 'Look here, I wonder if you could have made a mistake? Are you absolutely sure that the man you saw had red hair, big white teeth and white hands?'

"The children were indignant with their father. 'Why, of course, pa; we ain't made no mistake. We saw him as plain as day.'

"Later young Freddy's mind began to work like ketchup. His nights were haunted with terrible memories of the man with red hair, big white teeth and white hands, and the prolonged absence of his mother made him wonder and wonder. Presently he quite gratuitously developed the theory that his mother was dead. He knew about death. He had once seen a dead dog; also dead chickens, rabbits and mice. One day he asked his father: 'Pa, is ma ever coming back?'

"Jones said: 'Well, no, I don't think she is.' This answer confirmed the boy in his theory. He knew that dead people did not come back.

"The attitude of Jones toward this descriptive legend of the man with the axe was very peculiar. He came to be in opposition to it. He protested against the convictions of the children, but he could not move them. It was the one thing in their lives of which they were stonily and absolutely positive.

"Now that really ends the story. But I will continue for your amusement. The jury hung Jones as high as they could, and they were quite right, because Jones confessed before he died. Freddy is now a highly respected driver of a grocery wagon in Ogdensburg. When I was up there, a good many years afterward, people told me that when he ever spoke of the tragedy at all he was certain to denounce the alleged confession as a lie. He considered his father a victim to the stupidity of juries, and some day he hopes to meet the man with the red hair, big white teeth and white hands, whose image still remains so distinct in his memory that he could pick him out in a crowd of ten thousand."

No. 37   MANACLED

IN THE First Act there had been a farm scene, wherein real horses had drunk real water out of real buckets, afterward dragging a real wagon off stage, L. The audience was consumed with admiration of this play, and the great Theatre Nouveau rang to its roof with the crowd's plaudits.

The Second Act was now well advanced. The hero, cruelly victimized by his enemies, stood in prison garb, panting with rage while two brutal warders fastened real handcuffs on his wrists and real anklets on his ankles. And the hovering villain sneered.

"'Tis well, Aubrey Pettingill," said the prisoner. "You have so far succeeded, but, mark you, there will come a time——"

The villain retorted with a cutting allusion to the young lady whom the hero loved.

"Curse you," cried the hero, and he made as if to spring upon this demon, but, as the pitying audience saw, he could only take steps four inches long.

Drowning the mocking laughter of the villain came cries from both the audience and the people back of the wings. "Fire! Fire! Fire!" Throughout the great house resounded the roaring crashes of a throng of human beings moving in terror, and even above this noise could be heard the screams of women more shrill than whistles. The building hummed and shook; it was like a glade which holds some bellowing cataract of the mountains. Most of the people who were killed on the stairs still clutched their play-bills in their hands as if they had resolved to save them at all costs.

The Theatre Nouveau fronted upon a street which was not of the first importance, especially at night, when it only aroused when the people came to the theatre and aroused again when they came out to go home. On the night of the fire, at the time of the scene between the enchained hero and his tormentor, the thoroughfare echoed with only the scraping shovels of some street-cleaners who were loading carts with blackened snow and mud. The gleam of lights made the shadowed pavements deeply blue, save where lay some yellow plum-like reflection.

Suddenly a policeman came running frantically along the street. He charged upon the fire-box on a corner. Its red light touched with flame each of his brass buttons and the municipal shield. He pressed a lever. He had been standing in the entrance of the theatre chatting to the lonely man in the box-office. To send an alarm was a matter of seconds.

Out of the theatre poured the first hundreds of fortunate ones, and some were not altogether fortunate. Women, their bonnets flying, cried out tender names; men, white as death, scratched and bleeding, looked wildly from face to face. There were displays of horrible blind brutality by the strong. Weaker men clutched and clawed like cats. From the theatre itself came the howl of a gale.

The policeman's fingers had flashed into instant life and action the most perfect counter-attack to the fire. He listened for some seconds and presently he heard the thunder of a charging engine. She swept around a corner, her three shining enthrilled horses leaping. Her consort, the hose-cart, roared behind her. There were the loud clicks of the steel-shod hoofs, hoarse shouts, men running, the flash of lights, while the crevice-like streets resounded with the charges of other engines.

At the first cry of fire, the two brutal warders had dropped the arms of the hero and run off the stage with the villain. The hero cried after them angrily. "Where you going? Here, Pete —Tom—you've left me chained up, damn you!"

The body of the theatre now resembled a mad surf amid rocks, but the hero did not look at it. He was filled with fury at the stupidity of the two brutal warders, in forgetting that they were leaving him manacled. Calling loudly, he hobbled off stage, L, taking steps four inches long.

Behind the scenes he heard the hum of flames. Smoke, filled with sparks sweeping on spiral courses, rolled thickly upon him. Suddenly his face turned chalk-color beneath his skin of manly bronze for the stage. His voice shrieked. "Pete—Tom— damn you—come back—you've left me chained up."

He had played in this theatre for seven years, and he could find his way without light through the intricate passages which mazed out behind the stage. He knew that it was a long way to the street door.

The heat was intense. From time to time masses of flaming wood sung down from above him. He began to jump. Each jump advanced him about three feet, but the effort soon became heart-breaking. Once he fell, and it took time to get upon his feet again.

There were stairs to descend. From the top of this flight he tried to fall feet first. He precipitated himself in a way that would have broken his hip under common conditions. But every step seemed covered with glue, and on almost every one he stuck for a moment. He could not even succeed in falling down stairs. Ultimately he reached the bottom, windless from the struggle.

There were stairs to climb. At the foot of the flight he lay for an instant with his mouth close to the floor trying to breathe. Then he tried to scale this frightful precipice up the face of which many an actress had gone at a canter.

Each succeeding step arose eight inches from its fellow. The hero dropped to a seat on the third step and pulled his feet to the second step. From this position he lifted himself to a seat on the fourth step. He had not gone far in this manner before his frenzy caused him to lose his balance, and he rolled to the foot of the flight. After all, he could fall down stairs.

He lay there whispering. "They all got out but I. All but I." Beautiful flames flashed above him, some were crimson, some were orange, and here and there were tongues of purple, blue, green.

A curiously calm thought came into his head. "What a fool I was not to foresee this! I shall have Rogers furnish manacles of papier-mâché to-morrow."

The thunder of the fire-lions made the theatre have a palsy.

Suddenly the hero beat his handcuffs against the wall, cursing them in a loud wail. Blood started from under his finger-nails. Soon he began to bite the hot steel, and blood fell from his blistered mouth. He raved like a wolf.

Peace came to him again. There were charming effects amid the flames. . . . He felt very cool, delightfully cool. . . . "They've left me chained up."

No. 38 THE GHOST

[New York Public Library Typescript]

Play to be given in Brede School-house on December 28th, 1899.

The Ghost. I am the ghost. I don't admit this because I am proud. I admit it because it is necessary that my identity should be established. My identity has been disputed for many centuries—how many, I forget—anyhow, it was some time ago. It is difficult to be a ghost here. I would like to have an easier place. Tourists come here and they never give me a penny although I had my last pipe of 'baccy two hundred years ago and I drank my last pint of bitter in 1531.* * Ha, a noise! Perhaps some terrible tourist! Will I fly? No; despite my constitutional timidity, I will stand my ground.

(Enter tourist with white whiskers and his son.)

Tourist with white whiskers. Now, you see, my son, there is no such thing as a ghost. Really there is not. It is all a superstition. There is no such thing as a ghost.

The Ghost (approaching unnoticed). Aw——pardon?

Tourist with w. w. (jumping). Beg pardon?

Ghost. Oh, nothing. Only I thought I heard you denying the existence of ghosts.

T. with w. w. (excitedly). Well, you did. I can prove to you mathematically that it is impossible——

Ghost (holding up his hand). Don't. I couldn't bear to hear that there is no such thing as a ghost. I would begin to doubt my own existence.

T. with w. w. Why, I could easily prove it to you.

Ghost. Look here, do you deny the existence of any such thing as a tourist?

T. with w. w. No, I'm a tourist myself.

Ghost. Well, I'm——

T. with w. w. Well?

Ghost. Well!

(Enter care-taker followed by the three little maids from Rye and the remainder of company.)

Care-taker. Now ladies and gentlemen here you see the terrible room in which ten men have hanged themselves and eight men have been saved the trouble by others.

(Shudders by tourists; care-taker starts upon perceiving ghost.)

C.Taker (in swift aside to ghost). What are you doing here? I thought that I told you that you were only to appear on Tuesdays and Saturdays?

Ghost (apologetically). Well I don't want to appear. I'd disappear if I could. (aloud) It's no fun to be told that there's no such thing in existence as a ghost.

T. with w. w. (triumphantly). Well you were enquiring about the existence of tourists. What do you think of these three?

(The Three Little Maids from Rye down stage C & sing.)

Ghost. Very good, very good.

C.Taker. Oh, I don't think it's very good. When I was a girl I could sing much better than that.

Ghost. Yes, but that was in 1630.

T. with w. w. Why, is she as old as that? How wonderful is historic England.

C.Taker (aside). That will cost him another half-crown before he goes away.

Ghost (to C.Taker). Look here, you're not really going to sing? They'll think it's the groaning bridge.

C.Taker. Yes I am. I can sing as well as any three little maids from Rye who ever rode over on their bicycles.

Ghost. Well anyhow, I won't mind it nearly as much as the others. I've been rather deaf for the last 200 years.

(Care-taker advances down stage and sings "One at a time." [a])

C.Taker. Now, ladies and gentlemen I will take you to the dining-room.

Tourists. What? Luncheon?

C.Taker (hurriedly). No, no, no. Mere plain dining-room without anything to eat in it.

Tourists. Oh, I'm sorry.

One tourist. But anyhow we'll go and have a look at it.

(Exeunt all but Buttercup and Ghost.)

Buttercup. No, I don't want to go. I'd rather stay here and talk to you. You seem to know so much about the old place.

[a] "One at a time" *added in unidentified hand in pencil after deleted typed* "The Little Silver Ring"

Ghost. And you all seem to be so talented. Do you dance?

Buttercup. No, I don't dance—not very much.

Ghost. Do you play cricket?

Buttercup. Oh, really no.

Ghost. Do you sing?

Buttercup. Somebody must have told you?

Ghost. Well then, won't you please sing for me?

Buttercup. If I sing will you agree to tell me all you know about the giant?

Ghost. The giant? Why I'm——well please sing and I will tell you a lot about this house which you have never heard before.

Buttercup. Well on that bargain I will sing for you. (Buttercup sings.) And now what are all these strange things you are to tell me?

Ghost (rising from his chair speaks in clammy voice). At twelve o'clock tonight, in this room, I will tell you who I am.

Buttercup (terrified). Oh, you frighten me.

Ghost (rising out of his chair). I am—— (Buttercup shrieks.) I am the ghost and I come at twelve o'clock!

(Buttercup shrieks again. Enter all tourists and
sing—CHORUS "I'll be dar.")

Curtain

ACT II

Scene Same as Act I.

(Enter Trotter.)

Trotter (takes out watch). Ah! I see it's only half past 11. I wonder if everyone but me is afraid of the ghost, they all said they would come; I thought I should be late. Shall I go?— Here comes someone—— Ah! a pretty girl. She may be the village belle. I'll ask her.

(Enter Mistletoe. He advances towards her.) (bowing) I beg pardon but your face is familiar to me. Haven't we met before?

Mistletoe (sighing). I do not know. (sigh) All young men look alike to me—now.

Trotter. Why, how's that? Tell me your story.

Mistletoe. Listen. (She sings.)

(Then she walks off stage, Trotter following her.)

Trotter. Are you really so sad? Let [b] me console you.

(Exit R.)

(Enter Blotter, hurriedly.)

Blotter. No one here.—— Late ?——(looks watch) No, I'm too early. I'll sing to pass the time away. (Sings "Soldiers of the Queen.") (Enter Morning Glory.)

M. Glory. That *was* badly sung. Do you know I can dance better than you sing.

Blotter. Well I'd be very glad to have you do it. Will you —please?

(Morning Glory bows to him and dances. Business by
Blotter who watches her. After dance Blotter says.)

Blotter. Thank you, oh thank you. For reward, would you like to have me show you the gallows'-room? We have still time.

M. Glory. Will you take me there now? Let us go at once.

(Exeunt L.)

(Enter R. T. with w. w. and his son. They do
their act. Enter R. Daisy.)

Daisy. Oh, I'm awfully glad to find someone here. I was so afraid I would have to encounter the ghost all alone. You haven't seen it—him—have you? What have you been doing?

T. with w. w. We found ourselves the first here and we have been entertaining ourselves while we waited for the others. Tell us a story of Rye, won't you?

Daisy. I'll sing you one if you like.

T. w. w. w. & his son. Oh, do.

(Daisy sings "Fairly Caught.")

Both.

[b] Let] 'L' *typed over* 'l' *and preceding* 'Come' *x'd out*

[COLUMBIA UNIVERSITY MANUSCRIPT]

[NOTE: In this manuscript Buttercup's lines are underscored.]

Buttercup and Suburbia (together). No, we don't want to
go. We'd rather stay here and talk to you.

Buttercup. You seem to know so much about the old place.

Ghost. And you all seem to be so talented. Do you girls
dance? ᶜ

Buttercup. No, I don't dance, not very much. But little
Suburbia recites beautifully.

Ghost. Then what do you do? Do you play cricket?

Buttercup. Oh really ᵈ no!

Ghost. Do you sing?

Buttercup. Some one ᵉ must have told you.

Ghost. Then won't you please sing for me.

Buttercup. If I sing will you agree to tell us all you know
about the giant?

Ghost. The giant? Why I'm——. Well please sing and
Suburbia, recite, and I will tell you a lot about this house that
you've never heard before.

Buttercup. Well, on that bargain, I will sing ᶠ for you.
(Sings.) And now, what are all these strange things you are to
tell us?

*   *   *   *   *   *   *

Cue. Ghost rising from his chair speaks in a clammy
voice. At twelve o'clock tonight in this room I will tell you who
I am.

Buttercup and Suburbia together. Oh! You frighten us.

Ghost. I am——

Buttercup and Suburbia shriek.

Ghost. I am the ghost and I come at 12 o'clock.

ᶜ girls dance] *deleted in pencil and not necessarily in the same hand* 'sing'
interlined

ᵈ really] *preceded by deleted almost completed* 'dear'

ᵉ one] *written in ink over* 'body'

ᶠ sing] *in pencil the same hand as in c has deleted* 'sing' *and interlined* 'dance'

Buttercup and Suburbia shriek again. Enter
all the company and sing "We'll
be there."

Curtain

[UNIVERSITY OF VIRGINIA TYPESCRIPT]

THE TIRESOME GHOST OF SOMBERLY HALL, SUSSEX.

By Robert Barr.

This poem is not copyright. The original manuscript may be
had (in quantities to suit purchasers) for £500. It may be
recited by anyone having sufficient cheek and £5 which the
author will expend in charity on himself. The original manuscript has been typewritten regardless of expense, and none is
genuine that has a signature attached, for the author cannot
write his own name.

> Good Lord Preserveus paced his stately hall
> With haughty miene and with a noble step;
> He was the proudest noble of them all
> Who came from Normandy right through Dieppe
> Because this is the cheapest Continental line
> That plows the Channel's somewhat frothy brine.
>
> Along by His Lordship's starboard side
> Strode Viscount Pickles, his eldest son.
> They loved to walk thus in the eventide
> When the twelve hours hard day's work was done.
> He'd doff his jacket of corderoy
> To tramp the floor with his only boy.
>
> On the ancient gallery's timbered walls
> Hung priceless pictures and chromos rare;
> Fine forms that advertised music halls;
> And Barnum & Bailey's posters were there,
> With a huge three sheeter from Ameri-kay
> Announcing The Angelus by Millet.

To the youthful Viscount's great amaze
The head-bowed man stepped out of the print.
In his eyes the idiot's vacant gaze,
In his hands an agricultural implement.
"Don't fear" said His Lordship, "because, you know,
He's posing as Markham's Man with the Hoe."

The Hoe-man put questions inane and absurd,
Bidding the Plutocrats avow
Why they went First while he travelled Third,
And who bent back his sloping brow.
Said Lord Preserveus, "Blowed if I know,
But I'd like to see you at work with the hoe."

The Man grimly haunted these people of title;
Followed them slowly wherever they went;
Asking conundrums; imploring requital,
Till My Lord thought of letting his castle for rent.
"I wish," said Preserveus, "that you were as slow
With your blithering jaw as you are with the Hoe."

But the Noble at last got relieved of the strutting,
He found sweet repose when the weeds 'gan to grow;
As soon as the thistles cried loudly for cutting
Into his poster climbed the Man with the Hoe.
So this is the Moral of the song that I sing,
Snow shovels seek work when the flowers bloom in Spring.

[COLUMBIA UNIVERSITY MANUSCRIPT]

[NOTE: Miranda's lines are underscored.]
Miranda's part.

Cue. Tony speaks. It's a jolly cold world. I'll sing to warm myself. Sings "Soldiers of the Queen."

Enter Miranda.

Miranda. That *was* badly sung. Do you know, I can dance better than ⁵ you sing.

⁵ than] 'n' *over* 't'

Tony. Well, I'd be very glad to have you do it. Will you
—please?

Miranda bows to him and dances. Business by
Tony who watches her.

Tony. Thank you. Oh! thank you. For reward would
you like to have me show you the gallows room? We have still
time.

Miranda. Will you take me there now? Let us go at
once.

Both exit L.

[NEW YORK PUBLIC LIBRARY MANUSCRIPT]

FINALE CHORUS.

BREDE PLACE.   DECEMBER 28 '99

I've had more trouble than a heap of Sussex men,
Don't you tell, my Brede Hill Belle,
And I save all the money the silly tourists spend,
For my Belle, Brede Hill Belle.
If I try hard to drop her and to get a maid more gay,
Then she says, "O, my honey not today,
Don't you be a foolish ghost,
You are sure to love *me* most,"
Then she sighs, and she cries, Oh!
CHORUS
We're the tourists come to see the ghost,
We all come to hear you groan,
In your fine old Tudor home,
Come Sir Goddard I'm the girl you choose,
Don't forsake me, try and shake me,
You're too good to lose.
They came to a picnic in the lovely summer time,
Don't you tell, my Brede Hill Belle,
The tourist population of the very best kind,
They were there, everywhere.
[*continued on page* 175]

Finale Chorus.

Bride Place.   December 29'99

Miss Mrs H.G. Wells.   W^m & Wm W. Barr.

They paid for the hearing of some quite untruthful yarns,
How I used to eat children every day,
How the children made me drink,
Till I had no brain to think,
Then they sawed me in two, Oh!!!
CHORUS
We are children of Sussex East and West,
We enjoy your painful sighs,
You're our wicked Giant prize.
Come Sir Goddard don't you be a goose,
Don't forsake us, try and shake us,
You're too good to lose.

[*Sussex Express, Surrey Standard, & Kent Mail.*

Friday, January 5, 1900]

BREDE.
MR. STEPHEN CRANE ENLIVENS THE HOLIDAYS.

ON THURSDAY evening, December 28th, there was performed at the Brede Hill School-room, by an amateur company, an amusing little original play bearing the appropriate title of "The Ghost." The programme stated that the play was written by Messrs. Henry James, Robert Barr, George Gissing, Rider Haggard, Joseph Conrad, H. B. Marriott-Watson, H. G. Wells, Edwin Pugh, A. E. W. Mason, and Stephen Crane, and it is a fact that all these notable authors had contributed something towards the libretto.

The performers consisted of the Brede Place house party, assisted by a few friends, and Mr. Stephen Crane paid all the expenses incurred in producing the play. The children of the parish had attended a dress rehearsal on Wednesday afternoon, and on Thursday evening, in spite of the prevailing epidemic and bad weather, the room was filled by those who accepted Mr. Crane's invitations to see the performance.

Mr. J. F. Smith had enlarged the existing stage, and had fixed up a correct proscenium. The back scene, which had been cleverly painted by Miss Richie, represented an empty room in Brede Place showing a realistic fire-place and chimney corner, and the wings gave a very good effect of bare walls.

The plot of the play was, shortly, as follows:—In the first act the ghost (Mr. A. E. W. Mason), in disguise, is discovered in the empty room in Brede Place in the year 1950; he soliloquises on ghosts and tourists in general, and upon himself and tourists to Brede—"children of Sussex East and West"—in particular. Two of the latter presently appear—Dr. Moreau (Mr. F. L. Bowen) and his son, Peter Quint Prodmore Moreau (Mr. Cunningham)—and converse with him. They are afterwards joined by the caretaker (Miss Bray), an historical story-teller, and the rest of the tourists. Three little maids from Rye —Holly (Mrs. Mark Barr), Buttercup (Miss Bowen), and Mistletoe (Miss Richie)—sing a trio. After this, while the other tourists are conducted off to the dining-room, "but not for lunch," Suburbia (Miss Ethel Bowen) and Miranda (Miss Sylvia Bowen) remain behind to get further information from their unknown companion about the ghost. Suburbia recites and Miranda dances, by way of recompensing the gentleman for his trouble. They learn that the ghost appears at midnight.

In the second act Rufus Coleman (Mr. Cyril Frewer) appears on the scene half an hour too early; he meets Mistletoe, who sings to him, telling how her lover has been the first to enlist in the Sussex volunteers against the Boers. After singing a duet they go out. There appear next in order Tony Drunn (Mr. Ford Richie), who sings the "The Soldiers of the Queen," and Dr. Moreau who, after some business with Tony Drunn, imitates some of the best known denizens of the farmyard, and sings "Simon the Cellarer." Holly joins him and sings at his request, and his son Peter makes his appearance. While the father and son are disputing as to who shall look after the young lady, Tony Drunn walks off with the latter. As the hour of midnight approaches the tourists all return, and sing a chorus "We'll be there."

The third act opens with a chorus "Oh, ghost, we're waiting for you to come," sung on the darkened stage. He soon appears and discloses his identity. He tells his story, supported by music, prompted by the caretaker, and helped out by the questions of the tourists. The play ends with a final chorus, in which the company sings the praises of Sir Goddard, their "wicked giant prize."

The songs, most of which were encored, were tastefully accompanied on the piano by Mrs. H. G. Wells. At the close of the performance a vote of thanks to the performers, proposed by MR. HARVEY, in the name of the Rector, who was absent through illness, was carried by acclamation. The audience sang "For they are jolly good people," the original word being changed in consideration of the ladies among those acting.

[*South Eastern Advertiser*, Friday, January 5, 1900]

THEATRICALS AT BREDE.

PERFORMANCE OF "THE GHOST."

The inhabitants of Brede have every reason to be thankful to Mr. and Mrs. Stephen Crane, of Brede Place, for providing them with such a treat as they enjoyed on Thursday week, when a performance of "The Ghost" was given in the Brede Hill School-room by the Brede Place Christmas House Party and their friends. The play, which is a combination of farce, comedy, opera, and burlesque, is founded on a local legend, and was said to be the production of the following eminent literary men:—Mr. Henry James, Mr. Robert Barr, Mr. Geo. Gissing, Mr. Rider Haggard, Mr. Joseph Conrad, Mr. H. B. Marriott-Watson, Mr. H. G. Wells, Mr. Edwin Pugh, Mr. A. E. W. Mason, and Mr. Stephen Crane. The following authors were present at the performance: Mr. Robert Barr, Mr. H. G. Wells, Mr. Edwin Pugh, Mr. A. E. W. Mason, and Mr. Stephen Crane. The scene of the piece was "A Haunted Room at Brede Place," date 1950, and the following was the cast:—The Ghost, Mr. A. E. W. Mason; the Caretaker, Miss Bray; Rufus Coleman, Mr. Cyril Frewer; Peter Quint Prodmore Moreau, Mr. Cunningham; Holly,

Buttercup, and Mistletoe, three little maids from Rye: Mrs.
Mark Barr, Miss Bowen, and Miss Richie; Suburbia, Miss Ethel
Bowen; Miranda, Miss Sylvia Bowen; Tony Drum, Mr. Ford
Richie; Doctor Moreau, Mr. F. L. Bowen; accompanist, Mrs.
H. G. Wells. Mr. A. E. W. Mason, besides taking the principal
part of ghost, performed the duties of stage manager in a very
satisfactory manner. His representation of the character was
very realistic. He first introduces himself to the audience, the
inference being that he appears on special occasions at midnight for the special delectation of the antiquary or tourist, the
latter of whom is held in abomination by the said ghost. A
couple of tourists then appear, followed by "three little maids
from Rye," Holly, Buttercup, and Mistletoe, and these ladies
were rapturously encored for their rendering of the selection,
"Three Little Maids from Rye," which bore a suspicious resemblance to an air from a popular opera. Miss Bray, in the capacity
of caretaker, gave one the impression that the greater part of
her life had been spent in showing visitors over the place.
Miranda delighted the audience with a castanet dance, which
she was compelled to repeat. A poem was then recited by
Suburbia, which convulsed the audience, and so moved one of
the party that he wiped away tears with his ample whiskers. A
very amusing chorus, "We'll be there," was rendered, Miss
Ritchie singing the chorus capitally. In the next act Rufus
Coleman appears in the haunted room at 11.30, and whilst
waiting for the apparition Mistletoe enters and unbosoms her
sorrow to Rufus in an original, up-to-date song, "The Sussex
Volunteers," which depicts the call to arms of the "The Absent-
Minded Beggar," and the forlorn condition of the girl he left
behind him. The conversation between these two is carried on
by means of a comic duet, and eventually Rufus supplies the
place of the absent one, and leads Mistletoe away in triumph.
Tony Drum then comes on the scene, and sings the song of
the hour, "The Soldiers of the Queen," thus giving the male
portion of the audience the opportunity of displaying their lung
power. As the hour of midnight approaches Doctor Moreau
gives a correct imitation of cock-crowing, followed by "Simon
the Cellarer," and a pleasing selection by Miss Bowen. At midnight the company are paralysed by the sudden appearance of

the ghost from apparently nowhere, and he commences his weird history, but reminds himself that he can relate it better with soft musical accompaniment, and this is accorded him. He states that in the year 1531 he was sitting in that very same room, consuming six little Brede boys, and washed down his meal with an appropriate quantity of beer. This overcame him, and whilst in a stupor four courageous Brede men enter, and saw him asunder. This horrible statement is greeted with piercing shrieks from all the ladies on the stage except Mistletoe, who causes an amount of mirth by continually ejaculating: "Isn't he sweet?" The caretaker constantly corrects the ghost during the time he is making his statement, and she emphatically denies that it was beer he was drinking. She said he knew it should be "sack," and that he will get the "sack" from his post if he commits such glaring historical errors again. At this juncture the ghost makes a speedy exit, and re-appears partially divested of his ghostly raiment, when he causes laughter by going round with the hat, his fee to each batch of tourists being two "bob." A grand chorus and dance, taken part in by the ghost and tourists, concluded the piece.

No charge was made for admission, the whole of the expenses being defrayed by Mr. Stephen Crane, including an addition to the stage, which he has since presented to the School. Mr. J. F. Smith kindly gave his services as stage carpenter.

A dress rehearsal was given on Wednesday afternoon, to which the children in the parish were invited, and a large number attended.

At the close Mr. Harvey, on behalf of the delighted audience, expressed their hearty appreciation of the successful efforts of the various ladies and gentlemen, who had afforded them a most amusing entertainment. The singing of "For they are jolly good people," by the audience, concluded a most enjoyable evening.

No. 39 THE MAN FROM DULUTH

THE man from Duluth reproached his companions. "I don't see as we're having much fun," he said. "This is about the dreariest time I ever run up against."

One of the New York men waved his hand mournfully. "Well, you see, it is Sunday night, for one thing; and besides that, the town is about dead now, anyhow."

"That's what it is," said the others. They began plaintively to deplore the ravages of reform. Their voices filled with pathos, they spoke of the days that had been. It was the wail of the Tenderloin, the lamentation of the "rounders" who have seen their idols of men and places taken from them.

"Why, I can remember when——"

But the man from Duluth interrupted these tales. "Oh, I've no doubt it was all very great," said he, "but what are we going to do now? That's the point."

The five men stood on a street corner and reflected. Occasionally the visitor from the West prodded the others with accounts of the splendors of life in his country, and poked at them comments upon their slumbrous environment.

"It's dead slow," he told them, "dead slow. I'll never come East again expecting to play horse. I'll do my flying in Chicago. You fellows have all been turned down. You're buried. Come out and see me in Chicago and I'll show you real dives with electric lights out in front, and whole neighborhoods that get drunk by half-past three in the afternoon."

The others were eager to explain. "Well, you see, we——"

"Oh, I know you can still have fun in New York if you are a nervy spender," interrupted the man from Duluth; "but I guess you could do that in Mecca or Jerusalem, too. That's no sign of a red-hot town. It's the sign of a dead-slow town."

He stared severely at the New York men. They cast down their eyes and pondered in mournful silence.

At last one man suddenly spoke. He wore an air of having arrived at the only real golden suggestion. "Well, let's go and get a drink, anyhow." It was said with great vigor.

The party aroused at this. "All right, come ahead." "Where'll we go?" "Oh, anywhere; what's the matter with the little French concert hall?" "All right, come ahead."

Led by one, they paraded down the avenue. They were presently among the criss-cross streets of Greenwich. The river was in sight before they halted. Once the silence of their tongues had been broken by the voice of the man from Duluth: "This is a derned long ways to go for a drink."

The man who was in advance conducted the party up the steps of a private house. He rang the bell, and the door presently was opened a little way. A woman's head was thrust out warily. She exclaimed in French when she discovered the size of the band of invaders. She was about to slam the door, but two or three of the men burst forth in very bad but voluble French.

There was a rapid parley. The man from Duluth edged forward. If it came to the worst, he could put his foot where it would prevent the door from closing.

The conductor of the party was a painter who had studied in France. He volleyed prayers and entreaties in a way that he learned in that country. Presently the woman let them in quickly and then banged the door upon the form of some stranger who had tried to insinuate himself inside.

They passed down a mutilated hall-way. In the rear of the house, where no doubt had once been kitchens and dining room, there was now a little hall. A gallery occupied one end; at the other there was a tiny stage. There was a scenic arrangement in the form of *papier mâché* rocks and boulders. They looked indescribably dusty.

The ceiling was high; in it some little transoms were turned to let in the night air. At the tables that filled the floor space sat twoscore people babbling French. The polish of the surface of these tables had been worn away in spots by the contact of countless beer and wine glasses. There was an air of dilapidation in the room that imparted itself even to the waiters and to the youth over in the corner who thrummed the piano.

But with it all there was in the atmosphere, enwrapped, it may be, in thick clouds of cigarette smoke that hung and hovered overhead, the irresistible spirit of French carelessness.

It was an angel that had flown over-seas. There was the presence of a memory of Paris. Everything remained local save the thoughts; these were fleeting, reminiscent. There was something retrospective in the very way the men pounded tables with their glasses, the while humming in chorus with the clattering piano. It was a gayety that was inherited, and it recalled in a way that was meagre and sad the mother of it—Paris.

And one then could instantly see that little did it matter here if there were dust and suggestions of cobwebs, nor if the linen generally of the company was soiled, nor if the waiter who brought the wine had stains on his apron and only one eye. In blessed security from these things dwelt this assemblage. The environment was made rose-hued by the laughter of girls; the color of wine was a weapon with which to defy cobwebs and dust, stains and spots; whole legions of one-eyed waiters would fail to dampen the ardor of these existences.

Three men sat near the youth who played on the piano. At intervals one of them would arise, vanish for a moment in the bosom of the paper mountains, and then suddenly appear upon the little stage. They relieved each other with the regularity of sentries, and sang from the inexhaustible store of French comic songs. One was wretched, one was fair, and one was an artist. Even the man from Duluth, who comprehended less of French than he did of Sanscrit, enjoyed this latter performer. It is not always necessary to understand a language; sometimes one can be glad that he does not. But the man from Duluth revelled in the songs of him who was an artist. There were eloquent gestures and glances of the eyes that were full symbols. The man from Duluth was ignorant of details; that at which he grinned and giggled was the universal part. Good art of this kind cannot be confined to a language; there is something absorbingly intelligent to the thinking Zulu in the exhibition of a master of it.

One could wonder what he of the eloquent hands was paid. Probably he received the merest trifle. Some French customs are transported in completeness to certain portions of New York, and perhaps in France emotions are cheap. It is usually in the colder countries that publics pay fabulous prices for good emotions.

But the man from Duluth was not always satisfied with the universal part of art. When the audience would suddenly laugh he would lean forward and demand translation from the painter who had studied in France. The latter politely struggled with the difficulties of the task, but usually he failed.

"Say, what was that—what did he say then?" demanded once the man from Duluth.

"Oh—er—well," the painter replied. "Er—well—you see—he was going along the street with three chickens in a basket—and then—er—he, you know—he looked up at a window—and there was a girl in the window, you know—and he looked up at her and kissed his hand, and he said, 'Good-day, sweetheart' —and then he—he was walking backward when he said that— 'Good-day, sweetheart'—and then, you know, he didn't see where he was going—and he—he fell down and the chickens got away—and flew up to this girl's window, you know—and he began to—to yell at her, 'Oh, I say, sweetheart, return to me my chickens'—and she laughed at him, and then he said—he said—oh, I don't know what he said. It's funny in French, but it don't sound funny in English—I couldn't make you understand."

The man from Duluth seemed strangely puzzled.

Also, later in the evening, he began to grow weary of even the artistic performer. "Say," he demanded, "don't they ever have girls here that sing?" Everyone hastened to explain to him: "Well, you know, it's Sunday night——"

However, at frequent intervals after this time he would burst forth: "Say, this is pretty slow, ain't it?" "Ain't this slow, hey?" "Good Gawd, this is slow!"

"They always have a dance afterward—perhaps you will like that better," somebody said, to comfort him.

Presently, indeed, the performers ceased to pop out from behind the paper rocks. The one-eyed waiter and his fellows made a clear space by dragging away chairs and tables and stacking them in an end of the room. Then the young man at the piano suddenly attacked his instrument, and the ball began.

Couples emerged from all portions of the hall to go whirling about in reckless fashion. There was nothing uniform or sedate. It was all emotional. Each couple danced according to moods. Some went solemnly, some affectionately, and at all times a man would swirl his partner about the floor with a mad speed that would threaten to send her head flying. They were having lots of fun; almost everyone was laughing.

"It's dead slow," said the man from Duluth.

Then, suddenly, in the middle of the floor there was a fight. The music stopped with a shrill crash; the dancers scurried out of the way. The atmosphere of the place became instantly tense, ominous, battleful. A woman shrieked; another threw her hand up to her throat, as if feeling an agony of strangulation. The man from Duluth stood on a chair.

Two furious men had dropped from the ceiling, or come up through the floor or from somewhere. They appeared suddenly, like apparitions, in the very centre of the hall. It was all as quick as an explosion. There had been peace and jollity; in a flash it was changed to lurid war. Violent, red-faced, swift of motion, they were hammering at each other with their fists, and lunging with their feet in the manner of French infantry soldiers. Their eyes flashed tragic hatred. There was prodigal expenditure of the most vast and extraordinary emotions. The blows were delivered with the energy of mad murder. In that instant of silence that followed the first shrieks and exclamations of the women one could hear their breaths come quick and harsh from between their clenched teeth.

But the men were about eight feet apart from each other. Their savage fists cut harmlessly through the air; the terrific deadly lunges of their feet were mere demonstrations of some kind. The man from Duluth climbed down from his chair. "They're a pair of birds," he said with supreme contempt. He regarded them with eyes of reproach. Apparently he considered that they had swindled him out of something, and he was much injured.

The vivid picture was blurred in a few seconds. Everybody had been frozen for a minute; then all rushed forward. Friends of both parties took flying leaps to avert a dreadful tragedy. The floor became a surge of men, tussling, tugging, and gesticulating in tremendous excitement. The principals in the affair were dragged this way and that way. There arose a wild clamor of explanation, condemnation, and reiteration.

The women, left without escorts, stood trying to look in other directions. Some shuddered with fear; some incessantly tapped the floor with the tips of their boots. They turned to each other with little nervous remarks. And over at a table directly opposite the battle sat the man from Duluth and his friends, silent, motionless, absorbed, grinning with wild, strange glee.

It was impossible to look upon the jumble of men, emotions, and swift French oaths without expecting some sort of a deadly riot. There was an impending horror. Men, frenzied with rage, gestured in each other's faces, the quivering fingers threatened eyes. The lightning-blooded spirit of battle hovered over the swaying crowd. The man from Duluth and his friends were carven with interest. There was a great fight coming, and they were on the spot.

But the crowd finally finished their explanations, their condemnations, and their reiterations. Their fury expended itself in the air; the flaming words and gestures had absorbed the energy for war. Generally the men went back to their female friends. Their collars were wilted, from the grandeur of their emotions perhaps, but they had expressed themselves, and they were satisfied. Only a little mob of five or six people was left upon the scene. They still gestured and roared at each other.

"Oh, what a fake!" said the disgusted man from Duluth. "A great big fight in which nobody hits anybody else. It gives me a pain." He leaned back in his chair and stretched out his legs. He thrust his hands into his pockets and stared calmly, contemptuously, and with incredible insolence at the agitated group before him. "What a husky lot of willies!" Gradually he assumed a demeanor of the greatest importance and prowess. He sneered boldly and obviously at the wrangle. "Holy smoke! I could whip about eight hundred pounds of 'em." He was getting just a little bit drunk.

Downstairs from the gallery at that moment came a little, fat, tipsy Frenchman who was fated to play a great part. Evidently he was aware that there had been a difficulty, and he decided, of course, that with his peculiarly lucid intellect he could go over and straighten the whole thing. So he tottered uncertainly to the crowd, and, wedging his fat body among the gesticulators, he began to argue and explain in a slow, aimless, drunken fashion. No one paid attention to him at first, but it was not long before he had inaugurated an entirely new turmoil. He got one of the principals by the lapel and began another slow, distant harangue. This impassioned individual jerked away and swore in intense French.

Then came again the red apparition of war. There was renewed jostlings, gestures, oaths. Another tragedy impended, perhaps, but the man from Duluth stretched himself and said, "Oh, Gawd," in a tone from the profound and absolute depths of scorn.

Suddenly a woman came toward the crowd. Her hands were outstretched like the claws of an eagle. There was an unspeakable rage in her face, but her high and quavering voice held a burden of tears. "Ah, I kin lick you meself," she cried, with an accent that was from the street. She made a furious dive at the little, fat, tipsy Frenchman.

It seemed that this other man, a principal in the previous affair, was something to her. She had waited back there and trembled long enough. Now she was coming forward like a chieftainess of savages. That little, fat, tipsy Frenchman was the final exasperation; he had renewed the peril to her lover. She sprang at him. At last, at last there was war—real, red war. The man from Duluth climbed swiftly to an erect position upon his chair and cheered with valiant enthusiasm.

The little, fat, tipsy Frenchman was like a porpoise caught in a mighty human net. His face wore an expression of utter drunken woe and astonishment. There was one long crimson mark down his cheek. A dozen men held him and hauled him and berated him and fought at him. A half-dozen more beseeched the woman, holding her arms. Her shrill scream rose above the hoarse babble.

Then from an inner room came a large waiter. He was pushed on by the proprietress of the place, a dingy woman in a brown dress. She was giving him hurried directions, and he was nodding his head, "Yes, yes."

He made a violent charge and seized the little Frenchman,

who was casting despairing glances at the ceiling, praying for succor or at least explanation of this phenomenon. The large waiter grappled his coat collar. He gave a prodigious jerk. The little Frenchman's collar and necktie came off with a ripping sound. He was in the last agonies of bewilderment.

Two or three men were trying to pacify the woman. She was turning from them always to shriek at the little Frenchman, who was being noisily dragged out by the large waiter.

She replied in screams to her friends who intercepted her: "Well, no man dare call me a name like that, not any man here. I dare any johnnie in this room to call me a name like that."

"Hurrah!" shouted the man from Duluth from on top of his chair. "Hurrah! hurrah for America and the star spangled banner! No man here dare call the lady anything."

"What's that?" said the woman. She came ominously toward him. Her face was red and fierce. Her hands were held in the same peculiar claw-like manner. "What's that yeh say?"

"Madam," said the man from Duluth, suddenly sober and serious, "I didn't mean to reflect upon you in any way." His chair shook a little as he changed his weight from one leg to the other. His friends, down below at the table, were gazing solemnly at the ceiling. They were in deep thought.

"Well, yeh think yer jollyin' me, don't yeh?" burst out the woman with sudden violence. "I'll let yeh know——"

The man from Duluth looked down at his friends. He bowed swiftly, but with satirical ceremony. "This is too many for me, boys. I've got no further use for this place. Tra-la-loo! I'll see you next year." He made a flying leap and ran for the door. The woman made a grab at his coat-tails, but she missed him.

No. 40   THE SQUIRE'S MADNESS

LINTON was in his study remote from the interference of domestic sounds. He was writing verses. He was not a poet in the strict sense of the word because he had eight hundred a year and a manor-house in Sussex. But he was devoted, at any rate, and no happiness was for him equal to the happiness of an imprisonment in this lonely study. His place had been a semi-fortified house in the good days when every gentleman was either abroad with a bared sword hunting his neighbors or behind oak-and-iron doors and three-foot walls while his neighbors hunted him. But in the life of Linton it may be said that the only part of the house which remained true to the idea of fortification was the study which was free only to Linton's wife and certain terriers. The necessary appearance from time to time of a servant always grated upon Linton as much as if from time to time somebody had in the most well-bred way flung a brick through the little panes of his window.

This window looked forth upon a wide valley of hop-fields and sheep-pastures, dipping and rising this way and that way but always a valley until it reached a high faraway ridge upon which stood the up-right figure of a wind-mill, usually making rapid gestures as if it were an excited sentry warning the old grey house of coming danger. A little to the right, on a knoll, red chimneys and parts of red-tiled roofs appeared among trees and the venerable square tower of the village church arose above them.

For ten years, Linton had left vacant Oldrestham Hall and when at last it became known that he and his wife were to return from an incomprehensible wandering, the village which for four centuries had turned a feudal eye toward the Hall was wrung with a prospect of change, a proper change. The great family pew in Oldrestham church would be occupied each Sunday morning by a fat, poppy-faced, utterly squire-looking man who would also be dutifully at his post when the parish was stirred by a subscription-list. Then, for the first time in many years, the hunters would ride in the early morning merrily out through the park and there would be, also, shooting parties and in the summer, groups of charming ladies would be seen walking the terrace, laughing on the lawns and in the rose-gardens. The village expected to have the perfectly legal and fascinating privilege of discussing the performances of its own gentry.

The first intimation of calamity was in the news that Linton had rented all the shooting. This prepared the people for the blow and it fell when they sighted the master of Oldrestham Hall. The older villagers remembered then that there had been nothing in the youthful Linton to promise a fat, poppy-faced, dignified, hunting, shooting over-lord but still they could not but resent the appearance of the new squire. There was no conceivable reason for his looking like a gaunt ascetic who would surprise nobody if he borrowed a sixpence from the first yokel he met in the lanes.

Linton was in truth three inches more than six feet in height but he had bowed himself to five-feet-eleven inches. His hair shocked out in front like hay and under it were two spectacled eyes which never seemed to regard anything with particular attention. His face was pale and full of hollows and the mouth apparently had no expression save a chronic pout of the under-lip. His hands were large and raw-boned but uncannily white. His whole bent body was thin as that of a man from a long sick-bed and all was finished by two feet which for size could not be matched in the county.

He was very awkward but apparently it was not so much a physical characteristic as it was a mental inability to consider where he was going or what he was doing. For instance when passing through a gate it was not uncommon for him to knock his side viciously against one of the posts. This was because he dreamed almost always and if there had been forty gates in a row, he would not then have noted them more than he did the one. As far as the villagers and farmers were concerned, he never came out of this manner save in wide-apart cases when he had forced upon him either some great exhibition of stupidity or some faint indication of double-dealing and then this smouldering man flared out, encrimsoning his immediate surrounding with a brief fire of ancestral anger. But the lapse back to indifference was more surprising. It was far quicker than the flare in the beginning. His feeling was suddenly ashes at the moment when one was certain it would lick the sky.

Some of the villagers asserted that he was mad. They argued it long in the manner of their kind, repeating, repeating and repeating, and when an opinion confusingly rational appeared, they merely shook their heads in pig-like obstinacy.

Anyhow, it was historically clear that no such squire had before been in the line of Lintons of Oldrestham Hall and the present incumbent was a shock.

The servants at the Hall—notably those who lived in the country-side—came in for a lot of questioning and none were found too backward in explaining many things which they themselves did not understand. The household was most irregular. They all confessed that it was really so uncustomary that they did not know but what they would have to give notice. The master was probably the most extraordinary man in the whole world. The butler said that Linton would drink beer with his meals day in and day out like any carrier resting at a pot-house. It didn't matter even if the meal were dinner. Then suddenly he would change his tastes to the most valuable wines and in ten days make the wine-cellar look as if it had been wrecked at sea. What was to be done with a gentleman of that kind? The butler said for his part he wanted a master with habits and he protested that Linton did not have a habit to his name. At least, none that could properly be called a habit.

Barring the cook, the entire establishment agreed categorically with the butler. The cook did not agree because she was a very good cook indeed which she thought entitled her to be extremely aloof from other servants' hall opinions.

As for the squire's lady, they described her as being not much different from the master. At least she gave support to his most unusual manner of life and evidently believed that whatever he chose to do was quite correct.

II

Linton had written:

> "*The garlands of her hair are snakes*
> *Black and bitter are her hating eyes*
> *A cry the windy death-hall wakes*
> *O, love, deliver us.*
> *The flung cup rolls to her sandal's tip*
> *His arm——*"

Whereupon, his thought fumed over the next two lines, coursing like grey-hounds after a fugitive vision of a writhing lover with the foam of poison on his lips dying at the feet of the woman. Linton arose, lit a cigarette, placed it on the window ledge, took another cigarette, looked blindly for the matches, thrust a spiral of paper into the flame of the log fire, lit the second cigarette, placed it toppling on a book and began a search among his pipes for one that would draw well. He gazed at his pictures; at the books on the shelves; out at the green spread of country-side, all without taking mental note. At the window ledge he came upon the first cigarette and in a matter of fact way he returned it to his lips, having forgotten that he had forgotten it.

There was a sound of steps on the stone floor of the quaint little passage that led down to his study and turning from the window he saw that his wife had entered the room and was looking at him strangely. "Jack," she said in a low voice, "what is the matter?"

His eyes were burning out from under his shock of hair with a fierceness that belied his feeling of simple surprise. "Nothing is the matter," he answered. "Why do you ask?"

She seemed immensely concerned but she was visibly endeavoring to hide her concern as well as to abate it. "I—I thought you acted queerly."

He answered: "Why no. I'm not acting queerly. On the contrary," he added smiling, "I'm in one of my most rational moods."

Her look of alarm did not subside. She continued to regard him with the same stare. She was silent for a time and did not move. His own thought had quite returned to a contemplation of a poisoned lover and he did not note the manner of his wife. Suddenly she came to him and laying a hand on his arm said: "Jack, you are ill!"

"Why no, dear," he said, with a first impatience, "I'm not ill at all. I never felt better in my life." And his mind beleaguered by this pointless talk strove to break through to its old contemplation of the poisoned lover. "Hear what I have written." Then he read:

> "The garlands of her hair are snakes
> Black and bitter are her hating eyes
> A cry the windy death-hall wakes
> O, love, deliver us.

The flung cup rolls to her sandal's tip
His arm——"

Linton said: "I can't seem to get the lines to describe the man who is dying of the poison on the floor before her. Really I'm having a time with it. What a bore. Sometimes I can write like mad and other times I don't seem to have an intelligent idea in my head."

He felt his wife's hand tighten on his arm and he looked into her face. It was so a-light with horror that it brought him sharply out of his dreams. "Jack," she repeated tremulously, "you are ill."

He opened his eyes in wonder. "Ill? Ill? No, not in the least."

"Yes, you are ill. I can see it in your eyes. You—act so strangely."

"Act strangely? Why my dear what have I done? I *feel* quite well. Indeed I was never more fit in my life."

As he spoke he threw himself into a large wing chair and looked up at his wife who stood gazing at him from the other side of the black oak table upon which Linton wrote his verses.

"Jack dear," she almost whispered, "I have noticed it for days," and she leaned across the table to look more intently into his face. "Yes, your eyes grow more fixed every day—you—you—your head, does it ache, dear?"

Linton arose from his chair and came around the big table toward his wife. As he approached her, an expression akin to terror crossed her face and she drew back as in fear, holding out both hands to ward him off.

He had been smiling in the manner of a man reassuring a frightened child but at her shrinking from his outstretched hand, he stopped in amazement. "Why Grace, what is it, tell me!"

She was glaring at him, her eyes wide with misery. Linton moved his left hand across his face, unconsciously trying to brush from it that which alarmed her.

"O, Jack, you must see someone, I am wretched about you. You are ill!"

"Why, my dear wife," he said, "I am quite, quite well, I am anxious to finish these verses but words won't come somehow, the man dying——"

"Yes, that is it, you cannot remember, you see that you cannot remember. You must see a doctor. We will go up to town at once," she answered quickly.

'Tis true, he thought, that my memory is not as good as it used to be. I cannot remember dates, and words won't fit in somehow. "Perhaps I don't take enough exercise, dear, is that what worries you?" he asked.

"Yes, yes, dear, you do not go out enough," said his wife. "You cling to this room as the ivy clings to the walls—but we must go to London; you *must* see someone; promise me that you will go, that you will go immediately."

Again Linton saw his wife look at him as one looks at a creature of pity. The faint lines from her nose to the corners of her mouth deepened as if she were in physical pain; her eyes, open to their fullest extent, had in their expression the dumb agony of a mother watching her dying babe. What was this strange wall that had suddenly raised itself between them? Was he ill? No; he never was in better health in his life. He found himself vainly searching for aches in his bones. Again he brushed away this thing which seemed to be upon his face. There must be something on my face, he thought; else why does she look at me with despair in her eyes; those eyes that had hitherto been so quickly responsive to each glance of his own. *Why* did she think that he was ill? She who knew well his every mood. *Was he mad?* Did this thing of the poisoned cup that rolled to her sandal's tip—and her eyes, her hating eyes, mean that his—no it could not be. He fumbled among the papers on the table for a cigarette. He could not find one. He walked to the huge fire-place and peered nearsightedly at the ashes on the hearth.

"What, what do you want, Jack? Be careful! The fire!" cried his wife.

"Why, I want a cigarette," he said.

She started, as if he had spoken roughly to her. "I will get you some, wait, sit quietly. I will bring you some," she replied as she hastened through the small passage-way up the stone steps that led from his study.

Linton stood with his back still bent, in the posture of a man picking something from the ground. He did not turn from the fire-place until the echo of his wife's foot-fall on the stone floors had died away. Then he straightened himself and said: "Well I'm damned!" And Linton was not a man who swore.

III

A month later the Squire and his wife were on their way to London to consult the great brain specialist, Doctor Redmond. Linton now believed that 'something' *was* wrong with him. His wife's anxiety which she could no longer conceal, forced him to this conclusion; 'something' was wrong! Until these last few weeks Linton's wife had managed her household with the care and wisdom of a chatelaine of mediaeval time. Each day was planned for certain duties in house or village. She had theories as to the management and education of the village children and this work occupied much of her time. She was the antithesis of her husband. He was a weaver of dream-stories, she that type who has ideas of the emancipation of women and who believes the problem could be solved by training the minds of the next generation of mothers. Linton was not interested in these questions but he would smile indulgently at his wife as she talked of the equality of mind of the sexes and the public part in the world's history which would be played by the women of the future.

There was no talk of this kind now. The household management fell into the hands of servants. Night and day his wife watched Linton. He would awaken in the night to find her face close to his own, her eyes burning with feverish anxiety.

"What is it, Grace?" he would cry, "have I said anything? What is the reason you watch me in this fashion, dear?"

And she would sob: "Jack, you are ill, dear, you are ill, we must go to town, we must indeed."

Then he would soothe her with fond words and promise that he would go to London.

This present journey was the outcome of those weeks of watching and fear in Linton's wife's mind.

Linton's wife was trembling violently as he helped her down from the cab in front of Doctor Redmond's door. They had made an appointment so that they were sure of little delay before the portentous interview.

A small page in blue livery opened the door and ushered them into a waiting-room. Mrs. Linton dropped heavily into a chair, looking with a frightened air from side to side and biting her under lip nervously. She was moaning half under her breath: "O, Jack, you are ill, you are ill."

A short stout man with clean-shaven face and scanty black hair entered the room. His nose was huge and misshapen and his mouth was a straight firm line. Overhanging black brows tried in vain to shadow the piercing dark eyes, that darted questioning looks at everyone, seeming to search for hidden thoughts as a flash-light from the conning tower of a ship searches for the enemy in time of war.

He advanced toward Mrs. Linton with out-stretched hand. "Mrs. Linton?" he said. "Ah!"

She almost jumped from her chair as he came near her crying: "O, doctor, my husband is ill, very ill, very ill!"

Again Doctor Redmond with his eyes fixed upon her face ejaculated: "Ah!" Turning to Linton he said: "Please wait here, Squire, I will first talk to your wife. Will you step into my study, madam?" he said to Mrs. Linton, bowing courteously.

Linton's wife almost ran into the room which the doctor pointed toward as his study.

Linton waited. He moved softly about the room looking at the photographs of Greek ruins which adorned the walls. He stopped finally before a large picture of the Gate of Hadrian. He traveled once more into his dream-country. His fancy painted in the figures of men and women who had passed through that gate. He had forgotten his fear of the blotting out of this mind that could conjure these glowing colours. He had forgotten himself.

From this dream he was recalled to the present by a hand being placed gently upon his arm. He half turned and saw the doctor regarding him with sympathetic eyes.

"Come, my dear sir, come into my study," said the doctor, "I have asked your wife to await us here." Linton then turned fully toward the center of the room and found that his wife was seated quietly by a table. Doctor Redmond bowed low to Mrs.

Linton as he passed her and Linton waved his hand, smiled and said: "Only a moment, dear." She did not reply. The door closed behind them.

"Be seated, my dear sir," said the doctor drawing forward a chair, "be seated. I want to say something to you but you must drink this first." He handed Linton a small glass of brandy.

Linton sat down, took the glass mechanically and gulped the brandy in one great swallow. The doctor stood by the mantel and began slowly: "I rejoice to say to you, sir, that I have never met a man more sound mentally than yourself,——"

Linton half started from his chair.

"Stop!" said the doctor— "I have not yet finished—but it is my painful duty to tell you the truth—— It is your WIFE WHO IS MAD. MAD AS A HATTER!"

II SKETCHES

SULLIVAN COUNTY SKETCHES

Few of the old, gnarled and weather-beaten inhabitants of the pines and boulders of Sullivan County are great readers of books or students of literature. On the contrary, the man who subscribes for the county's weekly newspaper is the man who has attained sufficient position to enable him to leave his farm labors for literary pursuits. The historical traditions of the region have been handed down from generation to generation, at the firesides in the old homesteads. The aged grandsire recites legends to his grandson; and when the grandson's head is silvered he takes his corn-cob pipe from his mouth and transfixes his children and his children's children with stirring tales of hunter's exploit and Indian battle. Historians are wary of this form of procedure. Insignificant facts, told from mouth to mouth down the years, have been known to become of positively appalling importance by the time they have passed from behind the last corn-cob in the last chimney corner. Nevertheless, most of these fireside stories are verified by books written by learned men, who have dived into piles of mouldy documents and dusty chronicles to establish their facts.

This gives the great Sullivan County thunderbolt immense weight. And they hurl it at no less a head than that which once evolved from its inner recesses the famous Leatherstocking Tales. The old story-tellers of this district are continually shaking metaphorical fists at *The Last of the Mohicans* of J. Fenimore Cooper. Tell them that they are aiming their shafts at one of the standard novels of American literature and they scornfully sneer; endeavor to oppose them with the intricacies of Indian history and they shriek defiance. No consideration for the author, the literature or the readers can stay their hands, and they claim without reservation that the last of the Mohicans, the real and only authentic last of the Mohicans, was a demoralized, dilapidated inhabitant of Sullivan County.

The work in question is of course a visionary tale and the historical value of the plot is not a question of importance. But when the two heroes of Sullivan County and J. Fenimore Cooper, respectively, are compared, the pathos lies in the contrast, and the lover of the noble and fictional Uncas is overcome with great sadness. Even as Cooper claims that his Uncas was the last of the children of the Turtle, so do the sages of Sullivan County roar from out their rockbound fastnesses that their nondescript Indian was the last of the children of the Turtle. The pathos lies in the contrast between the noble savage of fiction and the sworn-to claimant of Sullivan County.

All know well the character of Cooper's hero, Uncas, that bronze god in a North American wilderness, that warrior with the eye of the eagle, the ear of the fox, the tread of the cat-like panther, and the tongue of the wise serpent of fable. Over his dead body a warrior cries:

"Why has thou left us, pride of the Wapanachki? Thy time has been like that of the sun when in the trees; thy glory brighter than his light at noonday. Thou art gone, youthful warrior, but a hundred Wyandots are clearing the briers from thy path to the world of spirits. Who that saw thee in battle would believe that thou couldst die? Who before thee has ever shown Uttawa the way into the fight? Thy feet were like the wings of eagles; thine arm heavier than falling branches from the pine; and thy voice like the Manitto when he speaks in the clouds. The tongue of Uttawa is weak and his heart exceedingly heavy. Pride of the Wapanachki, why hast thou left us?"

The last of the Mohicans supported by Sullivan County is a totally different character. They have forgotten his name. From their description of him he was no warrior who yearned after the blood of his enemies as the hart panteth for the waterbrooks; on the contrary he developed a craving for the rum of the white men which rose superior to all other anxieties. He had the emblematic Turtle tattooed somewhere under his shirtfront. Arrayed in tattered, torn and ragged garments which some white man had thrown off, he wandered listlessly from village to village and from house to house, his only ambition being to beg, borrow or steal a drink. The settlers helped him because they knew his story. They knew of the long line of mighty sachems sleeping under the pines of the mountains. He was a veritable "poor Indian." He dragged through his wretched life in helpless misery. No one could be more alone in the world than he and when he died there was no one to call him pride of anything nor to inquire why he had left them.

No. 42 HUNTING WILD HOGS

IF THE well-worn and faded ghost of many an old scout or trapper of long ago could arise from beneath the decayed shingle with awkward hunting-knife carvings where it lies, it could doubtless create a thrill by reciting tales of the panther's gleaming eyes and sharp claws. Mayhap, in a thousand varieties of chimney-corner, old, gnarled and knotted forty-niners curdle the blood and raise the hair of their listeners with legends of the ferocious and haughty grizzly bear. But it is certain that there are only three men in the United States to-day who have proper right to thrill anybody, curdle any blood, or raise any hair with tales of the hunting and killing of the famous wild hogs of ancient and modern Europe upon the territory of the United States. The hog of commerce and domesticity has escaped from broken pens and wrecked trains and lives in the wilds of Canada and Mississippi, and also, it is claimed, in some parts of this State, but they make no such sport as the long-haired, swift-running, powerful animals from Europe. The latter are prominent indeed in mythology and history. They are said to be the most wily and cunning of animals. They are very fleet of foot and make great speed through exceedingly rough country. The Sullivan County hunters say that when one of these animals "strikes a line" for a certain point they will not stop for obstructions that would make a bear turn out. They say that they have seen bunches of scrub-oaks as big as a man's wrist broken and bent aside like reeds where one of the wild hogs has charged through them. They turn out for no bush or little tree, but bolt directly at it. In the fields they root holes with their snouts that would flatter a plough.

Otto Plock, a wealthy New-York banker, has a country-seat in the Neversink Valley. He imported a number of wild hogs from Europe and turned them loose in his park. The shaggy beasts must have added a picturesqueness to Mr. Plock's grounds. But one morning they disappeared. They digged under the fences with their strong snouts and scattered over the country. They almost immediately began a series of night expeditions against the farmers' corn and potato fields. It is said that they did great damage. In a single night they would so root up a field with their powerful hoofs and snouts that it would be unrecognizable the next day. The farmers became agitated. They were aroused to action. They turned out in armed brigades. They spent certain sums for ammunition. In the corner stores they laid their plans, and individuals told what they were going to do. They then mustered their forces and attacked the surrounding hills. The wild hogs evaded the army with astonishing ease. The farmers then turned their attention to poison. They fixed up little meals and left them in open places but with no success. To one farm the hogs took a great liking. In its corn-fields they even tore down stalks by the dozen and heaped them in a fence-corner to sleep upon. A neighbor decided to make an investigation. He took a boy, a gun and a position behind a wall, and sat waiting one night for the appearance of the hogs. But he went to sleep. Then the boy, looking over the wall, discovered the wild hogs, not fifteen feet away. He cried out and the animals ran. The man groaned, grunted, stood up, rubbed his eyes, remembered about the hogs, and shot off his gun. The hogs went on. Later the skeleton of the wild boar was found on Shawangunk Mountain. The tusks were about eight inches in length.

The great liar appeared all over Orange and Sullivan Counties, and lots of wild hogs were seen. Children going to school were frightened home by wild hogs. Men coming home late at night saw wild hogs. It became a sort of fashion to see wild hogs and turn around and come back. But when the outraged farmers made such a terrific onslaught upon the stern and rock-bound land the wild hogs, it appears, withdrew to Sullivan County. This county may have been formed by a very reckless and distracted giant who, observing a tract of tipped-up and impossible ground, stood off and carelessly pelted trees and boulders at it. Not admiring the results of his labors he set off several earthquakes under it and tried to wreck it. He succeeded beyond his utmost expectations, undoubtedly. In the holes and crevices, valleys and hills, caves and swamps of this uneven country, the big game of the southern part of this State have made their last stand. Isolated wanderers are sometimes chased by everybody who owns a gun, and by every dog that has legs, in thickly-populated portions of other counties, but here is where the bear tears the bark from the pines devoid of the fear of hunters until he hears the yelp of the hounds on the ridges.

Here the wild hogs were in a country which just suited them. Its tangled forests, tumbled rocks and intricate swamps were for them admirable places of residence. Here they remained unmolested for a long time. The first man to kill one of them was Special County Judge William H. Crane, of Port Jervis. While on one of the Hartwood Park hunts, he was standing on a "runway" for deer. He suddenly heard a great scampering of feet and crackling of brush ahead and to the right of him. The next moment a small herd of what afterward proved to be the wild hogs dashed through the brush to his right. Turning quickly, he caught a glimpse of a brown body and fired. They carried home a wild hog weighing 200 pounds. The carcass was inspected, photographed and sketched. A magnificent skin, with stuffed head, now hangs in the club-house at Hartwood Park.

The last hog hunt resulted in untold glory and meat for the successful ones. Lew Boyd, the famous bear hunter, was the hero of the expedition. He is a six-foot-four-inch man, with broad shoulders, a good eye, and legs that have no superior for travel in a rough country. He chased one of the hogs in this hunt for over 200 miles, and the animal was shot by him on the seventh day of the chase. A party of hunters took the trail of two of the hogs and followed it for two days. They did not catch sight of the game. On the third day they met Lew Boyd. He joined them, and they followed the trails in the snow all day. Toward night, one by one, the party began to be discouraged and to drop out. Finally all had disappeared over the ridges but Boyd, who never disappears in such case, and Charles Stearns, of Oakland Valley. They plodded along together, endeavoring to get over a few miles more before sunset. As they were passing through a little gulch, Boyd, upon looking up the side of it, perceived both wild hogs in the bushes about 100 yards away. As he exclaimed to his companion, one of the hogs wheeled and tore through the bushes like a brown cyclone. Boyd whirled about and fired, but the animal did not stop. The other one came charging down the hill directly at the hunters. Stearns fired within forty yards, and that hog, too, then wheeled and scurried over the hill after her companion. The hunters followed as rapidly as possible. Some 400 yards from the scene of the shooting Boyd suddenly discovered that in their great haste they were following but one track. They turned back, and found where the two animals had separated. Following the new track they came to a dead hog in the brush. Stearns of course argued that this was his game. Boyd then went on after the other. Along the trail were great clots of blood from a wound in the throat. Yet the hog travelled with great speed, and Boyd was compelled to go home that night and leave his hog in the woods. The next day seven men turned out to assist in the search. The party trailed the wounded animal to White Cedar Swamp, a narrow, heavily-wooded marsh five miles in length. At the southern end Boyd placed three men on each side of the swamp. These, with two men to drive straight through, would form a very effective pocket. They were ordered to keep about seventy-five yards apart, and not to get behind or ahead, but to proceed slowly and all to keep their relative positions. In this manner Boyd was sure that he could get the hog. This was thought to be a sure mode of procedure, but the second man on the left pushed close to the first man on the same side and the hog passed out at railway speed between the second man and the third man.

They traced the animal to Beaver Dam Swamp and gave up the search for the night. In the morning they met near the place and Boyd placed his men about the swamp. There was a young man with a bulldog upon the scene, who said his dog would fight anything. Boyd told him, however, to hold the animal until the hunters were in their positions, but the young man succeeded with great difficulty in making the bulldog follow the track into the swamps some moments before he should have done so. As a result the hog escaped from the swamp, and Boyd sent the young man and his bulldog a safe distance to the rear. They followed the trail all the rest of that day. The hog's wound had ceased to bleed and it was making good time on its travels. The hunters could only count upon coming up with it once a day. At night it would make itself a bed by tearing down young trees and bushes and heaping them in a huge pile. Boyd says he has seen a quarter of an acre pretty well cleared of small growth to make one of these temporary couches. When once aroused the hog was good for a twenty-mile run over the rocks and fallen logs. The principal hunter had almost an entirely new lot of followers every day. Men would grow enthusiastic for twenty-four hours and join the hunt, and drop out next day to make room for some one else. Some were frozen away, some were wearied quickly and a number were scared away. Every night, except one or two, Boyd returned to his home from where he left the trail, always at least six miles away. In the morning he would walk back and resume it. On the fourth day the pursuers again were up with the hog, which had as before hidden itself in a swamp. Boyd placed his men and had the swamp beaten. Now, as above mentioned, some of these men thought the wild hog was a dangerous animal. In such cases men have great fancies for each other's society, and pairs of Boyd's men often feebly insisted upon being allowed to sit upon the same log. As the swamp was being beaten one of the hunters became lonesome and went over to see another hunter. The other hunter came half way to meet the first hunter. The hog left the swamp six feet from where the first hunter was told to stand. Boyd was angry. Three times had he laid careful plans and three times had a man who was in a hurry, a man with a bulldog and a man who was lonesome made all his efforts vain. He called the lonesome men and stated the case in forcible English, concluding with the remark: "Boys, if you are frightened, go home! Don't come into the woods and hunt an animal you are afraid of." The young men tilted their noses, shouldered their weapons and made large and defiant tracks in the snow over the hill.

The chase continued all that day and all the next. At the close of the fifth all the hunters gave up the hunt except Boyd.

They told him they were rapidly freezing to death, they were worn to skin and bone, and they could not keep up any longer. Boyd called them several names, but they were firm. They departed after impressing upon him the fact that he was doomed to certain death from cold, exposure or fatigue if he did not give up the hunt. In reply he hitched up his trousers and started on his lonely quest.

The hog now showed the first signs of giving out. It did not stop any more to make those elaborate preparations for a night of repose, but simply crawled under a slanting rock or fallen tree as if it had no time to spare. The fifth night was spent by Boyd in Oakland. There they tried to dissuade him. They told him he would never catch it, and if he did it would kill him. An old German told him frightful tales of the animal's powers in battle. He told how horses and men went down before the terrible tusk of the boar of Europe and Bengal. He said that in his native land the wild hogs used often to rip the bark from the pines, rub the pitch into their bristles and then go and roll in a soft clay, which, baked upon their sides by the sun, would make them impervious to bullets. Boyd failed to be impressed. The sixth day was a long and cold one. An icy north wind swept over the ridges and through the gulleys, and the snow drifted heavily. Long icicles hung on Boyd's mustache and his face was frozen blue as he clambered over logs, fell down rocks and plunged through snowbanks, the while keeping both eyes upon the tracks of the hog, which were rapidly being obliterated by the snow. The close of the day brought him no success.

The next day he again took up the chase. The drifting snow made the task of keeping the trail a difficult one. Several times he found himself off the track and lost time looking it up. About noon he discovered fresh blood. This made him, of course, redouble his exertions. Late in the day he discovered a fox standing in the track of the hog, sniffing at the blood on the snow. He fired at the fox and hit it behind the ear. Immediately after the report there was a grunt in the bushes twenty yards away; the wild hog bounded from a clump of bushes and swiftly plunged through the woods. Instantly Boyd turned and fired. Then he started on a run in pursuit. A hundred yards further on he found the hog lying stone dead. Half an hour later it would have been too dark to have shot correctly. He left the dead hog and walked eight miles in the dark through the woods and drifts to his home. In the morning he drove his team upon old logging roads to within a mile or so of his game. Then he and a boy tied a stick in its jaws and dragged it over the snow to the horses. On the afternoon of the eighth day the carcass was hung up in his barn and the struggle was over. Assuming that only five of the wild hogs were in Mr. Plock's park and escaped, the Hartwood Park hunters have accounted for all of them but one. Judge Crane took a second shot in the direction of the fast-lessening noise, after he had fired at the spot of brown in the brush, and it is believed by Boyd that a second pig received a fatal wound from that shot. This of course would end the hunting of the wild hog in the United States.

The people of Sullivan County are wonderful yarn-spinners and they have some great additions to their list of tales. Doubtless for years to come those that know the story will tell to admiring listeners how "Lew" Boyd chased the wounded wild hog for 200 miles.

No. 43   THE LAST PANTHER

So FAR as known, the last of the panthers which once were plentiful in this part of the country was killed in 1829 by a negro who, flushed with victory and panting with pride, received from the hands of the admiring authorities, in the presence of his friends, filled with sympathetic joy at his good fortune, the munificent reward of $15. In the old days entangled, disordered and intricate Sullivan County was the home of dozens of these animals. They, of course, were accounted to be more formidable and more dangerous than any of the other animals of the swamps and ridges. They frequently made depredations upon the cattle and sheep and sometimes attacked men. The settlers are said to have believed that the panthers would sometimes imitate the cries of children and thus lure victims away from the houses and to the woods. But, although the memories of the old inhabitants bristle with tales of battles with panthers, the tales contain no specific accounts of the panther's siren voice. They tell how individuals returning home late on moonless nights ran several miles in great haste and a cold perspiration upon hearing that wild, weird cry ring out, as if a woman were being murdered by a red-handed villain with a knife. But, either because of good roads or great speed, none of these men seems ever to have been caught. It is evident, too, that they spoke truly, for these hard-working, industrious mountaineers would never run four miles simply to receive nothing at the end but a soulful welcome and a chance to tell a thrilling story. And, in their gentle innocence and guilelessness, they have not the consummate art of the actor of lurid drama, who rushes upon the stage from a point six feet from the edge of the wing, and sinking down, pantingly cries that he has been pursued eighteen miles by a band of Indians. So it is apparent that travelling by night was once a dangerous practice in Sullivan County.

There were many stout-hearted and quick-shooting hunters in the region who used to like nothing better than a "brush with a painter." But it was difficult to get a good dog to follow the track. Most dogs, upon smelling a panther trail, would shrivel up and quake or mayhap howl in a distressing manner. But there were a few Sullivan County dogs who, confident of their own ability, would not hesitate to worry the retreating form of a man-eating tiger. These dogs were at a premium, although even they, when approaching the panther, would give a mournful tone to their howl.

Nelson Crocker, long since dead, is said to have seen seven panthers at once, a feat which probably surpasses the wildest dream of the most able and proficient delirium-tremens expert in the country. Crocker was hunting in "Painter Swamp" one day when he discovered the tracks of a number of panthers. His dog was a good one, and briskly followed the trail. At noon, the hunter sat down on a log to eat his luncheon. As he slowly put the last morsel in his mouth there was a chorus of howls from the surrounding bushes, and he saw seven panthers in rapid succession. He fired at one and killed it, while his dog was soundly thrashed by another. Crocker quickly decided that the sooner he emerged from the swamp the better, so he retreated, preceded by a very willing dog. The next day he went back to skin his game and recover his hat, which he had lost. After shooting a second panther, he and his dog were again forced to retreat by a third. This time, to accelerate his speed, he was forced to throw away his rifle. Having safely arrived on high ground, he decided to return for his weapon. He recovered it, and after a three-handed fight, in which he lost part of his dog, he killed a third panther. He skinned all three and proceeded joyously homeward.

Cyrus Dodge, down the dim vista of rural history, follows close with six panthers the shade of Nelson Crocker. At Long Pond he saw six panthers at once. He ran out into the pond and, standing in water up to his waist, shot four of them.

An old authority on hunting claims that a man by the name of Calvin Bush was the prince of panther-killers. Bush was a clear-headed, nervous-limbed, muscular hunter, who was as good for his inches as any man in the county. He had a dog that was nearly as famous as himself. He had many adventures with the animals, and killed a large number of them. It is said that once, when he and a friend were hunting together, they shot and wounded a panther which took refuge in the top of a tall tree. Bush remarked to his companion: "I'm going to have some fun with that beast." He then cut a pole and climbed a tree close to the one in which the panther crouched. Straddling a limb, and twining his legs to preserve his balance, the hunter poked the wounded animal in the ribs until, enraged and furious, it fell to the ground in an ineffectual attempt to spring upon its assailant. There it was dispatched by the other man. On that hunt of two days they killed five panthers.

Upon one occasion a wounded animal sprang at the hunter's dog. Bush's gun was empty, but he stood by his valorous and faithful canine friend. He aimed a blow at the panther's head with a hatchet. The animal dodged and caught the handle in its teeth. It wrenched the implement from the hunter's hand with the utmost ease, and then dropped it to fight the dog, which had begun a noisy attack in the rear. While the panther was mutilating the dog Bush loaded his gun and shot it through the head. He always carried a crooked finger, which was made by the panther's teeth when it grasped the hatchet-handle.

The people around Monticello were disturbed by two of these animals, which used to prowl around in the night and cry like children. They sent for Bush and his famous "painter-dog." The hunter chased and overtook the animals in a swamp and killed them both.

A score or so of hunters from Callicoon chased a huge panther into its den in a ledge of rocks. They closed up the entrance to the lair and departed, returning on the next day with reinforcements and a determination to kill the dread beast. It had retreated to a dark inner recess. After a council of war, in which every gentleman of the company told the others how to hunt panthers, they decided to place a lighted candle where the rays would gleam down a rifle-barrel. This was done and a man ventured in until he perceived the inevitable "fiery eye-balls." Then he pulled the trigger. The report was followed by howls from the wounded animal, which caused a retreat of the entire army. That which a moment before had been the scene of a well-planned campaign turned to one of the wildest confusion and disorder. Four hundred yards from the scene of the attack the little band rallied, and it was then perceived that nearly every member had been wounded. Bruised shins, lacerated feet and skinned elbows were plentiful as a result of the wild charge over rocks and logs and through brambles. One brave man had bumped his head on a rock right where the panther had once walked. Slowly they again approached the den wherein lurked the foe. It was necessary that every precaution be taken or they might be attacked in overwhelming numbers. They arrived safely with no accident. Another man ventured in and cracked away at the "fiery eyeballs" with the same result as before, excepting that the panther howled less and the army did not retreat quite so far. A third man followed and with his bullet prostrated the beast upon the floor of the den, where it roared so faintly that the army almost refused to retreat at all. The leading spirits then grappled with the question as to how to get the animal out. It had retreated so far back in the cave that it was possible only for a boy to get to it. A boy volunteered, took off his coat in the presence of his admiring friends, went in and came out again, making a remark irrelevant to the subject, about the weather, which none heeded. A small lad who had not figured very highly in the retreats owing to his short legs and boyish strength proceeded to pile his coat, vest and hat behind a bush, and then sneaked into the cave armed with a Spanish dirk and a hatchet. Through the dark and uneven passage he crept until he could see the yellow-green eyes of the wounded animal staring at him fixedly. Nearer he crawled until he could hear its slow, labored breathing and could see it evidently gathering its forces for a last desperate effort. Reaching forward, the lad sunk his hatchet-blade in the beast's skull, and as it writhed and struggled on the floor in its death agony he cut its throat with his dirk. When the animal's limbs gave their last convulsive quivers he seized it and dragged it forth into the presence of the army, who thereupon cheered and went home and told about the killing of the panther.

No. 44   NOT MUCH OF A HERO

IT IS supposed to be a poor tombstone that cannot sing praises. In a thousand graveyards the prevailing sentiment is: "Here lies a good man." Some years ago the people of this place erected a monument which they inscribed to "Tom Quick, the Indian Slayer, or the Avenger of the Delaware." After considerable speechmaking and celebrating, they unveiled the stone upon which was inscribed the following touching tribute to the life and character of the great Delaware Valley pioneer: "Tom Quick was the first white child born within the present borough of Milford."

As he has long been known in history as a righteous avenger inflamed with just wrath against his enemies, the silence of the marble upon those virtues which nearly all dead men are said to have possessed is astonishing. Why the worthy gentlemen who had the matter in hand failed to mention any of those qualities or deeds by which "Tom" Quick made fame, but simply mentioned a fact for which he apparently was quite irresponsible, is, possibly, an unintentional rebuke to those who have delighted to honor those qualities of pitiless cruelty which rendered him famous. His exemplary character has made his memory popular in many parts of the valley. A local writer in Port Jervis some years ago was asked to dramatize a life of "Tom" Quick. He agreed and began a course of reading on his subject. But after much study he was compelled to acknowledge that he could not make Quick's popular qualities run in a noble and virtuous groove. He gave up the idea of making Quick the hero and introduced him as a secondary character, as a monomaniac upon the subject of Indians. The little boys living about Milford must be much agitated over the coldness of the monument's inscription, for Quick was a boys' hero. He has been a subject for the graphic and brilliant pens of the talented novelists of the dime and five-cent school. Youths going westward to massacre the devoted red man with a fell purpose and a small-calibre revolver always carry a cheap edition of Tom Quick's alleged biography, which is, when they are at a loss how to proceed, a valuable book of reference. In these volumes all the known ways to kill Indians are practically demonstrated. The hero is pictured as a gory-handed avenger of an advanced type who goes about seeking how many Indians he can devour within a given time. He is a paragon of virtue and slaughters savages in a very high and exalted manner. He also says "b'ar" and "thar" and speaks about getting his "har riz." He is a "dead shot" and perforates Indians with great rapidity and regularity, while they, it seems, persist in offering themselves as targets with much abandon and shoot at him with desperate wildness, never coming within several yards of their aim.

Historians are, as a rule, unsentimental. The aesthetic people, the lovers of the beautiful, the poetic dreamers, have always claimed that Quick during his lifetime killed one hundred Indians. The local historians stoutly assert that he only killed fifteen at the most. But certainly there must be some glory in fifteen Indians and when the manner in which the historians say Quick killed his Indians is taken into consideration it is not surprising that Quick occupies a unique place in history. He was born in Milford as above-mentioned, where his parents had settled in 1733. His father built mills and owned other valuable real-estate in the town, but "Tom" loved the woods and the mountains and chose rather to spend his time wandering with red companions than staying in or near the settlements. He became a veritable Indian in his habits. Until the French and Indian War he lived in perfect amity with the savages, sharing their amusements and pursuits. During this war, however, some savages shot "Tom's" father from ambush. His friendship turned immediately to the deadliest hatred and he swore that he would kill every redskin that crossed his path; he would hunt them as long as one of them remained east of the Alleghanies. The first Indian to be killed by Quick was named Muskwink. After the French and Indian War this Indian returned to the Valley of the Neversink. One day Quick went to a tavern near the junction of the Neversink and Delaware rivers. There he met Muskwink, who was, as usual, intoxicated. The Indian approached "Tom" and told him with great glee that he was of the party that killed Quick's father. He said he had scalped the old man with his own hand. He described laughingly the dying agonies of Quick's father, and mimicked his cries and groans. "Tom" was immediately worked up to the convulsive fury of an enraged panther. He snatched an old musket from the wall and pointing it at Muskwink's breast, drove him out of the house in advance of himself. After proceeding with his prisoner about a mile from the tavern, he shot him in the back, dragged the body into the bushes and left it.

At another time "Tom" and two other white men went into ambush in a thicket which overlooked some rocks where Indians often fished. Three Indians came to the rocks and were attacked by the white men. One was killed by a blow on the head with a club. Another was shot through the head and through the hand, while the third jumped into the river to save his life.

On one occasion Quick and a number of other white hunters sought shelter for the night in the log cabin of a man named Showers. An Indian arrived later and asked permission to stay all night. Showers agreed and the Indian, rolling himself in his blanket, lay down among the white hunters. In the middle of the night there was an explosion. When the hunters hastily struck a light they discovered Quick with a smoking rifle in his hand standing over the body of the Indian, who had been shot dead in his sleep.

Some time after the killing of Muskwink, an Indian with his squaw and three children was paddling down the Delaware River in a canoe. When the family was passing through Butler's Rift "Tom" Quick rose from where he lay concealed in the tall reed-grass on the shore and aiming his rifle at them commanded them to come ashore. When they had come near he shot the man, tomahawked the woman and the two eldest children and knocked the babe's brains out against a tree.

Quick made a statement to his nephew that he had killed an indefinite number of Indians. He said he would lie in the woods and wait until he heard a rifle go off. Then he would creep stealthily in the direction of the sound and would often find an Indian skinning a deer or a bear. He said that it was an easy matter then to put a ball through the red man's head or heart.

Another tale told of him smacks somewhat of the impossible and yet should be recognized as a unique method of fighting Indians. It seems that the tribes used to send small parties of their young warriors to kill this implacable hater of their race. A party of these Indians once met Quick in the woods. He was splitting a long log. They announced to him their intention of killing him. He parleyed with them for some time. Finally he seemed to agree to their plan, but requested that he be allowed, as his last act on earth, to split that log. They agreed for certain reasons only known to themselves. He drove a wedge in the end and then he begged as another favor that they assist him in splitting the log. Again they innocently and guilelessly agreed. Arranging themselves in a long line down the side of the log, the imbecile redskins placed their fingers in the crack held open by the wedge and began to heave. "Tom" then calmly knocked out the wedge, the log closed up and their fingers were all caught tight and fast. They, of course, danced about like so many kittens whose claws were caught in balls of yarn. "Tom" enjoyed their peculiar gyrations and listened to their passionate comments for a while and then proceeded to cut them up in small pieces with his axe. It is a notable fact that no one in the history of the country has ever discovered that kind of an Indian except "Tom" Quick in this alleged adventure. Quick finally died from old age in his bed quietly.

Apparently, if these adventures of his can be taken as examples, "Tom" Quick was not an "Indian fighter." He was merely an Indian killer. There are three views to be taken of "Tom" Quick. The deeds which are accredited to him may be fiction ones and he may have been one of those sturdy and bronzed woodsmen who cleared the path of civilization. Or the accounts may be true and he a monomaniac upon the subject of Indians as suggested by the dramatist. Or the accounts may be true and he a man whose hands were stained with unoffending blood, purely and simply a murderer.

No. 45 SULLIVAN COUNTY BEARS

OLD settlers say that there are more bears in Sullivan County to-day than there were a generation ago. A number of facts make this statement one easy to be believed. Long ago the forests thronged with a race of brawny hunters who shouldered deadly rifles and were keen-eyed for the chase. The hills were dotted with the little homes and clearings of woodsmen who made their living with axes, were iron-nerved and clear-eyed, and could shoot true. Tanneries and sawmills giving employment to many men sat by the sides of all the streams. The woods were full of the sounds of axe-blows and the creakings of ox-chains. Youths grew up with desire for fame and they took rifles and went to seek it in the woods. A hardy race of huntsmen made terrible war on the game. With the vanishing of the great forests these men disappeared from the face of the earth. Not all men now are hunters. There are those surrounded by the best cover for game who never taste partridge or venison the year round.

When Sullivan County was covered with a growth of heavy forest-trees hunters walking through the woods had good travelling, and could see far, for the brush, under the shade of the great trees, was not thick. Now the huge forest monarchs have gone their ways to the river-rafts and the sawmills, and after them have come second-growth and brush, thick as the hair on a dog's back. The game finds excellent crouching places in the dense thickets, and escapes the hunter's eye with ease.

Contrary to general belief, the shyest of all the animals which naturally live in these woods is the bear, and not the deer. The oldest hunters of this region assert this fact positively. They say that it is a comparatively easy thing to get a shot at a deer, but a difficult one to get the chance of holding a rifle on a bear as a target. The bear is much keener. If he hears a hunter or hunters coming a quarter of a mile away he will immediately get up and dust, and the hunter may not find out that he has been in his vicinity at all. The old bears, however, are not inclined to be very shy. They grow confident in their own strength and prowess, and do not always flinch when they accidentally meet a human being. For instance, if one of these old warriors should happen to be confronted by a man when crossing the road, he would stop and look, with curiosity expressed in his eyes, and maybe snarl and show his teeth if the man made a sudden motion. Having satisfied his curiosity he would quietly move off into the brush, generally leaving the man in a limp state.

The bear makes his bed for the winter in a number of different ways. Sometimes he crawls down in a hole, crevice or cave and snuggles under dead leaves and sticks. At other times, when trees fall down and make tangled masses, he crawls in the thickest part. He has also been known to gather great bunches of laurel boughs and pile them in a heap; then climb on top and sleep, letting the snow fall right on him. When the bear is engaged in making his couch he makes a pile of brush six or eight feet in diameter and three or four feet high. He will often strip a young tree so bare of leaf and branch that it looks like a flagpole, with only a small tassel on top. In the summer he has a private bath. He goes to some swamp and with his strong claws digs down into the black mud until he has hollowed out a little place which soon filters full of a black ooze. Here the bear lies and wallows through the dead heat of a summer's day in the forest, when not a leaf in the woods stirs and the earth and the animals on it bake and swelter. Beaten paths are generally found to lead to each one of these, showing that the bear loves his slimy baths above all things.

He takes care of his claws in the same manner in which a cat does. Scarred trees can be found in the wilds, showing that the bears stand up on their hind legs and claw down the bark.

In the spring and early summer the bears live on roots and sprouts and tender leaves, together with the grubs and worms which they get by turning over the stones in the valleys. Boulders too heavy for a man to lift are found rolled recklessly about by bears in pursuit of grubs. Of course when a bear finds a bee tree he is a happy animal. In the late summer and fall he resorts to the berry patches and scrub-oak ridges and feasts on the berries and acorns.

But when he first comes out in the spring he is very hungry and will eat anything he can get. He will dine on dead horse, or will steal a pig from a pen or a calf from a stable. But when other food is plentiful the black bear will never touch flesh. Hunger will drive him to it, but of his own free will he prefers a diet of vegetables.

A bear-hunt in this region is in reality a chase from swamp to swamp. The bear, when hunted, always runs to a swamp and hides in its thickest and most inaccessible part. Here he will stay until driven out by the approach of a man or a dog on the trail. The hunters always do what they call "surrounding" the swamp, although, of course, they do not really do so, owing to the size of the swamp and the limit to the number of men. Then the guide and the dogs generally follow in on the trail, after leaving the rest of the party stationed at convenient points on the outskirts. The best spot to get a shot at a bear is at the place where he entered the swamp, for he is pretty sure to come out there. But he is a wary strategist. He crouches in the depths of a bog maybe and listens. He hears voices off to the north, as the hunters take up their positions on the "runways" in that direction. From the east come faint sounds of the snapping of a twig as a hunter makes room for the better sweep of his rifle barrel. To the south he may hear a man cautiously scramble up on a log or an old stump, and in the rear he hears faintly the whines of the hound on a warm trail and the low, directing voice of the guide. The hunters may be a long distance away, but the old bear hears them and interprets the sounds and lays his plans accordingly. He shows ability and skill in his effort to come unscathed from the tight place he is in. He runs some distance and then stops, perhaps, and listens intently. Maybe his ears tell him to take a new direction, and he starts rapidly off. Whether he gets out of the swamp now or not depends entirely upon what backwoods general has stationed the men, and who the men are. Even if they are expert shots, it will avail them nought unless they are placed by a leader, who knows the important posts, who can calculate on the bear's conclusions, and guard against errors of judgment. To be a strategist equal to emergencies which arise when hunting in Sullivan County takes a lifetime in the woods, a thirty years' study of the habits of animals.

After that difficulty is overcome there exists the one of shooting the bear. Some men can hit things with a gun and some men can't. So, even if a hunter on a "runway" gets a shot, the bear has a dozen chances to escape. He immediately starts for another swamp three or four miles away. It must not be supposed that he travels slowly. A bear can keep well ahead of a good dog all day, through bushes, swale or any kind of country, except in the open fields. These animals, which people call awkward and ungainly, run as easily as rabbits. Nor do they "shamble" or "wobble" or "flounder." They have an easy, rapid gait, which carries them swiftly and easily away from the pursuing dogs.

Not many dogs will follow bear. Some quake and shiver when they scent the trail. Some will run an old trail, but will turn back when it freshens. Others will run an old trail with rapidity, but will slow up and run poorly on the fresh scent, giving a mournful "sorry-like" tone to their yelps as they near the bear's possible crouching place. But there are stout-hearted hounds of good breed who will take a bear's track eagerly and run with a determination to overtake the animal. If such a dog comes up with a wounded bear, he will tackle him without a moment's hesitation. A good bear-hound seems to take the trail with a strange vindictiveness and bloodthirstiness. He seems eager for the bear's life and will follow until he is totally exhausted, the bear is killed, or his owner takes him off the scent. Old Scout, the former pride of Hartwood Park and the best bear-runner in Sullivan County, ran the game with the ferocity of a wolf. If he came up with a wounded bear, there ensued immediately a tremendous scuffle. His valiant heart never flinched at the sight of huge, gleaming teeth, nor great, spreading claws, nor at the sound of the fierce snarls. One of his human friends once stood over a whirling chaos of dog's feet and bear's feet and of dog's ears and bear's ears. From it there rose a haze of two different kinds of hair. Snarls and snaps, growls and roars, filled the forests. Soon the mass took shape, and the bear appeared with his forefeet planted on the dog's body, chewing and rending it with teeth and claws. Old Scout never whimpered nor made complaint. The bear left off and started to run away. The hound, gathering his bleeding form together, gave furious pursuit. The friend of Old Scout, who had not dared to fire at the mass of dog and bear, then dropped the game with a ball behind the ear. The dog plunged savagely upon the fallen foe, but, finding that there was no more fight in the animal, sat down and contentedly wagged his tail. When a bear is shot through the head, he "falls dead in his tracks." If the bullet happens to break the spinal column, he also then falls dead. But plant a bullet anywhere else, and the animal may run a mile with it in him. Most hunters prefer to aim at a point under the foreshoulder when the bear is moving rapidly through difficult cover. If one hits him there, it is almost certain that the bullet will pierce the heart, pass through the lungs, or sever an artery.

Although no one can doubt the great strength and fighting ability of the bear, yet it is difficult to reconcile the bear of fiction with the bear of reality. The black bear of the hunter's tales was a fighter. He had a fashion of rearing upon his hind legs and crushing men and guns in a passionate embrace. Story books bristle with accounts of his enthusiastic receptions of sportsmen. The books say that when the Indians and black bears roamed these hills the brave who possessed a necklace of the claws of this terrible animal was considered a great warrior. Save the dreaded panther, the bear was the monarch of the wilds. Indians were generally knocked rudely about when they ventured upon a hand-to-hand encounter with bruin.

The gentlemen who figure in fiction as "scouts" and "guides" and what not are reputed to have stood, attired in fringed buckskin, about the camp-fires and told of desperate attacks upon themselves by ferocious bears. They are supposed to have carried so many scars that their bodies looked like road-maps. But the black bear of to-day is not a fighter. Of course, when cornered he will make a fight for his life, as a gray squirrel will. A she bear will fight to protect her young. A wounded bear will turn and beat off the dogs. If exasperated in close quarters, a bear may let drive savagely with both paws and snarl and bite with great fierceness. In this case, it is advisable to retire, if convenient. An old bear encountering some one accidentally in the woods will show his teeth. If the man insists on a row he will get a fine one. But the modern black bear is not a fighter by choice. He depends more on his four feet and his keen senses for safety than he does upon his prowess.

No. 46   THE WAY IN SULLIVAN COUNTY

A COUNTRY famous for its hunting and its hunters is naturally prolific of liars. Wherever the wild deer boundeth and the shaggy bear waddleth, there does the liar thrive and multiply. Every man cultivates what taste he has for prevarication lest his neighbors may look down on him. One can buy sawlogs from a native and take his word that the bargain is square, but ask the same man how many deer he has killed in his lifetime and he will stop working, take a seat on the snake-fence and paralyze the questioner with a figure that would look better than most of the totals to the subscription lists for monuments to national heroes. The inhabitants grow up to regard each other with painful suspicion. So there is very little field for the expert liars among their fellows. They must keep to a certain percentage or they will lose caste, but there is little pleasure in it for them because everybody knows everybody else. The only real enjoyment is when the unoffending city man appears. They welcome him with joyful cries. After he recovers from a paroxysm of awe and astonishment he seizes his pen and with flashing eye and trembling, eager fingers, writes those brief but lurid sketches which fascinate and charm the reading public while the virtuous bushwhacker, whittling a stick near by, smiles in his own calm and sweet fashion.

Hence we have the tale of the farmer lad who rounded up the herd of seven bears and drove them to a pasture lot by means of a tin huckleberry pail and an iron nerve. Hence comes also the story of the young man who hitched the team of cubs to a soap-box, and trained them to drag him over the snow, with admirable success, until one day when chased by a dog they dragged him and the soap-box up into the top of a tall hemlock. The writer ended his tale at about that point, and so it is an open question whether the young man and the soap-box ever got down from the tree or are up there at this moment. Scores of tales of even more brilliancy than the two recited are prevalent.

It is inevitable that this should be the state of society in Sullivan County as well as in Pike County, and the vicinity of Scranton, Penn. In a shooting country, no man should tell just exactly what he did. He should tell what he would have liked to do or what he expected to do, just as if he accomplished it. And they all take the proper course, bringing the bump of creative genius up to a high point of development and adding little legends to the hunting lore of the region, which will undoubtedly go down the ages and impress coming generations with the fact that the Sullivan County bushwhackers were very great men indeed. Only two tales need be introduced to illustrate the lines of thought followed by these able and proficient gentlemen—one of great execution done by the liar, the other in which the liar figures as one who saw great things. Quite a number of men sometimes tell the same tale as part of their own individual experience. For instance, six men say that once when they, or he, was on a hunt, he was crawling cautiously through a thicket toward a huge fallen tree. Suddenly when he was some yards distant a bear raised its head over the log and peered at him. He aimed at it and fired. The bear disappeared behind the log. The hunter proceeded toward the log, when he saw the bear's head again. He fired and the head disappeared as before. He crawled on, when for the third time he perceived the bear's head. He fired again. Upon crawling to the log and looking over he found three dead bears.

Once upon a time two men slept all night in a cave. Upon waking up and peering out in the morning they perceived a huge bear and a panther some distance away. The animals were about forty yards apart. The bear was eating huckleberries from the bushes, while the panther was sharpening its claws on a tree like a cat. The men according to an agreement fired simultaneously, one at the bear and one at the other animal. There came a roar of astonishment from the bear and a snarl of surprise from the panther. Gazing around, they perceived each other and each decided that the other animal was the cause of its sudden pain. Filled with anger they furiously fell upon each other, bent on taking full revenge. They both seemed overcome with indignation at the insult offered them. They roared and snarled and fought furiously. Brown hair and tawny fur flew about in handfuls, and blood stained the stones. In the frantic fight, it was impossible to tell which was getting the better of it, so the brilliant-minded and philosophical hunters dangled their heels and smilingly looked on until the panther finished the bear. Then they shot the victor.

No. 47   A REMINISCENCE OF INDIAN WAR

IN JULY, 1779, a red wave of savages, with crest of bloody steel, swept down the Delaware Valley. The settlers fled before it to the crowded stockades and blockhouses where a legion of colonels and majors wrote letters and dispatched them to each other. The savages were led by Brandt. They burned and pillaged, while the colonels indited epistles. One wrote: "An express is just this moment come from Colonel Stroud's, bringing the melancholy account that the Tories and Indians in the upper part of the Minisink, in York Government, are burning and destroying all before them. It is said the enemy are six hundred strong and that the Tories join them every hour. It is not to be doubted that they will be in this State very soon, and the inhabitants above are all moving, and in the greatest distress and confusion. By a letter I have seen this morning from Captain Alexander Patterson, at Colonel Stroud's, stationed as quartermaster, it is mentioned that they have neither military stores or provisions, so that if they should suddenly attack that part of this country, destitute of help as they are, the country must fly before the enemy."

He was too busy with Indians to bother with pronouns. Another wrote: "Brant is Doing the mischief att Peainpack, and to my sorrow I acquaint you it has struck the People in general with such fear that they are moving away from the upper end of the Minisink very fast. If there is not some Means Taken To Stop the Enemy, the whole of the Inhabitance will move from this Place, and if so, pray what will be the Consiquence? Ruin and Destruction will Emediately Follow."

When the first of the fugitives reached Goshen, in Orange County, N.Y., Colonel Tusten who commanded the local militia, rallied his forces, with as many volunteers as could be raised, and held a council of war. The Indians, having devastated the valley and gorged themselves with plunder, had begun a retreat. Colonel Tusten said in the council that he doubted the expediency of a pursuit at that time, for the Indians outnumbered the whites two to one. But one man cried:

"Let the brave men follow me. The cowards may stay behind."

It was impossible for the prudent to say more. So they set out. They were joined by Colonel Hathorn, of the "Warwick Regiment," who had a few men with him. He, being the senior officer, took command. Thirty-four miles from their starting point they held another council of war, where the leaders were blistered by the words of valiant subordinates. So Colonel Hathorn decided to try to intercept Brandt at the Lackawaxen Ford of the Delaware, where they understood he was going to cross the river. Hathorn and his men made a bold dash for the ford, hoping to reach it first. But Brandt reversed his column, passed down a ravine and came upon the patriot force in the rear. The battle of the Minisink followed. The scene of the fight is a little over a mile from this town, across the river, in Sullivan County, N.Y.

The Americans were caught like a lot of kittens in a bag, but Hathorn was a gallant officer and a sagacious leader. He made a stout-hearted fight. On a plateau near the river the Americans took their position. They threw up an irregular breastwork of stones and logs. They used every crevice and boulder possible as a means of protection, and lay close to the earth. Ninety men, without water and with no provisions, held this position from 10 o'clock until sundown, on a sultry July day.

Before a shot was fired Brandt appeared in full view of the Americans and requested them to surrender. He said his force was superior to theirs, and he had them penned in. If they surrendered, he would protect them. He was interrupted by a bullet. He retired, and the Indians immediately began a furious fire. The little plateau was covered with black powder smoke, from which the little red flames leaped at the Indians like tongues of snakes. Brandt opened the battle with his usual cautiousness. His men made no targets of themselves, but crept warily toward the Americans, taking advantage of every feature of the ground and firing at every hand, head or shoulder which appeared above the rocks on the plateau. But they could not make the patriots yield an inch, though the Indian dead lay thickly on the slope. The panting, powder-grimed whites on the height held their ground. The Indians were repelled at every point. The band of Americans on the plateau had grown to manhood with rifles in their hands. They were of that bronzed and sturdy race who were hewing their way through the matted forests and making homes in the dense jungles of an American wilderness. If a part of the line flinched even for a moment, they would all die. Each man felt his responsibility as a link in the chain of defence, and yielded not an inch. The powder ran short, of course, and they had to make every bullet find a red, howling mark.

As the day wore on, and one after another of his whooping minions was bowled over without making any gap in the American line, Brandt grew disheartened. It is said that there was one brave hunter who held the key to the American position. It is not explained by any one how this could be. A careful investigation of the battlefield as it appears to-day fails to discover any spot where one man could hold the key to the plateau against nearly 300 Indians. Or, if there was such key, why leave it to the guardianship of one man, unsupported by the fire of his comrades, and with no reinforcing body? But, at any rate, the tradition runs that way. Near sundown the Indians shot this man, and Brandt with a body of warriors sprang through the gap. Immediately the Americans became demoralized. They began a retreat. Where the noble red man shines out in transcendent lustre is as a pursuer. The scalping-knife and the tomahawk took the place of the rifle. The Americans made a frantic rush for the river. The Indians sank their hatches in the body of every white man they could overtake. Captain Vail, of the militia, being wounded in the battle, was unable to retreat. While seated upon a rock, bleeding, he was slaughtered by the Indians. Seventeen wounded Americans and a surgeon were found behind a ledge of rocks. They were all killed. The Americans, scattered and broken, worn out with fighting against overwhelming numbers, fled madly. Many threw themselves into the Delaware and endeavored to escape by swimming as much as possible under the water. A small and decrepit band of those who had fought arrived home safely. There were thirty-three widows in the Presbyterian congregation at Goshen.

Fifty men had been cut off from the main body by Brandt's sudden attack. They took no part in the battle at all. It is said that they were led by the man who made the valorous oration at the council of war.

No. 48   FOUR MEN IN A CAVE

THE moon rested for a moment in the top of a tall pine on a hill.

The little man was standing in front of the camp-fire making oration to his companions.

"We can tell a great tale when we get back to the city, if we investigate this thing," said he, in conclusion.

They were won.

The little man was determined to explore a cave, because its black mouth had gaped at him. The four men took lighted pine-knots and clambered over boulders down a hill. In a thicket on the mountain-side lay a little tilted hole. At its side they halted.

"Well?" said the little man.

They fought for last place and the little man was overwhelmed. He tried to struggle from under by crying that if the fat, pudgy man came after, he would be corked. But he finally administered a cursing over his shoulder and crawled into the hole. His companions gingerly followed.

A passage, the floor of damp clay and pebbles, the walls slimy, green-mossed and dripping, sloped downward. In the cave-atmosphere the torches became studies in red blaze and black smoke.

"Ho!" cried the little man, stifled and bedraggled, "let's go back." His companions were not brave. They were last. The next one to the little man pushed him on, so the little man said sulphurous words and cautiously continued his crawl.

Things that hung, seemed to be upon the wet, uneven ceiling, ready to drop upon the men's bare necks. Under their hands the clammy floor seemed alive and writhing. When the little man endeavored to stand erect the ceiling forced him down. Knobs and points came out and punched him. His clothes were wet and mud-covered, and his eyes, nearly blinded by smoke, tried to pierce the darkness always before his torch.

"Oh, I say, you fellows, let's go back!" cried he. At that moment he caught the gleam of trembling light in the blurred shadows before him.

"Ho!" he said, "here's another way out."

The passage turned abruptly. The little man put one hand around the corner but it touched nothing. He investigated and discovered that the little corridor took a sudden dip down a hill. At the bottom shone a yellow light.

The little man wriggled painfully about and descended feet in advance. The others followed his plan. All picked their way with anxious care. The traitorous rocks rolled from beneath the little man's feet and roared thunderously below him. Lesser stones, loosened by the men above him, hit him in the back. He gained a seemingly firm foothold and turning half about, swore redly at his companions for dolts and careless fools. The pudgy man sat, puffing and perspiring, high in the rear of the procession. The fumes and smoke from four pine-knots were in his blood. Cinders and sparks lay thick in his eyes and hair. The pause of the little man angered him.

"Go on, you fool," he shouted. "Poor, painted man, you are afraid!"

"Ho!" said the little man, "come down here and go on yourself, imbecile!"

The pudgy man vibrated with passion. He leaned downward. "Idiot——"

He was interrupted by one of his feet which flew out and crashed into the man in front of and below him. It is not well to quarrel upon a slippery incline, when the unknown is below. The fat man, having lost the support of one pillar-like foot, lurched forward. His body smote the next man, who hurtled into the next man. Then they all fell upon the cursing little man.

They slid in a body down over the slippery, slimy floor of the passage. The stone avenue must have wibble-wobbled with the rush of this ball of tangled men and strangled cries. The torches went out with the combined assault upon the little man. The adventurers whirled to the unknown in darkness. The little man felt that he was pitching to death, but even in his convolutions he bit and scratched at his companions, for he was satisfied that it was their fault. The swirling mass went some twenty feet and lit upon a level dry place in a strong, yellow light of candles. It dissolved and became eyes.

The four men lay in a heap upon the floor of a gray chamber. A small fire smouldered in a corner, the smoke disappearing in a crack. In another corner was a bed of faded hemlock boughs and two blankets. Cooking utensils and clothes lay about, with boxes and a barrel.

Of these things the four men took small cognizance. The pudgy man did not curse the little man, nor did the little man swear, in the abstract. Eight widened eyes were fixed upon the centre of the room of rocks.

A great gray stone, cut squarely, like an altar, sat in the middle of the floor. Over it burned three candles in swaying tin cups hung from the ceiling. Before it, with what seemed to be a small volume clasped in his yellow fingers, stood a man. He was an infinitely sallow person in the brown checked shirt of the ploughs and cows. The rest of his apparel was boots. A long gray beard dangled from his chin. He fixed glinting, fiery eyes upon the heap of men and remained motionless. Fascinated, their tongues cleaving, their blood cold, they arose to their feet. The gleaming glance of the recluse swept slowly over the group until it found the face of the little man. There it stayed and burned.

The little man shrivelled and crumpled as the dried leaf under the glass.

Finally the recluse slowly, deeply spoke. It was a true voice from a cave, cold, solemn and damp.

"It's your ante," he said.

"What?" said the little man.

The hermit tilted his beard and laughed a laugh that was either the chatter of a banshee in a storm or the rattle of pebbles in a tin box. His visitors' flesh seemed ready to drop from their bones.

They huddled together and cast fearful eyes over their shoulders. They whispered.

"A vampire!" said one.

"A ghoul!" said another.

"A Druid before the sacrifice," murmured another.

"The shade of an Aztec witch doctor," said the little man.

As they looked, the inscrutable's face underwent a change. It became a livid background for his eyes, which blazed at the little man like impassioned carbuncles. His voice arose to a howl of ferocity. "It's your ante!" With a panther-like motion, he drew a long, thin knife and advanced, stooping. Two cadaverous hounds came from nowhere and, scowling and growling, made desperate feints at the little man's legs. His quaking companions pushed him forward.

Tremblingly he put his hand to his pocket.

"How much?" he said, with a shivering look at the knife that glittered.

The carbuncles faded.

"Three dollars," said the hermit, in sepulchral tones which rang against the walls and among the passages, awakening long-dead spirits with voices. The shaking little man took a roll of bills from a pocket and placed "three ones" upon the altar-like stone. The recluse looked at the little volume with reverence in his eyes. It was a pack of playing cards.

Under the three swinging candles, upon the altar-like stone, the gray-beard and the agonized little man played at poker. The three other men crouched in a corner and stared with eyes that gleamed with terror. Before them sat the cadaverous hounds, licking their red lips. The candles burned low and began to flicker. The fire in the corner expired.

Finally the game came to a point where the little man laid down his hand and quavered: "I can't call you this time, sir. I'm dead broke."

"What?" shrieked the recluse. "Not call me? Villain! Dastard! Cur! I have four queens, miscreant!" His voice grew so mighty that it could not fit his throat. He choked, wrestling with his lungs, for a moment. Then the power of his body was concentrated in a word: "Go!"

He pointed a quivering, yellow finger at a wide crack in the rock. The little man threw himself at it with a howl. His erstwhile frozen companions felt their blood throb again. With great bounds they plunged after the little man. A minute of scrambling, falling and pushing brought them to open air. They climbed the distance to their camp in furious springs.

The sky in the east was a lurid yellow. In the west the footprints of departing night lay on the pine trees. In front of their replenished camp-fire sat John Willerkins, the guide.

"Hello!" he shouted at their approach. "Be you fellers ready to go deer huntin'?"

Without replying, they stopped and debated among themselves in whispers.

Finally the pudgy man came forward.

"John," he inquired, "do you know anything peculiar about this cave below here?"

"Yes," said Willerkins at once, "Tom Gardner."

"What?" said the pudgy man.

"Tom Gardner!"

"How's that?"

"Well, you see," said Willerkins slowly, as he took dignified pulls at his pipe, "Tom Gardner was onct a fambly man, who lived in these here parts on a nice leetle farm. He uster go away to the city orften, and one time he got a-gamblin' in one of them there dens. He wentter the dickens right quick then. At

last he kum home one time and tol' his folks he had up and
sold the farm and all he had in the worl'. His leetle wife, she
died then. Tom, he went crazy, and soon after——"

The narrative was interrupted by the little man, who became
possessed of devils.

"Iwouldn'tgiveacussifhehadleftme'noughmoneytogethomeonth-
edoggonedgrayhairedredpirate," he shrilled, in a seething sentence. The pudgy man gazed at the little man calmly and
sneeringly.

"Oh well," he said, "we can tell a great tale when we get
back to the city after having investigated this thing."

"Go to the devil!" replied the little man.

No. 49 THE OCTOPUSH

FOUR men once upon a time went into the wilderness seeking
for pickerel. They proceeded to a pond which is different from
all other sheets of water in the world excepting the remaining
ponds in Sullivan County. A scrawny stone dam, clinging in
apparent desperation to its foundation, wandered across a wild
valley. In the beginning, the baffled waters had retreated to a
forest. In consequence, the four men confronted a sheet of
water from which there up-reared countless grey, haggard
tree-trunks. Squat stumps, in multitudes, stretched long, lazy
roots over the surface of the water. Floating logs and sticks
bumped gently against the dam. All manner of weeds throttled
the lilies and dragged them down. Great pine trees came from
all sides to the pond's edge.

In their journey the four men encountered a creature with
a voice from a tomb. His person was concealed behind an
enormous straw hat. In graveyard accents, he demanded that
he be hired to assist them in their quest. They agreed. From
a recess of the bank he produced a blunt-ended boat, painted a
very light blue, with yellow finishings, in accordance with
Sullivan aesthetics. Two sculls whittled from docile pine boards
lay under the seats. Pegs were driven into the boat's sides at
convenient row-lock intervals. In deep, impressive tones, the

disguised individual told the four men that, to his knowledge, the best way to catch pickerel was to " 'skidder' fur 'em from them there stumps." The four men clambered into the beautiful boat and the individual manoeuvered his craft until he had dealt out to four low-spreading stumps, four fishers. He thereupon repaired to a fifth stump where he tied his boat. Perching himself upon the stump-top, he valiantly grasped a mildewed corn-cob between his teeth, ladened with black, eloquent tobacco. At a distance it smote the senses of the four men.

The sun gleamed merrily upon the waters, the gaunt, towering tree-trunks and the stumps lying like spatters of wood which had dropped from the clouds. Troops of blue and silver darning-needles danced over the surface. Bees bustled about the weeds which grew in the shallow places. Butterflies flickered in the air. Down in the water, millions of fern branches quavered and hid mysteries. The four men sat still and 'skiddered.' The individual puffed tremendously. Ever and anon, one of the four would cry ecstatically or swear madly. His fellows, upon standing to gaze at him, would either find him holding a stout fish, or nervously struggling with a hook and line entangled in the hordes of vindictive weeds and sticks on the bottom. They had fortune, for the pickerel is a voracious fish. His only faults are in method. He has a habit of furiously charging the fleeting bit of glitter and then darting under a log or around a corner with it.

At noon, the individual corralled the entire outfit upon a stump where they lunched while he entertained them with anecdote. Afterward he redistributed them, each to his personal stump. They fished. He contemplated the scene and made observations which rang across the water to the four men in bass solos. Toward the close of the day, he grew evidently thoughtful, indulging in no more spasmodic philosophy. The four men fished intently until the sun had sunk down to some tree-tops and was peering at them like the face of an angry man over a hedge. Then one of the four stood up and shouted across to where the individual sat enthroned upon the stump.

"You had better take us ashore now." The other three repeated: "Yes, come take us ashore."

Whereupon the individual carefully took an erect position.

Then, waving a great yellow-brown bottle and tottering, he gave vent to a sepulchral roar.

"You fellersh—hic—kin all go—hic—ter blazersh."

The sun slid down and threw a flare upon the silence, coloring it red. The man who had stood up drew a long, deep breath and sat down heavily. Stupefaction rested upon the four men.

Dusk came and fought a battle with the flare before their eyes. Tossing shadows and red beams mingled in combat. Then the stillness of evening lay upon the waters.

The individual began to curse in deep maudlin tones. "Dern fools," he said, "dern fools! Why don'tcher g'home?"

"He's full as a fiddler," said the little man on the third stump. The rest groaned. They sat facing the stump whereon the individual perched, beating them with mighty oaths. Occasionally he took a drink from the bottle. "Shay, you'm fine lot fellers," he bellowed, "why blazersh don'tcher g'home?"

The little man on the third stump pondered. He got up finally and made oration. He, in the beginning, elaborated the many good qualities which he alleged the individual possessed. Next he painted graphically the pitiful distress and woe of their plight. Then he described the reward due to the individual if he would relieve them, and ended with an earnest appeal to the humanity of the individual, alleging, again, his many virtues. The object of the address struggled to his feet, and in a voice of far-away thunder, said: "Dern fool, g'home." The little man sat down and swore crimson oaths.

A night wind began to roar and clouds bearing a load of rain appeared in the heavens and threatened their position. The four men shivered and turned up their coat collars. Suddenly it struck each that he was alone, separated from humanity by impassable gulfs. All those things which come forth at night began to make noises. Unseen animals scrambled and flopped among the weeds and sticks. Weird features masqueraded awfully in robes of shadow. Each man felt that he was compelled to sit on something that was damply alive. A legion of frogs in the grass by the shore and a host of toads in the trees chanted. The little man started up and shrieked that all creeping things were inside his stump. Then he tried to sit facing four ways, because dread objects were approaching at his back.

The individual was drinking and hoarsely singing. At different times they labored with him. It availed them nought. "G'home, dern fools." Among themselves they broached various plans for escape. Each involved a contact with the black water, in which were things that wriggled. They shuddered and sat still.

A ghost-like mist came and hung upon the waters. The pond became a grave-yard. The grey tree-trunks and dark logs turned to monuments and crypts. Fire-flies were wisp-lights dancing over graves, and then, taking regular shapes, appeared like brass nails in crude caskets. The individual began to gibber. A gibber in a bass voice appals the stoutest heart. It is the declamation of a genie. The little man began to sob; another groaned and the two remaining, being timid by nature, swore great lurid oaths which blazed against the sky.

Suddenly the individual sprang up and gave tongue to a yell which raised the hair on the four men's heads and caused the waters to ruffle. Chattering, he sprang into the boat and grasping an oar paddled frantically to the little man's stump. He tumbled out and cowered at the little man's feet, looking toward his stump with eyes that saw the unknown.

"Stump turned inter an octopush. I was a-settin' on his mouth," he howled.

The little man kicked him.

"Legs all commenced move, dern octopush!" moaned the shrunken individual.

The little man kicked him. But others cried out against him, so directly he left off. Climbing into the boat he went about collecting his companions. They then proceeded to the stump whereon the individual lay staring wild-eyed at his "octopush." They gathered his limp form into the boat and rowed ashore. "How far is it to the nearest house?" they demanded savagely of him. "Four miles," he replied in a voice of cave-damp. The four men cursed him and built a great fire of pine sticks. They sat by it all night and listened to the individual who dwelt in phantom shadows by the water's edge dismally crooning about an "octopush."

No. 49a EARLY DRAFT (THE FISHERMEN)

FOUR men once upon a time came into the wilderness seeking for pickerel. They proceeded to a pond which is different from all other ponds in the world excepting the remaining ponds in Sullivan County. A scrawny stone dam, clinging in apparent desperation of its foundation, wandered aimlessly across a wild valley. In the beginning, the baffled waters had retreated to a dense forest. Consequently, the four men confronted a smooth sheet of water from which there up-reared countless grey, haggard tree-trunks. Squat stumps in multitudes, idly stretched lazy roots over the surface of the water. All manners of weeds throttled the lilies and dragged them down. Great pine trees came from all sides to the pond's edge. Floating logs and sticks bumped gently against the careening dam.

In their journey the four men encountered a creature with a voice as from a tomb. His person was concealed behind an enormous straw hat. In sepulchral accents, he demanded that he be hired to assist them in their quest. They agreed to accept his services. From an inner recess of the bank he then produced a blunt-ended boat, painted a very light blue, in accordance with Sullivan County aesthetics. Two sculls whittled from docile pine boards, with a jack knife, lay under the seats. Pegs were driven into the boat's sides at convenient row-lock intervals.

In deep, impressive tones, the disguised individual told the four men that, to his certain knowledge the best way to catch pickerel was to " 'skidder' fur 'em from them there stumps". So the four men climbed into the beautifully blue boat and the individual manoeuvered his craft over the waters until he had dealt out four large low-spreading stumps to the four men, with fishing tackle. He then repaired to a fifth stump to which he tied his boat, and perching himself upon the stump-top, valiantly attacked a worn and mildewed corn-cob, ladened with black tobacco which smote the chests of the four men, all within hailing distance.

The sun beamed merrily upon the riffled waters, the gaunt, towering tree-trunks, and the low-lying stumps. Troops of blue and silver needles darted over the surface of the pond. Down in the waters, millions of moss branches waved gently and hid mysteries. The four men sat and 'skiddered'. The individual puffed tremendously at his pipe. Ever and anon, one of the four would cry ecstatically or swear dreadfully; and his fellows, upon standing to gaze at him, would find him either holding in joyous fingers a stout fish, or struggling with a hook and line entangled in the hordes of grasping weeds, sticks, and stumps, at the bottom of the pond. They fished until the sun slunk down behind some tree-tops and peered at them like the face of an angry man over a hedge. They had good fortune, for the pickerel is a voracious fish, his only faults being in method. He has a habit of furiously charging the fleeting bits of glitter, and then darting under a log or around a corner with it. Each one of the four had mighty strings of fish.

The individual sat enthroned cross-legged on his stump all day, pipe in mouth. From time to time in hollow tones he would venture suggestions, relate anecdotes, ask questions or volunteer information about his domestic life with great abruptness as the inspiration struck him. About noontime he corralled the entire outfit on one huge stump where they lunched. Later he distributed them about, each to his personal stump. They fished. He contemplated the scene and made occasional observations which rang across the waters to them, in bass solos.

Toward the close of the day, he grew silent and, evidently, thoughtful. When the sun had slid down until it only threw a red flare among the trees, one of the four men stood up and shouted to the individual:

"You had better take us ashore now."

The other three repeated: "Yes, take us ashore now."

The individual raised himself on his stump suddenly and waving a black bottle around his head, roared: "You fellersh—hic—kin all go—hic—ter blazerish."

There were a few moments of intense silence. Then the man who had stood up, drew a long, deep breath and sat down heavily. The rest were frozen in silence.

The night came creeping over the tree-tops. The stillness of evening rested upon the waters. The individual began to curse in deep maudlin tones. "Dern fools," he said, "dern fools! Why don'tcher g'home?"

"He's full as a fiddler," said a little man on the third stump. The rest groaned in reply. They all sat facing the stump whereon the individual perched, beating them with gigantic oaths.

Occasionally he would take another drink from the inexhaustible bottle. "Shay, you'm fine lot fellers," he would cry, "why blazersh don'tcher g'home?"

The little man on the third stump had been deeply thoughtful for a few moments. He now got up and made oration. He, in the beginning, elaborated the many good qualities which, he alleged, the individual possessed. Then, he painted graphically the pitiful distress and utter woe of their plight. Later, he described the reward due to the individual if he would relieve them; and ended with an earnest plea to the humanity of the individual. The individual struggled to his feet and cried:

"G'home, dern fool."

The little man sat down and swore crimson oaths. Then, in chorus they entreated, threatened, cursed and berated. All to no purpose. He called them names and told them to "g'home". He drank deeply.

A night wind began to moan and clouds bearing a load of rain appeared in the lofty heavens. The four men shivered and turned up their coat collars. All those things which come forth at night began to make noises. Unseen animals scrambled and splashed among the debris on the water. Crooked, slimy sticks seemed to squirm like snakes. The four men began to feel that they were sitting on live things. A legion of frogs and tree-toads chanted a solemn dirge on the pond's edge. The little man started up and shrieked that all creeping things were crawling about inside his stump. Each felt himself alone and at the mercy of unseen horrors which were approaching at his back.

The individual was still drinking and hoarsely singing. At different times they labored with him. It availed them nought. To each other, they broached various plans for escape but they gazed down into the black waters and thought that it teemed with slimy life. They shuddered and sat still.

A ghost mist came and hung above the water. In the shadows, the pond began to look like a vast grave-yard, the grey tree-trunks turning to aged marble pillars and monuments. Fireflies began to look like wisp-lights dancing over the graves, and then, taking regular shapes, appeared like the brass nails in crude caskets. The individual began to gibber. A gibber in a bass voice appalls the stoutest heart. The little man began to sob; another groaned and the remaining two, being timid by nature, swore great lurid oaths which blazed against the sky.

Suddenly the individual sprang up and gave tongue to a dreadful yell which raised the hair on the four men's heads and caused the surface of the water to ruffle. Chattering frenziedly he sprang into the boat and grasping an oar paddled frantically to the little man's stump. He jumped out and cowered at the little man's feet.

"Stump turned inter an octopush. I was a-settin' on his mouth," he said.

The little man kicked him.

"Legs all commenced wriggle'n twine 'round me, dern octopush," moaned the shrunken individual.

The little man kicked him.

The others cried out against the little man; so he desisted and, climbing into the boat, sculled about and collected his companions. They proceeded then back to the stump whereon the individual lay staring wild-eyed across the water at his octopus. They gathered his limp form into the boat and rowed ashore.

"How far is it to the nearest house?" they demanded savagely of the individual.

"Four miles," he replied in a voice made of cave-damp.

They cursed at him and built a great fire of pine sticks. They sat by it all night and listened to the individual, who dwelt in phantom shadows by the water's edge, dismally crooning about an "octopush".

No. 49b   MANUSCRIPT FRAGMENTS

NOTE: The following trial sentences, some bearing on "The Octopush" and other Sullivan County sketches, are in three manuscript fragments (wove, 217 × 141.5 mm.) at Columbia.

[leaf 1] [*jottings*] [*above to the left*] [un *deleted*] regular shapes like | brass [brass *added*] nails in casket [233.9–10] [*below*] like an octopus | sitting on it's eyes [*to the right*] sepulchral | hollow | forlorn | dismal | melancholy | all creeping things [232.37–38] [*right corner*] wisp-light | over a grave [233.8–9] [*main inscription*] ghost-mist [233.6] [¶]An ill name it is to be charged with wickedness after having embraced the faith. [¶] Inquire not to curiously into other men's failings [¶] A roaring wind [*interlined*] [¶] Clouds bearing a load of rain. [232.27] [¶] Cast veils over their hearts.—lofty heavens— [¶] burdened soul bear the burden of another "Your watch gallops." [*quotation added*]

[leaf 2] pines hung their sprays to the waters edge. [230.24–25] [¶] diffused infection of a man red, sparkling eyes [¶] "The filaments which bind the body and soul together." [¶] "There's two of you! The devil make a 3ᵈ." [¶] A trembling gleam [¶] quailed | fixed teeth | cacodaemon [¶] "A poor painted queen | jewels in dead men's skulls | Medrick [*reversed at foot of page*] 12 [*page number*] | Here come

[leaf 2ᵛ] HARTWOOD PARK, SUL CO, N.Y. | [¶] When they wish to make a pond in this country, they build a [*followed by deleted* rather] stone wall [*cf.* 230.16–18]

[leaf 3] 2 [*page number*] | lay across a wild valley, clinging in apparent desperation [s *over* r] to it's [*altered from* is] foundation. The baffled waters had backed into [230.16–18]

No. 50   BEAR AND PANTHER

Two or three men known individually as positively the oldest inhabitants of the county can tell stories of the time when the panthers used to haunt these woods and make desperate hunting. A story of a disturbance between a bear and a panther is their favorite, and as each oldest inhabitant insists upon telling it whenever a listener heaves in sight, it may be said to be well authenticated.

Two young men in passing near a ledge while out upon a deer hunt discovered the entrance to a cave. Before it on the ground were the bones of a deer and other animals. Tracks made by a panther were plentiful. They concealed themselves a short distance away behind a fallen log and waited for the animal to either approach the cave or emerge from it.

Soon they heard a great grunting and puffing, accompanied by squeals and squeaks, down in the cave. The agitated hunters made ready and drew beads on the mouth of the cave. A big bear clambered slowly out and sat down on the ground before the cave. One hunter was about to shoot from his ambush, when the other man restrained him for he had observed that the bear had a little panther kitten in his mouth. The hunters then remained quietly in concealment and watched the proceedings.

The bear with a crunch of his jaws squeezed the little panther to death and then threw it out upon the ground. Perched upon his quarters, solemn and dignified, he watched the last writhings of the little panther with all the gravity of demeanor and close attention of a scientific investigator. When the little animal ceased struggling, he tapped it softly with his paw and seemed to be endeavoring to get it to wriggle some more. But as the kitten lay motionless and stiff, he turned about and waddled rather painfully through the aperture into the cave. There was a renewal of the gruntings and puffings, squealings and squeakings within the cave, and after a short time the bear reappeared with another kitten in his mouth. The first scene was repeated. The bear after remaining an interested spectator of the second little panther's last agonies, disappeared again within the cave and brought the third small victim. This one, however, seizing a moment when the pressure of the bear's jaws lessened, gave voice to a terrified little scream. It was immediately answered by the blood-curdling roar of the female panther some distance away.

The bear at once dropped the kitten as if in great dismay, and shambled awkwardly about in the most intense excitement and trepidation. The little panther lay on the ground and squealed. It was answered by the roars of its mother as she hurried to the rescue. The bear, now evidently considering that in his eagerness for scientific investigation he had put himself in a bad fix, cast a last despairing look at the open mouth of the kitten, and then started off in a rapid wobble in an opposite direction to the one from which the cries of the "she-painter" proceeded. A moment later a huge panther, with blazing yellow eyes and foam-dripping jaws, bounded into the open space, with every hair bristling on her tawny back, and her lithe limbs quivering and trembling with eagerness. The bear cast one look over his shoulder and made off faster than ever. The panther began an earnest pursuit, and gained rapidly.

The bear, seeing that the panther was overtaking him, hastily ascended a tree. The panther sprang into the lower branches, and in a second had ripped two big bunches of brown hair from the bear's back as that animal, in his terror, climbed the tree with the celerity of a schoolboy. He crawled out on a branch, but the panther followed. The bear was now in extremities. There was but one remedy. So he wound himself up in a brown ball and dropped to the ground. He struck with a sort of smash, unwound himself, and started on a frantic "lope" for safety. But, with two or three bounds the panther was down the tree and near to him. She sprang upon the bear, buried her teeth in his throat, and with her powerful claws tore out his entrails. The hunters then shot the panther. They found that the greater part of the bear's hide was literally torn to ribbons.

No. 51   A GHOUL'S ACCOUNTANT

IN A wilderness sunlight is noise. Darkness is a great, tremendous silence, accented by small and distant sounds. The music of the wind in the trees is songs of loneliness, hymns of abandonment, and lays of the absence of things congenial and alive.

Once a campfire lay dying in a fit of temper. A few weak flames struggled cholerically among the burned-out logs. Beneath, a mass of angry, red coals glowered and hated the world. Some hemlocks sighed and sung and a wind purred in the grass. The moon was looking through the locked branches at four imperturbable bundles of blankets which lay near the agonized campfire. The fire groaned in its last throes, but the bundles made no sign.

Off in the gloomy unknown a foot fell upon a twig. The laurel leaves shivered at the stealthy passing of danger. A moment later a man crept into the spot of dim light. His skin was fiercely red and his whiskers infinitely black. He gazed at the four passive bundles and smiled a smile that curled his lips and showed yellow, disordered teeth. The campfire threw up two lurid arms and, quivering, expired. The voices of the trees grew hoarse and frightened. The bundles were stolid.

The intruder stepped softly nearer and looked at the bundles. One was shorter than the others. He regarded it for some time motionless. The hemlocks quavered nervously and the grass shook. The intruder slid to the short bundle and touched it. Then he smiled. The bundle partially up-reared itself, and the head of a little man appeared.

"Lord!" he said. He found himself looking at the grin of a ghoul condemned to torment.

"Come," croaked the ghoul.

"What?" said the little man. He began to feel his flesh slide to and fro on his bones as he looked into this smile.

"Come," croaked the ghoul.

"What?" the little man whimpered. He grew gray and could not move his legs. The ghoul lifted a three-pronged pickerel-spear and flashed it near the little man's throat. He saw menace on its points. He struggled heavily to his feet.

He cast his eyes upon the remaining mummy-like bundles, but the ghoul confronted his face with the spear.

"Where?" shivered the little man.

The ghoul turned and pointed into the darkness. His countenance shone with lurid light of triumph.

"Go!" he croaked.

The little man blindly staggered in the direction indicated. The three bundles by the fire were still immovable. He tried to pierce the cloth with a glance, and opened his mouth to whoop, but the spear ever threatened his face.

The bundles were left far in the rear and the little man stumbled on alone with the ghoul. Tangled thickets tripped him, saplings buffeted him, and stones turned away from his feet. Blinded and badgered, he began to swear frenziedly. A foam drifted to his mouth, and his eyes glowed with a blue light.

"Go on!" thunderously croaked the ghoul.

The little man's blood turned to salt. His eyes began to decay and refused to do their office. He fell from gloom to gloom.

At last a house was before them. Through a yellow-papered window shone an uncertain light. The ghoul conducted his prisoner to the uneven threshold and kicked the decrepit door. It swung groaning back and he dragged the little man into a room.

A soiled oil-lamp gave a feeble light that turned the pine-board walls and furniture a dull orange. Before a table sat a wild, gray man. The ghoul threw his victim upon a chair and went and stood by the man. They regarded the little man with eyes that made wheels revolve in his soul.

He cast a dazed glance about the room and saw vaguely that it was dishevelled as from a terrific scuffle. Chairs lay shattered, and dishes in the cupboard were ground to pieces. Destruction had been present. There were moments of silence. The ghoul and the wild, gray man contemplated their victim. A throe of fear passed over him and he sank limp in his chair. His eyes swept feverishly over the faces of his tormentors.

At last the ghoul spoke.

"Well!" he said to the wild, gray man.

The other cleared his throat and stood up.

"Stranger," he said, suddenly, "how much is thirty-three bushels of pertaters at sixty-four an' a half a bushel?"

The ghoul leaned forward to catch the reply. The wild, gray man straightened his figure and listened. A fierce light shone on their faces. Their breaths came swiftly. The little man wriggled his legs in agony.

"Twenty-one, no, two, six and——"

"Quick!" hissed the ghoul, hoarsely.

"Twenty-one dollars and twenty-eight cents and a half," laboriously stuttered the little man.

The ghoul gave a tremendous howl.

"There, Tom Jones, dearn yer!" he yelled, "what did I tell yer! hey? Hain't I right? See? Didn't I tell yer that?"

The wild, gray man's body shook. He was delivered of a frightful roar. He sprang forward and kicked the little man out of the door.

No. 52 THE BLACK DOG

THERE was a ceaseless rumble in the air as the heavy rain-drops battered upon the laurel-thickets and the matted moss and haggard rocks beneath. Four water-soaked men made their difficult ways through the drenched forest. The little man stopped and shook an angry finger at where night was stealthily following them. "Cursed be fate and her children and her children's children! We are everlastingly lost!" he cried. The panting procession halted under some dripping, drooping hemlocks and swore in wrathful astonishment.

"It will rain for forty days and forty nights," said the pudgy man, moaningly, "and I feel like a wet loaf of bread, now. We shall never find our way out of this wilderness until I am made into a porridge."

In desperation, they started again to drag their listless bodies through the watery bushes. After a time, the clouds withdrew from above them and great winds came from concealment and went sweeping and swirling among the trees. Night also came very near and menaced the wanderers with darkness.

The little man had determination in his legs. He scrambled among the thickets and made desperate attempts to find a path or road. As he climbed a hillock, he espied a small clearing upon which sat desolation and a venerable house, wept over by wind-waved pines.

"Ho," he cried, "here's a house."

His companions straggled painfully after him as he fought the thickets between him and the cabin. At their approach, the wind frenziedly opposed them and skirled madly in the trees. The little man boldly confronted the weird glances from the crannies of the cabin and rapped on the door. A score of timbers answered with groans and, within, something fell to the floor with a clang.

"Ho," said the little man. He stepped back a few paces.

Somebody in a distant part started and walked across the floor toward the door with an ominous step. A slate-colored man appeared. He was dressed in a ragged shirt and trousers, the latter stuffed into his boots. Large tears were falling from his eyes.

"How-d'-do, my friend?" said the little man, affably.

"My ol' uncle, Jim Crocker, he's sick ter death," replied the slate-colored person.

"Ho," said the little man. "Is that so?"

The latter's clothing clung desperately to him and water sogged in his boots. He stood patiently on one foot for a time.

"Can you put us up here until to-morrow?" he asked, finally.

"Yes," said the slate-colored man.

The party passed into a little unwashed room, inhabited by a stove, a stairway, a few precarious chairs and a misshapen table.

"I'll fry yer some po'k and make yer some coffee," said the slate-colored man to his guests.

"Go ahead, old boy," cried the little man cheerfully from where he sat on the table, smoking his pipe and dangling his legs.

"My ol' uncle, Jim Crocker, he's sick ter death," said the slate-colored man.

"Think he'll die?" asked the pudgy man, gently.

"No!"

"No?"

"He won't die! He's an ol' man, but he won't die, yit! The black dorg hain't been around yit!"

"The black dog?" said the little man, feebly. He struggled with himself for a moment.

"What's the black dog?" he asked at last.

"He's a sperrit," said the slate-colored man in a voice of sombre hue.

"Oh, he is? Well?"

"He hants these parts, he does, an' when people are goin' ter die, he comes an' sets an' howls."

"Ho," said the little man. He looked out of the window and saw night making a million shadows.

The little man moved his legs nervously.

"I don't believe in these things," said he, addressing the slate-colored man, who was scuffling with a side of pork.

"Wot things?" came incoherently from the combatant.

"Oh, these-er-phantoms and ghosts and what not. All rot, I say."

"That's because you have merely a stomach and no soul," grunted the pudgy man.

"Ho, old pudgkins!" replied the little man. His back curved with passion. A tempest of wrath was in the pudgy man's eye. The final epithet used by the little man was a carefully-studied insult, always brought forth at a crisis. They quarrelled.

"All right, pudgkins, bring on your phantom," cried the little man in conclusion.

His stout companion's wrath was too huge for words. The little man smiled triumphantly. He had staked his opponent's reputation.

The visitors sat silent. The slate-colored man moved about in a small personal atmosphere of gloom.

Suddenly, a strange cry came to their ears from somewhere. It was a low, trembling call which made the little man quake privately in his shoes. The slate-colored man bounded at the stairway, and disappeared with a flash of legs through a hole in the ceiling. The party below heard two voices in conversation, one belonging to the slate-colored man, and the other in the quavering tones of age. Directly the slate-colored man reappeared from above and said: "The ol' man is took bad for his supper."

He hurriedly prepared a mixture with hot water, salt and beef. Beef-tea, it might be called. He disappeared again. Once more the party below heard, vaguely, talking over their heads. The voice of age arose to a shriek.

"Open the window, fool! Do you think I can live in the smell of your soup?"

Mutterings by the slate-colored man and the creaking of a window were heard.

The slate-colored man stumbled down the stairs, and said with intense gloom, "The black dorg'll be along soon."

The little man started, and the pudgy man sneered at him. They ate a supper and then sat waiting. The pudgy man listened so palpably that the little man wished to kill him. The wood-fire became excited and sputtered frantically. Without, a thousand spirits of the winds had become entangled in the pine branches and were lowly pleading to be loosened. The slate-colored man tiptoed across the room and lit a timid candle. The men sat waiting.

The phantom dog lay cuddled to a round bundle, asleep down the roadway against the windward side of an old shanty. The spectre's master had moved to Pike County. But the dog lingered as a friend might linger at the tomb of a friend. His fur was like a suit of old clothes. His jowls hung and flopped, exposing his teeth. Yellow famine was in his eyes. The wind-rocked shanty groaned and muttered, but the dog slept. Suddenly, however, he got up and shambled to the roadway. He cast a long glance from his hungry, despairing eyes in the direction of the venerable house. The breeze came full to his nostrils. He threw back his head and gave a long, low howl and started intently up the road. Maybe he smelled a dead man.

The group around the fire in the venerable house were listening and waiting. The atmosphere of the room was tense. The slate-colored man's face was twitching and his drabbed hands were gripped together. The little man was continually looking behind his chair. Upon the countenance of the pudgy man appeared conceit for an approaching triumph over the little man, mingled with apprehension for his own safety. Five pipes glowed as rivals of the timid candle. Profound silence drooped heavily over them. Finally the slate-colored man spoke.

"My ol' uncle, Jim Crocker, he's sick ter death."

The four men started and then shrank back in their chairs.

"Damn it!" replied the little man, vaguely.

Again there was a long silence. Suddenly it was broken by a wild cry from the room above. It was a shriek that struck upon them with appalling swiftness, like a flash of lightning. The walls whirled and the floor rumbled. It brought the men together with a rush. They huddled in a heap and stared at the white terror in each other's faces. The slate-colored man grasped the candle and flared it above his head. "The black dorg," he howled, and plunged at the stairway. The maddened four men followed frantically, for it is better to be in the presence of the awful than only within hearing.

Their ears still quivering with the shriek, they bounded through the hole in the ceiling, and into the sick room.

With quilts drawn closely to his shrunken breast for a shield, his bony hand gripping the cover, an old man lay, with glazing eyes fixed on the open window. His throat gurgled and a froth appeared at his mouth.

From the outer darkness came a strange, unnatural wail, burdened with weight of death and each note filled with foreboding. It was the song of the spectral dog.

"God!" screamed the little man. He ran to the open window. He could see nothing at first save the pine-trees, engaged in a furious combat tossing back and forth and struggling. The moon was peeping cautiously over the rims of some black clouds. But the chant of the phantom guided the little man's eyes, and he at length perceived its shadowy form on the ground under the window. He fell away gasping at the sight. The pudgy man crouched in a corner, chattering insanely. The slate-colored man, in his fear, crooked his legs and looked like a hideous Chinese idol. The man upon the bed was turned to stone, save the froth, which pulsated.

In the final struggle, terror will fight the inevitable. The little man roared maniacal curses, and, rushing again to the window, began to throw various articles at the spectre.

A mug, a plate, a knife, a fork, all crashed or clanged on the ground, but the song of the spectre continued. The bowl of beef-tea followed. As it struck the ground the phantom ceased its cry.

The men in the chamber sank limply against the walls, with the unearthly wail still ringing in their ears and the fear unfaded from their eyes. They waited again.

The little man felt his nerves vibrate. Destruction was better than another wait. He grasped a candle and, going to the window, held it over his head and looked out.

"Ho!" he said.

His companions crawled to the window and peered out with him.

"He's eatin' the beef-tea," said the slate-colored man, faintly.

"The damn dog was hungry," said the pudgy man.

"There's your phantom," said the little man to the pudgy man.

On the bed, the old man lay dead. Without, the spectre was wagging its tail.

No. 53   TWO MEN AND A BEAR

THE bear as a pugilist is a new discovery. He has never been associated with the phrases, "Break away" or "Go to your corner." He has no fame as a professional. Yet the oldest and most experienced hunters about here claim that the bears are the best boxers in the world. They say that an axe or a crowbar is perfectly useless in the hands of a man against the paws of a big bear. Sometimes when a bear is attacked by dogs he simply rears himself upon his haunches and strikes out with his forepaws deftly, swiftly and with tremendous force. He can hold his position against any number of dogs unless the smaller animals get around in the rear and make a desperate charge there. Every time a dog is hit by one of the powerfully swinging paws of the bear he topples over with broken ribs or a crushed skull. The bear deals swift blows right and left, straight from the shoulder, and he creates speedily a great mourning among the owners of the dogs. But it is happily a fact that there are few canines who are stout-hearted enough or foolish enough to wade in and attempt to grapple with the bear. Their general plan is to form a circle just without the reach of the mighty claws. From this safe position they keep up a prodigious barking and howling as if they were valiantly assaulting a regiment of Indians. The bear makes a little advance upon a certain portion of the circle and the uproar grows terrific as the dogs retreat hastily. Mayhap there may be a heavy dog among the crowd who is made of stern stuff. He watches his chance and bolts in at a vulnerable point. If he passes the bear's guard and gets a good grip, he encourages other dogs, who make a combined attack while the bear is engaged in wrenching loose the jaws of the first dog. The bear then has a bad quarter of an hour, but many of the dogs must weep and wail and gnash their teeth, for the bear crunches them and crushes them as if they were papier-mâché images. But this plan is not the general one used by the dogs. As before mentioned, their forte is to sit around and howl. Then, if the bear starts to make off, they are snapping at his heels like so many fiends, and the great creature is speedily forced to make a halt. He rears himself up and makes a number of fierce dabs at the more courageous dogs. In this manner, they have occasionally been known to delay the bear until the hunters arrive, but in the very few cases in which numbers of dogs have come up with a bear, it has been a bad year for dogs in that part of the country.

The tale-tellers say that once upon a time, two men chopping logs in these woods, discovered a bear very close to them, engaged in stripping some bushes of huckleberries. They cautiously approached him with up-lifted axes. He discovered them and started slowly over the rocks. They rushed upon him. He sat up on his haunches, squared off and whacked at the foremost man with a swiftness that nearly took their breaths away. The paw struck the axe-helve and completely shivered it. The bear then made a pass at the second man, clipped him alongside the head and knocked him, head over heels, over a fallen log with the blood starting from his nose and mouth, and a nice contusion that fitted the side of his head like a hat. By this time, the first man was up a tree. The bear went over and smelt of the man behind the log, and evidently satisfied himself that he was dead. He then turned about with the apparent intention of climbing the tree, but the first man sat on a branch and was very meek and quiet, so the bear changed his mind and shambled off over the ridge. He was watched out of sight by the man in the tree, who then climbed down and carried his unconscious companion on his back to a house one mile and a half away.

No. 54 KILLING HIS BEAR

IN A field of snow some green pines huddled together and sang in quavers as the wind whirled among the gullies and ridges. Icicles dangled from the trees' beards, and fine dusts of snow lay upon their brows. On the ridge-top a dismal choir of hemlocks crooned over one that had fallen. The dying sun created a dim purple and flame-colored tumult on the horizon's edge and then sank until level crimson beams struck the trees. As the red rays retreated, armies of shadows stole forward. A gray, ponderous stillness came heavily in the steps of the sun. A little man stood under the quavering pines. He was muffled to the nose in fur and wool, and a hideous cap was pulled tightly over his ears. His cold and impatient feet had stamped a small platform of hard snow beneath him. A black-barrelled rifle lay in the hollow of his arm. His eyes, watery from incessant glaring, swept over the snowfields in front of him. His body felt numb and bloodless, and soft curses came forth and froze on the icy wind. The shadows crept about his feet until he was merely a blurred blackness, with keen eyes.

Off over the ridges, through the tangled sounds of night, came the yell of a hound on the trail. It pierced the ears of the little man and made his blood swim in his veins. His eyes eagerly plunged at the wall of thickets across the stone field, but he moved not a finger or foot. Save his eyes, he was frozen to a statue. The cry of the hound grew louder and louder, then passed away to a faint yelp, then still louder. At first it had a strange vindictiveness and bloodthirstiness in it. Then it grew mournful as the wailing of a lost thing, as, perhaps, the dog gained on a fleeing bear. A hound, as he nears large game, has the griefs of the world on his shoulders and his baying tells of the approach of death. He is sorry he came.

The long yells thrilled the little man. His eyes gleamed and grew small and his body stiffened to intense alertness. The trees kept up their crooning, and the light in the west faded to a dull red splash, but the little man's fancy was fixed on the panting, foam-spattered hound, cantering with his hot nose to the ground in the rear of the bear, which runs as easily and as swiftly as a rabbit, through brush, timber and swale. Swift pictures of himself in a thousand attitudes under a thousand combinations of circumstances, killing a thousand bears, passed panoramically through him.

The yell of the hound grew until it smote the little man like a call to battle. He leaned forward, and the second finger of his right hand played a low, nervous pat-pat on the trigger of his rifle. The baying grew fierce and blood-curdling for a moment, then the dog seemed to turn directly toward the little man, and the notes again grew wailing and mournful. It was a hot trail.

The little man, with nerves tingling and blood throbbing, remained in the shadows, like a fantastic bronze figure, with jewelled eyes swaying sharply in its head. Occasionally he thought he could hear the branches of the bushes in front swish together. Then silence would come again.

The hound breasted the crest of the ridge, a third of a mile away, and suddenly his full-toned cry rolled over the tangled thickets to the little man. The bear must be very near. The little man kept so still and listened so tremendously that he could hear his blood surge in his veins. All at once he heard a swish-swish in the bushes. His rifle was at his shoulder and he sighted uncertainly along the front of the thicket. The swish of the bushes grew louder. In the rear the hound was mourning over a warm scent.

The thicket opened and a great bear, indistinct and vague in the shadows, bounded into the little man's view, and came terrifically across the open snowfield. The little man stood like an image. The bear did not "shamble" nor "wobble"; there was no awkwardness in his gait; he ran like a frightened kitten.

It would be an endless chase for the lithe-limbed hound in the rear.

On he came, directly toward the little man. The animal heard only the crying behind him. He knew nothing of the thing with death in its hands standing motionless in the shadows before him.

Slowly the little man changed his aim until it rested where the head of the approaching shadowy mass must be. It was a wee motion, made with steady nerves and a soundless swaying of the rifle-barrel; but the bear heard, or saw, and knew. The animal whirled swiftly and started in a new direction with an amazing burst of speed. Its side was toward the little man now. His rifle-barrel was searching swiftly over the dark shape. Under the fore-shoulder was the place. A chance to pierce the heart, sever an artery or pass through the lungs. The little man saw swirling fur over his gun-barrel. The earth faded to nothing. Only space and the game, the aim and the hunter. Mad emotions, powerful to rock worlds, hurled through the little man, but did not shake his tiniest nerve.

When the rifle cracked it shook his soul to a profound depth. Creation rocked and the bear stumbled.

The little man sprang forward with a roar. He scrambled hastily in the bear's track. The splash of red, now dim, threw a faint, timid beam on a kindred shade on the snow. The little man bounded in the air.

"Hit!" he yelled, and ran on. Some hundreds of yards forward he came to a dead bear with his nose in the snow. Blood was oozing slowly from a wound under the shoulder, and the snow about was sprinkled with blood. A mad froth lay in the animal's open mouth and his limbs were twisted from agony.

The little man yelled again and sprang forward, waving his hat as if he were leading the cheering of thousands. He ran up and kicked the ribs of the bear. Upon his face was the smile of the successful lover.

No. 55 A TENT IN AGONY

FOUR men once came to a wet place in the roadless forest to fish. They pitched their tent fair upon the brow of a pine-clothed ridge of riven rocks whence a bowlder could be made to crash through the brush and whirl past the trees to the lake below. On fragrant hemlock boughs they slept the sleep of unsuccessful fishermen, for upon the lake alternately the sun made them lazy and the rain made them wet. Finally they ate the last bit of bacon and smoked and burned the last fearful and wonderful hoecake.

Immediately a little man volunteered to stay and hold the camp while the remaining three should go the Sullivan county miles to a farmhouse for supplies. They gazed at him dismally. "There's only one of you—the devil make a twin," they said in parting malediction, and disappeared down the hill in the known direction of a distant cabin. When it came night and the hemlocks began to sob they had not returned. The little man sat close to his companion, the campfire, and encouraged it with logs. He puffed fiercely at a heavy built brier, and regarded a thousand shadows which were about to assault him. Suddenly he heard the approach of the unknown, crackling the twigs and rustling the dead leaves. The little man arose slowly to his feet, his clothes refused to fit his back, his pipe dropped from his mouth, his knees smote each other. "Hah!" he bellowed hoarsely in menace. A growl replied and a bear paced into the light of the fire. The little man supported himself upon a sapling and regarded his visitor.

The bear was evidently a veteran and a fighter, for the black of his coat had become tawny with age. There was confidence in his gait and arrogance in his small, twinkling eye. He rolled back his lips and disclosed his white teeth. The fire magnified the red of his mouth. The little man had never before confronted the terrible and he could not wrest it from his breast. "Hah!" he roared. The bear interpreted this as the challenge of a gladiator. He approached warily. As he came near, the boots of fear were suddenly upon the little man's feet. He cried out and then darted around the campfire. "Ho!" said the bear to himself, "this thing won't fight—it runs. Well, suppose I catch it." So upon his features there fixed the animal look of going—somewhere. He started intensely around the campfire. The little man shrieked and ran furiously. Twice around they went.

The hand of heaven sometimes falls heavily upon the righteous. The bear gained.

In desperation the little man flew into the tent. The bear stopped and sniffed at the entrance. He scented the scent of many men. Finally he ventured in.

The little man crouched in a distant corner. The bear advanced, creeping, his blood burning, his hair erect, his jowls dripping. The little man yelled and rustled clumsily under the flap at the end of the tent. The bear snarled awfully and made a jump and a grab at his disappearing game. The little man, now without the tent, felt a tremendous paw grab his coat tails. He squirmed and wriggled out of his coat, like a schoolboy in the hands of an avenger. The bear howled triumphantly and jerked the coat into the tent and took two bites, a punch and a hug before he discovered his man was not in it. Then he grew not very angry, for a bear on a spree is not a black-haired pirate. He is merely a hoodlum. He lay down on his back, took the coat on his four paws and began to play uproariously with it. The most appalling, bloodcurdling whoops and yells came to where the little man was crying in a treetop and froze his blood. He moaned a little speech meant for a prayer and clung convulsively to the bending branches. He gazed with tearful wistfulness at where his comrade, the campfire, was giving dying flickers and crackles. Finally, there was a roar from the tent which eclipsed all roars; a snarl which it seemed would shake the stolid silence of the mountain and cause it to shrug its granite shoulders. The little man quaked and shrivelled to a grip and a pair of eyes. In the glow of the embers he saw the white tent quiver and fall with a crash. The bear's merry play had disturbed the centre pole and brought a chaos of canvas about his head.

Now the little man became the witness of a mighty scene. The tent began to flounder. It took flopping strides in the direction of the lake. Marvellous sounds came from within—rips and tears, and great groans and pants. The little man went into giggling hysterics.

The entangled monster failed to extricate himself before he had frenziedly walloped the tent to the edge of the mountain. So it came to pass that three men, clambering up the hill with bundles and baskets, saw their tent approaching.

It seemed to them like a white-robed phantom pursued by hornets. Its moans riffled the hemlock twigs.

The three men dropped their bundles and scurried to one side, their eyes gleaming with fear. The canvas avalanche swept past them. They leaned, faint and dumb, against trees and listened, their blood stagnant. Below them it struck the base of a great pine tree, where it writhed and struggled. The three watched its convolutions a moment and then started terrifically for the top of the hill. As they disappeared, the bear cut loose with a mighty effort. He cast one dishevelled and agonized look at the white thing, and then started wildly for the inner recesses of the forest.

The three fear-stricken individuals ran to the rebuilt fire. The little man reposed by it calmly smoking. They sprang at him and overwhelmed him with interrogations. He contemplated darkness and took a long, pompous puff. "There's only one of me—and the devil made a twin," he said.

No. 56 THE CRY OF A HUCKLEBERRY PUDDING: A DIM STUDY OF CAMPING EXPERIENCES

A GREAT blaze wavered redly against the blackness of the night in the pines. Before the eyes of his expectant companions, a little man moved with stately dignity as the creator of a huckleberry pudding.

"I know how to make'm," he said in a confident voice, "just exactly right."

The others looked at him with admiration and they sat down to eat.

After a time, a pudgy man whose spoon was silent, said: "I don't like this much."

"What?" cried the little man, threateningly.

"I don't seem to get on with it," said the pudgy man. He

looked about for support in the faces of his companions. "I don't like it, somehow," he added slowly.

"Fool!" roared the little man, furiously. "You're mad because you didn't make it. I never saw such a beast."

The pudgy man wrapped himself in a great dignity. He glanced suggestingly at the plates of the two others. They were intact.

"Ho," cried the little man, "you're all idiots."

He saw that he must vindicate his work. He must eat it. He sat before them and, with ineffable bliss lighting his countenance, ate all of the huckleberry pudding. Then he laid aside his plate, lighted his pipe and addressed his companions as unappreciative block-heads.

The pipe, the fire and the song of the pines soothed him after a time and he puffed tranquilly. The four men sat staring vacantly at the blaze until the spirits of the tent at the edge of the fire circle, in drowsy voices began to call them. Their thoughts became heavily fixed on the knee-deep bed of hemlock. One by one they arose, knocked ashes from their pipes and treading softly to the open flaps, disappeared. Alone, the camp-fire spluttered valiantly for a time, opposing its music to the dismal crooning of the trees that accented the absence of things congenial and alive. A curious moon peered through locked branches at imperturable bundles of blankets which lay in the shadows of the tent.

The fragrant blackness of the early night passed away and grey ghost-mists came winding slowly up from the marshes and stole among the wet tree trunks. Wavering leaves dotted with dew drops glowed in a half-light of impending dawn. From the tent came sounds of heavy sleeping. The bundles of blankets clustered on the hemlock twigs.

Suddenly from off in the thickets of gloom, there came a cry. It seemed to crash on the tent. It smote the bundles of blankets. There was instant profound agitation, a whirling chaos of coverings, legs and arms; then, heads appeared. The men had heard the voice of the unknown, crying in the wilderness and it made their souls quaver.

They had slumbered through the trees' song of loneliness, and the lay of isolation of the mountain-grass. Hidden frogs had muttered ominously since night-fall, and distant owls, undoubtedly perched on lofty branches and silhouetted by the moon, had hooted. There had been an endless hymning by leaves, blades, and unseen live things, through which these men, who adored Wagner, had slept.

But a false note in the sounds of night had convulsed them. A strange tune had made them writhe.

The cry of the unknown instantly awoke them to terror. It is mightier than the war-yell of the dreadful, because the dreadful may be definite. But this whoop strikes greater fear from hearts because it tells of formidable mouths and great, grasping claws that live in impossibility. It is the chant of a phantom force which imagination declares invincible, and awful to the sight.

In the tent, eyes a-glitter with terror gazed into eyes. Knees softly smote each other and lips trembled.

The pudgy man gave vent to a tremendous question. "What was that?" he whispered.

The others made answer with their blanched faces. The group waiting in the silence that followed their awakening, wriggled their legs in the agony of fright. There was a pause which extended through space. Comets hung and worlds waited. Their thoughts shot back to that moment when they had started upon the trip and they were filled with regret that it had been.

"Oh, goodness, what was that?" repeated the pudgy man, intensely.

Suddenly, their faces twitched and their fingers turned to wax. The cry was repeated. Its burden caused the men to huddle together like drowning kittens. They watched the banshees of the fog drifting lazily among the trees. They saw eyes in the grey obscurity. They heard a thousand approaching foot-falls in the rustling of the dead leaves. They grovelled.

Then, they heard the unknown stride to and fro in the forest, giving calls, weighted with challenge, that could make cities hearing, fear. Roars went to the ends of earth and, snarls that would appall armies, turned the men in the tent to a moaning mass with forty eyes. The challenges changed to wailings as of a fever-torn soul. Later, there came snorts of anger, that sounded cruel, like the noise of a rampant bull on a babies' play ground. Later still, howls, as from an abandoned being, strangling in the waters of trouble.

"Great Scott," roared the pudgy man, "I can't stand this."

He wriggled to his feet and tottered out to the dying fire. His companions followed. They had reached the cellar of fear. They were now resolved to use weapons on the great destruction. They would combat the inevitable. They peered among the trees wherefrom an hundred assaulting shadows came. The unknown was shrieking.

Of a sudden, the pudgy man screamed like a wounded animal.

"It's got Billie," he howled. They discovered that the little man was gone.

To listen or to wait is the most tense of occupations. In their absorption they had not seen that a comrade was missing.

Instantly, their imaginations perceived his form in the clutch of a raging beast.

"Come on," shouted the pudgy man. They grasped bludgeons and rushed valiantly into the darkness. They stumbled from gloom to gloom in a mad rush for their friend's life. The key-note of terror kept clanging in their ears and guided their scrambling feet. Tangled thickets tripped them. Saplings buffeted heroically, and stones turned away. Branches smote their heads so that it appeared as if lightning had flapped its red wings in their faces.

Once, the pudgy man stopped. The unknown was just ahead.

The dim lights of early dawn came charging through the forest. The grey and black of mist and shadow retreated before crimson beams that had advanced to the tree-tops.

The men came to a stand, waving their heads to glance down the aisles of the wilderness.

"There he is," shouted the pudgy man. The party rushing forward came upon the form of the little man, quivering at the foot of a tree. His blood seemed to be turned to salt. From out his wan, white face his eyes shone with a blue light. "Oh, thunderation," he moaned. "Oh, thunderation."

"What!" cried his friends. Their voices shook with anxiety.

"Oh, thunderation," repeated he.

"For the love of Mike tell us, Billie," cried the pudgy man, "What is the matter."

"Oh, thunderation," wailed the little man. Suddenly he rolled about on the ground and gave vent to a howl that rolled and pealed over the width of forest. Its tones told of death and fear and unpaid debts. It clamored like a song of forgotten war, and died away to the scream of a maiden. The pleadings of fire-surrounded children mingled with the calls of wave-threatened sailors. Two barbaric tribes clashed together on a sun-burnt plain; a score of bare-kneed clansmen crossed claymores amid grey rocks; a woman saw a lover fall; a dog was stabbed in an alley; a steel knight bit dust with bloody mouth; a savage saw a burning home.

The rescuing party leaned weakly against trees. After the little man had concluded, there was a silence.

Finally, the pudgy man advanced. He struggled with his astonished tongue for a moment. "Do you mean to say, Billie," he said at last, "that all that tangled chaos emanated from you?"

The little man made no reply but heaved about on the ground, moaning: "Oh, thunderation."

The three men contemplating him suddenly felt themselves swell with wrath. They had been terrorized to no purpose. They had expected to be eaten. They were not. The fact maddened them. The pudgy man voiced the assembly.

"You infernal little jay, get up off'n the ground and come on," he cried. "You make me sick."

"Oh, thunderation," replied the little man.

The three men began to berate him. They turned into a babble of wrath.

"You scared us to death."

"What do you wanta holler that way for?"

"You're a bloomin' nuisance. For heaven's sake, what are you yellin' about?"

The little man staggered to his feet. Anger took hold of him. He waved his arms eloquently.

"That pudding, you fools," he cried.

His companions paused and regarded him.

"Well," said the pudgy man, eventually, "what in blazes did you eat it for then?"

"Well, I didn't know," roared the other, "I didn't know that it was that way."

"You shouldn't have eaten it, anyhow. There was the sin. You shouldn't have eaten it anyway."

"But I didn't know," shouted the little man.

"You should have known," they stormed. "You've made idiots of us. You scared us to death with your hollerin'."

As he reeled toward the camp, they followed him, railing like fish-wives.

The little man turned at bay.

"Exaggerated fools," he yelled. "Fools, to apply no salve but moral teaching to a man with the stomach-ache."

No. 57   THE HOLLER TREE

As THEY went along a narrow wood-path, the little man accidentally stumbled against the pudgy man. The latter was carrying a basket of eggs and he became angry.

"Look-out, can't you! Do you wanta break all these eggs? Walk straight—what's the matter with you," he said and passed on.

The little man saved his balance with difficulty. He had to keep from spilling a pail of milk. "T'blazes with your old eggs," he called out.

The pudgy man spoke over his shoulder. "Well, you needn't have any when we get to camp, then," he said.

"Who wants any of your infernal old eggs. Keep your infernal old eggs," replied the little man.

The four men trudged on into the forest until presently the little man espied a dead tree. He paused. "Look at that tree," he said.

They scrutinized it. It was a tall, gaunt relic of a pine that stood like a yellow warrior still opposing an aged form to blows in storm-battles.

"I bet it's got lots of nests in it and all sorts of things like that," murmured the little man.

The pudgy man scoffed. "Oh, fudge," he said.

"Well, I bet it has," asserted the other.

The four men put down their loads of provisions and stood around and argued.

"Yes, I bet it's a corner-stone with an almanac in it and a census report and a certified list of the pew-holders," said the pudgy man to the little man.

The latter swore for some time. "Put up even money," he demanded in conclusion. "Put up even money."

"Look out—you'll kick over the eggs," replied the pudgy man.

"Well, put up even money. You daren't."

The pudgy man scornfully kicked a stone. "Oh, fudge. How you going to prove it? Tell me that."

The little man thought. "Well," he said, eventually, "I'll climb up. That's how."

The pudgy man looked at the tree and at the little man. He thought.

"I'll go it," he suddenly decided.

The little man laid down his pipe, tightened his belt and went off and looked at the tree.

"Well——" he began, coming back.

"Go on and climb it," said the pudgy man. "You said you'd climb it."

The little man went off and looked at the tree again. "Well, I will," he said, finally. The pudgy man giggled. The little man tightened his belt more. He approached and put both arms around the tree.

"Say," he said, turning round. "You—I——"

"Go on and climb it," interrupted the pudgy man. "You said you'd climb it."

The little man began to climb school-boy fashion. He found many difficulties. The wood crumbled and rubbed into his clothes. He felt smeared. Besides there was a horrible strain upon his legs.

When about half way, he ceased wriggling and turned his head cautiously. "Say——"

The three men had been regarding him intently. They then burst out. "Go on! Go on! You've got that far—what's the use of stopping. I believe you're gettin' scared! Oh, my!"

He swore and continued up. Several times he seemed about to fall in a lump. The three below held their breath.

Once, he paused to deliver an oration and forgot his grip for a moment. It was near being fatal.

At last, he reached the top. "Well?" said the pudgy man. The little man gazed about him. There was a sombre sea of pines, rippling in a wind. Far away, there was a little house and two yellow fields.

"Fine scenery up here," he murmured.

"Oh, bother," said the pudgy man. "Where's your nests and all that. That's what I wanta know."

The little man peered down the hollow trunk. "They're in there."

The pudgy man grinned. "How do you know?"

The little man looked down the hole again. "It's all dark," he said.

The pudgy man complacently lit a fresh pipe. "Certainly, it is," he remarked. "You look great up there, don't you? What you goin' to do now, eh?"

The little man balanced himself carefully on the ragged edge and looked thoughtfully at the hole. "Well, I might slide down," he said in a doubtful voice.

"That's it," cried the other. "That's what you wanta do! Slide down!"

"Well," said the little man, "it looks pretty dangerous."

"Oh, I see! You're afraid!"

"I ain't!"

"Yes, you are, too! Else why don't you slide down?"

"Well, how th' devil do I know but what something's down there," shouted the little man in a rage.

His companion replied with scorn. "Pooh! Nothin' but a hollow tree. You're afraid of the dark."

"You must take me for a fool! What th' blazes do I wanta be slidin' down every hollow tree I see for?"

"Well, you climbed up, didn't you? What are you up there for? You can't find your little nests and things just settin' there an' cursin', can you? You're afraid, I bet."

"You make——"

"Oh, yes, you are. You know you are."

The little man flung his legs over and slid down until only his head and his gripping fingers appeared. He seemed to be feeling about with his feet.

"There's nothing to climb down with," he said, finally.

"Certainly not. Did you hope for a stairway. You're afraid."

The little man's face flushed and his eyes grew like beads. He glared from out of the hole.

"I am not, you big——"

"Oh, yes, you are. Anyone can see it."

"Thunderation, you're th'——"

"Oh, come, Billie, either climb down th' outside or slide down th' inside. There's no use of you sittin' up there, you know, if you ain't going to do something. You're afraid, that's what."

"I tell you I ain't. What th' devil——"

"Oh, yes, you are, too. You're pale with fright, Billie. We can see it down here. Oh, my! I'm surprised."

The little man raised a fist. "Thunder and blazes——"

He vanished down the hole.

The wood had crumbled and broken under the strain of the one hand. Hollow sounds of scratchings and thumpings came to the ears of his three companions. In agitation, they ran about the vibrating trunk and called to their comrade in many voices. They were fearful he had met his time.

Presently, they heard a muffled noise of swearing. They listened. Down near the ground, the little man was cursing under forced draft. The old tree shook like a smoke-stack.

The pudgy man approached and put near his ear.

"Billie!"

"What?"

"Are you inside the tree?"

The little man began to kick and clamor. His voice came in a dull roar. "Certainly I'm inside the tree. Where th' devil did you suppose I was? What th'——"

His voice died away in smothered thunder.

"Well, but, Billie," asked the pudgy man, anxiously, "how you going to get out."

The little man began to rage again. "What a fool you are. I

don't know how I'm going to get out. Don't suppose I've got plans made already do you?"

"Well, I guess you'll have to climb," mused the pudgy man. "That's the only way and you can't stay in there forever, you know."

The little man made some efforts. There was a sound of rending clothes. Presently he ceased.

"It's no go," he announced.

The three men sat down and debated upon theories.

Finally the little man began to roar at them and kick his prison wall. "Think I wanta stay in here while you fellows hold arguments for a couple of hours? Why th' thunder don't you do something instead of talking so much? What do you think I am anyway?"

The pudgy man approached the tree. "You might as well keep quiet," he said in a grim voice. "You're in there and you might as well keep quiet——"

The little man began to swear.

"Stop your howling," angrily cried the pudgy man. "There's no use of howlin'."

"I won't! It's your fault I'm in here. If it hadn't been for you, I wouldn't'a climbed up."

"Well, I didn't make you fall down inside, anyway. You did that yourself."

"I didn't either. You made me tumble, old pudgkins. If you had minded your own business it would have been all right. It's your stupidity that's got me in here."

"It was your own, you little fool. I——"

The little man began to rave and wriggle. The pudgy man went very near to the tree and stormed. They had a furious quarrel. The eloquence of the little man caused some tremors in the tree and presently it began to sway gently.

Suddenly, the pudgy man screamed. "You're pushin' th' tree overon me." He started away. The trunk trembled, and tottered, and began to fall. It seemed like a mighty blow aimed by the wrathful little man at the head of the fleeing pudgy man.

The latter bounded, light as a puff-ball, over the ground. His face was white with terror. He turned an agonized somersault into a thicket, as the tree, with a splintering cry, crashed near his heels. He lay in a bush and trembled.

The little man's legs were wagging plaintively from the other end of the trunk. The two remaining men rushed forward with cries of alarm and began to tug at them. The little man came forth, finally. He was of deep bronze hue from a coating of wet dead wood. A soft bed of it came with him. They helped him to his feet. He felt his shoulders and legs with an air of anxiety. After a time, he rubbed the crumbles from his eyes and began to stagger and swear softly.

Suddenly, he perceived the pudgy man lying pale in the bush. He limped over to him.

The pudgy man was moaning. "Lord, it just missed me by 'bout an inch."

The little man thoughtfully contemplated his companion. Presently, a smile was born at the corner of his mouth and grew until it wreathed his face. The pudgy man cursed in an unhappy vein as he was confronted by the little man's grins.

The latter seemed about to deliver an oration but, instead, he turned and, picking up his pail of milk, started away. He paused once and looked back. He pointed with his fore-finger.

"There's your eggs—under the tree," he said.

He resumed his march down the forest pathway. His stride was that of a proud grenadier.

No. 58   AN EXPLOSION OF SEVEN BABIES

A LITTLE man was sweating and swearing his way through an intricate forest. His hat was pushed indignantly to the far rear of his head and upon his perspiring features there was a look of conscious injury.

Suddenly he perceived ahead of him a high stone wall against which waves of bushes surged. The little man fought his way to the wall and looked over it.

A brown giantess was working in a potato patch. Upon a bench, under the eaves of a worn-out house, seven babies were wailing and rubbing their stomachs.

"Ho!" said the little man to himself.

He stood, observant, for a few moments. Then he climbed painfully over the wall and came to a stand in the potato patch. His eyes wandered to the seven babies wailing and rubbing their stomachs. Their mournful music fascinated him.

"Madam," he said, as he took off his hat and bowed, "I have unfortunately lost my way. Could you direct——" He suddenly concluded: "Great Scott!"

He had turned his eyes from the seven babies to the brown giantess and saw upon her face the glare of a tigress. Her fingers were playing convulsively over her hoe-handle and the muscles of her throat were swollen and wriggling. Her eyes were glowing with fury. She came forward with the creeping motion of an animal about to spring.

The little man gave a backward leap. Tremendous astonishment enwrapped him and trepidation showed in his legs.

"G-good heavens, madam," he stuttered. He threw up one knee and held his spread fingers before his face. His mouth was puckered to an amazed whistle.

The giantess stood before him, her hands upon her hips; her lips curled in a snarl. She followed closely as the little man retreated backward step by step toward the fence, his eyes staring in bewilderment.

"For the love of Mike, madam, what ails you," he spluttered.

He saw here an avenger. Wherefore, he knew not but he momentarily expected to be smitten to a pulp.

"Beast!" roared the giantess, suddenly. She reached forth and grasped the arm of the palsied little man, who cast a despairing glance at the high, stone wall. She twisted him about and then, raising a massive arm, pointed to the row of seven babies, who as if they had gotten a cue, burst out like a brass band.

"Well, what the devil——" roared the little man.

"Beast!" howled the giantess, "It made'm sick! They ate ut! That dum fly-paper!" The babies began to frantically beat their stomachs with their fists.

"Villain!" shrieked the giantess. The little man felt the winding fingers crush the flesh and bone of his arm. The giantess began to roar like a dragon. She bended over and braced herself. Then her iron arms forced the little man to his knees.

He knew he was going to be eaten. "Gawd," he moaned.

He arrived at the critical stage of degradation. He would resist. He touched some hidden spring in his being and went off like a fire-work. The man became a tumult. Every muscle in his body he made perform a wriggling contortion. The giantess plunged forward and kneaded him as if he were bread unbaked.

From over the stone wall came the swishing sound of moving bushes, unheard by the combatants. Presently the face of a pudgy man, tranquil in its wrinkles, appeared. Amazement instantly smote him in his tracks and he hung heavily to the stones.

From the potato patch arose a cloud of dust, pregnant with curses. In it he could dimly see the little man in a state of revolution. His legs flashed in the air like a pin-wheel. The pudgy man stared with gleaming eyes at the kaleidoscope. He climbed upon the wall to get a better view. Some bellowing animal seemed to have his friend in its claws.

It soon became evident to the little man that he could not eternally revolve and kick in such a manner. He felt his blood begin to dry up and his muscles turn to paste. Those talons were squeezing his life away. His mangled arms were turning weak. He was about to be subdued.

But here the pudgy man, in his excitement, performed the feat of his life. He fell off the wall, giving an involuntary shout, and landed, with a flop, in the potato patch. The brown giantess snarled. She hurled the little man from her and turned, with a toss of her dishevelled locks, to face a new foe. The pudgy man quaked miserably and yelled an unintelligible explanation or apology or prayer. The brow of the giantess was black and she strided with ferocious menace toward him.

The little man had fallen in a chaotic mass among the potato hills. He struggled to his feet. Somehow, his blood was hot in his veins and he started to bristle courageously in reinforcement of his friend. But suddenly he changed his mind and made off at high speed, leaving the pudgy man to his fate.

His unchosen course lay directly toward the seven babies who, in their anxiety to view the combat, had risen from the bench and were standing, ready as a Roman populace, to signify the little man's death by rubbing their stomachs. Intent upon the struggle, they had forgotten to howl.

But when they perceived the headlong charge of the little man, they, as a unit, exploded. It was like the sudden clang of an alarm bell to the brown giantess. She wheeled from the pudgy man, who climbed the wall, fell off, in his haste, into the bushes on the other side and, later, allowed but the half of his head to appear over the top of it. The giantess perceived the little man about to assault her seven babies, whose mouths were in a state of eruption. She howled, grabbed a hoe from the ground, and pursued.

The little man shied from the protesting babies and ran like a grey-hound. He flung himself over a high fence. Then he waited. Curiosity held him. He had been mopped and dragged, punched and pounded, bitten and scratched. He wished to know why.

The brown giantess, mad with rage, crashed against the fence. She shook her huge fist at the little man.

"Drat yeh!" she roared.

She began to climb the fence. It is not well to behold a woman climb a fence. The little man yelled and ran off.

He stumbled and tore through a brush lot and bounced terrifically into the woods. As he halted to get breath, he heard above the sound of the wind laughing in the trees, a final explosion by the seven babies as, perhaps, they perceived the brown giantess returning empty handed to the worn-out house.

As the little man went on into the woods, he perceived a crouching figure with terror-gleaming eyes. He whistled and drew near it. Directly, the little man, bedraggled, dirt-stained, bloody and amazed, confronted the pudgy man perspiring, limp, dusty and astonished. They gazed at each other profoundly.

Finally, the little man broke the silence.

"Devilish mysterious business," he said, slowly. The pudgy man had a thousand questions in his eyes.

"What in Heaven's name, Billie——" he blurted.

The little man waved his hand. "Don't ask me. I don't know anything about it."

"What?"

"No more'n a rabbit. She said something about fly-paper and the kids, that's all I know."

The pudgy man drew a long breath. "Great Lord," he said. They sat down on a log and thought.

At last, the little man got up and yawned. "I can't make head nor tail of the bloomin' business," he said wearily. They walked slowly off through the day-gloom of the woods. "I wish she hadn't called me a beast. I didn't like that," added the little man, musingly, after a time.

In a shady spot on a highway, they found their two companions who were lazily listening to a short stranger who was holding forth at some length and with apparent enthusiasm. At the approach of the little man and the pudgy man, the short man turned to them with a smile.

"Gentlemen," he said, "I have here a wonder of the age, which I wish to present to your intelligent notice. Smither's Eternal Fly Annihilating Paper is————"

The little man frothed at the mouth and cursed. Before his comrades could intervene he sprang forward and kicked the short man heavily in the stomach.

No. 59   THE MESMERIC MOUNTAIN

ON THE brow of a pine-plumed hillock there sat a little man with his back against a tree. A venerable pipe hung from his mouth and smoke-wreaths curled slowly sky-ward. He was muttering to himself with his eyes fixed on an irregular black opening in the green wall of forest at the foot of the hill. Two vague wagon ruts led into the shadows. The little man took his pipe in his hands and addressed the listening pines.

"I wonder what the devil it leads to," said he.

A grey, fat rabbit came lazily from a thicket and sat in the opening. Softly stroking his stomach with his paw, he looked at the little man in a thoughtful manner. The little man threw a stone and the rabbit blinked and ran through the opening. Green, shadowy portals seemed to close behind him.

The little man started. "He's gone down that roadway," he said, with ecstatic mystery to the pines. He sat a long time and contemplated the door to the forest. Finally, he arose and, awakening his limbs, started away. But he stopped and looked back.

"I can't imagine what it leads to," muttered he. He trudged over the brown mats of pine needles to where, in a fringe of laurel, a tent was pitched and merry flames caroused about some logs. A pudgy man was fuming over a collection of tin dishes. He came forward and waved a plate furiously in the little man's face.

"I've washed the dishes for three days. What do you think I am——"

He ended a red oration with a roar: "Damned if I do it anymore."

The little man gazed dim-eyed away. "I've been wonderin' what it leads to."

"What?"

"That road out yonder. I've been wonderin' what it leads to. Maybe, some discovery or something," said the little man.

The pudgy man laughed. "You're an idiot. It leads to ol' Jim Boyd's over on the Lumberland Pike."

"Ho!" said the little man, "I don't believe that."

The pudgy man swore. "Fool, what does it lead to, then?"

"I don't know just what but I'm sure it leads to something great or something. It looks like it."

While the pudgy man was cursing, two more men came from obscurity with fish dangling from birch twigs. The pudgy man made an obviously herculean struggle and a meal was prepared. As he was drinking his cup of coffee, he suddenly spilled it and swore. The little man was wandering off.

"He's gone to look at that hole," cried the pudgy man.

The little man went to the edge of the pine-plumed hillock and, sitting down, began to make smoke and regard the door to the forest. There was stillness for an hour. Compact clouds hung unstirred in the sky. The pines stood motionless, and pondering.

Suddenly, the little man slapped his knee and bit his tongue. He stood up and determinedly filled his pipe, rolling his eye over the bowl to the door-way. Keeping his eyes fixed he slid dangerously to the foot of the hillock and walked down the wagon-ruts. A moment later, he passed from the noise of the sunshine to the gloom of the woods.

The green portals closed, shutting out live things. The little man trudged on alone.

Tall tangled grass grew in the road-way and the trees bended obstructing branches. The little man followed on over pine-clothed ridges and down through water-soaked swales. His shoes were cut by rocks of the mountains and he sank ankle-deep in mud and moss of swamps. A curve, just ahead, lured him miles.

Finally, as he wended the side of a ridge, the road disappeared from beneath his feet. He battled with hordes of ignorant bushes on his way to knolls and solitary trees which invited him. Once he came to a tall, bearded pine. He climbed it and perceived in the distance a peak. He uttered an ejaculation and fell out.

He scrambled to his feet and said: "That's Jones's Mountain, I guess. It's about six miles from our camp as the crow flies."

He changed his course away from the mountain and attacked the bushes again. He climbed over great logs, golden-brown in decay, and was opposed by thickets of dark green laurel. A brook slid through the ooze of a swamp, cedars and hemlocks hung their sprays to the edges of pools.

The little man began to stagger in his walk. After a time, he stopped and mopped his brow.

"My legs are about to shrivel up and drop off," he said. . . . "Still if I keep on in this direction, I am safe to strike the Lumberland Pike before sun-down."

He dived at a clump of tag-alders and emerging, confronted Jones's Mountain.

The wanderer sat down in a clear place and fixed his eyes on the summit. His mouth opened widely and his body swayed at times. The little man and the peak stared in silence.

A lazy lake lay asleep near the foot of the mountain. In its bed of water-grass some frogs leered at the sky and crooned. The sun sank in red silence and the shadows of the pines grew formidable. The expectant hush of evening, as if some thing were going to sing a hymn, fell upon the peak and the little man.

A leaping pickerel off on the water created a silver circle that was lost in black shadows. The little man shook himself and started to his feet, crying: "For the love of Mike, there's eyes in this mountain! I feel 'em! Eyes!"

He fell on his face.

When he looked again, he immediately sprang erect and ran.

"It's comin'!"

The mountain was approaching.

The little man scurried sobbing through the thick growth. He felt his brain turning to water. He vanquished brambles with mighty bounds.

But after a time, he came again to the foot of the mountain.

"God!" he howled, "it's been follerin' me!" He grovelled.

Casting his eyes upward made circles swirl in his blood.

"I'm shackled I guess," he moaned. As he felt the heel of the mountain about to crush his head, he sprang again to his feet. He grasped a handful of small stones and hurled them.

"Damn you!" he shrieked, loudly. The pebbles rang against the face of the mountain.

The little man then made an attack. He climbed with hands and feet, wildly. Brambles forced him back and stones slid from beneath his feet. The peak swayed and tottered and was ever about to smite with a granite arm. The summit was a blaze of red wrath.

But the little man at last reached the top. Immediately he swaggered with valor to the edge of the cliff. His hands were scornfully in his pockets.

He gazed at the western horizon edged sharply against a yellow sky. "Ho!" he said. "There's Boyd's house and the Lumberland Pike."

The mountain under his feet was motionless.

New York City Sketches

No. 60 THE BROKEN-DOWN VAN

THE gas lamps had just been lit and the two great red furniture vans with impossible landscapes on their sides rolled and plunged slowly along the street. Each was drawn by four horses, and each almost touched the roaring elevated road above. They were on the uptown track of the surface road—indeed the street was so narrow that they must be on one track or the other.

They tossed and pitched and proceeded slowly, and a horse car with a red light came up behind. The car was red, and the bullseye light was red, and the driver's hair was red. He blew his whistle shrilly and slapped the horse's lines impatiently. Then he whistled again. Then he pounded on the red dash board with his car-hook till the red light trembled. Then a car with a green light crept up behind the car with the red light; and the green driver blew his whistle and pounded on his dash board; and the conductor of the red car seized his strap from his position on the rear platform and rung such a rattling tattoo on the gong over the red driver's head that the red driver became frantic and stood up on his toes and puffed out his cheeks as if he were playing the trombone in a German street-band and blew his whistle till an imaginative person could see slivers flying from it, and pounded his red dash board till the metal was dented in and the car-hook was bent. And just as the driver of a newly-come car with a blue light began to blow his whistle and pound his dash board and the green conductor began to ring his bell like a demon which drove the green driver mad and made him rise up and blow and pound as no man ever blew or pounded before, which made the red conductor lose the last vestige of control of himself and caused him to bounce up and down on his bell strap as he grasped it with both hands in a wild, maniacal dance, which of course served to drive uncertain Reason from her tottering throne in the red driver, who dropped his whistle and his hook and began to yell, and ki-yi, and whoop harder than the worst personal devil encountered by the sternest of Scotch Presbyterians ever yelled and ki-yied and whooped on the darkest night after the good man had drunk the most hot Scotch whiskey; just then the left-hand forward wheel on the rear van fell off and the axle went down. The van gave a mighty lurch and then swayed and rolled and rocked and stopped; the red driver applied his brake with a jerk and his horses turned out to keep from being crushed between car and van; the other drivers applied their brakes with a jerk and their horses turned out; the two cliff-dwelling men on the shelf half-way up the front of the stranded van began to shout loudly to their brother cliff-dwellers on the forward van; a girl, six years old, with a pail of beer crossed under the red car horses' necks; a boy, eight years old, mounted the red car with the sporting extras of the evening papers; a girl, ten years old, went in front of the van horses with two pails of beer; an unclassified boy poked his finger in the black grease in the hub of the right-hand hind van wheel and began to print his name on the red landscape on the van's side; a boy with a little head and big ears examined the white rings on the martingales of the van leaders with a view of stealing them in the confusion; a sixteen-year-old girl without any hat and with a roll of half-finished vests under her arm crossed the front platform of the green car. As she stepped up on to the sidewalk a barber from a ten-cent shop said "Ah! there!" and she answered "smarty!" with withering scorn and went down a side street. A few drops of warm summer rain began to fall.

Well, the van was wrecked and something had got to be done. It was on the busiest car track on Manhattan Island. The cliff-dwellers got down in some mysterious way—probably on a rope ladder. Their brethren drove their van down a side street and came back to see what was the matter.

"The nut is off," said the captain of the wrecked van.

"Yes," said the first mate, "the nut is off."

"Hah," said the captain of the other van, "the nut is off."

"Yer right," said his first mate, "the nut is off."

The driver of the red car came up, hot and irritated. But he had regained his reason. "The nut is off," he said.

The drivers of the green and of the blue car came along. "The nut," they said in chorus, "is off."

The red, green and blue conductors came forward. They examined the situation carefully as became men occupying a higher position. Then they made this report through the chairman, the red conductor:

"The nut is gone."

"Yes," said the driver of the crippled van, who had spoken first, "yes, the damned nut is lost."

Then the driver of the other van swore, and the two assistants swore, and the three car drivers swore and the three car conductors used some polite but profane expressions. Then a strange man, an unknown man and an outsider, with his trousers held up by a trunk-strap, who stood at hand, swore harder than any of the rest. The others turned and looked at him inquiringly and savagely. The man wriggled nervously.

"You wanter tie it up," he said at last.

"Wot yo' goin' to tie it to, you cussed fool?" asked the assistant of the head van scornfully, "a berloon?"

"Ha, ha!" laughed the others.

"Some folks make me tired," said the second van driver.

"Go and lose yourself with the nut," said the red conductor, severely.

"That's it," said the others. "Git out, 'fore we t'row you out."

The officiously profane stranger slunk away.

The crisis always produces the man.

In this crisis the man was the first van driver.

"Bill," said the first van driver, "git some candles." Bill vanished.

A car with a white light, a car with a white and red light, a car with a white light and a green bar across it, a car with a blue light and a white circle around it, another car with a red bullseye light and one with a red flat light had come up and stopped. More were coming to extend the long line. The elevated trains thundered overhead, and made the street tremble. A dozen horse cars went down on the other track, and the drivers made derisive noises, rather than speaking derisive words at their brother van-bound drivers. Each delayed car was full of passengers, and they craned their necks and peppery old gentlemen inquired what the trouble was, and a happy individual who had been to Coney Island began to sing.

Trucks, mail-wagons and evening paper carts crowded past. A jam was imminent. A Chatham Square cab fought its way along with a man inside wearing a diamond like an arc-light. A hundred people stopped on either sidewalk; ten per cent of them whistled "Boom-de-ay." A half dozen small boys managed to just miss being killed by passing teams. Four Jews looked out of four different pawnshops. Pullers-in for three clothing stores were alert. The ten-cent barber eyed a Division-st. girl who was a millinery puller-in and who was chewing gum with an earnest, almost fierce, motion of the jaw. The ever-forward flowing tide of the growlers flowed on. The men searched under the slanting rays of the electric light for the lost nut, back past a dozen cars; scattering drops of rain continued to fall and a hand-organ came up and began an overture.

Just then Bill rose up from somewhere with four candles. The leader lit them and each van man took one and they continued the search for the nut. The humorous driver on a blue car asked them why they didn't get a fire-fly; the equally playful driver of a white car advised them of the fact that the moon would be up in the course of two or three hours. Then a gust of wind came and blew out the candles. The hand-organ man played on. A dozen newsboys arrived with evening paper extras about the Presidential nomination. The passengers bought the extras and found that they contained nothing new. A man with a stock of suspenders on his arm began to look into the trade situation. He might have made a sale to the profane man with the trunk-strap but he had disappeared. The leader again asserted himself.

"Bill," he shouted, "you git a lager beer-keg." Bill was gone in an instant.

"Jim," continued the leader, in a loud voice, as if Jim were up at the sharp end of the mainmast and the leader was on the deck, "Jim, unhitch them hosses and take out the pole."

Jim started to obey orders. A policeman came and walked around the van, looked at the prostrated wheel, started to say something, concluded not to, made the hand-organ man move on, and then went to the edge of the sidewalk and began talking to the Division-st. girl with the gum, to the infinite disgust of the cheap barber. The trunk-strap man came out of a restaurant with a sign of "Breakfast, 13 cents; Dinner, 15 cents," where he had been hidden and slunk into the liquor store next door with a sign of "Hot spiced rum, 6 cents; Sherry with a Big Egg in it, 5 cents." At the door he almost stepped on a small boy with a pitcher of beer so big that he had to set it down and rest every half block.

Bill was now back with the keg. "Set it right there," said the leader. "Now you, Jim, sock that pole under the axle and we'll h'ist 'er up and put the keg under."

One of the horses began kicking the front of the van. "Here, there!" shouted the leader and the horse subsided. "Six or seven o' you fellers git under that pole," commanded the leader, and he was obeyed. "Now all together!" The axle slowly rose and Bill slipped under the chime of the keg. But it was not high enough to allow the wheel to go on. "Git a paving block," commanded the leader to Bill. Just then a truck loaded with great, noisy straps of iron tried to pass. The wheels followed the car track too long, the truck struck the rear of the van and the axle went down with a crash while the keg rolled away into the gutter. Even great leaders lose their self-control sometimes; Washington swore at the Battle of Long Island; so this van leader now swore. His language was plain and scandalous. The truckman offered to lick the van man till he couldn't walk. He stopped his horses to get down to do it. But the policeman left the girl and came and made the truckman give over his warlike movement, much to the disgust of the crowd. Then he punched the suspender man in the back with the end of his club and went back to the girl. But the second delay was too much for the driver of the green car, and he turned out his horses and threw his car from the track. It pitched like a skiff in the swell of a steamer. It staggered and rocked and as it went past the van plunged into the gutter and made the crowd stand back, but the horses strained themselves and finally brought it up and at last it blundered on to its track and rolled away at a furious rate with the faces of the passengers wreathed in smiles and the conductor looking proudly back. Two other cars followed the example of the green and went lumbering past on the stones.

"Tell them fellers we'll be out of their way now in a minute," said the leader to the red conductor. Bill had arrived with the paving block. "Up with 'er, now," called the leader. The axle went up again and the keg with the stone on top of it went under. The leader seized the wheel himself and slipped it on. "Hitch on them hosses!" he commanded, and it was done. "Now, pull slow there, Bill," and Bill pulled slow. The great red car with the impossible landscape gave a preliminary rock and roll, the wheel which had made the trouble dropped down an inch or two from the keg and the van moved slowly forward. There was nothing to hold the wheel on and the leader walked close to it and watched it anxiously. But it stayed on to the corner, and around the corner, and into the side street. The red driver gave a triumphant ki-yi and his horses plunged forward in their collars eagerly. The other drivers gave glad ki-yis and the other horses plunged ahead. Twenty cars rolled past at a fast gait. "Now, youse fellys, move on!" said the policeman, and the crowd broke up. The cheap barber was talking to a girl with one black eye, but he retreated to his shop with the sign which promised "bay rum and a clean towel to every customer." Inside the liquor store the trunk-strap man was telling a man with his sleeves rolled up how two good men could have put their shoulders under the van and h'isted it up while a ten-year-old boy put on the wheel.

No. 61 A NIGHT AT THE MILLIONAIRE'S CLUB

A DOZEN of the members were enjoying themselves in the library. Their eyes were for the most part fixed in concrete stares at the ceiling where the decorations cost seventy-four dollars per square inch. An ecstatic murmur came from the remote corners of the apartment where each chair occupied two thousand dollars worth of floor. William C. Whitney was neatly arranged in a prominent seat to impart a suggestion of brains to the general effect. A clock had been chiming at intervals of ten minutes during the evening, and at each time of striking, Mr. Depew had made a joke, per agreement.

The last one, however, had smashed a seven-thousand dollar vase over by the window and Mr. Depew was hesitating. He had some doubt whether, after all, his jokes were worth that much commercially. His fellow members continued to ecstatically admire their isolation from the grimy vandals of the world. The soft breathing of the happy company made a sound like the murmur of pines in a summer wind. In the distance, a steward could be seen charging up seven thousand dollars to Mr. Depew's account; all, otherwise, was joy and perfect peace.

At this juncture, a seventeen-cent lackey upholstered in a three hundred dollar suit of clothes, made his appearance. He skated gracefully over the polished floor on snow-shoes. Halting in the centre of the room, he made seven low bows and sang a little ode to Plutus. Then he made a swift gesture, a ceremonial declaration that he was lower than the mud on the gaiters of the least wealthy of those before him, and spoke: "Sirs, there is a deputation of visitors in the hall who give their names as Ralph Waldo Emerson, Nathaniel Hawthorne, George Washington and Alexander Hamilton. They beg the favor of an audience."

A slumbering member in a large arm chair aroused and said: "Who?" And this pertinent interrogation was followed by others in various tones of astonishment and annoyance. "What's their names?" "Who did you say?" "What the devil do they want here?"

The lackey made seven more bows and sang another little ode. Then he spoke very distinctly: "Sirs, persons giving their names as Ralph Waldo Emerson, Nathaniel Hawthorne, George Washington and Alexander Hamilton desire the favor of an audience. They——"

But he was interrupted. "Don't know 'em!" "Who the deuce are these people anyhow!" "By Jove, here's a go! Want to see us, deuce take me!" "Well, I'm——"

It was at this point that Erroll Van Dyck Strathmore suddenly displayed those qualities which made his friends ever afterward look upon him as a man who would rise supreme at a crisis. He asked one question, but it was terse, sharp, and skill-ful, a master-piece of a man with presence of mind:

"Where are they from?"

"Sir," said the lackey, "they said they were from America!"

Strathmore paused but a moment to formulate his second searching question. His friends looked at him with admiration and awe. "Do they look like respectable people?"

The lackey arched his eyebrows. "Well—I don't know, sir." He was very discreet.

This reply created great consternation among the members. There was a wild scramble for places of safety. There were hurried commands given to the lackey. "Don't let 'em in here!" "Throw 'em out!" "Kill 'em!" But over all the uproar could be heard the voice of the imperturbable Strathmore. He was calmly giving orders to the servant.

"You will tell them that as we know no one in America, it is not possible that we have had the honor of their acquaintance, but that nevertheless it is our pleasure to indulge them a little, as it is possible that they are respectable people. However, they must not construe this into permission to come again. You will say to them that if they will repair quietly to any convenient place, wash their hands and procure rubber bibs, they may return and look at the remains of a cigarette which I carelessly threw upon the door-step. Tell the steward to provide each man with a recipe for Mr. Jones-Jones Smith-Jones' terrapin stew and a gallery ticket for the Kilanyi living pictures, then bid them go in safety. Afterward, you will sponge off the front steps and give the door-mat to one of those down-town clubs. You may go."

As the servant skated forth on his errand, Mr. Whitney fell in a death-like swoon, unnoticed, as the company thronged about the adroit, the brave Erroll Van Dyck Strathmore. "Bravo, old man, you saved us!" "What skill, what diplomacy!" "Egad, but you have courage!"

Suddenly the clock noted the time of ten minutes after twelve. Mr. Depew sprang to his feet. A broad smile illuminated his face.

"Say, fellows, the other day——" But he was surrounded by

slumbering figures. His smile changed then to a glare of bitter disappointment. In a burst of rage he hurled a champagne bottle at the clock and broke it to smithereens. Its cost was $4,675. He strode over to the ex-secretary. When Mr. Whitney had become aroused, the following conversation ensued:

"Say, Willie, what are we doing here?"

"I don't know, Chauncey!"

"Well, let's float, then!"

"Float it is, Chauncey!"

On the sidewalk they turned to regard each other.

"An antidote, Willie?"

"Well, I should say, Chauncey!"

They started on a hard run down the avenue.

No. 62 AN EXPERIMENT IN MISERY

It was late at night, and a fine rain was swirling softly down, causing the pavements to glisten with hue of steel and blue and yellow in the rays of the innumerable lights. A youth was trudging slowly, without enthusiasm, with his hands buried deep in his trousers' pockets, toward the downtown places where beds can be hired for coppers. He was clothed in an aged and tattered suit, and his derby was a marvel of dust-covered crown and torn rim. He was going forth to eat as the wanderer may eat, and sleep as the homeless sleep. By the time he had reached City Hall Park he was so completely plastered with yells of "bum" and "hobo," and with various unholy epithets that small boys had applied to him at intervals, that he was in a state of the most profound dejection. The sifting rain saturated the old velvet collar of his overcoat, and as the wet cloth pressed against his neck, he felt that there no longer could be pleasure in life. He looked about him searching for an outcast of highest degree that the two might share miseries. But the lights threw a quivering glare over rows and circles of deserted benches that glistened damply, showing patches of wet sod behind them. It seemed that their usual freights had fled on this night to better things. There were only squads of well-dressed Brooklyn people who swarmed toward the Bridge.

The young man loitered about for a time and then went shuffling off down Park Row. In the sudden descent in style of the dress of the crowd he felt relief, and as if he were at last in his own country. He began to see tatters that matched his tatters. In Chatham Square there were aimless men strewn in front of saloons and lodging houses, standing sadly, patiently, reminding one vaguely of the attitudes of chickens in a storm. He aligned himself with these men, and turned slowly to occupy himself with the flowing life of the great street.

Through the mists of the cold and storming night, the cable cars went in silent procession, great affairs shining with red and brass, moving with formidable power, calm and irresistible, dangerful and gloomy, breaking silence only by the loud fierce cry of the gong. Two rivers of people swarmed along the sidewalks, spattered with black mud, which made each shoe leave a scar-like impression. Overhead elevated trains with a shrill grinding of the wheels stopped at the station, which upon its leg-like pillars seemed to resemble some monstrous kind of crab squatting over the street. The quick fat puffings of the engines could be heard. Down an alley there were sombre curtains of purple and black, on which street lamps dully glittered like embroidered flowers.

A saloon stood with a voracious air on a corner. A sign leaning against the front of the doorpost announced: "Free hot soup to-night." The swing doors snapping to and fro like ravenous lips, made gratified smacks as the saloon gorged itself with plump men, eating with astounding and endless appetite, smiling in some indescribable manner as the men came from all directions like sacrifices to a heathenish superstition.

Caught by the delectable sign, the young man allowed himself to be swallowed. A bartender placed a schooner of dark and portentous beer on the bar. Its monumental form upreared until the froth a-top was above the crown of the young man's brown derby.

"Soup over there, gents," said the bartender, affably. A little yellow man in rags and the youth grasped their schooners and went with speed toward a lunch counter, where a man with oily but imposing whiskers ladled genially from a kettle until he had furnished his two mendicants with a soup that was steaming hot and in which there were little floating suggestions of chicken. The young man, sipping his broth, felt the cordiality expressed by the warmth of the mixture, and he beamed at the man with oily but imposing whiskers, who was presiding like a priest behind an altar. "Have some more, gents?" he inquired of the two sorry figures before him. The little yellow man accepted with a swift gesture, but the youth shook his head and went out, following a man whose wondrous seediness promised that he would have a knowledge of cheap lodging houses.

On the side-walk he accosted the seedy man. "Say, do you know a cheap place t' sleep?"

The other hesitated for a time, gazing sideways. Finally he nodded in the direction of up the street. "I sleep up there," he said, "when I've got th' price."

"How much?"

"Ten cents."

The young man shook his head dolefully. "That's too rich for me."

At that moment there approached the two a reeling man in strange garments. His head was a fuddle of bushy hair and whiskers from which his eyes peered with a guilty slant. In a close scrutiny it was possible to distinguish the cruel lines of a mouth, which looked as if its lips had just closed with satisfaction over some tender and piteous morsel. He appeared like an assassin steeped in crimes performed awkwardly.

But at this time his voice was tuned to the coaxing key of an affectionate puppy. He looked at the men with wheedling eyes and began to sing a little melody for charity.

"Say, gents, can't yeh give a poor feller a couple of cents t' git a bed. I got five an I gits anudder two I gits me a bed. Now, on th' square, gents, can't yeh jest gimme two cents t' git a bed. Now, yeh know how a respecter'ble gentlem'n feels when he's down on his luck an' I——"

The seedy man, staring with imperturbable countenance at a train which clattered overhead, interrupted in an expressionless voice: "Ah, go t' h——!"

But the youth spoke to the prayerful assassin in tones of astonishment and inquiry. "Say, you must be crazy! Why don't yeh strike somebody that looks as if they had money?"

The assassin, tottering about on his uncertain legs, and at intervals brushing imaginary obstacles from before his nose, entered into a long explanation of the psychology of the situation. It was so profound that it was unintelligible.

When he had exhausted the subject the young man said to him: "Let's see th' five cents."

The assassin wore an expression of drunken woe at this sentence, filled with suspicion of him. With a deeply pained air he began to fumble in his clothing, his red hands trembling. Presently he announced in a voice of bitter grief, as if he had been betrayed: "There's on'y four."

"Four," said the young man thoughtfully. "Well, look-a-here, I'm a stranger here, an' if ye'll steer me to your cheap joint I'll find the other three."

The assassin's countenance became instantly radiant with joy. His whiskers quivered with the wealth of his alleged emotions. He seized the young man's hand in a transport of delight and friendliness.

"B'gawd," he cried, "if ye'll do that, b'gawd, I'd say yeh was a damned good feller, I would, an' I'd remember yeh all m' life, I would, b'gawd, an' if I ever got a chance I'd return th' compliment"—he spoke with drunken dignity—"b'gawd, I'd treat yeh white, I would, an' I'd allus remember yeh——"

The young man drew back, looking at the assassin coldly. "Oh, that's all right," he said. "You show me th' joint—that's all you've got t' do."

The assassin, gesticulating gratitude, led the young man along a dark street. Finally he stopped before a little dusty door. He raised his hand impressively. "Look-a-here," he said, and there was a thrill of deep and ancient wisdom upon his face, "I've brought yeh here, an' that's my part, ain't it? If th' place don't suit yeh yeh needn't git mad at me, need yeh? There won't be no bad feelin', will there?"

"No," said the young man.

The assassin waved his arm tragically and led the march up the steep stairway. On the way the young man furnished the assassin with three pennies. At the top a man with benevolent spectacles looked at them through a hole in the board. He collected their money, wrote some names on a register, and speedily was leading the two men along a gloom shrouded corridor.

Shortly after the beginning of this journey the young man felt his liver turn white, for from the dark and secret places of the building there suddenly came to his nostrils strange and unspeakable odors that assailed him like malignant diseases with wings. They seemed to be from human bodies closely packed in dens; the exhalations from a hundred pairs of reeking lips; the fumes from a thousand bygone debauches; the expression of a thousand present miseries.

A man, naked save for a little snuff colored undershirt, was parading sleepily along the corridor. He rubbed his eyes, and, giving vent to a prodigious yawn, demanded to be told the time.

"Half past one."

The man yawned again. He opened a door, and for a moment his form was outlined against a black, opaque interior. To this door came the three men, and as it was again opened the unholy odors rushed out like released fiends, so that the young man was obliged to struggle as against an overpowering wind.

It was some time before the youth's eyes were good in the intense gloom within, but the man with benevolent spectacles led him skillfully, pausing but a moment to deposit the limp assassin upon a cot. He took the youth to a cot that lay tranquilly by the window, and, showing him a tall locker for clothes that stood near the head with the ominous air of a tombstone, left him.

The youth sat on his cot and peered about him. There was a gas jet in a distant part of the room that burned a small flickering orange hued flame. It caused vast masses of tumbled shadows in all parts of the place, save where, immediately about it, there was a little gray haze. As the young man's eyes became used to the darkness he could see upon the cots that thickly littered the floor the forms of men sprawled out, lying in death-like silence or heaving and snoring with tremendous effort, like stabbed fish.

The youth locked his derby and his shoes in the mummy case

near him and then lay down with his old and familiar coat around his shoulders. A blanket he handled gingerly, drawing it over part of the coat. The cot was leather covered and cold as melting snow. The youth was obliged to shiver for some time on this affair, which was like a slab. Presently, however, his chill gave him peace, and during this period of leisure from it he turned his head to stare at his friend, the assassin, whom he could dimly discern where he lay sprawled on a cot in the abandon of a man filled with drink. He was snoring with incredible vigor. His wet hair and beard dimly glistened and his inflamed nose shone with subdued luster like a red light in a fog.

Within reach of the youth's hand was one who lay with yellow breast and shoulders bare to the cold drafts. One arm hung over the side of the cot and the fingers lay full length upon the wet cement floor of the room. Beneath the inky brows could be seen the eyes of the man exposed by the partly opened lids. To the youth it seemed that he and this corpse-like being were exchanging a prolonged stare and that the other threatened with his eyes. He drew back, watching his neighbor from the shadows of his blanket edge. The man did not move once through the night, but lay in this stillness as of death, like a body stretched out, expectant of the surgeon's knife.

And all through the room could be seen the tawny hues of naked flesh, limbs thrust into the darkness, projecting beyond the cots; up-reared knees; arms hanging, long and thin, over the cot edges. For the most part they were statuesque, carven, dead. With the curious lockers standing all about like tombstones there was a strange effect of a graveyard, where bodies were merely flung.

Yet occasionally could be seen limbs wildly tossing in fantastic, nightmare gestures, accompanied by guttural cries, grunts, oaths. And there was one fellow off in a gloomy corner, who in his dreams was oppressed by some frightful calamity, for of a sudden he began to utter long wails that went almost like yells from a hound, echoing wailfully and weird through this chill place of tombstones, where men lay like the dead.

The sound, in its high piercing beginnings that dwindled to

final melancholy moans, expressed a red and grim tragedy of the unfathomable possibilities of the man's dreams. But to the youth these were not merely the shrieks of a vision pierced man. They were an utterance of the meaning of the room and its occupants. It was to him the protest of the wretch who feels the touch of the imperturbable granite wheels and who then cries with an impersonal eloquence, with a strength not from him, giving voice to the wail of a whole section, a class, a people. This, weaving into the young man's brain and mingling with his views of these vast and somber shadows that like mighty black fingers curled around the naked bodies, made the young man so that he did not sleep, but lay carving biographies for these men from his meager experience. At times the fellow in the corner howled in a writhing agony of his imaginations.

Finally a long lance point of gray light shot through the dusty panes of the window. Without, the young man could see roofs drearily white in the dawning. The point of light yellowed and grew brighter, until the golden rays of the morning sun came in bravely and strong. They touched with radiant color the form of a small, fat man, who snored in stuttering fashion. His round and shiny bald head glowed suddenly with the valor of a decoration. He sat up, blinked at the sun, swore fretfully and pulled his blanket over the ornamental splendors of his head.

The youth contentedly watched this rout of the shadows before the bright spears of the sun and presently he slumbered. When he awoke he heard the voice of the assassin raised in valiant curses. Putting up his head he perceived his comrade seated on the side of the cot engaged in scratching his neck with long finger nails that rasped like files.

"Hully Jee dis is a new breed. They've got can openers on their feet," he continued in a violent tirade.

The young man hastily unlocked his closet and took out his shoes and hat. As he sat on the side of the cot, lacing his shoes, he glanced about and saw that daylight had made the room comparatively commonplace and uninteresting. The men, whose faces seemed stolid, serene or absent, were engaged in dressing, while a great crackle of bantering conversation arose.

A few were parading in unconcerned nakedness. Here and there were men of brawn, whose skins shone clear and ruddy.

They took splendid poses, standing massively, like chiefs. When they had dressed in their ungainly garments there was an extraordinary change. They then showed bumps and deficiencies of all kinds.

There were others who exhibited many deformities. Shoulders were slanting, humped, pulled this way and pulled that way. And notable among these latter men was the little fat man who had refused to allow his head to be glorified. His pudgy form, builded like a pear, bustled to and fro, while he swore in fishwife fashion. It appeared that some article of his apparel had vanished.

The young man, attired speedily, went to his friend, the assassin. At first the latter looked dazed at the sight of the youth. This face seemed to be appealing to him through the cloud wastes of his memory. He scratched his neck and reflected. At last he grinned, a broad smile gradually spreading until his countenance was a round illumination. "Hello, Willie," he cried, cheerily.

"Hello," said the young man. "Are yeh ready t' fly?"

"Sure." The assassin tied his shoe carefully with some twine and came ambling.

When he reached the street the young man experienced no sudden relief from unholy atmospheres. He had forgotten all about them, and had been breathing naturally and with no sensation of discomfort or distress.

He was thinking of these things as he walked along the street, when he was suddenly startled by feeling the assassin's hand, trembling with excitement, clutching his arm, and when the assassin spoke, his voice went into quavers from a supreme agitation.

"I'll be hully, bloomin' blowed, if there wasn't a feller with a nightshirt on up there in that joint!"

The youth was bewildered for a moment, but presently he turned to smile indulgently at the assassin's humor.

"Oh, you're a d—— liar," he merely said.

Whereupon the assassin began to gesture extravagantly and take oath by strange gods. He frantically placed himself at the mercy of remarkable fates if his tale were not true. "Yes, he did! I cross m' heart thousan' times!" he protested, and at the time his eyes were large with amazement, his mouth wrinkled in unnatural glee. "Yessir! A nightshirt! A hully white nightshirt!"

"You lie!"

"Nosir! I hope ter die b'fore I kin git anudder ball if there wasn't a jay wid a hully, bloomin' white nightshirt!"

His face was filled with the infinite wonder of it. "A hully white nightshirt," he continually repeated.

The young man saw the dark entrance to a basement restaurant. There was a sign which read, "No mystery about our hash," and there were other age stained and world battered legends which told him that the place was within his means. He stopped before it and spoke to the assassin. "I guess I'll git somethin' t' eat."

At this the assassin, for some reason, appeared to be quite embarrassed. He gazed at the seductive front of the eating place for a moment. Then he started slowly up the street. "Well, goodby, Willie," he said, bravely.

For an instant the youth studied the departing figure. Then he called out, "Hol' on a minnet." As they came together he spoke in a certain fierce way, as if he feared that the other would think him to be weak. "Look-a-here, if yeh wanta git some breakfas' I'll lend yeh three cents t' do it with. But say, look-a-here, you've gota git out an' hustle. I ain't goin' t' support yeh, or I'll go broke b'fore night. I ain't no millionaire."

"I take me oath, Willie," said the assassin, earnestly, "th' on'y thing I really needs is a ball. Me t'roat feels like a fryin' pan. But as I can't git a ball, why, th' next bes' thing is breakfast, an' if yeh do that fer me, b'gawd, I'd say yeh was th' whitest lad I ever see."

They spent a few moments in dexterous exchanges of phrases, in which they each protested that the other was, as the assassin had originally said, a "respecter'ble gentlem'n." And they concluded with mutual assurances that they were the souls of intelligence and virtue. Then they went into the restaurant.

There was a long counter, dimly lighted from hidden sources. Two or three men in soiled white aprons rushed here and there.

The youth bought a bowl of coffee for two cents and a roll for one cent. The assassin purchased the same. The bowls were webbed with brown seams, and the tin spoons wore an air of having emerged from the first pyramid. Upon them were black, moss-like encrustations of age, and they were bent and scarred from the attacks of long forgotten teeth. But over their repast the wanderers waxed warm and mellow. The assassin grew affable as the hot mixture went soothingly down his parched throat, and the young man felt courage flow in his veins.

Memories began to throng in on the assassin, and he brought forth long tales, intricate, incoherent, delivered with a chattering swiftness as from an old woman. "——great job out'n Orange. Boss keep yeh hustlin', though, all time. I was there three days, and then I went an' ask'im t' lend me a dollar. 'G-g-go ter the devil,' he ses, an' I lose me job.

——"South no good. Damn niggers work for twenty-five an' thirty cents a day. Run white man out. Good grub, though. Easy livin'.

——"Yas; useter work little in Toledo, raftin' logs. Make two or three dollars er day in the spring. Lived high. Cold as ice, though, in the winter——

"I was raised in northern N'York. O-o-o-oh, yeh jest oughto live there. No beer ner whisky, though, way off in the woods. But all th' good hot grub yeh can eat. B'gawd, I hung around there long as I could till th' ol' man fired me. 'Git t'hell outa here, yeh wuthless skunk, git t'hell outa here an' go die,' he ses. 'You're a hell of a father,' I ses, 'you are,' an' I quit 'im."

As they were passing from the dim eating place they encountered an old man who was trying to steal forth with a tiny package of food, but a tall man with an indomitable mustache stood dragon fashion, barring the way of escape. They heard the old man raise a plaintive protest. "Ah, you always want to know what I take out, and you never see that I usually bring a package in here from my place of business."

As the wanderers trudged slowly along Park Row, the assassin began to expand and grow blithe. "B'gawd, we've been livin' like kings," he said, smacking appreciative lips.

"Look out or we'll have t' pay fer it t' night," said the youth, with gloomy warning.

But the assassin refused to turn his gaze toward the future. He went with a limping step, into which he injected a suggestion of lamb-like gambols. His mouth was wreathed in a red grin.

In the City Hall Park the two wanderers sat down in the little circle of benches sanctified by traditions of their class. They huddled in their old garments, slumbrously conscious of the march of the hours which for them had no meaning.

The people of the street hurrying hither and thither made a blend of black figures, changing, yet frieze-like. They walked in their good clothes as upon important missions, giving no gaze to the two wanderers seated upon the benches. They expressed to the young man his infinite distance from all that he valued. Social position, comfort, the pleasures of living, were unconquerable kingdoms. He felt a sudden awe.

And in the background a multitude of buildings, of pitiless hues and sternly high, were to him emblematic of a nation forcing its regal head into the clouds, throwing no downward glances; in the sublimity of its aspirations ignoring the wretches who may flounder at its feet. The roar of the city in his ear was to him the confusion of strange tongues, babbling heedlessly; it was the clink of coin, the voice of the city's hopes which were to him no hopes.

He confessed himself an outcast, and his eyes from under the lowered rim of his hat began to glance guiltily, wearing the criminal expression that comes with certain convictions.

No. 63   AN EXPERIMENT IN LUXURY

"IF YOU accept this invitation you will have an opportunity to make another social study," said the old friend.

The youth laughed. "If they caught me making a study of them they'd attempt a murder. I would be pursued down Fifth avenue by the entire family."

"Well," persisted the old friend who could only see one thing at a time, "it would be very interesting. I have been told all my life that millionaires have no fun, and I know that the poor are always assured that the millionaire is a very unhappy person. They are informed that miseries swarm around all wealth, that all crowned heads are heavy with care, and——"

"But still——" began the youth.

"And, in the irritating, brutalizing, enslaving environment of their poverty, they are expected to solace themselves with these assurances," continued the old friend. He extended his gloved palm and began to tap it impressively with a finger of his other hand. His legs were spread apart in a fashion peculiar to his oratory. "I believe that it is mostly false. It is true that wealth does not release a man from many things from which he would gladly purchase release. Consequences cannot be bribed. I suppose that every man believes steadfastly that he has a private tragedy which makes him yearn for other existences. But it is impossible for me to believe that these things equalize themselves; that there are burrs under all rich cloaks and benefits in all ragged jackets, and the preaching of it seems wicked to me. There are those who have opportunities; there are those who are robbed of——"

"But look here," said the young man; "what has this got to do with my paying Jack a visit?"

"It has got a lot to do with it," said the old friend sharply. "As I said, there are those who have opportunities; there are those who are robbed——"

"Well, I won't have you say Jack ever robbed anybody of anything, because he's as honest a fellow as ever lived," interrupted the youth, with warmth. "I have known him for years, and he is a perfectly square fellow. He doesn't know about these infernal things. He isn't criminal because you say he is benefited by a condition which other men created."

"I didn't say he was," retorted the old friend. "Nobody is responsible for anything. I wish to Heaven somebody was, and then we could all jump on him. Look here, my boy, our modern civilization is——"

"Oh, the deuce!" said the young man.

The old friend then stood very erect and stern. "I can see by your frequent interruptions that you have not yet achieved sufficient pain in life. I hope one day to see you materially changed. You are yet——"

"There he is now," said the youth, suddenly. He indicated a

young man who was passing. He went hurriedly toward him, pausing once to gesture adieu to his old friend.

The house was broad and brown and stolid like the face of a peasant. It had an inanity of expression, an absolute lack of artistic strength that was in itself powerful because it symbolized something. It stood, a homely pile of stone, rugged, grimly self reliant, asserting its quality as a fine thing when in reality the beholder usually wondered why so much money had been spent to obtain a complete negation. Then from another point of view it was important and mighty because it stood as a fetich, formidable because of traditions of worship.

When the great door was opened the youth imagined that the footman who held a hand on the knob looked at him with a quick, strange stare. There was nothing definite in it; it was all vague and elusive, but a suspicion was certainly denoted in some way. The youth felt that he, one of the outer barbarians, had been detected to be a barbarian by the guardian of the portal, he of the refined nose, he of the exquisite sense, he who must be more atrociously aristocratic than any that he serves. And the youth, detesting himself for it, found that he would rejoice to take a frightful revenge upon this lackey who, with a glance of his eyes, had called him a name. He would have liked to have been for a time a dreadful social perfection whose hand, waved lazily, would cause hordes of the idolatrous imperfect to be smitten in the eyes. And in the tumult of his imagination he did not think it strange that he should plan in his vision to come around to this house and with the power of his new social majesty, reduce this footman to ashes.

He had entered with an easy feeling of independence, but after this incident the splendor of the interior filled him with awe. He was a wanderer in a fairy land, and who felt that his presence marred certain effects. He was an invader with a shamed face, a man who had come to steal certain colors, forms, impressions that were not his. He had a dim thought that some one might come to tell him to begone.

His friend, unconscious of this swift drama of thought, was already upon the broad staircase. "Come on," he called. When the youth's foot struck from a thick rug and changed upon the tiled floor he was almost frightened.

There was cool abundance of gloom. High up stained glass caught the sunlight, and made it into marvelous hues that in places touched the dark walls. A broad bar of yellow gilded the leaves of lurking plants. A softened crimson glowed upon the head and shoulders of a bronze swordsman, who perpetually strained in a terrific lunge, his blade thrust at random into the shadow, piercing there an unknown something.

An immense fire place was at one end, and its furnishings gleamed until it resembled a curious door of a palace, and on the threshold, where one would have to pass a fire burned redly. From some remote place came the sound of a bird twittering busily. And from behind heavy portieres came a subdued noise of the chatter of three, twenty or a hundred women.

He could not relieve himself of this feeling of awe until he had reached his friend's room. There they lounged carelessly and smoked pipes. It was an amazingly comfortable room. It expressed to the visitor that he could do supremely as he chose, for it said plainly that in it the owner did supremely as he chose. The youth wondered if there had not been some domestic skirmishing to achieve so much beautiful disorder. There were various articles left about defiantly, as if the owner openly flaunted the feminine ideas of precision. The disarray of a table that stood prominently defined the entire room. A set of foils, a set of boxing gloves, a lot of illustrated papers, an inkstand and a hat lay entangled upon it. Here was surely a young man, who, when his menacing mother, sisters or servants knocked, would open a slit in the door like a Chinaman in an opium joint, and tell them to leave him to his beloved devices. And yet, withal, the effect was good, because the disorder was not necessary, and because there are some things that when flung down, look to have been flung by an artist. A baby can create an effect with a guitar. It would require genius to deal with the piled up dishes in a Cherry street sink.

The youth's friend lay back upon the broad seat that followed the curve of the window and smoked in blissful laziness. Without one could see the windowless wall of a house overgrown with a green, luxuriant vine. There was a glimpse of a side street. Below were the stables. At intervals a little fox terrier ran into the court and barked tremendously.

The youth, also blissfully indolent, kept up his part of the conversation on the recent college days, but continually he was beset by a stream of sub-conscious reflection. He was beginning to see a vast wonder in it that they two lay sleepily chatting with no more apparent responsibility than rabbits, when certainly there were men, equally fine perhaps, who were being blackened and mashed in the churning life of the lower places. And all this had merely happened; the great secret hand had guided them here and had guided others there. The eternal mystery of social condition exasperated him at this time. He wondered if incomprehensible justice were the sister of open wrong.

And, above all, why was he impressed, awed, overcome by a mass of materials, a collection of the trophies of wealth, when he knew that to him their dominant meaning was that they represented a lavish expenditure? For what reason did his nature so deeply respect all this? Perhaps his ancestors had been peasants bowing heads to the heel of appalling pomp of princes or rows of little men who stood to watch a king kill a flower with his cane. There was one side of him that said there were finer things in life, but the other side did homage.

Presently he began to feel that he was a better man that many —entitled to a great pride. He stretched his legs like a man in a garden, and he thought that he belonged to the garden. Hues and forms had smothered certain of his comprehensions. There had been times in his life when little voices called to him continually from the darkness; he heard them now as an idle, half-smothered babble on the horizon edge. It was necessary that it should be so, too. There was the horizon, he said, and, of course, there should be a babble of pain on it. Thus it was written; it was a law, he thought. And, anyway, perhaps it was not so bad as those who babbled tried to tell.

In this way and with this suddenness he arrived at a stage. He was become a philosopher, a type of the wise man who can eat but three meals a day, conduct a large business and understand the purposes of infinite power. He felt valuable. He was sage and important.

There were influences, knowledges that made him aware that he was idle and foolish in his new state, but he inwardly reveled like a barbarian in his environment. It was delicious to feel so high and mighty, to feel that the unattainable could be purchased like a penny bun. For a time, at any rate, there was no impossible. He indulged in monarchical reflections.

As they were dressing for dinner his friend spoke to him in this wise: "Be sure not to get off anything that resembles an original thought before my mother. I want her to like you, and I know that when any one says a thing cleverly before her he ruins himself with her forever. Confine your talk to orthodox expressions. Be dreary and unspeakably commonplace in the true sense of the word. Be damnable."

"It will be easy for me to do as you say," remarked the youth.

"As far as the old man goes," continued the other, "he's a blooming good fellow. He may appear like a sort of a crank if he happens to be in that mood, but he's all right when you come to know him. And besides he doesn't dare do that sort of thing with me, because I've got nerve enough to bully him. Oh, the old man is all right."

On their way down the youth lost the delightful mood that he had enjoyed in his friend's rooms. He dropped it like a hat on the stairs. The splendor of color and form swarmed upon him again. He bowed before the strength of this interior; it said a word to him which he believed he should despise, but instead he crouched. In the distance shone his enemy, the footman.

"There will be no people here to-night, so you may see the usual evening row between my sister Mary and me, but don't be alarmed or uncomfortable, because it is quite an ordinary matter," said his friend, as they were about to enter a little drawing room that was well apart from the grander rooms.

The head of the family, the famous millionaire, sat on a low stool before the fire. He was deeply absorbed in the gambols of a kitten who was plainly trying to stand on her head that she might use all four paws in grappling with an evening paper with which her playmate was poking her ribs. The old man chuckled in complete glee. There was never such a case of abstraction, of want of care. The man of millions was in a far land where mechanics and bricklayers go, a mystic land of little, universal emotions, and he had been guided to it by the quaint gestures of a kitten's furry paws.

His wife, who stood near, was apparently not at all a dweller in thought lands. She was existing very much in the present. Evidently she had been wishing to consult with her husband on some tremendous domestic question, and she was in a state of rampant irritation, because he refused to acknowledge at this moment that she or any such thing as a tremendous domestic question was in existence. At intervals she made savage attempts to gain his attention.

As the youth saw her she was in a pose of absolute despair. And her eyes expressed that she appreciated all the tragedy of it. Ah, they said, hers was a life of terrible burden, of appalling responsibility; her pathway was beset with unsolved problems, her horizon was lined with tangled difficulties, while her husband—the man of millions—continued to play with the kitten. Her expression was an admission of heroism.

The youth saw that here at any rate was one denial of his oratorical old friend's statement. In the face of this woman there was no sign that life was sometimes a joy. It was impossible that there could be any pleasure in living for her. Her features were as lined and creased with care and worriment as those of an apple woman. It was as if the passing of each social obligation, of each binding form of her life had left its footprints, scarring her face.

Somewhere in her expression there was terrible pride, that kind of pride which, mistaking the form for the real thing, worships itself because of its devotion to the form.

In the lines of the mouth and the set of the chin could be seen the might of a grim old fighter. They denoted all the power of machination of a general, veteran of a hundred battles. The little scars at the corners of her eyes made a wondrously fierce effect, baleful, determined, without regard somehow to ruck of pain. Here was a savage, a barbarian, a spear woman of the Philistines, who fought battles to excel in what are thought to be the refined and worthy things in life; here was a type of Zulu chieftainess who scuffled and scrambled for place before the white altars of social excellence. And woe to the socially weaker who should try to barricade themselves against that dragon.

It was certain that she never rested in the shade of the trees. One could imagine the endless churning of that mind. And plans and other plans coming forth continuously, defeating a rival here, reducing a family there, bludgeoning a man here, a maid there. Woe and wild eyes followed like obedient sheep upon her trail.

Too, the youth thought he could see that here was the true abode of conservatism—in the mothers, in those whose ears displayed their diamonds instead of their diamonds displaying their ears, in the ancient and honorable controllers who sat in remote corners and pulled wires and respected themselves with a magnitude of respect that heaven seldom allows on earth. There lived tradition and superstition. They were perhaps ignorant of that which they worshiped, and, not comprehending it at all, it naturally followed that the fervor of their devotion could set the sky ablaze.

As he watched, he saw that the mesmeric power of a kitten's waving paws was good. He rejoiced in the spectacle of the little fuzzy cat trying to stand on its head, and by this simple antic defeating some intention of a great domestic Napoleon.

The three girls of the family were having a musical altercation over by the window. Then and later the youth thought them adorable. They were wonderful to him in their charming gowns. They had time and opportunity to create effects, to be beautiful. And it would have been a wonder to him if he had not found them charming, since making themselves so could but be their principal occupation.

Beauty requires certain justices, certain fair conditions. When in a field no man can say: "Here should spring up a flower; here one should not." With incomprehensible machinery and system, nature sends them forth in places both strange and proper, so that, somehow, as we see them each one is a surprise to us. But at times, at places, one can say: "Here no flower can flourish." The youth wondered then why he had been sometimes surprised at seeing women fade, shrivel, their bosoms flatten, their shoulders crook forward, in the heavy swelter and wrench of their toil. It must be difficult, he thought, for a woman to remain serene and uncomplaining when she contemplated the wonder and the strangeness of it.

The lights shed marvelous hues of softened rose upon the table. In the encircling shadows the butler moved with a mournful, deeply solemn air. Upon the table there was color of pleasure, of festivity, but this servant in the background went to and fro like a slow religious procession.

The youth felt considerable alarm when he found himself involved in conversation with his hostess. In the course of this talk he discovered the great truth that when one submits himself to a thoroughly conventional conversation he runs risks of being most amazingly stupid. He was glad that no one cared to overhear it.

The millionaire, deprived of his kitten, sat back in his chair and laughed at the replies of his son to the attacks of one of the girls. In the rather good wit of his offspring he took an intense delight, but he laughed more particularly at the words of the son.

Indicated in this light chatter about the dinner table there was an existence that was not at all what the youth had been taught to see. Theologians had for a long time told the poor man that riches did not bring happiness, and they had solemnly repeated this phrase until it had come to mean that misery was commensurate with dollars, that each wealthy man was inwardly a miserable wretch. And when a wail of despair or rage had come from the night of the slums they had stuffed this epigram down the throat of he who cried out and told him that he was a lucky fellow. They did this because they feared.

The youth, studying this family group, could not see that they had great license to be pale and haggard. They were no doubt fairly good, being not strongly induced toward the by-paths. Various worlds turned open doors toward them. Wealth in a certain sense is liberty. If they were fairly virtuous he could not see why they should be so persistently pitied.

And no doubt they would dispense their dollars like little seeds upon the soil of the world if it were not for the fact that since the days of the ancient great political economist, the more exalted forms of virtue have grown to be utterly impracticable.

No. 64 SAILING DAY SCENES

THE interior of the huge pier had been long thronged with trucks, merchandise and people. A great babble of voices and roar of wheels arose from it. Over all rang the wild incoherent shouts of the bosses, who directed the stevedores. These latter marched in endless procession, with bales and bags upon their shoulders. It was the last of the cargo. They ferreted their way stolidly through the noisy crowds of visitors and then up a wide gangplank in steady and monotonous procession.

Through the wide doors in the side of the pier could be seen the mighty sides of the steamer, and above little stretches of white deck, whereon people stood in rows gazing fixedly at the shore as if they expected at any moment to see it vanish. At the end of the passenger gangplank two sailors remained imperturbably at their station. An officer leaned on the railing near them. Near the shoreward end swarmed countless stewards, mingling their blue uniforms in with the gay colored clothes of the crowd and wondering assiduously about everybody's business.

From a position near the doors one could see that the enormous funnels of the steamship were emitting continual streams of black, curling smoke.

Gradually there was a vanishing of the stewards. The two sailors at the gangplank began to look serious and rather wild, as if the responsibility of their positions and the eye of the adjacent officer was too much for them. Rows of stevedores manned ropes and prepared to tug at the gangplanks. Meanwhile, from all along the line of the pier, extraordinary conversations were being held with people who leaned upon the railings of the decks above. A preliminary thrill went through the throng. The talk began to grow hurried, excited. People spoke wildly and with great speed, conscious that the last moments were upon them. And it devolved upon certain individuals to lose their friends at the final minute in the chaos of heads upon the decks, so that one could often hear the same typical formula coming from a dozen different sources, as if everybody was interested in the same person and had missed him. Two grayheaded New Yorkers held a frantic argument.

"There he is! There he is! Hurray! Goodby, ol' man!"

"Darn it all, I tell you that it isn't him at all!"

"It is, too!"

"It ain't, I tell you!"

"Ah, there he is now. Down there further! Goodby, ol' man, goodby!"

A man upon the steamer suddenly burst out in a fury of gesticulation. "Where's Tommie?" he bawled. "I can't see Tommie!"

His excitement was communicated to two women upon the pier. "Heavens!" said one with a nervous cry, "Where is that boy!" She could not omit some complainings of motherhood. "He's the greatest plague! Here's his father sailing for Europe and he's off somewhere! Tommie! Tommie! Come here!" They began to glance frenziedly through the crevices of the crowd. It was plain that they expected to detect him in some terrible, irrelevant crime.

Then suddenly above the clamor of farewells arose the wild shout of a little boy, undismayed by the crowds. "Papa! Papa! Papa! Here I am! Goodby, papa!" The man on the steamship made a tremendous gesture. The two women on the pier began to weep vaguely.

The faces on all sides beamed with affection and some sort of a suggestion of mournful reminiscence. There were plentiful smiles, but they expressed always a great tender sorrow. It was surprising to see how full of expression the face of a blunt, every day American business man could become. They were suddenly angels.

As for the women, they were sacred from stare through the purity of their grief. Many of them allowed the tears to fall unheeded down their faces. Theirs was a quality of sorrow that has a certain valor, a certain boldness.

The crowd began to swarm toward the end of the pier to get the last gesture and glance of their friends as the steamer backed out. It was coming toward the supreme moment.

At last some indefinite mechanism set the sailors and the stevedores in motion. Ropes were flung away and the heavy gangplanks were pulled back onto the dock with loud shouts. "Look out! Look out there!" The people were unheeding, for now uprose a great tumult of farewells, a song of affection that swelled into a vast incoherent roar. They had waited long for this moment, and now with a sense of its briefness they were frantic in an effort to think how best to use it. Handkerchiefs waved in white clouds. Men bawled in a last futile struggle to express their state of mind. Over all could often be heard the shrill wail of the little boy: "Oh, papa! Papa! Here I am!"

Back from the surging crowd around the huge doors was the motionless figure of a beautiful woman. She had been gazing long at the steamship with clear and unswerving eye and face as stoical as a warrior's. She remained carven, expressionless, as the huge panorama of black and white went slowly past the doors. When the bow went by with its burden of a few tranquil sailors busy with ropes, a faint flutter went over her rose tinted under lip. She put up her hands and took a long time to arrange the laces about her throat.

Out at the end of the pier the whole final uproar was in full motion. A tug loaded with gesturing, howling people bustled to and fro, celebrating everything with a barbaric whistle. A last great cry arose as steel-hued water began to show between the craft and the pier. It was a farewell with an undercurrent of despair of expression. The inadequacy of the goodbys seemed suddenly apparent to the crowd. The forlorn pathos of the thing struck their minds anew and many of the women began to weep again in that vague way, as if overcome by a sadness that was subtly more than the tangible grief of parting. A pompous officer, obviously vain of his clothes, strode before the agitated faces upon the ship and looked complacently at the pier. It was an old story to him, and he thought it rather silly. He regarded all such moments with the contempt of a man of very strong nature.

When the steamer had passed out of shouting distance a woman spoke to a man who was bowing in a profuse foreign fashion. "Well, he is gone. It was good of you to come this morning. You can't think how he liked the flowers." She was one of those women whose grief had a quality of valor. She did not understand that tears were shameful things to be hidden in houses. Her veil was high upon her forehead. She paid no heed to the tears upon her eyelids.

Further back within the pier a woman sat weeping disconsolately. A group of four children stood around her in an awed and puzzled circle. A little babe kept repeating in a dumb, uncomprehending tone: "Ma-ma ky! ma-ma ky!"

The beautiful woman who had stared imperturbably at the ship walked slowly by. The weeping woman looked up. They exchanged a long, friendly glance. It was the free masonry of two sorrows.

No. 65   MR. BINKS' DAY OFF

WHEN Binks was coming up town in a Broadway cable car one afternoon he caught some superficial glimpses of Madison square as he ducked his head to peek through between a young woman's bonnet and a young man's newspaper. The green of the little park vaguely astonished Binks. He had grown accustomed to a white and brown park; now, all at once, it was radiant green. The grass, the leaves, had come swiftly, silently, as if a great green light from the sky had shone suddenly upon the little desolate hued place.

The vision cheered the mind of Binks. It cried to him that nature was still supreme; he had begun to think the banking business to be the pivot on which the universe turned. Produced by this wealth of young green, faint faraway voices called to him. Certain subtle memories swept over him. The million leaves looked into his soul and said something sweet and pure in an unforgotten song, the melody of his past. Binks began to dream.

When he arrived at the little Harlem flat he sat down to dinner with an air of profound dejection, which Mrs. Binks promptly construed into an insult to her cooking, and to the time and thought she had expended in preparing the meal. She promptly resented it. "Well, what's the matter now?" she demanded. Apparently she had asked this question ten thousand times.

"Nothin'," said Binks, shortly, filled with gloom. He meant by this remark that his ailment was so subtle that her feminine mind would not be enlightened by any explanation.

The head of the family was in an ugly mood. The little Binkses suddenly paused in their uproar and became very wary children. They knew that it would be dangerous to do anything irrelevant to their father's bad temper. They studied his face with their large eyes, filled with childish seriousness and speculation. Meanwhile they ate with the most extraordinary caution. They handled their little forks with such care that there was barely a sound. At each slight movement of their father they looked apprehensively at him, expecting the explosion.

The meal continued amid a somber silence. At last, however, Binks spoke, clearing his throat of the indefinite rage that was in it and looking over at his wife. The little Binkses seemed to inwardly dodge, but he merely said: "I wish I could get away into the country for awhile!"

His wife bristled with that brave anger which agitates a woman when she sees fit to assume that her husband is weak spirited. "If I worked as hard as you do, if I slaved over those old books the way you do, I'd have a vacation once in awhile or I'd tear their old office down." Upon her face was a Roman determination. She was a personification of all manner of courages and rebellions and powers.

Binks felt the falsity of her emotion in a vague way, but at that time he only made a sullen gesture. Later, however, he cried out in a voice of sudden violence: "Look at Tommie's dress! Why the dickens don't you put a bib on that child?"

His wife glared over Tommie's head at her husband, as she leaned around in her chair to tie on the demanded bib. The two looked as hostile as warring redskins. In the wife's eyes there was an intense opposition and defiance, an assertion that she now considered the man she had married to be beneath her in intellect, industry, valor. There was in this glance a jeer at the failures of his life. And Binks, filled with an inexpressible rebellion at what was to him a lack of womanly perception and sympathy in her, replied with a look that called his wife a drag, an uncomprehending thing of vain ambitions, the weight of his existence.

The baby meanwhile began to weep because his mother, in her exasperation, had yanked him and hurt his neck. Her anger, groping for an outlet, had expressed itself in the nervous strength of her fingers. "Keep still, Tommie," she said to him. "I didn't hurt you. You needn't cry the minute anybody touches you!" He made a great struggle and repressed his loud sobs, but the tears continued to fall down his cheeks and his under lip quivered from a baby sense of injury, the anger of an impotent child who seems as he weeps to be planning revenges.

"I don't see why you don't keep that child from eternally crying," said Binks, as a final remark. He then arose and went away to smoke, leaving Mrs. Binks with the children and the dishevelled table.

Later that night, when the children were in bed, Binks said to his wife: "We ought to get away from the city for awhile at least this spring. I can stand it in the summer, but in the spring——" He made a motion with his hand that represented the new things that are born in the heart when spring comes into the eyes.

"It will cost something, Phil," said Mrs. Binks.

"That's true," said Binks. They both began to reflect, contemplating the shackles of their poverty. "And besides, I don't believe I could get off," said Binks after a time.

Nothing more was said of it that night. In fact, it was two or three days afterward that Binks came home and said: "Margaret, you get the children ready on Saturday noon and we'll all go out and spend Sunday with your Aunt Sarah!"

When he came home on Saturday his hat was far back on the back of his head from the speed he was in. Mrs. Binks was putting on her bonnet before the glass, turning about occasionally to admonish the little Binkses, who, in their new clothes, were wandering around, stiffly, and getting into all sorts of small difficulties. They had been ready since 11 o'clock. Mrs. Binks had been obliged to scold them continually, one after the other, and sometimes three at once.

"Hurry up," said Binks, immediately, "ain't got much time. Say, you ain't going to let Jim wear that hat, are you? Where's his best one? Good heavens, look at Margaret's dress! It's soiled already! Tommie, stop that, do you hear? Well, are you ready?"

Indeed, it was not until the Binkses had left the city far behind and were careering into New Jersey that they recovered their balances. Then something of the fresh quality of the country stole over them and cooled their nerves. Horse cars and ferryboats were maddening to Binks when he was obliged to convoy a wife and three children. He appreciated the vast expanses of green, through which ran golden hued roads. The scene accented his leisure and his lack of responsibility.

Near the track a little river jostled over the stones. At times the cool thunder of its roar came faintly to the ear. The Ramapo Hills were in the background, faintly purple, and surmounted with little peaks that shone with the luster of the sun. Binks began to joke heavily with the children. The little Binkses, for their part, asked the most superhuman questions about details of the scenery. Mrs. Binks leaned contentedly back in her seat and seemed to be at rest, which was a most extraordinary thing.

When they got off the train at the little rural station they created considerable interest. Two or three loungers began to view them in a sort of concentrated excitement. They were apparently fascinated by the Binkses and seemed to be indulging in all manner of wild and intense speculation. The agent, as he walked into his station, kept his head turned. Across the dusty street, wide at this place, a group of men upon the porch of a battered grocery store shaded their eyes with their hands. The Binkses felt dimly like a circus and were a trifle bewildered by it. Binks gazed up and down, this way and that; he tried to be unaware of the stare of the citizens. Finally, he approached the loungers, who straightened their forms suddenly and looked very expectant.

"Can you tell me where Miss Pattison lives?"

The loungers arose as one man. "It's th' third house up that road there."

"It's a white house with green shutters!"

"There, that's it—yeh can see it through th' trees!" Binks discerned that his wife's aunt was a well known personage, and also that the coming of the Binkses was an event of vast importance. When he marched off at the head of his flock, he felt like a drum-major. His course was followed by the unwavering, intent eyes of the loungers.

The street was lined with two rows of austere and solemn trees. In one way it was like parading between the plumes on an immense hearse. These trees, lowly sighing in a breath-like wind, oppressed one with a sense of melancholy and dreariness. Back from the road, behind flower beds, controlled by box-wood borders, the houses were asleep in the drowsy air. Between them one could get views of the fields lying in a splendor of gold and green. A monotonous humming song of insects came from the regions of sunshine, and from some hidden barnyard a hen suddenly burst forth in a sustained cackle of alarm. The tranquillity of the scene contained a meaning of peace and virtue that was incredibly monotonous to the warriors from the metropolis. The sense of a city is battle. The Binkses were vaguely irritated and astonished at the placidity of this little town. This life spoke to them of no absorbing nor even interesting thing. There was something unbearable about it. "I should go crazy if I had to live here," said Mrs. Binks. A warrior in the flood-tide of his blood, going from the hot business of war to a place of utter quiet, might have felt that there was an insipidity in peace. And thus felt the Binkses from New York. They had always named the clash of the swords of commerce as sin, crime, but now they began to imagine something admirable in it. It was high wisdom. They put aside their favorite expressions: "The curse of gold," "A mad passion to get rich," "The rush for the spoils." In the light of their contempt for this stillness, the conflicts of the city were exalted. They were at any rate wondrously clever.

But what they did feel was the fragrance of the air, the radiance of the sunshine, the glory of the fields and the hills. With their ears still clogged by the tempest and fury of city uproars, they heard the song of the universal religion, the mighty and mystic hymn of nature, whose melody is in each landscape. It appealed to their elemental selves. It was as if the earth had called recreant and heedless children and the mother word, of vast might and significance, brought them to sudden meekness. It was the universal thing whose power no one escapes. When a man hears it he usually remains silent. He understands then the sacrilege of speech.

When they came to the third house, the white one, with the green blinds, they perceived a woman, in a plaid sun bonnet, walking slowly down a path. Around her was a riot of shrubbery and flowers. From the long and tangled grass of the lawn grew a number of cherry trees. Their dark green foliage was thickly sprinkled with bright red fruit. Some sparrows were scuffling among the branches. The little Binkses began to whoop at sight of the woman in the plaid sun bonnet.

"Hay-oh, Aunt Sarah, hay-oh!" they shouted.

The woman shaded her eyes with her hand. "Well, good gracious, if it ain't Marg'ret Binks! An' Phil, too! Well, I am surprised!"

She came jovially to meet them. "Why, how are yeh all? I'm awful glad t' see yeh!"

The children, filled with great excitement, babbled questions and ejaculations while she greeted the others.

"Say, Aunt Sarah, gimme some cherries!"

"Look at th' man over there!"

"Look at th' flowers!"

"Gimme some flowers, Aunt Sarah!"

And little Tommie, red faced from the value of his information, bawled out: "Aunt Sah-wee, dey have horse tars where I live!" Later he shouted: "We come on a twain of steam tars!"

Aunt Sarah fairly bristled with the most enthusiastic hospitality. She beamed upon them like a sun. She made desperate attempts to gain possession of everybody's bundles that she might carry them to the house. There was a sort of a little fight over the baggage. The children clamored questions at her; she tried heroically to answer them. Tommie, at times, deluged her with news.

The curtains of the dining room were pulled down to keep out the flies. This made a deep, cool gloom in which corners of the old furniture caught wandering rays of light and shone with a mild luster. Everything was arranged with an unspeakable neatness that was the opposite of comfort. A branch of an apple tree moved by the gentle wind, brushed softly against the closed blinds.

"Take off yer things," said Aunt Sarah.

Binks and his wife remained talking to Aunt Sarah, but the children speedily swarmed out over the farm, raiding in countless directions. It was only a matter of seconds before Jimmie discovered the brook behind the barn. Little Margaret roamed among the flowers, bursting into little cries at sight of new blossoms, new glories. Tommie gazed at the cherry trees for a few moments in profound silence. Then he went and procured a pole. It was very heavy, relatively. He could hardly stagger under it, but with infinite toil he dragged it to the proper place and somehow managed to push it erect. Then with a deep earnestness of demeanor he began a little onslaught upon the trees. Very often his blow missed the entire tree and the pole thumped on the ground. This necessitated the most extraordinary labor. But then at other times he would get two or three cherries at one wild swing of his weapon.

Binks and his wife spent the larger part of the afternoon out under the apple trees at the side of the house. Binks lay down on his back, with his head in the long lush grass. Mrs. Binks moved lazily to and fro in a rocking chair that had been brought from the house. Aunt Sarah, sometimes appearing, was strenuous in an account of relatives, and the Binkses had only to listen. They were glad of it, for this warm, sleepy air, pulsating with the sounds of insects, had enchained them in a great indolence.

It was to this place that Jimmie ran after he had fallen into the brook and scrambled out again. Holding his arms out carefully from his dripping person, he was roaring tremendously. His new sailor suit was a sight. Little Margaret came often to describe the wonders of her journeys, and Tommie, after a frightful struggle with the cherry trees, toddled over and went to sleep in the midst of a long explanation of his operations. The breeze stirred the locks on his baby forehead. His breath came in long sighs of content. Presently he turned his head to cuddle deeper into the grass. One arm was thrown in childish abandon over his head. Mrs. Binks stopped rocking to gaze at him. Presently she bended and noiselessly brushed away a spear of grass that was troubling the baby's temple. When she straightened up she saw that Binks, too, was absorbed in a contemplation of Tommie. They looked at each other presently, exchanging a vague smile. Through the silence came the voice of a plowing farmer berating his horses in a distant field.

The peace of the hills and the fields came upon the Binkses.

They allowed Jimmie to sit up in bed and eat cake while his clothes were drying. Uncle Daniel returned from a wagon journey and recited them a ponderous tale of a pig that he had sold to a man with a red beard. They had no difficulty in feeling much interest in the story.

Binks began to expand with enormous appreciations. He would not go into the house until they compelled him. And as soon as the evening meal was finished he dragged his wife forth on a trip to the top of the hill behind the house. There was a great view from there, Uncle Daniel said.

The path, gray with little stones in the dusk, extended above them like a pillar. The pines were beginning to croon in a mournful key, inspired by the evening winds. Mrs. Binks had great difficulty in climbing this upright road. Binks was obliged to assist her, which he did with a considerable care and tenderness. In it there was a sort of a reminiscence of their courtship. It was a repetition of old days. Both enjoyed it because of this fact, although they subtly gave each other to understand that they disdained this emotion as an altogether un-American thing, for she, as a woman, was proud, and he had great esteem for himself as a man.

At the summit they seated themselves upon a fallen tree, near the edge of a cliff. The evening silence was upon the earth below them. Far in the west the sun lay behind masses of corn colored clouds, tumbled and heaved into crags, peaks and canyons. On either hand stood the purple hills in motionless array. The valley lay wreathed in somber shadows. Slowly there went on the mystic process of the closing of the day. The corn colored clouds faded to yellow and finally to a faint luminous green, inexpressibly vague. The rim of the hills was then an edge of crimson. The mountains became a profound blue. From the night, approaching in the east, came a wind. The trees of the mountain raised plaintive voices, bending toward the faded splendors of the day.

This song of the trees arose in low, sighing melody into the still air. It was filled with an infinite sorrow—a sorrow for birth, slavery, death. It was a wail telling the griefs, the pains of all ages. It was the symbol of agonies. It celebrated all suffering.

Each man finds in this sound the expression of his own grief. It is the universal voice raised in lamentations.

As the trees huddled and bended as if to hide from their eyes a certain sight the green tints became blue. A faint suggestion of yellow replaced the crimson. The sun was dead.

The Binkses had been silent. These songs of the trees awe. They had remained motionless during this ceremony, their eyes fixed upon the mighty and indefinable changes which spoke to them of the final thing—the inevitable end. Their eyes had an impersonal expression. They were purified, chastened by this sermon, this voice calling to them from the sky. The hills had spoken and the trees had crooned their song. Binks finally stretched forth his arm in a wondering gesture.

"I wonder why," he said; "I wonder why the dickens it—why it —why——"

Tangled in his tongue was the unformulated question of the centuries, but Mrs. Binks had stolen forth her arm and linked it with his. Her head leaned softly against his shoulder.

No. 66   THE ART STUDENTS' LEAGUE BUILDING

SINCE the Art Students' League moved to the fine new building on West 57th St., there remains nothing but the consolation of historical value for the old structure that extends from No. 143 to No. 147 East 23d St. This building with its commonplace front is as a matter of fact one of the landmarks of American art. The old place once rang with the voices of a crowd of art students who in those days past built their ideals of art-schools upon the most approved Parisian models and it is a fact generally unknown to the public that this staid puritanical old building once contained about all that was real in the Bohemian quality of New York. The exterior belies the interior in a tremendous degree. It is plastered with signs, and wears sedately the air of being what it is not. The interior however is a place of slumberous corridors rambling in puzzling turns and curves. The large studios rear their brown rafters over scenes of lonely quiet. Gradually the tinkers, the tailors, and the plumbers who have captured the ground floor are creeping toward those dim ateliers above them. One by one the besieged artists give up the struggle and the time is not far distant when the conquest of the tinkers, the tailors and the plumbers will be complete.

Nevertheless, as long as it stands, the old building will be to a great many artists of this country a place endeared to them by the memory of many an escapade of the old student days when the boys of the life class used to row gaily with the boys of the "preparatory antique" in the narrow halls. Every one was gay, joyous, and youthful in those blithe days and the very atmosphere of the old place cut the austere and decorous elements out of a man's heart and made him rejoice when he could divide his lunch of sandwiches with the model.

Who does not remember the incomparable "soap slides," of those days when the whole class in the hour of rest slid whooping across the floor one after another. The water and soap with which the brushes were washed used to make fine ice when splashed upon the floor and the hopes of America in art have taken many a wild career upon the slippery stretch. And who does not remember the little man who attempted the voyage when seated in a tin-wash-basin and who came to grief and arose covered with soap and deluged the studio with profanity.

Once when the women's life class bought a new skeleton for the study of anatomy, they held a very swagger function in their class room and christened it "Mr. Jolton Bones" with great pomp and ceremony. Up in the boys' life class the news of the ceremony created great excitement. They were obliged to hold a rival function without delay. And the series of great pageants, ceremonials, celebrations and fetes which followed were replete with vivid color and gorgeous action. The Parisian custom, exhaustively recounted in "Trilby" of requiring each new member of a class to make a spread for his companions was faithfully followed. Usually it consisted of beer, crackers and brie cheese.

After the Art Students' League moved to Fifty-Seventh St., the life classes of the National Academy of Design school moved in for a time and occasionally the old building was alive with its old uproar and its old spirit. After their departure, the corridors settled down to dust and quiet. Infrequently of a night one could pass a studio door and hear the cheerful rattle of half of a dozen tongues, hear a guitar twinkling an accompaniment to a song, see a mass of pipe smoke cloud the air. But this too vanished and now one can only hear the commercial voices of the tinkers, the tailors and the plumbers.

In the top-most and remotest studio there is an old beam which bears this line from Emerson in half-obliterated chalk marks: "Congratulate yourselves if you have done something strange and extravagant and broken the monotony of a decorous age." It is a memory of the old days.

No. 67 THE MEN IN THE STORM

AT about three o'clock of the February afternoon, the blizzard began to swirl great clouds of snow along the streets, sweeping it down from the roofs and up from the pavements until the faces of pedestrians tingled and burned as from a thousand needle-prickings. Those on the walks huddled their necks closely in the collars of their coats and went along stooping like a race of aged people. The drivers of vehicles hurried their horses furiously on their way. They were made more cruel by the exposure of their positions, aloft on high seats. The street cars, bound up-town, went slowly, the horses slipping and straining in the spongy brown mass that lay between the rails. The drivers, muffled to the eyes, stood erect and facing the wind, models of grim philosophy. Overhead the trains rumbled and roared, and the dark structure of the elevated railroad, stretching over the avenue, dripped little streams and drops of water upon the mud and snow beneath it.

All the clatter of the street was softened by the masses that lay upon the cobbles until, even to one who looked from a window, it became important music, a melody of life made necessary to the ear by the dreariness of the pitiless beat and sweep of the storm. Occasionally one could see black figures of men busily shovelling the white drifts from the walks. The sounds from their labor created new recollections of rural experiences which every man manages to have in a measure. Later, the immense windows of the shops became aglow with light, throwing great beams of orange and yellow upon the pavement. They were infinitely cheerful, yet in a way they accented the force and discomfort of the storm, and gave a meaning to the pace of the people and the vehicles, scores of pedestrians and drivers, wretched with cold faces, necks and feet, speeding for scores of unknown doors and entrances, scattering to an infinite variety of shelters, to places which the imagination made warm with the familiar colors of home.

There was an absolute expression of hot dinners in the pace of the people. If one dared to speculate upon the destination of those who came trooping, he lost himself in a maze of social calculations; he might fling a handful of sand and attempt to follow the flight of each particular grain. But as to the suggestion of hot dinners, he was in firm lines of thought, for it was upon every hurrying face. It is a matter of tradition; it is from the tales of childhood. It comes forth with every storm.

However, in a certain part of a dark West-side street, there was a collection of men to whom these things were as if they were not. In this street was located a charitable house where for five cents the homeless of the city could get a bed at night and, in the morning, coffee and bread.

During the afternoon of the storm, the whirling snows acted as drivers, as men with whips, and at half-past three, the walk before the closed doors of the house was covered with wanderers of the street, waiting. For some distance on either side of the place they could be seen lurking in doorways and behind projecting parts of buildings, gathering in close bunches in an effort to get warm. A covered wagon drawn up near the curb sheltered a dozen of them. Under the stairs that led to the elevated railway station, there were six or eight, their hands stuffed deep in their pockets, their shoulders stooped, jiggling their feet. Others always could be seen coming, a strange procession, some slouching along with the characteristic hopeless gait of professional strays, some coming with hesitating steps wearing the air of men to whom this sort of thing was new.

It was an afternoon of incredible length. The snow, blowing in twisting clouds, sought out the men in their meagre hiding-places and skilfully beat in among them, drenching their persons with showers of fine, stinging flakes. They crowded together, muttering, and fumbling in their pockets to get their red, inflamed wrists covered by the cloth.

Newcomers usually halted at one of the groups and addressed a question, perhaps much as a matter of form, "Is it open yet?"

Those who had been waiting inclined to take the questioner seriously and become contemptuous. "No; do yeh think we'd be standin' here?"

The gathering swelled in numbers steadily and persistently. One could always see them coming, trudging slowly through the storm.

Finally, the little snow plains in the street began to assume a leaden hue from the shadows of evening. The buildings up-reared gloomily save where various windows became brilliant figures of light that made shimmers and splashes of yellow on the snow. A street lamp on the curb struggled to illuminate, but it was reduced to impotent blindness by the swift gusts of sleet crusting its panes.

In this half-darkness, the men began to come from their shelter places and mass in front of the doors of charity. They were of all types, but the nationalities were mostly American, German and Irish. Many were strong, healthy, clear-skinned fellows with that stamp of countenance which is not frequently seen upon seekers after charity. There were men of undoubted patience, industry and temperance, who in time of ill-fortune, do not habitually turn to rail at the state of society, snarling at the arrogance of the rich and bemoaning the cowardice of the poor, but who at these times are apt to wear a sudden and singular meekness, as if they saw the world's progress marching from them and were trying to perceive where they had failed, what they had lacked, to be thus vanquished in the race. Then there were others of the shifting, Bowery lodging-house element who were used to paying ten cents for a place to sleep, but who now came here because it was cheaper.

But they were all mixed in one mass so thoroughly that one could not have discerned the different elements but for the fact that the laboring men, for the most part, remained silent and impassive in the blizzard, their eyes fixed on the windows of the house, statues of patience.

The sidewalk soon became completely blocked by the bodies of the men. They pressed close to one another like sheep in a winter's gale, keeping one another warm by the heat of their bodies. The snow came down upon this compressed group of men until, directly from above, it might have appeared like a heap of snow-covered merchandise, if it were not for the fact that the crowd swayed gently with a unanimous, rhythmical motion. It was wonderful to see how the snow lay upon the heads and shoulders of these men, in little ridges an inch thick perhaps in places, the flakes steadily adding drop and drop, precisely as they fall upon the unresisting grass of the fields. The feet of the men were all wet and cold and the wish to warm them accounted for the slow, gentle, rhythmical motion. Occasionally some man whose ears or nose tingled acutely from the cold winds would wriggle down until his head was protected by the shoulders of his companions.

There was a continuous murmuring discussion as to the probability of the doors being speedily opened. They persistently lifted their eyes toward the windows. One could hear little combats of opinion.

"There's a light in th' winder!"

"Naw; it's a reflection f'm across th' way."

"Well, didn't I see 'em lite it?"

"You did?"

"I did!"

"Well, then, that settles it!"

As the time approached when they expected to be allowed to enter, the men crowded to the doors in an unspeakable crush, jamming and wedging in a way that it seemed would crack bones. They surged heavily against the building in a powerful wave of pushing shoulders. Once a rumor flitted among all the tossing heads.

"They can't open th' doors! Th' fellers er smack up ag'in 'em."

Then a dull roar of rage came from the men on the outskirts; but all the time they strained and pushed until it appeared to be impossible for those that they cried out against to do anything but be crushed to pulp.

"Ah, git away f'm th' door!"

"Git outa that!"

"Throw 'em out!"

"Kill 'em!"

"Say, fellers, now, what th' 'ell? Give 'em a chanct t' open th' door!"

"Yeh damned pigs, give 'em a chanct t' open th' door!"

Men in the outskirts of the crowd occasionally yelled when a boot-heel of one of frantic trampling feet crushed on their freezing extremities.

"Git off me feet, yeh clumsy tarrier!"

"Say, don't stand on me feet! Walk on th' ground!"

A man near the doors suddenly shouted: "O-o-oh! Le' me out—le' me out!" And another, a man of infinite valor, once twisted his head so as to half face those who were pushing behind him. "Quit yer shovin', yeh ——" and he delivered a volley of the most powerful and singular invective straight into the faces of the men behind him. It was as if he was hammering the noses of them with curses of triple brass. His face, red with rage, could be seen; upon it, an expression of sublime disregard of consequences. But nobody cared to reply to his imprecations; it was too cold. Many of them snickered and all continued to push.

In occasional pauses of the crowd's movement the men had opportunity to make jokes; usually grim things, and no doubt very uncouth. Nevertheless, they are notable—one does not expect to find the quality of humor in a heap of old clothes under a snowdrift.

The winds seemed to grow fiercer as time wore on. Some of the gusts of snow that came down on the close collection of heads cut like knives and needles, and the men huddled, and swore, not like dark assassins, but in a sort of an American fashion, grimly and desperately, it is true, but yet with a wondrous under-effect, indefinable and mystic, as if there was some kind of humor in this catastrophe, in this situation in a night of snow-laden winds.

Once, the window of the huge dry-goods shop across the street furnished material for a few moments of forgetfulness. In the brilliantly-lighted space appeared the figure of a man. He was rather stout and very well clothed. His whiskers were fashioned charmingly after those of the Prince of Wales. He stood in an attitude of magnificent reflection. He slowly stroked his moustache with a certain grandeur of manner, and looked down at the snow-encrusted mob. From below, there was denoted a supreme complacence in him. It seemed that the sight operated inversely, and enabled him to more clearly regard his own environment, delightful relatively.

One of the mob chanced to turn his head and perceive the figure in the window. "Hello, lookit 'is whiskers," he said genially.

Many of the men turned then, and a shout went up. They called to him in all strange keys. They addressed him in every manner, from familiar and cordial greetings to carefully-worded advice concerning changes in his personal appearance. The man presently fled, and the mob chuckled ferociously like ogres who had just devoured something.

They turned then to serious business. Often they addressed the stolid front of the house.

"Oh, let us in fer Gawd's sake!"

"Let us in or we'll all drop dead!"

"Say, what's th' use o' keepin' all us poor Indians out in th' cold?"

And always some one was saying, "Keep off me feet."

The crushing of the crowd grew terrific toward the last. The men, in keen pain from the blasts, began almost to fight. With the pitiless whirl of snow upon them, the battle for shelter was going to the strong. It became known that the basement door at the foot of a little steep flight of stairs was the one to be opened, and they jostled and heaved in this direction like laboring fiends. One could hear them panting and groaning in their fierce exertion.

Usually some one in the front ranks was protesting to those in the rear: "O—o—ow! Oh, say, now, fellers, let up, will yeh? Do yeh wanta kill somebody?"

A policeman arrived and went into the midst of them, scolding and berating, occasionally threatening, but using no force but that of his hands and shoulders against these men who were only struggling to get in out of the storm. His decisive tones rang out sharply: "Stop that pushin' back there! Come, boys, don't push! Stop that! Here, you, quit yer shovin'! Cheese that!"

When the door below was opened, a thick stream of men forced a way down the stairs, which were of an extraordinary narrowness and seemed only wide enough for one at a time. Yet they somehow went down almost three abreast. It was a difficult and painful operation. The crowd was like a turbulent water forcing itself through one tiny outlet. The men in the rear, excited by the success of the others, made frantic exertions, for it seemed that this large band would more than fill the quarters and that many would be left upon the pavements. It would be disastrous to be of the last, and accordingly men with the snow biting their faces, writhed and twisted with their might. One expected that from the tremendous pressure, the narrow passage to the basement door would be so choked and clogged with human limbs and bodies that movement would be impossible. Once indeed the crowd was forced to stop, and a cry went along that a man had been injured at the foot of the stairs. But presently the slow movement began again, and the policeman fought at the top of the flight to ease the pressure on those who were going down.

A reddish light from a window fell upon the faces of the men when they, in turn, arrived at the last three steps and were about to enter. One could then note a change of expression that had come over their features. As they thus stood upon the threshold of their hopes, they looked suddenly content and complacent. The fire had passed from their eyes and the snarl had vanished from their lips. The very force of the crowd in the rear, which had previously vexed them, was regarded from another point of view, for it now made it inevitable that they should go through the little doors into the place that was cheery and warm with light.

The tossing crowd on the sidewalk grew smaller and smaller. The snow beat with merciless persistence upon the bowed heads of those who waited. The wind drove it up from the pavements in frantic forms of winding white, and it seethed in circles about the huddled forms, passing in, one by one, three by three, out of the storm.

No. 68 CONEY ISLAND'S FAILING DAYS

"DOWN here at your Coney Island, toward the end of the season, I am made to feel very sad," said the stranger to me. "The great mournfulness that settles upon a summer resort at this time always depresses me exceedingly. The mammoth empty buildings, planned by extraordinarily optimistic architects, remind me in an unpleasant manner of my youthful dreams. In those days of visions I erected huge castles for the reception of my friends and admirers, and discovered later that I could have entertained them more comfortably in a small two story frame structure. There is a mighty pathos in these gaunt and hollow buildings, impassively and stolidly suffering from an enormous hunger for the public. And the unchangeable, ever imperturbable sea pursues its quaint devices blithely at the feet of these mournful wooden animals, gabbling and frolicking, with no thought for absent man nor maid!"

As the stranger spoke, he gazed with considerable scorn at the emotions of the sea; and the breeze from the far Navesink hills gently stirred the tangled, philosophic hair upon his forehead. Presently he went on: "The buildings are in effect more sad than the men, but I assure you that some of the men look very sad. I watched a talented and persuasive individual who was operating in front of a tintype gallery, and he had only the most marvelously infrequent opportunities to display his oratory and finesse. The occasional stragglers always managed to free themselves before he could drag them into the gallery and take their pictures. In the long intervals he gazed about him with a bewildered air, as if he felt his world dropping from under his feet. Once I saw him spy a promising youth afar off. He lurked with muscles at a tension, and then at the proper moment he swooped. 'Look-a-here,' he said, with tears of enthusiasm in his eyes, 'the best picture in the world! An' on'y four fer a quarter. On'y jest try it, an' you'll go away perfectly satisfied!'

" 'I'll go away perfectly satisfied without trying it,' replied the promising youth, and he did. The tintype man wanted to dash his samples to the ground and whip the promising youth. He controlled himself, however, and went to watch the approach of two women and a little boy who were nothing more than three dots, away down the board walk.

"At one place I heard the voice of a popcorn man raised in a dreadful note, as if he were chanting a death hymn. It made me shiver as I felt all the tragedy of the collapsed popcorn market. I began to see that it was an insult to the pain and suffering of these men to go near to them without buying anything. I took new and devious routes sometimes.

"As for the railroad guards and station men, they were so tolerant of the presence of passengers that I felt it to be an indication of their sense of relief from the summer's battle. They did not seem so greatly irritated by patrons of the railroad as I have seen them at other times. And in all the beer gardens the waiters had opportunity to indulge that delight in each other's society and conversation which forms so important a part in a waiter's idea of happiness. Sometimes the people in a sparsely occupied place will fare more strange than those in a crowded one. At one time I waited twenty minutes for a bottle of the worst beer in Christendom while my waiter told a charmingly naive story to a group of his compatriots. I protested sotto voce at the time that such beer might at least have the merit of being brought quickly.

"The restaurants, however, I think to be quite delicious, being in a large part thoroughly disreputable and always provided with huge piles of red boiled crabs. These huge piles of provision around on the floor and on the oyster counters always give me the opinion that I am dining on the freshest food in the world, and I appreciate the sensation. If need be, it also allows a man to revel in dreams of unlimited quantity.

"I found countless restaurants where I could get things almost to my taste, and, as I ate, watch the grand, eternal motion of the sea and have the waiter come up and put the pepper castor on the menu card to keep the salt breeze from interfering with my order for dinner.

"And yet I have an occasional objection to the sea when

dining in sight of it; for a man with a really artistic dining sense always feels important as a duke when he is indulging in his favorite pastime, and, as the sea always makes me feel that I am a trivial object, I cannot dine with absolute comfort in its presence. The conflict of the two perceptions disturbs me. This is why I have grown to prefer the restaurants down among the narrow board streets. I tell you this because I think an explanation is due to you."

As we walked away from the beach and around one of those huge buildings whose pathos had so aroused the stranger's interest, we came into view of two acres of merry-go-rounds, circular swings, roller coasters, observation wheels and the like. The stranger paused and regarded them.

"Do you know," he said, "I am deeply fascinated by all these toys. For, of course, you perceive that they are really enlarged toys. They reinforce me in my old opinion that humanity only needs to be provided for ten minutes with a few whirligigs and things of the sort, and it can forget at least four centuries of misery. I rejoice in these whirligigs," continued the stranger, eloquently, "and as I watch here and there a person going around and around or up and down, or over and over, I say to myself that whirligigs must be made in heaven.

"It is a mystery to me why some man does not provide a large number of wooden rocking horses and let the people sit and dreamfully rock themselves into temporary forgetfulness. There could be intense quiet enforced by special policemen, who, however, should allow subdued conversation on the part of the patrons of the establishment. Deaf mutes should patrol to and fro selling slumberous drinks. These things are none of them insane. They are particularly rational. A man needs a little nerve quiver, and he gets it by being flopped around in the air like a tailless kite. He needs the introduction of a reposeful element, and he procures it upon a swing that makes him feel like thirty-five emotional actresses all trying to swoon upon one rug. There are some people who stand apart and deride these machines. If you could procure a dark night for them and the total absence of their friends they would smile, many of them. I assure you that I myself would indulge in these forms of intoxication if I were not a very great philosopher."

We strolled to the music hall district, where the sky lines of the rows of buildings are wondrously near to each other, and the crowded little thoroughfares resemble the eternal "Street Scene in Cairo." There was an endless strumming and tooting and shrill piping in clamor and chaos, while at all times there were interspersed the sharp cracking sounds from the shooting galleries and the coaxing calls of innumerable fakirs. At the stand where one can throw at wooden cats and negro heads and be in danger of winning cigars, a self reliant youth bought a whole armful of base balls, and missed with each one. Everybody grinned. A heavily built man openly jeered. "You couldn't hit a church!" "Couldn't I?" retorted the young man, bitterly. Near them three bad men were engaged in an intense conversation. The fragment of a sentence suddenly dominated the noises. "He's got money to burn." The sun, meanwhile, was muffled in the clouds back of Staten Island and the Narrows. Softened tones of sapphire and carmine touched slantingly the sides of the buildings. A view of the sea, to be caught between two of the houses, showed it to be of a pale, shimmering green. The lamps began to be lighted, and shed a strong orange radiance. In one restaurant the only occupants were a little music hall singer and a youth. She was laughing and chatting in a light hearted way not peculiar to music hall girls. The youth looked as if he desired to be at some other place. He was singularly wretched and uncomfortable. The stranger said he judged from appearances that the little music hall girl must think a great deal of that one youth. His sympathies seemed to be for the music hall girl. Finally there was a sea of salt meadow, with a black train shooting across it.

"I have made a discovery in one of these concert halls," said the stranger, as we retraced our way. "It is an old gray haired woman, who occupies proudly the position of chief pianiste. I like to go and sit and wonder by what mighty process of fighting and drinking she achieved her position. To see her, you would think she was leading an orchestra of seventy pieces, although she alone composes it. It is great reflection to watch that gray head. At those moments I am willing to concede that I must be relatively happy, and that is a great admission from a philosopher of my attainments.

"How seriously all these men out in front of the dens take their vocations. They regard people with a voracious air, as if they contemplated any moment making a rush and a grab and mercilessly compelling a great expenditure. This scant and feeble crowd must madden them. When I first came to this part of the town I was astonished and delighted, for it was the nearest approach to a den of wolves that I had encountered since leaving the West. Oh, no, of course the Coney Island of to-day is not the Coney Island of the ancient days. I believe you were about to impale me upon that sentence, were you not?"

We walked along for some time in silence until the stranger went to buy a frankfurter. As he returned, he said: "When a man is respectable he is fettered to certain wheels, and when the chariot of fashion moves, he is dragged along at the rear. For his agony, he can console himself with the law that if a certain thing has not yet been respectable, he need only wait a sufficient time and it will eventually be so. The only disadvantage is that he is obliged to wait until other people wish to do it, and he is likely to lose his own craving. Now I have a great passion for eating frankfurters on the street, and if I were respectable I would be obliged to wait until the year 3365, when men will be able to hold their positions in society only by consuming immense quantities of frankfurters on the street. And by that time I would have undoubtedly developed some new pastime. But I am not respectable. I am a philosopher. I eat frankfurters on the street with the same equanimity that you might employ toward a cigarette.

"See those three young men enjoying themselves. With what rakish, daredevil airs they smoke those cigars. Do you know, the spectacle of three modern young men enjoying themselves is something that I find vastly interesting and instructive. I see revealed more clearly the purposes of the inexorable universe which plans to amuse us occasionally to keep us from the rebellion of suicide. And I see how simply and drolly it accomplishes its end. The insertion of a mild quantity of the egotism of sin into the minds of these young men causes them to wildly enjoy themselves. It is necessary to encourage them, you see, at this early day. After all, it is only great philosophers who have the wisdom to be utterly miserable."

As we walked toward the station the stranger stopped often to observe types which interested him. He did it with an unconscious calm insolence as if the people were bugs. Once a bug threatened to beat him. "What 'cher lookin' at?" he asked of him. "My friend," said the stranger, "if any one displays real interest in you in this world, you should take it as an occasion for serious study and reflection. You should be supremely amazed to find that a man can be interested in anybody but himself!" The belligerent seemed quite abashed. He explained to a friend: "He ain't right! What? I dunno. Something 'bout 'study' er something! He's got wheels in his head!"

On the train the cold night wind blew transversely across the reeling cars, and in the dim light of the lamps one could see the close rows of heads swaying and jolting with the motion. From directly in front of us peanut shells fell to the floor amid a regular and interminable crackling. A stout man, who slept with his head forward upon his breast, crunched them often beneath his uneasy feet. From some unknown place a drunken voice was raised in song.

"This return of the people to their battles always has a stupendous effect upon me," said the stranger. "The gayety which arises upon these Sunday night occasions is different from all other gayeties. There is an unspeakable air of recklessness and bravado and grief about it. This train load is going toward that inevitable, overhanging, devastating Monday. That singer there to-morrow will be a truckman, perhaps, and swearing ingeniously at his horses and other truckmen. He feels the approach of this implacable Monday. Two hours ago he was engulfed in whirligigs and beer and had forgotten that there were Mondays. Now he is confronting it, and as he can't battle it, he scorns it. You can hear the undercurrent of it in that song, which is really as grievous as the cry of a child. If he had no vanity—well, it is fortunate for the world that we are not all great thinkers."

We sat on the lower deck of the Bay Ridge boat and watched the marvelous lights of New York looming through the purple mist. The little Italian band situated up one stairway, through two doors and around three corners from us, sounded in beautiful, faint and slumberous rhythm. The breeze fluttered again in the stranger's locks. We could hear the splash of the waves against the bow. The sleepy lights looked at us with hue of red and green and orange. Overhead some dust colored clouds scudded across the deep indigo sky. "Thunderation," said the stranger, "if I did not know of so many yesterdays and have such full knowledge of to-morrows, I should be perfectly happy at this moment, and that would create a sensation among philosophers all over the world."

No. 69 IN A PARK ROW RESTAURANT

"WHENEVER I come into a place of this sort I am reminded of the Battle of Gettysburg," remarked the stranger. To make me hear him he had to raise his voice considerably, for we were seated in one of the Park Row restaurants during the noon-hour rush. "I think that if a squadron of Napoleon's dragoons charged into this place they would be trampled under foot before they could get a biscuit. They were great soldiers, no doubt, but they would at once perceive that there were many things about sweep and dash and fire of war of which they were totally ignorant.

"I come in here for the excitement. You know, when I was Sheriff, long ago, of one of the gayest counties of Nevada, I lived a life that was full of thrills, for the citizens could not quite comprehend the uses of a sheriff, and did not like to see him busy himself in other people's affairs continually. One man originated a popular philosophy, in which he asserted that if a man required pastime, it was really better to shoot the sheriff than any other person, for then it would be quite impossible for the sheriff to organize a posse and pursue the assassin. The period which followed the promulgation of this theory gave me habits which I fear I can never outwear. I require fever and exhilaration in life, and when I come in here it carries me back to the old days."

I was obliged to put my head far forward, or I could never have heard the stranger's remarks. Crowds of men were swarming in from streets and invading the comfort of seated men in order that they might hang their hats and overcoats upon the long rows of hooks that lined the sides of the room. The finding of vacant chairs became a serious business. Men dashed to and fro in swift searches. Some of those already seated were eating with terrible speed or else casting impatient or tempestuous glances at the waiters.

Meanwhile the waiters dashed about the room as if a monster pursued them and they sought escape wildly through the walls. It was like the scattering and scampering of a lot of water bugs, when one splashes the surface of the brook with a pebble. Withal, they carried incredible masses of dishes and threaded their swift ways with rare skill. Perspiration stood upon their foreheads, and their breaths came strainedly. They served customers with such speed and violence that it often resembled a personal assault. The crumbs from the previous diner were swept off with one fierce motion of a napkin. A waiter struck two blows at the table and left there a knife and a fork. And then came the viands in a volley, thumped down in haste, causing men to look sharp to see if their trousers were safe.

There was in the air an endless clatter of dishes, loud and bewilderingly rapid, like the gallop of a thousand horses. From afar back, at the places of communication to the kitchen, there came the sound of a continual roaring altercation, hoarse and vehement, like the cries of the officers of a regiment under attack. A mist of steam fluttered where the waiters crowded and jostled about the huge copper coffee urns. Over in one corner a man who toiled there like a foundryman was continually assailed by sharp cries. "Brown th' wheat!" An endless string of men were already filing past the cashier, and, even in these moments, this latter was a marvel of self possession and deftness. As the spring doors clashed to and fro, one heard the interminable thunder of the street, and through the window, partially obscured by displayed vegetables and roasts and pies, could be seen the great avenue, a picture in gray tones, save where a bit of green park gleamed, the foreground occupied by this great typical turmoil of car and cab, truck and mail van, wedging their way through an opposing army of the same kind and surrounded on all sides by the mobs of hurrying people.

"A man might come in here with a very creditable stomach and lose his head and get indigestion," resumed the stranger, thoughtfully. "It is astonishing how fast a man can eat when he tries. This air is surcharged with appetites. I have seen very orderly, slow moving men become possessed with the spirit of this rush, lose control of themselves and all at once begin to dine like madmen. It is impossible not to feel the effect of this impetuous atmosphere.

"When consommé grows popular in these places all breweries will have to begin turning out soups. I am reminded of the introduction of canned soup into my town in the West. When the boys found that they could not get full on it they wanted to lynch the proprietor of the supply store for selling an inferior article, but a drummer who happened to be in town explained to them that it was a temperance drink.

"It is plain that if the waiters here could only be put upon a raised platform and provided with repeating rifles that would shoot corn-muffins, butter cakes, Irish stews or any delicacy of the season, the strain of this strife would be greatly lessened. As long as the waiters were competent marksmen, the meals here would be conducted with great expedition. The only difficulty would be when for instance a waiter made an error and gave an Irish stew to the wrong man. The latter would have considerable difficulty in passing it along to the right one. Of course the system would cause awkward blunders for a time. You can imagine an important gentleman in a white waist-coat getting up to procure the bill-of-fare from an adjacent table and by chance intercepting a hamburger-steak bound for a man down by the door. The man down by the door would refuse to pay for a steak that had never come into his possession.

"In some such manner thousands of people could be accommodated in restaurants that at present during the noon hour can feed only a few hundred. Of course eloquent pickets would have to be stationed in the distance to intercept any unsuspecting gentleman from the West who might consider the gunnery of the waiters in a personal way and resent what would look to them like an assault. I remember that my old friend Jim Wilkinson, the ex-sheriff of Tin Can, Nevada, got very drunk one night and wandered into the business end of the bowling alley there. Of course he thought that they were shooting at him and in reply he killed three of the best bowlers in Tin Can."

No. 69a   NOTEBOOK DRAFT

"WHENEVER I come into a place of this sort I am reminded of the Battle of Gettysburg," said the stranger. We were seated in one of the Park Row restaurants during the noon-hour. "I think if Pickett and his men charged in here they would be trampled under foot before they could get a biscuit. I come in here for the excitement. I feel a thrill and exhilaration during the noon hour in here such as I might have felt if I had stood upon the summit of Little Round Top and over-looked the battle in some safe manner. It is a frightful struggle. I have often wished to induce Detaille to come to this country and get a subject for a melee that would make his frenzied Franco-Prussian battle-scenes look innocent!"

We were obliged to put our heads close together or the stranger's remarks would have never been known. Even as he spoke more men were thronging in from the streets, clapping their hats upon pegs and sitting down with more or less violence. The men already seated were eating with terrible speed or else casting stormy glances after the waiters.

"Hey! Did you forget those chops?"

"Waiter! Here! A napkin, please!"

"Hurry up that pie, will you, old man!"

"Got that mutton-stew yet?"

"Butter-cakes and coffee! Certainly! About ten minutes ago!"

"You needn't mind the pie! I can't wait!"

"Bring me a ham-omelet, a cup of coffee, and some corn muffins! What? Well, send the right waiter here then! I can't wait all day."

Meanwhile the waiters dashed about the room as if something threatened them and they were trying to escape through the walls. They carried incredible masses of dishes and threaded their swift ways with rare skill. And always from afar back, at the communications to the kitchen, came hoarse roars and screams in a long chorus, vehement and excited, like the cries of the officers of a ship in a squall.

"You will perceive," said the stranger, "that if the waiters could only be put upon a raised platform and armed with repeating rifles loaded with corn-muffins, butter cakes, Irish stew or whatever was in particular demand, the public would be saved this dreadful strife each day and as long as the waiters were fairly competent marksmen, each man could cease his worry for the affair would be conducted with great expedition. The only great difficulty would be when for instance a waiter would make an error and give an Irish stew to the wrong man. This latter would have considerable trouble in passing it along to the right one. Everybody, I think, would grow dexterous in catching their meals in these derby hats which you wear so much in the east. Of course, like all innovations, it would cause awkward blunders for a time. You can imagine an important-looking gentleman in a white waist-coat getting up to procure the bill-of-fare from the adjacent table and by chance intercepting a hamburger-steak bound for a man down by the door. You see of course that the man down by the door would refuse to pay for a steak which had never come into his possession and this would entail a certain loss to the house. And then undoubtedly there would develop a certain class of unscrupulous persons, clever at catching liners right off the bat so to speak, who would stand up in the front rank and appropriate a good many orders that were meant for quiet citizens in the rear. But after a time the laws would arise that always come to control these new inventions and the system would settle into something neat and swift. At these places where butter cakes are at a premium, batteries of rapid-fire ordnance could be erected to command every inch of floor-space and at a given signal, a destructive fire could sweep the entire establishment. I estimate that forty-two thousand people could be fed by this method in establishments which can now accommodate but from one to three hundred during the noon rush. Of course eloquent pickets would have to be stationed in the distance to intercept any unsuspecting gentlemen from the west who might resent what would look to them like an assault and retort with western fervor. I remember that my old friend Jim Wilkinson, the sheriff of Tin Can, Nevada, got drunk one night and strolled into the business end of the bowling alley there. Of course he thought they were shooting at him and in reply he killed three of the best bowlers in Tin Can!"

No. 70   HEARD ON THE STREET ELECTION NIGHT

"Hully chee! Everything's dumped!"

———

"S'cuse me, g'l'men, fer bein' s'noisy, but, fact is, I'm Republican! What? Yessir! Morton by seventy-fi' thousan'. Yessir! I'm goin' holler thish time 'til I bust m' throat—tha's what I am."

———

"Can you tell me, please, if the returns indicate that Goff has a chance?"

"Who? Goff? Well, I guess! He's running like a race-horse. He's dead in it."

———

"That's all right. Wait 'til later. Then, you'll see. Morton never had a show. Hill will swamp him."

———

"Oh, hurry up with your old slide. Put on another. Good thing—push it along. Ah, there we are. 'Morton's-plurality-over-Hill-is-estimated-at-40,135.' Say, look at that, would you? Don't talk to me about the unterrified Democracy. The unterrified Democracy can be dog goned. There's more run than fight in them this trip. Hey, hurry up, Willie, give us another one. It's a good thing, but push it along."

———

"Say, that magic lantern man is a big fakir. Lookatim pushin' ads in on us. Hey, take that out, will yeh? You ain't no billposter, are yeh?"

———

"Strong has got a cinch. He wins in a walk. Ah there, Hughie, ah there."

———

"Well, I guess nit. If Hill wins this time, he's got to have ice-boats on his feet. He ain't got a little chance."

———

"Down in Fourteenth street,
"Hear that mournful sound;
"All the Indians are a-weeping,
"Davie's in the cold, cold ground."

———

"If Tammany wins this time, we might as well all quit the

town and go to Camden. If we don't beat 'em now, we're a lot of duffers and we're only fit to stuff mattresses with."

———

"Say, hear 'em yell 'Goff.' Popular? I guess yes."

———

"He won't, hey? You just wait, me boy. If Hill can't carry this State at any time in any year, I'll make you a present of the Brooklyn bridge, and paint it a deep purple with gold stripes, all by myself."

———

"Goff! Goff! John-W-Goff!
"Goff! Goff! John-W-Goff!"

———

"Voorhis and Taintor! They're the only two. The rest——"

———

"Well, this is what comes from monkeyin' with the people. You think you've got 'em all under a board when, first thing you know, they come out and belt you in the neck."

———

"Oh, everything's conceded. Yes, they admit the whole thing. They didn't get a taste. It's a walk-over."

———

"Hully chee!
"Who are we?
"The men who did up Tammanee!"

———

"I've only seen two Tammany Democrats to-night. There's another. That makes three."

———

"Oh, my, what a surprise! Little David Bennett Hill is now going down the backstairs in his stocking-feet."

———

"Who said Tammany couldn't be thrown down? Grady did. Ah there, Grady."

———

"There never was a minute
"Little Goffie wasn't in it."

———

"I'd like to see Dickie Croker now and ask him how he knew when to get in out of the wet. I tell you what it is—there's no use saying anything about Dickie's eyesight."

———

"Don't be too sure, sonny. I tell you, Dave Hill is a foxey man, and you better wait until it's a dead sure thing before you holler. I've seen a good deal of this sort of thing. In 1884——"

———

"Strong's got a regular pie."

———

"Ta-ra-ra-ra-boom-de-aye,
"Hughie Grant has had his day,
"Safely now at home he'll stay,
"Ta-ra-ra-boom-de-aye."

———

"Now, I'll tell you just one thing—if this don't prove to politicians that a man has got to be always on the level if he wants to hold his snap. Why, they're about as thick-headed a gang as there is on the face of the earth. The man who is always on the level is the man who gets there in the end. If you ain't on the level, you get a swift, hard throw-down sooner or later—dead sure."

———

"Hurray for Goff!"

———

" 'Eternal vigilance is the price of liberty.' That's what it is. The people lost their liberty because they went to sleep. Then all of a sudden they wake up and slug around and surprise all of the men who thought they were in a trance. They ought to have done it long ago. And now they are awake, they don't want to do a thing but sit up night and day and lay for robbers. This waking up every ten or twelve years gives me a pain."

———

"There never was a doubt of it. No, sir. It was playing a sure thing from start to finish. I tell you, when the avalanche starts, you want to climb a hill near by and put all your money on the avalanche."

———

"I'm a Tammany Hall man, but I put my vote on John W. Goff. I did. What? Hill. Well, any man would tumble if a brick steeple fell on him."

———

"Parkhurst was his Jonah."

———

"Who's all right? Strong! Hurrah for Strong!"

———

"Say, lookut d' blokie flashin' er patent-medicine ad on d' canvas. He's a Dimmycrat. Who won't be 'lected? Goff? I bet'che he will. Soitenly! Say, Jimmie, gimme change fer a nick! Ah, I bet'che Goff'll leave 'm at d' post. Say, who 'er yez fer, anyhow? Ah, he'll git it in d' troat. Goff'll smother 'im."

———

"By colly, I bed you Morton is elected by a hundret thousand votes. Suah! I am a Republican effery leetle minnet. I am so excited my hand shake."

———

"Oh, what a cinch they thought they had. Say, those fellers thought they had New York locked in a box. And they got left, didn't they?"

———

"Good-bye, Hughie! Good-bye, Hughie!
"Good-bye, Hughie, you'll have to leave us now."

———

"Well, they monkeyed with the band wagon and they got slumped. Good job. Very surprising way the American people have of throttling a man just when he thinks he's got 'em dead under his thumb."

———

"It was easy, after all, wasn't it? Truth is, New York has been held down by a great big, wire-edged bluff. Tammany said she couldn't be beaten, and everybody believed it."

———

"What? Git out! Entire Republican ticket, city and State? Well, for the love of Mike! Holy smoke, ain't we in it!"

———

"Is they any Democrats left?"

———

"Where's all the Tammany men?"

———

"Somebody tell Hill where he's at."

———

"Tammany's in the soup."

———

"Oh, what a roast!"

"Hully chee! Everyt'ings dumped!"

No. 70a NOTEBOOK DRAFT

"Huly gee! Everyting's dumped!"

"S'cuse me, gen'l'm'n fer-bein' so noisy but I'm Republican! See? I'm Republican! What? Yessir! Morton by seventy-fi' thousan', Yessir!

Can you tell me, please, do the returns indicate whether Goff has a chance?

"Who? Goff? Well I guess! He's running away ahead everywhere. He's dead in it!"

Not by a blame sight he didn't!

"Oh, hurry up your old slide! Put on another! Good thing—push it along! Ah, there we are! 'Morton's plurality over Hill is estimated at 40135.' Say, look at that, would you? Don't talk to me about the unterrified Democracy. There's more run than fight in that crowd, you bet. Hey, hurry up, Willie, give us another one. It's a good thing but push it along!"

Say, Strong has got a cinch! He wins in a walk! Ah, there, Hughey, ah there!"

"Well, I guess nit! If Hill wins this time, he's got to have ice-boats on his feet. He ain't got a little chance.

"If Tammany wins this time we might as well all quit the town and go live in Jersey. If we don't beat 'em now, we're a lot duffers and we ought to be used to stuff mattresses with!"

> Down in Fourteenth Street
> Hear that mournful sound
> All the Indians are a-weeping
> Davie's in the cold, cold ground

"Say, hear 'em yell for Goff! Popular? Well I should say!

Oh, what a roast——

Hully chee!
Who are we?
The men who did up Tammanee

He won't, hay? You just wait, me boy. If Hill can't carry this state at any time in any year, I'll make you a present of the Brooklyn bridge and paint it a deep purple with gold stripes all by myself."

I've only see two Democrats tonight. There's another one. That makes three!

I'd like to see Dickie Croker now and ask him how he knew when to get in out of the wet! I'll tell you what it is—there's no use saying anything about Dickie's eye-sight."

"Oh, my, what a surprise! Little David Bennett Hill is now looking at himself with opera-glasses to see if

Well, this is what comes from monkeying with the people.
"There never was a minute."
"Little Goffie wasn't in it!"

Now I'll tell you just one thing—if this don't prove to politicians that you got to be always on the level, why, they're about as thick-headed a gang as there is on the face of the earth.

"Voorhis and Taintor! They're the only two! The rest——"

Who said Tammany couldn't be thrown down?
Grady did!
Ah there, Grady!

No. 71   THE FIRE

WE WERE walking on one of the shadowy side streets, west of Sixth avenue. The midnight silence and darkness was upon it save where at the point of intersection with the great avenue, there was a broad span of yellow light. From there came the steady monotonous jingle of streetcar bells and the weary clatter of hoofs on the cobbles. While the houses in this street turned black and mystically silent with the night, the avenue continued its eternal movement and life, a great vein that never slept nor paused. The gorgeous orange-hued lamps of a saloon flared plainly, and the figures of some loungers could be seen as they stood on the corner. Passing to and fro, the tiny black figures of people made an ornamental border on this fabric of yellow light.

The stranger was imparting to me some grim midnight reflections upon existence, and in the heavy shadows and in the great stillness pierced only by the dull thunder of the avenue, they were very impressive.

Suddenly the muffled cry of a woman came from one of those dark, impassive houses near us. There was the sound of the splinter and crash of broken glass, falling to the pavement. "What's that," gasped the stranger. The scream contained that ominous quality, that weird timbre which denotes fear of imminent death.

A policeman, huge and panting, ran past us with glitter of buttons and shield in the darkness. He flung himself upon the fire-alarm box at the corner where the lamp shed a flicker of carmine tints upon the pavement. "Come on," shouted the stranger. He dragged me excitedly down the street. We came upon an old four story structure, with a long sign of a bakery over the basement windows, and the region about the quaint front door plastered with other signs. It was one of those ancient dwellings which the churning process of the city had changed into a hive of little industries.

At this time some dull grey smoke, faintly luminous in the night, writhed out from the tops of the second story windows, and from the basement there glared a deep and terrible hue of red, the color of satanic wrath, the color of murder. "Look! Look!" shouted the stranger.

It was extraordinary how the street awakened. It seemed but an instant before the pavements were studded with people. They swarmed from all directions, and from the dark mass arose countless exclamations, eager and swift.

"Where is it? Where is it?"

"No. 135."

"It's that old bakery."

"Is everybody out?"

"Look—gee—say, lookut 'er burn, would yeh?"

The windows of almost every house became crowded with people, clothed and partially clothed, many having rushed from their beds. Here were many women, and as their eyes fastened upon that terrible growing mass of red light one could hear their little cries, quavering with fear and dread. The smoke oozed in greater clouds from the spaces between the sashes of the windows, and urged by the fervor of the heat within, ascended in more rapid streaks and curves.

Upon the sidewalk there had been a woman who was fumbling mechanically with the buttons at the neck of her dress. Her features were lined in anguish; she seemed to be frantically searching her memory—her memory, that poor feeble contrivance that had deserted her at the first of the crisis, at the momentous time. She really struggled and tore hideously at some frightful mental wall that upreared between her and her senses, her very instincts. The policeman, running back from the fire-alarm box, grabbed her, intending to haul her away from danger of falling things. Then something came to her like a bolt from the sky. The creature turned all grey, like an ape. A loud shriek rang out that made the spectators bend their bodies, twisting as if they were receiving sword thrusts.

"My baby! My baby! My baby!"

The policeman simply turned and plunged into the house. As the woman tossed her arms in maniacal gestures about her head, it could then be seen that she waved in one hand a little bamboo easel, of the kind which people sometimes place in corners of their parlors. It appeared that she had with great difficulty saved it from the flames. Its cost should have been about 30 cents.

A long groaning sigh came from the crowd in the street, and from all the thronged windows. It was full of distress and pity, and a sort of cynical scorn for their impotency. Occasionally the woman screamed again. Another policeman was fending her off from the house, which she wished to enter in the frenzy of her motherhood, regardless of the flames. These people of the neighborhood, aroused from their beds, looked at the spectacle in a half-dazed fashion at times, as if they were contemplating the ravings of a red beast in a cage. The flames grew as if fanned by tempests, a sweeping, inexorable appetite of a thing, shining, with fierce, pitiless brilliancy, gleaming in the eyes of the crowd that were upturned to it in an ecstasy of awe, fear and, too, half barbaric admiration. They felt the human helplessness that comes when nature breaks forth in passion, overturning the obstacles, emerging at a leap from the position of a slave to that of a master, a giant. There became audible a humming noise, the buzzing of curious machinery. It was the voices of the demons of the flame. The house, in manifest heroic indifference to the fury that raged in its entrails, maintained a stolid and imperturbable exterior, looming black and immovable against the turmoil of crimson.

Eager questions were flying to and fro in the street.

"Say, did a copper go in there?"

"Yeh! He come out again, though."

"He did not! He's in there yet!"

"Well, didn't I see 'im?"

"How long ago was the alarm sent in?"

"'Bout a minute."

A woman leaned perilously from a window of a nearby apartment house and spoke querulously into the shadowy, jostling crowd beneath her, "Jack!"

And the voice of an unknown man in an unknown place answered her gruffly and short in the tones of a certain kind of downtrodden husband who rebels upon occasion, "What?"

"Will you come up here," cried the woman, shrilly irritable. "Supposin' this house should get afire——" It came to pass that during the progress of the conflagration these two held a terse and bitter domestic combat, infinitely commonplace in language and mental maneuvers.

The blaze had increased with a frightful vehemence and swiftness. Unconsciously, at times, the crowd dully moaned, their eyes fascinated by this exhibition of the strength of nature, their master after all, that ate them and their devices at will whenever it chose to fling down their little restrictions. The flames changed in color from crimson to lurid orange as glass was shattered by the heat, and fell crackling to the pavement. The baker, whose shop had been in the basement, was running about, weeping. A policeman had fought interminably to keep the crowd away from the front of the structure.

"Thunderation!" yelled the stranger, clutching my arm in a frenzy of excitement, "did you ever see anything burn so? Why, it's like an explosion. It's only been a matter of seconds since it started."

In the street, men had already begun to turn toward each other in that indefinite regret and sorrow, as if they were not quite sure of the reason of their mourning.

"Well, she's a goner!"

"Sure—went up like a box of matches!"

"Great Scott, lookut 'er burn!"

Some individual among them furnished the inevitable grumble. "Well, these——" It was a half-coherent growling at conditions, men, fate, law.

Then, from the direction of the avenue there suddenly came a tempestuous roar, a clattering, rolling rush and thunder, as from the headlong sweep of a battery of artillery. Wild and shrill, like a clangorous noise of war, arose the voice of a gong.

One could see a sort of a delirium of excitement, of ardorous affection, go in a wave of emotion over this New York crowd, usually so stoical. Men looked at each other. "Quick work, eh?" They crushed back upon the pavements, leaving the street almost clear. All eyes were turned toward the corner, where the lights of the avenue glowed.

The roar grew and grew until it was as the sound of an army, charging. That policeman's hurried fingers sending the alarm from the box at the corner had aroused a tornado, a storm of horses, machinery, men. And now they were coming in clamor and riot of hoofs and wheels, while over all rang the piercing cry of the gong, tocsin-like, a noise of barbaric fights.

It thrilled the blood, this thunder. The stranger jerked his shoulders nervously and kept up a swift muttering. "Hear 'em come!" he said, breathlessly.

Then in an instant a fire patrol wagon, as if apparitional,

flashed into view at the corner. The lights of the avenue gleamed for an instant upon the red and brass of the wagon, the helmets of the crew and the glossy sides of the galloping horses. Then it swung into the dark street and thundered down upon its journey, with but a half-view of a driver making his reins to be steel ribbons over the backs of his horses, mad from the fervor of their business.

The stranger's hand tightened convulsively upon my arm. His enthusiasm was like the ardor of one who looks upon the pageantry of battles. "Ah, look at 'em! Look at 'em! Ain't that great? Why it hasn't been any time at all since the alarm was sent in, and now look!" As this clanging, rolling thing, drawn swiftly by the beautiful might of the horses, clamored through the street, one could feel the cheers, wild and valorous, at the very lips of these people habitually so calm, cynical, impassive. The crew tumbled from their wagon and ran toward the house. A hoarse shout arose high above the medley of noises.

Other roars, other clangings, were to be heard from all directions. It was extraordinary, the loud rumblings of wheels and the pealings of gongs aroused by a movement of the policeman's fingers.

Of a sudden, three white horses dashed down the street with their engine, a magnificent thing of silver-like glitter, that sent a storm of red sparks high into the air and smote the heart with the wail of its whistle.

A hosecart swept around the corner and into the narrow lane, whose close walls made the reverberations like the crash of infantry volleys. There was shine of lanterns, of helmets, of rubber coats, of the bright, strong trappings of the horses. The driver had been confronted by a dreadful little problem in street cars and elevated railway pillars just as he was about to turn into the street, but there had been no pause, no hesitation. A clever dodge, a shrill grinding of the wheels in the street-car tracks, a miss of this and an escape of that by a beautifully narrow margin, and the hosecart went on its headlong way. When the gleam-white and gold of the cart stopped in the shadowy street, it was but a moment before a stream of water, of a cold steel color, was plunging through a window into the yellow glare, into this house which was now a den of fire wolves, lashing, carousing, leaping, straining. A wet snake-like hose trailed underfoot to where the steamer was making the air pulsate with its swift vibrations.

From another direction had come another thunder that developed into a crash of sounds, as a hook-and-ladder truck, with long and graceful curves, spun around the other corner, with the horses running with steady leaps toward the place of the battle. It was always obvious that these men who drove were drivers in blood and fibre, charioteers incarnate.

When the ladders were placed against the side of the house, firemen went slowly up them, dragging their hose. They became outlined like black beetles against the red and yellow expanses of flames. A vast cloud of smoke, sprinkled thickly with sparks, went coiling heavily toward the black sky. Touched by the shine of the blaze, the smoke sometimes glowed dull red, the color of bricks. A crowd that, it seemed, had sprung from the cobbles, born at the sound of the wheels rushing through the night, thickly thronged the walks, pushed here and there by the policemen who scolded them roundly, evidently in an eternal state of injured surprise at their persistent desire to get a view of things.

As we walked to the corner we looked back and watched the red glimmer from the fire shine on the dark surging crowd over which towered at times the helmets of police. A billow of smoke swept away from the structure. Occasionally, burned out sparks, like fragments of dark tissue, fluttered in the air. At the corner a steamer was throbbing, churning, shaking in its power as if overcome with rage. A fireman was walking tranquilly about it scrutinizing the mechanism. He wore a blasé air. They all, in fact, seemed to look at fires with the calm, unexcited vision of veterans. It was only the populace with their new nerves, it seemed, who could feel the thrill and dash of these attacks, these furious charges made in the dead of night, at high noon, at any time, upon the common enemy, the loosened flame.

No. 72   WHEN MAN FALLS, A CROWD GATHERS

A MAN and a boy were trudging slowly along an East-Side street. It was nearly six o'clock in the evening and this street, which led to one of the East River ferries, was crowded with laborers, shop men and shop women, hurrying to their dinners. The store windows were a-glare.

The man and the boy conversed in Italian, mumbling the soft syllables and making little quick egotistical gestures. They walked with the lumbering peasant's gait, slowly, and blinking their black eyes at the passing show of the street.

Suddenly the man wavered on his limbs and glared bewildered and helpless as if some blinding light had flashed before his vision; then he swayed like a drunken man and fell. The boy grasped his companion's arm frantically and made an attempt to support him so that the limp form slid to the sidewalk with an easy motion as a body sinks in the sea. The boy screamed.

Instantly, from all directions people turned their gaze upon the prone figure. In a moment there was a dodging, pushing, peering group about the man. A volley of questions, replies, speculations flew to and fro above all the bobbing heads.

"What's th' matter? What's th' matter?"

"Oh, a jag, I guess!"

"Nit; he's got a fit!"

"What's th' matter? What's th' matter?"

Two streams of people coming from different directions met at this point to form a crowd. Others came from across the street.

Down under their feet, almost lost under this throng, lay the man, hidden in the shadows caused by their forms which in fact barely allowed a particle of light to pass between them. Those in the foremost rank bended down, shouldering each other, eager, anxious to see everything. Others behind them crowded savagely for a place like starving men fighting for bread. Always, the question could be heard flying in the air. "What's the matter?" Some, near to the body and perhaps feeling the danger of being forced over upon it, twisted their heads and protested violently to those unheeding ones who were scuffling in the rear. "Say, quit yer shovin', can't yeh? What d' yeh want, anyhow? Quit!"

A man back in the crowd suddenly said: "Say, young feller, you're a peach wid dose feet o' yours. Keep off me!"

Another voice said: "Well, dat's all right——"

The boy who had been walking with the man who fell was standing helplessly, a terrified look in his eyes. He held the man's hand. Sometimes he gave it a little jerk that was at once an appeal, a reproach, a caution. And, withal, it was a timid calling to the limp and passive figure as if he half expected to arouse it from its coma with a pleading touch of his fingers. Occasionally, he looked about him with swift glances of indefinite hope, as if assistance might come from the clouds. The men near him questioned him, but he did not seem to understand. He answered them "Yes" or "No," blindly, with no apparent comprehension of their language. They frequently jostled him until he was obliged to put his hand upon the breast of the body to maintain his balance.

Those that were nearest to the man upon the side-walk at first saw his body go through a singular contortion. It was as if an invisible hand had reached up from the earth and had seized him by the hair. He seemed dragged slowly, relentlessly backward, while his body stiffened convulsively, his hands clenched, and his arms swung rigidly upward. A slight froth was upon his chin. Through his pallid half-closed lids could be seen the steel-colored gleam of his eyes that were turned toward all the bending, swaying faces and in the inanimate thing upon the pave yet burned threateningly, dangerously, shining with a mystic light, as a corpse might glare at those live ones who seemed about to trample it under foot.

As for the men near, they hung back, appearing as if they expected it to spring erect and clutch at them. Their eyes however were held in a spell of fascination. They seemed scarcely to breathe. They were contemplating a depth into which a human being had sunk and the marvel of this mystery of life or death held them chained. Occasionally from the rear, a man came thrusting his way impetuously, satisfied that there was a horror to be seen and apparently insane to get a view of it. Less curious persons swore at these men when they trod upon their toes.

The loaded street-cars jingled past this scene in endless parade. Occasionally, from where the elevated railroad crossed the street there came a rhythmical roar, suddenly begun and suddenly ended. Over the heads of the crowd hung an immovable canvas sign. "Regular dinner twenty cents."

After the first spasm of curiosity had passed away, there were those in the crowd who began to consider ways to help. A voice called: "Rub his wrists." The boy and some one on the other side of the man began to rub his wrists and slap his palms, but still the body lay inert, rigid. When a hand was dropped the arm fell like a stick. A tall German suddenly appeared and resolutely began to push the crowd back. "Get back there—get back," he continually repeated as he pushed them. He had psychological authority over this throng; they obeyed him. He and another knelt by the man in the darkness and loosened his shirt at the throat. Once they struck a match and held it close to the man's face. This livid visage suddenly appearing under their feet in the light of the match's yellow glare, made the throng shudder. Half articulate exclamations could be heard. There were men who nearly created a battle in the madness of their desire to see the thing.

Meanwhile others with magnificent passions for abstract statistical information were questioning the boy. "What's his name?" "Where does he live?"

Then a policeman appeared. The first part of the little play had gone on without his assistance but now he came swiftly, his helmet towering above the multitude of black derbys and shading that confident, self-reliant police face. He charged the crowd as if he were a squadron of Irish lancers. The people fairly withered before this onslaught. He shouted: "Come, make way there! Make way!" He was evidently a man whose life was half-pestered out of him by the inhabitants of the city who were sufficiently unreasonable and stupid as to insist on being in the streets. His was the rage of a placid cow, who wishes to lead a life of tranquillity, but who is eternally besieged by flies that hover in clouds.

When he arrived at the centre of the crowd he first demanded threateningly: "Well, what's th' matter here?" And then when he saw that human bit of wreckage at the bottom of the sea of men he said to it: "Come, git up outa that! Git outa here!"

Whereupon hands were raised in the crowd and a volley of decorated information was blazed at the officer.

"Ah, he's got a fit! Can't yeh see!"

"He's got a fit!"

"He's sick!"

"What th' ell yeh doin'? Leave 'm be!"

The policeman menaced with a glance the crowd from whose safe interior the defiant voices had emerged.

A doctor had come. He and the policeman bended down at the man's side. Occasionally the officer upreared to create room. The crowd fell away before his threats, his admonitions, his sarcastic questions and before the sweep of those two huge buckskin gloves.

At last, the peering ones saw the man on the side-walk begin to breathe heavily, with the strain of overtaxed machinery, as if he had just come to the surface from some deep water. He uttered a low cry in his foreign tongue. It was a babyish squeal or like the sad wail of a little storm-tossed kitten. As this cry went forth to all those eager ears the jostling and crowding recommenced until the doctor was obliged to yell warningly a dozen times. The policeman had gone to send an ambulance call.

When a man struck another match and in its meagre light the doctor felt the skull of the prostrate one to discover if any wound or fracture had been caused by his fall to the stone side-walk, the crowd pressed and crushed again. It was as if they fully anticipated a sight of blood in the gleam of the match and they scrambled and dodged for positions. The policeman returned and fought with them. The doctor looked up frequently to scold at them and to sharply demand more space.

At last out of the golden haze made by the lamps far up the street, there came the sound of a gong beaten rapidly, impatiently. A monstrous truck loaded to the sky with barrels scurried to one side with marvelous agility. And then the black ambulance with its red light, its galloping horse, its dull gleam of lettering and bright shine of gong clattered into view. A young man, as imperturbable always as if he were going to a picnic, sat thoughtfully upon the rear seat.

When they picked up the limp body, from which came little moans and howls, the crowd almost turned into a mob, a silent mob, each member of which struggled for one thing. Afterward some resumed their ways with an air of relief, as if they themselves had been in pain and were at last recovered. Others still continued to stare at the ambulance on its banging, clanging return journey until it vanished into the golden haze. It was as if they had been cheated. Their eyes expressed discontent at this curtain which had been rung down in the midst of the drama. And this impenetrable fabric suddenly intervening between a suffering creature and their curiosity, seemed to appear to them as an injustice.

No. 72a NOTEBOOK DRAFT

A MAN and a boy were trudging slowly along an east-side street. It was nearly six o'clock in the evening and this street, which led to one of the East River ferries was crowded with laborers, shop-men and shop women, hurrying to their dinners, made more eager by the recollections of their toil and by the shop-windows, glaring with light, suggesting those [page ends here]

The man and the boy conversed in Italian, mumbling the soft syllables and making little quick egotistical gestures. Suddenly, the man glared, and wavered on his limbs for a moment as if some blinding light had flashed before his vision; then he swayed like a drunken man and fell. The boy grasped his arm convulsively and made an attempt to support his companion so that the body slid to the side-walk with an easy motion like a corpse sinking in the sea. The boy screamed.

Instantly, in all directions people turned their gaze upon that figure prone upon the side-walk. In a moment there was a dodging, peering, pushing crowd about the man. A volley of questions, replies, speculations flew to and fro among all the bobbing heads.

"What's th' matter? What's th' matter?"

"Oh, a jag, I guess!"

"Aw, he's got a fit!"

"What's th' matter! What's th' matter?"

Two streams of people coming from different directions met at this point to form a great crowd. Others came from across the street.

Down under their feet, almost lost under this mass of people, lay the man, hidden in the shadows caused by their forms which in fact barely allowed a particle of light to pass between them. Those in foremost rank bended down eagerly anxious to see everything. Others behind them crowded savagely like starving men fighting for bread. Always, the question could be heard flying in the air. "What's th' matter?" Some, near to the body and perhaps feeling the danger of being forced over upon it, twisted their heads and protested violently to those unheeding ones who were scuffling in the rear. "Say, quit yer shovin', can't yeh? What do yeh want, anyhow? Quit!"

Somebody back in the throng suddenly said: "Say, young feller, cheese dat pushin'! I ain't no peach!"

Another voice said: "Well, dat's all right——"

The boy who had been with the Italian, was standing helplessly, a frightened look in his eyes and holding the man's hand. Sometimes, he looked about him dumbly, with indefinite hope, as if he expected sudden assistance to come from the clouds. The men about him frequently jostled him until he was obliged to put his hand upon the breast of the body to maintain his balance. Those nearest the man upon the side-walk at first saw his body go through a singular contortion. It was as if an invisible hand had reached up from the earth and had seized him by the hair. He seemed dragged slowly pitilessly backward, while his body stiffened convulsively, his hands clenched and his arms swung rigidly upward. Through his pallid half-closed lids one could see the steel-colored, assassin-like gleam of his eye that shone with a mystic light as a corpse might glare at those live ones who seemed about to trample it under foot.

As for the men near, they hung back, appearing as if they expected it might spring erect and grab them. Their eyes however were held in a spell of fascination. They scarce seemed to breathe. They were contemplating a depth into which a human being had sunk and the marvel of this mystery of life or death held them chained. Occasionally from the rear, a man came thrusting his way impetuously, satisfied that there was a horror to be seen and apparently insane to get a view of it. More self-contained men swore at these persons when they trod upon their toes.

The street-cars jingled past this scene in endless parade. Occasionally, down where the elevated road crossed the street one could hear sometimes a thunder, suddenly begun and suddenly ended. Over the heads of the crowd hung an immovable canvas sign. "Regular dinner, twenty cents."

The body on the pave seemed like a bit of debris sunk in this human ocean.

But after the first spasm of curiosity had passed away, there were those in the crowd who began to bethink themselves of some way to help. A voice called out: "Rub his wrists." The boy and a man on the other side of the body began to rub the wrists and slap the palms of the man. A tall German suddenly appeared and resolutely began to push the crowd back. "Get back there—get back," he repeated continually while he pushed at them. He seemed to have authority; the crowd obeyed him. He and another man knelt down by the man in the darkness and loosened his shirt at the throat. Once they struck a match and held it close to the man's face. This livid visage suddenly appearing under their feet in the light of the match's yellow glare, made the crowd shudder. Half articulate exclamations could be heard. There were men who nearly created a riot in the madness of their desire to see the thing.

Meanwhile others had been questioning the boy. "What's his name? Where does he live?"

Then a policeman appeared. The first part of the little drama had gone on without his assistance but now he came, striding swiftly, his helmet towering over the crowd and shading that impenetrable police face. He charged the crowd as if he were a squadron of Irish lancers. The people fairly withered before this onslaught. Occasionally he shouted: "Come, make way there. Come now!" He was evidently a man whose life was half-pestered out of him by people who were sufficiently unreasonable and stupid as to insist on walking in the streets. He felt the rage toward them that a placid cow feels toward the flies that hover in clouds and disturb her repose. When he arrived at the centre of the crowd he first said threateningly: "What's th' matter here." And then when he saw that human bit of wreckage at the bottom of the sea of men he said to it: "Come, git up outa that! Git outa here!"

Whereupon hands were raised in the crowd and a volley of decorated information was blazed at the officer.

"Ah, he's got a fit! Can't yeh see!"

"He's got a fit!"

"What th'ell yeh doin'? Leave 'im be."

The policeman menaced with a glance the crowd from whose safe precincts the defiant voices had emerged.

A doctor had come. He and the policeman bended down at the man's side. Occasionally the officer reared up to create room. The crowd fell away before his admonitions, his threats, his sarcastic questions and before the sweep of those two huge buckskin gloves.

At last, the peering ones saw the man on the side-walk begin to breathe heavily, strainedly as if he had just come to the surface from some deep water. He uttered a low cry in his foreign way. It was like a baby's squeal or the sad wail of a little storm-tossed kitten. As this cry went forth to all those eager ears the jostling, crowding, recommenced again furiously until the doctor was obliged to yell warningly a dozen times. The policeman had gone to send the ambulance call.

When a man struck another match and in its meagre light the doctor felt the skull of the prostrate man carefully to discover if any wound had been caused by his fall to the stone side-walk, the crowd pressed and crushed again. It was as if they fully expected to see blood by the light of the match and the desire made them appear almost insane. The policeman returned and fought with them. The doctor looked up occasionally to scold and demand room.

At last out of the faint haze of light far up the street, there came the sound of a gong beaten rapidly, impatiently. A monstrous truck loaded to the sky with barrels, scurried to one side with marvelous agility. And then the black wagon with its gleam of gold lettering and bright brass gong clattered into view, the horse galloping. A young man, as imperturbable always as if he were going on a picnic, sat thoughtfully upon the rear seat.

When they picked up the limp body, from which came little moans and howls, the crowd almost turned into a mob. When the ambulance started on its banging and clanging return, they stood and gazed until it was quite out of sight. Some resumed their ways with an air of relief. Others still continued to stare after the vanished ambulance and its burden as if they had been cheated, as if the curtain had been rung down on a tragedy that was but half completed and this impenetrable blanket intervening between a sufferer and their curiosity, seemed to make them feel an injustice.

No. 73   THE DUEL THAT WAS NOT FOUGHT

PATSEY TULLIGAN was not as wise as seven owls, but his courage could throw a shadow as long as the steeple of a cathedral. There were men on Cherry street who had whipped him five times, but they all knew that Patsey would be as ready for the sixth time as if nothing had happened.

Once he and two friends had been away up on Eighth avenue, far out of their country, and upon their return journey that evening they stopped frequently in saloons until they were as independent of their surroundings as eagles, and cared much less about thirty days on Blackwell's.

On lower Sixth avenue they paused in a saloon where there was a good deal of lamp glare and polished wood to be seen from the outside, and within the mellow light shone on much furbished brass and more polished wood. It was a better saloon than they were in the habit of seeing, but they did not mind it. They sat down at one of the little tables that were in a row parallel to the bar and ordered beer. They blinked stolidly at the decorations, the bar-tender and the other customers. When anything transpired they discussed it with dazzling frankness and what they said of it was as free as air to the other people in the place. At midnight there were few people in the saloon. Patsey and his friends still sat drinking. Two well-dressed men were at another table, smoking cigars slowly and swinging back in their chairs. They occupied themselves with themselves in the usual manner, never betraying by a wink of an eye-lid that they knew that other folk existed. At another table directly behind Patsey and his companions was a slim little Cuban with miraculously small feet and hands, and with a youthful touch of down upon his lip. As he lifted his cigarette from time to time his little finger was bended in dainty fashion and there was a green flash when a huge emerald ring caught the light. The bar-tender came often with his little brass tray. Occasionally Patsey and his two friends quarreled.

Once this little Cuban happened to make some slight noise and Patsey turned his head to observe him. Then Patsey made a careless and rather loud comment to his two friends. He used a word which is no more than passing the time of day down in Cherry street, but, to the Cuban, it was a dagger point. There was a harsh scraping sound as a chair was pushed swiftly back.

The little Cuban was upon his feet. His eyes were shining with a rage that flashed there like sparks as he glared at Patsey. His olive face had turned a shade of grey from his anger. Withal his chest was thrust out in portentous dignity, and his hand, still grasping his wine glass, was cool and steady, the little finger still bended, the great emerald gleaming upon it. The others, motionless, stared at him.

"Sir," he began ceremoniously. He spoke gravely and in a slow way, his tone coming in a marvel of self-possessed cadences from between those lips which quivered with wrath. "You have insult me. You are a dog, a hound, a cur. I spit upon you. I must have some of your blood."

Patsey looked at him over his shoulder. "What's th' matter wi'che?" he demanded. He did not quite understand the words of this little man who glared at him steadily, but he knew that it was something about fighting. He snarled with the readiness of his class and heaved his shoulders contemptuously. "Ah, what's eatin' yeh? Take a walk! You hain't got nothin' t' do with me, have yeh? Well, den, go sit on yerself."

And his companions leaned back valorously in their chairs and scrutinized this slim young fellow who was addressing Patsey.

"What's de little Dago chewin' about?"

"He wants t' scrap!"

"What!"

The Cuban listened with apparent composure. It was only when they laughed that his body cringed as if he was receiving lashes. Presently he put down his glass and walked over to their table. He proceeded always with the most impressive deliberation.

"Sir," he began again. "You have insult me. I must have s-s-satisfact-shone. I must have your body upon the point of my sword. In my country you would already be dead. I must have s-s-satisfact-shone."

Patsey had looked at the Cuban with a trifle of bewilderment. But at last his face began to grow dark with belligerency, his mouth curved in that wide sneer with which he would confront an angel of darkness. He arose suddenly in his seat and came toward the little Cuban. He was going to be impressive, too. "Say, young feller, if yeh go shootin' off yer face at me, I'll wipe d' joint wid yeh. What'cher gaffin' about, hey? Are yeh givin' me er jolly? Say, if yeh pick me up fer a cinch, I'll fool yeh. Dat's what! Don't take me fer no dead easy mug." And as he glowered at the little Cuban, he ended his oration with one elegant word, "Nit!"

The bar-tender nervously polished his bar with a towel, and kept his eyes fastened upon the men. Occasionally he became transfixed with interest, leaning forward with one hand upon the edge of the bar and the other holding the towel grabbed in a lump, as if he had been turned into bronze when in the very act of polishing.

The Cuban did not move when Patsey came toward him and delivered his oration. At its conclusion, he turned his livid face toward where, above him, Patsey was swaggering and heaving his shoulders in a consummate display of bravery and readiness. The Cuban, in his clear, tense tones, spoke one word. It was the bitter insult. It seemed to fairly spin from his lips and crackle in the air like breaking glass.

Every man save the little Cuban made an electric movement. Patsey roared a black oath and thrust himself forward until he towered almost directly above the other man. His fists were doubled into knots of bone and hard flesh. The Cuban had raised a steady finger. "If you touch me wis your hand, I will keel you."

The two well-dressed men had come swiftly, uttering protesting cries. They suddenly intervened in this second of time in which Patsey had sprung forward and the Cuban had uttered his threat. The four men were now a tossing, arguing, violent group, one well-dressed man lecturing the Cuban, and the other holding off Patsey, who was now wild with rage loudly repeating the Cuban's threat and maneuvering and struggling to get at him for revenge's sake.

The bar-tender, feverishly scouring away with his towel and at times pacing to and fro with nervous and excited tread, shouted out: "Say, for heaven's sake, don't fight in here. If yeh wanta fight, go out in the street and fight all yeh please. But don't fight in here."

Patsey knew only one thing and this he kept repeating, "Well, he wants t' scrap! I didn't begin dis! He wants t' scrap."

The well-dressed man confronting him continually replied: "Oh, well, now, look here, he's only a lad. He don't know what he's doing. He's crazy mad. You wouldn't slug a kid like that."

Patsey and his aroused companions, who cursed and growled, were persistent with their argument. "Well, he wants t' scrap!" The whole affair was as plain as daylight when one saw this great fact. The interference and intolerable discussion brought the three of them forward, battleful and fierce. "What's eatin' you, anyhow?" they demanded. "Dis ain't your business, is it? What business you got shootin' off your face?"

The other peacemaker was trying to restrain the little Cuban, who had grown shrill and violent. "If he touch me wis his hand I will keel him. We must fight like gentlemen or else I keel him when he touch me wis his hand."

The man who was fending off Patsey comprehended these sentences that were screamed behind his back and he explained to Patsey: "But he wants to fight you with swords. With swords, you know."

The Cuban, dodging around the peacemakers, yelled in Patsey's face: "Ah, if I could get you before me wis my sword! Ah! Ah! A-a-ah!" Patsey made a furious blow with a swift fist, but the peacemakers bucked against his body suddenly like football players.

Patsey was greatly puzzled. He continued doggedly to try to get near enough to the Cuban to punch him. To these attempts the Cuban replied savagely: "If you touch me wis your hand, I will cut your heart in two piece."

At last Patsey said: "Well, if he's so dead stuck on fightin' wid swords, I'll fight 'im. Soitenly! I'll fight 'im." All this palaver had evidently tired him, and he now puffed out his lips with the air of a man who is willing to submit to any conditions if he can only bring on the row soon enough. He swaggered, "I'll fight 'im wid swords. Let 'im bring on his swords, an' I'll fight 'im 'til he's ready t' quit."

The two well-dressed men grinned. "Why, look here," they said to Patsey, "he'd punch you full of holes. Why, he's a fencer. You can't fight him with swords. He'd kill you in 'bout a minute."

"Well, I'll giv' 'im a go at it, anyhow," said Patsey, stout-hearted and resolute. "I'll giv' 'im a go at it anyhow an' I'll stay wid 'im long as I kin."

As for the Cuban, his lithe, little body was quivering in an ecstasy of the muscles. His face radiant with a savage joy, he fastened his glance upon Patsey, his eyes gleaming with a gloating, murderous light. A most unspeakable, animal-like rage was in his expression. "Ah! Ah! He will fight me! Ah!" He bended unconsciously in the posture of a fencer. He had all the quick, springy movements of a skillful swordsman. "Ah, the b-r-r-rute! The b-r-r-rute! I will stick him like a pig!"

The two peacemakers, still grinning broadly, were having a great time with Patsey. "Why, you infernal idiot, this man would slice you all up. You better jump off the bridge if you want to commit suicide. You wouldn't stand a ghost of a chance to live ten seconds."

Patsey was as unshaken as granite. "Well, if he wants t' fight wid swords, he'll get it. I'll giv' 'im a go at it, anyhow."

One man said: "Well, have you got a sword? Do you know what a sword is? Have you got a sword?"

"No, I ain't got none," said Patsey, honestly, "but I kin git one." Then he added valiantly: "An' d—d quick, too."

The two men laughed. "Why, can't you understand it would be sure death to fight a sword duel with this fellow?"

"Dat's all right! See? I know me own business. If he wants t' fight one of dees d—n duels, I'm in it, understan'?"

"Have you ever fought one, you fool?"

"No, I ain't. But I will fight one, dough! I ain't no muff. If he wants t' fight a duel, by Gawd, I'm wid 'im! D' yeh understan' dat?" Patsey cocked his hat and swaggered. He was getting very serious.

The little Cuban burst out: "Ah, come on, sirs; come on! We can take cab. Ah, you big cow, I will stick you, I will stick you. Ah, you will look very beautiful, very beautiful. Ah, come on, sirs. We will stop at hotel—my hotel. I there have weapons."

"Yeh will, will yeh? Yeh bloomin' little black Dago," cried

Patsey in hoarse and maddened reply to the personal part of the Cuban's speech. He stepped forward. "Git yer d—n swords," he commanded. "Git yer swords. Git 'em quick! I'll fight wi'che! I'll fight wid anyting, too! See? I'll fight yeh wid a knife an' fork if yeh say so! I'll fight yeh standin' up er sittin' down! I'll fight yeh in h—l, see?" Patsey delivered this intense oration with sweeping, intensely emphatic gestures, his hands stretched out eloquently, his jaw thrust forward, his eyes glaring.

"Ah," cried the little Cuban joyously. "Ah, you are in very pretty temper. Ah, how I will cut your heart in two piece, my dear, d-e-a-r friend." His eyes, too, shone like carbuncles, with a swift, changing glitter, always fastened upon Patsey's face.

The two peacemakers were perspiring and in despair. One of them blurted out: "Well, I'll be blamed if this ain't the most ridiculous thing I ever saw."

The other said: "For ten dollars I'd be tempted to let these two infernal blockheads have their duel."

Patsey was strutting to and fro, and conferring grandly with his friends. "He took me fer a muff. He tought he was goin' t' bluff me out, talkin' 'bout swords. He'll get fooled." He addressed the Cuban: "You're a fine little dirty picter of a scrapper, ain't che? I'll chew yez up, dat's what I will."

There began then some rapid action. The patience of well-dressed men is not an eternal thing. It began to look as if it would at last be a fight with six corners to it. The faces of the men were shining red with anger. They jostled each other defiantly, and almost every one blazed out at three or four of the others. The bar-tender had given up protesting. He swore for a time, and banged his glasses. Then he jumped the bar and ran out of the saloon, cursing sullenly.

When he came back with a policeman, Patsey and the Cuban were preparing to depart together. Patsey was delivering his last oration: "I'll fight yer wid swords! Sure I will! Come ahead, Dago! I'll fight yeh anywheres, wid anyting! We'll have a large, juicy scrap, an' don't yeh forget dat! I'm right wid yez. I ain't no muff! I scrap wid a man jest as soon as he ses scrap, an' if yeh wanta scrap, I'm yer kitten. Understan' dat?"

The policeman said sharply: "Come, now; what's all this?" He had a distinctly business air.

The little Cuban stepped forward calmly. "It is none of your business."

The policeman flushed to his ears. "What?"

One well-dressed man touched the other on the sleeve. "Here's the time to skip," he whispered. They halted a block away from the saloon and watched the policeman pull the Cuban through the door. There was a minute of scuffle on the side-walk, and into this deserted street at midnight fifty people appeared at once as if from the sky to watch it.

At last the three Cherry Hill men came from the saloon and swaggered with all their old valor toward the peacemakers. "Ah," said Patsey to them, "he was so hot talkin' about this duel business, but I would a-givin' 'im a great scrap, an' don't yeh forgit it."

For Patsey was not as wise as seven owls, but his courage could throw a shadow as long as the steeple of a cathedral.

No. 73a   NOTEBOOK DRAFT

MIKE TULLIGAN and two friends went into a corner-saloon to get drinks. There was a good deal of polished wood to be seen from the outside and everything gleamed in the mellow rays of the lights. It was a better saloon than they were used to over in their own East Side but they did not mind it. They entered and sat down at one of the little tables that were in a row parallel to the bar. They ordered beer and then sat blinking stolidly at the decorations, the bar-tender and the other customers. When anything transpired they discussed it with dazzling frankness and what they said of it was as free as air to the other people in the saloon. When it became midnight there happened to be but three men besides themselves and the bar-tender in the place. Two of these were well-dressed New Yorkers who smoked cigars rapidly and swung back in their chairs occupying themselves with themselves in the usual manner and never betraying by a wink of an eye-lid that they knew anybody else existed. The third man was a lithe little Cuban with miraculously small feet and hands, and with the faintest touch of down upon his youthful upper lip. As he lifted his cigarette from time to time to his lips, his little finger crooked in dainty fashion and one could see the flashes of light in an emerald. He sat

[*ten leaves torn out*]

him with swords. He'd kill you in about a minute."

But never an inch did Patsey give way. "Well, I'll give 'im a go at it, anyhow," he said, stoutly. "I'll give 'im a go at it anyhow an' I'll stay wid 'im as long as I kin."

As for the Cuban, his lithe, little body was quivering in an ecstasy of the muscles. His face was radiant with joy and his eyes shot a murderous gloating gleam upon Patsey. "Ah! Ah! He will fight me! Ah!" He bended unconsciously in the attitude of a practised, skilful fencer. "Ah, the brrute! The brrute! I will stick him like pig."

The two well-dressed men, grinning broadly, were having a great time with Patsey. "Why, you infernal idiot, this man would slice you all up. You better jump off the bridge if you want to die. You wouldn't stand a ghost of a chance to live ten seconds."

Patsey made one persistent retort. "Well, if he wants to fight with swords, I'll give 'im a go at it anyhow."

One man said: "Well have you got a sword? Do you know what a sword is? Have you got a sword?"

"No, I ain't got none," said Patsey, honestly, "but I kin git one." Then he added valiantly "An' d—d quick, too."

The two men laughed. "Why, can't you understand that it would be pure suicide for you to fight with swords with this fellow?"

"Dat's all right! If he wants to fight with swords, he'll git it! Dat's all!"

The little Cuban burst out excitedly: "Ah, come on! Come on! We can take cab! Ah, you big calf, I will stick you very pretty! Ah, you will look very beautiful, very beautiful. Ah, come on, we will stop at my hotel. I have weapons there!"

"Yeh will, will yeh, yeh bloomin' little black Dago," cried Patsey in enraged reply to the personal part of the Cuban's speech. He stepped forward fiercely. "Git yer d—d swords! Git 'em I'll fight wi' che! Go ahn. Git 'em! I'll fight wid anyting! See? I'll fight yeh wid a knife an' fork if yeh say so, I'll fight yeh standin' up er sittin' down! I'll fight yeh in h—l, see?" This intense oration Patsey delivered with sweeping gestures, his hands stretched out eloquently, his body leaning forward, his jaw thrust out.

The wrath in the little Cuban's

No. 74   A LOVELY JAG IN A CROWDED CAR

THE crosstown car was bound for the great shopping district, and one side of it was lined with women who sat in austere silence regarding each other in occasional furtive glances and preserving their respectability with fierce vigilance. A solitary man sat in a corner meekly pretending that he was interested in his newspaper. The conductor came and went without discussion, like a wellbred servant. The atmosphere of the car was as decorous as that of the most frigid of drawing rooms.

However, the decorous atmosphere was doomed to be destroyed by a wild red demon of drink and destruction. He was standing on a street corner, swaying gently on his wavering legs and blinking at the cobbles. Frequently he regarded the passing people with an expression of the most benign amiability.

As the car came near to him he tottered greatly in his excitement. He waved his umbrella and shouted: "Stop sh' car! Stop sh' car!"

The driver pulled stoutly at the reins with his gloved left hand, and with his right one swung the polished brass of the brake lever. The car halted and, upon the rear platform, the conductor reached down to help the wild, red demon of drink and destruction aboard the car. He climbed up the steps with an important and serious air, as if he were boarding a frigate; then he went smiling in jovial satisfaction into the car. As he was about to sit down there were two sharp, clanging notes on the bell, the driver released his brake and again tightened his reins, and the car started with a sudden jerk that caused the man to be precipitated violently into a seat as if some one had struck him. He seemed to feel a keen humor in the situation for, upon recovering himself, he looked at the other passengers and laughed.

As for the women bound for the shopping district, they had suddenly turned into so many statues of ice. They stared out of the little windows which cut the street scenes in half and allowed but the upper parts of people to be seen, moving curiously without any legs. Whenever the eyes of the women were obliged to encounter the man they assumed at once an expression of the most heroic disgust and disdain. The man over in the corner grinned, urchin-like.

The drunken man put his hands on his knees and beamed about him in absolute unalloyed happiness. He seemed to believe that he was engaged in carousing with a convivial party and these friends were represented to his mind by the silent row of women who were going shopping. He had not the air of a man who was on a solitary spree; he was conducting a great celebration. The universe was engaged with him in a vast rakish song to flagon and cup, the sun had its hat over its eye, all of humanity staggered and smiled.

Presently his excited spirits overflowed to such an extent that he was obliged to sing. He began to beat time with his forefinger as if he was leading a grand chorus.

> But th' younger shon was er shon-of-a-gun,
> > He was! He was!
> 'E shuffle' cards an' 'e play fer mon,
> > He did! He did!
> He wore shilk hat an' er high stannin' collar,
> He'd go out with'er boys an' gi' full an' then
> > holler.
> Oh, he was er——

He was interrupted by the conductor, who came in and said in a heavy undertone: "Close that trap now or I'll put'che off!"

The injustice of the conductor was both an astonishment and a grief to the man. He had been on the best of terms with each single atom in space, and now here suddenly appeared a creature who gruffly stated a dampening fact. He spoke very loudly in his pain and disappointment:

"Pu' me off? What 'che go pu' me off fer? We ain't doin' er shing! G'wan way! Go shtand on er end z'car! Thash where you b'long! You ain' got no business talk me."

The conductor returned scowling to the rear platform. He turned and looked at the man with a glance that was full of menace.

Meanwhile, within the car, the inebriated passenger continued to conduct the grand celebration. "Hurray!" he said, at the conclusion of one of his little ballads. "Le's all haver drink!

Le's all haver noz' drink! Shay! Shay, look here a minute." He began to pound on the floor with his umbrella and make earnest gestures at the conductor. "Shay, look here!"

The conductor, watchful eyed but self contained, came forward. "Well," he said.

"Bringesh noz' round drinkshs," said the man. "Bringesh noz' round drinkshs."

"Say, you'll have to cool down some or I'll put'che off th' car. What d'yeh think?" said the conductor.

But the man was busy trying to find out the preference of each of the passengers. "What'll yeh take?" he demanded of each one, smiling genially. Whereupon the women opposite to him stared at the floor, at the ceiling, at the forward end of the car and at the rear end of the car, their lips set in stern lines.

Notwithstanding all these icy expressions, his face remained lit with a sunny grin, as if he were convinced that every one regarded him affectionately. He insisted that they should all take something.

"What'll yeh take? What? Ain'che drinkin'? What? Shay, yeh mus' take somethin'. What? Well, all ri'. I'll order Manhattan fer yeh! Shay, Jim," he called loudly to the conductor, "bringesh noz' Manhattan."

With infinite pains and thoroughness he canvassed the passengers, putting to each one the formidable question: "What'll yeh drink?" The faces of the women were set in lines of horror, dismay and disgust. No one uttered a syllable in reply save the man over in the corner, who said indulgently: "Oh, I guess I'll take a beer."

At the conclusion of his canvass the man spent some anxious moments in reflection, calculating carefully upon his fingers. Then he triumphantly ordered one beer and nine Manhattan cocktails of the conductor.

The latter, who was collecting fares at the time, turned and said: "Say, lookahere, now, you've got t' quit this thing. Just close your face or I'll throw yeh out in th' street."

"Tha's all ri'," said the other, nodding his head portentously and wisely. "Tha's all ri'. You ain't go' throw me out. I ain't doin' er shing. Wha' you throw me out fer? That's all ri'." Then he returned to his demeanor of command. "Come. Hur' up!

Bringesh nine Manhattans an'—an'—le's see—somebody order beer, didn' they? Who order beer?" He gazed inquiringly at the imperturbable faces. Finally he addressed the man over in the corner. "Shay, didn' you order beer?"

The man in the corner grinned. "Well, yes, I guess it was me."

"Look here, bringesh nine Manhattans an' er beer," called the celebrating man to the conductor. "Hur' up! Bringesh 'em quick."

The conductor looked scornfully away.

As the car passed through the region of the great stores the group of women gradually diminished until finally they disappeared altogether, and, as the car went on its way toward a distant ferry, there remained within only the celebrating individual and the man over in the corner. The celebrater became more jovial as time went forward. He rejoiced that the world was to him one vast landscape of pure rose color. The humming of the wheels and the clatter of the horses' hoofs did not drown the sound of this high quavering voice that sang of the pearl-hued joys of life as seen through a pair of strange, oblique, temporary spectacles. The conductor, musing upon the rear platform, had grown indifferent.

At last the celebrater seemed overcome by the wild thought that the car had passed the point where he had intended to leave it. He broke off in the midst of a ballad and scrambled for the door. "Stop sh' car," he yelled. The conductor reached for the bell strap, but before the car stopped the celebrater sprawled out upon the cobbles. He arose instantly and began a hurried and unsteady journey back up the street, retracing the way over which the car had just brought him. He seemed overwhelmed with anxiety.

The man in the corner came to the rear platform and gazed after the form of the celebrater. "Well, he was a peach," he said.

"That's what he was," said the conductor.

They both turned to watch him and they remained there deep in reflection, absorbed in contemplation of this wavering figure in the distance, until observation was no longer possible.

No. 75 OPIUM'S VARIED DREAMS

OPIUM smoking in this country is believed to be more particularly a pastime of the Chinese, but in truth the greater
number of the smokers are white men and white women.
Chinatown furnishes the pipe, lamp and yen-hock, but let a
man once possess a "layout" and a common American drug
store furnishes him with the opium, and afterward China
is discernible only in the traditions that cling to the habit.

There are 25,000 opium-smokers in the city of New York
alone. At one time there were two great colonies, one in the
Tenderloin, one of course in Chinatown. This was before the
hammer of reform struck them. Now the two colonies are
splintered into something less than 25,000 fragments. The
smokers are disorganized, but they still exist.

The Tenderloin district of New York fell an early victim to
opium. That part of the population which is known as the
sporting class adopted the habit quickly. Cheap actors, race
track touts, gamblers and the different kinds of confidence
men took to it generally. Opium raised its yellow banner over
the Tenderloin, attaining the dignity of a common vice.

Splendid "joints" were not uncommon then in New York.
There was one on Forty-second street which would have been
palatial if it were not for the bad taste of the decorations. An
occasional man from Fifth avenue or Madison avenue would
there have his private "layout," an elegant equipment of silver,
ivory, gold. The bunks which lined all sides of the two rooms
were nightly crowded and some of the people owned names
which are not altogether unknown to the public. This place
was raided because of sensational stories in the newspapers and
the little wicket no longer opens to allow the anxious "fiend"
to enter.

Upon the appearance of reform, opium retired to private
flats. Here it now reigns and it will undoubtedly be an extremely long century before the police can root it from these
little strongholds. Once, Billie Rostetter got drunk on whisky
and emptied three scuttles of coal down the dumb-waiter
shaft. This made a noise and Billie naturally was arrested. But
opium is silent. These smokers do not rave. They lay and

dream, or talk in low tones. The opium vice does not betray itself by heaving coal down dumb-waiter shafts.

People who declare themselves able to pick out opium-smokers on the street are usually deluded. An opium-smoker may look like a deacon or a deacon may look like an opium-smoker. One case is as probable as the other. The "fiends" can easily conceal their vice. They get up from the "layout," adjust their cravats, straighten their coat-tails and march off like ordinary people, and the best kind of an expert would not be willing to bet that they were or were not addicted to the habit.

It would be very hard to say just exactly what constitutes a "habit." With the fiends it is an elastic word. Ask a smoker if he has a habit and he will deny it. Ask him if some one who smokes the same amount has a habit and he will gracefully admit it. Perhaps the ordinary smoker consumes 25 cents worth of opium each day. There are others who smoke $1 worth. This is rather extraordinary and in this case at least it is safe to say that it is a "habit." The $1 smokers usually indulge in "high hats," which is the term for a large pill. The ordinary smoker is satisfied with "pin-heads." "Pin-heads" are about the size of a French pea.

"Habit-smokers" have a contempt for the "sensation-smoker." This latter is a person who has been won by the false glamour which surrounds the vice and who goes about really pre-tending that he has a ravenous hunger for the pipe. There are more "sensation-smokers" than one would imagine.

It is said to take one year of devotion to the pipe before one can contract a habit. As far as the writer's observation goes, he should say that it does not take any such long time. Sometimes an individual who has only smoked a few months will speak of nothing but pipe and when they "talk pipe" persistently it is a pretty sure sign that the drug has fastened its grip upon them so that at any rate they are not able to easily stop its use.

When a man arises from his first trial of the pipe, the nausea that clutches him is something that can give cards and spades and big casino to seasickness. If he had swallowed a live chimney-sweep he could not feel more like dying. The room and everything in it whirls like the inside of an electric light plant. There appears a thirst, a great thirst, and this thirst is so sinister and so misleading that if the novice drank spirits to satisfy it he would presently be much worse. The one thing that will make him feel again that life may be a joy is a cup of strong black coffee.

If there is a sentiment in the pipe for him he returns to it after this first unpleasant trial. Gradually, the power of the drug sinks into his heart. It absorbs his thought. He begins to lie with more and more grace to cover the shortcomings and little failures of his life. And then finally he may become a full-fledged "pipe fiend," a man with a "yen-yen."

A "yen-yen," be it known, is the hunger, the craving. It comes to a "fiend" when he separates himself from his pipe and takes him by the heart strings. If indeed he will not buck through a brick wall to get to the pipe, he at least will become the most disagreeable, sour-tempered person on earth until he finds a way to satisfy his craving.

When the victim arrives at the point where his soul calls for the drug, he usually learns to cook. The operation of rolling the pill and cooking it over the little lamp is a delicate task and it takes time to learn it. When a man can cook for himself and buys his own "layout," he is gone, probably. He has placed upon his shoulders an elephant which he may carry to the edge of forever. The Chinese have a preparation which they call a cure, but the first difficulty is to get the hop-fiend to take the preparation, and the second difficulty is to cure anything with this cure.

A "hop-fiend" will defend opium with eloquence and energy. He very seldom drinks spirits and so he gains an opportunity to make the most ferocious parallels between the effects of rum and the effects of opium. Ask him to free his mind and he will probably say: "Opium does not deprive you of your senses. It does not make a madman of you. But drink does! See? Who ever heard of a man committing murder when full of hop? Get him full of whisky and he might kill his father. I don't see why people kick so about opium smoking. If they knew anything about it they wouldn't talk that way. Let anybody drink rum who cares to, but as for me I would rather be what I am."

As before mentioned, there were at one time gorgeous opium

dens in New York, but at the present time there is probably not one with any pretense to splendid decoration. The Chinamen will smoke in a cellar, bare, squalid, occupied by an odor that will float wooden chips. The police took the adornments from the vice and left nothing but the pipe itself. Yet the pipe is sufficient for its slant-eyed lover.

When prepared for smoking purposes, opium is a heavy liquid much like molasses. Ordinarily it is sold in hollow li-shi nuts or in little round tins resembling the old percussion cap-boxes. The pipe is a curious affair, particularly notable for the way in which it does not resemble the drawings of it that appear in print. The stem is of thick bamboo, the mouthpiece usually of ivory. The bowl crops out suddenly about four inches from the end of the stem. It is a heavy affair of clay or stone. The cavity is a mere hole, of the diameter of a lead pencil, drilled through the centre. The "yen-hock" is a sort of sharpened darning-needle. With it the cook takes the opium from the box. He twirls it dexterously with his thumb and forefinger until enough of the gummy substance adheres to the sharp point. Then he holds it over the tiny flame of the lamp which burns only peanut oil or sweet oil. The pill now exactly resembles boiling molasses. The clever fingers of the cook twirl it above the flame. Lying on his side comfortably, he takes the pipe in his left hand and transfers the cooked pill from the yen-hock to the bowl of the pipe where he again molds it with the yen-hock until it is a little button-like thing with a hole in the centre fitting squarely over the hole in the bowl. Dropping the yen-hock, the cook now uses two hands for the pipe. He extends the mouthpiece toward the one whose turn it is to smoke and as this latter leans forward in readiness, the cook draws the bowl toward the flame until the heat sets the pill to boiling. Whereupon, the smoker takes a long, deep draw at the pipe, the pill splutters and fries and a moment later the smoker sinks back tranquilly. An odor, heavy, aromatic, agreeable and yet disagreeable, hangs in the air and makes its way with peculiar powers of penetration. The group about the layout talk in low voices and watch the cook deftly molding another pill. The little flame casts a strong yellow light on their faces as they cuddle about the layout. As the pipe passes and passes around the circle, the voices drop to a mere indolent cooing, and the eyes that so lazily watch the cook at his work glisten and glisten from the influence of the drug until they resemble flashing bits of silver.

There is a similarity in coloring and composition in a group of men about a midnight camp-fire in a forest and a group of smokers about the layout tray with its tiny light. Everything, of course, is on a smaller scale with the smoking. The flame is only an inch and a half perhaps in height and the smokers huddle closely in order that every person may smoke undisturbed. But there is something in the abandon of the poses, the wealth of light on the faces and the strong mystery of shadow at the backs of the people that bring the two scenes into some kind of artistic brotherhood. And just as the lazy eyes about a camp-fire fasten themselves dreamfully upon the blaze of logs so do the lazy eyes about an opium layout fasten themselves upon the little yellow flame.

There is but one pipe, one lamp and one cook to each smoking layout. Pictures of nine or ten persons sitting in arm-chairs and smoking various kinds of curiously carved tobacco pipes probably serve well enough, but when they are named "Interior of an Opium Den" and that sort of thing, it is absurd. Opium could not be smoked like tobacco. A pill is good for one long draw. After that the cook molds another. A smoker would just as soon choose a gallows as an arm-chair for smoking purposes. He likes to curl down on a mattress placed on the floor in the quietest corner of a Tenderloin flat, and smoke there with no light but the tiny yellow spear from the layout lamp.

It is a curious fact that it is rather the custom to purchase for a layout tray one of those innocent black tin affairs which are supposed to be placed before baby as he takes his high chair for dinner.

If a beginner expects to have dreams of an earth dotted with white porcelain towers and a sky of green silk, he will, from all accounts, be much mistaken. "The Opium Smoker's Dream" seems to be mostly a mistake. The influence of "dope" is evidently a fine languor, a complete mental rest. The problems of life no longer appear. Existence is peace. The virtues of a man's friends, for instance, loom beautifully against his own sudden perfection. The universe is re-adjusted. Wrong departs, injustice vanishes; there is nothing but a quiet, a soothing harmony of all things—until the next morning.

And who should invade this momentary land of rest, this dream country, if not the people of the Tenderloin, they who are at once supersensitive and hopeless, the people who think more upon death and the mysteries of life, the chances of the hereafter, than any other class, educated or uneducated. Opium holds out to them its lie, and they embrace it eagerly, expecting to find a definition of peace, but they awake to find the formidable labors of life grown more formidable. And if the pipe should happen to ruin their lives they cling the more closely to it because then it stands between them and thought.

No. 76 NEW YORK'S BICYCLE SPEEDWAY

THE Bowery has had its day as a famous New York street. It is now a mere tradition. Broadway will long hold its place as the chief vein of the city's life. No process of expansion can ever leave it abandoned to the cheap clothing dealers and dime museum robbers. It is too strategic in position. But lately the Western Boulevard which slants from the Columbus monument at the southwest corner of Central Park to the river has vaulted to a startling prominence and is now one of the sights of New York. This is caused by the bicycle. Once the Boulevard was a quiet avenue whose particular distinctions were its shade trees and its third foot-walk which extended in Parisian fashion down the middle of the street. Also it was noted for its billboards and its huge and slumberous apartment hotels. Now, however, it is the great thoroughfare for bicycles. On these gorgeous spring days they appear in thousands. All mankind is a-wheel apparently and a person on nothing but legs feels like a strange animal. A mighty army of wheels streams from the brick wilderness below Central Park and speeds over the asphalt. In the cool of the evening it returns with swaying and flashing of myriad lamps.

The bicycle crowd has completely subjugated the street. The glittering wheels dominate it from end to end. The cafes and dining rooms of the apartment hotels are occupied mainly by people in bicycle clothes. Even the billboards have surrendered. They advertise wheels and lamps and tires and patent saddles with all the flaming vehemence of circus art. Even when they do condescend to still advertise a patent medicine, you are sure to confront a lithograph of a young person in bloomers who is saying in large type: "Yes, George, I find that Willowrum always refreshes me after these long rides."

Down at the Circle where stands the patient Columbus, the stores are crowded with bicycle goods. There are innumerable repair shops. Everything is bicycle. In the afternoon the parade begins. The great discoverer, erect on his tall grey shaft, must feel his stone head whirl when the battalions come swinging and shining around the curve.

It is interesting to note the way in which the blasphemous and terrible truck-drivers of the lower part of the city will hunt a bicyclist. A truck-driver, of course, believes that a wheelman is a pest. The average man could not feel more annoyance if nature had suddenly invented some new kind of mosquito. And so the truck-driver resolves in his dreadful way to make life as troublous and thrilling for the wheelman as he possibly can. The wheelman suffers under a great handicap. He is struggling over the most uneven cobbles which bless a metropolis. Twenty horses threaten him and forty wheels miss his shoulder by an inch. In his ears there is a hideous din. It surrounds him, envelopes him.

Add to this trouble, then, a truckman with a fiend's desire to see dead wheelmen. The situation affords deep excitement for everyone concerned.

But when a truck-driver comes to the Boulevard the beautiful balance of the universe is apparent. The teamster sits mute, motionless, casting sidelong glances at the wheels which spin by him. He still contrives to exhibit a sort of a sombre defiance, but he has no oath nor gesture nor wily scheme to drive a three-ton wagon over the prostrate body of some unhappy cyclist. On the Boulevard this roaring lion from down town is so subdued, so isolated that he brings tears to the sympathetic eye.

There is a new game on the Boulevard. It is the game of Bicycle Cop and Scorcher. When the scorcher scorches beyond the patience of the law, the bicycle policeman, if in sight, takes after him. Usually the scorcher has a blissful confidence in his ability to scorch and thinks it much easier to just ride away from the policeman than to go to court and pay a fine. So they go flying up the Boulevard with the whole mob of wheelmen and wheelwomen, eager to see the race, sweeping after them. But the bicycle police are mighty hard riders and it takes a flier to escape them. The affair usually ends in calamity for the scorcher, but in the meantime fifty or sixty cyclists have had a period of delirious joy.

Bicycle Cop and Scorcher is a good game, but after all it is not as good as the game that was played in the old days when the suggestion of a corps of bicycle police in neat knickerbockers would have scandalized Mulberry street. This was the game of Fat Policeman on Foot Trying to Stop a Spurt. A huge, unwieldy officer rushing out into the street and wildly trying to head off and grab some rider who was spinning along in just one silver flash was a sight that caused the populace to turn out in a body. If some madman started at a fierce gait from the Columbus monument, he could have the consciousness that at frequent and exciting intervals, red-faced policemen would gallop out at him and frenziedly clutch at his coat-tails. And owing to a curious dispensation, the majority of the policemen along the Boulevard were very stout and could swear most graphically in from two to five languages.

But they changed all that. The un-police-like bicycle police are wonderfully clever and the vivid excitement of other days is gone. Even the scorcher seems to feel depressed and narrowly looks over the nearest officer before he starts on his frantic career.

The girl in bloomers is, of course, upon her native heath when she steers her steel steed into the Boulevard. One becomes conscious of a bewildering variety in bloomers. There are some that fit and some that do not fit. There are some that were not made to fit and there are some that couldn't fit anyhow. As a matter of fact the bloomer costume is now in one of the primary stages of its evolution. Let us hope so at any rate. Of course every decent citizen concedes that women shall wear what they please and it is supposed that he covenants with himself not to grin and nudge his neighbor when anything particularly amazing passes him on the street but resolves to simply and industriously mind his own affairs. Still the situation no doubt harrows him greatly. No man was ever found to defend bloomers. His farthest statement, as an individual, is to advocate them for all women he does not know and cares nothing about. Most women become radical enough to say: "Why shouldn't I wear 'em, if I choose." Still, a second look at the Boulevard convinces one that the world is slowly, solemnly, inevitably coming to bloomers. We are about to enter an age of bloomers and the bicycle, that machine which has gained an economic position of the most tremendous importance, is going to be responsible for more than the bruises on the departed fat policemen of the Boulevard.

No. 77   IN THE BROADWAY CABLE CARS

THE cable cars come down Broadway as the waters come down at Lodore. Some years ago Father Knickerbocker would have had convulsions if anyone had proposed to lay impious rails on his sacred thoroughfare. At the present day they, by force of color and numbers, almost dominate the great street and the eye of even an old New Yorker is held by these long yellow monsters which prowl intently, up and down, up and down, in a mystic search.

In the gray of the morning they come out of the uptown bearing janitors, porters, all that class which carries the keys to set alive the great downtown. Later they shower clerks. Later still they shower more clerks. And the thermometer which is attached to a conductor's temper is steadily rising, rising, and the blissful time arrives when everybody hangs to a strap and stands on his neighbor's toes. Ten o'clock comes to New York and the Broadway cars, as well as elevated cars, horse cars and ferryboats innumerable, heave sighs of relief. They have filled lower New York with a vast army of men who will chase to and fro and amuse themselves until almost nightfall.

The cable car's pulse drops to normal. But the conductor's pulse begins now to beat in split seconds. He has come to the crisis in his day's agony. He is now to be overwhelmed with feminine shoppers. They all are going to give him two-dollar bills to change. They all are going to threaten to report him. He passes his hand across his brow and curses his beard from black to gray and from gray to black.

Men and women have different ways of hailing a car. A man—if he be not an old choleric gentleman who owns not this road but some other road—throws up a timid finger and appears to believe that the King of Abyssinia is careering past on his war chariot and only his opinion of other people's Americanism keeps him from deep salaams. The gripman usually jerks his thumb over his shoulder and indicates the next car, which is three miles away. Then the man catches the last platform, goes into the car, climbs upon someone's toes, opens his morning paper and is happy.

When a woman hails a car there is no question of its being the King of Abyssinia's war chariot. She has bought the car for $3.98. The conductor owes his position to her and the gripman's mother does her laundry. No captain in the Royal Horse Artillery ever stops his battery from going through a stone house in a way to equal her manner of bringing that car back on its haunches. Then she walks leisurely forward and after scanning the step to see if there is mud upon it and opening her pocketbook to make sure of a two-dollar bill, she says: "Do you give transfers down Twenty-eighth street?"

Sometimes the conductor breaks the bell-strap when he pulls it under these conditions. Then as the car goes on he moves forward and bullies some person who had nothing to do with the affair.

The car sweeps on its diagonal path through the Tenderloin with its hotels, its theaters, its flower shops, its 10,000,000 actors who played with Booth and Barrett. It passes Madison square and enters the gorge made by the towering walls of great shops. It sweeps around the double curve at Union square and Fourteenth street, and a life insurance agent falls in a fit as the uncontrolled car dashes over the crossing, narrowly missing three old ladies, two old gentlemen, a newly-married couple, a sandwich man, a newsboy and a dog. At Grace church the conductor has an altercation with a brave and reckless passenger who beards him in his own car, and at Canal street he takes dire vengeance by tumbling a drunken man onto the pavement. Meanwhile the gripman has become involved with countless truck drivers and, inch by inch, foot by foot, he fights his way to City Hall park. On past the post-office the car goes with the gripman getting advice, admonition, personal comment, and invitation to fight from the drivers until Battery park appears at the foot of the slope and as the car goes sedately around the curve, the burnished shield of the bay shines through the trees.

It is a great ride, full of exciting action. Those inexperienced persons who have been merely chased by Indians know little of the dramatic quality which life may hold for them. These jungles of men and vehicles, these cañons of streets, these lofty mountains of iron and cut stone—a ride through them affords plenty of excitement. And no lone panther's howl is more serious in intention than the howl of a lone truck driver when the cable car bumps one of his rear wheels.

Owing to a strange humor of the gods that make our comfort, sailor hats with wide brims come into vogue whenever we are all engaged in hanging to cable car straps. There is only one more serious combination known to science but a trial of it is at this day impossible. Of course if a troop of Elizabethan courtiers in large ruffs should board a cable car the complication would be a very awesome one and the profanity would be in old English, but very inspiring. However, the combination of wide-brimmed hats and crowded cable cars is tremendous in its power to cause acute misery to the patient New York public.

Suppose you are in a cable car clutching for life and family a creaking strap from overhead. At your shoulder is a little dude in a very wide-brimmed straw hat with a red band. If you were in your senses you would recognize this flaming band as an omen of blood. But you are not in your senses; you are in a

Broadway cable car. You are not supposed to have any senses. From the forward end you hear the gripman uttering shrill whoops and running over citizens. Suddenly the car comes to a curve. Making a swift running start, it turns three hand-springs, throws a cart-wheel for luck, bounds into the air, hurls six passengers over the nearest building and comes down a-straddle of the track. That is the way in which we turn curves in New York.

Meanwhile during the car's gamboling, the corrugated rim of the dude's hat has swept naturally across your neck, and it has left nothing for your head to do but to quit your shoulders. As the car rears your head falls into the waiting arms of the proper authorities. The dude is dead; everything is dead. The interior of the car resembles the scene of the battle of Wounded Knee, but this gives you small satisfaction.

There was once a person, possessing a fund of uncanny humor, who greatly desired to import from past ages a corps of knights in full armor. He then purposed to pack the warriors in a cable car and send them around a curve. He thought that he could gain much pleasure by standing near and listening to the wild clash of steel upon steel, the tumult of mailed heads striking together, the bitter grind of armored legs bending the wrong way. He thought that this would teach them that war is grim.

Towards evening, when the tides of travel set northward, it is curious to see how the gripman and conductor reverse their tempers. Their dispositions flop over like patent signals. During the down trip they had in mind always the advantages of being at Battery park. A perpetual picture of the blessings of Battery park was before them, and every delay made them fume, made this picture all the more alluring. Now the delights of uptown appear to them. They have reversed the signs on the cars, they have reversed their aspirations. Battery park has been gained and forgotten. There is a new goal. Here is a perpetual il-lustration which the philosophers of New York may use to good purpose.

In the Tenderloin, the place of theaters and of the restau-rants where gayer New York does her dining, the cable cars in the evening carry a stratum of society which looks like a new one, but it is one of the familiar strata in other clothes. It is just as good as a new stratum, however, for in evening dress the average man feels that he has gone up three pegs in the social scale and there is considerable evening dress about a Broadway car in the evening. A car with its electric lamp resembles a brilliantly lighted salon and the atmosphere grows just a trifle strained. People sit more rigidly and glance sideways perhaps as if each was positive of possessing social value, but was doubtful of the others. The conductor said: "Aw, go ahn! Git off th' earth!" but this was to a man at Canal street. Here he shows his versatility. He stands on the platform and beams in a modest and polite manner into the car. He notes a lifted finger and grabs swiftly for the bell-strap. He reaches down to help a woman aboard. Perhaps his demeanor is a reflection of the manner of the people in the car. No one is in a mad New York hurry; no one is fretting and muttering; no one is perched upon his neighbor's toes. Moreover, the Tenderloin is a glory at night. Broadway of late years has fallen heir to countless signs illuminated with red, blue, green, gold electric lamps, and the people certainly fly to these as the moths go to a candle. And perhaps the gods have allowed this opportunity to observe and study the best dressed crowds in the world to operate upon the conductor until his mood is to treat us with care and mildness.

Late at night, after the diners and theater-goers have been lost in Harlem, various inebriate persons may perchance emerge from the darker regions of Sixth avenue and swing their arms solemnly at the gripman. If the Broadway cars run for the next 7000 years, this will be the only time when one New Yorker will address another in public without an excuse sent direct from heaven. In these cars late at night it is not impossible that some fearless drunkard will attempt to inaugurate a general conversation. He is quite willing to devote his ability to the affair. He tells of the fun he thinks he has had; describes his feelings; recounts stories of his dim past. None replies, although all listen with every ear. The rake probably ends by borrowing a match, lighting a cigar and entering into a wrangle with the conductor with an abandon, a ferocity and a courage that does not come to us when we are sober.

In the meantime the figures on the street grow less and less in number. Strolling policemen test the locks of the great dark-fronted stores. Nighthawk cabs whirl by the car on their mysterious errands. Finally the cars themselves depart in the way of the citizen and for the few hours before dawn a new sound comes into the still thoroughfare—the cable whirring in its channel underground.

No. 78 THE ROOF GARDENS AND GARDENERS OF NEW YORK

NEW YORK.—When the hot weather comes the roof-gardens burst into full bloom and if an inhabitant of Chicago should take flight on his wings over this city he would observe six or eight flashing spots in the darkness, spots as radiant as crowns. These are the roof-gardens and if a giant had flung a handful of monstrous golden coins upon the sombre-shadowed city he could not have benefited the metropolis more, although he would not have given the same opportunity to various commercial aspirants to charge a price and a half for everything. There are two classes of men—reporters and Central Office detectives—who do not mind these prices because they are very prodigal of their money.

Now is the time of the girl with the copper voice, the Irishman with circular whiskers and the minstrel who had a reputation in 1833. To the street the noise of the band comes down on the wind in fitful gusts and at the brilliantly illuminated rail there is suggestion of many straw hats.

One of the main features of a roof-garden is the waiter who stands directly in front of you whenever anything interesting transpires on the stage. This waiter is three hundred feet high and seventy-two feet wide. His little finger can block your view of the golden-haired soubrette and when he waves his arm, the stage disappears as if by a miracle. What particularly fascinates you is his lack of self-appreciation. He doesn't know that his length over all is three hundred feet and that his beam is seventy-two feet. He only knows that while the golden-haired soubrette is singing her first verse he is depositing beer on the table before some thirsty New Yorkers. He only knows that during the second verse he is making change. He only knows that during the third verse the thirsty New Yorkers object to the roof-garden prices. He does not know that behind him are some fifty citizens who ordinarily would not give three whoops to see the golden-haired soubrette, but who under these particular circumstances are kept from swift assassination by sheer force of the human will. He gives an impressive exhibition of a man who is regardless of consequences, oblivious to everything save his task which is to provide beer. Some day there may be a wholesale massacre of roof-garden waiters but they will die with astonished faces and with questions on their lips. Skulls so steadfastly opaque defy axes or any of the other methods which the populace occasionally use to cure colossal stupidity.

Between numbers on an ordinary roof-garden program, the orchestra sometimes plays what the more enlightened and wary citizens of the town call a "beer overture." But for reasons which no civil service commission could give the waiter does not choose this time to serve the thirsty. No; he waits until the golden-haired soubrette appears, he waits until the haggard audience has goaded itself into some interest in the proceedings. Then he gets under way. Then he comes forth and blots out the stage. In case of war, all roof-garden waiters should be recruited in a special regiment and sent out in advance of everything. There is a peculiar quality of bullet-proofness about them which would turn a projectile pale.

If you have strategy enough in your soul you may gain furtive glimpses of the stage despite the efforts of the waiters and then with something to engage the attention when the attention grows weary of the mystic wind, the flashing yellow lights, the music and the undertone of the far street's roar you should be happy.

Far up into the night there is a wildness, a temper to the air which suggests tossing tree boughs and the swift rustle of grass. The New Yorker whose business will not allow him to go out to nature perhaps appreciates these little opportunities to go up to nature, although doubtless he thinks he goes to see the show.

This season two new roof-gardens have opened. The one at the top of Grand Central Palace is large enough for a regimental drill room. The band is imprisoned still higher in a turreted affair and a person who prefers gentle and unobtrusive amusement can gain deep pleasure and satisfaction from watching the leader of this band gesticulating upon the heavens. His figure is silhouetted beautifully against the sky and every gesture in which he wrings noise from his band is interestingly accentuated.

The other new roof-garden is Oscar Hammerstein's Olympia which blazes on Broadway.

Oscar originally made a great reputation for getting out injunctions. All court judges in New York worked overtime when Oscar was in this business. He enjoined everybody in sight. He had a special machine made—"Drop a nickel in the judge and get an injunction." Then he sent a man to Washington for $22,000 worth of nickels. In Harlem where he then lived it rained orders of the court every day at twelve o'clock. The street-cleaning commission was obliged to enlist a special force to deal with Oscar's injunctions. Citizens meeting on the street never said: "Good morning, how do you feel to-day?" They always said: "Good morning, have you been enjoined yet to-day?" When a man perhaps wished to enter a little game of draw, the universal form was changed when he sent a note to his wife: "Dear Louise; I have received an order of the court restraining me from coming home to dinner to-night. Yours, George."

But Oscar changed. He smashed his machine, girded himself and resolved to provide the public with amusement. And now we see this great mind applying itself to a roof-garden with the same unflagging industry and boundless energy which had previously expressed itself in injunctions. The Olympia his new roof-garden, is a feat. It has an exuberance which reminds one of the Union Depot train-shed of some Western city. The steel arches of the roof make a wide and splendid sweep and over in a corner there are real swans swimming in real water. The whole structure glares like a conflagration with the countless electric lights. Oscar has caused the execution of decorative paintings upon the walls. If he had caused the execution of the decorative painters he would have done better but a man who has devoted the greater part of his life to the propagation of injunctions is not supposed to understand that wall-decoration which appears to have been done with a nozzle is worse than none. But if carpers say that Oscar failed in his landscapes none can say he failed in his measurements of the popular mind. The people come in swarms to the Olympia. Two elevators are busy at conveying them to where the cool and steady night-wind insults the straw hat and the scene here during the popular part of the evening is perhaps more gaudy and dazzling than any other in New York.

The bicycle has attained an economic position of vast importance. The roof-garden ought to attain such a position and it doubtless will as soon as we give it the opportunity it desires. The Arab or the Moor probably invented the roof-garden in some long-gone centuries and they are at this day inveterate roof-gardeners. The American surprisingly belated—for him— has but recently seized upon the idea and its development here has been only partial. The possibilities of the roof-garden are still unknown.

Here is a vast city in which thousands of people in summer half stifle, cry out continually for air, more air, fresher air. Just above their heads is what might be called a county of unoccupied land. It is not ridiculously small when compared with the area of New York county itself. But it is as lonely as a desert, this region of roofs. It is as untrodden as the corners of Arizona. Unless a man be a roof-gardener he knows practically nothing of this land.

Down in the slums necessity forces a solution of problems. It drives the people to the roofs. An evening upon a tenement roof with the great golden march of the stars across the sky and Johnnie gone for a pail of beer is not so bad if you have never seen the mountains nor heard, to your heart, the slow sad song of the pines.

No. 79   AN ELOQUENCE OF GRIEF

THE windows were high and saintly, of the shape that is found in churches. From time to time a policeman at the door spoke sharply to some incoming person. "Take your hat off!" He displayed in his voice the horror of a priest when the sanctity of a chapel is defied or forgotten. The court-room was crowded with people who sloped back comfortably in their chairs, regarding with undeviating glances the procession and its attendant and guardian policemen that moved slowly inside the spear-topped railing. All persons connected with a case went close to the magistrate's desk before a word was spoken in the matter, and then their voices were toned to the ordinary talking strength. The crowd in the court-room could not hear a sentence; they could merely see shifting figures, men that gestured quietly, women that sometimes raised an eager eloquent arm. They could not always see the judge, although they were able to estimate his location by the tall stands surmounted by white globes that were at either hand of him. And so those who had come for curiosity's sweet sake wore an air of being in wait for a cry of anguish, some loud painful protestation that would bring the proper thrill to their jaded, world-weary nerves —wires that refused to vibrate for ordinary affairs.

Inside the railing the court officers shuffled the various groups with speed and skill; and behind the desk the magistrate patiently toiled his way through mazes of wonderful testimony.

In a corner of this space, devoted to those who had business before the judge, an officer in plain clothes stood with a girl that wept constantly. None seemed to notice the girl and there was no reason why she should be noticed if the curious in the body of the court-room were not interested in the devastation which tears bring upon some complexions. Her tears seemed to burn like acid and they left fierce pink marks on her face. Occasionally the girl looked across the room where two well-dressed young women and a man stood waiting with the serenity of people who are not concerned as to the interior fittings of a jail.

The business of the court progressed and presently the girl, the officer and the well-dressed contingent stood before the judge. Thereupon two lawyers engaged in some preliminary fire-wheels which were endured, generally, in silence. The girl, it appeared, was accused of stealing fifty dollars' worth of silk clothing from the room of one of the well-dressed women. She had been a servant in the house.

In a clear way and with none of the ferocity that an accuser often exhibits in a police-court, calmly and moderately, the two young women gave their testimony. Behind them stood their escort, always mute. His part, evidently, was to furnish the dignity, and he furnished it heavily, almost massively.

When they had finished, the girl told her part. She had full, almost Afric, lips, and they had turned quite white. The lawyer for the others asked some questions, which he did—be it said, in passing—with the air of a man throwing flower-pots at a stone house.

It was a short case and soon finished. At the end of it the judge said that, considering the evidence, he would have to commit the girl for trial. Instantly the quick-eyed court officer began to clear the way for the next case. The well-dressed women and their escort turned one way and the girl turned another, toward a door with an austere arch leading into a stone-paved passage. Then it was that a great cry rang through the court-room, the cry of this girl who believed that she was lost.

The loungers, many of them, underwent a spasmodic movement as if they had been knived. The court officers rallied quickly. The girl fell back opportunely for the arms of one of them, and her wild heels clicked twice on the floor. "I am innocent! Oh, I am innocent!"

People pity those who need none, and the guilty sob alone; but innocent or guilty, this girl's scream described such a profound depth of woe—it was so graphic of grief, that it slit with a dagger's sweep the curtain of common-place, and disclosed the gloom-shrouded spectre that sat in the young girl's heart so plainly, in so universal a tone of the mind, that a man heard expressed some far-off midnight terror of his own thought.

The cries died away down the stone-paved passage. A patrol-

man leaned one arm composedly on the railing, and down below him stood an aged, almost toothless wanderer, tottering
and grinning.

"Plase, yer honer," said the old man as the time arrived for
him to speak, "if ye'll lave me go this time, I've niver been
dhrunk befoor, sir."

A court officer lifted his hand to hide a smile.

No. 80   IN THE TENDERLOIN: A DUEL BETWEEN AN ALARM CLOCK AND A SUICIDAL PURPOSE

EVERYBODY knows all about the Tenderloin district of New
York. There is no man that has the slightest claim to citizenship that does not know all there is to know concerning the
Tenderloin. It is wonderful—this amount of truth which the
world's clergy and police forces have collected concerning the
Tenderloin. My friends from the stars obtain all this information, if possible, and then go into this wilderness and apply it.
Upon observing you, certain spirits of the jungle will term you a
wise guy, but there is no gentle humor in the Tenderloin, so you
need not fear that this remark is anything but a tribute to
your knowledge.

Once upon a time there was fought in the Tenderloin a duel
between an Alarm Clock and a Suicidal Purpose. That such a
duel was fought is a matter of no consequence, but it may be
worth a telling, because it may be the single Tenderloin incident
about which every man in the world has not exhaustive
information.

It seems that Swift Doyer and his girl quarreled. Swift was
jealous in the strange and devious way of his kind, and at
midnight, his voice burdened with admonition, grief and deadly
menace, roared through the little flat and conveyed news of the
strife up the air-shaft and down the air-shaft.

"Lied to me, didn't you?" he cried. "Told me a lie and thought
I wouldn't get onto you. Lied to me! Lied to me! There's where
I get crazy. If you hadn't lied to me in one thing, and I hadn't

collared you flat in it, I might believe all the rest, but now—
how do I know you ever tell the truth? How do I know I ain't
always getting a game? Hey? How do I know?"

To the indifferent people whose windows opened on the air-
shaft there came the sound of a girl's low sobbing, while into it
at times burst wildly the hoarse bitterness and rage of the man's
tone. A grim thing is a Tenderloin air-shaft.

Swift arose and paused his harangue for a moment while he
lit a cigarette. He puffed at it vehemently and scowled, black as
a storm-god, in the direction of the sobbing.

"Come! Get up out of that," he said, with ferocity. "Get up
and look at me and let me see you lie!"

There was a flurry of white in the darkness, which was no
more definite to the man than the ice-floes which your reeling
ship passes in the night. Then, when the gas glared out
suddenly, the girl stood before him. She was a wondrous white
figure in her vestal-like robe. She resembled the priestess in
paintings of long-gone Mediterranean religions. Her hair fell
wildly on her shoulder. She threw out her arms and cried to
Swift in a woe that seemed almost as real as the woe of good
people.

"Oh, oh, my heart is broken! My heart is broken!"

But Swift knew as well as the rest of mankind that these
girls have no hearts to be broken, and this acting filled him
with a new rage. He grabbed an alarm clock from the dresser
and banged her heroically on the head with it.

She fell and quivered for a moment. Then she arose, and,
calm and dry-eyed, walked to the mirror. Swift thought she
was taking an account of the bruises, but when he resumed his
cyclonic tirade, she said: "I've taken morphine, Swift!"

Swift leaped at a little red pill box. It was empty. Eight
quarter-grain pills make two grains. The Suicidal Purpose was
distinctly ahead of the Alarm Clock. With great presence of
mind Swift now took the empty pill box and flung it through
the window.

At this time a great battle was begun in the dining-room of
the little flat. Swift dragged the girl to the sideboard, and in
forcing her to drink whisky he almost stuffed the bottle down
her throat. When the girl still sank to the depths of an infinite

drowsiness, sliding limply in her chair like a cloth figure, he dealt her furious blows, and our decorous philosophy knows little of the love and despair that was in those caresses. With his voice he called the light into her eyes, called her from the sinister slumber which her senses welcomed, called her soul back from the verge.

He propped the girl in a chair and ran to the kitchen to make coffee. His fingers might have been from a dead man's hands, and his senses confused the coffee, the water, the coffee-pot, the gas stove, but by some fortune he managed to arrange them correctly. When he lifted the girlish figure and carried her to the kitchen, he was as wild, haggard, gibbering, as a man of midnight murders, and it is only because he was not engaged in the respectable and literary assassination of a royal juke that almost any sensible writer would be ashamed of this story. Let it suffice, then, that when the steel-blue dawn came and distant chimneys were black against a rose sky, the girl sat at the dining-room table chattering insanely and gesturing. Swift, with his hands pressed to his temples, watched her from the other side of the table, with all his mind in his eyes, for each gesture was still a reminiscence, and each tone of her voice a ballad to him. And yet he could not half measure his misery. The tragedy was made of homeliest details. He had to repeat to himself that he, worn-out, stupefied from his struggle, was sitting there awaiting the moment when the unseen hand should whirl this soul into the abyss, and that then he should be alone.

The girl saw a fly alight on a picture. "Oh," she said, "there's a little fly." She arose and thrust out her finger. "Hello, little fly," she said, and touched the fly. The insect was perhaps too cold to be alert, for it fell at the touch of her finger. The girl gave a cry of remorse, and, sinking to her knees, searched the floor, meanwhile uttering tender apologies.

At last she found the fly, and, taking it, her palm went to the gas-jet which still burned weirdly in the dawning. She held her hand close to the flame. "Poor little fly," she said, "I didn't mean to hurt you. I wouldn't hurt you for anything. There now— p'r'aps when you get warm you can fly away again. Did I crush the poor little bit of fly? I'm awful sorry—honest, I am. Poor little thing! Why I wouldn't hurt you for the world, poor little fly——"

Swift was wofully pale and so nerve-weak that his whole body felt a singular coolness. Strange things invariably come into a man's head at the wrong time, and Swift was aware that this scene was defying his preconceptions. His instruction had been that people when dying behaved in a certain manner. Why did this girl occupy herself with an accursed fly? Why in the name of the gods of the drama did she not refer to her past? Why, by the shelves of the saints of literature, did she not clutch her brow and say: "Ah, once I was an innocent girl"? What was wrong with this death scene? At one time he thought that his sense of propriety was so scandalized that he was upon the point of interrupting the girl's babble.

But here a new thought struck him. The girl was not going to die. How could she under these circumstances? The form was not correct.

All this was not relevant to the man's love and despair, but, behold, my friend, at the tragic, the terrible point in life there comes an irrelevancy to the human heart direct from the Wise God. And this is why Swift Doyer thought those peculiar thoughts.

The girl chattered to the fly minute after minute, and Swift's anxiety grew dim and more dim until his head fell forward on the table and he slept as a man who has moved mountains, altered rivers, caused snow to come because he wished it to come, and done his duty.

For an hour the girl talked to the fly, the gas-jet, the walls, the distant chimneys. Finally she sat opposite the slumbering Swift and talked softly to herself.

When broad day came they were both asleep, and the girl's fingers had gone across the table until they had found the locks on the man's forehead. They were asleep, and this after all is a human action, which may safely be done by characters in the fiction of our time.

No. 81   THE "TENDERLOIN" AS IT REALLY IS

MANY requiems have been sung over the corpse of the Tenderloin. Dissipated gentlemen with convivial records burn candles
to its memory each day at the corner of Twenty-eighth street
and Broadway. On the great thoroughfare there are 4,000,000
men who at all times recite loud anecdotes of the luminous
past.

They say: "Oh, if you had only come around when the old
Haymarket was running!" They relate the wonders of this prehistoric time and fill the mind of youth with poignant regret.
Everybody on earth must have attended regularly at this infernal Haymarket. The old gentlemen with convivial records
do nothing but relate the glories of this place. To be sure, they
tell of many other resorts, but the old gentlemen really do their
conjuring with this one simple name—"the old Haymarket."

The Haymarket is really responsible for half the tales that
are in the collections of these gay old boys of the silurian
period. Some time a man will advertise "The Haymarket Restored," and score a clamoring, popular success. The interest in
a reincarnation of a vanished Athens must pale before the
excitement caused by "The Haymarket Restored."

Let a thing become a tradition, and it becomes half a lie.
These moss-grown columns that support the sky over Broadway
street corners insist that life in this dim time was a full joy.
Their descriptions are short, but graphic.

One of this type will cry: "Everything wide open, my boy;
everything wide open! You should have seen it. No sneaking
in side doors. Everything plain as day. Ah, those were the times!
Reubs from the West used to have their bundles lifted every
night before your eyes. Always somebody blowing champagne
for the house. Great! Great! Diamonds, girls, lights, music.
Well, maybe it wasn't smooth! Fights all over Sixth avenue.
Wasn't room enough. Used to hold over-flow fights in the side
streets. Say, it was great!"

Then the type heaves a sigh and murmurs: "But now? Dead
—dead as a mackerel. The Tenderloin is a graveyard. Quiet
as a tomb. Say, you ought to have been around here when the
old Haymarket was running."

Perchance they miss in their definition of the Tenderloin. They describe it as a certain condition of affairs in a metropolitan district. But probably it is in truth something more dim, an essence, an emotion—something superior to the influences of politics or geographies, a thing unchangeable. It represents a certain wild impulse, and a wild impulse is yet more lasting than an old Haymarket. And so we come to reason that the Tenderloin is not dead at all and that the old croakers on the corners are men who have mistaken the departure of their own youth for the death of the Tenderloin, and that there still exists the spirit that flings beer bottles, jumps debts and makes havoc for the unwary; also sings in a hoarse voice at 3 a.m.

There is one mighty fact, however, that the croakers have clinched. In the old days there was a great deal of money and few dress clothes exhibited in the Tenderloin. Now it is all clothes and no money. The spirit is garish, for display, as are the flaming lights that advertise theatres and medicines. In those days long ago there might have been freedom and fraternity.

Billie Maconnigle is probably one of the greatest society leaders that the world has produced. Seventh avenue is practically one voice in this matter.

He asked Flossie to dance with him, and Flossie did, seeming to enjoy the attentions of this celebrated cavalier. He asked her again, and she accepted again. Johnnie, her fellow promptly interrupted the dance.

"Here!" he said, grabbing Maconnigle by the arm. "Dis is me own private snap! Youse gitaway f'm here an' leggo d' loidy!"

"A couple a nits," rejoined Maconnigle swinging his arm clear of his partner. "Youse go chase yerself. I'm spieling wit' dis loidy when I likes, an' if youse gits gay, I'll knock yer block off —an' dat's no dream!"

"Youse'll knock nuttin' off."

"Won't I?"

"Nit. An' if yeh say much I'll make yeh look like a lobster, you fresh mug. Leggo me loidy!"

"A couple a nits."

"Won't?"

"Nit."

Blim! Blam! Crash!

The orchestra stopped playing and the musicians wheeled in their chairs, gazing with that semi-interest which only musicians in a dance hall can bring to bear upon such a scene. Several waiters ran forward, crying "Here, gents, quit dat!" A tall, healthy individual with no coat slid from behind the bar at the far end of the hall, and came with speed. Two well-dressed youths, drinking bottled beer at one end of the tables, nudged each other in ecstatic delight, and gazed with all their eyes at the fight. They were seeing life. They had come purposely to see it.

The waiters grabbed the fighters quickly. Maconnigle went through the door some three feet ahead of his hat, which came after him with a battered crown and a torn rim. A waiter with whom Johnnie had had a discussion over the change had instantly seized this opportunity to assert himself. He grappled Johnnie from the rear and flung him to the floor, and the tall, heathy person from behind the bar, rushing forward, kicked him in the head. Johnnie didn't say his prayers. He only wriggled and tried to shield his head with his arms, because every time that monstrous foot struck it made red lightning flash in his eyes.

But the tall, healthy man and his cohort of waiters had forgotten one element. They had forgotten Flossie. She could worry Johnnie; she could summon every art to make him wildly jealous; she could cruelly, wantonly harrow his soul with every device known to her kind, but she wouldn't stand by and see him hurt by gods nor men.

Blim! As the tall person drew back for his fourth kick, a beer mug landed him just back of his ear. Scratch! The waiter who had grabbed Johnnie from behind found that fingernails had made a ribbon of blood down his face as neatly as if a sign painter had put it there with a brush.

This cohort of waiters was, however, well drilled. Their leader was prone, but they rallied gallantly, and flung Johnnie and Flossie into the street, thinking no doubt that these representatives of the lower classes could get their harmless pleasure just as well outside.

The crowd at the door favored the vanquished. "Sherry!"

said a voice. "Sherry! Here comes a cop!" Indeed a helmet and brass buttons shone brightly in the distance. Johnnie and Flossie sherried with all the promptitude allowed to a wounded man and a girl whose sole anxiety is the man. They ended their flight in a little dark alley.

Flossie was sobbing as if her heart was broken. She hung over her wounded hero, wailing and making moan to the sky, weeping with the deep and impressive grief of gravesides, when he swore because his head ached.

"Dat's all right," said Johnnie. "Nex' time youse needn't be so fresh wit' every guy what comes up."

"Well, I was only kiddin', Johnnie," she cried, forlornly.

"Well, yeh see what yeh done t' me wit'cher kiddin'," replied Johnnie.

They came forth cautiously from their alley and journeyed homeward. Johnnie had had enough of harmless pleasure.

However, after a considerable period of reflective silence, he paused and said: "Say, Floss, youse couldn't a done a t'ing t' dat guy."

"I jest cracked 'im under d' ear," she explained. "An' it laid 'im flat out, too."

A complacence for their victory here came upon them, and as they walked out of the glow of Seventh avenue into a side street it could have been seen that their self satisfaction was complete.

Five men flung open the wicket doors of a brilliant cafe on Broadway and, entering, took seats at a table. They were in evening dress, and each man held his chin as if it did not belong to him.

"Well, fellows, what'll you drink?" said one. He found out, and after the ceremony there was a period of silence. Ultimately another man cried: "Let's have another drink." Following this outburst and its attendant ceremony there was another period of silence.

At last a man murmured: "Well, let's have another drink." Two members of the party discussed the state of the leather market. There was an exciting moment when a little newsboy slid into the place, crying a late extra, and was ejected by the waiter. The five men gave the incident their complete attention.

"Let's have a drink," said one afterward.

At an early hour of the morning one man yawned and said: "I'm going home. I've got to catch an early train, and——"

The four others awoke. "Oh, hold on, Tom. Hold on. Have another drink before you go. Don't go without a last drink."

He had it. Then there was a silence. Then he yawned again and said: "Let's have another drink."

They settled comfortably once more around the table. From time to time somebody said: "Let's have a drink."

Yes, the Tenderloin is more than a place. It is an emotion. And this spirit seems still to ring true for some people. But if one is ever obliged to make explanation to any of the old croakers, it is always possible to remark that the Tenderloin has grown too fine. Therein lies the cause of the change.

To the man who tries to know the true things there is something hollow and mocking about this Tenderloin of to-day, as far as its outward garb is concerned. The newer generation brought new clothes with them. The old Tenderloin is decked out. And wherever there are gorgeous lights, massive buildings, dress clothes and theatrical managers, there is very little nature, and it may be no wonder that the old spirit of the locality chooses to lurk in the darker places.

No. 82 IN THE "TENDERLOIN"

THE waiters were very wise. Every man of them had worked at least three years in a Tenderloin restaurant, and this must be equal to seven centuries and an added two decades in Astoria. Even the man who opened oysters wore an air of accumulated information. Here the science of life was perfectly understood by all.

At 10 o'clock the place was peopled only by waiters and the men behind the long bar. The innumerable tables represented a vast white field, and the glaring electric lamps were not obstructed in their mission of shedding a furious orange radiance upon the cloths. An air of such peace and silence reigned that one might have heard the ticking of a clock. It was as quiet as a New England sitting room.

As 11 o'clock passed, however, and time marched toward 12, the place was suddenly filled with people. The process was hardly to be recognized. One surveyed at one moment a bare expanse of tables with groups of whispering waiters and at the next it was crowded with men and women attired gorgeously and plainly and splendidly and correctly. The electric glare swept over a region of expensive bonnets. Frequently the tall pride of a top hat—a real top hat—could be seen on its way down the long hall, and the envious said with sneers that the theatrical business was booming this year.

Without, the cable cars moved solemnly toward the mysteries of Harlem, and before the glowing and fascinating refrigerators displayed at the front of the restaurant a group of cabmen engaged in their singular diplomacy.

If there ever has been in a New York cafe an impulse from the really Bohemian religion of fraternity it has probably been frozen to death. A universal suspicion, a thing of so austere a cast that we mistake it for a social virtue, is the quality that generally oppresses us. But the hand of a bartender is a supple weapon of congeniality. In the small hours a man may forget the formulae which prehistoric fathers invented for him. Usually social form as practised by the stupid is not a law. It is a vital sensation. It is not temporary, emotional; it is fixed and, very likely, the power that makes the rain, the sunshine, the wind, now recognizes social form as an important element in the curious fashioning of the world. It is as solid, as palpable as a fort, and if you regard any landscape, you may see it in the foreground.

Therefore a certain process which moves in this restaurant is very instructive. It is a process which makes constantly toward the obliteration of the form. It never dangerously succeeds, but it is joyous and frank in its attempt.

A man in race-track clothing turned in his chair and addressed a stranger at the next table. "I beg your pardon—will you tell me the time please?"

The stranger was in evening dress, very correct indeed. At the question, he stared at the man for a moment, particularly including his tie in this look of sudden and subtle contempt. After a silence he drew forth his watch, looked at it, and returned it to his pocket. After another silence he drooped his eyes with peculiar significance, puffed his cigar and, of a sudden, remarked: "Why don't you look at the clock?"

The race-track man was a genial soul. He promptly but affably directed the kind gentleman to a place supposed to be located at the end of the Brooklyn trolley lines.

And yet at 4:30 a.m. the kind gentleman overheard the race-track man telling his experience in London in 1886, and as he had experiences similar in beauty, and as it was 4:30 a.m., and as he had completely forgotten the incident of the earlier part of the evening, he suddenly branched into the conversation, and thereafter it took ten strong men to hold him from buying a limitless ocean of wine.

A curious fact of upper Broadway is the man who knows everybody, his origin, wealth, character and tailor. His knowledge is always from personal intercourse, too, and, without a doubt, he must have lived for ten thousand years to absorb all the anecdotes which he has at the tip of his tongue. If it were a woman, now, most of the stories would be weird resurrections of long-entombed scandals. The trenches for the dead on medieval battle fields would probably be clawed open to furnish evidence of various grim truths, or of untruths, still more grim. But if, according to a rigid definition, these men are gossips, it is in a kinder way than is usually denominated by the use of the word. Let a woman once take an interest in the short-comings of her neighbors, and she immediately and naturally begins to magnify events in a preposterous fashion, until one can imagine that the law of proportion is merely a legend. There is one phrase which she uses eternally. "They say——" Herein is the peculiar terror of the curse. "They say——" It is so vague that the best spear in the world must fail to hit this shadow. The charm of it is that a woman seldom relates from personal experience. It is nearly always some revolving tale from a hundred tongues.

But it is evident in most cases that the cafe historians of

upper Broadway speak from personal experience. The dove
that brought the olive branch to Noah was one of their number.
Another was in Hades at the time that Lucifer made his celebrated speech against the street-lighting system there. Another
is an ex-member of the New Jersey Legislature. All modes, all
experiences, all phases of existence are chronicled by these
men. They are not obliged to fall back upon common report for
their raw material. They possess it in the original form.

A cafe of the kind previously described is a great place for
the concentration of the historians. Here they have great
opportunities.

"See that fellow going there? That's young Jimmie Lode.
Knew his father well. Denver people, you know. Old man had a
strange custom of getting drunk on the first Friday after the
first Thursday in June. Indian reservation near his house. Used
to go out and fist-fight the Indians. Gave a twenty-dollar gold
piece to every Indian he licked. Indians used to labor like
thunder to get licked. Well, sir, one time the big chief of the
whole push was trying to earn his money, and, by Jove, no
matter what he did, he couldn't seem to fix it so the old man
could lick him. So finally he laid down flat on the ground and
the old man jumped on him and stove in his bulwarks. Indian
said it was all right, but he thought forty dollars was a better
figure for stove-in bulwarks. But the old man said he had
agreed to pay twenty dollars, and he wouldn't give up another
sou. So they had a fight—a real fight, you know—and the
Indian killed him.

"Well, that's the son over there. Father left him a million
and a half. Maybe Jack ain't spending it. Say! He just pours it
out. He's crushed on Dollie Bangle, you know. She plays over
here at the Palais de Glace. That's her now he's talking to. Ain't
she a peach. Say? Am I right? Well, I should say so. She don't
do a thing to his money. Burns it in an open grate. She's on the
level with him, though. That's one thing. Well, I say she is. Of
course, I'm sure of it."

In the meantime others pass before the historian's watchful
vision, and he continues heroically to volley his traditions.

The babble of voices grew louder and louder. The heavy

smoke clouds eddied above the shining countenances. Into the street came the clear, cold blue of impending daylight, and over the cobbles roared a milk wagon.

No. 83   YEN-HOCK BILL AND HIS SWEETHEART

THEY called him Yen-Hock Bill. He had been a book agent, a confidence man, a member of a celebrated minstrel troupe, a shoplifter, a waiter in a Bowery restaurant and other things. But he had never been guilty of a dishonest act in his life. He used to say so, solemnly.

"No sir," he often remarked. "I've lived at a pretty hot gait all my life, but I've always been on the level. Never did a crooked thing since I was born. No, sir!"

He did not stick at an occupation because he was fond of a certain delicate amusement of the Chinese. A most peculiar truth of life is the fact that, when a man gets to be an opium smoker, he has ill-fortune. Disaster comes upon his business schemes, and his valuable friends slide unaccountably away from him. And so it happened that, when Bill fell deadly ill with pneumonia, there was nobody to come to him and bid him a good journey through the skyland.

On the contrary, his dragon of a landlady paced the halls and wondered who was going to provide the $4 Bill owed for lodging. She was a woman with business principles, and she wanted her $4. She did not give three hurrahs in Hades whether Bill lived or died, so long as he did not put her to pecuniary loss. She was a just woman; her life had been a hard struggle for daily bread, and when anybody owed her $4, it was no more than fair that she should be paid.

Bill was a small man. He had a way of pulling the sheet up to his throat with one thin hand, and then coughing until his whole body jumped and writhed. When he was not coughing, he simply lay and rolled his eyes. In the days of his prosperity, when his particular confidence game was paying him a great deal of money, Bill had a sweetheart, and it becomes a most painful obligation to introduce her into this story.

When Julie heard of Bill's plight, she went there post haste. She flung herself down at the bedside and cried: "Oh, Billie!"

Bill raised himself and scanned her with a cold eye. "Why th'ell didn't you come before?" he demanded. "You're a nice one, you are. Leaving me here to die—leaving me here to die all alone—all alone—without a friend in the world." He shed tears.

Julie soothed him and flattered the man in the manner of woman, even in the face of his arrant injustice, and by the way the irritation in his voice was of a quality worse than knife blades. "I'll take you right to the flat, dear," cried Julie, sobbing. "There I can take care of you and 'tend you until you get well; poor, poor boy!"

But when she put out her hand to smooth his brow, he brushed her away savagely. "Oh, you make me tired, you fool! Tell me how I'm going to get around there, will you? You are an ass."

Thereupon Julie pleaded with him. "I'll call a cab, dear, and have it right here at the door, and the coachman can help you down stairs. I'll go around now and borrow Swift Doyer's Winter overcoat, and then I'll go home and have Mary fix everything ready for you. And then I'll have the doctor come right over. Won't you come, dear? Won't you?"

Bill turned his stern face toward the wall. "No," he answered. To one who had no interest in the proceedings it would have been plain that Bill lied, but since this woman loved this man, she could never tell when he lied to her. So she continued to beseech him. Always he answered: "No."

At last she went into the hall to beg the landlady to use her influence, but the door was no sooner closed behind her than Bill cried out, in a wild spasm of sick man's rage: "Julie, Julie!"

Julie returned in a flurry. "What, dear? What is it?"

"Why don't you order the cab?" he cried, shrilly. "Get a gait on you, will you! Think I want to lie here forever?"

"All right, Billie—all right," answered Julie. She kissed him and hurried away. Bill scowled at the wall and muttered sullenly to himself. Suddenly he had seemed possessed of some great grievance.

Julie returned, out of breath, and with Swift Doyer's Winter overcoat over her arm. "It's all right!" she cried. "The cab's at the door, and everything is all fixed."

But here the landlady appeared as a factor. Previously she had been concerned chiefly about her four dollars, but now her ideas of respectability were concerned. She evidently had concluded that it would be better for Bill to die alone in the hall bedroom. "He shan't be taken from my house until I know where he is going," she said, coldly and significantly to Julie.

The girl flashed upon her one of those tearful glances into which a woman can put scorn, rage and at the same time entreaty. Julie hesitated a moment, and the landlady never knew how near she came to a time of fire and the sword, whirlwind and sudden death. Better ask a ravenous wolf to sleep under your pillow than to stand between a woman who loves so completely and the man.

But Julie went calmly away with no word. Later a four-wheeler drew up before the house, and Swift Doyer and Jimmie the Mole emerged from it. "We want that sick man," said Swift to the landlady. "I'm his friend, and I'm going to take him home."

The landlady gracefully accepted four dollars from Swift, and led the way to the hall bedroom.

"Let 'er go easy, boys," said Bill, with a wan smile, as they carried him around the curve of the stairs. In daylight Bill was a sad figure. Two weeks' growth of red beard was on his leaden face, and his eyes swung and turned in a way that was at once childish and insane. But when they bundled him into the cab, Julie put her arms about his neck and cooed and murmured. The instant they were alone in Julie's flat he began to howl at her. Swift Doyer was a good fellow, but he used to remark that Bill's voice made him wish that he was a horse, so that he could spring upon the bed and trample him to death. And for many days thereafter Bill bullied and abused, rated and raged at the girl, until people whose windows opened on the air-shaft often remarked: "Say, why don't she kill him!"

Julie arrived at a point where she threw out her hands and

said: "Oh, be good to me; won't you, Billie, dear?" "No! Why should I?"

No. 84 STEPHEN CRANE IN MINETTA LANE

MINETTA LANE is a small and becobbled valley between hills of dingy brick. At night the street lamps, burning dimly, cause the shadows to be important, and in the gloom one sees groups of quietly conversant negroes with occasionally the gleam of a passing growler. Everything is vaguely outlined and of uncertain identity unless indeed it be the flashing buttons and shield of the policeman on post. The Sixth avenue horse cars jingle past one end of the Lane and, a block eastward, the little thoroughfare ends in the darkness of MacDougal street.

One wonders how such an insignificant alley could get such an absurdly large reputation, but, as a matter of fact, Minetta Lane, and Minetta street, which leads from it southward to Bleecker street, were, until a few years ago, two of the most enthusiastically murderous thoroughfares in New York. Bleecker street, MacDougal street and nearly all the streets thereabouts were most unmistakably bad, but when the Minettas started out the other streets went away and hid. To gain a reputation in Minetta Lane, in those days, a man was obliged to commit a number of furious crimes, and no celebrity was more important than the man who had a good honest killing to his credit. The inhabitants for the most part were negroes and they represented the very worst elements of their race. The razor habit clung to them with the tenacity of an epidemic, and every night the uneven cobbles felt blood. Minetta Lane was not a public thoroughfare at this period. It was a street set apart, a refuge for criminals. Thieves came here preferably with their gains, and almost any day peculiar sentences passed among the inhabitants. "Big Jim turned a thousand last night." "No-Toe's made another haul." And the worshipful citizens would make haste to be present at the consequent revel.

As has been said, Minetta Lane was then no thoroughfare. A peaceable citizen chose to make a circuit rather than venture through this place, that swarmed with the most dangerous people in the city. Indeed, the thieves of the district used to say: "Once get in the Lane and you're all right." Even a policeman in chase of a criminal would probably shy away instead of pursuing him into the Lane. The odds were too great against a lone officer.

Sailors and any men who might appear to have money about them, were welcomed with all proper ceremony at the terrible dens of the Lane. At departure, they were fortunate if they still retained their teeth. It was the custom to leave very little else to them. There was every facility for the capture of coin, from trap-doors to plain ordinary knock-out drops.

And yet Minetta Lane is built on the grave of Minetta Brook, where, in olden times, lovers walked under the willows of the bank, and Minetta Lane, in later times, was the home of many of the best families of the town.

A negro named Bloodthirsty was perhaps the most luminous figure of Minetta Lane's aggregation of desperadoes. Bloodthirsty, supposedly, is alive now, but he has vanished from the Lane. The police want him for murder. Bloodthirsty is a large negro and very hideous. He has a rolling eye that shows white at the wrong time and his neck, under the jaw, is dreadfully scarred and pitted.

Bloodthirsty was particularly eloquent when drunk, and in the wildness of a spree he would rave so graphically about gore that even the habituated wool of old timers would stand straight. Bloodthirsty meant most of it, too. That is why his orations were impressive. His remarks were usually followed by the wide lightning sweep of his razor. None cared to exchange epithets with Bloodthirsty. A man in a boiler iron suit would walk down to City Hall and look at the clock before he would ask the time of day from the single-minded and ingenuous Bloodthirsty.

After Bloodthirsty, in combative importance, came No-Toe Charley. Singularly enough, Charley was called No-Toe solely because he did not have a toe to his feet. Charley was a small negro and his manner of amusement was not Bloodthirsty's simple way. As befitting a smaller man, Charley was more wise, more sly, more round-about than the other man. The path of his crimes was like a corkscrew, in architecture, and his method led him to make many tunnels. With all his cleverness, however, No-Toe was finally induced to pay a visit to the gentlemen in the grim gray building up the river.

Black-Cat was another famous bandit who made the Lane his home. Black-Cat is dead. It is within some months that Jube Tyler has been sent to prison, and after mentioning the recent disappearance of Old Man Spriggs, it may be said that the Lane is now destitute of the men who once crowned it with a glory of crime. It is hardly essential to mention Guinea Johnson. Guinea is not a great figure. Guinea is just an ordinary little crook. Sometimes Guinea pays a visit to his friends, the other little crooks who make homes in the Lane, but he himself does not live there, and with him out of it there is now no one whose industry in unlawfulness has yet earned him the dignity of a nickname. Indeed, it is difficult to find people now who remember the old gorgeous days, although it is but two years since the Lane shone with sin like a new head-light. But after a search the reporter found three.

Mammy Ross is one of the last relics of the days of slaughter still living there. Her weird history also reaches back to the blossoming of the first members of the Whyo gang in the old Sixth ward, and her mind is stored with bloody memories. She at one time kept a sailor's boarding house near the Tombs prison, and accounts of all the festive crimes of that neighborhood in ancient years roll easily from her tongue. They killed a sailor man every day, and pedestrians went about the streets wearing stoves for fear of the handy knives. At the present day the route to Mammy's home is up a flight of grimy stairs that is pasted on the outside of an old and tottering frame house. Then there is a hall blacker than a wolf's throat and this hall leads to a little kitchen where Mammy usually sits groaning by the fire. She is, of course, very old and she is also very fat. She seems always to be in great pain. She says she is suffering from "de very las' dregs of de yaller fever."

During the first part of a reporter's recent visit, old Mammy seemed most dolefully oppressed by her various diseases. Her great body shook and her teeth clicked spasmodically during her long and painful respirations. From time to time she reached her trembling hand and drew a shawl closer about her shoulders. She presented as true a picture of a person undergoing steady, unchangeable, chronic pain as a patent medicine firm could wish to discover for miraculous purposes. She breathed like a fish thrown out on the bank, and her old head continually quivered in the nervous tremors of the extremely aged and debilitated person. Meanwhile her daughter hung over the stove and placidly cooked sausages.

Appeals were made to the old woman's memory. Various personages who had been sublime figures of crime in the long-gone days were mentioned to her, and presently her eyes began to brighten. Her head no longer quivered. She seemed to lose for a period her sense of pain in the gentle excitement caused by the invocation of the spirits of her memory.

It appears that she had had a historic quarrel with Apple Mag. She first recited the prowess of Apple Mag; how this emphatic lady used to argue with paving stones, carving knives and bricks. Then she told of the quarrel; what Mag said; what she said; what Mag said; what she said. It seems that they cited each other as spectacles of sin and corruption in more fully explanatory terms than are commonly known to be possible. But it was one of Mammy's most gorgeous recollections, and, as she told it, a smile widened over her face.

Finally she explained her celebrated retort to one of the most illustrious thugs that had blessed the city in bygone days. "Ah says to 'im, Ah says: 'You—you'll die in yer boots like Gallopin' Thompson—dat's what you'll do. You des min' dat, honey! Ah got o'ny one chile an' he ain't nuthin' but er cripple, but le'me tel' you, man, dat boy'll live t' pick de feathers f'm de goose dat'll eat de grass dat grows over your grave, man!' Dat's what I tol' 'im. But—lan' sake—how I know dat in less'n three day, dat man be lying in de gutter wif a knife stickin' out'n his back. Lawd, no, I sholy never s'pected noting like dat."

These reminiscences, at once maimed and reconstructed, have been treasured by old Mammy as carefully, as tenderly, as if they were the various little tokens of an early love. She applies the same back-handed sentiment to them, and, as she sits groaning by the fire, it is plainly to be seen that there is only one food for her ancient brain, and that is the recollection of the beautiful fights and murders of the past.

On the other side of the Lane, but near Mammy's house, Pop Babcock keeps a restaurant. Pop says it is a restaurant and so it must be one, but you could pass there ninety times each day and never know that you were passing a restaurant. There is one obscure little window in the basement and if you went close and peered in, you might, after a time, be able to make out a small dusty sign, lying amid jars on a shelf. This sign reads: "Oysters in every style." If you are of a gambling turn of mind, you will probably stand out in the street and bet yourself black in the face that there isn't an oyster within a hundred yards. But Pop Babcock made that sign and Pop Babcock could not tell an untruth. Pop is a model of all the virtues which an inventive fate has made for us. He says so.

As far as goes the management of Pop's restaurant, it differs from Sherry's. In the first place, the door is always kept locked. The wardmen of the Fifteenth precinct have a way of prowling through the restaurant almost every night, and Pop keeps the door locked in order to keep out the objectionable people that cause the wardmen's visits. He says so. The cooking stove is located in the main room of the restaurant, and it is placed in such a strategic manner that it occupies about all the space that is not already occupied by a table, a bench and two chairs. The table will, on a pinch, furnish room for the plates of two people if they are willing to crowd. Pop says he is the best cook in the world.

When questioned concerning the present condition of the Lane, Pop said: "Quiet? Quiet? Lo'd save us, maybe it ain't! Quiet? Quiet?" His emphasis was arranged crescendo, until the last word was really a vocal explosion. "Why, disher' Lane ain't nohow like what it uster be—no indeed, it ain't. No, sir! 'Deed it ain't! Why, I kin remember when dey des was a-cuttin' an' a-slashin' 'long yere all night. 'Deed dey was! My—my, dem times was diff'rent! Dat dar Kent, he kep' de place at Green Gate Cou't—down yer ol' Mammy's—an' he was a hard baby— 'deed, he was—an' ol' Black-Cat an' ol' Bloodthirsty, dey was a-roamin' round yere a-cuttin' an' a-slashin' an' a-cuttin' an' a-slashin'. Didn't dar' say boo to a goose in dose days, dat you didn't, less'n you lookin' fer a scrap. No, sir!" Then he gave information concerning his own prowess at that time. Pop is about as tall as a picket on an undersized fence. "But dey didn't have nothin' ter say to me! No, sir! 'Deed, dey didn't! I wouldn't lay down fer none of 'em. No, sir! Dey knew my gait, 'deed, dey did! Man, man, many's de time I buck up agin 'em. Yes, sir!"

At this time Pop had three customers in his place, one asleep on the bench, one asleep on the two chairs, and one asleep on the floor behind the stove.

But there is one man who lends dignity of the real bevel edged type to Minetta Lane and that man is Hank Anderson. Hank of course does not live in the Lane, but the shadow of his social perfections falls upon it as refreshingly as a morning dew. Hank gives a dance twice in each week, at a hall hard by in MacDougal street, and the dusky aristocracy of the neighborhood know their guiding beacon. Moreover, Hank holds an annual ball in Forty-fourth street. Also he gives a picnic each year to the Montezuma Club, when he again appears as a guiding beacon. This picnic is usually held on a barge and the occasion is a very joyous one. Some years ago it required the entire reserve squad of an up-town police precinct to properly control the enthusiasm of the gay picnickers, but that was an exceptional exuberance and no measure of Hank's ability for management.

He is really a great manager. He was Boss Tweed's body servant in the days when Tweed was a political prince, and anyone who saw Bill Tweed through a spy-glass learned the science of leading, pulling, driving and hauling men in a way to keep the men ignorant of it. Hank imbibed from this fount of knowledge and he applied his information in Thompson street. Thompson street salaamed. Presently he bore a proud title: "The Mayor of Thompson street." Dignities from the principal political organization of the city adorned his brow and he speedily became illustrious.

Hank knew the Lane well in its direful days. As for the inhabitants, he kept clear of them and yet in touch with them according to a method that he might have learned in the Sixth ward. The Sixth ward was a good place in which to learn that trick. Anderson can tell many strange tales and good of the Lane and he tells them in the graphic way of his class. "Why, they could steal your shirt without moving a wrinkle on it."

The killing of Joe Carey was the last murder that happened in the Minettas. Carey had what might be called a mixed-ale difference with a man named Kenny. They went out to the middle of Minetta street to affably fight it out and determine the justice of the question. In the scrimmage Kenny drew a knife, thrust quickly and Carey fell. Kenny had not gone a hundred feet before he ran into the arms of a policeman.

There is probably no street in New York where the police keep closer watch than they do in Minetta Lane. There was a time when the inhabitants had a profound and reasonable contempt for the public guardians, but they have it no longer, apparently. Any citizen can walk through there at any time in perfect safety unless, perhaps, he should happen to get too frivolous. To be strictly accurate, the change began under the reign of Police Captain Chapman. Under Captain Groo, the present commander of the Fifteenth precinct, the Lane has donned a complete new garb. Its denizens brag now of its peace, precisely as they once bragged of its war. It is no more a bloody lane. The song of the razor is seldom heard. There are still toughs and semi-toughs galore in it, but they can't get a chance with the copper looking the other way. Groo has got the poor old Lane by the throat. If a man should insist on becoming a victim of the badger game, he could probably succeed upon search in Minetta Lane, as indeed, he could on any of the great avenues, but then Minetta Lane is not supposed to be a pearly street in Paradise.

In the meantime, the Italians have begun to dispute possession of the Lane with the negroes. Green Gate Court is filled with them now, and a row of houses near the MacDougal street corner is occupied entirely by Italian families. None of them seems to be overfond of the old Mulberry Bend fashions of life, and there are no cutting affrays among them worth mentioning. It is the original negro element that makes the trouble when there is trouble.

But they are happy in this condition, are these people. The most extraordinary quality of the negro is his enormous capacity for happiness under most adverse circumstances. Minetta

Lane is a place of poverty and sin, but these influences cannot destroy the broad smile of the negro, a vain and simple child but happy. They all smile here, the most evil as well as the poorest. Knowing the negro, one always expects laughter from him, be he ever so poor, but it was a new experience to see a broad grin on the face of the devil. Even old Pop Babcock had a laugh as fine and mellow as would be the sound of falling glass, broken saints from high windows, in the silence of some great cathedral's hollow.

WESTERN SKETCHES

No. 85 NEBRASKA'S BITTER FIGHT FOR LIFE

EDDYVILLE, DAWSON CO., NEB., Feb. 22.—The vast prairies in this section of Nebraska contain a people who are engaged in a bitter and deadly fight for existence. Some of the reports telegraphed to the East have made it appear that the entire State of Nebraska is a desert. In reality the situation is serious, but it does not include the whole State. However, people feel that thirty counties in pain and destitution is sufficient.

The blot that is laid upon the map of the State begins in the north beyond Custer county. It is there about fifty miles wide. It slowly widens then in a southward direction until when it crosses the Platte River it is over a hundred miles wide. The country to the north and to the west of this blot is one of the finest grazing grounds in the world and the cattlemen there are not suffering. Valentine is in this portion which is exempt. To the eastward, the blot shades off until one finds moderate crops.

In June, 1894, the bounteous prolific prairies of this portion of Nebraska were a-shine with the young and tender green of growing corn. Round and fat cattle filled the barnyards of the farmers. The trees that were congregated about the little homesteads were of the vivid and brave hue of healthy and vigorous vegetation. The towns were alive with the commerce of an industrious and hopeful community. These mighty brown fields stretching for miles under the imperial blue sky of Nebraska had made a promise to the farmer. It was to compensate him for his great labor, his patience, his sacrifices. Under the cool, blue dome the winds gently rustled the arrays of waist-high stalks.

Then, on one day about the first of July there came a menace from the southward. The sun had been growing prophetically more fierce day by day, and in July there began these winds from the south, mild at first and subtle like the breaths of the panting countries of the tropics. The corn in the fields underwent a preliminary quiver from this breeze burdened with an omen of death. In the following days it became stronger, more threatening. The farmers turned anxious eyes toward their fields where the corn was beginning to rustle with a dry and crackling sound which went up from the prairie like cries.

Then from the southern horizon came the scream of a wind hot as an oven's fury. Its valor was great in the presence of the sun. It came when the burning disc appeared in the east and it weakened when the blood-red, molten mass vanished in the west. From day to day, it raged like a pestilence. The leaves of the corn and of the trees turned yellow and sapless like leather. For a time they stood the blasts in the agony of a futile resistance. The farmers helpless, with no weapon against this terrible and inscrutable wrath of nature, were spectators at the strangling of their hopes, their ambitions, all that they could look to from their labor. It was as if upon the massive altar of the earth, their homes and their families were being offered in sacrifice to the wrath of some blind and pitiless deity.

The country died. In the rage of the wind, the trees struggled, gasped through each curled and scorched leaf, then, at last, ceased to exist, and there remained only the bowed and bare skeletons of trees. The corn shivering as from fever, bent and swayed abjectly for a time, then one by one the yellow and tinder-like stalks, twisted and pulled by the rage of the hot breath, died in the fields and the vast and sometime beautiful green prairies were brown and naked.

In a few weeks this prosperous and garden-like country was brought to a condition of despair, but still this furnace-wind swept along the dead land, whirling great clouds of dust, straws, blades of grass. A farmer, gazing from a window was confronted by a swirling tempest of dust that intervened between his vision and his scorched fields. The soil of the roads turned to powder in this tempest, and men traveling against the winds found all the difficulties of some hideous and unnatural snow storm. At nightfall the winds always vanished and the sky which had glistened like a steel shield became of a soft blue, as the purple shadows of a merciful night advanced from the west.

These farmers now found themselves existing in a virtual desert. The earth from which they had wrested each morsel which they had put into their mouths had now abandoned them. Nature made light of her obligation under the toil of these men. This vast tract was now a fit place for the nomads of Sahara.

And yet, for the most part, there was no wavering, no absence of faith in the ultimate success of the beautiful soil. Some few despaired at once and went to make new homes in the north, in the south, in the east, in the west. But the greater proportion of the people of this stricken district were men who loved their homes, their farms, their neighborhoods, their counties. They had become rooted in this soil, which so seldom failed them in compensation for their untiring and persistent toil. They could not move all the complexities of their social life and their laboring life. The magic of home held them from traveling toward the promise of other lands. And upon these people there came the weight of the strange and unspeakable punishment of nature. They are a fearless folk, completely American. Their absolute types are now sitting about New England dinner tables. They summoned their strength for a long war with cold and hunger. Prosperity was at the distance of a new crop of 1895. It was to be from August to August. Between these months loomed the great white barrier of the winter of 1894–95. It was a supreme battle to which to look forward. It required the profound and dogged courage of the American peoples who have come into the West to carve farms, railroads, towns, cities, in the heart of a world fortified by enormous distances.

The weakest were, of course, the first to cry out at the pain of it. Farmers, morally certain of the success of the crop, had already gone into debt for groceries and supplies. The hot winds left these men without crops and without credit. They were instantly confronted with want. They stood for a time reluctant. Then family by family they drove away to other States where there might be people who would give their great muscular hands opportunity to earn food for their wives and little children.

Then came the struggle of the ones who stood fast. They were soon driven to bay by nature, now the pitiless enemy. They were sturdy and dauntless. When the cry for help came from their lips it was to be the groan from between the clenched teeth. Men began to offer to work at the rate of twenty-five cents a day, but, presently, in the towns no one had work for them, and, after a time, barely anyone had twenty-five cents a day which they dared invest in labor. Life in the little towns halted. The wide roads, which had once been so busy, became the dry veins of the dead land.

Meanwhile, the chill and tempest of the inevitable winter had gathered in the north and swept down upon the devastated country. The prairies turned bleak and desolate.

The wind was a direct counter-part of the summer. It came down like wolves of ice. And then was the time that from this district came that first wail, half impotent rage, half despair. The men went to feed the starving cattle in their tiny allowances in clothes that enabled the wind to turn their bodies red and then blue with cold. The women shivered in the houses where fuel was as scarce as flour, and where flour was sometimes as scarce as diamonds.

The cry for aid was heard everywhere. The people of a dozen States responded in a lavish way and almost at once. A relief commission was appointed by Governor Holcomb at Lincoln to receive the supplies and distribute them to the people in want. The railroad companies granted transportation to the cars that came in loaded with coal and flour from Iowa and Minnesota, fruit from California, groceries and clothing from New York and Ohio, and almost everything possible from Georgia and Louisiana. The relief commission became involved in a mighty tangle. It was obliged to contend with enormous difficulties.

Sometimes a car arrives in Lincoln practically in pawn. It has accumulated the freight charges of perhaps half a dozen rail-roads. The commission then corresponds and corresponds with railroads to get the charges remitted. It is usually the fault of the people sending the car who can arrange for free and quick transportation by telegraphing the commission in Lincoln a list of what their car, or cars, contain. The commission will then arrange all transportation.

A facetious freight agent in the East labelled one carload of food: "Outfit for emigrants." This car reached the people who needed it only after the most extraordinary delays and after many mistakes and explanations and re-explanations. Meanwhile, a certain minority began to make war upon the commission at the expense of the honest and needy majority. Men resorted to all manner of tricks in order to seduce the commission into giving them supplies which they did not need. Also various unscrupulous persons received donations of provisions from the East and then sold them to the people at a very low rate it is true, but certainly at the most obvious of profits. The commission detected one man selling a donated carload of coal at the price of forty cents per ton. They discovered another man who had collected some two thousand dollars from charitable folk in other States, and of this sum he really gave to the people about eight hundred dollars. The commission was obliged to make long wars upon all these men who wished to practice upon the misery of the farmers.

As is mentioned above, this stricken district does not include in any manner the entire State of Nebraska, but, nevertheless, certain counties that are not in the drought portion had no apparent hesitation about vociferously shouting for relief. When the State Legislature appropriated one hundred and fifty thousand dollars to help the starving districts, one or two counties in the east at once sent delegations to the capital to apply for a part of it. They said, ingenuously, that it was the State's money and they wanted their share of it.

To one town in the northern part of the State there was sent from the East a carload of coal. The citizens simply apportioned it on the basis of so much per capita. They appointed a committee to transport the coal from the car to each man's residence. It was the fortune of this committee finally to get into the office of a citizen who was fairly prosperous.

"Where do yeh want yer coal put?" they said, with a clever and sly wink.

"What coal?"

"Why, our coal! Your coal! The coal what was sent here."

"Git out 'a here! If you put any coal in my cellar I'll kill some of yeh."

They argued for a long time. They did not dare to leave

anyone out of the conspiracy. He could then tell of it. Having failed with him, they went to his wife and tried to get her to allow them to put the coal in the cellar. In this also they were not successful.

These are a part of the difficulties with which the commission fights. Its obligation is to direct all supplies from the generous and pitying inhabitants of other States into the correct paths to reach the suffering. To do this over a territory covering many hundreds of square miles, and which is but meagrely connected by railroads, is not an easy task.

L. P. Ludden, the secretary and general manager of the commission, works early and late and always. In his office at Lincoln he can be seen at any time when people are usually awake working over the correspondence of the bureau. He is confronted each mail by a heap of letters that is as high as a warehouse. He told the writer of this article that he had not seen his children for three weeks, save when they were asleep. He always looked into their room when he arrived home late at night and always before he left early in the morning.

But he is the most unpopular man in the State of Nebraska. He is honest, conscientious and loyal; he is hard-working and has great executive ability. He struggles heroically with the thugs who wish to filch supplies, and with the virtuous but misguided philanthropists who write to learn of the folks that received their fifty cents and who expect a full record of this event.

From a hundred towns whose citizens are in despair for their families, arises a cry against Ludden. From a hundred towns whose citizens do not need relief and in consequence do not get it, there arises a cry against Ludden. The little newspapers print the uncompromising sentence: "Ludden must go!" Delegations call upon the governor and tell him that the situation would be mitigated if they could only have relief from Ludden. Members of the legislature prodded by their rural constituents, arise and demand an explanation of the presence in office of Ludden. And yet this man with the square jaw and the straight set lips hangs on in the indomitable manner of a man of the soil. He remains in front of the tales concerning him; merely turns them into his bureau and an explanation comes out by the regular machinery of his system, to which he has imparted his personal quality of inevitableness. Once, grown tired of the abuse, he asked of the governor leave to resign, but the governor said that it would be impossible now to appoint a new man without some great and disastrous halt of the machinery. Ludden returned to his post and to the abuse.

But in this vast area of desolated land there has been no benefit derived from the intrigues and scufflings at Lincoln which is two hundred miles away from the scene of the suffering. This town of Eddyville is in the heart of the stricken territory. The thermometer at this time registers eighteen degrees below zero. The temperature of the room which is the writer's bedchamber is precisely one and a half degrees below zero. Over the wide white expanses of prairie, the icy winds from the north shriek, whirling high sheets of snow and enveloping the house in white clouds of it. The tempest forces fine stinging flakes between the rattling sashes of the window that fronts the storm. The air has remained gloomy the entire day. From other windows can be seen the snowflakes fleeing into the south, traversing as level a line as bullets, speeding like the wind. The people in the sod houses are much more comfortable than those who live in frame dwellings. Many of these latter are high upon ridges of the prairie and the fingers of the storm clutch madly at them. The sod houses huddle close to the ground and their thick walls restrain the heat of the scant wood-fire from escaping.

Eddyville is a typical town of the drought district. Approaching it over the prairie, one sees a row of little houses, blocked upon the sky. Most of them are one storied. Some of the stores have little square false-fronts. The buildings straggle at irregular intervals along the street and a little board sidewalk connects them. On all sides stretches the wind-swept prairie.

This town was once a live little place. From behind the low hillocks, the farmers came jogging behind their sturdy teams. The keepers of the three or four stores did a thriving trade. But at this time the village lies as inanimate as a corpse. In the rears of the stores, a few men perhaps, sit listlessly by the stoves. The people of the farms remain close in-doors during this storm. They have not enough warm clothing to venture into the terrible blasts. One can drive past house after house without seeing signs of life unless it be a weak curl of smoke scudding away from a chimney. Occasionally, too, one finds a deserted homestead, a desolate and unhappy thing upon the desolate and unhappy prairie.

And for miles around this town lie the countless acres of the drought-pestered district.

Some distance from here a man was obliged to leave his wife and baby and go into the eastern part of the State to make a frenzied search for work that might be capable of furnishing them with food. The woman lived alone with her baby until the provisions were gone. She had received a despairing letter from her husband. He was still unable to get work. Everybody was searching for it; none had it to give. Meanwhile he had ventured a prodigious distance from home.

The nearest neighbor was three miles away. She put her baby in its little ramshackle carriage and traveled the three miles. The family there shared with her as long as they could—two or three days. Then she went on to the next house. There, too, with the quality of mercy which comes with incredible suffering, they shared with her. From house to house she went pushing her baby-carriage. She received a meal here, three meals here, a meal and a bed here. The baby was a weak and puny child.

During this swirling storm, the horses huddle abjectly and stolidly in the fields, their backs humped and turned toward the eye of the wind, their heads near the ground, their manes blowing over their eyes. Ice crusts their soft noses. The writer asked a farmer this morning: "How will your horses get through the winter?"

"I don't know," he replied, calmly. "I ain't got nothing to give 'em. I got to turn 'em out and let 'em russle for theirselves. Of course if they get enough to live on, all right, an' if they don't they'll have to starve."

"And suppose there are a few more big storms like this one?"

"Well, I don't suppose there'll be a horse left round here by ploughin' time then. The people ain't got nothin' to feed 'em upon in the spring. A horse'll russle for himself in the snow, an' then when th' spring rains comes, he'll go all to pieces unless he gets good nursin' and feedin'. But we won't have nothin' to give 'em."

Horses are, as a usual thing, cheaper in this country than good saddles, but at this time, there is a fair proportion of men who would willingly give away their favorite horses if they could thus insure the animals warm barns and plenty of feed.

But the people cannot afford to think now of these minor affections of their hearts.

The writer rode forty-five miles through the country, recently. The air turned the driver a dark shade, until he resembled some kind of a purple Indian from Brazil, and the team became completely coated with snow and ice, as if their little brown bodies were in quaint ulsters. They became dull and stupid in the storm. Under the driver's flogging they barely stirred, holding their heads dejectedly, with an expression of unutterable patient weariness. Six men were met upon the road. They strode along silently with patches of ice upon their beards. The fields were for the most part swept bare of snow, and there appeared then the short stumps of the corn, where the hot winds of the summer had gnawed the stalks away.

Yet this is not in any sense a type of a Nebraska storm. It is phenomenal. It is typical only of the misfortunes of this part of the State. It is commensurate with other things, that this tempest should come at precisely the time when it will be remarkable if certain of the people endure it.

Eddyville received a consignment of aid recently. There were eighty sacks of flour and a dozen boxes of clothing. For miles about the little village the farmers came with their old wagons and their ill-fed horses. Some of them blushed when they went before the local committee to sign their names and get the charity. They were strong, fine, sturdy men, not bended like the Eastern farmer but erect and agile. Their faces occasionally expressed the subtle inner tragedy which relief of food and clothing at this time can do but little to lighten. The street was again lively, but there was an elemental mournfulness in the little crowd. They spoke of the weather a great deal.

Two days afterward the building where the remainder of the relief stores had been put away, burned to the ground.

A farmer in Lincoln county recently said: "No, I didn't get

no aid. I hadter drive twenty-five miles t' git my flour, an' then drive back agin an' I didn't think th' team would stand it, they been poor-fed so long. Besides I'd hadter put up a dollar to keep th' team over night an' I didn't have none. I hain't had no aid!"

"How did you get along?"

"Don't git along, stranger. Who the hell told you I did get along?"

In the meantime, the business men in the eastern part of the State, particularly in the splendid cities of Omaha and Lincoln, are beginning to feel the great depression resulting from extraordinary accounts which have plastered the entire State as a place of woe. Visitors to the country have looked from car-windows to see the famine-stricken bodies of the farmers lying in the fields and have trod lightly in the streets of Omaha to keep from crushing the bodies of babes. But the point should be emphasized that the grievous condition is confined to a comparatively narrow section of the western part of the State.

Governor Holcomb said to the writer: "It is true that there is much misery in the State, but there is not the universal privation which has been declared. Crop failure was unknown until 1890 when the farmers lost much of their labor, but at that time, and in 1893, when a partial loss was experienced, the eastern half of the State was able to take care of the western half where the failure was pronounced.

"This year has been so complete a failure as to reduce many to extreme poverty, but I do not think that there are more than twenty per cent at present in need. Great irrigation enterprises that are now being inaugurated will, no doubt, eliminate the cause of failure in large districts of the western part of the State. The grain that is produced and stock that is raised in this State put it in the front rank of the great agricultural commonwealths. I have no doubt that in a year or two her barns will be overflowing. I see nothing in the present situation nor in the history of the State as I have observed it for sixteen years that ought to discourage those who contemplate coming here to make homes. In the western part of the State, a vast amount of unwise speculation has caused great losses, but that part of the country cannot be excelled for grazing, and irrigation will, no doubt, render it safe and profitable for agriculture. In the greater part of the State, the people are suffering no more than a large percentage of the agricultural districts of other States. It has been brought about as much by the general national depression as by local causes."

It is probable that a few years will see the farms in the great Platte River valley watered by irrigation, but districts that have not an affluence of water will depend upon wind-mills. The wells in this State never fail during a drought. They furnish an abundance of cool and good water. Some farmers plan to build little storage reservoirs upon the hillocks of the prairie. They are made by simply throwing up banks of earth, and then allowing cattle to trample the interiors until a hard and water-tight bottom is formed. In this manner a farmer will be in a degree independent of the most terrible droughts.

Taking the years in groups of five the rainfall was at its lowest from 1885 to 1890 when the general average was 22.34 inches. The general average for 1891, 1892 and 1893 was 23.85 inches. But 1894 now enters the contest with a record of but 13.10 inches. People are now shouting that Nebraska is to become arid. In past years when rainfalls were enormous they shouted that Nebraska was to become a great pond.

The final quality of these farmers who have remained in this portion of the State is their faith in the ultimate victory of the land and their industry. They have a determination to wait until nature, with her mystic processes, restores to them the prosperity and bounty of former years. "If a man stays right by this country, he'll come out all right in the end."

Almost any man in the district will cease speaking of his woes to recite the beauties of the times when the great rolling prairies are green and golden with the splendor of young corn, the streams are silver in the light of the sun, and when from the wide roads and the little homesteads there arises the soundless essence of a hymn from the happy and prosperous people.

But then there now is looming the eventual catastrophe that would surely depopulate the country. These besieged farmers are battling with their condition with an eye to the rest and success of next August. But if they can procure no money with which to buy seed when spring comes around, the calamity that ensues is an eternal one, as far as they and their farms here are concerned. They have no resort then but to load their families in wagons behind their hungry horses and set out to conquer these great distances, which like walls shut them from the charitable care of other and more fortunate communities.

In the meantime, they depend upon their endurance, their capacity to help each other, and their steadfast and unyielding courage.

No. 86 SEEN AT HOT SPRINGS

HOT SPRINGS, ARK., March 3.—This town arises to defeat a certain favorite theory of all truly great philosophers. They have long ago proven that spring is the time when human emotion emerges from a covering of cynical darkness and becomes at once blithe and true. They have decided that the great green outburst of nature in the spring is essential to the senses before that mighty forgetfulness, that vast irresponsibility of feeling can come upon a man and allow him to enjoy himself.

The Hot Springs crowd, however, display this exuberance in the dead of winter. It has precisely the same quality as the gaiety of the Atlantic Coast resorts in the dead of summer. There is then proven that the human emotions are not at all guided by the calendar. It is merely a question of latitude. The other theory would confine a man to only one wild exuberant outbreak of feeling per year. It was invented in England.

As soon as the train reaches the great pine belt of Arkansas one becomes aware of the intoxication in the resinous air. It is heavy, fragrant with the odor from the vast pine tracts and its subtle influence contains a prophecy of the spirit of the little city afar in the hills. Tawny roads, the soil precisely the hue of a lion's mane, wander through the groves. Nearer the town a stream of water that looks like a million glasses of lemon phosphate brawls over the rocks.

And then at last, at the railway station, comes that incoherent mass of stage drivers and baggagemen which badgers all resorts, roaring and gesticulating, as unintelligible always as a row of Homeric experts, while behind them upon the sky are painted the calm turrets of the innumerable hotels and, still further back, the green ridges and peaks of the hills. Not all travellers venture to storm that typical array of hackmen; some make a slinking detour and, coming out suddenly from behind the station, sail away with an air of half relief, half guilt. At any rate, the stranger must circumnavigate these howling dervishes before he can gain his first glance of the vivid yellow sun-light, the green groves and the buildings of the springs.

When a man decides that he has seen the whole of the town he has only seen half of it. The other section is behind a great hill that with imperial insolence projects into the valley. The main street was once the bed of a mountain stream. It winds persistently around the base of this hill until it succeeds in join-ing the two sections. The dispossessed river now flows through a tunnel. Electric cars with whirring and clanging noises bowl along with modern indifference upon this grave of a torrent of the hills.

The motive of this main street is purely cosmopolitan. It un-doubtedly typifies the United States better than does any exist-ing thoroughfare, for it resembles the North and the South, the East and the West. For a moment a row of little wooden stores will look exactly like a portion of a small prairie village, but, later, one is confronted by a group of austere business blocks that are completely Eastern in expression. The street is bright at times with gaudy gypsy coloring; it is grey in places with dull and Puritanical hues. It is wealthy and poor; it is impertinent and courteous. It apparently comprehends all men and all moods and has little to say of itself. It is satisfied to exist without being defined nor classified.

And upon the pavement the crowd displays the reason of the street's knowledge of localities. There will be mingled an accent from the South, a hat and pair of boots from the West, a hurry and important engagement from the North, and a fine gown from the East.

An advantage of this condition is that no man need feel strange here. He may assure himself that there are men of his kind present. If, however, he is mistaken and there are no men of his kind in Hot Springs, he can conclude that he is a natural phenomenon and doomed to the curiosity of all peoples.

In Broadway perhaps people would run after a Turk to stare

at his large extravagant trousers. Here it is doubtful if he would excite them at all. They would expect a Turk; they would comprehend that there were Turks and why there were Turks; they would accept the Turk with a mere raise of the eyebrows. This street thoroughly understands geography, and its experience of men is great. The instructors have been New York swells, Texas cattlemen, Denver mining kings, Chicago business men, and commercial travellers from the universe. This profound education has destroyed its curiosity and created a sort of a wide sympathy, not tender, but tolerant.

It is this absence of localism and the bigotry of classes which imparts to the entire town a peculiarly interesting flavor. There has been too general a contribution to admit two identical patterns. They were all different. And from these the town and the people were builded. Some of the hotels are enormous and like palaces. Some are like farm houses. Some are as small and plain as pine shanties. This superior education has impressed upon the town the fact that pocketbooks differentiate as do the distances to stars.

The bath houses for the most part stand in one row. They are close together and resemble mansions. They seem to be the abodes of peculiarly subdued and home-loving millionaires. The medicinal water is distributed under the supervision of the United States government, which in fact has reserved all the land save that valley in which the town lies. The water is first collected from all the springs into a principal reservoir. From thence it is again pumped through pipes to the bath houses. The government itself operates a free bath house, where 900 people bathe daily. The private ones charge a fee, which ranges from 20 to 60 cents.

Crowds swarm to these baths. A man becomes a creature of three conditions. He is about to take a bath—he is taking a bath —he has taken a bath. Invalids hobble slowly from their hotels, assisted perhaps by a pair of attendants. Soldiers from the U. S. Army and Navy Hospital trudge along assisting their rheumatic limbs with canes. All day there is a general and widespread march upon the baths.

In the quiet and intensely hot interiors of these buildings men involved in enormous bath-robes lounge in great rocking chairs. In other rooms the negro attendants scramble at the bidding of the bathers. Through the high windows the sun-light enters and pierces the curling masses of vapor which rise slowly in the heavy air.

There is naturally an Indian legend attached to these springs. In short, the Kanawagas were a great tribe with many hunters and warriors among them. They swung ponderous clubs with which they handily brained the ambitious but weaker warriors of other tribes. But at last a terrible scourge broke forth, and they who had strode so proudly under the trees, crawled piteously on the pine-needles and called in beseeching voices toward the yellow sunset. After festivals, rites, avowals, sacrifices, the Spirit of the Wind heard the low clamor of his Indians and suddenly vapors began to emerge from the waters of what had been a cool mountain spring. The pool had turned hot. The wise men debated. At last, a courageous and inquisitive red man bathed. He liked it; others bathed. The scourge fled.

The servants at Hot Springs are usually that class of colored boys who come from the far South. They are very black and have good-humored, rolling eyes. They are not so sublime as Pullman-car porters. They have not that profound dignity, that impressive aspect of exhaustive learning, that inspiring independence, which the public admires in the other class. They are good-natured and not blessed with the sophistication that one can see at a distance. As waiters, they bend and slide and amble with consummate willingness. Sometimes they move at a little jig-trot.

And, in conclusion, there is a certain fervor, a certain intenseness about life in Hot Springs that reminds philosophers of the times when the Monmouth Park Racing Association and Phil Daly vied with each other in making Long Branch a beloved and celebrated city. It is not obvious, it is for the most part invisible, soundless. And yet it is to be discovered.

The traveller for the hat firm in Ogallala, Neb., remarked that a terrible storm had raged through the country during the second week in February. He surmised that it was the worst blizzard for many years. In New Orleans, the hackmen raised their fare to ten dollars, he had heard.

The youthful stranger with the blonde and innocent hair, agreed with these remarks.

"Well," said the traveller for the hat firm, at last, "let's get a drink of that What-you-may-call-it Spring water, and then go and listen to the orchestra at the Arlington."

In the saloon, a man was leaning against the bar. As the traveller and the youthful stranger entered, this man said to the bar-tender: "I'll shake you for the drinks?"

"Same old game," said the traveller. "Always trying to beat the bar-tender, eh?"

"Well, I'll shake you for the drinks? How's that suit you?" said the man, ruffling his whiskers.

"All right," said the traveller for the hat firm in Ogallala, Neb. "I tell you what I'll do—I'll shake you for a dollar even."

"All right," said the man.

The traveller won. "Well, I tell you. I'll give you a chance to get your money back. I'll shake you for two bones."

The traveller won. "I'll shake you for four bones."

The traveller won.

"Got change for a five? I want a dollar back," said the man.

"No," said the traveller. "But I've got another five. I'll shake you for the two fives."

When the traveller for the hat firm in Ogallala, Neb., had won fifty dollars from the man with ruffled whiskers, the latter said: "Excuse me for a moment, please. You wait here for me, please. You're a winner."

As the man vanished, the traveller for the hat firm in Ogallala, Neb., turned to the youthful stranger with the blonde and innocent hair, in an outburst of gleeful victory. "Well, that was easy," he cried ecstatically. "Fifty dollars in 'bout four minutes. Here—you take half and I'll take half, and we'll go blow it." He tendered five five-dollars to the youthful stranger with the blonde and innocent hair. The bar-tender was sleepily regardant. At the end of the bar was lounging a man with no drink in front of him.

The youthful stranger said: "Oh, you might as well keep it. I don't need it. I——"

"But, look here," exclaimed the traveller for the hat firm in Ogallala, Neb., "you might as well take it. I'd expect you to do the same if you won. It ain't anything among sporting men. You take half and I'll take half, and we'll go blow it. You're as welcome as sunrise, my dear fellow. Take it along—it's nothing.

What are you kickin' about?" He spoke in tones of supreme anguish, at this harsh treatment from a friend.

"No," said the youthful stranger with the blonde and innocent hair, to the traveller for the hat firm in Ogallala, Neb., "I guess I'll stroll back up-town. I want to write a letter to my mother."

In the back room of the saloon, the man with the ruffled beard was silently picking hieroglyphics out of his whiskers.

No. 87   GRAND OPERA IN NEW ORLEANS

NEW ORLEANS, LA., March 23.—In the heart of the French quarter, there uprears a building that has the closest identification with the life of New Orleans. One of the first local prides of the citizens of this city, is the French Opera House and its traditions of Parisian prime donne, its legends of ovations to famous tenors, all its memories of musical glory, which with its deeply scarred and worn exterior give it the dignity and the solemnity of a volume of history.

The approach to the opera house is through those quaint and narrow streets which are in themselves so graphic of tradition. Then suddenly appears among the low roofs, a taller edifice, grey and white and leaden with age. The pillars of the portico align the outer curb of the sidewalk.

In the evening the little street before the building is gay with people. The electric light at the corner chooses its own time for illumination and takes occasional sputtering vacations. The diverging streets, too, present, for the most part, the assassin-like gloom of some European cities. But under the old portico there is a wealth of light, and the blithe and joyous clatter of many tongues. In the yellow rays from the adjacent cafes, move innumerable figures.

Grand opera in New Orleans has a history of a hundred years. Davis, a French refugee from San Domingo, came here in 1790, and, with the true spirit of his nation, it was no trouble at all for him to change at once from a participant in the bloody scuffling at San Domingo, to a conductor of grand opera. In 1814, the Orleans theatre was built at the corner of Orleans and

Bourbon streets. Madame Devries was singing the role of Fides in "The Prophet" at this theatre, when she conceived the idea of naming her daughter after the title of her part, and this sudden inspiration is responsible for the name of the present famous Parisian singer. Mme. Witman, Mme. Colson, M. Du Luc, M. De La Grave, M. Le Croix, M. Crambade and M. Jenibrel were all imported from Paris to this house to satisfy the vast enthusiasm of the French New Orleans public.

This house was the heart of the social life of the city. All the existence of the old Creole aristocracy was centered in the opera. The spirited and earnest gentlemen of the day exchanged cards with a magnificent frequence in this building. In fact, it is said, that more duels were arranged there than in any other building in the world. And a certain great feature were the "loges grilles"—latticed boxes—where families in mourning could listen to the opera without being observed by the spectators.

In 1859, the present opera house was erected. The Orleans had become too small. Gradually, the opera had acquired a patronage that comprised the wealthy classes of both the French and American populations, as well as the masses of the people. Mathieu and Tournier were the two tenors who, at this time, soared to brilliant heights of popularity. Adelina Patti was the star of 1860. This was before she began her farewell tours; in fact, it was her American debut. Singer appeared in 1881, Gerster in 1882, De Murska in 1885, Martinez in 1889. There are, of course, veterans in opera attendance who love to tell of the memorable events of the past, and their favorite theme is of the time when Devoyod, the famous baritone, was fairly overwhelmed at his benefit in 1874, with flowers, kisses, jewelry, devotion, adoration. Men stood on each other's backs in the parquet and the management was obliged to remove the negroes out of the fourth tier in order to make room.

New Orleans is the only city in the United States that supports a continual and elaborate production of grand opera. And, as mentioned, New Orleans has done so for quite a hundred years. In New York it is, perhaps, always something of a venture. From time to time a manager acquires sufficient courage. He speculates long and deeply, and then afterward he wears the pious air of a man who has dared everything for the sake of a beloved art. And he is altogether entitled to wear this air of piety.

Here the opera is supported by the entire populace. The lights of the company are the deities of the masses. Their adherents wrangle over their merits. There is a vast and elemental interest and enthusiasm.

Above all, the prices are arranged so that building sites do not have to be exchanged for tickets. As a matter of fact, the opera can be seen for ten cents. The best seats in the house are purchased for one dollar and fifty cents. This does not make a taste for grand opera to be thorns in the flesh of a small vendor of olives or matches.

Perhaps these things adjust themselves. It may be that it is only when a public attains the cultivation of a New Orleans public that cheap opera can be given it. Perhaps it is necessary to charge a man the price of a schooner yacht in order to instruct him.

The company this year is headed by Madame Laville. She is a soprano who sings with a dramatic comprehension that is unusual. She renders the principal roles in all the weightier operas given, with an impressive emotional sincerity. Her fine voice and her artistic earnestness have caused her to be immensely popular. Anasty, the tenor, and Chavaroche, the basso, are usually associated with her in the productions.

The chorus is a commendable portion of the company. There is a distinct dash and vigor in their singing and acting which is not always observed in chorus. This air of spirit is more apparent in the male part of the chorus than in the female. For example, in the first act of "La Juive" there is a little terse quarrel of peasants, enduring just a few seconds, which the men of the chorus render with a sudden snap and intensity which is evidently impossible to the usual chorus men who conduct the same little vignette with the fire and fervor of a row of box-wood plants.

In all their appearances, they are in earnest, engrossed in the opera.

The orchestra is an organization of eighty pieces. The leadership is perfectly capable and wise, and the orchestra plays well,

animated by the single purpose of creating artistic performances.

The company often varies its grand opera with little interjections of light opera. Its public depends almost entirely upon it
for amusement as well as for musical thought. There are stars
enough to give three or four operas at one time and the chorus
is versatile.

In "Les Amours du Diable," "Les Dragons de Villars,"
"Madame Angot," and operas of this class, the principal role is
usually sung by Madame St. Laurent.

And this is another quite strange fact concerning localism of
the opera company. Madame St. Laurent, it may be said, is
absolutely unknown to the country at large. She is not supposed
to regret it, since her audience here appreciates her in that
proprietary way of people who are fellow-countrymen, but it
seems wonderful that such a marvelously clever woman's fame
for finesse and skill on the beloved comic opera boards should
go no farther than the limits of this city, when as a matter of
truth there are so many of the world's exalted in light comic
opera careers who could gain much instruction by a series of
attendances at Madame St. Laurent's school.

At present, the company is existing in a state that ordinarily
devours an operatic company in two days. In short it is without
a manager. However, the performances continue and there has
been no sign yet of the usual ear-splitting row. The company is
managing itself. It must be said again that this is the unique
opera company of the world.

When the great question of grand opera is agitated in other
cities, people can look toward New Orleans and see certain
incredible things. They can see grand opera that is an institution of a century. They can see grand opera given at cheap
prices and they can see grand opera patronized by all classes.

No. 88   THE CITY OF MEXICO

THE main streets of this city do not preserve the uniform uproar that marks the daily life of the important thoroughfares in
northern cities. Their life begins at an early hour and lasts until
almost noon. Then there is a period of repose. Few people appear upon the side-walks and barely a carriage obstructs the
assault of the glaring yellow sun-light upon the pave of the
street. At about 3.30, however, there is an awakening. Carriages
come from all directions. The walks are suddenly thick with
people and from that time until 9.00 the streets are a-whirl with
shining carriages, sombrero-ed coachmen, proud horses. A
mighty gathering of young men crowd the curbs and peer at
the occupants of the passing vehicles. The blue quivering light
of the modern electric lamp illuminates the fine old decorations
of the buildings and, above all, rings the clatter of innumerable
hoofs upon the concrete of the narrow streets.

Or perhaps instead of the period of glaring sun-light there
comes a swift and sudden rain with the premonitory winds, the
atmospheric coolness, the low-hanging deep-blue clouds, the
rumbling thunder of a spring shower in the North. Then as soon
as the rain ceases, the carriages, like some kind of congregating bugs, come flying again. In the parks, the vivid green of
the foliage turns dark from the shadows of the night.

The term "rainy season" in the City of Mexico merely means
that at a certain time every afternoon you can count upon a
shower that will last for an hour or more. It is as regular almost
as day and night and you have only to make your arrangements
according to it. During the winter, the weather is immovably
calm. Each day is the counterpart of the day that precedes it.
You could make picnic plans weeks in advance and be sure
of your weather. It is precisely like late spring as we of the
North know it.

This gives the belles of the city no opportunity to exploit
those enormous capes which make every woman look like a
full-rigged ship going before the wind. They would be smothered.
But still they can wear Easter bonnets all the time. In fact, one
is always able to see upon the streets those fresh and charming

toilettes which we associate with the new blossoming of woman-hood in the spring.

The Mexican women are beautiful frequently but there seems to be that quality lacking which makes the bright quick eyes of some girls so adorable to the contemplative sex. It has something to do with the mind, no doubt. Their black eyes are as beautiful as gems. The trouble with the gem however is that it cannot regard you with sudden intelligence, comprehension, sympathy. They have soft rounded cheeks which they powder without much skill, leaving it often in streaks. They take life easily, dreamily. They remind one of kittens asleep in the sunshine.

The stranger to the city is at once interested in the architecture of the buildings. They are not ruins but they have somehow the dignity of ruins. There is probably no structure in the city of the character that a man of the North would erect. Viewing them as a mass, they are two-storied and plain with heavily barred windows from which the senoritas can gaze down at the street. In the principal part of the town, however, there are innumerable fine old houses with large shaded courts and simple stern decorations that must be echoes of the talent of the Aztecs. There is nothing of the modern in them. They are never incoherent, never over-done. The ornamentation is always a part of the structure. It grows there. It has not been plastered on from a distance. Galleries wind about the sides of the silent and shadowed patios.

Commerce has however waged a long war upon these structures and a vast number of them have succumbed. Signs are plastered on their exteriors and the old courts are given over to the gentle hum of Mexican business. It is not unusual for the offices of a commission merchant or of a dealer of any kind to be located in a building that was once the palace of some Mexican notable and the massive doors, the broad stair-way, the wide galleries, have become in this strange evolution as familiar to messenger boys and porters as they were once perhaps to generals and statesmen. The old palace of the Emperor Iturbide is now a hotel over-run with American tourists. The Mexican National Railroad has its general offices in a building that was the palace of a bygone governor of the city and the

American Club has the finest of club-houses because it gained control of a handsome old palace.

There is a certain American aspect to the main business part of the town. Men with undeniable New England faces confront one constantly. The business signs are often American and there is a little group of cafes where everything from the aprons of the waiters to the liquids dispensed are American. One hears in this neighborhood more English than Spanish. Even the native business purpose changes under this influence and they bid for the American coin. "American Barber-shop," "The American Tailor," "American Restaurant" are signs which flatter the tourist's eye. There is nothing so universal as the reputation of Americans for ability to spend money. There can be no doubt that the Zulus upon the approach of an American citizen begin to lay all manner of traps.

Nevertheless there is a sort of a final adjustment. There is an American who runs a merry-go-round in one of the parks here. It is the usual device with a catarrhal orchestrion and a whirl of wooden goats, and ponies and giraffes. But his machine is surrounded at all times by fascinated natives and he makes money by the basketful. The circus too which is really a more creditable organization than any we see in the States, is crowded nightly. It is a small circus. It does not attempt to have simultaneous performances in fifty-nine rings but everything is first-class and the American circus people attain reputations among the populace second only to the most adored of the bull-fighters.

The bull-fighters, by the way, are a most impressive type to be seen upon the streets. There is a certain uniformity about their apparel. They wear flat-topped glazed hats like the seamen of years ago and little short jackets. They are always clean-shaven and the set of the lips wherein lies the revelation of character, can easily be studied. They move confidently, proudly, with a magnificent self-possession. People turn to stare after them. There is in their faces something cold, sinister, merciless. There is history there too, a history of fiery action, of peril, of escape. Yet you would know, you would know without being told that you are gazing at an executioner, a kind of moral assassin.

The faces of the priests are perhaps still more portentous, for the countenances of the bull-fighters are obvious but those of the priests are inscrutable.

No. 89 THE VIGA CANAL

THE Viga Canal leads out to the floating gardens. The canal is really a canal but the floating gardens are not floating gardens at all. We took a cab and rattled our bones loose over the stones of streets where innumerable natives in serape and sombrero thronged about pulque shops that were also innumerable. Brown porters in cotton shirts and trousers trotted out of the way of the cab, moving huge burdens with rare ease. The women seated upon the curb with their babes, glanced up at the rumble of wheels. There were dashes of red and purple from the clothes of the people against the white and yellow background of the low adobe buildings. Into the clear cool afternoon air arose the squawling cries of the vendors of melons, saints, flowers.

At the canal, there was a sudden fierce assault of boatmen that was like a charge of desperate infantry. Behind them, their boats crowded each other at the wharf and the canal lay placid to where upon the further shore, long lazy blades of grass bended to the water like swooning things. At the pulque shop, the cabman paused for a drink before his return drive.

The boatmen beseeched, prayed, appealed. There could have been no more clamor around the feet of the ancient brown gods of Mexico. They almost shed tears; they wriggled in an ecstasy of commercial expectation. They smote their bare breasts and each swore himself to be the incomparable boatman of the Viga. Above their howls arose the tinkle of a street-car bell as the driver lashed his mules toward the city.

The fortunate boatman fairly trembled in his anxiety to get his craft out into the canal before his freight could change their minds. He pushed frantically with his pole and the boat, built precisely like what we call a scow, moved slowly away.

Great trees lined the shore. The little soiled street-cars passed and passed. Far along the shimmering waters, on which details of the foliage were traced, could be seen countless boatmen, erect in the sterns of their crafts, bending and swaying rhythmically, prodding the bottom with long poles. Out from behind the corner of a garden-wall suddenly appeared Popocatepetl, towering toward the sky, a great cone of creamy hue in the glamor of the sunshine. Then later came Iztaccihuatl, the white woman, of curious shape more camel than woman, its peak confused with clouds. A plain of fervent green stretched toward them. On the other side of the canal, in the shade of a great tree, a mounted gendarme sat immovable and contemplative.

A little canoe made from the trunk of a single tree and narrower than a coffin, approached and the Indian girl in the bow advocated the purchase of tamales while in the stern a tall youth in scant clothing poled away keeping pace with the larger craft.

Frequently there were races. Reposing under the wooden canopies of the boats, people cried to their boatmen. "Hurry up! If you beat that boat ahead, I will give you another real." The laconic Spanish sentences, fortified usually with swift gestures, could always be heard. And under the impetus of these offers, the boatmen struggled hardily, their sandaled feet pattering as they ran along the sides of the boats.

There were often harmless collisions. These boatmen, apparently made blind by the prospective increase in reward, poled sometimes like mad and crashed into boats ahead. Then arose the fervor of Mexican oaths.

Withal, however, they were very skilful, managing their old wooden boxes better than anybody could ever expect of them. And indeed some of them were clever enough to affect the most heroic exertions and gain more pay when in reality they were not injuring their health at all.

At the little village of Santa Anita, everybody disembarked. There was a great babbling crowd in front of the pulque shops. Vivid serapes lighted the effect made by the modest and very economical cotton clothes of the most of the people. In the midst of this uproar, three more mounted gendarmes sat silently, their sabres dangling in their scabbards, their horses poising their ears intently at the throng.

Indian girls with bare brown arms held up flowers for sale, flowers of flaming colors made into wreaths and bouquets. Caballeros, out for a celebration, a carouse, strutted along with these passionate burning flowers of the southland serving as bands to their sombreros. Under the thatched roofs of the pulque shops, more Indian girls served customers with the peculiar beverage and stood by and bantered with them in the universal style. In the narrow street leading away from the canal, the crowd moved hilariously while crouched at the sides of it, a multitude of beggars, decrepit vendors of all kinds, raised unheeded cries. In the midst of the swarming pulque shops, resorts, and gardens, stood a little white church, stern, unapproving, representing the other fundamental aspiration of humanity, a reproach and a warning. The frightened laughter of a girl in a swing could be heard as her lover swung her high, so that she appeared for a moment in her fluttering blue gown and tossing locks, over a fence of tall cactus plants.

A policeman remonstrated with a tottering caballero who wished to kiss a waitress in a pulque shop. A boatman, wailing bitterly, shambled after some riotous youths who had forgotten to pay him. Four men seated around a table were roaring with laughter at the tale of a fifth man. Three old Indian women with bare shoulders and wondrously wrinkled faces squatted on the earthern floor of a saloon and watched the crowd. Little beggars beseeched everybody. "Niña! Niña! Deme un centavo!"

Above the dark formidable hills of the west there was a long flare of crimson, purple, orange, tremendous colors that, in the changes of the sunset, manoeuvred in the sky like armies. Suddenly the little church aroused and its bell clanged persistently, harshly and with an incredible rapidity. People were beginning to saunter back toward the canal.

We procured two native musicians, a violinist and a guitarist and took them with us in our boat. The shadows of the trees in the water grew more portentous. Far to the southeast the two peaks were faint ghostly figures in the heavens. They resembled forms of silver mist in the deep blue of that sky. The boatman lit the candle of a little square lantern and set it in the bottom of the boat. The musicians made some preliminary chords and conversed about being in tune.

Tall trees of some poplar variety that always resemble hearse plumes dotted the plain to the westward and as the uproar of colors there faded to a subtle rose, their black solemn outlines intervened like bars across this pink and pallor. A wind, cool and fragrant, reminiscent of flowers and grass and lakes came from those mystic shadows—places whence the two silver peaks had vanished. The boatman held his pole under his arm while he swiftly composed a cigarette.

The musicians played slumberously. We did not wish to hear any too well. It was better to lie and watch the large stars come out and let the music be merely a tale of the past, a recital from the possessions of one's own memory, an invoking of other songs, other nights. For, after all, the important part of these dreamful times to the wanderer is that they cry to him with emotional and tender voices of his past. The yellow glitter of the lantern at the boatman's feet made his shadow to be a black awful thing that hung angrily over us. There was a sudden shrill yell from the darkness. There had almost been a collision. In the blue velvet of the sky, the stars had gathered in thousands.

No. 90 THE MEXICAN LOWER CLASSES

ABOVE all things, the stranger finds the occupations of foreign peoples to be trivial and inconsequent. The average mind utterly fails to comprehend the new point of view and that such and such a man should be satisfied to carry bundles or mayhap sit and ponder in the sun all his life in this faraway country seems an abnormally stupid thing. The visitor feels scorn. He swells with a knowledge of his geographical experience. "How futile are the lives of these people," he remarks, "and what incredible ignorance that they should not be aware of their futility." This is the arrogance of the man who has not yet solved himself and discovered his own actual futility.

Yet, indeed, it requires wisdom to see a brown woman in one garment crouched listlessly in the door of a low adobe hut while a naked brown baby sprawls on his stomach in the dust of the roadway—it requires wisdom to see this thing and to see it a million times and yet to say: "Yes, this is important to the scheme of nature. This is part of her economy. It would not be well if it had never been."

It perhaps might be said—if any one dared—that the most worthless literature of the world has been that which has been written by the men of one nation concerning the men of another.

It seems that a man must not devote himself for a time to attempts at psychological perception. He can be sure of two things, form and color. Let him then see all he can but let him not sit in literary judgment on this or that manner of the people. Instinctively he will feel that there are similarities but he will encounter many little gestures, tones, tranquilities, rages, for which his blood, adjusted to another temperature, can possess no interpreting power. The strangers will be indifferent where he expected passion; they will be passionate where he expected calm. These subtle variations will fill him with contempt.

At first it seemed to me the most extraordinary thing that the lower classes of Indians in this country should insist upon existence at all. Their squalor, their ignorance seemed so absolute that death—no matter what it has in store—would appear as freedom, joy.

The people of the slums of our own cities fill a man with awe. That vast army with its countless faces immovably cynical, that vast army that silently confronts eternal defeat, it makes one afraid. One listens for the first thunder of the rebellion, the moment when this silence shall be broken by a roar of war. Meanwhile one fears this class, their numbers, their wickedness, their might—even their laughter. There is a vast national respect for them. They have it in their power to become terrible. And their silence suggests everything.

They are becoming more and more capable of defining their condition and this increase of knowledge evinces itself in the deepening of those savage and scornful lines which extend from near the nostrils to the corners of the mouth. It is very distressing to observe this growing appreciation of the situation.

I am not venturing to say that this appreciation does not exist in the lower classes of Mexico. No, I am merely going to say that I cannot perceive any evidence of it. I take this last position in order to preserve certain handsome theories which I advanced in the fore part of the article.

It is so human to be envious that of course even these Indians have envied everything from the stars of the sky to the birds, but you cannot ascertain that they feel at all the modern desperate rage at the accident of birth. Of course the Indian can imagine himself a king but he does not apparently feel that there is an injustice in the fact that he was not born a king any more than there is in his not being born a giraffe.

As far as I can perceive him, he is singularly meek and submissive. He has not enough information to be unhappy over his state. Nobody seeks to provide him with it. He is born, he works, he worships, he dies, all on less money than would buy a thoroughbred Newfoundland dog and who dares to enlighten him? Who dares cry out to him that there are plums, plums, plums in the world which belong to him? For my part, I think the apostle would take a formidable responsibility. I would remember that there really was no comfort in the plums after all as far as I had seen them and I would esteem no orations concerning the glitter of plums.

A man is at liberty to be virtuous in almost any position of life. The virtue of the rich is not so superior to the virtue of the poor that we can say that the rich have a great advantage. These Indians are by far the most poverty-stricken class with which I have met but they are not morally the lowest by any means. Indeed, as far as the mere form of religion goes, they are one of the highest. They are exceedingly devout, worshipping with a blind faith that counts a great deal among the theorists.

But according to my view this is not the measure of them. I measure their morality by what evidences of peace and contentment I can detect in the average countenance.

If a man is not given a fair opportunity to be virtuous, if his environment chokes his moral aspirations, I say that he has got the one important cause of complaint and rebellion against society. Of course it is always possible to be a martyr but then we do not wish to be martyrs. Martyrdom offers no inducements to the average mind. We prefer to be treated with justice and then martyrdom is not required. I never could appreciate those grey old gentlemen of history. Why did not they run? I would have run like mad and still respected myself and my religion.

I have said then that a man has the right to rebel if he is not given a fair opportunity to be virtuous. Inversely then, if he possesses this fair opportunity, he cannot rebel, he has no complaint. I am of the opinion that poverty of itself is no cause. It is something above and beyond. For example, there is Collis P. Huntington and William D. Rockefeller—as virtuous as these gentlemen are, I would not say that their virtue is any ways superior to mine for instance. Their opportunities are no greater. They can give more, deny themselves more in quantity but not relatively. We can each give all that we possess and there I am at once their equal.

I do not think however that they would be capable of sacrifices that would be possible to me. So then I envy them nothing. Far from having a grievance against them, I feel that they will confront an ultimate crisis that I, through my opportunities, may altogether avoid. There is in fact no advantage of importance which I can perceive them possessing over me.

It is for these reasons that I refuse to commit judgment upon these lower classes of Mexico. I even refuse to pity them. It is true that at night many of them sleep in heaps in doorways, and spend their days squatting upon the pavements. It is true that their clothing is scant and thin. All manner of things of this kind is true but yet their faces have almost always a certain smoothness, a certain lack of pain, a serene faith. I can feel the superiority of their contentment.

No. 91   STEPHEN CRANE IN MEXICO (I)

CITY OF MEXICO, May 18.— Two Americans were standing on a street corner in this city not long ago, gazing thoughtfully at the paintings on the exterior wall of a pulque shop—stout maidens in scant vestments lovingly confronting a brimming glass, kings out of all proportion draining goblets to more stout maidens—the whole a wild mass of red, green, blue, yellow, purple, like a concert hall curtain in a mining town.

Far up the street six men in white cotton shirts and short trousers became visible. They were bent forward and upon their shoulders there was some kind of an enormous black thing. They moved at a shambling trot.

The two Americans lazily wondered about the enormous black thing, but the distance defeated them. The six men, however, were approaching at an unvarying pace, and at last one American was enabled to cry out: "Holy poker, it's a piano!"

There was a shuffling sound of sandals upon the stones. In the vivid yellow sunlight the black surface of the piano glistened. The six brown faces were stolid and unworried beneath it.

They passed. The burden and its carriers grew smaller and smaller. The two Americans went out to the curb and remained intent spectators until the six men and the piano were expressed by a faint blur.

When you first come to Mexico and you see a donkey so loaded that little of him but a furry nose and four short legs appear to the eye, you wonder at it. Later, when you see a haystack approaching with nothing under it but a pair of thin human legs, you begin to understand the local point of view. The Indian probably reasons: "Well, I can carry this load. The burro, then, he should carry many times this much." The burro, born in slavery, dying in slavery, generation upon generation, he with his wobbly legs, sore back, and ridiculous little face, reasons not at all. He carries as much as he can, and when he can carry it no further, he falls down.

The Indians, however, must have credit for considerable ingenuity because of the way they have invented of assisting a fallen donkey to its feet. The Aztecs are known to have had many great mechanical contrivances, and this no doubt is part of their science which has filtered down through the centuries.

When a burdened donkey falls down a half dozen Indians gather around it and brace themselves. Then they take clubs and hammer the everlasting daylights out of the donkey. They also swear in Mexican. Mexican is a very capable language for the purposes of profanity. A good swearer here can bring rain in thirty minutes.

It is a great thing to hear the thump, thump, of the clubs and the howling of the natives, and to see the little legs of the donkey quiver and to see him roll his eyes. Finally, after they have hammered him out as flat as a drum head, it flashes upon them suddenly that the burro cannot get up until they remove his load. Well, then, at last they remove his load and the donkey, not much larger than a kitten at best, and now disheveled, weak and tottering, struggles gratefully to his feet.

But, on the other hand, it is possible to see at times—perhaps in the shade of an old wall where branches hang over and look down—the tender communion of two sympathetic spirits. The man pats affectionately the soft muzzle of the donkey. The donkey—ah, who can describe that air so sage, so profoundly reflective, and yet so kind, so forgiving, so unassuming. The countenance of a donkey expresses all manly virtues even as the sunlight expresses all colors.

Perhaps the master falls asleep, and, in that case, the donkey still stands as immovable, as patient, as the stone dogs that guarded the temple of the sun.

A wonderful proportion of the freight-carrying business of this city is conducted by the Indian porters. The donkeys are the great general freight cars and hay wagons for the rural districts, but they do not appear prominently in the strictly local business of the city. It is a strange fact also that of ten wagons that pass you upon the street nine will be cabs and private carriages. The tenth may be a huge American wagon belonging to one of the express companies. It is only fair to state, however, that the odds are in favor of it being another cab or carriage.

The transportation of the city's goods is then left practically in the hands of the Indian porters. They are to be seen at all times trotting to and fro, laden and free. They have acquired all manner of contrivances for distributing the weight of their burdens. Their favorite plan is to pass a broad band over their foreheads and then leaning forward precariously, they amble along with the most enormous loads.

Sometimes they have a sort of table with two handles on each end. Two men, of course, manage this machine. It is the favorite vehicle for moving furniture.

When a man sits down who has been traversing a long road with a heavy bundle he would find considerable agony in the struggle to get upon his feet again with his freight strapped to his back if it were not for a long staff which he carries. He plants the point of this staff on the ground between his knees, and then climbs up it, so to speak, hand over hand.

They have undoubtedly developed what must be called the carrying instinct. Occasionally you may see a porter, unburdened, walking unsteadily as if his centre of balance had been shuffled around so much that he is doubtful. He resembles then an unballasted ship. Place a trunk upon his back and he is as steady as a church.

If you put in his care a contrivance with fifty wheels he would not trundle it along the ground. This plan would not occur to him. No, he would shoulder it. Most bicycles are light enough in weight, but they are rather unhandy articles to carry for long distances. Yet if you send one by a porter he will most certainly carry it on his shoulder. It would fatigue him to roll it along the road.

But there are other things odd here beside the street porters. Yesterday some thieves stole three iron balconies from off the second-story front of a house in the Calle del Sol. The police did not catch the miscreants. Who, indeed, is instructed in the art of catching thieves who steal iron balconies from the second-story fronts of houses?

The people directly concerned went out in the street and assured themselves that the house remained. Then they were satisfied.

As a matter of truth, the thieves of the city are almost always petty fellows, who go about stealing trifling articles and spend much time and finesse in acquiring things that a dignified American crook wouldn't kick with his foot. In truth, the City of Mexico is really one of the safest cities in the world at any hour of the day or night. However, the small-minded and really harmless class who vend birds, canes, opals, lottery tickets, paper flowers and general merchandise upon the streets are able and industrious enough in the art of piracy to satisfy the ordinary intellect.

Those profound minds who make the guide books have

warned the traveler very lucidly. After exhaustive thought, the writer has been able to deduct the following elementary rules from what they have to say upon the matter:

I. Do not buy anything at all from street venders.

II. When buying from street venders give the exact sum charged. Do not delude yourself with the idea of getting any change back.

III. When buying from street venders divide by ten the price demanded for any article, and offer it.

IV. Do not buy anything at all from street venders.

It is not easy to go wrong when you have one of these protective volumes within reach, but then the guide book has long been subject to popular ridicule and there is not the universal devotion to its pages which it clearly deserves. Strangers upon entering Mexico should at once acquire a guide book, and then if they fail to gain the deepest knowledge of the country and its inhabitants, they may lay it to their own inability to understand the English language in its purest form. There are tourists now in this hotel who have only been in the city two days, but who, in this time, have devoted themselves so earnestly to their guide books that they are able to draw maps of how Mexico looked before the flood.

It is never just to condemn a class and, in returning to the street venders, it is but fair to record an extraordinary instance of the gentleness, humanity and fine capability of pity in one of their number. An American lady was strolling in a public park one afternoon when she observed a vender with four little plum-colored birds seated quietly and peacefully upon his brown hand.

"Oh look at those dear little birds," she cried to her escort. "How tame they are!"

Her escort, too, was struck with admiration and astonishment and they went close to the little birds. They saw their happy, restful countenances and with what wealth of love they looked up into the face of their owner.

The lady bought two of these birds, although she hated to wound their little hearts by tearing them away from their master.

When she got to her room she closed the door and the

windows, and then reached into the wicker cage and brought out one of the pets, for she wished to gain their affection, too, and teach them to sit upon her finger.

The little bird which she brought out made a desperate attempt to perch upon her finger, but suddenly toppled off and fell to the floor with a sound like that made by a water-soaked bean bag.

The loving vender had filled his birds full of shot. This accounted for their happy, restful countenances and their very apparent resolution never to desert the adored finger of their master.

In an hour both the little birds died. You would die too if your stomach was full of shot.

The men who sell opals are particularly seductive. They polish their wares and boil them in oil and do everything to give them a false quality. When they come around in the evening and unfold a square of black paper, revealing a little group of stones that gleam with green and red fires, it is very dispiriting to know that if one bought one would be cheated.

The other day a vender upholding a scarfpin of marvelous brilliancy approached a tourist.

"How much?" demanded the latter.

"Twelve dollars," replied the vender. "Cheap! Very cheap! Only $12."

The tourist looked at the stone and then said: "Twelve dollars! No! One dollar."

"Yes, yes," cried the vender eagerly. "One dollar! Yes, yes; you can have it for $1! Take it!"

But the tourist laughed and passed on.

The fact remains, however, that the hotels, the restaurants and the cabs are absolutely cheap and almost always fair. If a man consults reputable shopkeepers when he wishes to buy Mexican goods, and gives a proper number of hours each day to the study of guide books, the City of Mexico is a place of joy. The climate is seldom hot and seldom cold. And to those gentlemen from the States whose minds have a sort of liquid quality, it is necessary merely to say that if you go out into the street and yell: "Gimme a Manhattan!" about forty American bartenders will appear of a sudden and say: "Yes, sir."

No. 92 FREE SILVER DOWN IN MEXICO

CITY OF MEXICO, June 29.—Mexico is a free silver country. When travelers from the United States arrive at Laredo, or at Eagle Pass, or at El Paso, they, of course, exchange their American coin for the currency of Mexico. In place of the green bills of the United States they receive the rather gaudy script of Mexico. For the silver of the American eagle they receive dollars which bear imprints of the eagle, serpent and cactus of this brown republic of the South. It makes them feel very wealthy. The rate of exchange is always about two for one. For fifty American dollars they receive one hundred of the dollars of Mexico. It is a great thing to double money in this fashion. The American tourist is likely to keep his hand in his pocket and jingle his hoard.

However, when he boards the Pullman to ride to the City of Mexico he finds that the fare has become nine dollars in Mexican money, instead of the normal and expected $4.50. The traveler discovers that he has not as yet gained anything. Still greater is his disappointment when he learns that the usual tip to the porter is now fifty cents, instead of the almost universal quarter. He exclaims that he can as yet see no benefit in this money exchange.

The Americans who earn salaries in the City of Mexico are continually crying that if they could only get their pay in American money and spend it in Mexican money they would be happy. A Mexican dollar is a good dollar with which to buy things, unless those things be imported. Then there is trouble. Pullman cars, porters and a multitude of other things which will be enumerated hereafter come very high.

If a young Mexican clerk, who is, for instance, on a salary of $60 per month, but who, nevertheless, thinks considerable of himself, as young clerks are apt to do—if this young clerk wishes to purchase a suit of clothes commensurate with his opinions, he will have to spend something more than a month's pay to get it. If he wishes to buy a good pair of trousers, he is required to pay about $15. Hats are to be bought at about $10. A tie—an ordinary four-in-hand—comes at $1. A collar is a matter of 35 cents. The best brand costs 50 cents. A pair of cuffs can be obtained in exchange for 60 cents. Shoes, which are ordinarily of very poor quality, cost from $8 to $20. Young clerks do not become great dudes in Mexico.

It is to be noticed that the best-dressed men in Mexico are not nearly so well dressed as the men of an ordinary New York crowd. Of course, one would expect the styles to be old, but then there is to be observed a certain lack of quality to the cloths, an air of being fragile about the shoes, and as for the hats, anything goes in Mexico.

The lower classes in Mexico do not wear shoes. They seem contented enough in their sandals, but if one of them should save his money in order to buy a pair of shoes, it would take about ten years for him to get the required amount. That is to say, if he got paid at the usual Mexican rates.

If a man wishes to see his wife and his daughters well dressed and in the latest Mexican style, it costs him a very pretty penny. It is not in the power of the middle-class Mexican to buy gowns for the feminine part of his family, as a middle-class American may do. He would go broke shortly.

It costs 25 cents to get shaved in a Mexican city. However, there is one great point where the Mexicans head us. Cocktails are sold at the rate of two for a Mexican quarter. All the good brands of whisky are at the same rate. Reduced to an American standard, this is at the rate of 6¼ cents per cocktail or per whisky. Beer is sold for 10 cents a glass—in American terms 5 cents a glass. The beer is not imported, but the whiskies come straight from the United States and Canada. Still, whisky is cheaper in Oaxaca or Tehuantepec than it is in Kentucky. There are quite a number of Kentucky emigrants to Mexico who do not feel that longing to return to the homes of their fathers which one would naturally expect in a true-born son of the blue-grass State.

Railroad fares in Mexico are usually quoted at double the mileage in the United States. That is to say, reduced to a common basis, they are equivalent. This doubling of the rates, then, does not affect the tourist from the United States, because he thinks in American coin, but it plays havoc with the Mexican citizen, who earns his money in the coin of Mexico. The passenger trains of these railroads carry first, second and third class coaches. One can find very well-mannered and sensitive people in the second-class car. As for the Pullman, it is the resort of the Americans, and of the higher, perhaps only the very swellest and most wealthy, grade of Mexicans. Perhaps it should have been mentioned some distance back in this article that the lower classes can purchase pulque, the native beverage, at the rate of 3 cents per glass. Five glasses seem to be sufficient to floor the average citizen of the republic, so it happens that he can get howling, staggering and abusive for 15 cents, or, in our money, 7½ cents.

The author of this article is not supposed to be transfixed with admiration because of the above facility of jag. He merely recites facts. It is a national condition, for which he is in no wise responsible.

The cost of prepared foods in Mexico is, when reduced to a common basis, about the same as it is in the United States. If one goes to an American restaurant in Mexico, he gets robbed more or less, but then this is not important. The Mexicans themselves live cheaply. However, they do not have one-eighth of the comforts and luxury that are in the ordinary little American home. Their lives in their houses are bare and scant, when measured with American firesides.

The Mexican laborer earns from 1 real (6¼ cents United States) to 4 reals (25 cents United States) per day. He lives mostly on tortillas, which are beans. His clothing consists of a cotton shirt, cotton trousers, leather sandals, and a straw hat. For his wages he has to work like a horse.

No. 93   STEPHEN CRANE IN MEXICO (II)

CITY OF MEXICO, July 14.—The train rolled out of the Americanisms of San Antonio—the coal and lumber yards, the lines of freight cars, the innumerable tracks and black cinder paths —and into the southern expanses of mesquite.

In the smoking compartment, the capitalist from Chicago said to the archaeologist from Boston: "Well, here we go." The archaeologist smiled with placid joy.

The brown wilderness of mesquite drifted steadily and for

hours past the car-windows. Occasionally a little ranch appeared half-buried in the bushes.

In the door-yard of one some little calicoed babies were playing and in the door-way itself a woman stood leaning her head against the post of it and regarding the train listlessly. Pale, worn, dejected, in her old and soiled gown, she was of a type to be seen North, East, South, West.

"That'll be one of our best glimpses of American civilization," observed the archaeologist then.

Cactus plants spread their broad pulpy leaves on the soil of reddish brown in the shade of the mesquite bushes. A thin silvery vapor appeared at the horizon.

"Say, I met my first Mexican, day before yesterday," said the capitalist. "Coming over from New Orleans. He was a peach. He could really talk more of the English language than any man I've ever heard. He talked like a mill-wheel. He had the happy social faculty of making everybody intent upon his conversation. You couldn't help it, you know. He put every sentence in the form of a question. 'San Anton' fine town—uh? F-i-n-n-e—uh? Gude beesness there—uh? Yes gude place for beesness—uh?' We all had to keep saying 'yes,' or 'certainly' or 'you bet your life,' at intervals of about three seconds."

"I went to school with some Cubans up North when I was a boy," said the archaeologist, "and they taught me to swear in Spanish. I'm all right in that. I can——"

"Don't you understand the conversational part at all?" demanded the capitalist.

"No," replied the archaeologist.

"Got friends in the City of Mexico?"

"No!"

"Well, by jiminy, you're going to have a daisy time!"

"Why, do you speak the language?"

"No!"

"Got any friends in the city?"

"No."

"Thunder."

These mutual acknowledgements riveted the two men together. In this invasion, in which they were both facing the unknown, an acquaintance was a prize.

As the train went on over the astonishing brown sea of

mesquite, there began to appear little prophecies of Mexico. A Mexican woman, perhaps, crouched in the door of a hut, her bare arms folded, her knees almost touching her chin, her head leaned against the door-post. Or perhaps a dusky sheep-herder in peaked sombrero and clothes the color of tan-bark, standing beside the track, his inscrutable visage turned toward the train. A cloud of white dust rising above the dull-colored bushes denoted the position of his flock. Over this lonely wilderness vast silence hung, a speckless sky, ignorant of bird or cloud.

"Look at this," said the capitalist.

"Look at that," said the archaeologist.

These premonitory signs threw them into fever of anticipation. "Say, how much longer before we get to Laredo?" The conductor grinned. He recognized some usual, some typical aspect in this impatience. "Oh, a long time yet."

But then finally when the whole prairie had turned a faint preparatory shadow-blue, some one told them: "See those low hills off yonder? Well, they're beyond the Rio Grande."

"Get out—are they?"

A sheep-herder with his flock raising pale dust-clouds over the lonely mesquite could no longer interest them. Their eyes were fastened on the low hills beyond the Rio Grande.

"There it is! There's the river!"

"Ah, no, it ain't!"

"I say it is."

Ultimately the train manœuvered through some low hills and into sight of low-roofed houses across stretches of sand. Presently it stopped at a long wooden station. A score of Mexican urchins were congregated to see the arrival. Some twenty yards away stood a train composed of an engine, a mail and baggage car, a Pullman and three day coaches marked first, second and third class in Spanish. "There she is, my boy," said the capitalist. "There's the Aztec Limited. There's the train that's going to take us to the land of flowers and visions and all that."

There was a general charge upon the ticket office to get American money changed to Mexican money. It was a beautiful game. Two Mexican dollars were given for every American dollar. The passengers bid good-bye to their portraits of the national bird, with exultant smiles. They examined with interest the new bills which were quite gay with red and purple and green. As for the silver dollar, the face of it intended to represent a cap of liberty with rays of glory shooting from it, but it looked to be on the contrary a picture of an exploding bomb. The capitalist from Chicago jingled his coin with glee. "Doubled my money!"

"All aboard," said the conductor for the last time. Thereafter he said: "Vamanos." The train swung around the curve and toward the river. A soldier in blue fatigue uniform from the adjacent barracks, a portly German regardant at the entrance to his saloon, an elaborate and beautiful Anglo-Saxon oath from the top of a lumber pile, a vision of red and white and blue at the top of a distant staff, and the train was upon the high bridge that connects one nation with another.

Laredo appeared like a city veritably built upon sand. Little plats of vivid green grass appeared incredible upon this apparent waste. They looked like the grass mats of the theatrical stage. An old stone belfry arose above the low roofs. The river, shallow and quite narrow, flowed between wide banks of sand which seemed to express the stream's former records.

In Nuevo Laredo, there was a throng upon the platform— Mexican women, muffled in old shawls, and men, wrapped closely in dark-hued serapes. Over the heads of the men towered the peaked sombreros of fame. It was a preliminary picture painted in dark colors.

There was also a man in tan shoes and trousers of violent English check. When a gentleman of Spanish descent is important, he springs his knee-joint forward to its limit with each step. This gentleman was springing his knee-joints as if they were of no consequence, as if he had a new pair at his service.

"You have only hand baggage," said the conductor. "You won't have to get out."

Presently, the gentleman in tan shoes entered the car, springing his knee-joints frightfully. He caused the porter to let down all the upper berths while he fumbled among the blankets and mattresses. The archaeologist and the capitalist had their valises already open and the gentleman paused in his knee-springing flight and gently peered in them. "All right," he said approvingly and pasted upon each of them a label which bore some formidable Mexican legend. Then he knee-springed himself away.

The train again invaded a wilderness of mesquite. It was amazing. The travellers had somehow expected a radical change the moment they were well across the Rio Grande. On the contrary, southern Texas was being repeated. They leaned close to the pane and stared into the mystic south. In the rear, however, Texas was represented by a long narrow line of blue hills, built up from the plain like a step.

Infrequently horsemen, shepherds, hovels appeared in the mesquite. Once, upon a small hillock a graveyard came into view and over each grave was a black cross. These somber emblems, lined against the pale sky, were given an inexpressibly mournful and fantastic horror from their color, new in this lonely land of brown bushes. The track swung to the westward and extended as straight as a rapier blade toward the rose-colored sky from whence the sun had vanished. The shadows of the mesquite deepened.

Presently the train paused at a village. Enough light remained to bring clearly into view some square yellow huts from whose rectangular doors there poured masses of crimson rays from the household fires. In these shimmering glows, dark and sinister shadows moved. The archaeologist and the capitalist were quite alone at this time in the sleeping-car and there was room for their enthusiasm, their ejaculations. Once they saw a black outline of a man upon one of these red canvasses. His legs were crossed, his arms were folded in his serape, his hat resembled a charlotte russe. He leaned negligently against the door-post. This figure justified to them all their preconceptions. He was more than a painting. He was the proving of certain romances, songs, narratives. He renewed their faith. They scrutinized him until the train moved away.

They wanted mountains. They clamored for mountains. "How soon, conductor, will we see any mountains?" The conductor indicated a long shadow in the pallor of the afterglow. Faint, delicate, it resembled the light rain-clouds of a faraway shower.

The train, rattling rhythmically, continued toward the far horizon. The deep mystery of night upon the mesquite prairie settled upon it like a warning to halt. The windows presented black expanses. At the little stations, calling voices could be heard from the profound gloom. Cloaked figures moved in the glimmer of lanterns.

The two travellers, hungry for color, form, action, strove to penetrate with their glances these black curtains of darkness which intervened between them and the new and strange life. At last, however, the capitalist settled down in the smoking compartment and recounted at length the extraordinary attributes of his children in Chicago.

Before they retired they went out to the platform and gazed into the south where the mountain range, still outlined against the soft sky, had grown portentously large. To those upon the train, the black prairie seemed to heave like a sea and these mountains rose out of it like islands. In the west, a great star shone forth. "It is as large as a cheese," said the capitalist.

The archaeologist asserted the next morning that he had awakened at midnight and contemplated Monterey. It appeared, he said, as a high wall and a distant row of lights. When the capitalist awoke, the train was proceeding through a great wide valley which was radiant in the morning sunshine. Mountain ranges, wrinkled, crumpled, bare of everything save sage-brush, loomed on either side. Their little peaks were yellow in the light and their sides were of the faintest carmine tint, heavily interspersed with shadows. The wide, flat plain itself was grown thickly with sage-brush, but date palms were sufficiently numerous to make it look at times like a bed of some monstrous asparagus.

At every station a gorgeous little crowd had gathered to receive the train. Some were merely curious and others had various designs on the traveller—to beg from him or to sell to him. Indian women walked along the line of cars and held baskets of fruit toward the windows. Their broad, stolid faces were suddenly lit with a new commercial glow at the arrival of this trainful of victims. The men remained motionless and reposeful in their serapes. Back from the stations one could see the groups of white, flat-roofed adobe houses. From where a white road stretched over the desert toward the mountains, there usually arose a high, shining cloud of dust from the hoofs of some caballero's charger.

As this train conquered more and more miles toward its sunny destination, a regular progression in color could be noted. At Nuevo Laredo the prevailing tones in the dress of the people were brown, black and grey. Later an occasional purple or crimson serape was interpolated. And later still, the purple, the crimson and the other vivid hues became the typical colors, and even the trousers of dark cloth were replaced by dusty white cotton ones. A horseman in a red serape and a tall sombrero of maroon or pearl or yellow was vivid as an individual, but a dozen or two of them reposeful in the shade of some desert railway station made a chromatic delirium. In Mexico the atmosphere seldom softens anything. It devotes its energy to making high lights, bringing everything forward, making colors fairly volcanic.

The bare feet of the women pattered to and fro along the row of car windows. Their cajoling voices were always soft and musical. The fierce sun of the desert beat down upon their baskets, wherein the fruit and food was exposed to each feverish ray.

From time to time across this lonely sunbeaten expanse, from which a storm of fine, dry dust ascended upon any provocation at all, the train passed walls made of comparatively small stones which extended for miles over the plain and then ascended the distant mountains in an undeviating line. They expressed the most incredible and apparently stupid labor. To see a stone wall beginning high and wide and extending to the horizon in a thin, monotonous thread, makes one think of the innumerable hands that toiled at the stones to divide one extent of sage-brush from another. Occasionally the low roof of a hacienda could be seen, surrounded by outbuildings and buried in trees. These walls marked the boundary of each hacienda's domain.

"Certain times of year," said the conductor, "there is nothing for the Indian peons to do, and as the rancheros have to feed 'em and keep 'em anyhow, you know, why they set 'em to building these stone walls."

The archaeologist and the capitalist gazed with a new interest at the groups of dusty-footed peons at the little stations. The clusters of adobe huts wherein some of them dwelt resembled the pictures of Palestine tombs. Withal, they smiled amiably, contentedly, their white teeth gleaming.

When the train roared past the stone monument that marked the Tropic of Cancer, the two travellers leaned out dangerously.

"Look at that, would you?"

"Well, I'm hanged!"

They stared at it with awed glances. "Well, well, so that's it, is it?" When the southern face of the monument was presented, they saw the legend, "Zona Torrida."

"Thunder, ain't this great."

Finally, the valley grew narrower. The track wound near the bases of hills. Through occasional passes could be seen other ranges, leaden-hued, in the distance. The sage-bushes became scarce and the cactus began to grow with a greater courage. The young green of other and unknown plants became visible. Greyish dust in swirling masses marked the passage of the train.

At San Luis Potosi, the two travellers disembarked and again assailed one of those American restaurants which are located at convenient points. Roast chicken, tender steaks, chops, eggs, biscuit, pickles, cheese, pie, coffee, and just outside in blaring sunshine there was dust and Mexicans and a heathen chatter—a sort of an atmosphere of chili con carne, tortillas, tamales. The two travellers approached this table with a religious air as if they had encountered a shrine.

All the afternoon the cactus continued to improve in sizes. It now appeared that the natives made a sort of a picket fence of one variety and shade trees from another. The brown faces of Indian women and babes peered from these masses of prickly green.

At Atotonilco, a church with red-tiled towers appeared surrounded by poplar trees that resembled hearse plumes, and in the stream that flowed near there was a multitude of heads with long black hair. A vast variety of feminine garments decorated the bushes that skirted the creek. A baby, brown as a water-jar and of the shape of an alderman, paraded the bank in utter indifference or ignorance or defiance.

At various times old beggars, grey and bent, tottered painfully with outstretched hats begging for centavos in voices that expressed the last degree of chill despair. Their clothing hung in the most supernatural tatters. It seemed miraculous that such fragments could stay upon human bodies. With some unerring inexplainable instinct they steered for the capitalist. He swore and blushed each time. "They take me for an easy thing," he said wrathfully. "No—I won't—get out—go away." The unmolested archeologist laughed.

The churches north of Monterey had been for the most part small and meek structures surmounted by thin wooden crosses. They were now more impressive, with double towers of stone and in the midst of gardens and dependent buildings. Once the archaeologist espied a grey and solemn ruin of a chapel. The old walls and belfry appeared in the midst of a thicket of regardless cactus. He at once recited to the capitalist the entire history of Cortez and the Aztecs.

At night-fall, the train paused at a station where the entire village had come down to see it and gossip. There appeared to be no great lighting of streets. Two or three little lamps burned at the station and a soldier, or a policeman, carried a lantern which feebly illuminated his club and the bright steel of his revolver. In the profound gloom, the girls walked arm and arm, three or four abreast, and giggled. Bands of hoodlums scouted the darkness. One could hear their shrill cat-calls. Some pedlers came with flaring torches and tried to sell things.

In the early morning hours, the two travellers scrambled from their berths to discover that the train was high in air. It had begun its great climb of the mountains. Below and on the left, a vast plain of green and yellow fields was spread out like a checkered cloth. Here and there were tiny white villages, churches, haciendas. And beyond this plain arose the peak of Nevado de Toluca for 15,000 feet. Its eastern face was sun-smitten with gold and its snowy sides were shadowed with rose. The color of gold made it appear that this peak was staring with a high serene eternal glance into the East at the approach of the endless suns. And no one feels like talking in the presence of these mountains that stand like gods on the world, for fear that they might hear. Slowly the train wound around the face of the cliff.

When you come to this country, do not confuse the Mexican cakes with pieces of iron ore. They are not pieces of iron ore. They are cakes.

At a mountain station to which the train had climbed in some wonderful fashion, the travellers breakfasted upon cakes and coffee. The conductor, tall, strong, as clear-headed and as clear-eyed, as thoroughly a type of the American railroad man as if he were in charge of the Pennsylvania Limited, sat at the head of the table and harangued the attendant peon. The capitalist took a bite of cake and said "Gawd!"

This little plateau was covered with yellow grass which extended to the bases of the hills that were on all sides. These hills were grown thickly with pines, fragrant, gently waving in the cool breeze. Upon the station platform a cavalry officer, under a grey sombrero heavily ladened with silver braid, conversed with a swarthy trooper. Over the little plain, a native in a red blanket was driving a number of small donkeys who were each carrying an enormous load of fresh hay.

The conductor again yelled out a password to a Chinese lodge and the train renewed its attack upon these extraordinary ridges which intervened between it and its victory. The passengers prepared themselves. Every car window was hung full of heads that were for the most part surmounted by huge sombreros. A man with such a large roll of matting strapped to his back that he looked like a perambulating sentry-box, leaned upon his staff in the roadway and stared at the two engines. Puffing, panting, heaving, they strained like thoroughbred animals, with every steel muscle of their bodies and slowly the train was hauled up this tilted track.

In and out among the hills it went, higher and higher. Often two steel rails were visible far below on the other side of a ravine. It seemed incredible that ten minutes before, the train had been at that place.

In the depths of the valley, a brook brawled over the rocks. A man in dusty white garments lay asleep in the shade of a pine.

At last the whistle gave a triumphant howl. The summit—10,000 feet above the sea—was reached. A winding slide, a sort of tremendous toboggan affair began. Around and around among the hills glided the train. Little flat white villages displayed themselves in the valleys. The maguey plant, from which the Mexicans make their celebrated tanglefoot, flourished its lance-point leaves in long rows. The hills were checkered to their summits with brown fields. The train swinging steadily down the mountains crossed one stream thirteen times on bridges dizzily high.

Suddenly two white peaks, afar off, raised above the horizon, peering over the ridge. The capitalist nearly fell off the train. Popocatepetl and Ixtaccihuatl, the two giant mountains, clothed in snow that was like wool, were marked upon the sky. A glimpse was had of a vast green plain. In this distance, the castle of Chapultepec resembled a low thunder cloud.

Presently the train was among long white walls, green lawns, high shade trees. The passengers began their preparations for disembarking as the train manœuvered through the switches. At last there came a depot heavily fringed with people, an omnibus, a dozen cabs and a soldier in a uniform that fitted him like a bird cage. White dust arose high toward the blue sky. In some tall grass on the other side of the track, a little cricket suddenly chirped. The two travellers with shining eyes climbed out of the car. "A-a-ah," they said in a prolonged sigh of delight. The city of the Aztecs was in their power.

No. 94   A JAG OF PULQUE IS HEAVY

THE first thing to be done by the investigating tourist of this country is to begin to drink the national beverage, pulque. The second thing to be done by the investigating tourist is to cease to drink pulque. This last recommendation, however, is necessary to no one. The human inclination acts automatically, so to speak, in this case. If the great drunkard of the drama should raise his right hand and swear solemnly never to touch another drop of intoxicating pulque as long as he lived—so help him heaven—he would make himself ridiculous. It would be too simple. Why should a man ever taste another drop of pulque after having once collided with it?

But this does not relate to the Mexicans. This relates to the foreigner who brings with him numerous superstitions and racial, fundamental traditions concerning odors. To the foreigner, the very proximity of a glass of pulque is enough to take him up by the hair and throw him violently to the ground.

It resembles green milk. The average man has never seen green milk, but if he can imagine a handful of paris green interpolated into a glass of cream, he will have a fair idea of the appearance of pulque. And it tastes like—it tastes like— some terrible concoction of bad yeast perhaps. Or maybe some calamity of eggs.

This, bear in mind, represents the opinion of a stranger. As far as the antagonism of the human stomach goes, there can be no doubt but that pulque bears about the same relation to the uninitiated sense as does American or any kind of beer. But the first encounter is a revelation. One understands then that education is everything, even as the philosophers say, and that we would all be eating sandwiches made from door-mats if only circumstances had been different.

To the Mexican, pulque is a delirium of joy. The lower classes dream of pulque. There are pulque shops on every corner in some quarters of the city. And, lined up at the bar in conventional fashion, the natives may be seen at all times, yelling thirsty sentences at the barkeepers. These pulque shops are usually decorated both inside and out with the real old paintings done on the walls by the hand of some unknown criminal. Looking along the pale walls of the streets, one is startled at every corner by these sudden lurid interjections of pulque green, red, blue, yellow. The pulque is served in little brown earthern mugs that are shaped in miniature precisely like one of the famous jars of the Orient.

The native can get howling full for anything from twelve

cents to twenty cents. Twelve cents is the equivalent in American coinage of about six cents. Many men of celebrated thirsts in New York would consider this a profoundly ideal condition. However, six cents represents something to the Indian. Unless there are some Americans around to be robbed, he is obliged to rustle very savagely for his pulque money. When he gets it he is happy and the straight line he makes for one of the flaming shops, has never been outdone by any metropolitan iceman that drinks. In the meantime the swarm of pulque saloons are heavily taxed, and the aggregate amount of their payments to the government is almost incredible. The Indian, in his dusty cotton shirt and trousers, his tattered sombrero, his flapping sandals, his stolid dark face, is of the same type in this regard that is familiar to every land, the same prisoner, the same victim.

In riding through almost any part of this high country, you will pass acre after acre, mile after mile, of "century" plants laid out in rows that stretch always to the horizon whether it is at the hazy edge of a mighty plain or at the summit of a rugged and steep mountain. You wonder at the immensity of the thing. Haciendas will have their thousands of acres planted in nothing but the maguey, or as the Americans call it, the "century" plant. The earth is laid out in one tremendous pattern, maguey plants in long sweeping perspective.

Well, it is from this plant that the natives make pulque.

Pulque is the juice taken from the heart of the maguey and allowed to ferment for one day. After that time, it must be consumed within twenty-four hours or it is positively useless. The railroads that run through the principal maguey districts operate fast early-morning pulque trains in much the same fashion that the roads that run through Orange County, N.Y., operate early-morning milk trains to New York. From the depots it is hustled in wagons and on the backs of porters to the innumerable saloons and from thence dispensed to the public.

Mescal and tequila are two native rivals of pulque. Mescal is a sort of a cousin of whisky, although to the eye it is as clear as water, and tequila is to mescal as brandy is to whisky. They are both wrung from the heart of the maguey plant.

In a low part of the country where pulque cannot be produced the natives use mescal, for this beverage is of course capable of long journeys, and where a native can get pulque he usually prefers it.

The effects of pulque as witnessed in the natives, do not seem to be so pyrotechnic and clamorous as are the effects of certain other drinks upon the citizens of certain other nations. The native, filled with pulque, seldom wishes to fight. Usually he prefers to adore his friends. They will hang together in front of a bar, three or four of them, their legs bending, their arms about each other's necks, their faces lit with an expression of the most ideal affection and supreme brotherly regard. It would be difficult to make an impression on their feelings at these times with a club. Their whole souls are completely absorbed in this beatific fraternal tenderness.

Still, there are certain mixtures, certain combinations which invariably breed troubles. Let the native mix his pulque at three cents a glass with some of that vivid native brandy and there is likely to be a monstrous turmoil on little or no provocation. Out at Santa Anita, which is a resort for the lower classes on the Viga Canal, they used to have a weekly ceremony which was of the same order as the regular Sunday night murder in the old days of Mulberry Bend. And it happened because the natives mixed their drinks.

No. 95   THE FETE OF MARDI GRAS

IT RAINED toward the latter part of the week and the visitors who had already arrived began to shake their heads as they proceeded carefully over the thin coating of black mud that lay upon the uneven stones of the streets. The citizens, however, remained in serene and unshaken faith. No, it would not rain on Mardi Gras. It never rained then. There would be fine weather—just wait.

And, in truth, when Sunday appeared it was of the quality of spring, fair, soft and balmy with the singularly lucid atmosphere of the southland. On Canal street swarmed an expectant crowd dodging in and about the upright joists that had been placed to support the balconies. The windows of the hotels and clubs were filled with visitors from other cities taking a preliminary view of the wide street with its masses of people upon the sidewalks and upon the strip of yellow grass in the middle of the avenue where too at short intervals ran mule cars and electric cars and the cars of a steam tramway proceeding slowly through the throng and filling the air with the clamor of gongs. In the breeze that came over the housetops, decorations of purple and green and gold gently fluttered.

At noon on Monday the throng occupying the avenue had been largely augmented. People turned their eyes toward the levee where because the waters of the river could in no wise be seen, the avenue seemed to be projected into the air. In the steel-colored sky some black smoke drifted upward. Then at last the masts and two tan stacks of a steamer moved slowly into view, afar off, over the multitude of heads in the street. Later there could be seen the glitter of many approaching bayonets and the steady beat of martial music. The crowds on the sidewalk underwent an anticipatory convulsion. Rex, his majesty of the carnival time, had come. There was a sudden interpolation of crimson color into the black masses of people down the avenue.

All Tuesday morning, the usual sombre clothes of citizens in the street were brightened by the gypsy hues of the maskers. Small boys arrayed in wondrous garments to represent monkeys, gnomes, imps, parrots, anything but small boys, paraded in bands and reaped a deep delight when they found a victim for their skill in badinage. And much older boys temporarily represented as all manner of nondescript personages, rambled over the city in the full joy of being at their own devices with a sort of mild license to caper and crack jokes into the air. At noon, Canal street was a river of human bodies moving slowly. At dusk, it was a sea, in which contrary currents indolently opposed each other. The fronts of the clubs and principal buildings suddenly became outlined in the shine of electric lights and, in these brilliant frames, symbolistic initials appeared. The royal colors of green and purple and gold shone forth in bunting and silk and glass. Between a curb and one of the horse car tracks a deep row of people had collected and the small street cars came along at regular and monotonous intervals and scraped some of them away. The boxes and stands had already begun to fill up and the people in them turned their faces toward the darkness of the end of the street. In one of the stands was a space reserved for his majesty, Rex, his queen and court. From these stands, the avenue resembled a vast black sea save where here and there gleamed the costumes of a group of maskers or where a street car fought its irritatingly painful way through the throng.

Ultimately, the king, gorgeous in his royal robes and his jewels, and with his features behind a huge cossack beard, came slowly down the sloping stand with his queen, and followed by his glittering court. Instantly this vast black expanse of the street became an ocean of faces, a great stretch of eager human countenances in which the eyes rolled slowly. A hoarse rumble of voices arose; then, later, a shout as if a rocket had been seen to ascend. "A—a—ah!"

Then the patient crowd settled into a profound and silent contemplation of their carnival ruler. Occasionally a man stretched forth his neck to peer down the street for the procession and frequently maskers engaged in a tumultuous frolic. Too, as mentioned, the street cars scraped sightseers from the curbs that bounded the grass plots in the middle of the street but, for the most part, this great mass of people remained silent, patient, motionless.

Suddenly a man shouted: "Here it comes!" Far over the heads could be seen a banner that caught a vivid reflection from some lights beneath it. At the side of the street, a negro coachman had crawled into the gloom of a corner of his victoria and gone to sleep. An agitated bystander yelled at him: "Come, uncle, wake up! They're comin' and they'll chase you away from here." The old man hastily drew on his shoes again and crawled up on his box. "Yas, I raiken dey is. Dey'll done bully me outa year an' I better had be gittin'." But this was not the procession at all but some marauding company of maskers. When he had gathered up his reins and turned for a last glance to the rear, the banner had vanished. He made a gesture of deep scorn at the man who had aroused him. "Aw! Aw! dat wan no percession——"

In the middle of the street some little boys had created a riot. They were dressed as some strange kind of white apes but the tails of their suits were so long and so neatly stuffed with cotton that the ends could be pulled around in front and used very effectively as clubs. With these weapons they had belabored some little boys who were exhibiting as minstrels and an exciting combat had at once ensued between the minstrels and the apes.

Meanwhile, the street cars had become blocked, and, standing thus in the middle of the wide streets, they made fine and cheap stands from which to view the procession as it passed to the right of them. Women with numerous children, old couples, and people without these reasons presented an interminable row of faces at the windows of an interminable row of cars.

Around the gleaming place where sat their majesties and the court, a throng in milder raiment in which shone many white conventional shirt fronts, slowly gathered. Ladies with dainty gestures raised their lorgnettes to stare into the dark perspective of the avenue. The king lifted his sceptre and examined it with interest. The ladies of the court chatted, turning their heads from one to another, their eyes shining. With the vivid light upon this balcony, the scene of violet and white had all the distinctness of a marvelous painting. The procession was delayed. Some of the court seemed petulant. If the king was bored his weariness was hidden in his flowing beard.

Down in the democratic semi-gloom of the street stood a young girl, her hand upon the arm of a young man. This girl had remained for a long time, motionless, her eyes raised at an angle and fixed upon the queen. Her lips were a little way parted, her cheeks were subtly flushed. And into this glance there was a profundity of awe, admiration. She dreamed and this dream was so splendid, so full of rainbow glories, that even the scene before her was merely a guide. The dream was broken by a negro teamster who came through the crowd with three mules and a dray. He had become so ferocious toward a small boy who had dived between the lead mule and the wheel team that he could not have the ordinary care for people's safety. A large section of crowd had to scurry. There was some eloquent abuse.

Meanwhile the king, inscrutable behind his beard, looked down at his subjects. The queen, regal alike in fact and carnival, talked to her ladies. And turned always toward the royal pair was this waxen sea of faces. Above the arcs and squares of illumination hung a sky like black velvet.

Down the avenue there appeared a pale purple haze. Presently the forms of mounted policemen could be seen outlined in it. A rocket went slantingly upward. There was some mild and good-natured jostling. A voice cried out: "Ah, git off de eart' an' give de grass a chanct t' grow." A man with the shaven face and mobile lips of an actor immediately said: "Great Scott, I know that breed! What's he doing away down here?"

The strains of a march came plainly. The haze grew brighter and varied its color. In the background could be seen the form of one of the floats, but in the incoherent shadows it resembled a striding giant. A row of negro babies in their eagerness peered out too far and toppled from the curb. The gutter contained about two inches of water.

The solitary mounted policeman who formed the extreme advance guard was gaily assaulted by an Indian chief, a pirate, and some apes. His horse reared and plunged and he wrenched his arm free of them. He rode on laughing good naturedly. After him came others, insistent and perfectly serious in their business of clearing the street but apparently always good natured and civil.

After the police, the procession slowly came through between the two black lines of people. From the high stands it resembled a long monster of golden fire upon which gleamed frequently dazzling spots of purple and green. The glittering floats creaked slowly over the stones and the shining and enormous emblems in wood and paper and cloth gently vibrated with a persistent and endless motion. The luminous figures upon them hung on with one hand while they waved the other gaily at the crowd.

The floats looked in the distance like vast confections. Some were of a fine cool green like spring water seen in the sunlight, while others were of the hue of violets. These soft colors imparted to the great moving masses a fairy-like quality as if a wind might blow them, light and unresisting, high into the sky. In long lines at either side, marched negroes in blood-red gnome cloaks and bearing torches with reflectors which shed a strong and continual orange glare upon the floats. And dragging slowly at the traces, the mules too were hidden in red cloaks, although occasionally a thoughtful and indifferent countenance appeared, and upon it an expression of deep and far-away reflection. Girls leaned over balconies and shouted: "Ah, there's Comus! There he is! Comus, Comus, look this way!"

This night's prince, high in air and crowned, gestured and bowed amiably at the cheers. One found one's self staring at the mask and wondering, not of the features, but of the emotion, and feeling exasperated at the baffling cover.

Further down the gorgeous line the float of the great god Pan started from a halt with a sudden jerk and almost precipitated him from his high estate.

A masker in red and green expressed in pantomime from his perch on a float his great anxiety to present a certain box tied with ribbons to some young men in the street. The young men yelled: "Yes! Go ahead! Let'er come." The masker threw the box swiftly; the astonished young men dodged. But the masker had a string to it and it returned to his hand. A derisive howl came from the crowd. As the float moved on, the masker gestured mockingly. It seemed wonderful in some way that throughout this incident that mask should remain imperturbable, unchanged, with the same expression of extraordinary ferocity with which it had been created.

Vivid fires of red, yellow, purple, white, sputtered forth their luminous smoke. Bands clashed interminably. And because of the glare of light the faces of the crowd became pallid and in the immobility of expression, death like, save for the eyes which glinted with delight.

In the balconies near the king and queen, ladies leaned forward intently. Upon the floats, the glittering maskers turned at once toward this array of silent, deeply observant women. The display here found itself out displayed. And the occasional, the temporary royalties gazed at the eternal royalty of beautiful women. Occasionally from these high stands, a gloved hand lifted a handkerchief and waved it.

As soon as the procession had passed, the crowd swirled in one mass over the avenue as the waters close after the passage of a vessel.

Down in the French quarter, the narrow and gloomy street that leads to the famous opera house suddenly achieved all the radiance of light and splendor of hue which had illuminated Canal street. From the profoundly dark side streets the procession, as it passed the corners, bore the appearance of a wide and shining frieze upon which were painted marvelous moving figures in violet, gold, light green. In front of the solemn pillars of the opera house each float was suddenly made a bare splendor, as its imps, its knights and its flower girls clambered hastily down. Later, the tiny glow of carriage lamps was seen up the street. Their majesties were coming to Comus' grand ball.

In other gloomy streets, the negroes, still in their blood-red gnome cloaks, could be seen urging the mules in front of the deserted floats which gleamed like frost in the darkness.

No. 96   HATS, SHIRTS, AND SPURS IN MEXICO

THE hat is the main strength of the true Mexican dude. Upon these gorgeous sombreros the Mexican gentleman of fashion frequently spends fifty dollars or even a hundred dollars. And these splendid masses of gold braid and pearl grey beaver surmount the average masculine head with the same artistic value as would a small tower of bricks. In the first place, the true Mexican wears his trousers very tight in the leg, and as his legs are always small and wiry, he produces an effect of instability. When you see him crowned by one of those great peaked sombreros, you think he is likely to fall down upon slight occasion.

This same gentleman may run to spurs a good deal. There are for sale in the shops in the City of Mexico silver spurs that weigh a couple of pounds each—immense things that look more like rhinoceros traps than spurs to urge on a horse. He may, too, when he rides in the country, have a pair of elegantly decorated pistol holsters at his pommel. A double row of little silver buttons extend down each leg of his tight trousers and it is more than probable that his little jacket will be embroidered like mad. After all this, he will be seated upon a saddle that the sultan of a thousand Turkeys would never dare use for a foot-stool. Mounted then upon a charger that proceeds at mincing, restrained gait down the avenue crowded with fashionable carriages, he with his full chin, black mustache and vaguely sinister eye, is the true type of the Mexican caballero.

But, on the other hand, the true Mexican style has been combated subtly for years by the ideas from America and from Europe, which have flown into the country. In the rural districts the caballero is still supreme, but in the larger towns and in the capital, the men of the greatest wealth and position always resemble the ordinary type of American men of affairs. And the younger generation, who are yet of a mind to care for dress, study the fashions of New York and London with much diligence.

Here begins the conflict between the holy London creed of what is correct and an innate love of vivid personal adornment. They clash and the clash is sometimes to be heard for miles. The great distance which these mandates come also confuses matters.

Here is an attempt at a typical enumeration.

I. A black tie, a high white collar, a green opal stud in a shirt of crimson silk.

II. Cuffs of fine lace, a shirt bosom of more fine lace which falls in a beautiful cascade over the breast of a discreet black cutaway.

III. Four men in evening dress at 10:30 a.m.

IV. A shirt with green stripes two inches wide and red four-in-hand tie.

V. A tie of blue China silk, the ends of which fall to the waist.

These effects are to be seen from time to time. It would not be reasonable to quarrel with them or sneer at them. The first young man has an absolute right to wear his crimson shirt if it does not burn him. He no doubt finds it decorative and comfortable. Perhaps his sisters think it admirable and perhaps some senorita with flashing eyes thinks nothing so handsome as that little triangle of crimson, which glows above his coat lapels. It is never wise to deride the fashions of another people, for we ourselves have no idea of what we are coming to. Within two years, New York may be absolutely on fire with crimson shirts—blood red bosoms may flash in the air like lanterns.

Occasionally, in strolls about the streets, one is able to observe the final development of the English check. When a man sincerely sets out to have a suit of checked cloth, it is astonishing to what an extent he can carry his passion. There are suits of this description here that in the vivid sun-light of the country, throw a checkered shadow upon the pavement. They are usually upon Mexicans of the lower middle class, who save them for afternoon strolls. I distinctly remember some window shades to a store in upper Broadway that I thought displayed the most devastating checks in the universe. They do not.

But above all the reader must remember that the great mass of humanity upon the principal business street of Mexico City dress about the same as they do in other places. There is a little more variety perhaps, and of course there is an interpolation of Indians, who are utterly distinct. But in the main there is a great similarity. The streets do not blaze. If you wish blaze go into side streets where the Indians live.

The Indian remains the one great artistic figure. The caballero in his enormous sombrero and skin-tight trousers is top-heavy. But the Indian in his serape, with his cotton trousers, his dusty sandals upon which his bare toes are displayed, and his old sombrero pulled down over his eyes is a fascinating man.

Whether his blanket is purple or not or of some dull hue, he fits into the green grass, the low white walls, the blue sky as if his object was not so much to get possession of some centavos as to compose the picture.

At night when he crouches in a doorway with his sombrero pulled still further over his eyes, and his mouth covered by a fold of his serape, you can imagine anything at all about him, for his true character is impenetrable. He is a mystic and silent figure of the darkness.

He has two great creeds. One is that pulque as a beverage is finer than the melted blue of the sky. The other is that Americans are eternally wealthy and immortally stupid. If the world was really of the size that he believes it to be, you could put his hat over it.

No. 97   STEPHEN CRANE IN TEXAS

SAN ANTONIO, TEX., January 6, 1889. "Ah," they said, "you are going to San Anton? I wish I was. There's a town for you."

From all manner of people, business men, consumptive men, curious men and wealthy men, there came an exhibition of a profound affection for San Antonio. It seemed to symbolize for them the poetry of life in Texas.

There is an eloquent description of the city which makes it consist of three old ruins and a row of Mexicans sitting in the sun. The author, of course, visited San Antonio in the year 1101. While this is undoubtedly a masterly literary effect, one can feel glad that after all we don't steer our ships according to these literary effects.

At first the city presents a totally modern aspect to the astonished visitor. The principal streets are lanes between rows of handsome business blocks, and upon them proceeds with important uproar the terrible and almighty trolley car. The prevailing type of citizen is not seated in the sun; on the contrary he is making his way with the speed and intentness of one who competes in a community that is commercially in earnest. And the victorious derby hat of the North spreads its wings in the holy place of legends.

This is the dominant quality. This is the principal color of San Antonio. Later one begins to see that these edifices of stone and brick and iron are reared on ashes, upon the ambitions of a race. It expresses again the victory of the North. The serene Anglo-Saxon erects business blocks upon the dreams of the transient monks; he strings telegraph wires across the face of their sky of hope; and over the energy, the efforts, the accomplishments of these pious fathers of the early church passes the wheel, the hoof, the heel.

Here, and there, however, one finds in the main part of the town, little old buildings, yellow with age, solemn and severe in outline, that have escaped by a miracle or by a historical importance, the whirl of the modern life. In the Mexican quarter there remains, too, much of the old character, but despite the tenderness which San Antonio feels for these monuments, the unprotected mass of them must get trampled into shapeless dust which lies always behind the march of this terrible century. The feet of the years will go through many old roofs.

Trolley cars are merciless animals. They gorge themselves with relics. They make really coherent history look like an omelet. If a trolley car had trolleyed around Jericho, the city would not have fallen; it would have exploded.

Centuries ago the white and gold banner of Spain came up out of the sea and the Indians, mere dots of black on the vast Texan plain, saw a moving glitter of silver warriors on the horizon's edge. There came then the long battle of soldier and priest, side by side, against these stubborn barbaric hordes, who wished to retain both their gods and their lands. Sword and crozier made frenzied circles in the air. The soldiers varied their fights with the Indians by fighting the French, and both the Indians and the French occasionally polished their armor for them with great neatness and skill.

During interval of peace and interval of war, toiled the pious monks, erecting missions, digging ditches, making farms and cudgeling their Indians in and out of the church. Sometimes, when the venerable fathers ran short of Indians to

convert, the soldiers went on expeditions and returned dragging in a few score. The settlement prospered. Upon the gently
rolling plains, the mission churches with their yellow stone
towers outlined upon the sky, called with their bells at evening a multitude of friars and meek Indians and gleaming
soldiers to service in the shadows before the flaming candles,
the solemn shrine, the slow-pacing, chanting priests. And
wicked and hopeless Indians, hearing these bells, scudded off
into the blue twilight of the prairie.

The ruins of these missions are now besieged in the valley
south of the city by indomitable thickets of mesquite. They
rear their battered heads, their soundless towers, over dead
forms, the graves of monks; and of the Spanish soldiers not
one so much as flourishes a dagger.

Time has torn at these pale yellow structures and over-
turned walls and towers here and there, defaced this and
obliterated that. Relic hunters with their singular rapacity
have dragged down little saints from their niches and pulled
important stones from arches. They have performed offices of
destruction of which the wind and the rain of the innumerable
years was not capable. They are part of the general scheme of
attack by nature.

The wind blows because it is the wind, the rain beats because it is the rain, the relic hunters hunt because they are
relic hunters. Who can fathom the ways of nature? She
thrusts her spear in the eye of Tradition and her agents feed
on his locks. A little guide-book published here contains one
of these "Good friend, forbear——" orations. But still this
desperate massacre of the beautiful carvings goes on and it
would take the ghosts of the monks with the ghosts of
scourges, the phantoms of soldiers with the phantoms of
swords, a scowling, spectral party, to stop the destruction. In
the meantime, these portentous monuments to the toil, the
profound convictions of the fathers, remain stolid and unyielding, with the bravery of stone, until it appears like the
last stand of an army. Many years will charge them before
the courage will abate which was injected into the mortar by
the skillful monks.

It is something of a habit among the newspaper men and

others who write here to say: "Well, there's a good market for Alamo stuff, now." Or perhaps they say: "Too bad! Alamo stuff isn't going very strong, now." Literary aspirants of the locality as soon as they finish writing about Her Eyes, begin on the Alamo. Statistics show that 69,710 writers of the state of Texas have begun at the Alamo.

Notwithstanding this fact, the Alamo remains the greatest memorial to courage which civilization has allowed to stand. The quaint and curious little building fronts on one of the most populous plazas of the city and because of Travis, Crockett, Bowie and their comrades, it maintains dignity amid the taller modern structures which front it. It is the tomb of the fiery emotions of Texans who refused to admit that numbers and Mexicans were arguments. Whether the swirl of life, the crowd upon the streets, pauses to look or not, the spirit that lives in this building, its air of contemplative silence, is as eloquent as an old battle flag.

The first Americans to visit San Antonio arrived in irons. This was the year 1800. There were eleven of them. They had fought one hundred and fifty Spanish soldiers on the eastern frontier and, by one of those incomprehensible chances which so often decides the color of battles, they had lost the fight. Afterward, Americans began to filter down through Louisiana until in 1834 there were enough of them to openly disagree with the young federal government in the City of Mexico, although there was not really any great number of them. Santa Anna didn't give a tin whistle for the people of Texas. He assured himself that he was capable of managing the republic of Mexico, and after coming to this decision he said to himself that that part of it which formed the state of Texas had better remain quiet with the others. In writing of what followed, a Mexican sergeant says: "The Texans fought like devils."

There was a culmination at the old Mission of the Alamo in 1836. This structure then consisted of a rectangular stone parapet 190 feet long and about 120 feet wide, with the existing Church of the Alamo in the southeast corner. Colonel William B. Travis, David Crockett and Colonel Bowie, whose monument is a knife with a peculiar blade, were in this enclosure with a garrison of something like one hundred and fifty men when they heard that Santa Anna was marching against them with an army of 4,000. The Texans shut themselves in the mission, and when Santa Anna demanded their surrender they fired a cannon and inaugurated the most appalling conflict of the continent.

Once Colonel Travis called his men together during a lull of the battle and said to them: "Our fate is sealed. * * * Our friends were evidently not informed of our perilous situation in time to save us. Doubtless they would have been here by this time if they had expected any considerable force of the enemy. * * * Then we must die."

He pointed out to them the three ways of being killed—surrendering to the enemy and being executed, making a rush through the enemy's lines and getting shot before they could inflict much damage, or of staying in the Alamo and holding out to the last, making themselves into a huge and terrible porcupine to be swallowed by the Mexican god of war. All the men save one adopted the last plan with their colonel.

This minority was a man named Rose. "I'm not prepared to die, and shall not do so if I can avoid it." He was some kind of a dogged philosopher. Perhaps he said: "What's the use?" There is a strange inverted courage in the manner in which he faced his companions with this sudden and short refusal in the midst of a general exhibition of supreme bravery. "No," he said. He bade them adieu and climbed the wall. Upon its top he turned to look down at the upturned faces of his silent comrades.

After the battle there were 521 dead Mexicans mingled with the corpses of the Texans.

The Mexicans form a certain large part of the population of San Antonio. Modern inventions have driven them toward the suburbs, but they are still seen upon the main streets in the ratio of one to eight and in their distant quarter of course they swarm. A small percentage have reached positions of business eminence.

The men wear for the most part wide-brimmed hats with peaked crowns, and under these shelters appear their brown faces and the inevitable cigarettes. The remainder of their apparel has become rather Americanized, but the hat of romance is still superior. Many of the young girls are pretty, and all of the old ones are ugly. These latter squat like clay images, and the lines upon their faces and especially about the eyes, make it appear as if they were always staring into the eye of a blinding sun.

Upon one of the plazas, Mexican vendors with open-air stands sell food that tastes exactly like pounded fire-brick from hades—chili con carne, tamales, enchiladas, chili verde, frijoles. In the soft atmosphere of the southern night, the cheap glass bottles upon the stands shine like crystal and the lamps glow with a tender radiance. A hum of conversation ascends from the strolling visitors who are at their social shrine.

The prairie about San Antonio is wrinkled into long low hills, like immense waves, and upon them spreads a wilderness of the persistent mesquite, a bush that grows in defiance of everything. Some forty years ago the mesquite first assailed the prairies about the city, and now from various high points it can be seen to extend to the joining of earth and sky. The individual bushes do not grow close together, and roads and bridle paths cut through the dwarf forest in all directions. A certain class of Mexicans dwell in hovels amid the mesquite.

In the Mexican quarter of the town the gambling houses are crowded nightly, and before the serene dealers lie little stacks of silver dollars. A Mexican may not be able to raise enough money to buy beef tea for his dying grandmother, but he can always stake himself for a game of monte.

Upon a hillock of the prairie in the outskirts of the city is situated the government military post, Fort Sam Houston. There are four beautiful yellow and blue squadrons of cavalry, two beautiful red and blue batteries of light artillery and six beautiful white and blue companies of infantry. Officers' row resembles a collection of Newport cottages. There are magnificent lawns and gardens. The presence of so many officers of the line besides the gorgeous members of the staff of the commanding general, imparts a certain brilliant quality to San Antonio society. The drills upon the wide parade ground make a citizen proud.

No. 98   GALVESTON, TEXAS, IN 1895

IT IS the fortune of travellers to take note of differences and
publish them to their friends. It is the differences that are
supposed to be valuable. The travellers seek them bravely, and
cudgel their wits to find means to unearth them. But in this
search they are confronted continually by the resemblances
and the intrusion of commonplace and most obvious similarity
into a field that is being ploughed in the romantic fashion is
what causes an occasional resort to the imagination.

The winter found a cowboy in south-western Nebraska who
had just ended a journey from Kansas City, and he swore
bitterly as he remembered how little boys in Kansas City followed him about in order to contemplate his wide-brimmed hat.
His vivid description of this incident would have been instructive
to many Eastern readers. The fact that little boys in Kansas
City could be profoundly interested in the sight of a wide-hatted
cowboy would amaze a certain proportion of the populace.
Where then can one expect cowboys if not in Kansas City? As
a matter of truth, however, a steam boiler with four legs and a
tail, galloping down the main street of the town, would create no
more enthusiasm there than a real cow-puncher. For years the
farmers have been driving the cattlemen back, back toward the
mountains and into Kansas, and Nebraska has come to an almost universal condition of yellow trolly-cars with clanging
gongs and whirring wheels, and conductors who don't give a
curse for the public. And travellers tumbling over each other in
their haste to trumpet the radical differences between Eastern
and Western life have created a generally wrong opinion. No
one has yet dared to declare that if a man drew three trays in
Syracuse, N.Y., in many a Western city the man would be
blessed with a full house. The declaration has no commercial
value. There is a distinct fascination in being aware that in
some parts of the world there are purple pigs, and children who
are born with china mugs dangling where their ears should be.
It is this fact which makes men sometimes grab tradition in
wonder; color and attach contemporaneous date-lines to it. It is

this fact which has kept the sweeping march of the West from being chronicled in any particularly true manner.

In a word, it is the passion for differences which has prevented a general knowledge of the resemblances.

If a man comes to Galveston resolved to discover every curious thing possible, and to display every point where Galveston differed from other parts of the universe, he would have the usual difficulty in shutting his eyes to the similarities. Galveston is often original, full of distinctive characters. But it is not like a town in the moon. There are, of course, a thousand details of street color and life which are thoroughly typical of any American city. The square brick business blocks, the mazes of telegraph wires, the trolly-cars clamoring up and down the streets, the passing crowd, the slight fringe of reflective and reposeful men on the curb, all disappoint the traveller, and he goes out in the sand somewhere and digs in order to learn if all Galveston clams are not schooner-rigged.

Accounts of these variations are quaint and interesting reading, to be sure, but then, after all, there are the great and elemental facts of American life. The cities differ as peas—in complexion, in size, in temperature—but the fundamental part, the composition, remains.

There has been a wide education in distinctions. It might be furtively suggested that the American people did not thoroughly know their mighty kinship, their universal emotions, their identical view-points upon many matters about which little is said. Of course, when the foreign element is injected very strongly, a town becomes strange, unfathomable, wearing a sort of guilty air which puzzles the American eye. There begins then a great diversity, and peas become turnips, and the differences are profound. With them, however, this prelude has nothing to do. It is a mere attempt to impress a reader with the importance of remembering that an illustration of Galveston streets can easily be obtained in Maine. Also, that the Gulf of Mexico could be mistaken for the Atlantic Ocean, and that its name is not printed upon it in tall red letters, notwithstanding the legend which has been supported by the geographies.

There are but three lifts in the buildings of Galveston. This is not because the people are skilled climbers; it is because the buildings are for the most part not high.

A certain Colonel Menard bought this end of the island of Galveston from the Republic of Texas in 1838 for fifty thousand dollars. He had a premonition of the value of wide streets for the city of his dreams, and he established a minimum width of seventy feet. The widest of the avenues is one hundred and fifty feet. The fact that this is not extraordinary for 1898 does not prevent it from being marvellous as municipal forethought in 1838.

In 1874 the United States Government decided to erect stone jetties at the entrance to the harbor of Galveston in order to deepen the water on the outer and inner bars, whose shallowness compelled deep-water ships to remain outside and use lighters to transfer their cargoes to the wharves of the city. Work on the jetties was in progress when I was in Galveston in 1895—in fact, two long, low black fingers of stone stretched into the Gulf. There are men still living who had confidence in the Governmental decision of 1874, and these men now point with pride to the jetties and say that the United States Government is nothing if not inevitable.

The soundings at mean low tide were thirteen feet on the inner bar and about twelve feet on the outer bar. At present there is twenty-three feet of water where once was the inner bar, and as the jetties have crept toward the sea they have achieved eighteen feet of water in the channel of the outer bar at mean low tide. The plan is to gain a depth of thirty feet. The cost is to be about seven million dollars.

Undoubtedly in 1874 the people of Galveston celebrated the decision of the Government with great applause, and prepared to welcome mammoth steamers at the wharves during the next spring. It was in 1889, however, that matters took conclusive form. In 1895 the prayer of Galveston materialised.

In 1889, Iowa, Nebraska, Missouri, Kansas, California, Arkansas, Texas, Wyoming, and New Mexico began a serious pursuit of Congress. Certain products of these States and Territories could not be exported with profit, owing to the high rate for transportation to Eastern ports. They demanded a harbor on the coast of Texas with a depth and area sufficient for great sea-crossing steamers. The board of army engineers which was appointed by Congress decided on Galveston as the point. The plan was to obtain by means of artificial constructions a volume and velocity of tidal flow that would maintain a navigable channel. The jetties are seven thousand feet apart, in order to allow ample room for the escape of the enormous flow of water from the inner bar.

Galveston has always been substantial and undeviating in its amount of business. Soon after the war it attained a commercial solidity, and its progress has been steady but quite slow. The citizens now, however, are lying in wait for a real Western boom. Those products of the West which have been walled in by the railroad transportation rates to Eastern ports are now expected to pass through Galveston. An air of hope pervades the countenance of each business man. The city, however, exported 1,500,000 bales of cotton last season, and the Chamber of Commerce has already celebrated the fact.

A train approaches the Island of Galveston by means of a long steel bridge across a bay, which glitters like burnished metal in the winter-time sunlight. The vast number of white two-storied frame houses in the outskirts remind one of New England, if it were not that the island is level as a floor. Later, in the commercial part of the town, appear the conventional business houses and the trolly-cars. Far up the cross-streets is the faint upheaval of the surf of the breeze-blown Gulf, and in the other direction the cotton steamers are arrayed with a fresco upon their black sides of dusky chuckling stevedores handling the huge bales amid a continual and foreign conversation, in which all the subtle and incomprehensible gossip of their social relations goes from mouth to mouth, the bales leaving little tufts of cotton all over their clothing.

Galveston has a rather extraordinary number of very wealthy people. Along the finely-paved drives their residences can be seen, modern for the most part and poor in architecture. Occasionally, however, one comes upon a typical Southern mansion, its galleries giving it a solemn shade and its whole air one of fine and enduring dignity. The palms standing in the grounds of these houses seem to pause at this time of year, and patiently abide the coming of the hot breath of summer.

They still remain of a steadfast green and their color is a wine.

Underfoot the grass is of a yellow hue, here and there patched with a faint impending verdancy. The famous snow-storm here this winter played havoc with the color of the vegetation, and one can now observe the gradual recovery of the trees, the shrubbery, the grass. In this vivid sunlight their vitality becomes enormous.

This storm also had a great effect upon the minds of the citizens. They would not have been more astonished if it had rained suspender buttons. The writer read descriptions of this storm in the newspapers of the date. Since his arrival here he has listened to 574 accounts of it.

Galveston has the aspect of a seaport. New York is not a seaport; a seaport is, however, a certain detail of New York. But in Galveston the docks, the ships, the sailors, are a large element in the life of the town. Also, one can sometimes find here that marvellous type the American sailor. American seamen are not numerous enough to ever depreciate in value. A town that can produce a copy of the American sailor should encase him in bronze and unveil him on the Fourth of July. A veteran of the waves explained to the writer the reason that American youths do not go to sea. He said it was because saddles are too expensive. The writer congratulated the veteran of the waves upon his lucid explanation of this great question.

Galveston has its own summer resorts. In the heat of the season, life becomes sluggish in the streets. Men move about with an extraordinary caution as if they expected to be shot as they approached each corner.

At the beach, however, there is a large hotel which over-flows with humanity, and in front is, perhaps, the most com-fortable structure in the way of bath-houses known to the race. Many of the rooms are ranged about the foot of a large dome. A gallery connects them, but the principal floor to this structure is the sea itself, to which a flight of steps leads. Galveston's 35,000 people divide among themselves in summer a reliable wind from the Gulf.

There is a distinctly cosmopolitan character to Galveston's people. There are men from everywhere. The city does not represent Texas. It is unmistakably American, but in a general manner. Certain Texas differentiations are not observable in this city.

Withal, the people have the Southern frankness, the honesty which enables them to meet a stranger without deep suspicion, and they are the masters of a hospitality which is instructive to cynics.

IRISH SKETCHES

ONE by one, passengers in heavy rain-coats came on deck and
turned their eyes toward the dripping coast-line of Ireland. In
the thick rain-mist to the west gaunt capes were sleepily lifting
their heads from the sea, and on these headlands were sometimes little buildings, implacably severe and grim, which denoted that a government had built them. Afterward a red buoy
that appeared to be swimming against the tide shone amid the
dim streets of a terraced city on the hillside. The form of H.M.S.
Howe was flat against some long sheds at the water's edge. The
buoy which had challenged towers and steeples rapidly subsided to its usual meek size.

Queenstown, tilted sharply toward the bay, disclosed herself
through clouds of rain. In the meantime, on the bridge of the
packet, a very wet man with much gold lace on his cuffs was
pacing spiritedly to and fro, turning often with headlong violence, as if he had suddenly recalled something exciting and
important at the other end.

The packet began to wind through the channel of the river
Lee. This is a wide avenue to Cork, lined on both sides with
mansions and lawns. The rain made the savagely plain outlines
of these houses all the more dismaying, but as a prelude to
Cork a passenger of the heroic band drenching on the forward
deck of the steamer talked with all the gentle evasions and
slidings of the true brogue. Then a dismal water-front, attended
by dismal ships, appeared through the storm. It was a dreary
Ireland, with its eaves sending down sheets of rain and its
gutters turned into turbulent grey streams. There was a solitary
illumination. A jaunting-car driver, miraculously tied up in a
rubber blanket, stood on the dock making signs to the approaching boat. His enterprise would not allow him to merely compete
for fares with his fellow-drivers at the shore end of the prospec-

tive gang-plank. He desired to conduct all negotiations across the dwindling stretch of water.

In his wish to gain and keep the attention of the passengers he was led to make most extraordinary gestures. The decorous lift of the London cabby's finger, which portrays a fear that if he is too abrupt he may puncture the sky, is not related in any way to these gyrations. In comparison, the ambitious Celt was displaying the mad passion of a barbaric dance. Nevertheless, his movements were all comic. He did not evince any intention; he was simply and inevitably comic. The very crooking of his arm was enough for a smile. It could not be said that he was a type of the particular locality. The other waiting drivers were all merely men who were getting soaked with rain in the attempt to earn some shillings. One of them even came and smote his gesturing brother with the heavy end of a whip. This disapprobation, however, could not suppress true genius, and in the subsequent exhibition of discomfiture and pain he was still comic. The splendor of it lay in the fact that there was no aspiration. He was as natural as the sun or a tree.

Cork was weeping like a widow. The rain would have gone through any top-coat but a sentry-box. The passengers looked like specimens of a new kind of sponge as they separated to gloomy ways. From the dock to a railway station and thence to a hotel in Queenstown, the path of the traveller was lined with men not schooled merely in formulæ; car-drivers, porters and guards who could apparently rise beyond a law and understand a joke, a poem or even an idiosyncrasy. The difference from England did not here exist in a conformation nor yet in the color of the turf. It existed in the gleam of a man's eye.

From her high terraces Queenstown stares always at the coming and the going of great ships. She is eminently contemplative. Her business is to witness. To the mind the place is as strategic as a tower. Here one can almost hear the voice of the Western world and see the other millions. And the inhabitants seem to get from the fact a strange broad quality, a kind of egotism of vision, as if from their hills they could comprehend the gestures of a man in Denver. Because they are Irish and because of this pinnacled position they assimilate like lightning. Upon the appearance of a stranger they have a little accurate opinion which is a perfect bit of machinery, and the stranger does not have to explain himself if he wants something which is not usual. From his tower the Queenstown citizen sees patterns and kinds of men, and it is a good thing. He never says "It is not customary." He does not at once flee to this loft and pull the ladder of speech up after him. He is capable of making excursions into the domain of another man's habits. In short, he is a citizen of the world, a philosopher, an intelligence.

For prehistoric reasons the traveller invariably seeks to portray the differences. The resemblances, the eternal parallels, are sure to become lost amid these glib recitals of variations of form which are always illustrated by reproductions from photographs taken by the author's hand camera. The shape of a cloak is handier to the eye than is a point of view, and if the traveller rushes to chronicle another manner of striking a match, it is because he is unwise or lazy. That profound undercurrent that with terrific force compels these women to stand on a corner and gossip, or with its relentless energy obliges those men to work in that foundry, demands that this boy should kick a dog, is far beneath the feet of the people, and its temper is not to be registered by a hand camera.

And yet, who would not forget all this in the pursuit of Jerry? Jerry is in Queenstown, and Queenstown is in Jerry. His jaunting-car with sates for fure, is not very new, but his laugh is new. It is a fine, bold, generous laugh, preserved in brandy, a memory of those red-headed scoundrels whose laughter rang against the low ceils in the castle keeps, while cup followed cup and clouds of attendants galloped into the room with more drink. He is of that time, and he is not at all of that time. He is of it in his appearance of straight-out face-to-face courage of speech. He is a swashbuckler, a bearder of lions through force of habit. Then suddenly he is of the time of the elder prophets, when it is said there were some men who lived their lives to pity the others—no less. Many ramifications of human tenderness run through this little Irishman. He knows the by-roads of sympathy, how to pity him who is unfortunate in some unusual manner. Then immediately there comes upon all this antiquity the shadow of man's ordinary vanities, accentuated by a number of well-worn jokes which Jerry feels that the traveller demands of him. He is modern; he is akin to the steam-engine, the telephone, the electric lamp. In fact, his agile mind is a real type of the country; it moves with the rapidity of light from the past to the future, here, there and everywhere. It is the type that can in the same breath imagine a radiant idol out of a pewter mug and subtract ten shillings from a half crown. When it fails, it fails because it has eyes at the back and at the sides of its head, and thus merges twenty scenes in a confusing one. It would attempt forty games of chess at one time and play them all passably well.

The rain disclosed the bay at last, and from the hill one could look down upon the broad deck of the *Howe*. Against the slate-colored waters shone the white pennant of the English navy, emblem of the man who can play one game at a time.

No. 100   BALLYDEHOB

THE illimitable inventive incapacity of the excursion companies has made many circular paths throughout Ireland, and on these well-pounded roads the guardians of the touring public may be seen drilling the little travellers in squads. To rise in rebellion, to face the superior clerk in his bureau, to endure his smile of pity and derision, and finally to wring freedom from him, is as difficult in some parts of Ireland as it is in all parts of Switzerland. To see the tourists chained in gangs and taken to see the Lakes of Killarney is a sad spectacle, because these people believe that they are learning Ireland, even as men believe that they are studying America when they contemplate the Niagara Falls.

But afterwards, if one escapes, one can go forth, unguided, untaught and alone, and look at Ireland. The joys of the pig-market, the delirium of a little tap-room filled with brogue, the fierce excitement of viewing the Royal Irish Constabulary fishing for trout, the whole quaint and primitive machinery of the peasant-life, its melancholy, its sunshine, its humor—all this is then the property of the man who breaks like a Texan steer out of the pens and corrals of the tourist agencies. For what syndicate of maiden ladies—it is these who masquerade as tourist agencies—what syndicate of maiden ladies knows of the existence, for instance, of Ballydehob?

One has a sense of disclosure at writing the name of Ballydehob. It was really a valuable secret. There is in Ballydehob not one thing that is commonly pointed out to the stranger as a thing worthy of a half-tone reproduction in a book. There is no cascade, no peak, no lake, no guide with a fund of useless information, no gamins practised in the seduction of tourists. It is not an exhibit, an entry for a prize, like a heap of melons or a cow. It is simply an Irish village wherein live some three hundred Irish and four constables.

If one or two prayer-towers spindled above Ballydehob it would be a perfect Turkish village. The red tiles and red bricks of England do not appear at all. The houses are low, with soiled white walls. The doors open abruptly upon dark old rooms. Here and there in the street is some crude cobbling done with round stones taken from the bed of a brook. At times there is a great deal of mud. Chickens depredate warily about the doorsteps, and intent pigs emerge for plunder from the alleys. It is unavoidable to admit that many people would consider Ballydehob quite too grimy.

Nobody lives here that has money. The average English tradesman with his back-breaking respect for this class, his reflex contempt for that class, his reverence for the tin gods, could here be a commercial lord and bully the people in one or two ways, until they were thrown back upon the defence which is always near them, the ability to cut his skin into strips with a wit that would be a foreign tongue to him. For amid his wrongs and his rights and his failures, his colossal failures, the Irishman retains this delicate blade for his enemies, for his friends, for himself, the ancestral dagger of fast sharp speaking from fast sharp seeing—an inheritance which could move the world. And the Royal Irish Constabulary fished for trout in the adjacent streams.

Mrs. Kearney keeps the hotel. In Ireland male inn-keepers die young. Apparently they succumb to conviviality when it is presented to them in the guise of a business duty. Naturally honest temperate men, their consciences are lulled to false security by this idea of hard drinking being necessary to the successful keeping of a public-house. It is very terrible.

But they invariably leave behind them capable widows, women who do not recognize conviviality as a business obligation. And so all through Ireland one finds these brisk widows, keeping hotels with a precision that is almost military.

In Kearney's there is always a wonderful collection of old women, bent figures shrouded in shawls who reach up scrawny fingers to take their little purchases from Mary Agnes, who presides sometimes at the bar, but more often at the shop that fronts it in the same room. In the gloom of a late afternoon these old women are as mystic as the swinging, chanting witches on a dark stage when the thunder-drum rolls and the lightning flashes by schedule. When a grey rain sweeps through the narrow street of Ballydehob, and makes heavy shadows in Kearney's taproom, these old creatures, with their high, mournful voices, and the mystery of their shawls, their moans and aged mutterings when they are obliged to take a step, raise the dead superstitions from the bottom of a man's mind.

"My boy," remarked my London friend cheerfully, "these might have furnished sons to be Aldermen or Congressmen in the great city of New York."

"Aldermen or Congressmen of the great city of New York always take care of their mothers," I answered meekly.

On a barrel, over in a corner, sat a yellow-bearded Irish farmer in tattered clothes who wished to exchange views on the Armenian massacres. He had much information and a number of theories in regard to them. He also advanced the opinion that the chief political aim of Russia, at present, is in the direction of China, and that it behoved other Powers to keep an eye on her. He thought the revolutionists in Cuba would never accept autonomy at the hands of Spain. His pipe glowed comfortably from his corner; waving the tuppenny glass of stout in the air, he discoursed on the business of the remote ends of the earth with the glibness of a fourth secretary of Legation. Here was a little farmer, digging betimes in a forlorn patch of wet ground, a man to whom a sudden two shillings would appeal as a miracle, a ragged, unkempt peasant, whose mind roamed the world like the soul of a lost diplomat. This unschooled man believed that the earth was a sphere inhabited by men that are alike in the essentials, different in the manners, the little manners, which are accounted of such great importance by the emaciated. He was to a degree capable of knowing that he lived on a sphere and not on the apex of a triangle.

And yet, when the talk had turned another corner, he confidently assured the assembled company that a hair from a horse's tail when thrown in a brook would turn shortly to an eel.

No. 101   THE ROYAL IRISH CONSTABULARY

THE newspapers called it a Veritable Arsenal. There was a description of how the sergeant of Constabulary had bent an ear to receive whispered information of the concealed arms, and had then marched his men swiftly and by night to surround a certain house. The search elicited a double-barrelled breech-loading shot-gun, some empty shells, powder, shot, and a loading-machine. The point of it was that some of the Irish papers called it a Veritable Arsenal, and appeared to congratulate the Government upon having strangled another unhappy rebellion in its nest. They floundered and misnamed and misreasoned, and made a spectacle of the great modern craft of journalism until the affair of this poor poacher was too absurd to be pitiable, and Englishmen over their coffee next morning must have almost believed that the prompt action of the Constabulary had quelled a rising. Thus it is that the Irish fight the Irish.

One cannot look Ireland straight in the face without seeing a great many constables. The country is dotted with little garrisons. It must have been said a thousand times that there is an absolute military occupation. The fact is too plain.

The constable himself becomes a figure interesting in its isolation. He has in most cases a social position which is somewhat analogous to that of a Turk in Thessaly. But then, in the same way, the Turk has the Turkish army. He can have

battalions as companions and make the acquaintance of brigades. The constable has the Constabulary, it is true; but to be
cooped with three or four others in a small white-washed iron-
bound house on some bleak country side is not an exact parallel
to the Thessalian situation. It looks to be a life that is infinitely
lonely, ascetic, and barren. Two keepers of a lighthouse at a
bitter end of land in a remote sea will, if they are properly let
alone, make a murder in time. Five constables imprisoned 'mid
a folk that will not turn a face toward them, five constables
planted in a populated silence, may develop an acute and vivid
economy, dwell in scowling dislike. A religious asylum in a snow-
buried mountain pass will breed conspiring monks. A separated
people will beget an egotism that is almost titanic. A world
floating distinctly in space will call itself the only world. The
progression is perfect.

But the constables take the second degree. They are next to
the lighthouse keepers. The national custom of meeting stranger
and friend alike on the road with a cheery greeting like "God
save you" is too kindly and human a habit not to be missed. But
all through the South of Ireland one sees the peasant turn his
eyes pretentiously to the side of the road at the passing of the
constable. It seemed to be generally understood that to note the
presence of a constable was to make a conventional error. None
looked, nodded, or gave sign. There was a line drawn so sternly
that it reared like a fence. Of course, any policing force in any
part of the world can gather at its heels a riff-raff of people,
fawning always on a hand licensed to strike that would be larger
than the army of the Potomac, but of these one ordinarily sees
little. The mass of the Irish strictly obey the stern tenet. One
hears often of the ostracism or other punishment that befell
some girl who was caught flirting with a constable.

Naturally the constable retreats to his pride. He is commonly
a soldierly-looking chap, straight, lean, long-strided, well
set-up. His little saucer of a forage cap sits obediently on his
ear, as it does for the British soldier. He swings a little cane. He
takes his medicine with a calm and hard face, and evidently
stares full into every eye. But it is singular to find in the situation of the Royal Irish Constabulary the quality of pathos.

It is not known if these places in the South of Ireland are

called disturbed districts. Over them hangs the peace of Surrey, but the word disturbance has an elastic arrangement by which it can be made to cover anything. All of the villages visited garrisoned from four to ten men. They lived comfortably in their white houses, strolled in pairs over the country roads, picked blackberries, and fished for trout. If at some time there came a crisis, one man was more than enough to surround it. The remaining nine add dignity to the scene. The crises chiefly consisted of occasional drunken men who were unable to understand the local geography on Saturday nights.

The note continually struck was that each group of constables lived on a little social island, and there was no boat to take them off. There has been no such marooning since the days of the pirates. The sequestration must be complete when a man with a dinky little cap on his ear is not allowed to talk to the girls.

But they fish for trout. Isaac Walton is the father of the Royal Irish Constabulary. They could be seen on any fine day whipping the streams from source to mouth. There was one venerable sergeant who made a rod less than a yard long. With a line of about the same length attached to this rod, he haunted the gorse-hung banks of the little streams in the hills. An eight-inch ribbon of water lined with masses of heather and gorse will be accounted contemptible by a fisherman with an ordinary rod. But it was the pleasure of the sergeant to lay on his stomach at the side of such a stream and carefully, inch by inch, scout his hook through the pools. He probably caught more trout than any three men in the county Cork. He fished more than any twelve men in the county Cork. Some people had never seen him in any other posture but that of crowding forward on his stomach to peer into a pool. They did not believe the rumor that he sometimes stood or walked like a human.

No. 102   A FISHING VILLAGE

THE brook curved down over the rocks, innocent and white, until it faced a little strand of smooth gravel and flat stones. It turned then to the left, and thereafter its guilty current was tinged with the pink of diluted blood. Boulders standing neck-deep in the water were rimmed with red; they wore bloody collars whose tops marked the supreme instant of some tragic movement of the stream. In the pale green shallows of the bay's edge, the outward flow from the criminal little brook was as eloquently marked as if a long crimson carpet had been laid upon the waters. The scene of the carnage was the strand of smooth gravel and flat stones, and the fruit of the carnage was cleaned mackerel.

Far to the south, where the slate of the sea and the grey of the sky wove together, could be seen Fastnet Rock, a mere button on the moving, shimmering cloth, while a liner, no larger than a needle, spun a thread of smoke aslant. The gulls swept screaming along the dull line of the other shore of Roaring Water Bay, and, near the mouth of the brook, circled among the fishing boats that lay at anchor, their brown leathery sails idle and straight. The wheeling, shrieking, tumultuous birds stared with their hideous unblinking eyes at the Capers—men from Cape Clear—who prowled to and fro on the decks amid shouts and the creak of tackle. Shoreward, a little shrivelled man, overcome by a profound melancholy, fished hopelessly from the end of the pier. Back of him, on a hillside, sat a white village, nestled among more trees than is common in this part of southern Ireland.

A dinghy sculled by a youth in a blue jersey wobbled rapidly past the pier-head and stopped at the foot of the moss-green dank stone steps, where the waves were making slow but regular leaps to mount higher, and then falling back gurgling, choking, and waving the long dark seaweeds. The melancholy fisherman walked over to the top of the steps. The young man was fastening the painter of his boat in an iron ring. In the dinghy were three round baskets heaped high with mackerel. They glittered like masses of new silver coin at times and then other lights of faint carmine and peacock blue would chase across the sides of the fish in a radiance that was finer than silver.

The melancholy fisherman looked at this wealth. He shook his head mournfully. "Aw, now, Denny. This would not be a very good kill."

The young man snorted indignantly at his fellow townsman. "This will be th' bist kill th' year, Mickey. Go along now."

The melancholy old man became immersed in a deeper gloom. "Shure I have been in th' way of seein' miny a grand day whin th' fish was runnin' sthrong in these wathers, but there will be no more big kills here. No more. No more." At the last his voice was only a dismal croak.

"Come along outa that now, Mickey," cried the youth impatiently. "Come away wid you."

"All gone now! A–ll go–o–ne now!" The old man wagged his grey head, and, standing over the baskets of fishes, groaned as Mordecai groaned for his people.

" 'Tis you would be cryin' out, Mickey, whativer," said the youth with scorn. He was giving his baskets into the hands of five incompetent but jovial little boys to carry to a waiting donkey cart.

"An' why should I not?" said the old man sternly. "Me—in want——"

As the youth swung his boat swiftly out toward an anchored smack, he made answer in a softer tone. "Shure, if yez got for th' askin', 'tis you, Mickey, that would niver be in want." The melancholy old man returned to his line. And the only moral in this incident is that the young man is the type that America procures from Ireland, and the old man is one of the home types, bent, pallid, hungry, disheartened, with a vision that magnifies with a microscopic glance any fly-wing of misfortune and heroically and conscientiously invents disasters for the future. Usually the thing that remains to one of this last type is a sympathy as quick and acute for others as is his pity for himself.

The donkey with his cartload of gleaming fish, and escorted by the whooping and laughing boys, galloped along the quay and up a street of the village until he was turned off at the gravelly strand, at the point where the color of the brook was changing. Here twenty people of both sexes and all ages were preparing the fish for the market. The mackerel, beautiful as fire-etched salvers, first were passed to a long table, around which worked as many women as could have elbow room. Each one could clean a fish with two motions of the knife. Then the washers, men who stood over the troughs filled with running water from the brook, soused the fish until the outlet became a sinister element that in an instant changed the brook from a happy thing of the gorse and heather of the hills to an evil stream, sullen and reddened. After being washed, the fish were carried to a group of girls with knives, who made the cuts that enabled each fish to flatten out in the manner known of the breakfast table. And after the girls came the men and boys, who rubbed each fish thoroughly with great handfuls of coarse salt, which was whiter than snow, and shone in the daylight from a multitude of gleaming points, diamond-like. Last came the packers, drilled in the art of getting neither too few nor too many mackerel into a barrel, sprinkling constantly prodigal layers of the brilliant salt. There were many intermediate corps of boys and girls carrying fish from point to point, and sometimes building them in stacks convenient to the hands of the more important laborers.

A vast tree hung its branches over the place. The leaves made a shadow that was religious in its effect, as if the spot was a chapel consecrated to labor. There was a hush upon the devotees. The women at the large table worked intently, steadfastly, with bowed heads. Their old petticoats were tucked high, showing the coarse men's brogans which they wore—and the visible ankles were proportioned to the brogans as the diameter of a straw is to that of a half-crown. The national red under-petticoat was a fundamental part of the scene.

Just over the wall, in the sloping street, could be seen the bejerseyed Capers, brawny, and with shocks of yellow beard. They paced slowly to and fro amid the geese and the children. They, too, spoke little, even to each other; they smoked short pipes in saturnine dignity and silence. It was the fish. They who go with nets upon the reeling sea grow still with the mystery and solemnity of the trade. It was Brittany; the first respectable catch of the year had changed this garrulous Irish hamlet into a hamlet of Brittany.

The Capers were waiting for a high tide. It had seemed for a long time that, for the south of Ireland, the mackerel had fled in company with the potato; but here at any rate was a temporary success, and the occasion was momentous. A strolling Caper took his pipe and pointed with the stem out upon the bay. There was little wind, but an ambitious skipper had raised his anchor, and the craft, her strained brown sails idly swinging, was drifting away on the first oily turn of the tide.

On the tip of the pier the figure of the melancholy old man was portrayed upon the polished water. He was still dangling his line, hopelessly. He gazed down into the misty water. Once he stirred and murmured, "Bad luck to thim." Otherwise, he seemed to remain motionless for hours. One by one the fishing-boats floated away. The brook changed its color, and, in the dusk, showed a tumble of pearly white among the rocks.

A cold night wind, sweeping transversely across the pier, awakened perhaps the rheumatism in the old man's bones. He arose, and, mumbling and grumbling, began to wind his line. The waves were lashing the stones. He moved off toward the intense darkness of the village streets.

No. 103   AN OLD MAN GOES WOOING

THE melancholy fisherman made his way through a street that was mainly as dark as a tunnel. Sometimes an open door threw a rectangle of light upon the pavement, and within the cottages were scenes of working women and men, who comfortably smoked and talked. From them came the sounds of laughter and the babble of children. Each time the old man passed through one of these radiant zones the light etched his face in profile with touches flaming and sombre, until there was a resemblance to a stern and mournful Dante portrait.

Once a whistling lad came through the darkness. He peered intently for purposes of recognition. "Good avenin', Mickey," he cried cheerfully. The old man responded with a groan, which intimated that the lamentable reckless optimism of the youth had forced from him an expression of an emotion that he had been enduring in saintly patience and silence. He continued his pilgrimage toward the kitchen of the village inn.

This kitchen is a great and worthy place. The long range with its lurid heat continually emits the fragrance of broiling fish, roasting mutton, joints, and fowls. The high black ceiling is ornamented with hams and flitches of bacon. There is a long dark bench against one wall, and it is fronted by a darker table handy for glasses of stout. On an old mahogany dresser rows of plates face the distant range, and reflect the red shine of the peat. Smoke which has in it the odor of an American forest fire eddies through the air. The great stones of the floor are scarred by the black mud from the inn-yard. And here the gossip of a country-side goes on amid the sizzle of broiling fish and the loud protesting splutter of joints taken from the oven.

When the old man reached the door of this paradise, he stopped for a moment with his finger on the latch. He sighed deeply; evidently he was undergoing some lachrymose reflection. From somewhere overhead in the inn he could hear the wild clamor of dining pig-buyers, men who were come for the pig-fair to be held on the morrow. Evidently in the little parlor of the inn these men were dining amid an uproar of shouted jests and laughter. The revelry sounded like the fighting of two mobs amid a rain of missiles and the crash of shop windows. The old man raised his hand as if, unseen there in the darkness, he was going to solemnly damn the dinner of the pig-buyers.

Within the kitchen Nora, tall, strong, intrepid, approached the fiery stove in the manner of a boxer. Her left arm was held high to guard her face, which was already crimson from the blaze. With a flourish of her apron she achieved a great brown humming joint from the oven, and, emerging a glowing and triumphant figure from the steam and smoke and rapid play of heat, she slid the pan upon the table even as she saw the old man standing within the room and lugubriously cleaning the mud from his boots. " 'Tis you, Mickey?" she said.

He made no reply until he had found his way to the long bench. "It is," he said then. It was clear that in the girl's opinion he had gained some kind of strategic advantage. The sanctity of her kitchen was successfully violated, but the old man betrayed no elation. Lifting one knee and placing it over the other, he grunted in the blissful weariness of a venerable laborer returned to his own fireside. He coughed dismally. "Ah, 'tis no good a man gits from fishin' these days. I moind the toimes whin they would be hoppin' up clear o' the wather, there was that little room fur thim. . . . I would be likin' a bottle o' stout."

"Niver fear you, Mickey," answered the girl. Swinging here and there in the glare of the fire, Nora, with her towering figure and bare brawny arms, was like a feminine blacksmith at a forge. The old man, pallid, emaciated, watched her from the shadows of the other side of the room. The lines from the sides of his nose to the corners of his mouth sank low to an expression of despair deeper than any moans. He should have been painted upon the door of a tomb with wringing willows arched above him and men in grey robes slowly booming the drums of death. Finally he spoke. "I would be likin' a bottle o' stout, Nora, me girrl," he said.

"Niver fear you, Mickey," again she replied with cheerful obstinacy. She was admiring her famous roast, which now sat in its platter on the rack over the range. There was a lull in her tumultuous duties. The old man coughed and moved his foot with a scraping sound on the stones. The noise of dining pig-buyers, now heard through doors and winding corridors of the inn, was the roll of a far-away storm.

A woman in a dark dress entered the kitchen and keenly examined the roast and Nora's other feats. "Mickey here would be wantin' a bottle o' stout," said the girl to her mistress. The woman turned toward the spectral figure in the gloom, and regarded it quietly with a clear eye. "Have yez the money, Mickey?" she said.

This question seemed to strike the old man as the final point in human brutality. "A-ah," he said, stricken to the heart. He rolled his eyes toward the throne of heaven.

"Have yez the money, Mickey?" repeated the woman of the house.

Profoundly embittered, he replied in short terms. "I have."

"There now!" cried Nora, in astonishment and admiration.

Poising a large iron spoon, she was motionless, staring with open mouth at the old man. He searched his pockets slowly during a complete silence in the kitchen. He brought forth two coppers and laid them sadly, reproachfully, and yet defiantly on the table. "There now!" cried Nora, stupefied.

They brought him a bottle of the black brew, and Nora poured it for him with her own red hand, which looked to be as broad as his chest. A collar of brown foam curled at the top of the glass. With measured movements the old man filled a short pipe. There came a sudden howl from another part of the inn. One of the pig-buyers was at the head of the stairs bawling for the mistress. The two women hurriedly freighted themselves with the roast and the vegetables, and sprang with them to placate the pig-buyers. Alone, the old man studied the gleam of the fire on the floor. It faded and brightened in the way of lightning at the horizon's edge.

When Nora returned, the strapping grenadier of a girl was blushing and giggling. The pig-buyers had been humorous. "I moind the toime——" began the old man sorrowfully. "I moind the toime whin yez was a wee bit of a girrl, Nora, an' wouldn't be havin' words wid min loike thim buyers."

"I moind the toime whin yez could attind to your own affairs, ye ould skileton," said the girl promptly. He made a gesture which may have expressed his stirring grief at the levity of the new generation. He lapsed into another stillness.

The girl, a giantess, carrying, lifting, pushing, an incarnation of dauntless labor, changing the look of the whole kitchen with a moment's manipulation of her great arms, did not heed the old man for a long time. When she finally glanced toward him, she saw that he was sunk forward with his grey face on his arms. A growl of heavy breathing ascended. He was asleep.

She marched to him and put both hands to his collar. Despite his feeble and dreamy protestations, she dragged him out from behind the table and across the floor. She opened the door and thrust him into the night.

III Reports
News from Asbury Park

AVON-BY-THE-SEA, N.J., July 27 (Special).—The classes in art, elocution, oratory and aesthetic physical culture are all drawing large attendances on the Seaside Assembly grounds. The Kindergarten is also a great success. The School of Music, under Professor Albert W. Borst, will open on August 4. On August 6 the Rev. Dr. Charles F. Deems will be here, and the Summer School of the American Institute of Christian Philosophy will open. Some of the ablest speakers of the country are on the Institute lecture list.

Madame Le Prince's classes in art form a most interesting feature of the Seaside Assembly. Her particular work is the practical application of design to the trades. While she uses the best art principles, she gives art efforts commercial value. Besides treating of design, she teaches the technique of practical success. She was formerly principal of the Leeds Technical School of Design in England. While there her scholars took the honors at the Paris Exposition. The year previous to her connection with the New-York Institute for Artist Artisans she was in charge of the department of design of the New-York Institute for the Deaf and Dumb. Her pupils from there took the medals at the New-Orleans Exposition, and the bronze medal of superiority at the American Institute Fair.

Dr. H. C. Hovey, who delivered his course of lectures on caves here before the Seaside Assembly, is taking his summer outing at the Sylvan Lodge. For many years the Doctor has written about caves. His first article was for *The Tribune*. He is one of the foremost cave explorers in the country and can recite many stories of adventures underground.

Few accidents occur at the Avon bathing grounds. No fatal drowning has happened since bronzed and sturdy Captain

Kittell, formerly of the Life Saving Service, became the bathing master.

No. 105 AVON'S SCHOOL BY THE SEA

AVON-BY-THE-SEA, Aug. 3 (Special).—It has become an exceedingly popular notion of late years to found summer schools at seaside and mountain resorts, so that people in their thirst for knowledge might combine the cool breezes from hillside or ocean with useful instruction and entertainment. This idea has taken such root that dozens of summer schools are flourishing all over the country. It is a noticeable fact, too, that the students of our schools and colleges are not the ones that take all the advantages of the course in summer instruction, but the business and professional men and teachers themselves are present in large numbers. On the grounds of the Seaside Assembly here one may see—and learn a great lesson from the sight—a man with the sharp, keen eye of business, and, it may be, with gray hairs on his forehead, wending his way with his books to the Hall of Philosophy to take a lesson in French, or to Otis Hall to study art. It is a familiar scene anywhere to see the old man, who has battled with adversity, put his hand on a young man's head and say: "My boy, study hard; don't give up your books. How much more I might have been in the world if I had thought more of my Caesar's Commentaries and my geometry than I did of sleighride parties and corn huskings." But here the old man has a partial way out of his difficulties. Of course, many of his lost opportunities can never be regained, but if when he comes to a beautiful summer resort for his vacation he spends an hour a day taking a course in a language or in some study that concerns his business, he receives an immense benefit. The teachers here find that men and women in middle life make just as enthusiastic scholars as the young people who are satisfying their first cravings after knowledge.

In Madame Alberti's classes in physical culture, it is interesting to note the look of surprise on people's faces, many of them showing the marks of age, when they learn for the first time the proper way to pick up articles from the floor or the scientific method of taking a chair, or, as an old farmer said to a friend, when asked how he liked the lecture, "I'm going on sixty-six-year-old, an' I never knew how to shet a door or git out'n a wagon before."

The teachers and instructors here are all of recognized ability, and the lecturers that come here are men who stand at the head of their respective pursuits in science or art. On next Monday the session of the American Institute of Christian Philosophy opens. The Rev. Charles F. Deems, D.D., of New-York, the president, was here a few days ago, making the final arrangements for the opening. The learned members of the institute are already making their appearance with their baggage at the hotels and boarding houses. The guests claim that they can tell the members of the institute from afar by a certain wise, grave and reverend air that hangs over them from the top of their glossy silk hats to their equally glossy boots. A member gazes at the wild tossing of the waves with a calm air of understanding and philosophy that the poor youthful graduate from college, with only a silk sash and flannel suit to assert his knowledge with, can never hope to acquire. When he learns to row on the lake or river, to his philosophical mind he is only describing an arc from the rowlock as a centre, with a radius equal to the distance between the fulcrum or rowlock and the point of resistance, vulgarly known as the tip end of the oar. When he "catches a crab" and goes over backward, he gets up and, after rubbing the back of his head, he calmly returns anew to what he calls a demonstration of the principles of applied force. He watches the merry dancers at the hotel hops with an air that says: "Vanity, vanity, all is vanity." Yet he has no doubt in his own mind, from certain little geometric calculations of his own, that he could waltz in such a scientific manner, with such an application of the laws of motion, that the best dancers would, indeed, be surprised.

Professor L. C. Elson, of the Boston Conservatory of Music, gave two of the finest lectures here ever listened to on the Assembly grounds. He had with him several rolls of old music on parchment taken from monasteries in Europe more than 600 years ago, and now worth more than their weight in gold.

Among the noted teachers connected with the art department of the Seaside Assembly is Professor Conrad Diehl, of New-York. His genial manner has already made him many friends here and his lectures are of intense interest to his enthusiastic pupils. He began his career in art as an apprentice to some of the Art-Industries in Illinois. From there he went to the Art School in Munich for a five-years' course. He returned to Chicago with a large picture of the play scene in "Hamlet," which he presented to the Chicago Art Association in 1865. The same year he went to Paris and entered Gérôme's atelier classes at the Ecole des Beaux Arts. It was there he painted his large picture from "Macbeth," with which he came to Chicago in 1867. He assumed charge of the classes of the Chicago Academy of Design, which he conducted with but a short intermission up to the time of the great fire. He saved his picture by cutting the canvas out of the frame. Then he went to St. Louis and established an art school. The donation of the "Macbeth" picture to the city as a nucleus of a public art gallery called into existence the St. Louis Art Society. It was in the public schools of St. Louis that he developed his "Grammar of Form Languages." After serving some time as the head of the art department of the Missouri State University, he came to New-York and became the co-laborer of John Ward Stimson in the New-York Institute for Artist Artisans.

Among other prominent people connected with the Assembly is Mr. Albert G. Thies, the well-known New-York tenor. Mr. Thies has been spending his summer here, and while so doing has become identified with the Assembly in a musical capacity. He has a voice of great compass and sweetness, with which he has several times charmed the guests of the hotels and the Assembly audiences. He has had adventures and escapades in foreign lands such as fall to the lot of but few singers. He was educated first as a pianist, and made a tour of the Continent, playing in London, Paris, Vienna, Dublin and so on. In studying voice-culture to improve his phrasing, he discovered that he had a splendid tenor voice. So he abandoned the piano, became a singer, and finally made a tour of the world. After his return to London his adventuresome spirit took him to Africa. There he became a friend of Chinese Gordon, and was thrown in connection with Henry M. Stanley in a number of ways. He played and sang before all the British magnates of Southern Africa, and finally had the pleasure of playing before royalty, in the person of the old Chief Cetewayo, styled "King" of the Zulus, but at that time a prisoner in the hands of the English. The old "King" was much pleased with Mr. Thies's performance, and had about made up his mind to give one of his wives to the musician. In fact, he brought the four then with him in for Mr. Thies's inspection. They were all over six feet four inches in height. The "King" seemed rather dazed at finding his elegant gift "declined with thanks." The American musician was in Southern Africa at the time of the smallpox plague, when 9,000 people were down with the disease, and 3,000 deaths occurred. He helped to nurse the sufferers and escaped unscathed. He returned to America, settled in New-York, and began a musical career in America which has been very successful.

No. 106 BIOLOGY AT AVON-BY-THE-SEA

AVON-BY-THE-SEA, July 18 (Special).—The school of biology of the Seaside Assembly was opened for the first time this week, and people have not yet become familiar with the ways of the scientist when he is pursuing his favorite study. In the ignorant mind, the sight of a well-known college professor frenziedly pursuing a June-bug around the block is apt to arouse a question. But still they go their way, happy and contented, and return the contemptuous gaze of the summer youth who knows nothing with the scornful glance of knowledge.

The Assembly management point with pride to the faculty of the school of biology. The dean is George Macloskie, Sc.D., LL.D., the senior professor of biology in Princeton College. He is well known to all scientists as a writer on various subjects. He is the author of a botany used in many of the colleges of the country. He has written over twenty-five papers on insects. John E. Peters, A.M., Sc.D., another of the faculty, is a well-known naturalist and the author of books and pamphlets of scientific interest. He has made a careful study of the vegetable life of New-Jersey. He also regards the seaweeds as a favorite study. His name appears in all the official catalogues of plants as the discoverer of new forms. Arthur M. Miller, A.M., the professor of natural sciences at Wilson College, Chambersburg, Penn., is a thorough scientist. Francis E. Lloyd has been recently appointed assistant instructor of biology at Williams College. Curator A. Dumas Watkins, histological aid in Princeton College, is one of the most valuable assistants and is a first-class collector.

The new building of the school is situated upon the bank of Shark River. It is a compact structure built upon piles. During high tides the water under the building is about a foot deep. Steps lead down from the front of the building, and a small knot of boats tug at their chains there.

Within one is first impressed with the abundance of light and ventilation. Large windows on all sides of the building give sufficient light for all experiments. Long tables extend down the sides of the room for the convenience of the students, every one of whom has his separate racks, shelves and drawers, for the safe-keeping of his instruments and specimens. The tables are built with special regard to solidity, so that no vibrations will dislodge the most delicate specimens. On the walls are natural-history charts, covering typical forms of animal life. They were lent to the school by Princeton College. Great jars and glasses stand about, already filled with different forms of seaweeds and other growths.

In the library one finds the most valuable private library of its kind in the State. It was lent to the school by Dr. Peters. A huge case in this room holds the microscopes, of which there are a great number.

The herbarium, in another corner of the building, is furnished with all the necessary appliances for pressing and preserving plants. Particular regard is paid to the pine flora, which in this region is much diversified. While the collections are being made here, Dr. Peters has brought many fine collections from his home, so that the students may have the advantages of the specimens at once for study. A large and beautiful collection of the seaweeds of the coast of California is his pride.

This laboratory, with its efficient corps of scientists, will be of great value to the science of the State. It is the only school of the kind which offers instruction south of the one at Cold Spring Harbor, L.I. It is fully equipped for work. Nothing has been spared to render it so. The biological discoveries on this part of the coast have not been carried forward far. But the faculty of the new school intend making catalogues of the flowering plants and the lichens, ferns and mosses of the entire region. The marine algae will also be thoroughly investigated, as there have been no extensive lists made as yet. Enthusiastic workers are plentiful. Every one seems to enjoy his work to the utmost.

Dr. Samuel B. Lockwood, the superintendent of the public schools of Monmouth County, takes a great interest in the new school, and is in town often, observing the various plans go forward. Scientists in all parts of the country have read the accounts of the school and are writing to the secretary for information.

No. 107   HOWELLS DISCUSSED AT AVON-BY-THE-SEA

AVON-BY-THE-SEA, Aug. 17 (Special).—At the Seaside Assembly the morning lecture was delivered by Professor Hamlin Garland, of Boston, on W. D. Howells, the novelist. He said: "No man stands for a more vital principle than does Mr. Howells. He stands for modern-spirit, sympathy and truth. He believes in the progress of ideals, the relative in art. His definition of idealism cannot be improved upon, 'the truthful treatment of material.' He does not insist upon any special material, but only that the novelist be true to himself and to things as he sees them. It is absurd to call him photographic. The photograph is false in perspective, in light and shade, in focus. When a photograph can depict atmosphere and sound, the comparison will have some meaning, and then it will not be used as a reproach. Mr. Howells' work has deepened in insight and widened in sympathy from the first. His canvas has grown large, and has thickened with figures. Between *Their Wedding Journey* and *A Hazard of New Fortunes* there is an immense distance. *A Modern Instance* is the greatest, most rigidly artistic novel ever written by an American, and ranks with the great novels of the world. *A Hazard of New Fortunes* is the greatest, sanest, truest study of a city in fiction. The test of the value of Mr. Howells' work will come fifty years from now, when his sheaf of novels will form the most accurate, sympathetic and artistic study of American society yet made by an American. Howells is a many-sided man, a humorist of astonishing delicacy and imagination, and he has written of late some powerful poems in a full, free style. He is by all odds the most American and vital of our literary men to-day. He stands for all that is progressive and humanitarian in our fiction, and his following increases each day. His success is very great, and it will last."

The evening lecture was delivered by James Clement Ambrose, of Chicago. His subject was "The Sham Family."

No. 108 MEETINGS BEGUN AT OCEAN GROVE

OCEAN GROVE, N.J., July 1.—The sombre-hued gentlemen who congregate at this place in summer are arriving in solemn procession, with black valises in their hands and rebukes to frivolity in their eyes. They greet each other with quiet enthusiasm and immediately set about holding meetings. The cool, shaded Auditorium will soon begin to palpitate with the efforts of famous preachers delivering doctrines to thousands of worshippers. The tents, of which there are hundreds, are beginning to rear their white heads under the trees.

The clergymen of the New-Brunswick district of the New-Jersey Methodist Episcopal Conference held their regular meeting this week in the lecture-room of St. Paul's Church. Most of the morning was spent in the rendering of informal pastoral reports, after which the Rev. Dr. J. A. MacCauley, ex-president of Dickinson College, delivered an address on "The Results of the Higher Criticism." At noon the ministers and their wives sat down to a banquet in the dining-room of the Howland House. The Rev. D. B. Harris, of Ocean Grove, toasted "The Older Members of the New-Jersey Conference."

The Rev. John Handley, of Asbury Park, gave a toast to "The Younger Members." "The New-Brunswick District" was responded to by Presiding Elder W. C. P. Strickland; "The Ocean Grove Association," by its president, the Rev. Dr. Elwood H. Stokes; "The Women of Methodism," by Mrs. C. F. Garrison, of Cranbury, and "Our Deceased Members," by Professor John Wilson, D.D., of Ocean Grove.

Among the many clergymen present as visitors were

[List of names]

At 9 o'clock every morning hereafter the Rev. C. H. Yatman holds a meeting in the Young People's Temple and Mrs. Palmer holds services in the Jones Memorial Tabernacle.

During the session of the ministers' meeting an "association of pastors' wives" was formed at the suggestion of Mrs. Garrison, the wife of the Rev. C. F. Garrison, of Cranbury, N.J.

The Rev. George L. Barker, of Camden, N.J., is a guest at the Arlington.

The Rev. George W. Evans, the secretary of the Ocean Grove Association, has returned from a business trip through the Indian Territory. Mrs. Evans accompanied her husband.

Mr. and Mrs. A. D. Sturgis, the Gospel singers of East Orange, N.J., will sing in the Auditorium this season.

A reformed convict named "Big Frank" Carr addressed a large audience at the Bradley Beach surf meeting last Sunday night. He went considerably into the details when describing the lives and methods of "crooks."

[List of names]

No. 109   CROWDING INTO ASBURY PARK

ASBURY PARK, N.J., July 2 (Special).—Pleasure seekers arrive by the avalanche. Hotel-proprietors are pelted with hailstorms of trunks and showers of valises. To protect themselves they do not put up umbrellas, nor even prices. They merely smile copiously. The lot of the baggageman, however, is not an easy one. He manipulates these various storms and directs them. He is beginning to swear with a greater enthusiasm. It will be a fine season.

Asbury Park is rapidly acquiring a collection of machines. Of course there is a toboggan slide. Now, in process of construction, there is an arrangement called a "razzle-dazzle." Just what this will be is impossible to tell. It is, of course, a moral machine. Down by the lake an immense upright wheel has been erected. This will revolve, carrying little cars, to be filled evidently with desperate persons, around and around, up and down.

James J. Corbett, with his trainer and sparring partner, James Daly, of Philadelphia, is a prominent figure on the board-walk in the summer crowds. The big man has made hosts of friends because of his gentlemanly bearing and quiet manners. Even James A. Bradley came down momentarily from his pinnacle and conversed pleasantly with the boxer.

The grounds of the Asbury Park Athletic Association, in the northern part of the town, are being put in splendid condition. The main stand has been extended eighty-five feet, and is now 250 feet in length. Underneath the stand, dressing rooms, toilet rooms and a restaurant have been built. The tennis courts and baseball diamond have been put on a first-class footing. The bicycle track is already one of the best in the country, and no expense will be spared in the attempt to make it perfect. Fifteen thousand dollars has already been expended.

[Personal news]

No. 110   JOYS OF SEASIDE LIFE

ASBURY PARK, N.J., July 16.—This town is not overrun with seaside "fakirs," yet there are many fearful and wonderful types in the collection of them here. The man with the green pea under all or none of three walnut shells is not present, nor is any of his class. There is no fierce cry of "Five, five, the lucky five!" nor the coaxing call of "Come, now, gentlemen, make your bets. The red or the black wins." These men cannot pass the gigantic barriers erected by a wise government, which recognizes the fact that these things should not be.

However, the men who merely have things to sell can come and flourish. There are scores of them, and they do a big business. The summer guests come here with money. They are legitimate prey. The fakirs attack them enthusiastically.

Those who are the most persistently aggressive are the Hindoos, who sell Indian goods, from silk handkerchiefs to embroidered petticoats. They are an aggregation of little brown fellows, with twinkling bright eyes. They wear the most amazing trousers and small black surtouts, or coats of some kind. Apparently they are, as a race, universally bow-legged, and are all possessed of ancestors who were given to waddling. The Hindoos have soft, wheedling voices, and when they invade a crowded hotel-porch and unload their little white packs of silk goods they are very apt to cause a disturbance in the pocketbooks of the ladies present. They parade the streets in twos and threes. They all use large umbrellas of the rural pattern to protect their chocolate skins from the rays of the sun. A camera fiend was the first to discover an astonishing superstition or fear which possesses these men. Once she perceived three of them reclining in picturesque attitudes on a shady bank. Their bundles and umbrellas reposed beside them and they were fanning themselves with their caps. She approached them with an engaging smile and a camera levelled at their heads. Astonishment and terror swept over their faces. With one accord they gave a great shout and, raising their umbrellas, interposed them as a bulwark against the little glass eye of the camera. The fiend had her finger on the trigger, and she pulled it before she was aware of the bewildering revolution in the appearance of the objects of her ambition. As a result the picture is the most valued one in all the fiend's collection. There is the grassy bank and a few trees. In the foreground appear the tops of three large umbrellas. Underneath dangle three pairs of legs with also three pairs of feet. The picture is a great success and is the admiration of all beholders.

Of course the frankfurter man is prevalent. He is too ordinary to need more than mere mention. With his series of quick motions, consisting of the grab at the roll, the stab at the sausage and the deft little dab of mustard, he appears at all hours. He parades the avenues swinging his furnace and howling.

There is a sleight-of-hand Italian, with a courageous mustache and a clever nose. He manoeuvres with a quarter of a dollar and a pack of playing cards. He comes around to the hotels and mystifies the indolent guests. Nobody cares much to ask: "How does he do it," so the mustache takes a vain curve and the exhibition continues.

Tintype galleries are numerous. They are all of course painted the inevitable blue, and trundle about the country on wheels. It is quite the thing to have one's features libelled in this manner. The occupants of the blue houses make handsome incomes. Babies and pug dogs furnish most of the victims for these people.

Down near the beach are a number of contrivances to tumble-bumble the soul and gain possession of nickels. There is a "razzle-dazzle," invented apparently by a man of experience and knowledge of the world. It is a sort of circular swing. One gets in at some expense and by climbing up a ladder. Then the machine goes around and around, with a sway and swirl, like the motion of a ship. Many people are supposed to enjoy this thing, for a reason which is not evident. Solemn circles of more or less sensible-looking people sit in it and "go 'round."

On the lake shore is an "observation wheel," which is the name of a gigantic upright wheel of wood and steel, which goes around carrying little cars filled with maniacs, up and down, over and over. Of course there are merry-go-rounds loaded with impossible giraffes and goats, on which ride crowds of joyous children, who clutch for brass rings. All these machines have appalling steam organs run in connection with them, which make weird music eternally. Humanity had no respite from these things until the police made their owners tone them down a great deal, so that now they play low music instead of grinding out with stentorian force such airs as "Annie," the famous, so that they could be heard squares away.

The camera obscura is in Ocean Grove. It really has some value as a scientific curiosity. People enter a small wooden building and stand in a darkened room, gazing at the surface of a small round table, on which appear reflections made through a lens in the top of the tower of all that is happening in the vicinity at the time. One gets a miniature of everything that occurs in the streets, on the boardwalk or on the hotel-porches. One can watch the bathers gambolling in the surf or peer at the deck of a passing ship. A man stands with his hand on a lever and changes the scene at will.

These are the regular ways in which Asbury Park amuses itself. There is, however, a steady stream of transient fakirs, who stay a week, an hour, or perchance go at once away. This week an aggregation of five Italian mandolin and guitar players came to town. They are really very clever with their instruments, and have already made themselves popular with the hotel guests. One "Jesse Williams" is a favorite with everybody, too. He is very diminutive and very black. He has a disreputable silk-hat and a pair of nimble feet. He passes from house to house, and sings and dances. He accompanies both his dances and his songs on an old weather-beaten banjo. The entire populace adore him, because he sometimes discloses various qualities of the true comedian, and is never exactly idiotic. But the most terrific of all the fakirs, the most stupendous of all the exhibitions is that of the Greek dancer, or whatever it is. Two Italians, armed with a violin and a harp, recently descended upon the town. With them came a terrible creature, in an impossible apparel, and with a tambourine. He, or she, wore a dress which would take a geometrical phenomenon to describe. He, or she, wore orange stockings, with a bunch of muscle in the calf. The rest of his, or her, apparel was a chromatic delirium of red, black, green, pink, blue, yellow, purple, white and other shades and colors not known. There were accumulations of jewelry on different portions of his, or her, person. Beneath were those grotesque legs; above, was a face. The grin of the successful midnight assassin and the smile of the coquette were commingled upon it. When he, or she, with his, or her, retinue of Italians, emerged upon the first hotel veranda, there was a panic. Brave men shrunk. Then, he, or she, opened his, or her, mouth, and began to sing in a hard, high, brazen voice, songs in an unknown tongue. Then, he, or she, danced, with ballet airs and graces. The scowl of the assassin sat side by side with the simper and smirk of the country maiden who is not well-balanced mentally. The fantastic legs slid over the floor to the music of the violin and harp. And, finally, he, or she, passed the tambourine about among the crowd, with a villainously-lovable smile upon his, or her, features. Since then, he, or she, has become a well-known figure on the streets. People are beginning to get used to it, and he, or she, is not mobbed, as one might expect him, or her, to be.

No. 111 SUMMER DWELLERS AT ASBURY PARK AND THEIR DOINGS

ASBURY PARK, N.J., July 23 (Special).—The big "Observation Wheel" on Lake-ave. has got into a great lot of trouble, and it is feared that the awe-stricken visitor will be unable to see the "wheel go 'round" hereafter. Complaints were made by the hotel-owners in the neighborhood that the engine connected with the machine distributed ashes and sparks over their counterpanes. Also, residents of Ocean Grove came and said that the steam organ disturbed their pious meditations on the evils of the world. Thereupon the minions of the law violently suppressed the wheel and its attendants. The case comes before Chancellor McGill, of Jersey City.

Captain Minot, the popular proprietor of the Minot House on Third-ave., was, one evening this week, presented by his guests with a large Sevres plaque and two pitchers, on a table of carved oak.

Arthur Zimmerman, the famous American bicycle rider, who has been smashing English records, and who is, incidentally, the idol of Asbury Park wheelers, is to be here on August 5 and 6. He will race here on those days against some of the cracks of the country. It is certain that he will receive a tremendous ovation.

The thousands of summer visitors who have fled from the hot, stifling air of the cities to enjoy the cool sea breezes are not entirely forgetful of the unfortunates who have to stay in their crowded tenements. Jacob Riis, the author of *How the Other Half Lives*, gave an illustrated lecture on the same subject in the Beach Auditorium on Wednesday evening. The proceeds were given to the tenement-house work of the King's Daughters.

Over $300 was cleared, which, at $2 each, will give 150 children a two-weeks outing in the country.

The first annual convention of the Christian Alliance began to-day in Educational Hall. The convention will last until August 1, and is presided over by the Rev. A. B. Simpson. The first four days will be devoted to the subject of Christian Holiness, one day to the Lord's Coming, another to Divine Healing, and the remaining days will be given up to foreign missions.

Owing to the glut in the weakfish market this week, a splendid catch of 100,000 pounds in the Asbury Park nets was turned loose, after the local market was supplied at a very low rate.

[Personal news]

No. 112 ON THE BOARDWALK

ASBURY PARK, N.J., Aug. 13.—During the summer months the famous boardwalk at this resort takes a sudden leap into a prominence quite equal, it would seem, to that of any street, boulevard or plaza on the earth. Apparently the centre of the world of people, not of science nor art, is situated somewhere under the long line of electric lights which dangles over the great cosmopolitan thoroughfare. It is the world of the middle classes; add but princes and gamblers and it would be what the world calls the world.

In the evening it is a glare of light and a swirl of gayly attired women and well-dressed men. There is a terrific tooting by brass bands and a sort of roar of conversation that swells up continually from the throng. There are no clusters of "fakirs" adding their shrill cries to the clamor, nor none of the many noisy devices to catch the unwatched nickle. Only the crowds, the bands and the surf.

Occasionally philosophers ponder over the question why all these people come down to the beach evening after evening. There is the sea; but it is evident, at first glance, that no one ever looks at the sea or considers it in any way. The crowd at Asbury Park does not sit and gape at the sea. The Atlantic

Ocean is a matter of very small consequence. No doubt occasional glances are thrown at it. Lovers on the beach are supposed sometimes to contemplate it, when the moon peeps over the horizon, but it is apparent that the ocean is a secondary matter and is merely tolerated. It could not be the music, of course, because thousands of people would not congregate to hear indifferent bands play.

But the people come to see the people. The huge wooden hotels empty themselves directly after dinner; the boardinghouses seem to turn upside down and shake out every boarder; the cottagers make ready for an evening stroll, and up in the business part of the town the merchants and clerks bestir themselves and finish their work, roll down their sleeves and put on their coats. Then all hie to the big boardwalk. For there is joy to the heart in a crowd. One is in life and of life then. Nothing escapes; the world is going on and one is there to perceive it.

The walk itself is a heavy plank structure varying from 50 to 100 feet in width, and extending along the entire ocean frontage of the town. It is built on heavy pilings whose tops are usually from four to ten feet above the beach. Rows of immovable wooden benches stretch along the edge of the walk, and landward a lawn comes flush with it. Next to this is a brick walk and then the driveway, Ocean-ave. Statues, allegorical and memorial, occupy positions on the lawn, with also many little pavilions and summer houses. During certain hours this great passage is fairly choked with humanity. The whole space —one mile long by 50 to 100 feet wide—is alive and swarming with pedestrians. Confusion never reigns only because the general pace is leisurely and every one "keeps moving."

Day excursion trains sometimes bring down as many as 15,000 people to enjoy a few cool hours by the sea. This momentarily gives the resort a population of about 45,000. And they all appear on the beach. When great public meetings are held on the beach and boardwalk, audiences of 10,000 persons gather frequently. It is said that 20,000 people watched the participants in the annual baby parade as the nurse maids trundled their charges down the walk.

The average summer guest here is a rather portly man, with a good watch-chain and a business suit of clothes, a wife and about three children. He stands in his two shoes with American self-reliance and, playing casually with his watch-chain, looks at the world with a clear eye. He submits to the arrogant prices of some of the hotel proprietors with a calm indifference; he will pay fancy prices for things with a great unconcern. However, deliberately and baldly attempt to beat him out of fifteen cents and he will put his hands in his pockets, spread his legs apart and wrangle, in a loud voice, until sundown. All day he lies in the sand or sits on a bench, reading papers and smoking cigars, while his blessed babies are dabbling around throwing sand down his back and emptying their little pails of sea-water in his boots. In the evening he puts on his best and takes his wife and the "girls" down to the boardwalk. He enjoys himself in a very mild way and dribbles out a lot of money under the impression that he is proceeding cheaply.

However, the long-famous "summer girl" takes precedence in point of interest. She has been enshrined in sentimental rhyme and satirical prose for so long that it is difficult for one to tell just what she is and what she isn't. If one is to believe the satirists, a man would better encase himself in a barrel, put dinner-plates down his trousers' legs and shake hands with her by means of a very long-handled pitchfork. If the rhymers are to be relied on, she is a maiden with a bonny blue eye and a tender smile and with a red heart palpitant under fields of white flannel. At any rate, she is here on the boardwalk in overwhelming force and the golden youths evidently believe the poets.

The amount of summer girl and golden youth business that goes on around this boardwalk is amazing. A young man comes here, mayhap, from a distant city. Everything is new to him and in consequence, he is a new young man. He is not the same steady and, perhaps, sensible lad who bended all winter over the ledger in the city office. There is a little more rose-tint and gilt-edge to him. He finds here on the beach, as he saunters forth in his somewhat false hues, a summer girl who just suits him. She exactly fits his new environment. When he returns to the ledger he lays down his coat of strange colors and visions fade. Allah il Allah.

But she, with her escort or escorts, makes life at summer resorts. She is a bit of interesting tinsel flashing near the sombre hued waves. She gives the zest to life on the great boardwalk. Without her the men would perish from weariness or fall to fighting. Men usually fall to fighting if they are left alone long enough, and the crowd on the boardwalk would be a mob without the smile of the summer girl. She absent, the bands would play charges and retreats and the soda-water fountains would run blood. Man is compelled by nature to be either a lover or a red-handed villain.

Great storms create havoc with the heavy planking of the walk nearly every fall. The huge beams are torn and twisted and smashed by the breakers in a regardless manner, making an annual bill of expense of $15,000. This bill for repairs is met by James A. Bradley. He is a millionaire, who bought the land upon which this resort is situated years ago for a nominal price. He still has great possessions here. A part of them is the ocean front. Everybody knows him and everybody calls him "Founder Bradley." He is a familiar figure at any hour of the day. He wears a white sun-umbrella with a green lining and has very fierce and passionate whiskers, whose rigidity is relieved by an occasional twinkle in his bright Irish eye. He walks habitually with bended back and thoughtful brow, continually in the depths of some great question of finance, involving, mayhap, a change in the lumber market or the price of nails. He is noted for his wealth, his whiskers and his eccentricities. He is a great seeker after the curious. When he perceives it he buys it. Then he takes it down to the beach and puts it on the boardwalk with a little sign over it, informing the traveller of its history, its value and its virtues.

On the boardwalk now are some old boats, an ancient ship's bell, a hand fire engine of antique design, an iron anchor, a marble bathtub and various articles of interest to everybody. It is his boardwalk, and if he wants to put 7,000 fire engines and bathtubs on it he will do so. It is his privilege. No man should object to everybody doing as he pleases with his own fire engines and bathtubs.

"Founder" Bradley has lots of sport with his ocean front and boardwalk. It amuses him and he likes it. It warms his heart to see the thousands of people tramping over his boards, helter-skeltering in his sand and diving into that ocean of the Lord's which is adjacent to the beach of James A. Bradley. He likes to edit signs and have them tacked up around. There is probably no man in the world that can beat "Founder" Bradley in writing signs. His work has an air of philosophic thought about it which is very taking to any one of a literary turn of mind. He usually starts off with an abstract truth, an axiom, not foreign nor irrelevant, but bearing somewhat upon a hidden meaning in the sign—"Keep off the grass," or something of that sort. Occasionally he waxes sarcastic; at other times, historical. He may devote four lines to telling the public what happened in 1869 and draw from that a one-line lesson as to what they may not do at that moment. He has made sign-painting a fine art, and he is a master. His work, sprinkled broadcast over the boardwalk, delights the critics and incidentally warns the unwary. Strangers need no guide-book nor policemen. They have signs confronting them at all points, under their feet, over their heads and before their noses. "Thou shalt not" do this, nor that, nor the other.

He also shows genius of an advanced type and the qualities of authorship in his work. He is no mere bungler nor trivial paint-slinger. He has those powers of condensation which are so much admired at this day. For instance: "Modesty of apparel is as becoming to a lady in a bathing suit as to a lady dressed in silks and satins." There are some very sweet thoughts in that declaration. It is really a beautiful expression of sentiment. It is modest and delicate. Its author merely insinuates. There is nothing to shake vibratory senses in such gentle phraseology. Supposing he had said: "Don't go in the water attired merely in a tranquil smile," or "Do not appear on the beach when only enwrapped in reverie." A thoughtless man might have been guilty of some such unnecessary uncouthness. But to "Founder" Bradley it would be impossible. He is not merely a man. He is an artist.

No. 113   ALONG THE SHARK RIVER

AVON-BY-THE-SEA, N.J., Aug. 14 (Special).—The work of the Seaside Assembly continues here with unabated interest for the summer youths and maidens who are inclined to mingle useful lessons in the arts and sciences with the pleasure and expense usually attendant upon seaside life. The series of evening entertainments which are being given in the huge auditorium on the Assembly grounds are popular with the guests at the summer hotels and the classes during the day are composed of pupils from the hotels and cottages here and from the adjoining resorts.

The faculty and pupils of the Assembly's School of Biology are constantly engaged in inspecting great glass jars filled with strange floating growths in the laboratory on the banks of Shark River. Occasionally they vary this exciting pursuit by taking a boat and going to dig ecstatically for singular things in the mud flats of the outlet to the river. Microscopes and various instruments that vaguely resemble machine-guns and the entrails of alarm-clocks are to them, the world. But they are a good, jolly lot of fellows, who work with their sleeves rolled up and have sunburned noses. If they prefer rare sea-weeds to very scarce bottled beer, it is their privilege; if they choose to chase June-bugs around the block on warm nights, no one may interfere with their proper pursuit of happiness. The corps of instructors is a very learned and able one. Professor George Macloskie, Sc.D., LL.D., of Princeton College, is the dean of the school, and the working head of the department is Professor Julius Nelson, Ph.D., who occupies the chair of biology in Rutgers College.

The concerts which Frederic Dean, of the Scharwenka Conservatory, of New-York, has been giving in the Assembly auditorium, have been blessed with the presence of several lights of the musical world. Senor Gonzalo Nunez played at the one given last week. He is a New-York concert pianist who has been a favorite for nearly fifteen years. Although still a young man, he has had remarkable advantages in the way of musical education. He studied at the Paris Conservatoire under George Mathias, who was one of Chopin's pupils, and other masters. He has a European reputation both as performer and composer, and has made extensive tours through this country and Mexico. It is needless to say that his playing has proved a delight to Assembly audiences.

Probably the people who really have the most fun, not to omit a most thorough course of instruction, are the art students who are so fortunate as to compose the out-door sketching class, under the leadership of Madame S. E. Le Prince, of New-York. They go on long tours after the browns and grays and greens of Shark River scenery. Under white umbrellas, tilted conveniently, they perch in rows on campstools, and chatter and paint and paint and chatter. Sometimes they seem to do more of one than the other, but, notwithstanding this, when they arrive home they always contrive to produce for inspection a fair amount of work done. They sail on the river and picnic on its bank; they have clambakes in the pine woods and chase the blithesome crab among the sea-weeds at the river's bottom. Nevertheless, they sketch incidentally, and sketch understandingly and well. [Five paragraphs of personal items including the information "Hamlin Garland, of Boston, who is going to deliver a course of lectures here on American and English literature, will arrive at the Sylvan Lodge next week."]

No. 114   PARADES AND ENTERTAINMENTS

ASBURY PARK, N.J., Aug. 20 (Special).—The parade of the Junior Order of United American Mechanics here on Wednesday afternoon was a deeply impressive one to some persons. There were hundreds of the members of the order, and they wound through the streets to the music of enough brass bands to make furious discords. It probably was the most awkward, ungainly, uncut and uncarved procession that ever raised clouds of dust on sun-beaten streets. Nevertheless, the spectacle of an Asbury Park crowd confronting such an aggregation was an interesting sight to a few people.

Asbury Park creates nothing. It does not make; it merely amuses. There is a factory where nightshirts are manufactured, but it is some miles from town. This is a resort of wealth and leisure, of women and considerable wine. The throng along the line of march was composed of summer gowns, lace parasols, tennis trousers, straw hats and indifferent smiles. The procession was composed of men, bronzed, slope-shouldered, uncouth and begrimed with dust. Their clothes fitted them illy, for the most part, and they had no ideas of marching. They merely plodded along, not seeming quite to understand, stolid, unconcerned and, in a certain sense, dignified—a pace and a bearing emblematic of their lives. They smiled occasionally and from time to time greeted friends in the crowd on the sidewalk. Such an assemblage of the spraddle-legged men of the middle class, whose hands were bent and shoulders stooped from delving and constructing, had never appeared to an Asbury Park summer crowd, and the latter was vaguely amused.

The bona fide Asbury Parker is a man to whom a dollar, when held close to his eye, often shuts out any impression he may have had that other people possess rights. He is apt to consider that men and women, especially city men and women, were created to be mulcted by him. Hence the tan-colored, sun-beaten honesty in the faces of the members of the Junior Order of United American Mechanics is expected to have a very staggering effect upon them. The visitors were men who possessed principles.

A highly attractive feature of social entertainment at the Lake Avenue Hotel during the past week has been the informal piano recitals given by Miss Ella L. Flock, of Hackettstown, N.J., who is one of the guests of that house. Miss Flock won a gold medal for superiority in piano playing at the Centenary Collegiate Institute last spring by her fine performance of Beethoven's "Sonata Pathetique." She plays with singular power and grace of expression, and with the assured touch of a virtuoso.

Professor Milo Deyo and wife are spending the summer in the Park. Professor Deyo gave a delightful entertainment last week at the Lake Avenue Hotel, at which he played several of his original compositions.

The leader of the beach band has arranged Professor Deyo's very popular air de ballet "Enchantment," and this piece is now the greatest favorite of any that the band renders.

[List of names]

No. 115   THE SEASIDE ASSEMBLY'S WORK AT AVON

AVON-BY-THE-SEA, N.J., Aug. 28 (Special).—The rainy weather of last week has interfered but slightly with the routine of work on the grounds of the Seaside Assembly here. The lectures and entertainments have all been remarkably well attended, considering recent storms.

Mme. Alberti, of New-York, the principal of the school of expression here, gave one of her popular entertainments in the auditorium of the Assembly grounds this week. The "emotive gestures" as given by her were applauded long and heartily by the large audience. The pantomimic "Nearer, My God, to Thee" was also enthusiastically redemanded. On Wednesday evening of last week, the Rev. Dr. John E. Peters, of Atlantic City, gave a scientific lecture on "The Microscope and Its Revelations," and on Monday evening Frederic Dean, of the Scharwenka Conservatory of Music, of New-York, gave his "Midsummer Musical." Among those who took part were Mrs. Frederic Dean, contralto, of New-York; Mrs. A. A. Judd, soprano, of New-York, and the Avon Choral Society of forty voices.

Once more the question of widening and deepening Shark River, to make it navigable for yachts and passenger vessels, is being agitated. P. Sanford Ross, a wealthy summer resident of Belmar, offers to organize a stock company and put the matter successfully through if the town of Belmar will deed to him for a nominal consideration a strip of land near his residence. The subscription books of the company will be open to members of the Belmar Association, and they will be allowed to take as many shares as they wish. There is no port of entry for vessels in distress between Barnegat Inlet and Sandy Hook, and it is understood that the influence of Mr. Ross and others will be used to have Congress declare Shark River such a port. Most of the citizens of Belmar are favorable to the plan, but of this side of the inlet nothing has been said or done. In the days prior to the Revolution Shark River was a large deepwater bay. Pirates used to anchor their vessels in the deep channels and go ashore to eat oysters and hang prisoners. It is said Captain Kidd himself frequented the river in a villainous black-hulled schooner. But the sand bar at the inlet rose higher and higher until it poked its face out of the water, and still it grew, until a huge wall of sand interposed between the waters of the ocean and the waters of the river. Then the river gradually became what it now is—a shallow stream, the resort of the crab and the crabber. It still preserves its appearance of a magnificent harbor.

There is no doubt that if Shark River were made a harbor, all the resorts near would have a great boom, although some of them, like Asbury Park and Ocean Grove, do not need it. To have a town in the great resort region of the New-Jersey coast become the abiding place of yachtsmen would add much to coast interests.

[Personal news]

No. 116   THE SEASIDE ASSEMBLY (II)

AVON-BY-THE-SEA, N.J., Sept. 5 (Special).—The Seaside Assembly at this place is about closing its most successful season. The end of the session has left the Assembly in a thoroughly sound condition in every way, and the prospects for next year are all that could be desired. Although the Seaside Assembly has become well known among the scholars of the land, its aims are totally misunderstood by many persons. The object of the Assembly is an educational one. It is non-denominational in character. There are devotional services in the Auditorium every morning, but they are conducted in turn by the leading clergymen of all denominations from all parts of the land. There are over a dozen educational departments in the Assembly. There are schools of biology, art, music, expression, mathematics, literature, philosophy, chemistry, Bible study, geology, psychology, history, pedagogics, writing, phonography and cookery. On the Assembly grounds there are places for all these schools, and daily sessions are held from early in July until the end of the first week in September.

The grounds of the Assembly occupy a block between four of the most prominent avenues of the town. It is only a short distance from the sea and from Shark River, and is within a stone's throw of Sylvan Lake. The grounds are heavily shaded with a growth of pines. Near the centre of the block stands the Auditorium, a large building of the amphitheatrical pattern, with a spacious stage. The sides of this structure are open, but aprons of heavy canvas are attached to them, to be let down on rainy or windy nights. The stage has been made to represent the interior of a negro hut, to accommodate some minstrel troupe, made up from the jolly guests of one of the hotels, other times it merely becomes the sombre background for a silver-haired savant, lecturing on diatomes or bacteria. One can listen to learned lectures occasionally, and can also occasionally laugh over the jokes of an amateur minstrel. Musical entertainments are, however, the most numerous. On this stage have appeared from time to time some of the best-known singers and performers of the country.

Over in a corner of the grounds is the Hall of Philosophy, a quaint little building, once the abiding place of the members of the Summer School of the American Institute of Christian Philosophy. Here did the Rev. Dr. Charles F. Deems, of New-York, and his cohorts of learned men gather to sit in the noiseless gloom and discuss their pet tried and untried theories. But they are gone, and the noiseless gloom has also gone. The hall now rings with the merry voices of Mme. Alberti's pupils who come here to be taught Delsarte. Mme. Alberti is the dean of the School of Expression here. Dozens of young ladies come to this resort merely to attend her lectures. The "Delsarte Girls" are a familiar feature of the Avon-by-the-Sea landscape.

Directly in front of the Auditorium stands the little building in which Professor Marion Miller, of Princeton College, keeps one of the best libraries of its kind to be found in this country. Near this structure is the Kindergarten tent with its dozens of contrivances to delight the childish art. Here little babies and larger babies are taught for hours each day. And they advance steadily, too. They work hard over their little tasks at times, although they are quite unaware of it. Banks of sand are under the trees. On these the spectators can observe all manner of villages, cities, mills and factories, rivers, harbors, canals and lakes. In these strange countries the children carry on a miniature civilization. They also publish a paper called "The Weekly News" every Thursday. Every little pupil makes a copy of the paper, painfully putting in the illustrations with a crayon, and the reading matter with a pen and ink. Fearful and wonderful journalism is often developed in the pages of "The Weekly News." The infantile brains evolve strange and weird things. Some of the editions of this unique paper are valued at their weight in gold by parents whose offspring's amazing handiwork adorns its pages.

On the ocean side of the grounds is Otis Hall, the home of the Avon art student. The School of Art has been in charge of Charles A. Hulbert, of New-York, who had as his assistant Miss Katherine D. Allmond. They have made the school a popular feature of the Assembly. In Otis Hall is the studio of the school. The walls are hung with the work of pupils and instructors. An evening is occasionally devoted to a reception in the studio. The summer guests of the hotel and the cottagers then throng the building, and go into raptures over the work of the school.

The School of Music occupies for the most part the large Auditorium. This department has achieved considerable success this year under the leadership of Frederic Dean, of the Scharwenka Conservatory, of New-York. A special feature of the sessions this year was an illustrated course of forty lectures on the history of music. Mr. Dean organized the Avon-by-the-Sea Choral Union, which sang at many of the Assembly entertainments. All the young singers from the hotels and the cottages of the town joined the union, and it was a decidedly popular organization. The contralto of the Assembly is Mrs. Frederic Dean. She possesses a pure and strong voice, which she has under complete control.

The laboratory of the School of Biology is not upon the Assembly grounds proper. Over upon the bank of Shark River is a little building standing like a peak-roofed centipede upon its legs of pilings. During high tide the laboratory is up to its knees in the salt waters of the river, but a knot of boats that tug and haul at their chains at the foot of a long flight of steps shows the means of going and coming are at the command of the occupants. The interior of the building is a chaos of glass jars, in which swim various hideous animals, cans, and tubs, microscopes and instruments of all sizes and kinds. Among these a little group of scientists is completely and gloriously happy from all accounts. There they stay all day long with plenty of light coming in through the big windows and pore over quaint bugs and beasts. Professor George Macloskie, Sc.D., LL.D., who occupies the chair of biology in Princeton College, is dean of the school, and in the faculty are Professor Arthur M. Miller, A.M., late of Wilson College; Professor Julius Nelson, Ph.D., of Rutgers College; John E. Peters, A.M., Sc.D., Richard S. Lull, of Rutgers College, and A. Dumas Watkins, of Princeton College. Among the lecturers are Samuel Lockwood, Ph.D., superintendent of schools for Monmouth County, Principal Lyman Best, of Brooklyn, Professor Byron D. Halstead, of Rutgers College, and Miss Mary E. Murtfeldt, of St. Louis.

No. 117 THE SEASIDE HOTEL HOP

THE seaside hotel hop is an institution peculiar unto itself. It is generally held on Saturday evening when a few extra dancing men come down in the pursuit of Sunday rest(?). There are usually from 200 to 600 people looking on, and occasionally as many as six couples on the floor, though this highwater mark is not often reached. The music varies with the character of the hotel, but is likely to consist of a wailing cornet and a piano, which resemble a Christian who hath not charity, in that it long ago became as sounding brass and tinkling cymbal. The music plays right along by the hour whether anybody is dancing or not. Occasionally the hotel proprietor looks in, rubbing his hands and beaming on the scene with an air that says, "Enjoy yourselves, my people, these riotous festivities are given away with every package of twenty meal tickets."

Early in the evening the floor is taken up by skinny little girls with curls, short white dresses and a superabundance of blue ribbon, who perform "dancing in the barn" and other gems of the dancing-school, to the delight of admiring parents. After an army of nurses have cleared the floor of the small fry, the sunbrowned summer girl comes in from her retreat around on the dark side of the veranda. Her ball dress is evidently cut lower in the neck than her bathing suit, which makes her look like a doll with a bronze head on a porcelain body. She dances somewhat recklessly as one who is aware that the eyes of seventeen ancient and honorable spinsters in the front row are upon her, and has determined to show her contempt for, and independence of, "the horrid old things." Her partner is a young man with tender, yearning eyes, a struggling mustache, a tennis shirt and russet shoes. He holds her—well, as if he were afraid of losing her.

When a set is made up for the lancers it is composed of people from seven different States. As the figures for the lancers are never danced alike in any two localities, and there is no prompter, a general tangle results. "Brother Tom, from college," creates an additional ruction by pressing all the girls' hands in the "grand right and left," and swinging them off their feet at "balance the corners." A number of men in evening dress wander wearily about and do the "heavy standing around" but never dance. Only the men in tennis shirts dance.

In the hotel dining-room or parlor where the hop is going on it is as hot as a furnace. The windows are blocked up with people who are too old or too weary of life to dance, and with visitors from the neighboring boarding-houses which have not risen to the dignity of a hop. In a secluded corner of the veranda the coterie of dashing widows and young married women have ensconced themselves with their following of mature admirers. Throughout the evening they dispose of endless lemonades containing a certain percentage of woody fibre commonly called "stick."

At ten minutes to 12 o'clock the cornet wails its last wail and the piano thumps its last thump. The bronzed maidens of the dance drag themselves up stairs jingling their room-keys and dropping an occasional joke for the benefit of the night clerk. The men smoke their good-night cigars on the veranda while they cool off and listen to the booming breakers on the shore. A Sunday quiet settles down over the frail fabric of a summer hotel, unless the forty-seven babies wake up and howl their midnight chorus, or the fat man with the thirty-two foot diapason snore gets "cast" on his back and rouses the furthermost echoes of the whispering gallery into which 500 people are packed.

Possible Attributions

No. 118—Mr. Yatman's Conversions

Ocean Grove, Aug. 26 (Special).—The usual 9 o'clock meetings were held an hour earlier to-day, as the camp-meeting love feast had the right of way at that hour. At the young people's meeting a number were converted. The Rev. C. H. Yatman, the leader, possesses a strong personality and magnetism which, with a graphic way of putting things, wins souls to higher things. Mr. Yatman also conducts the training class and the twilight meeting daily. He goes from here to Jane-st., New-York, to open a meeting in September, and thence to Washington, D.C., and then to Galveston, Tex., and Youngstown, Ohio. Six thousand people filled every foot of space before 9 o'clock. Dr. Stokes asked the people to shake hands in token of brotherly love, which they did with shouts and tears. Four Christian Chinamen sent up a written testimony that they "loved Jesus better and better every day." The venerable Augustus Webster, eighty-three years of age, and many ministers were among the speakers. The Rev. Dr. O. H. Tiffany, of New-York, was the preacher of the morning.

[Personal news]

No. 119   A Prosperous Year at Asbury Park

Asbury Park, July 13 (Special).—Asbury Park is enjoying an unusally prosperous season. The cottages are all filled with summer visitors, and the hotels are being well patronized. Last evening there were fully 15,000 persons upon the famous board walk along the ocean front, which is one of the great attractions of this remarkable resort. This walk runs along the beach of Asbury Park and Ocean Grove, from Deal Lake to Ocean Park. Last winter's storms badly wrecked a portion of it between

Fifth and Sixth aves., but James A. Bradley, the founder of Asbury Park, is rebuilding it twenty feet further inland. The bathing-houses here are pushed to their utmost capacity in supplying the demands made upon them. Mr. Bradley has a Roman pool at the foot of Asbury-ave., where both hot and cold salt water baths attract many people. The swimming pool of this establishment is a popular institution.

The Atlas of Monmouth County, prepared and published by ex-Assemblyman Chester Wolverton, is being delivered to the cottages along the shore. It is the finest work of the kind ever issued. There are detail maps of every portion of the Monmouth shore with the property lines correctly shown, and the name of the owner of each plot of ground and cottage. In cases where the lines were disputed Mr. Wolverton had the cottage plots surveyed before the maps were drawn. This work will decide many disputed points. There is also a map of the county, which shows every drive along this section of the coast.

The popular Coleman House which was purchased two years ago by Justus E. Ralph, the treasurer and secretary of the Freehold and New-York Railroad Company, has been greatly improved and beautified this year. The nightly dances in the pretty amusement hall on the hotel property are enjoyable affairs. Benjamin H. Swope, for several years the manager of the Howland Hotel at Long Branch, is now the manager of the Coleman House. The hotel has a large annex at Third-ave. and Kingsley-st. and its own stables.

Samuel B. McIntyre, an old hotel proprietor of Long Branch and New-York, is the new proprietor of the Oriental Hotel, a well-appointed house near the beach.

Swan boats with propellers worked by the feet, like those on Central Park Lake, are a new and novel feature of Wesley Lake this season.

Sunset Hall, near the Ocean, on Fourth-ave., has been almost doubled in capacity since last season. The house is well patronized.

The Ocean Hotel, in Asbury-ave., has a new annex. The floors are arranged in family suites and all the modern hotel appliances make life there enjoyable to many city visitors.

[List of names]

No. 120 WORKERS AT OCEAN GROVE

OCEAN GROVE, Aug. 9 (Special).—The crowds here grow larger every day. A stranger within the gates of Ocean Grove wonders where all the people come from and where they are fed and lodged. A walk through several of the streets shows that the broad piazzas of the hotels, boarding-houses and cottages are filled with people, mostly portly matrons and pretty maidens. At the big Auditorium is seen an audience of 7,000 to 8,000 persons. There is a big crowd of people around the handsome brick postoffice, and the ice-cream shops are packed. Down on the beach the famous board walk and the broad sandy beach are literally covered with people. The crowd upon the beach is so big that it overflows into Asbury Park on the north and Ocean Park and Bradley Beach on the south. Daily excursion trains come here from all parts of New-York, New-Jersey and Pennsylvania, but the people who come here for a day are lost in the immense crowd of humanity which has come here for the season. One of the interesting features of the gathering is the baby element. Ocean Grove is, beyond all doubt, for the family, of the family and by the family. There are thousands of babies here. The plump and pretty infants swing in hammocks under the trees and upon cottage stoops, shout with glee as they roll and tumble upon the sands of the beach or gaze with supreme disdain upon those who have to walk while they ride in royal state in gay carriages propelled by demure nurse girls wearing coquettish little white caps. The joyful screams of the children are heard all day in all parts of the town. It is not an unusual thing for the babies to be taken to the services at the big Auditorium, and if they laugh and "crow" during the services no one seems to care. The babies here are fat and good-natured, and with their pretty faces and charming little tricks are the pride of their parents and the especial joy of this city by the sea.

The children who are able to walk and run about are here, too, in great numbers. They spend most of the day at the beach. Each little man and woman has a small pail and a shovel. They dig in the sand and build forts and lay out towns which are swept away by the tide at night only to be rebuilt the next day.

These youngsters revel in sand, chewing-gum, popcorn and toy balloons. They are well behaved and their wildest mode of dissipation is a drink of soda water and a ride in one of the merry-go-rounds over in Asbury Park or a trip up and down Wesley Lake.

[Personal news]

No. 121 JOYS OF THE JERSEY COAST

AVON-BY-THE-SEA, Aug. 25 (Special).—This has been a good year at this resort, and if all the plans proposed for its advancement and improvement are carried out it will be one of the most popular summer towns on the entire New-Jersey coast. The principles of temperance are strictly enforced here, and thus the hotels are kept entirely free from the element which has proven so obnoxious at some of the other summer towns. A project is already under way looking to the erection of a mammoth hotel for use next season.

There are a number of ardent fishermen here among the guests of the several hotels and cottages. They have been making big catches the entire season. They equip themselves in rubber boots, and standing in the edge of the water, cast their well-baited hooks far out into the surf. They favor the erection of a fishing pier like the one at Asbury Park. Several big sea bass have been caught here this season. The heaviest weighed nearly twenty-three pounds. Last season one of our prominent cottagers, James Ronan, of Trenton, hooked a big bass near Shark River Inlet. After a most exciting battle with his prize he succeeded in reeling it in and pulling it ashore. The fish tipped the scales at forty-two pounds. This is the biggest fish caught along this section of the New-Jersey coast for several years.

This week also the cottagers and hotel guests have been having merry times at their crabbing parties on Shark River. The student of human nature can spend several hours in watching these parties and studying the reasons why they use different kinds of bait by which to lure the toothsome shell-fish up to the top of the water, where he can be scientifically scooped up with a hand net. The summer visitors from each section of the country have their favorite bait. Those who register from Boston use skinned heads of sheep. The average Jerseyman is fond of using "job-lots" of beef, and the older the meat the better he likes it. The people from Baltimore use oysters and hard-shelled clams. It is a big task to convince any one from Chicago that the New-Jersey crab has such depraved tastes that it will prefer anything to pork, and pretty maidens and their young admirers from that city serenely bob for crabs with lines attached to the jaw-bones or spare-ribs of defunct porkers, as they sit side by side and hand in hand in the boats that rock to and fro in the channel. The people hailing from the West insist upon using pieces of liver, but when a girl from Omaha said to her lover, while they were out crabbing together yesterday: "I would liver die with you," the young man, it is said, jumped overboard and was rescued with great difficulty. People from New-York use fish-heads, while the Southern guests prefer fish-tails. This week two ingenious young men came here on a crabbing trip. They were from a New-England State and they fooled the crabs with an artificial bait and caught a boat-load of them.

[List of names]

No. 122   LIGHTNING'S PRANKS AT ASBURY PARK

ASBURY PARK, July 5 (Special).—The lightning played a number of pranks here last night during the heavy storm which began about 9:30 o'clock. A bolt struck an electric-light wire at the junction of Cookman and Asbury aves. and Kingsley-st., severing the wire and throwing it down into the street. John Robbins, of West Asbury Park, was caught by the wire and dragged for a distance of fifty feet. He was badly cut and bruised. Several women and children accidentally stepped upon the wire and were knocked down. They created intense excitement by screaming "Murder." A ball of fire flew from the wires to the porch of the Oriental Hotel, to the great alarm of the guests who were seated there watching the storm. Dr. Wildman, of New-York, who was on the porch, was struck in the face and slightly burned. The lightning followed the telephone wires into a number of cottages and burned the instruments out. Great alarm was caused by the big balls of red, white, blue and green colors which danced and sputtered about the telephone boxes. Several persons who were standing near the telephones were severely shocked. The lightning also ran over the wires into the offices of the Western Union Telegraph Company and gave heavy shocks to the operators. A young summer visitor to Ocean Grove named Spencer received a terrible shock while trying to board an electric car at Cookman-ave. and Bond-st. The injured persons had their injuries dressed at drug-stores and were sent home in stages. A heavy current ran on the fishing pier of James A. Bradley, the founder of the town, and gave paralyzing shocks to a number of persons.

Francis Ashworth, the engineer of the Sea Shore Electric Railway, received a shock yesterday afternoon while oiling one of the dynamos at the power station of the road. The shock was so severe that he was hurled upon his head on the floor. His hands were both burned to the bone.

No. 123 GUESTS AT AVON-BY-THE-SEA

AVON-BY-THE-SEA, N.J., July 6 (Special).—One of the prettiest sheets of water in New-Jersey is Shark River, between Avon-by-the-Sea and Belmar. It is one of the best fishing and crabbing places along the coast. There are a number of romantic stories told about the time when the noble redman wooed his dusky mate in the pine woods which skirt the water. Now the lake is daily the Mecca of hundreds of young lovers, who tie fishtails to strings and tell of their love as they and their charmers bob for crabs. A roadway is to be laid out around the water. It will make a fine drive.

The hotels are crowded with guests. Hops are held nightly to the great enjoyment of the younger guests.

[List of names]

No. 124 THRONGS AT ASBURY PARK

ASBURY PARK, N.J., July 12 (Special).—The hotels here are crowded with summer guests and the hotel proprietors look happy and contented. This afternoon the late comers had considerable difficulty in securing rooms. Judging by the immense number of arrivals and the demands for rooms sent by mail and wire this season will be an unusually prosperous one. There are not over twenty cottages left unrented. The rentals are about the same as last year.

James A. Bradley, the founder of Asbury Park, is one of the most energetic men in the State. He rises at daylight and works almost every night until after midnight. He personally supervises all his property here, and keeps a close watch upon his brush manufacturing establishment in New-York.

The Seashore Electric Railroad is slowly laying its second track through Kingsley-st. To-day passengers had to walk over a block from one car to another because of the idiotic manner in which the work is being performed. Nearly all of the cars are worn out and the stuffy box cars originally designed for winter use have been again brought into service.

The Ocean Plaza which extends along the beach from Deal Lake south through Asbury Park and Ocean Grove to Fletcher Lake was crowded with people this evening. Every seat on the Plaza, the pavilions and the piers was occupied.

Ralph's Coleman House, the Ocean, West End, Metropolitan, Oriental, Grand Avenue, Brunswick, Colonnade, St. James, Atalanta, Laurel and Albion hotels and Sunset Hall held their regular weekly hops this evening.

The city maidens and their gallant attendants have blossomed out in blazer jackets with caps to match which make them look like huge potato bugs.

Ralph's Coleman House flies an unique flag from the staff on the roof. The coat of arms of New-Jersey is shown in the centre of the blue union with forty-two stars grouped around it.

Founder Bradley has offered another set of prizes for the largest catches of fish made from his fishing pier, and the structure is crowded daily with men and women anglers.

Bond's Wave Power machine, which uses "Old Neptune's"

rollers to force salt water into the street sprinkling pipes of Ocean Grove, is an object of considerable interest to the hotel guests and cottagers.

The Salvation Army comes here to-morrow to hold services in Bradley's beach pavilion at the foot of Fifth-ave. The organization is reaping a harvest of dollars here while some of the churches are sadly in need of ready funds.

Frederick E. Walton, of New-York, has purchased a fine lot at Interlaken at the head of Deal Lake, and will erect a large cottage.

Mr. Bradley has had a Sunday flag made. It will be displayed on Sundays only from the pavilion at the foot of Asbury-ave. It bears the words "Peace on earth; good-will toward men."

Several persons who foolishly left their valuables in their bathing houses, have been robbed.

There are three yachts here that take merry parties out to sea on fishing and sailing trips.

Water polo is a new game here. It is played in the ocean with a big rubber ball, resembling a football. Goals are made with it as in polo. The Asbury Park team was defeated yesterday by a team from Ocean Grove.

[List of names]

No. 125   HIGH TIDE AT OCEAN GROVE

OCEAN GROVE, N.J., July 18 (Special).—The flannel shirt is a sine qua non at Ocean Grove. In the early days of the place it was a blue flannel affair most probably home-made, and often of the bathing-suit variety of flannel, twilled, thick and clumsy. That was in the remote past when the boys (and girls too) often went barefooted and conventionalities were few. The blue shirt gave way to a series of dark colors and the youngsters rejoiced in a new style, but still dark. Browns of various hues and maroons were the favorite colors. In the course of this evolution about ten years ago appeared the various shades of butternut and olive green. These toned down to lighter shades and more dainty material, until at last the flannel shirt is a thing of beauty and may be a joy for a hot day. The delicate silken fabrics that are affected as a substitute must be very pleasant to wear.

It took the Rev. Mr. Yatman, the popular leader of the Young People's Meeting, to find in the flannel shirt a means of grace. He noticed the absence of young men and boys from the meeting. Making inquiry among the girls for their brothers, he was informed that the boys did not want to "dress up" to come to the meeting. On the Pauline plan of being all things to all men (and some boys), he forthwith bought a light flannel shirt, and donning that with his blue coat and trousers went to the meeting. At the close he sent word to the boys to come, flannel shirts and all. The next morning there were 200 more boys than had been wont to attend.

[Personal news]

No. 126   THE BABIES ON PARADE AT ASBURY PARK

ASBURY PARK, N.J., July 21 (Special).—The most unique parade ever known here since the time when Asbury Park was a howling wilderness and the Indians marched in single file through the woods was seen this afternoon on the famous board walk of James A. Bradley, the founder of the town. It was a baby show on wheels. About 200 mothers and nurses wheeled babies in their little carriages in single file from the foot of Wesley Lake up the board walk to the big pavilion at the foot of Fifth-ave., and back again. The famous band from the United States steamship *Trenton* led the procession, under the general direction of Mr. Bradley, who acted as the godfather of all the youngsters. There were all kinds of babies. The little wagons were decorated with silk and satin flags, streamers and Japanese lanterns. Two Armenians carried a silk hammock hanging from bamboo poles on their shoulders, in which were Armenian twins. Several other carriages contained twins. Only one baby cried. The rest sucked their thumbs in great contentment, or cooed and smiled at the spectators and waved their rattles and other toys when the procession was applauded. The chief of police, Mr. Bailey, conceived the idea of the parade. It was witnessed by at least 15,000 people, and is to be repeated.

No. 127 "PINAFORE" AT ASBURY PARK

ASBURY PARK, Aug. 16 (Special).—The business of the hotels at this place was never better than it is this season, and in consequence the hotel-keepers are happy. The principal houses are all full, and visitors have been unable to get accommodations at some of them. The Coleman House has had all its rooms engaged for some weeks ahead, and the managers say that the house will have a full complement of guests until the end of the season. The West End Hotel is also doing the largest business of any season since it was opened, and in order to get rooms it is necessary to engage them ahead. All the other hotels are doing well. The crowds of people on the beach are greater than ever, and the electric railroad has been unable to accommodate all the traffic. Several times during the past week the cars stopped running, owing to breaks in the wires, and the people had to walk from the railroad depot to the shore, or patronize dilapidated stages. The railroad may last the balance of the season without falling to pieces. The electricity has a habit of going astray, but fortunately no one has yet been hurt by it. Many women have been badly scared by the big balls of blue and green light which dance about the front of the car when the wires get out of order.

The popular old opera "Pinafore" was given here twice this week in the new Casino of Founder James A. Bradley, at the foot of Sixth-ave., by well-known amateurs selected from the cottagers and hotel guests. The principal characters were taken by the Misses Sadie Ramsey, Lillian Ely and Maggie Neely, and Messrs. E. L. O'Connor, William S. Miller, Frank Watson, P. S. Flynn and William Taylor. The proceeds went to the payment of the band on the beach.

A concert was given here Thursday night in Educational Hall for the benefit of George W. O'Brien, who was for some years the police officer at North Asbury Park. He is now suffering from cancer of the face.

The Rev. F. C. Colby, the pastor of the Baptist Church, on Wednesday evening united in marriage William Riddell, the manager of the Dun Mercantile Agency in Washington, and Miss Jennie E. Griffith, of Brandon, Vt.

Several baseball nines have been organized here by the summer guests.

The surf has run unusually high this week, and a number of foolhardy persons who went bathing at the wrong hour have narrowly escaped drowning.

A number of petty robberies have occurred in Ocean Grove, in cases where cottages and tents have been left without caretakers.

A new fad here is elephant parties. The sport consists of trying to pin a tusk upon the picture of an elephant while blindfolded.

Hecker, the flour man, has opened a store on Kingsley-st. where his men give away daily several thousand pancakes. No goods are sold, and the store is crowded all day by women and girls, who eat sugared pancakes from paper plates.

This is the height of the excursion season, and the trains are long and the cars heavily packed.

[List of names]

No. 128 ASBURY PARK

ASBURY PARK, Aug. 23 (Special).—The opening of the Ocean Grove camp-meeting this week has been the means of attracting large crowds to this town, and the good people from all parts of the country have been shocked to find that rum-selling was a thriving business in this supposedly staid prohibition town. The arrest of the violators of the law has been as much talked about as the attractions at the Ocean Grove meeting-grounds. The principal offender's place of business was near the main artery of traffic between this town and the Grove, which is only separated from Asbury Park by a small lake a few hundred feet wide. As the poker players rattled the "chips," they could hear the sound from 5,000 throats singing the doxology. The founder of the town always goes away before the period of raids begins. He is now on his way to Europe. He sailed last Tuesday, and on Wednesday the first raid was made. They have been continued every night since that time.

Business at the hotels has been good, and many of the more

popular places have had to utilize their stock of cots on several occasions. Entertainments and balls have been given nightly at all the large hotels during last week. On Thursday night, during the heavy storm, there were hops at Ralph's Coleman House, the West End Hotel, the Oriental, Sunset Hall, the Ocean Hotel, Norwood Hall, the Colonnade, the Metropolitan Hotel and other large houses. There were also a number of progressive whist and euchre parties. At some of the houses the guests, while blindfolded, tried to pin tusks on elephants and tails on donkeys made of cloth, or engaged in the festive amusement of hunting the slippery button or firing the bean-bag at each other.

The Sea Shore Electric Railway Company's cars were badly demoralized by the heavy rainstorm of Thursday night. Some of the cars broke down, and their passengers were compelled to wade through mud in the pelting rain to other cars. Almost the entire equipment of the road is worn out. The officers of the road refuse to run their cars on Sunday, on the ground that they are opposed to violations of the Lord's Day. The truth of the matter is, that Sunday is the repair day of the line, and if the cars ran seven days a week there would be great danger of a complete collapse of the system. The company is now using a current which throws out big balls of colored fire whenever the "trolleys" strike the irons which support the cross wires of the overhead system which carries the current. While the employees of the company persist in telling the passengers that the current is harmless, yet they are much afraid of coming into contact with it, and the wires running from the "trolleys" to the cars are incased in thick rubber hose. When the wires break and fall into the street the ends snap and sizzle like the wires of an electric light company and throw out big showers of sparks. The men on wet days wear rubber boots and gloves, and it is no uncommon thing for a passenger to declare: "I felt a shock." The electricity has an unpleasant habit of meandering around the ironwork of the car. The conductors have been heard to say on these occasions: "Don't touch the guard-rail."

Fishing parties composed of pretty girls and gallant admirers are the order of the day at Barnegat Bay. Bluefish are running well, as are also bass. Big catches are being made every day.

[List of names]

No. 129 ASBURY PARK'S BIG BROAD WALK

ASBURY PARK, Aug. 30 (Special).—This has been the best season the Asbury Park hotel men have known in five years or more. The hotels have been packed with guests the entire season. The big board walk of James A. Bradley, the founder of the town, has been crowded every day and far into the night with the cottagers and hotel guests. The number of persons who take their daily promenade on the ocean plaza surpasses belief. This week the crowd has numbered at least twenty thousand persons every evening. The walk is from twenty to seventy feet wide. Two broad streams of people pass each other night and day upon the walk. A hotel guest or cottager who is looking for his or her friend goes down to the ocean front and waits until the one they are looking for comes along. All sorts and conditions of men are to be seen on the board walk. There is the sharp, keen-looking New-York business man, the long and lank Jersey farmer, the dark-skinned sons of India, the self-possessed Chinaman, the black-haired Southerner and the man with the big hat from "the wild and woolly plains" of the West. Here all find a genial and pleasant summer home. The Chinaman works all day long at his washtub, and at night goes down to the beach and jabbers with "Charlie Young" or "Ja Huah" on the beauties of living in America; the Hindoo comes to the beach to talk with his fellow-countrymen over the big profits he makes on rare pieces of lace manufactured in New-York; the stock brokers gather in little groups on the broad plaza and discuss the prospective rise and fall of stocks; the pretty girl, resplendent in her finest gown, walks up and down within a few feet of the surging billows and chatters away with the college youth, who wears "old mater's" colors in his blazer jacket and cap, or else sits hand in hand with her "own dear one" in a pavilion, and they two, "the world forgetting and by the world forgot," chew gum together in time to the beating of the waves upon the sandy beach. The beach plaza is the chief attraction of the Park, and so no one is surprised at the number of babies here. The youngsters are wheeled up and down the walk by comely maids with quaint little French caps. The little ones coo at the waves, dig in the sand, and when tired are lulled to sleep by old Neptune's roars on a sandy bed.

The hotel proprietors are frightened over the move made against the illegal liquor sellers. So far, with but one exception, all have escaped arrest. It is known beyond all possible question that wines and liquors can be obtained at the largest hotels, but the town authorities lack the necessary amount of backbone to prosecute them. The annual farce of arresting the druggists is being played daily, but the hotel men go free. The authorities have made no move to close the two gambling dens which exist in the town and they will no doubt remain open until the close of the season. Jersey justice here means persecution and not prosecution.

[List of names]

No. 130   IMPROVEMENTS AT OCEAN GROVE

OCEAN GROVE, N.J., June 9 (Special).—With the assistance of the beautiful spring-time, this Methodist Mecca is being adorned with all that nature and art can bring to brighten and beautify it.

Cottages and hotels are being enlarged and made bright with paint and paper, and refurnished in the finest style of decorative art.

The Campmeeting Association, not to be outdone by the people, have laid thousands of feet of concrete walks. New gates have been put up at the Main-st. entrance. These are painted green, with golden tips. On each side new concrete walks improve the entrance, while electric lights seem to say: "This is the way to rest and peace, walk ye in."

An iron pier, 500 feet long, 16 feet wide at the shore end, and widening out in the ocean to 32 feet, has been built by the Richmond Brothers, of Dupont, N.J., and is pronounced by experts to be constructed in the best possible manner.

The plank walk from Ross's Pavilion to Ocean Pathway has been widened to thirty-two feet, and built on new piling, placed so close together that an underview makes one think of the multitudinous tree trunks of a dense forest. Within the walk the ground has been filled in, graded and sloped landward, and is covered with a thrifty sodding of grass. It is hoped that this will prevent the washouts and gullies which used to occur in that vicinity.

The electric light plant has been increased and has been put in the best condition. The fishing pier will be well lighted.

There is considerable activity among real estate men in vieing with one another in their efforts to secure rentals.

[Personal news]

No. 131   LIGHTNING ON THE JERSEY COAST

ASBURY PARK, N.J., June 12 (Special).—A heavy electrical and rain storm visited the upper section of the New-Jersey coast this afternoon. The rain fell in torrents, washing out the streets, undermining many of the sidewalks and destroying the flower-beds of the summer cottages and hotels. A bolt struck the cottage of Dr. David S. Skinner, of Brooklyn, on the southwest corner of Seventh-ave. and Emery-st. Mrs. Skinner, her little daughter and her son were seated on the front porch, watching the lightning, when the house was struck. Madeline, the daughter, was partially stunned by the shock. The bolt ripped the walls in its passage through four bedrooms, throwing the plaster over the beds and floors. A picture hung on the walls where the bolt entered the house. The picture was shattered. The bolt tore open the blinds of a window and turning at right angles ran across Emery-st. over a dead wire into the kitchen of the cottage of Abram T. Lake, a contractor. It shivered timbers, punched a lot of holes in the walls and ceiling and then passed out on the east side and tore away a corner of the porch of the cottage of August L. Seighortner, slightly shocking Mrs. Seighortner and her servant. It will cost over $1,000 to repair Dr. Skinner's cottage. A ball of lightning ran along the wires of the Seashore Electric Railway in Kingsley-st. When it reached the trolley of a car it ran down the wires, burning them off. Another bolt ran into the office of the telephone company, fusing the brass and burning out the wires. A cottage in Fifth-ave. in the rear of Sunset Hall was struck and slightly damaged. Cusack's pharmacy in Mattison-ave. was flooded with water.

The storm was severe at Long Branch. The face of the bluff of Ocean-ave. was badly washed.

No. 132   ARRIVING AT OCEAN GROVE

OCEAN GROVE, June 28 (Special).—Great train-loads of pleasure-seekers and religious worshippers are arriving at the huge double railway station of Ocean Grove and Asbury Park. The beach, the avenues and the shaded lawns are once more covered with the bright-hued garments of the summer throng. The "old-timers," evading the crowds of hackmen, take leisurely routes to their hotels, and gaze at the improvements and new buildings of the twin cities; the newcomer falls a victim to the rapacity of the hackmen because of his great astonishment at the vast length of platform, the huge pile of trunks, the wide roadways and the wriggling, howling mass of humanity which declares itself ready to take him to "any hotel or cottage" at a moderate charge. Having escaped with the connivance of one of these weary toilers after the dollar of the summer traveller, he forgets the turmoil of the station as he rides through the high Main-st. gates and obtains a view of a long, quiet avenue, shaded by waving maples, with a vision of blue sea in the distance.

All the hotels have nearly full registers, and the private cottages are being rented rapidly.

The mammoth excursions for which these two resorts are noted have already begun. Eighteen cars came from Lafayette, N.J., on Saturday.

The Fourth of July will be celebrated with the usual appropriate ceremonies at the Auditorium. Bells will ring and cannons will be fired at sunrise. At 10:30 a.m. the Declaration of Independence will be read by the Rev. John Handley, of Asbury Park. The Rev. D. B. Harris, of Ocean Grove, will deliver an oration. The choir will be under the leadership of Mrs. George

M. Bennet. As usual the association has forbidden the burning of any kind of fireworks except on the beach east of the board walk.

[Personal news]

No. 133   STATUARY AT ASBURY PARK

ASBURY PARK, N.J., July 4 (Special).—The bathing facilities on the beach have been greatly enlarged and two handsome new pavilions have been erected. Founder Bradley's penchant for statuary is greatly improving the appearance of the lawns directly in front of the board walk.

Mr. Bradley has rebuilt and improved the famous ocean plaza at a cost of over $30,000. In some places the promenade is over 100 feet wide and there is ample room for the summer visitors to take their walk and listen to the roar of the surf. The beach is crowded daily with infants in charge of nurses.

[Personal news]

No. 134   IMPROVEMENTS AT AVON-BY-THE-SEA

AVON-BY-THE-SEA, N.J., July 4 (Special).—Many improvements have been made along the beach and in the town this year. New cottages have been erected, hotels renovated, roads placed in fine condition and new walks laid down. The whole town has gone through a parallel to that institution of the New-England housewife familiarly known as "spring house-cleaning." Hotel proprietors confidently look forward to the most successful season they have ever had. Nearly every cottage has been rented. Edward Bachelor, of Philadelphia, the widely-known proprietor of Avon, has had over 3,000 piles driven along the Shark River front, to keep the rapid current from eating away the bank.

The bronzed and sturdy Captain Kittell will be on hand as usual this year to protect the bathers from any straying "sea-puss." The Captain has been at the bathing grounds for eight years, and during that time there has not been a single drowning accident here.

The Seaside Assembly opens with a greatly extended programme this year, which includes schools of biology, mathematics, political science, languages, American literature, Bible study and Sunday-school work, art, writing and music. The famous American Institute of Christian Philosophy also holds its midsummer session in connection with the Assembly.

The Assembly was incorporated to promote the general interests of education, and it is a model school for the young student who needs the balm-laden breezes from ocean and pine forest, as well as useful instruction. Also, the healthy young student who craves boat-riding, crabbing, fishing, driving, cycling, hotel hops and card parties always finds Avon a place after his heart. The Assembly was planned to promote the best interests of education.

[Personal news]

No. 135   ON THE BANKS OF SHARK RIVER

AVON-BY-THE-SEA, July 10 (Special).—The Rev. A. Armstrong, of this place, led the morning devotional exercises on the Seaside Assembly grounds. In the School of Art, Professor Conrad Diehl, of New-York, lectured upon the elements of form, Madame Alberti, in the School of Expression, taught the correct use of the muscles of the arm and wrist. In the kindergarten the children were engaged in painting small flags of all nations, placing them upon ships and sailing these ships from imaginary ports, laden with imaginary products. The object was to impress geographical positions upon the mind of the child. The pupils of Madame Alberti have been rehearsing the Greek play "Electra," which is to be given in August.

The guests at this resort are delighted with the natural beauty of the surrounding country. Parties from the hotels go on long pedestrian tours along the banks of Shark River, and create havoc among the blithesome crabs and the festive oysters. Sketching parties from the Art School of the Seaside

Assembly also love the banks of the river, and they can be seen on fine afternoons painting industriously, while their white umbrellas keep off the rays of the sun and give the party the appearance of a bunch of extraordinary mushrooms.

The bass fishermen are out in force this year. A large group of them stand at the mouth of Shark River, dressed in oilskins, with the waves whirling around their booted legs. Symptoms of violent but partially suppressed excitement on the part of one of the fishermen, a sudden tightening of his line, and all eyes are turned in his direction. Amid ejaculations from the summer throng and while the fish throws little jets of foam into the air, the fisherman displays all his science and knowledge of the art, and finally with heroic tugs lands a huge wriggling fish. He occupies a prominent place, and the crowd watch him closely. The other fishermen standing with their pipes in their mouths watch their neighbor with jealous eyes as the crowd gaze at him and make admiring remarks. Suddenly a fisherman some distance up the beach shows the invariable symptoms which precede a catch. The crowd rush in the direction of the lucky one, and the first popular idol is left alone with his pipe and his boots.

On the Seaside Assembly grounds appearances proclaim a prosperous session. The number of students has never been larger than at present. All the schools are having great success.

The Rev. George C. Maddock, of Trenton, N.J., the president of the assembly, is a well-known clergyman of the Methodist Episcopal Church. He has been stationed in all the principal towns of Monmouth County as well as in important districts in the northern part of the State. He is popular as president, because of his sound sense and practical views of life.

Miss Carrie Maude Pennock, the New-York soprano soloist, is pleasing the assembly audiences with her voice.

The corps of instructors of the School of Biology have been busy this week unpacking their cases of supplies. By next Monday they expect to have their equipments in readiness. Shark River is pronounced admirable with its shallow water and sandy bottom, on which the forms of marine life can easily be seen.

The faculty of the School of Art have made the announcement that the general course in art is open to all special students under any of the teachers of the school. This course is intended to familiarize the student with the essential elements and vital principles of beauty, with form reasoning, historical styles and decorative design; also to cultivate intelligent observation of the native forms and colors appropriate to original application and composition. The analysis of elements and principles is accompanied by black-board and stereopticon illustrations. These lectures of the general course occupy the teachers, in regular rotation at 9 a.m. daily. The course will also include a series of lectures by Professor John Ward Stimson, the dean of the school and the superintendent of the New-York Institute for Artist-Artisans. He will lecture on fundamental forms and principles, on nature's art methods and on ancient, mediaeval and modern art. The last three subjects will be lectured upon in the auditorium in July.

Lester Shaffner, the New-York fencing expert, who has lectured here in Madame Alberti's School of Expression, has taught Assembly audiences many facts about the manner of fighting with swords from the fifteenth century to the present day. He has made a study of the use of this weapon and has learned the Italian, French and Spanish modes of fighting. He says that the duels and other combats on the stage are mere nonsense as to methods.

[List of names]

No. 136   ALL OPEN IN SPITE OF MR. BRADLEY

ASBURY PARK, N.J., July 19 (Special).—James A. Bradley, who founded and still owns the greater part of Asbury, was considerably troubled in mind to-day caused by doubt as to the result of his Sunday closing order. As president of the Board of Commissioners, he issued strict orders yesterday requiring all places of business, including barber-shops and cigar stores, to be closed to-day. Chief of Police Bailey instructed his men to see that no back doors were open. This injunction was entirely unnecessary for, despite Mr. Bradley's written orders, and the strict survelliance of the police, the front doors of the drug and cigar stores and restaurants were kept open as usual, and business was carried on without any attempt at concealment. There will doubtless be a large crop of arrests to-morrow. The druggists and cigar dealers say they are determined to make a fight.

No. 137 THE SEASIDE ASSEMBLY (I)

AVON-BY-THE-SEA, N.J., July 25 (Special).—The Seaside Assembly here is enjoying its most successful season. It has been most fortunate in the choice of its officers and directors. The projectors saw at the start that, though they needed enthusiasts and specialists in the several departments, these were not the men to manage the affairs. The result was that they elected an executive board of practical business men. The School of Art is one of the most interesting departments of the assembly. It occupies Otis Hall. The interior of the building is decorated with many sketches and paintings done by the teachers and pupils, and with plaster casts and wood-carvings. Wild flowers and grasses are always about in great profusion. Every evening the room is thrown open to the public and a crowd is always ready to come in and admire the work.

John Ward Stimson, the dean of the school, is well-known as the foremost exponent of industrial art in America. He is a quick, nervous man with eyes that never rest. He is always talking about the artist-artisan. His views radiate from him at all times. He is the pioneer and leader in the movement and his whole life is given to it. At his lectures one is at once struck by his deep earnestness and sincerity. He was born in Paterson, N.J., in 1850. The books he used while attending school there show the early development of his talent. Every available space in them is covered with all manner of drawings done in lead-pencil. He entered the class of 1872 at Yale. After graduation he went to Paris and studied under Cabanel at the Beaux-Arts. While there he received a medal from the French Government for draughtsmanship. He stayed six years in the French capital and then travelled extensively through Europe, studying in the old galleries of Italy and observing the art of all countries. He then came to New-York, where he made illustrations for magazines and painted for the exhibitions. He was called to Princeton College to take charge of the art department there. He left there to become the head of the school of the Metropolitan Museum of Art and finally founded the New-York Institute for Artist-Artisans. Professor Stimson was democratic in his belief. He did not see why art should be merely the fad of the aristocracy. His ambition is to develop a National art that will give the country what it greatly needs, and with this, aided by the inventive genius and brain of America, place her far ahead of her European rivals in the industrial arts.

Professor Conrad Rossi Diehl, of New-York, is a professor in the School of Art. He is an artist of note. Personally, he is a man of remarkable strength of character. He has a kindly blue eye, and like all great men in all professions, is simple and honest in his daily life. His dominant aim is truth and exactness in all that he undertakes. He was born near Landau, in Bavaria, in 1842. He had a fancy for drawing from earliest childhood. His father, being a leader in the revolution of 1848, was condemned to death and his estates were confiscated. He was compelled to seek refuge with his family in America. He settled on a farm in Illinois. Louis Schmolze, a historical painter of note, who was also a fugitive of the revolution, was a friend of the family and took a great interest in the child. The boy desired to emulate this artist in the painting of historical scenes. In 1851 he went to Philadelphia to attend public school. John Sartain, the president of the Philadelphia Academy of Fine Arts, accidentally discovered the talents of young Diehl and persuaded him to enter the evening classes of that institution. Leaving the Quaker City he went to Buffalo, and became an apprentice in a lithographing establishment. He also worked at this trade in Chicago. He became a decorator and designer. At the age of fifteen he did all the fresco painting in the new home of Governor Mattison, at Springfield, Ill. On the occasion of a Fourth of July celebration this mere boy painted a transparency larger than any picture he had ever seen, allegorically representing America and Germany joining in a celebration of the National holiday. This crude work created such a stir in St. Louis that his father finally decided to send him to Europe to study art. As Kaulbach was the boy's ideal, he went to Munich, and although Kaulbach tried to dissuade him from entering upon art as a profession, in less than three months he took him under his immediate charge, although he had not had a pupil for twenty years.

What Professor Diehl considers his greatest piece of good fortune was that he became a pupil of Philip Foltz, the bulwark of the Munich School, in whose composition class Diehl painted his first picture, "Hamlet." He came to America with his picture and placed it upon exhibition in the Darby Gallery in New-York, where it had an enthusiastic reception. From New-York he took his picture to Chicago, where he made it a free gift to the public as the nucleus of a city collection. At the instance of George P. A. Healy, the portrait painter, a fund was raised sufficient to defray the expense of two years' study for the young man in Paris. He attended Gérôme's atelier in the Beaux-Arts, where he painted his picture "Macbeth." This picture he also brought to Chicago. Soon after his arrival he painted three panels illustrating the life of St. Francis, in the church of that name in Chicago.

When the great fire broke out he rushed to the academy, and finding no other way to save his picture cut it from its frame and carried it through the burning city to a place of safety. He went with it to St. Louis, where an art society was forming. This society formed an art school, over which he presided. Through the influence of William T. Harris, at that time superintendent of public schools of St. Louis, who is now the head of the National Bureau of Education, the great artist's attainments were utilized in the public schools of the city. Here he developed his well-known grammar of form, language and art, which was further matured in Columbia, Mo., where he occupied the chair of art in the State University for six years. He then came to New-York, where he has been the co-worker of John Ward Stimson in building up an American art school in the true sense of the word. During his leisure hours he has painted a picture entitled "Love and Labor," modelled a statuette representing a floating figure of Christ, and worked out the plans for this new departure in form, study and art education.

Madam S. E. Le Prince is the head of the outdoor sketching and landscape painting department of the art school. She began her studies in South Kensington, England. She also studied the French methods of art instruction. She opened her first technical art school in Leeds, England. The work of the school and its branches in other cities excited great interest and gained many medals and certificates in both local and international exhibitions. Encouraged by her great success and knowing the great field for her work in America, Madame Le Prince came to New-York, where she organized the successful art department of the New-York Institute for the Deaf and Dumb. In connection with the New-York Society of Decorative Art, Madame Le Prince has directed classes for tapestry and lincrusta decorations. At the college for the training of teachers she has taught modelling and drawing. In her studio, in the historic Jumel mansion on Washington Heights, she designs for textiles and ceramics.

The kindergarten is in charge of Miss Marie Le Prince and Miss Aimee Le Prince, of New-York. This department is of great interest to grown folks as well as the children. Many of the parents and friends of the pupils come and watch them in their work on the huge sand-pile back of the kindergarten tent. This sand heap has as varied an existence as a soldier of fortune. One morning it will take the part of a city, with streets, houses and inhabitants; next it will be a desert island, with a clay Robinson Crusoe and a charcoal Man Friday. It will suddenly become a farm with garden-patches and hay fields, or an assembly grounds with an auditorium and numerous halls. The children are happy in kindergarten hours. The plan was made with regard for the season, the locality and fluctuating number of pupils. Each week of their work is a distinct link without disturbing the sequence of the whole course.

[Personal news]

No. 138   A BABY PARADE ON THE BOARD WALK

ASBURY PARK, Aug. 3 (Special).—Once or twice a year Founder Bradley and President Stokes come down from their perches, as it were, and atone in a measure for their ironclad actions. Yesterday was one of these times, and one of the most unique attractions on the entire Jersey coast was allowed to come off. It was a baby-parade, and for two hours the board walk running between Ocean Grove and Asbury Park was crowded with well-dressed babies, reclining comfortably in handsomely decorated carriages. The hour for the start was 2 o'clock, but long before that time the walk began to fill with spectators and with anxious mammas and proud papas who were intent upon securing a good place in the line and sure, of course, that their baby would get first prize. At 2 o'clock sharp the pavilion band began the march, and at this signal 300 baby-carriages were started on their way down the board walk. Besides this there was nearly 100 little toddlers, all under the age of five years, who walked two-by-two, hand-in-hand, like tasty viands sandwiched between the carriages. At the head of the line stood two of the members of the committee and into each carriage was thrown a pound box of mixed candies. One careless nurse forgot to relieve her infant in charge of his candy and he succeeded in opening it. When discovered he had smeared the contents over his face, and had so decorated his gown that he was taken from the parade in disgrace. Pleasant-faced mammas propelled some carriages while proud papas nobly took charge of others.

One of the most unique outfits was that of a miniature ship of the desert, made of pink canvas. In it rode three-year-old Frankie Force, as happy as a king. Miss Hortense Bohannan wore a pretty wreath of clover blossoms and reclined gracefully in her carriage amid a bed of clover, ferns and ivy. Blanche Sherman Boardman will soon be three months old. She was carried all through the parade in a clothes-basket lined with pink cheese cloth. Two-year-old Sylvia Truax was bedecked with wreaths of golden rod. The carriage was also prettily decorated with the same flowers. Elmer Clark is one year old. On the carriage in which she rode were seventy-five tiny lanterns and twenty-three parasols, covering wheels and all. Alice Beach Watkins attracted much attention in a carriage that was built like a fairy bower of roses, water-lilies and ferns.

No. 139   THE GUESTS ROSE TO THE OCCASION

AVON-BY-THE-SEA, Aug. 11 (Special).—Consternation reigned in the hearts of the 250 guests of the Norwood Inn here this morning. The servants of the hotel deserted their posts in a body immediately after breakfast. All the hotels in town were comfortably full, and upon the disappearance of the help the guests knew not where to go. They congregated on the porch and discussed their position. Persons connected with the house departed in every direction to look for help. The crowds on the porches became ravenous. At last a bright young man had an idea. He proposed to become a waiter himself for the time being. His speech was greeted with cheers. Other young men agreed to wait on the tables, and a corps of amateur cooks was also formed to assist the professional in the kitchen. These volunteers disappeared in the direction of the dining-room and the kitchen.

The reappearance of a volunteer waiter with a tray was the signal for applause. The other waiters entered with smiles upon their faces and napkins over their arms. A menu had been prepared which was a model of good penmanship and frankness. After the word "Coffee" came the significant N.B.: "We haven't much milk." "We are short of bread and go slow on the butter." By this time everybody was good-natured and thoroughly enjoyed the mishaps and antics of the amateur waiters. The young ladies at last decided that they, too, would do something for the commonwealth. As the men had served the dinner the women agreed to serve the supper. A code of rules was adopted for the occasion, prominent among which appeared: "Guests will not pay too much attention to the waitress."

In the evening the guests held a jubilee, and every one decided that they had spent a most happy day. The landlady smiled once more.

The runners who were dispatched after servants have been heard from, and it is hoped a new collection of assistants will occupy the servants' hall by to-morrow afternoon.

No. 140   ART AT AVON-BY-THE-SEA

AVON-BY-THE-SEA, Aug. 15 (Special).—Two bright women are at the head of two of the most popular departments here. They are Madame Alberti, of the School of Expression, and Madame S. E. Le Prince, of the School of Art. Madame Alberti is well known as one of New-York's leading teachers of Delsarte. Besides her large school in New-York, she has classes in Philadelphia and in many towns between the two cities. She has given a series of popular entertainments here this season. They have been attended thus far by the largest audiences ever seen on the Assembly grounds. The School of Expression is the Mecca of the awkward girl who wishes to become graceful, the stout girl who wishes to become thin, the thin girl who wishes to become stout, the graceful girl who wishes to become more graceful. In fact, every kind of girl who wishes to become some other description of girl joins this school. But of course the largest number of pupils come for healthful exercise and physical improvement. For one of Madame Alberti's entertainments given here this week every seat in the auditorium was taken long before the evening. Her pupils who took part gave abundant proof of the benefits of her training. The Grecian dance was the special feature.

[Names of participants]

Madame S. E. Le Prince holds undisputed sway in the art department. She, too, is a well-known New-York teacher. Upon her arrival from Europe she began teaching in New-York. She is now connected with the New-York Institute for Artist-Artisans. In china painting, ceramic and textile work Madame Le Prince excels. Her classes are enthusiastic and work industriously.

Otis Hall, the art building, is the most pleasantly located building upon the grounds. It is always cool and shady. It is, perhaps, a building whose interior could never seem heated on a warm day because of the soft harmony and beauty of the decorations. The work of the students is placed upon the walls, with a large number of plaster casts and other artistic ornaments brought from the School for Artist-Artisans in New-York.

[Personal news]

No. 141   FLOWERS AT ASBURY PARK

ASBURY PARK, June 18 (Special).—The beautiful trees that line the streets here are now covered with heavy foliage and the flowers are in full bloom. There is no place on the coast, with the exception of Elberon, where there are such elaborate floral displays seen during the entire season as they have here. For several blocks in many of the avenues, the hotel and cottage lawns are nearly hidden from sight by masses of blossoms of all hues and by valuable shrubbery. Many of the plants are imported by the property owners. The hotels and cottages too have put on their new summer coats of gay paint and their windows glisten. Asbury Park is a city of cottages, and contains summer homes of all styles of architecture, from costly structures of the most exaggerated Queen Anne style, with shingled sides and stained glass windows, to plain little buildings with bay windows gay with many flowers. Every cottage has plenty of piazza room for the use of the inmates. Here the people gather and swing in comfortable hammocks or "take things easy" in huge rocking-chairs. All newcomers to this charming place are interested in the names of the cottages. The people have a perfect mania for naming their summer homes. A number of the names are remarkably appropriate, while as many more seem to the wayfarer to be decidedly incongruous. A pretty cottage in Grand-ave. is known as "Shady Dell," as a tall elm tree grows up through the front porch and throws a delightful shade over the house. A large white building is the White House; the Crystal Palace is a "study" in white and pink; the Canary Cottage is painted a dark brown; one cottage is called the K. C. D. C. Cottage; then there are numerous others named after the birth-places of the owners, after Presidents, horses, actors, actresses, States, and young women who are dear to the owners of the property.

The little park in the centre of Fourth-ave., near the ocean, is the pride of the people who live in that beautiful thoroughfare. It has large beds of flowers and shrubs, and a fountain that keeps the air cool all day. The idea of laying out the park originated with Messrs. Morgan and Parsons, of the Hotel Brunswick. They worked hard in securing this beauty spot and now other avenues are to have them.

The formal opening of the Lake Avenue Hotel was held this evening. The feature of the affair was the fine vocal and instrumental music. The parlors of the hotel and the cottage annex were filled with guests who danced until midnight. Cut flowers and fruits frozen in cakes of ice ornamented the supper tables. . . . Mrs. Nellie C. Van Nortwick, the artist, has arrived at the Lake Avenue Hotel, where she will spend the summer. She is a sister of Judge William Howe Crane, of Port Jervis, who tried to prevent the lynching of Lewis by the mob.

No. 142   A MULTITUDE OF GUESTS AT ASBURY PARK

ASBURY PARK, N.J., July 9 (Special).—James A. Bradley is happy. He no longer carries the title deed to the whole of Asbury Park in his inside pocket, but his paternal interest in the famous resort is not diminished in the least, and the reason for his present cheerful state of mind may be found in the fact that the season has opened with a rush that exceeds even Mr. Bradley's fondest expectations. Most of the hotels and cottages are already filled with guests, and the crowds on the beach and the wide ocean plaza are larger by far than they have ever been before at this time of the year.

[Two paragraphs of personal news]

James J. Corbett, the pugilist, who is preparing for his fight with John L. Sullivan in a handsome Loch Arbour cottage, is now down to hard training, and his admirers, who used to haunt his footsteps as he tramped the Asbury Park board walk in the evenings, are at present somewhat at a loss. However, the day at Loch Arbour could consist of one long reception, so far as requisite guests are concerned. Little knots of spectators stand about the handball court and the wrist machine and the pulley-weights and the punching-bag, and watch the big man exercise. He will be in perfect condition on September 3.

[Personal news]

No. 143 BABY PARADE AT ASBURY PARK

ASBURY PARK, July 30 (Special).—The annual baby parade, one of the unique and interesting features of the season at Asbury Park, was held this afternoon on the board walk along the ocean front. Elaborate preparations had been made, under the direction of Mayor James A. Bradley and Mrs. Helen A. Miles, the latter acting as general manager of the novel parade. Nearly 400 babies were in line. Among them were representatives of all parts of the country, as well as of several foreign countries. One of the features of the parade was a little four-months-old papoose named Runaway, which was carried along slung on the back of its mother, who rejoiced in the name of Gray Buffalo Robe. They are a part of the Indian party connected with "Pawnee Bill's" Wild West, now exhibiting here. The parade formed under cover of the Asbury-ave. pavilion, from which the babies were wheeled up the long walk to the Fifth-ave. pavilion and back again. Fully 20,000 people crowded every available inch of space along the line. The prettily decorated carriages were divided into six sections, headed by the Trenton warship band and a tiny four-year-old policeman in full uniform and brass buttons. The judges, who occupied an elevated pavilion erected for the occasion, were Mrs. Justus E. Ralph, of Asbury Park; Mrs. Julius Chambers and Mrs. Depew. There was a long list of prizes. Every baby in the parade received a souvenir box of candy from Founder James A. Bradley, and a nursing bottle and toys from several business houses. Mr. Bradley also gave a handsome baby carriage as a prize for the best decorated carriage in line. William C. Roberts, of New-York, gave a handsome gold watch for the youngest mother, and the local Grand Army post offered a large silk flag for the grandchild of a veteran registered first. The prize for the prettiest baby was awarded to a representative of Chicago, little Sylvia Wilde. Among the entries were two little daughters of Julian Ralph, the magazine writer. The Burke triplets, of Trenton, were in a two-seated pony carriage, presented to them by Mr. Bradley, and were escorted by a company of about thirty little boys in bathing suits.

No. 144   SUMMER ATHLETIC SPORTS AT ASBURY PARK

ASBURY PARK, N.J., July 30 (Special).—This famous resort is rapidly becoming a great athletic centre. Corbett is here with his retinue of trainers and supporters; Zimmerman, the world's greatest bicycle rider, is a member of the Asbury Park Wheelmen, and is now here, ready to begin active training for his fall races; and a number of other athletes are here in training for various events. The grounds of the Asbury Park Athletic Association are among the finest in this State, while the track is said to be the best half-mile bicycle track in the country. One of the most important bicycle meetings of the year will be held on these grounds on Thursday and Friday of next week. Zimmerman, Munger, Taxis and a long list of other crack riders will be among the contestants for the valuable prizes offered. The athletic grounds at Camp Wanamassa are completed and in daily use, as are also the large gymnasium and bowling alley. It is probable that a single-scull regatta on Deal Lake, between a number of the leading oarsmen of the country, will be among the attractions here next month. All of which emphasizes the remark concerning Asbury Park's growing importance as a summer athletic centre.

Pawnee Bill and his "historical Wild West" have been here throughout the week, and thousands have enjoyed their performances.

In spite, however, of all these athletic sports and circuses, Asbury Park is not entirely given over to frivolity. One of the features of the week has been the Christian Alliance, which is holding its first annual meeting at Educational Hall. It is the intention of Dr. Simpson and his associates to establish here an annual meeting similar in character to the famous Old Orchard Convention.

[Personal news]

No. 145 THE HEIGHT OF THE SEASON AT ASBURY PARK

ASBURY PARK, N.J., Aug. 13 (Special).—The past week has been the banner bathing week of the season. The weather has just driven the people into the surf, where the water has been of the right temperature. The bathing suits are getting pretty giddy again, and some fears have been expressed that another mandate against short sleeves and shorter skirts would be issued by the authorities. However, there have been no unseemly exhibitions, and the girls look charming in their neat and natty attire.

One of those drug stores that really exist for the sole purpose of selling liquors in this "no license" town was raided last Monday evening, and the proprietor, clerk and some dozen patrons were arrested. The affair caused no little excitement in town, and no small inconvenience to those unfortunate ones who were arrested to appear as witnesses. Some women, unhappily, were in the party, but were not put under arrest.

[Personal news]

News, Commentary, and Descriptions

FOR many centuries the interior of the great continent of Africa was unknown and unexplored. The countries bordering on the Mediterranean had contributed to the history of the civilized world. The entire coast of the continent was known to commerce and travel, but the vast tract of land lying between the Desert of Sahara and the colonized districts in the south was a place unexplored, a land about which fabulous tales of powerful empires, beautiful cities and immense wealth were told. The rivers, lakes and mountains were mysteries unsolved.

The first explorer who contributed largely to the science and the geography of Africa was David Livingstone, the English missionary. He gave thirty years of his life to missionary work in Africa. In his endeavor to christianize even the most remote tribes, he made many valuable discoveries. His last great undertaking was an effort to discover the sources of the Nile. For months nothing was heard of him. He was supposed to be wandering somewhere among the jungles of Central Africa, no one knew where. The people of every enlightened nation of the globe were troubled over his fate. Rumors of his death filtered out from tribe to tribe until they reached the coast. England, for whose benefit he had invaded the Dark Continent, made no attempt at a rescue, and had virtually given him up as dead.

While people and press were wondering over the fate of the aged explorer, James Gordon Bennett, the editor of the New York *Herald*, conceived the idea of sending an expedition to find Livingstone. In looking about for a man who had qualities to command such an expedition he decided on Henry M. Stanley, then a war correspondent of the *Herald* in Spain during the Carlist insurrection. He sent for Stanley and in a short interview informed him of his scheme. The substance and, in fact, nearly the sum of his directions was: "Go and find Livingstone."

A short and concise sentence, but it meant over a year of peril and privation, of suffering and toil for Stanley and those who followed on his great journey into the unknown.

In six months he found Livingstone a lonely white man in the middle of Africa, very ill; probably dying. Livingstone refused to return with Stanley, because *he knew* he was dying and chose to remain and try to finish his work among the negroes. In vain Stanley plead with him—he preferred to die at his post. And reluctantly, because without his friend, Stanley commenced his march toward the coast. A little way from the village where Livingstone resided they parted. One turned toward home, friends, and country, the other turned his face toward the heart of Africa—away from all he loved except his duty.

In due time Stanley reached the coast and afterwards Europe and America. His fame had gone before him, and he was everywhere welcomed with applause and congratulations. But he was not destined to enjoy the rest after labor, for Mr. Bennett again sent him to Africa: this time to explore the Victoria Nyanza and other inland lakes. This he successfully accomplished and returned by the way of the Congo river, making one of the most remarkable journeys ever known. Then from 1879 to 1884 he was occupied with his great Congo undertaking, the result of which was the establishment of an independent nation on the western coast.

After this had been accomplished, he returned to America hoping to spend the remainder of his life in less arduous labors, but again he was asked to go to the interior of Africa, to rescue the imperilled Emin Pacha. After many privations and the loss of many men he reached Emin, but here the same difficulty interposed itself as with Livingstone. Emin, the faithful, refused to return with Stanley and desert his native followers. But finally circumstances changing he was induced to return. Stanley and he arrived at Zanzibar in December, 1889. The geographical results of this expedition are of even more importance than the preceding ones. The features of the country are now located and described with certainty and precision. The success of all these expeditions seems to have resulted from Stanley's indomitable will and faith in a Supreme Power, who guided him through the forests and valleys of the great continent. His black followers became deeply attached to him, and he never forgot their love. Even when he was being feted and flattered by kings he could remember the many lonely graves, under the equatorial sun, of followers who had died by the way. In his descriptive letters to the New York *Herald* and other papers, he gives himself no credit for the success of his expedition. He ends his letter with the sentence: "Praise be to God forever and ever." Such was a fitting end to his first letter after a return from the perils of the jungles and glades of Africa.

His simplicity and modesty form a prominent part of his character. He who had lived in constant peril of the javelins and poisoned arrows of hostile tribes for months; who, with his little band, had fought battles every day for weeks, gives no eloquent description of his exploits to an admiring world. But from his simple description the world easily sees the tremendous obstacles he must have overcome, and instantly lionizes him, giving him a place among the great men of the earth, where he should ever rank not only as a great christian explorer, but as a great statesman and a great general.

No. 147   BASEBALL

AT LAST the long looked for and cherished season has arrived, that of base-ball. Perhaps no other event in our midst is responded to with so much vigor and hearty cheer as this favored sport; at least there is none that brings together our small community so quickly and promptly as does the notice of "Base-Ball to-day." And here on the ball field one meets representatives of all classes, but however different their station in life, the one thought is displayed by all, namely, victory for their favorite. The village dominie, who ordinarily is looked upon with awe and reverence, sinks gloomily behind the pall of favoritism on these occasions, and may be seen to complacently stand for more than an hour beside the worst boy of boarding school fame, and look admiringly upon his sin stained brow as he explains a new feature in the game. And, too, the sedate President loses his sedateness and may be frequently seen to go through "very peculiar motions" with his plug hat on very slight pretext.

A noticeable change has been made in our ball-team this year from last, and though the new men seem to be of better material, a lack of strength at the bat seems to be the prominent weak point. The important feature of thorough organization has been attended to, but a more dominant spirit of enterprise would greatly add to the support. Crane, catcher, was tendered the office of captain, but declining, Jones, 1st base, was elected captain.

The game with the Chathams on the 23d resulted in the first victory for H. R. I. in the series. The game was hotly contested, and was conceded, by all, to be the most exciting held on these grounds for some time. The score is as follows:

CHATHAMS.	R.	B.H.	P.O.	A.	E.
Gardner, C.	1	0	12	5	4
Beebe W. C., 1st	1	0	8	0	0
Beebe W. J., 2d	1	0	3	2	1
Slighter, S. S.	0	0	0	0	0
Smyth, P.	1	0	0	10	1
Rosberry, 3d	0	2	0	1	2
W. Woolbridge, C. F.	1	1	0	0	1
Pulver, R. F.	1	0	0	0	0
H. Woolbridge, L. F.	1	0	1	0	0
	7	3	24	18	9

H. R. INST.	R.	B.H.	P.O.	A.	E.
Roberts, L. F.	2	0	2	0	0
Fabricius, 2d	0	0	0	1	1
Hines, S. S.	1	2	0	1	0
Melius, P.	0	1	0	20	0
Crane, C.	2	0	20	4	1
Knapp, 3d	3	1*	2	0	0
Leiva, C. F.	1	0	1	0	0
Underwood, R. F.	1	0	0	0	1
Jones, 1st	1	0	2	0	2
	11	4	27	26	5

* Home run.

May 3d with Athens scored an easy victory for H. R. I. The game was marked for improvement at the bat.

That with the Chathams, at Chatham, resulted in the third victory for H. R. I., and the work of the visiting battery was exceedingly commendable:

H. R. I. 23
Athens 4
Chatham 6
H. R. I. 11

A MEAN TRICK.

The unsportsmanlike manner in which the Hudson High School evaded defeat on the 10th is something unheard of before on grounds that have been accustomed to play with "men." Of course we claim a victory.

At the close of the ninth inning, with the score 10 to 10, H. R. I. at the bat, with a man on third, an excellent batter up, and only one out, these small pretenders refused to continue on account of a little rain that was insufficient to drive a number of young ladies from the grand stand, that was without protection. We would suggest that the next time the High School nine meets with defeat they take it like men.

Mr. Deaf and Dumb has become a "church goer."

Frobie had a "good eye" last game.

L—— wants to run the nine. Why not? But others are of a different opinion. Take warning.

No. 148   THE KING'S FAVOR

THE lives of all musicians do not glide on in a quiet flow of melody and unpaid music bills. It is popularly supposed that a musician is a long-haired individual who does nothing more exciting than fall in love with his loveliest pupil, dine on mutton chops and misery all his life; and finally become famous as a composer, after the name on his tombstone has been nearly obliterated by the moss and mould of years.

Mr. Albert G. Thies, a prominent New York tenor, proves by his history that such is not always the case. He has had adventures in many strange lands. The crowned heads of Europe and the furred backs of Africa have both taken a hand in chasing him from their dominions; the first, as an alleged political conspirator; the second, as a choice morsel of diet. He has sung before crowned heads and before heads in dilapidated old hats; before the gilded, tasseled boots of the German hussar and the ponderous, wooden sabots of the Hollandese peasant. In fact, he has had as varied an existence as a soldier of fortune. The frozen ice-fields of the North have made him cold and the scorched sands of the desert have made iced lemonade an absolute necessity.

About four years ago, Mr. Thies was giving a series of evenings of song in the principal cities of the British colonies in South Africa. In the height of a successful season, he was told that old King Cetewayo, the famous Zulu chief, had sent a request for a private musicale. The king was then a prisoner in the hands of the British. His dark-skinned *impis* had gone down, the red and purple of the waving plumes had fallen beneath the Enfield rifles of the scarlet-coated visitors from the sea. Cetewayo's captors did all in their power to make his captivity as comfortable as possible. He, with his wives, occupied a large and commodious farm-house, and was dealt out liberal allowances of provisions and supplies by the government. They even possessed a piano though, of course, it was of no use except as a means of recreation and wholesome amusement to the fair Mursala, one of the king's wives. She was very muscular; she was six-feet-two-inches high; and she played the piano by main strength. The hand-organ grinders of America, playing different tunes in chorus, would have felt insignificant if they could have listened to Mrs. Cetewayo. Her mode of amusement caused some discomfort in the family circle. If the three others had shown a like propensity for contrasting their dark fingers with the ivory keys, I fear there would have been direful murder done in that household. But the king had paid sixteen cows for Mursala, so she was a valuable piece of property; she had an intrinsic worth; a face value, although the last would never be noted except by a Zulu in an advanced stage of barbarism. And

she must be allowed to disturb the entire vicinity without reproach, or she might take herself off to the dim recesses of her
native jungle; and her dark fingers never more mingle in the
wool of her imperial lord and master; and he be at a dead loss
in cows.

Mr. Thies, accompanied by an English friend and a Hottentot
interpreter, appeared before the king. Cetewayo sat on the floor,
in front of his four wives. He arose and received the singer with
gracious dignity. After they had exchanged the usual compliments, through the interpreter, Mr. Thies went to the piano.
Mursala had caused sad havoc in the instrument, but the singer
did not allow that to disconcert him. He sang numbers of songs.
He did not choose highly classical music, but sang the simple
English ballads and American popular songs. The interpreter
explained the words of each number after it was rendered.
The king was delighted. He demanded to hear some of the
pieces over and over again.

For the last of the programme Mr. Thies chose an inspiring
war song. There was no need of an interpreter then; the king
recognized at once the sounds of battle, the clatter and din of
war, and the cries of victory.

His eye, grown sullen and down-cast from years of captivity,
again flashed, and his chest heaved. He was again a great chief,
leading his hundreds of brown-bodied warriors, snake-like
through the rustling grass to where the red coats and bayonets
of the stolid, calm Britons glimmered and shone in the sunlight.
He heard the swift rush of hundreds of naked feet, as his
warriors swept down on the immovable British square, and
writhed and twisted about it like a monstrous serpent. He heard
the low muttered war-chant of his followers, sounding to his
enemies in the distance as the most ominous and dreadful of
forebodings; the great, wild cry of battle as his swarthy demons
dyed their spears in the white man's blood; the yells and curses
of the Britons as they went down, blanched and pale and
bloody, to death. He saw the ghastly faces and gory bodies of
his enemies lie thick amongst the brown grass.

When the music ceased, he drew a long deep breath. He
associated closely the singer, his own thoughts of battle, and
the music. He stood up and extended his royal hand. "Thou art

a great warrior, oh, son of a wise father. Come with me, and we two will drive these English dogs into the sea."

Mr. Thies modestly declined to drive his half of several millions of people into anything.

The king was surprised that a great warrior who could stir people's hearts in such a manner would not accept the partnership. He thought he could get his people to rise once more for one great final struggle could they but hear the inspiring voice of this mighty warrior from an unknown land, whose warriors had defeated the red-coats in many battles. But he did not allow his disappointment to affect his attitude toward his guest. The musician stood high in the king's favor.

Suddenly a thought struck his imperial majesty. He would confer upon the great stranger the highest honor known to his race.

"Hearken, oh warrior, son of many warriors, the fallen king loves you," said Cetewayo, waving his hand graciously, "I, even I, king of the Zulus. And it becomes a great king to give honor to his friend, aye, even to as much as twenty cows. Then, oh great stranger, take Mursala, my wife, to be your wife, to follow you to the land of the setting sun and keep your hut and tend your cows until she die."

When the interpreter put the king's kindness and condescension into English, a solemn hush fell upon the two white men. The king and his four wives gazed expectantly.

The silence was horrible. Mr. Thies moved his feet restlessly and felt very uncomfortable. The Englishman, with his head down, laughed in an insane manner.

The king detected the giggle. He stood up and glanced fiercely at them. Was this the way to treat the gift of a monarch? His brow grew dark. He was a prisoner but he looked formidable. Standing six-feet-four-inches high, his massive shoulders and long, sinewy arms showed him to be indeed the king who had led his people in so many desperate battles. The two friends felt that it was an evil hour for them. They turned to the interpreter and implored him, by all he held sacred, to smooth the thing over some way and let them escape the royal displeasure. They begged him to make it known to Cetewayo that an American gentleman's views on connubial bliss were a little queer and old-fashioned, and differed from the prevailing modes of the jungle *elite*. Mr. Thies urged him to thank the monarch heartily and say that it would be Mr. Thies' pleasure to send a red and white sun-umbrella and a toy pistol to the king, from Capetown, the moment of his arrival there. The Englishman expressed his great desire to forward a pair of suspenders and an opera-glass by the first Hottentot express. The king could not be propitiated by these munificent offers. He smiled faintly. The two friends saw their advantage and followed it up with the promise of a jack-knife and a bottle of red ink. The great monarch smiled decidedly and irrevocably. When Mr. Thies heaped on, so to speak, a pack of cards and a silk handkerchief, the Englishman responding with a dozen clay pipes and a banjo, his imperial majesty became gleeful. They commenced to feel safe. The king grew cheerful and pleasant. His conversation became as courtly and affable as it had been in the first part of the interview. They considered it a good time to retreat and so made their adieus. The king seemed very sorry to have Mr. Thies leave. He inquired anxiously if he could not be counted on to change his mind about the insurrection scheme. Mr. Thies, however, assured him that no considerations could induce him to devote his talents to the extermination of the whites of Africa. So the old king bowed his head as if his last hope of revenge was taken from him, and reluctantly bade adieu. The two whites backed out the door. The last sight of Cetewayo was as he sat calm and immovable, with his stern old face set with the rigidity of a bronze cast, only the eyes seeming to say that his hope of being once more the ruler of a nation was gone forever.

When they reached open air, Mr. Thies heaved a sigh which is said to have shaken the more tender of the young sprouts on certain of the banyan trees, adjacent to him. Mursala, mayhap, pressed her face against the pane, and bade a sad farewell as the horses clattered down the road.

Mr. Thies always speaks of this adventure as the narrowest escape of his life. Daniel, mingling in a social way with the denizens of the den, could never have experienced the sensations that the singer did, as he stood before the king and felt, somehow, that he must refuse the royal gift.

Mr. Thies returned to America safely and was very glad

to put several thousand miles of water between him and the lovely Zulu. He has resolved upon a course of action when called to sing before savage kings. He will send a little circular with a blank to be filled in. The questions will be something as follows: 1–"Are you married?" 2–"How many?" 3–"Have you a natural affection for your wife?" 4–"Could any offer induce you to part with one?"

These questions being answered satisfactorily, Mr. Thies feels that he can trust himself.

No. 149   A FOREIGN POLICY, IN THREE GLIMPSES

First Glimpse

I

LONELYISLE'S white sands and green palms glimmer in the rays of a tropical sun. From the countless flowers, a heavy perfume, incense burned upon the altar of the earth, rises toward Heaven. Brown-bodied natives swarm in and out of the cone-shaped huts. In the shady dells, merry maidens toss blossoms to and fro; in the surf, young men gaily laugh as they breast the white-crested waves; upon the beach, fat little boys play games and settle infantile disputes. A sail, a dead black upon its shady and visible side, rears slowly above the horizon and seems to peer at the island. The natives perceive the sail and gather upon the beach to discuss it. It grows larger and larger until a small schooner comes to an anchor outside where the waves roar upon the reef. A boat puts off toward the crowd of wondering natives. It finally bumps upon the beach, and men with white faces step out. The innocent, guileless natives give a cordial welcome. The strangers offer valuable glass-beads and calico remnants for the products of Lonelyisle. The natives accept with alacrity, amazed at the sight of so much wealth and the simplicity of the white strangers. The traders laugh in their beards and gleefully swindle the natives. They camp upon the beach, awaiting the time when their vessel shall be filled, like a voracious animal, with spoil from the island.

All goes well for a few days. Then a shriek rings over the white sands and up to the blue sky above Lonelyisle. It is a woman's voice. A white hand grasps her throat and as she attempts to repeat her cry, her mouth is stuffed with a pocket-handkerchief. The male natives gather around the traders and their chief says quietly: "You must give up the girl, white men."

The only audible reply is: "Lookut 'is bloomin' chieflets. Hi say, where did you git them pants, now."

The sturdy natives gaze darkly upon the strangers. There is a discussion which ends in an altercation. There are blows exchanged. The girl kills herself with a dirk from a trader's girdle and the white men retreat leaving their leader dead upon the sand. The ship becomes a black speck and topples off the horizon.

II

Two black-hulled British gun-boats are at anchor off Lonelyisle. A crowd of natives watch them curiously from the shore.

Suddenly, a signal is run up to the mast-head of the foremost gun-boat, a streak of fire flashes from her bow, there is a thundering roar and a shell shrieks as it falls among the cone-shaped huts of the island. The natives die around in the grass as flash upon flash leaps from the sides of the men-of-war. After a couple of score are killed in this manner, the marines land and kill a few more with the bayonet. While they are thus employed, a group of chiefs advance from the shelter of the woods, holding up their hands in token of peace. The captain of the marines, who, while smoking a short brierwood, is engaged in thoughtfully prodding a writhing native with a sword looks casually up and observes them. The native seizes the opportunity to crawl behind a bunch of grass and die.

"Most noble king," says the principal chief to the captain, "we have come to ask why all this wanton slaughter for a brute who had committed an indignity upon one of our maidens and thus deserved his fate. Two score of our people lie cold in death."

"Why, my friend," replies the captain, "British interests must be protected—oh, I say, now, where's my native. This won't do, you know. He wriggled his legs great." The captain looks about for his writhing victim but, as mentioned, the native had quietly died behind the bunch of grass. "This won't do, you know. I've been regularly jewed out of some fun. I shall report this matter to my commanding officer."

"Most-noble and powerful chieftain," continues the chief, "you hold our poor lives in your cannon's mouth but we would crave, noble sir, that you produce for our inspection those British interests, you mention."

"Oh, that's all right, old ten-pin, British interests must be protected you know."

Slightly exasperated, the venerable chief says: "You confounded, insolent insignificant little prig, I'd like to bat you one with my war-club. What we want to know is, why in Heaven's name don't you go away? Ain't you satisfied, dern you. You have killed forty of us for a bloody-handed villain who reeked of no law but might. And, now, why don't you get out? We don't want you! See? Get out, that's all we ask. Hear?"

To this the captain calmly replies as he borrows a match from his first-serjeant and scratches it on the head of a dead native: "My friend, I think I have already informed you that British interests must be protected."

"But," frenziedly cries the chief, "where in the devil's name, are the British interests? And, if so, where are our interests?"

"British interests, b'gad, must be protected if we die for it," cry the sturdy soldiery as they go in to permanent camp.

III

It has been flashed to London that, "owing to the murder of Europeans it has been found necessary to occupy Lonely-isle with a British force, powerful enough to cope with the natives and afford adequate protection to foreign residents." In less than four hours after the receipt of this dispatch, there are thirteen companies organized for carrying on commerce with Lonelyisle. The representatives of these companies swoop down on the doomed native, they improve him, they rescue him, they enlighten him, they dicker with him and they beat him out of his senses, they rob him, they convert him, and when they get through with him, he has been manipulated out of everything but his blackened conscience and his toenails. He gets uproariously drunk on the worst rum England can produce and through the storm-doors of his clouded mind he has an impression that he will strike for liberty about twice a month.

He does so. There's a howl from Lonelyisle. "Oh, I say, now this won't do, you know. British interests predominate here, you know, British interests predominate here and we must have protection you know."

Gun-boats arrive again and kill all natives in sight. After which the British government puzzles over the Lonelyisle question. "How can we afford sufficient protection to our interests in Lonelyisle without annexing it? Why it can't be done! Of course, it can't! The only way to advance civilization and protect British interests is to annex Lonelyisle."

"But what is to become of the poor native. He owns it, you know. I don't see what right——"

"Oh, damn the native! British interests must be protected you know."

Glimpse II

The Czar of Russia to the British Lion in 1884: "By Jim, I have ideaovitch to cutski your throatovitch."

The Lion: "What's that? Oh, I say, Mr. Czar you didn't mean me, did you?"

The Czar: "Damnovitch if I didn'tski, by Jim."

The Lion: "Oh, I say now, I am really sorry, you know. I didn't mean it, you know."

The Czar: "Anyway, I believeovitch I'll breakski your faceovitch, you damnovitch cusski."

The Lion: "Oh, my dear, dear sir, you are mistaken, indeed, indeed you are. You have no idea how I hate to fight when my opponent is as big as you are. I am the most peaceable animal on earth in a case like this. I will not fight unless you insist on it and knock me down three times. Forgive me this once, and I'll never do so no more, s'elp me Gawd."

Glimpse III

Chorus from British Newspapers in 1892: "The attitude of the United States in the trouble with Chili is disgusting to all mankind. Never in history did a nation of the world give such an exhibition of the brutal coward and bully as is now afforded us by the ignorant, petty, and vain-glorious government at Washington. America's policy all along has been that of a stupid, big, fat and conceited republic which attempts to browbeat and coerce a little but liberty-loving truthful, and virtuous rival. America would never dare to assume such an attitude toward a nation of any importance, but her silly, vain president seeks a little insignificant country to bluster to and strut before. Language fails us—God save the queen, b'gad."

No. 150   GREAT BUGS IN ONONDAGA

A WILD-EYED man in overalls told a STANDARD reporter yesterday a story of the strangest character. The fellow was from the sand hills. He acted as well as talked strangely, and was evidently suffering from alcoholism. He gave his name as William Davis. This is in substance the story he told, frequently interrupting himself to insist that what he related was an actual fact:

"Southeast of Brighton Corners, between here and Jamesville, on the Delaware, Lackawanna & Western Railroad, are extensive limestone quarries, which have been in operation for many years and have penetrated deeply into the rock. Through the cut thus made and into the quarries a branch track has been laid from the Lackawanna road for the accommodation of the hewn stone. Night work being necessary a

large part of the time an arc light has been placed high over
the track at the darkest part of the cut. Several cars were
loaded with stone for shipment on Friday and left on the
switch pending the observance of Memorial Day. Last night
in preparation for drawing the cars out the electric light was
cut in, and an engine with the necessary crew left the city
for the quarries. What was the surprise of all hands upon
reaching the scene of operations to find the track beneath
the electric light completely thronged with strange insects of
immense proportions, some of them lying perfectly still, huddled in bunches, and some of them playing a sort of leapfrog
over their fellows' backs. They covered a space of not less
than sixty feet along the tracks, though toward either boundary of the occupied territory they grew fewer as the rays of
the light began to grow dimmer. These pickets or skirmishers
were one and all of a most lively disposition and scudded over
the ground with that lightning-like rapidity which characterized the movements of the electric-light bugs which made
their appearance all over the country soon after the system
of electric lighting became of general adoption. The locomotive
continued on its way, and as the drivers rolled over the insects
the things gave up the ghost with a crackling sound like the
successive explosions of toy torpedoes. But this was at the
beginning of the swarm; as the iron monster ploughed its way
along the bugs became more numerous and the crackling grew
to a monotonous din, as though some fire cracker storehouse
had been touched off in an hundred places, until in the thick
of the multitudinous swarm the engine was brought to a stop,
the drivers refusing to catch on the now slippery rails, greased
by the crushed vitals of the slaughtered bugs. An examination
of the insects showed a resemblance to the electric-light bug,
though they are somewhat larger than those bugs, the outer
shell of the back being about the size and shape of half a
shanghai-egg shell. It was this turtle-like armor with which
the insects are equipped that made the crackling sound as the
wheels passed over them. The shell is black and partakes of
the nature of stone, having a slatey structure and being brittle.
This property of the shell set the more thoughtful people to
thinking and observing, and after a time search along the

sides of the cut revealed innumerable small holes in the rock, which seemed to have been bored into it by some agency not that of man, and in them were traces of a peculiar ovula, some hatched and some apparently blighted. An erudite recluse whose abode is in the neighborhood of the quarries had by this time appeared, for news of the strange occurrence had spread rapidly. His opinion was that the bugs that had blocked the track were the issue of a rare species of lithodome —a rock-boring mollusk—crossed with some kind of predatory insect. To secure the shipment of the freight to-night it became necessary to let the loaded train from above in the quarry come down the grade of the cut. Gathering momentum all the time, its impetus when it came to the obstruction carried it by the bugs."

The story, of course, is too improbable for belief and could not be verified. Davis had perhaps in his sober moments read or heard the reports of caterpillars and other insects stopping trains in Minnesota and South Carolina and in his unfortunate mental condition yesterday believed that he had actually witnessed a spectacle of a similar nature.

No. 151   THE WRECK OF THE "NEW ERA"

Asbury Park, N.J.   The wreck of the *New Era* in 1854 was the worst disaster that has ever occurred on the New Jersey coast, the land of shipwrecks and summer resorts, of horror at sea and hilarity on land. On many parts of the shore, the rotting timbers of wrecked vessels lie thick, but none of these monuments to human suffering tell so much as that little path of foam which until a few years ago led away from a bunch of old timbers and marked the spot where the *New Era* went down. There are possibly three survivors now living and of those who witnessed the disaster from the shore, few are now alive. In consequence, after the event has been partially covered and obscured by the moss and mould of years, and the little track of foam over the grave has disappeared, expressed opinions have placed the scene of the wreck at a number of places on the coast and it would require quite a fleet of *New Eras* to verify their statements. However those who saw the wreck say that it occurred at the foot of what is now, Sixth Avenue of this town. So that the small monument erected further southward only saves its reputation for accuracy by the wording of its introduction: "Near this spot" —which allows the reader sufficient license, and room for the imagination.

The *New Era* was a packet ship built at Bath, Maine. She was 1328 tons burden and was valued at about seventy-five thousand dollars. She was on a voyage from Bremen to New York. Her consignees were Charles C. Duncan and Co. She had on board when she set sail from Bremen, three hundred and eighty steerage passengers, ten cabin passengers and a crew numbering twenty. The first part of the voyage was uneventful, although claims have been made that the captain did not give his entire attention to his ship owing to the presence of a beautiful young German girl among the passengers.

They sighted land on Sunday, November 12, 1854. A dense fog prevailed but in spite of this, the captain steered a northern course for New York Harbor. He lost his reckoning and early in the morning of the 13th, the ship struck with a thundering crash on the outer bar, opposite what is now North Asbury Park. The vessel stranded an hundred yards from the beach and in the midst of a heavy surf.

Asbury Park at that time appeared a desolate stretch of sandy beach with a back-ground of gloomy dwarf-pines and faded grass. There were no rows of hotels and miles of cottages in those days.

Indeed, James A. Bradley says graphically and eloquently in his justly-celebrated and altogether-admirable history: "In 1869, Asbury Park was a wilderness and a barren sand-waste." From this solemn thought, we surmise that the condition of Asbury Park in 1854, must have been very distressing indeed. But the fishermen from along the shore, the farmers from back in the pines, hastened to the beach as soon as the wreck could be seen.

Upon the ship, a scene of confusion ensued the moment

the ship struck. The panic-stricken emigrants hurried from their crowded cabins and besieged the officers and crew, rendering their efforts helpless. Every wave washed over the ship from stem to stern. Shrieks, groans and curses filled the air. Men fought with each other like wild beasts for the possession of stray spars or casks. Women and children clad only in their night-clothes ran about the flooded decks, adding their screams to the din. It was at low tide that the ship struck and as the night wore away, the waves of the rising tide swept over the deck carrying struggling men or women on their crests. Suddenly the vessel lurched nearly on her beam ends and those who were clinging to the lee shrouds were swept away at once. It was estimated by a survivor that forty persons were carried overboard by the wave that immediately followed the careening of the ship. A hatch was burst open and in a moment the cabins were flooded, drowning like kittens those who had sought shelter in them. The lower parts of the rigging were crowded with women and children who alarmed by the way in which the ship pitched and tossed, refused to proceed further aloft, thus keeping on deck many who tried to find safety there. Then before any of the terror-stricken emigrants could seek to prevent it, a boat was hastily manned and the captain and crew deserted the ship, unmindful of either the prayers or curses of the shivering shrieking wretches whose wild eyes peered at them from every part of the rigging.

On shore nearly all the inhabitants of the sparsely-settled coast had gathered on the beach and were cursing their inability to render assistance. Each time a man clinging to the rigging, loosed his hold and fell headlong into the sea, a cry went up from the shore that could be heard above the roar of the breakers by those on board the ship. The hardy life-savers gathered, with the meagre equipment of the day, and with great difficulty got a line to the vessel. Then those on the wreck drew out a boat by means of the line. Fourteen persons bundled into it and it started on its return drawn by the men on the shore. The huge life-boat was buffeted about like a chip. In the midst of the breakers, the part of the line connecting with the wreck became entangled and the course of the boat toward the shore was stopped. Those in the boat cut the line, thus severing the last connection between the ship and the shore for no more rope could be obtained. The boat capsized on its way three times and but five of the fourteen who started reached shore alive. It was impossible to launch a boat from the beach into that tremendous surf and so all turned eagerly to the bodies that were being washed ashore by each wave and attempted to resuscitate any who appeared to have a single spark of life remaining.

It is said the dead laid in windrows along the sand. All that day, men worked at gathering the bodies together, and at helping those few who reached shore alive to a place of safety. As night again settled down over the scene the cries of those still on board grew fainter and fainter. The clusters of human beings in the rigging had rapidly grown smaller and smaller as one after another, their strength gave out and they fell into the sea.

All the barns in the vicinity were turned into morgues that night. Regular patrols relieved each other on the beach and half-naked ghastly corpses were borne all night long, on improvised stretchers to the temporary dead-houses. And as the men worked on the beach, there came the moaning cries from the sea of those who were yet to die and were yet to be carried away. When dawn came, the storm cleared and the bright sun-rays fell upon the grey up-turned faces of many corpses. Whole families lay dead on the sands, from the white-haired grandsire to the little babies of two or three years. Out upon the bar, the *New Era* writhed and fought with the waves like an animal wounded sorely, and in the rigging were human bodies, some alive, and some holding on with the frozen grasp of death.

As soon as the surf went down boats were speedily launched and went to save all that could be saved. Upon the deck of the vessel, bodies washed to and fro; in the rigging the dead and the living grasped the ropes side by side. Some of the bodies were frozen stiff and coated with the ice from spray. Some of those alive were speechless from exhaustion; others welcomed the boats with frenzied expressions of joy. When the boats reached shore, the scene could not be described. Some fell on their knees and thanked God for deliverance; others rushed off in search of friends or relatives. Many wept over corpses of their loved ones and many were satisfied that they themselves lived.

Of the saved there were about one hundred and eighty; of the dead, nearly two hundred and thirty.

The job of building the coffins was let out by contract and the carpenters put up a temporary shop on the beach where they turned out the rough pine boxes by the score. The farmers came with their hay wagons and took great loads of bodies to the West Long Branch cemetery where they interred them in a huge trench extending one entire length of the grave-yard. Prominent German-Americans of the county and state have formed an organization calling it the *New Era* Monument Association. Their object is to erect a suitable memorial over this great long grave wherein lie the bodies of their unfortunate countrymen. All the German societies of the state have been communicated with and requested to send in contributions. Many of them, and private parties as well, have responded liberally.

No. 152   ACROSS THE COVERED PIT

REV. H. C. HOVEY D.D. of Bridgeport, Conn., has the grave and reverend look which betokens his profession. To see the gentleman dressed in shining black, in his pulpit on Sunday, one could never imagine that the devout minister of the gospel was one of the most daring cave explorers in this country. Yet all the noted caverns of this country have been visited by him. No cavern looks so gloomy and forbidding but that the doctor feels his boyish spirit of adventure seize him and he longs to tread its dark mysteries and explore its unknown recesses. The unknown region beyond the mouth of the Covered Pit in Mammoth Cave was a bug-bear to him. To any one's knowledge, the mass of tangled slippery slabs that was heaped over the mouth of the pit, had never been tread on.

As authorities had forbidden anyone to cross this dangerous place, its strength had never been tested. It might be strong enough to allow a train of cars to cross it and again the weight of a cat might cause the whole mass to tumble to the unknown depth.

The doctor had been to the edge of the pit several times. He would look at the huge patches of darkness that showed between the slabs which seem to have been thrown loosely over the mouth of the hole by a giant hand, and then glance at the dim outline of a wide tunnel which led away from the other side of the pit. A wistful look would come into his eyes, as he would wonder about that unknown land. He would speculate for awhile on the length and number of caverns the passage contained and then return to his hotel and dream of a large interrogation point framed in the mouth of the dark tunnel.

It finally became too much for the doctor and he attempted to bribe the guides by offering sums which came little short of being fabulous. Not one of them, however, would go with him.

At last, William, the famous colored guide, showed signs of his love of money predominating over his love of life and the doctor worried the poor darkey until he won his reluctant consent to accompany him.

The two provided themselves with the necessary articles and, one day, made their way stealthily along the passages toward the Covered Pit.

The uniqueness of the doctor's scheme is apparent at once. As the authorities had forbidden it, they must steal into the cave without their knowledge and, consequently, their fate would be unknown. No one would ever know what became of Dr. Hovey and William. The Covered Pit would withhold its story of the tragedy until the Resurrection Morn. A few pleasant thoughts like these crowded into the doctor's brain as he made his way along the cavern. He was half constrained to turn back and, at least, leave a letter telling where he had gone. He was half minded to turn back, anyhow. But there was William trudging stolidly along ahead of him and the doctor settled his nerves and pushed on.

They arrived at the edge of the pit and stood together trying to pierce the gloom in the openings between the slabs.

"It will make a right big grave," said William, contemplating the pit.

The doctor started but kept silent.

The two adventurers sat down on a boulder and made deliberate plans covering any casualty that might occur. It was also decided, with no indecent haggling whatever, that William should go first.

The guide tightened everything about him, and placed his torch in his hat that he might have both hands free.

Getting down on his hands and knees, he commenced to make his way like a cat on very tender ice. It was a moment of supreme suspense to both. The guide's labored breathing was plainly audible as he slowly moved along. The doctor shut his eyes at times and waited with almost a desire, the tension was so terrible, for the sudden grinding noise; then, the awful roar that would announce to him that the covering had fallen. But William's light gleamed on the other side and he was safe. It was now the doctor's turn. William shouted a few directions about the bad places. Then the doctor started. On his hands and knees as the guide had been, the doctor would thrust one hand forward and, finding a firm place, would bring the other one forward. Some of the slabs slanted frightfully and were damp and slippery. The doctor's life depended on the grip of his fingers.

When about half way across the doctor's hand loosened a slab ahead of him which had no connection with the structure of the cover but simply lay on one of the others.

With an awful sound the stone slid off the lower slab and plunged down into the pit. The explorer gave himself up for lost. As the movement of the stone was communicated to the slab on which he crouched, he thought he was gone. A second later when the sounds ceased he could hardly believe that he was still on the cover.

The sensations of the poor guide can only be imagined. Let alone the depressing effects on one's spirits the horrible death of a companion in the bowels of the earth would have, the guide would be in a sorry plight, indeed. With the doctor and the cover at the bottom of the pit, he was alive in his tomb.

His bridge was burned behind him. His only known means of exit was across the covering to the pit and if the cover broke, William was in a bad way. The darkey's teeth chattered as he heard the sound of the falling slab.

But the torch still flickered out over the pit and began to come nearer and nearer. A few more minutes of suspense and the doctor of divinity and the ignorant guide clutched each other's hands in the most affectionate manner possible.

The explorers proceeded along the tunnel. They were then on ground trod by no man before and the doctor was in his glory. They spent two days in the new regions and had some startling adventures but returned safely across the Covered Pit. When the sun light beamed on their delighted visions, they looked at each other for a moment without speaking. Then the doctor remarked that he guessed he wouldn't explore any more caves for awhile and William said he reckoned he needed a vacation, too.

No. 153 THE GRATITUDE OF A NATION

A SOLDIER, young in years, young in ambitions,
Alive as no grey-beard is alive,
Laid his heart and his hopes before duty
And went staunchly into the tempest of war.
There did the bitter red winds of battle
Swirl 'gainst his youth, beat upon his ambitions,
Drink his cool clear blood of manhood
Until at coming forth time
He was alive merely as the grey-beard is alive.
And for this——
The nation rendered to him a flower
A little thing—a flower
Aye, but yet not so little
For this flower grew in the nation's heart
A wet, soft blossom

From tears of her who loved her son
Even when the black battle rages
Made his face the face of furious urchin,
And this she cherished
And finally laid it upon the breast of him.
A little thing—this flower?
No—it was the flower of duty
That inhales black smoke-clouds
And fastens its roots in bloody sod
And yet comes forth so fair, so fragrant——
Its birth is sunlight in grimmest, darkest place.

Gratitude, the sense of obligation, often comes very late to the mind of the world. It is the habit of humanity to forget her heroes, her well-doers, until they have passed beyond the sound of earthly voices; then when the loud, praising cries are raised, there comes a regret and a sorrow that those ears are forever deaf to plaudits. It has almost become a great truth that the man who achieves an extraordinary benefit for the race shall go to death without the particular appreciation of his fellows. One by one they go, with no evident knowledge of the value of their services unless their own hearts tell them that in their fidelity to truth and to duty, they have gained a high success.

The men who fought in the great war for freedom and union are disappearing. They are upon their last great march, a march that ceases to be seen at the horizon and whose end is death. We are now viewing the last of the procession, the belated ones, the stragglers. A vast body of them have thronged to the grave, regiment by regiment, brigade by brigade, and the others are hurrying after their fellows who have marched into the Hereafter. There, every company is gradually getting its men, no soldier but what will be there to answer his name, and upon earth there will remain but a memory of deeds well and stoutly done.

If in the past there is any reflection of the future, we can expect that when the last veteran has vanished there will come a time of great monuments, eulogies, tears. Then the boy in blue will have grown to heroic size, and painters, sculptors and writers, will have been finally impressed, and strive to royally celebrate the deeds of the brave, simple, quiet men who crowded upon the opposing bayonets of their country's enemies. But no voice penetrates the grave, and the chants and shouts will carry no warmth to dead hearts.

Let us then struggle to defeat this ironical law of fate. Let us not wait to celebrate but consider that there are now before us the belated ones of the army that is marching over the horizon, off from the earth, into the sky, into history and tradition. The laws of the universe sometimes appear to be toying with compensations, holding back results until death closes the eyes to success, bludgeoning a man of benefactions, rewarding they who do evil. It is well that we do all in our power to defeat these things.

Do not then wait. Let not loud and full expression of gratitude come too late to the mind of the nation. Do not forget our heroes, our well-doers, until they have marched to where no little cheers of men can reach them. Remember them now, and if the men of the future forget, the sin is with them. They are ours, these boys in blue, their deeds and their privations, their wondrous patience and endurance, their grim, abiding faith and fortitude are ours. Let us expend our lungs then while they can hear; let us throw up our caps while they can see, these veterans whose feet are still sore from marches, in whose old grey hairs there still lingers the scent of victory. In the tremendous roll of events the pages and paragraphs of future histories are nothing. Our obligation exists in the present, and it is fit that we leave not too much to future historians.

Upon this day, those who are left go sadly, a little pitiable handful, to decorate the places of their comrades' rest. When the small solemn flower-ladened processions start for the graves, it is well to be with them. There are to be learned there lessons of patriotism that are good for us at this day. No harm would come if we allowed the trucks to be less roaring and busy upon this day, nor if we allowed the stores to have less rush and crowd. We cannot afford to neglect the spectacle of our bearded, bronzed and wrinkled men in blue tramping slowly and haltingly to bestow their gifts upon the sleeping places of those who are gone. And it is well then to think of the time when these men were in the flush of vigor and manhood and went with the firm-swinging steps of youth to do their duty to their God, their homes and their country.

When they are gone, American society has lost its most valuable element for they have paid the price of patriotism, they know the meaning of patriotism, and stars shot from guns would not hinder their devotion to the flag which they rescued from dust and oblivion. Let us watch with apprehension this departure of an army, one by one, one by one. Let the last words that they hear from us be words of gratitude and affection.

It is just and proper that we go with them to the graves, that they may see that when they too are gone, there will be many to come to their graves, that their camping grounds and battle fields will be remembered places and that the lesson of their lives will be taught to children who will never see their faces.

Great are the nation's dead who sleep in peace. May all old comrades gather at an eternal camp-fire. May the sweet, wind-waved rustle of trees be over them, may the long, lush grass and flowers be about their feet. Peace and rest be with them forever, for they have done well.

No. 154   IN THE DEPTHS OF A COAL MINE

THE breakers squatted upon the hillsides and in the valley like enormous preying monsters eating of the sunshine, the grass, the green leaves. The smoke from their nostrils had ravaged the air of coolness and fragrance. All that remained of the vegetation looked dark, miserable, half-strangled. Along the summit-line of the mountain, a few unhappy trees were etched upon the clouds. Overhead stretched a sky of imperial blue, incredibly far away from the sombre land.

We approached the colliery over paths of coal-dust that wound among the switches. The breaker loomed above us, a huge and towering frame of blackened wood. It ended in a little curious peak and upon its sides there was a profusion of windows appearing at strange and unexpected points. Through occasional doors one could see the flash of whirring machinery. Men with wondrously blackened faces and garments came forth from it. The sole glitter upon their persons was at their hats where the little tin lamps were carried. They went stolidly along, some swinging lunch-pails carelessly, but the marks upon them of their forbidding and mystic calling fascinated our new eyes until they passed from sight. They were symbols of a grim, strange war that was being waged in the sunless depths of the earth.

Around the huge central building clustered other and lower ones, sheds, engine-houses, machine-shops, offices. Railroad tracks extended in web-like ways. Upon them stood files of begrimed coal-cars. Other huge structures similar to the one near us up-reared their uncouth heads upon the hills of the surrounding country. From each, a mighty hill of culm extended. Upon these tremendous heaps of waste from the mines, mules and cars appeared like toys. Down in the valley, upon the railroads, long trains crawled painfully southward where a low-hanging grey cloud with a few projecting spires and chimneys indicated a town.

Car after car came from a shed beneath which lay hidden the mouth of the shaft. They were dragged creaking up an inclined cable-road to the top of the breaker.

At the top of the breaker, laborers were dumping the coal into chutes. The huge lumps slid slowly on their journey down through the building from which they were to emerge in classified fragments. Great teeth on revolving cylinders caught them and chewed them. At places, there were grates that bid each size go into its proper chute. The dust lay inches deep on every motionless thing and clouds of it made the air dark as from a violent tempest. A mighty gnashing sound filled the ears. With terrible appetite this huge and hideous monster sat imperturbably munching coal, grinding its mammoth jaws with unearthly and monotonous uproar.

In a large room sat the little slate-pickers. The floor slanted at an angle of forty-five degrees, and the coal having been masticated by the great teeth was streaming sluggishly in long iron troughs. The boys sat straddling these troughs and as the mass moved slowly, they grabbed deftly at the pieces of slate therein. There were five or six of them, one above another, over each trough. The coal is expected to be fairly pure after it passes the final boy. The howling machinery was above them. High up, dim figures moved about in the dust clouds.

These little men were a terrifically dirty band. They resembled the New York gamins in some ways but they laughed more and when they laughed their faces were a wonder and a terror. They had an air of supreme independence and seemed proud of their kind of villainy. They swore long oaths with skill.

Through their ragged shirts we could get occasional glimpses of shoulders black as stoves. They looked precisely like imps as they scrambled to get a view of us. Work ceased while they tried to ascertain if we were willing to give away any tobacco. The man who perhaps believes that he controls them came and harangued the crowd. He talked to the air.

The slate-pickers, all through this region, are yet at the spanking period. One continually wonders about their mothers and if there are any school-houses. But as for them, they are not concerned. When they get time off, they go out on the culm-heap and play base-ball, or fight with boys from other breakers, or among themselves, according to the opportunities. And before them always is the hope of one day getting to be door-boys down in the mines and, later, mule-boys. And yet later laborers and helpers. Finally when they have grown to be great big men they may become miners, real miners, and go down and get "squeezed," or perhaps escape to a shattered old man's estate with a mere "miner's asthma." They are very ambitious.

Meanwhile, they live in a place of infernal dins. The crash and thunder of the machinery is like the roar of an immense cataract. The room shrieks and blares and bellows. Clouds of dust blur the air until the windows shine pallidly, afar off. All the structure is a-tremble from the heavy sweep and circle of the ponderous mechanism. Down in the midst of it, sit these tiny urchins, where they earn fifty-five cents a day each.

They breathe this atmosphere until their lungs grow heavy and sick with it. They have this clamor in their ears until it is wonderful that they have any hoodlum valor remaining. But they are uncowed; they continue to swagger. And at the top of the breaker laborers can always be seen dumping the roaring coal down the wide, voracious maw of the creature.

Over in front of a little tool house, a man, smoking a pipe, sat on a bench. "Yes," he said, "I'll take yeh down, if yeh like." He led us by little cinder paths to the shed over the shaft of the mine. A gigantic fan-wheel, near by, was twirling swiftly. It created cool air for the miners, who on the lowest vein of this mine were some eleven hundred and fifty feet below the surface. As we stood silently waiting for the elevator, we had opportunity to gaze at the mouth of the shaft. The walls were of granite blocks, slimy, moss-grown, dripping with water. Below was a curtain of ink-like blackness. It was like the opening of an old well, sinister from tales of crime.

The black greasy cables began to run swiftly. We stood staring at them and wondering. Then of a sudden, the elevator appeared and stopped with a crash. It was a plain wooden platform. Upon two sides iron bars ran up to support a stout metal roof. The men upon it, as it came into view, were like apparitions from the centre of the earth.

A moment later, we marched aboard, armed with little lights, feeble and gasping in the daylight. There was an instant's creak of machinery and then the landscape that had been framed for us by the door-posts of the shed, disappeared in a flash. We were dropping with extraordinary swiftness straight into the earth. It was a plunge, a fall. The flames of the little lamps fluttered and flew and struggled like tied birds to release themselves from the wicks. "Hang on," bawled our guide above the tumult.

The dead black walls slid swiftly by. They were a swirling dark chaos on which the mind tried vainly to locate some coherent thing, some intelligible spot. One could only hold fast to the iron bars and listen to the roar of this implacable descent. When the faculty of balance is lost, the mind becomes a confusion. The will fought a great battle to comprehend something during this fall, but one might as well have been tumbling among the stars. The only thing was to await revelation.

It was a journey that held a threat of endlessness.

Then suddenly the dropping platform slackened its speed. It began to descend slowly and with caution. At last, with a crash and a jar, it stopped. Before us stretched an inscrutable darkness, a soundless place of tangible loneliness. Into the nostrils came a subtly strong odor of powder-smoke, oil, wet earth. The alarmed lungs began to lengthen their respirations.

Our guide strode abruptly into the gloom. His lamp flared shades of yellow and orange upon the walls of a tunnel that led away from the foot of the shaft. Little points of coal caught the light and shone like diamonds. Before us, there was always the curtain of an impenetrable night. We walked on with no sound save the crunch of our feet upon the coal-dust of the floor. The sense of an abiding danger in the roof was always upon our foreheads. It expressed to us all the unmeasured, deadly tons above us. It was a superlative might that regarded with the supreme calmness of almighty power the little men at its mercy. Sometimes we were obliged to bend low to avoid it. Always our hands rebelled vaguely from touching it, refusing to affront this gigantic mass.

All at once, far ahead, shone a little flame, blurred and difficult of location. It was a tiny indefinite thing, like a wisp-light. We seemed to be looking at it through a great fog. Presently, there were two of them. They began to move to and fro and dance before us.

After a time we came upon two men crouching where the roof of the passage came near to meeting the floor. If the picture could have been brought to where it would have had the opposition and the contrast of the glorious summer-time earth, it would have been a grim and ghastly thing. The garments of the men were no more sable than their faces and when they turned their heads to regard our tramping party, their eye-balls and teeth shone white as bleached bones. It was like the grinning of two skulls there in the shadows. The tiny lamps on their hats made a trembling light that left weirdly shrouded the movements of their limbs and bodies. We might have been confronting terrible spectres.

But they said "Hello, Jim" to our conductor. Their mouths expanded in smiles—wide and startling smiles.

In a moment they turned again to their work. When the lights of our party reinforced their two lamps, we could see that one was busily drilling into the coal with a long thin bar. The low roof ominously pressed his shoulders as he bended at his toil. The other knelt behind him on the loose lumps of coal.

He who worked at the drill engaged in conversation with our guide. He looked back over his shoulder, continuing to poke away. "When are yeh goin' t' measure this up, Jim?" he demanded. "Do yeh wanta git me killed?"

"Well, I'd measure it up t'-day, on'y I ain't got me tape," replied the other.

"Well, when will yeh? Yeh wanta hurry up," said the miner. "I don't wanta git killed."

"Oh, I'll be down on Monday."

"Humph!"

They engaged in a sort of an altercation in which they made jests.

"You'll be carried out o' there feet first before long."

"Will I?"

Yet one had to look closely to understand that they were not about to spring at each other's throats. The vague illumination created all the effect of the snarling of two wolves.

We came upon other little low-roofed chambers each containing two men, a "miner" who makes the blasts and his "laborer" who loads the coal upon the cars and assists the miner generally. And at each place there was this same effect of strangely satanic smiles and eye-balls wild and glittering in the pale glow of the lamps.

Sometimes, the scenes in their weird strength were absolutely infernal. Once when we were traversing a silent tunnel in another mine, we came suddenly upon a wide place where some miners were lying down in a group. As they up-reared to gaze at us, it resembled a resurrection. They slowly uprose with ghoul-like movements, mysterious figures robed in enormous shadows. The swift flashes of the steel-gleaming eyes were upon our faces.

At another time, when my companion, struggling against difficulties, was trying to get a sketch of the mule "Molly Maguire," a large group of miners gathered about us, intent upon the pencil of the artist. "Molly," indifferent to the demands of art, changed her position after a moment and calmly settled into a new one. The men all laughed and this laugh created the most astonishing and supernatural effect. In an instant, the gloom was filled with luminous smiles. Shining forth all about us were eyes, glittering as with cold blue flame. "Whoa, Molly," the men began to shout. Five or six of them clutched "Molly" by her tail, her head, her legs. They were going to hold her motionless until the portrait was finished. "He's a good feller," they had said of the artist, and it would be a small thing to hold a mule for him. Upon the roof were vague dancing reflections of red and yellow.

From this tunnel of our first mine we went with our guide to the foot of the main shaft. Here we were in the most important passage of a mine, the main gangway. The wonder of these avenues is the noise—the crash and clatter of machinery as the elevator speeds up-ward with the loaded cars and drops thunderingly with the empty ones. The place resounds with the shouts of mule-boys and there can always be heard the noise of approaching coal-cars, beginning in mild rumbles and then swelling down upon one in a tempest of sound. In the air is the slow painful throb of the pumps working at the water which collects in the depths. There is booming and banging and crashing until one wonders why the tremendous walls are not wrenched by the force of this uproar. And up and down the tunnel, there is a riot of lights, little orange points flickering and flashing. Miners stride in swift and sombre procession. But the meaning of it all is in the deep bass rattle of a blast in some hidden part of the mine. It is war. It is the most savage part of all in the endless battle between man and nature. These miners are grimly in the van. They have carried the war into places where nature has the strength of a million giants. Sometimes their enemy becomes exasperated and snuffs out ten, twenty, thirty lives. Usually she remains calm, and takes one at a time with method and precision. She need not hurry. She possesses eternity. After a blast, the smoke, faintly luminous, silvery, floats silently through the adjacent tunnels.

In our first mine we speedily lost all ideas of time, direction, distance. The whole thing was an extraordinary, black puzzle. We were impelled to admire the guide because he knew all the tangled passages. He led us through little tunnels three and four feet wide and with roofs that sometimes made us crawl. At other times we were in avenues twenty feet wide, where double rows of tracks extended. There were stretches of great darkness, majestic silences. The three hundred miners were distributed into all sorts of crevices and corners of the labyrinth, toiling in this city of endless night. At different points one could hear the roar of traffic about the foot of the main shaft, to which flowed all the commerce of the place.

We were made aware of distances later by our guide, who would occasionally stop to tell us our position by naming a point of the familiar geography of the surface. "Do yeh remember that rolling-mill yeh passed coming up? Well, you're right under it." "You're under th' depot now." The length of these distances struck us with amazement when we reached the surface. Near Scranton one can really proceed for miles, in the black streets of the mines.

Over in a wide and lightless room we found the mule-stables. There we discovered a number of these animals standing with an air of calmness and self-possession that was somehow amazing to find in a mine. A little dark urchin came and belabored his mule "China" until he stood broadside to us that we might admire his innumerable fine qualities. The stable was like a dungeon. The mules were arranged in solemn rows. They turned their heads toward our lamps. The glare made their eyes shine wondrously, like lenses. They resembled enormous rats.

About the room stood bales of hay and straw. The commonplace air worn by the long-eared slaves made it all infinitely usual. One had to wait to see the tragedy of it. It was not until we had grown familiar with the life and the traditions of the mines that we were capable of understanding the story told by these beasts standing in calm array, with spread legs.

It is a common affair for mules to be imprisoned for years in the limitless night of the mines. Our acquaintance, "China," had been four years buried. Upon the surface there had been the march of the seasons; the white splendor of snows had changed again and again to the glories of green springs. Four times had the earth been ablaze with the decorations of brilliant autumns. But "China" and his friends had remained in these dungeons from which daylight, if one could get a view up a shaft, would appear a tiny circle, a silver star aglow in a sable sky.

Usually when brought to the surface, these animals tremble at the earth, radiant in the sunshine. Later, they go almost mad with fantastic joy. The full splendor of the heavens, the grass, the trees, the breezes breaks upon them suddenly. They caper and career with extravagant mulish glee. Once a miner told me of a mule that had spent some delirious months upon the surface after years of labor in the mines. Finally the time came when he was to be taken back into the depths. They attempted to take him through a tunnel in the hillside. But the memory of a black existence was upon him; he knew that gaping mouth that threatened to swallow him. He had all the strength of mind for which his race is famous. No cudgellings could induce him. The men held conventions and discussed plans to budge that mule. The celebrated quality of obstinacy in him won him liberty to gambol clumsily about on the surface.

After being long in the mines, the mules are apt to duck and dodge at the close glare of lamps, but some of them have been known to have piteous fears of being left in the dead darkness. They seem then, somehow, like little children. We met a boy once who said that sometimes the only way he could get his resolute team to move was to run ahead of them with the light. Afraid of the darkness, they would trot hurriedly after him and so take the train of heavy cars to a desired place.

To those who have known the sun-light there may come the fragrant dream. Perhaps this is what they brood over when they stand solemnly in rows with slowly flapping ears. A recollection may appear to them, a recollection of pastures of a lost paradise. Perhaps they despair and thirst for this bloom that lies in an unknown direction and at impossible distances.

We were appalled occasionally at the quantity of mud we encountered in our wanderings through some of the tunnels. The feet of men and mules had churned it usually into a dull-brown clinging mass. In very wet mines all sorts of gruesome fungi grow upon the wooden props that support the uncertain-looking ceiling. The walls are dripping and dank. Upon them too there frequently grows a moss-like fungus, white as a druid's beard, that thrives in these deep dens but shrivels and dies at contact with the sun-light.

Great and mystically dreadful is the earth from a mine's depth. Man is in the implacable grasp of nature. It has only to tighten slightly and he is crushed like a bug. His loudest shriek of agony would be as impotent as his final moan to bring help from that fair land that lies, like Heaven, over his head. There is an insidious silent enemy in the gas. If the huge fan-wheel on the top of the earth should stop for a brief period, there is certain death and a panic more terrible than any occurring where the sun has shone ensues down under the tons of rock. If a man may escape the gas, the floods, the "squeezes" of falling rock, the cars shooting through little tunnels, the precarious elevators, the hundred perils, there usually comes to him an attack of "miner's asthma" that slowly racks and shakes him into the grave. Meanwhile he gets three dollars per day, and his laborer one dollar and a quarter.

In the chamber at the foot of the shaft, as we were departing, a group of the men were resting. They lay about in careless poses. When we climbed aboard the elevator, we had a moment in which to turn and regard them. Then suddenly the study in black faces and crimson and orange lights vanished. We were on our swift way to the surface. Far above us in the engine-room, the engineer sat with his hand on a lever and his eye on the little model of the shaft wherein a miniature elevator was making the ascent even as our elevator was making it. In fact, the same mighty engines give power to both, and their positions are relatively the same always. I had forgotten about the new world that I was to behold in a moment. My mind was occupied with a mental picture of this faraway engineer, who sat in his high chair by his levers, a statue of responsibility and fidelity, cool-brained, clear-eyed, steady of hand. His arms guided the flight of this platform in its mad and unseen ascent. It was always out of his sight, yet the huge thing obeyed him as a horse its master. When one gets upon the elevator down one of those tremendous holes, one thinks naturally of the engineer.

Of a sudden the fleeting walls became flecked with light. It increased to a downpour of sunbeams. The high sun was afloat in a splendor of spotless blue. The distant hills were arrayed in purple and stood like monarchs. A glory of gold was upon the near-by earth. The cool fresh air was wine.

Of that sinister struggle far below there came no sound, no suggestion save the loaded cars that emerged one after another in eternal procession and were sent creaking up the incline that their contents might be fed into the mouth of the breaker, imperturbably cruel and insatiate, black emblem of greed, and of the gods of this labor.

No. 154a FIRST DRAFT

THE breakers squatted upon the hillsides and in the valley like enormous preying monsters eating of the sunshine, the grass, the green leaves. The smoke and dust from their nostrils had devastated the atmosphere. All that remained of the vegetation looked dark, miserable, half-strangled. Along the summit-line of the mountain, a few unhappy trees were etched upon the clouds. Overhead stretched a sky of imperial blue, incredibly faraway from the sombre land.

We approached our first colliery over paths of coal-dust that wound among the switches. The breaker loomed above us, a huge and towering building of blackened wood. It quaintly resembled some extravagant Swiss chalet. It ended in a little curious peak and upon its side there was a profusion of windows appearing at strange and unexpected points. Through occasional doors one could see the flash of whirring machinery. Men with wondrously blackened faces sometimes came forth from it. The sole glitter upon their persons was at their hats where the little tin lamps were carried. They went stolidly along, some swinging lunch-pails carelessly but the marks upon them of their forbidding and mystic calling fascinated the new eye until they passed from sight. They were symbols of this grim, strange life in the sunless depths of the earth. They came like black, industrious beetles from a hole. A little girl was waiting to meet her father. She went away holding to his hand.

Around the huge central building clustered other and lower ones, sheds, engine-houses, machine shops, offices. The tracks extended in web-like ways. Upon them stood the rows of countless begrimed coal-cars.

Other huge structures, counterparts of the one near us, upreared their uncouth heads upon the hills of the surrounding country. From each, a mighty hill of culm extended. Upon these tremendous heaps of waste from the mines, mules and cars appeared like toys. Down in the valley, upon the railroads, long trains crawled southward where a low grey cloud with a few projecting spires and chimneys denoted the presence of a true town of the coal-districts.

We saw car after car of coal come from where the mouth of the shaft was hidden in a shed. They went creaking up an inclined cable-road to the top of the breaker. They suggested to us then the mystery of toil in the earth's heart. After certain experiences, they expressed the net-work of tunnels far below where the dim orange light gleams on the visages of the men laboring where roofs are as a menace and the sound of trickling water may send a chill to the untried blood.

At the top of the breaker, laborers were dumping the coal into chutes. The huge lumps slid slowly on their journey down through the building from which they were to emerge in classified fragments. Great teeth caught them and chewed them. At places, there were grates that bid each size to go into its proper chute. A mighty banging and clattering filled the ears. The dust lay inches deep on every motionless thing and clouds of it made the air dark as from a mad and violent tempest.

In a large room sat the little slate-pickers. The floor slanted at an angle of forty-five degrees, and the coal having been masticated by the teeth of the huge revolving cylinders was streaming sluggishly in long iron troughs. The boys sat straddling these troughs and as the mass moved slowly past them, they grabbed deftly at the pieces of slate. There were five or six of them seated in a row over each trough. The coal is expected to be reasonably pure after it passes the last boy.

They were a terrifically dirty band, and scoundrels every one of them. After I had come to know them better, I discovered that they took a higher pride in their villainy than any urchins I had yet experienced. They are a class unto themselves. They resemble the New York ragamuffin in some ways but they laugh more and when they laugh, their faces are a wonder and a delight and a terror.

They swagger with consummate valor. They are obviously independent of everything under the skies, excepting perhaps their own boss and he must be in a habitual state of surprise that he continues to exist. They swear long ponderous oaths with magnificent ease. They remind one of babes armed with great swords. And there is a considerable portion of them named: "Redny."

Through their ragged shirts we could get occasional glimpses of little bare shoulders black as stoves. They looked precisely like imps as they scrambled about to get a view of us and to ascertain if possible if we were willing to give away any tobacco.

The slate-pickers, all through this region, are yet at the spanking period. One wonders continually about their mothers and if there are any school-houses. But as for them, they are not concerned. When they get time off, they go out on the dump-heap and play base-ball, or fight with boys from other breakers, or among themselves, according to the opportunities. Perhaps, too, they can get to be door-boys down in the mines and, later, mule-boys. And after that laborers and helpers. And finally when they grow to be great big men they can become miners, real miners, and go down into the mines and get "squeezed," or perhaps escape with a mere attack of "miner's asthma." Meanwhile, they live in a place of infernal noises. The crash and thunder of the machinery is like the roar of an immense cataract. The room shrieks and blares and bellows. Clouds of dust blur the air until the windows shine pallidly, afar off. All the structure is a-tremble from the heavy sweep and dash and circle of the ponderous mechanism. And down in the midst of it, sit these tiny black urchins, breathing this atmosphere until their lungs grow heavy and having this clamor in their ears until they grow deaf as bats. Poor little ambitious lads, it is no wonder that to become miners, is the height of their desires.

Over in front of a little tool house, a man, smoking a pipe, sat on a bench. "Yes," he said, in reply to our letter, "I'll take yeh down, if yeh like." He led us by little cinder paths to the shed over the mouth of the mine. A gigantic fan-wheel, near by, was twirling swiftly. It created cool air for the miners, who on the lowest vein of this mine were seven hundred and fifty feet below the surface. As we stood silently waiting for the elevator, we had an opportunity to gaze at the mouth of the shaft. The walls were of granite blocks, slimy, moss-grown, and dripping with water. Below was a curtain of ink-like darkness. It was like the opening of an old well, sinister from tales of crime.

The black greasy cables began to run swiftly. We stood staring at them and wondering. Then of a sudden, the elevator appeared and stopped with a crash. The men upon it were like apparitions from the centre of the earth. A moment later, we stood upon it, a little group armed with flickering lights. There was an instant's creak of machinery and then that landscape that had been framed for us by the door-posts of the shed, disappeared in a flash. We were dropping with extraordinary swiftness straight into the earth. It was like a plunge, a fall. The noise of the machinery was an imposing thunder. The flames of our little lamps fluttered and flew and struggled like birds to release themselves from the wicks. "Hang on," roared our guide above the tumult.

The dead black walls slipped swiftly by. They were a swirling dark chaos on which the eye tried vainly to locate some coherent thing, some intelligible spot. One could only hold fast and listen to the roar of this implacable descent. It was a journey that held a threat of endlessness.

Then suddenly the dropping platform slackened its speed. It began to descend slowly and with caution. Presently, with a crash and a jar, it stopped. Before us stretched an inscrutable darkness, a soundless place of tangible loneliness. We were in the mines.

Our guide strode abruptly into this gloom. His lamp flared shades of yellow and orange upon the walls of the tunnel. Little points of coal caught the light and shone like diamonds. Before us, there was always the curtain of an impenetrable night. We walked on with no sound save the crunch of our feet upon the coal-dust of the floor.

All at once, far ahead shone a little flame, blurred and difficult of location. It was a little indefinite thing, like a wisp-light. We seemed to be looking at it through a great fog. Presently, there were two of them. They began to move to and fro and dance before us.

After a time we came upon two men crouching where the roof of the passage came near to meeting the floor. If the picture could have been brought to where it would have had the opposition and the contrast of the glorious summer-time earth, it would have been a grim and ghastly thing. Their garments were no more sable than their faces and when they turned their heads to regard our tramping party, their eye-balls and teeth shone white as bleached bones. It was like the grins of two skulls in the shadows. The tiny lamps on their hats made a trembling and weird light that left shrouded in mystery the movements of their limbs and bodies. We might have been confronting terrible spectres.

But they said "Hello, Jim" to our conductor. Their mouths expanded in smiles, wide and startling smiles.

In a moment they turned again to their work. When the lights of the party reinforced their two lamps, it could be seen that one was busily drilling into the coal with a long thin bar. The low ominous roof pressed his shoulders as he bended at his toil. The other knelt behind him on the loose lumps of coal.

He who worked at the drill engaged in conversation with our guide. He looked back over his shoulder, continuing to poke away. "When are yeh goin' t' measure this up, Jim?" he demanded. "Do yeh wanta git me killed?"

"Well, I'd measure it t'-day, only I ain't got me tape," replied the other.

"Well, yeh wanta hurry up," said the miner. "I don't wanta git killed."

"Oh, I'll be down on Monday."

"Humph!"

They engaged in a sort of an altercation. One had to look closely to discern that they were smiling at each other. The vague illumination created all the effect of snarls of hate.

Presently, we left them to their drear and lonely task. All along this passage we came upon other little low-roofed chambers each containing two men, a "miner" who makes the blasts and a "laborer" who loads the coal upon the cars and assists the miner generally. And at each place there was this same effect of strangely satanic smiles and eye-balls glittering in the pale glow of the lamps.

Sometimes, the scenes were absolutely infernal in their weird strength. Once when we were traversing a silent tunnel in another mine, we came suddenly upon a wide place where the miners were lying down in a group. As they up-reared to gaze at us, it was like a resurrection. They slowly arose like ghouls, mysterious figures robed in enormous shadows. The swift menacing flashes of the steel-gleaming eyes were upon our faces.

At another time, when my companion, struggling against great difficulties, was trying to get a sketch of the mule "China," a large group of miners gathered about us, intent upon the pencil of the artist. "China," indifferent to the demands of art, changed his position after a moment and calmly settled into a new one. The men all laughed and this laugh created the most astonishing and supernatural effect. In an instant, the gloom was filled with luminous smiles. Shining forth all about us were eyes, glittering as with threats. "Whoa, China," they began to shout. Upon the roof were vague reflections of red and yellow.

From this tunnel, we went with our guide to the foot of the main shaft. Here we were in the most important tunnel of the mine, the "main gang-way." The wonder of these avenues is the noise, the crash and clatter and clang of machinery as the elevators speed up-ward with the loaded cars and drop crashingly with the empty ones. The place resounds with the shouts of mule-boys and there can always be heard the noise of approaching cars, beginning in mild rumbles and then swelling down upon one in a tempest of sound. In the air is the slow painful throb of the pumps working at the water that collects in the depths. There is booming and blasting and crashing and banging until one wonders why the tremendous walls are not wrenched by the force of this uproar. And up and down the tunnel, there is a riot of lights, little orange points flashing and flickering. Miners stride along, in swift and sombre procession. But the meaning of it all is in the deep bass ominous rattle of a blast in some hidden part of the mine.

[Pages 12, 13, 14 of MS wanting]

We were appalled occasionally in our visits to the mines by the quantity of mud through which we were obliged to wade in our wanderings through the tunnels. The feet of men and mules had churned it usually into a dull-brown clinging mass. In very wet mines, all sorts of gruesome fungi grow upon the wooden props that support the uncertain-looking ceiling. The walls are dripping and dank. And upon them too there frequently grows moss-like fungi, white as a druid's beard, that thrive in these deep dens but shrivel and die at contact with the sun-light.

When I had studied mines and the miner's life underground and above ground, I wondered at many things but I could not induce myself to wonder why the miners strike and otherwise object to their lot.

Great and mystically dreadful is the earth from a mine's depth. Man is in the implacable grasp of nature. It has only to tighten slightly and he is crushed like a bug. His loudest shriek of agony would be as impotent as his dying moan to bring help from that fair land that lies, like Heaven, over his head.

There is an insidious silent enemy in the gas. If the huge fan-wheel on top of the earth should stop for a brief period, there is certain death in the mines. A panic wilder than any where the sun shines is the scene that ensues. To him that escapes the gas, "squeezes," the trundling cars, the precarious elevators, the hundred dangers, to his bent and gnarled form there comes an inevitable disease, the "mine asthma." He has the joy of looking back upon a life spent principally for other men's benefit until the disease racks and wheezes him into the grave.

In all our encounters with the Irish and more particularly the Welsh miners, we found them to be a brave and cheery people. The Hungarians, Polacs and Italians impressed us differently. In the mines they looked like assassins and on the surface they looked like thieves. We could catch glints of the eyes, cowering aspects of the heads that made one imagine a scene in a penitentiary for bandits, murderers, and cannibals. They live in temporary buildings, ramshackle affairs that are an outspoken declaration of their intention of never becoming permanent citizens.

But the Welsh and Irish miners appeared to us to be bold, hardy, warm-hearted fellows stout of limb and genial of face, men who lived perilous lives in a matter-of-fact, manly way. Their faces were frequently bright with intelligence and strength. They were erect of figure and muscular and straight of limb. To us they were men who worked hard and risked much in an endeavor to have certain lights of comfort glow in their homes. Some succeeded, others did not but it seemed to us that they all deserved some measure of warm contentment and peace. One cannot go down in the mines often before he finds himself wondering why it is that coal-barons get so much and these miners, swallowed by the grim black mouths of the earth day after day get proportionately so little.

While I was in Wilksbarre, there was an accident at a mine near there that threatened the lives of about twenty coal-brokers and other men who make neat livings by fiddling with the market. The elevator and the fan became paralyzed so that the visitors were menaced with death from gas in a mine ten hundred feet deep. The miners helped them up ladders to the surface. Upon their arrival, they promptly fainted or agitatedly drank whiskey, according to their dispositions. They were weak with the horror of it. The newspapers were deeply interested in the affair and told of it well. The reading public breathed a great sigh of relief at the escape of the coal-brokers.

I hasten to express my regards for these altogether estimable coal-brokers and there is of course no doubt that there was the usual proportion of good and generous men among them but I must confess to a delight at for once finding the coal-broker associated in hardship and danger with the coal-miner. I confess to a dark and sinful glee at the descriptions of their pangs and their agonies. It seemed to me a partial and obscure vengeance. And yet this is not to say that they were not all completely virtuous and immaculate coal-brokers.

If all men who stand uselessly and for their own extraordinary profit between the miner and the consumer were annually doomed to a certain period of danger and darkness in the mines, they might at last comprehend the misery and bitterness of men who toil for existence at these hopelessly grim tasks. They would begin to understand then the value of the miner, perhaps. Then maybe they would allow him a wage according to his part. They will tell you all through this country that the miner is a well-paid man. If you ask the miner about his condition he will tell you, if he can confide in you, that the impersonal and hence conscienceless thing, the company

[MS *page 19 ends mid-page and pages 20 and 21 are wanting*]

the study in black faces and crimson and orange flame, vanished.

We were on our swift way to the surface. Gradually the pungent odor of the mines, an odor of powder-smoke, kerosene, wet earth, went from out our nostrils. The cables slid rapidly and the platform swayed in a usual fashion. Of a sudden the fleeting walls became flecked with light. It increased to streams. Then before our eyes burst the radiance of the day. We closed our lids before the high splendor of the sun afloat in a sea of spotless blue. It was a new scene to us, and wondrous.

Of the sinister struggle far below there came no sound, no suggestion save the heavily loaded cars that emerged one after another with terrific monotony and were sent creaking up to feed the insatiate breaker.

No. 155   PIKE COUNTY PUZZLE || "HSTR WTH XZOASCVAR"
—*Senger.* || CAMP INTERLAKEN, PENN., AUGUST
28, 1894.   NO. I. |||

FRESH DETAILS.

NEW FACTS CONCERNING THE LATE TERRIBLE RIOT IN THE THIRD TENT.

The Situation Previous to the Outbreak.
The Scrap in Detail—Desperate Violence of Wicked Wickham
and Impious Hulse. Night of Stormy Tubbs.

It seems from the latest stories of the recent bloodshed here
that the whole dreadful affair wás caused by a dinnerhorn
in the careless hands of Mr. S. Energetic Brinson of Port
Jervis, N.Y. He has been arrested and is now suffering great
agony with his feet tied together while jig-music is pumped
automatically into his ears.

From the scattered and quite incoherent account of the
affair it seems that the situation upon that fatal morning was
about as follows: Within the tent, Stormy Tubbs, Wicked
Wickham, Pan-cake Pete and Ravenous Pierce were deluding
themselves with the idea that they were playing cards. Meanwhile Ontario Bradfield was stuffing straw softly down the
neck of Pan-cake Pete. Wild Bill Woodward was glowering
vindictively into the air and muttering something about the
girls, to the effect that he wished they were all in Seoul,
Corea. Impious Hulse was half-unconsciously using his smile
to tighten up the guy ropes of the canvass structure. Arlington,
N.J., Ambler was feverishly searching for his hand-mirror. Thus
stood the scene, calm, tranquil, typical of camp life, utterly
conventional. One had only to look at Ontario's evolutions
with the straw to see that everything was as usual.

But underneath this repose, this careless abandon of posture
and thought, lurked the grim, red spirit of hate and battle.
Only the touch of a match and the black rages that were
privately consuming these men would burst into the flame
of war. Would it come? Who could tell? The bystanders quivered with alarm and expectancy. It was a terrible crisis.

Without, just a step from this seething place of men's

passions, the glory of the mild and gentle summer was upon the earth. Over the green fragrant forest flickered the golden light of the sun and the waves of the lakes were touched with splendor. Upon the rocks, Kate Green and Sadie Sliter were hanging up the quilts and Bess Rogers was mournfully eating candy. Over in a distant hammock Larry lay sleeping. All was peace.

When the shock came it was like an electric contortion of the earth. Suddenly, without warning, as astounding and numbing as lightning from a blue sky, the wild, barbaric howl of the dinner horn rang upon the expectant stillness. The terrible moment had arrived.

Swift and lithe as panthers the desperados in the third tent leaped to their feet and plunged for the door. A tremendous and hideous struggle developed. To the shivering spectators came the sound of a wild, hoarse gritting roar as the battling men crashed together in the narrow door-way. It seems that little Arlington, Sussex Co., N.J., was the first to fall. Being directly in the track of the onward rush of the men and engrossed in his mirror, he was instantly overwhelmed. He fell, a writhing victim, and their unheeding feet were tangled in his face.

For a moment the terrific force of Stormy Tubbs' anger and appetite dominated the battle. Then Wicked Wickham who had been searching for a weapon of strength, began to use his personality as a wedge against the mass of foaming humanity. The crush and grind and bitter cut of bone and sinew came heavily to the ears of the watchers without. Impious Hulse, with a loud yell of baffled rage, was then seen to begin slicing a way for himself with his smile.

Old veterans of Napoleonic wars who stood regarding the battle said that it was a revelation to them. They declared that after all the Emperor of the French did not understand the first rudiments of war. In fact she herself, when observing the strife, came within a little inch of losing her self-possession and displaying interest.

The enormous effort could not be eternal. The weak must sink before the strong. Pan-cake Pete, Wild Bill Woodward and Wicked Wickham made a fierce and manful fight, but their defeat and destruction was of the inevitable things. They fell, and their appetites fell with them. Strong and bold, wild as a prairie wind, implacable as law, pitiless as fate, Impious Hulse, Ravenous Pierce, Ontario Bradfield and Stormy Tubbs swept toward the table. The scuffle on the threshold of success was short, fearful, thunderous. The spectators swooned around unheeded. Then at last from wreck and riot rose the form of Stormy Tubbs. A long wail, half dread, half admiration, came from the multitude. It was the form of the victory emerging from the crimson clouds of battle.

With one long muscle-enveloped arm he punched a hole in the sun. It was a gesture of triumph. The victor had announced himself. The strife was finished.

COLD WAVE.

HOWELLS, Orange Co., N.Y., Aug. 27.—A cold wave struck this place about six o'clock last night. It froze to death a valuable white rubber dog belonging to Reuben Watson, whose farm is near this place. The little children are skating in the streets. Isadore T. Billson was obliged to chop out his large crop of pumpkins with an axe. John T. Tanke, in his anxiety to get a drink, put his frozen bottle of whiskey under a steam pile driver. All four fingers of his left hand were mashed.

EMIGRATION TO CANADA.

MONTREAL, Aug. 13.—The Internation Association of the Amalgamated Fugitives from Justice, have admitted as members Wicked Wickham, Ontario Bradfield, the Two Knights in a Barroom, Accompanied by Royce and other popular anarchists of Middletown, N.Y. It is rumored that they have emigrated to this city because the sidewalks are constructed almost wholly of boards, and in Canada there is no tariff upon new sets of teeth.

LOST!

KANSAS CITY, Aug. 26.—A tired and dusty couple were seen wandering about in the outskirts of this city at a late hour last evening. They gave their names as Miss Pronk and Mr. Senger, both of Camp Interlaken. Upon Mr. Senger's person was found three quarts of milk and two dozen biscuits. They said they were lost and plaintively enquired the road home from Corson's. Corson is not known in this vicinity.

PROTEST IN PARLIAMENT.

OTTAWA, Aug. 14.—In the Canadian Parliament this morning Sir Duffer G. Duffy arose to enquire of the ministry why the hair oil the emigration laws with the United States were not made more stringent and prohibitive.

GRAND CONCERT.

A Brilliant Affair—Success of Miss Lawrence—Signor Pancako Peti's Alarming but Not Dangerous Display.

The concert given around the camp-fire here on the evening of August 13th was one of the most successful and paralyzing in the history of music. It is stated by well-informed spectators that it was really louder than any ten ordinary concerts. The excellent programme here is given:

I. Baritone Solo—"The Girl that Left Me Behind."
        Mr. Wicked Wickham Young.
II. Chorus . . . . "Ein Lieber Bier"
      The East Main Street Sengerbund, composed of
        Mr. Empty Senger and himself.
III. Mandolin Solo . . . . "Exit Quickstep"
        Dr. Burt.
IV. Tenor Solo, "Life on the Ocean Wave."
        Captain C. K. Linson.
V. Soprano Solo . . . . . . "Ancient Egyptian Ballad"
        Miss Agnes Lawrence.

This prominent soprano was so vociferously encored that she sang nine more of the ballads of the ancient Egyptians and twenty-six of the old Norse sagas. "Little Mary Green," "Sweet Marie," and "Two Little Girls in Blue," were among the number. In conclusion she touchingly rendered that favorite of Artaxerxes II, entitled "After the Ball." The enthusiasm of the audience was with difficulty restrained by the police. The regular programme was then continued:

VI. Soprano Solo . . . . . . "Two Little Girls in Blue."
    Miss Agnes Lawrence.
VII. Soprano Solo . . . . "Lizette"
    Miss Agnes Lawrence.
VIII. Soprano Solo . . . . "Mavourneen"
    Miss Agnes Lawrence.
IX. Soprano Solo . . . . "Lizette"
    Miss Agnes Lawrence.

At the conclusion of the programme, the first ten rows of orchestra chairs were moved back, and Signor Pancako Peti was introduced in his celebrated act with his trained voice. He first put it through such simple tricks as jumping, through his hands, running to fetch a thrown ball, standing on its head, etc. Later, they developed into more difficult feats. Signor Peti broke his voice across his knees, spliced it simply with a silk handkerchief and sang: "Give Me Back my Whisky Slings," with intense emotion and feeling. Next he held it between his thumb and finger in plain sight of the audience, when, presto, it was gone. The wondering multitude gaped when the Signor, passing down the centre aisle, laughed playfully and drew his voice from the left vest pocket of Ontario Bradfield's sweater. The Signor passed from one feat to another in his dazzling Italian manner, and as the curtain fell for the last time, all united in declaring that they had spent one of the most pleasant, enjoyable, and disastrous evenings of their lives.

CLOSE RACE.

PORT JERVIS, N.Y., Aug. 28.—Upon the arrival of the Milk train here this evening, the foot race to Geisenheimer's was won by Ray Tubbs in one second and two-thirds. Crane protested the decision.

HOTTENTOTS TRIUMPHANT.

WASHINGTON, D.C., Aug. 20.—It was learned here this evening that in the contest between the Japanese government and the Hottentot Base Ball Club for the services of Miss Beatrice Myers as mascot, the Hottentots were successful.

ACCIDENT.

Port Jervis, N.Y., Aug. 14.—As Stephen Crane was traversing the little rope ladder that ascends the right hand side of the cloud-capped pinnacle of his thoughts, he fell and was grievously injured.

HORRIBLE DISASTER.

A TREMENDOUS MISFORTUNE—NO LIVES LOST.

The Ship "Sarann" Meets a Gale—Wrecked within Sight of the Earth—Heroism of Captain Linson.

The survivors of the ill-fated ship "Sarann" reached port to-day, after one of the most tempestuous and quarrelsome voyages known to navigation. They were more than two hours and thirty minutes on the trip, which beats all records save those made when Frank Hulse held his celebrated slow races with himself. They were wan, thin, tired and foot-sore. It was with great difficulty that some of them walked from the boat to the dinner table.

The now famous captain of the ship received the congratulations of his friends with calm and simple dignity as befitted a hero. With no exaggeration, in honest manly fashion, he told the grim story of his fight with the sea, his victory over the elements. "You see," he said simply, "I don't like to row girls anyhow. I'll never do it again you bet."

The stories of the other survivors are told below.

Miss Myers:—"Bedad, we had nothing to eat but straw hats."

Miss Pronk:—"We were only gone a little while when the captain mutinied. It is quite unusual for the captain to mutiny, isn't it? Don't question me any more now please. Wait until after dinner."

Miss Hulse:—"He rowed about four miles, poor fellow. Now, at Syracuse and also at Harvard we—"

Miss F. Sliter:—"Oh it was all right."

PANIC IN GERMANY.

BERLIN, Germany, Sept. 18.—Captain Corwin Knapp Linson, the notorious American, was thrown into prison for debt here some weeks ago. In puzzling in solitude on some bitter revenge, he finally hit upon the project of ruining the country by consuming all their resources in brown bread and water. After an impressive fortnight, the courts hastily commuted his sentence to hanging. The Reichstag, at a special session, unanimously voted him the war budget as a testimonial of his worth and capacity. It was handsomely engraved with the American and German arms.

END OF THE FEUD.

RICHBURG, Miss., Aug. 10.—In the duel with ladders fought between Dr. F. M. Lawrence and Mr. R. Stormy Tubbs, the latter was easily the victor. In the first of the combat Lawrence aimed a frightful blow with his ladder at his opponent, but Tubbs' physical development passed easily between the seventh and eighth rounds of the weapon. He returned the blow and wedged his opponent securely between the sixth and seventh cross pieces. He was given the purse.

IMPROVEMENTS.

NEW YORK. Aug. 8.—Seward, Main & Co. have won the contract for laying the beer pipe line between Milwaukee and Camp Interlaken.

EXCITEMENT AT HOWELLS.

HOWELLS, Orange Co., N.Y., Aug. 27.—Miss F. Sliter passed through here on her way to Middletown at about 6.30 o'clock.

STRAYED:—A wall-eyed pipe with red chin-whiskers.

CRANE.

[*page 2*]

Pike County Puzzle.

INTERLAKEN, AUG. 28.

PROPRIETORS,

Mrs. W. T. Hulse,	F. M. Lawrence, M.D.,
Mrs. C. M. Lawrence,	Wickham W. Young,
Miss Gertrude A. Hulse,	Frank V. Hulse,
Miss Agnes Lawrence,	Arlington M. Ambler,
Miss Bessie L. Rogers,	William W. Woodward,
Miss Sadie L. Sliter,	Herbert S. Bradfield,
Miss Beatrice O. Myers,	S. R. Morgan,
Miss Julia F. Myers,	Richard R. Knight,
Miss Mary S. Pronk,	Samuel Knight,
Miss Florence M. Sliter,	Herbert B. Royce,
Miss Lizzie L. Royce,	Charles L. Pierce,
Miss C. Kate Green,	W. Ray Tubbs,
Corwin Knapp Linson,	Ellsworth Elliot.

In case the proprietor dies, the management of this paper shall descend to the office boy.

OFFICE BOY − − − STEPHEN CRANE.

All good shots who are infuriated at the appearance of this sheet are cordially and enthusiastically requested to consider the associate office boy to be responsible for it. Ring night-bell after 4.30 a. m. Please do not interrupt jack-pots.

ASSOCIATE OFFICE BOY—L. C. SENGER, Jr.

SUCSCRIPTION RATE AS FOLLOWS:

ONE YEAR − − − − $9,000,000.00

Blue stone or rattlesnakes will be taken in exchange. The editor wishes it to be expressly understood that he will *not* trade subscriptions for Erie Railway stock. The Milford red chips marked with a gilt horse-shoe are good in this office.

INTRODUCTION.

Having in this issue proven ourselves to be earnest, firm and intolerable representatives of the most advanced and exasperating types of rural journalism, we here take occasion to felicitate the universe upon our being present. This is the day of our first anniversary, beginning from next year. In looking over the coming months, we feel that we can justly point to the by-gone days with pride. It was only next January that a dispatch from Winnipeg, Man., reached us to the effect that a well-known forger of that section would have frozen to death if it had not been for a smelting furnace and twelve copies of this newspaper, which he chanced to have in his pocket. At nearly the same time we learned from reliable sources that the farmers of Wayne Co., were wintering their cattle on a bran composed of equal parts of condensed milk and our clever sheet. Meanwhile, the populace all about us was boiling over with enthusiasm and rage. It is the opinion of all incapable people that by 1883, we shall have developed a more incredible newspaper than any of which Pike county now boasts, and following in the illustrious foot-prints of those who come after us, shall stagger far into the land of journalistic success and infallibility.

It was a typographical error on the first page that caused us to say: "Seoul Corea" instead of "Seoul Japan."

The Weekly Hearth-Rug was misinformed in its statement that R. Stormy Tubbs' snore was run over by a bicycle and split. Our fellow citizen is as firm, healthy and elastic as ever.

Be sure and get our next Sunday's issue, and with it our colored supplement, a superb full-length portrait of the king of

Acrossthelake. It is not very tall, but it is as wide and willowy as thunder.

THE man who says our motto is a copy of our shot-gun load after we had emptied it into Pro Bono Publico, is a falsifying fiend. We wish some people around here would learn to understand the Chinese language.

As we surmised, our contemporary, the Curry Ear-Trumpet, was wrong in its wild tale that Stephen Crane, the celebrated pipe smoker, had broken out suddenly with virulent tobacco plants. It was a mere attack of cheroots.

IT was rumored in New York yesterday that Mr. Charles A. Dana, having caught one blinding glimpse of this issue of the PUZZLE, immediately gave a wild cry, set fire to the *Sun* office, and began a pilgrimage in our direction.

A MILLION years have passed since the introduction of fried-oat-meal into this country. We must judge the future in the light of the past. What assurances have we now of the further stomachial reduction of Ravenous Pierce?

WE hear this morning that Pro Bono Publico and Constant Reader are lurking in the woods that surround our office. The entire staff is massed in the second story windows with shotguns that are loaded with the word Riefensnyderspiel in heavy-faced Roman.

THE one-eighth of a spectator who disappeared directly after the roly-poly game has not yet been found. As the king of Acrossthelake has been arrested on a mysterious assault and battery charge, it is suspected that he has discovered the fraction alone in the woods and attempted to thrash it.

ONE of our most unreliable contemporaries, the Manayunk Cloud-burst, asserts that recently, at that place, Miss Pronk drove her team of hysterics around the track in 2.08 1–4. As a matter of fact, these swift flyers have not beaten 2.10 1–2 since the well-known record made at Princeton.

WE are glad to call attention to the work of one of our staff in his description of the roly-poly fight. He does not follow the vagaries and falsehoods of modern newspapers in his estimates of crowds. He remains in the realm of the absolute, careful, unswerving, conscientious to a degree. He simplifies the work of the census enumerator and renders turnstiles useless. With all our boasted progress, we have not yet invented a turnstile that can commute in fractions.

IT is with deep regret we learn that one day last week, as Mr. S. Energetic Brinson was running a lawn mower lightly over his beard, a blade caught and interfered with his features so seriously that he now closely resembles Mr. Willie Astor of London. The sympathy of his friends was extended to him at half-mast. His sister, Miss Charlotte Montague Brinson, the marvelous impersonator of activity, swooned and became paralyzed in both arms. It is said that she will not be able to wash dishes for four years.

COMMUNICATION FROM HENRY.

OUR friends advise us to print the following letter from Mr. Henry Labouchere as a special sign to our readers of our progress and our piety:

LONDON, ENG.
Aug. 29, '94.

EDITOR PUZZLE,

Dear Sir:—I don't like your newspaper at all. When I was a missionary among the Zulus, I saw many newspapers which I liked much better than I do yours. The rum was cheaper there, too. Since you insist upon printing your sheet, I shall return to Zululand.

Yours, terribly enraged,
H. L.

"HSTR WTH HZOASCVAR."

It was directly after the victories of Jena and Pittsburg Landing. Peter the Great was at the zenith of his power. One day
the king ordered forward his favorite regiment of stenographers
and commanded them to storm the position in their front. With
a loud cheer for their beloved emperor, the stenographers
bravely sprang forward, a squadron of mounted fire-engines
thundering into position to support them. Instantly every gun
along the whole Italian front opened a destructive fire. The
king bended forward anxiously in his saddle intent upon every
movement of his brave stenographers. It was a terrible struggle.
At last he saw the New Zealanders swarming in untold billions
upon them. No courage could withstand those hordes. The day
was lost. The emperor gave vent to a bitter sigh, and turning
to his chief of staff said sadly; "Hstr wth Xzoascvar!"

Whose conscience is not touched by these simple words coming from a man when his soul was dark with tribulation?
Others may do as they choose, but as for the editor of this
newspaper, when his stenographers fail in the attack, when
his mounted fire-engines sink in defeat, his soul shall turn in
fraternity to the great emperor of the Japanese, and his lips
however feeble, shall murmur: "Hstr wth Hzoascvar."

FOR SALE.

AN iridescent radiating, resplendent, illuminated canine who
never answers to the name of Don. Just the thing for a starving
Arab in the middle of Sahara at noon.

AGNES LAWRENCE.

Copies of the new ballad entitled "The Little Red Hammock
Under the Trees," are on sale at my restaurant.

W. W. Y,

A choice revolver, unused.

DR. BURT.

BUSINESS ANNOUNCEMENT.

Little Candy Carrier Catchem will carry candy as usual.

CANDY CARRIER CATCHEM

TELEGRAPHIC NEWS

CHICAGO, Ill., Aug. 20.—At a special meeting of the Enlightened Brothers of Anarchy, held here this evening, the following resolutions were adopted:

WHEREAS, We recognize the futility of human effort, the temporary element in human construction and general uncertainty of human plans, we hereby vest all power and control of this society in a more formidable being.

RESOLVED, That the president of this society, in whom all power and control is now vested, shall be Wicked Wickham.

NEW CREED.

TERRA HAUTE, IND., Aug. 10.—Hungry Elliot, the evangelist, is besieging this town. He asks why men should strive together. They waste their opportunities for progress in futile battles with each other, he says. He claims that the wrath of men should come to a focus upon some particular thing, and thus give everybody certain times in which they could do something besides grapple with the hostility of the world. He says that so many people have focussed their wrath upon him that he wouldn't mind the others. So to start the thing he offers himself as a first objective point. He agrees to remain in position until the Grant monument is finished. As an evidence of good faith, he allowed the crowd at the opera house last Sunday night to throw bricks and pieces of lead pipe at him. Later, Excelsior Hose Co. No. 9 played a three inch hose on him amid the delirious cheering of the populace.

THE DANCE AT CURRY'S,
(*From the Misleading Record.*)

One evening Pop threw open the doors of his palatial barn to the world, but as the inhabitants of Interlaken had a good start, nobody got in but them and Mr. George Elston, who gave the dance. Every loyal son of Interlaken at once contributed one white chip each to the everlasting memory of Mr. Elston as a benefactor of Pike County. Lanterns were hung from the rafters and the fiddler piped blithely in a corner. The clans departed from Interlaken when the camp-fire made crimson reflections on the amassed shadows of the trees and returned when these were swallowed by the grey and amber lights that shone in the east. The barn on the hill was decorated as farmers always decorate their barns, in a wealth of hay and shadow and beam. The wind blew from where the sombre-hued lake lay in the moon-light and across it, within the mystic gloom of the pines was the red shine of the camp-fire of Interlaken.

SNAKE MASSACRED.

BRADNER WOODS, Penn., Aug. 28.—L. C. Senger, Jr., and Stephen Crane, when passing through this city late this afternoon, killed a rattlesnake measuring over 93 feet and with 362 rattles.

PERSONAL ADVERTISEMENTS.

BESSIE.—"All yite."   WICK.

WICK.—"All yite."   BESSIE.

JULIE.—I'm mad at you.   FRANK.

AGNES.—Why have I not written? Thunderation! I *have* written! One-two-three-four letters! What d'you want?

A. N. J., A.

If the red-haired young man with the keen brain and the freckles will meet the mop-headed young gentleman in the mud-colored sweater by moonlight and alone he will hear something greatly to his disadvantage.

[*page 3*]

SPORT AT SPRING BEACH.

FASHIONABLE CROWD GATHER TO SEE.
THE ANNUAL ROLY-POLY CONTEST.

Appearance of the Athletes —Skillful Misses by Crane—
Constitutional Inaccuracy of Linson—Miss Hulse's Puzzling
Delivery—Fatal Termination of the Game.

The long looked-for event came off at Spring Beach yesterday. Hours before the time appointed, the beach was covered by throngs of fashionable people. The steam yacht of Dr. F. Mortimer Lawrence of Philadelphia, was one of the first of the pleasure boats to take prominent position. Her brass and mahogany shone gaily in the sun. Fourteen of the handsomely-attired crew were busily bailing out amidships. As she gracefully rounded to, the signals fluttered out at her fore with the news that the ship's cook had gone on strike.

Beautiful costumes abounded among the fashionable people who surged against the ropes. Miss L. C. Senger was attired in black crape man-o'-war sails, with corinthian columns and light-houses wreathed across the front. Miss Ontario Bradfield's pearl grey sentry box over-skirt was only matched by the Indian corn that grew exuberantly from her majolica ware hat. Miss W. W. Young's white satin corsage, with green blinds and a brick chimney, was well set off by a skirt of ornamental fire places, finished in hard maple. While the fashion reporter was gone for a drink, Miss Crane disappeared, so that part of the excitement which was furnished by her apparel, cannot be described.

Promptly at 11.15 two steam-boats rounded the point and a mighty shout went up from the vast crowd of thirteen spectators. A moment later twelve brawny and sun-burned athletes strode grimly up the beach.

The preliminaries were quickly arranged. Then Pan-Cake Pete, the veteran dispatcher of breakfasts, took the bean bag and toed the line. The audience breathlessly awaited the result of the first throw. It was a miss. One-fourth of the audience was carried fainting from the premises. The remaining three-fourths, or nine and three-fourths, cheered lustily as he next threw right at where Ravenous Pierce lived. With his usual panther-like swiftness, Ravenous discharged the bag directly at stalwart Captain Linson, who ducked his head so quickly that he threw two toes completely out of joint. The captain shoved the missile at Stormy Tubbs, who nailed Miss Hulse. The latter, in turn, bowled over Wicked Wickham. This talented young expert made a wild swipe at Empty Senger, but it seems that the brass wheels of his self-acting demeanor of superiority had not been oiled that morning, and a dropped cog tripped him badly just as he was edging up to throw. The referee said Senger was safe. One-half the crowd, or four and seven-eighths, howled "Yaller." A relative of the wounded man swooned in the grand stand. This left eight and three-quarters.

Wicked Wickham, on his second try, hit the lithe and agile representative of Coney Island, who began to prowl around after her ancient enemy, Pan-Cake Pete. She missed him, and in deploring her failure, allowed everyone else to get out of range. After this characteristic proceeding she made a skillful, unerring shot at Impious Hulse and struck Miss Pronk heavily. At this moment three of the injured spectators were announced as resusitated and led back into the grounds. This swelled the audience to eleven and three-quarters.

During the next play the referee made a decision which again divided the spectators into two opinions, four and five-eighths declaring for the referee, and the other seven and one-eighth protesting that his decision was absurd. At length, Miss A. L., enjoining her self-possession not to go too near the water, came hastily forward without it, and missed everything this side of Arlington, Sussex County, N.J. The disappointment broke the bean bag, and in the excitement that followed, eleven and five-eighths spectators, grown thin from suspense, fell through the railing of the grand stand and were instantly killed. The other one-eighth, with a maniacal cry, broke for the woods.

THE GAME OF THE CHAMPIONS.

Complete Record of the Whist Encounter as Witnessed by our Sporting Editor.

[EDITOR's NOTE—Our sporting reporter is dead. He died soon after the game herein described. When he returned to the office he was feeling badly. His voice shook. He said that he had always considered himself a sporting reporter of high degree but he knew now that there were some things too vast for his mind. He was discouraged. He said that he had better die. He died. Below is his last exertion. Wild Bill was a good sporting reporter. He is now dead. Good-by, Bill.]

[EDITOR's NOTE No. 2.—The public will please remember that Bill is dead and if this account seems incoherent and even visionary at times, they must send their complaints elsewhere than to this office.]

THE GAME.

Tubbs led from his flannel suit, which was his long suit, in fact, it was the longest suit in camp. On account of his familiarity with farm life, Senger played a spade, Pierce played La Serenata and Elliot took the trick, because he always took anything he could lay his hands on. Elliot and Tubbs disputed as to which should then lead. Tubbs claimed that Elliot's intellect was not of the grandeur which would properly entitle him to lead in such an assemblage. Whereupon Elliot cried that he had remained on the ground with everyone's feet upon him long enough. They had not permitted him to lead in even the record for getting fire wood. He was about to assert his rights, he said. After Elliot had asserted his rights Tubbs led.

Senger played another spade; Pierce played thunder with his partner's hand, and Elliott took the trick because he got there first. In the third inning Senger knocked the deuce of hearts into right field for a good single, and the jack of diamonds gracefully slid to second. The long waving curls of the king of spades floated upon the breeze as he sprinted for home plate. At this moment the trump three spot made an intricate carom on the red ball, and the ten of diamonds knocked down all nine pins with one wild, luxuriant sweep of his arm. The eight of hearts hit the first pigeon as it quartered to the right.

Above the furious clamor of the multitude arose the voice of Senger, telling his partner that he couldn't play lacrosse with a shad net. As the excitement in a measure subsided, Pierce woke up and said: "What's trumps."

The fourth round would have been the end of the bout and a walk-over for the queen of diamonds if it had not been for the ability of the queen of clubs to take punishment. She braced up in the fifth and sixth and punched her opponent all over the ring. At the end of the half hour Pierce was no less than seven laps ahead of Elliot, whose appetite weighed him down in a manner that made the whole thing a gigantic handicap. At this moment the four of spades declared that he could shoot all around Senger when it came to the game of miggles, and as the play became violent through the enthusiastic rivalry of the two experts, Tubbs pulled the stroke up to 39 and his boat took the lead. The nine of diamonds was playing right-half-back and his long run at this critical time was the feature of the game but Tubbs at once braced up and hit seven glass balls without a miss. It was then apparent that Senger would have to swing Indian clubs better or Elliot would win the yacht race. Throughout the game the pitching of the king of clubs was superb and behind the bat the five of diamonds played with a skill that delighted the bleachers, nailing the base-stealers with a regularity that was beautiful. Senger here neglected to put in his ante and the referee called the match off. In the excitement that ensued Pierce swallowed his pipe. This accident caused widespread horror and lamentation. It was a brand new pipe costing one dollar and a half. They hope to recover the stem which was of first-grade amber.

The game, as a matter of fact, was a season of misfortune and catastrophe. Mr. S. R. Morgan after watching the game for some time in morbid silence, went away and calmly drowned himself in the pond and Elliot fell down and fractured one of the finest appetites that this country has been able to produce. On account of the gathering darkness the ninth inning was not played out but at that time Pierce's boat had rounded the light-ship and was coming down the wind, a certain winner. The Senger colt was second under the wire.

ENQUIRY COLUMN.

All persons wishing to learn any of the undiscovered truths of the universe, will kindly address this newspaper, care of the ENQUIRY COLUMN. If there is any person who knows everything under the Heavens, it is the man who conducts this column. Providence has every faith in him. In fact, he often runs the earth for a while when times are slack during the summer months.

To the Editor:—Does Arlington Ambler conduct the Enquiry Column?

Anxious Reader.

No, Anxious, old stuff, not yet. You must reflect that there are some portions of the solar system, including Grover Cleveland, a part of South Africa, and this column, which Arly does not as yet conduct. Still, you may well be apprehensive. We are self-reliant, but we are not proud.

To the Editor:—Can you direct me on the road to Rigg's?

Mame Pronk.

We are obliged to refer you to Stephen Crane. We hate to refer even our enemies to Stephen Crane, but he is a person who knows all about the road to Rigg's. He don't say he made the road himself, mind you, but even the original maker of it would throw down his hand and quit if he once confronted the knowledge of the road to Rigg's possessed by Stephen Crane.

To the Editor:—What is your opinion of my silence. I have been where there are people who know about silences, and they say I am unusually silent.

Florence Sliter.

We should say that it is a great silence. In fact it is a heavy, white sand-stone stillness. When mingled with Pan-Cake Pete's wild profusion of invective and imprecation it makes what might be termed a happy balance.

To the Editor:—Do you recommend mixed drinks?

Kate Green.

Our sporting reporter was a man of fine discernment, and from the time he viewed a camp whist game until his tragic death, he preferred mixed drinks. He liked everything mixed, after that, Bill did. Nothing was right to him unless it was mixed. He adored Senger's metaphors and hash was heaven to him.

To the Editor:—Have you ever seen anything of my table manners?

Dr. F. Mortimer Lawrence.

No, we have never seen them. When we stated so valiantly in our introduction that persons wishing information concerning the undiscovered things of the universe could come to us, we never thought that a man would rise with this paralyzing question.

To the Editor:—Would you advise me to smile so freely?

Frank Hulse.

Yes, Frankie, your smile is everything that is adorable and peachy. We have seen your smile, however, when we have trembled for the bystanders, and we think if you erect a nice board fence at a protective distance, you can allow it to be as alluring, soft, and silken as you please. On second thought we might suggest that you build a snow shed over it during the winter months.

To the Editor:—What can I do with my voice?

Stephen Crane.

In the spring, Stephen, you can plough with it, but after corn ripens you will have to seek employment in the blue-stone works. We have seen voices like yours used very effectively as cider presses.

To the Editor:—Do you know a cure for a strong desire for rest. It effected me seriously during the last week of my stay in camp.

B. M.

A larger amount of sleep is a good cure for many of these complaints that effect us during the summer months.

HASTILY ANSWERED.

S. C.—In regard to your enquiry concerning the most imperturbable being in the universe, we should say that Napoleon, the great emperor of the French, is giving Jupiter Pluvius a rattling finish. The sphinx is lumbering along a very bad third.

F. H.—What would we do in case of a Manhattan cocktail? We would retire to a safe distance and throw stones at it.

R. T.—Yes, if we had the ace, king, queen, jack, ten, nine, eight, seven, deuce and tray of trumps in our hands we should certainly lead the four of diamonds.

S. C.—No, it would not be a good plan to make an asparagus bed in your hair. Asparagus needs nourishment. Summer, fallow it well and then plant poison ivy and wild cucumbers.

AN ADJUSTED QUARREL.

DRAMATIS PERSONAE.

A YOUTH · · · · · · · · · · · ·Who never fibs
A GIRL · · · · · · · · · · · ·Who never fibs

SCENE: Sunset Rock.—The grey rocks and green moss are in the shadows from the crimson and gold death of the sun over behind Pop Curry's barn. In the foreground the tranquil water is splashed with color. The youth and the girl are discovered disconsolately seated under a low, sighing hemlock.

THE GIRL (clearing her throat and speaking with feminine sternness.) "Now, I want to know why you did not keep your engagement with me?"

THE YOUTH (contritely) "Well, if I must tell you. I went to the theatre that evening and the curtain fell and sprained its ankle, so I—. But, look here, why didn't you keep your engagement with me last Tuesday?"

THE GIRL:—"Well, I meant to. Really I did, Frank, only when I was down to Paterson, the mill hands struck and I looked around to see who they had hit, and by that time—"

THE YOUTH (interrupting) "Never mind, Julie! Don't say another word about it."

[There is a great stillness while they both reflect. The youth moodily throws stones at the water while the girl stares fixedly but unseeing at the wondrous green tangle of forest that lays within reach of her arm.]

THE YOUTH:—"Well, now that we have so satisfactorily explained to each other, we might as well make up, hadn't we?"

[The girl nods her head; they make up.]

[CURTAIN.]

[page 4]

DINNER-TIME CONVERSATIONS.

Report from our stenographer, Mr. Empty Senger, who has had long experience as a treasurer, adopter, and appropriator of other people's remarks.

SCENE:—A long, narrow, board table on the rocks above the cooking stove. Trees, boulders, and water in the background. Over twenty ravenous citizens are about to eat.

HUNGRY ELLIOT:—"Hey, pass the butter!"

WICKED WICKHAM: (suavely)—"Will somebody please pass the butter to Elliot. He wants the butter."

[Julie Myers passes down the butter because she hates to see anybody starve.]

IMPIOUS HULSE:—"Oh, you oughter been swimming. Had more fun than a goat."

EMPTY SENGER:—"That's what we did. [Turning to J. M.] Julie, you'd learn to swim in about two thousand years."

JULIE MYERS:—"Oh, shut up, please."

F. M. LAWRENCE, M. D., the man whose interior is filled with caverns:—"Yes, Miss Royce, the centrifugal force of a gooseberry leaf rapidly revolved around an opaque cylinder of chloride of insomnia will eventually prove deadly to the sea serpents that so destroy the watermelon trees in this vicinity."

[He here encompasses nine slices of bread abruptly to compensate for the lost time.]

MISS ROYCE:—"I think so, too."

MRS. C. M. LAWRENCE:—"Is everybody getting enough to eat? I declare I feel that—"

F. M. LAWRENCE, M. D.:—"Mamma, pass the bread."

MISS PRONK (with a sudden rush of courage).—"Mr. Crane, don't you like the Lays of Ancient Rome? I think they are awfully sweet."

CRANE:—"My uncle had a hen named Ancient Rome, once,

and her eggs were popular all over the country. Yes, Miss Pronk, you are undoubtedly right. Agnes, will you please pass the sugar?"

AGNES LAWRENCE, (throwing up her hands tragically)—"Squelched again!"

(Falls limply in a heap.)

[*Stormy Tubbs* and *Ravenous Pierce* here exchange glances of sympathy with *Pan-Cake Pete*.]

KATE GREEN, (resolved to be good to everybody.) "Mr. Tubbs, don't you think it is fine up here?"

STORMY TUBBS, (fiercely) "What's that?"

MISS GREEN, (falteringly) "I say, don't you think it is fine up here?"

STORMY, (with gloomy scorn) "Of course, I do. What would I think of it?"

IMPIOUS HULSE:—"Come, now, children, don't get gay. Whoa, Bill! Hey, Arly, chase down that salt, will you? All yite, Stevie! All yite Bessie! All yite! O-o-oh, bird! Who is going to get a load of wood to-day? I ain't! No, Sir! My toe hurts! Well, it does! What the—hello, Bill! Huh!" (Smiles.)

MRS. HULSE:—(in a general way) "Oh, I don't know what I'll ever do with that boy. (Then to him.) Frank, don't be such a fool."

IMPIOUS HULSE:—"Well, my toe hurts!"

Miss Lawrence having recovered from her swoon, suddenly appears in a mood of wondrous gaiety, and leads the crowd in the following song:

See those banners gaily streaming
I'm a soldier now Lizette
I'm a soldier now Lizette
La la la la la la la
La la la la la la la la la la
With a sabre by my side
And a la la la la
I shall la la la la la
La la la la la la la
Oh it's glorious Lizette
La la la la la la la
The gay life of a soldier true
And the la la la la la la la etc., etc.

[Here Wicked Wickham seductively gets Pan-Cake Pete started on the Pilgrim's Chorus and then suddenly stops.]

PETE (to Wickham.) "You Digger Indian."

(Wicked Wickham turns on his superior smile.)

WILD BILL WOODWARD (suddenly inspired.) "All yite, Tevie?"

PAN-CAKE PETE:—"All yite, Bill!"

WILD BILL (continuing.) "All yite, Bessie?"

MISS B. MYERS:—"All yite!"

ALL TO EVERYBODY:—"All yite?"

EVERYBODY (in reply) "All yite!"

DR. LAWRENCE:—"Please pass the bread? What? Is it? Mamma, how did that happen? Here's the bread all gone and we're not half through dinner!"

MRS. LAWRENCE:—"Well, I don't know what we shall do. Here, we got two large loaves last night and three this morning, and now they are all gone. I declare I"—

DR. LAWRENCE:—"Will you pass the condensed milk, Bradfield, old man?"

GENERAL CHORUS:—"Who is going to Woods this afternoon? Ain't anybody?"

RAVENOUS PIERCE (after conferring with Stormy.) "We'll go!"

(They then exchange glances of mutual congratulation and admiration upon being superior to feminine fascination.)

MISS LAWRENCE:—"Oh, may I go with you?"

STORMY TUBBS:—"Certainly, you may!"

MISS LAWRENCE (in despair) "Squelched again!"

(She is carried away.)

MISS HULSE (suddenly impelled by an anecdote.) "Last – year – when – I – was – in – Syracuse – I – met – a – Harvard– man – who – said – he – knew – Sluggermason – as – well – as – he – knew – his – own – father – he – was – awfully – nice – he – told – me – all – about – some – nice – new – pool– tables – they – are – erecting – on – the – campus – at – Harvard – I – think – it's – great."

WICKED WICKHAM:—"What did you say, Gertrude?"

MISS HULSE:—"Oh, noneofyourbusiness."

EMPTY SENGER:—(Who has been furtively regarding Miss F. Sliter's Arctic atmosphere.) "May I pass you anything, Miss Sliter?"

Miss F. Sliter:—"No."

(Sudden dead silence.)

Hungry Elliot (afflicted with a thought,) "Say, Stevie, you had better get to bed earlier at night, hadn't you?" (Laughs with subtle appreciation of himself.)

Crane:—"Of course, you know, Hungry, that while your assistance is no doubt always of marvelous benefit to people, there are certain times when they would prefer to be left alone with their own meagre and simple devices for conducting themselves. As far as your insight and perception of events is concerned, I"—

Elliot:—(interrupting with one of his celebrated decisive retorts,) "Yaller! Yaller! Yaller!"

Miss S. Sliter (glancing at Crane and speaking in an undertone to Miss B. Myers,) "Isn't he terribly disagreeable sometimes!"

Bradfield:—"Gee-gerum!"

All (in wild chorus, and eloquent and masterly use of inflections). "Gee—gerum—gee! Goo! Gee! Yapin—gee—gerum—gee—gerum! Goo! What the—hello, Bill! What the hair-oil! Gee–gerum–gee! Gee–gerum!"

(The thing would be continued indefinitely if at that moment there did not appear that most beauteous and sacred of nature's wise creations, Don. Pan-Cake Pete, Wild Bill Woodward, Wicked Wickham, Impious Hulse, Stormy Tubbs and Ravenous Pierce all make private but swift and hard kicks at the imperial animal. There is a momentary clamor of excitement.)

Miss L.:—"Well, did the little love come all the way for his dinner without being called. Well, he was a bright little darling, so he was! Look, mamma! Look, Fred! Isn't he sweet?"

Mrs. L. (from deep conviction) "Well, he was!"

Larry, M.D., (sentimentally) "Um–m–m."

Miss L., (turning toward the unholy end of the table. She speaks with tremendous emphasis. Each word would do for a coin-dye.) "Well, I don't care. I think you boys are the *meanest things* to abuse my Don so."

Arlington:—"That's right. You fellows ought to quit!"

(Chorus of groans, howls and terrible glares at Arly. He evinces a sudden interest in his hash.)

Bradfield:—"Yapin–gee–gerum!"

CRANE:—"What the—where the—how the—"

WOODWARD:—"Hello, Bill!"

CRANE:—"Want any ice?"

YOUNG:—"No, Napoleon!"

CRANE:—"Git-ap!"

MISS ROGERS (speaking generally.) "You ought to know my brother. You'd like him, I know. He—"

LARRY, M.D. (interrupting) "Pass the sugar, please?"

MISS B. M. (precipitating into some incoherency at a distance) "Who did you say? Dick Knight? Of course, I admire him immensely."

MISS G.:—"Were you at the Pendennis Club spread, Mr. Crane?"

PAN-CAKE PETE:—"No!"

MISS G.:—"Were you, doctor?"

LARRY, M.D.:—"No!"

MISS G.:—"Were you, Mr. Senger?"

EMPTY S.:—"No!"

MISS G.:—"Weren't any of you there?"

TRIO:—"No!"

MRS. L.:—"Have you all had enough to eat? I declare it is a positively fearful undertaking, one of these meals. Have you all had enough?"

WICKED WICKHAM (courteously to Elliot.) "Have you had enough, old man?"

HUNGRY ELLIOT (gratefully, to Wicked) "Pass the potatoes, will you?"

(Here sailor Linson having eaten in dazed silence, fades shadow-like away toward the pond.) There is a gradual breaking of the battle line until all are gone but Larry M. D. and Gertrude. From the tent, where Wickham has gone to make a joke, come cries of "Yaller, Yaller!" Mr. S. Energetic Brinson and his sister, Miss Charlotte Montague Brinson, both of Port Jervis, N.Y., appear suddenly and charge violently toward the table.

MRS. HULSE (retrospectively.) "How those children do eat!"

MRS. L. (in awed tones.) "I never saw anything like it in my life!"

[FINIS.]

Stephen Crane,

Drink Mixer.

Whiskey Sours and Hot Slings a specialty.   .   .   .

Reference : Dr. Burt.

GRAND
SPECTACULAR
PRODUCTION
OF

" Two Knights in a Bar=Room. "

AT
GUNTHER'S
THEATRE.

W. W. Young, Restaurant.

BILL OF FARE

- Oat meal fried,
- Bread,
- Oat meal, fried,
- Butter,
- Oat meal, fried,
- Coffee,
- Oat meal, fried.

Meals served at all hours during the first and last weeks of camp.   .   .

No. 156   HOWELLS FEARS THE REALISTS MUST WAIT

WILLIAM DEAN HOWELLS leaned his cheek upon the two outstretched fingers of his right hand and gazed thoughtfully at the window—the panes black from the night without, although studded once or twice with little electric stars far up on the west side of the Park. He was looking at something which his memory had just brought to him.

"I have a little scheme," he at last said slowly. "I saw a young girl out in a little Ohio town once—she was the daughter of the carpet-woman there—that is to say, her mother made rag-carpets and rugs for the villagers. And this girl had the most wonderful instinct in manner and dress. Her people were of the lowest of the low in a way and yet this girl was a lady. It used to completely amaze me—to think how this girl could grow there in that squalor. She was as chic as chic could be and yet the money spent and the education was nothing—nothing at all. Where she procured her fine taste you could not imagine. It was deeply interesting to me. It over-turned so many of my rooted social dogmas. It was the impossible, appearing suddenly. And then there was another in Cambridge—a wonderful type. I have come upon them occasionally here and there. I intend to write something of the kind if I can. I have thought of a good title, too, I think—a name of a flower—'The Ragged Lady.' "

"I suppose that is a long ways off," said the other man reflectively. "I am anxious to hear what you say in 'The Story of a Play.' Do you raise your voice towards reforming the abuses that are popularly supposed to hide in the manager's office for use upon the struggling artistic playwright and others? Do you recite the manager's divine misapprehension of art?"

"No, I do not," said Mr. Howells.

"Why?" said the other man.

"Well, in the first place, the manager is a man of business. He preserves himself. I suppose he judges not against art but between art and art. He looks at art through the crowds."

"I don't like reformatory novels anyhow," said the other man.

"And in the second place," continued Mr. Howells, "it does no good to go at things hammer and tongs in this obvious way. I believe that every novel should have an intention. A man should mean something when he writes. Ah, this writing merely to amuse people—why, it seems to me altogether vulgar. A man may as well blacken his face and go out and dance on the street for pennies. The author is a sort of trained bear, if you accept certain standards. If literary men are to be the public fools, let us at any rate have it clearly understood, so that those of us who feel differently can take measures. But on the other hand a novel should never preach and berate and storm. It does no good. As a matter of fact a book of that kind is ineffably tiresome. People don't like to have their lives half cudgeled out in that manner, especially in these days, when a man, likely enough, only reaches for a book when he wishes to be fanned, so to speak, after the heat of the daily struggle. When a writer desires to preach in an obvious way, he should announce his intention—let him cry out then that he is in the pulpit. But it is the business of the novel——"

"Ah," said the other man.

"It is the business of the novel to picture the daily life in the most exact terms possible with an absolute and clear sense of proportion. That is the important matter—the proportion. As a usual thing, I think, people have absolutely no sense of proportion. Their noses are tight against life, you see. They perceive mountains where there are no mountains, but frequently a great peak appears no larger than a rat-trap. An artist sees a dog down the street—well, his eye instantly relates the dog to its surroundings. The dog is proportioned to the buildings and the trees. Whereas many people can conceive of that dog's tail resting upon a hill-top."

"You have often said that the novel is a perspective," observed the other man.

"A perspective—certainly. It is a perspective made for the benefit of people who have no true use of their eyes. The novel, in its real meaning, adjusts the proportions. It preserves the balances. It is in this way that lessons are to be taught and reforms to be won. When people are introduced to each other, they will see the resemblances, and won't want to fight so badly."

"I suppose that when a man tries to write 'what the people want'—when he tries to reflect the popular desire, it is a bad quarter of an hour for the laws of proportion."

"Do you recall any of the hosts of stories that began in love and end a little further on. Those stories used to represent life to the people and I believe they do now to a large class. Life began when the hero saw a certain girl, and it ended abruptly when he married her. Love and courtship was not an incident, a part of life—it was the whole of it. All else was of no value. Men of that religion must have felt very stupid when they were engaged at anything but courtship. Do you see the false proportion? Do you see the dog with his tail upon the hill-top? Somebody touched the universal heart with the fascinating theme—the relation of man to maid—and, for many years, it was as if no other relation could be recognized in fiction. Here and there an author raised his voice, but not loudly. I like to see the novelists treating some of the other important things in life—the relation of mother and son, of husband and wife, in fact all these things that we live in continually. The other can be but fragmentary."

"I suppose there must be two or three new literary people just back of the horizon somewheres," said the other man. "Books upon these lines that you speak of are what might be called unpopular. Do you think them to be a profitable investment?"

"From my point of view it is the right—it is sure to be a profitable investment. After that it is a question of perseverance —courage. A writer of skill cannot be defeated because he remains true to his conscience. It is a long serious conflict sometimes, but he must win, if he does not falter. Lowell said to me one time: 'After all, the barriers are very thin. They are paper. If a man has his conscience and one or two friends who can help him it becomes very simple at last.' "

"Mr. Howells," said the other man suddenly, "have you observed a change in the literary pulse of the country within the last four months. Last winter, for instance, it seemed that realism was almost about to capture things, but then recently I have thought that I saw coming a sort of a counter-wave, a flood of the other—a reaction, in fact. Trivial, temporary, perhaps, but a reaction, certainly."

Mr. Howells dropped his hand in a gesture of emphatic assent. "What you say is true. I have seen it coming. . . . I suppose we shall have to wait."

No. 157   GHOSTS ON THE JERSEY COAST

ASBURY PARK, N.J., Nov. 9.—Of all the brightly attired city people who throng this place during the summer months not one seems to care a penny for the ghosts that line New Jersey's famous stretch of seacoast. It is only in the fall, when the marshes around Barnegat turn a dreary brown and the gray autumn rains sweep among the sand hills that the slightest attention is paid to the numerous phantoms that dwell here. However, some parts of this coast are fairly jammed with hobgoblins—white ladies, gravelights, phantom ships, prowling corpses. In his cabin many an old fisherman, wagging his head solemnly, can tell sincere and fierce tales, well calculated to freeze the blood. Around the gay modern resorts these stories have lost weight, but in the little villages of the fishermen south of here, near the salt marshes of Barnegat, a man had better think three times before he openly scorns the legends of the phantoms. Even at Branchburg, too, there are people who will pummel your features well if you deny the dim bluish light that floats above the long grave wherein lie the dead of the *New Era*, flickering and spluttering in spectral wrath whenever any attempt is made after the gold which is said to have been buried with the bodies of the unfortunate sailors and emigrants. Too, if you go into the huckleberry region back of Shark River you had better not scorn the story of the great pirate ship that sails without trouble in twelve inches of water, and has skeletons dangling at the mastheads. Terrible faces peer over the bulwarks, and confound the visions of any who would witness the phantom movements from the shore.

In this region there is also an old Indian, dead a hundred years, who stalks through the land at night. He is looking, it is said, for his fair young bride, whom he buried in a previous century because she put too much salt in his muskrat stew. This ghost was once followed on his shadowy pilgrimage by some young men who had greatly fortified themselves with applejack, but when his pursuers came too near the ghostly Indian simply turned and looked at them. He had a stiletto-like glance, they asserted, which went straight through them as if they had been made of paper. So they ran away.

At Deal Beach a youth and a maiden, impalpable as sea mist, perambulate to and fro on the bluff, keeping their lovers' tryst while the wind swirls in the branches of the solitary tree and the stars shine through their forms of air.

Near Barnegat Light, wicked fishermen engaged in doing that which they ought not to do, hear low chuckles, and upon looking up quickly see an old crone, who chuckles at them for a moment and then goes off, looking back occasionally to chuckle.

At Long Beach, where men deep in slumber were killed by

brave Refugees and Tories from New York, few fishermen care to lie and sleep, for then the gray specter of the Tory captain, hideous from the ancient crimes, comes and holds a knife at the throat. When they flee they hear feet crunch in the sand at their heels, and no matter how fast they run they cannot shake off this invisible pursuer, who follows them to their threshold.

In fact, it can truly be said that more hair has risen on the New Jersey shore than at any other place of the same geographical dimensions in the world. The fishermen are never low in their imaginative faculties. They are poets, and although they create more ghosts than any other known place they turn no butchers into specters. No dead jeweler in these villages ever comes back to wind up his clocks. No departed cobbler returns to peg at his trade. It would be incompatible with the taste of the people. To make a good ghost a man has to be old and sinister; a crone, wrinkled and wicked; a maiden, beautiful and fragile. When such die, a serviceable phantom is added to the list.

An example of the discernment of the people in their choice of specters may be had in the famous legend of the black dog. They created a spectral black hound in this tale and they gave him red eyes. It was genius. No one knew better than they that a ghostly Yorkshire terrier could have no effect upon even the most timid. The specter must be a hound, and it must be black; no yellow dog would answer the purpose, nor a speckled one, nor a striped one. It must be black. Thus was built the legend.

The tradition of the black dog has been much obscured because of its great age. It relates away back prior to the Revolution, when the New Jersey coast was for the most part unpeopled. It was a desolate stretch of sand, pine forest and salt marsh. Upon the narrow strip of land that separates Barnegat Bay from the ocean there then lived men who were so villainous that they had made a business of luring ships to the shore by means of false lights that in stormy weather shone afar out to the jaded sailors, precisely as bright as the brightest beacons of hope. When a vessel would be wrecked, the pirates gayly plundered it. It was their habit to murder the crews.

One night there came a great storm which tossed the vessels

upon the sea like little chips. The Jersey coast was strewn with wreckage and many strong ships lay dying upon the bar. No coast has proved so formidable to navigation as this New Jersey shore, just a brown lip of land rearing from the sea. From a vessel the coast looks so low that one wonders why each wave has not swallowed it.

During this storm a fine full rigged ship struck the bar directly opposite the stronghold of the band of pirates. They ran down to the beach and cheered and caroused, for they had not even been put to the trouble of deceiving the pilot and decoying the ship upon the bar. The thing had happened without labor or plan. They gathered in a crowd at the edge of the surf and watched the ship's people clinging to the rigging and looking toward the shore. They clung in bunches, lines, irregular groups, reminding one of some kind of insects. Sometimes a monstrous white wave would thunder over the ship, bearing off perhaps two or three sailors whose grasp it had torn away and tumbling the bodies into the wide swirl of foam that covered the sea. Soon they grew so weary that they began to drop off one by one into the water, unable to stand the strain of the terrific rushes of the waves. The pirates on the shore laughed when they saw a mass of men try to launch the boats, for they knew that none could live in that sea. Presently, the bodies of sailors and passengers began to wash up at the feet of the pirates, who searched them for jewels and money. The hull of the ship was hidden in the white smothering riot of water, but the rigging, with its lessening burden of men, was faintly outlined upon the dead black sky. The pirates became busily engaged in overhauling the corpses.

At last a fine black hound emerged slowly from the water and crawled painfully up the beach. He was dragging the body of a young man by the shirt collar. The dog had fought a tremendous battle. It seemed incredible that he could have forced his way to shore with the body through the wild surf. The young man's face was ghastly in death. There was a grievous red wound in his temple where, perhaps, he had been flung against some wreckage by the waves. The dog hauled the body out of reach of the water and then went to whine and sniff at the dead man's hand. He wagged his tail expectantly. At last he settled, shivering, back upon his haunches and gave vent to a long howl, a dog's cry of death and despair and fear, that cry that is in the most indescribable key of woe. It made the pirates turn their heads instantly, startled. They gathered about the dead body and the dog to stare curiously. At the approach of this band of assassins, vagabonds and outcasts the hound braced himself, the hair of his neck ruffled and his teeth gleaming. For a moment they confronted each other, the pirates and the dog, guardian of his master's corpse. There stood the dog, a tempest of water behind him and the evil crowd of men before him, and not even a caress possible from the pallid hand at his feet. No doubt he did not comprehend the odds of his battle. He only knew one thing—to be faithful until he was dead.

Then one particularly precious villain perceived the glitter of gems upon the dead man's hand. He reached covetously forward, and the dog lunged for his throat. An instant later there were many curses and the thud of blows and then, suddenly, a human like scream from the dog. He crawled until he could lay his head upon the dead man's chest, and there he died, as the robbers were pulling the rings from his master's fingers.

The phantom of this black hound is what the fishermen see as they return home from their boats and nets late at night. There is a dreadful hatchet wound in the animal's head, and from it the phantom blood bubbles. His jaws drip angry foam and his eyes are lit with a crimson fire. He gallops continually with his nose to the ground as if he were trailing some one. If you are ever down upon the New Jersey coast at midnight and meet this specter, you had better run.

No. 158 MISS LOUISE GERARD—SOPRANO

MISS LOUISE GERARD first became prominent as a child violinist. She was but eight years of age when she attracted the attention of the public with her violin, and the prints of a dozen years ago contained frequent expressions of admiration for the talent of this little girl, who indicated in no way save by the tiny torch-like points in her large eyes the power, the maturity of thought necessary to comprehend fully the music that she played. The *St. Nicholas Magazine*, which, true to the publishing instinct, only adopts that which has been clamorously adopted by the public, printed a very charming picture of her. Since she has become well known as a soprano the result of her violin study still is evident in intonation and phrasing. Moreover, it is undoubtedly her early experiences upon the concert stage that enable her to appear now with an utter absence of the affectations and stupid mannerisms that so mar the performances of many famous people. She sings the quaint little English ballads as a girl might sing in the garden; not as if she knew she was an accomplished soprano, alone in a blaze of yellow light, with a multitude of eyes upon her. It is the finesse of experienced wisdom in a girl of twenty-two.

Miss Gerard has had opportunity for making a reputation in the musical capitals of Europe; her voice has easily gained for her a conquest enviably complete and final. Upon her first trip to London the journals of the city were astonished out of their lassitude and ceased to wear a bored air. They cried in chorus of the sweetness of her voice and of the excellence of her concerts. One newspaper enthusiastically advised British artists that they might to great advantage copy her method, informing them in a frank way that they had much to learn from her. In the meantime the concerts at St. James's Hall were well crowded by the critical people of London. The fact that the American colony appeared in force is a great proof that London was charmed with her, since the American colony are usually fearful of disclosing their patriotism until after they learn the attitude of the fashionable set. She returned to America from this first trip with a memory of the applause of London, and with the great prestige that a success across the sea gives to an American singer. Afterward in London she has been always assured of that profound attention that was granted her by the most intelligently critical part of London upon her first journey.

Later, in Paris, she was received with acclaim by the artistic French public. The Parisians crowded the fashionable drawing rooms to hear her sing. The American colony, which in Paris is a free agent and quite different from the American colony in London, welcomed her loudly. *Galignani's Messenger* said, in its review of her first recital: "Miss Gerard is the possessor of a pure soprano voice of excellent quality. * * * She was warmly applauded for her artistic rendering of Scotch and English ballads. Santuzza's aria, from *Cavalleria Rusticana,* was delivered with great dramatic power." Each Paris paper was obliged to conclude its review with a list of titled people and representative musicians who were in the audience. Less conservative journals than the *Messenger* caused intensely laudatory reviews to be written.

Miss Gerard has made quite a name for herself as a writer on both social and musical subjects. Her recent article in the *American Art Journal,* summing up all that is possible in musical interpretation under eleven philosophical rules, has been copied and indorsed by the leading musical papers of both Europe and America.

The dramatic quality is particularly strong in Miss Gerard's singing. She is careful of the meaning of those curious little cries of love, grief, war, which grow upon the hillsides of Scotland and in the meadows of England. She understands that they are not merely clever collections of notes to be faultlessly sung, but that they have a significance, a meaning that is as wide as the world, as universal as love, grief, war; that these songs, so often called "simple," are as simple as the human heart and no more. Hence she sings them with an intelligent comprehension. It is because of such interpretations that one is able to discern between the artist and the machinist.

The training which she has given her voice allows her to sing with no apparent effort, and the tale of the composer's reverie comes to the ear clear and pure as silver. The New York *Herald* recently described Miss Gerard as "one of the most charming and popular women prominent in artistic circles. Her exquisite voice would win her admiration everywhere, but added to this she possesses a cultured, lovely personality."

No. 159 THE GHOSTLY SPHINX OF METEDECONK

METEDECONK, N.J., Dec. 28.—About a mile south of here, on the low brown bluff that overlooks the ocean, there is an old house to which the inhabitants of this place have attached a portentous and grewsome legend. It is here that the white lady, a moaning, mourning thing of the mist, walks to and fro, haunting the beach at the edge of the surf in midnight searches for the body of her lover. The legend was born, it is said, in 1815, and since that time Metedeconk has devoted much breath to the discussion of it, orating in the village stores and haranguing in the post office, until the story has become a religion, a sacred tale, and he who scorns it receives the opprobrium of all Metedeconk.

It is claimed that when this phantom meets a human being face to face she asks a question—a terrible, direct interrogation. She will ask concerning the body of her lover, who was drowned in 1815, and if the chattering mortal cannot at once give her an intelligent answer, containing terse information relating to the corpse, he is forthwith doomed, and his friends will find him next day lying pallid upon the shore. So, for fear of being nonplussed by this sphinx, the man of Metedeconk, when he sees white at night, runs like a hare.

There have been those who have come here and openly derided the legend, but they have always departed wiser. Once a young man, who believed in the materialism of everything, came to town and perambulated up and down the beach during three midnights. He had requested the inhabitants to bring forth their phantom. She did not appear. During some following days the young man poked all of the leading citizens in the ribs and laughed loudly, but he was whipped within an inch of his life by an old retired sea captain named Josiah Simpson. Since then the legend has obtained a much wider credit, and for miles around Metedeconk the people evince a great faith in it.

The last man to assert definitely that he has encountered the specter is a bronzed and blasé young fisherman, who assures the world that the matter of its believing his story is of no consequence to him. He relates that one night, when swift scudding clouds flew before the face of the moon, which was like a huge silver platter in the sky, he had occasion to pass this old house, with its battered sides, caving roof and yard overgrown with brambles. The passing of the clouds before the moon made each somber shadow of the earth waver suggestively and the wind tossed the branches of trees in strange and uncouth gestures. Within the house the old timbers creaked and moaned in a weird and low chant. By a desperate effort the fisherman dragged himself past this dark residence of the specter. Each wail of the old timbers was a voice that went to his soul, and each contortion of the shadows made by the wind waved trees seemed to him to be the movement of a black and sinister figure creeping upon him.

But it was when he was obliged to turn his back upon the old house that he suffered the most agony of mind. There was a little patch of flesh between his shoulder-blades that continually created the impression that a deathlike hand was about to be laid upon him. His trembling nerves told him that he was being approached by a mystic thing. He gave an involuntary cry and turned to look behind him.

There stood the ghostly form of the white lady. Her hair fell in disheveled masses over her shoulders, her hands were clasped appealingly, and her large eyes gleamed with the one eternal and dread interrogation. Her lips parted and she was on the very verge of propounding the awful question, when the fisherman howled and started wildly for Metedeconk. There rang through the night the specter's cry of anger and despair, and the fisherman, although he was burdened with heavy boots, ran so fast that he fell from sheer exhaustion upon the threshold of his home. From that time forward it became habitual with him to wind up his lines when the sun was high over the pines of the western shore of Barnegat, and to reach his home before the chickens had gone to bed.

It seems that long ago a young lady lived in this house which then was gorgeous with green blinds and enormous red chimneys. The paths in the grounds had rows of boxwood shrubbery lined down their sides with exquisite accuracy, and each geometrical flower bed upon the lawn looked like a problem in polygons. This maiden had a lover who was captain of a ship that was given to long voyages. They loved each other dearly, and, in consequence of these long voyages, they were obliged to part with protestations of undying affection about three times a year. But once when the handsome sailor luffed his ship into the wind and had himself rowed ashore to bid good by to his love, she chose that time to pout. He spent a good deal of time in oration and argument, he proved to her in sixty ways that she was foolish to act thus at the moment of his departure, but she remained perverse, and during his most solemn abjurations she lightly and blithely caroled a little ditty of the day. Finally in despair he placed his hand upon his lacerated heart and left for Buenos Ayres.

But his ship had not passed Absecon Inlet before the maiden was torn with regret and repentance, and by the time the craft was a white glimmer upon the edge of the horizon she began to mourn and mourn in the way that has since become famous. As the days passed, her sorrow grew, and the fishermen used often to see her walking slowly back and forth, gazing eagerly into the southeast for the sail that would bear her lover to her. During great storms she never seemed able to remain quietly in the house, but always went out to watch the white turmoil of the sea.

The round, tanned cheeks grew thin and pale. She became frail, and would have appeared always listless if it were not for the feverish gleam of those large eyes, which eternally searched the sea for a belated sail.

One winter's day a storm came from the wild wastes of the unknown and broke upon the coast with extraordinary fury. The tremendous breakers thundered upon the beach until it seemed that the earth shook from the blows. Clouds of sand whirled along the beach. The wind blew so that it was nearly impossible to make headway, but still the young girl came out to stare at the impenetrable curtains of clouds in the southeast.

That evening as she made her difficult way along the beach, a rocket went up out at sea, leaving for a moment a train of red sparks across the black sky. Then she knew that sailor lads were in peril. After a time a green light flashed over the water, and finally she could perceive a large ship on the bar. Above the roar of the waves she imagined she could hear the cries of men.

The fishermen, notified by the rocket, came to the shore by twos and threes. No boat could live in such a sea and the sailors of the ship were doomed. The fishermen bustled to and fro, impatiently shouting and gesturing, but in those days their greatest efforts could consist in no more than providing fires, drink and warm blankets for any who by some astounding chance should escape through the terrible surf. From time to time seamen tried to swim to the shore, and for an instant a head would shine like a black bead on this wild fabric of white foam. Bodies began to wash up and the fishermen, congregating about huge fires devoted their attention to trying to recall the life in these limp, pale things that the sea cast up one by one.

The maiden paced the beach praying for the souls of the sailors, who, upon this black night, were to be swallowed in a chaos of waters for the unknown reasons of the sea.

Once she espied something floating on the surf. Because of the small grewsome wake, typical of a floating corpse, she knew what it was and she awaited it. A monstrous wave hurled the thing to her feet and she saw that her lover had come back from Buenos Ayres.

This is the specter that haunts the beach at the edge of the surf and who lies in wait to pour questions into the ears of the agitated citizens of Metedeconk.

No. 160 SIX YEARS AFLOAT

CAPTAIN WILLIAM B. HILLER sails the bark *Tillie B.* His ship now lies in Erie Basin and both the captain and the *Tillie B.* are just recovering from a most singular adventure of the sea. When questioned, the captain was reticent; he is a sane and honest captain in the American merchant marine and he objects to gaining reputation as a purveyor of sea yarns. But there are many old salts in his forecastle and no old salt that lives could let slip a chance to tell what they saw when 500 miles off the coast of Labrador on the 1st day of last July.

It seems that the *Tillie B.* was bowling along on her course before a fair wind when the man forward espied something long and black some two points off the star-board bow. It was monstrous in size and lay quietly on the water awaiting the ship. The man at the bow was non-plussed for a moment. The thing was not land. It was not a ship. It was not a whale. It was not anything that enters into the ordinary vocabulary of a man at the bow. It was a mystery; that is all it could be called. Recollecting his business the lookout cried: "Something mysterious, sir, pint off the sta'board!"

The mate went to the rail and looking at the thing said: "It is not land! It is not a ship! It is not a whale! Then what is it?"

Everybody on deck went to the rail and looking at the thing said: "It is not land! It is not a ship! It is not a whale! Then what is it?"

Meanwhile the *Tillie B.* was sailing nearer and nearer to this formidable object. Finally the mate grew nervous and going to the cabin stairs called down to Captain Hiller.

"We've sighted something, sir, and, it's not land, it's not a ship and it's not a whale and we don't know what it is."

The captain came on deck and going to the rail looked at the object and said: "It's not la——" But here he seized his speaking-trumpet and an instant later the wild orders roared through the vessel: "Slip the trolley! Throw the ship onto a switch—send a man back with a flag—wire the superintendant—helltopay—this here's a sea-serpent!"

Immediately all was panic on board the *Tillie B.* Men rushed to and fro dragging at ropes and blaspheming at their misfortune while the captain roared more orders than nine ship-loads of sailors could possibly have obeyed. But before they could stop the ship she had sailed very close to the thing and the captain going to the rail said: "It is not land! It is not a ship! It is not a whale! It is NOT a sea-serpent but may I have my own main-m'st stuffed down my throat if it is not the famous lumber raft which was lost in the North Atlantic some years ago and for which *U.S.S. Enterprise* and the revenue cutter *Grant* made such painful but useless search."

And so Captain William B. Hiller of the bark *Tillie B.*, now lying in Erie Basin, solemnly states that on July 1st he discovered the celebrated raft some 500 miles off the coast of Labrador. It was headed southwest, he says, but was not making much more way than a foundry. The raft is larger than any ocean-liner and it would be an ugly customer to meet under the conditions of a twenty knot gait and a dark night. The sea-serpents do not object to navigation by ships but lumber rafts are more unreasonable.

John Leary, the lumber expert who first conceived the plan of transporting lumber at sea by means of a raft was recently interviewed at his Newton Creek sawmill. "I think Captain Hiller's story to be very probable. I was employed personally in the construction of this raft and I know that it was constructed as strong—if not stronger—than many ocean steamers. Its general compactness and solidity made it almost as inseparable as one great massive log.

"This raft was the largest by some three hundred feet of any ever shipped by sea. In fact it was too large. Nothing like it is now attempted. It was constructed on an improvised dry-dock at Two Rivers, Nova Scotia, in the fall of 1890 and launched on the plan of an Atlantic liner's launching. The largest rafts we now undertake are three hundred feet long and weigh about four thousand tons. The one we lost was six hundred feet in length—longer than any liner. It weighed ten thousand tons. The method we used in constructing the monster was new and has been patented in this country, Canada and Europe. We now use it on a smaller scale. It took us just one day over six months to build the great raft and we required the steady employment of 55 men. The distinguishing feature of the system now patented—and what makes me feel positive that wherever the raft is, it is whole—is the method of fastening the structure together with chains. It is not a matter of merely bunching the logs and then binding them, as many might conclude. The method in fact is quite ingenious. For instance the strength is all concentrated in one long and powerful centre chain. The raft may be towed by either termination of this chain. Side chains placed diagonally to the centre are added at the ends so that the greater the force applied to the tow-line, the stronger the logs are drawn together and at every yard or so along the body, chains leading from the centre line are brought through to the surface and after being carried over a distance of about six feet return to the centre chain.

"The great 600 feet raft was 62 feet beam at its widest part. It was constructed like a monstrous cigar as this form seemed to us most sea-worthy. The necessary tapering to accomplish this design was mainly secured by arranging the timbers with the butts toward the centre.

"When completed the structure contained twenty-five thousand sticks of spruce and pine timber from thirty-five to ninety-five feet in length and a great quantity of beech, birch, and maple, making a total of four million, five hundred thousand feet of timber. The diameters of the logs ran from twelve inches to thirty-five at the butts, and from 6 inches to ten at the tips. At the time it was launched and ready to be towed the raft had cost us about thirty-two thousand dollars and the contract price for towing it to our Long Island yards was thirty-five hundred dollars.

"The launching of the raft was a most interesting event. A vast crowd came to see it. The ways upon which it was slid into the sea were twelve hundred feet in length. The raft at first moved slowly but its speed naturally increased until it cleared the 1,000 feet between it and the water in about thirty seconds without straining a chain or showing the slightest change in its form.

"When the cradle was removed, the raft was found to draw only 19½ feet of water.

"The object of bringing timber to New York in this manner is to get the longest logs here since vessels trading to Nova Scotia cannot handle sticks over sixty feet long. In the general market those of greater length come from Michigan and Ohio by rail which is very expensive.

"Having such full knowledge of the strength of the raft's structure I make little doubt of the truth of Captain Hiller's report."

At the offices of the various trans-Atlantic lines word had been received of the *Tillie B.'s* discovery and the report seemed to be generally credited.

Collector Kilbreth, however, is really the man who keeps

tabs on the sea-serpents and other ocean mysteries for the United States government and he was openly and shamelessly bored when the story was brought to his ears. "It's all right, my boy," he said, waving his hand wearily, "it's all right. Don't get excited. It is only another Menace to Navigation. Listen; have you ever heard of the phantom stove-factory which prowls the sea at midnight looking for unwary ships? No? Do you know that last April the ship *Actoronhisuppers* from Khartum heard the weird chortle of many frogs when seven hundred miles from land? Do you know that every possible combination of inventive imagination is worked on me every day? Talk about the wonders of the deep! Why I—well, as a matter of brevity I do not believe the raft story. Common sense tells me that by this time the celebrated monster is torn to pieces."

No. 161 ASBURY PARK AS SEEN BY STEPHEN CRANE

It is a sad thing to go to town with a correspondent's determination to discover at once wherein this particular town differs from all other towns. We seek our descriptive material in the differences, perhaps, and dismay comes upon the agile mind of the newspaper man when the eternal overwhelming resemblances smite his eyes. We often find our glory in heralding the phenomena and we have a sense of oppression, perhaps, when the similarities tower too high in the sky.

The variations being subtle, and the resemblances being mountainous, we revenge ourselves by declaring the subject unworthy of a fine hand. We brand it with some opportune name, which places it beyond the fence of literary art, and depart to earn our salaries describing two-headed pigs. Asbury Park somewhat irritates the anxious writer, because it persists in being distinctly American, reflecting all our best habits and manners, when it might resemble a town in Siberia, or Jerusalem, during a siege.

A full brigade of stages and hacks paraded to meet the train, and as the passengers alighted the hackmen swarmed forward with a rapacity that had been carefully chastened by the police. While their voices clashed in a mellow chorus, the passengers for the most part dodged their appeals and proceeded across the square, yellow in the sunlight, to the waiting trolley cars. The breeze that came from the hidden sea bore merely a suggestion, a prophecy of coolness, and the baggagemen who toiled at the hill of trunks sweated like men condemned to New York.

From the station Asbury Park presents a front of spruce business blocks, and one could guess himself in one of the spick Western cities. Afterward there is square after square of cottages, trees and little terraces, little terraces, trees and cottages, while the wide avenues funnel toward a distant gray sky, whereon from time to time may appear ships. Later still, a breeze cool as the foam of the waves slants across the town, and above the bass rumble of the surf clamor the shrill voices of the bathing multitude.

The Summer girls flaunt their flaming parasols, and young men, in weird clothes, walk with a confidence born of a knowledge of the fact that their fathers work. In the meantime, the wind snatches fragments of melody from the band pavilion and hurls this musical debris afar.

Coney Island is profane; Newport is proper with a vehemence that is some degrees more tiresome than Coney's profanity. If a man should be goaded into defining Asbury Park he might state that the distinguishing feature of the town is its singular and elementary sanity.

Life at Asbury Park is as healthy and rational as any mode of existence which we, the people, will endure for our benefit. This is, of course, a general statement, and does not apply to the man with seven distinct thirsts in one throat. He exists here, but he is minute in proportion. He labors unseen with his seven thirsts and his manners are devious. He only appears when he has opportunity to deliver his Ode to Liberty.

Besides the prohibition law, there are numerous other laws to prevent people from doing those things which philosophers and economists commonly agree work for the harm of society. It is very irksome to be confronted with an ordinance whenever one wishes for novelty or excitement to smash a canon to smithereens. Moreover, there are a number of restrictions here which are ingeniously silly and are not sanctioned by nature's plan nor by any of the creeds of men, save those which define virtue as a physical inertia and a mental death.

But in the main it is unquestionably true that Asbury Park's magnificent prosperity, her splendid future, is due to the men who in the beginning believed that the people's more valuable patronage would go to the resort where opportunity was had for a rational and sober existence.

On cloudy nights there is always one star in the sky over Asbury Park. This star is James A. Bradley. The storm forces discover that he cannot be dimmed. A heavy mist can vanquish gorgeous Orion and other kings of the heavens, but James A. Bradley continues to shine with industry.

Orion and other kings of the heavens complain that this is because they do not own an ocean front. He it was who in 1879 purchased a sand waste and speedily made it into Asbury Park, the seething Summer city. He has celebrated this marvel in a beautiful bit of literature in which he does not refer to himself at all, nor to Providence. He simply admits the feat to be an evolution instead of a personal construction.

This famous feature is not obvious at once. James A. Bradley does not meet all incoming trains. He is as impalpable as Father Knickerbocker. It is well known that he invariably walks under a white cotton sun umbrella, and that red whiskers of the Icelandic lichen pattern grow fretfully upon his chin, and persons answering this description are likely to receive the salaams of the populace.

He himself writes most of the signs and directions which spangle the ocean front, and natives often account for his absence from the streets by picturing him in his library flying through tome after tome of ancient lore in chase of those beautiful expressions which add so particularly to the effect of the Atlantic.

Then suddenly he will flash a work of philanthropy of so deep and fine a kind that it could only come from a man whose bold heart raised him independent of conventional or narrow-minded people, and his grand schemes for decorating the solar system with signs will be forgotten. Withal, he never poses, but carries his sublimity with the calmness of a man out of debt.

Of course there has long been a flourishing garden of humorists here who owe their bloom solely to the fact that Founder Bradley indulges sometimes in eccentricities, which are the sun of the morning and the rain of noon to any proper garden of humorists. But he is eccentric only in detail, this remarkable man.

The people should forget that, for purposes too mystic, too exaltedly opaque for the common mind, he placed a marble bathtub in the middle of a public park and remember only that he created the greatest Summer resort in America—the vacation abode of the mighty middle classes—and, better still, that he now protects it with the millions that make him power-ful and with the honesty that makes his millions useful.

Of late the Founder has been delivering lop-sided political orations from the tail-end of a cart to stage-drivers, newsboys, unclassified citizens and Summer boarders who have no other amusement. "I own the pavilions and the bath houses, and the fishing pier and the beach and the pneumatic sea lion, and what I say ought to go with an audience that has any sense." The firmament has been put to considerable inconvenience, but it will simply have to adjust itself to the conditions and await his return.

In the meantime the brave sea breeze blows cool on the shore and the far little ships sink, one by one past the horizon. At bathing time the surf is a-swarm with the revelling bathers and the beach is black with watchers.

The very heart of the town's life is then at the Asbury avenue pavilion, and the rustle and roar of the changing throng gives the casual visitor the same deep feeling of isolation that comes to the heart of the lone sheep herder, who watches a regiment swing over the ridge or an express train line through the mesquite.

As the sun sinks the incoming waves are shot with copper beams and the sea becomes a green opalescence.

No. 162 ADVENTURES OF A NOVELIST

THIS is a plain tale of two chorus girls, a woman of the streets and a reluctant laggard witness. The tale properly begins in a resort on Broadway, where the two chorus girls and the reluctant witness sat the entire evening. They were on the verge of departing their several ways when a young woman approached one of the chorus girls, with outstretched hand.

"Why, how do you do?" she said. "I haven't seen you for a long time."

The chorus girl recognized some acquaintance of the past, and the young woman then took a seat and joined the party. Finally they left the table in this resort, and the quartet walked down Broadway together. At the corner of Thirty-first street one of the chorus girls said that she wished to take a car immediately for home, and so the reluctant witness left one of the chorus girls and the young woman on the corner of Thirty-first street while he placed the other chorus girl aboard an uptown cable car. The two girls who waited on the corner were deep in conversation.

The reluctant witness was returning leisurely to them. In the semi-conscious manner in which people note details which do not appear at the time important, he saw two men passing along Broadway. They passed swiftly, like men who are going home. They paid attention to none, and none at the corner of Thirty-first street and Broadway paid attention to them.

The two girls were still deep in conversation. They were standing at the curb facing the street. The two men passed unseen—in all human probability—by the two girls. The reluctant witness continued his leisurely way. He was within four feet of these two girls when suddenly and silently a man appeared from nowhere in particular and grabbed them both.

The astonishment of the reluctant witness was so great for the ensuing seconds that he was hardly aware of what transpired during that time, save that both girls screamed. Then he heard this man, who was now evidently an officer, say to them: "Come to the station house. You are under arrest for soliciting two men."

With one voice the unknown woman, the chorus girl and the reluctant witness cried out: "What two men?"

The officer said: "Those two men who have just passed."

And here began the wildest and most hysterical sobbing of the two girls, accompanied by spasmodic attempts to pull their arms away from the grip of the policeman. The chorus girl seemed nearly insane with fright and fury. Finally she screamed:

"Well, he's my husband." And with her finger she indicated the reluctant witness. The witness at once replied to the swift, questioning glance of the officer, "Yes; I am."

If it was necessary to avow a marriage to save a girl who is not a prostitute from being arrested as a prostitute, it must be done, though the man suffer eternally. And then the officer forgot immediately—without a second's hesitation, he forgot that a moment previously he had arrested this girl for soliciting, and so, dropping her arm, released her.

"But," said he, "I have got this other one." He was as picturesque as a wolf.

"Why arrest her, either?" said the reluctant witness.

"For soliciting those two men."

"But she didn't solicit those two men."

"Say," said the officer, turning, "do you know this woman?"

The chorus girl had it in mind to lie then for the purpose of saving this woman easily and simply from the palpable wrong she seemed to be about to experience. "Yes; I know her" —"I have seen her two or three times"—"Yes; I have met her before——" But the reluctant witness said at once that he knew nothing whatever of the girl.

"Well," said the officer, "she's a common prostitute."

There was a short silence then, but the reluctant witness presently said: "Are you arresting her as a common prostitute? She has been perfectly respectable since she has been with us. She hasn't done anything wrong since she has been in our company."

"I am arresting her for soliciting those two men," answered the officer, "and if you people don't want to get pinched, too, you had better not be seen with her."

Then began a parade to the station house—the officer and his prisoner ahead and two simpletons following.

At the station house the officer said to the sergeant behind the desk that he had seen the woman come from the resort on Broadway alone, and on the way to the corner of Thirty-first street solicit two men, and that immediately afterward she had met a man and a woman—meaning the chorus girl and the reluctant witness—on the said corner, and was in conversation with them when he arrested her. He did not mention to the sergeant at this time the arrest and release of the chorus girl.

At the conclusion of the officer's story the sergeant said, shortly: "Take her back." This did not mean to take the woman back to the corner of Thirty-first street and Broadway. It meant to take her back to the cells, and she was accordingly led away.

The chorus girl had undoubtedly intended to be an intrepid champion; she had avowedly come to the station house for that purpose, but her entire time had been devoted to sobbing in the wildest form of hysteria. The reluctant witness was obliged to devote his entire time to an attempt to keep her from making an uproar of some kind. This paroxysm of terror, of indignation, and the extreme mental anguish caused by her unconventional and strange situation, was so violent that the reluctant witness could not take time from her to give any testimony to the sergeant.

After the woman was sent to the cell the reluctant witness reflected a moment in silence; then he said:

"Well, we might as well go."

On the way out of Thirtieth street the chorus girl continued to sob. "If you don't go to court and speak for that girl you are no man!" she cried. The arrested woman had, by the way, screamed out a request to appear in her behalf before the Magistrate.

"By George! I cannot," said the reluctant witness. "I can't afford to do that sort of thing. I—I——"

After he had left this girl safely, he continued to reflect: "Now this arrest I firmly believe to be wrong. This girl may be a courtesan, for anything that I know at all to the contrary. The sergeant at the station house seemed to know her as well as he knew the Madison square tower. She is then, in all probability, a courtesan. She is arrested, however, for soliciting those two men. If I have ever had a conviction in my life, I am convinced that she did not solicit those two men. Now, if these affairs occur from time to time, they must be witnessed occasionally by men of character. Do these reputable citizens interfere? No, they go home and thank God that they can still attend piously to their own affairs. Suppose I were a clerk and I interfered in this sort of a case. When it became known to my employers they would say to me: 'We are sorry, but we cannot have men in our employ who stay out until 2:30 in the morning in the company of chorus girls.'

"Suppose, for instance, I had a wife and seven children in Harlem. As soon as my wife read the papers she would say: 'Ha! You told me you had a business engagement! Half-past two in the morning with questionable company!'

"Suppose, for instance, I were engaged to the beautiful Countess of Kalamazoo. If she were to hear it, she would write: 'All is over between us. My future husband cannot rescue prostitutes at 2:30 in the morning.'

"These, then, must be three small general illustrations of why men of character say nothing if they happen to witness some possible affair of this sort, and perhaps these illustrations could be multiplied to infinity. I possess nothing so tangible as a clerkship, as a wife and seven children in Harlem, as an engagement to the beautiful Countess of Kalamazoo; but all that I value may be chanced in this affair. Shall I take this risk for the benefit of a girl of the streets?

"But this girl, be she prostitue or whatever, was at this time manifestly in my escort, and—Heaven save the blasphemous philosophy—a wrong done to a prostitute must be as purely a wrong as a wrong done to a queen," said the reluctant witness —this blockhead.

"Moreover, I believe that this officer has dishonored his obligation as a public servant. Have I a duty as a citizen, or do citizens have duty, as a citizen, or do citizens have no duties? Is it a mere myth that there was at one time a man who possessed a consciousness of civic responsibility, or has it become a distinction of our municipal civilization that men of this character shall be licensed to deprecate in such a manner upon those who are completely at their mercy?"

He returned to the sergeant at the police station, and, after asking if he could send anything to the girl to make her more comfortable for the night, he told the sergeant the story of the arrest, as he knew it.

"Well," said the sergeant, "that may be all true. I don't defend the officer. I do not say that he was right, or that he was wrong, but it seems to me that I have seen you somewhere before and know you vaguely as a man of good repute; so why interfere in this thing? As for this girl, I know her to be a common prostitute. That's why I sent her back."

"But she was not arrested as a common prostitute. She was arrested for soliciting two men, and I know that she didn't solicit the two men."

"Well," said the sergeant, "that, too, may all be true, but I give you the plain advice of a man who has been behind this desk for years, and knows how these things go, and I advise you simply to stay home. If you monkey with this case, you are pretty sure to come out with mud all over you."

"I suppose so," said the reluctant witness. "I haven't a doubt of it. But I don't see how I can, in honesty, stay away from court in the morning."

"Well, do it anyhow," said the sergeant.

"But I don't see how I can do it."

The sergeant was bored. "Oh, I tell you, the girl is nothing but a common prostitute," he said, wearily.

The reluctant witness on reaching his room set the alarm clock for the proper hour.

In the court at 8:30 he met a reporter acquaintance. "Go home," said the reporter, when he had heard the story. "Go home; your own participation in the affair doesn't look very respectable. Go home."

"But it is a wrong," said the reluctant witness.

"Oh, it is only a temporary wrong," said the reporter. The definition of a temporary wrong did not appear at that time to the reluctant witness, but the reporter was too much in earnest to consider terms. "Go home," said he.

Thus—if the girl was wronged—it is to be seen that all circumstances, all forces, all opinions, all men were combined to militate against her. Apparently the united wisdom of the world declared that no man should do anything but throw his sense of justice to the winds in an affair of this description. "Let a man have a conscience for the daytime," said wisdom. "Let him have a conscience for the daytime, but it is idiocy for a man to have a conscience at 2:30 in the morning, in the case of an arrested prostitute."

The officer who had made the arrest told a story of the occurrence. The girl at the bar told a story of the occurrence. And the girl's story as to this affair was, to the reluctant witness, perfectly true. Nevertheless, her word could not be accounted of any value. It was impossible that any one in the courtroom could suppose that she was telling the truth, save the reluctant witness and the reporter to whom he had told the tale.

The reluctant witness recited what he believed to be a true accounting, and the Magistrate discharged the prisoner.

The reluctant witness has told this story merely because it is a story which the public of New York should know for once.

No. 162a MANUSCRIPT FRAGMENT

PROSTITUTES walk the streets. Hence it is a distinction of our municipal civilization that blockheads shall be licensed to depredate upon the sensibilities of all who are out [a] late at night.

"Imprison them. Hang them! Brain them! Burn them. Do anything but try to drive them into the air like toy balloons, because," said the philosopher, "you can't do it." He also said that a [b] man who possessed a sense of justice was a dolt, a simpleton, and double-dyed idiot for [c] finally his sense of justice would get him into a corner and, if he obeyed it, make him infamous. There is such a thing as a moral obligation arriving inopportunely. The inopportune arrival of a moral obligation can bring just as much personal humiliation as can a sudden impulse to steal or any of the other mental suggestions which we account calamitous. For instance, suppose a business man of New York has a wife and thirteen children. In [d] the wee hours one morning he is on Broadway. He sees

---

[a] are out] *interlined above deleted* 'walk the streets'
[b] a] *interlined with a caret*
[c] for] *interlined above deleted* 'and'
[d] In] *preceded by deleted* 'One night'

No. 162b TYPESCRIPT FRAGMENT

<   > to be a woman <   [lagg]>ard ᵃ wit-
ness.

The tale properly begins in a <   > on Broadway where the
two chorus girls and the reluctant laggard witness sat the entire
evening. They were joined there by a girl, who seem to know one of
the chorus girls, and who said "why, how do you do? ᵇ I haven't seen
you since you were a member of the some thing or other company."
The chorus girl replied amiably to this greeting, and the third girl
took a seat and joined the ᶜ party. Finally the reluctant laggard
witness proposed something to eat, and the quartette left this place
and started to walk down Broadway. As they were approaching the
corner of 31st street one of the chorus girls, the one who had been
responsible for the introduction, said that she felt ill and that she
would go home in preference to having any ᵈ supper. She asked the
reluctant laggard witness to conduct her to a Broadway car. He
escorted this woman across the street leaving ᵉ the other two girls deep
in conversation on the west corner of ᶠ 31st street and ᵍ Broadway. He
was returning to the two girls whom he had left on the corne<[r]>

[about five lines torn off]

of the girls when suddenly a man grabbed them. The reluctant laggard witness's ʰ astonishment was so great that he hardly was aware
of what was transpiring for the next four second, until he heard the
officer charging the two girls for soliciting the two men who had
passed ⁱ the moment previously. The hysterical ʲ sobbing of one of
the girls, and the fact that in every probability he had never laid his
eyes on her before caused him to release her arm and devote his
entire and vigorous attention to the other girl. He had said, "you are
under arrest". The reluctant laggard witness said, "what in the world

---

ᵃ < > ard] Crane's *misspelling* 'laggered' *corrected in pencil by deletion of*
'ered' *and interlineation of* 'ard' *throughout except at* 663.20; 664.15
ᵇ do?] *question mark added in blue pencil*
ᶜ joined the] 'joinedthe' *separated by a line*
ᵈ having any] 'havingany' *separated by a blue pencil line*
ᵉ leaving] *final* 'g' *supplied in blue pencil*
ᶠ of] *followed by x'd-out* 'the'
ᵍ and] *written in pencil over* 'on' ; *mended in blue pencil*
ʰ witness's] *final* 's' *supplied in pencil*
ⁱ had passed] 'hadpassed' *separated by a line*
ʲ hysterical] *interlined in pencil above typed* 'historical' *of which the first* 'i'
had been altered in pencil to a 'y' *and some attempt made to alter the* 'o' ; *whole
then deleted in pencil*

for?" This man who was then seen to be an officer said, "for soliciting two men". "What two men?" "The two men that have just passed. She solicited those two men and I saw her." "She did not solicit those two men, because I also saw it", replied the reluctant laggard witness. "She was earnestly engaged in conversation with the other girl at the time and I am quite confident that she didn't even know that the two men passed."

"Well," [k] said the officer, turning upon the reluctant laggard witness [1] "do you know this woman? she is a common prostitute." "No", said the witness "I do not know her at all, but I am sure she did [m] solicit those two men. What are you arresting her for? Are you arresting her as a common prostitute?" "No", said the officer. "I am arresting her for soliciting the two men".

"Very well then" said the reluctant laggard witness. "I shall be compelled to go to the station house with you <
> two men, for I have been in sight of her ever since she left the Broadway garden, until the moment of the arrest."

Then there was a parade to the station house; a [n] parade of four people.

In the meantime the mind of the reluctant laggard witness was very uneasy. He said to himself "Now, this arrest is wrong. This girl may be nothing but a prostitute. I know nothing whatever as to that. I have no information on that subject, but as to the facts of her soliciting two men between the time she left the Broadway Garden and the moment of her arrest I know that to be untrue. I have a small reputation; not as light [o] as a feather perhaps, or not so heavy as a penny, but one which I have earned by hard work—the thing—a little structure which has taken me years to build up. Now, this common prostitute is being done a wrong. But shall I risk all this? Shall I risk all this for a girl who is alleged to be a common walker of the streets? I have friends who are conventionally particular. Citizens of New York, men of character and reputation, perhaps witness these things from time to time, but do they then interfere? No, they go home and attend seriously and solemnly to their own affairs. Shall I become a ridiculous figure for the benefit of a prostitute? Or, shall I too go home?

"Well" continued the reluctant laggard witness "this girl be she a prostitute or whatever, was under your protection and while in your

[k] "Well,"] *double quotes typed directly over comma*
[1] witness] *follows x'd-out* 'officer'
[m] did] *for* 'did' *read* 'did not'
[n] a] *interlined in pencil above deleted* 'the'
[o] light] 's' *of* 'slight' *struck out in pencil*

escort she has suffered an injustice, and a wrong to a prostitute is as great a wrong as to a wrong to a queen."

At the station house the officer said to the sergeant behind the desk that he had seen this girl come out of the resort on [p] Broadway alone and solicit two men while she walking to the corner of 31st street and that two men went on and paid no attention, and then at the corner of 33rd street she was joined by this man and this woman. The other woman, who had not been arrested, was all this time sobbing in the wildest form of hysteria, and the reluctant laggard witness had all he could do to prevent her from making an uproar, and he knew that the police station was not the [q] place for an uproar and so it was that he had no time at all to reply to the statements of the detective and at the conclusion of the detective's story the sergeant said "send her back" and the girls was sent back.

Then the reluctant laggard witness conducted the other girl home and leaving her indulged in another series of reflection.

Despite everything he felt dishonored; dishonored to himself in his heart. He had retreated before the presence of an injustice. He had saved his bauble [r] reputation rather than risk it in defending this woman. Consequently he returns to the station house. He talked to the sergeant and told him the story of the arrest as he believed it.

[page 5 wanting]

ward and told the story of the arrest as plainly and truthfully as was in his power and on hearing this version the magistrate discharged the girl.

[p] resort on] 'resorton' *separated by a line*
[q] not the] 'notthe' *separated by a line*
[r] bauble] *interlined in pencil above deleted* 'barble'

No. 163   THE DEVIL'S ACRE

I

THE keeper unlocked a door in a low gray building within the prison inclosure at Sing Sing. The room which he and his two visitors then entered was certainly furnished sparsely. It contained only one chair. Evidently this apartment was not the library of a millionaire.

The walls and ceiling were of polished wood and the atmosphere was weighted heavily with an odor of fresh varnish. This uncouth perfume here controlled the senses as it does in a carriage factory. The chair, too, was formed of polished wood. It might have been donated from the office of some generous banker.

A long, curved pipe swung from behind a partition, and at the end of it there hung a wire almost as thick as a cigar. Some straps, formidably broad and thick, were thrown carelessly over the arms of the chair.

The keeper was exceedingly courteous in his explanations. He waved his hand towards a steel door. "We bring him through there," said he, "and we calculate that the whole business takes about a minute from the time we go after him." His courtesy went still further. "If one of you cares to sit down in it, gentlemen, I'll strap you in and you can try to imagine how it feels." But his visitors protested that they understood perfectly that his time was very valuable and that nothing could be further from their minds than an idea of putting him to such great trouble.

It is a lonely room and silent. No sound comes to break the calm hush of this chamber. The same people who cannot know that an express train at full speed is one of the most poetic things in the world would morbidly object, in the sub-conscious way, to the smell of varnish here, and disapprove for the same reason of the comfortable and shining chair. There should be an effect a thousand times more hideous. For the room is the place for the coronation of crime and the chair is the throne of death.

We, as a new people, are likely to conclude that our mechanical perfection, our structural precision, is certain to destroy all quality of sentiment in our devices, and so we prefer to grope in the past when people are not supposed to have had any structural precision. As the terrible, the beautiful, the ghastly, pass continually before our eyes we merely remark that they do not seem to be correct in romantic detail.

But an odor of oiled woods, a keeper's tranquil, unemotional voice, a broom stood in the corner near the door, a blue sky and a bit of moving green tree at a window so small that it might have been made by a canister shot—all these ordinary things contribute with subtle meanings to the horror of this comfortable chair, this commonplace bit of furniture that waits in silence and loneliness, and waits and waits and waits.

It is patient—patient as time. Even should its next stained and sallow prince be now a baby, playing with alphabet blocks near his mother's feet, this chair will wait. It is as unknown to his eye as are the shadows of trees at night, and yet it towers over him, monstrous, implacable, infernal, his fate—this patient, comfortable chair.

II

They summoned the "Captain," because his memory was a mine of thirty years' experience with the men in gray and black. He had conducted convict funerals until they were as ordinary to him as breakfast, dinner and lunch. It was a habit with him. The dull fall of dirt on wood probably no more concerned his nerves than would the flying, shining water of a fountain in a public park. He slowly stroked his long, gray beard and presented a demeanor of superb indifference. He was really bored. That an interest should be manifested in such matters struck him as being rather absurd.

"Did you ever see a ghost up there, Captain?" asked one visitor, with dark insinuation.

"No," said the Captain, subtly scoffing. "I did not." He looked around at the other men in the room and grinned.

"Never had a white thing gibber at you, did you?" gently murmured the visitor.

"Oh,——no," replied the Captain.

When the visitors left, the Captain was still thoughtfully stroking his long, gray beard.

III

On the hillside there is a place of peace. The river is spread in a silver sheet before it and the little ships move slowly with their mystic energy past it. The splendid reaches of the valley of the Hudson are here so plain to the vision that no fable prince could find a spot more suitable for his palace. In the sunshine the river is spread like a cloth.

This fair place is the convicts' graveyard. Simple white boards crop out from the soil in rows. The inscriptions are abrupt. "Here lies Wong Kee. Died June 1, 1890." The boards front the wide veranda of a cottage of modern type. If people on this veranda ever lower their eyes from the wide river and gaze at these tombstones they probably find that they can just make the inscriptions out at the distance and just can't make them out at the distance. They encounter the dividing line between coherence and a blur. It is a most comfortable house, and yet a person properly superstitious would possibly not care to offer more than $3 for it. For, after all, it is impossible for the eye to avoid these boards, these austere tributes to the memory of men who died black souled, whose glances in life fled sidewise with a kind of ferocity, a cowardice and a hatred that could perhaps embrace the entire world.

At night one could assuredly hear at this place the laugh of the devil. One could see here the clutching, demoniac fingers. It is the fiend's own acre, this hillside. The far red or green lights of the steamers swing up or down the river in serenity, distant whistles shout their little warnings, but here on this hillside, with the solemnity of the night, with the wind swishing the long grass, there surely must be gruesome action. Over this convict graveyard, where the boards show wan in the darkness, there must hover gruesome figures.

Even in the day one can weave from masses of clouds a laughing shape, with eager claws, a thing that reaches down into the earth under the simple headboards.

It takes more than this to arouse the awe of a cow. A cow cares little for superstition. A cow cares for grass. Good grass grows here. Kind, motherly old cows wander placidly among these new and old graves. Ordinarily it would be very annoying to have tombstones constantly in one's way. A solemn inscription at every turn is sufficient to vex the most gentle spirit. But these matters cannot move the deep philosophy of a cow. It is not a question of sentiment; it is a question of pasturage. A certain Roman class taught magnificent indifference as the first rule of life. These cows are disciples of the Romans. If a convict's grave is trampled by a cow, what does it matter to the Brooklyn Bridge? If the last record of a long-dead criminal is butted by a playful heifer, is the price of wheat affected? Cows understand these things as well as does a Standard Oil magnate. It is not a question of sentiment; it is a question of pasturage. Somebody connected with the prison comprehends this point as completely as do the cows. The cows cannot appropriate all the wisdom. There has been another student of the Romans. Anybody can see that when long lush grass grows over graves there is a good feeding place for cows.

In Philadelphia, where everybody of historic consequence is interred, men come at certain periods and scrub the old stones with acid in order that the world may know again the best that friends could invent concerning the buried. At Sing Sing the author of the inscriptions preserves a gorgeous neutrality. When he formulated one he formulated them all. "Here lies at rest ——" After this prodigal expenditure he ceases.

This term was noble and sufficient until they cut the new road through the hill. Proper civil engineering then demanded that certain bones should not lie at rest at that particular spot, and the cow pasture was cut in half.

Time deals strokes of rain, wind and sun to all things, and a board is not strong against them.

Soon it falls. There is none here to plant it upright again. The men that lie here are of the kind that the world wishes to forget, and there is no objection raised to the assault of nature. And so it comes to pass that the dates on the boards are recent. These white boards have marched like soldiers from the southward end of the field to the northward. As they at the south became dim, rotted and fell, others sprang up at their right hand. As these in turn succumbed, still others appeared at their right. It is a steady travel towards the north. In the other end there are now no boards; only a sinister undulation of the earth under the weeds. It is a fine short road to oblivion.

In the middle of the graveyard there is a dim but still defiant board upon which there is rudely carved a cross. Some singular chance has caused this board to be split through the middle, cleaving the cross in two parts, as if it had been done by the demoniac shape weaved in the clouds, but the aged board is still upright and the cross still expresses its form as if it had merely expanded and become transparent. It is a place for the chanting of monks.

No. 164 HARVARD UNIVERSITY AGAINST THE CARLISLE INDIANS

CAMBRIDGE, MASS., Oct. 31.—There is sorrow in the lodge of Lone Wolf, and despair sits upon the brow of Cayou. Harvard defeated the Carlisle Indian School on Soldiers' Field this afternoon by the score of 4 to 0. It was understood beforehand that the Indians were sure winners. Everybody declared that the Harvard team was composed mainly of cripples, and everybody recited the glory of the aborigines.

Fifteen thousand people expected a surprise. They were there to observe how the red man could come from his prairies with a memory of four centuries of oppression and humiliation as his inheritance, with dark years, perhaps utter extinction before him, and yet make a show of the white warriors at their favorite sport.

The career of the lads from Carlisle has not been the least amazing feature of the amazing year of 1896. They have made history in a bland and simple fashion, but they have made it none the less satisfactorily. Apache Kid is great, and his name stands high in the minds of men of his kind, but he will have to look twice at his bloody laurels, to make sure that they are still laurels, if he ever sees the wreath that crowns the brow of Lone Wolf, the centre rush.

How old Geronimo would have enjoyed it! The point of view of the warriors was terse but plain: "They have stolen a continent from us, a wide, wide continent, which was ours, and lately they have stolen various touchdowns that were also ours. The umpire, on several occasions, has made monkeys of us. It is too much. Let us, then, brothers, be revenged. Here is an opportunity. The white men line up in their pride. If sacrifice of bone and sinew can square the thing, let us sacrifice, and perhaps the smoke of our wigwam camp fire will blow softly against the dangling scalps of our enemies."

Yet, as they sat in the corridors of their hotel and mused upon the past, none could tell that they were men of prowess; they spoke little, barely a word to each other; there was never a crowd around them. They sat quietly in their simple blue and red uniforms, and appeared to listen a great deal. They were remarkably modest in their ways. They were like children, mightily well-behaved and docile children. It required long observation to find in these serene countenances the nerve which the men have displayed to such a tremendous degree.

The composition of the line-up was as follows:

Harvard.	Positions.	Carlisle.
Lewis	Left end	Jamieson
Mills	Left tackle	H. Pierce
Bouve	Left guard	Wheelock
Doucette, F. Shaw	Centre	Lone Wolf
N. Shaw	Right guard	B. Pierce
Merriman, Lee	Right tackle	Morrison
Moulton	Right end	Miller
Beale, Cochran	Quarter-back	Hudson
Sullivan	Left half-back	Cayou
Dunlop	Right half-back	McFarlane
Brown	Full-back	Metoxen

Garfield, of Williams, was umpire, and Atherton, of Boston, was referee.

At 2:45 a sound of applause arose from the stands and about seventeen soiled and impassive individuals strolled onto the field and did a little practicing in an indifferent sort of way. If they knew that the attention of a multitude of palefaces was centred upon them they did not seem to care. Their sweaters made flaming heaps at the side line. They might have been camp fires on a Western reservation.

It was not by any means a model day for football. The sun was quite copper-like in its strength, and even light overcoats were not discernible until the latter half of the game. The mildness of the atmosphere made the practicing players seem like stuffed figures. High on the stands the waiting crowd had a great view of tenement houses and factories.

Harvard won the toss and took the wind. Metoxen kicked off for the Indians, and Harvard's back sharply returned the ball to the middle of the field. The Indians then began a campaign of mass plays on Harvard's tackles, which they continued throughout the game. The first Indian rush resulted in a fumble, and Harvard got the ball. Sullivan was sent through the Indian line for a gain of eight yards, and later for a gain of five yards. Bemis Pierce did some stopping in the next play, and Harvard dropped back for a kick. Brown hammered the ball over to the aboriginal fifteen-yard line. Here the Indians fought the ball forward by means of the cast-iron Metoxen, who moved with the force of a steam drill. From the Indians' thirty-five-yard line Cayou then made a beautiful run around Harvard's right end, and Sullivan saved a touchdown. On Harvard's twenty-yard line Doucette scooped the ball on a fluke and took it twenty yards, when he passed it to Dunlop, and the latter added thirty yards more.

The Crimson pushed Dunlop over the line for the only touchdown of the game. The time occupied was seven minutes and eleven seconds. Brown missed the goal. Brown returned the Indian kick-off, and at the middle of the field the Indians renewed their systematic and rather primitive mass playing. They banged away at the Harvard tackles until they had forced the ball well into the enemy's country. Harvard here got the ball on downs, however, and Brown kicked to the Indians' twenty-five-yard line. McFarlane then got the ball and the Indians were punching the Harvard line with considerable success when time was called.

Brown opened the second half with a long punt, and Lewis got handsomely through the noble red men and downed Metoxen with the ball on Carlisle's twenty-yard line, whereupon the Indians renewed their mass playing on the tackles. Bemis Pierce varied this occasionally by savage charges dead ahead. Doucette, the Crimson's centre, was hurt in one of these crushes, and lay and breathed to himself for a time. Then

Merriman fell a victim and Lee took his place. He got head over heels into the play, and it was Harvard's ball on downs.

At this moment a singular thing happened. An Indian got hurt. Cayou's head was cut. He recovered in a moment, however.

Harvard then kicked and its forwards got through neatly. The ball was downed in Indian territory. Whereupon these simple savages began their mass playing again. It resulted in the injury of Beale. Cochran took his place. Doucette got into a happy knack of bursting the Carlisle wedge plays into fragments. Sullivan was hurt in one of them, and Cozzens came into the game. He and Doucette caught a little revolving Indian wedge and spun around into a gain for Harvard. But, in the main, these terrific plunges of the Indians resulted in steady gains. Doucette was finally helped off the field.

With seventeen minutes to play and the ball at Harvard's forty-yard line, the Indians took a drink of water all around and began a ferocious series of masses. They banged away as coolly as a lot of blacksmiths. Slowly and steadily the Harvard line was forced back. A touchdown seemed inevitable and the vast crowd went mad. The thundering Harvard cheers roared over the field like a storm, and the men who fought for the Crimson heard five thousand of their friends call upon them to be steadfast. Still the impassive Indians bucked and bucked, and the Harvards went slowly backward.

It was a matter of ten yards; it was a matter of eight yards; it was a matter of five yards; it was a matter of less than five yards. The crowd at the side line turned into a howling mob of maniacs and ran and shrieked at their team. It was a dark and tense moment for the Crimson. But here it was that the Crimson showed at its best and greatest. The Harvard men played like fiends. The Indians crashed mightily into them twice, but the tangle of men whirled around and dropped without a gain. A kick carried the ball midfield. Metoxen returned it, and to Dunlop, who played splendidly throughout, came the delirious privilege of getting a chance at the ball and carrying it in a long and beautiful run to a point where it was safe for the remaining few seconds of play. After the game the Indians moved off through the dusk with all their old impassiveness.

No. 165 HOW PRINCETON MET HARVARD AT
CAMBRIDGE

Boston, Mass., Nov. 7.—Before the game and before the crowd
the huge new wooden stands resembled monstrous constructions of the Northwestern lumber region, but soon black clumps
of people began to dot these great slanting expanses, and the
crimson flags of Harvard flashed here and everywhere. The
silhouette of the vast crowd against the blue sky was a moving
and tremendous thing. The sun was bright, but a breeze that
gradually became more chilly swept across the field from the
north.

The swarming throng exhibited but a languid interest in the
little negro boy who cantered the Harvard collie around the
field, over and over the sacred chalk lines. In the certain section of the eastward stand, where yellow chrysanthemums
bloomed profusely, there was a general and expectant silence.
The orange and black flags rustled quietly and without emotion.

Suddenly a man with a great camera rushed out from a
corner of the field, stumbling backward over his legs. A band
hidden somewhere in the crowd blared forth. Princeton's cheers
rolled over the field, and the orange and black team trotted
into the field. The gorgeous shocks of hair bobbed around
after the ball, and the great orange capitals colored the dull
November grass.

They were grouped and consulting solemnly when the Harvard cheers pealed, crimson flags flamed out from the black
crowds and the Cambridge team came on at a fast run. There
seemed enough of them to make a battalion of infantry. Thereafter there was frequent and spasmodic cheering, until that
tense and still moment when the players stood motionless on
the field and Baird went slowly forward to kick for Princeton.

The silence was complete enough to allow the impact of the
full-back's foot to be heard everywhere. The ball spun into Harvard territory. There was a flurry of red legs, another punt,
and it came violently out again. In the first scrimmage of the
game Armstrong lay down on the ground, slightly writhing.
The crippled condition of the Harvard team had been heralded

with some industry, but in the next few rushes she began to appear more formidable than one would have judged from the rumors.

The Crimson forced the stripes into their country. Crowdis was hurt; then Church was hurt, and after pauses to enable these men to recover, Princeton evidently decided to gain something. Out of the swaying mass came Kelly for a brilliant run, and a Princeton roar banged into the sky. The experts, coachers and substitutes on the side lines, crouching forward in strained poses, called out eagerly: "Now, Princeton! Go in, Princeton!"

But it seemed at this time a quite equal struggle. The clashing of the teams was bitter and headlong. As the dark tangles of men separated at the blow of the whistle still figures were often revealed on the grass. Harvard was holding her own.

Dunlop flashed through Princeton's tackle for a good gain, and for some time afterward the fight raged in the middle of the field. If fate was anywhere, it seemed to be with Harvard. Brown, the full-back, kicked early and often, and the wind was his slave. Soon Princeton was obliged to make a stern and stubborn stand near her goal line. The savage hammering of the Harvard backs could not move her there, and Baird presently whirled this terrible bit of leather into a more peaceful neighborhood.

Here the ferocious Dunlop discouraged the chrysanthemums by whistling through the Princeton line like a harpoon, but they stopped him presently. The battle was again in Princeton's danger precinct, but finally a kick by the steady and immovable Baird carried it far toward Harvard's goal, and the singular fates that rule the game swung the chances into Princeton's hands.

Then the Crimson came to defend the walls of its city of success, and the chrysanthemums in the stand threw a series of convulsions. The campaign toward the Harvard goal was almost Roman. But Harvard flung back the invaders and Doucette carried the ball to the same old middle of the field. And until the end of the half these two groups of soiled canvas figures flung themselves together and bucked and crushed with mutual instruction and advantage, but with no scoring.

During the intermission the Harvard elation developed in

songs and cheers. The great living hillsides flared with crimson, and the college band played the triumphant march of Sousa.

"Bet you fifty to thirty we win," said a Harvard man at the side lines. The Princeton coachers and substitutes were saying to their men: "Never mind, boys; wait until the next half. Wait until we get the wind with us."

At the beginning of the second half the teams exchanged kicks, and Baird, relieved of the wind's objections, began to completely out-punt the Harvard back. The game proceeded without much noise from the gigantic crowd. The fortunes of the game changed too easily. The situation was too harrowing. Baird, however, awakened the Princeton legions by a kick of quite fifty-five yards, and the thousands of Harvard adherents broke forth a long and doleful groan as the oval soared high. Harvard's kicking standard was lowered to Baird. Cabot, the Harvard end, went out of the game, and Arthur Brewer took his place.

A messenger boy said:

"Say, is that Arthur?"

"Yes," said another messenger boy.

"Well, you just watch Arthur," said the first one. "Just watch Arthur."

The messenger boy had but concluded this encomium when the ball went into play, and Bannard, the Princeton quarterback, went through Harvard like a skyrocket, swept Brewer heels over head and swung through and around Harvard's backs. After a long and gallant run, aided by faithful interference, he went over the line to secure a touchdown for Princeton.

The Harvard flags were dead; the Harvard throats were silent. Everyone in the crimson stands might have been undergoing a surgical operation. But the Princeton crowd, minute proportionately, made havoc of the ears of the people across the bay in Boston. They howled and roared and raged. The enthusiasm of the orange and black for their team and their Bannard went to that acute stage which is almost the verge of tears.

A shadow of dusk came over the field at this moment to cover a grim time for Harvard. The Princeton team seemed more swift and lithe than at the beginning of the game. The glow of their victory was upon them, and although the men in the crimson contested with the energy of a final despair, they were not able to withstand the team from New Jersey. The college band at this time chose to break forth in sad and plaintive melody.

The Princeton crowd suddenly whooped joyously.

"There goes Wheeler."

"Who?" said the reporter from Oshkosh.

"Beef Wheeler's brother," said everyone impatiently.

There was a long halt at this period of the game, and the throng invented the amusement of pounding the boards with their feet. There was little Harvard cheering. Baird was kicking too well, and Princeton's line possessed some of the attributes of a row of Harlem flats. Every man for Harvard played for all that there was in him, but slowly the Crimson line went back. In the last few moments of the game they rallied, but it was to no great purpose.

Twelve minutes from the end of the game, Church got through the Harvard entrenchments, blocked Brown's kick, and Brokaw fell on the ball for another touchdown. Baird naturally kicked another goal.

The jubilant din increased as the day faded slowly to the twilight hour and the time of the final uproar neared. The Cambridge police walked slowly past these regardless Princeton rooters and looked at them sideways and with half-hidden scorn. For the last ten minutes Harvard continued her same furious and desperate opposition, but the sublime Church, the illustrious Baird and the inspiring Brokaw were too numerous and too present, and so at sunset the Harvard fortunes concluded in defeat and three hundred maniacal chrysanthemums danced weird joy in the gloom.

No. 166 A BIRTHDAY WORD FROM NOVELIST STEPHEN CRANE

IT IS a condition of most of us who are in journalism that we do not know how to define it because your newspaper seems to change and advance each day.

Stephen Crane

No. 167 OUIDA'S MASTERPIECE

MOST of us forget Ouida. Childhood and childhood's different ideal is often required to make us rise properly to her height of sentiment. The poetic corner in the human head becomes too soon like some old dusty niche in a forgotten church. It is only occasionally that an ancient fragrance floats out to us, and then, usually, we do not recognize it. We apply some strange name and grin from the depths of our experience and wisdom. Perhaps it is rather a common habit to mistake a sort of a worldly complacence for knowledge.

For my part I had concluded that I had outgrown Ouida. I thought that I recognized the fact that her tears were carefully moulded globules of the best Cornish tin and that her splendors were really of the substance of shadows on a garden wall. And yet a late reading of *Under Two Flags* affected me like some old and honest liquor. It is certainly a refreshment. The characters in this book abandon themselves to virtue and heroism as the martyrs abandoned themselves to flames. Sacrifice appears to them as the natural course. Pain, death, dishonor, is counted of no moment so long as the quality of personal integrity is defended and preserved. Certainly we may get good from a book of this kind. It imitates the literary plan of the early peoples. They sang, it seems, of nobility of character. To-day we sing of portières and champagne and gowns. *Under Two Flags* has to me, then, a fine ring in the gospel of life it preaches. I confess, of course, that I often find Beauty's perfections depressing. We men of doleful flaws are thrown into moods of profound gloom by the contemplation of such a bejewelled mind. We grow solemn and sad, and feel revengefully that we might like to touch a match to the hem of Beauty's sacred bath-robe, and see if we couldn't incite him to something profane and human—something like a real oath, or, at least, a fit of perfectly manly ill-temper.

Cigarette is finer. In Ouida's drawing of this secondary character we detect something accidental. With Cigarette the novelist did not take so much pains. She never intended Cigarette to be splendid, and perhaps this is why the girl appears to some of us as really the best character in the book. She is a figure of flesh among all these painted gods. She has imperfections, thank heaven, and it is very nice to come upon a good, sound imperfection when one is grown surfeited with the company of gods.

Nevertheless, with all the cavilling of our modern literary class, it is good to hear at times the song of the brave, and *Under Two Flags* is a song of the brave. To the eye of this time it is, of course, a thing of imperfect creation, but it voices nevertheless the old spirit of dauntless deed and sacrifice which is the soul of literature in every age, and we are not growing too tired to listen, although we try to believe so.

No. 168   NEW INVASION OF BRITAIN

LONDON, April 29.—One of the curious things about this metropolis is the number of bounders that inhabit it. It is impossible to go about at all without hearing of the perfectly incredible number of bounders. Bounders are here, there and everywhere. There are bounders that fly, others that swim, others that walk, crawl and wriggle. In all cases they occupy the whole of their element and their doings are published. London is simply alive with bounders. At the clubs the topic is solely bounders. On the street one can go no distance without hearing of a recent achievement of some bounder. The bounders have taken London's attention by assault.

Inquiry as to the dimensions and weight and complexion of a bounder would naturally be conducted by the average American with care. He will sit around and smoke and wait for some chance illumination, preferring to then suddenly shine forth as a man thoroughly conversant with bounders. He will wait for the definition to appear of its own volition, and then calmly talk about bounders as if he had gone to school with all the bounders in the world.

Good slang is subtle and elusive. If there is a quick equivalent for a phrase it is not good slang, because good slang comes to fill a vacancy. It comes to cover some hole in the language. Hence it is not easy to find out about bounders. One pins the word to a certain type of man and presently hears that a man of an utterly different type is a bounder. They have something in common, then. What is it? It is fearsome, this task of pitching upon the only real bounder.

One man remarks to another: "Do you know this Jones chap, now? Isn't he something of a bounder?"

The other man grows solemn with the stress of profound deliberation. "No-o-o," he answers finally. "I shouldn't say he was a bounder, exactly."

"Is he not, really? I thought he was rather a bounder."

"No, not precisely a bounder. He may be an outsider, perhaps, but he is not a bounder."

"Well, well, he appeared to me rather a bounder."

"Oh, maybe he is rather inclined to be a bounder about some things, but then taking him altogether he is not quite a bounder."

"Why, I met him out the other night and if he wasn't——"

"Oh, well, in that way? Yes. Sometimes."

"Nonsense. He is a bounder, he is. A bounder."

Here one gets a clear view of an important distinction.

"Why, you wouldn't care to meet him. He's an awful bounder, you know."

"You should meet Jones. He's a bit of a bounder, perhaps, but a very decent chap for all that."

Here is more distinction. One might insist on meeting Jones and saying: "Look here, now, Jones, you are a bounder. What

in blazes is a bounder?" Perhaps bounders can fight. If bounders came in sizes and Jones was a small one and enfeebled from
much bounding, the question might be practicable.

Still as affairs go, and if it strikes the ear as an entirely
new word, it requires a system of gradual absorption, a period
of education. One should listen to the experts on bounders and
obtain testimony of the best authorities. To it should be
devoted time and care, because the result pays. When one has
arrived at the grand consummation and can detect bounders
—joy in a whirl! It is a perfectly new weapon to use on your
friends. You can commit a series of new and wholly unexpected
devastations. This word is an axe that has an edge like a
Damascus. It can be used like a rapier, and yet it falls on your
victim with the enthusiasm of a brick chimney. It is everything,
and nothing, this word. It is the war-cry of a certain way, a
certain manner, and precisely as immaterial and absurd as any
war-cry of any way or any manner; or again, it is the objection
of a subtlety fine and worthy for other modes that are indefinable usually and usually as palpable as a handful of gravel
in the tea. All this makes the question of a bounder perfectly
clear.

Formerly you perhaps spent days in the destruction of a
single friend. Now you can obliterate him in an instant. One
revels in slaughter for a time. Many of your friends for whom
you had no suitable imprecation now appear as candidates
for the term, and it spins from your lips as easily as is the
lighting of a match. Men who are neither forgers, assassins,
roués, chumps nor cads may perhaps be bounders, and whereas
they have, because of your ignorance of bounders, enjoyed
long immunity from assault, you can now swing at them with
this new hatchet or rapier or chimney.

At first one feels that at least two-thirds of the British populace is formed by bounders, and that the remaining third
devote all their speech to so naming them. Later comes a
strong suspicion. A man calls another man a bounder and
afterward you hear the other man call the man a bounder,
and ultimately appears a man who calls both the man and the
other man a bounder. You begin to reflect upon elasticity and
point of view. This infernal word ends by making one quake.

No. 169 LONDON IMPRESSIONS

I

LONDON at first consisted of a porter with the most charming manners in the world and a cabman with a supreme intelligence, both observing my profound ignorance without contempt or humor of any kind observable in their manners. It was in a great resounding vault of a place where there were many people who had come home, and I was displeased because they knew the detail of the business, whereas I was confronting the inscrutable. This made them appear very stony-hearted to the sufferings of one of whose existence, to be sure, they were entirely unaware, and I remember taking great pleasure in disliking them heartily for it. I was in an agony of mind over my baggage or my luggage, or my—perhaps it is well to shy around this terrible international question, but I remember that when I was a lad I was told that there was a whole nation that said luggage instead of baggage, and my boyish mind was filled at the time with incredulity and scorn. In the present case it was a thing that I understood to involve the most hideous confessions of imbecility on my part, because I had evidently to go out to some obscure point and espy it and claim it and take trouble for it, and I would rather have had my pockets filled with bread and cheese and had no baggage at all.

Mind you this was not at all an homage that I was paying to London. I was paying homage to a new game. A man properly lazy does not like new experiences until they become old ones. Moreover I have been taught that a man, any man, who has a thousand times more points of information on a certain thing than have I, will bully me because of it, and pour his advantages upon my bowed head until I am drenched with his superiority. It was in my education to concede some license of the kind in this case, but the holy father of a porter and the saintly cabman occupied the middle distance imperturbably, and did not come down from their hills to clout me with knowledge. From this fact I experienced a criminal elation. I lost view of the idea that if I had been brow-beaten by porters and cabmen from one end of the United States to the other end, I should warmly like it because in numbers they are superior to me, and collectively they can have a great deal of fun out of a matter that would merely afford me the glee of the latent butcher.

This London, composed of a porter and a cabman, stood to me subtly as a benefactor. I had scanned the drama and found that I did not believe that the mood of the men emanated unduly from the feature that there was probably more shillings to the square inch of me than there were shillings to the square inch of them. Nor yet was it any manner of palpable warmheartedness or other natural virtue. But it was a perfect artificial virtue; it was drill—plain, simple drill. And now was I glad of their drilling, and vividly approved of it because I saw that it was good for me. Whether it was good or bad for the porter and the cabman I could not know; but that point, mark you, came within the pale of my respectable rumination.

I am sure that it would have been more correct for me to have alighted upon St. Paul's and described no emotion until I was overcome by the Thames Embankment and the Houses of Parliament, but as a matter of fact I did not see them for some days, and at this time they did not concern me at all. I was born in London at a railroad station, and my new vision encompassed a porter and a cabman. They deeply absorbed me in new phenomena, and I did not then care to see the Thames Embankment nor the Houses of Parliament. I considered the porter and the cabman to be more important.

II

The cab finally rolled out of the gas-lit vault into a vast expanse of gloom. This changed to the shadowy lines of a street that was like a passage in a monstrous cave. The lamps winking here and there resembled the little gleams at the caps of the miners. They were not very competent illuminations at best, merely being little pale flares of gas that at their most heroic periods could only display one fact concerning this tunnel—the fact of general direction. But at any rate I should have liked to have observed the dejection of a search-light if it had been called upon to attempt to bore through this atmosphere. In it each man sat in his own little cylinder of vision, so to speak. It was not so small as a sentry-box nor so large as a circus-tent, but the walls were opaque, and what was passing beyond the dimensions of his cylinder no man knew.

It was evident that the paving was very greasy, but all the cabs that passed through my cylinder were going at a round trot, while the wheels, shod in rubber, whirred merely like bicycles. The hoofs of the animals themselves did not make that wild clatter which I knew so well. New York, in fact, roars always like ten thousand devils. We have ingenious and simple ways of making a din in New York that cause the stranger to conclude that each citizen is obliged by statute to provide himself with a pair of cymbals and a drum. If anything by chance can be turned into a noise it is promptly turned. We are engaged in the development of a human creature with very large, sturdy and doubly-fortified ears.

It was not too late at night, but this London moved with the decorum and caution of an undertaker. There was a silence and yet there was no silence. There was a low drone, perhaps, a humming contributed inevitably by closely gathered thousands, and yet on second thoughts it was to me a silence. I had perched my ears for the note of London, the sound made simply by the existence of five million people in one place. I had imagined something deep, vastly deep, a bass from a mythical organ; but I found, as far as I was concerned, only a silence.

New York in numbers is a mighty city, and all day and all night it cries its loud, fierce, aspiring cry, a noise of men beating upon barrels, a noise of men beating upon tin, a terrific racket that assails the abject skies. No one of us seemed to question this row as a certain consequence of three or four million people living together and scuffling for coin with more agility, perhaps, but otherwise in the usual way. However, after this easy silence of London, which in numbers is a mightier city, I began to feel that there was a seduction in this idea of necessity. Our noise in New York was not a consequence of our rapidity at all. It was a consequence of our bad pavements.

Any brigade of artillery in Europe that would love to assemble its batteries and then go on a gallop over the land, thundering and thundering, would give up the idea of thunder at once if it could hear Tim Mulligan drive a beer wagon along one of the side streets of cobbled New York.

III

Finally, a great thing came to pass. The cab-horse, proceeding at a sharp trot, found himself suddenly at the top of an incline where through the rain the pavement shone like an expanse of ice. It looked to me as if there was going to be a tumble. In an accident of such kind a hansom becomes really a cannon in which a man finds that he has paid shillings for the privilege of serving as a projectile. I was making a rapid calculation of the arc that I would describe in my flight, when the horse met his crisis with a masterly device that I could not have imagined. He tranquilly braced his four feet like a bundle of stakes, and then, with a gentle gaiety of demeanor, he slid swiftly and gracefully to the bottom of the hill as if he had been a toboggan. When the incline ended he caught his gait again with great dexterity, and went pattering off through another tunnel.

I at once looked upon myself as being singularly blessed by this sight. This horse had evidently originated this system of skating as a diversion or, more probably, as a precaution against the slippery pavement; and he was, of course, the inventor and sole proprietor—two terms that are not always in conjunction. It surely was not to be supposed that there could be two skaters like him in the world. He deserved to be known and publicly praised for this accomplishment. It was worthy of many records and exhibitions. But when the cab arrived at a place where some dipping streets met, and the flaming front of a music-hall temporarily widened my cylinder, behold, there were many cabs, and as the moment of necessity came, the horses were all skaters. They were gliding in all directions. It might have been a rink. A great omnibus was hailed by a hand from under an umbrella on the sidewalk, and the dignified horses bidden to halt from their trot did not waste time in wild and unseemly spasms. They, too, braced their legs and slid gravely to the end of their momentum.

It was not the feat, but it was the word, which had at this time the power to conjure memories of skating parties on moonlit lakes, with laughter ringing over the ice, and a great red bonfire on the shore among the hemlocks.

IV

A terrible thing in nature is the fall of a horse in his harness. It is a tragedy. Despite their skill in skating, there was that about the pavement on the rainy evening which filled me with expectations of horses going headlong. Finally it happened just in front. There was a shout and a tangle in the darkness and presently a prostrate cab horse came within my cylinder. The accident having been a complete success and altogether concluded, a voice from the sidewalk said: "*Look* out now! *Be* more careful, cawn't you?"

I remember a constituent of a Congressman at Washington who had tried in vain to bore this Congressman with a wild project of some kind. The Congressman eluded him with skill, and his rage and despair ultimately culminated in the supreme grievance that he could not even get near enough to the Congressman to tell him to go to Hades.

This cabman should have felt the same desire to strangle this man who spoke from the sidewalk. He was plainly impotent; he was deprived of the power of looking out. There was nothing now for which to look out. The man on the sidewalk had dragged a corpse from a pond and said to it: "*Be* more careful, cawn't you? or you'll drown." My cabman pulled up and addressed a few words of reproach to the other. Three or four figures loomed into my cylinder, and as they appeared spoke to the author or the victim of the calamity in varied terms of displeasure. Each of these reproaches was couched in terms that defined the situation as impending. No blind man could have conceived that the precipitate phase of the incident was absolutely closed. "*Look* out now, cawn't you?" And there was nothing in his mind which approached these sentiments near enough to tell them to go to Hades.

However, it needed only an ear to know presently that these expressions were formulæ. It was merely the obligatory dance which the Indians had to perform before they went to war. These men had come to help, but as a regular and traditional preliminary they had first to display to this cabman their idea of his ignominy.

The different thing in the affair was the silence of the victim. He retorted never a word. This, too, to me, seemed to be an obedience to a recognized form. He was the visible criminal, if there was a criminal, and there was born of it a privilege for them.

They unfastened the proper straps and hauled back the cab. They fetched a mat from some obscure place of succor and pushed it carefully under the prostrate thing. From this panting, quivering mass they suddenly and emphatically reconstructed a horse. As each man turned to go his way he delivered some superior cautions to the cabman while the latter buckled his harness.

v

There was to be noticed in this band of rescuers a young man in evening clothes and a top-hat. Now in America a young man in evening clothes and a top-hat may be a terrible object. He is not likely to do violence, but he is likely to do impassivity and indifference to the point where they become worse than violence. There are certain of the more idle phases of civilization to which America has not yet awakened—and it is a matter of no moment if she remains unaware. This matter of hats is one of them. I recall a legend recited to me by an esteemed friend, ex-Sheriff of Tin Can, Nevada. Jim Cortright, one of the best gun-fighters in town, went on a journey to Chicago and while there he procured a top-hat. He was quite sure how Tin Can would accept this innovation, but he relied on the celerity with which he could get a six-shooter into action. One Sunday Jim examined his guns with his usual care, placed the top-hat on the back of his head, and sauntered coolly out into the streets of Tin Can.

Now, while Jim was in Chicago, some progressive citizens had decided that Tin Can needed a bowling alley. The carpenters went to work the next morning and an order for the balls and pins was telegraphed to Denver. In three days the whole

population was concentrated at the new alley betting their
outfits and their lives.

It has since been accounted very unfortunate that Jim
Cortright had not learned of bowling alleys at his mother's knee
nor even later in the mines. This portion of his mind was
singularly belated. He might have been an Apache for all he
knew of bowling alleys.

In his careless stroll through the town, his hands not far
from his belt and his eyes going sideways in order to see who
would shoot first at the hat, he came upon this long low
shanty where Tin Can was betting itself hoarse over a game
between a team from the ranks of Excelsior Hose Company No.
1 and a team composed from the habitués of the "Red Light"
saloon.

Jim, in blank ignorance of bowling phenomena, wandered
casually through a little door into what must always
be termed the wrong end of a bowling-alley. Of course he saw
that the supreme moment had come. They were not only shooting at the hat and at him, but the low-down cusses were using
the most extraordinary and hellish ammunition. Still perfectly
undaunted, however, Jim retorted with his two Colts and killed
three of the best bowlers in Tin Can.

The ex-Sheriff vouched for this story. He himself had gone
headlong through the door at the firing of the first shot with
that simple courtesy which leads Western men to donate the
fighters plenty of room. He said that afterward the hat was the
cause of a number of other fights, and that finally a delegation
of prominent citizens were obliged to wait upon Cortright and
ask him if he wouldn't take that thing away somewheres and
bury it. Jim pointed out to them that it was his hat and that
he would regard it as a cowardly concession if he submitted to
their dictation in the matter of his head-gear. He added that
he purposed to continue to wear his top-hat on every occasion
when he happened to feel that the wearing of a top-hat was a
joy and a solace to him.

The delegation sadly retired and announced to the town that
Jim Cortright had openly defied them and had declared his
purpose of forcing his top-hat on the pained attention of Tin

Can whenever he chose. Jim Cortright's Plug Hat became a phrase with considerable meaning to it.

However, the whole affair ended in a great passionate outburst of popular revolution. Spike Foster was a friend of Cortright, and one day when the latter was indisposed Spike came to him and borrowed the hat. He had been drinking heavily at the "Red Light," and was in a supremely reckless mood. With the terrible gear hanging jauntily over his eye and his two guns drawn, he walked straight out into the middle of the square in front of the Palace Hotel, and drew the attention of all Tin Can by a blood-curdling imitation of the yowl of a mountain lion.

This was when the long-suffering populace arose as one man. The top-hat had been flaunted once too often. When Spike Foster's friends came to carry him away they found nearly a hundred and fifty men shooting busily at a mark, and the mark was the hat. My informant told me that he believed he owed his popularity in Tin Can, and subsequently his election to the distinguished office of Sheriff, to the active and prominent part he had taken in the proceedings.

The enmity to the top-hat expressed by this convincing anecdote exists in the American West at present, I think, in the perfection of its strength; but disapproval is not now displayed by volleys from the citizens, save in the most aggravating cases. It is at present usually a matter of mere jibe and general contempt. The East, however, despite a great deal of kicking and gouging, is having the top-hat stuffed slowly and carefully down its throat, and there now exist many young men who consider that they could not successfully conduct their lives without this furniture.

To speak generally, I should say that the head-gear, then, supplies them with a kind of ferocity of indifference. There is fire, sword and pestilence in the way they heed only themselves. Philosophy should always know that indifference is a militant thing. It batters down the walls of cities and murders the women and children amid flames and the purloining of altar vessels. When it goes away it leaves smoking ruins where lie citizens bayoneted through the throat. It is not a children's pastime like mere highway robbery.

Consequently in America we may be much afraid of these young men. We dive down alleys so that we may not kow-tow. It is a fearsome thing.

Taught thus a deep fear of the top-hat in its effect upon youth, I was not prepared for the move of this particular young man when the cab-horse fell. In fact I grovelled in my corner that I might not see the cruel stateliness of his passing. But in the meantime he had crossed the street, and contributed the strength of his back and some advice, as well as the formal address to the cabman on the importance of looking out immediately.

I felt that I was making a notable collection. I had a new kind of porter, a cylinder of vision, horses that could skate, and now I added a young man in a top-hat who would tacitly admit that the beings around him were alive. He was not walking a churchyard, filled with inferior headstones. He was walking the world, where there were people, many people.

But later I took him out of the collection. I thought he had rebelled against the manner of a class, but I soon discovered that the top-hat was not the property of a class. It was the property of rogues, clerks, theatrical agents, damned seducers, poor men, nobles, and others. In fact, it was the universal rigging. It was the only hat; all other forms might as well be named ham, or chops, or oysters. I retracted my admiration of the young man because he may have been merely a rogue.

VI

There was a window whereat an enterprising man by dodging two placards and a calendar was entitled to a view of a young woman. She was dejectedly writing in a large book. She was ultimately induced to open the window a trifle. "What nyme, please?" she said wearily. I was surprised to hear this language from her. I had expected to be addressed on a submarine topic. I have seen shell fishes sadly writing in large books at the bottom of a gloomy aquarium who could not ask me what was my nyme.

At the end of a hall there was a grim portal marked "Lift." I pressed an electric button and heard an answering tinkle in the heavens. There was an upholstered settle near at hand and I discovered the reason. A deer-stalking peace drooped upon everything, and in it a man could invoke the passing of a lazy pageant of twenty years of his life.

The dignity of a coffin being lowered into a grave surrounded the ultimate appearance of the lift. The expert that we in America call the elevator-boy stepped from the car, took three paces forward, faced to attention and saluted. This elevator-boy could not have been less than sixty years of age; a great white beard streamed toward his belt. I saw that the lift had been longer on its voyage than I had suspected.

Later in our upward progress a natural event would have been an establishment of social relations. Two enemies imprisoned together during the still hours of a balloon journey would, I believe, suffer a mental amalgamation. The overhang of a common fate, a great principal fact, can make an equality and a truce between any pair. Yet, when I disembarked, a final survey of the grey beard made me recall that I had failed even to ask the boy whether he had not taken probably three trips on this lift.

My windows overlooked simply a great sea of night in which were swimming little gas fishes.

VII

I have of late been led to wistfully reflect that many of the illustrators are very clever. In an impatience which was denoted by a certain economy of apparel, I went to a window to look upon day-lit London. There were the 'buses parading the street with the miens of elephants. There were the police looking precisely as I had been informed by the prints. There were the sandwich-men. There was almost everything.

But the artists had not told me the sound of London. Now in New York the artists are enabled to portray sound because in New York a dray is not a dray at all; it is a great potent noise hauled by two or more horses. When a magazine containing an illustration of a New York street is sent to me I always know it beforehand. I can hear it coming through the mails. As I have said previously, this which I must call the sound of London was to me only a silence.

Later in front of the hotel a cabman that I hailed said to me: "Are you gowing far, sir? I've got a byby here and I want to giver a bit of a blough." This impressed me as being probably a quotation from an early Egyptian poet, but I learned soon enough that the word byby was the name of some kind or condition of horse. The cabman's next remark was addressed to a boy who took a perilous dive between the byby's nose and a cab in front. "That's roight! Put your head in there and get it jammed—a whackin' good place for it, I should think!" Although the tone was low and circumspect, I have never heard a better off-hand declamation. Every word was cut clear of disreputable alliances with its neighbors. The whole thing was as clean as a row of pewter mugs. The influence of indignation upon the voice caused me to reflect that we might devise a mechanical means of inflaming some in that constellation of mummers which is the heritage of the Anglo-Saxon race.

Then I saw the drilling of the vehicles by two policemen. There were four torrents converging at a point, and when four torrents converge at one point engineering experts buy tickets for another place. But here again it was drill, plain simple drill. I must not falter in saying that I think the management of the traffic—as the phrase goes—to be distinctly illuminating and wonderful. The police were not ruffled and exasperated. They were as peaceful as two cows in a pasture.

I remember once remarking that mankind with all its boasted modern progress had not yet been able to invent a turnstile that will commute in fractions. I have now learned that 736 rights of way cannot operate simultaneously at one point. Rights of way, like fighting women, require space. Even two rights of way can make a scene which is only suited to the tastes of an ancient public.

This truth was very evidently recognized. There was only one right of way at a time. The police did not look behind them to see if their orders were to be obeyed; they knew they were to be obeyed. These four torrents were drilling like four battalions. The two blue-clothed men manœuvred them in a solemn abiding peace, the silence of London.

I thought at first that it was the intellect of the individual, but I looked at one constable closely and his face was as afire with intelligence as a flannel pin-cushion. It was not the police and it was not the crowd. It was the police and the crowd. Again it was drill.

VIII

I have never been in the habit of reading signs. I don't like to read signs. I have never met a man who liked to read signs. I once invented a creature who could play the piano with a hammer, and I mentioned him to a professor in Harvard University whose peculiarity was Sanscrit. He had the same interest in my invention that I have in a certain kind of mustard. And yet this mustard has become a part of me. Or, I have become a part of this mustard. Further, I know more of an ink, a brand of hams, a kind of cigarettes and a novelist than any man living. I went by train to see a friend in the country, and after passing through a patent mucilage, some more hams, a South African Investment company, a Parisian millinery firm and a comic journal, I alighted at a new and original kind of corset. On my return journey the road almost continuously ran through soap.

I have accumulated superior information concerning these things because I am at their mercy. If I want to know where I am I must find the definitive sign. This accounts for my glib use of the word mucilage as well as the titles of other staples.

I suppose even the Briton in mixing his life must sometimes consult the labels on 'buses and streets and stations even as the chemist consults the labels on his bottles and boxes. A brave man would possibly affirm that this was suggested by the existence of the labels.

The reason that I did not learn more about hams and mucilage in New York seems to me to be partly due to the fact that the British advertiser is allowed to exercise an unbridled strategy in his attack with his new corset or whatever upon the defensive public. He knows that the vulnerable point is the informatory sign which the citizen must, of course, use for his guidance, and then with horse, foot, guns, corsets, hams, mucilage, investment companies and all he hurls himself at this point.

Meanwhile I have discovered a way to make the Sanscrit scholar heed my creature who plays the piano with a hammer.

No. 170 THE EUROPEAN LETTERS

No. 2 (August 15, 1897)

(a)

WHEN the King of Siam travels in America the baggage smashers will have the greatest opportunity of their lives. His baggage consists of several hundred huge boxes and it requires about a regiment of porters to move this potentate's private effects on and off trains and steamers. The language of the porters on such occasions has not been made public.

Fifty of these boxes contain the jewelry and gold and silver ornaments which are destined as presents to the friendly rulers who entertain the King. They are guarded day and night by armed men. He has taken a house that adjoins his villa in Switzerland for the especial shelter of these ornaments. It is an altogether new and original idea of the supply depot. When the King feels like giving something away he goes into this house and makes a choice from his treasure.

The personality of the King of Siam has never been of exciting interest to Europe and it created general surprise and satisfaction when this King did not appear in a palanquin and with some manner of small pagoda for a hat but on the other hand loomed up as a European gentleman coached thoroughly in the conventional attire. He has not yet mentioned the famous white elephant which was supposed to have been the main object of Siam's existence.

The Crown Prince and the other little Prince are two particularly bright and manly lads and compare more than favorably with English boys.

(b)

[Nine paragraphs by Cora about fashions for the
Goodwood Races]

(c)

It has been discovered very recently by Americans in Europe that one of the popular ballads, "Put Me Off at Buffalo," is an absolutely pure product of the New World. The phrase itself could not have originated in Europe for many reasons. In the first place, a sleeping-car is not in the vocabulary of the ordinary railway company and in the second place no one should direct the porter, or the guard, to perform an office of that kind. The other reasons relate to local prejudices against what we would call humor.

A citizen of Frankfort had occasion for a long journey, so he took a sleeping-car. He told the guard to arouse him in time to dress for alighting at a particular station. The guard neglected his business and carried the unfortunate Frankfort man off into some corner of the German Empire where he aroused and finally disembarked in high dudgeon. Here he assailed the station-master with a claim for a free ticket back to his original destination, passed because of the incapacity of a railway employee.

The solemn and granite-headed official in reply simply quoted a by-law of the company which declares that if a passenger lets his station go by, he alone is responsible.

Later this irate traveller penned a letter to the company in which he tried to show them that such a rule could properly apply only to day-coaches and that its application to sleeping-cars was nonsensical. No traveller could be expected to pay an exuberantly extra sleeping-car fare for the privilege of sitting up all night and keeping watch for his station. Being fortified by this plain reasoning, he reiterated his assertion that the whole thing was nonsense.

Officialdom of the Royal Prussian Railway was speechless for a moment. What? This dog of a passenger writing that one of His Imperial Majesty's rules was nonsense! It was treason! And then these wooded-pated inebriates actually sued this man in the courts where he was practically doomed until some providential technical loop-hole appeared just snatching him from the jaws of the law in time.

(d)

The terrible death of a lady in London from using the petroleum hair wash should be a warning to those women in America who use it. This Mrs. Samuelson went to the store of her hairdresser, in the middle of the day. Her hair was washed with the petroleum preparation. The hairdresser states that after gently wiping the hair downward, he prepared to wring it. Then suddenly there was a loud explosion, and both he and Mrs. Samuelson were set on fire. It was a warm day and her hair was long and very thick. She lingered for three weeks in horrible agony: but her confinement was imminent and she gave birth to a still born child barely surviving its birth twenty-four hours.

This particular process of cleaning the hair is in great vogue. It is so convenient, as the hair can be washed and dried in the space of a quarter of an hour without even uncurling it. The inflamable spirit which composes the new mixture gives out fumes of course and is dangerous in the extreme.

This accident has quite cured many women in England from a desire to use this method.

(e)

The American tourist who passes Buckingham Palace on foot or in a hansom cab does not dream of the beautiful garden inside the grimy-looking walls. Like most great gems the case that hides them from the public eye is time-worn and dirty. In all London there is no spot so lovely as these gardens. They who enter here leave all smoke and dirt and hurrying humanity behind. If it were not for the dim hum of traffic one could quite forget that this was the hub of London. These Royal precincts are not by any means vast, yet so cleverly have the landscape gardeners done their work, that in which ever direction one turns, groves, sweet smelling nooks, green swards and woodland shrubs greet one, and over all reigns the peace of the country interrupted only by the happy twittering of the birds. One can wander under the trees through the seemingly endless walks, while before one stretches lawn after lawn so artistically arranged as to give the impression of a vast park. It is an ideal place for a lawn party. Then pretty rowing boats flit about the large lake propelled by the Queen's watermen, each in his gorgeous red and gold livery a picturesque figure. The main front of the Palace faces this lake, beyond which is a mound, dividing the Royal stables from the grounds. Numbers of stately Peacocks sun themselves and spread their tails on the lawns, adding bits of bright color to the scene.

The Garden Party given the last of June by her Majesty out dazzled all former brilliant affairs; not only were all the Royal family present, as well as most of the beautiful women and noble members of society, but also the India Princes and their suites, in their gorgeous oriental costumes ablaze with gold and jewels. One or two Indian ladies, the cynosure of all eyes in their beautiful native draperies, were there also. Although 6000 were present the only uncomfortable crowding was perhaps about the Royal tent where her Majesty sat dressed in black and white silk, drinking tea and eating strawberries and chatting to those around her.

Much merriment was afforded by the beautiful little Prince Edward of York on the day of the Jubilee day. When he was allowed to go out on the balcony at Buckingham Palace, so anxious was he to be the most polite little gentleman in England, in his pretty white frock and blue sash, that he saluted with both little hands, and then laughingly looked up in his nurse's face for approval.

(f)

[Placed in MS here but deleted]

The most wonderful of the Jubilee celebrations was surely that on board the ill fated "Aden." Although for over a week the survivors knew the ship would break up beneath them they remembered the 22nd of July was the Queen's Diamond Commemoration Day and they drank to her health with soda water and sang God Save the Queen.

(g)

Ten years ago when everyone was talking of the Queen's Jubilee, says the *Spectator*, a gentleman heard the following conversation between two Scotchwomen: "Can ye tell me, wumman, what is it they ca' a Jubilee?"

"Weel, it's this," said her neighbor. "When folks has been mairred twenty five year, that's a silver waddin', and when they have been mairred fifty year, that's a gowden waddin'; but if the man's deid, then it's a Jubilee."

(h)

The Maison Virot of Paris is mainly responsible for the designs and combinations of color and materials of hats and bonnets which set the style of the day.

The founder of this business, Madame Virot, retired at the end of 1885 with an enormous fortune. It has now been formed into a stock company and the newspapers are heralding the appearance of the prospectus. Preference shares were offered at £1. and £2. Ordinary shares are from five to fifteen shillings. The Earl of Warwick heads the list of the directors. The net profits of the business are stated to have been £22,540. per annum. The prospectus was most attractive. Today I learn that the premium has suddenly run off, while the ordinary shares are quoted at a discount. The preference shares may for all practical purposes be deemed unsaleable.

It is the desire of American milliners to have Virot models, which they copy and again copy in different colors perhaps. They then sell the models at a fabulous price. American women visiting Paris buy direct from Virot who have a retail department.

[Rest of paragraph description by Cora of fashions in hats and prices]

Nevertheless if the new company expected to stampede English stock-buyers with their inviting prospectus in the *Times*, they failed dismally. An Englishman with two sovereigns in his pocket would rather spend them on the races. He has been gulled too often.

No. 3 (August 22, 1897)

(a)

Goodwood is probably the most beautiful race track in the world. The grass stretches out in emerald slopes almost as far as the eye can reach. It is set on the highest hill in Goodwood Park, the Duke of Richmond's country place. He is descended from Charles the II and I have an impression founded on some historical account to which I am not now able to refer that that cheerful monarch donated this portion of the Goodwood estate as a national racing place and the present Duke of Richmond preserves this traditionary gift as a kind of backhanded inheritance. This may not be exact in detail but it is some curious idea of preserving a tradition which causes the Duke to make Goodwood a kind of holy spot to which all the society people as well as the racing sharps make annual pilgrimages. However he likes this sport himself and that may be the chief reason after all for his willingness to allow London to invade his property once each year.

Luncheon for the elect is set out under some trees. A long time ago the Duke was overcome by the idea that it would be nice to serve this luncheon in true picnic style. He made it a law that the tables should be about as high from the ground as a foot-stool. But this law has been slowly and successfully undermined through the men who have got cricks in their knees and women who are afraid of their gowns. This revolt caused the tables to be almost two feet from the ground this year and it is supposed that in time the Duke will perceive that people who come to Goodwood in the best frocks or trousers that their money can buy don't care to wallow around on his lawn. A genuine picnic is another thing entirely and people dress for it. But no woman cares to appear in the grand stand after luncheon with grass stains where no grass stains ought to be.

The Duke has a private stand reserved for Goodwood House and his guests from other country houses and from London. This season the particular suns which beamed upon Goodwood were the Prince and Princess of Wales and the Duke and Duchess of York. The latter pair stayed at Goodwood House.

The Duke of Richmond drove them to the course in a state carriage with postillions and all the rest of it. The guests who were not entitled to postillions and all the rest of it arrived in various traps. The distance from the nearest railway station is about five miles and the crowd arrived in all manner of locomotives from the muscles of the legs to a prancing pair of cobs. The procession begins about noon and lasts for several hours. There is a tremendous hill to be surmounted and only the ardor of the British racegoer impels the great crowd upward. The country people line the route and all the beggars who can possibly invent a bettor's superstition to seduce coin from the throng are present with their beseeching cry and outstretched palms. It is a typical English scene that reminds one of the series of old prints celebrating the exodus of London to the race track and the only change is in the costumes and the modelling of the carriages. The assault on the high hill is very exciting. There is a great deal of dust and tangle about it. At various points draught horses are stationed to assist their brethren with the heaviest carriages. Finally at the top the road passes near the Duke of Richmond's house and his famous herd of Jersey cattle and his Birdless Wood and all his other wonders but if any of the notabilities are in sight the streaming crowd spends itself in a strenuous attempt to identify them. On the race track itself however there is always a good breeze and the dusty people find themselves upon one of the most comfortable, as well as the most beautiful race tracks in the world.

[Paragraph by Cora about the fashions]

It might be added that when the Duke and Duchess of York were guests at Goodwood House they breakfasted in their own apartments while luncheon was served in a private room under their host's grand stand at the race track. The whole party met at dinner which was served in the ball room owing to the large number of guests. It is moreover the most splendid room in Goodwood House. When members of the Royal family pay a visit to the house of one of their subjects the list of guests is submitted to them for their approval and if there is any name thereon for which they have no interest they are supposed to promptly cross it out and substitute another if they choose.

This is one of the advantages of being a member of the Royal family.

(b)

Several of the solemn newspapers of London have called attention to the fact that the sale of wines and spirits is increasing year by year. They call attention in terms, which are not pointed, to the statistical proof that women drink a great deal more than usual. The society papers timidly allude to this vice of the women in the smart set. The small crusade has gone on without anybody paying the least attention to it even as most crusades go on in England. This is true from the matter of the South African inquiry to another matter which simply involves the question as to whether or no poor clergymen shall be robbed.

It remains a fact however that the multiple engagements of a London season seem to require a considerable number of bracers. These bracers are usually in the form of glasses of champagne. A large number of the women as they fly from ball to ball during the height of the activity in London support themselves by various forms of stimulant and the stimulant is more likely to be champagne than tea. The papers are trying to brand it as a social evil and in time they might possibly succeed although it would be very unusual for a London newspaper to succeed in anything. If society wants a drink, society takes a drink and the newspapers are not to be mentioned in the matter at all. This is the advantage of being in London society.

(e)

A priest in Dublin who was delivering a temperance lecture to his flock concluded with a convincing argument. "What makes ye shoot at yer landlords? The drink!" he shouted. "Aye and what makes ye miss them? The drink!"

(d)

Whereas at Goodwood all England participates in one way or another either through magnificent show gowns or through the small bets of north countrymen who never expect to lay eyes on Goodwood, the Yachting Week at Cowes in the Isle of Wight is purely for the amusement of the exclusive upper class. It is only a little fragment of the British public that plays at Yachting. It creates no excitement whatever in the popular mind. The newspapers all make a frantic effort to print late news from the race tracks—in which they appear as very clumsy and inadequate medicines for the public disease—but as for Cowes only those journals which are supposed to know what society does and what it doesn't do pay particular attention to this fashionable event. To be allowed the privilege of the grounds of the Squadron Club is the main thing and the second social heaven is to be on a yacht. Of course there is a mob who fringe the stone jetty and stand and stand until one thinks that they are a part of the jetty but they are merely the people.

Ogden Goelet's new yacht has created considerable excitement. It is built regardless of cost and taken with all the silly and fabulous ideas which the British public has in regard to American millionaires this new boat causes a dull wonder which a British Peer could not manufacture by the expenditure of twice the cost of this boat. This is part of the popular Arabian nights. This is not merely a boat but it is a symbol of that vast power of wealth which amazes the people of England as it appears from South Africa or from America. The fact that Mr. Ogden Goelet has a finer steam yacht than any British Duke does not strike them here as inspiring at all. They look upon the owner as they look upon some popular chimpanzee in the Zoological Gardens. Here is a man who can own a yacht grander than any yacht owned by an Englishman. Consequently he is a prize, a wonder, a new thing and an altogether extraordinary person. In fact there is a peculiar disposition on the part of the English to regard as vulgar anything which is better than they have got themselves.

[One paragraph of fashion notes by Cora]

(e)

In England the Emperor of the Germans is so constantly pointed out as the last mad man of the Universe that it is refreshing to hear many of the newspapers saying that the Empress of Germany is a very charming woman. "It is her wise and gentle counsel, her never failing tact, her sound judgement which influence the Emperor more than anything." Of course this is the regular legend. It is to be supposed that all Queens who are never heard of, invariably influence the King by their wise and gentle counsel, their never failing tact, their sound judgement.

However when the Empress was only little Princess Augusta Victoria of Schleswig-Holstein, it is interesting to know that she was deadly afraid of Bismarck. If she was naughty her nurse simply mentioned the terrible name of this statesman and immediately there was peace. He shadowed over her like a monstrous ogre of fable and she passed in all her checks at a glance from his eye. The Man of Iron used all his influence to bring about a marriage between her and the present German Emperor. He did it. It was the work of his hands precisely as if he had made a clock. And I wonder if the childish terror of the little Princess had anything premonitory in it.

No. 4 (August 29, 1897)

(a)

In London at present a stranger may be surprised to hear that the city is empty, that everybody has gone away and left the stillness of a churchyard. The stranger will not be able to see any subtraction from the trampling millions. Then it will be explained to him that what is meant is that the society people have all gone away from town. While it is not true that they have left the void in the metropolis that they seem to suspect yet it is certainly true that they have gone. The phenomenon of their absence is observable in New Bond Street and in Hyde Park but otherwise London does not seem to mind it. The audiences at the theatres are quite as large and gay and they are also a trifle more courteous to the stage or the music. The occupants of the stalls and boxes at this time of year have not so much to tell each other during the progress of the performance.

Society is now scattered throughout hundreds of English

country houses and all over the Continent. To be seen in London at this time of year would really smite the conscience of the more punctilious of the elite. Any young man in society who is forced by circumstances to now come to London sneaks along in the shadow of the houses and dodges up alleys for fear some body will detect him in this frightful crime. If any body does catch him he tries to save his reputation by a dreary and tiresome wail of how dull London is at present.

But nevertheless life in an English country house is perhaps the most delightful manner of living in the world and society should be forgiven if it grows quite silly over it. The band of idiotic novelists who describe always the doings of alleged Lords and supposed Ladies have given information to America upon one point at least. Their descriptions of the homes of the aristocracy in the country convey a nearly correct impression although this is supposed to be unconsciously done. In their semi-instinctive mention of moors and the hunting fields, the morning-rooms, balls, servants and all that, they suggest the reality. This is not to their credit at all because if this pack of numskulls had any idea that they were conveying anything worth while they would probably change it. But one must admit at least that if the average American girl considers a knowledge of English country houses to be of any consequence at all she may console herself with the fact that she knows a lot about it.

Now is the time when the Prince of Wales usually goes to Homburg to take the waters and a whole troop of society people trail after him. In this throng are always a large number of Americans.

(b)

[Paragraph on fashions by Cora]

(c)

Five hundred warrants have been issued here in London and something less than five hundred constables are endeavoring to serve them on five hundred missing parents. This means that there are this number of families now dependent on public charity for food, clothes and shelter. The local boards who control the affairs of the various parishes of London have placed a price upon the heads of these deserters. In most of the parishes a reward of one pound is offered but the parish of St. Giles, Camberwell, has raised the price to two pounds. Naturally most of the delinquents are men but there are a few women who are also wanted for the crime of deserting their children. The police say that they would rather try to catch five hundred Jack the Rippers than to scour London for these run-a-way fathers and mothers.

(d)

A writer in a London newspaper has recently made an article on the beauty of London women. It reads very much like a florist's catalogue. Here we learn that all the women in London society possess beauty beyond the dreams of an artist. He makes no exceptions. He simply goes through the social register from end to end and to all the women there-on he donates beautiful complexions and swan-like throats and ruby lips and all the other stock terms of the cheaper poets. This would be ridiculous if it were not for the fact that the English public will surely take this thing seriously and the Englishman who has never been nearer to London society than to be on the sidewalk in front of some well known house, will immediately go forth into the world and solemnly swear that the Parisiennes and the Americans are no where. This kind of a fact goes into an English head like a pin into a cushion but unlike the pin it never comes out. It remains there forever and you might as well save your breath about it. You will only get apoplexy or fall in a series of swoons and you will have made no change.

Meanwhile I wonder how the real beauties like Lady Mar-and-Kellie, and Lady Warwick, Miss Enid Wilson and some few others like this catalogue.

(e)

The Turk has recently rehabilitated himself and the interest in him here has become of a keener kind. People have about finished calling him the Sick Man of Europe. He has recently displayed the fact that he is nothing of the kind. He has succeeded in astonishing the world and there is considerable speculation as to how he did it all.

In the first place the Turk has been misunderstood to rather a large extent. We have been taught that his chief characteristics are sensualism and a desire to commit murder on all sides. But after all the Turk is considerable of a man. I do not mean the Sultan but I mean those simple individuals in baggy trousers and fez who make up a certain part of the great ruler's subjects.

On a recent visit to Constantinople I was allowed to pay several visits to the Harem of a prominent citizen and I discovered that we are somewhat deluded in regard to our ideas of it. The word is understood by the average Western mind in rather a wrong way. It simply means that part of the house or household establishment devoted to the use of the women and is not necessarily a place of wickedness. It is easy to account for the large number of women as not only the wife of a man but all the female members of his wife's family and his own live in the Harem. He has always the pleasure of the company of his sisters and his cousins and his aunts as well as that of his mother and his grandmother if the latter are not dead. There is a regular swarm of them and they are so idle and lazy that they have to be supplemented by a horde of female attendants. Speaking generally I think that if I were a man and had a Harem I would keep religiously out of it.

The seclusion of women and the wearing of the veil has no meaning of under-handed profligacy to the Oriental. In thus secluding the women of his family he is in fact conforming to the most stringent social form and any change would strike him as absolute blasphemy. Home is too sacred a thing to be disclosed to the public eye and also gossiping of the other sex is not a practice of the Oriental class that corresponds to the Clubmen of the Western world.

In the Harem which I visited there were perhaps a hundred women. It was the establishment of a very high Turkish official who had several wives as well as sisters and cousins and aunts and nieces and all the rest of it. I was received by five or six of the principal members. They were all rather stout and stupid. They crowded about me and showed an infantile enthusiasm over my hat and wrap. Each of them in turn tried them on and laughed and chattered incessantly over the absurd appearance they made, the Western hat towering over one after another of the dear little head-dresses of velvet and pearls and a succession of soft silly baggy trousers holding a sort of a dispute with the modern wrap. Only one of these women wore stockings which were of pale pink silk. The bare feet of the others were thrust into tiny red embroidered slippers with the pointed toes turned up and pompoms on them.

Their house dress in detail was precisely what romance teaches us that they wear. One woman about twenty years of age, a fair creature with large blue eyes and almost white hair, evidently a Circassian, had trousers of the soft silk made by hand only in the East, Ciel blue in color. Over her white blouse of the finest muslin and lace was a zouave jacket of blue velvet almost covered by embroidery of silver and seed pearls. Fastened on her head and covering but not hiding her flowing hair was a gauze-like veil spangled with silver. A rope of pearls was wound several times about her neck and fell on her bosom and her bracelets and rings were without number. Her eyes were heavily blackened and her lips and finger nails stained bright red with Henna. Hers was the most beautiful costume but some of the others were more gorgeous.

The room in which I was received was long and low with two heavily latticed windows. There were no divans but the floor was six inches deep with Persian and Turkish rugs of all sizes and shapes and the walls were hung with them. There were innumerable hard and soft cushions upon which these women reclined. At every elbow was a little ebony pearl inlaid coffee stand. The only other furniture of the apartment was a Swiss music box. Each woman had near her an ivory hand mirror. The air was pervaded with an odor of perfumed cigarettes which the women smoked incessantly.

Coffee in priceless china cups without handles which rested in gold enameled stands about the size of an egg cup was served with Turkish sweets and hot-house fruit. It was not a very cheerful gathering. I confess that I have traveled too much in Europe to be able to pry without shame into the affairs of other people although it is a habit that besets the average tourist. We must make ourselves most infernal nuisances to the stranger peoples and I am not one to excuse such proceedings on the grounds of a craving thirst for knowledge. I simply learned that these women were fat and lazy and ignorant and contented. Their chief excitement seems to lie in veiled visits to the Bazaar or, it may be, in a sail on the Bosphorus in a steamboat on the deck of which they are cloistered in a sort of a pen. On some days closely guarded and attended they may make excursions to the stream called Sweet Waters of Europe where they partake of a form of enjoyment which reminds one of an attempt at an imitation of Coney Island inside of a prison. It is not a very thrilling existence and they seem to have the precise mental qualifications essential for a full appreciation of this kind of life.

But of course these are the women folk of a great swell. The common man, the peasant of Turkey, only has one wife and cheerfully gets along with as few sisters and cousins and aunts as Heaven will let him.

(f)

A terrible industry is reported as being carried on by professional beggars in South Russia. It is the wholesale mutilation of children in order to be able to exhibit them maimed and excite the pity of passers by and thus get their money. One case discovered is of a little girl eight years of age, stolen from her home by beggars, gagged and carried to a cellar. She heard them discussing whether they should blind her or cut off her hands and feet. At last they decided to make her blind which they did by throwing pitch into her face and setting fire to it. Her fingers were pulled out of joint and her feet cut sufficiently to make her limp when walking. This child remained two weeks in the cellar before she was taken out to beg. She was then recognized by some relations who reclaimed her and had the beggars arrested.

The evidence at their trial proved that the dead bodies of two young boys were in the cellar at the time they took the little girl there. They had probably succumbed to similar tortures.

(g)

[Fashion note by Cora for old ladies]

(h)

The visit of the Duke and Duchess of York to Ireland has turned out as was plainly indicated from the first. The Duke has gone to Ireland and met a small group of people which he usually meets in London. This is the whole story. That he was cheered in Londonderry and Belfast has nothing to do with the situation at all. These two northern Irish towns do not hold the people which the Royal Pair were supposed to come and see. The political plan of the visit was that the Duke should let the light of his countenance shine on the dissatisfied and turbulent south but the Lakes of Killarney are not the dissatisfied and turbulent south. This is the tourist route and has no Irish meaning. I think it will be found that this much applauded visit has simply done nothing at all either in one way or in the other way.

(i)

It may interest Americans to know that the women of old Flanders are very beautiful. They are tall and graceful with shining golden hair and blue eyes. They dress simply but often elegantly, particularly on Sundays when their dress is usually of a heavy silk.

Bruges is the only city in Flanders that has preserved its originality as it was in the marvellous middle ages. When one walks through the very narrow streets darkened by the heavy facades of the thirteenth century which seem to bend forward and down, one meets these Junoesque women, wrapped in long mantles with broad brimmed hats. These women

are very religious and ideal mothers of families. They have
no ambition, do not care for art, or music, and not a whisper
of rebellion against the husband and despot of the household
is ever heard. In her eyes he represents power next to God's
and is so worshiped. The new woman has not place in
Flanders.

(j)

The Drury Lane Theatre is soon to produce a play in which
the actors and actresses are to wear the actual costumes
worn by society beaus and belles at the fancy dress and historic ball given by the Duchess of Devonshire. There is a
pause in the proceedings owing to some of the ladies being
intent on driving hard bargains for their beautiful dresses.
They are evidently loath to part with their finery and it is
astonishing that the sale of their dresses was considered for
a moment. They call Americans vulgar but such a wholesale
example of bad taste has never been known in America to
my knowledge.

The costumes of the gentlemen were obtained without difficulty.

No. 8 (September 26, 1897)

(a)

I doubt if English shooting has any particular interest for the
American sportsman. I have seen considerable shooting in
America and I have found it always to be an utterly different
thing. It seems to my amateurish mind that in America the
bird has always a very good chance for his life whereas in
England the bird is almost invariably fat and tame and I
would agree to do more or less execution with an empty soda
water bottle. After witnessing the men of the hunt clubs in
the Adirondacks or in the north east counties of Pennsylvania
return to the club house utterly fagged out but cheerful in
the consciousness of having bagged maybe ten birds to each
gun by dint of the most superhuman labor through swale
and over hill I am made a bit ill by this casual and indolent

slaughter of about a ton of birds by men who really do not shoot well after all.

I was going to remark however that the hunting preserves of Scotland have just now reached the zenith of their value. Every body wants a shooting box in the Highlands. The southern Duke or Earl is willing to pay a frightful price for a season's rental of four thousand acres of heather which ten years ago hung like a mill stone around the neck of some Scottish Laird. An income from one of these places amounts now to fifty guineas or two hundred and fifty dollars a day during the season and many of the poorer families among the gentry are enabled to spend the season in London because some manufacturing Earl wants to spend his hunting season in Scotland.

The exodus to the moors begins on the 12th of August and for some weeks after that the northern trains from London are crowded with men bearing fishing rods and gun cases and women who begin to affect both trimmings, plaids and tam-o-shanters. The wily Scotchman doesn't let any of this money escape if he can help it. Even the Duke of Sutherland whose income is seven hundred thousand dollars a year is glad to let some of his moor to the Duke of Westminster who pays fifty thousand dollars for the season's rights over some deer forests. The Duke of Argyll has very many places in Scotland. One of them can even be let for one hundred and fifty thousand dollars a season and the Duke has this little bait out for some generous Londoner. The eye for "siller" which has made the Scotchman famous has not been lost in any of the internecine shuffling. But after all if one had it one would be willing to give even two thousand pounds a season to be able to own for a time a part of the wonders and glories of the forests and hills of Scotland.

(b)

The bill included 96 francs for champagne, 5 francs for coffee and 15 francs for liqueurs. The entire bill was 190 francs or $38.00. A ragged and unkempt man entered a

Parisian restaurant, ordered a dinner which amounted to this total and then tranquilly announced that he did not have a sou. Outside of this question of a sou he had no boots, no linen, no vest, no hat and was in miraculous rags. When the judge questioned the proprietor of the restaurant as to his temerity in serving this man the proprietor stated that he thought that the bill was to be paid by the two well dressed women who were with the vagabond. This is Paris.

(c)

Mr. Harold Frederic, one of the small group of American novelists who prefer to live in England, has just finished his new book. It has yet no name but I can say that Mr. Frederic has departed from his American working ground and has written a book which deals solely with English people. It is the story of the young inheritor of a Dukedom in the north of England and follows the English life most wonderfully for the work of a writer who is so typically American in all his other books and in all his manners. Every one who has read the manuscript is joyful and enthusiastic over it. "Strawberry Leaves" may be the title.

(d)

[Paragraph by Cora about Sarah Bernhardt's treatment of her hair]

(e)

Queen Marguerite of Italy some time ago asked a little girl to knit for her a pair of silk mittens giving her the money to purchase the silk. In a short time a lovely pair of mittens arrived at the palace. The Queen in return sent another pair to the little girl, one containing liras and the other candies with the following note. "Tell me, my dear child, which you like best." The reply was "Dearest Queen—Your lovely presents have made me shed many tears. Papa took the mitten with the money, my brother had the candies."

(f)

A short time ago Queen Victoria gave to the Sultan of Johore an order which in British eyes is held as a high mark of honor to be worn only by worthy persons. Yet the conduct of this sovereign has for some time been the subject of general comment.

He is constantly intoxicated and riotous, and finds amusement in assaulting harmless and inoffensive natives knowing full well that the law cannot interfere. His chosen companions are stable boys and questionable Europeans who frequent with him places that are not considered desirable resorts where brawls are of nightly occurrence. This conduct hardly befits a sovereign prince. And the people of Singapore are justified in airing their disgust and in objecting generally.

(g)

The Hungarians to whom scandal is as a sweetmeat have a sensation now after their own heart. The tombs of their ancient Kings have been plundered. And the sacred bones have disappeared.

The Turks were the first despoilers. But in 1869 researches were made in the Bishop's garden in Stuhlweissenberg and the bones were collected and identified as those of St. Emerich, the son of the first Hungarian King, St. Stephen (1031); King Stephen (1038); King Koloman (1114); Prince Almos, father of King Bela II (1137); King Bela II (1141), and Kings Geiza II and Ladislaus; Queen Marie, the first wife of Robert Carl (1317); Johann Zapolya (1540) whose body was thrown out in 1543 by order of Achmed Pasha. Each skeleton was catalogued, and inside each skull was pasted a label, the whole being placed in stone sarcophagi. Then the town took care of them so carefully that the stone sarcophagi were thrown on a dust heap and the bones stored in a loft in the town hall. There they were forgotten until 1872, when the police director was informed that some bones were strewn about upstairs.

Upstairs sure enough were the bones from the Bishop's garden, the labels still inside the skulls, proving that they were the remnants of the Royal house of Hungary. They were then placed in the vault of St. Stephen's Church. In 1893, Professor Török, with several officials, went into the vault for the purpose of removing the remains to Budapest in the interests of anthropology. To their horror they found all the skulls had disappeared and one entire skeleton was also gone. This has been kept secret but the story that a drunken caretaker had sold them to visitors for good sums has just leaked out. The general feeling is of bitterness and rage. Who has these Royal bones?

(h)

The people of Oberammergau have petitioned the Pope to allow them to have the Passion Play either in 1899 or 1901. They contend that the Paris Exposition which takes place in 1900 will serve to prevent people from coming to see the portrayal of the life of Christ. This looks as if the genial Oberammergauans were not altogether oblivious to the value of the tourist's shilling. Religious fervor alone is evidently not enough to incite them. The personal anxiety of every peasant to gain the elusive coin seems to figure rather strongly in this petition.

During the intervals between the great celebrations the little town is quite asleep. There are no visitors and no visitors' silver. Oberammergau has its chance at the pocketbooks of Europe at widely separated intervals and in the meantime she remains deep in somnolent quiet. Of course it is thrilling to watch for instance Pontius Pilate as he sits in front of a beer shop and consumes mug after mug of the beverage, but few come to see him do it. Also the country about Oberammergau is in itself very interesting and beautiful.

Landshut, near by, is an old Bavarian town unspoiled as yet by the traveling hundreds. On the heights over it is a venerable grey castle where once stopped Ludwig the mad King. To have it known that Ludwig once stopped in it is more credit to a castle than is usual with the old towers that brag that this or that King or Queen once spent a night within their walls. Ludwig had a most perfect sense of art. This was part of his madness. He flatly declined to have to do with anything but the beautiful. If he was absurd he was at least absurd in a way that has its attractions. His palace of Lindenhof is not too far away. It is really a small chateau but the garden is a masterpiece of the landscaper's skill. The Kiosk in the garden was a favorite resort of his insane majesty. It is fitted with genuine Turkish furniture. At Lindenhof too, is the blue grotto. It is very evidently fashioned after the celebrated blue grotto of the Isle of Capri. It is dug out of the mountain side. Half of the rocks are merely wood although nature is so well imitated that the effect is very startling. Lights shedding their rays through blue glass make exquisite color on the bosom of the small lake and the tumbling waterfall. Here the mad King used to play a great deal. One of his favorite dodges was to array himself as Lohengrin and navigate the lake in that fashion. He even had made two mechanical swans that would pull him in his boat triumphantly about the pool while his attendants dressed in much the same way paraded the shore and tried to show the requisite amount of enthusiasm.

Of course it is very silly but if a man must be mad I like to see him be mad in a way that makes him for instance enjoy dining tête-a-tête with a small marble bust of the first Napoleon. This is a kind of madness that has a certain charm. When Ludwig ended his gorgeous career by suicide he left behind him at any rate more fine subtle stories than a nation could make. He was just over the bounds from the most marvelous and invincible genius. The spectacle of his subjects manœuvring to get in front of a proper number of shillings would not have been greatly to the taste of Mad King Ludwig.

(i)

The most unique slot machine in the world is probably in the Brussels Exhibition grounds. There, in a café, it does the entire work of serving either hot or cold luncheons to the hungry. By placing a franc in the slot a chop or steak with potatoes, hot and well cooked, appears on a little platform. The investment of another franc will result in the uncanny sight of a pint of wine sliding into view. Half a franc will produce a plate of cold meat with salad and a roll; and ten centimes will give one a large piece of bread and butter and a bit of cheese or a "brioche." By expending another ten centimes a glass of excellent hock can be drawn from one of the two large vessels in the middle of this queer café. I recommend this automatic method to the reformers of the tip system.

(j)

The tramp who steals rides on the fronts of freight cars is almost an unknown creature in Europe. Cited as a wonderful case of daring is the ride of a man from London to Swindon on the buffers between the first and second class carriages. He was a foreigner and had his portmanteau with him and the railroad officials are marveling at his making the trip in safety.

(k)

It is understood that there is now in full force a new profession for women. It is that of a brides-maid. There are said to be women who sell a beautiful presence [never finished]

No. 9 (October 3, 1897)

(a)

One of the distinct figures in the London streets to a stranger is the professional nurse. Wherever one goes the woman in her long circular cloak, and small bonnet, trimmed with a flat Alsatian bow, and white strings which tie in a big bow under her chin, is in evidence. This bonnet and cloak may be of dark blue, green or brown and a long veil to match may hang from the back of the bonnet, but always one sees the same rather fine rosy cheeked woman. English women in large numbers are joining this profession. In fact the young girl who is of the middle classes seems to consider that this is one good way to defy the walls which surround her condition as a maiden who is born to be married to somebody, even anybody. As soon as she becomes a nurse she leaps a barrier and becomes free, a woman earning her own living. Of course this is true of the type writer girl and of the women who work in shops but then the true feminine quality finds more room in this occupation of nursing. It is purely a woman's business.

It is indeed a noble profession. It demands extreme tranquility and faithfulness, steady nerves and all that extraordinary deftness of touch which almost every woman owns. They say that the Red Cross nurses need courage. I would not personally wish to deny that all Red Cross women have remarkable courage but I do not believe that courage in the way of being able to endure shot and shell, is a necessary attribute of the Red Cross nurse.

The pictures which display a Red Cross nurse going out on the field and administering to the wounded under a hurricane fire must portray a pure accident. In the history of woman's work on the battle field it must have often happened that the nurses were under fire but to contend that they are constantly in the midst of the battle surging to and fro with the combatants and getting peppered at from every side would be absurd. As a matter of fact the position of the hospitals is so far in the rear that the battle to the nurses is merely a dull booming always in the air. To speak boldly of the matter, I should say that they were in no danger at all. I have seen young girls who dream of being nurses and following on after cavalry charges and mixing up with the melee of the infantry and being a part of the whole terrible romance of a battle. They had visions of themselves applying a cup of water to the lips of a dying soldier and gaining the reward of a last grateful look from his eyes. But this, I say, can only be the result of a fabulous accident. Some extraordinary shifting of divisions and batteries might suddenly place any Red Cross nurse in the thickest of the fight but as a usual thing this not only does not happen but a Red Cross nurse will soon get a more serene conviction that she will never even see the enemy. She will have horrors in plenty. She will see every thing that is built to turn a woman pale. But she will not see it on the field of battle itself. She will see it afterward.

It is far from me to wish to disparage the Red Cross nurses. They do their duty beautifully. But they do not do it on the field. I wish merely to destroy this idea that the part of a nurse's duties is to go forth and place a cup of water to the lips of the dying soldier. The dying soldier is usually about ten miles away.

(b)

At Oxford, next month, is to be held a congress of lady cyclists under the auspices of Lady Haberton the well known advocate of dress reform. It will be open to cyclists of both sexes but ladies not wearing divided skirts will not be admitted. Arguments against the ordinary skirt will be made, that it is the cause of many accidents, also that in a wind and on long rides it heavily handicaps the wearer. A Hotel has been taken for the visitors and a dinner, concert and other social gaieties are also to be used as persuasive arguments in favor of rational dress for women cyclists.

The dress reform people of the bicycle division recently held a meeting in Hyde Park. There were perhaps a score of women in attendance attired in the more advanced forms of cycling dress. It was expected that the noble and fashionable names involved in the advertisement of the event would bring out almost every woman who wanted to do as she liked in this matter of dress but beside the score of valiant wheel-women there appeared merely a great crowd of outsiders who gently but frankly guyed the little band of heroines. If the meeting at Oxford is an improvement on the Hyde Park affair I shall be much surprised. As a matter of truth this movement for reform in dress is in precisely the same stage of development as many other reforms with which we are all familiar. A great body of sensible women in England will let the cranks do all the hard work. The cranks do all the hard work and take all the insolence and ridicule in other reforms and of course they must in this one. For my part I do not see any signs of dress reform setting the world on fire at this particular time. It is undoubtedly a growing movement, sane and proper. This we can say philosophically, with due understanding that the world moves but as for anything which will astound the universe growing from these late agitations it is impossible. The mass of women are aimed in another direction and their indifference to a dress reform meeting at Hyde Park or at Oxford or anywhere is supreme.

(c)

Each autumn it is the custom for the children of the Royal House of Denmark to meet at Copenhagen. They have all made such brilliant marriages that it has caused the matter of etiquette and rule of precedence to be more strictly observed in this Court than in any in Europe.

It is told of the late Czar, who was a favorite of the Danes, that at a visit shortly before his death, his yacht arrived earlier than was expected in the sound. Consequently the King and the long line of carriages filled with members of the Court were not there to meet him. The Master of the harbor was in great distress and begged the Czar to remain on board until the King could be notified but he replied in Danish "I know the way to Amalienborg, don't disturb the King." And with the Czarina on his arm he walked off to the Palace as happy as a lad on his way from school.

In spite of the fact that etiquette and the rule of precedence reign more strongly over the Court of Denmark than over any other Court it remains true that the Royalties seem to consider Denmark as the great house. It is small wonder.

Alexander the Third particularly loved his visits to the Copenhagen Court and many other lesser potentates and Princes seem to gain much fun from visiting the Palace of that amiable King. Denmark will soon come to be called the nursery of European potentates.

(d)

[Five paragraphs of fashions by Cora]

(e)

Before the year is ended the Queen Regent of Holland will have given up her easy duties and Wilhelmina will take the scepter of the tight little Dutch Kingdom in her own hands.

Despite the pictures of a fat cheeked young girl which were reproduced often enough in American illustrated papers the little Queen's childhood was not a very healthy one. It was often doubted that she should come to reign over Holland. The past few years however have witnessed a great change in her and she now enjoys perfect health.

She has lived for the greater part of time in what is called The House in the Wood, a fine old mansion not far from the Hague. It resembles an English country house more than it does a Continental palace and the child led there a very simple sweet life. She was more under the immediate care of her mother than are most Royal children.

The House in the Wood owes its particular distinction to the fact that the late King's large collection of Japanese vertu is there. The Dutch were really the first of the European peoples to trade with Japan in a large way and the late King had the first whack at the art treasures of Tokio. The result is shown in this collection. Outside of the palaces of the Mikado no such array of embroideries and old Satsuma can be found.

Queen Wilhelmina is known to have a strong will of her own. This makes speculation concerning her future mate on the throne to be all the more interesting. The royalties of Europe grow shy over a proposition to marry a woman with a strong will of her own. That is not the kind of wife for which a Continental royalty is looking. It perfectly represents what he don't want at all. However within a few years there will naturally be what an American would call a "big deal" of some kind and Wilhelmina will be married in some way that will have all the dignity of a move in a game of chess.

(f)

In a list I recently saw of American girls who have married foreign Princes I noticed that of Her Serene Highness the

Princess Soltykoff. How many New Yorkers, I wonder, remember the beautiful woman in New York and Long Branch first known as Minnie Rose and afterward as Mrs. Minnie Edwards? As Mrs. Minnie Edwards she appeared in Paris in 1890. Her wonderfully beautiful dark face and queenly carriage attracted much attention as she drove in the Bois and many romantic stories were flying about as to who she was. One was of a young Jewish girl selling shoes in a retail shop in Chicago—and of her fitting the feet of a fairy prince who lifted her to his high estate years before. But the fairy prince died or lost his fortune or returned to the Pixies as is the custom of fairy princes and so the beautiful Jewess came to Paris and to St. Petersburg and met the real Prince. They were married only a few months when she was again a widow with an enormous fortune. Young Prince Soltykoff died in Egypt in 1891 I believe. And this is the story of one of our American Princesses.

(g)

It seems that Sir Edward Sassoon does not have the same appreciation of art that inspired the late Mr. Barnato to adorn the mansion which used to be his in Park Lane with the statues representing "Night," "Morning," "Truth," "Welcome" and "Fidelity" and which society used to delight in calling "the petrified bondholders." The municipality of the city of Brighton have been presented with them. Was Brighton selected to be the recipient of this handsome gift because of Mr. Barnato's fondness for the place? is the question many are asking. To society in London Mr. Barnato was "an impossible person"; not so at Brighton. Here he had a circle of friends as well as one of the finest houses on the sea front and it was his custom to be a regular visitor from Saturday to Monday.

The wiles of the executors to throw dust into the eyes of the tax collectors of Great Britain is causing much amused comment. They stated the fortune left at about one fourth of its real value. Then becoming frightened when the truth oozed out they made a statement to the public through the Press that although Mr. Barnato named no charities to be benefited by his will, they the executors knew his wishes on the subject and therefore in their desire to carry them out to the letter gave £16300. in sums, varying from £250. to £3000. to different hospitals and homes—the sum total of which is comparatively so small that they have utterly failed in their object to gain public sympathy—and the facts are related in clubs and drawingrooms as an amusing story of the cupidity of the Jews.

(h)

In the Welsch-Tyrol when a young girl is starting for the church to be married she stops for a moment on the threshold of her old home and her mother solemnly hands her a new pocket-handkerchief. The bride holds it during the marriage ceremony always crying a few tears which she wipes away with the handkerchief. So soon as the gaieties are finished the young wife puts the handkerchief carefully away in her linen chest, and there it stays unused as long as she lives. Nothing would induce a Tyrolese woman to use this sacred kerchief. It may be yellow with age ere it is taken from its place to fulfill the second and last part of its mission. When the wife dies the nearest of kin place the bridal handkerchief over the face of the dead woman and so is buried with her.

(i)

Cycling has reached the limit in England. The old story of an American cook asking if she could use the piano is now repeated by house-maids and cooks stating in their applications for situations that they cycled was the end of things we thought but it was a mistake. In a suburb of London there is a very dignified convent. At five A.M. the sound of < > sacred music chanted by the nuns tells the world that their day is well advanced. At 8 A.M. you can see some of these "holy women" with folded hands and downcast eyes, walking in the beautiful grounds of the convent.

Late at night the dim religious light from the < > chapel window speaks of prayers and vigils. The < >

and romance has been sadly shaken. On a fine morning the most extraordinary pairs ever seen on bicycles built for two can be seen in the grounds. Around and around the paths ride the sombre < > dressed nuns, their black veils flying out behind them and an expression of suppressed enjoyment on their faces. But why should they not ride?

No. 10 (October 10, 1897)

(a)

[Five paragraphs of fashions by Cora]

(b)

During their recent trip the Duke and Duchess of York were entertained for a time at Killarney House, the seat of Lord Kenmare in that beautiful lake region of Ireland which the American tourist knows so well. There can be no doubt that this house is one of the handsomest in the kingdom although it was only built about seventeen years ago. It was the creation of the present Lady Kenmare and the people of the surrounding country call it Kenmare's Folly, Castle Folly and various names of that description. It was known to have demanded the entire strength of the family purse and the tenants of the broad estate had this fact impressed so strongly on their minds that to this day there exist many fine stories about Kenmare's Folly. One of the finest of them is that every doorknob in the house is made from the back of a Dresden watch. The fortunes of the family were supposed to have been recouped by the marriage of the heir to Miss Baring a daughter of one of the members of the great banking firm of that name. Soon after the marriage the firm failed and from the present appearance of the Kenmare estate it looks as if the marriage portion had not been left in the banking house. It is one of the finest estates in Ireland.

The creation of this Peerage only dated from 1798. At that time a Lord Kenmare who merely held this title by courtesy became a great favorite of the government because of his success in maintaining loyalty and order in Kerry, whatever that may mean. He was then raised to the Peerage.

(c)

Despite the tales one hears of Queen Victoria's wealth it is not known how much she possesses nor can it be known even after her death. Her will is never to be probated. When people call her the wealthiest woman in the world it may or may not be true. There is a great deal of secrecy surrounding the private purse.

The Queen does not come from a very rich family so that her estates have not been built into a huge pile by inheritance as is the case with most of the monarchs of Europe. Her childhood and girlhood were spent in what would be called poverty I suppose by her Royal neighbors. The Duke of Kent her father left her only debts. However I do not suppose that Windsor will call for charitable contributions. 37372 acres of land in Great Britain is not calculated to allow anybody to starve to death even if we do not count the German properties. You could not prove in any way to the average Briton that the Queen was not a fabulously wealthy woman and the Royal method of keeping the size of the purse a secret impresses him more than an open declaration and I don't doubt that if an ability to save and a care for expense count for anything that when Her Majesty dies she will leave a very comfortable property behind her.

(d)

There is no particular discussion about the Queen of Italy's will and no body is led to wonder about her private fortune but she is however undoubtedly the most talented and well educated of the Queens of Europe. She talks German, English, French and Spanish besides the Italian and is also a student of Latin and Greek. She is familiar with all the literatures and has even written a small hand book on Shakespeare's heroines which she keeps for her own use. She reads Ruskin and Darwin and Spencer and when the Emperor William referred to her in his speech at Homburg as having "deigned to leave her peaceful life and her work on behalf of art and literature and graciously to appear in our soldiers' camp" the phrases really had some meaning.

(e)

If there is anybody in the world who has heard of "The Ladies' Kennel Journal" it would be surprising and yet "The Ladies' Kennel Journal" is a very prosperous paper and is filled each week with the most exciting news.

"Southampton Ghost succumbed to a ball of hair in the stomach. Mrs. Greenwood laments him deeply.

Mrs. Marriott has a fine young orange male coming on.

The Seraph, Mrs. Marriott's Chinchilla kitten, purchased at the C. P. Show last year, has grown into a big, solid cat.

Mrs. Waldegrave Brodie evidently does not suffer from want of buyers for her kittens for she wrote, 'I sell my kittens almost too rapidly, as some unborn are already sold.' She has put up a delightful cattery.

The Hon. Miss Montague has been most unlucky with her cats this last two years, losing several with influenza. She has now a handsome lot of eight kits, bred by the famous Wooloomooloo. She is thinking of selling her litters and keeping only Mousie. The kittens are priced at 35 shillings each—quite a giving away price but Miss Montague says she must sell them."

There is also a birth announcement column in which I find paragraphs of this kind:

"Mrs. Cary Elwes' Persian cat Billing Sapphire, six blue kittens, by Lady Marcus Beresford's Julu."

If information of this kind is not calculated to send a thrill down a nation's spine no European correspondence can do it.

(f)

Scotland as is usual at this time of year contains a great quota of society people who are drawn there by the heather and the mountains and the shooting and, it may be, by the number of Royal personages who just at this time are making visits there. The Grand Duke Michael of Russia with Countess Torby and Countess Adda have been staying with Lord and Lady Tweedmouth and also with Lord Elphinstone at Carbery Tower. The Prince of Wales is with the Duke and Duchess of Fife. Afterward he will visit Mr. and Mrs. Farquharson of Invercauld. The Duke and Duchess of York after their duties in Ireland were over went to gain rest at the homes of Lord Rosebery and a whole list of nobilities who are now in Scotland. As soon as the official trip in Ireland was finished and the Duke and Duchess could dispense with a large number of state gowns and uniforms, about half a ton of luggage was shipped at once back to England and the future King and Queen hied them to an unofficial peace.

(g)

The new Earl of Egmont was recently discovered enjoying himself as the hall keeper of the new town hall, Chelsea. Previously to this he had been a member of one of those slow and solemn fire brigades which decorate the British Isles. He is of a family which has a most tragic and romantic history and his career has conformed to it. One of the historic curses which some ancient witch flung at the family was "Beware of fire and water" and this no doubt was the reason that he joined the fire brigade. He was resolved to protect himself. It is said that his wife is an American woman and hails from South Carolina.

(h)

The English papers are always crowded with appeals to the men of Great Britain made on the behalf of various societies. This is the only way in which one discovers that such societies exist. They never reach the public ear save through appeals of some frantic and honorable secretary to the men of Great Britain. I know now that there is a "Society for the Assistance of Ladies in Reduced Circumstances."

The duty of this society is to dig out all the ladies in reduced circumstances from the masses of the people and give them whatever assistance is possible. This seems to be in the nature of half crowns dispensed from time to time through the treasury of the society. I suppose it will strike Americans as unnatural that there should be societies for the assistance of ladies in reduced circumstances instead of societies for the assistance of women in reduced circumstances. But this distinction is intended and I don't doubt that the proper officers of the society draw the line according to their lights. In the pathetic list which is presented to the press I see that one lady is supporting herself and an invalid brother entirely through her needle and the sale of a poem written by her father. The price of the poem is one shilling and one penny. The secretary of the society announces that if it were not for the kindness of friends this old lady would not be able to support herself and her brother. This brings to one's mind the picture of her heroic friends thronging forward week after week and purchasing renewed copies of her father's poem, at one shilling and one pence.

Unplaced Miscellaneous Item

(a)

During the social season London is blessed by a solemn and austere Sunday ceremony which is called Church Parade. It consists in a certain portion of the populace driving slowly along a certain prescribed route in Hyde Park and recognizing or ignoring members of another and larger portion of the populace that lines a rail to the left of the drive. Stated simply, it may seem unimportant but in reality it is one of the bits of social masonry whose destruction would totter the British Empire dangerously toward its fall. This is not an expanded remark. A sight of the Church Parade fills one with the truth of it. It is a pageant more solemn than the crowning of kings.

No. 171 HOW THE AFRIDIS MADE A ZIARAT

THOSE terrible Afridis who still hold the Khyber Pass against the British are creatures of infinite resources, and when they want a thing they generally get it one way or another. Before the recent outbreak the Afridis established a "Ziarat," or place of pilgrimage, in their country, and the way they did it amounted to a stroke of genius. The neighboring tribes all had Ziarats, and the people went on pilgrimages to them and boasted of the virtues emanating from the dead holy men who were buried beneath the shrine.

Now, there does not seem ever to have been any holy man among the Afridis, and in order to have a real Ziarat you must first have a holy man to bury. The Afridis had been busy so many centuries robbing caravans and stealing sheep that they had not had time to pay any profound attention to their spiritual welfare, and really did not feel the want of a place of pilgrimage.

Not long ago, however, some Mullahs appeared among them and began to point out their deficiencies in this respect. It was shown to them that they did not even have a Ziarat and were in a bad way generally. A wave of religious fervor swept over the tribe and it was resolved that something must be done at once or black eyes and lemonade would not be their portion in the Mahometan heaven. A council of the leading men was called, and, after much deliberation, it was decided that what was most needed was a Ziarat. If they could only get a Ziarat they would feel comparatively respectable and there would be no further cause for complaint on the part of the Mullahs.

Then the question arose as to getting a saint for the shrine. One of the chiefs said that he knew of a Khattak, who lived out among the hills who would fill the bill, but he was unfortunately still alive. The council thought that that might be remedied, and so the Khattak was sent for. He was put through a rigid examination as to his high principles and general virtues, and he brought a lot of testimony to prove how holy he was.

His examination being satisfactory, they slew the astonished

Khattak then and there and built a big pile of stones over his body. Then they proclaimed their deed, and in a week the pilgrims were flocking to the new Ziarat and the reproach was removed from the land. Naturally the men who planned and executed this pious "coup" were looked upon by the Afridis as public benefactors of approved piety.

Among the Afridis the man most respected is the man who is the most expert thief. In fact, thievery is the only road to distinction among them. The scheme by which until of late Britain muzzled these desperate folk is ingenious and worthy of note. To pay an Afridi to behave himself every day of the week is a course too expensive for any Government. But by arrangement they have undertaken, at a price, to behave after the fashion of Christians on two days a week. The other five are devoted to throat-cutting, pillaging and the usual business of life, but on the remaining two they have hitherto sat quietly on their hilltops and watched with watering mouths the rich caravans pass to and fro in the pass beneath.

If a shot was fired on those days the tribe on whose ground the outrage took place got 1,000 rupees stopped out of its allowance next quarter day. Of this sum the man fired at got 500 rupees, or his relations if it happened to be a good shot, while the Government was the richer for the rest.

No. 172   HAROLD FREDERIC

THE personality of Mr. Harold Frederic is probably the one least discussed of the better American novelists. The goings and comings, the manners and the countenances of our leading men of letters are commonly limned with glee and some precision by the popular journals. Frederic has escaped much of it through the fact that his duties of correspondence have obliged him to live the last fifteen years in London, and so has been beyond the range of our inferior artillery. It is probably not very graceful to appear now in the guise of an advanced patrol ultimately potting at a man who has enjoyed the finer kind of peace for fifteen years; and if it were impossible to use these paragraphs to write about the books, the potting of the man would not be done.

One approaches certain sections of the American colony in London with a stealthy footfall. In England, there is sometimes a cousinly outdoing of the English in those matters which are particularly unimportant. A certain sympathetic and singing chord of the mind induces one to advance upon the field with caution. It was my fault to conclude beforehand that, since Frederic had lived intimately so long in England, he would present some kind of austere and impressive variation on one of our national types, and I was secretly not quite prepared to subscribe to the change. It was a bit of mistaken speculation. There was a tall, heavy man, moustached and straight-glanced, seated in a leather chair in the smoking-room of a club, telling a story to a circle of intent people with all the skill of one trained in an American newspaper school. At a distance he might have been even then the editor of the Albany *Journal*.

The sane man does not live amid another people without seeking to adopt whatever he recognizes as better; without seeking to choose from the new material some advantage, even if it be only a trick of grilling oysters. Accordingly, Frederic was to be to me a cosmopolitan figure, representing many ways of many peoples; and, behold, he was still the familiar figure, with no gilding, no varnish, a great reminiscent panorama of the Mohawk Valley!

It was in Central New York that Frederic was born, and it is there he passed his childish days and his young manhood. He enjoys greatly to tell how he gained his first opinions of the alphabet from a strenuous and enduring study of the letters on an empty soap-box. At an early age he was induced by his parents to arise at 5:30 A.M., and distribute supplies of milk among the worthy populace.

In his clubs, details of this story are well known. He pitilessly describes the gray shine of the dawn that makes the snow appear the hue of lead, and, moreover, his boyish pain at the task of throwing the stiff harness over the sleepy horse, and then the long and circuitous sledding among the customers of the milk route. There is no pretense in these accounts; many self-made men portray their early hardships in a spirit of purest vanity. "And now look!" But there is none of this in Frederic. He simply feels a most absorbed interest in that part of his career which made him so closely acquainted with the voluminous life of rural America. His boyhood extended through that time when the North was sending its thousands to the war, and the lists of dead and wounded were returning in due course. The great country back of the line of fight—the waiting women, the lightless windows, the tables set for three instead of five—was a land elate or forlorn, triumphant or despairing, always strained, eager, listening, tragic in attitude, trembling and quivering like a vast mass of nerves from the shock of the far away conflicts in the South. Those were supreme years, and yet for the great palpitating regions it seems that the mind of this lad was the only sensitive plate exposed to the sunlight of '61–'65. The book, *In the Sixties*, which contains "The Copperhead," "Marsena," "The War Widow," "The Eve of the Fourth," and "My Aunt Susan," breathes the spirit of a Titanic conflict as felt and endured at the homes. One would think that such a book would have taken the American people by storm, but it is true that an earlier edition of *The Copperhead* sold less than a thousand copies in America. We have sometimes a way of wildly celebrating the shadow of a mullein-stalk against the wall of a woodshed, and remaining intensely ignorant of the vital things that are ours. I believe that at about the time of the appearance of these stories, the critics were making a great deal of noise in an attempt to stake the novelists down to the soil and make them write the impressive common life of the United States. This virtuous struggle to prevent the novelists from going ballooning off over some land of dreams and candy-palaces was distinguished by the fact that, contemporaneously, there was Frederic doing his locality, doing his Mohawk Valley, with the strong trained hand of a great craftsman, and the critics were making such a din over the attempt to have a certain kind of thing done, that they did not recognize its presence. All this goes to show that there are some painful elements in the art of creating an American literature by what may be called the rattlety-bang method.

The important figures, the greater men, rise silently, un-spurred, undriven. To be sure, they may come in for magnifi-cent cudgelings later, but their approach is noiseless, invinci-ble, and they are upon us like ghosts before the critics have time to begin their clatter.

But there is something dismally unfortunate in the passing of *Seth's Brother's Wife*, *In the Valley*, the historical novel, and *The Lawton Girl*. Of course, they all had their success in measure, but here was a chance and a reason for every American to congratulate himself. Another thing had been done. For instance, *In the Valley* is easily the best historical novel that our country has borne. Perhaps it is the only good one. *Seth's Brother's Wife* and *The Lawton Girl* are rimmed with fine portrayals. There are writing men who, in some stories, dash over three miles at a headlong pace, and in an adjacent story move like a boat being sailed over ploughed fields; but in Frederic one feels at once the perfect evenness of craft, the undeviating worth of the workmanship. The excel-lence is always sustained, and these books form, with *In the Sixties*, a row of big American novels. But if we knew it we made no emphatic sign, and it was not until the appearance of *The Damnation of Theron Ware* that the book audiences really said: "Here is a writer!" If I make my moan too strong over this phase of the matter, I have only the excuse that I believe the *In the Sixties* stories to form a most notable achievement in writing times in America. Abner Beech, the indomitable and ferocious farmer, with his impregnable dis-loyalty or conscience, or whatever; Aunt Susan always at her loom making rag-carpets which, as the war deepened, took on two eloquent colors—the blue of old army overcoats and the black of woman's mourning; the guileless Marsena and the simple tragedy of his death—these characters represent to me living people, as if the book breathed.

It is natural that since Frederic has lived so long in Eng-land, his pen should turn toward English life. One does not look upon this fact with unmixed joy. It is mournful to lose his work even for a time. It is for this reason that I have made myself disagreeable upon several occasions by my ex-pressed views of *March Hares*. It is a worthy book, but one has a sense of desertion. We cannot afford a loss of this kind. But, at any rate, he has grasped English life with a precision of hand that is only equaled by the precision with which he grasped Irish life, and his new book will shine out for English eyes in a way with which they are not too familiar. It is a strong and striking delineation, free, bold, and straight.

In the mean time he is a prodigious laborer. Knowing the man and his methods, one can conceive him doing anything, unless it be writing a poor book, and, mind you, this is an important point.

No. 173   CONCERNING THE ENGLISH "ACADEMY"

AT LEAST once in every three years in London some journal or clique is sure to turn up with a plan, more or less disguised, for an English Academy founded on the manner of the French Academy. Some of these attempts have been almost shamelessly financial, and others have been shamelessly made for advertisement, so much so, that even if England wanted an Academy of Art and Letters, she would be prevented by the criminal impudence of the projectors. Moreover, Anglo-Saxon people usually object to the labelling of one artist as being officially guaranteed superior to another. It would surely mean at first a dreadful game of throat-cutting and sand-bagging, from which would not emerge enough children of light to form a coroner's jury, let alone an Academy of Art and Letters. It seems to be a general idea that the arena should remain as a cleared place in which no distinctions are recognized, where every man falls to and grabs what wool he may. Even a description of the present situation does not sound attractive.

But still the English powers are toying with the matter. Many men of importance have sent for publication lists of forty intellects which to their minds would form the proper Academy. In each of these lists we have the sublime spectacle of the writer leaving his own name out. This display of wholesale generosity might have brought the London public to tears had it not appeared later that there might be an exchange of contracts. "You put me in your list, and I'll put you in mine."

Recently, a well-known critical journal, the London *Academy*, unanimously elected itself to the position of mentor, and offered a prize of one hundred guineas to the book of signal merit published in the year of 1897, and a prize of fifty guineas for the next best book. Failures in projects of this kind dot contemporaneous history, and they have always been accompanied by howls of execration from men who did not win a prize, and from men who thought they knew who should have won a prize. It was quite a daring thing on the part of the *Academy* people. They had to steer their craft through the inch-wide channel between ridicule and equally terrible indictments for unfairness and falsity. To thoughtful people herein lay the interest.

And now one comes to the result. Usually these affairs are absurd, but one must hasten to admit that the decision of *Academy* is at least perfectly sane. They have succeeded in delivering an opinion to which none can strongly object. It is too respectable. The *Academy* emerges in the most graceful fashion from the mists of its precarious venture. Not a single formidable voice will be raised in protest, and in this fact is victory.

The first prize of one hundred guineas was given to Mr. Stephen Phillips for his volume of *Poems*. The prize of fifty guineas was awarded to Mr. W. E. Henley for his *Essay on the Life, Genius and Achievement of Burns*, which is contained in the fourth volume of the Centenary edition of Burns. The *Academy* remarks: "It is not likely that the choice will please every one, but the most patient consideration of the whole matter convinces us that we have done well."

And that is precisely what they have done. Here is a task which few have been able to perform decently, mainly, perhaps, because few decent people have ever attempted it, but the *Academy* has carried it through, and the result is, in the artistic sense, respectable, inexorably respectable.

The novelists did not appear in great force in the discussions which were waged in the columns of the journal previous to the decisions. Many people suggested that the prizes should be given to Mr. Henry James for his *What Maisie Knew,* and to Mr. Joseph Conrad for his *The Nigger of the "Narcissus"*—a rendering which would have made a genial beginning for an English Academy of letters, since Mr. James is an American and Mr. Conrad was born in Poland. However, these two were the only novelists who figured prominently. They were not puny adversaries. Mr. James's book is alive with all the art which is at the command of that great workman, and as for the new man, Conrad, his novel is a marvel of fine descriptive writing. It is unquestionably the best story of the sea written by a man now alive, and as a matter of fact, one would have to make an extensive search among the tombs before he who has done better could be found. As for the ruck of writers who make the sea their literary domain, Conrad seems in effect simply to warn them off the premises, and tell them to remain silent. He comes nearer to an ownership of the mysterious life on the ocean than anybody who has written in this century.

Mr. Conrad was stoutly pressed for the prize, but the editors of the *Academy* judged the book to be "too slight and episodic," although they considered it "a remarkable imaginative feat marked by striking literary power." If one wanted to pause and quibble, one would instantly protest against their use of the word episodic, which as a critical epithet is absolutely and flagrantly worthless.

Mr. Rudyard Kipling's *Captains Courageous* was disqualified on grounds which are not, apparently, within the limits of the *Academy's* declared purpose. The paper says: "Mr. Kipling has himself fixed his standard too high for *Captains Courageous* to be satisfying." If a man is to be measured according to his books of previous years, then the *Academy* has no right to the use of the name "1897." This is not, then, a question of the best book in 1897. This is, rather, a question as to whether some man in 1897 has written a book which is better than all other books in 1897, and also better than a book which he himself had written in 1849 or whenever you like. Apply this theory still further, and you find that the decision of the *Academy* amounts to a declaration that Mr. Henley's essay on

Burns is the best thing ever from the pen of that gifted man—a declaration that will at least not gain a general assent.

The *Academy* also says: "Mr. William Watson's *Hope of the World* causes us to glance back to what he has done, rather than to look forward to what he may do."

Well, there you are. When a man or a paper elects to don a wig and sit on a bench to hear a case of art in all solemn finality, the world is not prepared to be dazzled by the wisdom of the decision. One can only hope for an artistically respectable result. The result in this case was artistically respectable. The *Academy* would have justified the entire complacence of its readers if it had not been thoughtless enough to give two columns of its reasons. The decisions themselves would have stood criticism with honor, even distinction, but the printed reasons often bewilder one with the agility with which the *Academy* apparently disregards the laws which the *Academy* has made. Perhaps they are too episodic. At any rate, they contain statements that are at variance with the original plan —at least in some eyes—and the affair was not, therefore, the success of esteem that it might have been.

No. 174   THE BLOOD OF THE MARTYR

ACT I

Scene: Kiao Chou. Time: 1898.

(Prince Henry of Prussia discovered, seated. Background of bay, with anchored squadron. Enter an aide.)

Prince Henry—Captain, has that new squad of missionaries been properly drilled?

Aide—Yes, Your Highness.

P. H.—Are they all resolved in the proper spirit?

Aide—Yes, Your Highness.

P. H.—Well, feed them up for a time on broken glass, copies of Xenophon's "Anabasis" and blood. Then turn them loose. Send them into every corner of China, and in time we will reap enough martyrs. You see, we need twenty-three more railway concessions and eight more ports. These missionaries are a noble people.

Aide—Pardon, Your Highness, but the missionary at Yen Hock has appealed for assistance. He says that the people are about to kill him.

P. H.—The missionary at Yen Hock, eh? Let me think. Isn't Yen Hock in that fertile Fan Tan Valley?

Aide—Yes, Your Highness. What shall be done for the man, Your Highness?

P. H.—Oh, send him a box of cigars and my compliments. Tell him he is the right man in the right place. How is the temper of the people there? Would they massacre more than one, do you think? Might send up three or four more, eh? Makes a stronger case.

Aide—Pardon, Your Highness, but we are growing awfully short of missionaries. Those we have are greatly overworked. I have in mind now one man who is due to be martyred in at least five desirable agricultural districts.

P. H. (impatiently)—This will not do at all. I must be well equipped with missionaries or I will not be able to accomplish my great civilizing task in the East. Send to Berlin for another consignment. In the meantime drill the present squad up to the highest point of efficiency. And, by the way, send that chap in Yen Hock two boxes of cigars and my compliments. Or, no! Send him a box of cigars and give him my compliments twice. The services of these men must receive proper recognition.

ACT II

Scene: The Tsung-li-Yamen in session. Time: Later.

First Mandarin (yawning)—I have studied Confucius until I am lame in the right leg, but I can't for the life of me discover what is a railway concession.

Second M.—Why, it is a thing made sometimes by the missionaries.

First M.—Yes, but what does it look like? Now, I fancy that it strongly resembles a tea-junk.

Third M.—No. It looks more like a horse, only that it is a pale purple in color and has red eyes.

Second M.—No, you are both wrong. A railway concession is a thing of two silver wheels, and it is bestrode by the white man, who can make it fly over the world at his will.

Fourth M.—And I tell you you are all wrong. You chaps better climb back over the great wall and resume the business of sheep-herding. A railway concession is merely what they take with those machines they call "kodaks." It——

(Discordant interruption. Enter Prince Henry.)

Prince Henry (nodding)—Good morning. I have to announce to you another outrage and demand satisfaction in the name of my Emperor. The German missionary at Yen Hock has been foully murdered.

First Mandarin—We hasten to express to you our poignant grief at the untimely death of this worthy man; but before developing a full description of our personal woe and pain I would like to ask what form your demand for redress is likely to take.

P. H.—His Majesty's Government has been pleased to inform me that, as a new missionary may possibly go to Yen Hock, they consider that a railway concession would be the only proper guarantee of his safety.

Second M. (interested)—And does each missionary need a railway concession for his own use?

First M. (arising and flinging out his hands in desperation)— Here! Take our railway concessions and go away. I think the curse of China is this surplus of railway concessions. Take them!

P. H. (formally)—Do you mean that you are offering to His Majesty a monopoly of the railway system of China?

Chorus of Mandarins—We don't know. We are very tired. We are very unhappy. We want to rest. We don't understand this devilish row. Go away, bold, bad man, and take the railway concessions with you. We wish to slumber, for all the towers are nodding and each tree sinks languidly. Go away! And, in Heaven's name, lay your hands on every railway concession in China if that will quiet you.

P. H.—Pardon me, but the blood of the martyr that fell——

Fifth M. (suddenly awakening in a corner)—Oh, is that man here yet? Why don't he go home? Somebody book him free for Khartum.

P. H.—The blood of the martyr——

Chorus (hastily)—Yes, yes, we understand all that.

P. H. (stiffly)—One would think I represented the only foreign Power that is now holding negotiations with China.

Chorus (wearily)—Oh, no! There are others.

P. H.—Well, then, the blood of the martyr calls for——

Chorus (sleepily)—Yes, yes. So it does; so it does.

P. H.—It calls for——

(Tsung-li-Yamen snores. Exit Prince Henry.)

ACT III

Scene: Kiao Chou. Time: Still later. Background of bay, as before.

(Prince Henry discovered pacing to and fro proudly.)

Prince Henry (alone)—Thus do the glorious eagles of Germany soar above their rivals. Yen Hock and the Valley of the Fan Tan will soon be ours. All is well.

(In the distance figure of the Yen Hock Missionary is discerned slowly approaching on crutches. Prince Henry continues to pace to and fro proudly.)

The Yen Hock Missionary (having arrived)—Your Highness!

(Prince Henry, turning, perceives the Missionary and falls back with a loud cry of horror.)

Prince Henry (hoarsely)—Do my eyes deceive me, or is this a cartoon in the Kladderadatsch? Wherefore art thou come, ghost?

Missionary—Your Highness, I am no ghost. I am the Yen Hock Missionary in the flesh.

P. H.—What, then, traitor? And this is a man in whom the Emperor placed his trust! Oh, unhappy man! Oh, unhappy Germany, to be served by such a son!

M. (humbly)—Your Highness, my parishioners cut off one of my ears.

P. H.—An ear! Paltry!

M.—Your Highness, they burned off one of my feet.

P. H.—A foot! Idle amusement!

M.—Your Highness, they sliced out one of my lungs.

P. H. (impatiently)—Oh, come now; get to the main story. Did they disembowel you?

M. (abashed)—No, Your Highness, I—I couldn't honestly say that they did. But (gaining courage) they garroted me and flayed me alive.

P. H. (suddenly and completely mollified)—Oh, well, that is quite sufficient—quite sufficient. Some day I'll let you ride a short distance on the engine of the Fan Tan Express, and, as a mark of gratitude for my royal favor, you can present to me that box of cigars. Ho! there, Captain! Take this man down to the kitchen and give him some beer.

(Curtain.)

No. 175 THE SCOTCH EXPRESS

THE entrance to Euston Station is of itself sufficiently imposing. It is a high portico of brown stone, old and grim, in form a casual imitation no doubt of the front of the temple of Nike Apteros with a recollection of the Egyptians proclaimed at the flanks. The frieze where of old would prance an exuberant processional of gods is in this case bare of decoration but upon the epistyle is written in simple stern letters the word: "Euston." This legend, reared high by the gloomy Pelagic columns, stares down a wide avenue.

In short, this entrance to a railway station does not in any way resemble the entrance to a railway station. It is, more, the front of some venerable bank. But it has another dignity which is not born of form. To a great degree it is to the English and to those who are in England, the gate to Scotland.

The little hansoms are continually speeding through the gate, dashing between the legs of the solemn temple; the four-wheelers, their tops crowded with baggage, roll in and out constantly; and the footways beat under the trampling of the people. Of course, there are the suburbs and a hundred towns along the line and Liverpool, the beginning of an important sea-path to America, and the great manufacturing cities of the North, but if one stands at this gate, in August particularly, one must note the number of men with gun cases, the number of women who surely have tam-o'-shanters and plaids concealed in their luggage ready for the moors. There is during the latter part of that month a wholesale flight from London to Scotland which recalls the July throngs leaving New York for the shore or the mountains.

The hansoms after passing through this impressive portal of the station bowl smoothly across a courtyard which is in the centre of the terminal hotel, an institution dear to most railways in Europe. The traveller lands amid a swarm of porters and then proceeds cheerfully to take the customary trouble for his luggage. America provides a contrivance in a thousand situations where Europe provides a man or perhaps a number of men and the work of our brass check is here done by porters directed by the traveller himself. The men lack the memory of the check; the check never forgets its identity. Moreover the European railways generously furnish the porters at the expense of the traveller. Nevertheless if these men have not the invincible business precision of the check and if they have to be tipped, it can be asserted, for those who care, that in Europe one half of the populace waits on the other half most diligently and well.

Against the masonry of a platform under the vaulted arch of the train house lay a long string of coaches. They were painted white on the bulging part which led half way down from the top and the bodies were a deep bottle green. There was a group of porters placing luggage in the van and a great many others were busy with the affairs of passengers, tossing smaller bits of luggage into the racks over the seats and bustling here and there on short quests. The guard of the train, a tall man who resembled one of the first Napoleon's veterans, was caring for the distribution of passengers into the various bins. There were no second-class compartments; they were all third and first-class.

The train was at this time engineless but presently a railway monster painted a glowing vermilion slid modestly down and took its place at the head. The guard walked along the platform and decisively closed each door. He wore a dark blue uniform thoroughly decorated with silver braid in the guise of leaves. The way of him gave to this business the importance of a ceremony. Meanwhile the fireman had climbed down from the cab and raised his hand ready to transfer a signal to the driver who stood looking at his watch.

In the meantime, there had something progressed in the large signal box that stands guard at Euston. This high signal house contains many levers standing in thick shining ranks. It perfectly resembles an organ in some great church if it were not that these rows of numbered and indexed handles typify something more acutely human than does a key-board. It requires four men to play this organ-like thing and the strains never cease. Night and day, day and night, these four men are walking to and fro, from this lever to that lever, and under their hands the great machine raises its endless hymn of a world at work, the fall and rise of signals and the clicking swing of switches.

And so as the vermilion engine stood waiting and looking from the shadow of the curve-roofed station, a man in the signal-house had played the notes which informed the engine of its freedom. The driver saw the fall of those proper semaphores which gave him liberty to speak to his steel friend. A certain combination in the economy of the London and North Western Railway, a combination which had spread from the men who sweep out the carriages through innumerable minds to the general manager himself, had resulted in the law that the vermilion engine with its long string of white and bottle-green coaches was to start forthwith toward Scotland.

Presently the fireman standing with his face toward the rear, let fall his hand. "All right," he said. The driver turned a wheel and as the fireman slipped back, the long train moved along the platform at the pace of a mouse. To those in the tranquil carriages this starting was probably as easy as the sliding of one's hand over a greased surface but in the engine there was more to it. The monster roared suddenly and loudly and sprang forward impetuously. A wrong-headed or maddened draught-horse will plunge into its collar sometimes when going up a hill. But this load of burdened carriages followed imperturbably at the gait of turtles. They were not to be stirred from their way of dignified exit by the impatient engine. The crowd of porters and transient people stood respectfully. They looked with the indefinite wonder of the railway-station sightseer upon the faces at the windows of the passing coaches. This train was off for Scotland. It had started from the home of one accent to the home of another accent. It was going from manner to manner, from habit to habit, and in the minds of these London spectators there surely floated dim images of the traditional kilts, the burring speech, the grouse, the canniness, the oatmeal, all the elements of the romantic Scotland.

The train swung impressively around the signal house and headed up a brick-walled cut. In starting this heavy string of coaches, the engine breathed explosively. It gasped and heaved and bellowed; once for a moment the wheels spun on the rails and a convulsive tremor shook the great steel frame.

The train itself however moved through this deep cut in the body of London with coolness and precision and the employees of the railway, knowing the train's mission, tacitly presented arms at its passing. To the travellers in the carriages, the suburbs of London must have been one long monotony of carefully-made walls of stone or brick. But after the hill was climbed, the train fled through pictures of red habitations of men on a green earth.

But the noise in the cab did not greatly change its measure. Even though the speed was now high, the tremendous thumping to be heard in the cab was as alive with strained effort and as slow in beat as the breathing of a half-drowned man. At the side of the track for instance the sound doubtlessly would strike the ear in the familiar succession of incredibly rapid puffs but in the cab itself this land-racer breathes very like its friend the marine-engine. Everybody who has spent time on ship-board has forever in his head a reminiscence of the steady and methodical pounding of the engines and perhaps it is curious that this relative which can whirl over the land at such a pace, breathes in the leisurely tones that a man heeds when he lies awake at night in his berth.

There had been no fog in London but here on the edge of the

city, a heavy wind was blowing and the driver leaned aside and yelled that it was a very bad day for travelling on an engine. The engine-cabs of England as of all Europe are seldom made for the comfort of the men. One finds very often this apparent disregard for the man who does the work, this indifference to the man who occupies a position which for the exercise of temperance, of courage, of honesty, has no equal at the altitude of prime-ministers. The American engineer is the gilded occupant of a salon in comparison with his brother in Europe. The man who was guiding this five hundred ton bolt aimed by the officials of the railway at Scotland could not have been as comfortable as a shrill gibbering boatman of the Orient. The narrow and bare bench at his side of the cab was not directly intended for his use because it was so low that he would be prevented by it from looking out of the ship's port-hole which served him as a window. The fireman on his side had other difficulties. His legs would have had to straggle over some pipes at the only spot where there was a prospect and the builders had also strategically placed a large steel bolt. Of course it is plain that the companies consistently believe that the men will do their work better if they are kept standing. The roof of the cab was not altogether a roof; it was merely a projection of two feet of metal from the bulk-head which formed the front of the cab. There was practically no sides to it and the large cinders from the soft coal whirled around in sheets. From time to time the driver took a handkerchief from his pocket and wiped his blinking eyes.

London was now well to the rear. The vermilion engine had been for some time flying like the wind. This train averages between London and Carlisle, forty-nine and nine-tenth miles an hour. It is a distance of 299 miles. There is one stop. It occurs at Crewe and endures five minutes. In consequence, the block-signals flashed by seemingly at the end of the moment in which they were sighted.

There can be no question of the statement that the road-beds of English railways are at present immeasurably superior to the American road-beds. Of course there is a clear reason. It is known to every traveller that peoples of the Continent of Europe have no right at all to own railways. Those lines of travel are too childish and trivial for expression. A correct fate would deprive the Continent of its railways and give them to somebody that knew about them. The Continental idea of a railway is to surround a mass of machinery with forty rings of ultra-military law and then they believe they have one, complete. The Americans and the English are the railway peoples. That our road-beds are poorer than the English road-beds is because of the fact that we were suddenly obliged to build thousands upon thousands of miles of railway and the English were obliged to slowly build tens upon tens of miles. A road-bed from New York to San Francisco with stations, bridges and crossings of the kind that the London and North Western owns from London to Glasgow would cost a sum large enough to support the German army for a term of years. The whole way is constructed with the care that inspired the creators of some of our now-obsolete forts along the Atlantic coast. An American engineer with his knowledge of the difficulties he had to encounter—the wide rivers with variable banks, the mountain chains, perhaps the long spaces of absolute desert, in fact all the perplexities of a vast and somewhat new country—would not dare spend a respectable portion of his allowance on seventy feet of granite wall over a gully when he knew he could make an embankment with little cost by heaving up the dirt and stones from here and there. But the English road is all made in the pattern that the Romans built their highways. After England is dead, savants will find narrow streaks of masonry leading from ruin to ruin. Of course this does not always seem convincingly admirable. It sometimes resembles energy poured into a rat-hole. There is a vale between expediency and the convenience of posterity, a mid-ground which enables men to surely benefit the hereafter-people by valiantly advancing the present and the point is that if some laborers live in unhealthy tenements in Cornwall, one is likely to view with incomplete satisfaction the record of long and patient labor and thought displayed by an eight foot drain for a non-existent, an impossible rivulet in the North. This sentence does not sound strictly fair but the meaning one wishes to convey is that if an English company spies in its dream the ghost of an ancient valley that later becomes a hill it would construct for it a magnificent steel trestle and consider that a duty had been performed in proper accordance with the company's conscience. But after all is said of it, the accidents and the miles of railway operated in England is not in proportion to the accidents and the miles of railway operated in the United States. The reason can be divided into three parts—older conditions, superior caution and road-bed. And of these the greatest is older conditions.

In this flight toward Scotland one seldom encountered a grade crossing. In nine cases out of ten there was either a bridge or a tunnel. The platforms of even the remote country stations were all of ponderous masonry in contrast to our constructions of planking. There was always to be seen as we thundered toward a station of this kind, a number of porters in uniform who requested the retreat of anyone who had not the wit to give us plenty of room. And then as the shrill warning of the whistle pierced even the uproar that was about us, came the wild joy of the rush past the station. It was something in the nature of a triumphal procession conducted at thrilling speed. Perhaps there was a curve of infinite grace, a sudden hollow explosive effect made by the passing of a signal box that was close to the track, and then the deadly lunge to shave the edge of a long platform. There was always a number of people standing afar with their eyes riveted upon this projectile and to be on the engine was to feel their interest and admiration in the terror and grandeur of this sweep. A boy allowed to ride with the driver of the band-wagon as a circus parade winds through one of our village streets could not exceed for egotism the temper of a new man in the cab of a train like this one. This valkyric journey on the back of the vermilion engine with the shouting of the wind, the deep mighty panting of the steed, the grey blur at the track side, the flowing quicksilver ribbon of the other rails, the sudden clash as a switch intersects, all the din and fury of this ride was of a splendor that caused one to look abroad at the quiet green landscape and believe that it was of a phlegm quite beyond patience. It should have been dark, rain-shot and windy; thunder should have rolled across its sky.

It seemed somehow that if the driver should for a moment take his hands from his engine it might swerve from the track as a horse from the road. Once indeed as he stood wiping his fingers on a bit of waste there must have been something ludicrous in the way the solitary passenger regarded him. Without those finely firm hands on the bridle, the engine might rear and bolt for the pleasant farms lying in the sunshine at either side.

This driver was worth contemplation. He was simply a quiet middle-aged man, bearded and with the little wrinkles of habitual geniality and kindliness spreading from the eyes toward the temple, who stood at his post always gazing out through his round window while from time to time his hands went from here to there over his levers. He seldom changed either attitude or expression. There surely is no engine-driver who does not feel the beauty of the business but the emotion lies deep and, mainly, inarticulate as it does in the mind of a man who has experienced a good and beautiful wife for many years. This driver's face displayed nothing but the cool sanity of a man whose thought was buried intelligently in his business. If there was any fierce drama in it there was no sign upon him. He was so lost in dreams of speed and signals and steam that one speculated if the wonder of his tempestuous charge and its career over England touched him, this impassive rider of a fiery thing.

It should be a well-known fact that, all over the world, the engine-driver is the finest type of man that is grown. He is the pick of the earth. He is altogether more worthy than the soldier and better than the men who move on the sea in ships. He is not paid too much, nor do his glories weight his brow, but for outright performance carried on constantly, coolly, and without elation by a temperate, honest, clear-minded man he is the further point. And so the lone human at his station in a cab, guarding money, lives and the honor of the road, is a beautiful sight. The whole thing is aesthetic. The fireman presents this same charm but in a less degree in that he is bound to appear as an apprentice to the finished manhood of the driver. In his eyes turned always in question and confidence toward his superior one finds this quality but his aspirations are so direct that one sees the same type in evolution.

There may be a popular idea that the fireman's principal

function is to hang his head out of the cab and sight interesting objects in the landscape. As a matter of fact he is always at work. The dragon is insatiate. The fireman is continually swinging open the furnace door—whereat a red shine flows out upon the floor of the cab—and shoveling in immense mouthfuls of coal to a fire that is almost diabolic in its madness. This feeding, feeding, feeding goes on until it appears as if it is the muscles of the fireman's arms that is speeding the long train. An engine running over sixty-five miles an hour, with five hundred tons to drag, has an appetite in proportion to this task.

View of the clear-shining English scenery is often interrupted between London and Crewe by long and short tunnels. The first one was disconcerting. Suddenly one knew that the train was shooting toward a black mouth in the hills. It swiftly yawned wider and then in a moment the engine dove into a place habitant with every demon of wind and noise. The speed had not been checked and the uproar was so great that in effect one was simply standing at the centre of a vast black-walled sphere. The tubular construction which one's reason proclaimed, had no meaning at all. It was a black sphere alive with shrieks. But then on the surface of it there was to be seen a little needle point of light and this widened to a detail of unreal landscape. It was the world; the train was going to escape from this cauldron, this abyss of howling darkness. If a man looks through the brilliant water of a tropical pool he can sometimes see coloring the marvels at the bottom the blue that was on the sky and the green that was on the foliage of this detail. And the picture shimmered in the heat-rays of a new and remarkable sun. It was when the train bolted out into the open-air that one knew that it was his own earth.

Once train met train in a tunnel. Upon the painting in the perfectly circular frame formed by the mouth, there appeared a black square with sparks bursting from it. This square expanded until it hid everything and a moment later came the crash of the passing. It was enough to make a man lose his sense of balance. It was a momentary inferno when the fireman opened the furnace door and was bathed in blood-red light as he fed the fires.

The effect of a tunnel varied when there was a curve in it. One was merely whirling then heels over head apparently in the dark echoing bowels of the earth. There was no needle point of light to which one's eyes clung as to a star.

From London to Crewe the stern arm of the semaphore never made the train pause even for an instant. There was always a clear track. It was great to see far in the distance a goods train whooping smokily for the north of England on one of the four tracks. The over-taking of such a train was a thing of magnificent nothing for the long-strided engine and as the flying express passed its weaker brother, one heard one or two feeble and immature puffs from the other engine, saw the fireman wave his hand to his luckier fellow, saw a string of foolish clanking flat-cars, their freights covered with tarpaulins, and then the train was lost to the rear.

The driver twisted his wheel and worked some levers and the rhythmical chunking of the engine gradually ceased. Gliding at a speed that was still high, the train curved to the left and swung down a sharp incline to move with an imperial dignity through the railway yard at Rugby. There was a maze of switches, innumerable engines noisily pushing cars here and there, crowds of workmen who turned to look, a sinuous curve around the longest train shed whose high wall resounded with the rumble of the passing express and then almost immediately it seemed, came the open country again. Rugby had been a dream which one could properly doubt.

At last the relaxed engine with the same majesty of ease swung into the high-roofed station at Crewe and stopped at a platform, lined with porters and citizens. There was instant bustle and in the interest of the moment no one seemed to particularly notice the tired vermilion engine being led away.

There is a five minute stop at Crewe. A tandem of engines slid up and buckled fast to the train for the journey to Carlisle.

In the meantime all the regulation items of peace and comfort had happened on the train itself. The dining-car was in the centre of the train. It was divided into two parts, the one being a dining-room for first-class passengers and the other a dining-room for the third-class passengers. They were separated by the kitchens and larder. The engine with all its rioting and roaring had dragged to Crewe a car in which numbers of passengers were lunching in a tranquility that was almost domestic on an average menu of a chop and potatoes, a salad, cheese and a bottle of beer. Betimes, they watched through the windows the great chimney-marked towns of northern England. They were waited upon by a young man of London who was supported by a lad who resembled an American bell-boy. The rather elaborate menu and service of the Pullman dining-car is not known in England or on the Continent. Warmed roast-beef is the exact symbol of a European dinner when one is travelling on a railway.

This express is named both by the populace and the company as the Corridor Train because a coach with a corridor is an unusual thing in England and so the title has a distinctive meaning. Of course in America where there is no car which has not what we call an aisle it would define nothing. The corridors are all at one side of the car. Doors open from thence to the little compartments made to seat four or perhaps six persons. The first-class carriages are very comfortable indeed being heavily upholstered in dark hard-wearing stuffs with a bulging rest for the head. The third-class accommodations on this train are almost as comfortable as the first-class and in this case carry a kind of people that are not usually seen travelling third-class in Europe. Many people sacrifice their habit in the matter of this train to the fine conditions of the lower fare.

One of the feats of this train is an electric button in each compartment. Commonly, an electric button is placed high on the side of the carriage as an alarm signal and it is unlawful to push it unless one is in serious need of assistance from the guard. But these bells also rang in the dining-car and were supposed to open negotiations for tea or whatever. A new function has been projected on an ancient custom. No genius has yet appeared to separate these two meanings. Each bell rings an alarm and a bid for tea or whatever. It is perfect in theory then that if one rings for tea the guard comes to interrupt the murder and that if one is being murdered the attendant appears with tea. At any rate, the guard was forever being called from his reports and his comfortable seat in the forward end of the baggage van by thrilling alarms. He often prowled the length of the train with hardihood and determination merely to meet a request for a sandwich.

The train entered Carlisle at the beginning of twilight. This is the border town and an engine of the Caledonian Railway manned by two men of broad speech came to take the place of the tandem. The engine of these men of the North was much smaller than the others but her cab was much larger and would be a fair shelter on a stormy night. They had also built seats with hooks by which they hang them to the rail and thus be still enabled to see through the round windows without dislocating their necks. All the human parts of the cab were covered with oil-cloth. The wind that swirled from the dim twilight horizon made the warm glow from the furnace to be a grateful thing.

As the train shot out of Carlisle, a glance backward could learn of the faint yellow blocks of light from the carriages marked on the dimmed ground. The signals were now lamps and shone palely against the sky. The express was entering night as if night were Scotland.

There was a long toil to the summit of the hills and then began the booming ride down the slope. There were many curves. Sometimes one could see two or three signal lights at one time twisting off in some new direction. Minus the lights and some yards of glistening rails, Scotland was only a blend of black and weird shapes. Forests which one could hardly imagine as weltering in the dewy placidity of evening sank to the rear as if the gods had bade them. The dark loom of a house quickly dissolved before the eyes. A station with its lamps became a broad yellow band that to a deficient sense was only a few yards in length. Below, in a deep valley, a silver glare on the waters of a river made equal time with the train. Signals appeared, grew and vanished. In the wind and the mystery of the night it was like sailing in an enchanted gloom. The vague profiles of hills ran like snakes across the sombre sky. A strange shape boldly and formidably confronted the train and then melted to a long dash of track as clean as sword blades.

The vicinity of Glasgow is unmistakable. The flames of pauseless industries are here and there marked on the distance.

Vast factories stand close to the track and reaching chimneys emit roseate flames. At last one may see upon a wall the strong reflection from furnaces and against it, the impish and inky figures of working men. A long prison-like row of tenements, not at all resembling London but in one way resembling New York, appeared to the left and then sank out of sight like a phantom.

At last the driver stopped the brave effort of his engine. The four hundred miles were come to the edge. The average speed of forty-nine and one-third miles each hour had been made and it remained only to glide with the hauteur of a great express through the yard and into the station at Glasgow.

A wide and splendid collection of signal-lamps flowed toward the engine. With delicacy and care, the train clanked over some switches, passed the signals, and then there shone a great blaze of arc-lamps defining the wide sweep of the station roof. Smoothly, proudly, with all that vast dignity which had surrounded its exit from London the express moved along its platform. It was the entrance into a gorgeous drawing-room of a man that was sure of everything. As the train definitely halted, a long harsh gasp burst from the engine and a jet of white steam feathered over-head. A loud panting could be heard.

The porters and the people crowded forward. In their minds there may have floated dim images of the traditional music-halls, the bobbies, the 'busses, the 'Arrys and 'Arriets, the swells of London.

No. 176   FRANCE'S WOULD-BE HERO

PARIS, Oct. 4.—When France shakes with some great national question the convulsion invariably flings to the surface a number of curious bubbles which glitter for a time in a false light, amid the quiet laughter of that great part of the nation which is not chronicled in the foreign press, or even in the Parisian press, for that matter. The most exciting bubbles of this year have undoubtedly been M. Guerin, of the Fort Chabrol, and M. Max Regis, one time Mayor of Algiers.

It is, of course, on the tip of the tongue to say that no other country can produce these strange personalities, which seem altogether moved by a dementia of sentimental ambition which causes them to burst into tears, cry loudly for Heaven's vengeance, shriek for the blood of their enemies, calmly and effectively state their determination to die for their principles, kiss good-by to their sobbing wives and children and—go to the nearest cafe for a drink. And this result, mark you, is without the slightest loss in dignity. The dignity—even the pomposity—all remains, and they possess without diminution that profound self-satisfaction which enables them to hold themselves so proudly. And they are never without followers, troops of them, men who hang upon the words of these garrulous heroes and fetch and carry for them, and—more marvellous than all—are never disaffected by the spectacle of the chieftains sitting quietly down to sausages, potato salad, lager and the evening paper at the very time they have named for a glorious sacrificial death on the steps of the Elysée. It would disconcert most followings, but not so this curious class in Paris which makes almost a profession of following the first showy, irresponsible, talkative ass that turns up to lead it.

During the siege of the Fort Chabrol it grew to be a kind of a fashion in Paris to almost daily jump in a cab and drive out to look at this curious thing. But it was not an interesting sight. On the top of a house could be seen just the busts of two or three men. In the street below were four lines of little red-legged soldiers looking exquisitely bored. Then there were many gendarmes, rather cross from the heat and the dust and the long duty. One day was much like another, save that on some days it rained.

Of the foreign journalists interested, I suppose that there was hardly one who did not at some time declare impatiently that if three resolute old women armed with wet mops should storm Fort Chabrol they would have M. Guerin out in the street in ten minutes. There was not a sensible person, French or foreign, who believed that Guerin had an ounce of fight in him, and everybody wondered that the Government did not simply blow down the door and send in some gendarmes to arrest him, like any other disturber of the public peace. The word of the Government was supposed to be this: "The forcible suppression of a mere great buffoon is not worth the blood of a single French soldier." But this weak sentence does not describe the position of the Government at all. The Government was not one whit afraid to shed the blood of several French soldiers.

Why, then, was this man allowed to conduct his curious performance in defiance of the State amid the amazement of the entire world? Not because the Government feared to shed the blood of soldiers, but because it feared that in the excitement of an assault M. Guerin might somehow manage to get himself hurt. In short, the Government was obliged to protect this absurdity as if it were a valuable jewel. They well knew that the turn of a hand would make a grand popular hero of M. Guerin, and in Paris a real grand, popular hero can sweep any Government into the Seine. Anything like a heroic scuffle in which M. Guerin should receive even a slight hurt would make a hero for the boulevards, a figure of ennobled desperation, a being who defied the lightning, a warrior without adequate strength but still fearless; to some a Lohengrin, to some a Bayard, and to others a Don Quixote. In short, a weeping and thrilled Paris would take him to her bosom.

But the Government saw clearly that if M. Guerin was only allowed a sufficient time to kick his heels helplessly in his terrible Fort Chabrol he would be sooner or later certain to affect the Parisian sense of humor, and they must have resolved to assist to that end to the best of their ability. It was amusing and instructive to note with what celerity the officials hurried to the journalists with repetitions of M. Guerin's great speeches. On the day when he roared through the hole in the wall that celebrated line—"Monsters! would you deprive starving men of cigarettes?"—the elate police transferred it so quickly to the ears of the newspaper men that its echo had hardly ceased to rumble in the Rue Chabrol.

"Monsters! Would you deprive starving men of cigarettes?" Ah, well, who could be a hero after having once committed his personality to an elocution so interesting? M. Guerin might have surrendered immediately to have saved himself trouble, for with the publication of that line ended his career as a hero.

The Government had not only won, but it had won in a manner quite consistent with its original plan.

M. Max Regis is a more sinister figure, for the reason that in the hot climate of Algiers the blood is more easily stirred to violence, and by his wild talk he has succeeded in getting himself and immediate followers implicated in a series of murders. He, too, retreated with a body of men into a house and declared his intention to die, if need came, in its defence. But one night he left hurriedly, leaving word that he had gone away because he did not like to kill any soldiers. The French army was no doubt deeply touched. During the Dreyfus trial M. Regis appeared at Rennes accompanied by a kind of bodyguard of two Arabs in their native dress. He announced that he would resist arrest. No one had asked him. The police paid no more heed than if he had been the manager of a small troupe of performing Arabs. This, of course, was before he was implicated in the murders.

The present Ministry is the first in years that has not attempted to kill with a steam hammer every beetle that waggled his jaws at it. At one time any egotist, by making some childish row, would be honored by the antagonism, active and public, of the whole Government, and naturally this stirred the Parisians, who saw in each incident the sublime spectacle of a mouse intrepidly fighting a lion.

In the meantime the Duc d'Orleans, obliged by the misfortunes of his cause to become the patron and fellow conspirator of almost any one who will try to shake the Republic, has been dodging up to the frontier, alive to hear that word from Paris which shall bid him rise to the throne of France on a wave created by—whom? M. Guerin, M. Déroulède and others. They occupy positions in France not unlike the position once occupied in the United States by that illustrious soldier and political economist, General Coxey. Only, as I remember it, American people and Government alike took Coxey and his army with a broad, tolerant grin. No one wanted to hurt Coxey, let alone seeing any necessity for it. Everybody knew that a certain rather pathetically weak mind was making a huge and very loud failure of an impossible plan. The newspapers found it picturesque and amusing, but the vein of accounts was invariably facetious. However, one regrets having classed Coxey absolutely with the Parisian egotists. Deep in him Coxey must have had some strong feeling that he was a Moses; in short, a leader and benefactor of humanity. Of course, that is egotism; and at any rate he was an egotist, or he would not have had faith of success in his colossal adventure. On the other hand, it may have been sheer simplicity of character and understanding. And one can finally say that it is not plain that Coxey was doing everything for Coxey.

But is M. Guerin at all interested in the future of M. Guerin? Somewhat. And did he start on his adventure with a childlike feeling that he would succeed? Not at all; he was perfectly aware that as soon as he became sufficiently dangerous the Government could blow his fort into ounce pieces. Did any observations concerning the welfare of humanity escape him when he harangued from a window? Not any. In these orations what was the principal topic, directly or indirectly? M. Guerin. Was there any evidence at all to show that M. Guerin considered the people of France as anything but an audience whose myriad eyes were fastened upon M. Guerin? No. Well, then, our poor Coxey, with his simple Utopian dream of taking money forcibly away from one man and dividing it among certain ragged others—our poor Coxey is a gentleman and an apostle beside this vain Parisian who paints his name on a banner and then carries the banner himself so that all people may read and say: "M. Guerin."

But fate puts to great uses men and events which the human mind is declaring at the time to be too silly and too small for speech. Republican France, herself on trial for her life at Rennes, was alternately weeping and raging; M. Guerin from time to time made her laugh.

No. 177 "IF THE CUP ONCE GETS OVER HERE . . ."

WHILE the *Columbia* and the *Shamrock* were racing or drifting off Sandy Hook it doubtless occurred to many Americans in England that it would not be unusual if the Cup remained on the American side of the Atlantic and those of us who make a point of knowing all we may of the English character sometimes amused ourselves in wondering what the average English-man would say if the *Shamrock* were defeated. We perfectly well knew that he would make some remark which would not bear an essential resemblance to a confession that an English champion had again been out-raced. It would, we thought, be the usual little screen behind which the Briton hides his chagrin in defeat from the world and perhaps from himself. But none of us could imagine for our lives what it would be. It would be something; it never fails; it ever arises to shield the English pride and incidentally to vex those of us whose prides are not English.

Directly after the third race I was informed of the shiboleth. In a railway carriage, an English friend announced to me jubilantly, triumphantly: "If the Cup once gets over here, you'll never get it back." And from this height of victory he looked down upon me with a proud and satisfied smile.

I bowed my head, I understood him; it was the empire builder talking to himself in the mirror. An inexperienced person would have moved with horse, foot and guns upon this imbecility of logic but I knew better. I held my peace.

Then this manifesto began to be issued in all directions. If you came to speaking terms with an Englishman, he said: "If the Cup once gets over here you'll never get it back." It was cried out in the coffee-rooms of hotels, in clubs, in busses, everywhere people meet. The last stroke arrived yesterday when a lady looked at me over her tea-cup and said: "If the Cup once gets over here you'll never get it back." I assented at once; I knew enough to assent at once. She didn't know a yacht from a motor-car but she had been given the pass-word, the national pass-word, by her husband who had said to her: "If the Cup once gets over here they'll never get it back." So she said to me: "If the Cup once gets over here you'll never get it back."

I had thought in my weakness that the *Columbia* had won because she was a superior boat to the *Shamrock* but I found nobody who cared to discuss the point. Everyone said to me: "If the Cup once gets over here you'll never get it back."

Who would care to disturb such colossal serenity? And even if there was a candidate who cared to try to disturb this colossal serenity, he couldn't.

At times somebody says: "I understand that many Americans build their racing yachts in English yards and then race them against English yachts."

Then you say: "No I hadn't heard of any such thing."

Then they reply: "Oh, but I'm sure of it."

And, speaking slowly, you reply: "I cannot understand that the ordinary rational American would imagine any possible reason for applying to an English yard for the building of a racing sloop since the American yards have so often and signally proved themselves superior in the making of racing sloops."

After a short silence, somebody says: "If the Cup once gets over here you'll never get it back." And then if you're old and wary and tired, you run away.

When old Bill Smithers wished to destroy a solid iron tombstone he hired boys to throw wet sponges at it and I hear that Bill's descendants are still carrying on this industry. He was a brave man and he did not care for odds. But I much doubt if he would have opposed himself to the phrase: "If the Cup once gets over here you'll never get it back."

This may not appear as a large point. The famous sentence of which I make such use may not appear in its full value. But I wish to indicate, as best I may, that the British government and people have a sort of constitutional inability to admit anything, and, second, that this inability is usually expressed in a phrase. When the Jameson raid shook the House of Commons into innumerable dissenting bodies, the word was passed: "The good name of the empire is at stake." And then Government and Opposition buckled together and when men like Courtney refuse to come into line, they are rebuked by men like Sir William Harcourt—who led the Opposition during the debates in Parliament on the Jameson raid—who displays a spirit which we cannot altogether admire nor feel its fidelity in any degree.

No. 178   STEPHEN CRANE SAYS: EDWIN MARKHAM IS HIS FIRST CHOICE FOR THE AMERICAN ACADEMY

THE question of an American Academy to foster the expansion of American literature occurs once a year, perhaps, in some period of inaction or laziness. In England the question of an English Academy is an institution. Annually every respectable person is supposed to send to some newspaper his choice of forty immortals. Nothing happens save that a number of people are amazed and grieved that their names were not included in any of the lists. It is a silly custom, but as it is an established custom, the English are not able to resent it. Customs in England are indestructible. The literary journals periodically worry over the question and fret at it and grow angry and hurt each other's feelings, and, in the end, nothing has happened.

I do not see why we should borrow this particular form of laceration. It is never amusing; it only hurts. And it accomplishes nothing.

However, the writer is willing to assert that the establishment of an American Academy would be a good thing if the proper number of immortals would care to entertain themselves in that way. If any forty men choose to elect themselves to positions of eminence in American literature it is purely their own affair, and there is no cause for any outsider to undergo a period of excitement. They would be a dignified body, and a photograph of them, taken in group, would be an honor to any nation. A tidy little sum might be raised from the sale of this photograph, for it is certain that we can show more fine old litterateurs with manes of snow white hair than any country on the face of the globe.

——"and whom you would suggest as the best ten men to start the thing on a big scale." At first this naturally stampedes the mind, but upon gaining courage to reapproach it circuitously and warily, one becomes able to see that it is very simple. There are a number of expeditious plans. First of all, it occurs that one could advocate the appointment of any ten college presidents. Every college president has written books, and they are habituated to wearing honors without a sense of personal discomfort. Furthermore they are known as a class, to be chaste and good. There would be no difficulty about persuading them to accept the distinction, because no college president in normal health ever abandons to another individual anything which by the due exercise of personal charm may be induced to remain under his benign care.

But the very simplicity of this solution may defeat it. These pious men probably should be left to the business of raiding Chicago's wealth.

And what then? One's thoughts instinctively turn to Edwin Markham. Mr. Markham is of that virile manhood which expresses itself by appearing in public in its shirt sleeves; a strong man, mark ye; no apish child of fashion; a veritable eagle of freedom, and, withal, kindly, tender to the little lame lamb—aye, bold, yet gentle, defiant of all convention, and yet simple in his manner even to kings. Such a man is Edwin Markham.

Very good. We have made a fair start. We have one leonine old man in his shirt sleeves. We proceed, much encouraged. Who is worthy to take a place by the side of the illustrious coatlessness? Let us make haste. The name of W. D. Howells occurs to somebody. But, no; he wears collars. It is known; it is common talk. He has never had his photograph taken while enwrapped in a carelessly negligent bath towel. In the name of God, let us have virility; let us look for the wild, free son of nature. Mark Twain? At first it seems that he would have a chance. He growls out his words from the very pit of his stomach and is often uncivil to strangers. But, no; he, too, wears collars and a coat.

For a moment we are stunned with a sense of defeat. But, no; an inspiration comes. Why have forty members to an American Academy? Let us have only one. Call Markham; frame him up; give him a constitution and a set of by-laws; let him convene himself and discuss literary matters. Then we have an American Academy.

Possible Attributions

LONDON, Nov. 20.—Londoners had an eye-opener yesterday, when the destruction of $20,000,000 worth of property by fire in the heart of the business district showed that the boasted superiority of their fire department has existed only in their imaginations and British conceit. The chief of the New York Fire Department could have told them that long ago if they had been in a mood to receive the information. This they are admitting to themselves, though they will not heap treason on humiliation by admitting it to a foreigner. To him they say that peculiar circumstances were responsible for the spread of the conflagration, with which you are already familiar by cable reports.

Suffice it only to add that it is the greatest fire that London has known since the historic one of 1666. In modern times it has been rivalled only by the great Chicago fire. Comparison of either instance with the present only reflects discredit upon the London Fire Department. In 1666 the buildings of London were of wood, the streets were narrow and the methods of fighting fire were limited to bucket brigades. Chicago's buildings were also of inflammable material, constructed with the haste of a new and growing city. Her fire department was poor indeed compared with the present departments of Chicago and New York.

The buildings which were gutted or destroyed in yesterday's fire were of stone and brick, only four to five stories in height. High buildings are tabooed in London as being firetraps. The rule is that no building may be of greater altitude than the width of the street where it stands.

Nothing in London strikes visiting Americans as being more quaint than the London fire engine. Compared with the great engines of New York they seem like toys.

"But our engines do the business required of them far better than yours. They will throw a stream as high as any of the buildings, and that is all that is required. And we have none of those flimsy sky-scraping fire-traps such as you have in New York," the Londoners said.

The American could not resist retorting: "It's a good thing that you haven't. Your little engines would be about as much use in quelling a fire on the seventh story as a garden hose."

The first time that the writer ever saw a London engine going to a fire he thought it was only an advertisement of some play like "The Still Alarm." There were three firemen on either side of the engine. On their heads were tremendous brass helmets, almost as large as the engine itself. They were swinging their arms and yelling with all their might. As the fire department originated before gongs, the engine men, in accordance with precedent, still use their voices to warn the crowd of their coming. Their "Hey, hey, hey!" is all very romantic, like the cries of the London costermongers, but in the hubbub of the city streets you can hear it only a few feet off, and consequently the engine horses, which are always on the heels of the crowd, cannot travel with the speed of the New York fire engines, which have the way cleared for them.

By the time they reach the fire the firemen are too worn out with their yelling to fight the flames with any vigor.

The alarm system is far inferior to that of the leading American cities; so are the arrangements at the engine house for a quick call. The men are not nearly as large and strong or as well paid as the American firemen. In England the army gets so many of the men of spirit who are inclined to enter government service that the fire department has to put up with what is left over. The uniforms are not so practical as those in New York, though more so than some of those on the Continent, which are more fitted to a dragoon on parade than to a man who is to swing an ax or handle a hose.

Speed is certainly the foremost requirement of any fire department. The department which can send engines to a fire the quickest after it originates is the best department. There was no hose playing on the fire yesterday for twenty minutes after it started. Owing to the poor fire patrol service it took some of the engines an hour to make their way through the crowds and the piles of merchandise that blocked the streets. Without a question the fire would have been confined within very small limits had it been in New York.

Some of the newspapers call urgently for reform. They are handling the new fire chief without gloves. He was a naval man who had never had any experience in fighting fires, which will be news to Americans, who supposed from the comments of English papers on New York municipal affairs that the merit system had full sway in London government. There was little adverse comment when he was appointed, however, and despite the supposed inferiority of municipal administration in America it is not likely that New York would have submitted with such good grace to the appointment of a retired naval officer who needed money as a practical chief of the New York Fire Department.

No. 180   ENGLAND A LAND OF ANXIOUS MOTHERS

LONDON, Nov. 27.—England is ever the land of anxious mothers. In the last five years there has never been a time when British soldiery in some part of the world was not advancing against some savage tribe. Only the deaths of prominent officers were telegraphed. Not until the troop-ship itself returned did the sweetheart of a private know if he was dead or alive.

"There would be a little satisfaction for me if he had died fighting the Germans," said a French mother who had lost her son in the conquest of Madagascar. "And he? He would have considered it glorious. But to die in a swamp of fever following up a black enemy that will not fight is too terrible. Had he fallen, sword in hand, fighting like a fiend, then I would have been reconciled. They tell me he is serving his country as much as if he had fallen on a European battlefield. He is serving it more, more, more, if my sacrifice and his sacrifice count for anything."

In other small wars, since the time of the Indian mutiny,

at least, the event has been decided in one or two fights. In all wars, battles are separated by considerable periods of time. On the Northwest frontier there has been fighting day after day for six months now. As a rule, governments are cruel machines which look upon men in wartime as so many pins to be knocked down or advanced. The British Government, on this occasion, has had the good sense to send daily from the front not only the names with the regiment and company of the officers, but also those of the privates who have been killed or wounded, no matter how slightly.

Every morning the newspapers have published this list. Crusty old gentlemen with side-whiskers have been heard to complain that it was d—d dry reading—but, bless 'em! they have no sons out there. To the outsider, who doesn't care whether it is Private Jones or Private Smith who was shot through the leg, there is something beautiful in this daily list of wounded and killed "plain Tommies" at the top, first column, foreign correspondence page always given over to what is the foremost event in the telegraphic world yesterday—the place of Czars, Emperors, Presidents and Parliaments—which greets the reader when he opens his *Times* at the breakfast table.

It seems to say: "You, you in your comfortable homes in old England, take notice of us who were killed and wounded for the sake of you and yours yesterday, and don't complain about your breakfast and your lot. They are much better than we have been accustomed to of late. And see that the army appropriations are increased, you beggars, if you don't want these niggers to get the best of you."

Thousands of people, however, scarcely dare to look at the list for fear they will see staring them in hard, cold type the name of a son, a husband, a father, or a sweetheart. What a difference it makes whether or not, if his name be there, it is among the killed or the wounded. If among the wounded, the relative is happier than if it was not down at all. For there is something glorious and satisfying to the relative as well as to the soldier in being wounded.

The man who returns from a hard-fought campaign, no matter how brave he may have been, without a scratch, is rather at a disadvantage. The joy of taking the bullet that has been extracted from your leg home for your sweetheart and daddy to look at beats anything in the world, young officers say. Daddy rushes off to show it to his friends and is willing to foot up any amount of debts.

A helmet or a tunic with a bullethole in it is also valuable. Some young officers have been so foolish as to leave these precious garments at home and rued the error forever afterward. Young officers have even been so foolish as not to bring the bullets back.

Needless to say officers are anxious for such chances as the Afridis have offered. It thins out the ranks and makes room for promotion and gives them a chance to distinguish themselves. More than one officer posted in India has cried like a baby because he had to be one of those who must remain behind for the sake of keeping order at the post in the interior. Who could blame them? As they say: "The niggers don't furnish us with a real big row more than once in a generation."

The officers of the poor big navy have no chance at all to distinguish themselves. It is rather hard lines, you will admit, for a full-blown commodore, who was never under fire in his life, to meet in a drawing room or at a country house a lieutenant of infantry scarcely yet able to raise a presentable mustache who knows the music of whistling bullets and has been wounded.

When a British cruiser was at Volo, during the operations of the Turks before Velestino, in the late Greco-Turkish war, three young officers took French leave, and went out to the Greek lines. For a few moments they were in the thick of shell fire, but escaped without any damages except a gravel cut or two and being covered with dust.

Their captain heard about it, and he told them that men had been reprimanded, even court martialed, for such indiscretion, to which one of them replied, dryly: "Yes, we know that a British naval officer isn't supposed to go where there is anything more dangerous than houseflies!"

Whoo! But what a reception the remnant of the Gordon Highlanders, which took the Dargai Ridge after two other companies had fallen back, will receive on their return. "Degenerating, are we?" the old bucks at the service clubs ask one another. "Degenerating, eh?" It looks as if England and Scotland would never stop talking about this heroic feat of arms.

The relatives of the surviving officers are the object of a sort of hero-worship at home. And the relatives of the dead officers find satisfaction in the glorious deaths of those who fell. Up in Scotland the other day, right in kirk, when the dominie mentioned the Highlanders, the canny folk burst out in a cheer, and the dominie, looking at first shocked, finally said, with a twinkle in his eye and one in his voice: "I dinna ken that I blame ye."

Probably no mothers receive the news of the deaths of their sons with more stoicism than English mothers. An old lady, who hadn't a penny to spare to buy a paper, was slowly spelling out the list of dead and wounded on one of the bulletins, when she suddenly said: "Yes, it's my Jim. They've killed him," and she put her handkerchief to her eyes. "Well, I expected it," she added, as she walked away.

THE TEXT: HISTORY AND ANALYSIS

THE TEXT: HISTORY AND ANALYSIS

I. TALES AND SKETCHES

No. 1. UNCLE JAKE AND THE BELL-HANDLE

If a note by Cora written in the upper left corner of the manuscript can be trusted, "Uncle Jake and the Bell-Handle" was written when Crane was fourteen years old, that is, in 1885. The holograph manuscript is preserved in the Special Collections of the Columbia University Libraries. It may have been among the manuscripts that Cora found at Hartwood in early July 1900 when she returned to the United States with Crane's body, a cache that included "A Desertion" and "The Fishermen," which is to say the early draft of "The Octopush." Or it may have been among the manuscripts sent to Crane in England from Hartwood at his request in late 1897.

The manuscript consists of fourteen pages of unwatermarked laid paper 255 × 204 mm., the chainlines 25 mm. apart, written in black ink, signed at the end. The full title is given as 'Sketches from Life. | By Stephen Crane. | Uncle Jake and the bell-handle.' The general title 'Sketches from Life' sounds as if the young Crane were contemplating a series. Here and there Cora has written in pencil corrections and revisions, apparently with some thought of making up a typescript for posthumous publication. The text of this tale was first printed by Thomas A. Gullason in *Complete Short Stories and Sketches* (1963).

No. 2. GREED RAMPANT

The typescript of this early work was purchased from Miss Edith Crane in 1961 for the University of Virginia–Barrett Collection, a provenience that establishes its date as somewhere in the 1890–91 range. Before the purchase of the original, the text had been known in at least two faulty typed transcripts which Miss Crane had permitted to be made. The blue ribbon typescript is on the backs of six leaves of Postal Telegraph Cables Press Despatch forms, 261 × 204 mm. The first page is unnumbered, pages 2 and 5 are numbered on the typewriter with parentheses, and pages 3, 4, and 6 in Crane's hand above semicircles. All numbering is in the top center. No significance appears to attach to this variation since a false start on page 2 is deleted but typed still in a faulty manner at the head of page 3 and then corrected. That is, no signs appear that certain pages represent one stage and others a different stage of the typing. The typing is naïve in that it repeats what seems to have been a number of misspellings in the lost original copy and may perhaps add some of its own. The title is written in black ink at the head of page 1 in Crane's large youthful hand. On page 6 he has signed the conclusion in black ink and appended the usual #. A number of autograph inked corrections have been made to correct misspellings, to supply missing words, and to add necessary letters at the ends of lines omitted because of the lack of a margin release. The asterisks in the text are made by crossing in ink a series of typed hyphens, so that they look like plus signs. One set is supplied by hand.

The piece was described by Stallman, with quotation, in the *Bulletin of the New York Public Library*, LXI (January, 1957), 37–39. As he suggests, it may date from Crane's Syracuse days (the paper procured from the *Syracuse Standard* or the *New York Tribune* for his work as correspondent). That it was ever intended for dramatic representation, however, is scarcely to be contemplated.

No. 3. THE CAPTAIN

Unsigned, "The Captain" appeared in the *New York Tribune*, Sunday, August 7, 1892, part II, page 19, headed ' *"THE CAPTAIN."* || HE IS A SAILOR AND A FIREMAN AND | HAS A MOST MARVELLOUS WIT.' Although Crane was reporting Asbury Park summer news for the *Tribune* at this time, "The Captain" is quite clearly intended to be a sketch, not a news-report description. The piece was attributed to Crane by Williams and Starrett in their *Bibliography* (1948).

No. 4. THE RELUCTANT VOYAGERS

The following fragment of text from "The Reluctant Voyagers" is found written on the original recto of the fourth leaf of the ledger-paper manuscript of "The Holler Tree" preserved in the University of Virginia–Barrett Collection:

The Reluctant Voyagers.
By Stephen Crane.

Two sad men sat by the waves.
"Well, I know I'm not handsome," said one, gloomily. He was poking holes in the sand with a discontented cane.

The companion was watching the waves play. He seemed over-come with perspiring discomfort as a man who is setting another man right.

Suddenly, his mouth turned into a straight line

The fifth and sixth leaves of this manuscript have on their original rectos a draft of the opening of *George's Mother*. Although "The Holler Tree" as a Sullivan County sketch should be associated with mid to late 1892, such a date would appear to be too early for a draft of *George's Mother* and even for "The Reluctant Voyagers," which on Corwin Linson's testimony was originally written in the spring of 1893. Obviously, in writing out "The Holler Tree" Crane was utilizing the backs of some pieces of paper on which he had previously begun trials of other works. Yet the use of such ledger paper is also found in other works to be dated in 1894, like "In the Depths of a Coal Mine," or perhaps "The Snake." The case is not wholly satisfactory but it may be that this manuscript of "The Holler Tree" is not the original but a later fair copy, revised, and that the inception of "The Reluctant Voyagers" should be set in 1893–94.[1]

At any rate, Crane took with him to England, or was sent, the manuscript, and in 1899 when pressed for money he seems to have refurbished the little story and sold it. The first reference we have is in a letter to Pinker of September 22, 1899, in which he remarks, "In your financial statement to me I note that you do not include 'The Reluctant Voyagers.' Should it be in?" (*Letters*, p. 231). It would seem from the terms of this query that the sale was recent. The purchaser was Tillotson's, or the Northern Newspaper Syndicate, in England. In mid-October, 1900, when Cora was raising money by serializing stories and putting together the copy for *Last Words*, she

---

[1] Corwin Linson gives a circumstantial account of Crane bringing him the story in what appears to be the spring of 1893 and asking him if he cared to make the illustrations for it. Linson drew some pictures and "Landed, a bulky package, in the office of a responsible magazine, it went into retirement and we waited. . . . For me, six months were spent in the wilds of Ramapo, while Steve put in a shorter time at his brother Edmund's. The story for some minor change was returned to Steve. On resubmission, the privilege of a responsible magazine was used to promptly lose all trace of my packet of drawings. They disappeared as it were from the earth, a total loss to me. . . . But it was not so bad for Stephen. 'The Reluctant Voyagers' survives in several printings" (*My Stephen Crane*, ed. E. H. Cady [1958], pp. 18–20). Professor Cady prints a photograph of Linson and Crane posing on a rooftop as the two voyagers. The extent of the delay in the office of the "responsible magazine" is not altogether clear. If it was extensive, the possibility exists that the manuscript we now have is the start of a fair copy of a revision made for resubmission in late 1893 or early 1894. The matter is very vague from Linson's account despite its interesting detail.

wrote Pinker from Milborne Grove, "Have you a copy of 'Dan Emmonds' and 'The Reluctant Voyagers'? If not please send me word where to address the Northern Syndicate who bought the last named," to which on October 17 Pinker replied that he did not have copies and enclosed the Syndicate's address. Finally, on November 8, [1900], Cora again addressed Pinker: "Have you sold the U.S. serial rights of 'The Reluctant Voyagers'—I understood that the N.N. Syndicate paid £9- for English serial. But a D. T. Pierce has copyrighted it in America." (Unpublished letters at Columbia and Dartmouth.)

The University of Virginia–Barrett Collection holds the Tillotson's galley proof that presumably dates from about September–October, 1899, and is headed 'NORTHERN NEWSPAPER SYNDICATE. ||| [ALL RIGHTS RESERVED.] | THE RELUCTANT VOYAGERS | BY | STEPHEN CRANE | (*Author of "The Red Badge of Courage," &c.*) || PART I. ||'. At the end of the fourth section is printed '(*To be Concluded.*)' followed by a thick-thin rule. The second part, beginning with the fifth section, has the same heading as for Part 1 except for the change in part number and the addition of 'V.' below it. The conclusion is marked by '[THE END.]' and a thick-thin rule. One would expect this proof to have served as copy for republication in provincial English newspapers, but such reprintings have not been recorded.

One then comes to a highly conjectural area. Cora's letter to Pinker of November 8 appears to have been written after she had been in touch with the Syndicate and received information from it, presumably including that of D. T. Pierce who had copyrighted the piece in the United States. It is unlikely that Pinker disposed of the American rights direct, for the textual evidence suggests that Tillotson's was in some manner behind the syndication in the United States. It is evident, moreover, from the dates, that Cora had no hand in anything but the *Last Words* appearance. The Northern Newspaper proof at the University of Virginia was part of the copy that Cora sent Reynolds for the American edition of *Last Words*. On the proof for the first part is a blue-pencil number 8 and Cora's coded minuscules *aa* at the lower left. On part 2 she penciled *Serial* (2) | *8000 words*, added the *aa*, and on the verso 2 *copies*. This was for the United States. She herself would have supplied Digby, Long with the copy for the English edition.

The lack of information about the sale of the piece is the more trying in that the copy for the United States printings represents something of a puzzle and certainly—in respect to newspaper syndication—an abnormality. The D. T. Pierce who acquired American copyright was Daniel T. Pierce, whose obituary in the *New York Times* for February 17, 1952, speaks of him as editor of *Public Opinion* from 1895 to 1905. His name is not on its masthead, however. *Public Opinion* was a digest magazine and had no part in the publication of "The Reluctant Voyagers." Whether Tillotson's sold the American rights to this magazine or to Pierce as a private speculation is not to be determined. It is possible, however, that Tillotson's did dispose of the rights to him personally and that Pierce acquired from the Syndicate several sets of the proofs and the typescript copy, which he was forced to use when he ran short of the Syndicate proofs that had been sent him, as will be suggested in the discussion of the text.

The piece was syndicated in the newspapers on Sunday, February 11 and February 18. The following examples have been observed:

N[1]: The Sunday Magazine of the *New York Press,* February 11, 1900, pages 6–12; February 18, pages 3–6. The title is given as 'THE RELUCTANT VOYAGERS. || BY STEPHEN CRANE. | Author of "The Red Badge of Courage," Etc. || CHAPTER I.' The part numbers are not provided and each section is labeled *CHAPTER.* Before the second part, on page 3, is a full-page illustration captioned *"As They Turned toward the Land They Saw That the Nearest Pier Was Lined with People."* | (*The Reluctant Voyagers.*) drawn by F. C. Underwood.

N[2]: *Philadelphia Press,* February 11, Color Supplement, page 2, run across the top half of the page headed 'STEPHEN CRANE'S LATEST AND BEST SHORT STORY. | "THE RELUCTANT VOYAGERS." ' Below the title is an illustration spread across the page showing the raft and the rescue by the schooner, from which depends an uncaptioned illustration of the two men on the deck before the captain. The text is headed 'PART I.' and the sections are marked off by roman numerals. Part II appeared on February 18, in the Sunday Magazine section, page 3, under the same headline but with different illustrations. The illustrative heading is gone but under the type heading depends an untitled drawing of the overturned boat. To the left is an illustration captioned *"If You Laugh Again, I'll Kill You" He Said* | *The Captain Gurgled and Waved his Arms* | *and Legs.* To the right of the central illustration is another captioned *" 'Driver' Breathed the Freckled Man* | *They Stood for a Moment and Gazed* | *Imploringly."* The parts are indicated and the sections are given roman numerals. The two central drawings are signed 'Williams'.

N[3]: *Chicago Times-Herald,* February 11, part III, page 4, occupying the upper half of a full page, headed 'THE RELUCTANT VOYAGERS. | BY STEPHEN CRANE, [on two lines] AUTHOR OF "THE RED | BADGE OF COURAGE," ETC.' Three illustrations are provided, captioned *"Wot th' Devil—" He Shouted; "Wot th' Devil Yeh Got On?", "Then He Turned a Shriveling Glance upon his Companion and Fled up the Beach.",* and *"This is Great," Said the Tall Man. His Companion Grunted Blissfully.*

The parts are numbered and roman numerals distinguish the sections. In part III, February 18, page 4, the piece was concluded with the second part. Here an illustrative heading was drawn containing the title 'The RELUCTANT | VOYAGERS. | by | STEPHEN | CRANE'. A single illustration was provided captioned *"Driver," Breathed the Freckled Man. They Stood for a Moment, and Gazed Imploringly.* The notation of the second part is missing but in its place appears within a wavy rule-frame a synopsis of the preceding installment. The sections are marked off by roman numerals.

N⁴: *New England Home Magazine*, February 11, pages 296–303, and February 18, pages 367–371, published as a supplement to the Sunday *Boston Journal*. The title was in the form of the Tillotson's proof: 'THE RELUCTANT VOYAGERS. | By Stephen Crane. | *Author of "The Red Badge of Courage," Etc.* | PART I.' The sections, or chapters, are given simple roman numbers. Above the title of each part is a half-page unsigned illustration. That for Part I is captioned *"The two wanderers stood up. Then they howled out a wild duet that rang over the waters of the sea.";* that for Part II *"The freckled man stood up and waved his arms."*

No United States version contains a copyright notice.

The final publication was in *Last Words* (1902), pages 1–32.

The copy for these various appearances presents a serious problem, for it does not appear to have been uniform, nor—so far as can be determined—were all the newspapers set from common copy. The simplest document appears to be *Last Words*. Despite the fact that Cora had a copy of the Tillotson proof to send to Reynolds, she seems to have given the English book printers a carbon copy of the typescript that she originally had made from the manuscript. Certain of the *Last Words* (E1) unique substantive variant readings are very likely errors and sophistications in the printing, such as, perhaps, *follow* at 20.1 for *foller, changing* for *charging* (23.26), or *sparkling* for *sparkled* (23.28). But some appear to be early readings that were subsequently revised. Prominent among these are such examples as E1 *"Haint got none," replied the captain promptly.* for *"Haint got 'em." The captain backed away.* (28.11); the doubtful grammar of *There was mysterious shadows* for *There were* (20.24) or *here comes our rescuers* for *here come* (21.26); or the mixup in the other documents about the position of the fourth section which seems to be consequent upon the addition of *He made another statement* wanting in E1. The correction of Crane's freewheeling grammar is suspicious, but enough other alterations are made in which all texts join against E1 to support the hypothesis that at least one range of authorial revision was undertaken in typescript but inadvertently was not transferred to the Crane file copy. *Last Words*, then, sets itself apart as representing the original substantially unrevised typescript. Joined to it, however, in accidentals although not in substantives (which are revised) is N^1, the *New York Press* text. The concurrence in punctuation of these two documents against the rest is so close and remarkable save for a certain amount of American newspaper styling as to enforce the further hypothesis that the copy behind the *Press* was the mate of the typescript behind E1, but authorially revised. The *Press,* then, was very likely set from the original ribbon typescript sent to Pinker and sold to Tillotson's but containing various Crane alterations. These two assignments of copy may be made with some confidence.

We now enter the area of speculation and conjecture. The *New England Home Magazine* (N^4), the *Philadelphia Press* (N^2), and the *Chicago Times-Herald* (N^3) join with the Tillotson's Northern Newspaper Syndicate Proof (T[p]) in certain overall characteristics that make something of a group that differs in its tradition from the texts of E1 and N^1. The tradition is in some part marked by externals, such as the appearance in this group of the notation *Part II* (but not in N^1)—although the synopsis takes its place in N^3. Joined with this is the lack of any roman numeral I to identify the first section under Part I; and also the use of a simple roman numeral for the sections instead of the E1 and N^1 formula *Chapter I,* etc., which, incidentally, was a favorite of Crane's even in short stories. The evidence of substantive readings is of little help. The proof T(p) never diverges uniquely from the agreement of all or of a majority of the other texts, nor do E1 and N^1 agree uniquely in substantives against the T(p) group. In short, the evidence suggests, first, that T(p) was set and proofed with absolute fidelity to the substantives of the revised copy and, second, that T(p) itself was not used as copy for a further typesetting from which would have radiated the American syndicated texts.

The simplest hypothesis would be that only two typescripts were ever made. One was revised and sold through Pinker to the Northern Newspaper Syndicate; the revisions of this particular range were not entered in the other copy, which was retained and eventually given to *Last Words.* That Cora used the T proof to send to Reynolds indicates that she had no other typescript copy left. If this hypothesis is sound, then with the odd exception of N^1, which we must suppose was set from the original typescript bought by the Syndicate, the other American texts would necessarily have used the T proof as their printer's copy. The evidence here is contradictory. Very strongly on the side of T proof as copy for N^3 and N^4 is their repetition at 26.30 of what may well be an uncorrected typo in T(p), the omission of the quotation marks after 'Place.' This would seem to be a real 'bibliographical link,' albeit the only one owing to the general correctness of $T(p)$. Against the hypothesis for common copy is the perhaps extraordinary diversity of styling given this proof by N^{2-4} if it were their common copy. On the one hand, N^2 is almost slavishly close to certain marked peculiarities of $T(p)$ punctuation, such as the setting off of inverted phrases with commas, and almost equally close in matters of word-division, two matters in which $T(p)$ and N^2 usually agree against N^3 and N^4 which are likely to follow N^1 and E1. It may be that the *Philadelphia Press* compositor was vitally affected by the accidentals of his copy in some respects. But the closeness of $T(p)$ and N^2 might be taken to suggest some peculiar relation between them not shared by N^3 and N^4. On the other hand, no particular signs of common copy join N^3 and N^4, except negatively, against $T(p)$ and N^2, and both often agree with American variation (less N^1) against the N^1 and E1 line of the text. It might not be fantasy to conjecture at least the possibility of some form of different copy for N^3 and N^4 from that behind N^2. There is, after all, the very odd case of N^1 set from typescript copy that appears by certain of its markings to have been the very same typescript used by $T(p)$ as printer's copy. Then there is an equally inexplicable anomaly within N^4. In the draft manuscript of the beginning, the penultimate sentence reads, *He seemed over-come with perspiring discomfort as a man who is setting another man right.* Except for N^4, all texts, including E1, read *as a man who is resolved to set another man right* (14.19–20); but N^4 agrees with MS in *who is setting.* Unless this is an editorial change by N^4 that by pure chance hit on the MS reading (not an utter impossibility, of course), N^4 could not derive from the T proof—even, on the evidence of E1, from a hypothetically uncorrected state.

However, it must be admitted that the cure is worse than the disease. If Tillotson's proof did not serve as printer's copy for all the observed American publications except for N^1, we should need to make a series of elaborate conjectures, such as Pinker had a fresh typescript and carbon(s) made from the typescript represented by the N^1 text, or—more likely—such a typescript and copies were made by the Northern Syndicate instead of sending Cora's typescript to their printer, a procedure that is certainly credible. If for unknown reasons they had decided at that time not to put the piece into type, they could have sent over various typescripts to the United States (neatly explaining the anomalous use of the Crane typescript for N^1), retaining one for later use as printer's copy for the proof. Yet if this were so, we should need to conjecture that one typist misread the Crane typescript, which had *setting* crossed out and *resolved to set* interlined. And such a multiplicity of typescripts instead of setting up the proof then and there is absurd. Moreover, one must recognize the peculiar importance of the bibliographical link that involves N^3 and N^4 with $T(p)$ at 26.30. It is easier to imagine N^4 objecting to *resolved to set* as awkward and by pure chance changing to restore the draft MS *setting* than it is to imagine an error like the omission of the quotation marks in the original typescript faithfully copied by the typist behind N^4 (and N^3?) and the compositor of $T(p)$, although automatically corrected by N^{1-2} and E1. The only reasonable hypothesis sets up the two lines of text represented by N^1 and E1 on the one side and $T(p)$ and its unauthoritative radiating derivatives on the other.

If this situation is the true one, then three basic authorities are present: E1, N^1, and Tillotson's proof. E1 has not been given the final revision and thus, except where this revision might have been in part unauthoritative (see below), its unique substantive readings represent a combination of its own errors and changes joined with the original typescript readings copied from holograph. The typescript ribbon or carbon that was the mate to that behind E1 was revised in part and became first the printer's copy for the T proof and subsequently the printer's copy for the *New York Press*. In this situation the substantive agreement of $T(p)$ and N^1 against E1 guarantees the reading of the typescript, since N^1 and E1 never agree substantively against $T(p)$. In short, the substantives of $T(p)$ may be taken as completely correct according to their reproduction of the copy. Both E1 and N^1 vary uniquely in error. The single exception to this principle comes in the question of the revision given the typescript behind N^1 and $T(p)$. That it was in the main authoritative is suggested by various of the readings. On the other hand, the alteration of the two shaky grammatical constructions at 20.24 and 21.26, to which may be added a third—the change at 25.14 from *comfortable* in E1 to *comfortably*—suggests the possibility of some other hand intervening in part by editorial markings in the typescript before it was set in proof. A few other of the changes in which N^1 and $T(p)$ agree against E1 could come in question. For instance, at 32.24–25, E1 reads, correctly, *Directly in front of it they found a row of six cabs*. That is, the row of cabs was placed directly in front of the dock. However, N^1 and $T(p)$ punctuate to give a meaning that might be different: *Directly, in front of it, they found a row*. However, it is probable that Crane's intention was not to use *directly* in a time sense as would be the literal interpretation of the punctuation, and instead that this is not a case of revision at all but of the original being parenthetically

punctuated and E1 unauthoritatively recognizing the possible ambiguity and removing the punctuation. At 25.40 it is a trifle odd to
find E1 more colloquial with *what's* than T(p) and N^1 with *what is*;
and at 29.34 for the captain to lean on *the railing* with E1 seems
preferable to N^1, T(p) *a railing*.[2] But these are small pickings. So
far as can be told, the revisions seem to be of a piece and all to be
accepted.

The case for the accidentals is not so clear-cut. No evidence is
available that these participated in the minor substantive revision
given the typescript sent to Pinker. Hence in this matter N^1, T(p),
and E1 are each independent and equal authorities subject, of course,
to their different kinds of styling. On the whole, however, the agreement of any two of these authorities against the third is more likely
to produce the typescript accidental than not, insofar as this recovery
can assist in the attempt to come as close to holograph as possible.
On some few occasions it may be that similar English styling has
made N^1 a minority witness although it might be the actual authority
if the truth were known; yet on other occasions the agreement between N$^{1-3}$, meaningless essentially since N$^{2-3}$ are derived texts, suggests the frequency of common newspaper styling. The *New York
Press* has been chosen as copy-text, however, chiefly on the ground
that its general styling is likely to have approximated Crane's American manner more faithfully than either T(p) or E1, even though considerable emendation would have been necessary with whichever one
of the three authorities was chosen. The eclectic text that results attempts to reproduce as closely as the evidence permits the lost original typescript but with the added substantive revisions.

In recognition of the fact that the reconstruction of the textual
transmission and authority of this piece is rather conjectural, the
apparatus has been expanded beyond the limits appropriate when a
family tree can be drawn with some certainty. In the emendations
the assumptions that have been made about the nonauthority of N^2,
N^3, and N^4 have not affected the record of their readings and they
have been treated, in respect to the recording of their variants, as if
each were an independent authority. In the Historical Collation, as is
usual with multiple radiating authoritative texts, the agreement in
accidentals of any two documents is recorded even though it is probable that all American prints except for N^1 are derivative and thus

---

[2] *The engineer of a passive tugboat hung lazily over a railing and watched,*
found in *Maggie,* 7.29, is not an exact parallel; nor is, perhaps, *a railing* in
"The Reluctant Voyagers" at 23.1, although both, of course, support the N^1
reading at 29.34 as against E1.

should be ignored. In view of the special relationship of E1 and T(p) to the other texts, as independently set from a slightly earlier stage of the typescript, all E1 and T(p) variants whether substantive or accidental have been recorded. The critic, thus, will have before him the entire body of evidence on which the present text has been reconstructed.

No. 5. WHY DID THE YOUNG CLERK SWEAR?

This narrative appeared in the New York humorous magazine *Truth*, XII (March 18, 1893), 4–5, and was reprinted in *Last Words* (1902), pages 306–314. Preserved in the University of Virginia–Barrett Collection is the black carbon of a typescript on three leaves of wove foolscap 327 × 202 mm., watermarked *Indian & Colonial*, paged at top center between spaced parentheses. Beneath the underlined typed title Cora wrote 'By | Stephen Crane || ' in ink, and on the back of page 3, in pencil, 'For Book | 2000 words'. Cumulative word counts in pencil appear on the versos of the first two pages. This posthumous typescript was among the group sent to Paul Reynolds in New York for the proposed American edition of *Last Words*. Its copy was a clipping of *Truth*, probably that preserved in one of the Crane scrapbooks in the Special Collections of Columbia University Libraries. The text of *Last Words* would have been set from the ribbon copy of this typescript. The sole authority and copy-text is the printing in *Truth*.

No. 6. AT CLANCY'S WAKE

"At Clancy's Wake" appeared in the New York humorous magazine *Truth*, XII (July 3, 1893), 4–5. A typescript black carbon copy is preserved in the University of Virginia–Barrett Collection that is one of the group that Cora made up after Crane's death to send to New York for the American edition of *Last Words*. It consists of four pages of wove foolscap 320 × 201 mm., watermarked *Indian & Colonial*, the pages numbered in top center with roman numerals between spaced parentheses. Cora wrote *By | Stephen Crane* under the typed title, added the code letter *s* in the lower-left corner, and supplied corrections in ink, with a last one in pencil. On the verso of the last page she wrote *Clancy's Wake | 1250 words | Book. ||*. The typist is uncertain (since Cora never numbered with roman numerals), but the Crane typewriter produced the typescript. The copy was a clipping of *Truth,* probably the one that is present in the Crane Collection in the Special Collections of the Columbia University Libraries. The ribbon copy of the Barrett TMs would have served as printer's copy for *Last Words* (1902), pages 288–293. Both the Barrett TMs and *Last Words* derive from the copy-text *Truth* and their variants thus, whether inadvertent or editorial, are without authority. In an undated letter from Milborne Grove, Cora wrote to her agent Perris, "I enclose you a short sketch 'Clancy's Wake' for book—1250 words," probably in the early winter of 1900 (Yale).

No. 7. SOME HINTS FOR PLAY-MAKERS

The humorous magazine *Truth,* XII (November 4, 1893), 4–5, printed "Some Hints for Play-Makers." It was never collected.

No. 8. AN OMINOUS BABY

To be grouped with the "Tommie" stories, "An Ominous Baby" first appeared in the *Arena,* IX (May, 1894), 819–821. Later, the *Philistine,* III (October, 1896), 133–137, reprinted it, and it was then collected in Heinemann's edition of *The Open Boat* (1898), pages 253–257. The *Philistine* used the *Arena* as copy, and *The Open Boat* was set from the *Philistine.* The *Arena,* thus, is the only document which has authority and can be selected as copy-text.

The Crane scrapbooks in the Special Collections of the Columbia University Libraries contain a puff for the story in the same issue of the *Arena,* worth quoting for what the editor saw in Crane:

I wish each reader of THE ARENA to peruse with care the vivid sketch by Stephen Crane in this issue. Read it carefully that you may enjoy its literary merit and note how simple the language and vivid the description of life. It is an admirable bit of work, even if viewed merely as a fine character study. But after you have perused the sketch from this point of view read it carefully as a social study. The little chap who had acquired the engine and who refused the gamin the pleasure of even playing with it for a few moments, places the toy behind him the moment there is danger. The "divine right" of property, as practically held by modern plutocracy, finds a striking expression in the involuntary action of the little aristocrat, who risks a thrashing by placing himself between the toy and danger. When he grows older he will probably become wiser in the way of the world and employ others to be bomb protectors; that is, if times do not change. But I believe they will change. The conscience of the nation is waking, and conscience, when aroused, is more powerful than avarice.

Keep your eyes on Stephen Crane. He will be a much-talked-of man long after many favorites of dilettanteism are forgotten.

In Corwin Linson's *My Stephen Crane*, ed. E. H. Cady (1958), pages 40–41, is an account of a now lost sequel written on ledger paper, which Linson describes as titled "An Ominous Baby—Tommie's Home Coming," with the following beginning:

A baby wended along a street. His little tattered dress showed the effects of some recent struggle. It disclosed his small thin shoulder. His blond hair was tousled. His face was still wet with tears, but in his hands he bore with an air of triumph a toy fire engine.

He avoided with care some men who were unloading some boxes from a truck, passed through knots of children playing noisily in front of tenements and went deeper into the slums. He kept his glittering possession concealed.

Linson also quotes a "stray sentence":

A wagon rattled dangerously near his tender legs. He scrambled up the curb and went on imperturbably.

According to Linson, Crane showed him this story in July, 1893, and asked him to draw illustrations for it. In Crane's autograph inventory of stories made about July, 1897, it appears as No. 15 and is noted as in the *Philistine*. See TALES OF ADVENTURE, *Works*, vol. v (1970) for a reproduction.

No. 9. A GREAT MISTAKE

This little story of the babe Tommie appeared first in the *Philistine*, 11 (March, 1896), 106–109. The first number of Hubbard's *Roycroft Quarterly*, May, 1896, pages 34–37, reprinted it exactly, line-for-line. The lack of any variation save for one simple misprint indicates that the text was derived immediately from the *Philistine*. Publication noticed in May, 1896, in *A Souvenir and a Medley* is the same as the *Roycroft Quarterly*. The last of the early publications came in the "Midnight Sketches" section of Heinemann's English edition of *The Open Boat* (1898), pages 261–263. General although not invariable agreement with the *Philistine* (and *Roycroft Quarterly*) paragraphing suggests that the English book edition derived from a clipping of one or the other, although it did not follow the *Roycroft* misprint *finger* at 52.13. The substantive variants in *The Open Boat* reprinting appear to have no authority and may represent only English editing.

Since all texts are derived from the initial *Philistine* printing, it becomes the copy-text and the only authority. In 1909 the journal *The Fra* reprinted the tale from the *Philistine* in its September issue, page 151.

In *My Stephen Crane*, edited by E. H. Cady (1958), page 39, Corwin Linson records that Crane gave him "A Great Mistake" to illustrate, at the same time as "An Ominous Baby," in July, 1893. Under the title "The kid who stole a lemon" it appears as No. 27, assigned to the *Philistine*, in the autograph inventory list of about July, 1897, at Columbia University, reproduced in TALES OF ADVENTURE, *Works*, vol. V (1970).

No. 10. A DARK-BROWN DOG

On December 7, 1899, Cora wrote probably to Reynolds—in Crane's name according to a copy in her hand in the Columbia University Libraries—"Dear Sir: I wrote you sometime ago in answer to your long delayed letter of June 30ᵗʰ '99. [¶] Please return to me the ms. of the 'Tale of a Dark Brown Dog.' I wrote it long ago and it is probably not quite rite for publication. [¶] Thanking you in anticipation, I am faithfully yours, Stephen Crane." It is possible that he revised it on receipt, for in a letter conjecturally dated January 7, 1900, Cora wrote to Pinker, "I mailed you this morning a little story—'The Tale of a dark-brown Dog'" (*Letters*, p. 259). On January 9 Pinker listed as unsold five stories and the 'story received this morning, 2,500' (*Letters*, p. 261). What appears to be a Pinker inventory (page 25) lists the story with the notation "£52.10 for all serial rights of 'An Illusion in Red & White' & Amer. ser'. rights of 'The Dark Brown Dog,' & 6 gs. for Eng. & Col. serial rights of 'A Xmas Dinner won in Battle.'"

The only publication was in the *Cosmopolitan*, xxx (March, 1901), 481–486, with various uncaptioned illustrations and also an illustrative heading by Thomas Mitchell Peirce. The "Tommie" stories, of which this is the third and last, seem to have been written in the summer of 1893.

No. 11. AN EXCURSION TICKET

Although better known from its *New York Press* headline as "Billy Atkins Went to Omaha," Crane's own title when he mounted the

Press clipping was "An Excursion Ticket," an authority that must be respected. The first and only publication was in the *New York Press*, Sunday, May 20, 1894, part IV, page 3, signed, headlined 'BILLY AT-KINS | WENT TO OMAHA || The Tale of a Great Yearning in | the Heart of a Hobo. || THROUGH FIRE AND WATER || Nothing Stopped Him, Although All | Hands Were Against Him. || A JOURNEY OF SACRIFICES || And the Reward at Its End Had Its | Drawbacks, Too —A Clever Study | of Tramp Character.' Two illustrations appeared, captioned *"Come Up Here," Said the Brakeman* and *He Looked at the Departing Train*, both signed by M. Stein.

With some idea of publication, perhaps when he was collecting pieces to add to Heinemann's edition of *The Open Boat* (1898), Crane took a clipping, pasted it on foolscap paper, numbered and titled each leaf, and in the margins added the cumulative word count. This clipping is preserved in the Crane Collection in the Special Collections of the Columbia University Libraries and thus has an impeccable pedigree. Unfortunately, only the first three of Crane's pages are preserved, through 62.35. In this part he made three substantive changes (two of these related) but did not touch any accidental.

In the Crane Collection are also preserved the black carbons of two four-page typescripts entitled "An American Tramp's Excursion," both corrected the same in black ink. The first consists of two leaves of laid paper 330 × 203 mm., watermarked *Britannia Pure Linen* with a head between the lines, and the remaining two of wove foolscap watermarked *Indian & Colonial*. On the back of the fourth page Cora wrote in pencil *An American Tramp's | Excursion | For E. Book || 3550 words ||*. The second carbon consists of only one leaf of the Britannia paper and the last three of Indian & Colonial. In pencil on its back Cora wrote *An American Tramp's Excursion | For A. Book | 3550 words ||*. Cora was not herself the typist, for the typescripts are not typical of her work, being numbered between parentheses in the upper left corner and single-spaced throughout. However, the paper as well as Cora's markings identify these typescripts as posthumous trials for *Last Words* in which, nevertheless, the sketch was not finally included. Since these typescripts—referred to collectively as TMs—incorporate the three revisions made in Crane's paste-up of the *Press* clipping and are otherwise influenced by the *Press*, there can be no doubt that they were typed from the Crane Collection copy of the clipping, revised. Obviously, the status of the TMs variants comes in question when the Crane clipping stops, for it is possible that he made further changes in the now lost pages. However, there is no sufficient internal evidence to permit an editor to select any of these TMs variants to emend the *Press* copy-text after 62.35. It seems evident from the various changes made in TMs when the clipping is a witness for the basic copy that the unknown typist was consciously revising while typing and in such touches as the substitution of *pot hat* for *derby* (61.15) and of *Memphis Tennessee* for *Memphis* (62.12) is thinking of English readers. The change in the title, certainly unauthoritative, also seems to have been made for an English audience.

No. 12. THE SNAKE

"The Snake" may have some associations with the Sullivan County sketches but it is not firmly established among them, its manuscript is written on a type of paper which is not identical but is associated with Crane's work in 1894, and it appears to come too late to be included in the 1892 series. The first printing was in syndicated form in the newspapers, distributed by Bacheller, Johnson and Bacheller, all on Sunday, June 14, 1896, except for N[5]. The following newspapers have been observed:

N[1]: *St. Louis Globe-Democrat*, June 14, 1896, page 36, headed ' "THE SNAKE." || BY STEPHEN CRANE.'

N[2]: *Galveston Daily News*, June 14, page 20, headed '[within a frame of linked type-orn.] THE SNAKE || BY STEPHEN CRANE. | [below the frame] For the News—Copyrighted.' In the same typesetting, including the copyright notice, it also appeared on the same date in the *Dallas Morning News*, page 9.

N[3]: *Cincinnati Commercial Gazette*, June 14, page 20, headed '[within a frame of type-orn.] The Man and the Snake. || By Stephen Crane. | [below the frame] (Written for the Commercial Gazette and | Copyrighted.)'.

N[4]: *Detroit Free Press*, June 14, page 17, headed '[within a frame of type-orn.] THE SNAKE. || By STEPHEN CRANE.' Above the title is placed a cut of Crane captioned 'STEPHEN CRANE. | Author of "The Red Badge of Courage," | and who is famous at 24. ||'.

N[5]: *Minneapolis Tribune*, July 6, 1896, page 4, headed '[within a frame of type-orn.] "The Snake." || By STEPHEN CRANE. ||'.

All newspapers printed from cuts furnished by Bacheller two illustrations, the first captioned *The Man Jumped Backward With a Convulsive Chatter* and the second *At the End the Man Clutched His Stick and Stood Watching.*

The little story also appeared in Bacheller's *Pocket Magazine*, II (August, 1896), 125–132, with the notice *Copyright, 1896, by the Bacheller Syndicate.* Its final publication was in *Last Words* (1902), pages 268–272.

In the University of Virginia–Barrett Collection, purchased from the Collamore Collection, is a holograph manuscript of "The Snake" that was used as printer's copy by the Bacheller Syndicate, written in black ink, with alterations in the same ink, on five pages of wove white ledger paper 311 × 201 mm., the rules 11 mm. apart. The title without quotation marks and Crane's signature head page 1, which is unnumbered, the other pages being numbered at top center above semicircles. In a strange hand, obviously from the Bacheller offices, is written in pencil 'Hold for orders', this deleted in ink and to the right of the title in the same ink, 'Please get into type at once', the *at once* underlined, to which are appended the initials *A. S.* Below this in pencil is written large the word count 1,142; separate counts appear on the versos of the first four pages. In the left margin a little above the halfway mark is a blue-crayon 53, which is repeated to 57 on page 5. The whole manuscript is smudged with inky fingerprints and was clearly the printer's copy for the Bacheller proof sent to the subscribing newspapers; thus it offers a most interesting example by which to test the general accuracy of other syndicated Bacheller texts. For this purpose, a table of variants has been placed after the Historical Collation that will permit the reconstruction of the proof and its variants. This table shows that the Bacheller compositor increased the weight of the punctuation by adding seven, possibly nine, commas. He removed one unusual hyphenation and corrected one real error in punctuation but otherwise did not alter the punctuation, sentence structure, or paragraphing. He corrected three Crane misspellings and two grammatical errors: one the usual Crane *it's* for the possessive pronoun and three of the four Crane uses of *was* for *were*, only one of which was positively required although the corrections were all technically appropriate. On the other hand, his substantive errors were serious indeed. He omitted one whole sentence and produced six omissions of words, misreadings, and sophistications. It seems clear that the proofreading was desultory and that copy was not consulted. The newspapers faithfully followed these errors with only one exception: N[3-5] returned to MS *sniffing* at 67.37 what seems to have been the proof sophistication *sniffling* as found in N[1-2]. One newspaper (N[3]) independently altered MS *was* to *were* at 67.15. An oddity exists in the omission of MS *full* by N[1,3,5] at 65.16. It is difficult to believe, given the context, that the proof also omitted this word but that N[2,4] supplied it. One is faced either with the dubious hypothesis that the proof was sent out in two stages, or the more probable explanation that independently N[1,3,5] omitted it on stylistic grounds in setting from the proof that read *full*.

Bacheller's *Pocket Magazine* (PM) in August seems to have been set independently from the same manuscript. No question can be raised about a lost typescript, and the PM text except for the normal alteration of *was* to *were* at 66.26 (^1was) and 67.15 (to which PM added a fourth alteration at 66.26 [^2was] not present in the proof) agrees with none of the $N variants (excepting N^3 at 67.15). The styling of the accidentals in PM was heavier but the setting of the MS substantives was much superior, only two related errors resulting from sophistication: the change of MS *backward* to *forward* at 66.9 and the omission of *backward* at 67.17, both evidently owing to a misunderstanding of the sense. No evidence exists to connect Crane with the proofs for the magazine text, and indeed the two changes noted were perhaps unauthorized proofreader's intervention.

The University of Virginia–Barrett Collection also owns a typescript of three pages numbered within parentheses, the (now laminated) laid paper measuring 330 × 203 mm., the chainlines 28 mm. apart, watermarked *Britannia Pure Linen* with a head between the two lines. This is a black carbon copy made on the Crane typewriter and can only doubtfully be attributed to Cora since the typed decoration about the title made up of colons and dashes is not characteristic of her typescripts. However, in the upper left corner of the first page she wrote in black ink *1150 words* and then, below, *Book*. A blue-crayon number 20 appears to the right of the title, and a minuscule letter which may be an *m* or more probably a *w* appears in the lower left corner. This typescript was purchased in the lot that came through the publisher Coates from Paul Reynolds, to whom Cora had sent typescripts for the American edition of *Last Words,* and it is therefore posthumous. This TMs makes three minor substantive changes, but its agreement with PM in the unique variants at 66.9 and 67.17 shows that the copy for TMs was a clipping from PM. In turn, the agreement of the Digby, Long *Last Words* (1902) in each substantive variant of TMs from PM indicates that it was set from the ribbon copy of the Barrett carbon.

The textual transmission, thus, is clear. The manuscript is the sole authority and copy-text since all published appearances derive from it without authorial review. The newspaper texts, deriving from the Bacheller proofs, are terminal. But *Pocket Magazine,* set independently from MS, was the ancestor of the typescript and thus of the *Last Words* text. The present text reprints the manuscript for the first time.

The story is listed as No. 23 and as being from the *Pocket Magazine* in Crane's inventory list of about July, 1897, preserved in the Special Collections of Columbia University Libraries.

No. 13. STORIES TOLD BY AN ARTIST

The only authoritative text of "Stories Told by an Artist" is that of its first appearance in the *New York Press,* unsigned, Sunday, October 28, 1894, part IV, page 6, with two illustrations captioned *"Here's Some Cake."* and *"Little Pennoyer Was Breezy."* The headline was 'STORIES TOLD | BY AN ARTIST || A Tale About How "Great Grief" | Got His Holiday Dinner. || AS TO PAYMENT OF THE RENT || How Pennoyer Disposed of His Sunday | Dinner. || '. From a clipping of this in Crane's scrapbook, now in the Special Collections of the Columbia University Libraries, Cora after his death made a typescript, the ribbon copy of which served as printer's copy for the story in *Last Words* (1902), pages 133–145. The black carbon of this typescript is preserved in the University of Virginia–Barrett Collection on 9 pages of cheap wove unwatermarked ruled paper 264 × 208 mm., the rules 9 mm. apart. In the black ink used for corrections within the typescript Cora added to the typed title 'in New York', which became the *Last Words* title "Stories Told by an Artist in New York." To the left of the title she wrote 2700 *words;* | *For book.* A blue-crayon figure 17 is placed to the right of the title. Cora's minuscule identification does not appear in the lower left corner. In pencil cumulative word counts are written on the versos up to 2680 on fol. 10^v. Cora paged the typescript within spaced parentheses at top center, omitting page 8. The *Press* version is the copy-text, corrected as necessary by reference to the other documents.

Crane later reworked these sketches to form part of chapters 19 and 20 of *The Third Violet* (1897). Although the same characters appear in "The Silver Pageant" (No. 14), that piece is not included in the novel. Since it has been the practice in this volume to publish early drafts only, we have not included a collation of *The Third Violet* against our Virginia text. This will appear in its proper place, as part of the apparatus to be published to volume III.

No. 14. THE SILVER PAGEANT

Although printed first in *Last Words* (1902), pages 145–148, "The Silver Pageant" probably dates from late 1894 when the other Great Grief stories were published. In the University of Virginia–Barrett Collection is preserved the black carbon of a typescript (now laminated) that Cora typed or had made up to send to Paul Reynolds for the proposed American edition of *Last Words* and perhaps for serialization in the United States. This consists of two leaves of laid paper 329 × 203 mm., the horizontal chainlines 28 mm. apart, watermarked *Britannia Pure Linen* with the helmeted head between the lines. Cora has reviewed the typing and marked corrections in pencil. In black ink she wrote *By* | *Stephen Crane* beneath the typed and underlined title and in the upper left corner placed the note *770 words.* A blue-crayon 22 is at the right of the title. A minuscule *v* is written in the lower left corner. On the back of page 2 she wrote in pencil *For book.* The ribbon copy of this typescript would have been used as printer's copy for *Last Words,* on the evidence of its reproduction of the TMs error *perface* (77.5) altered by Cora in the Barrett carbon to *preface.* This typescript is one step closer than *Last Words* to Crane's manuscript, which it seems to copy with considerable fidelity. The present edition uses this Barrett typescript as the copy-text for the first time.

No. 15. A DESERTION

A broken-off draft of the story in Crane's Notebook preserved in the University of Virginia–Barrett Collection dates the composition of this story in late 1894 or early 1895, since the fragment was inscribed just ahead of the draft of "When Man Falls, A Crowd Gathers" which was printed in the *New York Press* on December 2, 1894. The writing was on the versos of the turned-about Notebook, fols. 41ᵛ–38ᵛ. In this draft Crane originally wrote the title 'Discovery of the Crime' but deleted it; after his death Cora in blue pencil just above the deletion wrote 'First copy of a desertion'. The draft is reprinted from the Notebook in this edition after the final text, and its alterations appear following the Historical Collation. The emendations made to this draft are those which correct habitual Crane misspellings. The draft is too far removed from the final form to make a record in the Historical Collation practicable.

The first publication was in *Harper's Magazine,* CI (November, 1900), 938–939, and again in *Last Words* (1902), pages 245–251. Preserved in the University of Virginia–Barrett Collection is a blue ribbon typescript (now laminated) of five pages of laid paper 259 × 202 mm. The first leaf is watermarked *Brookleigh Fine* and has horizontal chainlines 26–27 mm. apart. Leaves 2–5 are unwatermarked and have vertical chainlines 26–27 mm. apart. In the black ink used for her alterations, Cora wrote in the upper left corner of page 1 'Stephen Crane | 1520 words', and on the verso of page 5 'A Desertion || 1500 words. | Dont know if ever sold | serially in U. S. No record |

To be used in book | of short stories.' Also in her hand, at upper right is written in pencil in a large script 'pub^d in "Harpers | Monthly" '. A blue-crayon figure 7 appears below this notation.

The typescript is one of the set that Cora sent to Reynolds in New York to serve as copy for the proposed American edition of *Last Words*. The English *Last Words* was definitely set from its carbon, perhaps marked in one or two places with small variants not added to the ribbon copy. The textual problem rests on the copy from which the typescript was made and its relation to that behind the *Harper's Magazine* version. Here some correspondence between Cora and Reynolds preserved in the Special Collections of the Columbia University Libraries is helpful. On July 9, 1900, Reynolds addressed Cora at Port Jervis:

I am returning to you herewith the originals of the two stories of your husband's.
I put the matter in hand at once and had them typewritten on Saturday, and I am sending back to you the originals to-day. . . .
[*handwritten postscript*]
I asked $100.00 for one story & $75.00 for other. This is about $50 a thousand.

Although "A Desertion" is not named in this letter, it was the short piece for which Reynolds proposed to ask $100, for the case of the $75 story, which was the fishermen sketch previously published as "The Octopush," is linked with "A Desertion" in the correspondence. Since the letter is addressed to Cora at Port Jervis, the implication is clear that she had found two early manuscripts of Crane's among his effects and had promptly put them on the market.

On September 4, 1900, Reynolds addressed Cora, now back in England, and in the course of a letter chiefly about the fishing story, he wrote, "With regard to the two stories which you sent me, 'A Desertion' I have not [as yet *interlined in ink*] been able to sell; [It is being considered *interlined in ink*]." Two days later, on September 6, Reynolds wrote:

I cabled you last night as follows: "Crane, Plant, 18 Bedford Row, London, Desertion sold provided unpublished serially or book England America Answer."
I have sold the story of Mr. Crane's entitled "A Desertion" for $150 to Harper, but they telephoned up to me that they had just learned that Mr. Heinemann had published a collection of Mr. Crane's stories under the Title "Bowery Stories" or "Stories of the Bowery," and that they were afraid that this might have been included in this collection; I, therefore, cabled you; and I have as yet no reply.

Finally, on September 22, Reynolds wrote once more: "I sold 'A Desertion' for $150. I sold the fishing story for $100., making a total of $250. You understand that in the case of 'A Desertion,' it was bought by Harper's Magazine and they bought the English and American serial rights, so the story must not be sold serially in England."

This correspondence explains the markings on the Barrett TMs. Cora would have brought the original manuscript, which Reynolds had returned after making his typed copy, to England as the only copy she owned. In the interval before the sale, she had begun to assemble copy for *Last Words* and had the manuscript typed in England (as shown by the English watermark of its title-page). Her original notation about serialization would necessarily precede the receipt of Reynolds' September 5 cable of sale and the handwritten title notation about *Harper's* is probably to be dated shortly after September 13, as suggested in the textual section on "The Octopush." Internal evidence of the Barrett TMs agrees with this reconstruction. Such Crane characteristics as *it's* for the possessive pronoun, and perhaps the curious *pro-cess* (79.10) which may have come from the division of the word between lines in the manuscript, all suggest derivation from manuscript. One may add to this the preservation in the typescript (TMs) of much of his characteristic punctuation system in a state that may just possibly reflect more closely his preferences in 1894 than in 1899 or 1900.[3] Finally, the typescript itself betrays some evidence for a state of the text earlier than the *Harper's* version. The *Harper's* editing was thorough, ranging from censorship of some profanity (80.3–4, 81.20) through such niceties as the substitution of *body* for *corpse* (81.7) to such stylistic matters as choices of words (81.3–4: *omit* 'terrible'; 'direct' *instead of* 'directed') and tinkering with the dialect as by the substitution of *wanter* for *wanta* and the normalization of *o'ny* to *on'y*. But there is no indication that it editorially expanded any part of the story. Thus it is significant that TMs was originally typed at 78.8–11 to read 'He ses she's too purty, Huh! My Sadie—O' my las' week, she' and that the added material from *Harper's* was interlined by Cora. This evidence combines with Cora's notation about *Harper's* publication added to page 1 later than her original disclaimer of knowledge about American publication to suggest that after the typescript had been prepared she received a

---

[3] That is, the use of commas to set off inverted introductory words and phrases, especially, was a trait that Crane largely dropped by 1900. The typescript retains other features of his characteristics, however, such as his refusal to punctuate between the two clauses of a compound sentence separated by *and*. On the other hand, TMs with only one exception punctuates adjectives in series. Crane seldom applied this punctuation in his late writing but he occasionally did so in the early 1890's.

clipping of the *Harper's* pages and—as she did with the typescript of "The Great Boer Trek" [4]—she brought the typescript into general conformity with the printed version in this marked difference. This material inserted in the dialogue would, apparently, represent a Crane revision in the typescript behind the *Harper's* text but one not then transferred back to the manuscript. If so, and the case of "The Great Boer Trek" is a strong analogy, something approaching demonstration is possible that *Harper's* and TMs radiate from the holograph manuscript and are therefore independent witnesses.

Since this working hypothesis places the Barrett typescript one stage closer to the manuscript by removing the housestyling and compositorial transmission of *Harper's*, TMs is the proper copy-text but emended as necessary by reference to the authority of the *Harper's* print. The resulting text alters a considerable amount of *Harper's* sophistication.[5] The text of *Last Words* is derived from the carbon of the Barrett typescript. Its variants show that the carbon had been marked substantially the same as the ribbon copy; thus the majority of E1's variants are editorial or compositorial.[6]

The present edition utilizes the Barrett authoritative typescript for the first time, with reference to the Notebook draft.

No. 16. A CHRISTMAS DINNER WON IN BATTLE

The story was first published as "A Christmas Dinner Won in Battle. A Tale by Stephen Crane" in the *Plumbers' Trade Journal, Gas, Steam and Hot Water Fitters' Review*, XVII (January 1, 1895), 26–27, with an illustration by T. C. Gordon captioned, *"You Fellows Can't Come*

---

[4] See REPORTS OF WAR, *Works*, IX (1971), 516–522.

[5] But perhaps not all, for the ink markings in TMs seem to be an indistinguishable mixture (in neutral cases) of Cora's review after typing and her subsequent comparison with the *Harper's* text, which may have influenced some of the punctuation like the exclamation marks. Thus the "List of Alterations in TMs" may have an added critical importance in this case.

[6] For instance, the addition made in TMs at 78.8–9 is found also in E1. Only two readings suggest markings in the carbon copy for E1 not present in the Barrett TMs. At 79.31 both *Harper's* and E1 read *paradin' through* for TMs *paradin'*. Except for the passage copied from *Harper's*, Cora in this TMs did not supply missing words. Thus it would seem more likely that in the carbon she interlined *through* from her *Harper's* copy but neglected to follow suit in the ribbon typescript than that *through* was an addition on her first review of an omitted word from manuscript that got into the carbon but not the ribbon copy. The word sounds like an editorial sophistication, moreover. The other instance is the exclamation mark in E1 after *me* at 80.22 for TMs period and *Harper's* question mark. All exclamation marks in Cora's typescripts had to be made by hand with the addition of a vertical stroke above the typed period. Although the E1 exclamation may be compositorial, it could instead represent its copy but the failure to make the mark in the Barrett TMs.

in Here!" The story was listed as No. 21 and as being from the *Trade Journal* in Crane's inventory of about July, 1897 at Columbia. In the University of Virginia–Barrett Collection is a clipping from the *Trade Journal* which Cora has annotated in the left margin as 2500 *words.* | *To use in book of short stories.* | *Courtesy of The Plumbers Trade Journal.* Across the top of the clipping a hand that is probably Paul Reynolds' wrote in blue pencil *Copyright by The Plumbers Trade Journal* | *New York City*— and added the figure *15*. This clipping was intended to serve as printer's copy for the American edition of *Last Words.* Two pencil marks of correction are present on it—the reduction to lower case of capital *He* (87.20) and the necessary addition of quote marks before *But* (87.28). In the lower left corner of the first page Cora wrote the minuscule *f* (followed by *1*) for her private inventory and on the second page a *2*. Reynolds listed this title in his inventory of October 23, 1900, at Columbia.

In the Special Collections of the Columbia University Libraries is preserved a set of galley proofs from the English syndicate of Tillotson's. In the upper left corner Cora wrote *Tillotsons* | *Evening News—* | *Bolton* and she marked nine proof-corrections, two substantive changes, one a correction of a misprint, and the remaining concerned with punctuation errors. Whether the text of this proof was set from an annotated clipping of the *Trade Journal* or from a revised typescript made from the *Journal* is not demonstrable. On the example of the two substantive changes that Cora made in the galleys, however, there is no reason not to suppose that she was responsible for the substantive variants that were set up by Tillotson's and which, almost certainly being posthumous, give no indication of authority. This marked proof is certainly the one referred to in an undated letter, probably in the early winter of 1900, sent by Cora from Milborne Grove to Perris in which she writes, "The proof of 'A Xmas Dinner won in Battle,' has been sent to me, and so I judge that it will shortly be published, therefore you can put it in the book of short stories— 'Last Words'" (Yale). It is also noted in an inventory that seems to be Pinker's when under the total sum of £52.10 for various serial rights is written "& 6 gs. for Eng. & Col. serial rights of 'A Xmas Dinner won in Battle.'" English publication was probably made in provincial newspapers but these have not been traced.

No. 17. THE VOICE OF THE MOUNTAIN

On May 22, 1895, this fable was syndicated in the newspapers by Bacheller, although only one example has been observed. This is N[1],

Nebraska State Journal, May 22, page 4, headlined 'MEXICAN TALES. || BY STEPHEN CRANE. || The Voice of the Mountain. | Copyright 1895 by Bacheller, Johnson & Bacheller'. Two illustrations were used, captioned *"Come and Consider With Me As To How I Shall Be Fed."* and *"How Much Will You Pay?"* (misprinted *Fay* in N[1]). A year and a half later Bacheller reprinted the tale in his *Pocket Magazine,* III (November, 1896), 136–142 as 'THE VOICE OF THE MOUNTAIN. || By Stephen Crane. ||'. The final appearance was in *Last Words* (1902), pages 301–305.

In the Special Collections of the Columbia University Libraries is preserved a black carbon copy (TMs[2]), two leaves of wove foolscap watermarked *Indian & Colonial;* its blue ribbon original on the same paper (TMs[1]) is in the University of Virginia–Barrett Collection. This typescript is paged 2 on the second leaf without parentheses. The typed title reads 'THE VOICE OF THE MOUNTAIN. || BY ||' and then in TMs[2] Cora wrote in black ink *Stephen Crane,* and the same but with a period and an underline in TMs[1]. Both copies have her note *1000 words* in the upper left corner of the first page and the concluding # on page 2 but no code letter in the lower left corner. On the back of page 2 in both copies she wrote *The voice of the | Mountains | Copy to Keep ||.* The Barrett TMs[1] came from the stock of typescripts assembled in New York for a possible American edition of *Last Words.* Another carbon must have been used as printer's copy for *Last Words.* This typescript, not of Cora's own typing, perhaps, used as copy a clipping from the *Pocket Magazine.* Both it and *Last Words,* therefore, are derived texts without authority.

Since it is known that from time to time Bacheller used the *Nebraska State Journal* to set up his syndicated proof for Crane's Western stories, the fact that only the *Journal* seems to have printed this fable, as well as the two other ones, suggests that in fact the *Journal* typesetting represents the proof typesetting from Crane's manuscript. Hence the almost exact agreement of the *Pocket Magazine* in every accidental with the *Journal* indicates the likelihood that it is a derived text set from the proof copy. The *Journal* becomes the copy-text, therefore, as almost certainly of primary authority.

No. 18. HOW THE DONKEY LIFTED THE HILLS

Although this fable was apparently syndicated by Bacheller, only one newspaper has been observed that printed it: the *Nebraska State Journal,* June 6, 1895, page 4, headed 'MEXICAN TALES. || BY STEPHEN CRANE. || How the Donkey Lifted the Hills. | [Copyright

1895.]'. Two illustrations accompanied the sketch captioned "*I Will Wager My Ears That You Cannot Carry a Range of Mountains On Your Back.*" and *The Donkey Limped Toward His Prison.* Bacheller waited two years before he published it in his *Pocket Magazine,* IV (June, 1897), 144–151. The final publication was in *Last Words* (1902), pages 252–257.

In the University of Virginia–Barrett Collection is found a blue ribbon typescript on three leaves of wove foolscap 330 × 204 mm., watermarked *Berkshire | Typewriter | Paper |USA.* This appears to be professional work and is not to be associated with Cora or with the Crane typewriter. It should be one of the typescripts sent to Reynolds, its carbon having been used to set the English edition of *Last Words,* although the use of the unique American typewriter paper is very odd. Yet Cora in pencil had circled word counts for each page on the versos, though not cumulated, and on the back of the third leaf wrote in pencil "*How The Donkey lifted the | Hills*" *for book | 1250 words.* The agreement of TMs and E1 in omitting *that* (92.3) and in substituting *a* for *the* (93.39) seems to demonstrate the use of the typescript for *Last Words.* But if so, it is odd that E1 makes so many independent errors and that it uses the American form *toward* (94.25) whereas TMs, like N[1] and PM, reads *towards.* The question of copy cannot be finally resolved.

On the same assumption as was made in "The Voice of the Mountain," it is probable that the *Nebraska State Journal* was used by Bacheller as the printer and hence that its text corresponds to the lost proof. N[1] is selected as copy-text, therefore, the more especially since PM appears to derive from its proof on the evidence of the extreme closeness of their accidentals.

No. 19. THE VICTORY OF THE MOON

Like the other fables that seem to have come from Crane's Mexican experiences, "The Victory of the Moon" appeared in the *Nebraska State Journal,* July 24, 1895, page 4, headed 'THE VICTORY OF THE MOON || BY STEPHEN CRANE. || [Copyright, 1895.]'. It was presumably a Bacheller-syndicated piece. Three illustrations accompanied it, captioned *The Strong Man Turned Upon Them So Furiously That Many Fell to the Ground., "Go to Yonder Brook and Bathe.",* and *The Moon Said No More, But Merely Smiled.* Two years later Bacheller reprinted the fable in his *Pocket Magazine,* IV (July, 1897), 144–152.

In the University of Virginia–Barrett Collection is the black carbon of a typescript of three numbered pages, on wove foolscap 329 × 202 mm., watermarked *Indian & Colonial*. In black ink Cora has written in the upper left corner *1325 words*, has double underlined the typed title, and below it written *By | Stephen Crane. ||*, but there is no code letter in the lower left corner. A few corrections appear in the same black ink. The typescript does not appear to be Cora's own work, and it is unusual in being single-spaced, with double-spacing only between paragraphs. However, that its ribbon copy was behind *Last Words* (1902), pages 315–320, is demonstrable from their readings. In turn, TMs was typed from a clipping of the *Pocket Magazine* and so is a purely derived text.

As with "The Voice of the Mountain" and "How the Donkey Lifted the Hills," the *Nebraska State Journal* typesetting is almost certainly that of the Bacheller proof set from Crane's manuscript, with PM derived from this proof. The *State Journal* is the only primary authority, therefore, and is the copy-text.

No. 20. THE JUDGMENT OF THE SAGE

The brief fable "The Judgment of the Sage" was published in *The Bookman*, II (January, 1896), 412. No other publication is known before modern reprints. This is probably not the piece listed under the title *The Wisdom of the Present* as No. 10 in an inventory list of about July, 1897, held by the Special Collections of the Columbia University Libraries and reproduced in TALES OF ADVENTURE, *Works*, V (1970), because Crane marked it in the group for which he had the manuscripts. Moreover, in his comprehensive inventory at Columbia, Crane gave the word count as 650 for *The Wisdom of the Present* whereas "The Judgment of the Sage" is somewhat less than 400 words. However, the 650 word count may have been a faulty recollection. In an earlier inventory (reproduced in vol. V) to be dated in July, 1897, the count is given as 500 words, which would be closer.

No. 21. ART IN KANSAS CITY

"Art in Kansas City" is reprinted from two leaves of holograph manuscript in the Special Collections of the Columbia University Libraries. The paper measuring 265 × 212 mm., with rules 9 mm. apart, is cheap wove unwatermarked. The second leaf is paged above a semi-circle. On the verso of the second leaf a strange hand, probably for inventory, has written *Uncle Clarence | Art in Kansas City | Unfinished*. Crane traveled to Kansas City on his Western trip after his visit to St. Louis in late January, 1895. The sketch was not necessarily written on the trip, however. It was never published and came to Columbia with the major collection of Crane's effects sold after his death. The mention of Uncle Clarence in the opening sentence associates this little piece with another tall-tale Uncle Clarence story, "The Camel," also unpublished. "Art in Kansas City" was first reprinted by R. W. Stallman in *Studies in Short Fiction*, 1, No. 2 (Winter, 1964), 147–152.

No. 22. A TALE OF MERE CHANCE

The only personal record of "A Tale of Mere Chance" that Crane preserved is in the last list of stories that he made up, probably in early January, 1900, where it is noted as "The Pursuit of the Tiles", as published by the Bacheller Syndicate, and as 1,250 words in length. The story was first published in a number of newspapers, copyrighted by Bacheller, Johnson and Bacheller,[7] on Sunday, March 15, 1896. The *Chicago Tribune* spread the tale on the upper half of its fifth part and had its own staff artist draw a page-wide decorative title based on the Bacheller cut and a new large illustration captioned *He Screamed—You Know That Scream—Mostly Amazement*. It also ran the portrait that Bacheller had supplied. To the tale it appended a lengthy account of Crane and of the story that appears to have been written by Bacheller. This same sketch was also run by the *Galveston Daily News* and, in the same typesetting, by the *Dallas Morning News*. Because of its personal interest, it is reprinted below. The other newspapers contented themselves with a decorative title containing the subtitle, an illustration captioned *I Ran Through the World at My Best Speed*, and a portrait of Crane, all signed by G. Y. Kauffman. The portrait is drawn from a photograph referred to by Crane as never used for publication in a letter to *The Critic* from Hartwood, February 15, 1896 (*Letters*, p. 117). These were all printed from cuts supplied by Bacheller with the copy. The standard Bacheller cut for the title, signed 'GYK', read: '[letters on winged tiles] A TALE OF MERE | [letters on tiles supported on legs]

---

[7] N[3,7] drop the notice; N[5] reads simply *For the News—Copyrighted.*

CHANCE | [remainder in script] Being an account of the pursuit of | the tiles, the statement of the clock, | and the grip of a coat of orange spots, | together with some criticism of | a detective said to be carved from an | old table-leg. | By | Stephen Crane ||'.

The following newspapers have been observed:

N^1: *Chicago Tribune,* March 15, 1896, page 41.
N^2: *Buffalo News,* March 15, page 9.
N^3: *St. Louis Globe-Democrat,* March 15, page 41.
N^4: *New Orleans Picayune,* March 15, page 26.
N^5: *Galveston Daily News,* March 15, page 12. This was reprinted in the same typesetting in the *Dallas Morning News,* March 15, page 12.
N^6: *Nebraska State Journal,* March 15, page 11.
N^7: *Minneapolis Tribune,* March 22, page 11. This reprint, one week later, was not set from the Bacheller copy but instead is a reprint of N^6. Whether the omission of the copyright notice indicates a piracy is not certain. The cuts would need to have come, like the clipping, from N^6 if the publication was unpaid for.

The sketch of Crane composed by Bacheller and sent out with the syndicated copy follows, the text being that from the *Chicago Tribune.*

We publish in this issue a new and extremely characteristic story by Stephen Crane, whose work, especially the "Red Badge of Courage," has attracted so much attention of late on both sides of the Atlantic. His success, when his age is taken into consideration—for he is only 24—has been phenomenal; yet undoubtedly, during the brief period that has sufficed him to win his way from obscurity to fame, he has experienced his full share of those trials and disappointments which few young authors escape and which even genius does not always surmount.

Mr. Crane is a native of New York State, and his home is at Hartwood, where he divides his time between writing and riding. That he is a lover of the horse no reader of his stories need be told.

The ancestry of a writer of marked originality is always interesting. The Cranes were a family of note in colonial days—a fact to which every line in the young author's face bears witness—and several of his progenitors played heroic parts in the great struggle for American independence. In view of this it seems a singular turn of fortune that Mr. Crane's work has received more general recognition in England than in the United States. Is it not rather humiliating? Why should we wait for London to report back to us that we have been entertaining a genius unawares?

On his mother's side Mr. Crane is descended from a long line of Methodist clergymen of the order of the saddlebag. Possibly this heredity, also, may be traced in his work; his style is curiously introspective and analytical.

Is this a betrayal of confidence? We trust not. We recall a certain story that Mr. Crane once showed us, in which two pistols were drawn, and on the trigger of each an angry finger trembled, but no explosion followed; those pistols hung fire for some twenty pages; the scene had shifted to the inner consciousness of one of the actors.[8] Who would not laugh—and admire, too? Like Nathaniel Hawthorne, this author, whatever his theme, always treats "the tragedy of a soul." This trait is very marked in "A Tale of Mere Chance," in which a murderer's maddening consciousness of his crime drives him to self-betrayal.

Mr. Crane studied more or less at Lafayette College and Syracuse University, but took no degree. Like several other authors not unknown to fame, he appears to have found it hard to stick to the curriculum. Perhaps it is precisely because college courses are so perfectly adapted to the average mind that exceptional minds rarely prosper with them.

Stephen Crane's mission was to write, and he began at the age of 16. At 20 he produced his first novel, "Maggie." It met, on the whole, a rather cold reception, but brought him the commendation and friendship of William Dean Howells, Hamlin Garland, and a few other appreciative critics. One of his sketches presently found its way into the Cosmopolitan.[9]

Of his remarkable "lines," published in the volume called "The Black Riders," it need only be said that they are original in the highest degree and as full of "reason" as they are lacking in "rhyme" and meter.

The credit of first recognizing the extraordinary merit of "The Red Badge of Courage" and giving its author an effective introduction to the American public is due to the Bacheller and Johnson Syndicate, which brought out this story, upon which Mr. Crane's reputation still chiefly rests, in December, 1894, in serial form. From that time his success was assured.

The story was republished in book form, crossed the sea, and has won the author much praise—and some British gold, we hope. He has just completed a novel entitled "The Third Violet," treating of art life in New York. May it prosper no less!

Mr. Crane is one of the founders of "The Sign o' the Lanthorn," a unique literary club in a historic building on William street, New York, the great attractions being "two fine old fire-places and good company." He is still an enthusiastic member; and among the many honors heaped upon him of late, none, probably, have been more acceptable than the invitation to be the guest of this club at a complimentary dinner to be given early in April.

Next in order was Bacheller's placement in the *English Illustrated Magazine*, xiv (March, 1896), 569–571 (EIM), with an illustration by Arthur Jule Goodman, dated 1896, captioned *He Fell Forward, and a Chair Threw Itself in my Way as I Sprang Toward the Door*. The Bacheller copyright notice is reproduced. Then it was printed in Bacheller's *Pocket Magazine*, i (April, 1896), 115–122 (PM). In June, *Current Literature*, xix (June, 1896), 516 (CL), reprinted the tale, copyrighted by Bacheller, with credit to its source, the *Buffalo News* (N²). The title here was "The White Tiles: A Tale of Mere Chance." In 1899 the compilation *Best Things from American*

---

[8] This story seems to be "One Dash—Horses," but Bacheller's memory betrays him. The protagonist held a pistol, but the Mexican bandit a knife. Twenty pages is certainly a hyperbole for the length of the scene.

[9] This would be "A Tent in Agony," *Cosmopolitan*, xiv (Dec., 1892), 241–244.

Literature (BT), put out by the *Christian Herald,* reprinted the piece, pages 69–71, its copy being the *Pocket Magazine.* Finally, *Last Words* (1902) collected it on pages 282–287 (E1).

A black carbon typescript (TMs) is preserved in the University of Virginia–Barrett Collection consisting of four leaves of wove foolscap paper 327 × 202 mm. watermarked *Indian & Colonial.* The typing is Cora's. Beneath the title she has written in black ink 'By | Stephen Crane.' underlined, and on the verso of the last leaf in pencil 'a Tale of mere chance | for book | 1250 words.' Three rounds of correction appear, the first in a thick grayish pencil, the second in black ink, and the third in a light thin pencil. The substantive alterations made in this review are listed in the Historical Collation. This is one of the typescripts that Cora made up to send to Reynolds as copy for the American edition of *Last Words.* Its copy was a clipping from the *Pocket Magazine.*[10] The ribbon typescript would have been used to set the Digby, Long *Last Words* (1902).

Most of the available documents are derived and can be discarded as without authority for the establishment of the text: CL was set from N^2, BT from PM, TMs from PM, and E1 from TMs in a slightly different state of correction from the Barrett copy. Only three texts remain, therefore, that have a claim to authority. These are the N newspapers insofar as their common proof copy can be recovered, EIM, and PM. The difficult question of the copy from which these authorities were set is involved with their interrelationship and cannot be settled for any one document without reference to the others.

The six observed newspapers that are substantive all radiate from a common source, the Bacheller proofs that were mailed for publication on March 15, 1896. This proof appears to have been uniform, in a single state of correction.[11] The newspapers agree in eight unique substantive variants against the joint readings of PM and EIM.[12] On

[10] The clipping from PM was probably sent her by Reynolds when she was assembling Crane's American magazine and newspaper writings in preparation for the book. Crane's listing of the story as "The Pursuit of the Tiles" suggests that he had no copy in January, 1900, when the list was written. The title is scarcely authoritative, therefore, since he was relying on his memory of the subject matter, and parallels to such paraphrases can be found in various of his lists.

[11] The only substantive variant shared by two newspapers is the plural *flocks,* printed in $N^{2,6}$ at 102.30. It would seem that the proof read, in error, *a long flocks* and that $N^{1,3-5}$ automatically corrected to the singular. The singular *troop* at 101.33 would show that the singular *flock* is correct even if the PM singular were not evidence.

[12] These are N *if it were not* for PM,EIM *were it not* (100.9), *servant* for *servants* (100.17), *retained* for *remained in possession of* (100.19–20), *smoothly; I* for *smoothly, and I* (101.6), *pursuing* for *following* (101.33), *of politics* for *in politics* (101.39), *vivid orange* for *vividly orange* (102.33), and *an effort* for PM *effort* but EIM *efforts* (102.38).

the other hand, PM has nine unique substantives against the N-EIM agreement.[13] Finally, EIM disagrees with the joint N-PM readings for six substantives.[14] Superficially this pattern might suggest radiation from common copy or else the radiation of two of the documents from one form of the copy and the derivation of the third from another form. In the first case we should need to conjecture that Crane submitted a holograph manuscript to Bacheller, who had a typescript and two carbons prepared.[15] In the second, Crane would have submitted either a manuscript or a typescript which served as printer's copy for one version, and Bacheller had a typescript and carbon prepared which was used to set the other two. The second is inherently improbable and does not satisfy the evidence without unnecessary complications.[16] The first is theoretically possible and cannot be disproved. If this were indeed the situation, then N, PM, and EIM would each radiate from the same source and would be of equal textual authority. If so, the editing would be greatly simplified, for in all cases of variation the agreement of any two prints (even in error) would generally demonstrate the authoritative reading of the lost common copy. On the other hand, a little over two months after syndication of "A Tale of Mere Chance," Bacheller also syndicated Crane's "An Indiana Story," on May 23 and 25, 1896, printed it in the *Pocket Magazine* for September, and sold it to the *English Illustrated Magazine* for December publication. In this case the evidence seems to point to the EIM copy being a set of the same proofs that

---

[13] These are PM *or sensitive* for N,EIM *and sensitive* (100.10–11), *old tall for tall old* (100.18), *these* for *those* (101.21), *desperate, fertile* for *desperately fertile* (101.26), *murders* for *murderers* (101.36), *detective* for *detectives* (102.4), *chance* for *chanced* (102.18), *were* for *was* (102.34), and *into* for *in* (103.1). In this last, PM is joined by N[4] *into*.

[14] These are EIM *sort of* for N,PM *sort of a* (100.16), *eye* for *eyes* (101.30), *street* for *streets* (101.37), *end* for *ends* (102.10), *Half-past* for *Half-after* (102.17), and *is* for *was* (103.6).

[15] Or a typescript and one carbon, one of these copies passing from the N-proof printers to the printers of PM, or vice versa, and the other going to England.

[16] That is, since the time taken to put this very brief tale into type would be little more than that required for typing, no purpose would be served by making up a typescript as printer's copy for the other two prints when a proof of one would have been available instead. If the N proof had been set from Crane's copy, and PM and EIM from a typescript and its carbon, a difficulty arises in that the EIM accidentals are much more closely related to N than to PM. Moreover, given the indication that the unique N variants are not authoritative, the problem arises when they appear in a print if it were conjecturally taken to have been set from Crane's copy although the typescript substantives conjecturally preserve the author's readings. On the other hand, if Crane's copy had set PM and a typescript and its carbon had been the copy for N and for EIM, the difficulties about the accidentals would be partly solved (only partly, because the N punctuation is in general closer to Crane's characteristics than PM's), but the problem of the N unique readings remains.

Bacheller had sent out to the newspapers.[17] Although the later date of this EIM printing might theoretically affect the nature of the copy that it utilized,[18] the possibility must be considered that EIM radiated, like $N, from such proof copy. (Proof from PM is contrary to the evidence and is almost impossible, anyway, because of the dates of publication.) However, even if such derivation of EIM from the N proof could be hypothesized (and the case is not demonstrable), the problem would still remain of the copy for N and for PM. Even here no certainty can obtain. We know from the preserved printer's copy manuscript of "The Snake," syndicated on June 14, 1896, that this piece was set directly into proof for the newspapers from its manuscript, and, moreover, that the manuscript itself, not a set of these proofs, was also the copy for the August *Pocket Magazine*. If this procedure may be taken as typical, then a Crane manuscript of "A Tale of Mere Chance" could have been the copy both for N and PM.[19]

----

[17] For a discussion of the evidence, see TALES OF WAR, *Works*, VI (1970), lxix–lxxv.

[18] In this matter one can only guess. Since EIM published "A Tale of Mere Chance" in March, the same month as American syndication, it is clear that copy must have been sent to it well ahead of time, no later than early February, and even then EIM would have had to make special arrangements to rush it into print in the forthcoming March issue. This evidence suggests that Bacheller must have held Crane's tale for an appreciable period before releasing it to the newspapers. One may speculate that at this point he was concerned to protect copyright in England and did not publish in the United States until EIM was safely in or near print. If this is so, time must be allowed for copy to be sent to England, to be accepted, and a mutual date agreed on. Under such circumstances it may be that "An Indiana Campaign," set in EIM from N proof, is not parallel evidence. The December EIM publication after May syndication could suggest not so much EIM holding accepted material as buying a story already in print, in which case the original typescript would no longer have been available. Yet the matter is obscure. Copy for the "Campaign" could not have been a clipping or proof of the September PM; hence it may be that EIM bought the rights and received its copy of the syndicated proof but decided to hold it for later publication, or else delayed a decision after receiving copy. The evidence is not really clear, therefore, whether Bacheller would normally make up a typescript for England or send proof. For "A Tale of Mere Chance" it is a question whether it was simpler for him to set up the story and mail proof as copy, knowing that the type would be standing for about two months, or to order a typescript to be made from Crane's manuscript and to delay setting the syndicated proof until he heard from England. For what it is worth, the evidence of "The Snake," syndicated by Bacheller on June 14, 1896, and published in the *Pocket Magazine* in August, does not suggest the mailing of a typescript, for this was set directly from Crane's manuscript. Of course, we do not know in this case whether Bacheller tried for an English sale and failed, for it was not published abroad until *Last Words*. What we do know, however, is that if he attempted an English sale—and this is not demonstrable—he must have sent proof as copy.

[19] The issue may only be confused by a speculation that "The Snake" could be atypical. The possibility that this is earlier work, more closely associated with the "Sullivan County Sketches," cannot be overlooked. It is at least theoretically

But this manuscript not being preserved, no textual evidence can assess whether the common copy for N and for PM was a manuscript or a typescript, and no family tree would distinguish them. It will be obvious, then, that the question of the EIM copy becomes important in two respects. As already remarked, if EIM were set from a typescript, then it has equal authority with N and PM, and its concurrence either with one or the other would be largely decisive. But if it derives from N proof, its authority would be limited to confirmation of whatever state of the proof was sent to England.

Here we come to the stumbling block for any textual hypothesis, the eight unique substantive variants that appear in $N and a scattering of transmissionally significant accidentals that are also unique. It seems clear that these N variants are in a different category from the unique readings either of PM or of EIM, for those in EIM, at least, can almost automatically be discarded as transmissional evidence, no matter whether EIM is derived or substantive.[20] Likewise, the PM variants are all clear-cut printing errors like *or* (100.10), *murders* (101.36), *detective* (102.4), and *chance* (102.18), or else certain sophistications like *old tall* for *tall old* (100.18), *desperate, fertile* for *desperately fertile* (101.26), *were* for *was* (102.34), or *into* for *in* (103.1).[21] On the other hand, at least some—and perhaps all—of the unique N variants go beyond printing errors and must represent attempted revision by some hand. The most obvious case is the alteration of the syntax at 101.6 from PM,EIM *smoothly, and I* to *smoothly; I,* which agrees (less N[5]) with the substitution of semicolons for commas (although without syntactical change) at 100.10, 100.28, and 101.23. Also obvious, one would think, is the change from the somewhat awkward *remained in possession of* to *retained*

possible that it was given to Bacheller in manuscript, if it was earlier work, whereas Crane might have had typescripts made for his later stories. But we do not know. Some evidence seems to exist, although not perhaps wholly certain, that a typescript was the copy for "An Indiana Campaign." On the other hand, the evidence suggests that "A Little Regiment" for McClure's was submitted in manuscript.

[20] If EIM is independent and substantive, its unique variants must necessarily be errors, on the evidence of the agreement of N and PM against them. If EIM is derived from N, the possibility would be present that in some part at least they might reflect errors in an early state of the proof, in which case we should need to conjecture that the corrected N proof returned the readings to authority as exemplified by PM. But the simplest and most natural view, given the nature of the EIM variants, is that they are the English printer's slips or his ideas of styling.

[21] For the order *tall old* see 102.19; for *desperately fertile* see *vividly orange* (102.33), which N altered to *vivid orange*; for *into* see the independent sophistication of N[4] to this reading from its copy *in*.

(100.19–20), of *vividly orange* to *vivid orange* (102.33), of *following* to *pursuing* (101.33)—this last picked up from 101.19 and 101.23—and probably of *were it not* changed to *if it were not* (100.9). An interesting case is the sophistication of PM *made effort* (a typical Crane locution) to *made an effort* (102.37–38). That the basic copy read with PM can be demonstrated by the EIM smoothing to *made efforts*. According to the theory of transmission adopted, this last example could be editorial, like most of those listed above, or compositorial. Similar cases would be the N change of copy *servants* to *servant* (100.17), and *in politics* to *of politics* (101.39). The direction of these changes is invariably toward smoothness and conventional idiom and away from Crane's own style. It is practically impossible to attribute them, as a group, to authorial revision at some stage.

The problem, then, resolves itself to this. If EIM is independent of the N proof, these eight substantive variants—and at least the semicolons at 100.10, 100.28, and 101.23—would need to have been marked in the copy for N(p) by a Bacheller editor or made in proof by a Bacheller editor or proofreader. On the other hand, if EIM derives from the N proof, they could be pinpointed not as editorial copy-markings but as changes made in the proofs at a late stage. In either case, owing to the agreement of PM and EIM they cannot have been present in the basic authorial copy (no matter what the transmission), even in the improbable circumstance that N was set from a unique typescript. The major textual problem is solved by this reasoning, for these variants in N must be discarded as nonauthoritative. If, then, on critical grounds the unique PM and EIM readings can also be discarded—for the substantives at least—an editor is relatively safe in selecting only those readings confirmed by two authorities. This editorial method is sound, in this particular case, without regard for the exact nature of the EIM text.[22]

However, the treatment of the accidentals is a trifle more dependent upon the transmission, and a brief consideration is worth while of the slender evidence that is available for the construction of a working hypothesis. The substantives alone can prove nothing about the

[22] That is, the isolation of the N substantive variants as unauthoritative changes either in the printer's copy or in a later stage of the proof promotes to authority the corresponding PM,EIM agreements since in any case these must be in different lines of the transmission from each other. Correspondingly, whether or not EIM derives from an independent typescript similar to N before its markings (and to PM), or else from an unaltered early state of N proof, its agreements with N against PM, in a different line, isolate the PM unique variants as unauthoritative.

relation of EIM to N, but the accidentals suggest the greater probability that EIM was set from a copy of the N newspaper proofs than from a common typescript. The statistics suggest, for instance, that EIM is much more closely related to N than to PM. For example, in accidentals of punctuation, capitalization, and word-division EIM agrees with N twenty-two times against PM whereas EIM joins PM against N only ten times.[23] A qualitative analysis increases the disproportion, for of these ten agreements three represent the special case of N semicolons (conjecturally part of the N special alterations), one concerns an exclamation point that would also be taken as an N special alteration,[24] and a fifth is a useful comma after *there* (102.10) that was already missing in the basic copy for PM and EIM but would be likely to attract the attention of a proofreader. The remaining five, then, represent the only *compositorial* differences in the accidentals between joint N and EIM on the one hand and PM on the other.[25] This extreme compositorial fidelity is most unlikely to have resulted from EIM and $N radiating from a common typescript copy and must almost certainly be assigned to the textual transmission of EIM from a proof of N.[26] This being so, except when

[23] Several cases of fifty-fifty division within the N newspapers are not included in these statistics.

[24] This is the odd case, perhaps the only real stumbling block to the EIM derivation from N proof. At 102.12 PM and EIM read *I should have escaped. Heavens, I should have escaped!* whereas N substitutes a period for the exclamation. That the N proofreader would reduce this exclamation to a period in order to be consistent with the first *escaped* is not impossible and is perhaps easier to conceive than that the basic copy had only a period in both places and the PM and EIM compositors independently selected only the second for special emphasis.

[25] The simplest of these five is the PM,EIM independent insertion of a comma after *long* (102.30) in an adjectival series where the absence of a comma in N is completely characteristic of Crane. Moreover, Crane did not capitalize *hell*, and thus the N *hades* (103.11) appears to represent the authoritative reading, though conventionally capitalized in PM,EIM. The removal of an N comma in PM,EIM after *them* (101.27) seems to go against the characteristic punctuation in such a respect found in the manuscript of "The Snake." The PM,EIM agreement in a comma after *imperturbability* (100.20) is an independent correction of a vestigial N attempt at a parenthesis with dashes that was not completed by a dash for a comma after *purpose* in the next line. Finally, the hyphen in *Half-after* in PM but *Half-past* in EIM where N has no hyphen seems to be merely a compositorial convention.

[26] Included in the N,EIM agreements in punctuation are some that seem to have significance as more likely to stem in EIM from N proof than from an independent typescript. The general EIM punctuation is the heaviest of all three prints, but it follows N in omitting a comma in an adjective series at 102.19 (although EIM, and PM, inserted such a comma in 102.30), in failing to surround a parenthetical phrase with commas in 101.11–12 and 102.19, and in setting no commas six other times (100.14, 101.1, 101.4, 102.16, 102.27, 102.37, including uncharacteristic EIM failure to punctuate the two clauses of a com-

EIM sets from the early state of the N proof and thus confirms PM, it has no independent authority in the accidentals or the substantives. Thus an editor, faced with variants between the single major stemma of N and PM, each of equal authority, must choose between them according to his knowledge of the probable manuscript readings characteristic of Crane, without regard for EIM agreements save where N proof-alteration is required to explain the variance of N from joint PM,EIM. The working textual hypothesis, then, is that N and PM radiate from common copy, which was probably Crane's manuscript, and that EIM derives from a copy of the N proof in a state earlier than that sent to the newspapers.

The present edition selects N¹, the *Chicago Tribune* version, as the copy-text instead of the equal authority of PM mainly because the N-line is more lightly punctuated in Crane's normal manner than is PM. The choice of N¹ is arbitrary, since any newspaper would do equally well,[27] but the *Chicago Tribune* is the most important and accessible newspaper of the group and is reasonably representative of the reconstructed Bacheller proof. Substantive emendation of the copy-text has been undertaken on the principle already discussed— that the unique readings of EIM can be disregarded in a derived text, that the unique N readings are confirmable as unauthoritative alterations of the basic copy, which can be recovered by the agreement of PM with the early state of the proof sent to EIM. Finally, the unique readings of PM are judged on critical grounds to be compositorial variants from the N,EIM substantives. The treatment of the accidentals has been more eclectic. Here the editor has chosen between the only two authorities, N and PM (once the N proof-alterations confirmed as such by EIM agreement with PM are discarded), according to his estimate of their association with Crane's usual practice as represented by the more usual fidelity of N to its copy in this respect both in the evidence here and in "The Snake."

---

pound sentence in 102.16–17) where PM—which had been heavier in "The Snake" than N—placed commas. EIM followed N in an exclamation point after *tiles* (101.10) where PM had a period; and N and EIM agree in parenthetical dashes for PM commas at 101.1–2. The twenty-three unique EIM accidentals variants must of course be taken as unauthoritative. Most represent the usual English styling such as the use of a comma instead of a colon to introduce dialogue, a freer use of exclamation points, several extra semicolons, and a generally heavier punctuation with commas contrary to Crane's style.

[27] The reconstructed proof possible from $N cannot be usefully taken as copy-text principally because of some doubt in perhaps three or four internal variants as to the exact readings of the Bacheller N proof. Any attempt to use such a reconstruction would also create considerable complexity of notation in the List of Emendations.

However, on some few occasions the punctuation system of "The Snake" has been replaced by heavier punctuation found in PM when, on the evidence of "The Snake" manuscript it would appear that N had removed commas in constructions that at this time Crane would normally have punctuated. The result is the closest approximation possible by combined bibliographical and critical reasoning of the lost manuscript that probably formed the printer's copy for both the Bacheller proof and for the *Pocket Magazine,* as found in "The Snake."

No. 23. THE CAMEL

This tall tale, designed to be part of a series of "Uncle Clarence Stories" with "Art in Kansas City," is preserved in a blue ribbon-copy typescript in the Special Collections of the Columbia University Libraries, the carbon of this typescript being in the University of Virginia–Barrett Collection. The piece consists of two leaves of wove foolscap 329 × 202 mm., watermarked *Indian & Colonial.* The second page is numbered at the upper right in parentheses. The typist was someone other than Cora; the typewriter appears to be that used for the typing of " 'And If He Wills, We Must Die'." The first page is headed 'THE CAMEL. | —BY— | STEPHEN CRANE.' Each copy has a separately typed title-page prefixed, making three leaves in all. That for the Columbia original reads 'THE CAMEL. | ---BY--- | STEPHEN CRANE. | UNCLE CLARENCE STORIES.' Then in the lower left corner is typed 'From Mrs Stephen Crane. | 6 Milborne Grove. | The Boltons. | South Kensington. | 700 Words'. The Barrett carbon has the same title, retyped in blue ribbon, but in the lower left corner reads only '700 words.' The Barrett copy has no markings, but the Columbia ribbon copy was corrected by Cora three times on page 2 to supply missing letters or punctuation at the ends of lines omitted because of the lack of a margin release. Cora also appended the # sign. On the verso of page 2 she wrote 'the Camel | for book England'.

This typescript must have been made from Crane's manuscript sometime after August, 1900, when Cora was assembling copy for *Last Words.* The Barrett carbon would have been in the lot sent to Reynolds for the proposed American edition.

The copy-text is the Columbia University ribbon copy compared with the Barrett carbon. No variants appear except for the several ink corrections on page 2 of the original. The only interesting alteration made in the course of typing is the false start *int* x'd-out after *walked* at 103.34. The text of this tale was first printed by Gullason in *Complete Short Stories and Sketches* (1963).

No. 24. A FREIGHT CAR INCIDENT

Copyrighted and syndicated by Bacheller, Johnson and Bacheller, on Sunday, April 12, 1896, "A Freight Car Incident" had wide circulation. The following newspaper versions have been observed:

N¹: *Nebraska State Journal*, April 12, 1896, page 11, signed, headlined 'A FREIGHT CAR INCIDENT. || Stephen Crane Tells of a Nerve-Shaking | Encounter With a Texas Desperado. || TRAPPED IN BLACK DARKNESS || In Momentary Expectation of a Bul-|let From an Unseen Pistol—A | Blaspheming Torpedo—|How It Ended. || (Copyright 1896, by Bacheller, Johnson & Bacheller.)'.

N²: *Buffalo Sunday News*, April 12, page 9, signed, headlined 'A FREIGHT CAR INCIDENT. || Stephen Crane Tells of a Nerve-|Shaking Encounter With a | Texas Desperado. || TRAPPED IN THE DARKNESS || In Momentary Expectation of a Bullet | From an Unseen Pistol—A Blas-|pheming Torpedo—How | It Ended. ||'. The Bacheller copyright notice appears at the foot following the signature.

N³: *St. Louis Globe-Democrat*, April 12, page 41, headlined 'A FREIGHT CAR INCIDENT. || BY STEPHEN CRANE.'

N⁴: *Louisville Courier-Journal*, April 12, sec. III, page 8, signed, headlined '[within a frame of type-orn.] A FREIGHT CAR INCIDENT | [below the frame] || BY STEPHEN CRANE. ||'.

N⁵: *Brooklyn Daily Eagle*, April 12, page 19, signed, headlined '[within a frame of type-orn.] A FREIGHT CAR INCIDENT | [below the frame] (Copyright, 1896.)'.

N⁶: *Philadelphia Press*, April 19, page 37, signed, headlined 'CAGED WITH A | WILD MAN || Stephen Crane Relates an | Exciting Incident of Life in the | Far West. ||'.

N⁷: *Rochester Democrat and Chronicle*, April 12, page 16, signed, headlined 'LIVELY ENCOUNTER | IN A FREIGHT CAR || Stephen Crane Tells of an Experi-|ence With a Texas Desperado. || MADE HIS NERVES SHAKE || Trapped in Black Darkness—In Mo-|mentary Expectation of a Bullet | From an Unseen Pistol—A | Blaspheming Torpedo. || Written for the Democrat and Chronicle. | (Copyright.)'.

An illustration signed G. Y. Kauffman accompanied the texts except in N⁴⁻⁶ captioned *Where's All These Galoots What Was Goin' T' Shoot at Me?*

In the Special Collections of the Columbia University Libraries is preserved a galley proof, uncorrected, in the same typesetting as the *Nebraska State Journal*. At the head is set in type 'Hold for Orders.' and beneath this is a somewhat different set of headlines beginning 'A FREIGHT CAR INCIDENT. || Trapped in the Darkness With a Texan Desperado. || A NERVE-SHAKING ENCOUNTER ||' with the same final set as in the *State Journal.* In his own hand in the Columbia copy Crane has added omitted *him* at 108.38; this is the only marking on the Columbia example, but collation with the *State Journal* text discloses that a missing comma after *pain* in the proof at 105.33 was supplied and at 107.10 the proof misprint *The'* was corrected to *Th'.* In addition one can add a dropped 'a' in N¹ at 107.11, the correction to single quotes at 106.15, and the correct *board* for *broad* at 108.13. This appears to be another of the Bacheller syndications of Crane's Western articles which had its proof set by the *State Journal.*

Under the title "A Texas Legend" the *English Illustrated Magazine,* xv (June, 1896), 273–275, printed the sketch with an illustration by Arthur Jule Goodman, *"Let 'Er Go," He Said.* Since what evidence we have indicates that Crane was accustomed to sending Bacheller a holograph fair copy, not a typescript, and that Bacheller was accustomed to having the proof set from this manuscript, the odds favor the hypothesis that EIM was set from a copy of the common newspaper syndicate proofs, not from a carbon of a typescript that provided the copy for the proofs typesetting. On the other hand, EIM shows some evidence of independence. The most notable example is what must be the correct *erside* at 107.26 for $N *enside,* an inspired guess by the English editor if without authority. This editor—if EIM were set from the proofs—went over the dialect with some care, although he mistook the meaning of *yer* which was changed from $N ²*yeh* at 106.19 and again at 107.17. That he would change *ye* to *yeh* at 106.20 is without significance; considerably odder is the change at 107.27 of $N *er* to *a'* but it might have been picked up from the use of *'a* at 107.15. Oddest of all is the agreement of N⁴ and EIM in the form *wa'n't* at 106.15 where the other texts read *wasn't.* On the whole, however, although there do exist these one or two anomalies, not enough positive evidence appears to suggest that EIM was set from a typescript carbon of one behind the Bacheller proof instead of from the proof itself, or from an earlier stage of the proof. It would seem, then, to have no special authority different from the newspapers.

The Special Collections of the Columbia University Libraries also houses two black carbon copies of a typescript that Cora had made up in preparation for *Last Words* but did not use. One consists of five pages of wove foolscap 329 × 202 mm., watermarked *Indian & Colonial,* the pages numbered within close parentheses in the upper left corner. Cora was not herself the typist although someone with an uncertain spelling and no special expertise made up the copy.

However, Cora interlined the word *Sale* after *Auction* in the typed title "An Auction of Real Estate in Texas U.S.A." and added —*By*— | *Stephen Crane.* Her minuscule indicator does not appear in the lower left corner of the first page. The versos contain cumulative word counts in pencil up to 1,535 on fol. 5^v. On this same page Cora wrote, vertically, *A Sale of Real Estate | in Texas U.S.A. | for a book England | 1550 words.* The copy for this typescript was evidently the *State Journal* proof now preserved at Columbia on the evidence of the omission of the comma after *pain* at 105.33 and the reading in TMs *The* for the proof uncorrected *The'* but corrected *Th'*. Only the authority of the variant title can come in question, then, and in this matter one can only guess that just as EIM had found the proof title unacceptable for English readers, so Cora recognized that "A Freight Car Incident" would have little meaning and changed it with *Last Words* and English publication in view. On fol. 5^v the second carbon (on the same paper) has the same notation as the first except for *for a book U.S.* Cora's ink corrections differ slightly in these two copies.

The copy-text is N^1(p), proof for the *Nebraska State Journal*.

No. 25. A PROLOGUE

Printed in the *Roycroft Quarterly*, May, 1896, page 38, and reprinted without variation in the *Philistine*, III (July, 1896), 39.

No. 26. A YELLOW UNDER-SIZED DOG

So far as observed, only three newspapers picked up this sketch, which was syndicated by S. S. McClure Co. and published on Sunday, August 16, 1896.

N^1: *Denver Republican*, August 16, 1896, page 18, headlined 'YELLOW UNDERSIZED DOG || But He Gives Warnings of Coming | Dynamite Blasts. | BY STEPHEN CRANE.'

N^2: *Boston Globe*, August 16, supplement, page 2, headlined 'ONLY A YELLOW DOG. || He Keeps Tabs on Dynamite and Gives Warning | of Coming Blasts. || By STEPHEN CRANE. ||'. At the end is noted '(Copyright, 1896, by the S. S. McClure Co.)'.

N^3: *Pittsburgh Leader*, August 16, page 21, headlined 'A YELLOW UNDER-SIZED DOG. || But He Keeps Tab on the Dynamite | and Gives Warning of a Coming Blast. || BY STEPHEN CRANE. | (Copyrighted, 1896, by S. S. McClure Co.)'.

The copy-text is N[1], the *Denver Republican*, which in general seems closest to what may be recognized as Crane's accidentals, but emended as necessary from the evidence of joint N[2-3]. On a few occasions the agreement of N[2-3] in accidentals against N[1] has been ignored when in a manner uncharacteristic of Crane they added a comma between the two clauses of a compound sentence separated by *and*. It is possible that the McClure proof punctuated as do N[2-3]; on the other hand, it is also possible that these agreements come only from independent housestyling. The Historical Collation records each case of N[2-3] disagreement in accidentals against the copy-text when the information is not noted in the emendations record. In two places where N[2] has been cut, the single disagreement of N[3] has been added. N[3] ran an illustration of the dog captioned *Giving the Alarm*.

In a post-1896 list Crane noted this under "Syndicate" pieces as "Dog that does blasting," and in another list as "A Knowing Canine."

No. 27. A DETAIL

The tiny vignette was first syndicated by Bacheller on Sunday, August 30, 1896. It has been observed in the following newspapers:

N[1]: *Chicago Daily News*, August 31, 1896, page 8, signed, headed 'A DETAIL. || [Copyright, 1896, by the Bacheller Syndicate.]'.

N[2]: *Buffalo Evening News*, August 30, page 9, headed '[within a frame of type-orn.] A DETAIL | [within a similar attached frame] BY STEPHEN CRANE.'

N[3]: *Nebraska State Journal*, August 30, page 10, headed 'A DETAIL. || (By Stephen Crane.)'. At the end is the notation '(Copyright, 1896.)'.

N[4]: *Galveston Daily News*, August 30, page 18, headed 'A DETAIL || BY STEPHEN CRANE. | For The News—Copyright.' In the identical typesetting this was also printed in the *Dallas Morning News*, August 30, page 16.

All newspapers except N[1] ran an illustration captioned *The Old Lady Dictated Her Address*.

Once the syndicated period was over, Bacheller printed the sketch in his *Pocket Magazine*, II (November, 1896), 145–148, without illustration and with the notice *Copyright, 1896, by the Bacheller Syndicate*. Crane thereupon reprinted the piece to fill out the Heinemann edition of *The Open Boat* (1898), pages 299–301. It was subsequently picked up and reprinted in *Best Things from American Literature* (1899), pages 415–416, published by the *Christian Herald*, and finally in the *Academy*, LVIII (June 9, 1900), 491, where it was prefaced by an obituary notice.

An unrecorded manuscript of an early draft is privately owned by Comdr. Melvin H. Schoberlin, USN (Ret.), to whose courtesy in granting permission to reprint this text for the first time the editor is especially obliged. This consists of seven leaves, numbered at top center, of ruled notebook paper 129 × 218 mm., the rules 12 mm. apart, written in pencil on one side of the paper. It would seem to represent the earliest form of the text and thus has a peculiar interest as illustrating the reworking that Crane gave his manuscripts.

Insufficient evidence appears in the brief sketch to demonstrate the precise textual transmission. It is clear that Crane rewrote the Schoberlin draft and sold the final manuscript to Bacheller. However, one cannot determine whether Bacheller had a typescript made from this manuscript which was used as copy for the syndicated newspaper proof (N) as well as the *Pocket Magazine* (PM), or whether, as more likely, the manuscript itself was used by both printers. More important, the derivation of *The Open Boat* (E1) text is also in doubt, whether it was set from Crane's manuscript returned by Bacheller, or from proofs or a clipping from PM or from some newspaper. Neither N nor PM has any substantive variant between them to give a clue as to the E1 copy, and the few substantive variants of E1 appear to be editorial or compositorial. Even the accidentals are of little or no assistance. It is true that PM, $N, and E1 agree at 112.6 in *time. Then* versus MS *time; then.* But whether in such an agreement (and in various similar but more ambiguous examples, since subject to independent styling) E1 independently reproduced the variants of the lost final manuscript that differed from the draft or else simply followed the readings of N or of PM is not to be determined. The paragraphing, also, is of little assistance. The consistent E1 styling of dialogue makes its agreement with the generally nonstyled MS at 112.7 of no account. Moreover, the agreement of all three prints in no paragraph at 111.27 versus the MS paragraph presents no evidence, for again the lost final manuscript may not have paragraphed at this point; and indeed the MS indentation of *Frequently* may just possibly be no paragraph but instead enforced by the rounding of the corner of the paper in the last line of the page.

Under these circumstances only opinion can rule, and the present editor has opted for the hypothesis that E1 was more likely to have been set from printed copy—probably from PM—than from a returned manuscript or from a carbon of some hypothetical typescript whether made by Crane or by Bacheller. If so, common agreement against MS in the half dozen or so accidentals variants that are in question cannot be demonstrated to derive from the superior authority of the printer's-copy manuscript; hence the accidentals of the draft MS have been used to emend the PM copy-text in the direction of what authority we have. The *Pocket Magazine* is unlikely to stand at a greater distance than the reconstructed N proofs from the lost manuscript and may by a shade seem to reproduce Crane's accidentals with greater faithfulness, the more particularly since the N proofs are not to be recovered with complete accuracy. E1 is disqualified as copy-text because of its uncertain and probably derived origin.

Best Things from American Literature and the *Academy* are both derived texts of no authority. *Best Things* appears to take its copy from a newspaper, not from PM, but the evidence suggests that the newspaper was some other than the observed four examples, although in some respects *Best Things* is so close to the *Buffalo News* (which was the copy for its reprint of *A Tale of Mere Chance*) that if it were not for the failure of BT to follow the variant N^2 paragraphing one could feel relatively confident of its source. On the other hand, the substantive agreements demonstrate that the English *Academy* text was a reprint of *The Open Boat*.

"A Detail" is edited here for the first time from the *Pocket Magazine* version, assisted by the evidence from the newspaper syndication and particularly from the early MS, both of which have not been previously known. In Crane's inventory list of about July, 1897, the story is numbered 24 and credited to the *Pocket Magazine*.

No. 28. DIAMONDS AND DIAMONDS

The period from late 1896 to early 1897 may perhaps be assigned to "Diamonds and Diamonds" on the fragile evidence of the appearance of its central character Jimmie the Mole in "Yen-Hock Bill and His Sweetheart" printed in the *New York Journal* on November 29, 1896. It is known only in a typescript preserved in the University of Virginia–Barrett Collection and was not made available until Robert Stallman printed it in the *Bulletin of the New York Public Library*, LX (October, 1956), 482–486. The typescript is a carbon copy of five leaves of text, numbered between spaced parentheses in the upper right corners, the first leaf wove foolscap 329 × 202 mm., watermarked *Indian & Colonial*, and the remaining four laid foolscap 330 × 203 mm., watermarked *Britannia Pure Linen* with a helmeted head between the lines. To this text is prefixed a typed title on the Britannia laid paper, a blue ribbon copy, reading 'DIAMONDS AND DIAMONDS. | BY | Stephen Crane.', which repeats the title on the first page of text *'Diamonds and Diamonds.* | --By-- | *Stephen Crane.'* The typing does not seem to be by Cora although apparently performed on the Crane typewriter. However, Cora made corrections by hand in black ink and on the verso of the last page she wrote *to sell serially* | *& copy for* | *book, if think* | *best.* This typescript was sent to Reynolds for the American edition of *Last Words*, but the story never appeared in print in England or in the United States so far as is known. The copy-text is the Barrett TMs, which was probably made up direct from Crane's holograph manuscript and, apparently, with some faithfulness to the copy.

No. 29. THE AUCTION

The only publication of "The Auction" was among the sketches that filled out Heinemann's London edition of *The Open Boat* (1898), in the section called "Midnight Sketches," pages 273–277. It appears in Crane's inventory list of about July, 1897, at Columbia, as No. 8, with the note "Ms with me". The book text could well have been set from this manuscript.

No. 30. A MAN BY THE NAME OF MUD

Since its title is not present in the inventory list of about July 1897, preserved in the Columbia University Libraries, "A Man by the Name of Mud" would appear to be later than "The Wise Men" and "The Five White Mice," which appear in the list and are to be dated in 1896 with a revision in late 1897. Presumably if it had been available at the time the English edition of *The Open Boat* was being made up for publication in April, 1898, it would have been included. On the other hand, although the story may have paralleled the revision of "The Five White Mice," Crane may not have been satisfied with it and withheld it, for no record exists of its being offered for sale and the first appearance in print was in *Last Words* (1902), pages 258–262.

The University of Virginia–Barrett Collection holds a black carbon typescript of four leaves of cheap wove unwatermarked paper 264 × 208 mm., the rules 9 mm. apart, typed by Cora Crane, who added *By Stephen Crane* in black ink under the title and on the back of the fourth page, in pencil, *Book* | *1000 words.* She also placed in the lower left corner a minuscule *l* or *e*. A large blue-crayon 18 is next to the title. Cora went over this typescript in black ink and later in pencil with considerable care and evidently with reference back to Crane's manuscript. The Barrett carbon was sent to Paul Reynolds for the American edition of *Last Words* and possible serialization and was listed by him on October 23, 1900. The mate of this TMs, wanting a few of the corrections in the Barrett example, but possibly with a few not written there, was the printer's copy for *Last Words*. The Barrett TMs is one step closer to the lost manuscript than *Last Words* and hence becomes, for the first time, the copy-text for an edition of this story.

No. 31. A SELF-MADE MAN

An interesting textual situation holds for "A Self-Made Man." The first publication was in the English *Cornhill Magazine*, n.s., VI (March, 1899), 324–329, followed by the collection *Last Words* (1902), pages 273–281. The University of Virginia–Barrett Collection preserves a blue ribbon-copy typescript consisting of eight pages, numbered within spaced parentheses, typed on the Crane typewriter, laid paper 259 × 202 mm., the chainlines 26–27 mm. apart, watermarked *Brookleigh Fine*. Cumulative word counts appear on each verso. On the back of the eighth page Cora wrote *A Self-made Man* | 2000 *words*. | *Don't know if ever sold* | *serially in U.S. No record.* | *to be used in book* | *of short stories*. At the end of the story, on page 8 recto, some hand, probably not Cora's, has signed the story *Stephen Crane* in ink and added below (*Copy*). This typescript comes from the lot sent Reynolds in New York when Cora was putting together copy for the American edition of *Last Words*, with possible serialization of pieces unpublished in the United States. A few corrections are made in this typescript with the fine pen used to sign it, and others in a different hand, probably Cora's. The typescript exhibits to the full the atrocious spelling of which Cora was capable when she was not copying printed matter and it also has her characteristic of breaking words with a hyphen at the end of the line, followed by a hyphen and the continuation on the next line. Also, it exhibits her difficulty in completing words at the end of a line without a marginal release. It would seem reasonably clear that she was the typist.

The readings and the frequent closeness of the accidentals indicate that the *Cornhill* and *Last Words* texts were set from the same lost typescript and its carbon (E1 could not have derived from a clipping of C). As for TMs, although there are exceptions Cora usually made up the typescripts for the English and American editions of *Last Words* from clippings or proofs, but this Barrett typescript is not related to E1 and it is not a copy of the *Cornhill* printing, in part because of some variant readings not to be imputed merely to typescript corruption but most obviously because the last four paragraphs (129.11–29) present in both C and E1 are wanting in this TMs. It would seem to be a reasonable hypothesis that in this case the carbon of the original typescript sent to *Cornhill* was preserved and used for *Last Words* printer's copy. Hence a different typescript had to be sent to Reynolds for the proposed *Last Words* collection by Stokes and then by Coates. Since this other typescript—the Barrett TMs—clearly does not derive from the carbon used for *Last Words,* it must go back for its copy to some anterior document. We may take it that this document was the original manuscript. The absence of the later ending (presumably added in the pair of typescripts for publication) agrees with this hypothesis (unless we are to conjecture a fortuitously lost final leaf). Also in agreement is Cora's unusually bad spelling, characteristic of her typing from manuscript, added to Crane's own spelling idiosyncrasies. Against this hypothesis is the curious appearance of the strange hand that signed the piece, as if the writer had been the typist and had been copying some other document than a manuscript.

It could be argued, also, that certain links between this TMs and the details of the texts of C and of E1 might be more readily explained on the theory that all three documents are linear and do not radiate in two lines from manuscript. What might be called a 'bibliographical link' occurs at 128.1. The typist elsewhere used a single hyphen for a dash that a contemporary printer would normally set as a one-em dash. A longer dash, which a printer would set as a two-em dash, appears at the end of a broken-off speech in line 128.34; and in line 128.1 three hyphens—clearly intended for a long dash—come between the second *we'll* and the parenthetical narrative description until the quoted speech resumes after *side* with a typed hyphen-dash and *"we'll put the screws on you."* Although E1 makes this long dash at 128.1 a normal one-em to correspond to the other dashes in the story, C observes the distinction as in TMs and sets a two-em dash. Possibly this small detail could derive from two independent typescripts made from a manuscript, but the observance of this distinction would be easier to explain as coming from a typescript copying another. Although both C and E1—largely because of the similarity of their independent styling, it would seem—agree in punctuation a number of times against TMs, yet many TMs punctuation traits appear either in C or in E1 to indicate that in the accidentals the typescript and its carbon behind C and E1 must have been very close indeed in its characteristics to the Barrett TMs. In substantives there is the mistake thrice repeated in C,E1 of *sage bush* (126.1; 129.3,15), in which TMs concurs at 126.1 but correctly reads *sage brush* at 129.3. If TMs were to derive from a manuscript, that error must have been present in the holograph at 126.1. Various other small links appear. The ungrammatical *out-laying* in TMs at 126.1 is repeated in E1 although corrected in C. Both TMs and C join in *fer* at 125.18 (E1 sophisticates to *for*) although four words later and thereafter all texts agree in *fur*. Then there is the notation in a strange hand that TMs is a copy—if that is the meaning. If Cora were herself not the typist of TMs, but some other person, that typist could not have derived all the misspellings, some of them familiar as Cora's common mistakes, from the manuscript, whereas a faithful copy of a Cora typescript would have produced them. On the other hand, the notation that TMs is a copy was not necessarily made by the typist, and it is easier to account for the TMs peculiarities by the hypothesis that Cora herself made up the document.

Nonetheless, these difficulties—and they are real ones—are less serious than the textual problems that would be encountered in conjecturing that Cora had typed up a trial typescript which became the basis for the final copies of the typescript sent to C and to E1 and was in turn used to make up the new Barrett TMs. Moreover, except for the ending, the texts of C and of E1 show no signs of anything that could be called Crane's revision, as distinguished from correction,[28] so that the whole reason for a trial vanishes if it were made up only to secure a preliminary copy for Crane to work over.

We are faced, then, with a paradox. Almost beyond question the Barrett TMs must be a copy made directly from Crane's manuscript, and by Cora. Ordinarily one would assume that, like other of the Barrett typescripts, it had been typed up specifically for Reynolds

---

[28] C and E1 join, probably from their common copy, in supplying the article *a* missing in error in TMs at 127.23,27 and in an almost certainly authoritative *only* at 128.15 omitted in TMs. They are probably correct in *'im* for TMs *him* (128.33), in *defeat* for TMs *defeats* (127.8), and in *forwarded* for TMs *have forwarded* (125.33), a mistake probably by contamination from *have as yet received* in 125.32, or possibly by anticipation of *have sold* in 125.35. They must be right in *large bales* at 127.6 for TMs *larger valves*, which could only come from handwriting misreading (or mishearing from dictation). For the rest, they agree only in what seems to be the error *railings* for TMs *railing* (125.22) and in *bush* for TMs *brush* (129.3). Correction there is, therefore, but no revision except for the ending.

and the American edition of *Last Words*, a clipping of the *Cornhill* apparently being unavailable as copy or—less likely—its publication forgotten by her.[29] In some respects there is no difficulty in the parallel hypothesis that the typescript for *Cornhill* and for *Last Words* had been made earlier from this manuscript but expanded by the new ending at some point after the manuscript had been written.[30] Yet there is serious textual evidence against this theory of transmission by radiation of C and Eı on the one hand and of the Barrett TMs on the other from the holograph. The high incidence of error in TMs as against the relatively few errors in the copy for joint C,Eı (not all of these corrections of TMs mistakes being possible as separate editorial operations) is difficult to explain if Cora—as she almost certainly would have been—was the typist for both documents. The numerous small points of punctuation agreement, and agreement occasionally in unusual hyphenation, go well beyond what would be anticipated from two independent copies of the manuscript, and to these must be added the extremely significant bibliographical link in the transmission of the unique three-hyphen dash as found in TMs and in C. The accuracy of copying necessary to secure the agreement in two documents of the first *fer* for *fur* (if indeed this was a manuscript reading) is unusual. The case of *sage bush* is interesting. One will recall that this appears first in TMs as *sage bush* and then once more as *sage brush*. But C and Eı read *sage bush* both times, and *sage bush* again in the added ending missing from TMs. It is difficult to believe that Crane ever wrote *sage bush* here and that the typescript behind C and Eı ever copied it from his manuscript (see the Textual Note).

The textual idiosyncrasies present in TMs on the one hand, repeated in C and Eı on the other, do not encourage a hypothesis for the radiation of their texts from the manuscript. Radiation from a trial typescript would satisfy the evidence, but too many difficulties attach to this hypothesis for it to be seriously entertained. In the first place, as has been indicated in footnote 28 above, Crane never used this trial as a basis for a revision of the typescript behind C and Eı. In the second place, if the Barrett TMs were a fresh copy of this

[29] Cora's correspondence with Pinker and with Reynolds after Crane's death indicates very clearly that she had little idea where many of Crane's magazine pieces had been published, or even if they had been published except for the rough lists of titles that Crane had kept as casual records. In this case, however, she had received notice of payment on April 20, 1899, from Pinker (Columbia).

[30] The ending could not have been added to the original manuscript else it would have appeared in the Barrett TMs. It was probably written on a separate piece of paper and, not being attached to the manuscript, got itself mislaid.

lost trial made up to supply Reynolds with a third and perhaps fourth typed copy,[31] no reason would apparently hold why the trial itself could not have been sent to Reynolds instead. Finally, the extraordinary number of errors present in the TMs suggest not only an example of Cora's early typing but also her typing from manuscript, not at a later date in 1900–1901 making a faithful copy of a most imperfect trial.

Under these conditions only one hypothesis remains. In short, the Barrett TMs sent to Reynolds must have been the trial copy itself from which the typescript for C and E1 had derived with its revised ending.[32] The straight-line derivation of the copy for C and E1 from the Barrett TMs not only satisfies the evidence for textual transmission but also the derivation of the TMs from manuscript and the external reasons why the trial itself came into Reynolds' hands. The closeness of detail between C, E1, and TMs is explained by this direct derivation. In this connection the anomaly of *sage bush* becomes clearer. It would seem that *sage bush* at 126.1 was a typing error that was got right at 129.3. On the evidence, the typescript for C,E1 repeated the error from TMs on its first appearance at this point. We can only guess whether having retyped it once as *sage bush* Cora continued the error in the new typescript at 129.3 and, from manuscript, *sage brush* at 129.15, or whether in the retyping the error fixed itself in her mind throughout; or whether indeed the conformity with 126.1 was the independent work of the editors of C and of E1. (Sage brush does not grow in England.) No other explanation can relieve Crane of writing in its context the almost impossible term *bush*, whereas Cora would scarcely know of the distinction.

To the question of who signed *Stephen Crane* and added (*Copy*) at the end of the trial, and probably made at least one correction in the body of the typescript, no firm answer can be given that would be at all satisfactory, and guesses are idle in view of the lack of all evidence. (Perhaps the word *Copy* is no more than a suggestion.) On the other hand, some reasonable explanation can be provided for the presence of an apparently unsigned trial typescript. The Cranes did not acquire a typewriter until about January, 1899. This typescript, then, would represent one of Cora's first attempts, and one

[31] The use of a copy for *Cornhill* prevented the usual distribution of a ribbon and carbon, one to Digby, Long and the other to Reynolds.

[32] The new ending would have been written on a separate piece of paper, as suggested, and the C,E1 typescript would have copied it from this manuscript. We must suppose that the separate manuscript had been lost or else that Cora forgot about it since she did not append it to the trial typescript mailed to Reynolds.

must say that it looks it, as a glance at the List of Emendations will confirm. Especially noticeable are the frequent omission of letters and the numerous transpositions, unusual even for Cora and betraying the inexperienced typist, as well as the numerous misspacings. When Crane wrote a new ending to the story it might well have been apparent that the necessary corrections beyond those already inserted would make the typescript unsuitable for submission to magazines and that a new one needed to be made up. On the evidence of *Cornhill* and of *Last Words* such a second typescript was produced on a more careful basis than this trial, one that incorporated a handful of necessary corrections to the substantives as well as the expanded conclusion. Whether an extra carbon of this was ever sent to Reynolds for serial sale in the United States, as one would expect, we have no information, or whether it was he who ordered a copy made of the Barrett TMs. If so, he failed to place it.

The reconstruction of the second typescript from the evidence of C and E1 is simple for the substantives but almost impossible for the accidentals. In these latter, agreement between magazine and book seems usually not to reproduce the typescript so much as the independent conventional English styling of the two editors or compositors. The punctuation is made noticeably heavier in a way that is often contrary to Crane's usual characteristics. The Barrett TMs preserves much of his light punctuation but is sometimes heavier than the manuscripts of this period illustrate. However, C and E1 join twenty-two times in adding commas not present in TMs but they subtract only three (six more removals are of obvious TMs errors). The spelling is anglicized, of course. Four hyphens are removed but three added. No evidence exists that can be used to discriminate what differences in the accidentals Crane might have made if and when he read over TMs, correcting it for the second typing. He does not seem to have troubled himself with the accidentals.

Under these circumstances it is not safe to assume that any single accidental in the prints is authoritative in origin or to attempt to utilize the details of the texture of C,E1 agreement except to correct the deficiencies of TMs. The copy-text, of course, must be the Barrett TMs—the first time the work has so been edited—since this TMs is the sole surviving document that appears to have a direct link with the lost manuscript. It has been emended from C and E1 only in respect to substantive corrections that are necessary even if not positively authoritative, and in the accidentals purely on the basis of the conservative correction of real errors. For the ending, *Last Words* is taken as the copy-text. Only three punctuation variants (no comma after *articles* at 129.22; the hyphenation of E1 *sage bush* [129.15]; and the use of double for E1 single quotes [129.27–29]) distinguishes the *Cornhill* text in this area.

One interesting common error has been emended. In all three documents the date of Jones's letter in line 125.29 is given as *May 19*. But Miss Gillian Kyles points out to me that since the bank draft is three times mentioned as sent on *June 25*, this May date must be wrong, for on such an urgent matter Jones would not have waited almost thirteen months. It seems clear that Crane intended about three weeks to intervene between the draft and the letter, but he moved the letter date back a month to May instead of forward a month to July.

Only two references in correspondence are preserved to this story. On April 20, 1899, Pinker wrote to Cora, "Messrs Morrisons & Nightingale have received from me £19–16–10. This represents the amounts received from the *Cornhill* for 'A Self-Made Man' and from *Black & White* for 'The Clan of No Name.'" Since it is known that the price for "The Clan of No-Name" was fifteen guineas, this would make the price of "A Self-Made Man" in the neighborhood of six to seven guineas, depending upon what extras Pinker had deducted in expenses in addition to his 10 percent. If, for example, he deducted an even pound in addition to his commission, the figure would be seven guineas precisely. In the second reference, Reynolds wrote Cora on October 23, 1900, giving "A Self-Made Man" in the list of sixteen stories he had on hand for *Last Words*.

No. 32. AT THE PIT DOOR

Although this sketch was published posthumously in the *Philistine*, XI (September, 1900), 97–104, the date would have permitted Crane to have sent "At the Pit Door" to Hubbard before his death. At least, Cora did not know of the sale, for on October 17, 1900, she wrote to Hubbard: "Will you kindly tell me from whom your magazine 'The Philistine,' got the little sketch signed Stephen Crane? Of course all these things belong to my late husbands estate until all obligations are settled and then to myself." Nevertheless, the date of composition would still be uncertain since placement in the *Philistine* might represent earlier work finally sent to an unremunerative source. All that can be said is that the odds favor composition at some time following the collection made for the Heinemann edition of *The Open Boat*, published in April, 1898.

Two references in Cora's correspondence might be to "At the Pit Door," although the details do not wholly fit. In an undated letter from Milborne Grove in early September, 1900, Cora sent to her agent Perris four short pieces but warned him that whereas the other three could be sold in both the United States and England, " 'The Crowds from N.Y. Theatres' to be sold only in England." One would be tempted to think this a careless mistake in setting the sketch in New York instead of London were it not for another letter to Perris, this one dated September 13, 1900, in which among various matters she approves of the title "After the Theatre" he has given to a sketch. Since the reference must be to the same theater sketch she sent him, Perris' proposed title does not seem to fit "At the Pit Door"; thus the references may be to some unpublished and unpreserved short piece. Finally, in Crane's comprehensive list, "The Crowds from New York Theatres" is given as 2,075 words, whereas "At the Pit Door" is approximately 1,490 (first letter at Yale, second letter and list at Columbia).

TALES OF THE WYOMING VALLEY, NOS. 33–35

What is known of the composition and publishing history of the three Wyoming Valley Tales "The Battle of Forty Fort," "The Surrender of Forty Fort," and " 'Ol' Bennet' and the Indians," is best considered as a whole, not in connection with the textual analysis of the different stories. The major reason is, in part, that their history is closely associated, but also that the individual titles are never referred to in the correspondence and Cora's identification of them by numbers is itself confused. The specific story that is in question, therefore, can be something of a conjectural matter.

So far as the preserved records go, the history begins when on September 30, 1899, Crane wrote Pinker: "Here is the first story of a series which will deal with the struggles of the settlers in the Wyoming Valley (Pennsylvania) in 1776–79 against the Tories and Indians. Perhaps you had better hold it until I finish two or three more and then deal with some wealthy persons for the purchase of the lot, eh? For the U.S., they exactly fit Harper's Weekly, Phila Sat Evening Post, Youth's Companion (they pay *big*, once offered me £22 per 1000) or Lippincott's" (*Letters*, pp. 232–233). This story was, judging from the chronology of events in the tales, "The Battle of Forty Fort." The fact that " 'Ol' Bennet' " was published first has no significance for the order of composition, as *Cassell's* probably bought them both at the same time and without the intervening "Surrender" the chronology is difficult to establish. Cora herself at one time correctly labeled " 'Ol' Bennet' " No. 3. when she marked the *Cassell's* proof to send to Reynolds for *Last Words* copy but deleted her marking. The three stories were complete and in Pinker's hands before October 21, when Cora wrote to him, "In looking over Mr. Crane's accounts with you, I find that you now have 'Moonlight on the Snow' and three 'Wyoming Stories' which mean, when sold, I judge £115" (*Letters,* p. 235). A few days later, conjecturally on October 26, she queried Pinker, "Have you tried the American 'Youth Companion' for the Early Settlers stories? I think they might like them" (*Letters,* p. 238), and again on conjectured November 7, "Mr. Crane says: to offer 'The Wyoming Stories'—if the Youth's Companion don't want them, to *Harper's* young people" (*Letters,* p. 241). On January 9, 1900, Pinker reported "three 'Wyoming' tales, making together 6,700 words" in his possession among unsold stories (*Letters,* p. 260). But Pinker made no progress in their sale. From Dover on May 23, 1900, Cora added a desperate postscript in a letter to him: "*Write!* Please, Wyoming Tales should bring big prices. It will be a long time before there are more" (*Letters,* p. 285), and on May 29 from Badenweiler, "I'm sure Mr. Reynolds could sell the Wyoming stories in U.S. Do try him with them" (*Letters,* p. 286). Pinker does not seem to have pushed these stories, for he did not get in touch with Reynolds, and the Reynolds listing of two of them in an inventory letter he sent to Cora on October 23, 1900, with a braced memorandum "ms to sell serially" derived from Perris' initiative after he had taken over Cora's affairs. Reynolds never succeeded in placing these stories in the United States despite their subject matter.

From this point all references are posthumous. Pinker reported to Plant, the solicitor who was in charge of the estate, on June 15, 1900, "I have still to dispose of the British and American serial rights . . . in the three Wyoming Valley Tales" (Columbia). On August 28, 1900, Cora broke finally with Pinker and requested the return to her of all manuscripts (Dartmouth); and in an undated letter from 22 Montague Place she thanked him for the return of the typed copies of stories and for the manuscripts, adding "I have sold the *Wyoming* Stories, the money for them will be paid to the estate" (Dartmouth). Some delay must have ensued between her request and Pinker's answer, for on September 6, 1900, McClure's London office wrote to Pinker, "I am sending you back enclosed the three short stories by Mr. Stephen Crane which Mr. Robert McClure has read and finds unsuitable for any of our channels of publication" (University of Virginia). Although no titles are mentioned, the odds greatly favor these rejected three stories being the Wyoming Tales. However, on September 13 Cora in a business letter to her new agent Perris remarks that the titles he has "given to the 'Wyoming Valley' stor[ies] suit me. . . . I would like all proofs sent to me and I will then return them to you" (Columbia). In the manuscript of "'Ol' Bennet' and the Indians" and the Barrett TMs of "The Battle of Forty Fort" the titles have been added in a strange hand, which may well have been Perris'. It would seem that Perris sold to *Cassell's Magazine* in fairly short order the two stories "'Ol' Bennet'" and "The Battle" which he had received from Cora, had himself titled, and had sent to Reynolds in time for the latter to list them by these titles among his holdings on October 23. Cora's letter of acknowledgment to Pinker and her statement that she had sold the Wyoming stories probably was not sent until late September or early October. Pinker must have been concerned about protecting his own rights and informed Plant of the sale, for on October 8, 1900, Plant wrote him "I have not yet seen Mrs Crane with reference to the sale of the Wyoming Stories but have an appointment with her for this afternoon" (Virginia).

That Pinker had, in fact, returned only the two stories in September seems evident from an undated letter Cora addressed to him from Milborne Grove inquiring about what she believed to be his sale of "Dan Emmonds" and adding a postscript, "Please return me the 'Wyoming' ms" (Schoberlin). This letter does not seem to refer to the previous request, for on November 2, 1900, Cora wrote to Perris a detailed discussion of the status of the Wyoming tales: "I send you *No. 2* of the Wyoming Tales. I think that this is the one, I did not send before. See Cassels they ought to print this one second. And also see if they would be likely to take more of the series if I do them. I have notes as I wrote you. [¶] Have you sent these stories to Reynolds to sell in America? Please let me know. The proof of No. 3 of these stories I think I have corrected & returned to you. [She evidently kept a copy of this: Cs(p) now in the Virginia–Barrett Collection.] But No. 1 has not been sent me. Please tell Cassels to send it to me. I really must have proofs to correct or look over" (Columbia). Cora wrote in the margin, "Reynolds has No. 2", no doubt at a later time. Since *Cassell's* printed "'Ol' Bennet' and the Indians" in December, 1900, and were not to print "The Battle of Forty Fort" until May, 1901, it would seem probable that the No. 3 which Cora had read in proof was "'Ol' Bennet' and the Indians" and the No. 1 she was expecting was "The Battle of Forty Fort," which would mean that the No. 2 she was only then sending Perris was "The Surrender of Forty

Fort" which she had recovered from Pinker but which Perris never sold. This conjecture would seem to be confirmed by the University of Virginia–Barrett TMs of "The Surrender" which originally she had labeled No. 2 but then at a later time deleted and renumbered as 3. The marginal memorandum on her letter may refer to this renumbered "Surrender" story. Oddly, the order in *Last Words* was one that resembled none of her numbers, being "The Surrender," " 'Ol' Bennet'," and "The Battle of Forty Fort."

Crane's source for these tales was *Wyoming; Its History, Stirring Incidents, and Romantic Adventures,* by George Peck, D.D. (New York, 1858). Peck was Crane's maternal grandfather and he was related by marriage to the Bennets who figure largely in these tales. Crane adapted certain of his grandfather's accounts by combining various events and characters.

No. 33. THE BATTLE OF FORTY FORT

In May, 1901, *Cassell's Magazine,* n.s., XXIII, 591–594, published "The Battle of Forty Fort" with an illustrative heading, the subtitle *A Tale of Wyoming Valley,* and a drawing by H. R. Millar captioned "*I Watched the Scene on the River*". In 1902 it was collected in the Wyoming Tales section of *Last Words,* pages 99–109. The failure of *Last Words* (E1) to follow the various plausible variants from *Cassell's* (Cs) shows that *Cassell's* was not its copy but instead that Cs and E1 were set from a typescript and its carbon, a hypothesis made relatively certain by the agreements in certain accidentals such as the use of quotation marks up to the same point for *Indian Butler* and not thereafter.

The typescript and carbon would have been made from the part-holograph, part-dictated original manuscript preserved in the University of Virginia–Barrett Collection on three leaves of cheap wove unwatermarked paper, now laminated, 262 × 204 mm., the rules 9 mm. apart. The title, which corresponds to that in *Cassell's,* is written in pencil in a strange hand (Perris?). The cumulative word count is given on the verso of each page, and occasionally marked in the text, ending on 3^v with centered 2690 and the word *Wyoming* in the right margin. Crane began to write in a violet ink and after completing page 1 he continued over halfway down on page 2 to line 139.21. Starting then with the next paragraph he dictated the rest to Edith Richie, who completed page 2 in a medium hand but on page 3 reverted to her favorite tiny script. She wrote in a blue-black ink.

Crane corrected his own part as he went along but reviewed it later and made three revisions in an ink now turned brown. It is possible that he made one small revision, at 140.16, in Edith Richie's part, but nowhere else. Edith Richie may have read her dictated part aloud to Crane and inserted a few revisions that seem to have been made later, most notably the short sentence at 142.11–12 which was added after the original word count had been written in at the end of the paragraph before it. One word—*elegancies* for *delicacies* (142.17)—seems to be in Cora's hand. This word may have been entered at Crane's suggestion, as is conjectured here, although the possibility is always present that it was a change she made before typing, if she and not Edith Richie were the typist.

Substantive agreement of Cs and E1 against MS reveals the altered readings of the lost typescript on twelve occasions, including one variant at 140.33, a word that had been deleted in MS—but perhaps not before typing. The possibility must be considered that at least some of these readings were ordered by Crane, but if so they cannot be identified and the general run are either inadvertent typist errors or else sophistications, perhaps Cora's. In short, emendation on the hypothesis that any of the typescript variants are authoritative cannot be made with confidence. Hence the text is edited here for the first time from the Barrett manuscript as copy-text but with a few corrections from the prints. The preservation of the manuscript is apparently due to Cora's having sent it to Reynolds in New York for serialization and copy for the American *Last Words* instead of making up a typescript and carbon herself. The manuscript seems to have come to the Barrett Collection as part of the major purchase of the *Last Words* copy typescripts, and in the lower left corner it shows a lower-case letter *r*, which indicates Cora's inventory code.

No. 34. THE SURRENDER OF FORTY FORT

Without having been sold, "The Surrender of Forty Fort" became eventually a part of the Wyoming Tales section of *Last Words* (1902), pages 81–88. Preserved in the University of Virginia–Barrett Collection is a ribbon copy typescript (TMs^a) and a carbon (TMs^b), on five pages of laid foolscap 330 × 203 mm., the chainlines 28–29 mm. apart, watermarked *Britannia Pure Linen*, numbered at top center within spaced parentheses. In TMs^a Cora has underlined the typed title *Wyoming Valley Tales* and added, in black ink, *By Stephen Crane*, under which she then wrote *No. II* marking off this last line with facing arrows. On the verso of the last page she wrote in pencil 'Sell serially | 1750 words'. In the upper left corner of TMs[b] she wrote *B. Serial*, added to the title *By Stephen Crane*; then, later, in pencil, she placed a *III* after the title. The ribbon copy and its carbon are corrected identically in black ink save for a few trifling oversights. These two documents were part of the copy sent to Reynolds for the American edition of *Last Words* and whatever serialization was possible. On the evidence he failed to place the story.

The printer's copy for *Last Words* was another carbon of this typescript, corrected in a similar manner. Since *Last Words* is a derived text, therefore, the copy-text selected is Barrett TMs[a], the closest we can come to the lost manuscript and the first time the story has been edited from this single authoritative source.

No. 35. "OL' BENNET" AND THE INDIANS

Publication first occurred in *Cassell's Magazine*, n.s., XXII (December, 1900), 108–111, for which an illustrative title was drawn by H. R. Millar, ' "OL' BENNET" | and the INDIANS.' being a part of this title and 'A Tale of Wyoming | Valley.' below in type. At the foot of the first page is the notice ** *Copyright, 1900, in the United States of America.* The University of Virginia–Barrett Collection holds a copy of the *Cassell's* galley proofs with no markings except for an ink 'No. 3' to the right of the title, deleted in ink, and a small typo correction in black ink, altered by a mark that Cora often used in proofs. The copyright notice seems to have been a pure formality, for the story never appeared in the United States and its second and last publication was in *Last Words* (1902), pages 88–98, in the section "Wyoming Tales."

Preserved in the Syracuse University Library is the untitled holograph manuscript of four leaves of cheap wove ruled paper 264 × 208 mm., the rules 9 mm. apart. Cumulative word counts in ink to 2,540 appear on the versos. On the recto of page 4 at the foot is the figure 420 in red ink, not to be explained. The inscription is in black ink with alterations in the same ink except for a single pencil correction of a misspelling, perhaps by the same stranger (Perris?) who wrote the title in pencil on the first page in the form as found printed in *Cassell's*.

The Special Collections of the Columbia University Libraries contains among its materials from Brede an uncompleted manuscript in the hand of Edith Richie, also untitled, written in black ink on four pages of the same paper as the Syracuse holograph, the pages numbered in the upper left corners. The inscription stops in mid-sentence at the end of the second line on the fourth page (150.13 Andrew rode the |). Nothing is written on the versos save for the usual inscription of the inventory, 'Wyoming | unfinished'.

The Syracuse University holograph manuscript (MS^1) is of course the prime authority and is made the copy-text for this edition, the first time that the tale has been edited from the manuscript. The fragment of the Edith Richie inscription (MS^2) is without question the start of a copy of the holograph. Its purpose is unknown. One could guess that the first proposal was to send MS^1 out for sale, or for professional typing, and that Edith Richie was asked to make a transcript for Cora's file (the Crane machine perhaps being out of order). It is possible that this scheme was abandoned and that either Cora or Edith did in fact type up a ribbon copy and carbon, although the fact that the manuscript was not preserved among the Brede papers might suggest that it had not been retained by Cora, for some reason. At any event, MS^2 has no independent authority. It follows MS^1 in small stylistic matters changed in the prints, and its single substantive alteration in the course of writing restores the MS^1 reading *a bend* (150.12) for the slip *the bend*.

That a typescript and carbon were made, however, is attested by the evidence of *Cassell's* (Cs) and *Last Words* (E1), which must have been set from these copies. If we except such agreements between Cs and E1 as the correction of Crane's misspellings like *principal* for *principle* (151.20–21) or of his grammar like *lie* for *lay* (152.15), Cs and E1 join in fifteen substantive variants from MS^1. E1 agrees with MS^1 and the *Cassell's* proof (Cs[p]) in the four substantive changes at 148.22, 150.4, 150.37, and 151.34 made between this early proof and the final magazine text, as well as in one Cs(p) spelling at 150.6 and a missing comma after *valley* (149.23) also corrected in the print. But neither the *Cassell's* proof nor a clipping could have been the printer's copy for E1, since E1 does not follow the five substantive variants from MS^1 that were editorially or compositorially made by Cs and found in the proof, nor does it capitalize *Redskins* as did the *Cassell's* version. Thus the fifteen common substantive variants in Cs and E1, but the failure of E1 to agree with what is unique Cs substantive variation, demonstrate that both must radiate from some lost transcript of MS^1 like a typescript and its carbon. If this is so, the fifteen substantives in which Cs and E1 agree against MS^1 must have been made either in the typing or by hand in both copies from a review of the typescript before it was sent off to

Pinker for sale. Some of these variants are simple inadvertent errors that were probably made in the typing, such as the plural *Indians* for MS[1] *Indian* (152.7) or *other* for *others* (153.13). In this category may come, also, the singular *kicking* for MS[1] *kickings* (148.24) and the plural *mountains* for *mountain* (150.33). Since these typescripts would have been manufactured while Crane was alive, the variants need to be scrutinized for possible authorial revisions, but signs of authority are wanting. The nearest, perhaps, is the variant *camp* for MS[1] *encampment* (152.15) or the substitution of neutral *that* for *which* (150.2). No variant, then, offers any positive evidence that it derived from Crane's surveying the typescript, although a few are not impossible as alterations. In this edition all substantive variation from MS[1] has been rejected *en bloc* as more probably errors than authorial revision.

One of the oddities of the textual transmission of this tale is the relatively large number of substantive variants—eleven in all—that are unique with E1. On the evidence of other material in *Last Words* it is clear that either the Digby, Long editor or the compositor, or both, occasionally tried to improve the text by unauthoritative emendation. Such variants as the omission of *all* (150.34) or the substitution of *the* for *a* (153.11) might be compositor's slips. But the change of MS[1], Cs *outright* to *downright* (149.15) and perhaps the misunderstanding that altered *fight* to *flight* (153.2) sound editorial, in which case *ill-used* for *abused* (149.15) in the same line as the change to *downright* is also editorial. On the other hand, the specification at 153.8 of *three Indians* for *some Indians* might be thought to go beyond editorial discretion and could represent an alteration made in the typescript for E1 but not in that for *Cassell's*. If so, the odds would favor Cora's preparing the final carbon copy for E1 after Crane's death, for otherwise the change should ordinarily have been made in the primary typescript as well. In this connection one interesting E1 variant does suggest that the two typescripts were not prepared at the same time for all markings. At 148.18–19 MS[1] read *I cannot tell why they hated him so bitterly*, whereas E1 has the nonsense *paled* for *hated*. Reference to MS[1] shows that *paled* is a quite possible misreading of *hated* in this place since the Crane *p*'s have high ascenders and the *t*'s in this piece are, for the most part, uncrossed. But since E1 could itself have no immediate connection with the manuscript, it seems probable that the typist misread the word and that the correction to *hated* was made in the copy for Cs but overlooked in that for E1. Another variant reading between Cs and E1 is a little more difficult to interpret. MS[1] reads *Well, this slaughter in*

the red glare of the fire on the lonely mountain-side endured until
. . . but both Cs and E1 tinkered with this, *Cassell's* by substituting
went on for *endured* but E1 by rearranging to *Well, this slaughter*
continued in the red glare of the fire. . . . Possibly it was the use of
the verb *endure* that made each English editor reach for his blue
pencil. Otherwise, one has the overcomplicated hypothesis that Cs's
went on was a hand alteration in the typescript not simultaneously
made in the carbon and that when Cora prepared the carbon a year
or so later for E1 she vaguely remembered that some alteration had
been made at this point but did not recall its exact terms. At any
rate, the upshot is that any unique E1 reading presumed to derive
from an alteration in the typescript copy cannot be authoritative
since it would have been posthumously made and from no documentary source. A unique Cs reading must necessarily be the result of
the markings of the *Cassell's* editor, Cora's proofreading, or—what
cannot be shown—an alteration in its typescript copy not made simultaneously in carbon. The readings in which Cs and E1 join against
MS are, with only one or two exceptions of independent styling, unauthoritative alterations made in the course of the typing, although
it is possible that a minimum may represent hand changes of doubtful authority in that typescript. The authority of the holograph manuscript in its substantives, as in its accidentals, is nowhere challenged
by the other documents. The Richie MS[2] has a few unique readings
that appear to be slips in the copying.

The *Cassell's* proof was purchased by Mr. Barrett among the lot of
typescripts and proofs that Cora had sent to Paul Reynolds in New
York as copy for an American edition of *Last Words.* Since the original ribbon typescript and its carbon had been used by *Cassell's* and
Last Words, this proof was mailed to take the place of a freshly typed
transcript.

No. 36. AN ILLUSION IN RED AND WHITE

The earliest reference to "An Illusion in Red and White" occurs in a
letter from Pinker to Cora of January 9, 1900, in which he lists the
story among those in his possession that are unsold (*Letters*, pp. 260–
261). It first appeared on Sunday, May 20, 1900, syndicated through
the *New York World.* Only two examples have been observed. The
first is the *World* (N[1]), which ran the story across the top half of its
Sunday supplement, page 2, with a decorative heading and an illustration captioned *"That's the man I saw up the road," said Jones to*

Freddy. "*Yes, sir; it seems like it must have been him.*" The accompanying advertisement states that it is No. 3 in the *Sunday World's Ten Complete Short Stories by Famous Authors.* From proof sent out by the *World* it was also printed on May 20 by N^2, the *St. Louis Post-Dispatch*, page 6. The title is enclosed in a frame of type-ornaments, Crane is puffed as 'Author of "The Red Badge of Courage" ', and below a wavy rule is the notice 'Copyright, 1900, by the Press Publishing Co—Reproduction Forbidden.' Cora seems to have known of the American sale when in an undated letter (probably in early August, 1900) from Gower Street to Pinker she inquires whether "An Illusion in Red and White" (among other stories) has been sold in Great Britain and adds, "Is there no chance of selling any of these now?" (Dartmouth).

On October 3, 1900, from Milborne Grove, Cora wrote to Pinker, "Please send copies of the following stories to Harpers for them to include in the English edition of 'The Monster.'" On February 23, 1901, Harper's included the story in the English edition of *The Monster and Other Stories*, pages 243–252.

Preserved in the University of Virginia–Barrett Collection is a set of galley proofs headed 'REVISED. || [PUBLISHED BY SPECIAL ARRANGEMENT.] || AN ILLUSION IN RED AND | WHITE. | BY STEPHEN CRANE. || [COPYRIGHT.] ||'. A blue-crayon 16 appears to the right of the title and at the left in Cora's hand is penciled *2000 words*. Below is her code notation, doubtful *ff*. It is certain that Cora sent this proof to Reynolds and that it was numbered for the proposed American edition of *Last Words*. The standing type of this proof (or its plates) was used to print the tale without change, except for the omission of the note 'REVISED.' in the heading, in Tillotson's Lancashire *Bolton Evening News* (N^3) on Saturday, December 28, 1901. This proof, then, is from the Tillotson Syndicate which had been in touch with Cora about Crane's stories. *An Illusion* would have been syndicated in the English provincial newspapers, but such Tillotson records were destroyed after the sale of the Syndicate over thirty years ago to Newspaper Features Limited of London. The Tillotson proof (and the *Bolton Evening News* printing) derive with relative faithfulness from a clipping or proof of the text in the Harper edition of *The Monster*. In what seems to be a Pinker undated inventory (page 25) is listed "£52.10 for all serial rights of 'An Illusion in Red & White' & Amer. ser^1. rights of 'The Dark Brown Dog,' & 6 gs. for Eng. & Col. serial rights of 'A Xmas Dinner won in Battle.' "

The *St. Louis Post-Dispatch* text would have been set from an early proof pulled from the *New York World* typesetting (subsequently revised at 157.25) and is thus derived, without authority, as is the Tillotson's proof. The two substantive texts, therefore, are the *World* and the Harper's *Monster,* which appear to have been set from a typescript and its carbon and are therefore of equal authority for the accidentals. On the whole the *World* seems to follow Crane's usual punctuation system with greater fidelity, although the paragraphing of E2 is to be preferred as not in the newspaper style. The *World,* thus, becomes the copy-text but with such emendations from E2 as appear to represent N^1 editorial or compositorial alterations of the typescript more faithfully reproduced in *The Monster.*

No. 37. MANACLED

The earliest publication of "Manacled" was in England, posthumously, in *Argosy,* LXXI (August, 1900), 364–366. In the United States it was published in *Truth,* XIX (November, 1900), 265–266, with two illustrations by R. G. Vosburgh captioned *"Here Pete—Tom—You've Left Me Chained Up, Damn You!"* and *"They All Got Out But Me—All But Me."* An unrecorded appearance for the discovery of which the editor is indebted to Professor Bernice Slote was in the *Index of Pittsburg Life,* VI (November 3, 1900), 15, a weekly magazine, in which it was advertised as *By the Late Stephen Crane.* Finally, the story was collected in Harper's *The Monster and Other Stories* (1901), pages 235–240. In the University of Virginia–Barrett Collection are preserved the torn-out leaves from the *Argosy,* with Cora's writing in the upper left corner of the first page *1200 words* and her notation QQ (just possibly *oo*) in the lower left corner. A blue-crayon *13* is placed to the right of the title, and above it is a circled pencil *2.* No markings are present in the clipping, which must have been among the batch of copy sent Reynolds for the American edition of *Last Words.*

The texts in *Index of Pittsburg Life* and *The Monster* present no problems since both are mere reprints of the *Argosy.* The closeness of certain of the accidentals, including the use of semicolons, indicates that the *Argosy* and *Truth* versions have a common source, no doubt a typescript and its carbon. But the authority of their substantive variants is less clear. Certain of the *Truth* readings appear to be editorial, such as the tinkering at 160.19–20 that got around an awkward sentence and the repetition of *when,* or the correction of the position of the modifier *only* at 160.6–7, and possibly the sophistication of the plural *crashes* at 160.11 to the singular. Although the image is obscure, the *Truth* reading *plume-like* at 160.26 for *Argosy plum-like* is automatically suspicious as a sophistication, for the gleams from the streetlights would presumably fall on the pavement in round yellow circles. Other readings, like the repeated *off the stage* at 159.27 and 161.18 for the more professional *off stage,* are likely to be editorial. In fact, were it not for the appearance in *Truth* of the passage *He began to blubber. "Damn them! They've left me chained up!" He moved down a passage, taking steps four inches long* which is wanting in *Argosy* and might be thought odd as an editorial addition, not much question of basic authority in *Truth* might be raised. But the passage does not appear to be a cut in *Argosy,* for little sign of editorial work is present in the text of the English magazine. It might have been omitted for space requirements, of course.

Unfortunately we have no means of knowing whether the story had been sold to *Argosy* before Crane's death. The only pertinent reference occurs in a letter of Pinker to Cora on January 9, 1900, in which he lists "Manacled" as among the stories he has that are unsold (*Letters,* pp. 260–261). If Crane had himself reviewed the typescript for *Argosy* before its sale but not the copy for the United States (which one assumes was mailed promptly), it is possible that at least some of the *Argosy* readings represent authorial changes whereas the original readings have been preserved in *Truth.* But, in fact, no such hypothesis is positively required, since the *Truth* editing seems to have been heavy. One way or another, the substantives of *Argosy* seem superior. More important for copy-text purposes, on the whole the texture of the accidentals in *Argosy* despite its English origin gives the impression of a source deriving from Crane with relative fidelity, whereas the *Truth* accidentals seem to have been editorially altered. *Argosy,* therefore, becomes the copy-text, emended on a few occasions when *Truth* seems better to preserve specific Crane characteristics of punctuation and, of course, of American spellings.

Only a few posthumous references to the story are preserved. In an undated letter from Gower Street, probably in August, 1900, Cora asks Pinker whether "Manacled" among other stories has been sold in England and, "Is there no chance of selling any of these now?" On October 3, 1900, Cora requests Pinker to send certain stories to Harper for the English edition of *The Monster,* among these being "Manacled." About this time, in an undated letter, Cora addresses Pinker, "Will you also let me know, if 'The Schrapnel of Their Friends' or 'And if He Wills We Must Die' or if 'Manacled' were ever sold by you here serially and if so to whom" (Dartmouth).

No. 38. THE GHOST

On the night of Thursday, December 28, 1899, members of a Christmas house party at Brede performed "The Ghost" in the Brede Hill School Room. The children of the parish had attended the dress rehearsal on the preceding afternoon, but for the Thursday evening performance invitations were issued.[33] Crane had prepared for the play by asking a number of prominent writers to contribute a few words so that he could print their names on the program as the authors.[34] In Cora's scrapbook at the University of Virginia are preserved several answers. Marriott-Watson wrote five words on separate pieces of paper pasted out of order in his reply, reading "most", "are", "publishers", "fools", "d—d".[35] Joseph Conrad contributed 'This is a jolly cold world'; George Gissing, 'He died of an indignity caught in running after his hat down Piccadilly'; Edwin Pugh, 'A bird in the hand *may* be worth two in the bush, but the birds in the bush don't think so.' H. Rider Haggard sent a note on November 17 saying only 'Good luck to your playing!' and may have enclosed some sentence unless this sentiment was supposed to stand for the contribution. His, as well as the contributions of Henry James, H. G. Wells, and A. E. W. Mason, have not been preserved. Robert Barr on November 18 wrote a letter regretting that he could not attend but enclosing the poem "The Tiresome Ghost of Somberly Hall, Sussex," that seems

[33] A ticket is preserved in Cora Crane's scrapbook at the University of Virginia along with other memorabilia. No admission was charged.

[34] The only preserved letter begging for a contribution seems to be the one of November 15, 1899, to H. B. Marriott-Watson, author of *The Heart of Miranda*: "We of Brede Place are giving a free play to the villagers at Christmas time in the school-house and I have written some awful rubbish which our friends will on that night speak out to the parish. [¶] But to make the thing historic, I have hit upon a plan of making the programmes choice by printing thereon a terrible list of authors of the comedy and to that end I have asked Henry James, Robert Barr, Joseph Conrad, A. E. W. Mason, H. G. Wells, Edwin Pugh, George Gissing, Rider Haggard and yourself to write a mere word—any word 'it,' 'they,' 'you,'— any word and thus identify themselves with this crime. [¶] Would you be so lenient as to give me the word in your hand writing and thus appear in print on the programme with this distinguished rabble. Yours faithfully, Stephen Crane" (*Letters*, p. 243).

[35] His letter of November 18 in the scrapbook reads in part: "Dear Stephen Crane, (I utterly refuse to 'Mister' you) I think I am invited to contribute to a comedy, but I do not quite gather how extensively. Never mind—I am equal to the work, and no doubt you will find the accompanying contribution full of cheer, atmosphere and music. I trust I do not clash with the well-known sentiments and works of Mr Henry James. If so share the glory between us. I wish the play a huge success and shall confidently look forward to heavy and continuous royalties."

to have been recited by Suburbia. It was Crane, obviously, who invented the idea of using the Brede ghost, the gigantic Sir Goddard, as the central theme for the burlesque and sketched out the action and the dialogue. According to H. G. Wells, he and Mason were also involved, but that would be in the revision and amplification stage.

The preserved documents are as follows:

1. The first page of the play written by Crane in his own hand on a leaf of cheap wove ruled paper 260(?) × 208 mm., headed in Cora's hand 'Stephen Crane's ms.' (University of Virginia).

2. Seven pages of revised typescript for all of Act I and the start of Act II, incomplete, the ribbon copy typed on wove unwatermarked foolscap 328 × 204 mm., page 1 unnumbered, pages 2–3, 5, 7 numbered within parentheses in the upper left corner, page 4 numbered at center within parentheses, page 6 heading Act II unnumbered, and page 7 misnumbered 6. This is headed 'Play to be given in Brede School-house on December 28th, 1899.' with a decorative row of typewriter symbols beneath (New York Public Library).

3. The black carbon copy of the first two pages of this typescript, on the same paper (Columbia University).

4. Two pages of manuscript in an unidentified hand written in black ink on the same paper headed 'Buttercup's part' and containing the end of Act I (Columbia University).

5. One page of typescript of Robert Barr's poem entitled "THE TIRESOME GHOST OF SOMBERLY HALL, Sussex" (University of Virginia).

6. One page of manuscript in the same hand as no. 4 and on the same paper headed 'Miranda's part' from the early dialogue of Act II (Columbia University).

7. Four leaves of foolscap ruled in musical staves, the first containing the title 'FINALE CHORUS. | BREDE PLACE. DECEMBER 29 '99'. At the foot, centered, is written 'MR AND MRS M. BARR' and to the left, in a different hand, is the deleted 'MR AND MRS H. G. WELLS.' The same title heads the second leaf except that December 29 is mended to December 28, followed by the piano score, the two verses of the song written in an unidentified hand below a third stave containing the vocal line (New York Public Library).

8. The printed program, four pages, the last blank. The first page reads 'THE GHOST. | Written by | MR. HENRY JAMES, MR. ROBERT BARR, | MR. GEORGE GISSING, MR. RIDER HAGGARD, | MR. JOSEPH CONRAD, MR. H. B. MARRIOTT-|WATSON, MR. H. G. WELLS, MR. EDWIN PUGH, | MR. A. E. W. MASON AND | MR. STEPHEN CRANE. | [short rule] | BREDE SCHOOL HOUSE, | DECEMBER 28TH, 1899. | 7.45 P.M.'

Page 2: 'ACT I. | EMPTY ROOM IN BREDE PLACE. | TIME—1950. | [short rule] | ACT II. | PLACE: SAME AS BEFORE.' Page 3: 'CHAR-ACTERS. | [short rule] | The Ghost ... MR. A. E. W. MASON. | The Care-Taker ... ... MISS BRAY. | Rufus Coleman ... MR. CYRIL FREWER. | Peter Quint Prodmore Moreau   MR. CUNNINGHAM. | [the next three lines braced to the right and left between 'Three Little | Maids from | Rye'] Holly   MRS. MARK BARR | Buttercup   MISS BOWEN. | Mistletoe   MISS RICHIE. | Suburbia ... MISS ETHEL BOWEN. | Miranda ... MISS SYLVIA BOWEN. | Tony Drunn ... MR. FORD RICHIE. | Doctor Moreau ... MR. F. L. BOWEN. | Accompanist ... MRS. H. G. WELLS.' (University of Virginia). This program is pasted on a larger fold of paper. On the verso of this fold facing the title-page is a written list of the characters in Cora's hand with the signatures of A. E. W. Mason, Florence Bray, Mabel Barr, Edith K. Richie, Ford Richie, and Frederick L. Bowen. In this list what is printed as 'Drunn' looks very like Tony Drum, which is the form in the *South Eastern Advertiser* newspaper account. The name *Drum* is especially appropriate for the song this character sings, and it seems likely that the form *Drunn* in the program is a misreading of the handwritten copy provided the printer. This view is confirmed by the fact that the reference is apparently to Edwin Pugh's book *Tony Drum, Cockney Boy.* (Rufus Coleman is taken from Crane's *Active Service*, Doctor Moreau from Wells's *Island of Doctor Moreau*, Peter Quint Prodmore Moreau stems from James's *Turn of the Screw* and Conrad's *Nigger of the Narcissus*, Suburbia comes from Pugh's *Street in Suburbia*, and Miranda from Marriott-Watson's *Heart of Miranda* and Mason's *Miranda of the Balcony*.) Above the title-page of the program Cora wrote 'Mr. Beerbohm Tree asked Mr. A. E. W. Mason if "The Ghost" couldn't follow "Midsummer Nights Dream" at Her Majestys Theatre. 1900. Mason said no.' There are also clippings from the *Sussex Express*, January 5, 1900, in the margin of which Cora wrote 'In the time of Stephen Crane. Brede Place', from the *South Eastern Advertiser* of the same date, as well as brief humorous comments from the *Academy*, January 6, the *Daily Chronicle*, January 8, and the *Brede and Udimore Church Magazine* for January, as well as the *Manchester Guardian*, January 13. Two handwritten requests are pasted in from the *Ladies' Field* asking for information and whether photographs were available.

From the newspaper accounts one can reconstruct the actual performance and relate its parts to the preserved drafts in manuscript and in typescript.

PERFORMANCE	DRAFTS
Act I	Act I
Soliloquy of the disguised Ghost	Soliloquy. ViU MS; NN TMs
Dialogue of Ghost with Dr. Moreau and Peter Moreau	Dialogue of Ghost with Tourist with White Whiskers and wife. Begins in ViU MS (incomplete); NN TMs
Episode of Caretaker, Tourists, Three Maids, to their exit [36]	Episode to exit (*Tourist with son*). NN TMs
Dialogue of Ghost with Suburbia and Miranda, their recitation and dance.	Dialogue of Ghost with Buttercup and her song. NN TMs
	Dialogue of Ghost with Buttercup and Suburbia, their song and recitation. NNC MS of Buttercup's part (partly revised for Miranda)
Act II	Act II
Rufus Coleman awaits Ghost; to him Mistletoe who sings, has duet with Rufus, and exeunt	Trotter awaits Ghost; to him Mistletoe, her song, their exeunt. NN TMs (incomplete)
Tony Drum enters, sings. Dr. Moreau enters, gives imitations; Holly enters and sings; entrance of Peter, dispute with father; exit of Tony with Holly. Chorus of Tourists	Blotter enters, sings. To him Miranda who dances and they exit. NNC MS of Miranda's part
Entrance of Ghost, his narrative, final Chorus [37]	Final Chorus. NN MS

This comparison assists in determining the order of composition of the incomplete documents. The New York Public Library TMs was made up from Crane's University of Virginia MS, of which only the first page is preserved. This manuscript presumably continued and sketched in the whole entertainment in draft form. The NN TMs on page 7 ends with the speech-prefix 'Both'; hence it is more likely that the manuscript is defective at this point than that typing was sus-

[36] The *Express* is explicit that only Suburbia and Miranda remain behind and that the dance and recitation are then presented. The *Advertiser* does not distinguish any exit before the end of the act and places the song "We'll Be There," in which Mistletoe sings the chorus, after the dance and recitation.

[37] Since the program provides for only two acts, the *Express* account that opens Act III with the chorus of tourists must be in error. The act is not mentioned in the *Advertiser*.

pended. The two manuscript parts for Buttercup and Miranda are later versions than that represented by the typescript and not necessarily by Crane, who in general may be credited with the text in the NN TMs. However, from the newspaper accounts it is obvious that the entertainment was further altered before performance in a version now lost.

The texts are presented in this edition first in the New York Public Library revised typescript (emended from the University of Virginia holograph manuscript to restore various of the original accidentals), followed by Buttercup's revised part in the Columbia University manuscript, then the Barr poem recited by Suburbia, the revision represented by the Columbia MS of Miranda's part, and then concluded with the text for the Final Chorus. The music for this Chorus is reproduced in facsimile from the New York Public Library manuscript. For convenience of reading, purely formal matters that would correspond to typography have been normalized silently. Of this text only the Crane holograph page has previously been reprinted. The accounts of the performance from the *Sussex Express* and the *South Eastern Advertiser* are appended to complete the details of the entertainment as it was actually performed.

No. 39. THE MAN FROM DULUTH

In an undated letter from Milborne Grove to her agent Perris, probably to be placed in early September, 1900, after her sale of "The Squire's Madness" on August 28, Cora wrote that she was sending him four short pieces of Crane's and hoped for a £10 advance. Among these was "The Man from Duluth." Perris seems to have acquiesced in what was actually a private sale to him, for on September 13, 1900, Cora wrote to him: "I enclose reciept for your cheque for ten pounds for the English and American serial rights in the story written by my late husband and revised by myself entitled 'The Man from Deluth'. I am very much obliged to you for your courtesy in making me this advance payment." If it were not for the information of this unpublished letter from the Special Collections of the Columbia University Libraries, we should have had no information that this story had been left in something of a draft state at Crane's death and that Cora had had a hand in the present text. On the same date, September 13, Perris on the letterhead of the Literary Agency of London addressed Reynolds in New York: "I send under separate cover two further Stephen Crane fragments: The first—THE MAN FROM DU-

LUTH, 3500 words,—seems to me to be a most capital story. We have bought the serial rights from Mrs Crane but she retains the book rights and will, I suppose, want the stuff copyrighted." On October 23, 1900, the story is in a list of Reynolds' holdings that he sent Cora; and on December 28, 1900, Reynolds wrote to Cora direct, "I enclose draft for 10 pounds 17 shillings. I sold 'The Man from Duluth' for $60.00 and this is the balance due less my commission and some postage charges" (Columbia).

This tale or sketch, however one views it, was first published in the United States in the *Metropolitan Magazine*, XIII (February, 1901), 175–181, where it is stated in the illustrative heading to be *The Last Story of New York Life by the Author of "The Red Badge of Courage," "Secret Service,"* etc. The illustrative title is captioned *"There Was a Rapid Parley. The Man from Duluth Edged Forward."* Three other illustrations appear captioned *"Say, This Is Pretty Slow, Ain't It?", "'Hurrah!' Shouted the Man from Duluth.",* and *"Her Hand Was Held in the Same Claw-like Manner."* Without illustrations the story later appeared in England in *Crampton's Magazine*, XVII (May, 1901), 353–360.

The printer's copy is not altogether certain, but the evidence suggests that each magazine was set independently from the typescript and its carbon that had been made—probably by Perris—from Crane's manuscript. The copy-text is the *Metropolitan Magazine* because of its American styling, but this text is emended from the equal authority of *Crampton's*, which seems to have preserved a handful of purer readings both in the accidentals and the substantives. The Historical Collation provides a complete account of all variants so that both of these substantive texts can be reconstructed in exact detail.

No. 40. THE SQUIRE'S MADNESS

The original untitled draft manuscript of "The Squire's Madness," begun by Stephen but finished by Cora, is preserved in the Special Collections of the Columbia University Libraries. The first six pages are written in blue ink on cheap wove pad paper 265 × 212 mm., the rules 9 mm. apart. The left margins are slightly charred from fire. The remaining three leaves, pages 7–9, are written on unruled laid paper 259 × 212 mm., with horizontal chains 26–27 mm. apart and the watermark *Brookleigh Fine*. The first four pages are in Crane's autograph with corrections and alterations in his own hand. These pages, numbered top center above a semicircle, comprise 187.30–

191.10. Starting on page 5 a strange hand takes over in black ink, numbering the pages within circles. This person, who is taking dictation from Crane, continues on page 6, until the last sentence of the paragraph at 192.8. In the same black ink Crane made two changes in the dictated part and then wrote the next line of dialogue (192.12) as his final act before abandoning the story. From line 192.13, MS page 6, to the end the text is entirely Cora's own composition written in black ink with a small hand and very heavily revised. Through fol. 3ʳ Crane wrote the cumulative word counts to 1,160. When he broke off on page 4 he left the lower third blank but gave what he had written the provisional word count 180 on the verso, without cumulation, as if he intended to continue. Dictated page 5 on its verso adds the word count of 240 to 180 for a total of 420, in Crane's hand, but still no cumulation with the counts for pages 1–3. Thereafter word counts do not appear on the versos when Cora started her work on different paper after completing the lower part of page 6 with the beginning of her own composition.

Crane evidently dictated instructions for the conclusion of the story. In the central panel of folded fol. 6ʳ, Cora wrote in pencil 'Linton || —wife thinks husband mad—makes him think he is mad —he goes with her to a doctor to see if its' true & Dr says wife is mad ||'. Below this, in black ink, Cora wrote 'Story finished by Mrs Stephen Crane called "The Squire's Madness." sold to London Literary agency for £10—both U.S. & B. Serial rights'. In the panel to the left of the initial pencil inscription is written in pencil, in Cora's hand, 'The Squir's Madness || Finished By Mrs Stephen Crane all serial right sold to the London Literary Agency || Aug. 1900 || £10—'. This writing on the verso of the last leaf of the wove pad paper combines with the char in the margins but no char on fols. 7–9 to suggest that Cora filed her leaves apart and used the original six leaves—albeit with the beginning of her own writing at the foot of page 6—as if it were a separate manuscript.

Cora's note on fol. 6ʳ gives August 1900 as the date of sale, but the date can be fixed more precisely from a letter from her to Perris on August 28, 1900, from Gower Street: "I have qualified your form of receipt for the story 'The Squire's Madness,' as I cannot believe you offer only £10—for *all* rights. I need the money, at once, and so if you think that is all you can offer for both commercial and English *serial* rights, I will accept the £10—but I cannot let you have book rights as well. If I had time I am sure Mr. Reynolds who is my agent in U.S. could get more than £10 for the American serial rights alone" (Dartmouth). This seems to be another of Perris' speculations in which he bought for cash and sold for his own profit, not on commission. Reynolds listed the story in the material in his possession on October 23, 1900, but since this was chiefly for the collection of *Last Words* he almost certainly had nothing to do with the sale of the story in the United States. The typescript in Reynolds' possession came from Cora, not from Perris.

The initial publication was in England in *Crampton's Magazine*, XVI (October, 1900), 93–99 (the volume is misnumbered XVII). The title is within a double rule-frame and reads 'THE SQUIRE'S MADNESS | BY STEPHEN CRANE | Author of "The Red Badge of Courage," "Active Service," etc. | A pathetic interest attaches to this, one of the last fragments which fell from | Mr. Crane's pen before his death last July. It was revised and completed by | his widow, to whom we are now indebted for the opportunity of publishing it.' This well-intentioned statement has its moments of weakness, for Crane died in June, not July, and Cora did not revise his first half of the tale.

In the United States the story was syndicated on Sunday, June 2 in some papers and June 7 in others, 1901. The following newspaper versions have been observed:

N[1]: *Washington Post,* June 2, 1901, page 35, headed '[within a double rule-frame] The Squire's Madness | [three leaf type-orns.] | By Stephen Crane, | Author of "The Red Badge of Courage." '.

N[2]: *San Francisco Chronicle,* June 9, 1901, page 26, with a decorative drawn heading 'STEPHEN CRANE'S LAST STORY | [to the left] THE SQUIRE'S | MADNESS.' A staff artist has drawn a large uncaptioned illustration of the wife facing Linton across a table, with a picture of Linton's head with downcast eyes, below, signed 'LANGGUTH'.

N[3]: *Minneapolis Tribune,* June 2, supplement, page 3, with an illustrative heading, a vignette of Oldrestham within a frame to the left and, the whole within a drawn rule-frame, 'The Squire's | Madness | By Stephen Crane | Author of "The Red Badge of Courage," | Etc.,'.

N[4]: *Cincinnati Commercial Tribune,* June 2, page 22, with an illustrative heading 'THE SQUIRE'S MADNESS. || [within a rule frame] By STEPHEN CRANE. | [below frame] A Posthumous Story, By the Au-|thor of "The Red Badge of Cour-|age," "Wounds in the Rain," | "Mollie," Etc. ||'. As a part of the heading are three illustrations captioned *"Jack, What is the Matter?"*, *"Was He Ill?"*, and *"The Front of Dr. Redmond's Door."*

N[5]: *Buffalo Morning Express,* June 9, page 2, headed 'The Squire's Madness. || BY STEPHEN CRANE. | Author of "The Red Badge of Courage," "Active | Service, etc.||'.

N[6]: *New Orleans Times-Democrat,* June 2, part II, page 8, headed 'The Squire's | Madness. || By Stephen Crane, | Author of "The Red Badge of Courage," Etc. || For The Times-Democrat.'.

Preserved in the University of Virginia–Barrett Collection is a blue ribbon typescript on ten leaves of wove ruled foolscap, unwatermarked, 264 × 208 mm., the rules 8.5 mm. apart, with the typed title 'The Squire's Madness. | (By Stephen Crane, finished by Mrs Stephen Crane.)'. In the upper left corner Cora wrote *3230 words* and in the lower left corner what appears to be a lower-case letter *x*. To the right of the title is the blue-crayon number 14. This is one of the group of typescripts and other forms of printer's copy that Cora sent to the United States in preparation for an American edition of *Last Words*.

The final publication came in the English *Last Words* (1902), pages 231–244.

The textual history of the story is complex but can be unraveled with fair certainty. The first point of importance is that the University of Virginia–Barrett ribbon typescript is the original of the lost carbon which was used to set *Last Words*. That the two copies of this same typescript were not brought into exact agreement by hand correction and revision, including a comparison back against the copy from which the typing was made, is evident from the variants between the Barrett TMs (*i.e.*, the omission of *placed . . . cigarette,* at 191.1–2) and *Last Words* (E1) as recorded in the Historical Collation, but the relation of this TMs to the printer's copy for E1 is certain. On the other hand, this preserved typescript is not in the line of the copy—which must have been an earlier typescript and its carbon—from which was set the text of *Crampton's Magazine* (Cr) and the syndicate proof for the American newspapers (N). It would seem, then, that after Crane's death Cora finished the story and typed a ribbon copy and carbon which were sold for £10 to Perris' London Literary Agency which was to control serial rights in both countries. Later, when she was putting together copy for *Last Words*, Cora seems not to have been aware of the *Crampton's* publication (or else it had not yet appeared) and she retyped from manuscript copy a typescript and carbon now represented by the Barrett TMs. The line of Cr and N, thus, radiates independently of the line of TMs and E1, but both lines go back to the identical manuscript copy. No other connection exists between them except for their reference at different times back to this common copy.

It is clear, however, that at least for Cora's part the manuscript from which the two lines of typescripts derive was not the preserved draft but instead a considerably revised fair copy. The scores of important readings in this part in which both Cr-N and TMs-E1 agree with each other against the Columbia MS demonstrate that two separately made typescripts could not so frequently have chosen the same revisions. Whether Cora also made a fair copy of Crane's part is less certain although the general evidence suggests that she did. Fortunately the point is of no concern for the establishment of Crane's text, since this must rest exclusively on the holograph authority and his dictated portion of the manuscript. The hypothesis of fair copy merely explains some of the agreements of the two lines against the manuscript but gives them no authority, of course.

The editing of Cora's conclusion is quite another matter. The preserved manuscript of this section is so much in a draft state as to offer only partial assistance in determining the text of the revised fair copy, the substantives of which can be recovered with greater accuracy from the concurrence of the Cr-N and the TMs-E1 lines. The identification of these revisions in which both lines agree against MS is an important forward step; yet it by no means establishes the text as a whole. Moreover, even when one line agrees with MS against the other, not all such variation exposes error. The evidence is perfectly clear in the Barrett TMs that as she typed, Cora (assuming she was the typist) sometimes revised the copy. For instance, in 195.5 she first typed *in a frightened manner*, which is the reading of MS followed by Cr and N; but then, before continuing, she decided to revise the phrase, continued with *air* after *manner*, and then, by hand, deleted *manner* and interlined *with* above deleted *in*. With this example in mind it is difficult to estimate how many of her departures were designed and how many in error. For instance, at 195.22 she first typed *he said bowing courteously* and ended with a period. But her fair copy seems to have read *he said to Mrs Linton, bowing courteously*. On the evidence of the typescript she continued after the period with *to Mrs Linton,* including its comma, and then drew a line to indicate its proper position. Here we cannot be sure whether she omitted the phrase in error or intentionally and then changed her mind. Somewhat similarly, at 196.1–2 MS and all printed texts read *Linton waved his hand, smiled and said,* but TMs alone reads, as typed, *hand, smiling and said*. From the E1 reading *smiled* it is clear that Cora subsequently altered the word back to copy in that document although not in the Barrett TMs; but whether the *smiling* was an inadvertent error or a designed revision at the moment of typing (which she may have thought to be an error when she reviewed the E1 printer's copy) is scarcely demonstrable. (For another case where her review seems to have altered a quite possible revision back to the reading of copy, see the Textual Note to 193.22.) In addition, Cora departed in TMs from her copy not only in the typing but also in the later review of the copy when some unique readings were inserted. At 196.9, for instance, she crossed out typed *dear* before *sir* although *dear sir* is the reading in MS, Cr, and N. The most prominent example of this post-typing revision is in the addition by hand in TMs of the final phrase MAD AS A HATTER, not present, again, in MS, Cr, or N. In the two above examples Cora would have transferred the same revisions to both copies of the second typescript so that E1 agrees with the revised TMs reading. But she did not always do so. At 188.33, for instance, the perfectly plausible plural *terraces* remains in TMs as typed although E1 and all other texts read the singular *terrace*, and so with TMs *gentlemen* but the others *a gentleman* (190.16). These two examples come from her typing of Crane's manuscript. In her own share one may point out the variant way in which she worked over the possible revision at 193.22, her failure to restore *the* in TMs before *figures* (195.29), and her possible removal in the E1 printer's copy of italics present in TMs at 194.6 and 194.8, as well as the question of *smiling* versus *smiled* at 196.1.

The process that may be observed at work in the Barrett TMs had evidently been preceded by exactly the same sort of double revision in the typing and by hand in the lost typescript behind Cr and N and its carbon. When Cr and N disagree we can sometimes be no wiser whether the departure from MS (or from TMs-E1) in the one is a compositorial error, a typed error not corrected, or else a revised Cora reading entered in one copy but not in the other. Whenever Cr and N agree against the other authorities there can be no doubt that Cora typed this Cr-N reading. Some few of such concurrences are errors, such as the omission of a line from her copy at 193.39, but various others give every sign of being planned revisions as she typed, as for instance, the alteration at 194.14–15 of *He, a weaver of dream-stories, she of that type of woman who*, which became a version that partly reverts to the original of the revised MS-TMs reading in the Cr-N *He was a weaver of dream-stories, she that type who*.

The difficulty of establishing a text in a situation like this is that priority of inscription means little when both lines go back independently at different times to Cora's fair copy and she could treat each typing in a different manner. It is possible to say, of course, that when she added MAD AS A HATTER by hand to TMs, she knew that this was a revision of a previously invariant reading. On the other hand, when in TMs she returns to her copy and thus aborts revisions made in the earlier typescript from which Cr and N derive, no assurance is possible that in typing or correcting TMs she recalled that she had revised copy earlier in such and such a way so that, later, in TMs, one could describe her return to copy as a preferential decision. An example is the cluster of connected revisions in 193.22–23 that were certainly made with conscious intention in the first typescript but appear in their original form in the second. As with Dr. Johnson before her in the revision of his Preface to Shakespeare, Cora having kept no record of the revisions she had made in the typing of the first typescript, or by hand alteration, was ignorant when she followed her manuscript copy in the second typescript that she had earlier preferred a revised reading. Hence chronology is meaningless when both typescripts were manufactured within such a short time, and the fact that the revisions in the preserved TMs are later than those in the lost first typescript gives them no more authority than the revisions in the first that were not followed in the second. When the change was not in error or so indifferent as very likely to be inadvertent, each must be taken as representing her conscious intention to revise her work; and if one is to be observed, the other must be respected as well. In such a situation an editor cannot with any logic retreat behind the concept of the author's 'final intentions' when the chronological order of the versions has no significance for conscious intention.

Thus the present edition essays an eclectic text for Cora's section. The only possible copy-text for Crane's part is his holograph, of course, to which must be added the portion that he dictated and reviewed. But Cora's draft in her share of the preserved manuscript was so thoroughly rewritten in the lost fair copy as to be of little service substantively as a copy-text. As for the accidentals, if she did her own typing of the preserved TMs (as seems probable but not wholly certain), her changes in these—certainly inadvertent—acquire as much authority as the forms in the original manuscript and often greater authority because of the altered context. The Barrett TMs, then, becomes the copy-text for Cora's conclusion, not the Columbia MS.[38] When errors are assumed to be present, this TMs copy-text is emended by reference to MS, to Cr-N agreement, and then to E1, in that order. However, certain of the Cr-N revisions are also introduced

[38] Because there is some slight doubt whether Cora actually was the typist, this choice of copy-text would not have been made if MS had been close enough to the fair copy to enable an editor to utilize its accidentals with any consistency. But it is not. The Barrett TMs has the puzzling feature that in general it is spelled better than Cora's usual work and that it corrects, partly in the typing and partly by hand on review, many of the manuscript errors, although by no means all of them. Whether Cora sought help to correct her fair copy is not to be determined although this would be an interesting point since such an adviser might also have made suggestions about the substantives. It may be remarked, however, that even though it is a rough draft, the MS is in general better spelled than is usual with her.

into the text even though, in the nature of the case, they could not be confirmed in the typing up of the preserved TMs. Some principles for the admission of these readings must be evolved, however, and the present editor has, perhaps arbitrarily, adopted the following criteria. In ordinary cases, and especially in clusters, the Cr-N revisions are admitted. On the other hand, when MS and TMs agree in a reading that is so indifferent as to lead one to suppose the typed variant in Cr-N was inadvertent, the MS-TMs reading has been preferred, and so with Cr-N errors in the typing such as clear-cut unintentional omissions. When MS is not a witness, no norm can be established, in which case—arbitrarily—TMs is preferred. Independent readings from Cr or from N might well represent Cora's separate revision by hand, but no bibliographical tests can be contrived to evaluate these with precision as other than possible compositorial divergences, and hence they have been ignored. Similarly, unique E1 readings could have resulted from independent revision of that copy of TMs although not transferred to the Barrett copy; nevertheless, such readings cannot be separated from compositorial or editorial sophistications when they are quite unique.

The substantives of all the printed documents, as well as those of MS, can be consulted by a critic in the Historical Collation. Any alteration in the accidentals of the TMs copy-text will be recorded in the List of Emendations. However, in order that the choice of TMs as the copy-text should not obscure the evidence for the accidentals of Cora's share of the MS, the Historical Collation also includes a complete record of all accidentals variants in MS not listed among the Emendations. From this list, as well as the separate account of the alterations made in this MS, the reader can reconstruct this document at pleasure.

II. SKETCHES

SULLIVAN COUNTY SKETCHES

No. 41. THE LAST OF THE MOHICANS

Printed in the *New York Tribune,* Sunday, February 21, 1892, page 12, unsigned, headed 'THE LAST OF THE MOHICANS. || HIS ASPECT IN FICTION CONTRADICTED BY HIS | FAME IN FOLKLORE.' The dateline was *Hartwood, Sullivan County, N.Y., Feb. 15.* First attributed to Crane by Robert Stallman in 1957.

No. 42. HUNTING WILD HOGS

Printed in *New York Tribune*, Sunday, February 28, 1892, page 17, unsigned, headlined 'HUNTING WILD HOGS. || IMPORTED GAME IN SULLIVAN COUNTY. || THE ANIMALS ESCAPED FROM A PRIVATE PARK—|ONE OF THEM WOUNDED LEADS ITS PUR-|SUERS A CHASE OF TWO HUNDRED | MILES—A RARE FORM OF SPORT | IN THE UNITED STATES.' The dateline was *Hartwood, Sullivan County, N.Y., Feb. 24.* First attributed to Crane by T. A. Gullason and Robert Stallman, independently, in 1968.

No. 43. THE LAST PANTHER

Printed in the *New York Tribune*, Sunday, April 3, 1892, part ii, page 17, unsigned, headlined 'THE LAST PANTHER. || AN AN-CIENT MEMORY OF SULLIVAN COUNTY. || CONFLICTS WITH OTHERS OF ITS SPECIES THAT | ARE STILL RECALLED IN TRADITION—|THE CREATURE'S CRY AT NIGHT.' The dateline was *Hartwood Park, N.Y., March 26 (Special)*. First attributed to Crane by T. A. Gullason and Robert Stallman, independently, in 1968.

No. 44. NOT MUCH OF A HERO

Printed in the *New York Tribune*, Sunday, May 1, 1892, page 15, unsigned, headlined 'NOT MUCH OF A HERO. || EXAMINING THE RECORD OF "TOM" QUICK, | INDIAN SLAYER. || A NOTORIOUS CHARACTER OF PIONEER TIMES | IN PENNSYLVANIA—HIS MONUMENT DIS-|CREETLY SILENT AS TO HIS VIRTUES.' The dateline was *Milford, Penn., April 4.* T. A. Gullason in 1968 first attributed this article to Crane.

No. 45. SULLIVAN COUNTY BEARS

The sketch appeared unsigned in the *New York Tribune*, Sunday, May 1, 1892, page 16, headlined 'SULLIVAN COUNTY BEARS. || GAME HARD TO CAPTURE—THEIR CUNNING | IN ESCAPING THE HUNTERS.' The dateline was *Hartwood Park, N.Y., April 19.*

First attributed to Crane by T. A. Gullason and Robert Stallman, independently, in 1968.

No. 46. THE WAY IN SULLIVAN COUNTY

Printed in the *New York Tribune,* Sunday, May 8, 1892, page 15, unsigned, headed 'THE WAY IN SULLIVAN COUNTY || A STUDY IN THE EVOLUTION OF THE HUNT-|ING YARN.' The dateline was *Fowlerville, Sullivan County, N.Y., May 4.* First attributed to Crane by T. A. Gullason and Robert Stallman, independently, in 1968.

No. 47. A REMINISCENCE OF INDIAN WAR

Printed in the *New York Tribune,* Sunday, June 26, 1892, page 17, unsigned, headed 'A REMINISCENCE OF INDIAN WAR. || BRANDT'S MURDEROUS VICTORY AT LACKA-|WAXEN FORD.' The dateline was *Lackawaxen, Pike County, Penn., June 10.* In 1968 T. A. Gullason was the first to attribute this article to Crane.

No. 48. FOUR MEN IN A CAVE

In the Special Collections of the Columbia University Libraries are preserved three unnumbered pages of a fragment of an early draft of "Four Men in a Cave." Crane wrote this in pencil on wove buff butcher's paper, 220 × 143 mm. The first leaf is headed by a geometrical doodle. Insofar as the situation can be recovered from this trial that is scarcely more than a series of notes, perhaps, the poker game with the hermit, though outdoors, was to be the central incident: the episode of the cave would seem to be a later development. A diplomatic transcript of this fragment follows:

A long, scrawny, yellow hand reached forth and clutched moss-grown poker-chips. Four [a] men watched it with consternation in their eyes. The proprietor of the yellow hand leaned back against a tree and cackled. He was an [b] infinitely sallow person with a brown check shirt and uncertain whiskers. The rest of him was boots. His laugh was the rattle of pebbles in a tin-box.
—The little man swore tremelously—
—The four [c] men dismally regarded him.—
He was not an excellent player
He was merely the favored of the fates.

A few more chips sat in front of the four men. The little man had ^d one red chip ^e remaining which he looked at as if it were his heart ^f
Steel-blue water was visible through green branches and over the brown of the pine-needles.

a   Four] *preceded by deleted* 'Forth'
b   an] *final* 'n' *inserted*
c   four] 'f' *over* 'l'
d   had] 'h' *over* 'r'
e   chip] *preceded by deleted* 'on'
f   heart] *preceded by deleted start of an* 'h'

The final form was published in the *New York Tribune*, Sunday, July 3, 1892, page 14, unsigned, headed 'FOUR MEN IN A CAVE. || LIKEWISE FOUR QUEENS; AND A SULLIVAN | COUNTY HERMIT.' Preserved in the University of Virginia–Barrett Collection is a black carbon typescript on seven pages of cheap wove ruled paper 264 × 208 mm., the rules 9 mm. apart, typed apparently by Cora from a clipping of the *Tribune* sketch, including the full form of the headlines. Under the title she wrote *By Stephen Crane* double underlined and in the upper left corner *1700 words*. To the right of the title has been added the number 19 in blue crayon. On the verso of the final leaf Cora wrote 'Four men in a | Cave | 1700 words | Book ||'. This typescript was made up for *Last Words* (1902), pages 217–224, and the mate of the Barrett copy was used by the English printer. The Barrett was among the batch sent to Paul Reynolds in New York for the proposed American edition of *Last Words*. Since the Barrett TMs derives from the *Tribune*, and *Last Words* from its equivalent, only the *Tribune* text has authority.

The appearance of this sketch (and of "The Mesmeric Mountain") in *Last Words* might encourage the speculation that they may have been among Crane's early work, whatever it was, that Cora discussed with Pinker in 1898, only to receive from him on November 10 the following discouragement, "I do not think it would be possible to dispose of the stories on the understanding that it should be announced that they were written when Mr. Crane was a lad, and it seems to me that, if Mr. Crane does not think them good enough to stand on their merits, it would be better not to let them go out" (Columbia). The reference seems to be to a series, and the "Sullivan County Sketches" would fit the situation perfectly.

No. 49. THE OCTOPUSH

"The Octopush" was printed in the *New York Tribune*, Sunday, July 10, 1892, page 17, unsigned and without dateline, headed 'THE

OCTOPUSH. || A SULLIVAN COUNTY NOCTURNE.' This has previously been the only known text, but in the University of Virginia–Barrett Collection is preserved the blue ribbon copy of a typescript of seven pages of text numbered at top center between hyphens. The title on page 1 is 'THE FISHERMEN. || By Stephen Crane. | Author of "Active Service", | "The Red Badge of Courage" etc.' The tale ends on page 7 with a centered row of twenty-six colons. Prefixed to the text is a separate ribbon-copy title-page 'THE FISHERMEN. || By Stephen Crane.' On this special title at the top is a blue-crayon number 8, and in the lower left corner a minuscule pencil *c*. Below the title, in Cora's hand is penciled *pub*^{d} *in Colliers* | *Weekly.* On page 7 below the decorative colons is the blue-crayon word count 1,000. The typescript paper, now laminated, is unwatermarked laid 254 × 204 mm., the chainlines 27 mm. apart.

The history of the copy for this typescript can be traced in letters between Cora and Paul Reynolds preserved in the Special Collections of the Columbia University Libraries. On July 9, 1900, Reynolds addressed Cora at Port Jervis, New York, where she was visiting after bringing Stephen's body to the United States for burial. Reynolds writes:

I am returning to you herewith the originals of the two stories of your husband's.

I put the matter in hand at once and had them typewritten on Saturday, and I am sending back to you the originals today. I shall have to put some title on the fishing story, as there does not seem to be any title on it now. [*handwritten postscript*]

I asked $100.00 for one story & $75.00 for other [Fishermen]. This is about $50 a thousand

On September 4 Reynolds wrote Cora, now back in England:

I have your letters of August 21st and 22d. . . . With regard to the two stories which you sent me . . . the other story had no title but described three men who went out fishing. I have sold it to Collier's Weekly for $100 but have not yet received the money. I find among the list of short stories which you send me and which you wish to arrange to have published in a book, one entitled "The Octopush." The fishing story which I have just sold dealt a good deal with an octopush and might have had this title, and I am afraid it may be the same story. The story as it came to me had no title on it and I put on it the title "A Fishing Adventure." If it was the same story I can only hope that there will be no trouble about it.

Cora's marginal annotation on this letter reads *Ans. Sept. 13 saying* . . . *"The Fishing Adventure" not published.* This statement was made, presumably, on her conviction that the finding of the manuscript at Port Jervis precluded the possibility of publication. From

Reynolds' letter it is clear that she had taken the title "The Octopush" from some list but did not have the clipping to send to him and thus had no means of comparing the text of the two pieces. On the same day, the 13th, she wrote her agent Perris enclosing a receipt for his advance on "The Man from Duluth" and adding: "Mr. Reynolds has written me by the last post, recieved this morning that he has sold the American serial rights of 'A fishing Adventure' to Colliers Weekly. He has no copies of any of the other stories and sketches which I have sent you."

It would seem that by pure chance her letter crossed one that Perris wrote to Reynolds on September 13: "I send under separate cover two further Stephen Crane fragments: The first—THE MAN FROM DULUTH, 3500 words,—seems to me to be a most capital story. We have bought the serial rights from Mrs Crane but she retains the book rights and will, I suppose, want the stuff copyrighted. THE FISHERMEN (1680 words) (which when I received it had the following enigmatical headline—'HARTWOOD PARK, SUL. CO. N. Y.') we are dealing with in the ordinary way, on commission. It seems a rattling piece of American humour." This reference to "Hartwood Park" illuminates an otherwise odd bit in an undated letter of Cora from Milborne Grove to Perris (Yale University), which apparently was sent only a few days before September 13: "I enclose four short things of Mr. Crane's. 'Hartwood Park', 'The Man from Duluth' and the little play can be sold both in England and U. S. . . . I have several more stories, but have been too ill to go over them. Will you buy these things outright or let me have an advance of £10-? If so please let me have cheque by the bearer, Mr. Richie. This will be a *great* accomodation. The other stories which I will bring or send you shortly you can sell on the usual commission."

On September 22 Reynolds again wrote Cora:

I sold "A Desertion" for $150. I sold the fishing story for $100., making a total of $250. . . .
Taking out my commission of 10%, and the cost of a cable to you (which cost $4.00) and some minor charges for postage, etc., it leaves $219.06 with which I bought this draft for 44 pounds 18 shillings 3 pence. Please acknowledge receipt.

Finally, in his letter to Cora of October 23, 1900, in which he lists the stories he has on hand for *Last Words*, Reynolds includes as ninth " 'The Fishermen' (this is the same story I sold under the title of 'A Fishing Adventure.')".

The pieces of this puzzle now begin to fall into place. While at Port Jervis, Cora had come upon the manuscripts for an untitled fishing story, which had the notation *Hartwood Park, Sul. Co. N. Y.,* and "A Desertion." These she rushed off to Reynolds for immediate sale. Reynolds had typescripts prepared and sent the manuscripts back to Cora, who returned with them to England. Reynolds sold "A Desertion" to *Harper's* and the fishing story, which he had entitled "A Fishing Adventure," to *Collier's*, this news being sent to Cora in a letter mailed on September 4 and received on September 13. Once Cora was in England, she occupied herself with raising money by selling Crane's unpublished stories. Shortly before September 13 she sent to Perris the manuscripts of "The Man from Duluth" and the untitled fishermen story noted as *Hartwood Park* with a request for an advance or outright sale. Perris paid £10 for "The Man from Duluth" and accepted the other material on regular commission. He then promptly wrote Reynolds about "The Man from Duluth" and "The Fishermen" (the title he had given to the 'Hartwood' piece) offering them for sale, while he was having typescripts prepared of them—his letter remarks that they are being sent under separate cover. The day after his letter to Reynolds had gone off Cora wrote him that "The Fishing Adventure" had been sold to *Collier's*. Presumably when the typescripts were ready, he then took out that for "The Fishermen" to give to Cora since it was no longer up for sale in the United States. She made the annotation on the title-page of "The Fishermen" and on that of "A Desertion" in an identical manner and perhaps at the very same time. It is likely that she then mailed "The Fishermen" to Reynolds for *Last Words*, who had received it before October 23, although curiously he did not also list "A Desertion" as in his hands on that date. Search of *Collier's Weekly* has failed to disclose the publication of the piece. It may be that when Reynolds received the manuscript of "The Fishermen" and recognized it to be the same as the story he had sold *Collier's* he warned *Collier's*, although his note on the title in the letter of October 23 does not seem to betray any real concern. It is possible that *Collier's* themselves discovered the prior newspaper publication, or simply lost interest and never printed the sketch. No record is preserved of any action by Reynolds, or any refund to the magazine.

What is of textual and critical importance here is the fact that the typescript ordered by Reynolds in New York has been lost, and the Barrett TMs as indicated by its title is one that was made up at the instance of Perris from the manuscript sent him by Cora in mid-September. This manuscript, which Cora had recovered from Port Jervis, was Crane's original draft that had been considerably worked over before he made a new fair copy for sale to the *Tribune* as "The Octopush." This transformation of the untitled manuscript behind the Barrett "Fishermen" is a relatively early example of the revision that lies behind much of Crane's writing at this date, and thus it is an important addition to the documents that offer evidence about the development of his work in the prepublication stages.

In the present edition "The Octopush" from the *Tribune* is the copy-text but edited with reference to the Barrett TMs in order to restore various of the more authoritative accidentals preserved in the typescript but modified in the newspaper styling. The *Tribune* accidentals can be readily reconstructed, however, from the list of these emendations. The Historical Collation for "The Octopush" carries a complete collation both for substantives and for accidentals of all "The Fishermen" variants not accepted and recorded in the emendations listing. The nature of the revisions in the newspaper may be recovered there in convenient and systematic form. Finally, in order that the first-draft version in its derived typescript form may be read for itself, "The Fishermen" has been reprinted with a minimum of editing. Following its brief list of emendations in the apparatus appears a description of the typing and handwritten corrections and revisions in the typescript so that the document may be completely reconstructed. Newly identified manuscript fragments at Columbia follow "The Fishermen."

No. 50. BEAR AND PANTHER

Printed in *New York Tribune*, Sunday, July 17, 1892, page 18, unsigned, on the same page as Crane's "Joys of Seaside Life.", headed 'BEAR AND PANTHER. || VENGEANCE FOR THE WRONGS OF A KITTEN.' The dateline was *Hartwood, N.Y., July 12*. First attributed to Crane by T. A. Gullason and Robert Stallman, independently, in 1968.

No. 51. A GHOUL'S ACCOUNTANT

Printed in the *New York Tribune*, Sunday, July 17, 1892, part II, page 17, unsigned, headed 'A GHOUL'S ACCOUNTANT. || THE STORY OF A SULLIVAN COUNTY PROD-|UCE DEAL.' No dateline appeared. The piece was attributed to Crane in the Williams and Starrett *Bibliography* of 1948.

No. 52. THE BLACK DOG

On Sunday, July 24, 1892, the *New York Tribune*, page 19, unsigned, printed 'THE BLACK DOG. || A NIGHT OF SPECTRAL TERROR.' No further publication has been observed. However, in the Special Collections of the Columbia University Libraries are preserved two different typescripts of the tale. The earlier is a blue ribbon copy (TMs[1]) consisting of six foolscap pages of wove paper watermarked *Indian & Colonial,* measuring 329 × 202 mm., the pages numbered within parentheses in the upper left corner. Although the Crane typewriter was used, Cora was not the typist, for the consistent English spellings are not customary with her, nor is the position of the pagination. However, the hand that wrote —*By—* | *Stephen Crane* to the right of the title is probably hers, as are the ink alterations. The typist was not a professional, as indicated by the number of misspellings. The versos of the pages have cumulative word counts in pencil ending with 1,940 on the back of the fifth page (only three words appearing on page 6). Written vertically on the back of page 6 in Cora's hand is *The Black Dog* | *For a book England.* | 2000 *words.* The second typescript (TMs[2]) is clearly a copy of the first since it repeats the errors and the English spellings of TMs[1] but is by a different typist who is particularly careless and adds a number of other errors. The spelling is worse than in TMs[1]. To the right of the title and probably in the same hand as TMs[1] is written the signature in imitation of TMs[1]. Some literals are corrected in ink, but the only substantive change is the deletion in ink of *groaned* (245.27) and the interlineation of *sighed,* which had been altered similarly in TMs[1] and hence seems a later revision in both. However, all the other of the substantive changes in ink in TMs[1] are accepted in the typing of TMs[2]. No word counts appear but in Cora's hand on the verso of page 5 is written *The Black Dog* | *for a book U.S.* | 2000 *words.* The paper of TMs[2] is the same *Indian & Colonial* foolscap as TMs[1].

The paper of these typescripts and the notations on their last pages indicate that they are posthumous copies prepared for *Last Words.* One may conjecture that the carbon of TMs[1] was making the rounds for English publication [39] and hence when a duplicate was needed to mail to Reynolds in New York, the second typescript had to be prepared from the copy intended for the Digby, Long *Last Words.* That both typescripts are preserved in the Crane Collection at Columbia suggests that the tale was not, after all, sent out for the two book publications; and the absence of the story from Reynolds'

[39] Cora's attempts to dispose of Crane's early work, even before his death, elicited the following remarks addressed to her by Pinker, "I do not think it would be possible to dispose of the stories on the understanding that it should be announced that they were written when Mr. Crane was a lad, and it seems to me that, if Mr. Crane does not think them good enough to stand on their merits, it would be better not to let them go out" (Nov. 10, 1898; Columbia).

list of October 23, 1900, and of the ribbon copy of TMs² from the University of Virginia–Barrett Collection—which owns the printer's copy Cora sent to New York for the American edition of *Last Words* —appear to confirm the hypothesis.

The central textual problem concerns the copy for TMs¹, whether it was a clipping of the *Tribune* or a Crane manuscript. General probability would suggest that Crane did not submit typed copy for the "Sullivan County Sketches" but instead his fair-copy manuscripts, as he seems to have done to Bacheller later. A draft manuscript is precluded by the closeness of the two texts. The typed title imitates that of the newspaper and both have the common error *quivering* for *quavering* at 244.39. Crane invariably wrote *quavering* for the tones of the voice but at least once a printer made this into the more familiar *quivering*.⁴⁰ Another common error is the absence of a necessary comma after *Without* (245.16) supplied in TMs¹ in ink after the completion of the typing. One may notice, too, that *tiptoed* (245.19) in TMs¹ was originally typed broken at the end of a line and hyphenated in both lines, but the corrector deleted the first hyphen to make the word agree with the unhyphenated *tiptoe* of the *Tribune*. Among other evidence it is significant that in the newspaper and in TMs¹ every appearance of the little man's *Ho* is followed by a comma, but both agree in the exclamation at 247.10. The only evidence in favor of a possible manuscript origin for TMs¹ is its slightly lighter punctuation, and particularly its removal in Crane's characteristic manner of commas in an adjective series. The TMs¹ misspellings are sometimes characteristic of Crane, such as *percieved* at 246.30; and the dialect is more consistent in TMs¹.⁴¹ Such mistakes as TMs¹ *skirted* for N¹ *skirled* (243.9), *droping* for N¹ *drooping* (242.24), and *dropped* for N¹ *drooped* (246.1) might suggest handwriting misreading. But various slips like the start of typed *slic* (for *slice*) before correct *side* (244.16) and *on* added to *slept* (245.27) but immediately corrected show that the typist from time to time proceeded on her own assumptions and had to check herself. This tendency may explain such variants as TMs¹ *the wind-waved* for N¹ *wind-waved* (243.5) or TMs¹ *said* for N¹ *replied* (246.5) without calling on a hypothesis of manuscript copy. The ambiguous evidence

---

⁴⁰ See the Textual Note to 15.31 in TALES OF ADVENTURE, *Works*, v (1970), 199.

⁴¹ The typist was clever at catching on to the dialect. For example, at 244.11 ¹*and* was typed following N¹ but altered later in ink to *an'*; thereafter later in the same line and also in 244.18 one finds typed *an'* for N¹ *and*. At 244.10 the typist wrote *ter* for N¹ *to*. If it were not for the slip at 244.11 these might be used as evidence against derivation from N¹; but they seem to represent the adaptation of the typist to dialect consistency.

in TMs[1] is not strong enough to overturn the normal assumption, supported by concrete evidence, that the typescript TMs[1] was made from a clipping of the *Tribune*. Thus the *Tribune* is the only authority and copy-text and the two derived typescripts are without textual significance. A few corrections to N[1] are drawn from TMs[1], but these are simple corrections and not revisions relying on authority. The ink alterations in the typescripts, being posthumous and without reference to any other document than N[1], cannot be accepted as of any value other than as occasional desirable corrections.

No. 53. TWO MEN AND A BEAR

Printed in *New York Tribune*, Sunday, July 24, 1892, page 17, unsigned, headed 'TWO MEN AND A BEAR. || A LIVELY SPARRING MATCH.' The dateline was *Hartwood, N.Y., July 12*. T. A. Gullason in 1968 was the first to attribute this piece to Crane.

No. 54. KILLING HIS BEAR

Printed in the *New York Tribune*, Sunday, July 31, 1892, part II, page 18, unsigned, headed 'KILLING HIS BEAR. || A WINTER TRAGEDY WITH THREE ACTORS.' No dateline was present. The piece was attributed to Crane in the Williams and Starrett *Bibliography* of 1948.

No. 55. A TENT IN AGONY

This sketch was printed, signed, in the *Cosmopolitan*, XIV (December, 1892), 241–244. An artist signing himself 'Chip' drew an illustrative title 'A TENT IN AGONY, | A SULLIVAN | COUNTY | SKETCH' and a series of uncaptioned humorous illustrations of the events.

No. 56. THE CRY OF A HUCKLEBERRY PUDDING

The date of December 23, 1892, when Crane had stopped writing "Sullivan County Sketches" for the *New York Press*, and the place of publication, the Syracuse *University Herald*, XXI, 51–54, signed, suggest that this is a later piece that finally found its place outside the commercial area. Its errors indicate that it was set with considerable faithfulness direct from holograph.

No. 57. THE HOLLER TREE

The holograph manuscript of "The Holler Tree" was not published until 1934 when the *Golden Book Magazine,* XIX (February, 1934), 188–191, secured a copy and printed it as "from his Unpublished Intimate Notebooks". This manuscript, now in the University of Virginia–Barrett Collection, consists of nine pages written in black ink on cheap white wove ledger paper 319 × 198 mm., the rules 10 mm. apart. The title is present on page 1 but the piece is not signed; the pages are numbered at top center above semicircles. Several of the pages are written on the versos of drafts of other material. Page 3 is written on the turned-around original foot of an unnumbered page containing the words ' "Certainly I do" ', which may be a false start in making the present fair copy; but its verso holds a draft of part of "The Reluctant Voyagers." On the verso of page 4 appears the false start of some piece 'In a small grey room there was a dead room.', and the versos of pages 5 and 6 contain a draft of part of Chapter 1 of *George's Mother.* The manuscript may be a fair copy dating from 1894. The paper, in fact, is composed of three different batches. Leaves 1, 2, 5, and 6 are on Paper C found in *The Red Badge of Courage* manuscript, and leaves 7–9 on a variant of this with 29 ruled lines instead of 28. Leaves 3–4, which utilized discarded leaves from some false starts of other work, are on paper with rules running through the left margin and with other differences from Paper C.

No. 58. AN EXPLOSION OF SEVEN BABIES

Although clearly dating from the "Sullivan County Sketches" period of 1892, "An Explosion of Seven Babies" was not published until after Crane's death, and then under the title of "A Sullivan County Episode" in the *Home Magazine of New York,* XVI (January, 1901), 77–80, but not again. The magazine provided an ornamental initial of two crying babies and three illustrations captioned *"Great Scott.",* *"Performed the Feat of his Life",* and *"The Little Man Frothed at the Mouth",* the first signed 'RAG'.

The holograph manuscript is preserved in the University of Virginia–Barrett Collection, written on the backs of eight pages of Postal Telegraph Cable Co. Press Despatch forms 263 × 199 mm., but different from those used for the inscription of "Greed Rampant," written in black ink with ink corrections and a final round of revision in pencil. The pages are numbered in top center above a semicircle. In Crane's own hand the title is given as 'An Explosion of Seven Babies. | A Sullivan County Sketch | By Stephen Crane.' Page 8 is written on the recto of a turned-around leaf discarded from another manuscript. This discard was paged 3 above a semicircle and begins 'There came a tremendous silence, heavy enough | to throttle life'. No closing punctuation appears. The preservation of this manuscript is due to the fortunate circumstance that Cora sent it, instead of a typescript, to Reynolds for the American *Last Words* and serialization in the United States. The evidence is her private code letter *u* in the lower left corner of the first page and on the back of the last page her notation, *An Explosion | of Seven Babies || Unpublished | Either in | England or | U.S.?.* Cumulative word counts total 1,428. This is the copy listed by Reynolds in his letter to Cora of October 23, 1900, about *Last Words* and its contents, prefaced by his disapproving, "Some of the stories don't seem to me fully up to Mr. Crane's standard. Such as, for instance, the story about the seven babies."

Nevertheless, Reynolds seems to have had a typescript made from this manuscript, with several carbons, the purple ribbon copy of which (TMs[1]) in the possession of Comdr. Melvin H. Schoberlin USN (Ret.) consists of eight pages of laid quarto 224 × 200 mm., watermarked *Marcus Ward*. The carbon of this was sold to *Home Magazine* and was the copy from which that magazine version was set. At 267.5, for instance, TMs[1] in error omitted MS *brown*, which is also missing in HM; at 267.7 TMs[1] by anticipation typed the error *top* for MS *half*, a mistake faithfully repeated in HM. The most striking evidence, however, comes at 267.22 where MS reads *tore* and HM *fell*. But the source of the HM variant is obvious when one notices that TMs[1] has typed *fell* corrected by hand to *tore,* a correction evidently not made in the duplicate sold to *Home Magazine.*

In the Special Collections of the Columbia University Libraries is found another typescript, a black carbon on eight pages of wove quarto paper, unwatermarked, 264 × 206 mm., the pages numbered at the foot. A note that the story appeared in the *Home Magazine* now written above the title is a later addition in an unknown hand. This typescript must once have belonged to Cora because of its presence in the Crane Collection at Columbia, but it has none of her usual markings and is a professional typing job that bears no re-

semblance to the typescripts she usually had made up for *Last Words.*
Moreover, just as the Schoberlin TMs[1] was copied from the manuscript, so this English TMs[2] is demonstrably a copy of TMs[1]. The
same sort of evidence holds as that which established the connection
between MS and TMs[1]. The subtitle in TMs[1] has been deleted by hand
and does not appear in TMs[2]. TMs[2] is missing *brown* and has the
error *top.* In addition, it reads *strode* at 266.31 where MS has Crane's
typical *strided;* one then notices that TMs[1] first typed *strode* but altered it by hand to *strided,* a change evidently not made in the copy
behind TMs[2]. Similarly, at 267.5 TMs[2] reads *wheeled round* whereas
MS has simply *wheeled;* TMs[1], however, first read *wheeled round* but
the *round* appears to have been x'd-out on the typewriter although in
a manner that leaves some doubt about the intention, perhaps. It
would appear, then, that when Cora sent Reynolds the manuscript
Reynolds ordered a typescript and several carbons prepared. One
carbon he sold to the *Home Magazine* and another he sent back to
Cora who, needing extra copies perhaps for *Last Words* and possible
English magazine sale, had the English TMs[2] made up, one copy of
which she retained.

The establishment of this family tree is comforting because it
disposes of any possibility that variants in HM, TMs[1], or TMs[2], or
any combination of them, can have any authority. Hence the Barrett
manuscript becomes the copy-text and the text appears for the first
time in this edition without the errors of the derived magazine version. The few alterations made from TMs[1-2] or HM are in the nature
of corrections only, not revisions. In the present text the paragraphing of MS has been somewhat reordered according to what seem to be
Crane's intentions although obscured by the method of writing out
the manuscript. That is, although dialogue in MS is usually given a
separate indented line, often only a few words, yet the next line of
narrative although not run-on is not indented as well but started at
the full left margin. The part-line of dialogue seems to indicate the
intention clearly enough, and thus emendation has been attempted
in the present text according to the evidence.

No. 59. THE MESMERIC MOUNTAIN

A Barrett typescript consisting of five pages of unwatermarked laid
paper 258 × 202 mm., the chainlines 27 mm. apart, paged within
spaced parentheses at top center, has the title typed as 'The Mesmeric
Mountain. | A tale of Sullivan County.' to which Cora added in black
ink *By the late Stephen Crane* double-underlined. In the upper left

corner she wrote *1200 words*, and inscribed in the lower left corner the minuscules *ee*. A blue-crayon number 23 is placed to the right of the title.

Cora herself seems to have typed this tale posthumously from Crane's manuscript, corrected it in black ink, and sent this copy to Reynolds in New York for the American edition of *Last Words*. The sketch appeared in the English *Last Words* (1902), pages 225–230, set quite obviously from the ribbon copy of the Barrett TMs carbon but without all of the corrections found in the latter. The copy-text is the Barrett TMs since *Last Words* is a purely derived text. In *My Stephen Crane*, edited by E. H. Cady (1958), page 7, Corwin Linson records Crane's own mention of this tale, and on page 40 he quotes from it, showing that he had read the text.

NEW YORK CITY SKETCHES

No. 60. THE BROKEN-DOWN VAN

The forerunner of Crane's series of New York sketches for the *Press* in 1894 and the *Journal* in 1896 is "The Broken-Down Van," printed in the *New York Tribune,* Sunday, July 10, 1892, part I, page 8, unsigned, headed 'TRAVELS IN NEW-YORK. || THE BROKEN-DOWN VAN.' The heading *TRAVELS IN NEW-YORK* should not suggest that Crane had in mind a series that did not materialize: this was a heading used by the *Tribune* under which appropriate articles by various writers were printed. The piece was attributed to Crane in the Williams and Starrett *Bibliography* of 1948.

No. 61. A NIGHT AT THE MILLIONAIRE'S CLUB

The sketch was printed in the New York humorous magazine *Truth,* XIII (April 21, 1894), 4, signed. A clipping is pasted in the Crane scrapbooks in the Special Collections of the Columbia University Libraries.

No. 62. AN EXPERIMENT IN MISERY

The first printing of "An Experiment in Misery" was in the *New York Press,* Sunday, April 22, 1894, part III, page 2, signed, headlined 'AN EXPERIMENT | IN MISERY || An Evening, a Night and a Morn-|ing with Those Cast Out. || THE TRAMP LIVES LIKE A KING || But His Royalty, to the Novitiate, Has | Drawbacks of Smells and Bugs. || LODGED WITH AN ASSASSIN || A Wonderfully Vivid Picture of a | Strange Phase of New York Life, | Written for "The Press" by | the Author of "Maggie." ' Two illustrations accompanied the article, captioned *A Place of Ghastly Shapes* and *They Breakfast,* both drawn by M. Stein. This was listed as No. 19 in the inventory Crane made about July, 1897, noted as being in the *Press* and having 3,000 words.

The original opening and conclusion of the *New York Press* version follows:

Two men stood regarding a tramp.

"I wonder how he feels," said one, reflectively. "I suppose he is homeless, friendless, and has, at the most, only a few cents in his pocket. And if this is so, I wonder how he feels."

The other being the elder, spoke with an air of authoritative wisdom. "You can tell nothing of it unless you are in that condition yourself. It is idle to speculate about it from this distance."

"I suppose so," said the younger man, and then he added as from an inspiration: "I think I'll try it. Rags and tatters, you know, a couple of dimes, and hungry, too, if possible. Perhaps I could discover his point of view or something near it."

"Well, you might," said the other, and from those words begins this veracious narrative of an experiment in misery.

The youth went to the studio of an artist friend, who, from his store, rigged him out in an aged suit and a brown derby hat that had been made long years before. And then the youth went forth to try to eat as the tramp may eat, and sleep as the wanderers sleep. It was late at night, and a fine rain was swirling softly down, covering the pavements with a bluish luster. He began a weary trudge toward the downtown places, where beds can be hired for coppers. By the time he had reached City Hall Park he was so completely plastered with yells of "bum" and "hobo," and with various unholy epithets that small boys had applied to him at intervals that he was in a state of profound dejection, and looked searchingly for an outcast of high degree that the two might share miseries. But the lights threw a quivering glare over rows and circles of deserted benches that glistened damply, showing patches of wet sod behind them. It seemed that their usual freights of sorry humanity had fled on this night to better things. There were only squads of well dressed Brooklyn people, who swarmed toward the Bridge.

HE FINDS HIS FIELD.

The young man loitered about for a time, and then went shuffling off down Park row. In the sudden descent in style of the dress of the crowd he felt relief. He began to see others whose tatters matched his tatters. In Chatham square there were aimless men strewn in front of saloons and lodging houses. He aligned himself with these men, and turned slowly to occupy himself with the pageantry of the street.

The mists of the cold and damp night made an intensely blue haze, through which the gaslights in the windows of stores and saloons shone with a golden radiance. The street cars rumbled softly, as if going upon carpet stretched in the aisle made by the pillars of the elevated road. Two interminable processions of people went along the wet pavements, spattered with black mud that made each shoe leave a scar like impression. The high buildings lurked a-back, shrouded in shadows. Down a side street there were mystic curtains of purple and black, on which lamps dully glittered like embroidered flowers.

[Conclusion]

"Well," said the friend, "did you discover his point of view?"

"I don't know that I did," replied the young man; "but at any rate I think mine own has undergone a considerable alteration."

The piece was not printed again until it was used in the "Midnight Sketches" section that pieced out the Heinemann edition of *The Open Boat* (1898), pages 211–226. Here it is footnoted as *From the Press, New York* but Crane has dropped the framework introduction and conclusion of the *Press* sketch as unsuitable for the book form and in the process has rewritten the beginning up to the point where the youth enters the saloon for hot soup. The result is to take out the masquerade and, it would appear, to make the youth a genuine bum undergoing a genuine experience. It is true that the title thereby becomes inapposite, and there might be a question of the import of the sentence, partly revised from the *Press*, that *He was going forth to eat as the wanderer may eat, and sleep as the homeless sleep* (283.21–22). But when to the *Press* sentence *In the sudden descent in style of the dress of the crowd he felt relief* the revision adds *and as if he were at last in his own country* (284.4–6), the intention would seem to be to describe the familiar feel of a real drifter for the crowds of the slums. The revisions tighten the sketch although the result is also to create a certain ambiguity and lack of motivation for the youth's subsequent generosity after his declaration that ten cents a night is too expensive for a lodging. With the start of the paragraph at 284.25, the printer's copy which was presumably a manuscript for the revision, or a typescript, changes and becomes the *Press*, with only a few verbal changes of authority up to the end, when it was a simple matter to delete the last two sentences.

That Crane to provide copy for *The Open Boat* had to revert to an early manuscript as his only source is not a tenable hypothesis, as it is for Cora's printer's copy for, say, "The Fishermen" instead of the printed "Octopush." A clipping from the *Press* is pasted in the Crane scrapbook in the Special Collections of the Columbia University Libraries and labeled in Crane's hand from the *Press,* although his added attribution of the *Buffalo Express* may be inaccurate since it cannot be located. The writing of the *Open Boat* new beginning is not that of a draft, nor would a draft suddenly come into so great conformity thereafter with the printed version.

The problem of a copy-text is not a simple one. Crane's final literary intentions manifestly were to reject the framework device, and it would appear that these should be respected. But thereafter save for a few casual alterations *The Open Boat* becomes a derived text. The present editor, then, has followed classic principles in making *The Open Boat* his copy-text for its revised opening (283.14–284.24), although with reference back to the *Press* for restoration of accidentals that come from English styling. From 284.25 to the end of the narrative with 293.24 the copy-text is the *Press,* which alone stands in direct relationship to the lost manuscript. In a sense the book then becomes the copy-text authority for the omission of the last two sentences. In the *Press* texture of accidentals are inserted as emendations those few book variants believed to have been Crane's revisory markings in the copy, whatever it was—handwritten transcript of the clipping or typescript. A number of the smaller book variants are clearly errors, whether of this preprinting stage of transcription or of the compositor is not to be determined. The result is an eclectic text that reproduces the original and its revision as faithfully as the evidence permits for Crane's final intentions.

No. 63. AN EXPERIMENT IN LUXURY

The companion piece to "An Experiment in Misery" appeared in the *New York Press,* Sunday, April 29, 1894, part III, page 2, signed, headlined 'AN EXPERIMENT | IN LUXURY || The Experiences of a Youth Who | Sought Out Croesus. || IN THE GLITTER OF WEALTH || A fuzzy Acrobatic Kitten Which Held | Great Richness at Bay. || LIFE OF THE WOMAN OF GOLD || Are There, After All, Burrs Under | Each Fine Cloak and Benefits | in all Beggars' Garb? ||'. Two illustrations accompanied the article, captioned *"He Began to Feel That He Was Better Than Other People."* and *"He Was Absorbed in the Gambols of a Kitten.",* both drawn by M. Stein. A clipping of this piece is in the Crane scrapbooks in the Special Collections of the Columbia University Libraries, but no attempt was later made to collect it.

No. 64. SAILING DAY SCENES

The unsigned sketch "Sailing Day Scenes" appeared in the *New York Press*, Sunday, June 10, 1894, part IV, page 2, headlined 'SAILING DAY SCENES || On the Dock of a Big Ocean Liner | Just Before the Start. || SMILES AND TEARS MINGLE || Roar, Bustle, Confusion, Conviviality | and Aching Hearts. ||'. A clipping is pasted in the Crane scrapbooks in the Special Collections of the Columbia University Libraries headed in Crane's hand *The Press, New York*. The date and page number have not previously been known.

No. 65. MR. BINKS' DAY OFF

Printed in the *New York Press*, Sunday, July 8, 1894, part IV, page 2, signed. Headlined 'Mr. Binks' Day Off || A Study of a Clerk's Holiday.' It was not reprinted but was listed as No. 20 in Crane's inventory of about July, 1897, as "Bink's Day in the Country", 2,000 words, in the *Press*.

No. 66. THE ART STUDENTS' LEAGUE BUILDING

Never published and known only from the draft in the Notebook preserved in the University of Virginia–Barrett Collection, this untitled sketch was written on the rectos of folios 4–14 in pencil, probably after April, 1894, by which time the League had moved. The title assigned here is a variant on that given it by R. A. Stallman who first described and quoted from this piece in the *Bulletin of the New York Public Library*, LX (September, 1956), 457–459, and subsequently reprinted it in his *New York City Sketches* (1966), pp. 14–16.

No. 67. THE MEN IN THE STORM

This sketch was published first in the *Arena*, x (October, 1894), 662–667 and then reprinted in the *Philistine*, IV (January, 1897), 37–48, and in the Heinemann edition of *The Open Boat* (1898), pages 227–238. It appeared as No. 14 in Crane's inventory of about July, 1897, credited to the *Philistine* and as 2,000 words. The *Arena* was set presumably from Crane's holograph manuscript. The agreement of accidentals indicates that the *Philistine* used the *Arena,* and that *The Open Boat* was set from a clipping of the *Philistine.* The only authority and copy-text, therefore, is the *Arena.* In the same issue, the editor of the *Arena* commented on the sketch in a puff preserved in the Crane scrapbooks at Columbia University: "Mr. Stephen Crane's little story is a powerful bit of literature. This young writer belonging to the new school is likely to achieve in his own field something like the success Hamlin Garland has attained in his."

No. 68. CONEY ISLAND'S FAILING DAYS

In the Crane scrapbooks in the Special Collections of the Columbia University Libraries is a clipping of this sketch, but without notation. It appeared in the *New York Press,* Sunday, October 14, 1894, part v, page 2, signed, headlined 'CONEY ISLAND'S | FAILING DAYS || What One of Them Held for a | Strolling Philosopher. || NOT WHOLLY WITHOUT JOY || The Advantages of Great Toys and the | Unimportance of Bugs. ||'. Four illustrations accompanied the article, captioned *He Went Away Satisfied, The Elusive Negro's Head, Everybody Eats Frankfurters,* and *The Musician.*

No. 69. IN A PARK ROW RESTAURANT

The Crane scrapbooks in the Special Collections of the Columbia University Libraries have a clipping of this piece that was printed in the *New York Press,* Sunday, October 28, 1894, part v, page 3, signed at the foot, headlined 'IN A PARK ROW | RESTAURANT || The Nevadan Sheriff Went There | for Excitement. || LIKE A BATTLE OF BAD MEN || He Suggests That Repeating Rifles | Might Take the Place of Spoons. ||'. In Crane's 1894 Notebook preserved in the University of Virginia–Barrett Collection on the versos of fols. 58–49 (the Notebook being reversed) is a draft of this sketch written in pencil with alterations in pencil. Cora inserted the title 'The Park Row Restaurant' when, despite the scrapbook clipping, she made up a typescript from the Notebook and wrote in the Notebook margin *Sent to P. R.,* that is, to Paul Reynolds. It may be, in fact, that when she made this typescript she was not aware of the scrapbook clipping and thought that she had an unpublished piece she could sell. The blue ribbon copy of this typescript is also present in the Barrett Collection, consisting of three pages, numbered within spaced parentheses in top center, of cheap wove ruled paper 264 × 208 mm., the rules 9 mm. apart. In black ink Cora added the title to the typescript 'The Park Row Restaurant' and then *By Stephen Crane*. A large blue-crayon number 26 appears to the right of the title, and to the left the mutilated remains of the word count 700. In the lower left corner of the first page is Cora's minuscule marking *g*. The word counts are written on the backs of pages 1 and 2, with the total 700. This posthumous typescript is completely derived and of course has no authority. Paul Reynolds noted it as in his possession on October 23, 1900.

The differences between the draft and the final newspaper version that would have been set from a revised fair copy are so great as to make it worth while to print both versions. However, for the record the Historical Collation of the *Press* version contains a complete listing of the variants of the Notebook text (except those accepted as emendations to the *Press* version). The *Press* is the copy-text; but whenever the two versions are close enough for comparison of the accidentals, emendation has been made from the Notebook holograph.

No. 70. HEARD ON THE STREET ELECTION NIGHT

Something of a mystery inheres to this piece in that its clipping is found in the Crane scrapbooks in the Special Collections of the Columbia University Libraries, it is clearly from the *New York Press*, the names of the candidates identify the election as in November, 1894, but the *Press* has been searched in vain. Just possibly some different edition that is not preserved in the usual collections carried the article. The clipping is headlined 'HEARD ON THE STREET | ELECTION NIGHT || Passing Remarks Gathered in Front | of "The Press" Stereopticon. || HOW THEY TOOK THE GOOD NEWS || Human Nature Had Full Swing on | Park Row Tuesday Evening. ||'. The clipping contains no signature.

In the University of Virginia–Barrett Collection is preserved a Notebook that Crane used for drafts of material in 1894. On the rectos of fols. 12–17 Crane wrote in pencil a complete draft of the newspaper sketch, which he then must have redone in a fair copy, revised, for the *Press*. The differences between the Notebook and the printed forms are so extensive that the Notebook text is printed separately. For the record the Notebook is given a Historical Collation against the *Press* clipping copy-text; accidentals have been ignored in this collation due to the cursory and inconsistent punctuation of the Notebook.

No. 71. THE FIRE

That this vivid sketch seems to be an imaginative composite and not a play-by-play description of an actual fire is of little account, of course, so that Stallman's use of the word "hoax" is perhaps unduly strong, especially since no claim for it as a news report was made by the *Press*. It appeared in the *New York Press*, Sunday, November 25, 1894, part IV, page 6, signed, headlined 'WHEN EVERY ONE | IS PANIC STRICKEN || A Realistic Pen Picture of a Fire | in a Tenement. || THE PHILOSOPHY OF WOMEN || Fright and Flight—The Missing Baby|—A Commonplace Hero. || FIRE!'.

In the Special Collections of the Columbia University Libraries are preserved two carbons of a four-page typescript made up by Cora Crane for possible use in *Last Words* and perhaps for independent sale in England. These are on the wove foolscap watermarked *Indian & Colonial* used for so many of the typescripts. The two carbons are identically corrected in black ink except for one variant: on page 1, line 40 (339.35) in the second carbon the final s has not been added by hand to *countles* at the end of a line. Both are titled in black ink, the first as 'The Fire || by | Stephen Crane. ||' and the second the same except for variant periods and no underline of the title. The pages are numbered within parentheses at top center. Cora probably was the typist. The first carbon on fol. 3ᵛ has Cora's note *The Fire | for B. Book* and on fol. 4ᵛ another note *The Fire | U.S. Book | words.* No word counts are present on any of the versos. The copy for this typescript was certainly a clipping of the *Press* text. That being so, it is possible that Cora did not send a copy to Reynolds for American sale and—since no example is present in the University of Virginia–Barrett Collection—she perhaps did not even mail one for the American edition of *Last Words*. Since the English edition omitted it, whether copies were sent to Digby, Long and to her London agent is uncertain. The sole authority and copy-text is the *New York Press* version. However, the title *The Fire* given the piece seems to represent Crane's own preference, when it appears as No. 18, credited to *The Press*, 2,000 words, in his inventory list of about July, 1897.

No. 72. WHEN MAN FALLS, A CROWD GATHERS

The first publication of "When Man Falls" was in the *New York Press*, Sunday, December 2, 1894, part III, page 5, signed, headlined 'WHEN MAN FALLS | A CROWD GATHERS || A Graphic Study of

New York | Heartlessness. || GAZING WITH PITILESS EYES ||
"What's the Matter?" That Too Fa-|miliar Query. ||'. It next appeared
in the *Westminster Gazette,* in England, October 9, 1900, pages 1–2,
headed 'A STREET SCENE IN NEW YORK | BY THE LATE STEPHEN
CRANE.', with a reprint from standing type (except for a reset first
paragraph) without variation in the *Westminster Budget,* November
9, 1900, page 10. In *Last Words* (1902) it was placed on pages 148–
154 among the New York Sketches and titled 'A STREET SCENE IN
NEW YORK.' A clipping from the *Press,* the headline removed to another page, is pasted in Crane's scrapbook now in the Special Collections of the Columbia University Libraries, with Crane's notation
'When Men Stumble' and the date 'Dec. 2ᵈ | The Press'. On another
page is a clipping of an answer by Eugen Sandow defending the com-
passion and helpfulness of New York crowds at accidents, which was
printed in the *Press* Letters to the Editor.

Preserved in the University of Virginia–Barrett Collection is Crane's
Notebook which on fols. 37ᵛ–18ᵛ (the Notebook being filled on its
versos after having been reversed) contains the original draft of the
sketch, untitled. On fol. 36ᵛ and the second paragraph, which Cora
took to be the beginning of the piece, she wrote in pencil '4 copies
made Sep 18–1900 Two sent Reynolds serial & book'. The figure 4 is
written over what may be the word 'Two'. Before typing, Cora made
several pencil alterations which appear in her typescript. Two carbons
of this posthumous typescript have been preserved, one in the University of Virginia–Barrett Collection and one in the Special Collections in the Columbia University Libraries. Both consist of five
leaves of cheap wove ruled paper 264 × 208 mm., the rules 9 mm.
apart, paged within parentheses at top center. Both are titled by Cora
in ink, *A Street Scene in New York* and both in the upper left corner
read, in her hand, *By | Stephen Crane || 1430 words.* Above the rule
and word count is deleted *finished by Mrs | Stephen Crane.* The basis
for this statement is obscure, since on the evidence of the *Press* the
Notebook version is complete. The only original contribution by Cora
is the elaboration of one sentence at 352.25 which she subsequently
deleted. Each typescript is corrected in black ink, with a few additional pencil alterations in the Barrett copy. On the versos of the
Columbia carbon Cora wrote in pencil the cumulative word counts
for each page up to 1,433 on fol. 5ᵛ. A blue-crayon 24 appears on page
1 of the Barrett copy, and in the lower-left corner a pencil *ll.* The
corrections differ slightly in the two carbons, the variants being noted
in the List of Alterations in the Typescripts that follows the list for
the Notebook after the Historical Collation. It is clear that Cora did
not know of the earlier newspaper appearance when after Crane's

death she typed out the copy from the Notebook to use in *Last Words* and possibly for separate sale. Whether she actually sent two copies to Reynolds is doubtful, for the *Westminster Gazette* and *Last Words* were set independently from two typescript copies, one of which was presumably the ribbon. The *Gazette* variants are not followed in *Last Words*. Since the typescripts and the texts set from them derive without authority from the Notebook, they cannot be considered as substantive texts.

The Notebook holograph is in too much of a draft state to permit its use as a copy-text in any efficient manner; hence the *New York Press* version is selected although it is at one remove from the holograph of the revised sketch. However, it has been emended in its accidentals from the superior authority of the Notebook draft when in these respects the *Press* seems to have been housestyled. The *Press* title is retained since it is that customarily listed in bibliographies (although "A Street Scene in New York" sometimes confusingly appears). Of course it has no more authority than the title that Cora invented for her typescript. Crane's own title in the Columbia scrapbook might be taken as the most authoritative, but it is perhaps incomplete. Moreover, the use of the word 'Stumble' is odd, and the title may be merely a careless guess when the separated *Press* headline was not identified as belonging to the clipping. In fact, when the piece appears as No. 16 in the holograph inventory list of about July, 1897, its title is given as "When Man Falls—" and it is credited to *The Press*, with a word count of 1,500. Reynolds lists it in his October 23, 1900, inventory but of course under the TMs title of "A Street Scene in New York."

The sketch is undoubtedly the one referred to in a letter of October 3, 1900, from the editor of the *Westminster Gazette* to Cora, "I will gladly use the article by your late husband which you sent me to-day, though I may have to wait a few days for its insertion" (Columbia). Its appearance on October 9 immediately excited the interest of Alfred Plant, the executor of Crane's estate, who on October 10 wrote to Pinker: "I saw there was a short article by Mr. Crane in the Westminster Gazette yesterday. I should like to know if they obtained same from you or Mrs. Crane" (University of Virginia).

No. 73. THE DUEL THAT WAS NOT FOUGHT

This sketch was first printed in the *New York Press*, Sunday, December 9, 1894, part III, page 2, signed, headlined 'THE DUEL THAT |

WAS NOT FOUGHT || Patsey Tulligan Almost Had His | Heart Cut in Two in the Middle. || A LITTLE CUBAN'S WRATH || Only Blood Would Appease It, but | It Went Unappeased. ||'. Two illustrations accompanied it, captioned *"You Have Insult Me."* and *"It's None of Your Business."* To piece out the Heinemann edition of *The Open Boat* (1898) Crane added the story to the "Midnight Sketches" section, pages 241–250. The printer's copy was a clipping of the *Press* as indicated not only by the close agreement of the punctuation but also by the English edition misinterpreting the newspaper's typo *per* (355.5) as *fer*, whereas the correct reading is *yer*. In addition to this obvious error, the only other significant variant is the book's *eloquent* for the newspaper's *elegant* (355.10), more likely to be an English sophistication destroying the American humor than an authorial revision. It would seem that Crane turned the clipping over to Heinemann with no attempt at revision.

In Crane's Notebook preserved in the University of Virginia– Barrett Collection is part of the original untitled draft of this story written on the rectos of fols. 46–53 (preserved) but with ten leaves torn out between fols. 48 and 49. These missing leaves constitute a puzzle. It is unlikely that they were so close to the final form of what Crane wanted that he was able to utilize them as part of the manuscript sent to the *Press*; instead, it was presumably something on their versos (the Notebook being written first on the rectos and then on the versos) that was removed, to our loss. This draft is printed following the final text, and an account of the alterations made during its inscription appears in Historical Collation.

Particularly because of the fragmentary nature of the draft it is unsuited for use as copy-text, which instead is the final printed form in the *Press*. However, a few useful emendations to the accidentals are possible from the Notebook, and one or two instances of profanity have been inserted in the *Press* text from it on the hypothesis that they were censored by the newspaper.

The piece appears in Crane's holograph inventory of about July 1897 as No. 17, titled "The Duel", given as 2,000 words and credited to the *Press*.

No. 74. A LOVELY JAG IN A CROWDED CAR

In the Special Collections of the Columbia University Libraries is preserved an unmarked proof of "A Lovely Jag" which was printed in the *New York Press*, Sunday, January 6, 1895, part v, page 6, signed at the foot, headlined 'A LOVELY JAG | IN A CROWDED CAR || A Blithe Episode of the Busy | Shopping Days. || JOY UNCORKED AND EXUBERANT || This Man Had a Great Time All by | Himself. ||'. The proof and the printed sketch are without differences. The printed version was accompanied by three illustrations captioned *"He Seemed to Feel a Keen Humor in the Situation."*, *"We Ain't Doin' a Thing!"*, and *"Shay, What'll Ye Take?"*.

No. 75. OPIUM'S VARIED DREAMS

Some change in Crane's dealings with the McClure syndicate may just possibly be indicated by the appearance in several newspapers of the copyright notice in his own name. This study of New York life was widely syndicated on Sunday, May 17, 1896, and has been observed in seven newspapers as follows:

N^1: *Detroit Free Press*, May 17, 1896, page 20, headlined '[within a frame of type-orns.] Opium Smokers. | [decorative double rule with pendant] | [to the left] Effects of the Insidious Drug | Upon Its Victims. | [to the right] Devotees of the Vice Described | by........... | STEPHEN CRANE. | [below the frame] || (Copyright, 1896, by Stephen Crane.)'.

N^2: *Portland Oregonian*, May 17, page 17, headlined 'SLAVE OF THE POPPY || ONCE THE "YEN-YEN" SEIZES A MAN | THERE IS NO HOPE. || There are Twenty Five Thousand | Opium-Smoking in New York Alone. |—By Stephen Crane. || (Copyright, 1896, by Stephen Crane.)'.

N^3: *New York Sun*, May 17, part III, page 3, headlined 'OPIUM'S VARIED DREAMS. || THE HABIT, THE VICTIM, THE RE-|LIEF, AND THE DESPAIR. || This City's 25,000 Opium Smokers and | Their Ways Since Reform Broke Up | Their Resorts—The Pipe and Its Han-|dling, and the Habitue's Defence.' Nothing in this version attributes the article to Crane.

N^4: *Kansas City Star*, May 17, page 16, signed, headlined 'THEY WHO SMOKE OPIUM || STEPHEN CRANE TELLS OF THE VICE | AND ITS VICTIMS. || There are 25,000 "Dope" Smokers in New | York City Alone, but Reform has Brok-|en Up the Luxurious Opium Joints|—The Effects of the Drug. ||'. At the foot, with the signature, is *Copyright, 1896*.

N^5: *Buffalo Express*, May 17, sec. II, page 3, headlined 'The Opium Smokers of New-York. || BY STEPHEN CRANE, | Author of "The Red Badge of Courage," etc. || (*Copyright, 1896, by Stephen Crane.*)'. Accompanying the article is a brief biography headed 'Stephen Crane. ||' and a captioned portrait.

N^6: *Philadelphia Inquirer*, May 17, page 28, headlined 'Slaves [on two lines] OF THE [continuation] Opium Habit || BY STEPHEN CRANE. ||'.

N^7: *Denver Republican*, May 17, page 21, signed, headlined 'WHITE SMOKERS OF OPIUM || There Are Many More of Them Than | Is Suspected. || THE JOINTS IN THE TENDERLOIN || The Opium Smoker Is

Hard for the | Police to Detect and Raid—How | the Habit Is Formed, Cultivated | and Defended by Its Devotees—|The Scene in an Opium Joint Is | Not as It Is Most Often Repre-|sented. ||'. This paper alone prefixed a dateline, *New York, May 12.—(Special Correspondence.)*

Two cuts accompanied the syndicate proofs. One was of two men and was captioned *Inside a "Joint," Watching the Cook.* The second pictured two women with a pipe. N[1,2,4,6] captioned this *Victims of Despair*; N[5] *Fair Victims of the Pipe*; and N[7] *Foolish Victims of the Harmful Drug.* N[3] used no illustrations, and N[4,6] only the second.

The copy-text chosen is N[1], the *Detroit Free Press*, which has perhaps the most representative text for accidentals and is without the heavy editorial sophistication that disqualifies the *New York Sun*, or the cuts that occur in the *Kansas City Star* or the *Philadelphia Inquirer*. The copy-text has been emended on the evidence of the other newspapers when they seem to represent more faithfully than N[1] the syndicate proofs which the present edition endeavors to reconstruct. Because a small number of readings in the accidentals is still in legitimate doubt, the Historical Collation records all agreements of two or more newspapers, from the seven collated, that have not been listed in the account of emendations. For simple convenience, the traditional title from the *New York Sun* given in bibliographies has been retained. Although a few details from the suggested headlines in the proofs can be reconstructed, the main title escapes identification, but it may have begun *Slaves of.*

In an (August?) 1896 Crane list at Columbia of McClure pieces this sketch is noted as "Dope Smokers" and the entry is annotated "part payment".

No. 76. NEW YORK'S BICYCLE SPEEDWAY

The McClure proof for this syndicated article on Sunday, July 5, 1896, is preserved in the Special Collections of the Columbia University Libraries, so that the basic copy set from Crane's lost manuscript brings us as close to authority as we can get. In addition, three newspaper versions of this proof have been observed:

N(p): McClure galley proof, unmarked, signed, headed 'For July 5. | NEW YORK'S | BICYCLE SPEEDWAY. || The Boulevard, Once a Quiet Avenue, Now | the Scene of Nightly Carnivals—Here | All Gotham Comes Together and | Rolls Along in an Endless, | Shimmering Panorama. || BY STEPHEN CRANE. || (Copyright, 1896, S. S. McClure Co.)'. The dateline is *New York, July 3, 1896.*

N[1]: *New York Sun*, July 5, 1896, section III, page 5, signed, headlined

'THE TRANSFORMED BOULEVARD. || Bicycling Has Made It the Most Interest-|ing of City Streets.' No dateline appears.

N²: *Boston Globe,* July 5, page 30, signed, headlined 'MIGHTY ARMY OF WHEELS. || Stephen Crane Writes of | Gotham's Speedway. || He Thinks the World is Slowly But | Surely Coming to Bloomers. || Game of "Bicycle Cop and Scorcher" as | Played in New York. ||'. The dateline is *New York, July 3,* and the McClure copyright notice follows the signature.

N³: *Pittsburgh Leader,* July 5, 1896, page 22, headlined 'A BICYCLE SPEEDWAY. || WHEELMEN'S NIGHTLY CARNIVALS | ON A NEW YORK STREET. || The Boulevard Once a Quiet Ave-|nue Now Dominated by Glittering | Wheels From End to End—All | Gotham Comes Together and Rolls | Along in an Endless Shimmering | Panorama. || BY STEPHEN CRANE. | (Copyright, 1896, S. S. McClure Co.)'. The dateline copies the McClure proof.

Since the newspapers all radiate from the Columbia proof, this is the copy-text, corrected in a few respects from the newspapers. No agreement in all newspaper readings suggests that Crane altered the copy of the proof returned to McClure. The extensive revisions in the *New York Sun* are typical of its treatment of Crane's articles and are unauthoritative. The piece is given as "Bicycle Boulevard" in Crane's list of his McClure 1896 articles, preserved in the Columbia Crane Collection with Cora's memorandum on the verso, *Business Notes.*

No. 77. IN THE BROADWAY CABLE CARS

The date and original place of publication of this piece have previously been unknown, the only evidence for the text being *Last Words* (1902), pages 173–180. However, in the University of Virginia–Barrett Collection is a newspaper clipping on which Cora has written in ink *For book 1665 words,* and, at the foot, her private code assignment *cc.* In blue pencil she wrote *N.Y. Press 2 copies,* and in ink she crossed out the headlines below the title. This is evidently intended to be the copy for the American edition of *Last Words,* and Cora has made one unauthorized change which was followed by *Last Words* from the duplicate kept for England. A number 28 is assigned the article. Cora's belief that the piece came from the *Press* was mistaken, for search discloses that the clipping is from the *New York Sun* of Sunday, July 26, 1896, and that this is a McClure piece syndicated in other newspapers, which must be the one referred to as "Broadway" in the list Crane made of his 1896 McClure syndications, a document preserved in the Special Collections of the Columbia University Libraries.

The following newspapers have been observed:

N¹: *Pittsburgh Leader,* July 26, 1896, page 22, headlined 'THE BROAD-WAY CABLE CARS. || The Exciting Drama Enacted Daily | on New York's Great Thorough-|fare. || BY STEPHEN CRANE. | (Copyright, 1896. The S. S. McClure Co.) | Dramatis Personae—The Gripman, the | Conductor, the Passenger and an Oc-|casional Truckman.' This *Dramatis Personae* is missing from the two other observed newspapers. One cannot be sure whether it was intended as part of the article or as part of the headline, possibly misplaced from the syndicate proof in N¹, as suggested by the headline of N³.

N²: *Denver Republican,* July 26, page 24, headlined 'ON A BROADWAY CABLE CAR || Stephen Crane Describes Life on the | Great Thoroughfare. || IT IS FULL OF EXCITING INCIDENTS || Thoughts Suggested by the Bustle | and Hurry in the Steady Stream | of Cars on the Center of Traffic | in New York City—New Phases of | the City's Life as the Time of Day | Progresses. ||'. A dateline is given, *New York, July 22.—(Special Correspondence.).*

N³: *New York Sun,* July 26, section II, page 3, unsigned, headlined 'IN THE BROADWAY CARS. || *HOW LIFE STRIKES A MAN WITH A | PICTURESQUE IMAGINATION.* || Panorama of a Day from the Down-town | Rush of the Morning to the Uninter-|rupted Whirr of the Cable at Night—The Man, and the Woman, and the Conductor.'

In its characteristic way the *Sun* tinkered extensively with the style and is the least trustworthy witness. The copy-text is N¹, the *Pittsburgh Leader,* which seems to be set with greatest fidelity to Crane's accidentals as they have been filtered through the lost McClure proof typesetting. Indeed, it may be that some of the emendations that add punctuation on the authority of joint N²⁻³ agreement may only mark independent conventional styling so that the N¹ text could be more authoritative in fact if one but had more witnesses to confirm. *Last Words,* being set from a duplicate of the Barrett clipping from the *Sun,* is derived and without authority. As "In a Broadway Car" the piece is listed in Paul Reynolds' inventory of *Last Words* material as of October 23, 1900.

No. 78. THE ROOF GARDENS AND GARDENERS OF NEW YORK

Preserved in the University of Virginia–Barrett Collection is a galley proof of "Roof-Gardens" headed 'For August 9. | THE ROOF GAR-DENS AND GAR-|DENERS OF NEW YORK. || A Phase of New York Life as Seen | by a Close Observer. ||'. The dateline reads simply *New York,* leaving the newspapers to supply whatever date they pleased. In the observed syndicated newspapers one omits the dateline, and in the others the dates range from August 4 to August 7. Although no notice is made in the proof, on the evidence of N³ the piece was distributed by McClure's for whom Crane was writing at this time. The preservation of this important proof⁴² is due to the good fortune that it was the copy sent by Cora to Paul Reynolds for the American edition of *Last Words*. On the second sheet of the proof Cora wrote *For book* in blue pencil, and she made a few corrections in ink, two of them to remove timely language.⁴³ The blue-pencil number 25 is written on the first sheet in the right margin, and *z* below the first column. A word count in blue pencil is deleted in blue and 2 *copies* is written in.

The sketch was syndicated for appearance on Sunday, August 9, 1896. The following examples have been observed:

N¹: *Cincinnati Commercial Tribune,* Sunday, August 9, 1896, page 18, signed, headlined 'THE ROOF GARDEN || Novel Phase of Life in the | Metropolis. || MIDSUMMER NIGHT SCENES || HOW NEW YORKERS MANAGE TO | AMUSE THEMSELVES. || VIVID PICTURES OF REAL LIFE || Taken by a Close Observer, Toned in | Lively Colors and Full of | Inspiration. || Special Correspondence Commercial Tribune.' The dateline is *New York, Aug. 5.*

N²: *Washington Post,* August 9, page 20, signed and copyrighted 1896, headlined 'EVENING ON THE ROOF || Flashing Spots in Darkness Where | New York Gets Fresh Air. || GOLDEN HAIRED SOUBRETTE || The Girl with a Copper Voice and the Irish-|man with Circular Whiskers Have Their | Innings at Entertaining and the Crowds | Guzzle Beer, While Waiters Obstruct the | View—Gardens Where People Most Do | Congregate—Invention of Arab and Moor. ||'. The dateline is *New York, Aug. 7.*

N³: *Portland Oregonian,* August 9, page 16, signed, headlined 'Roof Gardens | of New York || A Phase of New York Life, as Seen | by a Close Observer. || (Copyright, 1896, by S. S. McClure Co.)'. The dateline is *New York, Aug. 4.*

N⁴: *Pittsburgh Leader,* August 9, page 20, signed, headlined 'THE ROOF GARDENS. || Stephen Crane Describes an Interest-|ing Place of New York Life. ||'. The dateline is *New York, August 8, 1896.*

N⁵: *Denver Republican,* August 9, page 21, signed, headlined 'ROOF GARDENS OF NEW YORK || Stephen Crane Describes a Peculiar | Type

---

⁴² This is a rare example of a preserved syndicated proof for a Crane piece published by a series of newspapers; hence their accidental and substantive variants offer a student an excellent exercise in the reconstruction of a text from multiple radiating documents since the results can be checked against the exact copy that was furnished these newspapers.

⁴³ The proof and all newspapers read *This season* at 380.4, which Cora altered in ink to *One season;* at 380.13 she changed *is* to *was.* For the rest, she miscorrected the typo *abvious* (379.11) to *obvious* (which should be *oblivious*) and she passed the missing required comma after *consequence* (379.11) and the misspelling *propogation* (381.6) although correcting the typo *watis* to *waits* (379.22).

of Amusement. || THE WAITER A LEADING FEATURE || He Brings Beer and Then Stead-|fastly Stands in the Way and | Shuts Off All View of the Stage | From the Spectators—Oscar Ham-|merstein and His Injunction Ma-|chine—The Great Roof Garden | Which Is Not Artistic, but Is | Popular, Nevertheless. ||'. The dateline is *New York, Aug. 6.—(Special Correspondence.)*.

Cuts for three illustrations accompanied the McClure's proofs and were used by the newspapers, usually uncaptioned. With doubtful authority N[1] captions them *The Grand Central Palace, The Arabian,* and *The Olympia.* These cuts are not present in the University of Virginia–Barrett proof. N[4] only prints *The Arabian* without caption, and N[5] groups the three illustrations with the caption *Typical Scenes at New York's Swell Roof Gardens.*

After Crane's death Cora sold the piece in England and it appeared in the *Westminster Gazette,* October 17, 1900, pages 1–2, headed 'THE ROOF-GARDENS AND GARDENERS OF | NEW YORK. | A PHASE OF NEW YORK LIFE AS SEEN BY A CLOSE OBSERVER. | BY THE LATE STEPHEN CRANE.' The same typesetting (except for a rearranged first paragraph to accommodate an ornamental initial) was used to print the sketch in the *Westminster Budget,* November 2, 1900, page 14. Finally, it was printed in *Last Words* (1902), pages 166–171, in the section "New York Sketches."

The only authority, and copy-text, is the McClure's proof (N[p]) from which all the newspapers derive by radiation. The appearance of the misprint at 379.11 in two of the newspapers indicates that the syndicated proof had not been corrected from its University of Virginia state. The *Westminster Gazette* (WG) also radiates from this proof in a duplicate copy that seems to have been altered by Cora as in the University of Virginia copy since it repeats her changes of *This* to *One* (380.4) and *was* to *is* (380.13). *Last Words* (E1) follows N(p) instead of the unique WG variants at 380.4 and 381.25 ('stifled') and repeats the Cora miscorrection of N(p) *abvious* to *obvious* (379.11) whereas WG correctly makes it *oblivious.* On the other hand, at 378.25, 378.28, 379.3–4, 380.20, and 381.25 (*omit* 'more air') WG and E1 agree in unique substantive variants. This evidence is contradictory, for if E1 were to radiate also from another copy of N(p) one would need to take it that these four joint variant readings represent further alterations of the proof by Cora, evidence that would clash with the changes she made in the University of Virginia–Barrett example. More to the point, whereas the change from N(p) *a roof-* to WG,E1 *the roof-* (378.25) and just possibly the omission of *more air* (381.25) might be explicable as Cora's tinkerings, the omission of *little* (378.28) is more difficult to understand, and the omission of a whole sentence *He . . . change* (379.3–4) has no literary explanation but might very well be due to compositorial eyeskip since the preceding sentence begins with the same words *He only knows that*. The simplest explanation would be that Cora (not having more than two copies of N[p]) used one McClure's proof for the *Westminster Gazette* sale, sent the second to Reynolds, and utilized an early proof of the *Gazette* as copy for *Last Words*. If this is so, the WG variant readings not passed on to E1 (*a suggestion* [378.24], *oblivious* [379.11], and *opened* [380.4]) would be editorial changes made in the WG proof at a later stage than the copy sent to Cora, and the joint variant readings of WG and E1 would represent WG compositorial mistakes not caught in the proofing. This is a more credible hypothesis than the one for Cora's continued alterations in two copies of N(p) and it would mean that E1 is a derived text from WG whereas $N and WG radiate from N(p).

In a holograph list of McClure pieces preserved in the Columbia University Libraries Special Collections this sketch is noted as "Roof Garden" under the heading "Syndicate". It appears in Paul Reynolds' inventory of *Last Words* material in his possession in a letter to Cora of October 23, 1900, titled as in the proof. This is undoubtedly the sketch referred to by the editor of the *Westminster Gazette* in a letter to Cora dated October 12, 1900: "I think, for the present, I will choose one of the articles you send me and return you the other in case you may care to use it quickly elsewhere. I should be very much obliged if you would kindly let me know what price you think is fair for these articles" (Columbia).

No. 79. AN ELOQUENCE OF GRIEF

Preserved in the University of Virginia–Barrett Collection is a leaf from the draft holograph manuscript of this sketch. The text is written in pencil on a page of cheap wove ledger paper 312 × 200 mm., its rules 10 mm. apart. The page is numbered 3 and includes the text from 382.27–383.8, *constantly . . . exhibits* (*shows* in MS); the letters *jj* appear at the lower left corner. The leaf reads:

constantly. None seemed to notice the girl and there was no reason why she should be noticed if [a] the curious, rearward, were not interested in the devastation which tears bring to some complexions. Her tears however seemed to burn like acid and they left fierce pink marks on her face.

Occasionally this girl looked across the room where two well-dressed young [b] women and a man stood waiting with the serenity of people who are not concerned as to the [c] interior fittings of jails.

The business of the court progressed and presently the girl, the policeman and the [d] well-dressed party stood before the judge. Thereupon two lawyers engaged [e] in some prelimary rockets [f] and fire-wheels which were endured, generally, in silence. The [g] girl, it appeared, was accused of stealing fifty dollar's worth of silk underwear from the room of one of the well-dressed woman. She [h] had been a servant in the house.

In a clear way and with none of the ferocity that a plaintiff often shows,

a if] *interlined above independently deleted* 'unless' *and* 'unless'
b young] *interlined with a caret*
c the] *interlined with a caret above deleted* 'f'
d the] *followed by deleted* 'group'
e engaged] *preceded by deleted* 'embarked'
f rockets] *preceded by independently deleted* 'ren' *and* 'exchanges'
g The] *inserted before* 'Th' *deleted at paragraph point*
h She] *preceded by deleted* 'Soon a'

The chief importance of this leaf is that it enables us to date the sketch with some accuracy. The paper, pencil, and hand are identical with another leaf in the Barrett Collection on which are written notes for "Adventures of a Novelist," Crane's account of the arrest of Dora Clark and of his intervention. The two must have been inscribed at approximately the same date. Moreover, the *New York Journal* statement prefixed to "Adventures of a Novelist" published on Sunday, September 20, 1896, remarks that on the preceding Monday (which would be September 14) Crane had sat all day on the bench with Magistrate Cornell at the Jefferson Market Police Court and had observed the disposition of the various cases as part of his preparation for a series of *Journal* articles on New York life. The coincidence of paper and writing of the two leaves suggests very strongly that "An Eloquence of Grief" derives from some case he observed on September 14, 1896, and that it was written in close proximity to his notes for the *Journal* article published September 20. Thus a date of late September or early October 1896 for "An Eloquence of Grief" should be accurate. It appears as No. 9 in Crane's inventory of about July, 1897, and is listed as 'Ms with me' and of 1,000 words.

However, the sketch was not published and did not appear until Crane expanded the Heinemann edition of *The Open Boat* (1898), pages 267–270, by including it in the series called "Midnight Sketches." No other publication is known. The copy-text is *The Open Boat* but with emendation of the English styling of the accidentals in the section where the manuscript is preserved. The Historical Collation gives the variant MS readings.

No. 80. IN THE TENDERLOIN: A DUEL BETWEEN AN ALARM CLOCK AND A SUICIDAL PURPOSE

First printed in *Town Topics*, XXXVI (October 1, 1896), 14, this narrative was reprinted then in *Tales from Town Topics*, no. 33 (September, 1899), pages 119–123. The latter was a straight reprint without authority. Swift Doyer, one of the protagonists of this tale, appears briefly in "Yen-Hock Bill and His Sweetheart" (No. 83). This sketch seems to go back to 1894, at least in its genesis, as evidenced by the appearance of a draft of part of the dialogue on the rectos of fols. 37–39 in the Crane Notebook preserved in the University of Virginia–Barrett Collection. The Notebook reads as follows:

In the midnight silence of the bed-chamber, a man's voice rang angrily while from the other pillow over next to the wall, there came a sound of low sobbing.

"You haven't got any sense at all," said the man. "If you were ever born with any, you've lost it in the shuffle somehow. What did you want to lie to[a] me for,[b] hey?" He sat up suddenly and sent[c] this question forward fiercely. Then his voice dropped again to a monotone of intense bitterness, menace, despair, rage. "You lied, didn't you? Lied—lied like a common woman of the streets. Didn't you, now? Didn't you?" He paused a moment.[d] Finally a woful girl's voice said: "Yes."

"Yes, lied to me! Didnt you know I'd catch you?[e] Didnt you know I'd catch you, blast your wooden head.[f] Yet you lied! Like[g] a thief! How do[h] you ever expect me to take your word again? Say? Do you expect[i] me to trust you? Do you know what your word is worth to me now? Do you know? It isnt worth that?

a to] *interlined above deleted* 'for'
b for] *interlined*
c sent] *preceded by deleted* 'swung'
d moment.] *period altered from comma, followed by* 'and' *not deleted in error*
e you?] *question mark altered from exclamation point*
f head.] *period altered from question mark*
g Like] 'L' *over* 'l'
h do] 'o' *over* 'id'
i expect] *followed by deleted* 'to'

No. 81. THE "TENDERLOIN" AS IT REALLY IS

The first of a series that Crane wrote for the *Journal*, "The 'Tenderloin' As It Really Is" was given a full-page spread in the *New York Journal*, Sunday, October 25, 1896, pages 13–14. The headline, across the width of the page, read 'THE "TENDERLOIN" AS IT REALLY IS - - - BY STEPHEN CRANE.' Below is one of three full-width sets of drawings of Tenderloin life that space the text, and beneath this is 'The First of a Series of Striking Sketches of New York Life by the Famous Novelist.' On page 14 the continuation is headed 'CRANE IN THE | TENDERLOIN. ||' and the sketch is signed at the foot. The article must have excited some interest, for the *Literary Digest,* XIV (November 7, 1896), 13, reprinted the episode at 391.26–392.10 without substantive change, headed 'A Picture of the Tenderloin.—Mr. Stephen Crane, who has, as the newspapers have told us all, been making some pretty close studies of life in the "tenderloin" and "slum" districts of New York, comes forth with the following scene, which has rather more of verity than animation, of men trying to "see the town" and not knowing exactly how to do it. We quote from *The Journal:*'. The first sentence undoubtedly refers to the Dora Clark affair written up by Crane in "Adventures of a Novelist" in the *Journal,* September 20, 1896.

No. 82. IN THE "TENDERLOIN"

Following "The 'Tenderloin' As It Really Is," the first of an advertised series of sketches of New York Life, the *New York Journal* in its Sunday American magazine section, on November 1, 1896, page 25, ran the signed article on a whole page with three large illustrations, headed 'IN THE "TENDERLOIN," BY STEPHEN CRANE. | The Second of a Series of Sketches of New York Life by the Famous Novelist'. The lengthy captions for the illustrations quote from the first three sentences of the third paragraph, 393.4–9, from the passage represented by the paragraph at 394.11–17, and from the paragraph represented by 395.28–35. One illustration is signed 'Kerr' or 'Ferr' and the other two are signed 'Jameson'.

No. 83. YEN-HOCK BILL AND HIS SWEETHEART

The *New York Journal* printed this sketch on Sunday, November 29, 1896, page 35, giving it a full-page spread and a large illustration captioned *"Why th' ell didn't you come before? You're a nice one, leaving me here to die."* The headline was 'A TENDERLOIN STORY, BY NOVELIST STEPHEN CRANE. | [to the left] YEN-NOCK BILL | AND | HIS SWEETHEART. | [to the right] The Distinguished Author of "The Red Badge of Courage" Writes a Character Sketch of a Famous | Tenderloin Confidence Man and Shoplifter, a Man "Who

Never Did | a Crooked Thing Since He Was Born." ' No variants were observed in a collation of the sketch in the city and the out-of-town editions of the *Journal*. The *Journal's* 'Yen-Nock' is a misreading of 'Yen-Hock', for which see the Textual Note to 396.3.1. The illustration is signed 'Kerr' or 'Ferr'.

No. 84. STEPHEN CRANE IN MINETTA LANE

When it was syndicated, probably by Bacheller, on Sunday, December 20, 1896, a number of newspapers were interested in this account of New York's crime-ridden district. The following have been observed:

N[1]: *Nebraska State Journal,* December 21, 1896, page 3, signed, headlined 'MURDEROUS MINETTA LANE || Stephen Crane Describes One of New York's | Notorious Streets. || WORST DAYS HAVE PASSED AWAY || But Its Negro and Italian Denizens | Still Include Many Whose Deeds | Are Evil—Resort of Mammy | Ross. ||'. At the foot appears the simple notice *Copyright, 1896.*

N[2]: *Galveston Daily News,* December 20, page 24, signed, headlined 'IN MINETTA LANE || Stephen Crane Describes One of New York City's Most | Notorious Thoroughfares. || ITS WORST DAYS HAVE PASSED || But Its Inhabitants Still Include Many Whose Deeds are Evil—The | Celebrated Resort of Mammy Ross. || For the News—Copyrighted.' This version was printed, from standing type, without variation in the *Dallas Morning News,* December 20, page 11.

N[3]: *Philadelphia Press,* December 20, page 34, signed, headlined 'STEPHEN CRANE IN MINETTA LANE, | One of Gotham's Most Notorious Thoroughfares. || The Novelist Tells What He Saw and Heard on a Street Where the Inhabitants Have | Been Famous for Evil Deeds. Where the Burglar and the Shoplifter, and | the Murderer Live Side by Side. The Noted Resort of | Mammy Ross and Others of Her Kind. ||'.

N[4]: *San Francisco Chronicle,* January 10, 1897, page 2, signed, headlined '[type-orn.] STEPHEN CRANE IN MINETTA LANE. [type-orn]'.

N[5]: *New York Herald,* December 20, 1896, sec. v, page 5, signed, headlined 'WHAT LIFE WAS LIKE | In Bloody Days Gone By | IN MINETTA LANE. || Stephen Crane's Description of the His-|toric Old Locality as It Is | and as It Was. || THE OLD INHABITANTS MOURN. ||'.

N[6]: *Minneapolis Tribune,* December 20, page 21, signed, headlined 'STEPHEN CRANE | IN MINETTA LANE || The Novelist Describes One of New York's Most No-|torious Thoroughfares. || ITS WORST DAYS HAVE NOW PASSED AWAY || But Its Inhabitants Still Include Many Whose Deeds Are Evil—The | Celebrated Resort of Mammy Ross. ||'.

Two illustrations are common to all the newspapers except N[5]: one is captioned *Minetta Lane* and the other *Mammy Ross. The New York Herald* had its staff artist draw three different illustrations, captioned, *Minetta Street, Minetta Lane,* and *Minetta Lane at Night.*

The University of Virginia–Barrett Collection holds a black carbon typescript of ten leaves of cheap wove paper 264 × 208 mm., the rules 9 mm. apart, the pages numbered at top center within spaced parentheses. Its title is 'MINETTA LANE. | NEW YORK | ITS WORST DAYS HAVE PASSED AWAY. | But Its Inhabitants Still Include Many Whose Deeds Are Evil. | The Celebrated Resort of Mammy Ross. | By Stephen Crane.' In this title the words 'NEW YORK' and 'By Stephen Crane.' (the latter double underlined) are written in ink, not typed, and the periods after 'LANE' and 'Evil' have been added in ink. To the left is Cora's underlined *words,* the number not filled in. A blue-crayon 27 appears at the top right and in the lower left corner is a small letter *k.* The usual # concludes page 10. On the verso of page 10 Cora wrote in pencil *Minetta Lane | Sketches of N.Y. | For book. | 3000 words.* This typescript, among the group sent to Paul Reynolds in New York for the American edition of *Last Words,* was made from a clipping of the article in N⁶, the *Minneapolis Tribune,* the copy of which is pasted in the Crane scrapbooks in the Special Collections of the Columbia University Libraries. The final appearance in print, in *Last Words* (1902), pages 154–166, was set from the mate of this typescript, its title being 'MINETTA LANE, NEW YORK' with the subheadings as in the typescript and its N⁶ copy.

The nearest one can get to the lost manuscript is the partial reconstruction of the lost syndicate proof from the evidence of the six independent newspapers that radiate from this proof. The *Nebraska State Journal* (N¹) text has been selected as copy-text since it is representative and in its texture of accidentals is fairly close to what can be made of the characteristics of the proof. Emendation from other newspapers is made to construct an eclectic text, however, when in particular respects the readings of N¹ appear to diverge from those of the proof insofar as it can be recovered. In this respect the only major problem is the curious appearance in N⁵, the *New York Herald,* of a unique paragraph following 405.28 (see the Historical Collation) which reports information given the writer by Hector Worden, one of the district's plainclothesmen. Nothing in the style of this paragraph would prevent one from attributing the paragraph to Crane, but the physical circumstances lead to another conclusion. That is, it is impossible to believe that the paragraph was present in the syndicated proof and was independently omitted by the other five newspapers. Hence the only conjecture to be drawn is that the *New York Herald* took the opportunity to add on its own account some extra information not present in Crane's article, with the spice of a bit of moralizing. A small amount of tinkering with the article may be observed in the *Herald* to adapt the language to New York publication, but there are no signs of Crane's unique revision elsewhere in the *Herald* text to warrant any fantastic speculation that he was personally concerned with the *Herald's* version in any way.

WESTERN SKETCHES

No. 85. NEBRASKA'S BITTER FIGHT FOR LIFE

This first of Crane's Western sketches was syndicated by Bacheller, Johnson and Bacheller on Sunday, February 24, 1895, and had wide distribution. A proof of the article is preserved in Crane's scrapbook in the Special Collections of the Columbia University Libraries in the identical typesetting except for a few corrections as the text in the *Nebraska State Journal*. Other preserved proofs of these Western sketches also in the *State Journal* setting indicate beyond question that Bacheller had the *Journal* set up the articles from Crane's manuscripts. In this piece, as in the rest, little or no reason exists to suggest that these proofs were read and corrected by Bacheller; instead it seems evident that the rough proofs were sent out to subscribing newspapers in the same form as those preserved in the scrapbook, with no more proofreading than was given by the *Journal's* workmen in contrast to its editorial staff. The headlines in the proof read as follows: 'NEBRASKA'S BITTER | FIGHT FOR LIFE || The People of Thirty Coun-|ties Destitute and | Starving. || STEPHEN CRANE'S REPORT || Waiting in the Bitter Cold of Winter | for the Spring, When They'll | Have No Seed Corn---The | Relief Commission--- | Exempt Counties. || (Copyright, 1895, by Bacheller, Johnson | & Bacheller.)'. The syndicate furnished an illustrative initial and three drawings captioned *Helpless With No Weapon Against This Terrible Wrath of Nature, Secretary Ludden Works Early and Late,* and *She Travelled the Three Miles.* These proofs have no subheadings, and are signed. Their dateline is *Eddyville, Dawson Co., Neb., Feb. 22.*

The following newspapers have been observed:

N[1]: *Nebraska State Journal,* February 24, 1895, page 14, signed, headlined 'WAITING FOR THE SPRING || A Bitter Winter for the People of | Thirty Counties. || MR. STEPHEN CRANE'S REPORT || The Results of the Drought Have | Been Exaggerated, But the Situ-|ation Is Serious— Work of | the Relief Commission. || (Copyright, 1895, by Bacheller, Johnson | & Bacheller.)'. The dateline is the same as the proof's.

N[2]: *Salt Lake City Tribune,* February 24, page 14, signed, headlined 'NEBRASKA'S BITTER FIGHT || The People of Thirty Counties | Destitute and Starving. || STEPHEN CRANE'S REPORT. || Efforts for Relief De-layed or | Thwarted by Carelessness, Selfish-|ness or Greed—Sufferers Waiting | in the Bitter Cold of the Winter | for the Spring—No Seed for Corn—|The Commission. || [Copyright, 1895, by Bacheller, Johnson & | Bacheller.]'. The dateline is the same as the proof's. The third caption in N² reads *She Traveled with Her Baby Three Miles.*

N³: *Buffalo Morning News*, February 24, page 5, signed, headlined 'NEBRASKA'S BITTER | FIGHT FOR LIFE. || The People of 30 Counties Des-|titute and Starving. || STEPHEN CRANE'S REPORT. || Waiting in the Bitter Cold of Winter for | the Spring, When They'll Have No | Seed Corn---The Relief Commis-|sion-- Exempt Counties. ||'. The dateline is the same as in the proof.

N⁴: *New Orleans Times-Democrat*, February 23, page 9, signed, head-lined 'NEBRASKA'S FIGHT. || THE PEOPLE OF THIRTY COUN-|TIES DESTITUTE. || Waiting in the Bitter Cold of | Winter for the Spring, When | They'll Have No Seed Corn—|The Relief Commission—Ex-|empt Counties. || Correspondence of The Times-Democrat.' The dateline is the same as in the proof.

N⁵: *Galveston Daily News*, February 24, page 10, signed, headlined 'A FIGHT FOR LIFE. || The People of Thirty Counties | Destitute and Starving | in Nebraska. || STEPHEN CRANE'S REPORT. || Waiting in the Bitter Cold of Winter for | the Spring, When They'll Have | No Seed Corn. || For the News—Copyright.' The dateline is the same as in the proof. In the identical typesetting the article appeared in the *Dallas Morning News*, February 24, page 18.

N⁶: *Cincinnati Commercial Gazette*, February 24, pages 17–18, signed 'S. C.', headlined 'DISTRESS IN NEBRASKA || The Area of Acute Destitu-tion Covers | Some Thirty Counties. || A SPECIAL CORRESPONDENT'S REPORT || Scoundrels That Have Pilfered from | Relief Funds and Sup-plies—Condi-|tion of the Farmers—Work and | Needs of the Relief Com-mission. || Special Correspondence Commercial Gazette.' The dateline is the same as in the proof. The initial and the illustrations do not appear.

N⁷: *Philadelphia Press*, February 24, page 25, signed, headlined 'NE-BRASKANS' BITTER FIGHT FOR LIFE || Stephen Crane's Graphic Report on the Conditions in the | Thirty Counties Where the People Are Destitute | Yet Full of Courage and Hope. || Special Correspondence of "The Press." ' The date in the dateline is changed to *Feb.* 20. The illustrations but not the initial appear.

N⁸: *New York Press*, February 24, sec. v, page 2, signed, headlined 'A STATE'S HARD FIGHT || The Weather Had a Grudge | Against Nebraska Farmers. || THIRTY COUNTIES STARVING || The Storms of Winter Were as Bad | as the Summer's Scorching. || And the Greed of Those Who Are Not Des-|titute Is Almost as Appalling as the | Need of Those Who Are Starving—|Worse Yet, Where Will Seed Corn | Come from in the Spring?' The date is altered from the proof to *Feb.* 20. The illustrations are used but not the initial.

N⁹: *Rochester Democrat and Chronicle*, February 24, page 7, unsigned, headlined 'DISTRESS IN NEBRASKA || People of Thirty Counties Starving —Stephen | Crane's Report—Waiting in the Bitter | Cold of Winter for the Spring—|The Relief Commission. || Written for the Democrat and Chronicle (Copyright).' The dateline is the same as in the proof. The illustrations are used but not the initial.

The Columbia proof has several interesting features. It would seem that the first paragraph was set up at first without the illustrative initial, for at the end of the paragraph appear six lines of text in a different setting that repeat the last nine lines of the paragraph in the setting with the initial. It is obvious that these repeated lines were from an earlier setting left in the proof by mistake. No differences in text are present here. A resetting with textual implications occurs later at 418.6–7. Here the setting reads:

> "How did you get along?"
> "Don't git along, stranger. Who the
> "How do you get along?"

It seems clear that the third line *"How do you get along?"* is the original line which an alert proofreader detected as differing from the manuscript. However, when the correction line was inserted, in some inexplicable manner the original was retained in place of the completion of the sentence. The *State Journal* reads here:

> "How did you get along?"
> "Don't git along, stranger. Who the
> hell told you I did get along?"

This is a later correction, however, and presumably from the manuscript; but that the uncorrected proof was sent out is shown by the different versions the newspapers invented for the continuation whenever they did not simply omit it. The *State Journal* text faithfully repeats the misprints of the proof but in two places in addition to the above has reset the proof. The simplest is the resetting at 419.19–20 of two lines in the proof *were . . . pond* into three lines in order to avoid the division *Ne-|braska*. The second affected the text. At 412.39 the proof line read *A faceteous freight agent in the east* which was reset correcting *east* to *East* but omitting *facetious* to produce the N[1] form *A freight agent in the East*.

The copy-text and only authority is the proof, or rather the same typesetting in the *State Journal* which contains the corrections at 409.7.1 and 418.6–7 but needs the restoration, in correctly spelled form, of *facetious* at 412.39.

With the title "Sketches of Nebraska Life" the piece appears as No. 25 in Crane's holograph list of about July 1897, with the notation 'ms to be recovered from Bacheller'. The assigned word count of 1,000 is clearly a bad guess.

No. 86. SEEN AT HOT SPRINGS

Preserved in the Special Collections of the Columbia University Libraries is Crane's scrapbook containing a proof of "Seen at Hot Springs" which, except for some modification of the headlines, is in the same typesetting as the text as printed in the *Nebraska State Journal* for the syndicated date of Sunday, March 3, 1895. This is the second of several indications that from time to time the Bacheller syndicate employed the *State Journal* to set the type for the proofs that it sent out to subscribing newspapers, another being the preservation by Crane of the proof for "Grand Opera in New Orleans" and for "The Fete of Mardi Gras" which also correspond in their typesetting with the *State Journal* for March 24, 1895, and February 16, 1896, respectively. Except for cuts in the *State Journal* the newspaper and the proof are identical in their text. The headlines of the proof, however, read 'SEEN AT HOT SPRINGS || Crane Writes of a Pictur- | esque Winter Resort. || THE JOYS OF INVALIDISM || Bath Houses that Are Like the | Abode of Subdued Millionaires---|A Town Not Tender, | But Tolerant. || (Copyright, 1895, by Bacheller, Johnson | & Bacheller.)'. The dateline in the proof is *Hot Springs, Ark., March 3*. The syndicate supplied an ornamental initial and two illustrations captioned *Bath House Row* and *The Indian Legend*.

The following newspapers have been observed:

N[1]: *Nebraska State Journal*, March 3, 1895, page 10, signed, headlined 'SEEN AT HOT SPRINGS || Stephen Crane Writes of a Picturesque | Winter Resort || AND OF THE JOYS OF INVALIDISM || Bath Houses that Are Like the | Abodes of Subdued Millionaires---|A Town Not Tender, | But Tolerant. || (Copyright, 1895, by Bacheller, Johnson | & Bacheller.)'. The dateline is March 3 as in the proof.

N[2]: *Galveston Daily News*, March 3, page 11, signed, headlined 'HOT SPRINGS SCENES || Stephen Crane Writes of a Pictur-|esque Winter Resort in | Arkansas. || THE JOYS OF INVALIDISM. || Bath Houses That Are Like the Abode of Sub-|dued Millionaires—A Town Not | Tender, But Tolerant. || For the News—Copyright.' The dateline is *Hot Springs, Ark., March 1*. The piece in the same typesetting appeared in the *Dallas Morning News*, March 3, page 16.

N[3]: *Cincinnati Commercial Gazette*, March 3, page 17, signed 'S. C.', headlined 'ARKANSAS' HOT SPRINGS || A Picturesque Winter Resort in the | Southwest Pine Forests. || SOME OF THE JOYS OF INVALIDISM || Bath-Houses That Are Like the Abodes | of Subdued Millionaires—A Town | Not Tender, but Tolerant—The Baths | and the Black Servants. || Special Correspondence Commercial Gazette.' The dateline was *Hot Springs, Ark., Feb. 27*. Only the first illustration was used, and the ornamental initial does not appear.

N⁴: *Buffalo News,* March 3, page 8, signed, headlined 'SEEN AT HOT SPRINGS. || Crane Writes of a Picturesque | Winter Resort. || THE JOYS OF INVALIDISM. || Bath Houses That Are Like the Abode | of Subdued Millionaires---A | Town Not Tender, But | Tolerant. || [SPECIAL CORRESPONDENCE SUNDAY NEWS.]'. The dateline was *Hot Springs, Ark., March* 2. The ornamental initial does not appear.

N⁵: *Philadelphia Press,* March 3, page 29, signed, headlined 'THE MERRY THRONG | AT HOT SPRINGS. || Stephen Crane Writes of the | Picturesque and Cosmo-|politan Winter Resort. || JOYS OF A VALETUDINARIAN. || Bath Houses That Suggest the Abodes | of Subdued Millionaires—A Tol-|erant Town—Experience with | a Festive Sharper. || Special Correspondence of "The Press." ' The dateline was *Hot Springs, Ark., March* 1. The second illustration was omitted.

N⁶: *Rochester Democrat and Chronicle,* March 3, page 7, unsigned, headlined 'SEEN AT HOT SPRINGS || A Picturesque Winter Resort—The Joys of | Invalidism—Bath Houses that Are Like | the Abode of Subdued | Millionaires. || Written for the Democrat and Chronicle (Copyright).' The dateline was *Hot Springs, Ark., March* 1. The ornamental initial was not used.

The copy-text is the *State Journal* proof, N¹(p), which is the only authority.

No. 87. GRAND OPERA IN NEW ORLEANS

In the Crane scrapbook preserved in the Special Collections of the Columbia University Libraries is pasted a proof of "Grand Opera in New Orleans" that is identical with the typesetting of the syndicated article, save for a cut and some rewording of the headlines, in the *Nebraska State Journal* for Sunday, March 24, 1895. It seems clear that, as was true for "Seen at Hot Springs" on March 3, Bacheller used the *State Journal* to set up the proof that he mailed to subscribing newspapers. This proof is in uncorrected state, and the *State Journal,* on the evidence of its own typesetting, never seems to have had corrections returned from Bacheller to incorporate. As a consequence, errors such as *Armours* for *Amours* at 428.8 and *be* for *see* at 428.31 were passed on to other newspapers, and the serious mistake at 428.1–2 by which a line of type reset to correct an error displaced a line of the text was never rectified. Whether *opera* for the error *open* at 426.27, the missing comma after *baritone* at 426.29, and *thorns* for *thrones* at 427.12 were independent corrections in all other newspaper versions or handwritten alterations in some of the proofs is not to be determined. An uncaptioned illustration of the four major singers, three in operatic roles, signed by G. Y. Kauffman, was sent out by Bacheller, as was an illustrative initial. The following appearances have been observed:

N¹: *Nebraska State Journal,* March 24, 1895, page 11, signed, head-lined 'OPERA IN NEW ORLEANS || Music With History of More Than One | Hundred Years. || A MOST UNIQUE COMPANY || The Only City in the Country That | Supports a Continual and Elab-|orate Production of | Grand Opera. ||'. The dateline, as in the proof, is *New Orleans, La., March* 23. N¹ makes a cut at 428.3–7 but is otherwise identical with the proof except for the headlines and copyright notice, which read as follows in the proof, N¹(p): 'GRAND OPERA | IN NEW ORLEANS || Music With a History of | More Than 100 Years. || A MOST UNIQUE COMPANY || The Only City in the Country That | Supports a Continual and Elab-|orate Production of | Grand Opera. || (Copyright, 1895, by Bacheller, Johnson | & Bacheller.)'.

N²: *Philadelphia Press,* March 24, page 25, signed, headlined 'GRAND OPERA | IN NEW ORLEANS. || Music with an Uninterrupted | History of More Than a | Century. || THE COMPANY IS UNIQUE. || Continual and Elaborate Productions of | Grand Opera Boasted by the Cres-|cent City as No Other City | Can Boast It. || Special Correspondence of "The Press." ' The initial was used but not the illustration. The dateline copies the proof.

N³: *Galveston Daily News,* March 25, page 4, signed, headlined 'A CENTURY OF MUSIC. || Grand Opera in New Orleans Has a | History of More Than | 100 Years. || A MOST UNIQUE COMPANY. || The Only City in the Country That Supports | a Continual and Elaborate Produc-|tion of Grand Opera. || For the News—Copyright.' The dateline copies the proof. In the identical typesetting the article appeared in the *Dallas Morning News,* March 24, page 16.

N⁴: *Minneapolis Tribune,* March 24, page 17, signed, headlined 'UNIQUE. || Music With a History of | More Than One Hun-|dred Years. || New Orleans the Only City in | the Country That Supports | Continuous Grand Opera. || Special Correspondence to the Tribune.' The dateline is as in the proof except for the date *March* 22. The illustrative initial is omitted.

N⁵: *Rochester Democrat and Chronicle,* March 24, page 10, unsigned, headlined 'MUSIC IN NEW ORLEANS || Grand Opera Given There for More | Than One Hundred Years. || A VERY UNIQUE COMPANY || The Only City in the Country That | Supports a Continued and Elaborate | Production of Grand Opera—|History of Music There. || Written for the Democrat and Chronicle.' The dateline agrees with the proof.

PO: *Public Opinion,* xviii (July 4, 1895), 770, an excerpt headed 'Grand Opera for the People | Stephen Crane, in Galveston *News.*' A clipping is pasted in the Crane scrapbook.

The only authority, and hence the copy-text is the proof, which is to say the *Nebraska State Journal* except for the cut paragraph.

No. 88. THE CITY OF MEXICO

This article is preserved only in an untitled holograph manuscript, with two others of the same date, in the Special Collections of the Columbia University Libraries. The manuscript is numbered above semicircles at top center (except for the unnumbered first page) and is written in black ink on four pages of cheap wove unwatermarked paper 332 × 228 mm., the rules 8 mm. apart. The conclusion is signed on page 4. The word count for each page is circled on its verso and cumulated to 1,070 on the back of the last page. The person making the inventory has written on the last leaf verso *City of Mexico | 1070 words.* Before the first sentence appears the start of a dateline *City of Mexico,* followed by an empty space to be filled in and then a colon. Although Crane seems to have written various of his articles on his Western trip at a somewhat different time and place from that announced in the dateline, these three articles in manuscript probably date close to his stay in Mexico City in April, 1895. Stallman first reprinted the text from manuscript in the *Bulletin of the New York Public Library,* LXXI (1967), 555–557.

No. 89. THE VIGA CANAL

This sketch, dating presumably from about April, 1895, is preserved only in an untitled holograph manuscript in the Special Collections of the Columbia University Libraries. It consists of five pages (of which 2 through 5 are numbered above a semicircle) written in black ink on cheap wove unwatermarked paper 332 × 228 mm., the rules 8 mm. apart. The extensive autograph corrections that are not part of the original inscription are made also in a black ink but with a different pen and at a later time, and so are the signatures in the upper left corner of page 1 and at the end of page 5. The first sentence is preceded by a dateline *City of Mexico,* with a considerable space left for filling in the date. In pencil on the verso of the fifth leaf, in a strange hand probably that of the person who made the inventory, is written *Viga Canal.* Stallman first reprinted the text from manuscript in the *Bulletin of the New York Public Library,* LXXI (1967), 557–560.

No. 90. THE MEXICAN LOWER CLASSES

The untitled manuscript of this article is preserved in the Columbia University Libraries Special Collections, written in black ink on four pages of cheap wove unwatermarked paper 332 × 228 mm., the rules 8 mm. apart. Pages 2 through 4 are numbered above semicircles. Crane's signature appears in the upper left corner of the first page and at the conclusion on page 4. At the start is a partial dateline beginning *City of Mexico,* followed by a space to be filled in and then a colon and dash. The word total for each page is written in black ink on its verso, cumulated to 1,295 on the back leaf. This verso contains Cora's note *City of Mexico—Book | 1295 words,* a probable reference to a plan to include these sketches in *Last Words* (1902), but so far as is known no typescript was made from these manuscripts nor did Crane, so far as is known, ever attempt to publish them. Stallman first reprinted the text from manuscript in the *Bulletin of the New York Public Library,* LXXI (1967), 560–562.

No. 91. STEPHEN CRANE IN MEXICO (I)

Copyrighted by the Bacheller, Johnson and Bacheller syndicate, "Stephen Crane in Mexico" was printed in most newspapers on Sunday, May 19, 1895, although one was as early as May 16 and another as late as June 6. The following newspapers have been observed:

N[1]: *Nebraska State Journal,* May 19, 1895, page 13, signed, headlined 'STEPHEN CRANE IN MEXICO || Author of "The Black Riders" on Street | Porters and Venders. || THE PATIENT, PATHETIC BURRO || A City Where Many Things Are Pass-|ing Strange, but Where You | Can, After All, Get a Man-|hattan Cocktail. || (Copyright, 1895.).'. The dateline was *City of Mexico, May 18.*

N[2]: *Galveston Daily News,* May 19, page 13, signed, headlined 'CRANE SEES MEXICO. || The Author of "The Black Riders" | on Street Porters and | Venders. || PATIENT, PATHETIC BURRO. || A City Where Many Things Are Strange, But | Where You Can, After All, Get a | Manhattan Cocktail. || For the News—Copyright.' The dateline had *May 18.* From the same setting of type this text was also printed in the *Dallas Morning News,* May 19, page 18.

N[3]: *Buffalo Morning News,* May 19, page 11, signed, headlined 'CRANE IN MEXICO. || Author of "The Black Riders" | on Street Porters and | Venders. || PATIENT, PATHETIC BURRO || A City Where Many Things Are Passing | Strange, But Where You Can, | After All, Get a Manhat-|tan Cocktail. || [SPECIAL CORRESPONDENCE SUNDAY NEWS.]'. The dateline was *May 18.*

N[4]: *Louisville Courier-Journal,* May 19, part II, page 7, signed, headlined 'IN OLD MEXICO. || Some Sights Seen By An | American. || STREET PORTERS AND VENDERS || A City Where Many Things Are | Passing Strange. || THE PATIENT BURRO. ||'. The date in the dateline was *May 14.*

N[5]: *Philadelphia Press,* May 19, page 33, signed, headlined 'MEXICAN SIGHTS | AND STREET SCENES || The Author of "The Red | Badge of Courage" in the | Aztec Capital. || PATHETIC, PATIENT BURROS. || A City Where Many Things Are Pass-|ing Strange, but Where You Can, |

After All, Get a Manhattan | Cocktail. || Special Correspondence of "The Press." ' The dateline date is *May 13*.

N⁶: *Chicago Daily News*, June 6, page 10, signed, with '(Copyright 1895 by Bacheller, Johnson & | Bacheller.)' following the signature at the foot, headlined 'IN THE CITY OF MEXICO. || Stephen Crane Writes of the Amusing | Rascality and Dishonesty of | the Natives. || THE PATIENT, PATHETIC LITTLE BURRO. || Cheating Methods of Street Venders—|But After All One Can Get a | Manhattan Cocktail. || Special Correspondence of the Chicago Daily News.' The date in the dateline was *May 18*.

N⁷: *Rochester Democrat and Chronicle*, May 19, page 9, unsigned, headlined 'IN THE CITY OF MEXICO || Stephen Crane, Author of "The Black Riders," | on Street Porters and Venders—The | Patient Pathetic Burro—The | City's Strange Sights. || Written for the Democrat and Chronicle. (Copyright.)'. The dateline was given as *May 15*.

N⁸: *Savannah Morning News*, May 16, page 9, signed, headlined 'STEPHEN CRANE IN MEXICO. || AUTHOR OF "THE BLACK RIDERS" | ON STREET PORTERS AND | VENDERS. || The Patient, Pathetic Burro—A City | Where Many Things Are Passing | Strange, But Where You Can, After | All, Get a Manhattan Cocktail.'. The dateline date is *May 18*.

The dateline *May 18* in N⁸, published on May 16, confirms the same date in the *Nebraska State Journal* as that of the proof. All newspapers except N⁸ printed an illustrative initial with an Indian porter bearing a burden, and all newspapers except N⁶ and N⁸ printed three illustrations signed 'G. Y. Kauffman' and captioned *Two Lumber Wagons, Burro Loaded with Wood*, and *Palm-Mat Sellers*. N⁶ used only the second illustration, whereas N⁸ omitted all. Although the proof is not preserved in the Crane scrapbook, it is practically certain that the *Nebraska State Journal* represents the lost syndicate proof setting (although not necessarily the exact headlines) as in most of the other Western sketches. The evidence of the textual variants supports this hypothesis. The *State Journal*, therefore, is selected as copy-text and would appear to represent the only true authority, all other newspapers being derived from its form of the typesetting.

No. 92. FREE SILVER DOWN IN MEXICO

The Bacheller proof for this article, set by the *Nebraska State Journal* and identical with its text of Sunday, June 30, 1895, save for the copyright notice, is preserved in the Special Collections of the Columbia University Libraries. In the *Journal* the copyright notice is merely (*Copyright, 1895.*) but in the proof one finds, instead, (*Copyright, 1895, by Bacheller, Johnson & | Bacheller.*). The syndicate furnished an illustrative ornamental initial and four illustrations drawn by G. Y. Kauffman captioned *Cocktails Are Cheap, A Hat Costs $10, The Porter Wants Fifty Cents*, and *You Double Your Money*. The dateline in the proof is *City of Mexico, June 29*. The following news-papers have been observed:

N¹: *Nebraska State Journal*, June 30, 1895, page 13, signed, headlined 'IN FREE SILVER MEXICO || How the White Metal Standard Affects | Wages and Living. || AN IMPORTANT MATTER DISCUSSED || Stephen Crane Finds that Twice as | Many Jingling Dollars Won't | Begin to Buy Twice as | Many Things. || (Copyright, 1895.)'. The dateline is *City of Mexico, June 29*. The article was reprinted from standing type in the semi-weekly *Journal* on July 5, page 7.

N²: *Cincinnati Commercial Gazette*, June 30, page 9, signed, headlined 'WAGES AND LIVING | IN | FREE SILVER MEXICO. || Stephen Crane Finds That Twice | as Many Silver Dollars Won't | Buy Twice as Many Things. || Special Correspondence Commercial Gazette.' The dateline was *City of Mexico, June 24*.

N³: *Chicago Daily News*, July 23, page 2, signed, headlined 'IN FREE-SILVER MEXICO. || Living Is Very High and One Cannot | Have Very Many Com-|forts. || THE ONE CHEAP ARTICLE IS A COCKTAIL. || A Clerk on a Salary of $60 Per | Month Cannot Be a | Dude. || Special Correspondence of the Chicago Daily News.' Below the signature at the foot is the Bacheller copyright notice. The dateline was *City of Mexico, July 10*.

N⁴: *Minneapolis Tribune*, June 30, page 4, signed, headlined 'THE LAND OF | FREE SILVER || How the White Metal Stand-|ard Affects Wages | and Living. || Twice as Many Jingling Dollars | Won't Begin to Buy Twice | as Many Things. ||'. The dateline was *City of Mexico, June 29*. The illustrations were used but not the special initial.

N⁵: *Galveston Daily News*, July 1, page 4, signed, headlined 'FREE SILVER MEXICO. || How the White Metal Standard | Affects Wages and Living. | Matter Discussed. || Stephen Crane Finds that Twice as Many | Jingling Dollars Won't Begin to Buy | Twice as Many Things. || For The News—(Copyrighted).'. The dateline was *City of Mexico, June 29*. The article in the identical typesetting appeared in the *Dallas Morning News*, June 30, page 12.

N⁶: *Philadelphia Press*, June 30, page 31, signed, headlined 'FREE SILVER | DOWN IN MEXICO. || Stephen Crane's Picturesque | Account of the Effect of | the White Metal. || WAGES AND LIVING AFFECTED || Twice as Many Jingling Dollars Will | Not Begin to Buy Twice as Many | Things Because Their Cost | Is Just Double. || Special Correspondence of "The Press." ' The dateline was *City of Mexico, June 22*.

The only authority is the proof, corresponding to the text of N¹, the *Nebraska State Journal*, which becomes the copy-text.

No. 93. STEPHEN CRANE IN MEXICO (II)

This article is another in the group of Crane's Western sketches for which the Bacheller proof was set up by the *Nebraska State Journal*, as shown by an incomplete proof preserved in the Crane scrapbook in the Special Collections of the Columbia University Libraries, which breaks off with *upon the mes-|* at 451.2. This proof is headed (*For July 21.*) and is in the exact typesetting as the *State Journal* for Sunday, July 21, 1895, save that for the *Journal's* line beneath the headlines (*Copyright, 1895.*) the proof had read (*Copyright, 1895, Bacheller, Johnson & Bachel-|ler.*). Bacheller furnished an ornamental initial and two illustrations captioned *Waiting for the Train* and *The Popocatipetl and Ixtaccihuatl*, drawn by G. Y. Kauffman. N[3-4] changed the caption spelling to 'Popocatapetl.' The proof (and the *Journal*) text is not in a finally proofed state but appears to be in the condition of the other copies that were mailed out to subscribing newspapers. The following newspapers have been observed:

N[1]: *Nebraska State Journal*, July 21, 1895, page 13, signed, headlined 'STEPHEN CRANE IN MEXICO, || From San Antonio to the Ancient City of the | Aztecs. || THROUGH CACTUS AND MESQUITE. || The Author of "The Black Riders" | Describes a Trip as Picturesque as | any to be Taken in America. || (Copyright, 1895.)'. The dateline was *City of Mexico, July 4*, as in the proof.

N[2]: *Galveston Daily News*, July 21, page 10, signed, headlined 'FROM STEPHEN CRANE || An Interesting Trip From San An-|tonio to the Ancient City | of the Aztecs. || CACTUS AND MESQUITE. || The Author of "The Black Riders" | Describes a Trip as Picturesque | as Any To Be Taken in America. || For The News—Copyright.' In the same typesetting the article appeared in the *Dallas Morning News*, July 21, page 8. The dateline was *City of Mexico, July 4*.

N[3]: *Cincinnati Commercial Gazette*, July 21, page 18, signed, headlined '[within a frame of type-orn.] Two Tourists in Mexico. || The Author of "The Black Riders" Describes a Trip as | Picturesque as Any in the World. | [below the frame] Correspondence of Commercial Gazette.' The dateline was *City of Mexico, July 4*.

N[4]: *Philadelphia Press*, July 21, page 32, signed, headlined 'ANCIENT CAPITAL | OF MONTEZUMA. || Stephen Crane Describes the | Journey from San Antonio | to Mexico. || 'MID CACTUS AND MESQUITE. || The Brilliant Author of "The Black | Riders" Describes a Trip as Pic-|turesque as Any to Be Taken | in America. || Special Correspondence of "The Press."' The dateline was *City of Mexico, July 12*.

N[5]: *New Orleans Times-Democrat*, July 23, page 8, signed, headlined 'CRANE IN MEXICO. || FROM SAN ANTONIO TO THE AN-|CIENT CITY OF THE AZTECS. || Through Cactus and Mesquite—The | Author of "The Black Riders" | Describes a Trip as Picturesque | as Any To Be Taken in America. || Correspondence of the Times-Democrat.' The dateline was *City of Mexico, July 4*.

N[6]: *Rochester Democrat and Chronicle*, July 21, page 16, unsigned, headlined 'THE CITY OF THE AZTECS || Stephen Crane's Picturesque Trip in Mexico | From San Antonio to the Ancient City | of an Ancient People—Through | Cactus and Mesquite. || Written for the Democrat and Chronicle. (Copyright.)'. The dateline was *City of Mexico, July 4*.

Since all newspaper texts radiate from the proof as represented by the preserved fragment and, in identical form by N¹, the *Nebraska State Journal*, this becomes the copy-text and only authority.

No. 94. A JAG OF PULQUE IS HEAVY

Bacheller syndicated this Mexican report in various newspapers on Sunday, August 11, 1895, although a few adopted other dates. The following newspaper versions have been observed:

N¹: *Nebraska State Journal*, August 12, 1895, page 5, signed, headlined 'A JAG OF PULQUE IS HEAVY. || A Country Where a Drink Will Fill One's | Vision With Sea Serpents. || Stephen Crane Describes the Hor-| rors of Pulque and Registers a | Few Eloquent Vows—Inebriety | in the City of Mexico. ||'. The dateline was *City of Mexico, Aug. 4, 1895.*

N²: *Salt Lake City Tribune*, August 11, page 15, signed, headlined 'A JAG OF PULQUE IS HEAVY || A Drink that Will Fill One's | Vision with Serpents. || HORRORS OF THE VILE DRINK. || But It Is a Dream of Joy to the Mex-|ican Indian and Peon—The Stuff | Is Revolting to the Palate and | Stomach of the Foreigner—It is | Made in Haste and Must Be Con-| sumed in a Day. || [Copyright, 1895, by Bacheller, Johnson & Bacheller.]'. The dateline agrees with N¹.

N³: *Cincinnati Commercial Gazette*, August 11, page 17, signed, headlined '[within a frame of type-orn.] A Jag on Pulque. | A Drink That Will Create Sea Serpents. | Inebriety in Old Mexico. | [below frame] Correspondence of Commercial Gazette.' The dateline agrees with N¹.

N⁴: *Philadelphia Press*, August 11, page 26, signed, headlined 'JAGS OF PULQUE | DOWN IN MEXICO. || A Country Where One Drink | Will Fill the Vision with | Sea Serpents. || JUICE OF CENTURY PLANTS. || Stephen Crane Describes the Horrors | of Pulque and Registers a Few | Eloquent Vows—Inebriety | in the City of Mexico. || Special Correspondence of "The Press." '. The dateline agrees with N¹.

N⁵: *Galveston Daily News*, August 10, page 9, signed, headlined 'PUL-QUE JAG IS HEAVY. || A Country Where a Drink Will Fill | One's Vision with Sea | Serpents. || IN THE LAND OF THE AZTECS || Stephen Crane Describes the Horrors of Pulque | and Registers a Few Eloquent Vows. | Inebriety in Mexico. || For The News—Copyrighted.' The dateline agrees with N¹. From the same typesetting the sketch was printed, also, in the *Dallas Morning News*, August 10, page 8.

N⁶: *Rochester Democrat and Chronicle*, August 11, page 10, headlined 'DRINKING IN MEXICO || The National Beverage, Pulque, | and Its In-toxicating Powers. || A JAG FROM ONE QUAFF || Stephen Crane Describes the Horrors | of Pulque and Registers a Few | Eloquent Vows—Inebriety | in the City of Mexico. || Written for the Democrat and Chronicle. | (Copyright.)'. The dateline agrees with N¹. The piece is unsigned.

All newspapers except N⁴ ran the five humorous illustrations that Bacheller provided captioned *Swearing Off, Indian Going for a Drink of Pulque, The Human Inclination Acts Automatically, But It Is a Delirium to the*

Mexican, and *To the Foreigner It Tastes Like*——. N⁴ ran only the last two illustrations and prefaced its dateline with the illustrative initial also printed in Crane's piece of June 30 (No. 92).

Although no proof of this piece is preserved in the Crane scrapbooks, little doubt obtains that as in various other of Crane's Western sketches, the *Nebraska State Journal* was used to set up the syndicated proof. The textual evidence agrees with this conclusion, including the N¹ repetition of Crane's usual misspelling *familar* at 458.14. The *Journal* thus becomes the copy-text as, in all likelihood, the only authoritative document.

No. 95. THE FETE OF MARDI GRAS

Copyrighted by Bacheller, Johnson and Bacheller, "The Fete of Mardi Gras" was syndicated in various newspapers on Sunday, February 16, 1896. Accompanying the sketch were two illustrations by Archie Gunn captioned *The King Approaches with his Attendants* and *The Grotesque Figure Throwing a Box Tied with String to the People.* The following newspaper appearances have been observed:

N¹: *Nebraska State Journal,* February 16, 1896, page 11, signed, headlined 'THE FETE OF MARDI GRAS. || Stephen Crane Describes the Celebration of | This Remarkable Festival. || VERY HIGH JINKS IN NEW ORLEANS || The Extraordinary Pageant With | Its Display of Color and Gayety|—The Main Show and the | Side Shows. || (Copyright 1896, by Bacheller, Johnson & Bacheller.)'.

N²: *Philadelphia Press,* February 16, page 30, signed, headlined 'Mardi Gras |.....Festival || New Orleans' remarkable an-|nual fete, with its wealth of | display and gayety, described | by Stephen Crane. The main | show and the side entertain-|ments. [four dotted squares] ||'. The second illustration is captioned *One of the Grotesque Groups.*

N³: *Cincinnati Commercial Gazette,* February 23, page 19, signed, headlined '[within a frame of scroll rules] The Fete of Mardi Gras. || Very High Jinks in New Orleans—The Extraordinary Pa-|geant with Its Display of Color and Gayety.' A dateline *New Orleans, Feb. 21* is provided and above it appears *Correspondence Commercial Gazette.* Only the first illustration was used.

N⁴: *New Orleans Times-Democrat,* February 17, page 9, signed, headlined 'THE FETE OF MARDI GRAS. || STEPHEN CRANE DESCRIBES THE | CELEBRATION OF THIS | FESTIVAL. || The Extraordinary Pageant with | Its Display of Color and Gayety|—The Main Show and the Side | Shows. || For the Times-Democrat.' The illustrations do not appear.

N⁵: *Rochester Democrat and Chronicle,* February 16, page 9, signed, headlined 'FETE OF MARDI GRAS || Stephen Crane Describes the Celebration of This | Remarkable Festival in New Orleans—The | Extraordinary Pageant With Its Dis-|play of Color and Gayety. || Written for the Democrat and Chronicle. (Copyright.)'.

Preserved in the Special Collections of the Columbia University Libraries is a final proof for this piece headed *For Feb. 16* but otherwise identical with the text and headlines as printed in N¹. The copy-text, of course, becomes the proof of the *Nebraska State Journal*, which was probably set direct from Crane's manuscript and is the only authority.

No. 96. HATS, SHIRTS, AND SPURS IN MEXICO

This article appeared on Sunday, October 18, 1896, with three illustrations captioned *A Mexican Gentleman of Fashion, Some Swells for an Afternoon Stroll*, and *A Mystic Figure of the Night*. Only the *Chicago Daily News* carried the Bacheller, Johnson and Bacheller copyright notice. The following newspapers have been observed:

N¹: *Detroit Free Press*, October 18, 1896, page 20, signed, headlined 'STEPHEN CRANE IN MEXICO. || THAT VIVID WRITER DESCRIBES | SOME AMAZING THINGS. || HOW THE MEXICAN DUDE DECO-|RATES HIMSELF. || A CRIMSON SHIRT IS AN ESPECIAL | ATTACH-MENT. || His Hat, However, is His First and | Best Love. ||'.

N²: *Louisville Courier-Journal*, October 18, sec. III, page 2, signed, head-lined '[within a frame of type-orn.] HAT, SHIRT AND SPUR: | MEXICAN REQUISITES. | [below frame] || (Special Correspondence Courier-Jour-nal.)'. A dateline reads *City of Mexico, Oct. 13*. No illustrations.

N³: *Buffalo Evening News*, October 18, page 9, signed, headlined 'SWELLS AND | SPURS IN MEXICO. || Stephen Crane Says the Cha-|peau Is the Blossom of the | Mexican's Character. || AMAZING SHIRTS AND TIES. || To His Mind the World Is So | Small That He Could | Cover It With His | Hat. ||'.

N⁴: *San Francisco Chronicle*, October 18, page 12, signed, headlined 'Hats, Shirts and Spurs in Mexico. || Stephen Crane Declares the Chapeau Is the Blossom of Mexican | Character. || (Copyright, 1896. All Rights Reserved.)'.

N⁵: *Galveston Daily News*, October 18, page 10, signed, headlined 'THE MEXICAN DUDE. || STEPHEN CRANE SAYS THE MEX-|ICAN'S CHA-PEAU IS THE BLOS-|SOM OF HIS CHARACTER. || HATS, SHIRTS AND SPURS. || To His Mind the World Is So Small | That He Could Cover It With | His Hat. || For the News—Copyright.' The article was printed from the same typesetting omitting the illustrations in the *Dallas Morning News*, October 18, page 10.

N⁶: *Nebraska State Journal*, October 18, page 9, signed, headlined 'THE DRESS OF OLD MEXICO || Stephen Crane Writes of Amazing Hats, | Shirts and Spurs. || THE MEXICAN'S LARGE CHAPEAU || American and English Ideas Slowly | Reaching the People of the Towns|—Color Still

Supreme in | the Country. ||'. After the signature at the foot is *Copyright,*
1896.

N[7]: *Philadelphia Press,* October 18, page 34, signed, headlined 'HATS,
SHIRTS AND | SPURS IN MEXICO. || Stephen Crane Says the Mex-|ican's
Chapeau Is the Blos-|som of Character. || SOME AMAZING NECKTIES. ||
To His Mind the World Is So Small | That He Could Cover It with His |
Headgear. ||'.

N[8]: *Chicago Daily News,* October 29, page 5, signed, headlined 'A MEXI-
CAN DUDE'S HAT. || Stephen Crane Declares That It Is the | Blossom of
His Char-|acter. || MOST AMAZING SHIRTS AND NECKTIES. || The
Indian Remains the One Great Ar-|tistic Feature—A Fascinating, | Mystic
Figure. || Special Correspondence of the Chicago Daily News.' A dateline
appears *City of Mexico, Oct. 12.* After the signature at the foot is printed
[*Copyright, 1896, by the Bacheller Syndicate.*].

N[9]: *St. Louis Globe-Democrat,* October 18, page 33, signed, headlined
'MEXICAN CABALLEROS. || The Glass of Fashion on the Streets of |
Mexico. || The Extreme of Taste Is a Monster Hat, | Skin-Tight Trousers
and Gigantic | Spurs—A Mystic Figure of the | Night—Amazing Lin-
gerie. ||'.

N[10]: *Rochester Democrat and Chronicle,* October 18, page 9, signed,
headlined 'HATS, SHIRTS AND | SPURS IN MEXICO || The Mexican
Chapeau is the Blos-|som of His Character. || SO SAYS STEPHEN CRANE
|| Amazing Shirts and Neckties of the | Howling Swells Who Think the |
World so Small it Could be Cov-|ered by One of Their Hats. || Written for
the Democrat and Chronicle. | (Copyright.)'.

Possibly the N[8] dateline—on the evidence of N[2]—was a part of the
syndicated Bacheller proof but was omitted by the other newspapers
as too far out of line with publication, although—if so—it is odd that
they did not instead alter the date. The copy-text is N[1], the *Detroit
Free Press* which, although it is substantively faulty, is about as close
as any to the reconstructed accidentals of the lost Bacheller proof
possible from the ten witnesses.

No. 97. STEPHEN CRANE IN TEXAS

This article was first discovered by Professor Bernice Slote in the
versions in the *Omaha Bee* and the *Pittsburgh Leader* for January 8,
1899, and reprinted from the former in the *Prairie Schooner,* XLIII
(1969), 176–183. Since then three more newspaper texts have been
found. The five observed appearances are as follows:

N[1]: *Pittsburgh Leader,* Sunday, January 8, 1899, page 23, unsigned,
headlined 'STEPHEN CRANE IN TEXAS. || WHIMSICAL IMPRESSIONS
OF SAN | ANTONIO AND THE ALAMO. || Evidences of the Victorious
Derby | Hat of the North and the Trolley | Car — How Spain Came to

Texas. | When the Priests Ran Short of In-|dians to Convert—67,710 Writers of | Texas Began on the Alamo. || BY STEPHEN CRANE.'

N[2]: *Savannah Morning News*, January 8, page 10, unsigned, headlined 'STEPHEN CRANE WRITES OF TEXAS. || Whimsical Impressions of San Antonio and | the Alamo. || Evidence of the Victorious Derby Hat of the North and the Trolley Car. | How Spain Came to Texas—When the Priests Ran Short of Indians | to Convert—67,710 Writers of Texas Begun on the Alamo—How | Bowie and Crockett Met Santa Anna—Three Ways of Be-|ing Killed—Food like "Pounded Fire-|Brick From Hades." | BY STE-PHEN CRANE.'

N[3]: *Omaha Daily Bee*, January 8, page 15, signed, headlined 'PATRIOT SHRINE OF TEXAS || Stephen Crane's Impressions of San Antonio | and the Alamo. || EVIDENCE OF A NORTHERN INVASION || Derby Hats and Trolley Cars Disturb | an Atmosphere of Romance—How | Bowie and Crockett Met | Santa Ana. ||'.

N[4]: *Louisville Courier-Journal*, January 8, sec. III, page 4, unsigned, headlined '[within a frame of type-orn.] Some Lively Impressions [leaf] | [leaf] Of the Lone Star State. || By STEPHEN CRANE. | [below the frame] [Correspondence of the Courier-Journal.]'. Text starts with decorative initial.

N[5]: *St. Louis Globe-Democrat*, January 8, sec. III, page 6, signed, head-lined '[within a decorative frame] STEPHEN CRANE IN TEXAS. || Whim-sical Impressions of San Antonio and the Alamo. | [below the frame] || Special Correspondence of the Globe-Democrat.'

All the newspapers have a dateline *San Antonio, Tex., Jan. 6.* N[1,3-4] run an illustration captioned *Church of the Alamo.*

Although no newspaper mentions the syndicate, it is almost certain that S. S. McClure bought the article and distributed it. The syndicate headlines in the common proofs that would have been mailed to sub-scribing newspapers can be reconstructed almost verbatim. The copy for the McClure printer would have been a holograph manuscript in all probability. The five observed newspapers that radiate from the common proof enable one to reconstruct its substantives exactly, and many of its accidentals, the latter having been subjected to heavy housestyling. As among the first discovered examples, and one suffi-ciently representative in its accidentals, the *Pittsburgh Leader* version has been chosen as the copy-text but emended as advisable from the majority evidence of the other four witnesses. Since five versions are not enough to establish various of the accidentals with certainty, the agreement of any two newspapers in a rejected accidentals reading not noticed in the emendations listing is provided in the Historical Collation in order to avoid concealing evidence that might be of value in case other texts are discovered. Although corrected once by the *Omaha Bee,* the popular Americanization *Santa Anna* has been re-tained.

No. 98. GALVESTON, TEXAS, IN 1895

On October 19, 1900, the editor of the *Westminster Gazette* wrote to Cora, "I shall be very pleased to publish the article on Galveston by your husband which you sent me to-day" (Columbia). "Galveston, Texas, in 1895" appeared in the *Gazette*, November 6, 1900, pages 1–2, and in the same typesetting except for a rearranged first paragraph and a deep cut of lines 478.14–478.37 in the *Westminster Budget*, November 16, 1900, page 22. Undoubtedly the copy was of a much earlier piece, probably dating from 1895–96, which had remained in manuscript without attempt at sale like the unpublished trio beginning with "The City of Mexico." Whether Cora made a typescript to send to the *Gazette* for printer's copy is not to be determined.

IRISH SKETCHES

No. 99. QUEENSTOWN

The first of the series of five Irish Notes appeared in the *Westminster Gazette* on October 19, 1897, pages 1–2, reprinted in the same typesetting in the *Westminster Budget*, without textual change, on October 20, pages 7–8. The *Gazette* heading was standard for the series: 'IRISH NOTES. | I.—QUEENSTOWN. | *Copyright U.S.A., 1897.*]'. The pieces were signed at the end. One day earlier, on Monday, October 18, page 6, the *New York Journal* had printed "Queenstown" on its editorial page, signed, headed 'Stephen Crane's | Irish Notes. ||'. The next week, on Sunday, October 24, page 5, the *Kansas City Star* reprinted the article from a mail copy, headed 'STEPHEN CRANE'S IRISH NOTES || A Dripping View of Queenstown—Jerry and | His Jaunting Car. | Stephen Crane in the New York Journal.'

"Queenstown" is not mentioned by name, but a letter from Crane to Reynolds of about October, 1897 (*Letters*, p. 145) must refer to it when Crane remarks "As for the *Journal* I have quite a big misunderstanding with them and can't get it pulled out straight. They say I am over-drawn. I say I am not. I have sent them an installment of my Irish Notes. . . . My idea was that they would go in with that stuff on the editorial page." In a letter of October 29, 1897, to his brother William, Crane added, "The Irish Notes and so on, which appear in the Journal are written really for the Westminster Gazette"

(*Letters*, p. 148). The *Journal* was presumably sent more in the series, although this hypothesis is not certain, but at any rate printed only "Queenstown." The *Kansas City Star* text is a simple reprint of the *Journal* without authority. The letter sounds as if Crane had sent copy to the *Journal* himself, without going through Reynolds. The dates of appearance make it practically certain that the copy for the *Journal* must have been the carbon of a typescript sent to the *Gazette*. Since both authorities radiate from a common typescript in this manner, they are of equal textual weight. The *Journal* has been chosen as copy-text, however, because its lighter punctuation system is more characteristic of Crane than the heavy *Gazette* editorial pointing. On the other hand, a cut in the *Journal* must be taken from the *Gazette*, and many of the *Gazette* hyphenated compounds appear to be more faithful to what we may suppose to have been Crane's own copy than the general *Journal* refusal to hyphenate. The Historical Collation records all variants between N^1 and WG.

No. 100. BALLYDEHOB

The second in the series of *Irish Notes*, "Ballydehob," appeared in the *Westminster Gazette*, October 22, 1897, pages 1–2, and from the same typesetting but with a substantive correction and the omission of 489.8–10 it was reprinted in the *Westminster Budget*, November 5, page 15. *Last Words* (1902), pages 198–203, collected it under the section title of *Irish Notes*. The University of Virginia–Barrett Collection holds a blue ribbon copy typescript consisting of four pages of laid paper 259 × 202 mm., the chainlines 26–27 mm. apart, watermarked *Brookleigh Fine*. The typed title is *Irish Notes*, but in the black ink used for the corrections and alterations Cora has placed parentheses about this title and added to the right 2nd *Ballydehob*, the name double-underlined. A blue-crayon 30 is to the left. In the lower left corner is Cora's minuscule *q*. The word count 1,100 is placed at the foot of page 4 in blue crayon. The typescript was made on the Crane typewriter and appears to be Cora's work, one of the batch of printer's copy sent to Reynolds for the American edition of *Last Words* and possible syndication. The general faithfulness to its copy, the unusual accuracy of Cora's spelling, which was likely to improve when typing from a print, and her reproduction of certain typographical features like typing *trades-man* (487.26) when the word was broken between lines in the print, indicate that she made up the typescript from a clipping, and indeed a clipping is present in the Crane Collection in the Special Collections of the Columbia University Libraries.

It should be noted, however, that if the editor's hypothesis for the date in early 1899 of the Barrett typescript of the tale "A Self-Made Man" is correct, this typescript is linked to that of "Ballydehob" and "The Royal Irish Constabulary" by its Brookleigh watermarked paper. This would mean that these two Irish sketches, the only ones for which typescripts sent to Reynolds are preserved, were made up during Crane's lifetime and for some other purpose than *Last Words*. It may be no accident that these two sketches are the only two not published in the United States. Thus the possibility is present that they were typed in early 1899 for an attempted American sale.

The *Westminster Gazette* is the copy-text, then, being the only version with a direct connection with Crane's manuscript; in fact it was probably set from the holograph.

No. 101. THE ROYAL IRISH CONSTABULARY

This third in the series of *Irish Notes* appeared in the *Westminster Gazette*, November 5, 1897, pages 1–2, and was reprinted in the *Westminster Budget*, November 12, page 23 from standing type. *Last Words* (1902) collected it on pages 203–207. *Last Words* is clearly set from a clipping of the *Gazette* and is thus a derived text. No textual problem would seem to be present were it not for a typescript in the University of Virginia–Barrett Collection, a blue ribbon copy on four pages of laid paper 259 × 202 mm., the chainlines 26–27 mm. apart, watermarked *Brookleigh Fine*. The series and article titles are typed as in the *Gazette* save that the roman 'III.—' before the article title is wanting and after the title line has been added by hand a 3 and period within parentheses. A blue-crayon 31 is placed above and to the left of the title. Cumulative word counts appear on the versos of the pages for a total of 1,015. Although missing the minuscule that Cora customarily placed in the lower left corner of the first page, this is clearly a typescript that Cora marked up for the American edition of *Last Words*, as well as possible serialization, and sent to Reynolds in New York. The pages are numbered within spaced parentheses in Cora's manner, and the typing is corrected in black ink in her hand. Six substantive variants occur between WG and TMs, mostly questions of singular or plural and the omission of articles. Only one, the plural *strangers and freinds* at 490.17–18 for the WG singulars could have any claim for consideration on its own merits. The punctuation system of the two texts is almost identical, with only three or four cases of lightening the punctuation in TMs. The question of TMs copy arises, of course, for if Cora had turned to a manuscript instead of to a clipping as her copy, TMs would have independent authority. At first sight it might appear that she had, for her spelling is atrocious in a manner unexampled when she was typing from printed copy. On the other hand, the fact that point for point WG and TMs are likely to agree in a punctuation that is editorial in its system and opposed to Crane's own practice leads the present editor to the conclusion that Cora did indeed make up the Barrett typescript from a WG clipping at the same time in early 1899 as "Ballydehob." The anomaly of the spellings as against the almost correct typescript, say, for "Ballydehob," is inexplicable except, perhaps, from a particular haste, although the same difficulty is also found in the TMs of "A Self-Made Man" of the same date. The *Gazette*, thus, remains the only possible copy-text and authority. In the December 3, 1897, number of the *Gazette*, pages 1–2, was printed a good-humored point-by-point rebuttal by retired Constable Michael F. Morahan, reprinted from standing type in the *Budget* on December 10, page 20.

No. 102. A FISHING VILLAGE

Fourth in the *Irish Notes* series is "A Fishing Village," printed in the *Westminster Gazette*, November 12, 1897, pages 1–2, and reprinted from standing type, but with rearrangement of the first paragraph to admit an illustrative initial and a textual variant, in the *Westminster Budget*, November 19, page 13. In the United States the *Philistine* reprinted the piece in IX (August, 1899), 71–77, using as its copy the version in the *Westminster Budget*. *Last Words* (1902), pages 207–213, was set from the *Gazette* text. It is a real oddity that the proportion of E1 substantive variation rises sharply in this sketch, particularly in the omission of articles. Yet to conjecture that a lost typescript was the copy for *Last Words*, and not a clipping of the *Gazette*, is to go contrary to the visible evidence of the two texts. So far as can be determined, only the *Gazette* text has authority.

In the Reynolds inventory of October 23, 1900, "A Fishing Village" is listed, and in the University of Virginia–Barrett Collection is preserved this clipping from the *Westminster Gazette*, marked number 32 in blue crayon and in black ink, to the right of the title, in Cora's hand *For book 1450 | words,* underlined (with ink *words* traced over a pencil *words,* also underlined). No minuscule appears.

No. 103. AN OLD MAN GOES WOOING

The fifth and last of the *Irish Notes* was printed in the *Westminster Gazette,* November 23, 1897, pages 1–2, with a reprint from standing type except for a rearranged first paragraph in the *Westminster Budget,* November 26, page 6. Hubbard's *Philistine,* IX (July, 1899), 44–50, reprinted the sketch from the *Gazette* or *Budget* with the variant title "An Old Man Goes A-Wooing." Finally, it was collected in *Last Words* (1902), pages 193–198. "An Old Man Goes Wooing" is like "A Fishing Village" in that *Last Words* contains an unusual number of substantive variants, but the general indication is that, like "A Fishing Village," it was set from a clipping in the *Gazette.* The general system of accidentals is very close. Perhaps the strongest evidence is the appearance of the American form *toward* in both WG and E1 at 496.4 and 498.29 but their agreement in *towards* (with the *Philistine*) at 497.30,35, a situation difficult to attribute to chance. The copy-text, then, is the *Westminster Gazette.*

On September 4, 1900, Paul Reynolds in answer to a lost query from Cora Crane wrote, "I cannot place the 'Irish Notes' you sent me, as I do not think there will be any demand for them now." And on September 29 he wrote again: "With regard to the 'Irish Notes,' you say that Mr. Crane considered 'When an Old Man goes A' Wooing' as one of the very best things that he had ever done. I don't find it in the things that you have sent me; you sent me only two, and neither of them has this title. If you will send me the sketch, and it is as good as you say, I will try to place it. My feeling was that those sketches were local in character and that they would not have especial interest over here, and I am still of that opinion." Both letters are at Columbia University. This correspondence is difficult to understand. Reynolds, in response to Cora's title, calls the sketch "When an Old Man goes A' Wooing," which is the special form of the title adopted by the *Philistine* when it printed the story in July, 1899. Yet how Cora could think Reynolds could sell the story after it had appeared in the *Philistine* is difficult to understand, although she may not have been aware of Hubbard's reprint. In the Reynolds list of his holdings of October 23, 1900, is listed "When an Old Man goes a' Wooing," indicating that Cora had sent him a copy. It is odd that the *a'* is added in ink to the typed letter, especially since the

Reynolds copy seems to have been a clipping of the *Westminster Gazette*. This clipping is preserved in the University of Virginia–Barrett Collection. It has a blue-crayon number 33 at the top and Cora's minuscule *j* in pencil to the left of the title. In black ink she wrote to the right *To use in book*. An ink blot over the title has caused Cora to write *Wooing* in black ink (after deleting the partially visible 'A-Wooing.' of the *Gazette*). Above the title is written in pencil *1ˢᵗ article Queenstown Oct 19–1897*.

III. REPORTS

NEWS FROM ASBURY PARK

No. 104. AVON SEASIDE ASSEMBLY

Printed in the *New York Tribune*, July 28, 1890, page 4, unsigned, headlined 'AVON SEASIDE ASSEMBLY. || SUMMER SCHOOLS BY THE SURF. || MUSIC—CHRISTIAN PHILOSOPHY—APPLIED ART—|CAVES—SOCIETY.' The dateline was *Avon-by-the-Sea, N.J., July 27*. What may connect this item with Crane is the paragraph on H. C. Hovey, whose talk on caves was reported in the *Tribune* for July 26, 1890, page 3, datelined July 25, under "Lectures at Avon-by-the-Sea": "In the evening the Rev. Dr. H. C. Hovey, of Bridgeport, Conn., lectured in the auditorium on the 'Mazes and Marvels of Mammoth Cave.'" This lecture seems to have given rise to Crane's "Across the Covered Pit" (No. 152) just as his hearing Albert G. Thies during the same summer produced "The King's Favor" (No. 148). Not previously reprinted.

No. 105. AVON'S SCHOOL BY THE SEA

The basis for attributing to Crane this lengthy report on the activities of the Seaside Assembly's school is the paragraph about the tenor Albert Thies which was expanded into the article "The King's Favor" in the Syracuse *University Herald* for May, 1891. The report appeared in the *New York Tribune*, August 4, 1890, page 5, unsigned, headlined 'AVON'S SCHOOL BY THE SEA. || NEVER TOO LATE TO LEARN. || HOW TO PICK UP A PIN—THE PHILOSOPHER AT | PLAY—OLD MUSIC—ART—SONG.' The dateline was *Avon-by-the-Sea, Aug. 3*. It may be of more than casual interest that whereas in this news report and also in "The King's Favor" the singer's name is spelled *Thies,* in three other references to him in the *Tribune* this summer (see the textual section to "The King's Favor") it is *Theiss* twice and *Theis* once. The correct form for this date is *Thies,* as listed in 1895 in *Trow's New York City Directory.* In 1896–97 the *Directory* notes him as *Albert Thiers-Gerard,* in 1897–98 as *Albert G. Thiers,* and from 1898–1899 *Albert Gerard-Thiers.* For more about Crane's connection with this musician, see No. 158, "Miss Louise Gerard—Soprano."

No. 106. BIOLOGY AT AVON-BY-THE-SEA

This unsigned article is attributed to Crane and reprinted here for the first time from the *New York Tribune,* Sunday, July 19, 1891, page 22, headlined *'BIOLOGY AT AVON-BY-THE-SEA.* || ENTHUSI-ASTIC BEGINNING—A CONVENIENT | BUILDING—THE CORPS OF INSTRUCTORS.' The dateline was July 18. Certain features of the style suggest the young Crane's hand; but the best piece of evidence is the reference to 'the sight of a well-known college professor frenziedly pursuing a June-bug around the block', which links this article with "Along the Shark River," a piece generally assigned to Crane, which the *Tribune* printed on August 15, 1892. This reads in a paragraph about the School of Biology, 'if they choose to chase June-bugs around the block on warm nights, no one may interfere with their proper pursuit of happiness.'

No. 107. HOWELLS DISCUSSED AT AVON-BY-THE-SEA

The *New York Tribune,* August 18, 1891, page 5, printed this unsigned report, datelined August 17 and headed 'HOWELLS DIS-CUSSED AT AVON-BY-THE-SEA.' John Berryman in *Stephen Crane* (1950), page 28, first attributed this report to Crane by reprinting three sentences. He was followed by Donald Pizer, who in "Crane Reports Garland and Howells," *Modern Language Notes,* LXX (1955), 37–39, reprinted the whole.

No. 108. MEETINGS BEGUN AT OCEAN GROVE

The *New York Tribune,* July 2, 1892, page 4, printed this unsigned news item headlined *'MEETINGS BEGUN AT OCEAN GROVE.* ||

MANY MINISTERS HAVE ARRIVED—PREACHERS | OF THE NEW-BRUNSWICK DISTRICT—| ASSOCIATION OF PASTORS' WIVES.' The dateline was *Ocean Grove, N.J., July 1*. Joseph J. Kwiat, in "The Newspaper Experience: Crane, Norris, and Dreiser," *Nineteenth-Century Fiction*, VIII (1953), 99–117, seems to have been the first to attribute this piece (or, more properly, the last paragraph) to Crane. The wry understatement of this paragraph and the tone of the first paragraph sound authentic. The account of the meetings, otherwise, may or may not be by a different hand.

No. 109. CROWDING INTO ASBURY PARK

The unsigned report appeared in the *New York Tribune*, Sunday, July 3, 1892, page 28, headed 'CROWDING INTO ASBURY PARK. | HOTELS AND COTTAGES FILLING UP RAPIDLY | WITH SUMMER VISITORS.' The dateline was *Asbury Park, N.J., July 2*. The Williams and Starrett *Bibliography* (1948) attributes this piece to Crane, joined in the same year by Victor A. Elconin, in "Stephen Crane in Asbury Park," *American Literature*, XX (1948), 275–289.

No. 110. JOYS OF SEASIDE LIFE

Printed in the *New York Tribune*, Sunday, July 17, 1892, page 18, unsigned, headed '*JOYS OF SEASIDE LIFE*. || AMUSEMENTS, STATIONARY AND PERIPA-|TETIC.' The dateline was *Asbury Park, N.J., July 16*. The Williams and Starrett *Bibliography* (1948) attributes this piece to Crane, joined in the same year by Victor A. Elconin.

No. 111. SUMMER DWELLERS AT ASBURY PARK AND THEIR DOINGS

This unsigned report was printed by the *New York Tribune* on July 24, 1892, page 22, headlined 'ON THE NEW-JERSEY COAST || SUMMER DWELLERS AT ASBURY PARK AND | THEIR DOINGS. || THE WHEEL THAT GOES AROUND NO MORE—THE | BICYCLE CHAMPION—PERSONAL AND SOCIAL.' The first paragraph seems to have Crane's touch. The rest is uncertain. This report was first attributed to Crane by Elconin in 1948 and is usually printed under its series title "On the New-Jersey Coast," which was the general headline for many such reports. The dateline was *Asbury Park, N.J., July 23*.

No. 112. ON THE BOARDWALK

Unsigned, this report appeared in the *New York Tribune*, Sunday, August 14, 1892, page 17, headed 'ON THE BOARD WALK. || "FOUNDER" BRADLEY'S COSMOPOLITAN | DOMAIN.' The dateline was *Asbury Park, N.J., Aug. 13*. The piece was attributed to Crane by Williams and Starrett and by Elconin, both in 1948.

No. 113. ALONG THE SHARK RIVER

Datelined August 14, "Along the Shark River" was printed in the *New York Tribune* on August 15, 1892, page 4, unsigned, headlined 'ALONG THE SHARK RIVER. || THE PLEASURES OF BIOLOGY AND OF SKETCH-|ING FROM NATURE.' It was first attributed to Crane by Elconin in 1948.

No. 114. PARADES AND ENTERTAINMENTS

For the background of this unsigned report that caused Crane shortly to stop assisting his brother Townley with summer-resort news for the *Tribune*, one may consult the *Tribune's* editor, Willis Fletcher Johnson, "The Launching of Stephen Crane," *Literary Digest International Book Review*, IV (April, 1926), 288–290. Under the general heading used before for resort news, the report appeared in the *New York Tribune*, Sunday, August 21, 1892, page 22, unsigned, headlined 'ON THE NEW-JERSEY COAST. || GUESTS CONTINUE TO ARRIVE IN LARGE | NUMBERS. || PARADES AND ENTERTAIN-MENTS—WELL-KNOWN | PEOPLE WHO ARE REGISTERED AT | THE VARIOUS HOTELS.' The dateline was *Asbury Park, N.J., Aug. 20*. The piece is clearly Crane's through line 522.23; the rest is uncertain.

As narrated by Johnson, the reaction was serious because of the political situation. In the August 24 issue of the *Tribune*, page 9, under *Selections from the Mail* appeared the following communication:

Sir: I, as a member of the Junior Order of American Mechanics, take the liberty of writing to The Tribune in the name of all who belong to this patriotic American organization, in answer to the uncalled-for and un-American criticism published in The Tribune on Sunday, August 21, in regard to the annual outing of the order at Asbury Park, on Wednesday, August 17.

Personally I do not think The Tribune would publish such a slur on one of the largest bodies of American-born citizens if it knew the order, its objects, or its principles. In the strictest sense, we are a National political organization, but we do not recognize any party. Our main objects are to restrict immigration, and to protect the public schools of the United States and to prevent sectarian interference therein. We also demand that the Holy Bible be read in our public schools, not to teach sectarianism but to inculcate its teachings. We are bound together to promote Americans in business and shield them from the depressing effects of foreign competition. We are not a labor organization, nor are we a military company, drilled to parade in public and be applauded for our fine appearance and precision; but we were appreciated for our Americanism and we were applauded for it.

As a body we recognize no society, party or creed. We are brothers, one and all, bound together to honor and protect our country and to vow allegiance to the Stars and Stripes.

E. A. CANFIELD,
Clinton Council, No. 187, Jr. O. U. A. M.

New-York, Aug. 23, 1892.

Appended to this communication was the *Tribune's* apology:

(We regret deeply that a bit of random correspondence, passed inadvertently by the copy editor, should have put into our columns sentiments both foreign and repugnant to The Tribune. To those who know the principles and policy of this paper in both its earlier and later years, its devotion to American interests and its abhorrence of vain class distinctions, it can scarcely be necessary to say that we regard the Junior Order of United American Mechanics with high respect and hold its principles worthy of all emulation. The offence which has been unintentionally given by the correspondence referred to is as much deplored by The Tribune as it is resented by the members of the Order.—Ed.)

No. 115. THE SEASIDE ASSEMBLY'S WORK AT AVON

This news item is probably the work of Crane since it comes at the right date and exhibits not only his interest in Shark River but also in pre-Revolutionary history. It was printed in the *New York Tribune*, unsigned, on August 29, 1892, page 4, headlined 'THE SEASIDE ASSEMBLY'S WORK AT AVON. || RENEWED AGITATION OF THE PLAN TO WIDEN | AND DEEPEN SHARK RIVER.' This report was first attributed to Crane by Elconin in 1948 but has not previously been reprinted. The dateline is *Avon-by-the-Sea, N.J., Aug. 28.*

No. 116. THE SEASIDE ASSEMBLY (II)

Printed in the *New York Tribune*, September 6, 1892, page 4, unsigned, headed 'THE SEASIDE ASSEMBLY. || GRATIFYING SUCCESS OF THE SCHOOLS OF ART, | MUSIC AND BIOLOGY.' The dateline was *Avon-by-the-Sea, N.J., Sept. 5*. Two illustrations accompanied the article captioned *Entrance to the Grounds* and *New Library Building*. First attributed to Crane by Elconin in 1948, but not previously reprinted.

No. 117. THE SEASIDE HOTEL HOP

On Sunday, September 11, 1892, page 15, the *New York Tribune* printed this unsigned report, headed 'THE SEASIDE HOTEL HOP. || AN INSTITUTION THAT FLOURISHES MILDLY | IN CERTAIN NEIGHBORHOODS.' No dateline was present. The piece was attributed to Crane by Williams and Starrett and by Elconin, both in 1948.

POSSIBLE ATTRIBUTIONS

No. 118. MR. YATMAN'S CONVERSIONS. The tone of deadpan satire that seems to be present in this item contrasts with the bland approval usually manifest in the reports of the religious doings at Ocean Grove and may represent Crane's own scepticism. Printed in the *New York Tribune*, August 27, 1888, page 2, unsigned, headed 'MR. YATMAN'S CONVERSIONS. || RELIGIOUS SERVICES AT OCEAN GROVE AND ASBURY | PARK.' The dateline is *Ocean Grove, Aug. 26*. Not previously reprinted.

No. 119. A PROSPEROUS YEAR AT ASBURY PARK. Printed in the *New York Tribune*, July 14, 1889, page 16, unsigned, headlined 'A PROSPEROUS YEAR AT ASBURY PARK || MANY IMPROVEMENTS IN THE HOTELS—PER-|SONAL NOTES.' The dateline was *Asbury Park, July 13*. No particular evidence associates this report with Crane except perhaps for the youthful hyperbole like *It is the finest work of the kind ever issued* to which he was subject. But the report is typical of the descriptive items found in the *Tribune* from the resort and is presented on that basis. Not previously reprinted.

No. 120. WORKERS AT OCEAN GROVE. Printed in the *New York Tribune*, August 10, 1889, page 4, unsigned, headlined 'WORKERS

AT OCEAN GROVE. || SOME OF THE LEADERS IN EVANGELIS-
TIC | WORK. || POPULARITY OF THE MEETINGS—"BILLY" COR-
|BETT'S LUSTY SHOUT—WELL-KNOWN | WOMEN WHO ARE
HEARD ON | THE PLATFORM.' The dateline was *Ocean Grove,
Aug. 9.* The description of the religious meetings that follow the
opening two paragraphs about the babies could well be by another
hand, but some possibility exists that Crane wrote the beginning.
The similarities of language indicate that the same person who wrote
these paragraphs was also responsible for "The Babies on Parade at
Asbury Park" in the *Tribune* on July 22, 1890, and "Asbury Park's
Big Broad Walk" on August 31, 1890. That this person was Crane is
purely speculative, however. Not previously reprinted.

No. 121. Joys of the Jersey Coast. Printed in the *New York
Tribune*, August 26, 1889, page 5, unsigned, headlined 'JOYS OF
THE JERSEY COAST || SUMMER GUESTS FISHING AND CRAB-
BING | AT AVON-BY-THE-SEA. || FAVORITE KINDS OF BAIT
USED ON THE SHARK | RIVER—PROJECTED IMPROVEMENTS
—|LATE ARRIVALS AT THE HOTELS.' The dateline was *Avon-by-
the-Sea, Aug. 25.* Crane seems to have had a special interest in
Shark River, as indicated by reports that are more clearly his. The
amused catalogue of baits may perhaps be in his manner. Not previously reprinted.

No. 122. Lightning's Pranks at Asbury Park. Printed in the
New York Tribune, July 6, 1890, page 19, unsigned, headlined
'LIGHTNING'S PRANKS AT ASBURY PARK || IT STRIKES THE
ELECTRIC WIRES—MANY PER-|SONS INJURED.' The dateline was
Asbury Park, July 5. The pleasure in the colors—*big balls of red,
white, blue and green colors which danced and sputtered*—and the
jocular details may just possibly show Crane's hand. (One is reminded of the burning chemicals in *The Monster.*) It is probable,
owing to the similarity of language, that the same person also wrote
the first paragraph of " 'Pinafore' at Asbury Park" in the *Tribune* on
August 17, 1890, and the third paragraph of "Asbury Park" on August 24. Not previously reprinted.

No. 123. Guests at Avon-by-the-Sea. Printed in the *New York
Tribune*, July 7, 1890, page 4, unsigned, headlined 'GUESTS AT
AVON-BY-THE-SEA || FISHING AND FLIRTATION AMONG THE
PROMI-|NENT INDUSTRIES—WHERE PEOPLE | ARE STAYING.'
The dateline was *Avon-by-the-Sea, N.J., July 6.* It may be that the
reference to *the noble redman* comes from Crane's interest in the
early days of the locality. A similar reference is found in "The Babies
on Parade at Asbury Park" in the *Tribune* on July 22, 1890. Not
previously reprinted.

No. 124. Throngs at Asbury Park. Printed in the *New York
Tribune*, July 13, 1890, page 22, unsigned, headlined 'THRONGS
AT ASBURY PARK. || HOTELS FULL AND FEW COTTAGES TO
LET. || SEA GAZERS ON THE PLAZA—HOPS BEGIN—TWO |

FLAGS IN ONE.' The dateline was *Asbury Park, N.J., July* 12. The remarks about the electric railroad agree with the criticism of the service in other possible Crane reports; the use of the strong word *idiotic* in a news item is characteristic of the personal involvement sometimes found even in Crane's late reporting. Not previously reprinted.

No. 125. HIGH TIDE AT OCEAN GROVE. Printed in the *New York Tribune,* July 19, 1890, page 3, unsigned, headlined 'HIGH TIDE AT OCEAN GROVE || EVOLUTION OF THE FLANNEL SHIRT. || REMARKABLE CAREER—A SOLDIER METHODIST|—MODEL OF THE JEWISH TABERNACLE.' The dateline was *Ocean Grove, N.J., July* 18. The first two paragraphs of this lengthy report may suggest the private amusement sometimes found in items more clearly by Crane. Not previously reprinted.

No. 126. THE BABIES ON PARADE AT ASBURY PARK. Printed in the *New York Tribune,* July 22, 1890, page 7, unsigned, headlined 'THE BABIES ON PARADE AT ASBURY PARK || SCORES OF YOUNGSTERS WHEELED ALONG THE | STREETS IN GAY PROCESSION.' The dateline was *Asbury Park, N.J., July* 21. Links exist between this item and two other possibles, "Workers at Ocean Grove" in the *Tribune* on August 10, 1889, and "Guests at Avon-by-the-Sea" on July 7, 1890. Not previously reprinted.

No. 127. "PINAFORE" AT ASBURY PARK. Printed in the *New York Tribune,* August 17, 1890, page 5, unsigned, headlined '"PINAFORE" AT ASBURY PARK. || NARROW ESCAPES FROM DROWNING— ELEPHANT | PARTIES THE RAGE.' The dateline was *Asbury Park, Aug.* 16. Some links exist between this item and other reports such as "Lightning's Pranks at Asbury Park," in the *Tribune* on July 6, 1890, or "Throngs at Asbury Park," on July 13, or "Asbury Park," on August 24. The latter also contains the same information about elephant parties. Not previously reprinted.

No. 128. ASBURY PARK. Printed in the *New York Tribune,* August 24, 1890, page 13, unsigned, headlined 'ASBURY PARK. || MANY PEOPLE ATTRACTED BY THE CAMP-|MEETING. || ARRESTS OF LIQUOR-SELLERS—THE ELECTRIC | RAILWAY—PICKPOCK-ETS ABUNDANT—|GUESTS AT THE HOTELS.' The dateline was *Asbury Park, Aug.* 23. It is probable that the same writer of this item also wrote "Lightning's Pranks at Asbury Park" in the *Tribune* on July 6, 1890, "Throngs at Asbury Park" on July 13, 1890, and possibly " 'Pinafore' at Asbury Park" on August 17, 1890. Not previously reprinted.

No. 129. ASBURY PARK'S BIG BROAD WALK. Printed in the *New York Tribune,* August 31, 1890, page 13, unsigned, headlined 'ASBURY PARK'S BIG BROAD WALK. || HOTEL-KEEPERS AND THE ILLEGAL SALE OF | LIQUORS.' The dateline was *Asbury Park, Aug.*

30. Similarity of language and of detail associates the writer of this item with that of "Workers at Ocean Grove" in the *Tribune* on August 10, 1889, and "The Babies on Parade at Asbury Park" on July 22, 1890. Not previously reprinted.

No. 130. IMPROVEMENTS AT OCEAN GROVE. Like many of these news items, this is only doubtfully to be suggested as Crane's. It was printed in the *New York Tribune*, June 10, 1891, page 4, unsigned, as perhaps his first report of the season, headlined '*IMPROVE-MENTS AT OCEAN GROVE.* || READY FOR THE MEETINGS OF THE SUMMER—|HOTELS OPEN AND SEVERAL COT-|TAGES OCCUPIED.' The dateline was *Ocean Grove, N.J., June 9.* Not previously reprinted.

No. 131. LIGHTNING ON THE JERSEY COAST. From the *New York Tribune*, June 13, 1891, page 1, unsigned, headlined 'LIGHTNING ON THE JERSEY COAST.' The dateline was *Asbury Park, N.J., June 12.* This seems to be something of a standard story: one may compare it with "Lightning's Pranks at Asbury Park," July 6, 1890. Not previously reprinted.

No. 132. ARRIVING AT OCEAN GROVE. From the *New York Tribune*, June 29, 1891, page 5, unsigned, headlined 'ARRIVING AT OCEAN GROVE. || GREAT NUMBERS OF GUESTS AT THE | HOTELS. || COTTAGES FILLING UP—THE PROGRAMME FOR | THE SUMMER—A NEW FISHING PIER.' The dateline was *Ocean Grove, June 28.* The account of the difficulties of arriving guests with the hackmen has some relation to that in the later "Seen at Hot Springs," March 3, 1895. This last could have been using material previously exploited, as here. Not previously reprinted.

No. 133. STATUARY AT ASBURY PARK. Printed in the *New York Tribune*, July 5, 1891, page 22, unsigned, headlined '*STATUARY AT ASBURY PARK.* || FOUNDER BRADLEY'S METHOD OF ORNA-MENT-|ING THE PARKS—OTHER IMPROVEMENTS.' The dateline was *Asbury Park, N.J., July 4.* Not previously reprinted.

No. 134. IMPROVEMENTS AT AVON-BY-THE-SEA. From the *New York Tribune*, July 5, 1891, page 22, unsigned, headlined '*IM-PROVEMENTS AT AVON-BY-THE-SEA.* || CHANGES ON THE BEACH—NEW COTTAGES—|PLANS OF THE ASSEMBLY.' The dateline was *Avon-by-the-Sea, N.J., July 4.* This appears to be a companion piece to "Statuary at Asbury Park," printed on the same page on July 5, and very likely by the same hand. Not previously reprinted.

No. 135. ON THE BANKS OF SHARK RIVER. Printed in the *New York Tribune*, July 11, 1891, page 5, unsigned, headlined 'ON THE BANKS OF SHARK RIVER. | ACTIVITY AT THE SEASIDE ASSEM-BLY—BASS-|FISHING A FAVORITE SPORT.' The dateline was

Avon-by-the-Sea, July 10. The interest in Shark River may associate this item with what seems to be Crane's own "Biology at Avon-by-the-Sea," July 19, 1891, and the later "Along the Shark River," August 15, 1892. Not previously reprinted.

No. 136. ALL OPEN IN SPITE OF MR. BRADLEY. From the *New York Tribune*, July 20, 1891, page 7, unsigned, headed '*ALL OPEN IN SPITE OF MR. BRADLEY.*' The dateline was *Asbury Park, N.J., July 19.* 'Founder' Bradley's attempts to close down Asbury Park's businesses on Sundays while keeping his own concessions open on the beach provoked a number of reports, not necessarily by the same correspondent. The present has more humor in it than the rest. Not previously reprinted.

No. 137. THE SEASIDE ASSEMBLY (I). Although clearly written up from a handout, this account has some links with "Art at Avon-by-the-Sea" a little over two weeks later and may be by Crane. It was published in the *New York Tribune*, July 26, 1891, page 19, unsigned, headed 'THE SEASIDE ASSEMBLY. || PLANS AND ACHIEVEMENTS OF THE SCHOOL OF | ART—THE KINDERGARTEN.' The dateline was *Avon-by-the-Sea, N.J., July 25.* Not previously reprinted.

No. 138. A BABY PARADE ON THE BOARD WALK. Printed in the *New York Tribune*, August 4, 1891, page 5, unsigned, headlined 'A BABY PARADE ON THE BOARD WALK. | THREE HUNDRED CARRIAGES IN LINE—THOU-|SANDS VIEW THE UNIQUE PROCESSION.' The dateline was *Asbury Park, Aug. 3.* The annual baby parade produced an annual news item. For parallels, see the doubtful "The Babies on Parade at Asbury Park," July 22, 1890, and "Baby Parade at Asbury Park," July 31, 1892. Not previously reprinted.

No. 139. THE GUESTS ROSE TO THE OCCASION. From the *New York Tribune*, August 12, 1891, page 2, unsigned, headlined '*THE GUESTS ROSE TO THE OCCASION.* || THE SERVANTS WENT ON STRIKE, BUT DINNER | WAS SERVED NOTWITHSTANDING.' The dateline was *Avon-by-the-Sea, Aug. 11.* There is nothing particularly distinctive of Crane in this item, but it comes from Avon-by-the-Sea and is the sort of human interest story he had an eye for. Not previously reprinted.

No. 140. ART AT AVON-BY-THE-SEA. One note of wry humor may perhaps suggest that Crane wrote this item, despite the difficulty of identifying most of the 1891 news reports. It appeared in the *New York Tribune*, August 16, 1891, page 19, unsigned, headlined 'ART AT AVON-BY-THE-SEA. || THE SCHOOLS OF EXPRESSION AND DELINERA-|TION—MANY GUESTS AT THE HOTELS.' The dateline was *Avon-by-the-Sea, Aug. 15.* Not previously reprinted.

No. 141. FLOWERS AT ASBURY PARK. Partly because of amusement at incongruities and partly because of the personal plug for his family, the article is worth considering as Crane's. This piece was printed in the *New York Tribune*, June 19, 1892, page 22, unsigned, headed 'FLOWERS AT ASBURY PARK. || THE RESORT A BOWER OF GREEN LEAVES AND | BRIGHT BLOSSOMS.' The dateline was *Asbury Park, June 18*. Not previously reprinted.

No. 142. A MULTITUDE OF GUESTS AT ASBURY PARK. Probably to be attributed to Crane is this news item printed in the *New York Tribune*, July 10, 1892, page 24, headlined 'ON THE NEW-JERSEY COAST. || A MULTITUDE OF GUESTS AT ASBURY PARK. || A RECORD-BREAKING SEASON—SOME OF THE | DWELLERS IN HOTELS AND COTTAGES.', unsigned, with the dateline *Asbury Park, N.J., July 9*. Not previously reprinted.

No. 143. BABY PARADE AT ASBURY PARK. This piece comes in the area of Crane's reporting of Asbury Park events and may possibly be attributed to him. It appeared unsigned in the *New York Tribune*, July 31, 1892, page 9, headlined 'BABY PARADE AT ASBURY PARK. || TWENTY THOUSAND PEOPLE WATCH THE IN-|FANTS AS THEY ARE WHEELED BY.' The dateline was *Asbury Park, July 30*. Not previously reprinted.

No. 144. SUMMER ATHLETIC SPORTS AT ASBURY PARK. This possible Crane item was printed in the *New York Tribune*, July 31, 1892, page 31, unsigned, headlined 'ON THE NEW-JERSEY COAST. || SUMMER ATHLETIC SPORTS AT ASBURY | PARK. || AN ARMY OF GUESTS AT THE VARIOUS HOTELS | AND COTTAGES.' The dateline was *Asbury Park, N.J., July 30*. Not previously reprinted.

No. 145. THE HEIGHT OF THE SEASON AT ASBURY PARK. Possibly Crane's is this item printed in the *New York Tribune*, August 14, 1892, page 8, unsigned, headlined 'ON THE NEW-JERSEY COAST || THE HEIGHT OF THE SEASON AT ASBURY | PARK. || BATHING SUITS—REPUBLICAN CLUB—PERSONAL | AND SOCIAL NOTES.' The dateline was *Asbury Park, N.J., Aug. 13*. Not previously reprinted.

NEWS, COMMENTARY, AND DESCRIPTIONS

No. 146. HENRY M. STANLEY

The earliest known signed and published piece of Crane's writing is "Henry M. Stanley," what may have been a classroom exercise printed in the Claverack school magazine, the *Vidette*, February, 1890, pages 8–9.

No. 147. BASEBALL

If a split infinitive is to be taken as evidence, the attribution of this schoolboy piece to Crane is accurate. It was printed in the *Vidette*, May, 1890, page 11.

No. 148. THE KING'S FAVOR

Signed S. C., this piece was printed in the Syracuse University's *University Herald*, xix (May, 1891), 128–131. The *Herald* text seems to have been set with especial fidelity to Crane's manuscript, including several of his favorite misspellings.

Crane may have met Thies (later Gerard-Thiers) in Avon-by-the-Sea in the summer of 1890. On July 14, 1890, page 4, under the heading "Avon-by-the-Sea. Seaside Assembly Opens this Week" the *New York Tribune* recorded from Avon-by-the-Sea that "The first evening entertainment will be given by Albert G. Theiss, the well-known New-York tenor." On July 21 the *Tribune* reported, on page 5, that "Albert G. Theiss, the prominent New-York tenor, is a guest at the Sylvan Lodge," and on August 22, page 7, "Albert G. Theis, of New-York, tenor; Miss Louise Gerrard, soprano, and Mrs. Kate Vashti Baxter, pianist, gave one of the best concerts of the season here this afternoon." However, the really interesting news report, which may well have been written by young Crane himself, in view of the use made of it in "The King's Favor," is No. 105, "Avon's School by the Sea," printed in the *Tribune* on August 4, 1890, page 5, the last paragraph of which, before the concluding list of names, contains a long account of Thies's experiences in Africa. Although much of this, and perhaps of "The King's Favor," may have derived from press-agent handouts, the close relation of "The King's Favor" to the paragraph makes it clear where the subject came from. The publicity piece "Miss Louise Gerard—Soprano" that Crane wrote in 1894 for Thies's wife, Louise Gerard, who was performing with her husband at Avon-by-the-Sea, suggests that he had met the two during the summer and had heard from Thies's own lips the details of the African adventure that he wrote up, perhaps in 1890, although it was not published until May, 1891. The writeup of another of his experiences in the summer of 1890—"Across the Covered Pit"— seems to have been done almost immediately, also.

The copy-text is the *University Herald*. One leaf of a typescript preserved in the Syracuse University Library seems to be a copy of the *Herald*.

No. 149. A FOREIGN POLICY, IN THREE GLIMPSES

The manuscript of this unpublished early essay on politics was purchased in 1961 from Miss Edith Crane for the University of Virginia—Barrett Collection. It is written in black ink on the rectos of seventeen leaves of cheap white wove unwatermarked and unruled paper 227 × 176 mm. Crane signed the manuscript at an angle in the upper left corner of the first page and subscribed it on page 17, adding a concluding #. All leaves but 1 and 14 are paged at top center above a semicircle. On the verso of page 17 is written the page number 10 but no text. The text was first printed by Stallman, but from a faulty typescript Miss Crane had commissioned, in the *Bulletin of the New York Public Library*, LXI (1957), 41–46, with an introductory essay. The piece dates from Crane's undergraduate days, in 1890 or 1891.

No. 150. GREAT BUGS IN ONONDAGA

Crane's youthful tall tale appeared simultaneously in the *Syracuse Daily Standard*, Monday, June 1, 1891, page 6, unsigned, headlined 'HUGE ELECTRIC LIGHT BUGS. || What a Wild-Eyed Patriot from the Sand | Hills Thought He Saw.' and in the *New York Tribune*, June 1, page 1, unsigned, headlined 'GREAT BUGS IN ONONDAGA. || THEY SWARM IN A QUARRY AND STOP A | LOCOMOTIVE. || A RARE CHANCE FOR NATURAL HISTORIANS—|LIKE ELECTRIC LIGHT BUGS, BUT LARGER.' No dateline was present in the *Standard* (N^1) but the story in the *Tribune* (N^2) was datelined *Syracuse, May 31*. At this time Crane was serving as Syracuse University correspondent for the *Tribune*.

That the Syracuse text was set from a holograph manuscript seems clear; but the nature of the copy for the *Tribune* is more conjectural. The extremely light punctuation in the *Tribune* which generally follows that in the *Standard* with only a few additions might suggest that it was set from a proof, or from a wired account; but on the whole a holograph copy of the original manuscript behind the *Standard* text seems to fit the total evidence with least difficulty. A number of the *Tribune* variants are no doubt editorial, such as *great size* for *immense proportions* (579.10), *insects died* for *things gave up the ghost* (579.22), or *ran* for *scud* (579.16) and *began* for *begun* (579.15). The omission of the introductory and concluding material surrounding the narrative is understandable. Why N¹ *huddled* (579.-10–11) should be omitted is less clear; and one may query whether the added phrase *in cities* (579.20) and the substitution of *iron monster* for *engine* (579.24) are more likely to be editorial or perhaps authorial variants created when Crane recopied the piece.[44] The description of the insects in N² at 579.30–580.14 may be a cut in N¹ but just as possibly, perhaps, new matter added in the recopied version.

Although it would seem that both texts are independent and stem from different manuscripts, the *Syracuse Standard* has been chosen as copy-text because it appears to be less edited than the *Tribune*. However, the description of the bugs has been introduced from N² and—in order not to confuse the bibliographies which have listed the article under its *Tribune* title "Great Bugs in Onondaga"—the N² title has been substituted for the N¹ headline. The article has not previously been reprinted with the introduction and conclusion found in the *Standard*, or with its more authoritative substantives.

With tongue in cheek the *Tribune* the next day printed an editorial comment, June 2, 1891, page 6, headed 'THE SYRACUSE BUGS.' The *Tribune* text of this sequel must have been wired to Syracuse, where it appeared in the *Syracuse Daily Journal*, June 2, page 5, headed 'The Syracuse Bugs. | New York Tribune.' Although the possibility cannot be overlooked that the 'apology' was also written by Crane and the two parts planned as an elaborate whole, the writing does not sound like him, and in such a case the *Journal*, a rival to the *Standard*, would not have printed its version from that of the *Tribune*. It would seem, then, that some member of the *Tribune* staff, perhaps Willis Fletcher Johnson, as suggested by Ames Williams, amused himself with extending the joke. The text from the *Tribune* follows:

It is seldom necessary to apologize for a newspaper man. The stainless life, the high integrity, the nobleness of aim, the breadth of mind and the depth of scholarship of the journalist are so well known to the intelligent

---

[44] That the writer of the June 2 *jeu* in the *Tribune* made fun of the phrase *iron monster* may be evidence that it had not originally been editorial, since it would seem to be the only example of the extravagance of language being touched up by the *Tribune* instead of reduced. The odds may favor the conjecture that this is an authorial revision in the copying-out of the manuscript for the *Tribune*. *Monster* for a locomotive appears twice in "The Scotch Express" manuscript at 740.39 and 741.37, although the first is altered (perhaps editorially) to "*flier*" in the magazine text. The addition of the phrase *in the cities* has been rejected, however, as more likely to be the work of an editor disturbed by the possibility of misunderstanding *all over the country* as applying to 'countryside'.

readers of The Tribune that it would be an impertinence to dwell upon them here. But sometimes, after all, the journalist will make a mistake; he is but human. An instance of this was seen yesterday morning in the published accounts of the appearance of swarms of great bugs nearly three inches long and two inches wide near Syracuse. It was evident that the able correspondent had intended producing a series, beginning with ordinary bugs, running along through the summer with a gradual increase in size, and ending in October with these giant, mudturtle-like bugs which stopped a railroad train and dumbfounded the local scientists; but through some mistake the last account was sent first, and we shall probably hear nothing from the preliminary, cumulative bugs. It scarcely seems possible (though to genius nothing is impossible) that this could be the beginning of a series, and that October will find great bugs ten feet long and weighing half a ton galloping about Onondaga County, and in strange, unnatural cries voicing their horrid craving for human gore; but to this it may come after all.

In either case a moment's glance at the tale of the new Sinbad, of Syracuse, may not be out of place. The bugs were discovered in a deep cut which enters a stone quarry and covered the railroad track for sixty feet. The iron monster (locomotive) could not plough through them. They had hard shells of the nature of slaty stone, as big as half of a very large hen's egg shell and they moved about with lightning-like rapidity (very fast). An erudite recluse (weather prophet) living in the neighborhood pronounced them a cross between a rock mollusk and some kind of insect. (He is the same man who last summer so successfully crossed the common honey-bee and the lightning-bug, getting a species of bee which can work all night by its own light.) When the locomotive (iron monster) ran over one of these stone insects there was a loud report like a toy torpedo. But it is a hint dropped further along which will give people the best idea of this strange new bug. It is, says the correspondent, much like the well-known electric-light bug, now common all over the country, only larger. This is more to the point. Everybody knows the electric-light bug. It superseded the old gas-light bug, which took the place of the kerosene-lamp bug, which had itself driven out the tallow-candle bug. While not so large as the lighthouse bug or the bonfire bug, the electric-light bug is nevertheless a formidable bug, and has even been known, when suffering from hunger, to attack and kill the great oil-warehouse fire bug, which frequently comes out and chases the firemen around the corner and devours the hose. We would suggest, the oldest inhabitant (erudite recluse) to the contrary notwithstanding, that perhaps this new Syracuse insect is nothing, after all, but the well-known iron-monster head-light bug. They are larger than either the arc-light bug or the incandescent bug and have stone shells. When run over by a locomotive, however, they give out a report which sounds more like a toy pistol than a toy torpedo, so our surmise may be incorrect.

In closing we can only say that if Dr. Lintner expects another term as State entomologist he must board a monster of steel and iron, hurry to Syracuse and report on this new bug.

The attribution of "Great Bugs" to Crane, with supporting opinions from Olov Fryckstedt, Edwin H. Cady, and Walter Sutton, together with the texts of the *Tribune* story and editorial, was first printed in Lester G. Wells, "The Iron Monster, the Crackling Insects of Onondaga County, and Stephen Crane," *The Courier* (Syracuse University Library Associates), March, 1963, pages 1–7, followed by a further discussion by Ames Williams in "Stephen Crane's Bugs," *The Courier,* September, 1963, pages 22–31, including the demonstration of its source as a news item about caterpillars in Minnesota delaying a train that had come out in the *Syracuse Sunday Herald* on May 24, 1891.

No. 151. THE WRECK OF THE "NEW ERA"

The text of the unpublished "Wreck of the New Era" was first printed by Robert Stallman in the *Connecticut Campus Fine Arts Magazine,* April 28, 1956, pages 1–2, 19–20, the copy being a typescript in the University of Virginia–Barrett Collection that had been made at the instance of Miss Edith Crane from the manuscript in her possession. This copy (retyped?) notes that on the original typescript was deleted *A. T. Vance, N.Y. Press Club, N.Y. City.* In 1961, however, Mr. Barrett purchased from Miss Crane the original holograph manuscript, which consists of fourteen numbered pages (page 3 altered from 2) of cheap wove unwatermarked and unruled paper 253 × 204 mm., written in black ink on the rectos only. An oddity is the number of x-crosses that stand for periods as well as Crane's usual circled dots. The # sign is placed at the conclusion. The only signature is in the upper left corner of the first page, at an angle. The handwriting is large but well-formed. The reference in 584.13–20 to contributions being made for a monument to commemorate the dead from the wreck helps to date this piece as written probably in 1891, for the monument was not completed and erected until May 29, 1892, although the *New Era* Monument Association was formed in 1891.

The present edition prints the text from the manuscript for the first time.

No. 152. ACROSS THE COVERED PIT

The unpublished youthful essay "Across the Covered Pit" was first printed by Robert Stallman in "Stephen Crane: Some New Stories," in the *Bulletin of the New York Public Library,* LXI (January, 1957), 39–41, his copy being a retyped copy in the University of Virginia–Barrett Collection of a lost typescript made for Miss Edith Crane.

This ribbon typescript and its carbon had typed on its fourth and last leaf *Marked on typed copy: (two copies)* | *From S. Seth* | *Acting for A. T. Vance* | *1133 Broadway.* | [space] | *29 handwritten pages, thin, yellow tint, 6-⅜″ × 10″.* Whatever the significance of these names they have nothing to do with Crane's own publishing history since they seem to be associated only with the typescripts that Miss Crane had made at a late date from her stock of manuscripts.

In 1961 Mr. Barrett purchased the various original manuscripts from Miss Crane that had previously been known only from the inaccurate typed copies she had authorized. Among these was 'Across the covered pit.', the title double underlined, the piece signed *S. C.* at the end. The manuscript consists of twenty-nine leaves of cheap wove unruled paper without watermark, 250 × 160 mm., written in black ink in a very large hand, a minuscule *i* in the lower left corner of the first page. The first paragraph is unmarked, but thereafter to each indented paragraph is prefixed a ¶ sign. Corrections are made in the same ink during the course of writing, although a few may perhaps have been added on review. However, the last correction, that on 587.18, was made in pencil, and this pencil also deleted the ink initials *S.C.* underlined twice in ink in the manuscript. The opening words on page 1 *Rev. H. C. Hovey D. D. of Bridgeport, Conn.,* are lightly crossed through in pencil, and on page 13 *Dr. Hovey* (585.32) is similarly deleted. No substitution is made, but one may speculate that this removal of Hovey's name was intended to take the piece from the category of a news story and to turn it more toward that of a sketch.[45] This manuscript, once folded in thirds horizontally, is now laminated.

On July 14, 1890, in a report headed "Avon-by-the-Sea" about the Seaside Assembly's summer programs, the *New York Tribune,* page 4, noted that "On the evenings of July 23 and 25 the Rev. H. C. Hovey, D.D., of Bridgeport, Conn., will lecture on 'Subterranean Scenery, Wonderful Luray and Arabia Petra, and the Mazes and Marvels of Mammoth Cave,'" and on July 26 in "Lectures at Avon-by-the-Sea," page 3, datelined July 25 the *Tribune* reported, "In the evening the Rev. Dr. H. C. Hovey, of Bridgeport, Conn., lectured in the auditorium on the 'Mazes and Marvels of Mammoth Cave.'" On July 28, page 4,

[45] The minuscule letter *i* in the lower-left corner of the manuscript might be taken as associating this manuscript at one time with Cora Crane, who so marked the manuscripts, proofs, and typescripts in her possession after Crane's death, as may be seen frequently in copies she sent Reynolds for *Last Words.* If so, the pencil deletions may be unauthoritative, However, how the manuscript could pass from her after Crane's death to Miss Edith Crane is difficult to envisage.

in No. 104, a news story perhaps by Crane headlined "Avon Seaside Assembly," the *Tribune* printed a brief news account of Hovey. Just as "The King's Favor" grew out of stories told by the singer Albert Thies at Avon in the summer of 1890, so it is probable that "Across the Covered Pit" had its genesis in Hovey's lecture on July 25, 1890. The attempts to make something of a news article from the narrative might well place this manuscript in August, 1890, a date consistent with the formation of the handwriting.

No. 153. THE GRATITUDE OF A NATION

The Special Collections of the Columbia University Libraries preserves this untitled holograph manuscript of six pages, the first four of wove ledger paper, unwatermarked, measuring 318 × 204 mm., the rules 11 mm. apart. The poem occupies page 1, and the prose starts on numbered page 2 (each page except 1 being numbered above a semicircle). The first four pages are browned by age. The fifth and sixth leaves are on lighter colored paper measuring 318 × 198 mm. The ink was probably blue-black originally, with the alterations in the same ink. The sixth leaf was written on the verso of a page containing two different trials of other material. At the present top is written in pencil 'The name of this club | shall be the'; then, turned end for end, at the other top appears in black ink 'Once a man clambering to the house tops | Cried there to the imperturbab', a false start for a poem found in *War is Kind*. Below this, in pencil is the start 'Once'. Then below this, in pencil, but not in Crane's hand, is written 'Stephen Crane | Hartwood Club | Port Jervis N.Y.' Despite the alterations, the care with which this manuscript is written, and its general correctness, indicates that it is probably a fair copy of a worked-over earlier draft.

The notation *Hartwood Club* on the verso of the last leaf suggests that this article may have been a manuscript that Cora recovered from Port Jervis when she visited there after returning to the United States with Crane's body for burial. The date of the manuscript can be fixed with some precision from a letter Crane wrote to Hamlin Garland in May, 1894, from Chicago: "Everything is coming along nicely now. I have got the poetic spout so that I can turn it on or off. I wrote a Decoration Day thing for the *Press* which aroused them to enthusiasm. They said in about a minute, though, that I was firing over the heads of the soldiers" (Garland, *Roadside Meetings* [1930], pp. 200–201). Hence the piece remained unpublished until modern times.

No. 154. IN THE DEPTHS OF A COAL MINE

On a McClure's commission, Crane and Corwin Linson, his artist friend, journeyed to Scranton, Pennsylvania, in early June, 1894.[46] The result was "In the Depths of a Coal Mine," which was first syndicated by S. S. McClure in a number of newspapers on Sunday, July 22, 1894. The following examples have been observed:

N¹: *Detroit Free Press*, July 22, 1894, page 2, headlined 'DOWN IN A COAL MINE. || TO THE VISITOR IT IS A WEIRD AND MYSTERIOUS SCENE—TO | THE MINER A PLACE TO EARN HIS BREAD. || BY STEPHEN CRANE. ||'.

N²: *St. Paul Pioneer Press*, July 22, page 13, signed, headlined 'DEPTHS OF A | COAL MINE. || EXPERIENCES FAR BENEATH THE | SURFACE OF EARTH. || Through Mile Upon Mile of Hewn | Streets Which the Rays of the | Sun Can Never Reach—Wierd Im-|pression of a Visitor in These | Plutonian Depths—What a Min-|ing Life Means for Men and Mules | Under the Veil of Impenetrable | Night. ||'.

N³: *Buffalo Express*, July 22, page 17, headlined 'The Depths of a Coal Mine. || By STEPHEN CRANE.'

N⁴: *Philadelphia Inquirer*, July 22, page 21, headlined 'The Depths of a Coal Mine || BY STEPHEN CRANE || THROUGH MILES OF HEWN STREETS | FAR UNDER GROUND || What a Mining Life Does For Men and Mules. | Weird Impressions of a Visitor. || Copyright, 1894, by S. S. McClure, Limited.' A dateline appears of *Scranton, July 20.*

N⁵: *St. Louis Republic*, July 22, part III, page 17, signed, headlined 'DOWN IN A COAL MINE. || THROUGH MILES OF HEWN STREETS | FAR UNDERGROUND. || What a Mining Life Does for Men and | Mules —Weird Impressions of a Visi-|tor—A Curtain of Impenetrable | Night— Wonders of the Subterranean | Avenues. || Written for The Republic.'

Three cuts accompanied the McClure proofs sent out to subscribing newspapers, taken from Linson's drawings for *McClure's Magazine*. These were captioned *Entrance to the Elevator, A Breaker Boy,* and *The Breaker.* The *Buffalo Express* used none, and the *St. Paul Pioneer Press* omitted *A Breaker Boy*; otherwise the noted newspapers utilized all three.

In August, 1894, *McClure's Magazine*, III, 195–209, ran the article, entitled "In the Depths of a Coal Mine," with fourteen illustrations by Corwin Linson, captioned *A Few Projecting Spires and Chimneys Indicated a Town, The "Breaker", In a Large Room Sat the Little Slate-Pickers, The "Fan" and Entrance to Shaft, The Engineer, Feed-*

---

[46] For a personal account of this trip, see Corwin K. Linson, *My Stephen Crane*, ed. E. H. Cady (1958), pp. 65–70.

ing the Furnace, "The Dead Black Walls Slipped Swiftly By", "Two Men Crouching Where the Roof of the Passage Came Near to Meeting the Floor", "He Who Worked at the Drill Engaged in Conversation with our Guide", *Mule Stables. Putting in a Team,* "Whoa, Molly", *Last Sight of the* "Breakers" *from the Town,* together with a self-captioned sketch *Breaker Boy. A Type* and an untitled sketch of a bearded miner with pipe.

In the University of Virginia–Barrett Collection is preserved the holograph manuscript for most of an early draft, once owned by H. Bacon Collamore. This consists of seventeen leaves, plus one containing a false start, of *Red Badge* Paper C, 317 × 202 mm., the rules 10 mm. apart. The pages, written in black ink on one side of the paper, and corrected in the same ink and later in pencil, are numbered [1] 2–11, 15–19, 22. The manuscript is untitled. Evidently Crane gave this draft to his friend Linson as a memento of their expedition, for in Linson's hand on page 1 is inscribed in pencil 'Original MS. by Stephen Crane. | written in The Valley House, at Scranton. Pa.' and then below and to the left 'First | draft of | "In the Depths of a Coal Mine" | McClure's—Aug. 1894'. On fol. 7ᵛ are the word counts for five pages totaling 1,023 and on 9ᵛ five more totaling 1,124. Linson made various marginal notes. On page 3 opposite 'suggested . . . blood.' (601.20–25) he wrote 'Omitted from printed article—|CKL.', and on page 4 opposite 'They . . . themselves.' (601.42–602.3) 'omitted', and 'out' opposite the final sentence of paragraph 602.6–11. On page 10 opposite the opening lines of the paragraph 604.37–605.4 he wrote 'For some | reason, "China" | as here named, | was changed to "Molly Maguire" | in the printed | article. | CKL.'; and at the foot of the page below 605.4, '(a paragraph | added here, the holding of the mule)'. At the foot of page 11 he noted 'missing pages of ms. here | given in type. | CKL';[47] and on page 15 he wrote 'out' and 'omitted' opposite 'We . . . mass.' (605. 21–24) and 'When . . . lot.' (605.30–33). On page 16 he noted 606.9–17 as 'omitted', and marked the sentence 'He . . . grave.' (606.6–8) as 'omitted' and added 'Flattened out to "Meanwhile, he gets three dollars | per day, and his laborer one dollar | and a quarter."!' Page 17 (606.18–36) is noted as 'This whole | page | omitted in | printed | article'; page 18 (606.36–607.10), 'All this |

---

[47] The manuscript leaves for this missing material have not been preserved. The University of Virginia Library owns three typed pages presumably made by Linson, for his note appears on the first page: *Pages 12, 13, 14 of ms. missing— here typed from published article.* The third page corresponds to the conclusion of the published article.

omitted | also in | printed | article'; and page 19 has the brackets and 'omitted' for 607.10–16. The opening of page 22 with 'the study' (607.17) he prefaced with 'Then suddenly' drawn from *McClure's* and bracketed the text from 'We' (607.18) to the end of the paragraph with 'altered in text.' Passages on pages 9 and 11 are marked in pencil with a double vertical stroke and the figures 6 and 8 (the latter erased). These may refer to Linson's proposed illustrations.

On Linson's testimony this manuscript was written in Scranton before Crane returned to New York. The very considerable differences between this and the published version, added to the preservation and gift of the manuscript after it had fulfilled its purpose, indicates that Crane used it as the basis for a much revised fair copy. The missing pages 12–14, evidently, needed less revision and were removed to form part of the final manuscript. The function of the false-start page is obscure. The full page 15, altered from 14, begins 'We were appalled occasionally' (605.21), in which 'W' is written over 'In' and the first 'p' of 'appalled' is inserted. Since the single leaf—inscribed only with 'We were occasi'—is correctly numbered 15, it is possible that Crane contemplated recopying and revising the page at some point but gave up the idea after the opening words. The status of leaf 22 is conjectural. Since Crane broke off on page 19 in the middle of a sentence (607.16), it is possible that he recognized his editorializing was unsuitable and that he needed to get on with the business of the departure from the mine, or else he simply ran out of energy or of time. Pages 20–21, then, would need to have contained much more than the fifty-eight words 599.26–31—'Meanwhile . . . regard them.'—that was new material. Hence one may suppose that these two pages 20–21 are wanting because they were a part not of the original but instead of the new and revised manuscript. The simplest explanation is that Crane ended his writing at Scranton with page 19 as we have it. It is possible that when he returned to New York he continued in the editorial vein, picking up on a new page 19 or 20 and continuing through more material later rejected until writing what we now have as 599.26–31 at the foot of page 21 before concluding with page 22. On the other hand, it is perhaps more probable to conjecture that in New York he started his revision without completing the article and continued it through the present page 22, only to reject this last page, marked with his usual concluding #, in favor of a rewritten and revised conclusion such as we have in the prints. If so, the preserved page 22 is not from the original draft but instead ended the revised version, and pages 21–22 are wanting because they were part of the final submitted manuscript—in short, they would include roughly the two hundred and fifty-eight revised words in 'We were appalled . . . dollar and a quarter' (599.4–27) which would have been added to the abstracted pages 12–14 (renumbered, of course, when added to the preceding revised pages) to end the article. If so, the revised manuscript would have consisted of 22 pages.[48]

One of the important problems of this text concerns the differences between the preserved draft manuscript and the printed texts and how much these represent the form of Crane's lost revised manuscript and how much editorial changes that might have been made in the McClure office. Linson in his reminiscences (pp. 69–70) blames the major revision toward the end on *McClure's*:

> The *McClure's* editors thought the end of the article much too caustic of "big business." Crane had etched a picture of Capital and Labor with a sharp needle and bitten the plate deep in a nitric bath. There was a brief description of the miners, Polack, Hungarian, Italian, Irish, and Welsh. . . . Following this study of the miners came a contrasting excoriation of "men who make neat livings by fiddling with the market.". . .
> But this never saw print. Instead it was made tamely innocuous. When Stephen read his article in type, he grunted and tossed it aside. "The birds didn't want the truth after all. Why the hell did they send me up there then? Do they want the public to think the coal mines gilded ballrooms with the miners eating ice-cream in boiled shirt-fronts?" To Steve, this soft-pedal of editorial policy was a thing to be smashed with a crowbar.

The newspaper versions (N) and the *McClure's Magazine* (McC) texts are almost identical up to 598.15 (*Once a miner . . .*) where *McClure's Magazine* starts to cut, in part to avoid offense to business interests and in part to fit the article into the assigned space; and in this process of cutting it also pays more attention than hitherto to small editorial changes intended to improve the style. If one ignores the preliminary cut in the newspaper version 590.24–591.11, eighteen substantive variants appear in this area between the reconstructed N proof and McC. Of these it is evident that the N compositor or copy was in error at 591.18, 591.18–19, 591.26, 593.17 (*the tales*), 593.34, 594.12, 594.14, 594.27, 595.11, 595.25, and 597.34. The McC compositor was in error at 593.17, and he probably sophisticated *was* to *were* at 592.3. Of the remaining, the McC dialect 'th'' for $N^{2,4-5}$ 'the' (597.19) may be a McC improvement, but it is certain that the $N^{1,3-4}$ agreement with MS at 592.27 in

[48] Ordinarily in this manuscript Crane wrote about 230 words per page. Since material conjectured to have occupied pages 20–21 in the revised numbering consists only of 243 words, it may have been that the revision of original Scranton pages 12–14 occupied a part of page 20. On the other hand, editorial cuts may have removed some of this material.

mule-boys. And makes McC,N[5] run-on sentence an unauthoritative change. Only three readings remain that might not be compositorial. These are the McC sophistication *us, as if the roof were* for N *us. It was* (594.18), McC *the mules* for N *these animals* (598.11), and the McC omission of *Once* (598.15). The latter is so close to the point where the McC editor took over in proof to reduce the article and, in the process, to revise its style, that it is probable he picked up this alteration in reading over the proof to determine where to start the cuts: the McC form seems to be away from what Crane would likely have written. Since no other variant between McC and N seems to be editorial save for the possibility at 594.18, this may be credited to the compositor as well. The conclusion is that the copy for N and for McC was not independently edited up to 598.15, or more likely up to 598.11, but instead that it was identical save for the preliminary N cut that was designed. The McC variants at 592.3, 592.27, and 594.18 were either the compositor's or the proofreader's. The editing of McC after 598.15 was, of course, done not in the copy but in the proof.

The nature of the copy for each print is in part involved in this matter, for if both were set from identical copy then any editing of Crane's second manuscript would necessarily have been done before the common copy was sent to the two printers. That the N proof was not the copy for McC seems clear from the absence of detectable common error, and particularly the McC agreement with manuscript readings against N variation when MS is a witness. That an early state of the McC proof was not copy for N is probable. If the McC variants at 592.3, 592.27, and 594.18 were proofreader's variants, the case would hinge on the single reading *crimes* at 593.17 where MS and N read *crime* and a correction by N of the McC error is not likely. This alone is a strong piece of evidence; but if we can add to it the variants at 592.3, 592.27 and 594.18 as the McC compositor's, it would be a certainty that McC proof, in early or in late state, did not serve as copy for N. The question then resolves itself into whether both were set from Crane's manuscript or from a typescript prepared from it. On the whole the evidence strongly favors a common typescript, probably the ribbon copy and its carbon. Although in some details such as hyphenation the styling of the accidentals in N and McC may differ, and the use of commas is not uniform by any means (N usually having lighter punctuation than McC), yet the number of times that both agree in differing from the system of the draft manuscript would seem to go beyond independent styling that happened to coincide. The influence of a copy that often varied from the punctuation system of the MS both toward lightening and toward increasing the weight—in either case away from Crane's characteristics at this date—appears to be influential in the frequent agreements of N and McC in contrast to MS. No doubt some of these common agreements derive from the lost fair-copy manuscript, but the systematic differences are too great to permit this manuscript to have been the common copy. It is worth remarking that the punctuation characteristics of MS are the same as those in the preserved manuscript of "The Snake," which may date before 1896, and there is no reason to believe that Crane would adopt a widely variant system from these two in making a fair copy. It is possible that a few of the McC,N substantive variants from MS that are queried as perhaps representative of preliminary editing could instead be typist's changes. In this category one can point particularly to the repetition of *measure . . . up* at 595.13 in the guide's response to the miner's *measure . . . up* of 595.11 whereas MS has simply *measure* for the response, which seems to be the intended reading. A working hypothesis for a typescript and carbon made from the manuscript best fits the total evidence, in which case the presence of another intermediary increases the likelihood that not all of the McC,N joint readings are authoritative.

The question of the amount of editing of Crane's manuscript before typesetting can never be finally settled. That some editing would be given the manuscript goes without saying, and the hypothesis can be supported by changes made in Crane's work for *McClure's Magazine* in stories where something of a control is present to enable one to detect it. One thing seems relatively certain, however. The uniformity of the two texts up to 598.15 except for the few compositorial variants indicates the strong probability that the editing was done on the manuscript and not on the respective typescripts.[49] One piece of evidence demonstrates that the manuscript was marked for the typist at 591.12. All N texts begin at 591.12 with *Around a huge central building clustered other and lower ones,* and this is the McC reading, whereas MS has *Around the huge central building,* since this was the breaker building described in the preceding paragraph. In context with the full beginning, McC's *a . . . building* removes the reference to the breaker and fixes it to some indeterminate building in a manner that is clearly wrong. The change of MS *the . . . building* to *a . . . building,* it is clear, was enforced by

---

[49] Of course, if only one typescript served first for one and then for the other printer's copy, this could have been the document that was edited. But see below for one piece of important evidence that the manuscript itself was marked.

the opening of the N text, not by anything in the McC text. It follows that McC repeats a change made for the purpose of providing a suitable new opening for N. One may conjecture, then, that Crane's manuscript was marked for the typist to take account of the proposed N opening sentence.[50] Since this change was made in the manuscript, not in the typed copy for N (on the evidence of McC agreement), it is natural to suppose that the McC editor worked over the manuscript itself before the typist made up the copy for the printers. If this is so, the variants from MS in the first two paragraphs may give a critic a partial insight into the nature of some of the editorial changes. In this category the alteration of MS *our first colliery* to *the colliery* (590.32) is a good possibility, as is the substitution of *a grim, strange war* for *this grim, strange war* (591.10). Crane's persistent use of *this* was often changed by editors, and just such another variant occurs at 594.10. Possibly the change at 590.33 from MS *The "breaker"* to McC *A "breaker"* was similarly motivated. At 591.1 the McC plural *sides* would seem to be called for as against MS *side*, a change not likely to have been drawn from the second manuscript.[51] One cannot be sure whether Crane or the editor struck out MS *sometimes* before *came* at 591.5 or altered *the new eye* to the rather awkward *our new eyes* (591.9), a change somewhat like those made at 590.33 and 591.10. Whether it was Crane or the editor who cut the comparison to a Swiss chalet after *blackened wood* (590.34) and at the end of the second paragraph removed the detail of the beetles and of the little girl waiting for her father is scarcely to be determined, although one may legitimately suspect a certain amount of editorial pruning of detail throughout in order to speed up the descriptions.

The general evidence would suggest that there was little thorough editorial rewriting of the manuscript but, instead, a cutting of what seemed excess detail and the usual smoothing of what were always viewed as Crane's awkwardnesses of style and the forms of individual

[50] It is not to be determined whether the typist began with this third paragraph, and McC's opening was set from the manuscript, or whether the typist in fact typed the regular opening, which was deleted in the copy for N. The point is of no great significance except as it might bear on the matter of the manuscript being marked at 590.24–591.11 where McC editorial revision of the MS text may be suspected in these two paragraphs. What is important is the evidence that the McC,N reading *a* for *the* originated necessarily in a marking of the manuscript.

[51] A good analogy is Crane's *side* in "The Octopush" 230.33 where in the TMs of the early draft "The Fishermen" the reading is *sides of the boat* but in the *Tribune* later version it is, incorrectly, *side of the boat,* making one wonder whether the typescript sophisticated the reading or Crane altered it inadvertently when he revised the sketch in making a new fair copy.

words.[52] That the editorial work, with these exceptions, was not particularly heavy may perhaps be conjectured from the changes that were made after 598.15 once the McC editor found himself scrutinizing the text with greater care, in proof, when he had to adjust it to the given space. These really do tinker with the expression in a manner presumably not engaged in when the manuscript was marked, else they would have been revised at that time. One would expect heavier editorial work on a commissioned article, of course, than on a piece of fiction. On the other hand, if page 22 of the Barrett manuscript is—as conjectured—the final page of the revision, a comparison of what would have been the approximate word count of the second manuscript with the full printed form of the text does not suggest the possible cutting of more than a few hundred words in the editorial working over of the manuscript.

Because of the marked differences between the draft version in the Barrett MS and the final revised and then edited version in print, both forms of the text have been reprinted. For the printed version, *McClure's Magazine* has been taken as the copy-text, supplemented when necessary by the extra material found in reconstructed N. However, the accidentals of MS in parallel text are, of course, more authoritative than those of either print, and these holograph accidentals have been used to emend the copy-text in all cases where the McC text accidentals seem to reflect the styling of editor, typist, and compositor, it being assumed that the punctuation system of the fair-copy revision would not have differed materially from that of MS. In various cases the concurrence of N with MS against the McC styling may be taken as confirming the nature of the basic typescript copy and exposing McC's compositorial variation. The result, then, represents an attempt by the evidence of MS, $N, and McC to reconstruct as closely as may be the accidentals of the revised second manuscript that Crane submitted to S. S. McClure.[53] When MS is wanting, the evidence of N may affect the emendation of the McC copy-text, for there are some signs that in accidentals the com-

---

[52] Whether it was the typist or editor, for example, who changed Crane's characteristic *bended* to *bent* (595.6) is unknown but it certainly was not Crane.

[53] In fact, this eclectic form of the text is easier to reconstruct with credible accuracy than would have been the form of the typescript from the joint evidence of N and McC because of the numerous cases of their variation when MS would not be a witness. Of course, when MS is wanting or is not parallel, this attempt must be made as a means of returning to an authority closer to the revised manuscript—even though at one remove—than either McC or N individually. A more or less exact reprint of the McC accidentals would have been just that, a reprint of an authority at two removes from the manuscript and with no better credentials than $N.

positor of the N proof was more faithful to his typescript copy than the McC compositor.

Although for the accidentals an eclectic text is aimed at, the treatment of the substantives is more conservative. Because of the radiation of N and McC from a common typescript in an already edited form, the variation between the two points only to error in one or the other, not to variation of the text in different stages of transmission. In this situation to attempt to isolate and discard suspected examples of the editorial changes made before typing would be wholly speculative even when departures from characteristic Crane locutions found in MS may arouse suspicion. Hence in contrast to the treatment of the accidentals, the substantives are presented with very few alterations when McC and N agree, and disagreements before 598.11 are treated as cases of error in one or other of two equal authorities. Individual variation within the N-line can signify only the unauthoritative changes of the different newspaper compositors. All N texts except for N[5], the *St. Louis Republic,* cut the article in varying degrees whereas up to 598.15 *McClure's Magazine* gives the full text of the edited form, which, however, may have removed some amount of legitimate manuscript description drawn in revised form from MS. However, the N-texts bulk large in importance after this point when McC started not only to cut to meet space requirements but also to edit the style from time to time. It is unfortunate that the cuts decided on by the McC editor in this late proof stage are such natural ones that they may overlap with more extensive cuts in the various newspapers, so that on one occasion N[5] is the sole authority for the reconstructed text of the revised manuscript reprinted here, this being in an area where MS is not parallel, or is wanting. These parts of the text cut by McC, as well as the originals of its other alterations in this section, are restored in the present text from the N authorities. As a consequence, this edition prints material stemming from the revised Crane manuscript that has not previously been known.

The University of Virginia–Barrett manuscript has not heretofore been printed. It offers another example to add to that of "The Octopush" of Crane's thorough and careful methods of revision both in style and in content, well worth critical study. This MS has been edited with a minimum of editorial emendation, all of which has been separately recorded.

For the convenience of the reader wishing to survey the differences between McC and MS, the Historical Collation has been keyed to the McC copy-text version and contains a record of every substantive variation in MS, as well as every accidental variation not recorded in the List of Emendations. In addition, this Collation lists not only the complete record of substantive variation in the five newspapers but also every accidental variant whenever two or more of the newspapers agree in any reading. Unique N accidental variation has been ignored in the Collation since it could have no possible claim to authority in respect to the typescript.

The discrepancy between the McC and N titles, slight though it is, suggests the possibility that Crane's revised manuscript was untitled like his draft. The agreement between N^1 and N^5 in the title "Down in a Coal Mine" is probably fortuitous. The suggested headlines sent out as part of the McClure syndicated proof can be reconstructed in major part from $N^{2,4-5}$.

No. 155. PIKE COUNTY PUZZLE

This Vol. I, no. I of a four-page printed newspaper of August 28, 1894, was a summer-vacation joke. Crane seems to have been the moving spirit, joined by Senger, but whether the two were responsible for the whole contents as seems likely, or whether contributions were solicited from their companions, is not known. The newspaper was a four-column affair with advertisements occupying the bottom of the third column and all of the fourth on page 4. A facsimile of 300 copies was published by the *Stephen Crane Newsletter*, on January 26, 1967, out of series.

No. 156. HOWELLS FEARS THE REALISTS MUST WAIT

Crane's interview with William Dean Howells was syndicated by S. S. McClure for newspaper publication on Sunday, October 28, 1894. Fortunately, the original McClure galley proof has been preserved in the Crane scrapbooks in the Special Collections of the Columbia University Libraries. On the scrapbook page in Crane's hand is the notation *N.Y. Times*, and a single but important substantive correction—*art* for *act* at 636.21—also written on the page. Since all observed newspapers printed the error *act*, it would seem that Crane was wise after the event. The newspapers agree in no substantive variant, an indication that corrected proof may not have been returned, or at least that the later noted error was overlooked.

In its own proofreading McClure no doubt altered Crane's misspelling *concieve* found in the proof at 637.13, and probably also the position of the quotation marks in respect to the dash at 637.2. The printed versions observed are as follows:

N(p): Galley proof, headlined 'For Oct. 28 | Howells Fears the Realists Must Wait || A SUGGESTIVE TALK WITH THE | EMINENT NOVELIST. || He Still Holds a Firm Faith in Realism | But Confesses a Doubt if Its Day Has | Yet Come. || [Copyright, 1894, by S. S. McClure, Limited.]'. The dateline has blanks to be filled in by each newspaper: *New York,* — —. —, *1894.*—. The proof is signed at the end. The first 'S.' of 'S. S. McClure' is uncertain since the letter in the proof has been altered by hand and then deleted, obscuring the printed letter.

N¹: *New York Times,* October 28, 1894, page 20, signed, headlined 'FEARS REALISTS MUST WAIT || AN INTERESTING TALK WITH | WILLIAM DEAN HOWELLS. || The Eminent Novelist Still Holds a | Firm Faith in Realism, but Con-|fesses a Doubt if Its Day Has Yet | Come—He Has Observed a Change | in the Literary Pulse of the Coun-|try Within the Last Few Months—A | Reactionary Wave. | [Copyright, 1894, by L. S. McClure, Limited.]'. No dateline was used.

N²: *Philadelphia Inquirer,* October 28, page 9, signed, headlined 'Realists Must Wait, | Says W. Dean Howells || A SUGGESTIVE TALK WITH THE EMINENT | NOVELIST || He Still Holds a Firm Faith in Realism, But Confesses | a Doubt if Its Day Has Yet Come. || Copyright, 1894, by S. S. McClure, Ltd.' The dateline was *New York, Oct. 27.*

N³: *Louisville Courier-Journal,* October 28, page 20, signed, headlined 'HOWELLS TALKS OUT. || The Novelist's "Little Scheme' | About the Ohio Carpet-Wom-|an's Daughter. || He Views the Writer's Art As Des-|tined To Teach Men the Per-|spective of Life. ||'. No copyright notice appeared; the dateline was *New York, Oct. 27.*

N⁴: *Boston Globe,* Sunday, November 4, page 32, unsigned, headlined 'REALISTS MUST WAIT. || Howells Fears a Reaction | Has Come in Fiction. || Suggestive Talk With the Novelist | on Literary Tendencies. || Love But an Episode—Writers Should | Preserve Life's Perspective. ||'. No dateline was used; the McClure copyright notice was printed at the end.

N⁵: *St. Paul Pioneer Press,* November 6, page 4, signed, headlined 'THE REALISTS | MUST WAIT. || ACCORDING TO THE APPRNEHE|SIONS OF MR. HOWELLS. || A Highly Suggestive Talk With the | Eminent Novelist—The Author of | "A Hazard of New Fortunes" Still | Holds a Firm Faith in Realism, | but Confesses a Doubt as to | Whether Its Day Has Yet Come—|Every Novel Should Have an In-|tention. | (Copyright, 1894, by S. S. McClure, Limited.)'. The dateline was *New York, Oct. 25.*

All newspapers except for the galley proof and N¹ used a cut of Howells captioned *William Dean Howells at his Desk.*

The interview is here printed for the first time from the McClure galley proof as copy-text instead of what turns out to be the most corrupt text of all, that of the *New York Times.*

No. 157. GHOSTS ON THE JERSEY COAST

"Ghosts on the Jersey Coast" appeared in the *New York Press*, Sunday, November 11, 1894, part IV, page 2, unsigned, headlined 'GHOSTS ON THE | JERSEY COAST || Here Are Spooks and Specters to | Suit All Tastes. || A BLACK DOG WITH RED EYES || The Wicked Tory Captain, Too, Still | Keeps His Knife Sharp. ||'. The dateline was *Asbury Park, N.J., Nov. 9*. Three illustrations were captioned *"Dragged His Master to the Shore."*, *A Queer Scene on the Beach*, and *The Indian with the Dreadful Eyes*. The third was initialed T. P. Although unsigned, the sketch can be authenticated by its appearance in the Crane scrapbooks in the Special Collections of the Columbia University Libraries.

No. 158. MISS LOUISE GERARD—SOPRANO

Crane had the chance to meet Louise Gerard and her husband Albert Thies (later Gerard-Thiers) in the summer of 1890 at Avon-by-the-Sea. On July 14, 1890, page 4, under the heading "Avon-by-the-Sea: Seaside Assembly Opens this Week" the *New York Tribune* reported that in the program of evening entertainments the first "will be given by Albert G. Theiss, the well-known New-York tenor; Miss Louise Gerrard, soprano; and Mlle. Brousil, the Bohemian violinist." On July 28, page 4, in the lists of guests the *Tribune* records that "Miss Louise Gerrard, the well-known New-York soprano, is a guest at the Sylvan Lodge." Finally, on August 22, page 7, under dateline of August 21, we read that "Albert G. Theis, of New-York, tenor; Miss Louise Gerrard, soprano, and Mrs. Kate Vashti Baxter, pianist, gave one of the best concerts of the season here this afternoon."

In one of the Crane scrapbooks in the Special Collections of the Columbia University Libraries is pasted a clipping in two columns, following the clipping of "The Red Badge of Courage" newspaper serialization. In the center, between the columns, Crane wrote *The | Musical | News | Dec., 94* and at the foot of the last column, *The Musical Courier | Dec. 94*. The clipping is, in fact, from the *Musical News*, I (December, 1894), 3, with a reproduction of a photograph by Aime Dupont captioned *Louise Gerard* removed. The same article also appeared in the *Musical Courier*, XIX (December 26, 1894), 30, with only slightly differing text. The appearance in the scrapbook would seem to authenticate Crane's writing of this piece, for it would be unlikely for him to note its double appearance if she were merely someone who had interested him: besides, this scrapbook is of his own writings. How it was that he was persuaded in 1894 to write this puff, chiefly it would seem, from press-agent handouts, is not known, nor has any connection between the two persons been established. The two musical journals have different addresses and would seem to have been under separate management. It is more probable, then, that Miss Gerard's press-agent had a typescript made of Crane's manuscript and that the two texts were set from the ribbon copy and its carbon than that one was set from the proof or a clipping of the other, although the late-December publication of the *Courier* might not make the latter an impossibility. The *Musical Courier,* despite its later appearance, has been chosen as copy-text since though edited in substantives it is very much closer to Crane's light punctuation and to his customary word-division than is the *News.* The final sentence in the *Courier,* a quotation from the *New York Herald,* was omitted in the *News* for lack of space.

No. 159. THE GHOSTLY SPHINX OF METEDECONK

The proof for this article is pasted in the Crane scrapbooks in the Special Collections of the Columbia University Libraries. The article itself was published in the *New York Press,* Sunday, January 13, 1895, part v, page 1, unsigned, headlined (as in the proof) 'THE GHOSTLY SPHINX | OF METEDECONK || One Musts Needs Flee for His Life | When She Confronts Him. || A MOURNING THING OF THE MIST || What Comes of Pouting at the Pleadings | of One's Sailor Lover. || From a Special Correspondent of The Press.' In the proof the dateline is *Metedeconk, N.J., Dec. 28,* but since the piece was delayed in appearance, when it was printed on January 13 the *Press's* dateline was changed to *Jan. 12.* No differences exist between the proof and the printed text, but for the sake of the record the proof is here taken as the copy-text.

No. 160. SIX YEARS AFLOAT

First newspaper syndicated publication of this article was on Sunday, August 2, 1896; so far as is known only two newspapers found the piece sufficiently interesting to print. A holograph manuscript, almost certainly a fair copy, is preserved in the Berg Collection of the

New York Public Library. This consists of eight leaves of cheap wove ruled paper 310 × 203 mm., the rules 9 mm. apart, the first page not numbered, and pages 2–5, 7–8 numbered at top center above a semicircle. The usual # is placed at the end. The article is untitled but at an angle in the upper left corner Crane wrote 'Stephen Crane ||—Raft Story— ||'. The manuscript is written in pencil, with darker pencil alterations for changes made subsequent to inscription, various of these over erasures. In the Special Collections of the Columbia University Libraries is found a copy of the galley proof, with one correction of a misprint, not necessarily in Crane's hand. It is somewhat odd that the galley proof gives no indication of the syndicating agent, which at this date would have been S. S. McClure; nor does either of the observed newspapers print a copyright notice. Yet that Crane was not trying a private venture for himself may very likely be indicated not only by the date—within the range of his McClure articles—but also by the mention of 'Great Raft' under the heading 'Syndicate' in an 1896 list of pieces which were all for McClure.

The printed versions are as follows:

N(p): Galley proof headed '(For August 2.) | SIX YEARS AFLOAT. || The Captain of the Tillie B. Reports | That He Sighted, Five Hun-|dred Miles Off the Coast of | Labrador, the Famous Lumber | Raft Lost in the North Atlantic in | the Fall of 1890. At First He and | His Crew Thought It Was a Huge | Sea Serpent. | The Largest Raft Ever Floated—It | Contained Four Million Five Hun-|dred Thousand Feet of Timber and | Was Built Cigar Shape. || BY STEPHEN CRANE. ||'.

N¹: *Pittsburgh Leader*, August 2, 1896, page 20, headlined 'SIX YEARS AFLOAT. || THE FAMOUS LUMBER RAFT LOST | IN THE FALL OF 1890. || The Captain of the Tillie B. Reports | That He Sighted It Off the Coast | of Labrador—The Largest Raft | Ever Floated—It Contained 4,500,-|000 Feet of Timber and Was Built | Cigar Shape. || BY STEPHEN CRANE.'

N²: *Portland Oregonian*, August 2, page 18, headlined 'Six Years Afloat. || By Stephen Crane. ||'. An illustration is present captioned "*It is not land! It is not a ship! It is not a whole. Then what is it?*"

As the most generally authoritative document, the Berg manuscript becomes the copy-text. One must assume that it was the printer's copy for the galley proof, and this hypothesis would seem to be confirmed by the N(p) misreading *this* at 652.15 for MS *the* written over *this* in a manner easily mistaken for the reverse. The galley proof is set with quite unusual fidelity to Crane's punctuation in the MS. One advisable substantive difference in N(p)—*largest* for *longest* (650.22)—may actually be editorial although just as possibly it could have been marked by Crane in the master proof but not in the Columbia duplicate copy, especially if the single correction there of *handled* to *headed* (650.4) is not his. The two observed newspapers derive independently from the galley proof and have no authority. The article is printed here for the first time from the holograph manuscript.

No. 161. ASBURY PARK AS SEEN BY STEPHEN CRANE

On Sunday, August 16, 1896, page 33, the *New York Journal* printed this signed article on a page devoted to news of summer resorts. The headline was distributed in three lines at even intervals interrupting the text, 'ASBURY PARK | as Seen by | STEPHEN CRANE.' On August 22, page 2, the *Kansas City Star* picked it up and reprinted it with the introductory line 'Stephen Crane in the New York Journal' below the headline '*STEPHEN CRANE AT ASBURY PARK* || The Most American of Towns and Its Pic-|turesque Tyrant.' The copy-text is the *Journal* since the *Star* offers only a derived reprint without authority.

No. 162. ADVENTURES OF A NOVELIST

Crane's account of the Dora Clark affair [54] was given a large spread by the *New York Journal* on Sunday, September 20, 1896, all of page 17 being devoted to it with a run-over on page 18, headed 'STEPHEN CRANE'S | NARRATIVE. ||' and signed. The *Journal* headlined the article 'ADVENTURES OF A NOVELIST. | by STEPHEN CRANE. || THE DISTINGUISHED AUTHOR'S NARRATIVE OF HOW HE SOUGHT | "MATERIAL" IN REAL LIFE IN THE "TENDERLOIN" AND | FOUND MORE THAN HE BARGAINED FOR.' Five illustrations accompany the article, one of Crane at his desk captioned *Mr. Stephen Crane in His Study*, another captioned *Dora Clark. (From a Photograph Taken for the Sunday Journal.)*, and three illustrating the text captioned *Studying a Type of New York Life*, *The Arrest of the Girl*, and *Novelist Crane Narrating the Facts in Court*. The first two were signed *Jameson*, the last three—arranged in a cluster— were signed *Travis*. The *Journal* prefaced Crane's account with the following statement:

Last week the Journal arranged with Mr. Stephen Crane, the novelist whose "Red Badge of Courage" everybody has read, to write a series of

[54] An account of this confrontation is given by Robert Stallman in *Stephen Crane: A Biography* (1968), pp. 218–232, and various documents concerning it are reprinted in Stallman's *New York City Sketches* (1966), pp. 217–260.

studies of life in New York. He chose the police courts as his first subject.

Bright and early Monday morning Mr. Crane took a seat beside Magistrate Cornell at the Jefferson Market Police Court, and observed the machinery of justice in full operation. The novelist felt, however, that he had seen but a kaleidoscopic view of the characters who passed rapidly before the judicial gaze of the presiding Magistrate. He must know more of that throng of unfortunates; he must study the police court victims in their haunts.

With the scenes of the forenoon still flitting through his mind, the novelist sought out a Broadway resort that evening. He was soon deeply interested in the women who had gathered at his table—two chorus girls and a young woman of uncertain occupation. The novelist cared not who they were. It was enough that he had found the types of character that he was after.

Later in the evening the party separated, and the novelist courteously escorted one of the women to a Broadway car. While his back was turned for a moment a policeman seized one of the party—Dora Wilkins. Mr. Crane at once protested, and, following the officer to the station house, explained that a mistake had been made.

Bright and early next morning the novelist was once more at Jefferson Market Court. This time he was a witness. The novelist had sought a closer knowledge of the unfortunate creatures of the courts, and he found himself in the midst of them.

Preserved in the University of Virginia–Barrett Collection are two fragmentary documents that relate to the early stages of Crane's *Journal* article. The first is an unnumbered page, doubtless of notes, with a space between two items, the first paragraph written in blue ink and the rest in pencil on cheap wove ledger paper 312 × 200 mm., the rules 10 mm. apart. The continuation on the next page is missing.

The second document is a part of an original six-page black typescript that seems to represent an intermediate draft, or the typed version of the earliest complete draft. The paper is yellow wove 319 × 203 mm. Its first page is torn at top and bottom, affecting the text. Comparison of its contours with those of the succeeding leaves shows that 80 mm. are missing at the top and 55 mm. at the bottom. It may be that the small amount of preserved text at the top was part of a heading or title of some sort, since the first paragraph (of which only the latter part of the end of the first line is mutilated) begins as does the *Journal* article. An estimated five typewritten lines are missing at the foot. The top of page 3 is also mutilated, removing about half of the first line, and page 5 is wanting altogether. In this typescript most of the typed paragraph indentions have been marked in pencil with ¶ signs, and Crane's invariable spelling *laggered* has been corrected in pencil with only two oversights. One or two minor changes are made by the same hand, which does not appear to be

Crane's, but only casual editing is present and indeed a few errors are not corrected. Some possibility exists that this hand was preparing a typescript for the printer even though, on the evidence, it was withdrawn and a revision substituted. The typescript is certainly not so detailed or finished a work as the final account that was printed in the *Journal*. The interest of this early unpublished version is such that its extant text has been printed at the conclusion of "Adventures of a Novelist," prefaced by a transcript of the leaf of notes also in the Barrett Collection. The only emendations made to these drafts are those which correct Crane's habitual misspellings, and in this particular case the MS and TMs fragments are too divergent from the final printed version to make a record in the Historical Collation practicable.

No. 163. THE DEVIL'S ACRE

This special article appeared in the *New York World*, Sunday Magazine, October 25, 1896, page 23. A very large drawing extends across the top and then takes up the right-hand half of the page, signed Pruitt Shaw, depicting the graveyard, the Hudson River in the distance, and in the clouds the Devil carrying an armload of dead stripe-suited convicts. In the upper left is lettered in the illustration 'THE DEVIL'S ACRE | WRITTEN FOR THE SUNDAY WORLD MAGAZINE | [in outlined letters] BY STEPHEN CRANE.' Heading the first column, in type, is '*This Weird and Powerful Sketch Was Written | by Stephen Crane for the Sunday World | Magazine After a Visit to Sing Sing, | Where, with a Sunday World | Artist, He Inspected the Elec-|tric Chair and the Con-|victs' Graveyard on | the Hill.* | [wavy rule] | (Copyright, 1896, by the Press Publishing Company, the | New York World. All rights reserved.)'. The end of the article is signed with a facsimile signature 'Stephen Crane' and beneath it appears the notice 'Stephen Crane's first love story, "The Third | Violet," will begin in the Evening Edition of | The World Nov. 4 next. It will be illustrated by | Powers.' So far as is known, the article was not syndicated.

No. 164. HARVARD UNIVERSITY AGAINST THE CARLISLE INDIANS

Crane's debut as a sports reporter was made in the *New York Journal*, Sunday, November 1, 1896, page 5. Across the top of the full page was the headline 'HARVARD UNIVERSITY AGAINST THE CARLISLE INDIANS, DESCRIBED BY STEPHEN CRANE.' Below this was a series of five photographs of athletes in loincloth or (rear view) without, with their names, captioned in the Greater New York (or city) edition: *Members of the Wonderful Carlisle Indian School Football Team. | These young red men played against the Harvard University eleven yesterday before admiring thousands, | and after an exciting contest were beaten by a score of four to nothing. The picture was made from a snap-|shot photograph.* The out-of-town edition varied slightly by reading *pictures were taken from snap-|shot photographs.* The fifth photograph is signed 'Ben.' Below the first illustration, to the left, was the headline 'Red Men Put Up a Gallant | Fight-- Were Beaten by a | Score of Four to Nothing. || [out-of-town edition: BY STEPHEN CRANE.]'. The dateline was *Cambridge, Mass., Oct. 31.* An oval portrait of Crane without caption was inset in the first paragraph. The *Journal's* city and out-of-town editions have been collated but are without variation except as described above, and with a single variation in subheadings (see Historical Collation).

No. 165. HOW PRINCETON MET HARVARD AT CAMBRIDGE

On Sunday, November 8, 1896, the *New York Journal* devoted most of page 1 to the Harvard-Princeton football game with the headline across the whole page 'HOW PRINCETON MET HARVARD AT CAMBRIDGE AND WON, 12 TO 0. | STEPHEN CRANE AND J. K. MUMFORD DESCRIBE THE GREAT FOOTBALL MATCH.' Below this was a half-page drawing captioned *Captain Cochran Makes a Mighty Effort to Score for the Princeton Tigers,* its frame surrounded by vignettes of figures from the crowds. The illustration is signed 'Haydon Jones'. Two columns in the lower left of the front page were headlined 'Tigers Scored in the Second by | Bannard Passing Brewer and | by Brokaw's Run. || Delirious Multitude Applauded the Brilliant | Team Work of Princeton and the | Gallant Resistance of Harvard. || By Stephen Crane.' The story was continued on page 2 headed 'PRINCETON MET HARVARD. ||'. The dateline was *Boston, Mass., Nov. 7.* The Greater New York and the out-of-town editions of the *Journal* have been collated but no variants appeared.

No. 166. A BIRTHDAY WORD FROM NOVELIST STEPHEN CRANE

This little puff is an addition to the Crane canon. It appeared in the *New York Journal,* Sunday, November 8, 1896, page 14, on a page devoted to congratulatory messages from contributing writers and artists on the first anniversary of Hearst's acquisition of the *Journal*. The page was headlined 'NOTABLE CONTRIBUTORS TO THE JOURNAL SEND GREETING. | No Other Newspaper Ever Gave Its Readers the Work of So Many Famous Men in a Single Year.' Below are oval portraits of Henry George, J. L. Ford, Edgar Saltus, Stephen Crane, W. D. Howells, Julian Ralph, and R. K. Munkittrick. To the left is a congratulatory note from Murat Halstead and to the right one from Edgar Saltus, followed by a brief note from Julian Hawthorne subscribed Lincoln, Nebraska, November 7. Centered between these is a facsimile of a holograph letter from John J. Ingalls, subscribed Atchison, Kansas, October 28, 1896, with the message set in type below. Beneath, centered between congratulatory drawings from two artists is a facsimile of Crane's holograph note headed 'A BIRTHDAY WORD FROM | NOVELIST STEPHEN CRANE.' At the foot of the page are portraits in ovals of six artists who drew for the *Journal*.

No. 167. OUIDA'S MASTERPIECE

The review, or appreciation rather, appeared, signed, in the *Book Buyer*, n.s., XIII (January, 1897), 968–969. Two illustrations signed with the monogram 'CM', the 'C' imposed upon the 'M', and labeled *From "Under Two Flags"*, with a credit-line to J. B. Lippincott Co. accompanied it, with the captions "*'Run for Your Life, and Do Just What I Bid You!'*" and *"Then, Like Arrows from a Hundred Bows, They Charged."*

No. 168. NEW INVASION OF BRITAIN

Syndicated by McClure as indicated by the notice found in the *Pittsburgh Leader*, "New Invasion of Britain" must have been written shortly after Crane's return from Greece. The earliest dateline is *April 29* in the *Chicago Record*, which—given the time necessary for mail to cross the Atlantic and for the article to be set up and distributed for publication on May 9, 1897—may just possibly represent the date in the McClure syndicated proof but of course not the date of composition or even of dispatch. The article has been found in the following newspapers:

N¹: *Omaha Daily Bee*, Sunday, May 9, 1897, page 20, unsigned, headlined 'NEW INVASION OF BRITAIN || The "Bounder" Shadows the Land

Like a | Cloud of Grasshoppers. || A SPECIMEN OF FOG-LADEN SLANG || Unknown Origin and Inexplicable | Habits of the Species—One Word | on All Lips of the Metropo-|lis of the World. ||'. It was reprinted from standing type without variation except for the omission of the second and third lines of the headline in the *Omaha Weekly Bee,* May 12, 1897, page 11. No dateline is present.

N[2]: *Pittsburgh Leader,* May 9, page 22, headlined 'NEW INVASION OF BRITAIN. || THE "BOUNDER" THICK AS KANSAS | GRASSHOPPERS. || A Species of Unknown Origin and In-|explicable Habits and Characteris-|tics—His Name the One Word on All | Lips in the Metropolis of the World. | London's Latest Slang Term of | Obliquy. || BY STEUHEN CRANE. | (Copyright, 1897, by S. S. McClure Co.)'. The dateline is *London, May 1, 1897.*

N[3]: *Chicago Record,* May 8, page 4, signed, headlined 'STEPHEN CRANE ON BOUNDERS ||'. The dateline is *London, April 29.*

The general coincidence of the N[1-2] headlines indicates the nature of the McClure headlines in the proof-pulls that served as printer's copy for the subscribing newspapers, with the slight possibility that N[2] repeats the proof more faithfully than N[1]. Several difficulties at 679.6, 679.31, and 680.19 that had to be solved individually by the newspapers without authority suggest that the McClure proof was not carefully corrected or else too faithfully repeated the deficiencies of Crane's manuscript. Since the three observed newspapers radiate from this lost proof, no one has technically any greater authority than the other, but for convenience the *Omaha Daily Bee* has been selected as copy-text since on the whole it appears to be somewhat more representative of Crane's accidentals as they filtered through the McClure proof. However, when the concurrence of N[2-3] suggests not fortuitous agreement in their styling but perhaps a closer reprinting of the McClure proof than in N[1], emendation has been made; and very occasionally a reading has been taken from N[2] or N[3] alone when it seems of greater authority according to our knowledge of Crane's characteristics, or when textual difficulties in the proof need ironing out.

No. 169. LONDON IMPRESSIONS

Weekly between July 31, 1897, and August 14, the English *Saturday Review,* LXXXIV, 105–106, 132–133, 158–159, printed the eight sections of "London Impressions." The first three sections appeared on July 31, the fourth and fifth on August 7, and the sixth, seventh, and eighth on August 14. This series was later collected in *Last Words* (1902), pages 110–130, where the sections are called *chapters.*

The *Saturday Review* would very likely have been set directly from Crane's manuscript, as the characteristic misspelling of *principal* as *principle* at 690.16 may perhaps attest. The copy for *Last Words* was a typescript that was the mate of two preserved copies in the University of Virginia–Barrett Collection. In a letter to be dated perhaps in October, 1897 (*Letters,* p. 145), Crane wrote to Reynolds about his financial difficulties with the *New York Journal*: "I would send you . . . my London Impressions from the *Saturday Review*—for the *Journal,* if we could get some definite statement from them. My idea was that they would go in with that stuff on the editorial page. Twenty-five dollars per installment would be enough." So far as is known, the "London Impressions" were not offered for sale in the United States during Crane's lifetime, or if so were never accepted.

The Barrett typescripts consist of a fifteen-page blue ribbon copy and its black carbon. The ribbon copy was typed for fols. 1–9 on laid foolscap 329 × 203 mm. watermarked *Britannia Pure Linen* and for fols. 10–15 on wove foolscap watermarked *Indian & Colonial.* The pages are numbered in spaced parentheses 2–10 but then, oddly, XI–XV, also in spaced parentheses. Corrections in the text are made in black ink. On the back of fol. 15 Cora wrote *London Impressions | for Serial | 5200 words.* The black carbon copy uses the Britannia Pure Linen paper for fols. 1–10 and then the Indian & Colonial for fols. 11–15. At top left on the first page Cora wrote in pencil *5200 words,* and after underlining the title in both ribbon and carbon added *By | Stephen Crane.* The cumulative word counts in pencil appear on the versos up to 5,180 on the last, on which Cora also noted in pencil *London Impressions | for book | 5200 words.* The copy for the typescripts was the *Saturday Review.* They would seem to have been sent to Reynolds for sale and as copy for *Last Words* after October 23, 1900, since the title does not appear in his inventory of that date.

See "In a Park Row Restaurant" for another version of the bowling alley incident to be found in the fifth of these sketches.

The *Saturday Review* is the only authority and copy-text.

No. 170. THE EUROPEAN LETTERS

The main document relating to Crane's participation in the "European Letters" of August–October 1897 is the undated letter he wrote from Ravensbrook, probably in late October, 1897, to his New York agent Paul Reynolds (*Letters*, pp. 144–146). There, after discussing the sale of "The Monster" and "The Bride Comes to Yellow Sky," he comes to the possibility of syndicating future articles in newspapers, particularly in the *New York Press*. He writes:

> Then on the other hand instead of fooling with the big newspapers, here is another scheme. You might go to Curtis Brown, Sunday Editor of the *Press* and say how-how from me. Then tell him this *in the strictest confidence*, that a lady named Imogene Carter whose work he has been using from time to time is also named Stephen Crane and that I did 'em in about twenty minutes on each Sunday, just dictating to a friend. Of course they are rotten bad. But by your explanation he will understand something of the manner of the articles I mean to write only of course they will be done better. Ask him if he wants them, signed and much better in style, and how much he will give.

Imogene Carter was the pen name adopted by Cora for her several war dispatches from Greece to the *New York Journal* (reprinted in REPORTS OF WAR, *Works*, Vol. IX), which seem to have been generally supervised by Crane. The series of Imogene Carter articles mentioned in the above letter appeared, in part, in the *New York Press*, unsigned, between August 15 and October 10, 1897. Despite Cora's brave statements in the several preserved form letters designed to accompany the copy sent to various newspapers, search has failed to disclose that they were published elsewhere than in the *Press*. It is true that only Letters 2, 3, 4, 8, 9, and 10 have been preserved in manuscript to provide identification and that the nature of the anonymously published material makes it difficult to isolate these columns from other foreign gossip and comment appearing in newspapers; yet the absence of any of the known material from all other of the newspapers that were sent copy except for the *Press* makes it unlikely that the missing Letters 1, 5, and 6,[55] appeared elsewhere although not printed in the *Press*. With some confidence, then, it can be assumed that despite Cora's efforts to sell the "European Letters" on a syndicated basis, she failed in securing general distribution other than in the *Press*, which itself appears to have rejected (with or without pay) Letters 1, 5, 6, and 7.[56] So far as is known the Cranes abandoned the project after Letter No. 10 of October 10, 1897. The preserved unassigned manuscript material may or may not represent

[55] For the possibility that Letter No. 7 was printed, at least in part in the *Press* on September 19, 1897, see the textual section for "How the Afridis Made a Ziarat."

[56] It would be idle speculation even to suggest that the suspicious circumstance that (with the doubtful exception of "How the Afridis Made a Ziarat") no letter not preserved in manuscript can be identified in the *Press* might signify that none was written but that the Cranes preserved the sequence in order to give the illusion of a continuous weekly column.

an accumulation for a proposed Letter No. 11, or material originally prepared for the preserved Letters but not utilized, or (less likely) items from the missing Letters. The fact that the unassigned material is all unpaged suggests that it was never incorporated in any formally arranged Letter. Most of the manuscripts were written on separate pieces of paper except for very short items or items of related interest, and paged as the last operation.

The manuscripts of the Letters are at present preserved in eight basic folders in the Special Collections of the Columbia University Libraries. These folders arrange the material under Cora's numbered form letters, or under the first pages with the Letter number written at the top, but only one is really complete and the large folder of thirty-two miscellaneous items contains material that can readily be assigned to other folders. In this matter of assignment the prime evidence is of course that of the printed columns in the *Press*; but when material was omitted from the *Press* it can usually be identified by a combination of its pagination and its physical appearance. Most of the pages are charred (and some water-stained) along the right edges and occasionally the top by a fire of unknown origin. Matching the degree of this char and its configuration will often restore unprinted pages to the right Letter as it was constituted and filed in a batch at the time of the damage. The disarray in the Columbia folders, thus, seems to represent not an original out-of-order mixture but instead some shuffling of the pages at a later time and after some period of storage as a single unit.

These manuscripts represent the basic copy that was assembled for duplication. Thus it is a reasonable inference that the missing Letters were not preserved because the copy for them had itself been sent out to supplement the transcribed examples originally planned. It is nonetheless mysterious—even though apparently fortuitous, on the example of Letter No. 9—that the missing Letters do not appear to have been printed, unless identification of them in the *Press* has failed. Whether Cora had this basic copy typed up—the Cranes did not at this time own a typewriter—or transcribed by hand is not known.

Cora's earliest preserved form letter (that covering Letter No. 2) is on Ravensbrook stationery, is undated, and reads:

> Ravensbrook,
> Oxted,
> Surrey.
> England

Dear Sir: I enclose another of my letters from London and if the last one did not please you I hope this one will have better luck.

The price of the letter remains $4.00.

Yours Very Truly

P.S. This letter is syndicated for Aug 15th to the following newspapers.

San Francisco Chronical	—	New York Press
Pittsburg Despatch	—	Phila Press
Atlanta Constitution	—	Buffalo Express
Detroit Free Press	—	Baltimore Sun
Minneapolis Tribune	—	Boston Herald

Probably in Crane's hand, at an angle is written '(10 copies of this)'. Since ten newspapers are named (most of which had printed Crane's Bacheller-syndicated articles in 1895–1896), it is obvious that the statement about syndication was not one of accomplished fact aimed at newspapers other than those listed but instead that it constituted a statement to the ten newspapers to whom copy was being sent of the date of publication and the information that they alone were being offered the rights to the material.

In this edition the copy-text for all Letters is the Columbia manuscript file.

Letter No. 2 (August 15, 1897). The *New York Press* printed items *a, c, e,* and *g* on Sunday, August 15, 1897, page 23, unsigned, headlined 'FRESH BITS OF GOSSIP ON | EUROPEAN AFFAIRS. || From a Special Correspondent of The Press.' The dateline was *London, Aug. 1.* The Columbia folder for this Letter contains only the form letter and item *a*, two pages of laid paper with vertical chainlines, and with rules 8 mm. apart, watermarked 'CARISBROOK SUPREME', severely charred at the right. The average size of this foolscap paper is 328 × 205 mm. The first page is headed in Cora's hand, to the left *Aug 15/97*, and to the right *Letter No 2.*

(a) The first item is written in large script in Cora's normal slightly cursive hand, ending with two lines on page 2 and the usual concluding #. The pages were originally numbered with a centered small figure above a semicircle but have been renumbered with larger figures within a circle. Crane made a single alteration, the substitution of *boys* for *lads* at 693.29. The style and language indicate that this item is Crane's. However, it is possible that the manuscript represents a fair copy. In such cases he may have dictated the item or else written it out in his own hand (as he did item *c* in this letter and item *a* in the unassigned pieces). No word count appears.

(b) Filed with Letter No. 8 is an item of nine paragraphs by Cora on fashions, beginning *Most women have a certain sum on which to dress,* written in her normal cursive hand and originally intended (on the evidence of its pagination circled *3* and *4* and also the degree of its charring) as the second item in Letter No. 2. It would appear to be entirely her own composition and consists of three paragraphs of advice about economical dressing followed by six paragraphs describing the dresses ordered by society ladies for Goodwood. A circled word count *565* appears in the upper left corner of page 3. The *Press* omitted this item.

(c) The anecdote of the Prussian railway system was written by Crane in his own hand on two leaves of Carisbrook paper, badly charred, pages 5 and 6 in circles. At the upper left on page 5 is the circled word count *365*, which is also present in pencil on the verso of page 6. This manuscript is filed separately in the Crane Collection at Columbia.

(d) Filed with Letter No. 8, this unprinted item, paged 7 in a circle, is written in Cora's normal hand but with the last sentence added by Crane in his own hand; Crane also made five alterations in Cora's text. One may conjecture that Cora herself wrote up this item and that it was only reviewed by Crane. The circled word count *180* appears at the upper left.

(e) Filed with Letter No. 9 but printed in Letter No. 2 by the *Press*, this account of the Buckingham Palace gardens starts out in Cora's normal hand but beginning with *These Royal precincts* at 695.30–31 the hand grows considerably more cursive, as if from haste, and so continues to the end. No clear indications of Crane's language are present, although he was capable of imitating the society-reporter style and suppressing his own when the subject was neutral and his feelings were not involved. On the whole, the evidence of the change in the writing suggests the possibility that Cora took it down from dictation. Crane reviewed the work and made six alterations. This item is paged 8 and 9, circled, with a circled word count *455* at the upper left of page 8 and a # at the foot of page 9.

(f) This rejected beginning of an item heads a page numbered with a circled *10*. A horizontal line was drawn at its foot. It is in Cora's normal hand and is probably her work exclusively. No word count appears. The text has been deleted.

(g) Below item *f* on page 10 is the Jubilee anecdote that ended the *Press's* brief column. It is written in Cora's normal hand without notation by Crane. Whether it was dictated or simply copied by Cora from the *Spectator* is not to be determined. A horizontal line is placed beneath it. No word count appears.

(h) Filed in the folder for Letter No. 3, this item was clearly the last intended for Letter No. 2 although it was cut by the *Press*. The first leaf is paged *11* within a circle, and the second is *12* crowded in at the top above a semicircle. A circled word count *400* is at the upper left of page *11*. The paper is similarly charred at the right in the same contours as the other leaves in Letter No. 2. Cora started this item with a hand more upright than usual but after the first paragraph reverted to her normal script. Crane added the last paragraph 697.28–32 in his own hand and subscribed the column *Imogene Carter*; in addition, he reviewed Cora's inscription and made nine alterations. This item may represent a combination of Crane's dictation and Cora's own work but could perhaps be entirely hers save for the last paragraph.

Letter No. 3 (August 22, 1897). This Letter is filed with the undated form letter for No. 3 which has the publication date *Aug 22/97* at upper left, and at right *Letter No 3* addressed by Cora to the same ten newspapers and reading simply, 'Dear Sir: I enclose no. 3. of my letters from London. if you do not care for them I would be glad if you would let me know.' The paper is severely charred at the right, with pages 5–6 only slightly less so except at the upper right corner. The leaves are numbered *1* to 6, within semicircles, the numbers for leaves 4–6 starting with item *b* being larger. Except for a cut in the opening paragraph of item *d* the Letter was printed by the *New York Press*, Sunday, August 22, 1897, page 23, unsigned, headlined 'EUROPEAN GOSSIP | OF DRESS AND SPORT || Goodwood, the Duke of Rich-|mond's Great Race Track. || LONDON WOMEN'S BRACERS || Society Can't Get Through with Its | Arduous Tasks Without the | Help of Stimulants. || From a Special Correspondent of The Press.' The dateline was *London, Aug. 12.*

(a) This piece paged *1–3* starts out in Cora's normal hand but the writing grows progressively smaller in the lower third of page *1*. The same smaller script heads page 2. However, within the thirteenth line starting the sentence *The assault* [spelled *assult*] *on the high hill* (699.16–26) Cora shifts to a finer pen and changes her hand to a more formal upright script much resembling Crane's in its slight lean to the left. This continues to the end of the paragraph, at which point is pasted over the original leaf the lower three-quarters of a normal foolscap page, written with a wider pen in Cora's large cursive hand, beginning the section on fashions with *The Princess of Wales looked* and continuing with six lines on page 3. Below this is a paragraph (699.27–700.2) written again with the fine pen and with the left-leaning script to conclude the page with # about half way down. The word count *1160* appears at the left below #.

There is nothing inscribed under the paste-over leaf. It would seem that Cora added her own fashions section by this paste over, continuing it on the full leaf paged 3 and then, oddly perhaps, changed from her cursive hand to the fine pen and very upright script for the last paragraph. The full account except for the fashions seems to have been dictated by Crane although it is not impossible to speculate that the intrusive fine pen and upright script marks her copying of Crane holograph pieces; however, a worked-over version of his original dictation is also possible. The hand is completely unsuited for taking down dictation, at any rate, and it inscribes material that is Crane's.

(b) Written in the same very upright script on page 4 is the item about the drinking habits of society women, which must be Crane's, a fair copy made by Cora of his dictation or of his holograph, followed by the circled word count 250 altered from 248 and #.

(c) Below, to fill the page, is written in the same script the anecdote of the Irish priest with a word count of 40 altered from 30. The authorship is not to be determined, and Cora is apparently making a fair copy of an item taken from some journal. A # ends the page.

(d) The account of Cowes is contained on page 5, numbered within a semicircle like 4, written with the fine pen and small upright hand, not only the parts that seem to derive from Crane's dictation but also Cora's own final paragraph on fashions which shows no sign of later inscription. The circled word count 425 and # end the page.

(e) The final item in the Letter is written on page 6, semicircled, in the same smaller script and fine pen as before. At its foot Cora gave the circled word count 220 over 221, added #, and then signed it *Imogene Carter*, indicating that no further material was planned for the column. This item may be a fair copy of Cora's own work with a revision or two by Crane now concealed.

Letter No. 4 (August 29, 1897). Parts of this fourth letter appeared in the *New York Press*, Sunday, August 29, 1897, page 21, unsigned, headlined 'LONDON MIGRATES | TO COUNTRY HOUSES || Several Millions Remain, but | They Are Not Society. || GOWNS FOR THE CONTINENT || Some of the Creations the Belles | Will Wear— London's Beauties | Catalogued. || From a Special Correspondent of The Press.' The dateline was *London, Aug. 20*. Prefixed to the Columbia manuscripts is the form letter to the same ten newspapers containing the request, 'I hope if they do not suit your columns you will let me know at once or if you do care to recieve them I would be glad to recieve your advice anytime as to what kind of stuff your readers prefer'.

(a) This item on uncircled page *1* is prefixed at the upper left by

Aug 29/97 and at the right by *Letter No 4*. It is written in Cora's normal hand with a medium fine pen and has ten alterations or corrections by Crane. It is clearly his, by dictation, and is very likely a fair copy. No word count appears.

(b) Cora's long paragraph of fashion notes appears in the same hand on page 2, uncircled. The first sentence reads *I have seen some lovely creations ordered for the Continent*. No word count appears.

(c) Heading page 3, uncircled, is item *c* in the same script, apparently a fair copy of a paragraph dictated by Crane. Its circled word count is given as *135* over *134* in the upper left corner.

(d) After an intervening # item *d* follows on page 3, in the same hand, again probably a fair copy of a dictated Crane paragraph. Its circled word count 235 appears above the beginning of the item and then is added at the foot of the page to *135* to total 370 for the page, all within a circle. This was the last item printed by the *Press*.

(e) Since no signature appears at the end of page 3, and the newspaper column is a short one, other items were very likely appended in the original Letter. The piece given here as conjectural item *e* matches the charred contours very closely of item *d* and it is paged 4–6, although with semicircles under the numbers as an indication that the paging was made at a later time than that for 1–3. However, this fact appears to be of no importance for the assignment since the *4* is written over *1*, the *5* is written over *2*, and *6* is beside deleted *3*, indicating that when it was written it was either separately paged as a convenience or else it had initially been intended to begin a Letter. A # is inscribed at the end of the item. No word count appears. The medium fine pen is used and Cora's hand is identical with that of the preceding items. Nine alterations or corrections by Crane are present. The status of this curious section is uncertain owing to a question about the source of its material, although it is apparently the result of a personal experience before or after the Cranes were in Greece. It would appear to be a combination of Crane dictation and of Cora's own work preserved in a fair copy reviewed by Crane. For instance—although such evidence is notoriously tricky—at 707.12 the manuscript *Sund* deleted and followed by *some* may be an initial mishearing, corrected. Some of Cora's own alterations not only in this piece but elsewhere in these Letters may have been made if she read it aloud to Crane and wrote in his suggestions.

(f) Items *f-j* are more doubtfully to be associated with this Letter. The chief evidence is the important fact that they are continuously paged with the preceding material, and the char (if the leaves are reversed) is similar to that of the earlier leaves. Item *f* is written in the same hand as before and on a separate page numbered 7 above a semicircle, this being to the left of deleted circled 6 or 8 and the word *Insert*. The circled word count *190* and a # are written at the end of the text. This abstract of a news item cannot be assigned either to Cora herself or to Crane's dictation with any certainty.

(g) Cora's fashion note, a part of every column, follows on a page numbered 8, over a possible 6 in the same hand. It consists of the top half of a leaf, the lower having been cut off through the bottom part of a # sign. The circled word count *170* is at the left above the cut-off.

(h) Paged *9* (beside a false start of a *9*) with a semicircle, this item, alone on its page, is written in Cora's extremely cursive hand as though under especial pressure. It is pure Crane and would seem to represent the original inscription of his dictation. The writing grows progressively more slanting to the right and hastily formed as the paragraph progresses. The circled word count *155* and the # follows. The page seems to represent the upper two-thirds of a full leaf but the contours of the scissoring cannot be matched with other preserved part pages.

(i) This item returns to Cora's normal hand, a combination of upright and slight cursiveness that characterizes the other items except for *h*. The page number is *10* within a semicircle, and the circled word count *175* and # follow. The authorship is uncertain although the last sentence may be Crane's, especially since in these letters he sometimes seems to have provided the concluding snap-the-whip sentences. If so, the item is more likely to be a fair copy than a piece of original dictation like *h*.

(j) Below item *i* on page 10 appears this little note which may or may not be from Crane's dictation. The script is the same as in item *i* above it. It has a circled word count *120* and a # at the end, but no signature.

Letter No. 8 (September 26, 1897). It is odd that Letters 5–7 are not preserved in manuscript and apparently were not published in the *New York Press* (except perhaps for part of Letter No. 7—see No. 171, "How the Afridis Made a Ziarat"). The next recorded document is Letter No. 8 which appeared in the *Press* on Sunday, September 26, 1897, page 23, unsigned, headlined 'ENGLISH SOCIETY IS | SHOOTING ON THE MOORS || Any Old Price is Paid for a | Highland Estate. || CURRENT TALK OF EUROPE || Passion Player Folk Fear a Rival in | the Paris Exposition—Who Has | the Bones of Hungary's Saints? || From a Special Correspondent of The Press.'

The dateline was *London, Sept. 16.* This Letter consists of nine pages: page 1 unnumbered and pages 2–6, 8–10 lightly numbered (page 6 being numbered to the left of deleted 7) plus an unnumbered page containing the start of an uncompleted item. The *Press* omitted the last items *i* and *j* and altered the order of *b, c,* and *f.* In the blank space on page 4 below item *d* Cora wrote the word count for eleven items in a column as follows: 310, 165, 125, 115, 170, 305, 410, 200, 100, 120, 160, with a line and the total 2180. This list is evidently a trial for a series of assembled sections not yet put into their final order. The first figure 310 is unidentifiable and was certainly not paged at the start of the completed Letter. Item *a* is 165, item *b* is 125, item *c* is 115, item *g* is 305, and *h* is 410 (a figure squeezed into the column later). The 200-word item that follows was perhaps on missing page 7 (originally page 6), although the missing 170- and 310-word pieces would also qualify. Item *e* is 100, item *f* is 120, and item *d* is 160. Items *i* of 150 words and *j* of 68 words do not appear. None of the unassigned preserved manuscripts fits the missing 310-, 170-, or 200-word notations. One possibility for the 200-word piece would be item *f* in Letter No. 9, the note about Princess Soltykoff. Its char is not inconsistent with a filing position at the end of Letter 8. However, its word count is noted as 205, although actually it is 200 if one does not count every digit of the dates *1890* and *1891* as separate words as Crane sometimes did. It could not have been the missing page 7, however, for it is unnumbered, and clearly page 7 was withdrawn after numbering. It is true that a 170-word item not printed in the *Press* has been conjecturally assigned to Letter No. 4 as item *g.* However, this page has a large 8 at its head in ink, whereas the Letter 8 pagination is in light pencil, and the chances are remote that this item belongs in Letter 8, not in Letter 4 where its pagination fills the sequence of inked numbers.

(a) The manuscript of the unnumbered first page is headed *Letter No. 8 Sep 26ᵗʰ.* The first few words begin in Cora's normal hand but then become increasingly more cursive and slanting to the right, apparently under the pressure of haste. The piece would seem to be entirely Crane's, and the two pages that it occupied—the second numbered 2—were apparently dictated by Crane in this original. Crane made nine alterations upon review. The circled word count *165* over *164* and # appear at the end of this item.

(b) This paragraph heading page 3 is written in Cora's large normal hand but becomes more cursive toward the end. The last sentence is written with a finer pen and seems to have been added later. One may speculate that this paragraph is a fair copy of Crane's dictation

—although Cora's copying of some journal item is not impossible—
with the last sentence perhaps added by dictation. The *Press* reversed
the order of items *b* and *c* and printed this paragraph in the third
place. The circled word count is *125* and a # intervenes between this
and the next item.

(c) This paragraph is written in Cora's large normal hand below
item *b* on page 3. It very likely represents Crane's dictation, and the
evidence suggests that it is a fair copy, especially since items would
not normally be placed on the same page until their final order had
been decided. The last sentence adjusts its wording around a previously drawn # and the circled word count has been changed from
110 to *115* to take account of this added sentence, which seems to
have been inscribed with a different pen and a slightly more compact
script.

(d) Cora's paragraph about Sarah Bernhardt's treatment of her
hair is written in a rather upright hand, the circled word count *160*
appearing at its conclusion. At the foot is jotted the column of figures
for the various word counts proposed for the Letter.

(e) This item heads page 5, written in the same sort of hand as
d, a circled word count *100* and the # appearing below it. The authorship of this copied item from some journal is uncertain.

(f) In the lower half of page 5 comes *f,* written with a different
pen and starting with a larger hand of the same characteristics as *e*
but then reducing itself to moderate size after the first three lines.
The authorship is uncertain, although the final sentence may be
Crane's. The item was printed last by the *Press* apparently by its own
rearrangement. The circled word count is *120* with a # to its right.

(g) The account of the Hungarian kings starts in Cora's usual
fairly upright hand on page 6, renumbered from 7, but grows somewhat more cursive in the second paragraph. The authorship of this
item, which must be largely a copied-out piece from a journal, can
scarcely be determined. The circled word count *305* and # conclude
the item.

(h) The pen of this section occupying pages 8 and 9 (page 7 being
skipped) may be slightly finer than in the preceding items. The hand
is largely upright but grows more cursive on page 9. The piece appears to be a fair copy of Crane's dictation and was reviewed by him
since he added in his own hand six corrections of spellings. Only
the concluding # appears.

(i) This item—and *j* that follows on the same page—does not appear in the word count column and can be associated with the letter
only by the faint pagination 10 at its head and the charring that

shows it was filed after page 9. It starts in Cora's usual upright hand but grows slightly more cursive with the penultimate sentence, possibly when Crane could have begun dictation. It is in rough form with many alterations by Cora, some *currente calamo* but others made later on review, possibly when she read the section aloud to Crane. The word count *150* in parentheses and the # follow.

(j) This little paragraph in Cora's normal hand is of uncertain authorship although its subject matter would associate it with Crane's interests. No word count appears but the # follows.

(k) The appended unnumbered leaf containing this abortive start of an item is filed in the same folder with Letter No. 8 and is charred roughly the same. It is written in Cora's normal hand. No word count appears.

For the form letter for No. 8, see under Letter No. 10.

Letter No. 9 (Unpublished). No record of publication of Letter No. 9 has been preserved. The first page of the Columbia manuscript is headed *Letter No 9.* [*Sep* deleted] *Oct 3ʳᵈ.* The assignment of its complete contents must remain in part conjectural.

(a) This opening section perhaps consisted originally of two different items, one devoted to the professional nurse and the other to the Red Cross nurse. The first page is a single fragment ending with *rosy cheeked woman* (715.28) at the end of the seventh line, below which the paper has been cut off. A few tops of letters from the original eighth line appear above the irregular scissoring, but these do not match the first line of any other page, nor indeed do other pages have scissored tops. One may conjecture that the rest of the paragraph concluded the professional-nurse account and began that of the Red Cross nurse, probably after an interval and # but was cut away to join the two parts in one, with some inconsequential loss of text in the Red Cross nurse part. Although this fragment is headed *Letter No 9*, it is unnumbered. On its verso is the letterhead of the Charing Cross Hotel. The next three pages of this item are written on the versos of similar paper. The second page of the Letter is unnumbered (and was undoubtedly intended to be associated with the fragment as if pasted to it except for lack of space), and the third has a deleted illegible number above a semicircle with a half-circled 2 written at the upper right corner squeezed in at the end of the first line of text; there is also a 2 written at top right center of the page. The fourth page is numbered 3. above a semicircle; it contains the last four lines of text and is followed by the # and a word count 620 prefixed at the left by a parenthesis that may be intended for a half-circle. The writing on the fragment is in Cora's normal hand but on the second (unnumbered) leaf the writing begins to grow more cursive and by the time the paragraph at 716.18 is reached it shows all the signs of hasty writing that may be taken as indicating the pressure of dictation. The opening about the professional nurse may be Cora's own contribution, but from *English women* at 715.28 the item can be assigned with some confidence to Crane's dictation.

(b) This item is paged *4* and carries over to a conclusion on page 5 with five lines of text. Page 4 is on the usual foolscap paper and initially consisted of two items, spaced. But the # and circled word count *105* at the end of the paragraph after *cyclists* (717.19) have been deleted in order to join the Hyde Park meeting to that at Oxford as one unit. On the concluding leaf 5 in a semicircle was crowded in at the head later than the text and might be overlooked; hence a large *Page 5* was added below the circled word count 375 and the #. At the start on page 4 the writing is in Cora's normal fairly upright hand but becomes somewhat more cursive in the last sentence of the original first item. In the second part beginning with *If the meeting* (717.28–29) the writing grows much more cursive in its haste. Regardless of the authorship of 717.10–19 it would seem that Crane probably dictated the remainder and that this is the original version and not a fair copy. The evidence indeed suggests, given the original paging of item *c*, that page 4 initially contained only the paragraph about the Oxford meeting and that the Hyde Park account was added later.

(c) This item paged with a large *6* within a semicircle to the left of deleted *5* starts in Cora's normal large hand. This item originally ended at 718.23 with *school*. A # followed on the line below. Beginning with the paragraph at 718.24 the hand writes over the graph and changes markedly as if she were writing more hastily at Crane's dictation, although the authorship of this item may rest in some reasonable doubt save for this evidence. The word count 350 is at the foot, but this is an error for 250. The figures were originally enclosed in parentheses later made into a circle. There is no #.

(d) The association of the remaining items with this Letter is entirely conjectural since they are all unpaged and filed in the miscellaneous folder at Columbia. The evidence is in part the roughly similar pattern of char at the right and, for some, the use of parentheses to enclose the word count, a practice usual apparently with this Letter and first seen in item *c*. (However, see item *i* conjecturally assigned to Letter 8 which uses parentheses. This item could as well appear in Letter 9.) Cora's note on fashions comprising the conjecturally assigned item *d* begins *The fashions for the coming winter are regal.* It is written in her usual fairly upright hand and is much worked over; curiously, Crane reviewed this section and made six minor alterations and corrections of spelling in his own hand. The word count 355 is circled at the upper left corner, but no #.

(e) This unnumbered page is written in Cora's normal hand, fairly upright, and large. The circled word count 350 and a # follows. Since this item was no doubt mainly copied from some journal the authorship is uncertain although Crane may have added the last sentence, at least.

(f) The char and the water staining at the right seem to associate this item with *e* above in the original filing. Its word count 205 is within parentheses at the foot, but no #. Whether this is a dictated item or one that Cora largely abstracted from some journal is obscure.

(g) This note starts in the upright hand but grows slightly more cursive toward the end. The word count 280 over 282 within parentheses is added at the foot but no #. The authorship is uncertain although the piece may just possibly have been dictated. For example, the manuscript *costom* altered incorrectly to *costume* may just possibly be a mishearing of the correct *custom* and not a Cora eccentric spelling.

(h) Rather closely associated by its char with *g*, this item is written throughout at leisure in Cora's normal upright hand. Obviously copied from some journal, it is difficult to assign but may well be Cora's own work. This is the sort of item that often ended a Letter, but the lack of pagination and of any signature makes the position uncertain. The circled word count 150 and # appear at the foot.

(i) The extreme char at the right of this page shows that it was not filed with the rest of Letter 9. On the other hand, the parentheses about its word count 190 associate it with this peculiar practice mostly associated with Letter 9, and its subject, on cycling, suggests the possibility that it was originally present in the Letter as a follow-up to the Oxford section of item *b* but was removed when the Hyde Park meeting was added at a later time below this Oxford paragraph. It is written in Cora's large upright hand and is followed by #.

Letter No. 10 (October 10, 1897). The *New York Press* published this Letter on Sunday, October 10, 1897, page 18, unsigned, head-lined 'LONDON FASHIONS | RUN TO LIGHT COLORS || Some Winter Street Gowns | and Stage Costumes. || SMALL TALK FROM EUROPE || No Probate of Queen Victoria's Will|—Society Folk in

Scotland—|Famous Egmont Curse. || From a Special Correspondent of The Press.' The dateline was *London, Oct. 1.*

(a) Cora's five paragraphs on fashions begin *Society women are about to adopt much lighter colors for their winter street dresses.* The various paragraphs are written in different scripts, some leaning to the left in her imitation of Crane's manner, others upright, and others slanting to the right but with well-formed letters and no signs of haste. The first page is unheaded and unnumbered, the second is paged 2 above a semicircle; a word count 335 for page [1] is added to *145* for page 2 and the total *480* is circled and placed at the end; there is no #.

(b) This item on page *3* starts in the upright script but becomes slightly more cursive after the third sentence. The authorship is uncertain although some touches that sound like Crane appear, particularly in the final paragraph. No word count is present but only the # sign.

(c) This page numbered *4* starts in Cora's upright hand but with the second paragraph grows increasingly more cursive. It was probably dictated by Crane. The circled word count 235 and a # are placed at the foot.

(d) The hand of this item on page numbered *5* follows the pattern of item *c* and the paragraph may also have been dictated by Crane. The circled word count *135* and # are appended.

(e) This page numbered *6*, which seems to show Crane's sense of humor, was not printed by the *Press*. It starts as do the preceding items with Cora's upright hand but grows cursive. The indentation of the quoted excerpts may indicate a fair copy. Crane corrected one misspelling in his own hand. The circled word count *245* and the # end the piece.

(f) This paragraph on page numbered *7* is written throughout in Cora's normal cursive hand. Cora probably contrived this item herself. The circled word count *185* and the # sign follow.

(g) Of uncertain authorship this paragraph heads page numbered 8, written chiefly in Cora's upright hand. It is separated from *h* below by the circled word count *110* and #.

(h) Almost certainly dictated by Crane, item *h* starts with Cora's upright hand but grows markedly cursive with signs of haste. It ends on page numbered *9* with # and the circled word count 290.

The form letter for No. 10 seems to represent that for No. 8 of September 26 modified to serve as copy for No. 10. The address is followed by a date that originally read *Sep 26th*, with the S written over an *A*, then 26th (which may be 6th) deleted, and finally a following *12*th deleted. The letter reads:

Dear Sir: Enclosed is No 10 [*interlined above deleted* 8] of my European letters which remains at the usual Price of four dollars. Please [*altered from* Plese] notify me if you do not care to recieve them.

Very truly Yours
Imogene Carter

This Article has been syndicated for Sunday Oct 9th [*substituting for deleted* Sep. 26th] to the following newspapers:

San Francisco Chronicle	[Buffalo Express *deleted*]
New York Press	[Minneapolis Tribune *deleted*]
Phila Press	St Louis Globe Democrat
[Boston Herald *deleted*]	Pittsburg Despatch
[Chicago Inter Ocean *deleted*]	[Detroit Free Press. *deleted*]
St Paul Pioneer Press	New Orleans Piccayune
Boston Globe	Omaha Bee
	Galveston News.

That the deleted papers had in the interval shown a lack of interest seems reasonable to conjecture. The added papers were those which had published Crane's syndicated articles in 1895 and 1896. Presumably these alterations were made for No. 10, not for No. 8, and they reflect the ill-success of the column.

Unplaced Miscellaneous Item. The working hypothesis held by the present editor is that the preserved manuscript material is all (or in the main) to be identified with known Letters, not with missing Letters 1, 5, 6, and 7. No example occurs of an unpaged item being present in a printed column, and the fact of their lack of pagination may be taken as evidence that they were not actually arranged and copied as a part of the known columns although they had been assembled with relatively definite columns in view, according to the evidence of their filing and of such characteristics as the use of parentheses, in Letter 9, for the word counts. The only item for which all evidence is wanting for placement is the present, written out in Crane's own hand without word count or #. If its opening sentence is supposed to be a contemporary reference, the item would need to be placed somewhere in the first four Letters, but if it is retrospective, then no assumptions about position can be made.

The text of these European Letters (to borrow the phrase used by Cora in her eighth/tenth form letter) offers few serious difficulties. The manuscripts represent only the material that was used as the basis for making the formal copies sent out to the ten newspapers; but in themselves they cover a wide range from the original dictated or composed inscriptions to some that appear to be fair copies. In the transcription a few inadvertent variants and (if Cora made the transcripts) perhaps even a few improvements might occur. These are difficult to distinguish from the relatively light editing that the *New York Press* gave the columns. For instance, in No. 3 item *a* one cannot be certain that N^1 *racing holy of holies* is editorial or a change in the transcript of manuscript *holy spot* (698.12); but the inference would be that differences are more likely than not to be editorial, and it is clear that the *Press* often reduced to conventional language unusual phrases like manuscript *exuberantly extra* changed to *extravagant* (694.26) or *called . . . the fact* altered to *been muttering* (700.3–4), and it could invent when it did not understand the original, as probably in *heather trimmings* for Cora's *both trimmings* (710.18). The editing omitted matters of minor interest and sometimes even whole items. Stylistically it cut down on Crane's too colloquial and sometimes awkward language, and particularly on his excessive use of *very*. On the whole, however, the manuscripts are represented in print with reasonable faithfulness although with an increase in blandness.

The generally feminine cast of the items may represent only the audience aimed at in the United States, but it may also reflect the collection by Cora of items of possible interest from the journals of society doings like the *Illustrated London News* or the retrieval of information from the *Times* and *Spectator*. One may guess that the Cranes discussed the suitability of the various clippings and—usually on separate pages for convenience—either Cora wrote out the item in a paraphrase of her source or else Crane took the clipping and dictated from it. It may well be that some items represent a combination of the two methods, like the description of the Turkish harem in which Cora and Crane seem to have collaborated. Certainly Crane seems to have supplied the summary comment of the last sentence on several occasions, and there are indications that he was likely to review the items either by his own handwritten corrections or by hearing them read to him. Some of the manuscripts appear to be the originally transcribed or dictated material, but others give every sign of being fair copies. Finally, the items were sorted out and the pages numbered. The successive columns seem to have been stored together.

Because of the difficulty of assigning the precise authorship to various of the items, all of the preserved material except for Cora's fashion notes is printed in this edition for the first time although it is certain that not every word can be the unaided work of Crane himself. On the other hand, the occasional evidence from Cora's script that she was taking dictation may combine with one's estimate of the nature of the contents and of the characteristics of Crane's language, and prejudices, to assign to him perhaps more of these Letters than has commonly been suspected.

No. 171. HOW THE AFRIDIS MADE A ZIARAT

This previously unattributed article appeared in the *New York Press*, Sunday, September 19, 1897, page 23, unsigned, headlined 'HOW THE AFRIDIS | MADE A ZIARAT || Live Saint Wouldn't Do, So | They Killed One. || THEN HE WAS WORSHIPED || Unique Scheme of British Rulers | to Keep the Tribe | from Stealing. ||'. The editor is grateful to Comdr. Melvin H. Schoberlin USN (Ret.) for suggesting to him this attribution, one in which he has considerable confidence. The humor seems most typical of Crane, and there are several favorite Crane locutions such as *pay any profound attention* (727.14), but particularly *It was shown to them* (727.19). One may remark that the date favors this being a part of the otherwise unprinted and unknown European Letter No. 7, a conjecture that may help to explain the subject and possibly the tone.

No. 172. HAROLD FREDERIC

In a letter known from a typed transcript in the Syracuse University Library, dated November 3, [1897], Crane wrote to Paul Reynolds: "I am sending you a fifteen hundred word essay on Harold Frederic and his work. The Cosmopolitan begins his new novel in January and I have written this at his request with a definite view of it's going into their December number. However it has not been mentioned to them. Please see them at once. The price is not a particular point at this time. I enclose photograph. If Walker will not take it place it where you can."

The *Cosmopolitan* evidently was not interested, for the puff did not appear until March, and then in *The Chap-Book*, VIII (March 15, 1898), 358–359, signed, with the photograph of Frederic that Crane had enclosed.

No. 173. CONCERNING THE ENGLISH "ACADEMY"

This piece was a late bloomer among the newspaper articles that Crane occasionally wrote about English affairs after the collapse of the "European Letters" venture of Imogene Carter with Cora in October, 1897. It appeared in *The Bookman,* VII (March, 1898), 22–24, and was signed, of course. Crane had sent it to Paul Reynolds on December 20, [1897], according to a Syracuse University typed transcript: "I enclose you a short newspaper article on the recent prize-giving by the London *Academy.* Let me know if The Press is taking these articles."

No. 174. THE BLOOD OF THE MARTYR

This essay in political satire appeared in the *New York Press Magazine,* Sunday, April 3, 1898, pages 9–11, signed.

No. 175. THE SCOTCH EXPRESS

As early as October or November of 1897 Crane had a contract from S. S. McClure to 'write an article on an engine ride from London to Glasgow' (*Letters,* p. 144), but "The Scotch Express" was not published until 1899 simultaneously in England and the United States in *Cassell's Magazine,* n.s., XVIII (January, 1899), 163–171, and in *McClure's Magazine,* XII (January, 1899), 273–283. Under the illustrative title in *McClure's* is printed 'The illustrations are from drawings by the late W. L. Sonntag, Jr., who made the journey in company with Mr. Crane, expressly for | McCLURE's MAGAZINE. It was only a short time after these drawings were completed that Mr. Sonntag died—in the very prime of his fine | powers and to the deep regret of all who knew him or his work.' *Cassell's* used the illustrative title, an illustrative initial not present in *McClure's,* and eight illustrations captioned "*A Railway 'Flier' . . . Took its Place at the Head*", "*The Wild Joy of the Rush Past a Station*", *The Conductor, Driver, and Fireman, Taking Up Water, While Going at Full Speed, The Guard,* "*Paper, Sir!*", *Overtaking a Goods Train,* and *Over the Bridge to Glasgow.* The fourth and sixth of these do not refer to anything in the text. *McClure's* used these eight—sometimes with differing captions—and added three more captioned "*A Moment Later*

Came the Crash of the Passing", *Through the Iron District,* and *The End of the Journey—In the Station at Glasgow.* The *Cassell's* first page noted at its foot '⁂ Copyright 1899 in the United States of America by the S. S. McClure Co.' Under Crane's name *McClure's* advertised him as 'Author of "The Red Badge of Courage," "The Open Boat," etc.'

The untitled holograph manuscript for the article is preserved in the Special Collections of the Columbia University Libraries consisting of twelve pages numbered above a semicircle at top center. The first four leaves are laid foolscap 328 × 204 mm., vertical chainlines, rules 9 mm. apart, watermarked with a seated Britannia in a medallion supporting a crown. The remaining eight leaves are of wove foolscap watermarked *Carisbrook Supreme.* The writing is in black ink and alterations are made in the same ink. In pencil Cora made one addition *the grouse* (742.11) and in two places marked doubtful readings with a pencil cross (744.29, 746.21): both were altered in the printed versions. The status of Cora's addition is uncertain, for it may have been made on her own initiative; but since she did not engage herself to alter the two errors marked by crosses we may take it that *the grouse* had Crane's approval. On the verso of each page in Crane's hand is the cumulative word count ending with a notation in Cora's hand, on fol. 12ᵛ, *5125 words.* The paper has been folded horizontally in quarters but must have been kept for some time folded in half, for the upper half is soiled. On this half, in a strange hand that is probably that of the taker of the inventory, is written vertically 'London to Scotland | Corridor train'.

The preservation of the manuscript by the Cranes suggests that a typescript had been made from it either at Crane's instance or at Robert McClure's—perhaps the latter's—with return of the manuscript. (At the time this typescript would need to have been made outside, for Crane had not bought a typewriter for Cora.) No printer's markings appear on the manuscript. The evidence that *McClure's* follows the *Cassell's* heavy English styling slavishly, including words (but not spellings) anglicized by *Cassell's* from Crane's manuscript, indicates that *Cassell's* was set from this typescript but that a proof— with a set of the illustrations—was mailed through the McClure London office to New York for printer's copy. Synchronized publication for copyright protection was arranged, obviously. That this *Cassell's* proof was an as yet unedited one, at least in part, is demonstrated by the ten substantive variants (741.27; 744.12; 745.4; 747.-16,30,31(2); 748.19; 749.23; 751.1) appearing later in *Cassell's Magazine* where MS and *McClure's* differ, together with such unique accidentals as Cs *North Western* but MS,McC *Northwestern* (741.25–

26), *"bins"* but MS,McC *bins* (740.35), and Cs *menu* in italic but MS,McC in roman (749.3,8). The first text-cut in Cs (739.30–740.9) appears to have no significance, but the second (744.27–745.2) excised comments by Crane unflattering to the English. Both must have been present in the original proof, however. The McC cut at 751.19–22 seems to have been made to fit the ending into the available space.

Since the holograph manuscript is in existence it becomes the copy-text as preserving Crane's individualistic accidentals. The question of the variant substantives is more troublesome. McClure's being a completely derived text, has no authority whatever save as a confirmation of the readings of the early *Cassell's* proofs that differ in the *Cassell's Magazine* print from MS,McC agreement. The first problem is the status of these ten substantives. The reading at 747.16 is a clear case of editorial misunderstanding and sophistication. Others, as at 745.4, 747.31, and 749.23, improve Crane's grammar. Only two might be questioned as authorial: *traverses* for *owns* at 744.12 and *retching* for *reaching* at 751.1. Neither of these appears to represent a Crane proof-alteration. The first corrects a factual mistake and the second appears to be an ingenious sophistication by an editor who did not understand that *reaching* was intended to mean 'towering'. No evidence, then, suggests that Crane read or marked *Cassell's* proof at a stage after it had been mailed to McClure in New York; thus the unique *Cassell's* variants can be ignored except for the correction at 741.25–26 of *Northwestern* to *North Western*.

More difficult is the problem of the fifty-two substantive variants in which Cs and McC agree against MS. Theoretically these could be separated into four categories: (1) unauthoritative variants made in the typing that were not recognized when the typescript was read over; (2) Crane's authoritative revisions made in the typescript on review or else—less likely—in an earlier proof than the state that was mailed to McClure; (3) the *Cassell's* editor's changes made in the typescript before it was sent to the printer; and (4) compositorial departures from copy. In the nature of the case the kind of anglicization of style and words would be impossible to separate with any confidence as between the third and fourth categories, and if the unconscious changes in typing were sufficiently neutral these would be difficult to weed out from minor compositorial alterations. The question resolves itself then to the major distinction of the variants arising from the *Cassell's* editing and printing and those that might be supposed to represent Crane's own revisions made in the typescript.

A large number of readings are readily assignable to *Cassell's*.

Typical examples are the changes from Crane's *this* to *the* starting with 739.23 and repeated in 746.34, 747.7, and 749.27. Other stylistic changes correct errors of different sorts in MS and might have been written in the typescript although the odds might favor the editorial care of *Cassell's*, such as the wrong tense *bowled* in MS at 740.11 and of *became* at 744.39, the alteration of *doubtlessly* to *doubtless* (742.30), of *was* to *were* (743.24, 745.23), of *that* to *who* (744.3), *ten* to *tens* (744.10), paragraph (739.85; 741.8) to no paragraph, *to particularly* to *particularly to* (748.30–31), and so on. Positive errors in MS such as *train* for *the train* (747.14), *vast* for *a vast* (747.19), or the omission of *swung* (748.28)—less certainly the omission of *an hour* (747.9)—could readily have been detected during the typing. Not much doubt rests in the Cs substitution of *luggage* for *baggage* (739.32, 750.1) that the editorial hand is at work. Editorial or compositorial improvement is certain behind such minor idiomatic or stylistic variants as *within* for MS *in* (740.6), *a romantic* for *the romantic* (742.12), *a station* for *the station* (745.18), *little* for *the little* (749.18), and the like.

Some uncertainty must always inhere to any editor's choice between MS and joint Cs,McC in a handful or so of more significant variants. Was the addition of *important* at 740.1 Crane's or the *Cassell's* editor's; did the editor substitute *"flier"* for *monster* at 740.39 because of the use of *monster* later at 741.37 or to improve by a popular term;[57] at 741.8 was *interval* substituted by the editor or by Crane because of the echo of *Meanwhile* at 741.5, and *house* for *signal house* at 741.9–10 because of the clash with *signal box* at 741.9; was *long* dropped in 741.33 before *train* because of *long string of coaches* (740.27) and *long string of . . . coaches* (741.29–30) or was it perhaps a typing error; at 742.1–2 was the repetition of

[57] In this case the captions are no indication of authority. The illustration both in *Cassell's* and in *McClure's* has the word *'flier'* in the caption. Yet the fact that in the caption *The Wild Joy of the Rush Past a Station* for another illustration the reading is *a station* with Cs and McC against MS *the station* (a difference taken to be editorial) suggests that the captions were written from proofs that had these two altered readings. All these captions show, then, is that *'flier'* like *a station* was probably present in the text copy from which the compositor originally set. That in the second caption the marking appears to be editorial does not in any sense indicate whether the change from *monster* to *'flier'* was made in the typescript by Crane or by the editor. It is only a straw that whereas the editor inserted quotation marks around special words, as immediately before about *bins,* that Crane did use in the manuscript, it is less likely that Crane would have added the quotes about *flier* if the word had been his own substitute. Of course, to take a scrupulous view, Crane could have added the word *flier* in typescript and the editor could have added the quotes to it. For Crane's use of *iron monster* in "Great Bugs of Onondaga," see the discussion in its textual section.

pace of mice from *pace of a mouse* (741.34) too much for Crane or for the editor; did the awkwardness of *habitant with* at 747.17 as well as *in this case carry* at 749.22–23 offend the editor or author; did the editor or Crane find *populace* at 749.12 a misused word; did *mean* at 749.16 trouble the editor or the author? In fact, although there are several advisable changes that might have been either editorial or authorial, like the removal of the repetition of *pace of a mouse,* though in the plural, by substituting the *gait of turtles* (742.1–2), better editorial than authorial arguments can be found for almost every substantive change. Indeed, if it were not for the two pencil crosses that Cora made in the manuscript, at which point different words are found in *Cassell's,* it would be a reasonable conjecture that Crane had not looked over the typescript at all before sending it off. But since the evidence seems good that he did review it, though with little care, one may accept a handful of necessary corrections, from whatever source, and to these add a very few conjecturally authorial changes in the typescript like the characteristic *define* [58] for *mean* at 749.16 even though it may well be that the avoidance of an echo of *meaning* ending the preceding sentence could actually have led the editor to this substitution. There can be little doubt that on the whole the manuscript affords the most trustworthy substantive readings free from editorial attention, no matter how expert as indeed this was.

In the University of Virginia–Barrett Collection is a clipping of the *McClure's* pages without alterations. This is the copy listed by Reynolds in his possession on October 23, 1900, for it has a number *11* written at the top in blue crayon and the notation in ink *5125 words.*

"The Scotch Express" is edited here for the first time from the manuscript.

No. 176. FRANCE'S WOULD-BE HERO

This previously unrecorded piece of journalism appeared in the *New York Journal* (N¹) on Sunday, October 15, 1899, page 25, signed, headlined 'France's Would-be Hero. ∴ By Stephen Crane. | Being the Full Truth About the Celebrated M. Guerin, Professional Hero.' A photograph of Crane accompanied the article. It must have been telegraphed to the *San Francisco Examiner* (N²) where it was

---

[58] See, for instance, *It simply defined our misfortune* in " 'Ol' Bennet' and the Indians" (150.28–29).

printed, also on October 15, on page 15, headlined '[to the left] A JOKE OF FRANCE = = [to the right] BEING THE TRUTH ABOUT THE NOTORIOUS | M. GUERIN, PROFESSIONAL HERO || [centered] By Stephen Crane.' Although each paper datelined the article from Paris, October 4, the copy must have been a manuscript or typescript sent across the ocean by mail. The *New York Journal* furnishes the copy-text since it was printed without the extra stage of telegraphic transmission, but since the *Examiner* may be taken to radiate from common copy it is theoretically of equal authority. However, the N^2 variants appear to be corruptions and are rejected except for one correction of an N^1 misprint and two passages that were cut in N^1 either for editorial reasons or for lack of space. Publication seems to have been confined to these two Hearst newspapers.

No. 177. "IF THE CUP ONCE GETS OVER HERE . . ."

This unpublished news comment preserved in manuscript in the Special Collections of the Columbia University Libraries is written from Crane's dictation by Edith Richie in black ink on three pages of cheap wove unwatermarked paper 264 × 208 mm., the rules 9 mm. apart. It is untitled. Miss Richie marked off the word count in pencil by hundreds within the lines and wrote in black ink on the back of the first two leaves the totals, but no word count appears on the verso of the third leaf. On this verso in what appears to be Cora's hand is written in black ink *Journal* | *Oct. 31ˢᵗ '99* || followed in pencil by *Journal* | *did not* | *print it* ||. The copy for the *Journal* would have been a typescript or manuscript fair copy made up from the present original. The last race between *Columbia* and *Shamrock* was on October 20, 1899, and thus the composition can be dated with some precision as on October 20–21. This manuscript has not previously been printed.

Of possible interest is the fact that "Bill Smithers" is a name given also to a soldier in *The Red Badge of Courage*.

No. 178. STEPHEN CRANE SAYS: EDWIN MARKHAM IS HIS FIRST CHOICE FOR THE AMERICAN ACADEMY

Printed in the *New York Journal*, March 31, 1900, page 8, as a feature of the editorial page, signed, headlined 'STEPHEN CRANE SAYS: [in two lines to the right] Edwin Markham Is His First Choice

| for the American Academy. ||'. A portrait of Crane within a circle is inset in the first paragraph. The only correspondence preserved about this article is a letter in the Special Collections of the Columbia University Libraries from Paul Reynolds to Cora, dated May 4, 1900: "Answering your letter of April 17th, the check that I sent to Mr. Crane was for articles regularly sent to the Journal by Mr. Crane. He agreed to send one every month. One was an article about an American Academy, one had to do with the South African War, and the third was an article which had no title to it. I have nothing left unsold of Mr. Crane's."

POSSIBLE ATTRIBUTIONS

After the collapse of the "European Letters," Crane continued his interest in writing occasional columns for the American newspapers. In a letter probably to be dated in late October, 1897, he asked Reynolds to see if the Sunday *New York Press* would be interested in signed articles (*Letters*, pp. 144–146). "Concerning the English 'Academy' " is one of these, sent to Reynolds on December 20, 1897, with the request, "Let me know if The Press is taking these articles." In this case the *Press* apparently was not interested, for the piece was not published until March, 1898, and then in the *Bookman*. On January 14, 1898, Crane wrote Reynolds, "I enclose you a thousand words on the Alfridi business. It might go to the *Press* and be syndicated, or else to the *Journal*" (*Letters*, p. 168). As of a letter to his brother William on October 29, 1897, Crane had shown an interest in the frontier war against the Afridis begun on October 18, 1897, and—if the attribution is correct—had already written a humorous column on the Afridis published unsigned by the *Press* as "How the Afridis Made a Ziarat" on September 19, 1897. It is natural, on this evidence, to take it that he sent to Reynolds from time to time in late 1897 and early 1898, until the Spanish-American War captured his interest, at least several articles on matters of English or international concern that would not have been signed if accepted by the *New York Press* but credited merely to 'a Special Correspondent.' The present editor has read through a file of the *Press* in these months with the hope of identifying such possible articles. A number would not be inconsistent with what Crane could write, but only two— "London's Firemen Fall from Grace" and "England a Land of Anxious Mothers"—seemed to have any tinge of positive evidence in favor of his authorship. In particular, the thousand words on the Afridis sent to Reynolds on January 14, 1898, does not seem to have been printed in the *Press*. Articles published in the *New York Journal* would have been signed, but in spite of a special search none has been identified in this area.

No. 179. LONDON'S FIREMEN FALL FROM GRACE. This previously unattributed article was printed in the *New York Press*, Sunday, November 28, 1897, page 15, unsigned, headlined 'LONDON'S FIREMEN | FALL FROM GRACE || Latest Big Fire Shows Their | Weaknesses. || 20 MINUTES TO GET WATER || Answering an Alarm with One of | Their Toy Engines—Newspapers | Demand a Reform. || From a Special Correspondent of The Press.' The dateline was *London, Nov. 20*. In the letter of late October, 1897, from Crane to Reynolds (*Letters*, pp. 144–146) Crane discusses plans to syndicate future articles in American newspapers, particularly the *New York Press*, reveals that he has been concerned with the Imogene Carter articles the *Press* has been printing, and asks Reynolds to query Curtis Brown, the Sunday editor, whether he wants better-written signed articles. So far as is known no agreement was reached with the *Press*, but it is possible that Crane tried them through Reynolds with an occasional article which they printed unsigned. Of these, "London's Firemen Fall from Grace" could very well be Crane's. The critical tone of things British is his, and the selection of detail, as well as the general style, may be thought characteristic. It is worth note that there is an almost gratuitous reference to the inefficiency of the London fire brigade in the big fire introduced into Crane's "Little Stilettos" piece published by the *New York Journal* on April 24, 1898, page 21, as if he had had a special interest in the handling of the fire (see REPORTS OF WAR, *Works*, IX [1971], 235–240).

No. 180. ENGLAND A LAND OF ANXIOUS MOTHERS. The editor is grateful to Comdr. Melvin H. Schoberlin USN (Ret.) for calling his attention to Crane's possible authorship of this article, which was printed in the *New York Press*, Sunday, December 5, 1897, page 13, unsigned, headlined 'ENGLAND A LAND | OF ANXIOUS MOTHERS || Britain's Never Ending Wars | Keep Them So. || FIVE YEARS OF FIGHTING || Has Been Going on Relentlessly All That | Time— Deaths Make Promotions|—How the Women Take It. || From a Special Correspondent of The Press.' The dateline was *London, Nov. 27*. The observation that battles are not continuous in war but separated by intervals of time, although scarcely original, is found in "Crane at Velestino," No. 5(1), REPORTS OF WAR, *Works*, IX

(1971), 21. The sympathy with the private soldier is a feature of his Spanish-American War reporting, as in No. 42, "Regulars Get No Glory," or No. 53, "The Private's Story" (*ibid.*, pp. 170–173, 196–198). The incident of the three British naval officers at Volo would have been known only to someone like Crane who had been present at Velestino and the retreat on Volo.

APPENDIXES

TEXTUAL NOTES

No. 4. THE RELUCTANT VOYAGERS

30.29 wabbled] According to the *O.E.D.*, 'wabble' is given as an alternative spelling for the more common 'wobble'. Hence, it is possible that in Vol. IX, p. 396.34–35, the copy-text 'wobbling' should have been emended to the A1,E1 concurrence 'wabbling'.

No. 14. THE SILVER PAGEANT

77.11 feverish] The 'f' is very unclear in the Barrett typescript carbon, and evidently the ribbon must have been equally uncertain for E1 sets this as *Coverian,* the 's' being badly smudged in TMs and the top of the 'h' dim.

No. 31. A SELF-MADE MAN

126.1 sage-brush] TMs concurs with C and E1 in reading 'sage-bush' here but disagrees with their 'sage-bush' at 129.3, and is absent when at 129.15 C and E1 again repeat 'sage-bush'. It would seem that 'sage-bush' is an error in all three places, perhaps stemming, as suggested in the History and Analysis section, from an original typing error perpetuated by the English editors. The context requires 'sage-brush'. The distinction is made perfectly clear in "Stephen Crane in Mexico (II)," when at 451.25,28, and 452.32 *sage-brush* is consistently used in a general sense for an expanse. However, at 453.17 'sage-bushes' appears when, in contrast, Crane is talking about individual bushes of the sage-brush.

No. 36. AN ILLUSION IN RED AND WHITE

155.33–34 They . . . walnut.] In the N[1] text the order of the description is broken here by hair, hands, teeth instead of the E2 sequence, found elsewhere, of hair, teeth, hands. If there were reason to suspect eyeskip and repair in N[1], the E2 text might be taken not as an editorial correction but instead as representing the typescript. This may be so, but Crane could presumably vary the order at this place if he were subtly demonstrating what is presently to be stated, that the children's story was delivered 'without . . . parroty sameness'. The case for emendation is not strong enough, based on consistency of repetition. Just so, for example, E2 at 156.6 and

158.38 is consistent in repeating 'the red hair' but N^1 varies with the form 'red hair', taken by the editor not to be N^1 compositorial departure from copy but instead E2 editing. It is true, however, that at 155.20 the N^1 omission of 'white', which seems required by the sense as well as by the repetitive formula, is emended as an N^1 error of omission. The E2 reading 'walnuts' for N^1 'walnut' seems to be a sophistication caused by a slight misunderstanding of Crane's awkward use of 'black walnut' as a color, meaning the wood of the black walnut tree.

156.2 without . . . suspicion] The E2 variant 'would excite' for N^1 'excited' is clearly a sophistication since it is difficult to imagine N^1 as a compositorial error if the copy read with E2. The whole phrase is awkward, however. Crane evidently wanted to say what the E2 editor had him say, but the reading of the typescript would appear to be represented by N^1. The temptation to substitute 'with' for 'without' should be resisted. The idea is certainly: the children deviated occasionally but in no important detail and in so doing never told the story as if it had been memorized, always a suspicious matter. In this the art of Jones at 159.8–12 may be seen, for the arguments he would have with the children while confirming their consistency in the important details would lead to some flexibility of narrative.

157.7 senses] The E2 reading 'sense' emphasizes the meaning that Crane actually intended but is clearly a sophistication, for Crane by the plural intended not to refer to the children's five senses but instead to the 'sense' or understanding of each child.

No. 40. THE SQUIRE'S MADNESS

193.22 with despair] Little question can hold that Cora's fair copy read with MS (where 'such hopeless' was a substitute for 'sad'). It would seem that in the first typescript Cora became aware that 'such hopeless' was far too strong for a look directed at something in the squire's face and omitted it. In the second typescript she dropped the intensifying 'such', perhaps from partly the same motives; but in final review for the E1 printer's copy she seemed to have restored it after a comparison. In the light of the original reading 'sad', one may say that her first instinct in the second typescript was perhaps the soundest.

No. 49. THE OCTOPUSH

231.2 skidder] This appears to be a dialect form of 'skitter', defined in *A Dictionary of Americanisms*, ed. Mitford M. Mathews (1951), as "To cause (an object) to skim or skip along a surface." Various of the *Dictionary's* illustrations use the word as a verb or adjective in connection with the manipulation of bait in angling.

No. 59. THE MESMERIC MOUNTAIN

269.36 unstirred] TMs originally read 'unstired' but in the Barrett carbon the 's' was deleted, apparently at a later time than some of the other corrections. It would seem that the second round of correction was not present, at least in part, in the ribbon copy that was used to set *Last Words*. For example, a comma after 'swamp' at 270.24 in E1 repeats the TMs(u) comma altered in ink to a semicolon; and at 271.19 E1 omits the 'to' interlined in the Barrett copy. Thus when E1 altered TMs(u) 'unstired' to 'unstirred' it was no doubt correcting the original misspelling. The present editor takes it that Cora's second round of alteration in TMs was probably engaged in without reference back to the manuscript and hence that TMs(c) 'untired' is wrong, the result of a misunderstanding on her part of the intent of what had been typed.

No. 67. THE MEN IN THE STORM

319.18 shovin', yeh——" and] In the *Arena* reading 'yeh"—' 'yeh' is in the vocative and the short dash takes the place of a comma as a syntactical mark of punctuation. But in this particular sentence structure the use of such a syntactical dash would not be characteristic of Crane before 'and', and 'yeh' in the nominative—'will yeh' would be more natural. Although the case is conjectural, the context seems to call for a long dash standing for some profane word followed by a clause describing the further invective. It would seem that some agent—typist (if there was one) or compositor—misunderstood the intention and moved the quotation marks forward. Crane would not normally write a comma before 'and' in a sentence like this; hence the syntax might easily have been mistaken.

319.28 are] The copy-text reading 'are' is correct, and the 'were' of unauthoritative Ph (followed by E1) is a sophistication. Crane means not that the remarks at the time *were* especially good remarks but instead that they *are* worth the notice and attention, of the reader, in the present because in such conditions the men were, nevertheless, humorous.

No. 83. YEN-HOCK BILL AND HIS SWEETHEART

396.3.1;396.4 Yen-Hock Bill] On the evidence of "Opium's Varied Dreams" (365.4 *et seq.*) Yen-Hock is adopted here for the first time. The 'yen-hock' or 'yen-hok' is the needle instrument that is used by the 'cook' when preparing opium. In the present story Bill is stated as being an opium addict and therefore the appellation seems correct. Reference to the 'yen-hok' can be found in Bingham Dai, *Opium Addiction in Chicago* (Shanghai, 1937), p. 204. 'Yen-Nock' may be a simple misreading of Crane's handwriting, or a slip of memory on his own part. For a substantiation of Crane's use of the form 'yen-hock', see his satirical application of the term to an imaginary locale in No. 174, pp. 735–739.

No. 87. GRAND OPERA IN NEW ORLEANS

427.24 Chavaroche] The editor of the *Galveston Daily News* alone looked at the illustration, where Chavaroche's name is correctly spelled, and altered the error *Chavaroach* in the Bacheller proof.

428.1–2 performances] In the proof a line of type set to correct the misspelling of *engrossed* as 'ingrossed' at 427.36 has by error been substituted for a line following *artistic*. Some such word as *performances* needs to be supplied to conclude the paragraph.

No. 92. FREE SILVER DOWN IN MEXICO

446.25 tortillas] Crane's memory fails him here. It is *frijoles* which are beans.

No. 137. THE SEASIDE ASSEMBLY (I)

554.2 plans] N^1 'plates' agrees with the art produced in painting a picture and modeling a statuette and could be accurate if the reference were to a book in which plates were to be used to illustrate Diehl's theories. But no mention is made of such a book, and the reference appears to be to 'his well-known grammar of form, language and art' developed in St. Louis and 'further matured' in Columbia, Missouri. Presumably this 'grammar' was still being worked out in his leisure time, in which case, 'plans' would seem to be a necessary emendation.

554.16 lincrusta] *Webster's Third New International Dictionary* enters a definition for 'Lincrusta Walton', the trademark of a covering for walls and ceilings, 'a heavy fabric coated with thickened and colored linseed oil, stamped with decorative designs'. 'Lincrusta' appears to relate to the type of decoration that Frederick Walton developed in the 1860's when he introduced his method of making linoleum.

No. 154. IN THE DEPTHS OF A COAL MINE

591.12 the] The substitution in McC of 'a', which in the full context destroys the identification of this central building as the breaker, seems to have resulted from the beginning of the N-text with 591.12; as a consequence, the referent 'the' in the opening sentence of N would have been confusing and a change to 'a' was required. See the discussion in the Text: History and Analysis.

591.31 go] Like 591.12, the change of MS 'the' to 'a', the McC,N alteration of MS 'to go' is probably an editorial service.

591.33–36 A . . . uproar.] That this Crane addition in McC,N to substitute for MS 'A . . . ears.' (601.30–31) is authorial is self-evident and constitutes an interesting illustration of his reworking of the article. One may observe that 'gnashing' had first come to his mind at 601.29 where the false start 'g' appears before 'chewed'.

592.3 were] The agreement of N^{3-5} in 'was' indicates that this was the reading set up in the N proof and sophisticated to 'were' in N^{1-2}. Whether

McC 'were' is also a compositorial sophistication is not demonstrable but is probable on the evidence of N^{1-2}. The odds favor the possibility of the characteristic reading 'was' in the second manuscript, therefore, despite the evidence of 'were' in the Barrett MS. Nevertheless, the text is not emended at this point because the chance still exists that the shift in words was a personal aberration of the compositor of the N proof.

592.21 One wonders continually] This looks very much like an editorial smoothing of characteristic MS 'One continually wonders'.

592.27 mule-boys. And] The agreement of $N^{1,3-4}$ with MS in this reading indicates that it was present in Crane's second manuscript as well as in his first. The construction of a compound sentence with semicolons would seem to have been the work of the McC compositor or proofreader; just as N^5's choice of a compound sentence with commas seems to be compositorial. The absence of a comma after 'later' in $N^{1,4}$ suggests, also, that the comma here in McC and $N^{3,5}$ is compositorial.

592.28 Finally] This is another case of possible editorial intervention, here to remove the repetition of two sentences beginning with 'And' as in MS 'And finally'. See also the same possibility at 592.38 where McC,$N read 'Down' but MS 'And down'.

592.30–31 to a . . . estate] The agreement of N^3 with MS in omitting this phrase must be fortuitous. N^3 has a short cut, also, at 592.35, and the omission at 592.30–31 may be related.

593.9 mouth] At 593.14 all texts read 'the mouth of the shaft'. It is possible that the McC editor made the change at 593.9 from MS 'mouth' to 'shaft' in order to secure an exactness of reference confused by MS.

593.14 opportunity] The omission of MS 'an' before 'opportunity' may perhaps have been a reading of the second manuscript and not an editorial deletion. Crane liked to omit the article 'a' in such phrases, as in his habitual 'take seat'. For an example, see the sophistication in "A Tale of Mere Chance" (102.38) of PM 'made effort' to 'made an effort' in $N and 'made efforts' in EIM.

594.18 It was a] The reading of $N provides us with a characteristic Crane looseness of reference, the 'It' (the roof) of 594.18 being different from the 'It' (the danger) that began the preceding sentence. No compositor or editor would reverse the McC reading 'us, as if the roof were'; hence McC is exposed as a compositor's or proofreader's change. It is of some account that N^1, which cuts here and there, omitted the text from this point to the end of the paragraph. No other N^1 omission begins in mid-sentence and with a dependent clause as would have occurred here, but always with the start of a sentence. The reading of $N is established, then, as that of the copy that Crane submitted. (MS is wanting at this point.)

595.13 up] The repeat of this word in McC,N, when it is not present in MS, seems very likely to be an unauthoritative typist or editorial repetition of the 'up' of 595.11. There is no necessity for the guide to repeat the colloquial phrase of the miner.

595.36 uprose] This word in McC,N for MS 'arose' is suspicious as an editorial change influenced by 'upreared' in the preceding question. The word is not characteristic of Crane, who preferred 'arose'.

597.19 th'] The concurrence only of N³ with McC in this form whereas N²,⁴⁻⁵ (N¹ is missing) have 'the' indicates the reading of the proof, which could have been that of the manuscript. For instance, at 597.17 where it is clear that the copy read, also inconsistently, 'you', N³ alone printed 'yeh' to conform with 597.18, whereas N²,⁴⁻⁵ conservatively followed copy. Thus it is as possible that the McC and N³ reading 'th'' is an independent compositorial sophistication as that 'the' was the N compositor's mistake.

598.11 these animals] This is the first appearance of a marked variation between the readings of McC and N. The evidence favors this phrase in $N (N⁴ wanting) not as a trick of elegant variation by the N compositor but instead as the McC editor's notation in the proof when he was reading it over to decide where to start his reduction of the material to space requirements. See the discussion in the Text: History and Analysis. See also the similar case at 598.15 where McC substitutes 'A' for $N 'Once a' which is not strictly apposite in context (and also the McC omission of 'once' at 598.31).

600.16 were sent] McC 'went' is an odd variant. MS at first read 'went', but the 's' was written over 'w' and then 'were' interlined before 'sent' with a caret. How the original reading 'went' could get into McC but the revised reading 'were sent' into N is inexplicable, especially considering that this MS would have been recopied before submission and thus was not the final manuscript. Evidently the same forces worked on the McC editor as on Crane in the original reading, but the coincidence is curious.

No. 170. THE EUROPEAN LETTERS

724.29 Julu] The handwriting is not certain here, since the name could be 'Julie' with an undotted 'i'. On the other hand, it is probable that Cora is here copying an actual magazine item, in which case 'by' must indicate the male cat. If 'Julie' is the name, the item would have read 'out of'. *Julu* is an odd name, but it may just possibly be right.

EDITORIAL EMENDATIONS IN THE COPY-TEXT

[NOTE: Every editorial change from the copy-texts—whether manuscript, typescript, newspaper, or magazine versions, as chosen—is recorded for the substantives, and every change in the accidentals as well save for such silent typographical alterations as are remarked in "The Text of the Virginia Edition," prefixed to Volume I of this collected edition, with slight modification as indicated in the headnotes to the present apparatus. Only the direct source of the emendation, with its antecedents, is noticed; the Historical Collation may be consulted for the complete history, within the texts collated, of any substantive readings that qualify for inclusion in that listing. However, when as in syndicated newspaper versions a number of texts have equal claim to authority, all are noted in the Emendations listing. Moreover, all documents are listed with their readings when a Virginia edition (V) emendation supersedes documentary authority. An alteration assigned to V is made for the first time in the present edition if *by the first time* is understood *the first time in respect to the texts chosen for collation.* In cases of only one text, V is the understood authority for emendation. Asterisked readings are discussed in the Textual Notes. The note *et seq.* signifies that all following occurrences are identical in that particular text, and thus the same emendation has been made without further notice. The wavy dash ($\sim$) represents the same word that appears before the bracket and is used exclusively in recording punctuation or other accidentals variants. An inferior caret ($_\wedge$) indicates the absence of a punctuation mark. The dollar sign ($) is taken over from a convention of bibliographical description to signify *all* editions so identified. That is, if N represents newspaper versions in general, and N^{1-6} the six collated newspapers, then $N would be a shorthand symbol for all of these six texts and would be used even if one text owing to a more extensive cut than simple omission (always recorded in the Historical Collation) did not contain the reading in question. Occasionally a text subsumed under the $ notation may be excluded from agreement by the use of the minus sign. Thus such a notation as $N(-N^4)$ would mean that all of the N texts agree with the noted reading to the left of the bracket except for N^4 which, by its absence from the $N list of agreements, must therefore agree with the reading to the right of the bracket unless otherwise specified. A lengthier way of expressing the same situation would be $N^{1-3,5-6}$. A plus sign may be used as a shorthand indication of the concurrence of all collated editions following the cited edition. For instance, if E1, listed after A1, agrees in a reading with A1, the note may read A1+ instead of A1,E1. Rarely, in dealing with accidentals when only general concurrence of the following editions is in question and exactness of detail would serve no useful purpose, the $\pm$ symbol may be used. Thus if an emendation line read 'said:] $N±; ∼, WG' one should understand that the majority of the N texts have a colon instead of the WG comma, but some might have a period or some even a comma. The exact readings of these variant N texts would not, however, affect the conclusion that the basic proof from which the N texts radiate had the colon. If it seemed important to indicate that certain of these variant texts had such and such punctuation, then the listing would do so as most convenient. In this volume, all subheadings, chapter indications, acts in the playlets, and information supplied by the editor in brackets in the body of the texts are ignored in the page and line references, with the exception of No. 155. In the early drafts appearing in this volume, no more emendations have been made than are strictly required by a reading edition, such as those which correct Crane's habitual misspellings or supply necessary punctuation.]

No. 1. UNCLE JAKE AND THE BELL-HANDLE

[The copy-text is MS: manuscript in the Special Collections of Columbia University Libraries.]

3.7   considering∧] ∼ , MS
3.14   sun-flowers] ∼ ∧ ∼ MS
3.16   might] *interlined by* Cora
       in pencil
3.31   sun-bonnet] ∼ ∧ ∼ MS
4.3   views] veiws MS
4.4   grimy, smoky] grimey,
       smokey MS
4.5   freight] frieght MS
4.14   who] whom MS
4.21   were] where MS
4.24   of clothes,] , ∼ ∼ MS ('of
       clothes' *interlined in error fol-*
       lowing the comma)
4.25   Street] St MS
4.26   lying] MS(u); lieing MS(c)
4.27   prices."] ∼ ". MS (*see al-*
       terations)
4.30 *et seq.* Mr.] ∼ ∧ MS
4.30 *et seq.* Co.] ∼ ∧ MS
4.32–33 Perkins,] ∼ ∧ MS
4.37   cucumber] cucumbers MS
5.12   imminent] eminent MS

5.23   anyone] *possibly* any one *in*
       MS
5.27   its] it's MS
5.31   bell-handle] ∼ ∧ ∼ MS
5.34   some time] sometime MS
6.8   ¶ The] *not indented in* MS
       (*but preceding line short*)
6.15   fire∧department] ∼ - ∼ MS
6.16   corps] corp MS
6.20   ¶ His] *not indented in* MS
       (*but preceding line short*)
6.33   into] in to MS
6.34   be] *interlined in pencil with*
       a caret by Cora
6.35   ¶ The] *not indented in* MS
       (*but preceding line short*)
6.35   said] says MS
6.36   may be] maybe MS
7.4   companion] companions MS
7.4   around] arround MS
7.7   Chinese] chinese MS (*capi-*
       tal doubtful)
7.8   reins] rains MS
7.16   solemnly] solomnly MS

No. 2. GREED RAMPANT

[The copy-text is TMs: typescript in the UVa.–Barrett Collection.]

7.27   ¶ Mr.] *not indented in* TMs
7.30   ¶ He] *not indented in* TMs

8.1 *et seq.* Mr. St.] ∼ ∧ ∼ ∧ TMs
8.5   intruded.] ∼ . . TMs

8.8   develops] developes TMs
8.11   turnstile.] ~ ‸ TMs
8.11   without] with|out TMs
8.26   valuable] valueable TMs
9.1   metal] mettle TMs
9.1   from] fron TMs
9.7   bleed] bled TMs
9.8   themselves] themsevles TMs
9.8   animals.] ~ ‸ TMs
9.11   .********] ‸ *uncrossed hy-*
        phens TMs
9.12   up,] ~ ‸ TMs
9.16   fringe.] ~ ‸ TMs
9.17   turnstile] turnstiles TMs

9.23   can't] cant TMs
9.26   seventy-three] ~ ‸ ~ TMs
9.26   **********] *uncrossed hy-*
        phens TMs
9.33   Paradise] Paridise TMs
9.33   J.,] ~ ‸ , TMs
10.1   clothing] clotheing TMs
10.4   DOWN] DoWN TMs
10.8   headlong.] head long. . TMs
10.10   fresco] frescoe TMs
10.13   tempestuous]   tempestous
        TMs
10.19   ¶ In] *not indented in* TMs

No. 3. THE CAPTAIN

[The copy-text is N¹: *New York Tribune,* Aug. 7, 1892, part II, p. 19.]

10.24 *et seq.* *Anna*] Anna N¹
12.11   coming?] ~ ! N¹
12.23   fire‸department] ~ - ~ N¹
12.36   Captain] captain N¹

13.2–3 a bucketful] bucketful N¹
13.14–15 tantalizing] tantailzing
        N¹
14.11   there'll] their'll N¹

No. 4. THE RELUCTANT VOYAGERS

[The copy-text is N¹: the Sunday Magazine of the *New York Press,* Feb. 11,
1900, pp. 6–12, and Feb. 18, pp. 3–6. The other texts collated are N²: *Philadelphia Press,* Feb. 11, Color Supplement, p. 2, and Feb. 18, Sunday Magazine section, p. 3; N³: *Chicago Times-Herald,* Feb. 11, part III, p. 4, and
Feb. 18, part III, p. 4; N⁴: "New England Home Magazine," supplement to
Boston Sunday Journal, Feb. 11, pp. 296–303, and Feb. 18, pp. 367–371;
T(p): Tillotson's proof for the Northern Newspaper Syndicate; E1: *Last
Words,* Digby, Long, London, 1902, pp. 1–32. Lines 14.15–21 are preserved
in manuscript draft on the original recto of fol. 4 of "The Holler Tree" in
the UVa.–Barrett Collection.]

14.16   one,] MS; ~ ‸ N¹+
14.16–17 He . . . cane.] N²+;
        omit N¹
14.19   over-come] MS; overcome
        N¹+
14.21   Suddenly,] T(p),MS; ~ ‸
        $N,E1
14.24–25 wall paper] N²⁻³,E1;
        wallpaper N¹; ~ - ~ N⁴;
        ~ - |~ T(p)
14.28   sea-kittens] N⁴; ~ ‸ ~
        N¹⁻²; seakittens N³; ~ - |~
        T(p),E1
14.30   he,] N²+; ~ ‸ N¹

14.31   it,] N²+; ~ ? N¹
14.32;15.39;16.1 bathing-suit]
        N⁴+; ~ ‸ ~ N¹⁻³
15.7,10 bath-clerk] N⁴+; ~ ‸ ~
        N¹⁻³
15.10   Eventually,] N²,⁴+; ~ ‸
        N¹,³
15.24   cell‸] N²⁻⁴,T(p); ~ ,
        N¹,E1
15.26   bathing-dress] N⁴,E1;
        ~ ‸ ~ N¹⁻³,T(p)
15.33   he,] N²+; ~ ; N¹
16.3   bathing-suit] N⁴,E1; ~ ‸ ~
        N¹⁻³,T(p)

16.6 door,] N^2+; ~$_\wedge$ N^1
16.8 there,] N^2+; ~$_\wedge$ N^1 (*unclear*)
16.8 he,] $N^{2,4}$+; ~$_\wedge$ $N^{1,3}$
16.21–22 procession,] $N^{2,4}$+; ~$_\wedge$ $N^{1,3}$
16.24 was] N^2+; were N^1
16.26 wind,] N^2+; ~$_\wedge$ N^1
16.33 laughed,] $N^{2,4}$+; ~$_\wedge$ $N^{1,3}$
16.34; 19.7 bathing-suit] $N^{2,4}$+; ~$_\wedge$~ $N^{1,3}$
17.6 heel.] N^2+; ~ ! N^1
17.8 bathing-dress] $N^{2,4}$+; ~$_\wedge$~ $N^{1,3}$
17.13 murmuring.] $N^{2,4}$,T(p); ~, N^1; ~ : N^3,E1
17.20 a solitary . . . and] N^2+; *omit* N^1
17.21 bathing-dress] N^4,E1; ~$_\wedge$~ N^{1-3},T(p)
17.22 made . . . spars] N^2+; *omit* N^1
18.1 bathing-dress] N^4,E1; ~$_\wedge$~ N^{1-3},T(p)
18.5 over-come] V; overcome N^1+
18.7 of summer] N^2+; *omit* N^1
18.11 sea-songs] $N^{2,4}$+; ~$_\wedge$~ $N^{1,3}$
18.17 fish-hawk] N^2+; ~$_\wedge$~ N^1
18.26 scream.] N^2+; ~ : N^1
18.27 matter] N^2+; the matter N^1
18.31 up-reared] T(p),E1; upreared $N^{1-2,4}$; ~-|~ N^3
18.32 Lord,] N^2+; ~ ! N^1
18.32 roared,] N^2+; ~$_\wedge$ N^1
19.1 man$_\wedge$] N^{2-4},T(p); ~, N^1,E1
19.8 friend.] N^2+; ~ ! N^1
19.11 "Tom,] N^2+; "~— N^1
19.15 Landward,] $N^{2,4}$+; ~$_\wedge$ $N^{1,3}$
19.18 boy,] $N^{2,4}$+; ~ ! $N^{1,3}$
19.19 me.] N^2+; ~ ! N^1
19.20 not,] N^2+; ~ ! N^1
19.29 and$_\wedge$] N^3+; ~, N^{1-2}
19.32 waters,] N^2+; ~$_\wedge$ N^1
19.33 jelly-fish] N^4+; jellyfish N^1; jelly fish N^2; ~-|~ N^3
19.35 cogwheels] N^{2-3}; ~$_\wedge$~ N^1; ~-|~ N^4+

19.35 greyed] N^2,T(p),E1; grayed $N^{1,3-4}$
20.3 bottle,] $N^{2,4}$+; ~$_\wedge$ $N^{1,3}$
20.7 darkness,] N^2+; ~$_\wedge$ N^1
20.19 them,] $N^{2,4}$+; ~$_\wedge$ $N^{1,3}$
20.21 encase] $N^{2,4}$+; incase $N^{1,3}$
20.21 bathing-dress] N^4+; ~$_\wedge$~ N^{1-3}
20.27 man$_\wedge$] N^2+; ~, N^1
20.29 bosom,] N^2+; ~$_\wedge$ N^1
20.29 heart-bells] $N^{2,4}$+; ~$_\wedge$~ $N^{1,3}$
21.11 Then,] N^2,T(p),E1; ~$_\wedge$ $N^{1,3-4}$
21.12–13 us! . . . do! . . . us!] N^2+; ~. . . . ~. . . . ~. N^1
21.17 sea-wanderers] $N^{2,4}$,T(p); ~$_\wedge$~ $N^{1,3}$,E1
21.20 -like] N^2+; *omit* N^1
21.27 hand!] N^2+; ~ . N^1
21.32 around,] N^2+; ~$_\wedge$ N^1
21.35 black$_\wedge$] N^2+; ~, N^1
22.4 flappings,] $N^{2,4}$+; ~$_\wedge$ $N^{1,3}$
22.10 Hello,] N^2+; ~ ! N^1
22.11 shout.] N^2+; ~ : N^1
22.14 other,] N^2+; ~$_\wedge$ N^1
22.23 limbs$_\wedge$] N^2+; ~, N^1
22.26 silence,] N^2+; ~$_\wedge$ N^1
22.37 Oh,] N^{2-3},T(p),E1; ~ ! $N^{1,4}$
22.39 Later,] N^2,T(p),E1; ~$_\wedge$ $N^{1,3-4}$
23.10 suspender$_\wedge$] N^2+; ~, N^1
23.13 *Mary Jones*] V; Mary Jones N^1+(−E1); '~~' E1
23.19 Suddenly,] N^{2-3},T(p); ~$_\wedge$ $N^{1,4}$,E1
23.20 shouted, "wot] N^2+; ~. "Wot N^1
23.20.1 *omit*] E1; CHAPTER IV. N^1; IV. N^{2-4},T(p)
23.21 Bathing-suits] E1; ~$_\wedge$~ N^1+(−E1)
23.22.1 CHAPTER IV] E1(IV.); *omit* N^1+(−E1)
23.25 away,] N^2+; ~$_\wedge$ N^1
23.25 grey] N^2,T(p),E1; gray $N^{1,3-4}$
23.29; 24.26 bathing-dress] $N^{2,4}$+; ~$_\wedge$~ N^{1-3}
23.32 -hanged,] N^2+; ~ ! N^1
23.36 break,] N^2+; ~ ! N^1

24.4 deck,] N^{2,4}+; ∼ ∧ N^{1,3}
24.20 out.] N^{2,4}+; ∼ : N^{1,3}
25.1 quick,] N^2+; ∼ — N^1
25.4–5 suspender] V; suspenders N^1+
25.7 some!] N^2+; ∼ . N^1
25.9 Ted,] N^2+; ∼ — N^1
25.10 beds∧] N^2+(E1: bed); ∼ , N^1
25.32 rigging∧] N$^{3-4}$,T(p); ∼, N$^{1-2}$,E1
26.2 said,] N^2+; ∼ — N^1
26.2 bathing-suits] N^4,E1; ∼ ∧ ∼ N$^{1-3}$,T(p)
26.12 other,] E1; ∼ ∧ N^1+(−E1)
26.25 Harlem,] N^2+; ∼ ! N^1
26.26 are we to] N^2+; omit N^1
26.29 asked,] E1; ∼ ∧ N^1+(−E1)
26.30,32; 31.21 Place] N^{2,4}+; place N^{1,3}
27.4 captain] N^2+; Captain N^1
27.9 people,] N^{2,4}+; ∼ ∧ N^{1,3}
27.13 dock] N^2+; pier N^1
27.20 prodigiously snore] N^2+; snore prodigiously N^1
27.32 at the freckled man] N^2+; omit N^1
27.35 again∧] N^3,E1; ∼ , N$^{1-2,4}$, T(p)
28.11 Hain't] N^4; Haint N^1+ (−N^4)
28.15 Hain't] E1; Haint N^1+ (−E1)
28.16 over-came] V; overcame N^1+
28.20 plot.] N$^{2-4}$,T(p); ∼ ! N^1; ∼ , E1

28.33 daresay] N^3+; ∼ ∧ ∼ N^1; ∼ - | ∼ N^2
28.36 at all] N^2+; omit N^1
28.39 stern∧] N^2+; ∼ , N^1
29.1–2 in the air] N^2+; omit N^1
29.24 into] N^2+; in N^1
29.27 bright,] N^2+; ∼ ∧ N^1
29.31 companion,] N^2+; ∼ ∧ N^1
30.1; 32.1,11,24 dock] N^2+; pier N^1
30.3 heavens,] N$^{2-3}$,T(p),E1; ∼ ! N^{1,4}
30.10 Thunderation,] N^2+; ∼ ! N^1
30.10 around] N^2+; round N^1
30.11 —turn] N^2+; —— Turn N^1
30.12 hear.] N$^{2-3}$,T(p),E1; ∼ ? N^{1,4}
30.24 docks] N^2+; piers N^1
*30.29 wabbled] stet N^1
30.30 oarsman, "just] N^2+; ∼ . "Just N^1
30.31 you.] N^{2,4}+; ∼ ? N^{1,3}
30.31 to,] N^2+; ∼ ∧ N^1
30.35 th'] N$^{2-4}$,T(p); the N^1,E1
31.6 down,] N^2+; ∼ ! N^1
31.6 roar∧] N^2+; ∼ , N^1
31.11 dock] N^2+; wharf N^1
31.20 is?"] N^2+; ∼ ? ' N^1
31.24 wasn't] N^2+; isn't N^1
31.38 remarked] N^2+; said N^1
32.24–25 Directly∧ . . . it∧] N^3, E1; ∼ , . . . ∼ , N$^{1-2,4}$,T(p)
32.31 then] N^2+; omit N^1
33.6 quick.] N^2+; ∼ ! N^1

No. 5. WHY DID THE YOUNG CLERK SWEAR?

[The copy-text is Tr: *Truth*, XII (March 18, 1893), 4–5. The other texts collated are TMs: typescript in the UVa.–Barrett Collection; E1: *Last Words*, Digby, Long, London, 1902, pp. 306–314. TMs and E1 are derived texts without authority.]

34.8–9 comfortably] V; comfortable Tr+
35.10 handkerchief] V; Handkerchief Tr+
37.22 ∧struck] V; —struck Tr+
37.34 Silvere.] TMs+; ∼ ∧ Tr

No. 6. AT CLANCY'S WAKE

[The copy-text is Tr: *Truth*, XII (July 3, 1893), 4–5. The other texts collated are TMs: typescript in the UVa.–Barrett Collection; E1: *Last Words*,

Digby, Long, London, 1902, pp. 288–293. TMs and E1 are derived texts without authority.]

39.14 *disarranged*] TMs,E1; *dis-ar*∧|*ranged* Tr
41.15 -poker.] E1; ~∧ Tr; ~? TMs
42.8 I-I'm] E1 ; ~∧~ Tr,TMs

No. 7. SOME HINTS FOR PLAY-MAKERS

[The copy-text is Tr: *Truth,* XII (Nov. 4, 1893), 4–5.]

43.5 VILLAIN.] ~∧ Tr
43.7 Merryweather] ~∧|~ Tr (*space for hyphen which seems to have dropped out*)
46.18 *obbligato*] *obligato* Tr
46.35 *re-enters*] ~∧~ Tr

No. 8. AN OMINOUS BABY

[The copy-text is Ar: *Arena,* IX (May, 1894), 819–821. The other texts collated are Ph: *Philistine,* III (Oct., 1896), 133–137; E1: *The Open Boat,* Heinemann, London, 1898, pp. 253–257. Both Ph and E1 are derived texts without authority.]

48.2–3 nursery ∧ maids] Ph,E1; ~-|~ Ar
49.34 mine!"] V; ~," Ar+

No. 11. AN EXCURSION TICKET

[The copy-text is N¹: *New York Press,* May 20, 1894, part IV, p. 3. The other texts collated are N¹(c): *New York Press* with Crane's holograph revisions (wanting after 62.35); TMs: typescript in the Special Collections of Columbia University Libraries. The latter is a derived text, without authority. The designation N¹ without suffix indicates an agreement between N¹ and N¹(c).]

58.23 Northern] V; northern N¹,TMs
59.6 thought,] N¹(c); thought of Omaha N¹
59.7 to Omaha] N¹(c); *omit* N¹
59.29 rushed] N¹(c); rushed out of the shadow of the mountains and N¹
59.34 eight] TMs; 8 N¹
60.4 neck.∧] V; ~." N¹,TMs
60.10 "But] V; ∧~ N¹,TMs
63.16 throw] TMs; thow N¹
63.25 ¶ "Got] TMs; *no indentation in* N¹ (*but short preceding line*)
64.22 trembled.] TMs; ~, N¹
64.28 kin] V; can N¹,TMs
64.29 What?"] TMs; ~?' N¹
64.30 so's] TMs; so N¹
65.5 gave] TMs; give N¹
65.10 Hully] TMs; Huly N¹

No. 12. THE SNAKE

[The copy-text is MS: manuscript in the UVa.–Barrett Collection. The other texts collated are N¹: *St. Louis Globe-Democrat,* June 14, 1896, p. 36; N²: *Galveston Daily News,* June 14, p. 20; N³: *Cincinnati Commercial Gazette,* June 14, p. 20; N⁴: *Detroit Free Press,* June 14, p. 17; N⁵: *Minneapolis Tribune,* July 6, p. 4; PM: *Pocket Magazine,* II (Aug., 1896), 125–

132; TMs: typescript in the UVa.–Barrett Collection; E1: *Last Words,* Digby, Long, London, 1902, pp. 268–272. TMs and E1 are derived texts, without authority.]

66.27 maneuvered] N^{1-3}; maneuvered MS; maneuvred N^4; manoeuvred N^5; manœuvered PM

66.34 incur] $N+; incurr MS
66.35 friends,] $N+; ~ ∧ MS

67.7 *et seq.* its] $N+; it's MS
67.7 potency] $N+; potentcy MS
67.23 attack, it∧] $N+; ~ ∧ ~ , MS
67.39 were] $N+; was MS

No. 13. STORIES TOLD BY AN ARTIST

[The copy-text is N^1: *New York Press,* Oct. 28, 1894, part IV, p. 6. The other texts collated are TMs: typescript in the UVa.–Barrett Collection; E1: *Last Words,* Digby, Long, London, 1902, pp. 133–145. E1 is a derived text and without authority.]

68.26 head] TMs,E1; his head N^1
68.29 *Monthly Amazement*] E1; Monthly Amazement N^1,TMs
69.3 twenty-eight] E1; 28 N^1; ~ ∧ ~ TMs
69.12 grey] E1; gray N^1,TMs
69.37 stove,] E1; ~ ; N^1,TMs
71.1 thirty dollars] TMs; $30 N^1
71.2 red.] TMs; ~ ∧ N^1
71.15 fellow] TMs; fellaw N^1
71.21.1 As . . . Rent] E1; THE RENT N^1,TMs
71.32 "Finance."] TMs; " ~ .' N^1
71.34 six dollar] TMs; $6 N^1
71.35 seventy-five dollars] TMs; $75 N^1
72.6,7 ten . . . seven] TMs; 10

. . . 7 N^1
72.20 discovery,] E1; ~ ∧ N^1, TMs
72.35,38 *Amazement*] E1; Amazement N^1,TMs
73.3–4 *Established Magazine*] E1; Established Magazine N^1,TMs
73.29.1 How . . . Dinner] V; A DINNER ON SUNDAY EVE-NING N^1+
74.7 six] TMs; 6 N^1
74.10,12 *Gamin*] E1; Gamin N^1; "Gamin" TMs
74.16,19,29 ten] TMs; 10 N^1
74.30 three] TMs; 3 N^1
75.3 Penny.] TMs; ~ : N^1
75.33 out,∧] TMs; ~ , — N^1

No. 14. THE SILVER PAGEANT

[The copy-text is TMs: typescript in the UVa.–Barrett Collection. The other text collated is E1: *Last Words,* Digby, Long, London, 1902, pp. 145–148.]

76.4 said] E1; sai| TMs
76.13 asked:] E1; ~ . TMs
76.24 manner—] E1; ~ — — TMs

77.10 picture."] E1; ~ . ∧ TMs
*77.11 feverish] *stet* TMs
77.12 stretched] E1; streched TMs

No. 15. A DESERTION

[The copy-text is TMs: typescript in the UVa.–Barrett Collection. The other texts collated are HM: *Harper's Magazine,* CI (Nov., 1900), 938–939; E1: *Last Words,* Digby, Long, London, 1902, pp. 245–251. E1 is completely derived and without authority.]

77.34 gabbling] HM; gabbi|ling TMs

77.34 They] HM; they TMs

78.3 *et seq.* ain't] HM; aint TMs

78.5 t' fool 'im,] HM; it' fool 'in. TMs

78.5 An'] HM; ~ ∧ TMs

78.6 foolin'] HM; ~ ∧ TMs

78.6 now?"] HM; ~ ? ∧ TMs

78.7 keepin'] HM; *apostrophe over 'n'* TMs

78.8 purty∧] HM; ~ , TMs

78.9 purty!] HM; ~ ' ! TMs

78.10 "Well] HM; ∧ ~ TMs

78.10 'er,] HM; ~ ∧ TMs

78.10 On'y] HM; Only TMs

78.12–13 'Dorter . . . here!' "] HM; "~ . . . ~ ! ∧" TMs

78.23 dangers∧] E1; ~ , TMs(*ink*),HM

78.25 top floor] MS,HM; ~ - ~ TMs

78.29 Daddie!"] HM; ~ ! ∧ TMs

78.36; 79.5 Daddie!"] HM; ~ " ! TMs

78.38 daddie!"] HM; Daddie"! TMs

78.39 familiar] HM; familar TMs

79.1 cussin'-] HM; ~ ∧ - TMs

79.1 dad,"] HM; ~ " , TMs

79.7 re-assured] HM (reassured); re-asured TMs

79.7 daddie!"] HM; ~ . " TMs

79.10 process] HM; pro-cess TMs

79.12 in this] in the light of this TMs

79.17 *et seq.* on'y] HM; o'ny TMs

79.18 ye'd] HM; yed TMs

79.20 corner, and∧] HM; ~ ∧ ~ , TMs

79.29 an'] HM; ~ ∧ TMs

79.29 advice—] HM; ~ , TMs

79.30 Nell,'] HM; ~ , ∧ TMs

79.33 I'm a] HM; I'na a TMs

79.34 yeh!'] HM; ~ ' ! TMs

79.34 'bout] HM; ∧ ~ TMs (*i.e.*

'b' *typed over apostrophe*)

79.34,36 business,'] HM; buis-ness, ∧ TMs (*quote present at* 79.36)

79.34 ses.] HM; ~ , TMs

79.34 know] HM; knew TMs

79.34 He's] HM; His TMs

79.35 'You] HM; " ~ TMs

79.37–38 will,' . . . 'yeh] E1; ~ , ∧ . . . . ∧ ~ TMs; ~ ! ' . . . 'Yeh HM

79.39 'round] HM+; ∧ ~ TMs

79.39 place.] HM; ~ , TMs

80.1 advice.'] HM; ~ . ∧ TMs

80.3 'Well,'] HM; ' ~ , ∧ TMs

80.3 I'll] HM; ' ' ~ TMs (*first quote not deleted in error*)

80.5 takin'] HM; ~ ∧ TMs

80.7 time.' "] HM; ~ . " TMs

80.11 its] HM; it's TMs

80.13 inauguration] HM; inauge-ration TMs

80.16 Oh,] HM; ~ ∧ TMs

80.18 usually] HM; usaly TMs

80.19 lips,] HM; ~ ∧ TMs

80.19 were] HM; was TMs

80.21 Daddie] HM; Daddy TMs

80.21 daddie,] HM; ~ ∧ TMs

80.22 me!] E1; ~ . TMs; ~ ? HM

80.23 touched] HM; tuched TMs

80.32 featureless] HM; featur-les TMs

81.6 arm] HM; arms TMs

81.6 its] HM; it's TMs

81.9 from] HM; form TMs

81.10.1 [*space*]] V; *line of* x's TMs,E1 (*asterisks*); *no space* HM

81.13 stairway] HM; stair-way TMs

81.19 damned] E1; dammed TMs; *omit* HM

81.19 drivin' 'er] HM; drivin'er TMs

81.20 doin'.] V; doin∧, TMs; doin.' HM

81.20 He's drivin' 'er] HM; He' drivi' er TMs

No. 15a. NOTEBOOK DRAFT

[The copy-text is MS: the Crane Notebook in the UVa.–Barrett Collection.]

81.21   women] woman MS
81.27   temporarily] temporaryily
        MS

82.4   familiar] familar MS
82.5   its] it's MS

No. 16. A CHRISTMAS DINNER WON IN BATTLE

[The copy-text is PTJ: *Plumbers' Trade Journal, Gas, Steam and Hot Water Fitters' Review*, XVII (Jan. 1, 1895), 26–27. The other text collated is T(p): corrected proof Tillotson's.]

82.16   aldermen] T(p); alderman
        PTJ
82.31   violently] T(p);   violenty
        PTJ
83.22   to] T(p); t PTJ
83.28   sound-minded,   fearless-
        eyed] T(p);   ~ ∧ ~ , ~ ∧ ~
        PTJ
83.30   called∧ "My dear man."]
        T(p); ~ : [¶] "My dear man."
        PTJ
83.38   Fortmans] V;   Fortman's
        PTJ,T(p)
84.5   5.30] V;   5:30 PTJ;   5–30
        T(p)
84.7   don't] V; Don't PTJ,T(p)
84.16   grey] V; gray PTJ,T(p)
84.19–20 foretelling] T(p);   for-
        telling PTJ

85.7   grey] T(p); gray PTJ
85.11   blood-thirsty] V;   ~ ∧ ~
        PTJ,T(p) (*in* PTJ ~ ∧ | ~ *not
        flush with right margin, hy-
        phen possibly fell out*)
85.28   violence] T(p); viol nce
        PTJ
86.2   out,] T(p); ~ ∧ PTJ
86.13   "Break] T(p); ' ~ PTJ
86.19   faced] T(p); fa ed PTJ
86.24   seized] T(p);   siezed PTJ
87.24   dining-room] T(p); ~ ∧ ~
        PTJ
87.28   "But] PTJ (c[Cora]), T(p);
        ∧ ~ PTJ(u)
87.37   it's——"] T(p); ~ ∧" PTJ
88.3   Tom,"] T(p); ~ ∧" PTJ
88.8   Mildred.] T(p); ~ ∧ PTJ

No. 17. THE VOICE OF THE MOUNTAIN

[The copy-text is N[1]: *Nebraska State Journal*, May 22, 1895, p. 4. The other texts collated are PM: *Pocket Magazine*, III (Nov., 1896), 136–142; TMs: typescript in the Special Collections of Columbia University Libraries; E1: *Last Words*, Digby, Long, London, 1902, pp. 301–305. Both TMs and E1 are derived texts and without authority.]

88.21 *et seq.*   Popocatepetl] PM
        (*except* 'Popocatapetl' *at* 91.8);
        Popocatapetl N[1]
89.8   will] PM; wi l N[1]
89.15   wise."] TMs;   ~ . ∧ N[1],PM
89.22   you!"] PM; ~ ! ' N[1]

90.13   bargain] PM; b rgain N[1]
90.28   joy] PM; oy N[1]
91.2   brutes!] TMs; ~ ? N[1],PM
91.4–5   indeed——"] PM; ~ "——
        N[1]
91.5.1   [*space*]] V; * * * * * N[1]+

No. 18. HOW THE DONKEY LIFTED THE HILLS

[The copy-text is N[1]: *Nebraska State Journal*, June 6, 1895, p. 4. The other texts collated are PM: *Pocket Magazine*, IV (June, 1897), 144–151;

TMs: typescript in the UVa.–Barrett Collection; E1: *Last Words*, Digby, Long, London, 1902, pp. 252–257. TMs and E1 are derived texts, without authority.]

93.6   interrupted] PM; nterrupted   93.18   your] PM; you N¹
        N¹

No. 19. THE VICTORY OF THE MOON

[The copy-text is N¹: *Nebraska State Journal*, July 24, 1895, p. 4. The other texts collated are PM: *Pocket Magazine*, IV (July, 1897), 144–152; TMs: typescript in the UVa.–Barrett Collection; E1: *Last Words*, Digby, Long, London, 1902, pp. 315–320. TMs and E1 are derived texts without authority.]

95.5   pink,] PM; ~ . N¹   97.3   ecstasy] PM; ecstacy N¹
95.34   not] PM; nnt N¹   97.17   grey] E1; gray N¹,PM,TMs
96.13   ²the] PM; tne N¹   97.25   in] PM; by N¹
96.15   still,] PM; ~ ∧ N¹   97.39   doubtless   have] TMs,E1;
96.19   you!"] PM; youl" N¹   have doubtless have N¹,PM
96.31   cried:] PM; ~ , N¹

No. 21. ART IN KANSAS CITY

[The copy-text is MS: manuscript in the Special Collections of Columbia University Libraries.]

99.17   West] west MS   100.4   community] cummunity
99.22   amateur] ameteur MS   MS
99.29   water-colours] ~ ∧ ~ MS

No. 22. A TALE OF MERE CHANCE

[The copy-text is N¹: *Chicago Tribune*, March 15, 1896, p. 41. The other texts collated are N²: *Buffalo News*, March 15, p. 9; N³: *St. Louis Globe-Democrat*, March 15, p. 41; N⁴: *New Orleans Picayune*, March 15, p. 26; N⁵: *Galveston Daily News*, March 15, p. 12; N⁶: *Nebraska State Journal*, March 15, p. 11; N⁷: *Minneapolis Tribune*, March 22, p. 11 (reprint of N⁶); PM: *Pocket Magazine*, I (April, 1896), 115–122 (PM is independently authoritative); EIM: *English Illustrated Magazine*, XIV (March, 1896), 569–571 (EIM's independent authority is somewhat doubtful except on a partial basis); CL: *Current Literature*, XIX (June, 1896), 516; BT: *Best Things from American Literature*, 1899, pp. 69–71; TMs: typescript in the UVa.–Barrett Collection; E1: *Last Words*, Digby, Long, London, 1902, pp. 282–287. N⁷, CL, BT, TMs and E1 are derived texts without authority; their readings appear only in the Historical Collation. Prominent disagreements in the N-line are noted below when they do not involve emendation of N¹. PM variation is always noted since it is an equal authority with $N and EIM.]

100.9   were it not] PM,EIM; if it   100.10   and] *stet* $N,EIM; or PM
         were not $N   100.13   of contact] *stet* $N,EIM;
100.10   deed,] N⁵,PM,EIM;   ~ ;   of the contact PM
         $N(−N⁵)

100.14 morning,] N⁴,PM; ~ ∧ $N(−N⁴),EIM

100.15 rate∧] N²,⁴⁻⁶; ~ , N¹,³,PM, EIM

100.15 him,] N²⁻⁶,PM; ~ ∧ N¹, EIM

100.17 servants] PM,EIM; servant $N

100.17–18 drawing room] N²⁻³, PM; ~ - ~ $N(−N²⁻³),EIM

100.18 tall old] stet $N; old tall PM

100.19–20 remained . . .¹of] PM,EIM; retained $N

100.20 imperturbability,] PM, EIM; ~ — $N

100.20 although∧ . . . course∧] PM; ~ , . . . ~ , $N,EIM

100.21 purpose, but] PM; ~ ; ~ $N; ~ . But EIM

100.23 ¶ Presently] stet $N,EIM; no ¶ PM

100.27 ticking∧] PM; ~ , $N,EIM

100.28 sentence,] N⁵,PM,EIM; ~ ; $N(−N⁵)

101.1 later∧] stet $N,EIM; ~ , PM

101.1–2 —tranquil, . . . understand—] stet $N,EIM; , ~ , . . . ~ , PM

101.4 thing∧] stet $N,EIM; ~ , PM

101.6 smoothly, and I] PM,EIM; smoothly; I $N

101.8 me,] N³,⁴,⁶,PM; ~ ∧ N¹⁻²,⁵, EIM

101.10 tiles!] stet $N,EIM; ~ . PM

101.11 me∧] PM; ~ , $N,EIM

101.11–12 and, . . . back,] N³,PM; ~ ∧ . . . ~ ∧ N¹⁻²,⁵,EIM; ~ ∧ . . . ~ , N⁴,⁶

101.12 blood-stained] N⁴⁻⁵,PM, EIM; ~ - | ~ N¹; ~ ∧ ~ N²⁻³,⁶

101.12 impassioned,] stet N¹,⁴⁻⁵, PM,EIM; ~ ∧ N²⁻³,⁶

101.20 blood-stained] N²⁻⁶,PM, EIM; bloodstained N¹

101.21 those] stet $N,EIM; these PM

101.23 ox,] N⁵,PM,EIM; ~ ; $N (−N⁵)

101.26 desperately fertile] stet $N,EIM; desperate, fertile PM

101.27 them,] stet $N; ~ ∧ PM, EIM

101.31 saying:] N²⁻⁶,PM; ~ , N¹, EIM

101.33 following] PM,EIM; pursuing $N

101.34 tiles∧] stet $N,EIM; ~ , PM

101.34 give] $N(−N¹),PM,EIM; gave N¹

101.34 glances,] stet $N,EIM; ~ ∧ PM

101.36 murderers] stet $N,EIM; murders PM

101.39 in] PM,EIM; of $N

102.1 Oh] $N(−N¹),PM,EIM; O N¹

102.4 detectives] stet $N,EIM; detective PM

102.4 stone boats] stet $N,EIM; stoneboats PM

102.5 Tamaulipas] stet N¹; Taumalipas $N(−N¹),PM; Taumanipas EIM

102.10 there∧] PM,EIM; ~ , $N

102.12 escaped!] PM,EIM; ~ . $N

102.16 morning∧] stet N¹⁻²,⁵⁻⁶, EIM; ~ , N³⁻⁴,PM

102.17 once:] stet $N,EIM; ~ , PM

102.17 Half-after] $N(−N¹),EIM (Half-past); ~ ∧ ~ N¹,PM

102.17 eight] $N(−N¹),PM,EIM; 8 N¹

102.18 chanced] stet $N,EIM; chance PM

102.19,21 nine] $N(−N¹),PM, EIM; 9 N¹

102.19 And∧ . . . course∧] stet $N(−N³),EIM; ~ , . . . ~ , N³,PM

102.19 tall∧ old] stet $N,EIM; ~ , ~ PM

102.20 drawing room] N²⁻³,PM; ~ - ~ $N(−N²⁻³),EIM

102.27 atmosphere,] N²⁻³,PM; ~ ∧ $N(−N²⁻³),EIM

102.29 table-leg] N²⁻³,PM,EIM; ~ ∧ ~ $N(−N²⁻³)

102.30 long₍ₐ₎] *stet* $N; ~ , PM, EIM

102.30 flock] *stet* $N(−N²·⁶),PM, EIM; flocks N²·⁶

102.32 weazels] $N(−N¹); weasels N¹,PM,EIM

102.33 vividly] PM,EIM; vivid $N

102.34 course,] N²⁻³·⁵,PM,EIM; ~ ₍ₐ₎ N¹·⁴·⁶

102.34 was] *stet* $N,EIM; were PM

102.35 table-leg] *stet* N¹·³·⁶,PM (~ - | ~),EIM; ~ ₍ₐ₎ ~ N²·⁴⁻⁵

102.36 plague,] *stet* $N(−N⁵), EIM; ~ ₍ₐ₎ N⁵,PM

102.37 them₍ₐ₎] $N(−N¹·⁶),EIM; ~ , N¹·⁶,PM

102.38 effort] PM; an effort $N; efforts EIM

103.1 in] *stet* $N(−N⁴),EIM; into N⁴, PM

103.4 to-day] N⁴·⁶,PM,EIM; today N¹⁻²; ~ - | ~ N³·⁵

103.8 shrieking₍ₐ₎] *stet* $N(−N²·⁴), EIM; ~ , N²·⁴,PM

103.9 ¶ Yes] *stet* $N,EIM; *no* ¶ PM

103.10 muttering₍ₐ₎] $N(−N¹), PM,EIM; ~ , N¹

103.11 hades] *stet* $N; Hades PM,EIM

No. 23. THE CAMEL

[The copy-text is TMs: typescript in the Special Collections of Columbia University Libraries. The carbon of this typescript is in the UVa.–Barrett Collection. The ribbon copy has end-of-line letters supplied in ink; the carbon does not.]

103.15 man,] ~ ₍ₐ₎ TMs

103.20 during] durning TMs

103.21 men,] ~ ₍ₐ₎ TMs

103.33 seizing] siezing TMs

104.1 "There] ₍ₐ₎ ~ TMs

104.7 county] country TMs

104.14 "Now] ₍ₐ₎ ~ TMs

104.21 perceived] percieved TMs

104.28 "As] ₍ₐ₎ ~ TMs

104.30–31 clergymen.] ~ ₍ₐ₎ | TMs

104.38 committee] commitee TMs

105.2 -air."] - ~ . ₍ₐ₎ TMs

No. 24. A FREIGHT CAR INCIDENT

[The copy-text is N¹(p): proof for the *Nebraska State Journal*, April 12, 1896, p. 11, in the Special Collections of Columbia University Libraries. The other texts collated are N¹: *Nebraska State Journal*; N²: *Buffalo Sunday News*, April 12, p. 9; N³: *St. Louis Globe-Democrat*, April 12, p. 41; N⁴: *Louisville Courier-Journal*, April 12, sec. III, p. 8; N⁵: *Brooklyn Daily Eagle*, April 12, p. 19; N⁶: *Philadelphia Press*, April 19, p. 37; N⁷: *Rochester Democrat and Chronicle*, April 12, p. 16; EIM: *English Illustrated Magazine*, xv (June, 1896), 273–275; TMs: typescript in the Special Collections of Columbia University Libraries. It should be noted that the designation N¹ applies to both the proof and the final published version, and only where they differ will the symbol N¹(p) appear.]

105.3 Major] N³⁻⁴·⁶,EIM; major N¹⁻²·⁵·⁷,TMs

105.33 pain,] $N(−N¹[p]),EIM; ~ ₍ₐ₎ N¹(p),TMs

106.15 here?'] $N(−N¹[p]); ~ ?"

N¹(p),EIM

107.10 Th'] $N(−N¹[p]); The' N¹(p); The TMs

107.13 'Ain't] N²·⁴⁻⁵; ₍ₐ₎ ~ N¹·³·⁶⁻⁷, TMs; " ~ EIM

107.21 cat-like] N[3],EIM; ~ ∧ ~ N[1,4-7],TMs; catlike N[2]

107.22 door.'] N[3-5]; ~ ." N[1-2,6-7], EIM,TMs

107.25 said, 'es] N[2-3,5],EIM (" ~); ~ . 'Es N[1,4,6-7],TMs (" ~)

107.26 erside] EIM; enside $N; inside TMs

107.28 here——'] EIM(——"); ~ '— $N(-N[2,5]); ~ ,' N[2,5]; ~ " — TMs

107.29 hain't] N[7]; haint

$N(-N[7]),EIM,TMs

107.37 sale——'] N[2-3,5]; ~ ' —— N[1,4,6],EIM; ~ , —— N[7]; ~ " — TMs

107.39 the——'] N[2-3,5],EIM (——"); ~ ' —— N[1,6-7]; ~ " — TMs

108.13 board] $N(-N[1][p]),EIM, TMs; broad N[1](p)

108.38 him] N[1](p[c])+; omit N[1] (p[u])

No. 26. A YELLOW UNDER-SIZED DOG

[The copy-text is N[1]: *Denver Republican*, Aug. 16, 1896, p. 18. The other texts collated are N[2]: *Boston Globe*, Aug. 16, supplement, p. 2; N[3]: *Pittsburgh Leader*, Aug. 16, p. 21.]

109.22 whin] V; with N[1]; when N[3]

109.26 distance,] N[2-3]; ~ ∧ N[1]

110.16 whooping,] N[2-3]; ~ ∧ N[1]

110.24 man,] N[2-3]; ~ ∧ N[1]

110.28 illy-] N[2-3](N[2]: ~ ∧); ill- N[1]

110.29 off,] N[2-3]; ~ ∧ N[1]

110.36 closed,] N[2-3]; ~ ∧ N[1]

111.16 say,] N[2-3]; ~ ∧ N[1]

No. 27. A DETAIL

[The copy-text is PM: *Pocket Magazine*, II (Nov., 1896), 145–148. The other texts collated are MS: manuscript draft in the private collection of Comdr. Melvin H. Schoberlin USN (Ret.); N[1]: *Chicago Daily News*, Aug. 31, 1896, p. 8; N[2]: *Buffalo Evening News*, Aug. 30, p. 9; N[3]: *Nebraska State Journal*, Aug. 30, p. 10; N[4]: *Galveston Daily News*, Aug. 30, p. 18; E1: *The Open Boat*, Heinemann, London, 1898, pp. 299–301; BT: *Best Things from American Literature*, 1899, pp. 415–416; A: *Academy*, LVIII (June 9, 1900), 491. BT and A are derived texts without authority.]

111.23 district,] $N,E1; ~ ∧ PM

111.25 turns∧] $N,E1; ~ , PM

112.3 because, obviously,] MS; ~ ∧ ~ ∧ PM,$N,E1

112.6 time; then] MS; ~ . Then PM,$N,E1

112.8 me∧] MS; ~ , PM,$N,E1

112.11 but∧ . . . moment∧] MS, N[1,4] ; ~ , . . . ~ , PM,N[2-3],E1

112.15 little∧] MS; ~ , PM,$N,E1

112.15 soft∧] MS; ~ , PM,$N,E1

112.19 course∧] MS,E1; ~ , PM, $N

112.20 much∧] MS; ~ , PM,$N, E1

112.20 well∧] MS,$N; ~ , PM; ~ ; E1

112.21 folks,] MS,E1; ~ ∧ PM, $N

112.25 last,] MS; ~ . PM,$N; ~ ; E1

112.26 anyone] MS,N[2-4]; any one PM,N[1],E1

112.28 said∧] MS; ~ , PM,$N,E1

112.29 brave∧] N[2,4]; ~ , PM,N[1,3], E1

112.31 some one] MS,N[1],E1; someone PM,N[2,4]; anyone N[3]

112.31 one∧] MS; ~ , PM,$N,E1

No. 27a. EARLY DRAFT

[The copy-text is MS: manuscript of the original draft in the private collection of Comdr. Melvin H. Schoberlin USN (Ret.).]

113.19 et seq.   its] it's MS

No. 28. DIAMONDS AND DIAMONDS

[The copy-text is TMs: typescript in the UVa.–Barrett Collection.]

114.22   went] went went TMs
114.35 et seq.   can't] cant TMs
115.18; 118.3   won't] wont TMs
115.21;   117.17   courtly] curtly TMs
115.22   no,] ~ ∧ TMs
115.24   stone,] ~ . TMs
115.24   ex-alderman] exalderman TMs
115.25   "Yes,"] "~", TMs
116.7   bartender] bar-tender TMs
116.19   say—"] ~ "— TMs
116.19   ²"You] ∧ You TMs
116.21   But—"] ~ "— TMs
116.26   "Um,"] "~", TMs
116.34   tell] ell TMs (possibly a light impression of the 't')
116.37   ceiling] cieling TMs
117.12   person.∧] ~ ." TMs
117.20   you,"] ~ ", TMs
117.20   "I'd] ∧ ~ TMs
117.22   Say,"] ~ ", TMs
117.23   hadn't——"] ~ "—— TMs
117.35   endured] endeured TMs (the second 'e' being lightly struck was perhaps unintentional)
118.1   East-] east- TMs
118.2   again."] ~ . ∧ TMs
118.3   ring.∧] ~ ." TMs
118.9   jeweler] jewelry TMs

No. 29. THE AUCTION

[The copy-text is E1: The Open Boat, Heinemann, London, 1898, pp. 273–277.]

118.22   splendors] splendours E1
119.28–29   stairway] stair-way E1
120.23   odor] odour E1

No. 30. A MAN BY THE NAME OF MUD

[The copy-text is TMs: typescript in the UVa.–Barrett Collection. The other text collated is E1: Last Words, Digby, Long, London, 1902, pp. 258–262.]

121.24   evidently] E1; evdently TMs
121.30   What's] E1; Whats TMs
121.31   thirst."] E1; ~ ∧ " TMs
122.1   persistently] E1; presistently TMs
122.4   I saw] E1; Isaw TMs
122.4   night."] E1; ~ . ∧ TMs
122.9   Great—] V; ~, — TMs (dash added by Cora); ~ , E1
122.15   absence] E1; abscence TMs
122.21   achieved] E1; acheived TMs
122.29   'Why] E1; " ~ TMs
122.29   boy,] E1; ~ ∧ TMs
122.31   , etc.,'] E1; –ect.," TMs
122.31   went.] E1; ~ : TMs (altered by Cora to ~ ;)
122.32   'Here's . . . prowl.'] E1; " ~ . . . ~ ." TMs
122.34   beforehand] E1; before hand TMs
123.1   don't] E1; dont TMs

123.4 'Who . . . back?'] E1;
" ~ . . . ~ ?" TMs

123.4–5 'Oh . . . he——'] E1;
" ~ . . . ~ '—— TMs (Cora
added double quotes after
dash)

123.6 question] E1; questions
TMs

123.6–7 'Why . . . me?'] E1;
" ~ . . . ~ ?" TMs

123.7–8 'Damned . . . know.']
V; "Dammed . . . ~ ." TMs;
' ~ . . . ~ .' " E1

123.9 "Later] V; ∧ ~ TMs,E1

123.14 superiority] E1; superi-

orty TMs

123.16–17 Displays, . . . feels,]
V; ~ ∧ . . . ~ ∧ TMs(commas
added by Cora); ~ ∧ . . . ~ ∧
E1

123.19–20 'Good- . . . chap.'
'Good-night.'] V; " ~ - . . .
~ ." " ~ - ~ " TMs,E1

123.23–24 'Narrow . . . people.']
V; " ~ . . . ~ ." TMs,E1

123.26 "Kid] V; ∧ ~ TMs,E1

123.34 occasionally] E1; occas-
sionally TMs

123.36 "Time] V; ∧ ~ TMs,E1

123.36 to∧] E1; ~ , TMs

No. 31. A SELF-MADE MAN

[The copy-text is TMs: typescript in the UVa.–Barrett Collection. The other
texts collated are C: Cornhill Magazine, n.s., vi (March, 1899), 324–329;
E1: Last Words, Digby, Long, London, 1902, pp. 273–281. E1 is the copy-
text for lines 129.11–29. C has single quotes throughout.]

124.4.2 Example] C(Example),
E1; example TMs

124.8 although] C,E1; althuogh
TMs

124.11–12 temporary] C,E1;
temparary TMs

124.21 successfully] C,E1; suc-
cessfuly TMs

124.22;127.13 deuce] C,E1; duce
TMs

124.25 Although∧] C,E1; ~ ,
TMs

124.27 increased] C,E1; encreased TMs

124.32 perceived] C,E1; percieved TMs

125.2 unusual] C,E1; unusal
TMs

125.3 clay∧pipes] C,E1; ~ - ~
TMs

125.4 surprise∧] C,E1; ~ , TMs

125.10 approached] C,E1; ap-
proched TMs

125.11 match?"] C,E1; ~ "?
TMs

125.18 lookin'] C; lookim' TMs;
looking E1

125.18 fur an] V; fer an TMs,C;
for an E1

125.24 forbidden] C,E1; for-
biden TMs

125.26 hurry∧] C,E1; ~ , TMs

125.28 R.] C,E1; ~ ∧ TMs

125.28 Jones,] C,E1; ~ ∧ TMs

125.29 July] V; May TMs+

125.29 19,] C,E1; ~ ∧ TMs

125.30 Esq.] C,E1; ~ : TMs

125.33 forwarded] C,E1; have
forwarded TMs

126.1 out-lying] C (outlying);
out-laying TMs,E1

*126.1 -brush] V; ∧bush TMs,E1;
-bush C

126.2; 127.25 Mr.] C,E1; ~ ∧
TMs

126.3,16 West] C; west TMs,E1

126.10 Eastern] V; eastern
TMs+

126.11 Western] V; western
TMs+

126.11 good] C,E1; god (actually
'godd' with second 'd' very
lightly struck) TMs

126.16 metropolis] C,E1; metrop-
lis TMs

126.16–17 rose-hued] C,E1; ~ ∧
~ TMs

126.17.1–18 [space] [¶] Tom] E1;

[*no space*] *no* ¶ TMs, C

126.18 important] C,E1; impor-
tiant TMs

126.20 Yes,"] C,E1; ~ ", TMs

126.20 I've] C,E1; Ive TMs

126.20 heard] C,E1; herd TMs

126.27 really?"] C,E1; ~ "? TMs

126.29 enthusiasm.] E1; ~ ,
TMs; ~ ; C

126.30 one."] C,E1; ~ ". TMs

126.32 Well,"] C,E1; ~ ", TMs

126.34 What,"] E1; ~ ", TMs;
~ !' C

126.35 reader?"] C,E1; ~ . ∧
TMs

127.1 seized] C,E1; siezed TMs

127.6 large bales] C,E1; larger
valves TMs

127.8 defeat] C,E1; defeats TMs

127.9 time∧] C,E1; ~ , TMs

127.11 possession] C,E1; posse-
sion TMs

127.12 ²and∧] C,E1; ~ , TMs

127.14 didn't] C,E1; diden't TMs

127.18 -stone] C(∧~),E1;
-stoned TMs

127.23,27 a] C,E1; *omit* TMs

127.25 here's] C,E1; Here's
TMs(c); her's TMs(u)

127.25 ah–Smith] C,E1; ~ ∧ ~
TMs

127.36 you] C,E1; yuo TMs

127.36 totally] C,E1; totaly TMs

128.1 or we'll] C,E1; or we-ll
TMs

128.1 we'll——"] C; ~ "——
TMs; ~ "— E1

128.3 screws] C,E1; screw|TMs

128.11 latter] C,E1; later TMs

128.14 Well,"] C,E1; ~ ", TMs

128.14 finally] C,E1; finaly TMs

128.15 only] C,E1; *omit* TMs

128.16 don't] C,E1; dont TMs

128.24 attorney's] C,E1; *apostrophe over* 's' TMs

128.24 privately] C,E1; privetely
TMs

128.26 highly] C,E1; hightly
TMs

128.31 cried∧] C,E1; ~ . TMs

128.32 slowly] C,E1; slowely
TMs

128.33 murmured] C,E1; mur-
mered TMs

128.33 man.] C,E1; ~ , TMs

128.33 see 'im] C,E1; ~ him
TMs

128.33 dersert 'im] V; desert 'im
C,E1; desert [*deleted* 'himim']. |
dersert'im TMs

128.34 and——"] C,E1; ~ "——
TMs

128.35 I know] C,E1; I'know
TMs (*originally* 'know' *over* 'll'
of 'I'll'; *apostrophe not deleted
in error*)

128.36 up,] C,E1; ~ . TMs

128.37 man∧] C,E1; ~ , TMs

128.37 lived,] V; ~ ∧ TMs+

128.38 boarding-house] C,E1; ~
∧ ~ TMs

129.3 sage-brush] V; ~ ∧ ~ TMs;
sage-bush C; sage∧ bush E1

129.4 virtues] C,E1; virtures TMs

129.4–5 literature] C,E1; liter-
ture TMs

129.5 opinion] C,E1; opinon
TMs

129.5 Also,] C,E1; ~ . TMs

129.6 ¹who] C,E1; who who TMs

129.11–29 So . . . match."] C,
E1; *omit* TMs

129.15 -brush] V; -bush C,E1
(∧~)

No. 32. AT THE PIT DOOR

[The copy-text is Ph: *Philistine*, XI (Sept., 1900), 97–104.]

131.21 Rouge] Rogue Ph

132.33 and] & Ph

133.10 I'm] I 'm Ph

133.17 ¶ "But] (*no* ¶) ∧ ~ Ph

No. 33. THE BATTLE OF FORTY FORT

[The copy-text is MS: manuscript in the UVa.–Barrett Collection in both Crane's and Edith Richie's hands. The other texts collated are Cs: *Cassell's Magazine*, n.s., XXIII (May, 1901), 591–594; E1: *Last Words*, Digby, Long, London, 1902, pp. 99–109.]

137.2,14;138.38   its] Cs,E1;   it's MS

137.29   drunkenness] Cs,E1; drunkeness MS

138.5   defenceless] Cs,E1; defencless MS

138.19;139.14–15   command] Cs, E1; cammand MS

138.30   hours'] Cs,E1; hours MS

138.32   familiar] Cs,E1; familar MS

138.34;139.23   Fort] E1; fort MS, Cs

139.12   acquaintances] Cs,E1; acquintances MS

139.21   *Dictation to* Edith Richie *begins with this paragraph*

139.32 *et seq.* ¹Continental] Cs, E1; continental MS

139.39–140.1   Continentals] Cs, E1; continentals MS

140.5   affairs] Cs,E1; affair MS

140.21   3rd] Cs,E1; 3ᵈ MS

140.27   myself] Cs,E1;   my self MS

140.35   King] E1; king MS,Cs

142.26   Quarter."] V;   ~ ".   MS; ~ !" Cs; Quarte." E1

143.22   dependence] Cs,E1;   dependance MS

143.24   bible] V; Bible MS+

No. 34. THE SURRENDER OF FORTY FORT

[The copy-text is TMsᵃ: ribbon typescript in the UVa.–Barrett Collection. The other texts collated are TMsᵇ: carbon of TMsᵃ also in the UVa.–Barrett Collection; E1: *Last Words*, Digby, Long, London, 1902, pp. 81–85. The designation TMs without superior letter indicates an agreement of TMsᵃ and TMsᵇ. E1 is a derived text and without authority.]

143.29; 145.23   3rd] E1; 3d TMs

143.30; 144.6   Fort] E1; fort TMs

144.7   father,] E1; ~ ∧ | TMs

144.34   fear∧ . . . suppose∧] TMs(u); ~ , . . . ~ , TMs(c)

144.36   luxury,] E1; ~. TMs

145.1   nights] E1; night TMs

145.25   well,] E1; ~ : TMs

145.28   nor] E1; or TMs

145.30   before] befero TMs

145.31   stockade] E1; stocade TMs

146.3   importance] E1; importiance TMs

146.3   Denison's] E1; Denison'| TMs

146.4   linen] E1; Linen TMs

146.16   Continental] E1; continental TMs

146.28   mother] TMsᵇ(c),E1; Mother TMsᵃ

146.30   preliminary] E1; perliminary TMs

147.9   afterward] V; afterwards TMs,E1

147.13   Mr.] E1; ~ ∧ TMs

147.34   inadvertently] E1; inadvertantly TMs

No. 35. "OL' BENNET" AND THE INDIANS

[The copy-text is MS¹: Crane's manuscript in the Syracuse University Library. The other texts collated are MS²: Edith Richie's manuscript in the Special Collections of Columbia University Libraries (stops at 150.13 with 'rode the'); Cs(p): *Cassell's Magazine* proof; Cs: *Cassell's Magazine*, n.s., XXII (Dec., 1900), 108–111; E1: *Last Words*, Digby, Long, London, 1902, pp. 88–98. The designation MS without superior number indicates an agreement between the two manuscripts; this is also true of Cs which unless otherwise specified denotes Cs and its proof. E1 is a derived text without authority.]

148.11   Northern] V;   northern MS+

148.14   upon] MS+;   *query intended:* upon oath

148.21   drunkenness] Cs; drunkeness MS

148.32 *et seq.*   commanded] MS², Cs; cammanded MS¹

148.32 *et seq.*   Its] MS²,Cs; It's MS¹

149.13; 151.3   red-skins] V; redskins MS+

149.14   inexplicable] MS²(c),Cs; inexplicible MS¹

149.28   Loyalists_∧] MS²(c); ~ , MS¹,Cs

151.20–21   principal] Cs; principle MS

151.39   perceived] Cs; percieved MS

152.15   lie] Cs; lay MS

152.36   then_∧] MS *follows with what may just possibly be a comma*

152.38   inefficient] Cs; inefficent MS

153.5   crackling] Cs; crack_∧|ling MS

153.33   appallingly] Cs; apallingly MS

153.34   the leader] Cs; leader MS

154.19   its] *stet* MS

No. 36. AN ILLUSION IN RED AND WHITE

[The copy-text is N¹: *New York World*, May 20, 1900, supplement, p. 2. The other texts collated are E2: *The Monster and Other Stories*, Harper, London, 1901, pp. 243–252; N²: *St. Louis Post-Dispatch*, May 20, p. 6; N³: *Bolton* (England) *Evening News*, Dec. 28, 1901; N³(p): proof for N³. N²⁻³ are derived texts without authority.]

154.21   small_∧] E2 (small); ~ , N¹

154.30 *et seq.*   "Now] E2; N¹ *does not enclose narrative in quotation marks*

154.32   I (*no* ¶)] E2; ¶ N¹

155.2   sparkling] E2; *omit* N¹

155.3   ¶ "It] E2; *no* ¶ N¹

155.5–6   and_∧ . . . children_∧] E2; ~ , . . . ~ , N¹

155.20   big white] E2; big N¹

155.33,34,36   They (*no* ¶)] E2; ¶ N¹

155.33 *et seq.*   grey] E2; gray N¹

*155.33–34   They . . . walnut.] *stet* N¹

*156.2   without . . . suspicion] *stet* N¹

156.5   Always (*no* ¶)] E2; ¶ N¹

156.7   Jones (*no* ¶)] E2; ¶ N¹

156.7   in] E2; is N¹

156.12   Had (*no* ¶)] E2; ¶ N¹

156.15   What (*no* ¶)] E2; ¶ N¹

156.19   To (*no* ¶)] E2; ¶ N¹

156.22   He (*no* ¶)] E2; ¶ N¹

156.25   ¶ "Of] E2; *no* ¶ N¹

156.30   these] E2; theese N¹

156.32   I (*no* ¶)] E2; ¶ N¹

156.34   limpid_∧] E2; ~ , N¹

156.37   imagine] E2; imagined N¹

156.38   Some (*no* ¶)] E2; ¶ N¹

156.39   Seeing (*no* ¶)] E2; ¶ N¹

157.2   'Where (*no* ¶)] E2; ¶ N¹

157.2   The (*no* ¶)] E2; ¶ N¹

157.3   'Why (*no* ¶)] E2; ¶ N¹

157.4   'Me (*no* ¶)] E2; ¶ N¹

*157.7   senses] *stet* N¹

157.25 seemed to incline] E2; seemed inclined N¹
157.31 and housework.] N²; ~ ~ ∧ N¹; *omit* E2
158.1 white——'] E2; ~ ." N¹
158.7 solemnly:] N²; ~ : : N¹; ~ , E2
158.7 yed] E2; red N¹
158.15 For (*no* ¶)] E2; ¶ N¹
158.19 a barn] E2; the barn N¹
158.19–20 And what . . . there?] E2; *omit* N¹
158.20 actions and] E2; *omit* N¹

158.22 If (*no* ¶)] E2; ¶ N¹
158.25 Little (*no* ¶)] E2; ¶ N¹
158.29 'Look (*no* ¶)] E2; ¶ N¹
158.39 Presently (*no* ¶)] E2; ¶ N¹
159.4 'Pa (*no* ¶)] E2; ¶ N¹
159.5 This (*no* ¶)] E2; ¶ N¹
159.14 The (*no* ¶)] E2; ¶ N¹
159.16 Freddy (*no* ¶)] E2; ¶ N¹
159.17 When (*no* ¶)] E2; ¶ N¹
159.19 He (*no* ¶)] E2; ¶ N¹
159.24 thousand."] E2; ~ . ∧ |
THE END. N¹

No. 37. MANACLED

[The copy-text is Ag: *Argosy*, LXXI (Aug., 1900), 364–366. The other texts collated are Tr: *Truth*, XIX (Nov., 1900), 265–266; PL: *Index of Pittsburg Life*, VI (Nov. 3, 1900), 15; E2: *The Monster and Other Stories*, Harper, London, 1901, pp. 235–240. PL and E2 are derived texts without authority.]

159.27 wagon] Tr; waggon Ag
159.31 victimized] Tr; victimised Ag
159.32 rage∧] Tr; ~ , Ag
160.2 succeeded,] Tr; ~ ; Ag
160.6 demon,] Tr; ~ ; Ag
160.24 -cleaners∧] Tr; ~ , Ag
160.25–26 pavements] Tr; pave-

ment Ag
161.5 seconds∧] Tr; ~ , Ag
161.22 -color] Tr(∧ ~); -colour Ag
162.8 step∧] Tr; ~ , Ag
162.12 down stairs] Tr; downstairs Ag

No. 38. THE GHOST

[The copy-text is TMs: typescript in the New York Public Library. The other text collated is MS: Crane's one-page manuscript in the UVa.–Barrett Collection. In this TMs and in the following manuscripts, many periods have been inserted, without noted emendation, to preserve consistency in the form of the play; none interfere with original meaning.]

162.31 many,] MS; ~ ∧ TMs
163.3 'baccy] MS; ∧baccy TMs
163.5 No;] MS; ~ , TMs
163.7 Enter] MS; enter TMs
163.8 Tourist . . . whiskers.] MS (whiskers:); *Tourist w.w.w.* TMs
163.8 Now,] MS; ~ ∧ TMs
163.11 *The*] MS; *omit* TMs
163.11 ∧Aw——pardon?∧] V; "~ —— ~ ?" TMs, MS
163.12,15 *with*] MS; *w.* TMs
163.12 ∧Beg pardon?∧] MS; " ~ ~ ?" TMs

163.15 T.] MS; *Tourist* TMs
163.15 Well,] MS; ~ ∧ TMs
163.16 impossible——] V; ~ " —— TMs; ~ —— " MS
163.18 hear that] *last words of* MS
163.29 here] V; her TMs
163.32 Shudders] V; shudders TMs
164.20; 165.7; 166.31 won't] V; wont TMs
164.22 Care-taker] V; care-taker TMs
164.32 Exeunt] V; exeunt TMs

165.15 me?] V; ~ ∧ | TMs   *son* TMs
165.18 Oh,] V; ~ . TMs   166.25 Daisy] V; *Daisy* TMs
165.31 Enter] V; enter TMs   166.27 afraid] V; afrid TMs
166.24 T. . . . son] V; *T. . . .*

[The copy-text is MS: "Buttercup's part," manuscript in the Columbia University Libraries.]

167.1,2,15,16,24,26,27; 168.1,2   167.22,27 o'clock] V; oclock MS
    and] V; & MS   168.1 Suburbia] V; Surbia MS
167.8 cricket?] V; ~ ∧ MS

[The copy-text is TMs: typescript in the UVa.–Barrett Collection.]

169.5 Don't] V; Dont TMs   169.17 wish,] V; ~ ∧ TMs

[The copy-text is MS: "Miranda's part," manuscript in the Columbia University Libraries.]

169.25 It's] V; Its MS   170.3,8 Miranda] V; Mirandal
169.26 "Soldiers . . . Queen."]   MS
    V; ∧ ~ . . . ~ · ∧ MS   170.3 and] V; & MS

[The copy-text is MS: "Finale Chorus," manuscript in the New York Public Library.]

170.12,28 Don't] V; Dont MS   175.4 Till] V; till MS
170.14 ¹Belle] V; Brlle MS   175.12 lose.] V; ~ ∧ MS
170.18 You] V; you MS

[The copy-text is N¹: *South Eastern Advertiser,* Jan. 5, 1900.]

178.33 then] V; them N¹

No. 39. THE MAN FROM DULUTH

[The copy-text is MM: *Metropolitan Magazine,* XIII (Feb., 1901), 175–181. The other text collated is Cr: *Crampton's Magazine,* XVII (May, 1901), 353–360.]

180.2 dreariest] V; dreamiest   184.4 times∧] Cr; ~ ; MM
    MM+   186.1 tottered] Cr; tootered MM
181.27 *papier*∧*mâché*] Cr; papier-   186.9 was] Cr; were MM
    maché MM   186.12 depths] Cr; depth MM
182.16 dust,] Cr; ~ ∧ MM   187.17 claw-like] Cr; clawlike
183.27 *et seq.* Everyone] Cr; ~ ∧   MM
    ~ MM

No. 40. THE SQUIRE'S MADNESS

[The copy-text for 187.30–192.12 is MS: Crane's manuscript in the Special Collections of Columbia University Libraries, at 192.13 the copy-text becomes TMs: Cora's typescript in the UVa.–Barrett Collection. The other texts collated are Cr: *Crampton's Magazine,* XVI (Oct., 1900), 93–99; N¹: *Washington Post,* June 2, 1901, p. 35; N²: *San Francisco Chronicle,* June 9, p. 26; N³: *Minneapolis Tribune,* June 2, supplement, p. 3; N⁴: *Cincinnati Commercial Tribune,* June 2, p. 22; N⁵: *Buffalo Morning Express,*

June 9, p. 2; N⁶: *New Orleans Times-Democrat,* June 2, part II, p. 8; E1: *Last Words,* Digby, Long, London, 1902, pp. 231–244.]

187.32 the strict] Cr+; strict MS, TMs

188.28 be] TMs+; be | be MS

188.35 privilege] TMs(c)+; previlege MS,TMs(u)

188.35 *et seq.* its] TMs(c)+; it's MS,TMs(u)

189.6 conceivable] TMs(c)+; concievable MS,TMs(u)

189.15 raw-boned] TMs+(−N³); row-boned MS,N³

190.13 didn't] Cr+; didnt MS; did not TMs

190.15 look] TMs+; looked MS

190.15 it] TMs+; he MS

190.19 properly be] TMs,$N,E1; be properly be MS; probably be Cr

190.23 servants'] $N,E1;   servant's MS,TMs,Cr

190.27 chose] TMs(c),$N,E1; choose MS,TMs(u),Cr

190.34 *arm*——"] TMs,$N,E1; *arm*"—— MS,Cr

190.36 writhing] TMs(c),Cr,$N; writheing MS; writhening TMs(u),E1

[Crane's *dictation*]

191.15 matter?"] TMs+; ~ "? MS

191.18 ask?"] TMs+; ~ "? MS

191.19–20 endeavoring] TMs, $N; indeavoring MS; endeavouring Cr,E1

191.30 Jack,] Cr+; ~ ∧ MS,TMs

191.30 ill!"] V; ~ "! MS; ~ ?" TMs,Cr,E1; ~ ." $N

191.32 beleaguered] Cr+;   beleaguered MS,TMs

191.33 its] Cr+; it's MS,TMs

191.35 Then] TMs+; then MS

191.36–192.2 *"The . . . arm* ——"] TMs,Cr; roman in MS, $N,E1

191.39 O, love,] TMs+; ~ ∧ ~ ∧ MS

191.39 us.] TMs±; ~ ∧ MS

192.1 sandal's] TMs+;   sandals MS

192.6 don't] TMs+; dont MS

192.11 you] TMs+; You MS

[Cora's *composition; copy-text* TMs, *emendations made from* MS *and* Cr–N–E1 *in that order.*]

192.15 Why] TMs(c)+; why TMs(u),MS

192.31 me!] MS (*seems to be altered from a question mark*), N⁵; ~ ? TMs,Cr,N¹,⁴; ~ . N²,³,⁶, E1

193.1 remember] MS,Cr,$N,E1; remenber TMs

193.4 'Tis] MS(c),Cr,$N; " 'Tis TMs,MS(u),E1

193.8 yes,] MS,Cr,$N,E1; ~ ∧ TMs

193.15–16 their . . . agony] Cr, $N; them the expression TMs, MS,E1

193.21 thought;] MS(face;); ~ ∧ | TMs; ~ , Cr,$N,E1

*193.22 despair] Cr,$N; hopeless despair TMs; such hopeless despair MS,E1

193.22 those] TMs(u),Cr,$N; those kindly TMs(c); the MS; these kindly E1

193.23 quickly] Cr,$N(−N²); omit TMs,MS,N²,E1

193.31 cried] Cr+; Cried TMs

194.3.1 III] MS (*possibly deleted*); * * * * TMs+(−MS,N²); omit N²

194.14 He was] Cr,$N; He, TMs, MS,E1

194.15 that] Cr,$N; of that TMs, MS,E1

194.15 type] Cr,$N; type of

woman TMs,MS,E1

194.16 believes] V; believe
TMs+(−MS); belived MS
194.27 fashion,] Cr+; ~ ?, TMs
194.30 soothe] Cr+; sooth TMs,
MS
194.33.1 [*space*]] V; * * * *
TMs+
195.4 *et seq.* Mrs.] Cr+; Mrs⌄
TMs,MS(M^rs)
195.9 misshapen] Cr+; mis-
hapen MS,TMs
195.16 "Ah] MS+; —"Ah TMs
195.19 upon] MS+; upo TMs
195.22 madam] TMs(u),MS,N^2-3,
E1; madame TMs(c),Cr,N^1,4-6
195.23 almost] MS,Cr,$N; *omit*

TMs,E1

195.29 the] MS+; *omit* TMs
195.36 "Come] MS+; ⌄ ~ TMs
195.37 here."] Cr+; ~ . ⌄ TMs,
MS
196.1 smiled] MS+; smiling TMs
196.7 mechanically] Cr+; ma-
chanically TMs; machacally
MS
196.8 mantel] Cr+; mantle TMs,
MS
196.9 began] Cr,$N; said TMs,
MS,E1
196.12 said] MS+ (N^4: exclaimed); Said TMs
196.12 "I] Cr+; ⌄ ~ TMs,MS

No. 41. THE LAST OF THE MOHICANS

[The copy-text is N^1: *New York Tribune*, Feb. 21, 1892, p. 12.]

199.24 *The Last of the Mohicans*] "The Last of the Mohicans" N^1

199.31–32 demoralized] demors-
lized N^1

No. 42. HUNTING WILD HOGS

[The copy-text is N^1: *New York Tribune*, Feb. 28, 1892, p. 17.]

201.29 scrub-oaks] scruboaks N^1

207.7 snow] stone N^1

No. 43. THE LAST PANTHER

[The copy-text is N^1: *New York Tribune*, April 3, 1892, part II, p. 17.]

208.39 while] wile N^1

210.17 the trigger] trigger N^1

No. 45. SULLIVAN COUNTY BEARS

[The copy-text is N^1: *New York Tribune*, May 1, 1892, p. 16.]

217.30 bog] log N^1
218.11 years'] yars' N^1

220.12 will] wil N^1

No. 47. A REMINISCENCE OF INDIAN WAR

[The copy-text is N^1: *New York Tribune*, June 26, 1892, p. 17.]

224.23 the] tse N^1

No. 48. FOUR MEN IN A CAVE

[The copy-text is N^1: *New York Tribune*, July 3, 1892, p. 14. The other
texts collated are TMs: typescript in the UVa.–Barrett Collection; E1:

Last Words, Digby, Long, London, 1902, pp. 217–224. TMs and E1 are derived texts without authority.]

229.23   camp-fire] V; ~ ∧ ~ N¹+

No. 49. THE OCTOPUSH

[The copy-text is N¹: *New York Tribune*, July 10, 1892, p. 17. The other text collated is TMs: typescript of "The Fishermen" in the UVa.–Barrett Collection.]

230.15   world∧] TMs; ~ , N¹
230.20   up-reared] TMs; upreared N¹
230.20   grey] TMs; gray N¹
230.26   journey∧] TMs; ~ , N¹
230.30   bank∧] TMs; ~ , N¹
230.32   sculls∧] TMs; ~ , N¹
230.32   boards∧] V; ~ , N¹,TMs
230.33   sides∧] TMs; side, N¹
230.34   row-lock] TMs; rowlock N¹
231.1   men∧] TMs; ~ , N¹
*231.2   'skidder'] TMs; ∧kidder∧ N¹
231.4   manoeuvered] TMs; maneuvered N¹
231.7–8 corn-cob] TMs; corncob N¹
231.10   gleamed] V; gleaned N¹; beamed TMs
231.16   'skiddered'] TMs; ∧ ~ ∧ N¹
231.18   ecstatically∧] TMs; estatically, N¹
231.26   corralled] V; corraled N¹, TMs
231.27   stump∧] TMs; ~ , N¹
231.28   Afterward∧] TMs (Later∧); ~ , N¹
231.37   ashore∧] TMs; ~ , N¹
231.37–38 repeated:] TMs; ~ . N¹
232.11   dern] TMs; Dern N¹
232.11   don'tcher] TMs; don't'cher N¹
232.16   don'tcher] TMs; dontcher N¹
232.16   home?] TMs; ~ . N¹
232.37   shrieked] V; sheieked N¹; shreiked TMs
233.2   labored] TMs; labired N¹
233.2   availed] TMs; availtd N¹
233.7   grave-yard] TMs; graveyard N¹
233.8   Fire-flies] TMs; Fireflies N¹
233.16   heads] TMs; head's N¹
233.21   a-settin'] TMs; a|settin∧ N¹
233.32   miles,] TMs; ~ ∧ N¹

No. 49a. EARLY DRAFT (THE FISHERMEN)

[The copy-text is TMs: typescript in the UVa.–Barrett Collection. The other text collated is N¹: *New York Tribune*, July 10, 1892, p. 17.]

234.24   was] N¹; we TMs
235.12   corralled] V; corraled TMs,N¹
235.17   Toward] N¹; Towards TMs
235.23   "You] N¹; : You TMs
235.26   stood] N¹; sttod TMs
235.34   inexhaustible] V; inexhaustable TMs
236.14   shrieked] V; shreiked TMs; sheieked N¹
236.28   appalls] V; apalls TMs; appals N¹
237.2   sculled] V; aculled TMs

No. 51. A GHOUL'S ACCOUNTANT

[The copy-text is N¹: *New York Tribune*, July 17, 1892, part II, p. 17.]

240.3   hymns of] hymns on N^1
240.34   the] The N^1

241.8   were] was N^1
242.2   an'] 'an N^1

No. 52. THE BLACK DOG

[The copy-text is N^1: *New York Tribune*, July 24, 1892, p. 19. The other texts collated are TMs^1: ribbon typescript in the Special Collections of Columbia University Libraries; TMs^2: carbon of a later typescript, also in the Special Collections at Columbia.]

244.9   Well?"] TMs^1; ∼ ?' N^1
244.10   ter] TMs^1; to N^1
244.11   an' . . . an'] TMs^1; and . . . and N^1
244.36   stairway] TMs^2; st irway N^1; atairway TMs^1

244.39   quavering] V; quivering N^1+
245.7   ²the] TMs^1; teh N^1
245.16   Without,] TMs^1; ∼ ∧ N^1
246.1   candle] TMs^1; cadle N^1

No. 53. TWO MEN AND A BEAR

[The copy-text is N^1: *New York Tribune*, July 24, 1892, p. 17.]

247.19   "Break] (∼ N^1
248.15   papier-mâché] papier-mache N^1

248.20   courageous] corageous N^1
248.30   whacked] wacked N^1
248.34   alongside] along side N^1

No. 54. KILLING HIS BEAR

[The copy-text is N^1: *New York Tribune*, July 31, 1892, part II, p. 18.]

249.21   numb] dumb N^1
250.12   panoramically] panoram-

icaly N^1
251.10   rifle-barrel] ∼ ∧ | ∼ N^1

No. 56. THE CRY OF A HUCKLEBERRY PUDDING

[The copy-text is UH: *University Herald*, XXI (Dec. 23, 1892), 51–54.]

254.32   threateningly] threatingly UH
255.10   ineffable] eneffable UH
256.29; 258.5   Its] It's UH
257.25   its] it's UH

258.26   cried.∧] ∼ ." UH
258.26   sick."] ∼ .' UH
258.31   wanta] want a UH
259.1   "I] ∧ ∼ UH
259.6   "You've] ∧ ∼ UH

No. 57. THE HOLLER TREE

[The copy-text is MS: manuscript in the UVa.–Barrett Collection.]

259.34   ¶ The] *no indentation* MS (*but short preceding line*)
260.5   the pew-] ∼ - ∼ - MS
260.20   *et seq.* Well——"] ∼ "—— MS ("*et seq.*" *in this instance refers to the two-em dash followed by double quotes*)
260.24   will] well MS

261.27   *et seq.* ain't] aint MS
261.31   ¶ His] *no indentation* MS (*but short preceding line*)
261.35   didn't] didnt MS
262.2   slid] slide MS
262.34   th'] ∼ ∧ MS
263.8   It's] Its MS
264.11   perceived] percieved MS

No. 58. AN EXPLOSION OF SEVEN BABIES

[The copy-text is MS: manuscript in the UVa.–Barrett Collection. Other texts collated are TMs¹: typescript in Comdr. Melvin Schoberlin's private collection; TMs²: typescript in the Special Collections of Columbia University Libraries; HM: *Home Magazine of New York*, XVI (Jan., 1901), 77–80. HM and TMs² are derived texts without authority.]

264.27; 267.30 perspiring] TMs¹; perpiring MS

264.29 *et seq.* perceived] TMs¹; percieved MS

265.2 ¶ He] HM; *no* ¶ MS,TMs¹⁻²

265.7 direct——"] TMs¹; ~ "— MS

265.9,25 ¶ He] TMs¹; *no* ¶ MS

265.10 a] TMs¹; an MS ('n' *undeleted*)

265.27,33 ¶ Beast] TMs¹; *no* ¶ MS

265.32 devil——"] TMs²; ~ "— MS,TMs¹; ~ ," HM

265.36 Villain] TMs¹; Villian MS

266.8 ¶ From] TMs¹; *no* ¶ MS (*but preceding line short*)

266.8 stone‸wall] TMs¹; ~ - ~ MS

266.10,18 its] TMs¹; it's MS

266.19 It] TMs¹; It is MS

266.27 snarled.] HM; ~ ! MS, TMs¹⁻²

266.39 populace,] TMs²,HM; ~ ‸ MS,TMs¹

267.15 bitten] TMs¹; biten MS

267.15 wished] TMs¹; wish MS

267.19 yeh!] TMs¹; ~ ‸ MS

267.20 ¶ She] TMs²,HM; *no* ¶ MS,TMs¹

267.30 amazed,] TMs²,HM; ~ ‸ MS,TMs¹

267.34 ¶ "Devilish] TMs¹; *no* ¶ MS

267.36 Billie——"] TMs²,HM; ~ "— MS,TMs¹

267.37 ¶ The] HM; *no* ¶ MS, TMs¹⁻² (TMs² *no indentation, but short preceding line*)

268.3 ¶ The] TMs¹; *no* ¶ MS

268.10 ¶ In] TMs¹; *no* ¶ MS

268.17 is——"] TMs¹; ~ "— MS

No. 59. THE MESMERIC MOUNTAIN

[The copy-text is TMs: typescript in the UVa.–Barrett Collection. The other text collated is E1: *Last Words*, Digby, Long, London, 1902, pp. 225–230.]

269.7 where,] E1; ~ ‸ TMs

269.13 am——"] E1; ~ " —— TMs

269.14 Damned] E1; Dammed TMs

*269.36 unstirred] E1; untired TMs(c); unstired TMs(u)

270.5 ¶ The] E1; *no* ¶ TMs (*but preceding line short*)

270.17 perceived] E1; percieved TMs

270.19,32 Jones's] E1; Joneses TMs

270.24 swamp,] E1; ~ ; TMs

270.28 said. . . .] E1; ~ . * * * * * * TMs

270.36 foot] TMs(u),E1; feet TMs(c)

270.36 its] E1; it's TMs

271.3 water‸] E1; ~ , TMs

271.15 foot] E1; feet TMs

No. 60. THE BROKEN-DOWN VAN

[The copy-text is N¹: *New York Tribune*, July 10, 1892, part 1, p. 8.]

276.8   brake] break N[1]
276.11   out;] ~ : N[1]
276.15   necks] neck N[1]
277.2   chorus,] ~ . N[1]
277.17   wanter] wanter to N[1]
277.34   were] are N[1]
278.23,38 hand-organ]

handorgan N[1]
278.29;279.3 trunk-strap]
   trunkstrap N[1]
279.4   13] 18 N[1]
279.23   lose] loose N[1]
280.17   ki-yi] Ki-yi N[1]
280.18   ki-yis] Ki-yis N[1]

No. 61. A NIGHT AT THE MILLIONAIRE'S CLUB

[The copy-text is Tr: *Truth*, XIII (April 21, 1894), 4.]

282.23   bibs,] ~ . Tr

283.4   He] H Tr

No. 62. AN EXPERIMENT IN MISERY

[The copy-text for 283.14–284.24 is E1: *The Open Boat*, Heinemann, London, 1898, pp. 211–226. The copy-text for 284.25–293.24 is N[1]: *New York Press*, April 22, 1894, part III, p. 2. In lines 283.14–284.24 the N[1] variants will be found in the Historical Collation; from 284.25–293.24 the rejected E1 variants appear only in the Historical Collation.]

283.18   trousers'] V; trouser's E1
283.18;284.1 toward] N[1]; towards E1
283.18   downtown] N[1]; ~ - ~ E1
283.30   the two] N[1]; they too E1
283.31   miseries. But] N[1]; ~ , but E1
284.2   Bridge] N[1]; bridge E1
284.8   lodging∧houses] N[1]; ~ - ~ E1
284.16–17 side-walks] V; ~ ∧| ~ E1
284.28   smacks∧] E1; ~ , N[1]
284.28   as] E1; as if N[1]
284.28   gorged] E1; were gorging N[1]
284.29–31 , eating . . . superstition] E1; *omit* N[1]
285.1   ladled] E1; ladeled N[1]
285.13   side-walk] E1; sidewalk N[1]
285.18   much?"] E1; ~ ?' N[1]
286.5   obstacles] E1; cobwebs N[1]
286.34   ain't] E1; aint N[1]
287.6   man] E1; *omit* N[1]

287.37   death-like] E1; deathlike N[1]
288.1   his] V; *omit* N[1]; an E1
288.18   corpse-like] E1; ~ ∧ ~ N[1]
288.27   up-reared] V; upreared N[1],E1
289.2   man's] E1; mans N[1]
289.24   shadows] E1; mystic shadows N[1]
289.31   their] E1; ther N[1]
289.33   shoes and hat] E1; clothes N[1]
292.2   moss-like] E1; ~ ∧ ~ N[1]
292.12,15,18 *no closing quotes*] V; *closing quotes* N[1],E1
292.24   hell of a] E1; fine N[1]
292.32   Row] E1; row N[1]
293.1   lamb-like] V; lamblike N[1],E1
293.8   frieze-like] E1; ~ ∧ ~ N[1]
293.24   convictions.] E1; *for* N[1] *frame conclusion see* Historical Collation

No. 63. AN EXPERIMENT IN LUXURY

[The copy-text is N[1]: *New York Press*, April 29, 1894, part III, p. 2.]

294.17   benefits] benfits N[1]
294.18,23 opportunities] oppor-

tuities N[1]
295.2.1 [*space*]] ****** N[1]

296.28   them] him N¹
296.32   genius] genuis N¹
297.14   collection] colection N¹

298.13   "he's] ' ~ N¹
299.14   millions—] ~ , N¹
301.20   solemnly] solmenly N¹

No. 64. SAILING DAY SCENES

[The copy-text is N¹: *New York Press*, June 10, 1894, part IV, p. 2.]

302.4   directed] |rected N¹
303.38   gangplanks] gang planks
         N¹

304.36   liked] *lines* 304.34–36
         'bowing . . . liked' *repeated*
         in N¹

No. 65. MR. BINKS' DAY OFF

[The copy-text is N¹: *New York Press*, July 8, 1894, part IV, p. 2.]

305.21   faint∧] ~ , N¹
305.30   Well] Will N¹
307.2   needn't] neen't N¹
307.14   spring——"∧] ~ ——".

N¹
308.30   there."] ~.' " N¹
312.36   air.] ~ ∧ N¹
313.17   centuries] cetnuries N¹

No. 66. THE ART STUDENTS' LEAGUE BUILDING

[The copy-text is MS: manuscript to be found in Crane's Notebook in the UVa.–Barrett Collection.]

313.19; 314.38   Students'] Stu-
         dent's MS
313.21–22   No. . . . No.]
         ~ ∧ . . . ~ ∧ MS
313.22   *et seq.*   its] it's MS
313.27   a] *omit* MS
314.7   will] *omit* MS
314.15   divide] devide MS
314.15   sandwiches] sandwhiches

MS
314.15   model.] ~ ∧ MS
314.26   women's] woman's MS
314.28   Mr.] ~ ∧ MS
314.29   boys'] boy's MS
314.32   were] *omit* MS
315.2   spirit.] MS(u); ~ ∧
         MS(c)

No. 67. THE MEN IN THE STORM

[The copy-text is Ar: *Arena*, x (Oct., 1894), 662–667. The other texts collated are Ph: *Philistine*, IV (Jan., 1897), 37–48; E1: *The Open Boat*, Heinemann, London, 1898, pp. 227–238. Ph and E1 are derived texts without authority.]

*319.18   shovin', yeh ——" and]
         V; shovin', yeh"—and Ar+

*319.28   are] *stet* Ar

No. 68. CONEY ISLAND'S FAILING DAYS

[The copy-text is N¹: *New York Press*, Oct. 14, 1894, part V, p. 2.]

322.34   On'y] O'ny N¹
323.9   market] maket N¹
324.14   know,"] ~ , " N¹
324.32   tailless] tailess N¹

325.30   discovery] discoverey N¹
325.30   halls,"] ~ , " N¹
326.2   voracious] voracous N¹
327.30–31   engulfed] ingulfed N¹

No. 69. IN A PARK ROW RESTAURANT

[The copy-text is N¹: *New York Press,* Oct. 28, 1894, part v, p. 3. The other text collated is MS: manuscript draft in the Crane Notebook in the UVa.–Barrett Collection.]

328.12 sort$_\wedge$] MS; ~ , N¹
328.13 Battle] MS; battle N¹
328.15 Row] MS; row N¹
328.15 noon-hour] MS; ~ $_\wedge$ ~ N¹
329.8 speed$_\wedge$] MS; ~ , N¹
329.11 them$_\wedge$] MS; ~ , N¹
329.20 two] V; too N¹
329.33 latter] V; later N¹
330.11 atmosphere] V; asmos-phere N¹
330.12 consommé] V; consomme N¹
330.21 corn-muffins] MS; ~ $_\wedge$ ~ N¹

330.24 marksmen,] MS; ~ $_\wedge$ N¹
330.25 $_\wedge$ for instance$_\wedge$] MS; , ~ ~ , N¹
330.27 latter] MS; later N¹
330.30 waist-coat] V; waistcoat N¹; ~ - | ~ MS
330.31 bill-of-fare] MS; ~ $_\wedge$ ~ $_\wedge$ ~ N¹
330.32 hamburger-steak] MS; Hamburger steak N¹
330.39 unsuspecting] MS; unsupecting N¹
331.6 him$_\wedge$] MS; ~ , N¹

No. 69a. NOTEBOOK DRAFT

[The copy-text is MS; manuscript draft in Crane's Notebook in the UVa.–Barrett Collection. The other text collated is TMs: Cora's typescript made from the Notebook, also in the UVa.–Barrett Collection.]

331.19 stranger's] V; strangers MS,TMs
331.30 can't] V; cant MS,TMs
332.1–2 communications] V; cummunications MS,TMs
332.5 perceive] V; percieve MS; precive TMs
332.16 like] TMs(c); look MS,TMs(u)

332.23 develop] TMs; develope MS
332.30 command] V; cammand MS; comiand TMs
332.33 fed] TMs; feed MS
332.33–34 accommodate] V; accomadate MS,TMs
332.34 to] TMs; of MS

No. 70. HEARD ON THE STREET ELECTION NIGHT

[The copy-text is N°: newspaper clipping, probably from the *New York Press,* in the Crane scrapbook in the Special Collections of the Columbia University Libraries. The other text collated is MS: manuscript draft in the Crane Notebook in the UVa.–Barrett Collection.]

336.3 ad$_\wedge$] V; ad. N°

336.5 bet'che] V; bet 'che N°

No. 70a. NOTEBOOK DRAFT

[The copy-text is MS: manuscript draft version in the Crane Notebook in the UVa.–Barrett Collection.]

337.7 whether] wether MS
337.21 ain't] aint MS

337.23; 338.18 don't] dont MS
338.4 up] uf MS

338.5 can't] cant MS
338.8 There's] Theres MS
338.13 Bennett] Bennet MS

338.18 politicians] politicans MS
338.21 rest——"] ~ "—— MS

No. 71. THE FIRE

[The copy-text is N¹: *New York Press*, Nov. 25, 1894, part IV, p. 6. The other text collated is TMs: typescript in the Special Collections of Columbia University Libraries. TMs is a derived text and without authority.]

339.15 timbre] V; timber N¹+
339.27 grey] V; gray N¹+
340.18 fire-alarm] V; ~ ∧ ~ N¹+
340.23 thrusts.] TMs; ~ .. N¹
341.20 in] TMs; it N¹
341.29 afire——"] V; ~ "—

N¹+
341.32 maneuvers] V; manuvers N¹+
343.32 pillars] V; pillers N¹+
344.17 sprung] V; sprang N¹+
344.30 blasé] V; blaise N¹; blázé TMs

No. 72. WHEN MAN FALLS, A CROWD GATHERS

[The copy-text is N¹: *New York Press*, Dec. 2, 1894, part III, p. 5. The other texts collated are MS: manuscript draft in the Crane Notebook in the UVa.–Barrett Collection; TMs: Cora's typescript derived from MS (one carbon in the Special Collections of Columbia University Libraries and one in the UVa.–Barrett Collection); WG: *Westminster Gazette*, Oct. 9, 1900, pp. 1–2; E1: *Last Words*, Digby, Long, London, 1902, pp. 148–154. TMs, WG, and E1 are derived texts without authority.]

345.1 East-Side] MS(east-side); ~ ∧ ~ N¹
345.2 six] MS; 6 N¹
345.2 street,] MS; ~ ∧ N¹
345.3 ferries,] V; ~ ∧ N¹,MS
345.4 women,] MS; ~ ∧ N¹
345.6 Italian,] MS; ~ ∧ N¹
345.9 at] V; a N¹
345.12 vision; then] MS; ~ . Then N¹
345.14–15 et seq. side-walk] MS; sidewalk N¹
345.17 directions∧] MS; ~ , N¹
345.22 guess!] MS; ~ . N¹
345.23 fit!] MS; ~ . N¹
345.24 matter?"] MS (*for quotes only*); ~ ?' N¹
345.29–30 forms∧ which∧ in fact∧] MS; ~ , ~ , ~ ~ , N¹
345.32 Others∧ behind them∧] MS; ~ , ~ ~ , N¹
345.34 Always,] MS; ~ ∧ N¹
345.34 air.] MS; ~ : N¹
345.35 Some,] MS; ~ ∧ N¹

346.5 said:] MS; ~ , N¹
346.5 right——"] MS(~ "——); ~ ! N¹
346.12 Occasionally,] MS(Sometimes,); ~ ∧ N¹
346.23–24 hands clenched] MS; hand clenched N¹
346.25 pallid∧] MS; ~ , N¹
346.25 half-closed] MS; ~ ∧ ~ N¹
346.26 steel-colored] MS; ~ ∧ ~ N¹
346.27 in the] V; in this N¹
346.32–33 eyes∧ however∧] MS; ~ , ~ , N¹
346.35 sunk∧] MS; ~ , N¹
346.36 Occasionally (*no* ¶)] MS; ¶ N¹
346.36 rear,] MS; ~ ∧ N¹
347.3 ¶ The] MS; *no* ¶ N¹
347.3 street-cars] MS; ~ ∧ ~ N¹
347.5 street∧] MS; ~ , N¹
347.7 sign.] MS; ~ , N¹
347.7 dinner∧] MS; ~ , N¹

347.8   away,] MS; $\sim_\wedge$ N[1]
347.20 glare,] MS; $\sim_\wedge$ N[1]
347.28 assistance$_\wedge$] MS; $\sim$, N[1]
347.30 self-reliant] V; $\sim_\wedge \sim$ N[1]
347.34 half-pestered] MS; $\sim_\wedge \sim$
        N[1]
348.1   centre] MS; center N[1]
348.1–2 demanded$_\wedge$] MS(said$_\wedge$);
        $\sim$, N[1]
348.3   then$_\wedge$] MS; $\sim$, N[1]
348.4   men$_\wedge$] MS; $\sim$, N[1]
348.4–5 outa that . . . outa

here] MS; out a-that . . . out
a-here N[1]
348.8   see!] MS; $\sim$? N[1]
348.11 th' ell] MS; *omit* N[1]
348.16 away] MS; way N[1]
348.19 last,] MS; $\sim_\wedge$ N[1]
348.23 squeal$_\wedge$] MS; $\sim$, N[1]
348.24 ears$_\wedge$] MS; $\sim$, N[1]
348.28 meagre] MS; meager N[1]
349.14 fabric$_\wedge$] MS(blanket$_\wedge$);
        $\sim$, N[1]

No. 72a. NOTEBOOK DRAFT

[The copy-text is MS: manuscript draft in the Crane Notebook in the UVa.–Barrett Collection. The other texts collated are N[1]: *New York Press*, Dec. 2, 1894, part III, p. 5, and TMs: Cora's typescript derived from MS and therefore without authority (one carbon in the Special Collections of Columbia University Libraries and one in the UVa.–Barrett Collection).]

349.29   in] *stet* MS(u); into
            MS(c[Cora])+
349.31   Instantly, in] *stet* MS(u);
            Instantly, people from
            MS(c[Cora])+
349.31   people] N[1]; *omit* MS
349.35; 350.2   [2]matter?]
            N[1](*omits at* 350.2); $\sim_\wedge$ | MS
350.14   can't] N[1]; cant MS
350.16   ain't] N[1]; aint MS
350.17   right——"] N[1]; $\sim$ "——
            MS
350.26   seized] N[1]; siezed MS
350.40   trod] N[1]; tred MS
351.1   sometimes] N[1];
            some$_\wedge$|times MS

351.23   striding] N[1]; strideing
            MS
351.29   sufficiently] N[1]; suffi-
            cently MS
351.31   her] UVa.-TMs(c); their
            MS,TMs(u)
351.38   Can't] N[1]; Cant MS
352.7   foreign] N[1]; foriegn MS
352.8   sad] N[1]; sade MS ('a' *over*
            'i' *and final* 'e' *not deleted in
            error*)
352.13 *et seq.*   its] N[1]; it's MS
352.21   rapidly,] N[1]; $\sim_\wedge$ MS
352.25   imperturbable] *stet*
            MS(u) (*deleted by an
            unknown hand*)

No. 73. THE DUEL THAT WAS NOT FOUGHT

[The copy-text is N[1]: *New York Press*, Dec. 9, 1894, part III, p. 2. The other texts collated are MS: manuscript draft in Stephen Crane's Notebook in the UVa.–Barrett Collection; E1: *The Open Boat*, Heinemann, London, 1898, pp. 241–250. E1 is a derived text, without authority.]

353.1   Patsey] V; Patsy N[1],E1
353.4 *et seq.* Patsey] *stet* MS,N[1]
353.18 *et seq.* bar-tender] MS;
            bartender N[1]
353.20   frankness$_\wedge$] MS; $\sim$, N[1]
353.23 *et seq. until* 357.1 well-
            dressed] MS; $\sim_\wedge \sim$ N[1]

353.26   eye-lid] MS; eyelid N[1]
353.28   Cuban$_\wedge$] MS; $\sim$, N[1]
353.31   fashion$_\wedge$] MS; $\sim$, N[1]
354.7   grey] E1; gray N[1]
354.9   still] E1; stlil N[1]
354.13   self-possessed] E1; $\sim_\wedge \sim$
            N[1]

354.27   chewin'] E1; ~ ∧ N¹
354.33   always] E1; alawys N¹
354.36   satisfact-] V; satisfac-
    N¹,E1
355.2   curved] V; curve N¹,E1
355.5   yer] V; per N¹; fer E1
355.6   gaffin'] E1; ~ ∧ N¹
355.36   ²and] E1; *blank* N¹(*possibly mutilated*)
357.5   it∧ anyhow∧] MS; ~ , ~ ,
    N¹

357.7   lithe,] MS; ~ ∧ N¹
357.10   murderous] MS; murder-
    our N¹
357.25   d—d] MS; *omit* N¹
358.3   'em] E1; ∧ ~ N¹,MS
358.5   ²yeh] MS; yer N¹
358.5-6   I'll fight yeh in h—l,
    see?] MS; *omit* N¹
358.17   ten dollars] E1; $10 N¹
358.32   policeman,] E1; ~ ∧ N¹

No. 73a. NOTEBOOK DRAFT

[The copy-text is MS: manuscript draft in the Crane Notebook in the UVa.–
Barrett Collection. The other text collated is N¹: *New York Press,* Dec. 9,
1894, part III, p. 2.]

359.26   discussed] N¹; dicussed
    MS
359.33   anybody else] V;
    anybodyelse MS
360.9   with] V; was MS
360.11   unconsciously] MS(u);

unconscously MS(c)
360.21   ain't] N¹; aint MS
360.33   'em] N¹; ∧ ~ MS
360.33-34   wi'che] N¹; wi che
    MS
360.34   ahn. Git] V; ~ ∧ | ~ MS

No. 74. A LOVELY JAG IN A CROWDED CAR

[The copy-text is N¹(p): unmarked proof of *New York Press,* Jan. 6, 1895,
part V, p. 6. The other text collated is N¹: the published version. No
differences were observed between N¹ and its proof.]

363.6   ²"Bringesh] ∧ ~ N¹

363.36   the] *omit* N¹

No. 75. OPIUM'S VARIED DREAMS

[The copy-text is N¹: *Detroit Free Press,* May 17, 1896, p. 20. The other
texts collated are N²: *Portland Oregonian,* May 17, p. 17; N³: *New York
Sun,* May 17, part III, p. 3; N⁴: *Kansas City Star,* May 17, p. 16; N⁵:
Buffalo Express, May 17, sec. II, p. 3; N⁶: *Philadelphia Inquirer,* May 17,
p. 28; N⁷: *Denver Republican,* May 17, p. 21.]

365.1   this country] $N(−N¹);
    the United States N¹
365.5   layout] N³,⁵; ~ - ~
    N¹⁻²,⁶⁻⁷; ~ - | ~ N⁴
365.8   opium-smokers] N² (*unclear*); ~ ∧ ~ $N(−N²)
365.10   one∧ of course∧] N⁴,⁶⁻⁷;
    ~ , ~ ~ , N¹⁻³,⁵
365.13   disorganized,] $N(−N¹);
    ~ ∧ N¹
365.23   avenue∧] N³⁻⁵,⁷; ~ ,
    N¹⁻²,⁶

365.32   reigns] N²⁻³,⁵⁻⁶; reins
    N¹,⁴,⁷
365.37   lay] $N(−N¹); lie N¹
366.4   street] $N(−N¹);   streets
    N¹
366.7   layout] N²⁻³,⁵; ~ ∧ ~
    N¹,⁶⁻⁷; ~ - ~ N⁴
366.14   some one] N²⁻³,⁷;
    someone N¹,⁴⁻⁶
366.15   habit∧] $N(−N¹); ~ ,
    N¹
366.19   smokers . . . indulge]

$N^{2-4,7}$; smoker . . . indulges $N^{1,5-6}$

366.35 pipe,] $N(-N^1)$; $\sim_\wedge N^1$
367.1 a thirst,] $N(-N^1) \sim \sim_\wedge |$ N^1
367.3 it] $N^{3,5-6}$; *omit* $N^{1-2,4,7}$
367.7 Gradually,] $N^{2,4-5,7}$; $\sim_\wedge$ $N^{1,3,6}$
367.14 If$_\wedge$ indeed$_\wedge$] N^{4-7}; $\sim$, $\sim$, N^{1-3}
367.20 task$_\wedge$] $N^{2,4-6}$; $\sim$, $N^{1,3,7}$
367.38 to,] $N(-N^{1,6})$; $\sim_\wedge N^{1,6}$
368.15 lead pencil] $N^{3-4,7}$; leadpencil N^{1-2}; $\sim$ - $\sim N^{5-6}$

368.16 *et seq.* centre] $N^{3,6}$; center $N(-N^{3,6})$
368.26 $_\wedge$yen-hock$_\wedge$] $N^{3,7}$; " $\sim$ - $\sim$ " $N(-N^{3,7})$
368.28 two] $N(-N^1)$; both N^1
368.30 readiness,] $N(-N^1)$; $\sim_\wedge N^1$
369.2 work$_\wedge$] N^{4-6}; $\sim$, $N(-N^{4-6})$
369.9 height] $N(-N^1)$; hight N^1
369.25 arm-chair] $N^{2,5}$; $\sim_\wedge \sim$ $N^{1,7}$; armchair N^{3-4}

No. 76. NEW YORK'S BICYCLE SPEEDWAY

[The copy-text is N(p): *McClure's* proof. The other texts collated are N^1: *New York Sun*, July 5, 1896, part III, p. 5; N^2: *Boston Globe*, July 5, p. 30; N^3: *Pittsburgh Leader*, July 5, p. 22.]

371.14 shaft,] N^{1-2}; $\sim_\wedge$ N(p),N^3
371.36–37 three-ton] N^{1-3}; 3 ton

N(p)
373.11 choose."] N^2; $\sim$?" N^1; $\sim$. $_\wedge$ N(p),N^3

No. 77. IN THE BROADWAY CABLE CARS

[The copy-text is N^1: *Pittsburgh Leader*, July 26, 1896, p. 22. The other texts collated are N^2: *Denver Republican*, July 26, p. 24; N^3: *New York Sun*, July 26, section 2, p. 3; E1: *Last Words*, Digby, Long, London, 1902, pp. 173–180. E1 is a derived text, without authority.]

373.19 Lodore] N^3; Ladore N^{1-2}
374.25 Artillery] N^{2-3}; artillery N^1
374.36 10,000,000] N^{2-3}; 1,000,000 N^1
375.1 street,] N^{2-3}; $\sim_\wedge N^1$
375.10 City] N^{2-3}; Citl N^1
375.14 car] N^{2-3}; cars N^1
375.19 cañons] E1; canons $N
375.28 Elizabethan] N^{2-3}; Elizabethian N^1
375.31 English,] N^{2-3}; $\sim_\wedge N^1$
375.36 overhead] N^{2-3}; $\sim_\wedge \sim N^1$
376.9 gamboling,] N^{2-3}; $\sim_\wedge N^1$
376.10–11 neck, . . . quit your] N^{2-3}; *omit* N^1
376.13 dude] N^{2-3}; due N^1

376.30 them,] N^{2-3}; $\sim_\wedge N^1$
376.32 signs] N^{2-3}; sign N^1
377.3 up] N^{2-3}; *omit* N^1
377.4 and] N^{2-3}; and and N^1
377.7 just] N^{2-3}; *omit* N^1
377.8 as] N^{2-3}; *omit* N^1
377.9 the] N^2; *omit* N^1; all N^3
377.14–15 Perhaps . . . car.] N^{2-3}; *omit* N^1
377.19 lamps,] N^{2-3}; $\sim_\wedge N^1$
377.22 best$_\wedge$dressed] N^{2-3}; $\sim$ - $\sim$ N^1
377.29 7000] N^{2-3}; seven thousand N^1
377.35 replies,] N^{2-3}; $\sim_\wedge N^1$
378.7 underground] N^{2-3}; $\sim_\wedge \sim$ N^1

No. 78. THE ROOF GARDENS AND GARDENERS OF NEW YORK

[The copy-text is N(p): *McClure's* proof. The other texts collated are N^1: *Cincinnati Commercial Tribune*, Aug. 9, 1896, p. 18; N^2: *Washington*

Post, Aug. 9, p. 20; N³: *Portland Oregonian*, Aug. 9, p. 16; N⁴: *Pittsburgh Leader*, Aug. 9, p. 20; N⁵: *Denver Republican*, Aug. 9, p. 21; WG: *Westminster Gazette*, Oct. 17, 1900, pp. 1–2; E1: *Last Words*, Digby, Long, London, 1902, pp. 166–172. E1 is a derived text without authority.]

379.11   consequences,] N^{1,3,5},WG; ~ ₐ N(p),N^{2,4}
379.11   oblivious] N^{1,3,5},WG; abvious N(p); obvious N^{2,4}
379.22   waits] $N,WG; watis

N(p)
380.37   Western] $N(−N⁴),WG; western N(p),N⁴
381.6   propagation] $N,WG; propogation N(p)

No. 79. AN ELOQUENCE OF GRIEF

[The copy-text is E1: *The Open Boat*, Heinemann, London, 1898, pp. 267–270. The other text collated is MS: manuscript fragment in the UVa.–Barrett Collection present at 382.27–383.8 'constantly . . . exhibits'.]

382.27   girlₐ] MS; ~ , E1
382.28   noticedₐ] MS; ~ , E1
382.31   acidₐ] MS; ~ , E1
382.32   roomₐ] MS; ~ , E1
382.36   progressedₐ] MS; ~ , E1
383.1   officerₐ] MS (police-

manₐ); ~ , E1
383.3   -wheelsₐ] MS; ~ , E1
383.3   endured,   generally,] MS; ~ ₐ ~ ₐ E1
383.7   wayₐ] MS; ~ , E1

No. 80. IN THE TENDERLOIN: A DUEL

[The copy-text is TT: *Town Topics*, XXXVI (Oct. 1, 1896), 14. The other text collated is TTT: *Tales from Town Topics*, No. 33 (Sept., 1899), pp. 119–123. TTT is a derived text without authority.]

385.8   a] TTT; *omit* TT
386.24   stupefied] TTT; stupified TT
387.2   fly——"] V; ~ "—— TT;

~ !" TTT
387.11   girl"?] V; ~ ?" TT; ~ !" TTT

No. 81. THE "TENDERLOIN" AS IT REALLY IS

[The copy-text is N¹: *New York Journal*, Oct. 25, 1896, pp. 13–14.]

388.8   Haymarket] Hay'|market N¹ (*apostrophe not clear*)
388.20   Restored."] ~ .' N¹
388.25   Everything] Every thing N¹
389.19.1; 392.10.1   [*space*]] *** N¹

389.34,38   Won't] Wont N¹
390.24   Flossie] Fossie N¹
391.13   kiddin'] ~ ₐ N¹
391.20   An'] ~ ₐ N¹
391.25.1   [*space*]] *text continued on different page* N¹
392.4   and——"] ~ "—— N¹

No. 82. IN THE "TENDERLOIN"

[The copy-text is N¹: *New York Journal*, Nov. 1, 1896, p. 25.]

393.20   thing] hing N¹
393.35.1; 394.17.1; 395.37.1   [*space*]] ******** N¹
394.12   race-track] racetrack N¹

394.33,34   say——"] ~ "— N¹
395.29   ain't] aint N¹
395.31   Ain't] Aint N¹

No. 83. YEN-HOCK BILL AND HIS SWEETHEART

[The copy-text is N¹: *New York Journal*, Nov. 29, 1896, p. 35.]

*396.3.1; 396.4 Yen-Hock] Yen-Nock N¹
396.9 No] Nor N¹
396.17 him] his N¹
397.20 'T'll] ∧ ~ N¹
397.25(*twice*) Won't] Wont N¹

397.26 No,] ~ . N¹
398.1 seemed] seem N¹
398.23 home."] ~ . ∧ N¹
398.30 insane] in-|insane N¹
399.1 won't] wont N¹

No. 84. STEPHEN CRANE IN MINETTA LANE

[The copy-text is N¹: *Nebraska State Journal*, Dec. 21, 1896, p. 3. The other texts collated are N²: *Galveston Daily News*, Dec. 20, p. 24; N³: *Philadelphia Press*, Dec. 20, p. 34; N⁴: *San Francisco Chronicle*, Jan. 10, 1897, p. 2; N⁵: *New York Herald*, Dec. 20, 1896, sec. v, p. 5; N⁶: *Minneapolis Tribune*, Dec. 20, p. 21; TMs: typescript in the UVa.–Barrett Collection; E1: *Last Words*, Digby, Long, London, 1902, pp. 154–166. TMs and E1 are derived texts without authority.]

399.15 Bleecker] $N(−N¹); Bleecher N¹
399.19 out∧] N³,⁵; ~ , N¹⁻²,⁴
399.23 inhabitants∧ . . . part∧] N²,⁴⁻⁵; ~ , . . . ~ , N¹,³,⁶
399.33 said,] $N(−N¹); ~ ∧ N¹
400.7 Sailors∧] N²,⁴⁻⁵; ~ , N¹,³,⁶
400.24 Bloodthirsty] $N(−N¹); Bloodthirty N¹
400.25 gore∧] N²,⁴⁻⁵; ~ , N¹,³,⁶
400.32 ingenuous] N³⁻⁶; ingenious N¹⁻²
401.1 corkscrew] $N(−N¹,⁶); ~ - ~ N¹,⁶
401.5 *et seq.* Black-Cat] $N(−N¹,⁵); ~ ∧ ~ N¹,⁵
401.7 prison,] $N(−N¹); ~ ∧ N¹
401.14 it∧] $N(−N¹,³); ~ , N¹,³
401.28 day∧] $N(−N¹,⁴); ~ , N¹,⁴
401.39 respirations] $N(−N¹); respiration N¹
402.2 of a] $N(−N¹); of N¹
402.11 and presently] $N(−N¹); presently N¹
402.28 ain't] N²⁻³; aint N¹,⁴⁻⁶
402.35 tenderly,] N³⁻⁶; ~ ∧ N¹⁻²
403.16 Pop's] $N(−N¹); Pops's N¹
403.28 condition] $N(−N¹); conditions N¹

403.29 ain't] N⁴⁻⁶; aint N¹⁻³
403.32 ¹ain't] N²,⁵⁻⁶; aint N¹,³⁻⁴
403.32 uster] N²,⁴⁻⁶; useter N¹,³,⁵
403.32 ²ain't] N⁴⁻⁵; aint N¹⁻³,⁶
403.33 ain't] N²,⁴⁻⁵; aint N¹,³; haint N⁶
403.33 des] $N(−N¹); *omit* N¹
403.35 diff'rent] N²; dif'frent N¹,⁴; dif-|frent N³; diff'ent N⁵; different N⁶
403.37 'deed,] N²⁻⁴; ~ ∧ N¹,⁵⁻⁶
404.2 No,] $N(−N¹); ~ ∧ N¹
404.2 sir!] $N(−N¹); ~ . N¹
404.2 gave] $N(−N¹); gave the N¹
404.7 Yes,] $N(−N¹); ~ ∧ N¹
404.15 week,] $N(−N¹,⁵); ~ ∧ N¹,⁵
404.19 Montezuma] $N(−N¹); Monetzuma N¹
404.19 Club] $N(−N¹⁻²); club N¹⁻²
404.28 spy-glass] N²,⁴,⁶; ~ ∧ ~ N¹; spyglass N³; ~ -|~ N⁶
404.30 ignorant] $N(−N¹); ignortant N¹
404.32 salaamed] N²⁻³,⁵; salammed N¹,⁶; salamed N⁴
404.33 Mayor] $N(−N¹); mayor N¹

404.33   street."] $N(−N¹); ~ .".
N¹

405.2   Why,] $N(−N¹,⁴); ~ ₍
N¹,⁴

405.9   quickly₍] N²⁻³; ~ , $N
(−N²⁻³)

405.20   denizens] $N(−N¹);

deizens N¹

405.26   succeed₍] N²⁻³,⁵; ~ ,
N¹,⁴,⁶

405.30   Court] N³⁻⁶; court N¹⁻²

405.37   , are these people]
$N(−N¹); omit N¹

No. 85. NEBRASKA'S BITTER FIGHT FOR LIFE

[The copy-text is N¹(p): proof for the *Nebraska State Journal*, Feb. 24,
1895, p. 14, in the Special Collections of Columbia University Libraries.
The other texts collated are N¹: *Nebraska State Journal* (it should be
noted that the designation N¹ applies to both the proof and the final published version and only where they differ will the symbol N¹[p] appear);
N²: *Salt Lake City Tribune*, Feb. 24, p. 14; N³: *Buffalo Morning News*,
Feb. 24, p. 5; N⁴: *New Orleans Times-Democrat*, Feb. 23, p. 9; N⁵: *Galveston Daily News*, Feb. 24, p. 10; N⁶: *Cincinnati Commercial Gazette*, Feb.
24, p. 17; N⁷: *Philadelphia Press*, Feb. 24, p. 25; N⁸: *New York Press*, Feb.
24, sec. v, p. 2; N⁹: *Rochester Democrat and Chronicle*, Feb. 24, p. 7.]

409.4   East] $N(−N¹,⁵); east
N¹,⁵

409.7−8   sufficient. [¶ The]
N¹⁻²,⁴⁻⁹; sufficient.|east . . .
sufficient. [*lines* 409.4−7 *re-
peated*] | [¶ The N¹(p)

409.11   River] N⁶⁻⁸; river N¹⁻⁵,⁹

411.27   West] N²,⁴,⁶⁻⁷,⁹; west
N¹,⁵,⁸

412.23   Governor] N²,⁵,⁷⁻⁹; Gov.
N¹,³⁻⁴,⁶

412.23   Holcomb] V; Halcombe
N¹,³,⁵,⁷,⁹; Holcombe N²,⁴,⁶,⁸

412.33   and corresponds] N²⁻³,⁷⁻⁹;
and correspnds N¹; omit N⁴⁻⁶

412.34   railroads] $N(−N¹); rail-
rads N¹

412.39   facetious] N²⁻⁹; faceteous N¹(p); omit N¹

412.39   East] $N(−N¹[p],N⁵);
east N¹(p),N⁵

413.6   commission] $N(−N¹);
commision N¹

413.9,28   East] $N(−N¹,⁵); east
N¹,⁵

413.12   ton.] $N(−N¹); ~ ₍ N¹

413.38   yeh."] $N(−N¹); ~ .' N¹

414.31   uncompromising] N²⁻⁵,⁹;
uncomprising N¹,⁶⁻⁸

415.21   sod houses] N²⁻⁶,⁸; ~ - ~
N¹,⁹; ~ - | ~ N⁷

416.3   chimney] $N(−N¹); chin-
mey N¹

416.9 et seq.   State] N²⁻⁴,⁶⁻⁸; state
N¹,⁵,⁹

416.20   which] $N(−N¹); wich
N¹

416.32   out] $N(−N¹); out out
N¹

417.7   cannot] $N(−N¹); connot
N¹

417.18   were₍] N⁴,⁸; ~ , N¹⁻³,⁶⁻⁷,⁹;
omit N⁵

417.20   winds₍] $N(−N¹); ~ ,
N¹

417.22   phenomenal] $N(−N¹);
phenominal N¹

417.31   Eastern] $N(−N¹,⁵);
eastern N¹,⁵

417.39   said:] $N(−N¹,⁹); ~ ₍
N¹; ~ . N⁹

418.4   an'] N⁴⁻⁸; ~ ₍ N¹⁻²,⁹; and
N³

418.6−7   Who   the   hell . . .
along?"] N¹; Who the | [¶
"How do you get along?" N¹(p);
Who the h— tol' you I got
along?" N²; omit N³⁻⁸; Who
the —— can get along?" N⁹

418.16   grievous] N³⁻⁶,⁸; grevious
N¹⁻²,⁷,⁹

418.18   Holcomb] N²; Holcombe

N[1,3-4,6-9]; Halcombe N[5]
418.25 "This] N[3-4,7-9]; ∧ ~
N[1-2,5-6]

418.27 cent∧] N[2,4-5]; ~ . N[1,3,6,8];
~ , N[7,9]

No. 86. SEEN AT HOT SPRINGS

[The copy-text is N[1](p): proof for the *Nebraska State Journal*, March 3, 1895, p. 10, in the Special Collections of Columbia University Libraries. The other texts collated are N[1]: *Nebraska State Journal* (it should be noted that the designation N[1] applies to both the proof and the final published version and only where they differ will the symbol N[1][p] appear); N[2]: *Galveston Daily News*, March 3, p. 11; N[3]: *Cincinnati Commercial Gazette*, March 3, p. 17; N[4]: *Buffalo News*, March 3, p. 8; N[5]: *Philadelphia Press*, March 3, p. 29; N[6]: *Rochester Democrat and Chronicle*, March 3, p. 7.]

420.21 England.] $N(−N[1]); ~ ,
N[1]
420.31 badgers] N[3-4]; badges
$N(−N[3-4])
421.4 air of] N[3-4]; air $N(−N[3-4])
421.23 Eastern] N[3-6]; eastern
N[1-2]
421.32 ²and] $N(−N[1]); nd N[1]

423.1 sun-light] V; sunlight
N[1](p),N[2-6]
423.4 springs] N[2-5]; Springs N[1,6]
424.9 man,] $N(−N[1]); ~ . N[1]
424.10 traveller∧] N[5-6]; ~ , N[1,3]
424.13 Well,] N[3-6]; ~ . N[1]
424.36 Neb.,] N[3-6]; ~ ∧ , N[1](p)

No. 87. GRAND OPERA IN NEW ORLEANS

[The copy-text is N[1](p): proof for the *Nebraska State Journal*, March 24, 1895, p. 11, in the Special Collections of Columbia University Libraries. The other texts collated are N[1]: *Nebraska State Journal* (it should be noted that the designation N[1] applies to both the proof and the final published version and only where they differ will the symbol N[1][p] appear); N[2]: *Philadelphia Press*, March 24, p. 25; N[3]: *Galveston Daily News*, March 24, p. 4; N[4]: *Minneapolis Tribune*, March 24, p. 17; N[5]: *Rochester Democrat and Chronicle*, March 24, p. 10; PO: *Public Opinion*, XVIII (July 4, 1895), 770.]

425.14 scarred] N[2-3,5]; scared
N[1,4]
426.18 opera house] N[3-5]; ~ - ~
N[1]
426.27 opera] N[3-4]; open N[1,5]
426.29 baritone,] N[3-5]; ~ ∧ N[1]
427.12 thorns] N[2-5]; thrones N[1]
*427.24 Chavaroche] N[3]; Chava-
roach N[1-2,4-5]
427.36 engrossed] N[2-5]; ingrossed N[1]
427.39 perfectly] N[2-5]; perfacty

N[1]
*428.1−2 performances] V; artis-
tic earnest, engrossed in the
opera N[1-2,5]; artistic interest,
engrossed in the opera N[3]; artistic earnestness and are engrossed in the opera N[4]
428.8 Amours] N[2,4]; Armours
N[1,3,5]
428.8 Dragons de Villars] V;
Dragon de Villar $N
428.31 see] N[4-5]; be N[1,3],PO

No. 88. THE CITY OF MEXICO

[The copy-text is MS: the untitled manuscript in the Special Collections of Columbia University Libraries.]

429.1   The] City of Mexico,   :
   The MS
429.19,31; 430.16   North] north
   MS
429.33   make] makes MS
430.34   familiar] familar MS
430.38   its] it's MS

431.22   States] states MS
431.23–24   simultaneous] simal-
   taneous MS
431.34   sinister,] ~ ∧ | MS
431.39   portentous] portentious
   MS

No. 89. THE VIGA CANAL

[The copy-text is MS: manuscript in the Special Collections of Columbia University Libraries.]

432.3   The] City of Mexico, The
   MS
432.7   pulque∧shops] ~ - ~ MS
432.16   boatmen] boatman MS
433.3   rhythmically] rythmically
   MS
433.5   Popocatepetl] Popocatapetl
   MS
433.8 et seq.   its] it's MS

433.10–11   contemplative.] ~ ∧
   MS
433.14   tamales] tomales MS
433.15   clothing] clotheing MS
434.28   manoeuvred] manoevred
   MS
434.34   portentous] portentious
   MS

No. 90. THE MEXICAN LOWER CLASSES

[The copy-text is MS: manuscript in the Special Collections of Columbia University Libraries.]

435.21   Above] City of Mexico,   :
   —Above MS
435.21   foreign] foriegn MS
435.27   "How] ' ~ MS
435.28   remarks,] ~ ∧ MS (the
   following quotes are doubtful)
436.26   its] it's MS

436.39   not] omit MS
437.2 et seq.   perceive] percieve
   MS
438.3   run] ran MS
438.9   Rockefeller] Rockafeller
   MS
438.25   clothing] clotheing MS

No. 91. STEPHEN CRANE IN MEXICO (I)

[The copy-text is N¹: Nebraska State Journal, May 19, 1895, p. 13. The other texts collated are N²: Galveston Daily News, May 19, p. 13; N³: Buffalo Morning News, May 19, p. 11; N⁴: Louisville Courier-Journal, May 19, part II, p. 7; N⁵: Philadelphia Press, May 19, p. 33; N⁶: Chicago Daily News, June 6, p. 10; N⁷: Rochester Democrat and Chronicle, May 19, p. 9; N⁸: Savannah Morning News, May 16, p. 9.]

439.36   daylights] N²,⁶⁻⁸; day∧|
   lights N¹ (not flush at right
   margin, hyphen possibly fell
   out); ~ - | ~ N³⁻⁴; ~ -|light
   N⁵
440.21   conducted∧] $N(−N¹);
   ~ , N¹

441.6   then] $N(−N¹); them N¹
441.22   de] V; de $N
441.32   wouldn't] $N(−N¹);
   wouldnt N¹
442.37   little] $N(−N¹); lit-|the
   N¹

No. 92. FREE SILVER DOWN IN MEXICO

[The copy-text is N[1](p): proof for the *Nebraska State Journal*, June 30, 1895, p. 13, in the Special Collections of Columbia University Libraries. The other texts collated are N[1]: *Nebraska State Journal* (it should be noted that no differences have been observed between N[1] and its proof, and that the designation N[1] in this instance refers to both the proof and the final published form); N[2]: *Cincinnati Commercial Gazette*, June 30, p. 9; N[3]: *Chicago Daily News*, July 23, p. 2; N[4]: *Minneapolis Tribune*, June 30, p. 4; N[5]: *Galveston Daily News*, July 1, p. 4; N[6]: *Philadelphia Press*, June 30, p. 31.]

444.8   South] N[2,6]; south $N(−N[2,6])

444.13   hoard] N[3]; horde $N(−N[3])

444.30   nevertheless] $N(−N[1]); neverthless N[1]

*446.25   tortillas] *stet* $N

No. 93. STEPHEN CRANE IN MEXICO (II)

[The copy-text to 451.2 is N[1](p): proof for the *Nebraska State Journal*, July 21, 1895, p. 13, in the Special Collections of Columbia University Libraries. After 451.2 the copy-text is N[1]: *Nebraska State Journal* (it should be noted that no differences have been observed between N[1] and its proof, and that the designation N[1] in this instance refers to both the proof and the final published form); N[2]: *Galveston Daily News*, July 21, p. 10; N[3]: *Cincinnati Commercial Gazette*, July 21, p. 18; N[4]: *Philadelphia Press*, July 21, p. 32; N[5]: *New Orleans Times-Democrat*, July 23, p. 8; N[6]: *Rochester Democrat and Chronicle*, July 21, p. 16.]

447.7   North, East, South, West] N[3-4]; north, east, south, west $N(−N[3-4])

447.21   uh?'] $N(−N[1,4]); ~ ?" N[1,4]

447.21   yes,] $N(−N[1]) (N[4,6]: Yes,); ~ . N[1] (*single quotes very faint*)

447.21   certainly] N[2,5]; Certainly N[1,3-4,6]

447.23   ˄up] $N(−N[1,4]); " ~ N[1]; ' ~ N[4]

447.23   North] N[4]; north $N(−N[4])

447.24   "and] $N(−N[1,4]); ˄ ~ N[1,4]

447.25   can——"] $N(−N[1,3]); ~ —— ˄ N[1]; ~"—— N[3]

447.31   you're] $N(−N[1,6]); you've N[1,6]

448.18   shadow-blue] V; ~ —— ~ $N

448.27   manœuvered] V; manœvered N[1]; maneuvered $N(−N[1])

448.33   is,] $N(−N[1,6]); ~ ˄ N[1,6]

448.34   Limited] V; limited $N

449.1   passengers] $N(−N[1]); passenger N[1]

449.11   and] $N(−N[1]); aud N[1]

449.32   consequence] $N(−N[1]); conseqnence N[1]

450.2   approvingly] $N(−N[1]); approviugly N[1]

450.21   paused] N[3]; passed $N(−N[3])

451.1   rhythmically] N[2-4]; rythmically N[1,5-6]

451.15   portentously] N[2-3,5]; portentiously N[1,4,6]

451.16   train] N[6]; trains $N(−N[6])

451.25   sage-brush] V; ~ ˄ ~ $N

451.33   traveller] V; traveler $N

452.3   caballero's] V; cabellero's $N

452.4   toward] N[2-4]; towards N[1,5-6]

453.7,22,28   travellers] V; travelers $N

453.9   you?"] $N(—N[1]); ~ ?' N[1]

453.28   tamales] N[2]; tomales $N(—N[2])

454.36   Nevado] V; Nevada $N(—N[5]); the Nevada N[5]

455.7   [2]iron ore] $N(—N[1]); ironore N[1]

455.14   harangued] N[2-4]; haranged N[1,6]; harranged N[5]

456.8   maguey] N[3]; mague N[1-2,4,6]; bague N[5]

456.15   ridge.] $N(—N[1]); ~ , N[1]

456.22   manœuvered] V; manœvered N[1,3-4](N[3-4]: manoevered); maneuvered N[2,6]; manoeuvered N[5]

No. 94. A JAG OF PULQUE IS HEAVY

[The copy-text is N[1]: *Nebraska State Journal*, Aug. 12, 1895, p. 5. The other texts collated are N[2]: *Salt Lake City Tribune*, Aug. 11, p. 15; N[3]: *Cincinnati Commercial Gazette*, Aug. 11, p. 17; N[4]: *Philadelphia Press*, Aug. 11, p. 26; N[5]: *Galveston Daily News*, Aug. 10, p. 9; N[6]: *Rochester Democrat and Chronicle*, Aug. 11, p. 10.]

457.16   appearance] $N(—N[1]); appearence N[1]

457.26   circumstances] $N(—N[1]); circumstaces N[1]

457.37   miniature] $N(—N[1]); minerature N[1]

457.38   Orient] N[2-4,6]; orient N[1,5]

458.14   familiar] $N(—N[1]); familar N[1]

458.24   maguey] N[2-5]; maguery N[1,6]

458.31   County] $N(—N[1])(N[2,5-6]: county); Co. N[1]

458.39   maguey] $N(—N[1]); maquey N[1]

459.5   do] V; does $N

459.21   Canal] V; canal $N

No. 95. THE FETE OF MARDI GRAS

[The copy-text is N[1](p): proof for the *Nebraska State Journal*, Feb. 16, 1896, p. 11, in the Special Collections of Columbia University Libraries. The other texts collated are N[1]: *Nebraska State Journal* (it should be noted that no differences have been observed between N[1] and its proof, and that the designation N[1] in this instance refers to both the proof and the final published form); N[2]: *Philadelphia Press*, Feb. 16, p. 30; N[3]: *Cincinnati Commercial Gazette*, Feb. 23, p. 19; N[4]: *New Orleans Times-Democrat*, Feb. 17, p. 9; N[5]: *Rochester Democrat and Chronicle*, Feb. 16, p. 9.]

461.17   eyes[∧]] N[2-4]; ~ — N[1,5]

461.36   an'] $N(—N[1]); ~ [∧] N[1]

461.36   gittin'] N[3-5]; ~ [∧] N[1-2]

463.5   inscrutable] V; inscrutible $N

464.22   pantomime] N[3-4]; pantomine N[1-2,5]

464.31   imperturbable] N[2,4-5]; imperturbable N[1,3]

465.20   Comus'] N[4]; their N[1-2,5]

No. 96. HATS, SHIRTS, AND SPURS IN MEXICO

[The copy-text is N[1]: *Detroit Free Press*, Oct. 18, 1896, p. 20. The other texts collated are N[2]: *Louisville Courier-Journal*, Oct. 18, sec. III, p. 2;

N³: *Buffalo Evening News*, Oct. 18, p. 9; N⁴: *San Francisco Chronicle*, Oct. 18, p. 12; N⁵: *Galveston Daily News*, Oct. 18, p. 10; N⁶: *Nebraska State Journal*, Oct. 18, p. 9; N⁷: *Philadelphia Press*, Oct. 18, p. 34; N⁸: *Chicago Daily News*, Oct. 29, p. 5; N⁹: *St. Louis Globe-Democrat*, Oct. 18, p. 33; N¹⁰: *Rochester Democrat and Chronicle*, Oct. 18, p. 9.]

465.27 grey] N³,⁶; gray $N(−N³,⁶)

465.28 artistic] $N(−N¹); art stic N¹

466.1 This] $N(−N¹); The N¹

466.2 Mexico_∧] N²,⁴,⁶⁻⁹; ~ , N¹,³,⁵,¹⁰

466.25 holy] $N(−N¹); *omit* N¹

466.26 innate] $N(−N¹,⁶); inate N¹,⁶

466.26 vivid] $N(−N¹); *omit* N¹

466.31 *et seq.* I.] N³,⁶⁻⁸,¹⁰; 1. N¹,⁵,⁹; First N²,⁴

467.1 China] $N(−N¹,⁷); china N¹; hina N⁷

467.14 lanterns] $N(−N¹); lantern N¹

467.19 here] $N(−N¹); in the

city of Mexico N¹

467.20 country,] N²⁻⁷,⁹; ~ _∧ N¹,⁸,¹⁰

467.29 variety_∧] $N(−N¹,⁵); ~ , N¹,⁵

467.30–31 But . . . similarity.] $N(−N¹); *omit* N¹

467.32 side] $N(−N¹); the side N¹

468.1 or not] $N(−N¹,⁴,⁸); *omit* N¹,⁸; or red, N⁴

468.1 or of] $N(−N¹,¹⁰); or N¹,¹⁰

468.6 by] $N(−N¹); with N¹

468.8 mystic] $N(−N¹); majestic N¹

468.11 the melted] $N(−N¹) melted N¹

468.13 of] $N(−N¹); *omit* N¹

No. 97. STEPHEN CRANE IN TEXAS

[The copy-text is N¹: *Pittsburgh Leader*, Jan. 8, 1899, p. 23. The other texts collated are N²: *Savannah Morning News*, Jan. 8, p. 10; N³: *Omaha Daily Bee*, Jan. 8, p. 15; N⁴: *Louisville Courier-Journal*, Jan. 8, sec. III, p. 4; N⁵: *St. Louis Globe-Democrat*, Jan. 8, sec. III, p. 6.]

468.30 uproar_∧] N²⁻⁵; ~ , N¹

469.1,6 North] N⁴⁻⁵; north N¹⁻³

469.25 not] N²⁻⁵; *omit* N¹

469.26 ago_∧] N³⁻⁵; ~ , N¹⁻²

469.30 stubborn_∧] N²⁻⁵; ~ , N¹

469.37 farms_∧] N³⁻⁵; ~ , N¹⁻²

470.24 relic_∧hunters] N²⁻³,⁵; ~ - ~ N¹,⁴

470.25 relic_∧hunters] N²⁻⁵; ~ - | ~ N¹

470.29 on_∧] N²⁻⁴; ~ , N¹,⁵

470.33 meantime,] N²,⁴⁻⁵; ~ _∧ N¹,³

470.33 portentous] N⁴⁻⁵; porten-tious N¹⁻²; pretentous N³

471.2 stuff,] N²⁻⁴; ~ _∧ N¹,⁵

471.3 strong,] N²⁻⁴; ~ _∧ N¹,⁵

471.10 populous] N²,⁴⁻⁵; popular N¹,³

471.15 pauses] N²⁻⁵; pause N¹

471.20; 472.1–2 one hundred and fifty] N⁴; 150 N¹⁻³,⁵

471.21 frontier_∧] N²⁻³,⁵; ~ , N¹,⁴

471.21 chances] N²⁻⁵; chanches N¹

471.23 Afterward,] N²⁻⁵; ~ _∧ N¹

471.24 Louisiana_∧] N²⁻³,⁵; ~ , N¹,⁴

471.36 parapet_∧] N²⁻⁵; ~ , N¹

472.5–6 appalling] N²⁻⁵; appaliing N¹

472.8 sealed. * * *] N²⁻⁵; ~ . . . . N¹

472.11–12 enemy. * * *] N²⁻⁵; ~ . . . . N¹

472.22–23 There is] N²⁻⁵; There's N¹

472.29 mingled] N²⁻⁵; m ngled N¹

472.34 eight_∧] N²⁻⁵; ~ , N¹

472.34 quarter$_\wedge$ . . . course$_\wedge$]
N$^{2-5}$; $\sim$, . . . $\sim$, N^1
473.4 faces$_\wedge$] N$^{2-4}$; $\sim$, N^{1,5}
473.7 plazas,] N$^{2-4}$(N^2: piazzas);
$\sim$ $_\wedge$ N^1
473.9 hades] N$^{2-3}$; Hades N^{1,4}
473.9 chili con carne] V; Chili
concarne $N
473.9 tamales] V; tomales $N
473.9 frijoles] V; frjoles $N

473.10 atmosphere] $N($-N^1);
atmbosphere N^1
473.10 night,] N$^{2-4}$; $\sim$ $_\wedge$ N^1
473.11 crystal$_\wedge$] N$^{2-4}$; $\sim$, N^1
473.14 long$_\wedge$] N^{2,4}; $\sim$, N^{1,3}
473.31 artillery$_\wedge$] N$^{2-3}$; $\sim$, N^{1,4}
473.35 besides] V; beside N$^{1-4}$
473.36 general,] N$^{2-4}$; $\sim$ $_\wedge$ N^1
473.37 make] N$^{2-4}$; inake N^1

No. 98. GALVESTON, TEXAS, IN 1895

[The copy-text is WG: *Westminster Gazette*, Nov. 6, 1900, pp. 1–2. The *Westminster Budget* reprints this on Nov. 16, p. 22, cutting out three paragraphs 478.14–37 in order to print the article on one page.]

474.9 south-western] South-
Western WG
474.28–29 in Syracuse] to Syracuse WG
474.29 city$_\wedge$] $\sim$, WG
474.35 *et seq.* color] colour WG

475.13 clamoring] clamouring
WG
476.12,38 harbor] harbour WG
476.38; 477.13 Eastern] eastern
WG

No. 99. QUEENSTOWN

[The copy-text is N^1: *New York Journal*, Oct. 18, 1897, p. 6. The other texts collated are WG: *Westminster Gazette*, Oct. 19, pp. 1–2; N^2: *Kansas City Star*, Oct. 24, p. 5. N^2 is a derived text without authority.]

483.1 rain-coats] WG; $\sim$ $_\wedge$ $\sim$ N^1
483.2 coast-line] WG; $\sim$ $_\wedge$ $\sim$ N^1
483.3 rain-mist] WG; $\sim$ $_\wedge$ $\sim$ N^1
483.9 *et seq.* Howe] WG; Howe
N^1
483.24 water-front] WG; $\sim$ $_\wedge$ $\sim$
N^1
483.27 grey] WG; gray N^1
483.28 *et seq.* jaunting-car] WG;
$\sim$ $_\wedge$ $\sim$ N^1
483.31 fellow-drivers] WG; $\sim$ $_\wedge$
$\sim$ N^1
484.1 gang-plank] WG;
gangplank N^1
484.19 natural] WG; natuarl N^1
484.21 top-coat] WG; topcoat N^1
484.21 sentry-box] WG; $\sim$ $_\wedge$ $\sim$
N^1

484.25 formulæ] WG; formulae
N^1
484.25 car-drivers] WG; $\sim$ $_\wedge$ $\sim$
N^1
484.36 strange$_\wedge$] WG; $\sim$, N^1
485.10 intelligence.] WG; $\sim$ $_\wedge$ N^1
485.11–24 For . . . Jerry?] WG;
omit N^1
485.14 form$_\wedge$] V; $\sim$, WG
485.25 ^{1}Jerry (*no* ¶)] WG; ¶ N^1
485.26 -car$_\wedge$] WG; $_\wedge$ $\sim$, N^1
485.26 $_\wedge$sates for fure$_\wedge$] WG; " $\sim$
$\sim$ $\sim$ " N^1
485.37 by-roads] WG; byroads
N^1
486.3 steam-engine] WG; $\sim$ $_\wedge$ $\sim$
N^1

No. 100. BALLYDEHOB

[The copy-text is WG: *Westminster Gazette*, Oct. 22, 1897, pp. 1–2. The other texts collated are WB: *Westminster Budget*, Nov. 5, p. 15; TMs:

typescript in the UVa.–Barrett Collection; E1: *Last Words,* Digby, Long, London, 1902, pp. 198–203. The two latter texts are completely derived and without authority.]

486.34 humor] V; humour WG+
487.12–13 a cow] WB; cow WG

488.6 recognize] V; recognise WG+

No. 101. THE ROYAL IRISH CONSTABULARY

[The copy-text is WG: *Westminster Gazette,* Nov. 5, 1897, pp. 1–2. The other texts collated are TMs: typescript in the UVa.–Barrett Collection; E1: *Last Words,* Digby, Long, London, 1902, pp. 203–207. Both TMs and E1 are derived texts with no authority.]

491.32 rumor] V; rumour WG+

No. 102. A FISHING VILLAGE

[The copy-text is WG: *Westminster Gazette,* Nov. 12, 1897, pp. 1–2. The other texts collated are WB: *Westminster Budget,* Nov. 19, p. 13; Ph: *Philistine,* IX (Aug., 1899), 71–77; E1: *Last Words,* Digby, Long, London, 1902, pp. 207–213.]

493.18 " 'Tis] E1; "∧ ∼ WG,WB, Ph
493.23 want——"] WB+; ∼ ——." WG
493.26 'tis] E1; ∧tis WG,WB,Ph
494.1; 495.16 color] V; colour

WG+
494.23 laborers] V; labourers WG+
494.26 labor] V; labour WG+
495.21 toward] V; towards WG+

No. 103. AN OLD MAN GOES WOOING

[The copy-text is WG: *Westminster Gazette,* Nov. 23, 1897, pp. 1–2. The other texts collated are Ph: *Philistine,* IX (July, 1899), 44–50; E1: *Last Words,* Digby, Long, London, 1902, pp. 193–198.]

495.33 avenin',] E1; avenin,' WG,Ph
496.12 odor] V; odour WG+
496.21 clamor] V; clamour WG+
496.23 parlor] V; parlour WG+
497.4 laborer] V; labourer WG+
497.29 o'] E1,Ph; 'o WG

497.30,35 toward] V; towards WG+
498.2 pockets] E1; pocket WG, Ph
498.9 movements] V; moments WG+
498.27 labor] V; labour WG+

No. 104. AVON SEASIDE ASSEMBLY

[The copy-text is N[1]: *New York Tribune,* July 28, 1890, p. 4.]

501.26 *The Tribune*] The Tribune N[1]

No. 105. AVON'S SCHOOL BY THE SEA

[The copy-text is N[1]: *New York Tribune,* Aug. 4, 1890, p. 5.]

504.10 Gérôme's] Gerome's N[1]

504.23 co-laborer] colaborer N[1]

No. 106. BIOLOGY AT AVON-BY-THE-SEA

[The copy-text is N¹: *New York Tribune*, July 19, 1891, p. 22.]

506.8   Princeton] Princ_∧|ton N¹   507.1   efficient] efficent N¹

No. 107. HOWELLS DISCUSSED AT AVON-BY-THE-SEA

[The copy-text is N¹: *New York Tribune*, Aug. 18, 1891, p. 5.]

507.20   Hamlin] Hamblin N¹   *roman enclosed in single quotes*
507.32   Howells'] Howells's N¹   508.6   Howells'] Howell's N¹
507.34–508.4   *Their . . . For-*   508.8   Howells] Howell's N¹
tunes] N¹ *prints each title in*

No. 108. MEETINGS BEGUN AT OCEAN GROVE

[The copy-text is N¹: *New York Tribune*, July 2, 1892, p. 4.]

508.20   enthusiasm] enthusiam   508.31   address] oddress N¹
N¹   508.34   Grove,] ∼ ∧ N¹

No. 110. JOYS OF SEASIDE LIFE

[The copy-text is N¹: *New York Tribune*, July 17, 1892, p. 18.]

511.17   she] he N¹   514.1   villainously-] villanously-
512.39–513.1   hotel-porches] ∼ ∧   N¹
∼ N¹

No. 111. SUMMER DWELLERS AT ASBURY PARK AND THEIR DOINGS

[The copy-text is N¹: *New York Tribune*, July 24, 1892, p. 22.]

514.18   a large] alarge N¹   "How the Other Half Lives," N¹
514.29–30   *How . . . Lives,*]

No. 112. ON THE BOARDWALK

[The copy-text is N¹: *New York Tribune*, Aug. 14, 1892, p. 17.]

516.25   pavilions] pavlions N¹   519.30   or∧] ∼ , N¹
516.37   trundled] trundle N¹

No. 113. ALONG THE SHARK RIVER

[The copy-text is N¹: *New York Tribune*, Aug. 15, 1892, p. 4.]

520.1   (Special] ∧ ∼ N¹   521.6   fortunate] fortuntte N¹
520.21   privilege] previlege N¹   521.16   sea-weeds] ∼ ∧ ∼ N¹
520.25   LL.D.] L.L.D. N¹

No. 115. THE SEASIDE ASSEMBLY'S WORK AT AVON

[The copy-text is N¹: *New York Tribune*, Aug. 29, 1892, p. 4.]

523.8   of] or N¹   523.36   villainous] villanous N¹
523.16   Mrs.] ∼ ∧ N¹

No. 116. THE SEASIDE ASSEMBLY (II)

[The copy-text is N[1]: *New York Tribune*, Sept. 6, 1892, p. 4.]

526.19   Frederic] Frederick N[1]

No. 117. THE SEASIDE HOTEL HOP

[The copy-text is N[1]: *New York Tribune*, Sept. 11, 1892, p. 15.]

527.17   couples] couple N[1]   528.9,10   lancers] lanciers N[1]

No. 119. A PROSPEROUS YEAR AT ASBURY PARK

[The copy-text is N[1]: *New York Tribune*, July 14, 1889, p. 16.]

531.22   persons] prsons N[1]   532.36   in] is N[1]
532.18   House∧] ~ . N[1] (*doubt-fully*)

No. 121. JOYS OF THE JERSEY COAST

[The copy-text is N[1]: *New York Tribune*, Aug. 26, 1889, p. 5.]

534.22   pounds.] ~ , N[1]   535.19   -load] -loat N[1]

No. 124. THRONGS AT ASBURY PARK

[The copy-text is N[1]: *New York Tribune*, July 13, 1890, p. 22.]

537.11   every] very N[1]

No. 126. THE BABIES ON PARADE AT ASBURY PARK

[The copy-text is N[1]: *New York Tribune*, July 22, 1890, p. 7.]

539.23   *Trenton*] Trenton N[1]

No. 128. ASBURY PARK

[The copy-text is N[1]: *New York Tribune*, Aug. 24, 1890, p. 13.]

542.25   employees] employes N[1]

No. 129. ASBURY PARK'S BIG BROAD WALK

[The copy-text is N[1]: *New York Tribune*, Aug. 31, 1890, p. 13.]

543.12   until] untill N[1]

No. 132. ARRIVING AT OCEAN GROVE

[The copy-text is N[1]: *New York Tribune*, June 29, 1891, p. 5.]

546.24–25   cottages] cottagers N[1]   546.27   begun] began N[1]

No. 137. THE SEASIDE ASSEMBLY (I)

[The copy-text is N[1]: *New York Tribune*, July 26, 1891, p. 19.]

551.13 School of Art] school of art N¹
553.19 Gérôme's] Gerome's N¹

*554.2 plans] plates N¹
*554.16 lincrusta] *stet* N¹
554.28 island] inland N¹

No. 139. THE GUESTS ROSE TO THE OCCASION

[The copy-text is N¹: *New York Tribune,* Aug. 12, 1891, p. 2.]

556.23 "Coffee"] ∧ ~ " N¹

556.24 haven't] havn't N¹

No. 140. ART AT AVON-BY-THE-SEA

[The copy-text is N¹: *New York Tribune,* Aug. 16, 1891, p. 19.]

557.10–11 Besides] Beside N¹

557.21 pupils] puipls N¹

No. 141. FLOWERS AT ASBURY PARK

[The copy-text is N¹: *New York Tribune,* June 19, 1892, p. 22.]

558.29 decidedly] deciddly N¹

No. 143. BABY PARADE AT ASBURY PARK

[The copy-text is N¹: *New York Tribune,* July 31, 1892, p. 9.]

560.15 papoose] pappoose N¹

No. 146. HENRY M. STANLEY

[The copy-text is Vd: *Vidette,* Feb., 1890, pp. 8–9.]

566.16 congratulations] con-| ratgulations Vd

566.37 seems] seem Vd

No. 147. BASEBALL

[The copy-text is Vd: *Vidette,* May, 1890, p. 11.]

567.21 base-ball] ~ ∧ ~ Vd
567.31 worst] worse Vd

568.16 C] c Vd

No. 148. THE KING'S FAVOR

[The copy-text is UH: *University Herald,* XIX (May, 1891), 128–131.]

569.28 loveliest] lovliest UH
570.26 possessed] posessed UH
570.29 six-feet-two-inches] ~ ∧
~ ∧ ~ ∧ ~ UH
571.6 accompanied] accom-
panyed UH

571.7 interpreter] intrepreter UH
571.8 received] recieved UH
572.20 Mursala] Marsula UH
572.24 men.] ~ ∧ UH
572.35 interpreter] intepreter UH

No. 149. A FOREIGN POLICY, IN THREE GLIMPSES

[The copy-text is MS: manuscript in the UVa.–Barrett Collection.]

574.9.1 *et seq.* Foreign] Foriegn
MS

574.15 men∧] ~ , MS
574.18 *et seq.* its] it's MS

574.19   perceive] percieve MS
574.27   alacrity] alcrity MS
575.3 *et seq.*   shriek] shreik MS
575.10,20;   576.24,30;   577.24,28, 30,31   *Indention doubtful, but a space appears to separate two paragraphs*
575.17.1   II] Chapter II MS
575.22   shrieks] shreiks MS
575.30; 576.6   writhing] writheing MS
575.30   native_∧] ~ , MS
576.3,32; 577.22,26,33; 578.5   *Indention doubtful, line heads page*

576.9   officer] officier MS
576.10   chieftain,] ~ _∧ MS
576.15   know."] ~ . _∧ MS
576.16,28; 577.35   *Indention doubtful, but preceding line is short and paragraph appears to be spaced*
576.20   villain] villian MS
576.28   devil's] devils MS
577.18   sufficient] sufficent MS
577.28   Mr.] ~ _∧ MS
578.4.1   Glimpse] Glimpe MS
578.7   a] *omit* MS
578.11   conceited] concieted MS
578.16   b'gad."] ~ . _∧ MS

No. 150. GREAT BUGS IN ONONDAGA

[The copy-text is N[1]: *Syracuse Daily Standard*, June 1, 1891, p. 6. The other text collated is N[2]: *New York Tribune*, June 1, 1891, p. 1.]

578.25   Railroad] N[2]; railroad N[1]
579.4   Day] N[2]; day N[1]
579.13   sixty] N[2]; 60 N[1]
579.13   the tracks] N[2]; the the tracks N[1]
579.15   began] N[2]; begun N[1]
579.16   scudded] V; scud N[1]; ran N[2]

579.18   electric-light] V; ~ _∧ ~ N[1-2]
579.24   iron monster] N[2]; engine N[1]
579.30–580.14   An examination . . . bugs.] N[2]; *omit* N[1]
580.14   bugs."] N[1] (*from* 579.30); ~ . _∧ N[2]

No. 151. THE WRECK OF THE "NEW ERA"

[The copy-text is MS: manuscript in the UVa.–Barrett Collection.]

580.21   J._∧] ~ . , MS
580.21 *et seq.*   New Era] New Era MS
581.4   Avenue] Ave MS
581.5 *et seq.*   its] it's MS
581.7   sufficient] sufficent MS
581.7   license] lincense MS
581.9,20,31; 584.7   *Indention doubtful, but preceding line is short, and this line in MS heads page*
581.13   three_∧hundred] ~ - ~ MS
581.31   A.] ~ _∧ MS
581.34   solemn] solomn MS
582.2   cabins] cabin MS

582.2   besieged] beseiged MS
582.2   officers] officiers MS
582.4   Shrieks] Shreiks MS
582.24   shrieking] shreiking MS
582.32–33   life-savers] live-savers MS
583.1   stopped.] ~ _∧ MS
583.4   capsized] cap-sized MS
583.8   resuscitate] resusicate MS
583.10   windrows] winrows MS
583.19   relieved] releaved MS
583.20   borne] born MS
583.38   boats] boat MS
584.18   communicated] cummunicated MS

No. 152. ACROSS THE COVERED PIT

[The copy-text is MS: manuscript in the UVa.–Barrett Collection.]

584.21	Conn.,] $\sim_\wedge{}_\wedge$ MS
584.23	Sunday,] $\sim_\wedge$ MS
584.29	^{2}its] it's MS
585.2,32	its] it's MS
585.7	huge] hugh MS
585.19	however,] $\sim_\wedge$ MS
585.21	William, . . . guide,] $\sim_\wedge$ . . . $\sim_\wedge$ MS
585.26	stealthily] stealthly MS
585.29	they] They MS

585.35	cavern.] $\sim_\wedge$ MS
586.2	pierce] peirce MS
586.7	casualty] casuality MS
586.7	might] might a MS
586.7	occur] occurr MS
586.27	doctor's] doctors MS
586.36	of] of	of MS
586.38	earth$_\wedge$] $\sim$, MS
587.10	possible.] $\sim$ # MS
587.19	too.] $\sim$ # MS

No. 153. THE GRATITUDE OF A NATION

[The copy-text is MS: manuscript in the Special Collections of Columbia University Libraries.]

587.20	ambitions,] $\sim_\wedge$ MS
587.21	alive,] $\sim_\wedge$ MS
587.28	grey-beard] greybeard MS
588.9; 590.5	its] it's MS

588.11	Its] It's MS
588.11	grimmest] grimest MS
589.13	is] *omit* MS
589.32	solemn] solomn MS

No. 154. IN THE DEPTHS OF A COAL MINE

[The copy-text is McC: *McClure's Magazine*, III (Aug. 1894), 195–209. The other texts collated are MS: manuscript draft version in the UVa.– Barrett Collection; N^1: *Detroit Free Press*, July 22, 1894, p. 2; N^2: *St. Paul Pioneer Press*, July 22, p. 13; N^3: *Buffalo Express*, July 22, p. 17; N^4: *Philadelphia Inquirer*, July 22, p. 21; N^5: *St. Louis Republic*, July 22, part III, p. 17.]

590.24	$_\wedge$breakers$_\wedge$] MS (*quotes deleted*); " $\sim$ " McC
590.25	monsters$_\wedge$] MS; $\sim$, McC
590.28	the vegetation] MS; vegetation McC
590.29	summit-line] MS; $\sim_\wedge\sim$ McC
590.29	mountain,] MS; $\sim_\wedge$ McC
590.32	coal-dust] MS; $\sim_\wedge\sim$ McC
590.33	The] MS; A McC
590.33	$_\wedge$breaker$_\wedge$] V; " $\sim$ " MS, McC
591.1	peak$_\wedge$] MS; $\sim$, McC
591.1	sides] *stet* McC; side MS
591.6	hats$_\wedge$] MS; $\sim$, McC
591.7	carelessly,] V; $\sim_\wedge$ MS; $\sim$; McC
*591.12	the] MS; a McC,$N
591.15	coal-cars] MS; $\sim_\wedge\sim$ McC,$N

591.16	us$_\wedge$] N$^{1-4}$; $\sim$, MS,McC, N^5
591.16	up-reared] V; upreared MS,McC
591.17	each,] MS; $\sim_\wedge$ McC,$N
591.20	southward$_\wedge$] MS; $\sim$, McC,$N
591.21	grey] MS,N^2; gray McC, $N(−N^2)$
591.21–22	cloud$_\wedge$ . . . chimneys$_\wedge$] MS,$N(−N^4)$; $\sim$, . . . $\sim$, McC,N^4
591.24	dragged$_\wedge$ creaking$_\wedge$] MS (went); $\sim$, McC,$N
591.25	cable-road] MS,N^3; $\sim_\wedge$ $\sim$ McC,$N(−N^3)$
591.25	$_\wedge$breaker.$_\wedge$] MS,N^3; " $\sim$." McC,$N(−N^3)$
591.26	$_\wedge$breaker,$_\wedge$] MS; " $\sim$," McC; " $\sim_\wedge$ " $N(−N^{3-4})$; $_\wedge\sim{}_\wedge{}_\wedge$ N$^{3-4}$

591.28 building‸] MS,$N; ~ ,
McC
591.30 places,] MS; ~ ‸ McC,$N
*591.31 go] stet McC; to go MS
591.32 thing‸] MS,N¹; ~ , McC,
$N(−N¹)
*591.33–36 A . . . uproar.] stet
McC,$N; omit MS
591.38 coal‸] MS,N¹,⁴; ~ , McC,
N²⁻³,⁵
591.39 teeth‸] MS(cylinders‸),
N¹,⁴; ~ , McC,N²⁻³,⁵
592.1 troughs‸] MS; ~ , McC,$N
*592.3 were] stet McC,MS,N¹⁻²;
was N³⁻⁵
592.9 ways‸] MS; ~ , McC,$N
592.10 more‸] MS; ~ , McC,$N
592.11 independence‸] N¹,³⁻⁵;
~ , McC
592.20 -pickers, . . . region,]
MS; ~ ‸ . . . ~ ‸ McC,$N
*592.21 One . . . wonders] stet
McC; One wonders continually
MS
592.21 mothers‸] MS,N¹,³⁻⁴; ~ ,
McC, N⁵
592.24 culm-heap] MS(dump-
heap); ~ ‸ ~ McC,$N
592.24 base-ball] MS; baseball
McC,$N
592.25 ‸breakers,‸] MS; " ~ ‸ "
McC,N¹,⁴⁻⁵; ‸ ~ ‸ ‸ N³
592.27 mines‸] MS,N¹; ~ ; McC;
~ , N³⁻⁵
*592.27 -boys. And] MS,N¹,³⁻⁴; ~ ;
and McC; ~ ‸ and N⁵
592.28 later‸] MS(after that‸),
N¹,⁴; ~ , McC,N³,⁵
*592.28 Finally‸] MS(And fi-
nally‸); ~ , McC,$N
592.29 men‸] MS,N¹,³; ~ , McC,
N²,⁵
*592.30–31 to a . . . estate] stet
McC,N¹,⁴⁻⁵; omit MS,N³
592.33 Meanwhile,] MS; ~ ‸
McC,$N
592.36 pallidly,] MS; ~ ‸ McC,
$N (MS possibly , pallidly,)
592.38 it,] MS; ~ ‸ McC,$N
593.5 ‸breaker‸] N³; " ~ " McC,
N⁵

593.7 tool house] MS,N¹⁻²,⁴; ~ -
~ McC,N³; toolhouse N⁵
593.7 house,] MS,N⁴⁻⁵; ~ , McC,
N¹⁻³
593.7 man, . . . pipe,] MS; ~ ‸
. . . ~ ‸ McC,$N
593.8 down,] MS; ~ ‸ McC,$N
*593.9 shaft] stet McC,$N; mouth
MS
593.10 -wheel, . . . by,] MS;
~ ‸ . . . ~ ‸ McC,$N
593.13 elevator,] MS; ~ ‸ McC,
$N
*593.14 opportunity] stet McC,$N;
an opportunity MS
593.17 crime] MS,$N; crimes
McC
593.18 black‸] MS,N⁴; ~ , McC,
$N(−N⁴)
593.19 sudden,] MS; ~ ‸ McC,$N
593.23 centre] MS,N⁴; center
McC,$N(−N⁴)
593.24 later,] MS; ~ ‸ McC,$N
593.26 machinery‸] MS,$N
(−N⁵); ~ , McC,N⁵
593.26 landscape‸] MS,N³⁻⁵; ~ ,
McC,N¹⁻²
594.13 us,] MS; ~ ‸ McC,$N
*594.18 us. It was a] $N; us, as
if the roof were McC
594.24 tiny‸] MS(little‸),N³; ~ ,
McC,$N(−N³)
594.26 Presently,] MS; ~ ‸ McC,
$N
594.33 faces‸] MS; ~ , McC,$N
594.35 et seq. eye-balls] MS;
eyeballs McC,$N
594.37 on] MS; in McC,$N
595.1 said‸] MS,N¹,³; ~ , McC,
N²,⁵; ~ : N⁴
595.1 Jim‸] MS; ~ , McC,$N
595.6 bended] MS; bent McC,$N
*595.13 up] stet McC,$N; omit MS
595.26 chambers‸] MS; ~ , McC,
$N
595.27 miner‸] MS; ~ , McC,$N
595.27 blasts‸] MS; ~ , McC,$N
595.28 laborer‸] MS; ~ , McC,
$N
595.32 Sometimes,] MS; ~ ‸
McC,$N

595.33 Once₍ₐ₎] MS,$N; ~ , McC
595.35 up-reared] MS; upreared McC,$N
*595.36 uprose] *stet* McC; arose MS
596.2 mule₍ₐ₎] MS,N¹,³; ~ , McC, N⁵
596.3 us,] MS; ~ ₍ₐ₎ McC,$N
596.6 laughed₍ₐ₎] MS; ~ , McC, $N
596.8 instant,] MS; ~ ₍ₐ₎ McC,$N
596.9 eyes,] MS; ~ ₍ₐ₎ McC,$N
596.20 up-ward] MS; upward McC,$N
596.22 -boys₍ₐ₎] MS; ~ , McC,$N
596.27 crashing₍ₐ₎] MS,$N; ~ , McC
596.29 tunnel,] MS; ~ ₍ₐ₎ McC,$N
597.17 yeh] N³; you McC,N²,⁴⁻⁵
*597.19 th'] *stet* McC,N³; the N²,⁴⁻⁵
597.31 wondrously,] $N; ~ ₍ₐ₎ McC
*598.11 these animals] $N; the mules McC
598.12 earth,] $N; ~ ₍ₐ₎ McC
598.14 breezes₍ₐ₎] $N; ~ , McC
598.15 Once a] $N; A McC
598.18–19 into the . . . the hill-side] $N(N²: to the; N¹⁻²: a hillside); *omit* McC
598.21–22 He had . . . famous.] $N; *omit* McC
598.30 They . . . children.] $N; *omit* McC
598.31 once] $N; *omit* McC
598.32 resolute] $N; *omit* McC
598.33–35 trot . . . place.] $N; follow. McC
598.36 sun-light] V; sunlight McC,$N
598.37 dream.] N⁵; dream of a lost paradise. McC
598.37 when] N⁵; as McC
598.38–599.1 in rows . . . para-dise.] N⁵; flapping their ears. McC
599.1 bloom] N⁵; bloomland McC
599.4–7 We . . . mass.] MS,N³,⁵; *omit* McC
599.7–8 (*no* ¶) In . . . grue-some] MS,N³,⁵(N⁵: grewsome); ¶ In wet mines, gruesome McC
599.10 ₍ₐ₎ too₍ₐ₎ there] MS; , too, McC; , too, there N³,⁵
599.11 dens₍ₐ₎] MS; ~ , McC,$N (*i.e.* N³,⁵)
599.12 sun-light] MS; sunlight McC,$N(*i.e.* N³,⁵)
599.15 slightly₍ₐ₎] MS,$N; ~ , McC
599.18 insidious₍ₐ₎] MS,N³⁻⁴; ~ , McC,N¹⁻²
599.19 fan-wheel] MS; fanwheel McC,$N
599.20–22 death₍ₐ₎ and . . . rock.] $N±; death. McC
599.22 may] $N; *omit* McC
599.37–38 In . . . always.] $N (–N²)(N¹: gave); *omit* McC, N²
599.38–600.7 I had . . . eleva-tor] N³⁻⁴; *omit* McC,N¹⁻²
600.7 down] N³⁻⁴; Down McC
*600.16 were sent] MS(c),$N; went McC,MS(u)
600.18 ₍ₐ₎breaker₍ₐ₎] MS,N³; " ~ " McC,N¹,⁴⁻⁵

No. 154a. FIRST DRAFT

[The copy-text is MS: manuscript first draft in the UVa.–Barrett Collection.]

600.28 breaker] V; " ~ " MS, McC
600.31 *et seq.* its] McC; it's MS
601.38 past] V; passed MS(u); passt MS(c[*second 's' unde-leted in error*])
602.2 villainy] V; villiany MS
602.25 "squeezed,"] McC; " ~ ", MS(*doubtfully*)
602.32 breathing] V; breatheing MS
603.1 slimy] McC; slimey MS

604.11   drill₍ₐ₎] McC; ~ , MS
     (*doubtfully*)
604.13   Jim?"] McC; ~ "? MS
604.15   ain't] McC; aint MS
604.38   "China,"] V; " ~ ", MS
     (*doubtfully*)
605.3   China,"] V; ~ ", MS

605.26   ceiling] McC; cieling MS
605.28   shrivel] V; shrivels MS
605.34   mine's] McC; mines MS
606.4   squeezes,"] McC; ~ ", MS
606.24   succeeded,] V; ~ ₍ₐ₎ | MS
607.22   increased] V; encreased
     MS

No. 155. PIKE COUNTY PUZZLE

[The copy-text is P: *Pike County Puzzle*, Aug. 28, 1894, pp. 1–4. Most of the numerous typographical errors in the original have been silently corrected, such as wrong-font letters, turned letters, commas for periods and the reverse, and semicolons for colons. Transposed letters forming misspellings are probably typographical but have been recorded on the odd chance that they were intended. Due to the form of this piece, all written lines (other than editorial information supplied in brackets) are numbered.]

608.27   -mirror] -miror P
609.6   mournfully] monrnfully P
610.2   prairie] prarie P
615.24   enthusiastically] enthui-
     astically P
615.25   responsible] responsiele P
616.13   Winnipeg] Winnepeg P
616.21   enthusiasm] enthuriasm
     P
618.21   advise] advises P
619.12   billions] billons P
620.24   agrees] agress P
621.19   ADVERTISEMENTS] AD-
     VERTISDMENTS P
622.9   yacht] yatch P
622.24   fire] flre P
623.15   -eighths] -eigths P

623.16   howled] howeled P
623.20   Pan-Cake Pete] Pan-cake
     Pete P
625.30   misfortune] misiortune P
627.8   valiantly] vailantly P
628.5   sphinx] sphnix P
628.24   sternness] sterness P
629.22   "Oh] ₍ₐ₎ ~ P
629.33   "Mamma] ₍ₐ₎ ~ P
629.35   don't] dont P
630.8   *Pan-Cake*] ~ ₍ₐ₎ ~ P
631.6   "All] ₍ₐ₎ ~ P
631.11   "Please] ₍ₐ₎ ~ P
631.35   it's] its P
631.36   "What] ₍ₐ₎ ~ P
633.24   (courteously] ₍ₐ₎ ~ P

No. 156. HOWELLS FEARS THE REALISTS MUST WAIT

[The copy-text is N(p): *McClure's* galley proof. The other texts collated are N[1]: *New York Times*, Oct. 28, 1894, p. 20; N[2]: *Philadelphia Inquirer*, Oct. 28, p. 9; N[3]: *Louisville Courier-Journal*, Oct. 28, p. 20; N[4]: *Boston Globe*, Nov. 4, p. 32; N[5]: *St. Paul Pioneer Press*, Nov. 6, p. 4.]

636.21   and art] N(p[c]); and
     act N(p[u]),$N
637.2   novel——"] $N; ~ " — —
     N(p)
637.13   conceive] $N;   concieve

N(p)
637.16   man. ₍ₐ₎] $N; ~ ." N(p)
638.25   coming. . . .] N[4]; ~ .
     * * * * N(p),$N(–N[1,4]); ~ .
     * * * N[1]

No. 157. GHOSTS ON THE JERSEY COAST

[The copy-text is N[1]: *New York Press*, Nov. 11, 1894, part IV, p. 2.]

639.11 *New Era*] New Era N¹   640.34 lights∧] ~ , N¹

No. 158. MISS LOUISE GERARD—SOPRANO

[The copy-text is MC: *Musical Courier*, XIX, No. 26 (Dec. 26, 1894), 30. The other text collated is MN: *Musical News*, I, No. 3 (Dec., 1894), 3.]

642.29 Gerard∧] MN; Gerard, whose picture is printed on the first page of this issue of THE MUSICAL COURIER, MC
642.33 this] MN; the MC
643.2–4 The . . . her.] MN; *omit* MC
643.5 Since (*no* ¶)] MN; ¶ MC
643.23 In (*no* ¶)] MN; ¶ MC
643.24 James's] V; James' MC; James MN
643.39 *Galignani's*] V; "Galignani's MC; Galignana's MN

643.39 *Messenger*] MN; Messenger" MC
644.4 *Cavalleria Rusticana*] V; 'Cavalleria Rusticana' MC; ∧ ~ ~ ∧ MN
644.8 *Messenger*] MN; "Messenger" MC
644.10 quite] MN; *omit* MC
644.11 Her] MN; A MC
644.11–12 in . . . *Journal*] MN; from her pen MC
644.30 *Herald*] V; " ~ " MC

No. 159. THE GHOSTLY SPHINX OF METEDECONK

[The copy-text is N¹(p): proof for *New York Press*, Jan. 13, 1895, part v, p. 1, in the Crane scrapbook in the Special Collections of Columbia University Libraries. No differences were observed between N¹ and its proof.]

645.12 opprobrium] approbrium N¹(p)
645.29 loudly] londly N¹(p)

645.35 blasé] blase N¹(p)
647.14 Absecon] Abescom N¹(p)

No. 160. SIX YEARS AFLOAT

[The copy-text is MS: manuscript in the Berg Collection of the New York Public Library. The other texts collated are N(p): galley proof in the Special Collections of Columbia University Libraries; N¹: *Pittsburgh Leader*, Aug. 2, 1896, p. 20; N²: *Portland Oregonian*, Aug. 2, p. 18. N¹⁻² are derived texts without authority.]

648.28 *et seq. Tillie B.*] V; Tillie B. MS,N²; Lillie B. N(p),N¹ (*except* 'Tillie' *after* 649.3)
649.3; 650.1 *B.*] N(p) (*not italicized*); ~ ∧ MS
649.14 land!] N(p); ~ . ! MS
649.22 don't] N(p); dont MS
649.24 seized] N(p); siezed MS
649.38 *U.S.S. Enterprise*] V; U. S. S. Enterprise MS,N(p),N¹; United States steamship Enterprise N²
649.39 *Grant*] V; Grant MS+
650.1 bark] N(p); Bark MS

650.6 customer] N(p); costumer MS
650.10 conceived] N(p); concieved MS
650.18 "This] V; ∧ ~ MS+
650.21 Scotia,] N(p); ~ ∧ MS
650.22 largest] N(p); longest MS
650.23 three hundred] N(p); 300 [*circled*] MS
650.24 four thousand] N(p); 4000 [*circled*] MS
650.24 six hundred] N(p); 600 [*circled*] MS

650.25 length—] N(p); ~ ∧ | MS
650.25 ten thousand] N(p);
    10000 [*circled*] MS
651.4 centre∧chain] N(p); ~ - ~
    MS
651.5,19,28 "The] V; ∧ ~ MS+
651.5 *et seq.* its] N(p); it's MS
651.10,26 "When] V; ∧ ~ MS+
651.10–11 twenty-five thousand]
    N(p); 25000 [*circled*] MS
651.11–12 thirty-five . . . ninety-
    five] N(p); 35 . . . 95
    [*circled*] MS
651.12 beech] V; beach MS+
651.13 four . . . thousand]

N(p); 4500000 [*circled*] MS
651.18 thirty-five] N(p); ~ ∧ ~
    MS
651.22 increased] N(p); en-
    creased MS
651.23 1,000] N(p); 1000 MS
651.33 "Having] V; ∧ ~ MS+
651.37 received] N(p); recieved
    MS
651.37 B.'s] N(p) (*not itali-
    cized*); B∧'s MS
652.4 Don't] N(p); Dont MS
652.8 *Actoronhisuppers*] V; Ac-
    toronhisuppers MS+

No. 161. ASBURY PARK AS SEEN BY STEPHEN CRANE

[The copy-text is N[1]: *New York Journal*, Aug. 16, 1896, p. 33. The other text collated is N[2]: *Kansas City Star*, Aug. 22, p. 2.]

652.18 differences] N[2]; dif-
    fernces N[1]

655.9 middle] N[2]; midde N[1]

No. 162. ADVENTURES OF A NOVELIST

[The copy-text is N[1]: *New York Journal*, Sept. 20, 1896, pp. 17–18.]

657.27 before——"] ~ "—— N[1]
658.32 I——"] ~ "—— N[1]
659.7–9 'We . . . girls.']

" ~ . . . ~ ." N[1]
659.14 "Suppose] ∧ ~ N[1]
659.26 "But] ∧ ~ N[1]

No. 162a. MANUSCRIPT FRAGMENT

[The copy-text is MS: manuscript fragment in the UVa.–Barrett Collection.]

661.21 can't] cant MS

No. 162b. TYPESCRIPT FRAGMENT

[The copy-text is TMs: typescript fragment in the UVa.–Barrett Collection.]

662.16 across] accross TMs
663.20; 664.15 laggard] laggered
    TMs

No. 163. THE DEVIL'S ACRE

[The copy-text is N[1]: *New York World*, Sunday Magazine, Oct. 25, 1896, p. 23.]

666.10.1 II] [*short rule*]|II. N[1]
666.29.1 III] [*short rule*]|III. N[1]
667.17 world] word N[1]

668.17 rest——"] ~ "—— N[1]
668.33 boards;] ~ : N[1]

No. 164. HARVARD UNIVERSITY AGAINST THE CARLISLE INDIANS

[The copy-text is N¹: *New York Journal,* Nov. 1, 1896, p. 5.]

669.31 much.] ~ , N¹
670.9 well-behaved] ~ ∧ ~ N¹
670.17 Shaw] Sha w N¹
671.16 -five-yard] - ~ ∧ | ~ N¹
671.18 twenty-yard] ~ ∧ | ~ N¹

671.30 McFarlane] MacFarland N¹
671.35 Metoxen∧] ~ , N¹
672.30(*twice*) Crimson] crimson N¹

No. 165. HOW PRINCETON MET HARVARD AT CAMBRIDGE

[The copy-text is N¹: *New York Journal,* Nov. 8, 1896, p. 1–2.]

674.18 full-back] ~ ∧ ~ N¹
674.24 discouraged] descouraged N¹
674.31 Crimson] crimson N¹
675.2 march] *omit* N¹
675.25–26 quarter-back] ~ ∧ ~

N¹
675.31 Everyone] ~ ~ N¹
676.13 well,] ~ . N¹
676.18 game,] ~ . N¹
676.30 maniacal] maniacical N¹

No. 167. OUIDA'S MASTERPIECE

[The copy-text is BB: *Book Buyer,* n.s., XIII (Jan., 1897), 968–969.]

677.18 *et seq. Under Two Flags*]
    "Under Two Flags" BB

No. 168. NEW INVASION OF BRITAIN

[The copy-text is N¹: *Omaha Daily Bee,* May 9, 1897, p. 20. The other texts collated are N²: *Pittsburgh Leader,* May 9, p. 22; N³: *Chicago Record,* May 8, p. 4.]

678.22 LONDON, April 29.—]
    N³; *omit* N¹; LONDON, May 1,
    1897. N²
678.22–23 this metropolis] N²⁻³;
    London N¹
678.27 cases∧] N²⁻³; ~ , N¹
679.6 definition . . . volition]
    N³; definition, appear of its
    volition N¹; definition, appear-
    ance of its volution N²
679.10 phrase∧] N³; ~ , N¹⁻²
679.10 slang,] N²⁻³; ~ ∧ N¹
679.21 bounder,] N²⁻³; ~ ∧ N¹
679.31 bounder, . . . bounder."]
    N³; bounder." N¹; bounder, he

is a bounder." N²
679.36 chap∧] N²⁻³; ~ , N¹
680.4 go,] N²⁻³; ago∧ N¹
680.18 worthy∧] N²; ~ , N¹,³
680.19 ¹usually] N²⁻³; *omit* N¹
680.23 friend.] N²⁻³; ~ ∧ N¹
680.24–25 friends∧ . . . impre-
    cation∧] N²⁻³; ~ , . . . ~ , N¹
680.28 roués] V; roues N¹,³;
    rogues N²
680.28 and∧ whereas∧] N²⁻³; ~ ,
    ~ , N¹
680.36 afterward] N²⁻³; after-
    wards N¹

No. 169. LONDON IMPRESSIONS

[The copy-text is SR: *Saturday Review,* LXXXIV (July 31, Aug. 7, Aug. 14, 1897), 105–106, 132–133, 158–159. The other texts collated are TMs: typescript in the UVa.–Barrett Collection; E1: *Last Words,* Digby, Long,

London, 1902, pp. 110–130. TMs and E1 are derived texts without authority.]

681.4 humor] V; humour SR+

682.26.1 II] V; [*space*] SR; CHAPTER II. TMs,E1

*683.10 ingenious] V; ingenuous SR+

684.1 wagon] V; waggon SR+

684.13 demeanor] V; demeanour SR+

685.11,23 cawn't] V; cawnt SR,TMs; can't E1

685.30 cawn't] V; cawnt SR+

686.9 succor] V; succour SR+

686.24 ex-Sheriff] E1; ex-sheriff SR,TMs

688.31 head-gear] V; headgear SR,TMs; head-|gear E1

690.16 principal] TMs(u),E1; principle SR,TMs(c)

690.31 portray] V; pourtray SR+

691.14 neighbors] V; neighbours SR+

No. 170. THE EUROPEAN LETTERS

[No. 2: the copy-text for 693.5–29 is MS: manuscript in Cora's hand; copy-text for 694.1–695.3 is Stephen's manuscript; copy-text for 695.4–697.27 is Cora's manuscript; 697.28–32 is completed by Stephen. All manuscripts are in the Special Collections of Columbia University Libraries. The other text collated is N[1]: *New York Press*, Aug. 15, 1897, p. 23. In numbering, all section initials and material in brackets have been ignored.]

693.6 opportunity] N[1]; opp< > MS

693.7 hundred] N[1]; hund< > MS

693.8 of] N[1]; o< > MS

693.11 ²and] N[1]; a< > MS

693.12 ornaments] N[1]; orniments MS

693.14 adjoins] N[1]; ajoins MS

693.14 villa] N[1]; Villa MS

693.19 never] N[1]; ne< > MS

693.22 pagoda] N[1]; pogoda MS

693.25 was] N[1]; has MS

693.26 Siam's existence] N[1]; Siams existance MS

693.28 ¹and] N[1]; a< > MS

693.29 boys] N[1]; bo< > MS

694.2 Me Off] N[1]; me off MS

694.2 Buffalo,"] N[1]; ∼ ∧" MS

694.3 New World] N[1]; new world MS

694.10 journey,] N[1]; ∼ ∧ MS

694.20 by-law] N[1]; bye-law MS

694.24 its] N[1]; it's MS

694.26 privilege] N[1]; previlege MS

695.1 in] N[1]; MS *mutilated*

695.4 using] V; us< > MS

695.6 Samuelson] V; Samue< > MS

695.9 hair] V; ha< > MS

695.11 were] V; w< > MS

695.12 long] V; lo< > MS

695.15 -four] V; -f< > MS

695.18 quarter] V; quater MS

695.18 without] V; with out MS

695.23 Buckingham] N[1]; Bucking< > MS

695.25 grimy-looking] N[1]; grimey-look< > MS

695.28 hurrying] N[1]; hurring MS

695.28 humanity] N[1]; huma< > MS

695.29 traffic] N[1]; traff< > MS

695.32 landscape gardeners] N[1]; landscap garden< > MS

695.33 turns,] V; ∼ < > MS;

$\sim_\wedge$ N[1]
696.1 interrupted] N[1]; interuted MS
696.7 gorgeous] N[1]; georgeoug MS
696.9 dividing] N[1]; dividi< > MS
696.12 Party] V; party MS
696.14 women] V; wom< > MS
696.16 gorgeous] V; georgeous MS
696.18 draperies,] V; $\sim_\wedge$ MS
696.21 [2,3]and] V; & MS
696.28 and] V; & MS
696.29 nurse's] V; nurses' MS
696.30 was] V; w< > MS
696.31 Aden."] V; $\sim$ ". MS
696.31 Although] V; Althou< > MS
696.32 survivors] V; survivers MS
696.32 would] V; wou< > MS
696.33 22nd of] V; 22< > MS

696.33 Queen's] V; Queens MS
696.34 Day] V; D< > MS
696.35 water] V; watter MS
697.1 Queen's] N[1]; Queens MS
697.2 *Spectator*] V; Spectator MS+
697.3 between] N[1]; betwen MS
697.3 Scotchwomen:$_\wedge$] N[1]; $\sim$:" MS
697.5 Weel,] N[1]; $\sim$ < > MS
697.5 it's] N[1]; its' MS
697.6 that's] N[1]; thats' MS
697.7 that's] N[1]; tha< > MS
697.8 it's] N[1]; i< > MS
697.12 Madame] V; Madam MS
697.13 enormous] V; enormuus MS (*doubtfully*)
697.16 at] V; < > MS
697.16 shillings.] V; shilling< > MS
697.17 [1]The] V; The The Ms
697.23 Virot] V; < >irot MS
697.25 a] V; < > MS
697.30 sovereigns] V; soveriegns MS

[No. 3: the copy-text is MS: manuscript in Cora's hand in the Special Collections of Columbia University Libraries. The other text collated is N[1]: *New York Press*, Aug. 22, 1897, p. 23.]

698.4 Park] N[1]; park MS
698.4 Richmond's] N[1]; Richmonds MS
698.13 annual] N[1]; anual MS
698.13–14 pilgrimages] N[1]; prilgrimages MS
698.25 perceive] V; percive MS; see N[1]
698.27 don't] N[1]; dont MS
698.30 where] N[1]; were MS
698.36; 699.27 Duchess] N[1]; Dutchess MS
698.36; 699.28 House] N[1]; house MS
699.6 muscles] N[1]; mucles MS
699.8 tremendous] N[1]; tremendious MS
699.9 racegoer] N[1]; goer MS
699.9 impels] N[1]; impells MS
699.11 bettor's] N[1]; bettors MS
699.13 outstretched] N[1]; out

stretched MS
699.13 scene] V; scean MS
699.14 exodus] V; exidous MS
699.16 modelling] V; moddling MS
699.16 assault] V; assult MS
699.17 exciting. There] V; $\sim_\wedge$ there MS
699.19 brethren] V; brethern MS
699.20 Richmond's] V; Richmonds MS
699.22 notabilities] V; notibilities MS
699.29 apartments] N[1]; appartments MS
699.30 host's] N[1]; hosts MS
699.30 grand] N[1]; Grand MS
699.31 owing] N[1]; oweing MS
699.36 interest] V; intrest MS
700.3 solemn] N[1]; solome MS

700.5   year. They] N¹; ∼ ∧ they MS
700.12 involves] V; involvs MS
700.12 whether] V; wether MS
700.12 clergymen] V; clergemen MS
700.18 height] N¹; hight MS
700.19(*twice*) stimulant] N¹; stimulent MS
700.22 unusual] N¹; unsual MS
701.1   expect] N¹; expec< > MS
701.2   Week] V; week MS+
701.2   Wight] N¹; Weight MS
701.8   disease] V; desease MS
701.10 doesn't] V; doesent MS
701.11 privilege] V; priviledge MS
701.16–17 excitement. It] N¹; ∼ ∧ it MS

701.19 millionaires] N¹; million-nairs MS
701.28 Gardens] N¹; gardens MS
701.30–31 extraordinary] N¹; exterordinary MS
702.6   invariably] V; invaribly MS
702.9   Augusta] N¹; Auguste MS
702.11 Bismarck] N¹; Bismark MS
702.15 Man of Iron] N¹; man of iron MS
702.16 between] N¹; betwen MS
702.17 precisely] N¹; precicely MS
702.19 anything] N¹; |thing MS
702.19 premonitory] N¹; preminatory MS

[No. 4: the copy-text is MS: manuscript in Cora's hand in the Special Collections of Columbia University Libraries. The other text collated is N¹: *New York Press*, Aug. 29, 1897, p. 21.]

702.27 phenomenon] N¹; phe-nomena MS
702.30 theatres] N¹; Theatres MS
702.32 occupants] N¹; occupant MS
703.1,9 country] N¹; Country MS
703.14 descriptions] N¹; discrip-tions MS
703.17 semi-instinctive] N¹; ∼ ∧ ∼ MS
703.19 if] V; *omit* MS
703.21 But] *possible paragraph opening in* MS
703.22 least] N¹; last MS
703.27 waters] V; watters MS
703.30 warrants] V; warrents MS
703.30 issued] N¹; ussued MS
703.32 parents] N¹; parrents MS
703.33 families] N¹; famlies MS
704.1   food,] N¹; ∼ ∧ MS

704.2   control] N¹; controll MS
704.5   St.] N¹; ∼ ∧ MS
704.5   Camberwell,] N¹; ∼ ∧ MS
704.11 writer] N¹; writter MS
704.13 florist's catalogue] N¹; florests cattalogue MS
704.19 ridiculous] N¹; rediculous MS
704.23 solemnly swear] N¹; solomly sware MS
704.24 Parisiennes] N¹; Parisians MS
704.28 apoplexy] V; appoplexy MS
704.32 catalogue.] V; ∼ ∧ MS
704.33 interest] V; intrest MS
705.3   world] V; World MS
705.6   taught] V; tought MS
705.11 ruler's] V; rulers MS
705.20 female] V; feamale MS
705.20 wife's] V; wifes MS
705.26 horde] V; hord MS
705.26 attendants] V; attendents MS

705.36   Western] V; western MS
706.1,28   received] V;   recieved MS
706.4   enthusiasm] V; enthusism MS
706.5   incessantly] V; incessently MS
706.14   precisely] V; precicely MS
706.16   age,] V; ~ ∧ MS
706.17   Circassian] V; Cirssas-sian MS
706.27   gorgeous] V; goreous MS
706.34   apartment] V; appart-ment MS
706.36   odor] V; order MS
706.37   cigarettes] V;   cigerettes MS
707.14   Waters] V; Watters MS
707.15   imitation] V; immitation MS
707.20   peasant] V; pesant MS
707.29   whether] V; wether MS
707.34   weeks] V; week MS
708.1,22; 709.13   their] V; thir MS

708.3   succumbed] V; seccumed MS
708.5   Duchess] V; Dutchess MS
708.10   situation] V;   sutuation MS
708.10,16   Irish] V; irish MS
708.13   countenance] V; counta-nance MS
708.14   Killarney] V;   Killernay MS
708.15   tourist] V; tourest MS
708.25   as it was] V; as is as ['s' over 't'] it was MS
708.29   women] V; woman MS
709.2   music,] V; ~ ∧ MS
709.4   ever] V; every MS
709.4   God's] V; Gods MS
709.5   and] V; as MS
709.7   Theatre] V; theatre MS
709.8   wear] V; were MS
709.9   belles] V; bells MS
709.9   fancy] V; Fancy MS
709.11   owing] V; oweing MS
709.12   bargains] V; bargins MS
709.13   loath] V; loathe MS

[No. 8: the copy-text is MS: manuscript in Cora's hand in the Special Collections of Columbia University Libraries. The other text collated is N¹: *New York Press*, Sept. 26, 1897, p. 23.]

709.20   interest] N¹; intrest MS
709.21   sportsman] N¹; sportman MS
709.23   amateurish] N¹; amatur-ish MS
709.30   maybe] N¹; may-be MS
710.5–6   southern] V;   southron MS,N¹
710.7,23   season's] N¹; seasons MS
710.8   some] N¹; some some MS
710.10   dollars] N¹; dallars MS
710.13   manufacturing] N¹; man-ufactoreing MS
710.16   northern] N¹; northen MS
710.18   affect] V; effect MS,N¹
710.18   trimmings,] N¹; ~ ∧ MS

710.19   Scotchman] V;   Scotch-men MS
710.19   doesn't] N¹; does not MS
710.20   whose] N¹; whos MS
710.25–26   one hundred and fifty thousand   dollars] N¹($150,-000); one hundred and fifty dollars MS
710.27   "siller"] N¹; ∧ ~ ∧ MS
710.31   and] V; & MS
710.32   forests] V; forrests MS
710.35   and] V; an MS,N¹
710.35   unkempt] N¹; unkept MS
711.1   restaurant,] N¹; resturant∧ MS
711.2   announced] N¹; annouced MS

711.4 linen] N¹; linnen MS
711.5 restaurant] N¹; resturant MS
711.9,11 Frederic] N¹; Fredric MS
711.10 novelists] N¹; novlests MS
711.10 England,] N¹; ~ ∧ MS
711.18–19 "Strawberry Leaves"] N¹; ∧ ~ ~ ∧ MS
711.20 some time] V; sometime MS
711.24 girl,] V; ~ ∧ MS
711.24 liras] V; lires MS
711.28 candies."] V; ~ . ∧ MS
712.2 Johore∧] V; ~ , MS
712.4 sovereign] N¹; soverign MS
712.4 some time] N¹; sometime MS
712.6–7 amusement] N¹; amusment MS
712.7 inoffensive] N¹; inofensive MS
712.11 occurrence] N¹; occurrance MS
712.12 sovereign] N¹; soereign MS
712.15 ²their] N¹; thir MS
712.17 disappeared] N¹; disapeared MS
712.18 despoilers] N¹; dispoliers MS
712.18 researches] N¹; researchers MS
712.20 as∧ those of] N¹; as, MS
712.20 et seq. St.] N¹; ~ ∧ MS
712.22 1031)] N¹; ~ ∧ MS
712.22 (1038] N¹; ∧ ~ MS
712.25 whose] N¹; whos MS
712.28 label] N¹; lable MS
712.34 Bishop's] N¹; Bishops MS
712.35 garden, the] N¹; ~. The MS
712.35 labels] N¹; lables MS
713.2 Stephen's] N¹; Stephens MS

713.5 interests] N¹; intrests MS
713.5 horror] N¹; horrow MS
713.11 et seq. Oberammergau] V; Ammergau MS,N¹
713.13 Exposition] N¹; exposition MS
713.16 Oberammergauans] V; Ammergauns MS; Ammergauans N¹
713.21 between] N¹; betwen MS
713.23 visitors'] N¹; visitor's MS
713.24 separated] N¹; seperated MS
713.27 ²mug∧] N¹; ~ , MS
713.32 heights] N¹; hights MS
714.5 too] N¹; to MS
714.5 chateau] N¹; chatteau MS
714.6 landscaper's] V; landscapers MS; landscape gardener's N¹
714.12 imitated] N¹; immitated MS
714.14 bosom] N¹; bossom MS
714.14–15 waterfall] N¹; watterfall MS
714.16 array] N¹; aray MS
714.20 paraded] N¹; peraded MS
714.20 requisite] N¹; requsite MS
714.21 enthusiasm] N¹; enthusism MS
714.24 tête-a-tête] V; tate-a-tate MS; tete-a-tete N¹
714.29 spectacle] N¹; specticle or spectecle MS
714.30 manœuvring] N¹; manuvring MS
714.34 Exhibition] V; exhibition MS
715.1 platform.] V; ~ : MS
715.2 uncanny] V; uncany MS
715.5 centimes] V; centime MS
715.8 vessels] V; Vessels MS
715.11 freight] V; frieght MS
715.12 Cited] V; Sited MS
715.14 between] V; betwen MS
715.19 is] V; omit MS

[No. 9: the copy-text is MS: manuscript in Cora's hand in the Special Collections of Columbia University Libraries.]

715.24 Alsatian] V; Alsacian MS
715.25 may$_\wedge$] V; ∼ , MS
715.26 veil] V; vail MS
715.27 bonnet,] V;
bonn< > MS
716.1 is] V; *omit* MS
716.2 surround] V; suround MS
716.8,21 woman's] V; womans MS
716.11–12 extraordinary] V; ex-terdornay MS
716.13 *et seq.* Red Cross] V; red cross MS
716.16 necessary] V; necesse-sary MS
716.23 surging] V; surgin MS
716.24 the] V; *illegible word at edge of* MS
716.24 combatants] V; combat-ance MS
716.27 To] V; It MS
716.29,31 being] V; bing MS
716.30 cavalry] V; cavelry MS
716.32 visions] *final 's' doubtful*
716.32 applying] V; apply MS
716.32; 717.7 water] V; watter MS
716.33; 717.8 *(twice)* dying] V; diing MS
716.35 extraordinary] V; exteror-dinary MS
717.6 destroy] V; distroy MS
717.7 nurse's] V; nurses MS
717.13 divided] V; devided MS
717.16 rides] V; ride MS
717.18 arguments] V; argue-ments MS
717.19 cyclists] V; cycleists MS
717.20 bicycle] V; bycicle MS
717.20 division] V; devision MS
717.22 attendance] V; attend-ence MS
717.26 valiant] V; valient MS
717.35 ridicule] V; rediculε MS
718.12 precedence] V; priced-ence MS
718.15 yacht] V; Yacht MS
718.16–17 and the] V; and MS
718.21 don't] V; dont MS
718.26 remains] V; remain MS
718.28 Third] V; third MS

718.30 Princes] V; Prices MS
719.2 *et seq.* Wilhelmina] V; Wilhelminia MS
719.3 scepter] V; septer MS
719.6 Queen's] V; Queens MS
719.8 witnessed] V; wittenessed MS
719.9 enjoys] V; enjoyes MS
719.13 Continental palace] V; continental Palace MS
719.17 King's] V; Kings MS
719.17 Japanese] V; Japanesse MS
719.22 embroideries] V; em-broderies MS
719.29 Continental] V; continen-tal MS
719.30 don't] V; dont MS
719.30 all. However] V; ∼ $_\wedge$ however MS
720.1 Yorkers,] V; ∼ $_\wedge$ MS
720.6 Bois] V; bois MS
720.8 Jewish] V; jewesh MS
720.9 Chicago] V; Chiacago MS
720.10 prince] V; Prince MS
720.11 Pixies] V; Pixes MS
720.12 Jewess] V; jewess MS
720.13 St.] V; ∼ $_\wedge$ MS
720.21 Night," "Morning," "Truth,"] V; ∼ $_\wedge$" "∼ $_\wedge$" "∼ $_\wedge$" MS
720.25 recipient] V; recipeant MS
720.25 handsome] V; handsom MS
720.26 Barnato's] V; Barnotos MS
720.28 person"; not] V; ∼ "$_\wedge$ no MS
720.30 custom] V; costom (*al-tered from* 'costume') MS
720.32 wiles] V; whiles MS
720.33 Britain] V; Brittian MS
721.1 Barnato] V; Barnoto MS
721.4 varying] V; varieing MS
721.4–5 different] V; differently MS
721.5 the] V; The MS
721.5–6 comparatively] V; com-paritively MS
721.6 utterly] V; utter MS

721.6 their] V; thir MS
721.9 Jews] V; jews MS
721.16 linen] V; linnen MS
721.21 dies] V; died MS
721.21 ³the] V; the the MS
721.24 of an] V; <   > MS
721.24 American] V; american MS
721.24 piano] V; paino MS
721.25 repeated] V;
rep<   > MS
721.25–26 applications] V;
applica<   > MS
721.27 thought] V;
th<   > MS

721.28 is a] V; <   > MS
721.29 tells] V; tell MS
721.29 ²the] V; <   > MS
721.30 you] V; You MS
721.30 can] V; <   > MS
721.31 downcast] V;
dow<   > MS
721.34 chapel] V; chaple MS
721.34 vigils] V; virgils MS
722.2 extraordinary] V; exterordinary MS
722.4 nuns,] V; ~ ₗ MS
722.4 veils] V; vails MS
722.5 them] V; th<   > MS

[No. 10: the copy-text is MS: manuscript in Cora's hand in the Special Collections of Columbia University Libraries. The other text collated is N¹: *New York Press*, Oct. 10, 1897, p. 18.]

722.7 Duchess] N¹; Dutchess MS
722.8 House,] N¹; ~ ₗ MS
722.10 tourist] N¹; tourest MS
722.11 kingdom] N¹; *possibly* Kingdom MS
722.13 present] N¹; *possibly* prenent MS
722.14 surrounding] N¹; surounding MS
722.14,19 Kenmare's Folly] N¹; Kenmares folly MS
722.14 ²Folly] N¹; folly MS
722.15 description] N¹; discription MS
722.17 tenants] N¹; tennants MS
722.17 estate] N¹; estates MS
722.21 of the family] N¹; *omit* MS
722.23 Baring] N¹; Barring MS
722.25 appearance] N¹; apperance MS
722.30 government] N¹ (Government); goverment MS
723.3 Victoria's] N¹; Victorias MS
723.4 possesses] N¹; posseses MS
723.15 Windsor] N¹; windsor MS

723.16 Britain] N¹; Brittian MS
723.18 Briton] N¹; Brittian MS
723.21 don't] N¹; dont MS
723.24 her.] N¹; ~ ₗ MS
723.25 Italy's] N¹; Italys MS
723.30 familiar] N¹; familliar MS
723.31 a small] N¹; asmall MS
723.31 Shakespeare's] N¹; Shakespeares MS
723.33 Emperor] N¹; emperor MS
724.1 referred] N¹; refered MS
724.3 soldiers'] N¹; solders MS
724.3 the] N¹; The MS
724.5–6 "The Ladies'] V; the "Ladies ₗ MS
724.7 Ladies'] V; Ladies ₗ MS
724.11 Marriott] V; Marriot MS
724.17 sold.'] V; ~ . ₗ MS
724.29 Beresford's] V; Beresford' MS
*724.29 Julu] *stet* MS
724.31 nation's] V; nations MS
724.31 European] V; Eureopean MS
724.33 quota] N¹; qouta MS
724.34 and, it] N¹; ~ ₗ ~ , MS
725.5,7,11 Duchess] N¹; Dutchess MS

725.15 recently] V; when MS; once N¹
725.16 hall, Chelsea] N¹; ~ ∧ Chelsia MS
725.18 solemn] N¹; soloemn MS
725.24 It is said that his] N¹; His MS
725.24 woman] N¹; women MS
725.27,31 Britain] N¹; Britian MS
725.30 and] N¹; & MS
725.30; 726.13 secretary] N¹; secetary MS

726.7 don't] N¹; dont MS
726.8 society] N¹; soceity MS
726.9 their] N¹; thir MS
726.10 lady] N¹; ladie MS
726.10 invalid] N¹; invilade MS
726.13 penny] N¹; pennie MS
726.16 one's] N¹; ones MS
726.16 thronging] N¹; throning MS
726.17 purchasing] N¹; purchassing MS
726.18 father's] N¹; fathers MS

[Unplaced: the copy-text is MS: manuscript in Crane's hand in the Special Collections of Columbia University Libraries.]

726.20 Parade] V; parade MS

726.27 its] V; it's MS

No. 172. HAROLD FREDERIC

[The copy-text is CB: *The Chap-Book*, VIII (March 15, 1898), 358–359.]

729.18 *Journal*] Journal CB
730.17 *et seq. In the Sixties*] In the Sixties CB
730.17–19 "The . . . Susan,"] *no quotes in* CB
730.22 *The Copperhead*] The Copperhead CB

731.7–8 *et seq. Seth's . . . Girl*] Seth's . . . Girl CB
731.22 *The Damnation of Theron Ware*] The Damnation of Theron Ware CB
731.39 *March Hares*] March Hares CB

No. 173. CONCERNING THE ENGLISH "ACADEMY"

[The copy-text is B: *The Bookman*, VII (March, 1898), 22–24.]

732.22 emerge] merge B
732.25 recognized] recognised B

735.14 honor] honour B

No. 175. THE SCOTCH EXPRESS

[The copy-text is MS: the untitled manuscript in the Special Collections of Columbia University Libraries. The other texts collated are Cs: *Cassell's Magazine*, n.s., XVIII (Jan., 1899), 163–171; McC: *McClure's Magazine*, XII (Jan., 1899), 273–283. McC is a derived text without authority but is used for corrections where Cs is wanting.]

739.16 sufficiently] Cs; sufficently MS
740.1 an important] McC; a MS
740.3 *et seq.* North] McC; north MS
740.3 particularly,] McC; ~ ; MS
740.5 -o'-] McC; -o∧- MS

740.11 bowl] Cs; bowled MS
740.19 *et seq.* its] Cs; it's MS (*except at* 741.29)
740.19 identity] Cs; indentity MS
740.34 Napoleon's] Cs; Napoleon MS
740.37 first-class] Cs; ~ ∧ ~ MS

741.13 than] Cs; that MS

741.25–26 North Western] Cs; Northwestern MS

742.2 gait of turtles] Cs; pace of mice MS

742.11 the grouse,] *interlined by* Cora *in pencil*

742.31 familiar] Cs; familar MS

743.7 temperance,] Cs; ~ ∧ MS

743.19 bolt] Cs; boat MS

743.28 *et seq.* vermilion] Cs; vermillion MS

743.30 forty-nine . . . -tenth] Cs; 49⁹⁄₁₀ MS

743.32 occurs] Cs; occurrs MS

743.38 *et seq.* Continent] Cs; continent MS

743.39 railways.] Cs; ~ ∧ MS

744.3 Continental] V; continental MS+

744.10 tens upon] Cs; ten upon MS

744.12 North Western] V; Northwestern MS; North-| Western Cs, McC(western)

744.29 vale] McC; vane MS (*preceded by* Cora's *pencil cross*)

744.38 spies] McC; spys MS

744.39 later] McC; latter MS

744.39 becomes] McC; became MS

745.36 phlegm] Cs; phelgm MS

746.3 ludicrous] Cs; ludicrius MS

746.10 toward] Cs; towards MS

746.10 temple,] Cs; ~ ∧ MS

746.21 speculated] Cs; wondered MS (Cora's *pencil* 'X' *placed above*)

746.25 engine-driver] Cs; ~ ∧ ~ MS

746.28 much,] V; ~ ; MS+

746.28 do] Cs; *omit* MS

746.28 brow,] V; ~ ∧ MS; ~ ; Cs,McC

746.32 road,] Cs; ~ ∧ MS

746.39 principal] Cs; principle MS

747.9 An] Cs; A MS

747.9 an hour,] Cs; *omit* MS

747.10 drag] Cs; bring MS

747.14 the train] Cs; train MS

747.19 a vast] Cs; vast MS

748.14 freights] Cs; frieghts MS

748.17 rhythmical] Cs; rythmical MS

748.28 swung] Cs; *omit* MS

748.30 the moment] Cs; moment MS

748.34 regulation] Cs; regulations MS

749.6 by] Cs; *omit* MS

749.6 London] Cs; a ~ MS

749.16 define] Cs; mean MS

749.21 accommodations] Cs; accomadations MS

749.29 as] Cs; is MS

749.31 also rang] Cs; rang also rang MS

750.3 sandwich] Cs; sandwhich MS

750.21 then] Cs; then | then MS

750.26 Forests∧] Cs; ~ , MS

750.27 dewy] Cs; dewey MS

751.9 forty- . . . -third] Cs; 49⅓ MS

No. 176. FRANCE'S WOULD-BE HERO

[The copy-text is N¹: *New York Journal*, Oct. 15, 1899, p. 25. The other text collated is N²: *San Francisco Examiner*, Oct. 15, p. 15.]

752.18 Elysée] Elysee N¹

752.36 that] N²; the N¹

754.22–24 , and naturally . . . lion] N²; *omit* N¹

754.30 Déroulède] V; Deroulede N¹; Deroulode N²

755.3–8 Of course . . . for Coxey.] N²; *omit* N¹

No. 177. "IF THE CUP ONCE GETS OVER HERE . . ."

[The copy-text is MS: untitled manuscript in the hand of Edith Richie in the Special Collections of Columbia University Libraries.]

755.31 *et seq.* *Columbia . . . Shamrock*] Columbia . . . Shamrock MS

757.26 Jameson] Jaimeson MS

757.32 displays] displays with MS

No. 178. STEPHEN CRANE SAYS: EDWIN MARKHAM IS HIS FIRST CHOICE FOR THE AMERICAN ACADEMY

[The copy-text is N¹: *New York Journal,* March 31, 1900, p. 8.]

758.29 scale."] ~ . ∧ N¹

No. 179. LONDON'S FIREMEN FALL FROM GRACE

[The copy-text is N¹: *New York Press,* Nov. 28, 1897, p. 15.]

763.31 engines] egines N¹

No. 180. ENGLAND A LAND OF ANXIOUS MOTHERS

[The copy-text is N¹: *New York Press,* Dec. 5, 1897, p. 13.]

766.13 'em] ∧ ~ N¹

766.21 *Times*] Times N¹

768.7 canny] cannyj N¹

WORD-DIVISION

1. *End-of-the-Line Hyphenation in the Virginia Edition*

[NOTE: No hyphenation of a possible compound at the end of a line in the Virginia text is present in the copy-texts except for the following readings, which are hyphenated within the line in the copy-texts. Except for these readings, all end-of-the-line hyphenation in the Virginia text may be ignored except for hyphenated compounds in which both elements are capitalized.]

8.26	dollar-|and-	215.20	ox-|chains
20.26	to-|morrow	225.16	thirty-|three
21.30	quarter-|deck	225.30	pine-|knots
21.35	froth-|filled	228.37	altar-|like
37.5	shopping-|woman	234.20	row-|lock
45.19	*Picket-|fence*	234.26	low-|spreading
47.18	*rolling-|mill*	240.35	pickerel-|spear
53.8	dark-|brown	242.17	rain-|drops
67.19	steel-|colored	244.15; 245.18	slate-|colored
80.21	really-|truly	257.21	key-|note
85.18	snow-|covered	258.7	fire-|surrounded
101.33	blood-|stained	270.8	pine-|clothed
102.31	frothy-|mouthed	270.10	ankle-|deep
104.34	corner-|stone	276.5	left-|hand
115.34	pawn-|shops	276.23	half-|finished
119.30	²twenty-|one	280.26	ten-|year-
122.27	good-|natured	283.20	dust-|covered
123.19	Good-|night	284.16	side-|walks
126.16	rose-|hued	284.34	up-|reared
132.6	semi-|circle	313.22	common-|place
138.7	God-|speed	345.14; 348.30	side-|walk
144.7	living-|room	354.35	-s-|satisfact-
154.18	camp-|fire	357.4	stout-|hearted
155.11	long-|distance	358.24; 382.32; 390.7	well-|
160.32	box-|office		dressed
162.22	finger-|nails	366.3	opium-|smokers
164.27	dining-|room	366.5	opium-|smoker
189.14	under-|lip	368.9	cap-|boxes
200.31	water-|brooks	371.36	three-|ton
200.34	shirt-|front	376.6	a-|straddle
201.21	long-|haired	378.2	dark-|fronted
202.36	rock-|bound	380.25; 613.11	to-|day

383.38	patrol-|man	575.24	-of-|war
385.4	air-|shaft	575.29	brier-|wood
398.19	four-|wheeler	577.7	toe-|nails
402.10	long-|gone	582.32	life-|savers
403.38	a-|slashin'	583.26	white-|haired
419.11	water-|tight	584.12	grave-|yard
425.24	assassin-|like	594.24	wisp-|light
431.24	first-|class	597.23	mule-|stables
441.24	second-|story	602.21	door-|boys
443.6	water-|soaked	603.2	ink-|like
445.18	middle-|class	605.39	fan-|wheel
446.19	one-|eighth	607.5	coal-|brokers
448.5	tan-|bark	617.15	fried-|oat-
448.7	dull-|colored	617.21	shot-|guns
449.9	There-|after	617.22	heavy-|faced
464.6	blood-|red	623.3	three-|fourths
485.18	under-|current	625.16	-half-|back
489.15	breech-|loading	649.31	ship-|loads
490.3	iron-|bound	650.7	sea-|serpents
490.11	snow-|buried	651.11	ninety-|five
492.4	neck-|deep	651.14	thirty-|five
497.24	pig-|buyers	654.36	narrow-|minded
505.33	well-|known	656.15	Thirty-|first
506.23	natural-|history	675.25	quarter-|back
512.12	tumble-|bumble	682.10	warm-|heartedness
512.39	hotel-|porches	694.24	sleeping-|cars
516.9	boarding-|houses	695.14	twenty-|four
518.39	helter-|skeltering	698.9	back-|handed
520.21	June-|bugs	704.30	Mar-|and-
523.36	black-|hulled	710.18	tam-|o-
535.16	fish-|tails	729.14	smoking-|room
536.20	Avon-|by-	739.31	four-|wheelers
538.12	Asbury-|ave.	743.35	road-|beds
545.13	flower-|beds	744.10	road-|bed
547.27	widely-|known	747.19	black-|walled
547.32	"sea-|puss"	749.7	bell-|boy
551.30	lead-|pencil	752.26	red-|legged
555.14	baby-|carriages	757.15	tomb-|stone
555.24	Pleasant-|faced		

2. *End-of-the-Line Hyphenations in the Copy-Texts*

[NOTE: The following compounds, or possible compounds, are hyphenated at the end of the line in the copy-texts. The form in which they have been transcribed in the Virginia text, listed below, represents the practices of the respective copy-texts so far as can be determined, and in cases of doubt the form is that generally found in the Crane manuscripts.]

3.14	sun-bonnet	8.27	-and-a-
8.13	turnstile	10.16	footfalls
8.15	iron-railing	10.27	sun-burned

11.5	"wind-burn"	183.16	sweetheart
13.34	boat-hook	185.3	reiteration
19.15	Landward	190.36	grey-hounds
21.13	sun-kissed	195.13	flash-light
21.14	Sun-kissed	199.23	story-tellers
33.31	horse-car	201.11	chimney-corner
34.20	frock-coat	202.21	fence-corner
35.15	gray-haired	203.3	earthquakes
35.16	dog-fight	203.25	club-house
35.17	slaughter-houses	203.28	six-foot-
36.8	Night-shirts	206.33	redouble
36.27	fireplace	207.16	yarn-spinners
37.15	good-day	209.17	panther-killers
41.4	hand-runnin'	212.14	five-cent
41.15	shtove-poker	215.15	keen-eyed
46.1	Butterflies	217.10	scrub-oak
51.10	pocket-handkerchief	218.5	backwoods
53.17; 57.14,22; 58.21		220.21	lifetime
	dark-brown	220.22	snake-fence
55.13	household	221.1	bushwhacker
58.6	flower-pot	221.7	soap-box
58.18	backward	224.4	sundown
60.30,38	brakeman	226.9	bedraggled
61.20	superhuman	227.10	pillar-like
62.36	trainmen	231.28	redistributed
74.30	faint-hearted	232.1	yellow-brown
81.25	up-stairs	233.32	cave-damp
84.9; 737.8,37	railway	235.30	don'tcher
84.10	foreshadowed	239.15	foam-dripping
97.11	good-for-	240.26	up-reared
101.12; 103.13	blood-stained	241.1	mummy-like
102.24	blockhead	245.16	wood-fire
102.24	dust-eating	250.36	snowfield
106.21	wildcat	251.13	rifle-barrel
109.5	SWORD-BLADE	251.16	gun-barrel
114.15	intermingling	252.12	farmhouse
116.23	ranchman	253.22	bloodcurdling
118.7	-hundred-dollar	256.9	war-yell
126.6	projected-horse-	260.30	school-boy
126.14	car-wheel	262.6	stairway
131.30	good-looking	263.37	puff-ball
132.36	handkerchief	270.4	sunshine
144.27	blackberries	278.12	ever-forward
149.13	broadcast	281.16	snow-shoes
157.31	housework	282.9	eyebrows
160.26	plum-like	282.32	death-like
162.19	papier-mâché	283.4	ex-secretary
179.11	caretaker	284.1	well-dressed
181.23	hall-way	284.37	bartender
182.1	over-seas	286.32	-a-here

291.2	²nightshirt		398.4	overcoat
292.19	-o-o-		398.24	landlady
302.20	steamship		399.26	uneven
302.23	gangplank		400.20; 403.37	Bloodthirsty
302.26	gangplanks		402.25	bygone
303.18	farewells		403.21	wardmen's
308.36	drum-major		403.34	a-slashin'
312.19	un-American		404.4	undersized
315.18	needle-prickings		405.33	overfond
323.7	popcorn		409.13	cattlemen
327.28; 551.4; 557.5	to-morrow		412.4	twenty-five
332.18	waist-coat		414.21	hard-working
333.21	billposter		415.13	bedchamber
334.22	backstairs		418.1	hadter
334.29	eyesight		420.21	outbreak
335.12	thick-headed		424.26	outburst
336.3	patent-medicine		424.29	five-dollars
339.19	fire-alarm		424.30	bar-tender
340.39	half-dazed		429.16; 598.36	sun-light
343.37	gleam-white		439.21	haystack
349.32; 359.10	side-walk		440.20	freight-carrying
350.39	self-contained		445.4	best-dressed
356.24	peacemakers		445.32	blue-grass
356.28	football		448.5	sheep-herder
362.2	urchin-like		449.36	knee-joints
365.35	dumb-waiter		450.1	knee-springing
366.21	"pin-heads"		450.38	rain-clouds
368.8	li-shi		452.33	outbuildings
370.27; 371.4	billboards		453.35	red-tiled
371.18	truck-drivers		454.4	outstretched
371.30; 372.8	wheelmen		454.28	cat-calls
374.23	gripman's		455.24	password
375.32; 472.36	wide-brimmed		458.28	twenty-four
377.17	Moreover		462.36	rainbow
378.3	Nighthawk		464.12	far-away
378.12	roof-gardens		466.35	cutaway
378.25; 381.16	roof-garden		470.28	forbear
379.34	undertone		473.28	outskirts
380.16	overtime		477.24	trolly-cars
381.7	wall-decoration		478.15	¹seaport
381.20	roof-gardeners		483.8	hillside
382.12	court-room		485.28	red-headed
383.35	gloom-shrouded		486.15	slate-colored
385.10	storm-god		486.34	peasant-life
385.32	quarter-grain		487.26	tradesman
386.35	gas-jet		491.22	gorse-hung
391.16	homeward		494.17	diamond-like
394.11	overheard		494.33	bejerseyed
395.4	street-lighting		504.35	voice-culture
396.2	daylight		506.26	seaweeds

510.23	overrun	618.9	turnstile
514.2	well-known	621.3	everlasting
514.7	awe-stricken	621.6	camp-fire
514.32	tenement-house	621.11	sombre-hued
517.22	long-handled	621.24	One-two-
520.17	machine-guns	621.28	mud-colored
520.20	sunburned	622.13	amidships
521.29	nightshirts	623.15	seven-eighths
522.20	sun-beaten	623.28	five-eighths
525.8	background	625.27	widespread
525.13	best-known	628.20	foreground
527.28	superabundance	629.11	background
528.35	forty-seven	629.27	watermelon
531.2	camp-meeting	638.30	seacoast
534.32	shell-fish	639.17	mastheads
541.13	pancakes	641.8	stronghold
544.7	backbone	646.16	shoulder-blades
544.33	underview	647.33	headway
546.13	newcomer	650.12	sawmill
550.8	black-board	651.17	thirty-two
551.24	artist-artisan	651.36	trans-Atlantic
555.33	clothes-basket	652.1	sea-serpents
558.25	rocking-chairs	655.15	tail-end
559.1	birth-places	658.11	Thirty-first
560.24	-year-old	668.24	upright
561.6	two-seated	671.35	twenty-yard
571.24	snake-like	672.19	blacksmiths
574.13	Brown-bodied	676.20	touchdown
574.26	glass-beads	681.2	cabman
580.9	rock-boring	683.16	doubly-fortified
580.10	to-night	686.25	gun-fighters
580.23	shipwrecks	686.28	six-shooter
591.7	lunch-pails	691.13	off-hand
591.37	slate-pickers	692.3	pin-cushion
592.22	school-houses	695.26	time-worn
595.26	low-roofed	727.4	outbreak
597.27	broadside	731.29	rag-carpets
599.10	moss-like	746.8	middle-aged
600.25	Overhead	746.30	clear-minded
601.11	counterparts	754.13	bodyguard
606.27	coal-barons	756.30	pass-word
606.31	coal-brokers	764.18	costermongers
608.11	dinnerhorn	764.23	firemen
608.25	half-unconsciously		

3. *Special Cases*

[NOTE: In the following list the compound is hyphenated at the end of the line in the copy-texts and in the Virginia edition.]

44.29   play-|thing (i.e., plaything)

48.3   hob-|nobbed (i.e., hobnobbed)

54.12   stair-|ways (i.e., stair-ways)

56.13   over-|whelmed (i.e., overwhelmed)

98.6   -for-|nothingness (i.e., -for-nothingness)

112.39   inter-|mingling (i.e., intermingling)

119.8   second-|hand (i.e., second-hand)

176.14   story-|teller (i.e., story-teller)

250.29   swish-|swish (i.e., swish-swish)

252.2   pine-|clothed (i.e., pine-clothed)

253.19   black-|haired (i.e., black-haired)

275.20   street-|band (i.e., street-band)

308.1   ferry-|boats (i.e., ferryboats)

317.2   hiding-|places (i.e., hiding-places)

338.19   thick-|headed (i.e., thick-headed)

362.13   fore-|finger (i.e., fore-finger)

418.12   car-|windows (i.e., car-windows)

467.34   top-|heavy (i.e., top-heavy)

476.39   sea-|crossing (i.e., sea-crossing)

486.30   pig-|market (i.e., pig-market)

494.31   under-|petticoat (i.e., under-petticoat)

495.15   fishing-|boats (i.e., fishing-boats)

528.1   some-|what (i.e., somewhat)

546.1   Fifth-|ave. (i.e., Fifth-ave.)

547.19   house-|cleaning (i.e., house-cleaning)

604.35   steel-|gleaming (i.e., steel-gleaming)

606.40   coal-|brokers (i.e., coal-brokers)

610.25   Bar-|room (i.e., Barroom)

622.12   handsomely-|attired (i.e., handsomely-attired)

635.9   rag-|carpets (i.e., rag-carpets)

675.31   under-|going (i.e., undergoing)

751.24   music-|halls (i.e., music-halls)

HISTORICAL COLLATION

[NOTE: Substantive variants from the Virginia text are listed here, together with their appearances in the collated texts. In cases where there are several texts of equal authority, the rejected accidental readings have been recorded here if two or more texts agree in a particular reading. Collated texts not noted for any reading agree with the Virginia-edition reading to the left of the bracket. Paragraphing variants are listed for authorative texts only, and in the case of multiple texts of equal authority, are listed only if there is an agreement of two or more texts. Where there is only one text and a substantive emendation has been made, no record in the historical collation will appear for that item, and reference should be made to the Emendations to the Copy-Text. In the Alterations to the Typescripts no mention is made of ink completion of words or the addition of punctuation at the end of the typing line, or the supplying of the downward stroke to a period to form an exclamation point; typed letters altered in ink are not listed unless a substantive difference is created by the alteration, nor are typed letters over typed letters recorded unless they should happen to form an acceptable word. Words typed together and then separated by a slash are not usually recorded, nor are false-starts. No alterations are given for typescripts which are derived. Variants in date-lines are not recorded here but can be found in the textual history to each item. In the notation a plus sign indicates concurrence of all collated editions following the one cited. For this and for other conventions of shorthand notation, see the general headnote to the list of Editorial Emendations. In this volume, all subheadings, chapter indications, acts in the playlets, and information supplied by the editor in brackets in the body of the texts are ignored in the page and line references, with the exception of No. 155.]

No. 1. UNCLE JAKE AND THE BELL-HANDLE

[The copy-text is MS: manuscript in the Special Collections of Columbia University Libraries.]

Alterations in the Manuscript

3.1 ¹was] *followed by* Cora's *interlined* 'called' *in pencil with a pencil caret*

3.1 a . . . soul] *single quotes inserted in pencil about this phrase by* Cora

3.2 man] *preceded by deleted*

'old'

3.5 niece] 'ie' *over* 'ei'

3.7 considering] *following comma added in pencil by* Cora

3.10 about] *interlined with a caret*

3.11 at sunrise] *interlined with a caret which deleted a comma beneath it*

3.12 black] 'l' *interlined with an insertion line*

3.13 and put on] *interlined with a caret*

3.13 cotton mitts] *hyphen deleted*

3.15 a good deal of] *interlined above deleted* 'some'

3.16 city] *originally* 'cities' *with* 'ies' *deleted and* 'y' *added after*

3.16 might] *interlined in pencil by* Cora

3.18 seat,] *following* 'of his wagon' *interlined with a caret in pencil by* Cora *with comma deleted after* 'seat'

3.20 and] *interlined above deleted* 'and'

3.22 trotted] *second* 't' *inserted*

3.24 on another] 'the other' *interlined in pencil by* Cora *above deleted* 'on another'

3.25 fat] *deleted in pencil by* Cora

3.29 each] *preceded by deleted* 'she'

4.3 washes] Cora *deleted* 'washes' *and interlined* 'wet clothes' *above a caret*

4.4 lines] *preceded by* 'the' *interlined with a caret in pencil by* Cora

4.4 grimy] MS 'grimey' *with* 'e' *inserted*

4.4 smoky] MS 'smokey' *preceded by* 'som' *altered to* 'sm' *then deleted*

4.9–10 gentlemen] *originally* 'gentleman' *with* 'a' *altered to* 'e'; 'gentle' *deleted in pencil by* Cora

4.10 standing . . . them] *squeezed in at bottom of page with directional arrow*

4.10 ²their] *preceded by deleted* 'thi'

4.13 these] *first* 'e' *over* 'i' *and second* 'e' *added*

4.16 gentlemen] *third* 'e' *over* 'a'

4.16 in] *preceded by deleted* 'at'

4.18 winked] *followed by deleted* 'a'

4.18 eyes] 's' *added later*

4.24 of clothes] *interlined with a caret after the comma following* 'line'

4.26 man] *followed by deleted* ''s price'

4.26 lying] MS 'lieing' *preceded by deleted* 'lieing' *of which the* 'ie' *was over* 'y'

4.27 prices.] 's' *over original period and second period added later*

4.27 spent] *followed by deleted* 'to work'

4.29 would] *preceded by deleted* 't'

4.29 niece] *interlined above deleted* 'daughter' *with* 'ie' *over* 'ei'

4.31 board. After] *period added later;* 'After' *squeezed in at end of line with* 'A' *over* 'a'

4.32 little] *interlined with a caret*

4.33 was] *preceding double quotation marks added in pencil by* Cora

4.34 know] *preceded by deleted* 'wel'

4.36 George] 'G' *over* 'g'

4.36 sir.] *following double quotation marks added in pencil by* Cora

5.1 had] *preceded by deleted* 'was'

5.2 had] *squeezed in at end of line*

5.5 Mr.] MS 'Mr‸' *preceded by deleted* 'he ev'

5.6 Perkinses] 'i' *over* 'e'

5.10 good-bye] *preceded by deleted* 'adeu'

5.12 of . . . between] *interlined with a caret above deleted* 'of'

5.12 ²the] *squeezed in later*

5.14 Uncle Jake] *interlined, indented, on the second line above* 'old man' *of deleted* '¶

The good | old man'

5.16 deferentially] *an 'i' preceding the third 'e' deleted and 'i' inserted before 'a'*

5.16 his] *preceded by deleted* 'the old'

5.18 and] *squeezed in later at the end of line*

5.18 him,] *followed by deleted* 'and calle'

5.18 old man] 'old' *preceded by deleted* 'good m'; 'gentle' *deleted to leave* 'man'

5.19 from] *deleted and* 'through' *interlined in pencil by* Cora

5.20 glasses] *preceded by deleted* 'very'

5.24 ³the] *preceded by deleted* 'a'

5.28 magnificence] *preceded by deleted* 'magnifince'

5.31 In] *paragraph sign inserted before*

5.31 bell-] MS 'bell‸' *with* 'e' *over* 'i'

5.32 It] *paragraph sign inserted at left margin to clarify brief indention*

5.32 brass] *interlined above deleted* 's' *and the beginning of*

an upstroke, possibly a 'k'

5.33 which] *interlined with a caret*

5.36 a] *preceded by deleted* 'the'

5.37 was] *preceded by deleted* 'f' *and* 'it'

6.1 Uncle] *preceded by deleted* 'The sound'

6.3 did!] *exclamation point over question mark*

6.3 Mackerel] *second 'e' over 'i'*

6.11 suppressed] *preceded by deleted* 'as p'

6.16 that's] ' 's' *added*

6.22 now] *immediately preceded by deleted* 'k'

6.23 from] *preceded by deleted* 'of'

6.34 be] *interlined with a caret in pencil by* Cora

6.35 Come] 'C' *over* 'c'

7.3 and] *squeezed in later*

7.4 the] *final* 'y' *deleted*

7.4 companion] MS 'companions', *its* 's' *added later; followed by deleted* 'made'

7.14 in] *preceded by deleted* 'at'

7.17 touch] 'o' *over* 'u'

No. 2. GREED RAMPANT

[The copy-text is TMs: typescript in the UVa.–Barrett Collection.]

Alterations in the Typescript

[Alterations are in ink unless otherwise specified; three typed alterations in spelling appear in this list since they may reflect characteristics of the MS.]

7.32 lights] 'ts' *over* 't' *at end of line*

7.32 dim,] *comma added*

7.32 soft,] *comma added*

8.3 roar] 'o' *over illegible letter*

8.4 tempest,] *comma added*

8.5 guardian] 'ua' *over* 'au'

8.6 a] *altered from* 'an' *and followed by deleted* 'attitude of list'

8.18 themselves] 'lv' *over* 'vl'

8.18 shrill] *final* 'l' *added at end of line*

8.22 fierce] 'ie' *over* 'ei'

8.25 Finally,] *comma added*

8.26 Jew,] *comma added*

8.27–28 the palpitating] *interlined above deleted* 'thepalpitating' *in which third* 't' *typed over* 'y'; *preceded on line above by deleted* 'thepa'

8.31; 9.5 They] 'y' *added*

8.33 has] 's' *over* 'a'

8.37 head. With] *period inserted;* 'W' *over* 'w'

8.37 end,] *comma added*

8.39; 9.3   ²a] *interlined with a caret*

9.2   seethes] *second 'e' over 'a'*

9.4   * * * * *] *not formed from hyphens; supplied by hand*

9.7   tatters] *interlined above deleted* 'taters'

9.13   tears out] *interlined with a caret*

9.14   head.] *period added*

9.18   in] *preceded by deleted* 'in,' *followed by type x'd-out* 'in'

9.18   modest] *final* 'ly' *deleted*

9.18   manner,] *comma added*

9.19   they] *interlined with a caret*

9.19   good] *preceded by deleted* 'god'

9.20   ¹is] 'Is' *with slash through* 'I'

9.21   diamonds.] *spaced period preceded by type x'd-out* 'an'

9.22   tremendous] 'trem|' *interlined above deleted* 'trm|'

9.23   for] 'o' *over* 'i'

9.24   look] *interlined with a caret*

9.24   scorn] *following period deleted*

9.26–27   confer] 'o' *over* 'i'

9.27,28   Gentile] *final* 's' *deleted*

9.31   cloth] *final* 'e' *deleted*

9.33   melee] *preceded by type x'd-out* 'mell'

9.36   exhibits] *preceded by type x'd-out* 'exibits'

10.7   again tumble] *caret separates run-together words*

10.12–13   trembles beneath] *caret separates run-together words*

10.17   it] 'It' *with slash through* 'I'

10.17   Mr.] TMs 'Mr∧' *inserted*

No. 4. THE RELUCTANT VOYAGERS

[The copy-text is N¹: the Sunday Magazine of the *New York Press*, Feb. 11, 1900, pp. 6–12 and Feb. 18, pp. 3–6. The other texts collated are N²: *Philadelphia Press*, Feb. 11, Color Supplement, p. 2, and Feb. 18, in Sunday Magazine section, p. 3; N³: *Chicago Times-Herald*, Feb. 11, part III, p. 4, and Feb. 18, part III, p. 4; N⁴: "New England Home Magazine," supplement to *Boston Sunday Journal*, Feb. 11, pp. 296–303, and Feb. 18, pp. 367–371; T(p): Tillotson's proof for the Northern Newspaper Syndicate; E1: *Last Words*, Digby, Long, London, 1902, pp. 1–32. Lines 14.15–21 are preserved in manuscript draft on the original recto of fol. 4 of "The Holler Tree" in the UVa.–Barrett Collection. Since all texts are of equal authority, any accidental agreement of two or more texts is recorded here. All T(p) and E1 variants are listed.]

14.14.2   CHAPTER I] PART I N²⁻⁴, T(p); *omit* MS

14.15   men] sad men MS

14.15   sea] *omit* MS

14.16–17   He . . . cane.] *omit* N¹

14.19–20   resolved to set] setting MS,N⁴

14.21   "To (*no* ¶)] ¶ N⁴

14.25   it!] ~ . E1

14.26   plate!] ~ . E1

14.27   time∧] ~ , T(p),N²

14.31   "What . . . it,"] " ' ~ . . . ~ ,' " N²⁻⁴,T(p)

15.24   too-small] ~ ∧ ~ N²,⁴; ~ - | ~ N³,T(p),E1

15.25–26   arrived, finally,] ~ ∧ ~∧ E1

15.26   Immediately∧] ~ , N²,T(p)

15.30   Then∧] ~ , N²,T(p)

15.31   clamor] clamour T(p),E1

15.33   "Tom . . . Tom——"] N³ *places after line* 15.35

15.35   blazes.] ~ ! E1

16.2   ballroom] ~ - ~ N⁴; ~ - | ~ T(p)

16.2   ballroom∧] ~ , E1

16.11   storming∧] ~ , N⁴,T(p)

16.11   opened∧] ~ , E1

16.12   way∧] ~ , E1

16.17   bare] *omit* E1

16.18   riveted] rivetted T(p)
16.22   steps$_\wedge$] ~ , E1
16.24   was] were N[1]
16.25   sea-gull] seagull N[2],E1
16.36   changed$_\wedge$ . . . moment$_\wedge$]
    ~ , . . . ~ , N[2,4],T(p)
16.38   shriveling] shrivelling
    T(p),E1
17.1   tingled] tinged N[3]
17.4   he$_\wedge$] ~ , E1
17.7   tall] all T(p[u])
17.7   trance$_\wedge$] ~ , N[4],E1
17.9–10   [2]I . . . suit!] omit E1
17.9   [2]such] omit N[2]
17.15   into] to N[4]
17.15.1   CHAPTER] omit N[2-4],T(p)
17.16   cool$_\wedge$] cold$_\wedge$ N[2]; cool, E1
17.18   [1]in$_\wedge$] ~ , E1
17.19   endeavoring] endeavouring
    T(p),E1
17.20   a solitary . . . and] omit
    N[1]
17.22   made . . . spars] omit N[1]
17.24   raft$_\wedge$] ~ , E1
17.25   shoreward] shorewards
    N[4],T(p),E1
17.25   [2]around$_\wedge$] ~ , E1
17.28   practiced] practised
    T(p),E1
17.30   warily] wearily E1
17.35   length$_\wedge$] ~ , N[2,4],T(p)
18.7   of summer] omit N[1]
18.25   He . . . shore.] omit N[3]
18.25   had] has E1
18.25   arisen$_\wedge$] ~ , E1
18.26   [3]Ted!] omit N[4]
18.27   matter] the matter N[1]
18.28   birdshot] ~ $_\wedge$ ~ N[2,4],T(p);
    ~ - ~ E1
18.30   tall] omit N[4]
18.31   shoreward] shorewards
    N[4],T(p)
18.36   erect$_\wedge$] ~ , N[2,4],T(p),E1
19.3   Suddenly$_\wedge$] ~ , N[2,4],T(p)
19.7   idiocy! You] ~ ; you E1
19.11–12   beseeching] beseech-
    ingly E1
19.21   fiercely] omit E1
19.25   exploded.] ~ $_\wedge$ T(p)
19.32   little] like N[3]
19.36   land,] ~ $_\wedge$ N[4],E1

19.36   colors] colours T(p),E1
19.37   voyagers,] ~ $_\wedge$ N[2,4],T(p)
19.38   quarreled] quarrelled
    T(p),E1
20.1   foller] follow E1
20.4.1   CHAPTER] omit N[2-4],T(p)
20.5   away$_\wedge$] ~ , E1
20.13   toward] towards
    N[4],T(p),E1
20.24   were] was E1
20.26   dress$_\wedge$suit] ~ - ~ E1
20.29   little$_\wedge$] ~ , N[2-4],T(p)
20.33   man,] ~ $_\wedge$ N[2-3],T(p)
21.7   he,] ~ $_\wedge$ N[2-4],T(p)
21.10   south] South N[2,4]
21.11   devilment$_\wedge$] ~ , E1
21.13   palm$_\wedge$trees] ~ - ~ N[2],T(p)
21.14   that.] ~ ! N[2-4],T(p)
21.16   distance$_\wedge$] ~ , N[2,4],T(p)
21.18   watched$_\wedge$] ~ , N[2-4],T(p)
21.20   Directly$_\wedge$] ~ , N[2],T(p)
21.20   -like] omit N[1]
21.21   eye$_\wedge$] ~ , N[2,4],T(p)
21.26   Ha!] ~ , N[2-4],T(p)
21.26   come] comes E1
21.26   rescuers!] ~ . $N(−N[1,4])+
21.31   -deck,] ~ $_\wedge$ N[2-3],T(p)
21.31   captain$_\wedge$] ~ , E1
21.33   Havanas] Havana's E1
21.37   Then$_\wedge$] ~ , N[2],T(p)
21.38   sea] the sea N[4]
22.6   meantime$_\wedge$] ~ , N[2,4],T(p)
22.7   in] of N[3]
22.7   blackness$_\wedge$] ~ , N[2,4],T(p)
22.11   "Hello (no ¶)] ¶ N[4]
22.14   wanderers] wanders N[2]
22.17   immediately$_\wedge$] ~ , T(p);
    omit E1
22.17   bawled] brawled E1
22.18   and,] ~ $_\wedge$ E1
22.25   darkness$_\wedge$] ~ , N[2],T(p),E1
22.25   clamor] clamour T(p),E1
22.28   time$_\wedge$] ~ , N[2],T(p)
22.31   gloom$_\wedge$] ~ , N[2,4],T(p)
22.33   raft$_\wedge$] ~ , N[2],T(p)
22.33   "Who (no ¶)] ¶ N[4]
23.1   side] sides N[4]
23.1   vessel$_\wedge$] ~ , N[2-3],T(p)
23.1   a] the E1
23.5; 29.26,36   inquired] enquired
    T(p)

23.7 bronzed] bronze N⁴,E₁
23.7 a solitary whisker] solitary whiskers E₁
23.9 bare₍] ~ , E₁
23.10 Fearful (no ¶)] ¶ E₁
23.13 capt'in₍] ~ , E₁
23.14–15 boun' . . . N.Y.,] omit E₁
23.14 Nyack] N'yack N²⁻⁴,T(p),E₁
23.16 Ah,] ~ ! N⁴,E₁
23.20.1 omit] CHAPTER IV. N¹; IV. N²⁻⁴,T(p)
23.21–22 He . . . statement.] omit E₁
23.22.1 CHAPTER IV] omit $N,T(p)
23.23 down₍] ~ , T(p)
23.24 time₍] ~ , T(p)
23.26 Soon₍] ~ , T(p)
23.26 charging] changing E₁
23.27 sky₍] ~ , N⁴,E₁
23.27 Highlands] highlands E₁
23.28 sparkled] sparkling E₁
23.31 suspender₍] suspenders₍ N³; suspender, E₁
24.3 recovered₍] ~ , N⁴,T(p),E₁
24.5 square,] ~ ₍ E₁
24.8 table,] ~ ₍ N²⁻⁴,T(p)
24.9 builded] built N³
24.9 Overhead] ~ - | ~ N²,⁴; ~ - ~ T(p)
24.13 broiled] boiled N⁴
24.20 Suddenly₍] ~ , N²,T(p),E₁
24.21 blazes] the blazes E₁
24.25 the bench] a bench E₁
24.32,35 coffee₍pot] ~ - ~ N²,⁴, T(p)
24.36 carefully₍] ~ , N²⁻³,T(p), E₁
24.39 excitement₍] ~ , E₁
25.1 goin'] going N⁴,E₁
25.4–5 suspender] suspenders $N+
25.6 et] eat E₁
25.9 look,] ~ ₍ E₁
25.10 at the] a E₁
25.10 beds] bed E₁
25.10 on] in N³
25.13 blankets,] ~ ₍ E₁
25.14 comfortably] comfortable E₁

25.16 suspender] suspenders E₁
25.17 cry₍] ~ , E₁
25.18 insistent,] ~ ₍ N³⁻⁴,T(p)
25.18 and₍ shortly₍] ~ , ~ , N²⁻³, T(p)
25.20 it₍] ~ , N²⁻⁴,T(p)
25.26 polka₍dots] ~ - ~ E₁
25.31 A] An N⁴,T(p),E₁
25.32 and₍ . . . voices₍] ~ , . . . ~ , N²,T(p),E₁
25.36 wan] wane E₁
25.39 up.] ~ , N⁴,T(p)
25.40 what is] what's E₁
26.4–5 man, . . . astrologer₍] ~ ₍ . . . ~ , N²⁻⁴,T(p)
26.6.1 CHAPTER V] PART II. | V. N²⁻⁴,T(p)
26.7 Directly₍] ~ , N²,⁴,T(p)
26.9 for] omit E₁
26.10 quarreled] quarrelled T(p), E₁
26.11 man,] ~ ₍ N²⁻⁴,T(p)
26.14,16 thunder] the thunder E₁
26.16 he,] ~ ₍ N²⁻⁴,T(p)
26.17 man,] ~ ₍ N³,E₁
26.26 are we to] omit N¹
26.27 Well,] omit E₁
26.28 any one] anyone N³⁻⁴,T(p)
26.30 Place."] ~ . ₍ N³⁻⁴,T(p)
27.2–3 ²What's that?] omit E₁
27.4 maybe₍] ~ , N²⁻⁴,T(p)
27.5 'im?] ~ . E₁
27.7 oilskins] ~ - ~ N²,⁴,T(p); ~ - | ~ N³
27.7 and] an N³
27.7 sou'wester] sou'-wester E₁
27.8 ²not!] ~ . E₁
27.11 can't] can E₁
27.11 There (no ¶)] ¶ N²
27.13 dock] pier N¹
27.15 here] her N²
27.16(twice),17,18 ain't] aint T(p)
27.16 ²ain't!] ~ . E₁
27.16 not!] ~ . E₁
27.17 thing! I ain't!] ~ . ~ ~ . E₁
27.19 lyin'] lying E₁
27.20 prodigiously snore] snore prodigiously N¹
27.21 vigor] vigour E₁

27.22 time͵] ~ , N²˙⁴,T(p)
27.23 the] omit E1
27.28 York,] ~ ͵ E1
27.31 ¶ He] no ¶ E1
27.32 at the freckled man] omit N¹
28.3 are?] ~ , E1
28.3 Philadelphia,] ~ ͵ N²⁻⁴,T(p)
28.7 here] omit E1
28.11 'em.] none, E1
28.11 The . . . away.] replied the captain promptly. E1
28.12 red͵] ~ , E1
28.13 man,] ~ ͵ N²˙⁴,T(p)
28.13 advancing,] omit E1
28.20 plot. And] ~ , and E1
28.22 acrobatics] acrobatic feats E1
28.23 demon͵] ~ , N²˙⁴,T(p)
28.30 man͵ then͵] ~ , ~ , T(p)
28.32 So! You've] So, you've E1
28.36 things,] ~ ͵ N³,E1
28.36 at all] omit N¹
28.39 opprobrious] approbrious N³
29.1–2 in the air] omit N¹
29.3 put] push N³
29.7,9 said͵] ~ , E1
29.11 "I'd (no ¶)] ¶ E1
29.11 repeated͵] ~ , E1
29.12 into] in E1
29.17 won't!] ~ , E1
29.18 won't.] ~ ! N²,E1
29.19 expostulated] expostoated T(p)
29.24 into] in N¹
29.27 ¶ "So] no ¶ N⁴
29.27 bright] mighty N²
29.27 boat͵] ~ , E1
29.33 rubber] the rubber N³
29.34 dock] shore E1
29.34 went͵] ~ , N⁴,T(p),E1
29.34 a] the E1
29.35 very] omit N³
30.0.1 CHAPTER] omit N²⁻⁴,T(p)
30.1 dock͵] pier͵ N¹; dock, N²˙⁴, T(p)
30.5 Tommie] Tommy E1
30.10 around] round N¹
30.19 other] other man E1
30.24 docks] piers N¹
30.29 wabbled] wobbled N²+
30.31 thunder] the thunder E1
30.34 th'] the E1
30.35 the blazes] in th' blazes E1
30.35 th'] the N¹,E1
30.37 boat] omit E1
31.2 fear͵] ~ , E1
31.2 great] omit N²,E1
31.3 orders,] ~ ͵ N²⁻⁴,T(p)
31.6 man͵] ~ , E1
31.10 astonishment͵] ~ , E1
31.11 dozing] dosing E1
31.11 dock͵] wharf͵ N¹; dock, N⁴, T(p)
31.12 ferryboat] ~ ͵ ~ N³; ~ - ~ N⁴,T(p),E1
31.19 839.] 839! E1
31.24 "It . . . companion.] line repeated in N³
31.24 wasn't] isn't N¹
31.25 gesticulate,] ~ ͵ N⁴,T(p)
31.26 boat͵] ~ , E1
31.26 their] the E1
31.28 been] omit N³
31.30 up͵] ~ , N²˙⁴,T(p),E1
31.38 remarked] said N¹
31.39 land͵] ~ , N²˙⁴,T(p)
32.1,11,24 dock] pier N¹
32.6 ²it] omit N²
32.8 rubber] the rubber E1
32.9 fro͵] ~ , E1
32.13 leveled] levelled T(p),E1
32.16 sea-wanderers] ~ ͵ ~ N³⁻⁴
32.17–19 They . . . man.] omit N³
32.20 pummeling] pummelling N²,T(p); pumbling E1
32.22 legs] leg E1
32.23 softly;] ~ , N²⁻⁴,T(p)
32.24 Together,] ~ ͵ N³,E1
32.24–25 Directly͵ . . . it͵] ~ , . . . ~ , N¹⁻²˙⁴,T(p)
32.26 drivers, on top,] ~ ͵ ~ ~ ͵ N³,E1
32.31 detour͵] ~ , E1
32.31 then] omit N¹
32.32 toward] towards E1
32.38 goner] gonner N²+
32.38 said͵] ~ , E1
33.1 groaned͵] ~ , N²˙⁴,T(p)
33.4 in͵] ~ , E1

33.5 of] *omit* E1
33.6 roared‸] ~ , E1
33.6 839‸] ~ , N², T(p)
33.7 cabman] driver E1
33.8 Oh] oh N³⁻⁴

33.9 off‸] ~ , N²ʼ⁴,T(p)
33.18 moment,] ~ ‸ T(p)
33.20 temper‸] ~ , E1
33.21 own self] ownself E1

No. 5. WHY DID THE YOUNG CLERK SWEAR?

[The copy-text is Tr: *Truth*, XII (March 18, 1893), 4–5. The other texts collated are TMs: typescript in the UVa.–Barrett Collection; E1: *Last Words*, Digby, Long, London, 1902, pp. 306–314. TMs and E1 are derived texts without authority.]

34.4 awaited] waited E1
34.8–9 comfortably] comfortable Tr+
34.18 *et seq.* Eloise] Heloise TMs(c),E1
34.25 morning, silly.' Silvere] morning, silly Silvere TMs; morning. Silly Silvere E1
34.27 on] at E1
35.34 am] am so E1
35.39 shirts] shirt E1

36.13 I'm] I am TMs,E1
37.8 differently] different TMs, E1
37.39 feller] fellow TMs
38.10 the place] his place TMs,E1
37.11 always] only TMs,E1
37.14 at?‸Haven't . . . idea?‸ Well] ~ ?" "~ . . .~ ?" " ~ E1
38.13 -pots] -plots E1

No. 6. AT CLANCY'S WAKE

[The copy-text is Tr: *Truth*, XII (July 3, 1893), 4–5. The other texts collated are TMs: typescript in the UVa.–Barrett Collection; E1: *Last Words*, Digby, Long, London, 1902, pp. 288–293. TMs and E1 are derived texts without authority.]

39.7 ¹in] *omit* TMs,E1
39.9 jest] jes' E1
39.28 the] *The* TMs(c)
39.30 domned] damned E1
40.13 th'] the E1
40.34 shtarvin'] starvin' TMs,E1
41.3 loife] life E1
41.4 furniter] furnitir E1

41.4 hand-runnin'] hard-runnin' E1
41.5 sowl] soul E1
41.14 the] th' E1
41.17 cit'zen] sit'zen E1
41.23–24 ²is— . . . know] *omit* TMs,E1

No. 8. AN OMINOUS BABY

[The copy-text is Ar: *Arena*, IX (May, 1894), 819–821. The other texts collated are Ph: *Philistine*, III (Oct., 1896), 133–137; E1: *The Open Boat*, Heinemann, London, 1898, pp. 253–257. Both Ph and E1 are derived texts without authority.]

48.28 powder] with powder E1
49.8 An . . . ablaze.] *omit* Ph, E1

49.31 thin] fat Ph,E1
50.19 swallowing] *omit* E1

No. 9. A GREAT MISTAKE

[The copy-text is Ph: *Philistine*, II (March, 1896), 106–109. The other texts collated are RQ: *Roycroft Quarterly*, I (May, 1896), 34–37; E1: *The Open Boat*, Heinemann, London, 1898, pp. 261–263. E1 is a derived text, without authority.]

50.28   laid] had laid E1
50.30   treasure] treasures E1
51.34   ²the] a E1
51.39   the Italian] this Italian E1

52.1   him] the babe E1
52.1–2   the vendor] this monarch E1
52.13   fingers] finger RQ

No. 11. AN EXCURSION TICKET

[The copy-text is N¹: *New York Press*, May 20, 1894, part IV, p. 3. The other texts collated are N¹(c): *New York Press* with Crane's holograph revisions (wanting after 62.35); TMs: typescript in the Special Collections of Columbia University Libraries. The latter is a derived text, without authority.]

59.6   thought,] thought of Omaha N¹
59.7   to Omaha] *omit* N¹
59.17   the nozzle] a nozzle TMs
59.29   rushed] rushed out of the shadow of the mountains and N¹
60.1   motionin'] motinnin' TMs
60.25   little] *omit* TMs
60.29   of the car] *omit* TMs(c)
60.39–61.1   ladder and] ladder an| TMs
61.14   were] was TMs
61.15   derby] pot hat TMs
61.18   I'll] I'will TMs
61.28   requires] requir| TMs(u); required TMs(c)
61.35   growing] grain TMs
62.5   thought] thought that TMs
62.12   Memphis] Memphis Ten-

nessee TMs
62.18   seems] seemed TMs
62.25   car] freigh car TMs
63.4   have been] be TMs
63.8   disarranging] disturbing TMs
63.19   on] upon TMs
63.32   changing] *omit* TMs
64.13   nor] or TMs
64.17   kind] sort TMs
64.24   pawn] a pawn TMs
64.26   an officer] a policeman TMs
64.27,34; 65.3   yeh] yer TMs
64.28   kin] can N¹,TMs
64.30   so's] so N¹
64.34   ways] way TMs
65.5   They] The TMs
65.5   gave] give N¹
65.5   an] *omit* TMs

No. 12. THE SNAKE

[The copy-text is MS: manuscript in the UVa.–Barrett Collection. The other texts collated are N¹: *St. Louis Globe-Democrat*, June 14, 1896, p. 36; N²: *Galveston Daily News*, June 14, p. 20; N³: *Cincinnati Commercial Gazette*, June 14, p. 20; N⁴: *Detroit Free Press*, June 14, p. 17; N⁵: *Minneapolis Tribune*, July 6, p. 4; PM: *Pocket Magazine*, II (Aug., 1896), 125–132; TMs: typescript in the UVa.–Barrett Collection; E1: *Last Words*, Digby, Long, London, 1902, pp. 268–272. TMs and E1 are derived texts, without authority.]

65.13 curling] curying N[2]
65.14 the] a TMs,E1
65.16 full] *omit* N[1,3,5]
65.18 unending] unbending N[3]
65.20 ²the] *omit* N[5]
65.31 drooping] dropping E1
66.6 warily] warly N[5]
66.8 as from] as if from TMs,E1
66.9 backward] forward PM,TMs, E1
66.17 no] not $N
66.17 slink] sink $N
66.19 approaching] approaching him N[4]
66.26 ¹was] were $N+
66.26–27 In the snake's . . . fear.] *omit* $N
66.26 ²was] were PM,TMs,E1
66.28 battle] a battle TMs,E1
66.28 of] *omit* $N

66.28 a] *omit* N[2]
66.36 caress] carcass N[1]
66.38 nature] Nature E1
66.39 that] *omit* $N
67.2 colorings] colouring E1
67.6 ¶ As] *no* ¶ N[4]
67.6 this] the N[2]
67.7 *et seq.* its] $N+; it's MS
67.15 was] were N[3], PM,TMs,E1
67.17 backward] *omit* PM,TMs, E1
67.22 steaming] streaming N[3]
67.25 ²of] for $N
67.34 its] his E1
67.35 his] the N[1]
67.37 sniffing] sniffling N[1-2]
67.37 neck and back] back and neck N[5]
67.39 were] was MS
68.5 show the] show to the N[5]

Reconstruction of the Bacheller *Proof*

[The proof agrees with MS except in the following cases where the majority of the five newspapers indicate that the proof reading differed. Please note that the MS reading to the left of the bracket is in unemended form.]

65.33 bushes∧] ∼ , $N
66.2 unguided∧] ∼ , $N
66.17 no wit] not wit $N
66.17 slink] sink $N
66.20 incredibly-swift] ∼ ∧ ∼ $N
66.26 ¹was] were $N
66.26–27 In the snake's . . . fear.] *omit* $N
66.27 manuvered] maneuvered N[1-3]; maneuvred N[4]; manoeuvred N[5]
66.28 of] *omit* $N
66.34 incurr] incur $N
66.35 friends∧] ∼ , $N

66.39 that] *omit* $N
67.5 skilful] skillful $N
67.7 *et seq.* it's] its $N
67.7 head∧] ∼ , $N(−N[3])
67.7 potentcy] potency $N
67.17 low∧ straight∧] ∼ , ∼ , $N
67.23 attack∧ it,] ∼ , ∼ ∧ $N
67.24 despairing∧] ∼ , $N
67.25 ²of] for $N
67.30 fore-fathers] forefathers $N
67.37 sniffing] sniffling N[1-2]
67.39 was] were $N

Alterations in the Manuscript

65.14 a] *interlined with a caret*
65.15 sun] *final 's' deleted*
65.22 tranquilly] *preceded by deleted* 'soberly'
65.28 change] *preceded by deleted* 'smite him'
65.33 hands] *'s' added later*

66.1 turn] *interlined above deleted* 'change'
66.4 him] *interlined*
66.34 strife] *interlined above deleted* 'war'
67.1 these] *first 'e' over 'i'; second 'e' added later*

67.4 formidable] *interlined above deleted* 'relentless'

67.7 its] MS 'it's' *preceded by deleted* 'h'

67.8 with] *interlined above deleted* 'in'

67.17 spring.] *followed by deleted* 'It h' *and deleted* 'This attack was in some way despairing but yet gallant, impetuous, ferocious, of the same quality as the charge of the lone chief when the walls of white faces close upon him in the mountains.'

67.18 blind, sweeping] *interlined with a caret above deleted* 'blindin'

67.19 blow] *followed by deleted* 'did not'

67.21 bended] *interlined with a caret*

67.22 steaming] *preceded by deleted* 'h'

67.22 made] *possibly added later at end of line*

67.31 his] *interlined above deleted* 'it's'

67.32 anguish] *interlined above deleted* 'agony'

67.36 came] *followed by deleted* 'forward'

67.36 with] *followed by deleted start of* 'h'

68.2 foes] 'es' *over* 'e'

68.2 once] *beginning stroke of* 'o' *over a comma with intent to delete*

68.4 man,] *followed by deleted* 'wit'

68.9 tranquilly] *preceded by deleted* 'soberly'

No. 13. STORIES TOLD BY AN ARTIST

[The copy-text is N¹: *New York Press,* Oct. 28, 1894, part IV, p. 6. The other texts collated are TMs: typescript in the UVa.–Barrett Collection; E1: *Last Words,* Digby, Long, London, 1902, pp. 133–145. TMs and E1 are derived texts without authority.]

68.12 is] are TMs(c),E1

68.26 head] his head N¹

69.19 at] in E1

69.19 shadows] shadow TMs,E1

69.24 the dusk] dusk TMs,E1

69.28 sketches] scratches TMs,E1

69.34 ceiling] ceilings TMs,E1

70.14 toward] towards E1

70.18 calmly] *omit* TMs,E1

70.34 I'm] I'd E1

71.21.1 As . . . Rent] THE RENT N¹,TMs ('As . . . Rent' *appeared as a subtitle in* TMs *at* 68.10.4)

71.24 Afterward] Afterwards TMs,E1

71.30 he had] *omit* TMs,E1

71.30 was] had was TMs

72.4 then] *omit* TMs,E1

72.14 deal of] *omit* TMs,E1

72.15 neat] great TMs,E1

72.35 *Amazement*] Amazement Magazine TMs,E1 (*italicized in* E1)

73.7 weeks] weeks' E1

73.8 day of] *omit* TMs,E1

73.29.1 How . . . Dinner] A DINNER ON SUNDAY EVENING N¹+ ('How . . . Dinner' *appeared as a subtitle in* TMs *at* 68.10.4)

73.33 then] had TMs,E1

74.26 Afterward] Afterwards E1

75.14 tramping] trampin' TMs, E1

75.14 a] *omit* TMs,E1

75.23 give] gave E1

No. 14. THE SILVER PAGEANT

[The copy-text is TMs: typescript in the UVa.–Barrett Collection. The other text collated is E1: *Last Words,* Digby, Long, London, 1902, pp. 145–148.]

76.2–3   Great   Contribution . . .
    Art] great   contribution . . .
    art E1

76.33   yet.] ~ , E1
77.5   preface] perface TMs(u),E1
77.11   feverish] Coverian E1

Alterations in the Typescript

[All alterations are in pencil unless otherwise indicated.]

76.4   Gaunt] *altered from* 'Grant'
76.13   ²was] *preceded by type x'd-out* 'that' *which was then struck through in ink*
76.25   last] 'l' *inserted*
76.35   don't] *apostrophe inserted*
77.1   see——"] *quotes supplied in ink*
77.3   superstitious] *type altered from* 'superstition'

77.5   preface] *altered from* 'perface'
77.9   men] *type altered from* 'man'
77.17   Gaunt] 't' *added in ink*
77.21   a] *over* 'a'
77.23   finally] 'a' *interlined with a caret*
77.27   going] *final* 'g' *added*

No. 15.   A DESERTION

[The copy-text is TMs: typescript in the UVa.–Barrett Collection. The other texts collated are HM: *Harper's Magazine*, CI (Nov., 1900), 938–939; E1: *Last Words*, Digby, Long, London, 1902, pp. 245–251. E1 is completely derived and without authority.]

77.31   gaslight] yellow gas-light E1
78.2   conflict] effect HM
78.5   t' fool 'im,] it' fool 'in. TMs
78.5   An'] ~ ₄ TMs
78.8   ses] says HM
78.10   On'y] Only TMs; O'ny E1
78.12   begin] begun HM
78.12   t'] to E1
78.15   expressions] expression E1
78.18   into] in HM
78.22   effects] effect HM
78.27   ideas] idea E1
78.38   ¶ "Oh] *no* ¶ HM
79.5   ¶ Again] *no* ¶ HM
79.12   in this] in the light of this TMs,E1
79.17   on'y] o'ny TMs
79.22   ¹the] a HM
79.26   'a] 'a' HM
79.26   home] *omit* HM
79.26,35   on'y] o'ny TMs,E1
79.27   'til] till HM
79.28,29,32,33   wanta] wanter HM
79.30   Yer] Yeh HM
79.31   paradin'] paradin' through

HM+
79.31   th'] the E1
79.34   know] knew TMs
79.34   He's] His TMs
79.36   sed] ses E1
79.37   he'd] he HM
80.1   th'ell] th' 'ell E1
80.3–4   in, b'Gawd . . . ain't] *omit* HM
80.5,6   'a] o' HM
80.8   ¶ After] *no* ¶ HM
80.19   The (*no* ¶)] ¶ HM
80.19   were] was TMs
80.21–22   *mad . . . mad*] mad . . . mad E1
80.21–22   really-truly] ~ , ~ HM; ~ — ~ E1
80.23,27   ¶ She] *no* ¶ HM
80.28   toward] towards HM
80.29   that] *omit* HM
80.35   splattered] spattered E1
80.36   fire. Her] fire, her HM
81.3   ¶ Again] *no* ¶ HM
81.3   terrible] *omit* HM
81.4   directed] direct HM
81.6   arm] arms TMs
81.6   its] it's TMs

81.7 corpse] body HM
81.8 arising] rising HM
81.9 from] form TMs
81.9 hers] her HM
81.10.1 [space]] *line of* x's *in*
TMs; *no space* HM; *line of as-*
terisks in E1
81.17 anythin'] anything HM
81.19 damned] dammed TMs;
omit HM
81.20 He's drivin' 'er] He' drivi'er
TMs

Alterations in the Typescript

[All alterations were made in black ink unless otherwise specified.]

78.1 gestures] *final 's' added*
78.6 'im] *apostrophe prefixed*
78.7 keepin'] *final 'g' deleted*
78.7 'er] *interlined with a caret*
78.7 bad,] *comma inserted*
78.8–9 t' let . . . purty!] *inter-*
lined above a caret and a de-
leted illegible letter; 't' ' altered
from 'to'
78.9 Sadie——"] *quotes and dash*
added
78.10 "Well . . . On'y] *inter-*
lined with a caret and preceded
by paragraph sign above de-
leted 'O' my'; TMs variant read-
ings are '∧Well', ' 'er∧', and
'Only'
78.12 Dorter, dorter,] *'o' over 'a'*
in each case
78.12–13 'Dorter . . . here!' "]
TMs ' "Dorter . . . here!" '
with the double quotes added
78.20 her] *preceded by two de-*
leted 'h's' (one above and one
below the line)
78.23 dangers] *final 's' and a*
comma added
79.11 parts] *final 's' added*
79.12 blood-red] *preceding 'red'*
deleted
79.14 toward] *final 's' deleted*
79.17 on'y] TMs 'o'ny' *interlined*
with a caret above deleted
typed 'ony' with an apostrophe
inserted in ink first before and
then after the 'o'
79.18 somewheres."] *quotes*
added
79.20 it where it] 'where' *imme-*
diately followed by deleted 'i'
and then followed by deleted
'it where' of which 'where' type
x'd out
79.22 Presently] 'P' *over* 'p'
79.29 advice'] *quote added*
79.34 yeh!'] TMs 'yeh'!' *with ex-*
clamation point altered from a
comma
79.34 business,] *comma added*
79.34 'im.] 'm' *over* 'n' *and period*
altered from comma
79.35 'im.] *period altered from*
comma
79.36 ses.] *period inserted*
79.39 girl] *final 's' deleted*
80.1 advice.] *period altered from*
comma
80.1 What] 'W' *over* 'w'
80.1 father?'] *final 's' deleted and*
quote added
80.2 What's] 'W' *over* 'w'
80.2 me?' 'If] *quotes added; the*
second above a deleted quote
80.3 'im,'] *comma and quote*
added
80.4 in.'] *quote added*
80.5 either.] *period over comma*
80.9 We'll] *preceded by type*
x'd-out 'Will'
80.11–12 posture] *preceded by*
type x'd-out 'positio'
80.18 moods] *preceded by type*
x'd-out 'weerd'; *followed by*
type x'd-out 'usaly'
80.22 me!"] TMs 'me."' *preceded*
by type x'd-out 'me"' with
quotes separately deleted
80.24 then] *inserted at end of*
line
80.25 own.] *preceded by type*
x'd-out ' "Oh, daddie!'
81.13 stairway] TMs 'stair-way'
with hyphen over 's'

No. 15a. NOTEBOOK DRAFT

[The copy-text is MS: manuscript draft in the Crane Notebook in the UVa.–Barrett Collection.]

Alterations in the Manuscript

81.20.2   [*blank*]] *deleted original title* 'Discovery of the Crime'

81.22   animatedly.] *period altered from semicolon; followed by deleted* 'and'

81.22   Their] 'T' *over* 't'

81.24   came] *followed by deleted* 'back'

81.24   her] *over* 'on'

81.28   It] *preceded by deleted* 'Mary'

81.28   ²was] *preceded by deleted* 'must'

81.30   a] *over illegible letter*

81.32   near] *interlined above deleted* 'on'

81.35   four] 'f' *over a possible* 'l'

82.1   I] *over* 'P'

82.1   where] *a final* 's' *deleted*

82.7   joyous] *preceded by deleted* 'cry'

82.8   pouting] *followed by deleted* 'at once now'

No. 16. A CHRISTMAS DINNER WON IN BATTLE

[The copy-text is PTJ: *Plumbers' Trade Journal, Gas, Steam and Hot Water Fitters' Review*, XVII (Jan. 1, 1895), 26–27. The other text collated is T(p): corrected proof Tillotson's.]

82.10   learned] began T(p)

82.15   to a] into a T(p)

82.16   aldermen] alderman PTJ

82.26   and] *omit* T(p)

82.31   already] *omit* T(p)

82.33   to once] once to T(p)

82.34 *et seq.*   5.30] five-thirty T(p) (*except* 5–30 *at* 84.5)

83.17   green] great T(p)

83.26   could] should T(p)

83.33   dare to] *omit* T(p)

83.35   knew that] knew T(p)

83.38   Fortmans] Fortman's PTJ, T(p)

83.39   grades] grade T(p)

85.6   town] the town T(p)

85.16   evidences] evidence T(p)

85.21   Parisians] the Parisians T(p)

85.22   revolution] Revolution T(p)

85.36   a] *omit* T(p)

85.38–39   A . . . line:] *omit* T(p)

86.1,2,3   th'] the T(p)

86.6   ²the] this T(p)

86.9   hesitated] hesitated for T(p)

86.25   outa] out a T(p)

87.3   a] an ancient T(p[c])

87.14   dragons] wild beasts T(p[c])

87.20   He] he PTJ(c) (*reduced to lower case by* Cora), T(p)

87.26   minute] moment T(p)

87.30   said Mildred] Mildred said T(p)

88.5   as] *omit* T(p)

88.15   are] are going T(p)

88.19   damnitall] damitall T(p)

No. 17. THE VOICE OF THE MOUNTAIN

[The copy-text is N¹: *Nebraska State Journal*, May 22, 1895, p. 4. The other texts collated are PM: *Pocket Magazine*, III (Nov., 1896), 136–142; TMs: typescript in the Special Collections of Columbia University Libraries; E1: *Last Words*, Digby, Long, London, 1902, pp. 301–305. Both TMs and E1 are derived texts and without authority.]

88.21 *et seq.* Popocatepetl] Popocatapetl N¹ (PM *at* 91.9)
88.28 islands] island TMs,E1
89.21 Popocatepetl] Popcatepetl
TMs
90.14 head of the] *omit* TMs,E1
90.20 Popocatepetl] Popocateptel

90.35 performances] performance TMs,E1
91.6 summoned] summonsed
TMs
91.13 this] the TMs,E1

No. 18. HOW THE DONKEY LIFTED THE HILLS

[The copy-text is N¹: *Nebraska State Journal*, June 6, 1895, p. 4. The other texts collated are PM: *Pocket Magazine*, IV (June, 1897), 144–151; TMs: typescript in the UVa.–Barrett Collection; E1: *Last Words*, Digby, Long, London, 1902, pp. 252–257. TMs and E1 are derived texts, without authority.]

91.21 him] *omit* E1
91.22 wrong] *omit* E1
92.3 man] men TMs
92.3 that] *omit* TMs,E1
92.26–27 mountains] mountain
E1
93.18 your] you N¹
93.33 the stones] stones E1

93.39 the heap] a heap TMs,E1
94.2–3 The . . . mountains.]
omit E1
94.4 new] *omit* E1
94.23 him] them PM
94.25 towards] toward E1
94.26 the leaves] leaves E1

No. 19. THE VICTORY OF THE MOON

[The copy-text is N¹: *Nebraska State Journal*, July 24, 1895, p. 4. The other texts collated are PM: *Pocket Magazine*, IV (July, 1897), 144–152; TMs: typescript in the UVa.–Barrett Collection; E1: *Last Words*, Digby, Long, London, 1902, pp. 315–320. TMs and E1 are derived texts without authority.]

95.3 sun's] sun PM+
95.7 truth] the truth TMs,E1
95.14 man] *omit* TMs,E1
95.33 Afterwards] Afterward
PM+
96.10 knew] know TMs,E1
96.25 a] *omit* TMs,E1
96.25 then] seen E1
96.36 yet] *omit* E1

97.1 The (*no* ¶)] ¶ PM
97.3–4 there will] will there PM+
97.10 think] think that TMs,E1
97.23 appear] to appear TMs,E1
97.25 in] by N¹
97.39 doubtless] have doubtless
N¹,PM
98.5 ¹my] *omit* TMs,E1
98.6 my stupidity] *omit* TMs,E1

No. 21. ART IN KANSAS CITY

[The copy-text is MS: manuscript in the Special Collections of Columbia University Libraries.]

Alterations in the Manuscript

99.22 remarkable] *preceded by deleted* 'quite'
99.25 that her] *interlined above deleted* 'of the thinness'

99.27 fancy.] *interlined above deleted* 'spirit.'
99.27 a] *interlined with a caret*
99.28–29 his cow to sketch] *in-*

terlined with a caret
99.29 ¹to] interlined with a caret

100.1 -colour] 'u' altered from 'r'
100.7 not] interlined with a caret

No. 22. A TALE OF MERE CHANCE

[The copy-text is N¹: *Chicago Tribune*, March 15, 1896, p. 41. The other texts collated are N²: *Buffalo News*, March 15, p. 9; N³: *St. Louis Globe-Democrat*, March 15, p. 41; N⁴: *New Orleans Picayune*, March 15, p. 26; N⁵: *Galveston Daily News*, March 15, p. 12; N⁶: *Nebraska State Journal*, March 15, p. 11; N⁷: *Minneapolis Tribune*, March 22, p. 11 (reprint of N⁶); PM: *Pocket Magazine*, 1 (April, 1896), 115–122; EIM: *English Illustrated Magazine*, XIV (March, 1896), 569–571 (EIM's independent authority is somewhat doubtful except on a partial basis); CL: *Current Literature*, XIX (June, 1896), 516; BT: *Best Things from American Literature*, 1899, pp. 69–71; TMs: typescript in the UVa.–Barrett Collection; E1: *Last Words*, Digby, Long, London, 1902, pp. 282–287. N⁷, CL, BT, TMs, and E1 are derived texts without authority.]

100.7.2–5 Being . . . -leg.] *omit* CL

100.9 were it not] if it were not $N,E1

100.10 and] or PM,BT

100.13 of contact] of the contact PM,BT,TMs,E1

100.16 sort of a] sort of N⁷,EIM, CL,BT,TMs(c)

100.17 servants] servant $N,CL

100.18 tall old] old tall PM,BT, TMs,E1

100.19–20 remained . . . ¹of] retained $N,CL

100.20 imperturbability] imperturbality N⁶⁻⁷

100.28 gasp] grasp TMs(u)

101.6 smoothly, and I] smoothly; I $N,CL

101.12 them] then TMs(u)

101.14 so] *omit* TMs,E1

101.21 clash-clash] ~ , ~ , EIM

101.21 those] these PM,BT,TMs, E1

101.25–32 I am . . . murdered."] *omit* CL

101.26 desperately fertile] desperate, fertile PM,BT,TMs,E1

101.28–29 blaze . . . would] *omit* N²

101.30 eyes] eye EIM

101.33 following] pursuing $N, CL

101.33 troop] troupe EIM; troops TMs,E1

101.34 give] gave N¹

101.36 murderers] murders PM, TMs

101.37 streets] street EIM

101.38 clamoring] clamorous N², CL

101.39 in] of $N,CL

102.4 detectives] detective PM, BT,TMs,E1

102.5 Tamaulipas] Taumalipas $N(−N¹),PM,CL,BT,TMs,E1; Taumanipas EIM

102.6–8 I . . . dream.] *omit* CL

102.7 what's] Whats's TMs(u)

102.8 friend] friends N⁴

102.10 ends] end EIM

102.11 birds] little birds TMs,E1

102.14 which . . . intricate] *omit* CL

102.15 hunt] huning TMs(u); hunting TMs(c),E1

102.15 of] for CL

102.17 -after] -past EIM

102.18 chanced] chance PM,BT, TMs(u)

102.26 credit] a credit N⁵

102.26 pervading] prevading TMs

102.29 At] In the N²,CL

102.30 a long] along N²; long CL, E1

102.30	flock] flocks $N^{2,6-7}$,CL
102.31	things, they] things. In the day they N^2,CL (things,— in)
102.33	vividly] vivid $N,CL
102.34	was] were PM,BT,TMs,E1

102.38	effort] an effort $N,CL; efforts EIM
102.39	the grip] a grip TMs,E1
103.1	in] into N^4,PM,BT,TMs,E1
103.6	was] is EIM
103.13	to them] the them N^2

No. 24. A FREIGHT CAR INCIDENT

[The copy-text is N^1(p): proof for the *Nebraska State Journal*, April 12, 1896, p. 11, in the Special Collections of Columbia University Libraries. The other texts collated are N^1: *Nebraska State Journal*; N^2: *Buffalo Sunday News*, April 12, p. 9; N^3: *St. Louis Globe-Democrat*, April 12, p. 41; N^4: *Louisville Courier-Journal*, April 12, sec. III, p. 8; N^5: *Brooklyn Daily Eagle*, April 12, p. 19; N^6: *Philadelphia Press*, April 19, p. 37; N^7: *Rochester Democrat and Chronicle*, April 12, p. 16; EIM: *English Illustrated Magazine*, xv (June, 1896), 273–275; TMs: typescript in the Special Collections of Columbia University Libraries. It should be noted that the designation N^1 applies to both the proof and the final published version, and only where they differ will the symbol N^1(p) appear. TMs is a derived text without authority.]

105.10	open] open up EIM
105.10	free] *omit* EIM
105.24	this] his $N^{2,4}$
105.25	that] *omit* EIM
105.25	had] *omit* EIM
105.33	wishing] wishing that EIM
106.11	th'] the EIM
106.11	hell] h—l N^6
106.14–17	"He . . . corner.] *omit* TMs
106.15	supposed] supposed that N^3; suppose $N^{4,6}$; suppose that EIM
106.15	wasn't] wa'n't N^4,EIM
106.19	er yeh] er yer EIM; er yen TMs
106.20	now] naw N^5
106.20	ye] yeh EIM
106.28	you] yeh EIM
106.30	Give] Give me N^5
106.31	of] of a EIM
106.34	yeh] yer N^5,TMs
107.10	Th'] The' N^1(p); The TMs
107.10	hain't] ain't N^2
107.11	a goner] goner N^1 (N^1[p]:

	a goner)
107.15	damned] durned N^5
107.15	fellow] follow N^5
107.16	make er] make a N^2
107.17	yeh] yer EIM
107.25	as] es EIM
107.25	th'] the EIM
107.26	erside] enside $N; inside TMs
107.27	er] a' EIM
107.38–39	"But . . . the——'] *omit* N^4
107.39	damn'] damned N^3; durn N^5; damn$_\wedge$ EIM
107.39	'a] o' N^5; a' EIM
108.13	board] broad N^1(p)
108.18	respectful] respectable N^6
108.20	away] a way EIM
108.21	th'] the N^4
108.27	there's] ther's EIM
108.31–32	th' door . . . hisself,] *omit* N^3
108.32	hisself] hissel N^6
108.36	around] *omit* EIM
108.38	him] *omit* N^1(p[u])

No. 26. A YELLOW UNDER-SIZED DOG

[The copy-text is N^1: *Denver Republican*, Aug. 16, 1896, p. 18. The other texts collated are N^2: *Boston Globe*, Aug. 16, supplement, p. 2; N^3: *Pitts-*

burgh Leader, Aug. 16, p. 21. Since all texts are of equal authority, accidental agreements of N$^{2-3}$ against N^1 are recorded here.]

109.17; 110.36	The (*no* ¶)] ¶ N^2	110.12	course$_\wedge$] ~ , N^3
109.20–22	"Mulligan . . . off."]	110.14	whoop$_\wedge$] ~ , N$^{2-3}$
	omit N^2	110.15,18,29	He (*no* ¶)] ¶ N^2
109.21	home$_\wedge$] ~ , N^3	110.17	he] *omit* N^2
109.22	whin] with N^1; when N^3	110.21	blasting$_\wedge$] ~ , N$^{2-3}$
109.23	But] *omit* N^2	110.27	preparing] prepared N^3
109.24	mind$_\wedge$] ~ , N$^{2-3}$	110.28	illy-] ill- N^1
109.26	He (*no* ¶)] ¶ N^2	111.5	dogs$_\wedge$] ~ , N$^{2-3}$
110.3	Now (*no* ¶)] ¶ N^2	111.9–12	He . . . attention.] *omit*
110.4	this] the N^3		N^2
110.6	of the] in the N^3	111.9	under-sized;] ~ , N^3
110.6	The (*no* ¶)] ¶ N^2	111.16	Many (*no* ¶)] ¶ N^2
110.11	too$_\wedge$] ~ , N$^{2-3}$	111.17	"There (*no* ¶)] ¶ N^3
110.12–13	Of . . . but] *omit* N^2		

No. 27. A DETAIL

[The copy-text is PM: *Pocket Magazine,* II (Nov., 1896), 145–148. The other texts collated are MS: manuscript draft in the private collection of Comdr. Melvin H. Schoberlin USN (Ret.); N^1: *Chicago Daily News,* Aug. 31, 1896, p. 8; N^2: *Buffalo Evening News,* Aug. 30, p. 9; N^3: *Nebraska State Journal,* Aug. 30, p. 10; N^4: *Galveston Daily News,* Aug. 30, p. 18; E1: *The Open Boat,* Heinemann, London, 1898, pp. 299–301; BT: *Best Things from American Literature,* 1899, pp. 415–416; A: *Academy,* LVIII (June 9, 1900), 491. BT and A are derived texts without atuhority. An agreement in an accidental of two or more of the authoritative texts is recorded here.]

111.19	tiny] *omit* MS	111.30	this] this way N$^{3-4}$
111.19–20	in the . . . bonnet]	111.31; 112.5	at] *omit* N^1
	omit MS	111.32–112.1	They were . . .
111.21	But] *omit* MS		set.] *omit* MS
111.21	later$_\wedge$] ~ , MS	111.32	well-dressed] ~ $_\wedge$ ~ N^{2,4}
111.21–22	about . . . tempest]	111.33	full-rigged] ~ $_\wedge$ ~ N^{2,4}
	them when she came upon the	112.2	they . . . window.] they
	turmoil MS		proceeded leisurely. MS
111.21	about] all about N^3,BT	112.3	tiny . . . much] her MS
111.22	for] and N^3	112.4	tremendously] *omit* MS
111.22	Avenue] avenue $N,BT	112.5	She (*no* ¶)] ¶ MS
111.23–24	where . . . torrents]	112.5	them] the young women
	omit MS		MS; the girls E1,A
111.24	from] from the N^4	112.7	"Excuse (*no* ¶)] ¶ MS,N^2,
111.25–26	She . . . river.] Some-		E1,A
	times she seemed to doubt her	112.7	The (*no* ¶)] ¶ N^2,E1,A
	own wisdom; MS	112.7	girls] young women MS
111.26	impetuous] *omit* N^4	112.8 *et seq.*	its] it's MS
111.27	Frequently (*no* ¶)] ¶ MS	112.8	toward] towards E1,A
111.28	of a sudden] suddenly MS	112.8	"Excuse (*no* ¶)] ¶ N^2,E1,A
111.29–30	evidently . . . way.]	112.8	but] *omit* E1,A
	lose courage and pass on. MS	112.10	girls] young women MS

112.10 stared. Then they] *omit* MS

112.11 smile_∧] ~ , $N,E1

112.11 checked it.] intercepted this significant look because MS

112.12 tiny] *omit* MS

112.12 them.] their faces and MS

112.13 serious, . . . expectant.] serious and innocent. MS

112.13 She made] She seemed like a flower carried by the winds of destiny through a world of lies and she made MS

112.15 innocent] *omit* MS

112.15 glance_∧] ~ , $N,E1,BT,A

112.16 trustfulness] truthfulness N[3]

112.19 I'm not] I am not very MS

112.21 was] were N[1]

112.23 The young] Then the two young MS

112.23 did then] then did N[3]

112.23 then] *omit* MS

112.23 smile_∧] ~ , $N,E1,BT,A

112.24 subtly] subtle E1,A

112.24 verge] edge E1,A

112.25 madame] madam N[1-2],BT

112.25 hesitatingly] *omit* MS

112.27,33 tiny] *omit* MS

112.27 a] the MS

112.28 disappointment] first disappointment MS

112.28 "Don't (*no* ¶)] ¶ N[2],E1,A

112.28–29 a little . . . voice.] an attempt at courage. MS

112.30 girl] young woman MS

112.31 address,] ~ _∧ N[1,4]

112.31 some one] anyone N[3]

112.31 do,] ~ _∧ N[1,4]

112.34 girl] other MS

112.34 write] write it MS

112.36 smiling] smilingly N[2]

112.37 As . . . curb] The two girls went to the edge of the side-walk MS

112.37 girls_∧] ~ , $N,E1

112.37 went] walked E1,A

112.37 this] the N[4]

112.38 small] tiny MS

112.38 gown] dress MS

112.39 last,] ~ _∧ $N(−N[3]),A

113.1–2 suddenly engulfed it.] swallowed it, as if the mouth of a monster had opened. The girls stood wondering. MS

No. 27a. EARLY DRAFT

[The copy-text is MS: manuscript draft in the private collection of **Comdr. Melvin H. Schoberlin USN (Ret.).**]

Alterations in the Manuscript

113.3 the] *interlined with a caret*

113.3 made] 'ma' *over* 'her'

113.6 so] *preceded by deleted* 'so |'

113.13 window] 'indo' *over illegible letters, possibly* 'indow'

113.20 work?] *question mark altered from period*

113.27 were] 'w' *over* 's'

113.28 trustfulness] *preceded by deleted* 'ignor'

113.30 continued] 'con' *over* 'wa' *and the beginning of another letter*

113.32 can sew] *interlined above deleted* 'am a good sewer'

113.36 subtly] 'y' *over* 'e'

114.3 shade] 'e' *over* 'o'

114.4 "Don't] *quotes written over an* 'A'

114.10 visiting] *interlined above deleted* 'business'

114.14 aged] *preceded by deleted* 'tiny'

114.17 stood] 'sto' *over doubtful* 'wat'

No. 28. DIAMONDS AND DIAMONDS

[The copy-text is TMs: typescript in the UVa.–Barrett Collection.]

Alterations in the Typescript

[All alterations are in black ink unless otherwise specified.]

114.33–115.1 "You . . . bundle."] *quotes supplied*

115.13 ring?] *question mark altered from a period*

115.14–15 nothing . . . No."] *typed in at the foot of p. 1 when the carbon did not come through clearly*

115.22,28,34; 118.12 don't] *apostrophe inserted*

116.11 it's] *followed by 'g' struck through on the typewriter*

117.5 away.] *interlined with a caret by* Cora *above deleted* 'down the sidewalk. When he stopped he said: "Well, [quote supplied] I'll take the ring at a hundred." [period over 'd'];*

this repaired the typist's eye-skip

117.9 "I'll] *in TMs begins a new paragraph at head of p. 4, but an arrow is drawn at the foot of p. 3 after partially erased opening double quotes to indicate the run-on*

117.14 your] 'r' *inserted*

117.19 boy,"] *quotes supplied*

117.35 endured] TMs 'endeured' *with 'u' typed over 'd' of* 'ended'

118.10 ward,] *following* 'ward' *deleted*

118.11 make you] *final 'r' after* 'you' *struck through on typewriter*

No. 30. A MAN BY THE NAME OF MUD

[The copy-text is TMs: typescript in the UVa.–Barrett Collection. The other text collated is E1: *Last Words*, Digby, Long, London, 1902, pp. 258–262.]

122.17 then] them E1
123.6 question] questions TMs
123.7 Damned] Dammed TMs

123.25 own] *omit* E1
123.29 maybe] may be E1

Alterations in the Typescript

[Original readings not recoverable after deletion or alteration are ignored. All alterations are in black ink unless otherwise specified.]

121.26–27 and when . . . unapproachable] *interlined with a caret by* Cora

122.2 stare] *period deleted following*

122.5 "In back."] *final quotes added; preceded by ' "In back.' typed out and ink deleted*

122.9 Great—eh] *dash inserted in pencil after comma but in suitable space*

122.11 a contemplation] *preceded by typed out* 'the'

122.12 fell] *second 'l' over 't'*

122.14 friend's] 's' *following 'd' typed out*

122.15 absence] TMs 'abscence' *with final 's' deleted*

122.16 perceive] *altered in pencil from typed* 'preceived'

122.23 the] *over probable* 'The'

122.25,26 Comique] 'm' *interlined in pencil above deleted* 'n'; *at* 122.26 *interlined in ink*

122.25 probably] *second 'b' interlined with a caret*

122.31 went.] TMs *colon altered to semicolon in pencil without change of 'C' of 'Chorus'*

122.32 prowl.'] TMs *double quotes supplied*

122.35 thing] *preceded by typed out* 'word'

123.1 don't] TMs 'dont' *preceded by typed out* 'don't'

123.4 back?'] TMs *double quotes supplied*

123.5 he——'] *typed single quote after* 'he' *not altered but double quotes supplied after dash*

123.5 virtues—] *interlined with a caret by* Cora

123.7 me?'] TMs *double quotes supplied*

123.7–8 'Damned . . . know.'] TMs *double quotes supplied* (TMs: Dammed)

123.9 Not wildly] 'N' *over* 'n'; 'wildly' *preceded by typed out* 'willingly'

123.13 ²ambitions] *pencil* 'n' *over* 'u'

123.16–17 Displays, and feels,] *commas inserted in pencil*

123.17 faintly] *altered in pencil from* 'faithly'

123.17 heard] 'a' *interlined with*

a caret

123.18 They] *preceded by typed out* 'Part at last in front'

123.19 front of] *comma following deleted in pencil*

123.19–20 'Good . . . chap.' 'Good-night.'] TMs *double quotes supplied*

123.21 good-night] *period following struck through on typewriter*

123.22 desire] *final* 's' *struck through on typewriter*

123.24 ignorant,] *comma inserted*

123.27 supper] *following period deleted on typewriter as part of following typed out* 'reguarly and reguarly.'

123.31 Lays] *preceded by typed out and ink deleted* 'Lays f< > them < >'

123.31 'em] *apostrophe added after deleted possible apostrophe*

123.38 girl] *final* 's' *deleted followed by deleted* 'of'

123.39 stunning] *preceded by typed out, ink deleted* 'stunning'

124.1 and] 'd' *added*

No. 31. A SELF-MADE MAN

[The copy-text is TMs: typescript in the UVa.–Barrett Collection. The other texts collated are C: *Cornhill Magazine*, n.s., VI (March, 1899), 324–329; E1: *Last Words*, Digby, Long, London, 1902, pp. 273–281. E1 is the copy-text for lines 129.11–29. Agreement between C and E1 in rejected accidentals as well as in substantives is recorded, except for English spellings.]

124.4.2 Anyone] ~ ∧ ~ C,E1
124.8 dollars∧] ~ , C,E1
124.12 sole∧] ~ , C,E1
124.15 ability∧] ~ , C,E1
124.24 of] off E1
124.24 land-lady] landlady C,E1
124.26 him∧] ~ , C,E1
125.1 hurry∧] ~ , C,E1
125.5 face∧] ~ , C,E1
125.10 pocket∧] ~ , C,E1
125.11 enquired] inquired C,E1
125.11 The (*no* ¶)] ¶ C,E1

125.18 lookin'] looking E1
125.18 fur an] fer an TMs,C; for an E1
125.22 railing] railings C,E1
125.26 elbow∧] ~ , C,E1
125.28 attorney∧at∧law] Attorney-at-Law C,E1
125.29 July] May TMs+
125.29 18—∧] ~ —. C,E1
125.31 sir: | [¶ I] Sir,—I C(SIR),E1
125.33 forwarded] have for-

warded TMs

125.34; 126.9   June 25th] June 25
C; 25th June E1

126.1   out-lying] out-laying
TMs,E1

126.1   -brush] ∧bush TMs+ (C:
-bush)

126.2   ∧ of Boston∧] , ∼ ∼ , C,E1

126.3   ∧ no doubt∧] , ∼ ∼ , C,E1

126.7   ¶ Inform] no ¶ C

126.10   Eastern] eastern TMs+

126.11   Western] western TMs+

126.20   heard] herd TMs

127.6   large bales] larger valves
TMs

127.8   defeat] defeats TMs

127.9   house∧] ∼ , C,E1

127.10   ware-houses] warehouses
C,E1

127.12   half of] half C

127.14   Too,] omit E1

127.18   -stone] -stoned TMs

127.19   earth-works] earthworks
C,E1

127.23,27   a] omit TMs

127.25   ∧ Mr. . . . Smith∧]
, ∼ . . . ∼ , C,E1

127.26   June 25th] 25th June E1

127.28   table-cover∧] ∼ - ∼ ,
C,E1(tablecover)

127.36   George∧] ∼ , C,E1

128.3   screws] screw TMs

128.7   Tom∧] ∼ , C,E1

128.8   There (no ¶)] ¶ C

128.11   latter] later TMs

128.13   more∧] ∼ , C,E1

128.15   'though] though C

128.15   only] omit TMs

128.17   threats∧] ∼ , C,E1

128.20   ¶ Tom] no ¶ C

128.28   side-walk,] ∼ - ∼ ∧
C(sidewalk),E1

128.33   see'im] see him TMs

128.33   dersert] desert | dersert
TMs; desert C,E1

128.37–38   , at advanced rates,]
∧ ∼ ∼ ∼ ∧ C,E1

128.39   proprietress'] proprietress's C

128.39   smiles∧] ∼ , C,E1

129.3,15   -brush] -bush C,E1(∧ ∼)

129.6   who] who who TMs

129.11–29   So . . . match."]
omit TMs

Alterations in the Typescript

[Alterations are in ink unless otherwise specified.]

124.21   (king,] *parenthesis and
comma added*

124.26   had] *interlined with a
caret, probably by* Cora

124.26   him] *'m' typed over 's'*

125.2   thing] *preceded by typed
'sight' deleted by typed x's*

125.17   honest,] *typed comma inserted with a caret placed over
a period*

125.18   a'most] *preceded by typed
'six' deleted by typed x's*

125.35   my] *typed 'm' over* 'I'

125.35   the] *interlined with a
caret with a fine pen and perhaps by the writer of the signature at the end*

125.38   four] *interlined with a
caret probably by* Cora

126.1   acres] *'re' written over* 'er'

126.3   shrewd] *'e' after 'w' struck
through*

126.6   projected-horse-] *preceded
by typed 'project-horse-' deleted
by typed x's*

126.15   Methodist] *'M' over 'm'
and 't' added*

126.16   The] *preceded by typed
'There' deleted by typed x's*

126.17   not——] *dash altered
from a period*

126.24   now,"] *quote marks added
in ink; followed by typed
' "Brace u' deleted by typed x's*

126.34   "are] *' "are' ending a line
is followed by a whole typed
line deleted by typed x's reading 'you a lawyer as well as a
reader' with ' "Well", said Tom
again, "I might appear to advantage' typed over; ' "Well"
. . .' begins on 'lawyer' since
indented to start a new paragraph*

126.37 front] 'u' *after* 'o' *struck through*

127.1 seized him] *preceded by typed* 'sized him u' *deleted by typed* x's

127.14 didn't] TMs 'diden't' *preceded by typed* 'dident' *deleted by typed* x's

127.22 had] *preceded by typed* 'was' *deleted by typed* x's

127.22 diamond] 'a' *interlined with a caret, perhaps with the fine pen*

127.25 here's] TMs *originally read* 'her's' *then* 'H' *over* 'h'; 'e' *and apostrophe added over apostrophe*

127.28 musket] *this word beginning a line is preceded at the end of the line above by typed* 'a shot' *deleted, which by mistake excises the necessary* 'a'

128.3 you."] *quotes added*

128.13 stare.] *period altered from a comma*

128.15,16 you] *altered from* 'yuo'

128.23 arose] 'u' *after* 'o' *struck through*

128.24 attorney's] 's' *typed over apostrophe*

128.29 admiring] *preceded by typed* 'endearing' *deleted by typed* x's

128.33 see] *interlined with a caret possibly with the fine pen*

128.33 dersert] *preceded by typed* 'desert himim.|' *of which only* 'himim' *was deleted*

128.35 I know] 'kn' *typed over* 'll'; *preceding apostrophe not deleted*

129.3 thought] *typed as* 'through' *and altered*

129.7 highly] *followed by typed* 'and' *deleted*

129.8 latter] 'te' *typed over* 'er'

129.8 he had] *preceded by typed* 't' *and* 'he' *deleted*

129.9 who] *preceded by typed* 'who did not' *deleted*

No. 33. THE BATTLE OF FORTY FORT

[The copy-text is MS: manuscript in the UVa.–Barrett Collection in both Crane's and Edith Richie's hands. The other texts collated are Cs: *Cassell's Magazine*, n.s., XXIII (May, 1901), 591–594; E1: *Last Words*, Digby, Long, London, 1902, pp. 99–109.]

137.14 beside] besides E1
137.30 to] of Cs
138.5 and] *omit* E1
138.7 Stroudsburg] Stroudsberg Cs,E1
138.11 rather would] would rather MS(u),Cs
138.23 on] of E1
138.30 hours'] hours MS
138.35 from] at Cs,E1
139.4 could] would Cs,E1
139.11 people] men Cs,E1
139.21 *Dictation to* Edith Richie *begins with this paragraph*
139.24 learnt] learned Cs,E1
139.25 these] those Cs
139.27 heels] the heels Cs
139.29 if he had] had he Cs

139.29 me] us Cs,E1
140.5 affairs] affair MS
140.11 think I] think that I Cs, E1
140.15–16 Fort and Camp] camp and fort Cs
140.24 the] a Cs,E1
140.25 old] *omit* Cs,E1
140.33 Indians] the Indians MS(u),Cs,E1
140.36 afterward] afterwards Cs, E1
141.5 that] the Cs,E1
141.16 in] into Cs
141.25 eye] eyes Cs
141.33 1778] 1878 Cs
142.6 ²so] *omit* Cs

142.17 elegancies]   delicacies
MS(u) *alteration is by* Cora
142.25 toward] towards Cs
142.25 which] that Cs,E1
142.26 Quarter] Quarte E1

143.1 ¶ In] *no* ¶ E1
143.5 Afterward] Afterwards Cs
143.7 own] *omit* Cs
143.22 toward] towards Cs
143.28 Aye] Ay Cs

Alterations in the Manuscript

137.1 voted] *interlined above deleted* 'given'
137.3 that] *followed by deleted possible* 't' *or* 'l'
137.6 found] *interlined in pencil above pencil-deleted* 'could find'
137.9 two] *originally* 'to'; 'wo' *over* 'o'
137.10 the] 'th' *over* 'ou'
137.13 Wyoming Valley] *preceded by deleted* 'town'
137.14 its] MS 'it's' *preceded by deleted* 'his'
137.16 the] *interlined with a caret*
137.25 fighting] 'fi' *over possible* 't'
137.26 raided] 'ed' *interlined above deleted* 'ing'
137.28 wandering] *interlined with a caret above deleted* 'the'
137.29 extreme] *followed by deleted* 'and'
137.30 men] *interlined with a caret*
138.1 family,] *followed by deleted* 'to se'
138.2 coolness] *followed by deleted period*
138.3 we] *followed by deleted* 'also'
138.5 declaring] 'i' *over* 'e'
138.7 father] *final* ' 's' *deleted*
138.7–8 God-speed] *followed by deleted period*
138.10 Finally] *preceded by deleted* 'As the'
138.11 rather] *preceding* 'would' *deleted and* 'would' *interlined with a caret following*
138.17 A] *over* 'T'
138.24 milking] 'm' *over* 'w'
138.27 churn] *preceded by de-*

leted 'church'
138.28 before] *preceded by deleted* 'at'
138.32 ²with] *inserted in the line with a caret in different ink, possibly not by* Crane
138.33 Indians] *preceded by deleted* 'soldiers'
138.33 to] *interlined with a caret*
138.35 one morning] *interlined with a caret in different ink, possibly not by* Crane
138.36 ladder] *preceded by deleted* 'table'
138.36 Andrew] *preceded by deleted* 'Ad'
138.37 the] *interlined above deleted* 'my'
138.39 Son,] *comma over semicolon*
139.1 father?] *question mark altered from period*
139.6 risk] *followed by deleted* 'my'
139.11 itself] 't' *over* 's'
139.18 tell] *interlined*
139.21 I joined] Edith Richie's *hand begins here*
139.23 in] 'i' *over* 'o'
139.26 and] 'a' *over comma, with intent to delete*
140.10 opposition] *first* 'o' *mended or over illegible letter*
140.16 a] *interlined with a caret in* Crane's *hand* (?) *above deleted* 'the'
140.22 amid] *preceded by deleted* 'with'
140.22 drums] 's' *added*
140.24 close] *interlined above deleted* 'vivid'
140.25 which] 'wh' *over* 'tha'
140.33 whom] *made from* 'home'

with 'w' appended and 'e' deleted

140.33 Indians] *preceding 'the' deleted in same medium as the deleting stroke at 140.16*

140.37 decency] *second 'c' mended or over possible 's'*

140.38 dead] 'ad' *over* 'bt'

141.3 rode along the] 'rode' *interlined above deleted* 'wrote'; 'along' *preceded by a deleted* 'a'; 'the' *interlined with a caret*

141.4 once] 'c' *over* 'e'

141.6 now] *interlined with a caret*

141.30 contend] *preceded by deleted* 'do'

141.34 But] 'B' *over illegible letter or letters; possibly an* 'F' *is visible*

141.35 shadows] *final* 's' *added*

142.1 wounded] 'ou' *over illegible letters*

142.10 as if] *followed by deleted*

'it had'

142.11–12 In . . . well.] *added later*

142.17 elegancies] *inscribed in left margin in* Cora's *hand before deleted* 'delicacies'

142.18 Such was the] *interlined with a caret following deleted* 'The'

142.19 us] *followed by deleted* 'was such'

142.24 direction] *interlined with a caret above deleted* 'quarter'

142.24 cries] 's' *over* 'd'

142.27 think] 'k' *mended*

142.31 Denison] MS 'Dennison' *with first* 'n' *deleted*

143.4 things] 's' *added*

143.10 muscle] 's' *over* 'c'

143.24 bible] MS 'Bible' *with* 'B' *over* 'b'

143.28 it."] *followed by deleted* 'And it'

No. 34. THE SURRENDER OF FORTY FORT

[The copy-text is TMsᵃ: ribbon typescript in the UVa.–Barrett Collection. The other texts collated are TMsᵇ: carbon of TMsᵃ also in the UVa.–Barrett Collection; E1: *Last Words*, Digby, Long, London, 1902, pp. 81–88. The designation TMs without superior letter indicates an agreement of TMsᵃ and TMsᵇ.]

143.29; 145.23 July 3rd] 3rd July E1

144.19 Stroudsburg] Stroudsberg E1

145.1 nights] night TMs

145.26 a] the E1

145.28 nor] or TMs

146.3 Denison's] Denison'| TMs

147.9 afterward] afterwards TMs,E1

147.19 afterward] afterwards E1

147.28 transpiring] happening E1

Alterations in the Typescript

[All alterations are in black ink unless otherwise specified.]

143.31 ²not] 't' *added*

144.7 this] 'i' *typed over* 'e'

144.7–8 living-room] *hyphen inserted with a caret*

144.9 bids] 'i' *typed over* 'a'; 's' *typed over* 'e'

144.9 John Bennet] 'J' *typed over* 'B'

144.17 if] *added at end of typing*

line in ink

144.31 grey] *interlined with a caret in* TMsᵃ *preceding deleted typed* 'grea' *to which a* 't' *had been added;* 'y' *inserted over typed* 'a' *of* 'grea' *in* TMsᵇ

145.4 my] *preceded by type-deleted* 'the'

146.2 stolen.] *preceded by type-*

*deleted 'spoken' followed by de-
leted period in TMs*[a]

146.12   his] *typed over 'the'*

146.13   be] *preceded by type-de-*

leted 'give'

147.27   camp] *a final 's' type-deleted*

148.5   mainly] 'ma' *typed over* 'of'

No. 35. "OL' BENNET" AND THE INDIANS

[The copy-text is MS[1]: Crane's manuscript in the Syracuse University Library. The other texts collated are MS[2]: Edith Richie's manuscript in the Special Collections of Columbia University Libraries (stops at 150.13 with 'rode the'); Cs(p): *Cassell's Magazine* proof; Cs: *Cassell's Magazine*, n.s., XXII (Dec., 1900), 108–111; E1: *Last Words*, Digby, Long, London, 1902, pp. 88–98. The designation MS without superior number indicates an agreement between the two manuscripts; this is also true of Cs, which unless otherwise specified denotes Cs and its proof. Every variation between Cs and Cs(p) is listed here.]

148.11   throughout] through Cs, E1

148.19   hated] paled E1

148.22   singular] singularly Cs (Cs[p]: singular)

148.24   scenes] scene Cs

148.24   kickings] kicking Cs,E1

148.32 *et seq.* Its] It's MS[1] (*except at* 154.19)

149.5   Afterward] Afterwards Cs, E1

149.11   plough handles] plough-handle Cs

149.12   ol'] Ol' Cs,E1

149.13   red-skins] Redskins Cs

149.14   is] was MS[2]

149.15   abused] ill-used E1

149.15   outright] downright E1

149.17–18   sense of] *omit* E1

149.23   valley∧] ~ , Cs (Cs[p]: ~ ∧)

150.2   which] that Cs,E1

150.4   contending him] contending with him Cs (Cs[p]: contending him)

150.5   begun] began E1

150.6   Aye] Ay Cs (Cs[p]: Aye)

150.7   that] *omit* Cs,E1

150.8–9   a law] law MS[2]

150.13   rode the] *last words of* MS[2]

150.24   sun-down] ~ ∧ ~ Cs(p)

150.32   this] the Cs,E1

150.33   mountain] mountains Cs, E1

150.34   all] *omit* E1

150.37   [2]was] were Cs (Cs[p]: was)

151.1   afterward] afterwards Cs, E1

151.20–21   principal] principle MS

151.29   had] have Cs

151.33   ol'] Ol' Cs,E1

151.34   try] should try Cs (Cs[p]: try)

151.38   this] that Cs,E1

152.7   Indian] Indians Cs,E1

152.15   encampment] camp Cs, E1

152.15   lie] lay MS

153.1   chests] chest Cs

153.2   fight] flight E1

153.8   ¶ At] *no* ¶ Cs,E1

153.8   some] three E1

153.11   a] the E1

153.13   others] other Cs,E1

153.18   a] the Cs,E1

153.34   the leader] leader MS

154.7   slaughter in] slaughter continued in E1

154.8   endured] went on Cs; *omit* E1

154.10   strength] staength Cs(p)

154.10   in] on E1

Alterations in MS[1]

148.9.1 Bennet] *second 'n' over* 'e'

148.11 a sign] *interlined above deleted* 'known'

148.16 tomahawk] *followed by deleted period*

148.18 and] *an extended stroke of 'a' deleted preceding comma*

148.23 of] *followed by deleted* 'In'

148.28 had] *interlined with a caret*

149.2 snows.] *final 's' inserted*

149.2 fed] *followed by deleted* 'and'

149.5 soul] *followed by deleted* 'forever'

149.25 force] *final 's' deleted*

149.26 finding] *preceded by deleted* 'then'

149.28 but] *upstroke of 'b' extended to delete preceding comma*

149.35 It was] *interlined above deleted* 'They were'

149.38 chafed] *a second 'f' struck out in pencil*

150.16 apprehension] 're' *over* 'ree'

150.26 out] *preceded by deleted* 'out' *altered possibly from start of* 'and'

151.5 father's] *preceded by deleted* 'my'

151.21 [1]with] 'w' *over* 'a'

151.28 horse] *followed by deleted* 'in the'

151.28 its] MS 'it's' *interlined above deleted* 'his'

152.3 accidentally] *first 'a' over* 'u'

152.10 now] *interlined above deleted* 'not'

152.14 At] 'A' *over probable* 'I'

152.15 they] *following* 'la[*and beginning of* 'y']' *deleted*

152.17 My father] *interlined with a caret above deleted* 'He'

152.23 did] *interlined with a caret*

152.23 him] *interlined with a caret*

152.28 consultations,] *following period deleted and comma inserted*

152.37 guard] 'ua' *interlined above deleted* 'au'

152.39 captives] 'ives' *over* 'ain'

153.5 peeped] *followed by deleted* 'down'

153.9 prisoners] *interlined above deleted* 'Indians'

153.10 warrior] *followed by deleted* 'by the'

153.12 had] *interlined with a caret*

153.13 others] 's' *added*

153.18 at] *interlined above deleted* 'a'; *followed on the next line by deleted* 'a'

153.18 short] *followed by deleted* 'middle-aged'

153.19 too] *second 'o' added*

153.20 and] 'a' *over semicolon*

153.22 that] *altered from* 'the'

153.25 tugging] *preceded by deleted* 'pull'

153.28 my] *preceded by deleted* 'fa'

153.33 Hammond] *preceded by deleted* 'One'

154.9 trees] *followed by deleted period*

154.10 fleeing] *interlined with a caret*

154.11 on] *interlined with a caret*

154.16 six] *interlined above deleted* 'five'

154.16 had] *interlined with a caret*

154.19 career] *interlined above deleted* 'life'

154.19 dead.] *a deleted new paragraph begins after* 'dead.': 'In six days they reached [they reached *deleted*] from the'

Alterations in MS²

149.16   could] *followed by deleted*
        'be'
149.28   Loyalists] *followed by de-*
        leted comma
150.12   ²a] *interlined above de-*
        leted 'the'

No. 36. AN ILLUSION IN RED AND WHITE

[The copy-text is N¹: *New York World*, May 20, 1900, supplement, p. 2.
The other texts collated are E2: *The Monster and Other Stories*, Harper,
London, 1901, pp. 243–252; N²: *St. Louis Post-Dispatch*, May 20, p. 6;
N³: *Bolton* (England) *Evening News*, Dec. 28, 1901; N³(p): proof for
N³. N²⁻³ are derived texts without authority. No difference has been ob-
served between N³ and its proof.]

154.20–29   *Nights . . . journal-
           ism.*] *roman type in* E2+
154.30   imagine] imagined N³
155.2   sparkling] *omit* N¹⁻²
155.6   had] *omit* E2+
155.7   this] the N²
155.20   big white] big N¹⁻²
155.33–34 They . . . walnut.] *in*
           E2+ *this follows* small and
           brown, *line* 155.36
155.33   that] *omit* E2+
155.34   Jones's] Jones' N²
155.34   walnut] walnuts E2+
156.1   this] their E2+
156.2   excited] would excite E2+
156.6   the red] red E2+
156.7   in] is N¹
156.30   on a system] *omit* E2+
156.37   imagine] imagined N¹⁻²
156.39   to] into E2+
157.4   the] an N²
157.7   senses] sense E2+
157.11   Freddy (*no* ¶)] ¶ E2+

157.25   seemed to incline] seemed
           inclined N¹
157.25   'His (*no* ¶)] ¶ E2+
157.31   and housework] *omit* E2+
157.34   'Well (*no* ¶)] ¶ E2
158.2   Freddy] Freddie N²
158.7   yed] red N¹⁻²
158.8   hands] hand E2+
158.11   in complete confusion]
           completely muddled E2+
158.19   a barn] the barn N¹⁻²
158.19–20 And what . . . there?]
           omit N¹⁻²
158.20   actions and] *omit* N¹⁻²
158.21   estate] state N²
158.29   the] his E2+
158.29–31 Look . . . man] *lines
           set in error (between* 'con-|'*and*
           'cerned' *of* 158.27*)* N²
158.38   red] the red E2+
159.17   afterward] afterwards
           E2+

No. 37. MANACLED

[The copy-text is Ag: *Argosy*, LXXI (Aug., 1900), 364–366. The other texts
collated are Tr: *Truth*, XIX (Nov., 1900), 265–266; PL: *Index of Pittsburg
Life*, VI (Nov. 3, 1900), 15; E2: *The Monster and Other Stories*, Harper,
London, 1901, pp. 235–240. PL and E2 are derived texts without authority.]

159.27; 161.18   stage] the stage
                Tr
159.32   rage] futile rage Tr
159.32   warders] wardens PL
160.6–7   only take steps] take
           steps only Tr

160.9   "Fire (*no* ¶)] ¶ Tr
160.10   Throughout (*no* ¶)] ¶ Tr
160.11   crashes] crash Tr
160.12–13 women‸ more] ~, ~
           Tr
160.19–20 night . . . aroused]

night. It aroused Tr
160.20 when] when when PL
160.20 again] *omit* Tr
160.24 with] with the Tr
160.25–26 pavements] pavement Ag,PL,E2
160.26 plum-like] plume-like Tr
160.32 of] to Tr
161.1 clutched] scrambled Tr
161.5 he] *omit* Tr
161.12 run] ran Tr
161.13 cried] called Tr
161.13 "Where] "Where are Tr, E2

161.24 up."] up!" He began to blubber. "Damn them! They've left me chained up!" He moved down a passage, taking steps four inches long. Tr
161.36 that . . . conditions.] that, under common conditions, would have broken his hip. Tr
161.35–162.3 he tried . . . flight] *omit* PL
162.13 I . . . I] me . . . me Tr
162.18 furnish] make Tr
162.27 "They've (*no* ¶)] ¶ Tr

No. 38. THE GHOST

[The copy-text is TMs: New York Public Library typescript. The other authority is MS: UVa.–Barrett holograph preserved through line 163.18. All variants and alterations in this MS are listed here.]

162.28 Ghost.] *ghost:* MS
162.28 ¹I] "I MS
162.28 don't] dont MS
162.29 identity] indentity MS
163.4 1531] '531' *over* '815' MS
163.7 son] wife MS
163.8 *Tourist . . . whiskers.*] *Tourist w.w.w.* TMs
163.8 Now] "Now MS
163.8 son] dear MS
163.9 thing] things MS ('s' *possibly added later*)
163.9 a ghost] ghosts MS
163.10 a] *interlined* MS

163.11 The] *omit* TMs
163.11 Ghost~] MS 'Ghost:' *with* 'h' *over* 'o'
163.11 unnoticed).] ~ .) MS
163.12,15 with] w. TMs
163.12 (jumping).] (~)~ TMs, MS
163.13 *et seq.* Ghost.] ~ ~ TMs, MS
163.15 T.] *Tourist* TMs
163.15 excitedly).] ~)~ TMs,MS
163.17 hand).] ~)~ TMs,MS (*unclear*)
163.29 here] her TMs

Alterations in the Finale Chorus *Manuscript*

[The copy-text is MS: New York Public Library manuscript.]

170.10.3 28] '8' *over* '9'
170.13 money] 'ey' *over* 'y'
170.14 ¹Belle] MS *reads* 'Brlle' *with* 'lle' *over* 'ede'
170.21 tourists] 'r' *over* 'i'
170.22 all] 'll' *over* 're'

170.23 Tudor] MS *reads* 'Tud—or' *with dash over* 'or'
175.3 children] MS *reads* 'chil—dren' *with dash over* 'd'
175.12 lose] *written after a space following partially erased* 'lose'

No. 39. THE MAN FROM DULUTH

[The copy-text is MM: *Metropolitan Magazine*, XIII (Feb., 1901), 175–181. The other text collated is Cr: *Crampton's Magazine*, XVII (May, 1901), 353–360. Since MM and Cr are of equal authority, any variant is recorded here.]

180.1 *et seq.* man] Man Cr (*except lower case at* 180.28 *and* 184.31)

180.1 companions.] ~ : Cr

180.2 dreariest] dreamiest MM+

180.5 thing; and₄] ~ , ~ , Cr

180.8 pathos,] ~ ; Cr

180.10 Tenderloin] tender-lion Cr

180.10 "rounders₄"] " ~ ," Cr

180.15 now? That's] ~ ; that's Cr

180.15 point."] ~ ?" Cr

180.18 splendors] splendours Cr

180.19 slumbrous] slumberous Cr

180.20 slow. I'll] ~ ; ~ Cr

180.21 East] out Cr

180.23 Chicago₄] ~ , Cr

180.24 neighborhoods] neighbourhoods Cr

180.28 nervy spender,] nervey ~ ! Cr

180.28 Duluth;] ~ , Cr

180.28 "but] ₄ ~ Cr

180.35 It . . . vigor.] *omit* Cr

181.1 anywhere; what's] ~ ! What's Cr

181.7 go] do Cr

181.20 Presently₄] ~ , Cr

181.21 quickly₄] ~ , Cr

181.24 ₄no doubt₄] , ~ ~ , Cr

181.25 end;] ~ , Cr

181.26–27 arrangement₄] ~ , Cr

181.29 turned₄] ~ , Cr

181.30 floor₄space] ~ - ~ Cr

181.31 twoscore] two-score Cr

181.31 surface] surfaces Cr

181.34 room₄] ~ , Cr

181.36 But₄ . . . all₄] ~ , . . . ~ , Cr

181.37 smoke₄] ~ , Cr

182.3 fleeting] fleeing Cr

182.6 gayety] gaiety Cr

182.7 it—] ~ , Cr

182.15 color] colour Cr

182.17 ardor] ardour Cr

182.30 details;] ~ , Cr

182.32 language;] ~ , Cr

182.38 and₄ perhaps₄] ~ , ~ , Cr

183.5 laugh₄] ~ , Cr

183.8 that—] ~ , Cr

183.10 replied. "Er] ~ , "er Cr

183.14 said,] ~ : Cr

183.14–15 sweetheart'—] ~ ;' Cr

183.17 down₄] ~ , Cr

183.19 her,] ~— Cr

183.20 chickens₄'] ~ !' Cr

183.21 said. It's] ~—it's Cr

183.28 him:] ~ . Cr

183.30 is] *omit* Cr

183.32 afterward—] afterwards; Cr

183.36 space₄] ~ , Cr

184.1 hall₄] ~ , Cr

184.2–3 sedate. It] ~ , it Cr

184.7 fun;] ~ , Cr

184.8 slow,] ~ ! Cr

184.9,16 floor₄] ~ , Cr

184.10 crash;] ~ , Cr

184.12 shrieked;] ~ , Cr

184.13 throat,] ~ ₄ Cr

184.21 feet₄] ~ , Cr

184.21 infantry] Infantry Cr

184.32 said₄] ~ , Cr

184.34 something,] ~ ₄ Cr

184.39 tussling] tusselling Cr

185.2 clamor] clamour Cr

185.9 wild,] wild and Cr

185.23 perhaps,] ~ ; Cr

185.27 fight₄] ~ , Cr

185.29 into] in Cr

185.29 pockets₄] ~ , Cr

185.32 demeanor] demeanour Cr

185.33 smoke!] ~ , Cr

185.34 'em.] ~ ! Cr

185.36 Downstairs₄] ~ , Cr

185.36 gallery₄] ~ , Cr

185.37 Frenchman₄] ~ , Cr

185.39 that₄] ~ , Cr

185.39 intellect₄] ~ , Cr

186.3 explain₄] ~ , Cr

186.6 lapel₄] ~ , Cr

186.9 was] were MM

186.11 said,] ~ : Cr

186.12 Gawd,] ~ ! Cr

186.12 depths] depth MM

186.17 meself,] ~ ! Cr

186.19,23,28 little, fat] ~₄ ~ Cr

186.25 last₄] ~ , Cr

186.25 war—] ~ , Cr

186.25 real,] ~ ∧ Cr
186.27 chair∧] ~ , Cr
186.31–32 him∧ . . . him∧ . . .
    him∧] ~ , . . . ~ , . . . ~ , Cr
186.32 half-dozen] half a dozen
    Cr
186.35 an] the Cr
186.39 charge∧] ~ , Cr
187.2 succor∧] succour, Cr
187.2 phenomenon] phenomena
    Cr

187.7 them∧] ~ , Cr
187.9 her:] ~ , Cr
187.10 that, not] ~ ! Not Cr
187.10 here.] ~ ! Cr
187.11 johnnie] Johnnie Cr
187.11 that.] ~ ! Cr
187.13 chair.] ~ , Cr
187.13 hurrah] Hurrah Cr
187.13 star∧spangled] ~ - ~ Cr

No. 40. THE SQUIRE'S MADNESS

[The copy-text for 187.30–192.12 is MS: Crane's manuscript in the Special Collections of Columbia University Libraries; at 192.13 the copy-text becomes TMs: Cora's typescript in the UVa.–Barrett Collection. The other texts collated are Cr: *Crampton's Magazine*, XVI (Oct., 1900), 93–99; N[1]: *Washington Post*, June 2, 1901, p. 35; N[2]: *San Francisco Chronicle*, June 9, p. 26; N[3]: *Minneapolis Tribune*, June 2, supplement, p. 3; N[4]: *Cincinnati Commercial Tribune*, June 2, p. 22; N[5]: *Buffalo Morning Express*, June 9, p. 2; N[6]: *New Orleans Times-Democrat*, June 2, part II, p. 8; E1: *Last Words*, Digby, Long, London, 1902, pp. 231–244. At 192.13 when copy-text changes, all variants from MS are listed, but accidentals elsewhere are not noted.]

187.32 the strict] strict MS,TMs
188.4 three-foot] three-feet
    TMs(u),E1
188.8 The (no ¶)] ¶ $N
188.14 a valley] valley N[4]
188.15 the . . . of] omit $N
188.18 trees] the trees N[2,6]
188.19 venerable] venerate N[3]
188.19 arose] rose N[6],E1
188.21 vacant . . . Hall] Old-
    restham Hall vacant TMs(c)
188.24 a] [space] N[2]
188.27; 189.3 poppy-faced]
    happy-faced TMs+
188.28 also] omit TMs+
188.28 be] be | be MS
188.32 ladies] women N[5]
188.33 terrace] terraces TMs
188.35 privilege] privileges N[3]
188.35 et seq. its] it's MS,TMs(u)
189.2 remembered then that]
    then that said Cr; knew then
    that $N
189.4 over-lord] lord N[6]
189.8 lanes] lane Cr,$N
189.11 two] too TMs(u)

189.15 raw-boned] row-boned
    MS,N[3]
189.16 bent] omit TMs
189.19 very] omit $N
189.24 had been] were N[4]
189.25 then] omit $N
189.30 encrimsoning] crimson-
    ing N[5]
189.31 surrounding] surround-
    ings TMs,$N
189.32 more] most N[6]
189.32 far] omit N[4]
189.33 ashes] as ashes Cr,$N
189.38 merely] omit N[3]
190.2 Lintons] Linton Cr,$N
190.2 present] omit N[4]
190.5 were] was N[1]
190.6 they] them N[3]
190.10 master] matter N[5]
190.12 meals] meats N[4]
190.12 any] and N[4]
190.13 didn't] did not TMs
190.14 tastes] taste TMs(c)
190.15 make] would make TMs+
190.15 look] looked MS
190.15 it] he MS

190.16   What (*no* ¶)] ¶ $N

190.16   a gentleman]. gentlemen
TMs; a man N⁵

190.19   properly be] be properly
be MS; probably be Cr

190.21   did not] didn't TMs
(did'nt)+

190.23   other] the other TMs+

190.23   servants'] servant's MS,
TMs,Cr

190.24   squire's] squires' N¹

190.24   squire's lady] ' ~ ~ ' Cr;
" ~ ~ " $N

190.27   chose] choose MS,TMs(u),
Cr

190.27.1   II] *omit* TMs+; [*asterisks*] Cr,$N(−N¹); [*no space*]

TMs,Eɪ,N¹

190.31;   191.38   *wakes*]   *makes*
TMs+($N,Eɪ *not italic*)

190.35   thought] thoughts N⁶

190.36   writhing]   writhening
TMs(u),Eɪ

191.1   Linton (*no* ¶)] ¶ $N

191.1–2   placed . . . cigarette,]
omit TMs

191.3   of paper] paper N³

191.3   the log] log Cr

191.5   his] the N³

191.5   pipes] books $N

191.5   gazed] glanced N³

191.7   country-] the country- TMs

191.9   ¹he] *omit* N⁴

[Crane's *dictation begins at* 191.11 *with* 'There']

191.14   "Jack (*no* ¶)] ¶ TMs+

191.17   feeling] feelings N⁴

191.18   "Nothing (*no* ¶)] ¶ $N

191.19   seemed] seemed so N⁶

191.19   she] also N⁶

191.20   "I (*no* ¶)] ¶ Cr,$N,Eɪ

191.20   "I—I] "—I Cr; "I $N

191.21   thought]. though TMs

191.23   smiling] smilingly $N

191.23   I'm] I am N⁴

191.24   moods] ways Cr

191.27   thought] thoughts TMs+

191.29   and] any N³

191.30   ill!] ~ ? TMs,Cr,Eɪ; ~ .
$N

191.32   my] all my Cr,$N

191.33   this] his N²,⁴

192.1   *sandal's*] sandals MS

192.10   "Jack (*no* ¶)] ¶ $N

192.12   Ill? Ill?] ~ ! ~ ? Cr,$N,
Eɪ

[Cora's *composition begins at* 192.13 *with* ' "Yes'; *copy-text is* TMs]

192.13   You—] You—you MS

192.15   *feel*] feel MS,$N,Eɪ

192.16   Indeed] Inded MS

192.16   was . . . fit] never was
better MS

192.17   into] in Cr,$N

192.17   wing chair] winged chair
MS; armchair N⁶

192.18   stood] now stood MS

192.20   I have] I've MS

192.21   days," and] ~ ." And MS

192.21   look] looked MS

192.23   ache,] ~ ∧ MS

192.24   around]   round   Cr,$N
(−N⁴); 'round N⁴

192.25   toward] towards Cr

192.25   akin to] of MS

192.26   as in] in MS; as if in $N

192.27   both] her N³

192.27   to] as if to MS

192.32   him,] ~ ∧ MS

192.32   Linton] he MS

192.33   moved] *omit* Cr; passed
$N

192.33   face,] ~ ∧ MS

192.36   You] you MS

192.36   ill!] ~ . MS

192.37   ¹am] am MS

192.38   words] the words N⁶

192.38   won't] wont MS

193.1   Yes,] ~ ∧ MS

193.1   is] *omit* MS

193.1   ²that] *omit* MS

193.2   remember. You] ~ , you
MS

193.2   doctor. We] ~ , we MS

193.3   once," she] ~ ." She MS

193.4   my memory is] his memory was N[1,3]

193.5   I cannot] He could not N[1]

193.5   won't] would not N[1]

193.6   somehow.] ~ — MS

193.6   Perhaps] perhaps MS

193.8   said his wife] omit MS

193.10   must] must $N

193.10   someone;] ~ , MS

193.11   go,] go dear, MS

193.12   Linton_∧] ~ , (comma undeleted) MS

193.13   her] the Cr

193.15   [1]their] the N[2]

193.15–16   their expression the dumb agony] them the expression TMs,MS,E1

193.16   watching] watching at MS; watching beside Cr,$N

193.17   between] betwen MS

193.17   them?] ~ . MS

193.18   health] Health MS

193.21   There (no ¶)] ¶ $N

193.21   on] upon Cr,$N(−N[3]); about N[3]

193.21   he thought] omit MS

193.21   does] did MS

193.22   despair] hopeless TMs; such hopeless despair MS,E1

193.22   those] those kindly TMs; the MS; these kindly E1

193.22–23   had hitherto] hitherto had MS

193.23   quickly] omit TMs,MS,N[2], E1

193.23   each glance of] omit MS

193.24   Why] Why $N

193.24   She_∧] ~ ; MS

193.24   who knew well] who knew his TMs(u); had answered to MS

193.25   mood.] ~ ? MS

193.25   Was he mad?] Was he mad? $N

193.25–26   _∧poisoned . . . tip_∧] " ~ . . . ~ ' MS

193.25   cup] drug N[6]

193.27   the papers] his papers Cr, $N

193.29   nearsightedly] ~ - ~ MS

193.29   at] in at MS

193.31–32   cried his wife.] omit MS

193.34   started,] ~ _∧ MS

193.35   wait,] omit Cr,$N

193.36   as] and Cr,$N(−N[2])

193.36   hastened] hasten MS

193.36   up] & up MS

193.38   bent,] ~ ; MS

193.38   posture] position MS

193.39   ground. He did not_∧] ~ _∧ he ~ ~ , MS

193.39   ground . . . from the] omit Cr,$N

194.1   fire-place] fireplace MS

194.1   his wife's] wife MS

194.1   foot-fall] footfall MS

194.1   floors] floor Cr,$N

194.3   damned!] ~ . MS; — —! N[2]

194.3   And] and MS

194.3   swore] swore often N[6]

194.3.1   III] **** TMs±

194.4   their] thier MS

194.6   now] omit Cr,$N

194.6   'something' was wrong_∧] ' ~ _∧ ~ ~ ' MS

194.6   was] was MS,$N+

194.7   wife's] wifes' MS

194.8   'something'] 'something' MS,Cr+ (double quotes)

194.8   Until (no ¶)] ¶ $N

194.8   last few] few last MS,Cr,E1

194.8   wrong!] ~ . MS

194.9,22   household] houshold MS

194.10   mediaeval] mediaval MS

194.10   time] times E1

194.11   planned] planed TMs(u),MS

194.11,12   village] villiage MS

194.12   village] village of N[4]

194.14   He was] He, TMs,MS,E1

194.14   she_∧] ~ , MS

194.15   that] of that TMs,MS,E1

194.15   type] type of woman TMs, MS,E1

194.15   has] have $N

194.15   women] woman $N

194.16   believes] believe TMs+ (−MS); belived MS

194.16 problem . . . solved] question would be settled MS
194.19 the equality] equality MS
194.19 mind of] mind betwen MS
194.20 world's] worlds MS
194.23 servants] the servants N⁶
194.24 awaken] be awaken MS
194.24 her] his her MS
194.26 it, Grace?] ~ₐ ~, MS
194.27 in this fashion,] like this ₐ MS
194.28 sob: "Jack,] ~ ₐ " ~ ₐ MS
194.28 ¹ill,] ~ ₐ TMs(u),MS
194.29 town,] ~ ₐ MS
194.30 soothe] sooth TMs,MS
194.30 words ₐ] ~ , MS
194.30 promise] promises N¹
194.31 would] *would* MS
194.32 present] *omit* MS
194.33 Linton's wife's] Lintons wifes MS
194.33.1 [*space*]] **** TMs+
194.35 Doctor] Doctor's Cr
194.35 Redmond's] Redmonds MS
195.2 portentous] portentious MS
195.4 waiting-room] ~ ₐ|~ MS
195.5 with a frightened air] in a frightened manner TMs(u), MS,Cr,$N
195.7 Jack,] ~ ₐ MS
195.8 man ₐ] ~ , MS
195.8 clean-shaven] ~ ₐ ~ MS
195.8 black] back MS
195.9 ¹and] & MS
195.9 misshapen ₐ] ~ ; MS
195.11 shadow] shadowed MS
195.11 piercing] pierceing MS
195.11 dark] black N³
195.11 eyes, that] eyes, eyes that MS
195.12 questioning looks] *omit* MS
195.12 everyone] ~ ₐ ~ MS
195.12 seeming to] turning to MS
195.12 hidden] their hidden MS

195.13 flash-light] searchlight N⁶
195.13 conning] coning TMs(u), MS; coming E1
195.14 searches] seeks MS
195.15 out-stretched] outstretched MS
195.16 Ah] *Ah* TMs
195.17 as . . . her] *omit* MS
195.18 is] his Cr
195.19 Redmond] Redmonds MS
195.19 his] *omit* $N
195.19 face ₐ] ~ , MS
195.20 here,] ~ ₐ MS
195.21 first talk] talk first MS
195.21 study,] ~ ₐ MS
195.22 he said to] *omit* MS; he asked Cr,$N
195.22 to . . . courteously.] bowing courteously to Mrs ₐ Linton. TMs(u),MS(Bowing; Linton ₐ)
195.23 almost] *omit* TMs,E1
195.23–24 which . . . study.] toward which the doctor pointed. $N (N⁶: door pointed)
195.24 toward] to MS
195.28 dream-country] ~ ₐ ~ MS
195.27 Gate] Gates Cr
195.28–29 painted ₐin] ~ - ~ TMs(u),MS
195.29 the] *omit* TMs
195.30 this] his N⁴,E1
195.31 colours. He] ~ ; he MS
195.34 upon] on MS
195.34 half ₐturned] ~ - ~ MS
195.37 Linton then] Then Linton MS
196.1 smiled] smiling TMs
196.2 Only] only MS
196.2 moment,] ~ ₐ MS
196.2 She . . . reply.] *omit* MS
196.4–5 Be seated, . . . be seated.] Sit down ₐ . . . sit down. MS
196.7 down,] ~ ₐ MS
196.7 glass] glass & MS (*undeleted*)
196.7 and gulped] gulpping MS

196.9   began] said TMs,MS,E1
196.9   slowly] *omit* MS
196.9   sir] dear sir TMs(u),MS,
    Cr,$N
196.10   yourself,——"] ~ ,"——
    MS
196.12   Stop!] ~ , MS

196.12   said] exclaimed N⁴
196.12   yet] *omit* MS
196.13–14 WIFE . . . MAD.ʌ]
    wife, who is Mad!" MS; wife
    who is mad!" $N
196.14   MAD . . . HATTER!"]
    omit TMs(u),MS,Cr,$N

Alterations in the Manuscript

187.34   of] *preceded by deleted*
    'to'
188.1   lonely] 'ly' *added*
188.1   study.] *altered from* 'stu-
    dents'
188.3   sword] *interlined above de-
    leted* 'horse'
188.14   high] *interlined with a
    caret*
188.22   it] *preceded by deleted*
    'he'
188.23   the village] *interlined
    with a caret*
188.26   Oldrestham] *preceded by
    deleted* 'old'
188.28   parish] *preceded by de-
    leted* 'squire'
188.33   walking the] *upstroke of
    't' deletes with intent a comma
    after* 'walking'
188.33   lawns] *followed by de-
    leted comma*
188.34   perfectly] *preceded by de-
    leted* 'old previlege'
188.37   intimation] *preceded by
    deleted* 'blow'
189.3,6 a] *interlined with a caret*
189.5   appearance] *preceded by
    deleted* 'app'
189.7   sixpence] *first* 'e' *over* 'i'
189.12   eyes] *inserted*
189.13   hollows] *followed by de-
    leted period*
189.14   under-] *preceded by de-
    leted* 'upper-'
189.16   His] *preceded by deleted*
    'The'
189.17   by] *interlined with a caret*
189.17   feet] *preceded by deleted*
    'immense'

189.25   he] *interlined above de-
    leted* 'they'
189.26   far as] 'far' *altered from*
    'for' *and* 'as' *squeezed into the
    line*
189.37   when] *interlined with a
    caret*
190.1   before] *interlined*
190.2   Hall] *followed by deleted
    period*
190.6   explaining] *interlined
    above deleted* 'telling of'
190.7   themselves] *interlined with
    a caret*
190.8   was really] *preceded by de-
    leted* 'really was al all'
190.11   that] *followed by deleted*
    'the'
190.12   his] *interlined with a
    caret*
190.13   matter] *interlined with a
    caret*
190.14   to] *preceded by deleted*
    'and i'
190.15   ten] 't' *over* 'd'
190.18   Linton] *preceded by de-
    leted* 'he'
190.23   aloof] *preceded by deleted*
    'careful'
190.29   "The] *preceded by deleted*
    ' "Bl'
190.35   his thought] *interlined
    with a caret above deleted* 'he'
190.36   grey-hounds] *followed by
    deleted period*
190.37   ¹of] 'f' *over* 'n'
191.3   thrust] *preceded by deleted*
    'lit'
191.6   ³at] *squeezed into the line*

[Crane's *dictation*]

191.11   ¹the] *ink blot covers assumed* 'the'

191.13   wife] *ink blot covers all but lower portion of* 'fe'

191.20   hide] *interlined by* Crane *above deleted* 'conceal' *of which the* 'e' *has been inserted*

191.20   well] 'w' *over* 'a' *and beginning of* 's'

191.27   contemplation] MS 'contemp-|lation' *with hyphen over* 'a'

[Cora's *composition*]

192.16   more fit] MS 'better' *with second* 'e' *over* 'r'

192.17   As . . . ²he]'As he spoke' *added before* 'He' *with* 'H' *struck to lower case;* 'spoke' *has* 's' *mended*

192.17   a large] 'a' *interlined with a caret above deleted* 'the'; 'large' *then interlined above deleted* 'great'

192.18   stood] MS 'now stood' *with* 'now' *inserted*

192.19   oak] 'a' *over* 'k'

192.19   upon] *over* 'on'

192.21   look] MS 'looked' (*the* 'ed' *added*) *interlined with a caret above deleted* 'gaze'; *possibly a* 'g' *now deleted was begun before* 'looked'

192.24   Linton] *inserted before deleted* 'He'

192.26   in fear,] *preceded by deleted* 'as if'; *the comma may be altered from a period*

192.28   He] *preceded by deleted* 'His look[d?] chan', *which is followed by* 'His smile', *also deleted*

192.28   in the manner of a man] *interlined with a caret above deleted* 'as if'

192.28   reassuring] *altered from* 'to reassure'; *preceded by deleted* 'to'

192.30   amazement.] *altered from*

191.31   dear,] *interlined by* Crane *with a caret mistakenly placed before comma after* 'no'

191.32   beleaguered] MS 'beleagured' *with* 'u' *over* 'e'

191.38   cry] 'y' *over undotted* 'i'

192.1   rolls] 'll' *over* 'se'

192.4   poison] *final* 'ed' *deleted*

192.8   arm] *followed by deleted period*

192.10   tremulously] 'lo' *over start of* 'b'

'amazed' *which was followed by deleted* 'wonder'; *period after* 'wonder' *not deleted in error*

192.31   me!"] *quotes inserted later; followed by deleted* 'have I'

192.32   glaring] *interlined as* 'now glaring' *with a caret above deleted* 'yet looking'; *then* 'now' *written over* 'was' *deleted*

192.32   her] *interlined with a caret above deleted* 'with wide'

192.32   Linton] MS 'he' *inserted after deleted* 'He unconsciously'

192.33   unconsciously trying] *interlined with a caret before deleted* 'as if' *which is followed by another caret*

192.37   quite] *interlined with a caret*

192.37   ²I] ''m' *deleted*

193.1   cannot] 'not' *inserted*

193.2   cannot] *preceded by deleted* 'cant'

193.3   she] MS 'She' *with* 'S' *over* 's'

193.3   quickly.] *added after a deleted period*

193.4   'Tis] *preceded by deleted double quotes*

193.4   he] *ink blot covers assumed* 'e'

193.5 in] *interlined with a caret*

193.6 take] *interlined with a caret above deleted* 'have'

193.9 cling] *followed by deleted* 'like the ivy to'

193.9 clings] *interlined with a caret above deleted* 'does'

193.10 London] *interlined above deleted* 'town'

193.10 someone;] MS *comma inserted before deleted exclamation mark*

193.12 Again] *followed by deleted* 'as he saw he'

193.12 Linton] *followed by undeleted comma and deleted* 'as he' *above which is deleted* 'when' *interlined with a caret*

193.12 as one looks at] 'as' *followed by* 'if he were' *which is then deleted so that* 'one looks at' *may be interlined with a caret; following* 'were' *is independently deleted* 'a thing of'

193.13 pity.] *period inserted before deleted* 'and he who' *which is followed by deleted* 'she seemed to him to be in physical pain because of her fear for him.' *of which* 'to be in' *is interlined with a caret;* 'physical' *has a final* 'ly' *deleted;* 'pain' *is preceded by deleted* 'a' *and is followed by deleted* 'from'

193.13 faint] *preceded by deleted* 'lines'

193.13 to] *followed by deleted* 'her mouth'

193.14 physical] 'cal' *over* 'al'

193.15 extent,] *second* 'e' *over* 'a'; *followed by deleted* 'gazed at him'

193.16 watching] *interlined above deleted* 'gazing'

193.17 that] *interlined with a caret above deleted* 'which'

193.18 health] MS 'Health' *interlined above deleted* 'physical condition'

193.18 He] *squeezed in after two deleted false starts:* 'There was' *followed by* 'He suffered no ache nor pain—yet, he'

193.19 aches] *preceded by deleted* 'pain'

193.21 my] *interlined above deleted* 'his'

193.22 me] *interlined above deleted* 'him'

193.22 despair] MS 'such hopeless' *interlined with a caret preceding* 'despair' *and after deleted* 'that sad'

193.22 had] 'd' *over* 's'

193.24 knew well] MS 'had ['d' *over* 's'] answered to' *with* 'answered to' *interlined with a caret above deleted* 'always been so responsive to'

193.24 every] *interlined with a caret*

193.25 mad?] *possibly a mending is intended to turn question mark into an exclamation*

193.25 poisoned] 'ed' *squeezed in at end of word over illegible letters*

193.26 sandal's tip] *final* 's' *added and a final* 's' *struck from* 'tip'

193.28 to] *preceded by deleted* 'on'

193.29 nearsightedly] *interlined with a caret*

193.29 at] *interlined above deleted* 'to'

193.33 cigarette,] *comma altered from period*

193.34 She] *preceded by deleted* ' "A cigarette'

193.36 through] *interlined above deleted* 'to'

193.36 stone] *interlined with a caret*

193.37 study.] *period inserted before deleted* 'into the H'

193.38 Linton] *preceded by deleted* 'Linton'

193.38–39 in the posture . . . did not] *interlined with a caret above deleted* 'as he had' *fol-*

lowed by the alteration of 'turned' *to* 'turn'; *originally the interlineation began with* 'in the position' *to which* 'stooping' *was added by interlineation with a caret after* 'the' *but then deleted and* 'posture' *written over* 'position'

194.1 fire-place] MS 'fireplace' *with* 'place' *interlined*

194.1 his wife's] MS 'wife' *interlined above deleted* 'her'

194.1 floors] *preceded by deleted* 'falls'

194.4 ¶ A month] *inserted before deleted* ¶ 'Three weeks'

194.5 London] *preceded by deleted* 'way'

194.5 brain] *interlined with a caret*

194.8 conclusion;] *followed by deleted* 'that'

194.8 wrong] *followed by deleted closed quotes*

194.8 few] *interlined with a caret*

194.9 had] *interlined with a caret*

194.10 Each] *interlined above deleted* 'Her'

194.12 management] *followed by deleted* 'of other peoples children'

194.12 the village] MS 'the villiage' *interlined with a caret*

194.14 He was a] 'was' *deleted and comma inserted after* 'He'

194.14 she] *comma inserted after* 'she' *followed by deleted* 'was of' *and another* 'of' *interlined*

194.15 the] *interlined with a caret*

194.16 could be solved] MS 'would be settled' *with* 'would' *interlined with a caret after deleted* 'could only'

194.16 training] *preceded by deleted* 'the education'

194.17 next] *preceded by deleted* 'followin'

194.18 but] *preceded by deleted* 'an'

194.19 talked] 'ed' *added; preceded by deleted* 'would'

194.20–21 ²the . . . future] *interlined above deleted* 'future women'

194.23 into] 'in' *squeezed in before* 'to'

194.23 his wife] *interlined above deleted* 'she'

194.24 He] *preceded by deleted* 'In the night'

194.24 awaken] MS 'be awaken' *with* 'be' *interlined with a caret*

194.24 her] MS 'his her' *with* 'her' *interlined with a caret above deleted* 'wife'

194.26 he would cry,] *interlined with a caret*

194.30 he] *preceded by deleted* 'would'

194.30 soothe] *preceded by deleted* 'try to'

194.30 with . . . and] *interlined with a caret above deleted* 'and'

194.31 London.] *period added; followed by deleted* 'and'

194.32 This] *run-on after* 'London' *but preceded by inserted paragraph symbol*

194.32 those] *altered from* 'these'

194.33 watching] *preceded by deleted caret-interlined* 'the'

194.33 in] 'i' *over* 'o'

194.33 Linton's wife's] MS 'Lintons wifes' *with* 'Lintons' *interlined above deleted* 'his' *and* 's' *added to* 'wife'

194.35 They] *altered from* 'He'

195.2 portentous interview.] MS *originally read:* 'interview which was so portentous.'; *then the three middle words were deleted, a period was inserted after* 'interview', *and lines were drawn in to indicate the present reading*

195.3 blue] *interlined with a caret after deleted* 'black livery'

of which 'black' *was inter-*
lined with a caret

195.4 Mrs. Linton] *interlined*
with a caret above deleted 'She'

195.5 a] *interlined with a caret*

195.5 air] MS 'manner' *inter-*
lined with a caret above de-
leted 'way'

195.8 short] *interlined with a*
caret above deleted 'small'

195.8 with] *preceded by deleted*
'in'

195.9 nose] *preceded by deleted*
'huge'

195.9–10 was . . . line.] *inter-*
lined with a caret above de-
leted 'and over'

195.10 black] 'bl' *over doubtful*
'da'

195.11 tried . . . to] *interlined*
with a caret (originally 'seemed
trying . . .' *altered to present*
reading); preceding this is de-
leted 'seem to' *with also de-*
leted 'could not' *interlined*
above it

195.11 shadow] MS 'shadowed'
with 'ed' *over* 's'

195.11 eyes, that] MS 'eyes, eyes
that' *with* 'eyes that' *interlined*
with a caret above deleted
'that seemed'; '²eyes' *preceded*
by deleted 'apparently'

195.12 everyone,] MS 'every one,'
followed by deleted 'he looks
at' *before comma, and after*
comma is deleted 'as a stream
of water darts from a ho' *and*
'flash-light'

195.12 seeming to] MS 'turning
to' *or possibly* 'burning to' *in-*
terlined with a caret; 'to' *pos-*
sibly over 'in'

195.12 search] *final* 'ing' *deleted*

195.12 hidden] MS 'their hidden'
with 'their' *interlined with a*
caret

195.13 the] *interlined above de-*
leted 'some'

195.14 searches] MS 'seeks' *writ-*
ten over 'searches' *with an-*

other deleted 'searches' *inter-*
lined above the first

195.15 toward] 'ward' *inserted*

195.18 doctor] *second* 'o' *over* 'e'

195.19–20 with . . . ejaculated]
interlined with a caret above
deleted 'said'

195.20 Turning] 'T' *over* 't'; *pre-*
ceded by deleted 'And'

195.21 Squire] *interlined with a*
caret

195.22 to . . . courteously.] MS
'Bowing courteously to Mrs.
Linton‿' *squeezed in at the bot-*
tom of the page

195.23 Linton's wife] *altered*
from 'Mrs Linton'; 'wife' *inter-*
lined with a caret

195.24 pointed toward] MS
'pointed to' *interlined with a*
caret above deleted 'indicated'

195.26 Greek] *preceded by de-*
leted 'the ancient'

195.27 finally] *interlined with a*
caret

195.27 before] *second* 'e' *over* 'a'

195.27 ¹of] *followed by deleted*
'Hadrian'

195.27 Gate] 'G' *over* 'g'

195.28 traveled . . . into] *inter-*
lined with a caret above de-
leted 'went into'

195.28 dream-country.] MS
'dream country.' *originally*
'dreamland' *with* 'land' *deleted*
and 'country.' *interlined above*
it; followed by deleted 'before
this ['is' *over* 'e'] gate,'

195.28 His] *inserted*

195.28 painted] 'ed' *over* 'ing'

195.29 the] *interlined with a*
caret

195.29 men] *preceded by deleted*
'the' *interlined with a caret*

195.30 ¹of] *followed by deleted*
'ma'

195.31 that] *interlined with a*
caret following deleted 'that'

195.31 conjure] *interlined with a*
caret preceding deleted 'conger
up these'

195.31 these] *inserted*

195.33 From] *preceded by paragraph symbol inserted later*

195.33 this dream] *altered from* 'these dreams'

195.33 a] *interlined with a caret after deleted* 'the Doctors'

195.34 arm] *preceded by deleted* 'sho'

195.34 half‸] MS 'half-' *inserted*

195.34 saw] *followed by deleted* 'that'

195.35 him] *preceded by deleted* 'wi'

195.36 "Come] *preceded by deleted* 'Do'

195.37 here] *preceded by deleted* 'in the private d'

195.38 that] *interlined; caret sign misplaced after* 'his'

195.38 was] *interlined with a caret*

195.39 a table.] *interlined above deleted* 'the door.'

196.1 her] *interlined with a caret*

196.2 door] 'd' *over* 'c'

196.7 sat down,] *interlined with a caret, comma deleted*

196.7 the glass] MS 'the glass &' *interlined with a caret above deleted* 'it'

196.7 mechanically] *following* 'and' *deleted*

196.7–8 gulped the brandy] MS 'gulpping the brandy' *with* 'ping' *over* 'ed' *and* 'the brandy' *interlined with a caret above deleted* 'it down'

196.9 have] *interlined with a caret*

196.10 more] *interlined with a caret above deleted* 'so'

196.10 than] *interlined above deleted* 'as'

196.11 Linton] *preceded by deleted* 'Lin' *over which is interlined a paragraph symbol*

196.12 "Stop] *preceded by deleted* ' "But'

196.13 It] *preceded by deleted* 'Your wife is mad!'

Alterations in the Typescript

[Unless otherwise specified, all alterations are in pencil.]

188.4 -foot] *no hyphen in* TMs, *and ink* 'oo' *over* 'ee'

188.10 had] *interlined with a caret*

188.14 faraway] *a hyphen is inserted with a caret in* TMs

188.21 had . . . Hall‸] TMs 'vacant' *is circled and indicated with a caret to be positioned following* 'Hall'; *a semicolon has been inserted after the caret*

188.34 rose-gardens] *hyphen inserted in ink*

188.35 its] *pencil corrected from typed* 'it's'

189.10 five-feet-] *hyphens are deleted in* TMs

189.11 hay] *a comma is inserted following*

189.11 two] *interlined above deleted typed* 'too' *of which the first* 'o' *over* 'w'

189.24 always] *a comma is inserted following*

189.30 out,] *comma inserted*

189.36 long] *a comma is inserted following*

189.37 repeating,] *pencil semicolon over typed comma*

190.5 questioning] *type altered from* 'questions'

190.8 was] *interlined with a caret*

190.14 tastes] TMs 'taste' *with pencil* 'e' *over typed* 's'

190.14 wines] *a comma is inserted following*

190.20 establishment] *immediately preceded by type x'd-out* 'servants'

190.24 lady,] *comma inserted in*

pencil beneath deleted typed apostrophe

190.27 chose] *altered from* 'choose'

190.30 hating] 'e' *interlined with a caret after* 'i', *and then deleted*

190.36 writhing] *altered from* 'writhening'

191.6 green] *interlined with a caret*

191.22; 192.5; 194.3 I'm] *apostrophe inserted*

191.23 'I'm] *quotes and apostrophe inserted*

191.37 hating] 'e' *interlined with a caret before* 'i', *and then deleted*

192.4 her.] *interlined with a caret which deletes a period in ink*

192.9 a-light] *two words in TMs, joined to one word*

192.10 sharply] *altered in ink from* 'shortly'

192.11 you] *a final* 'r' *deleted*

192.25 akin] 'ak' *typed over* 'of'

193.4 'Tis] *apostrophe inserted in ink*

193.14 eyes,] *comma inserted*

193.15 extent,] *comma inserted*

193.20 away] *interlined with a caret*

193.22 those] TMs 'those kindly' *with* 'kindly' *interlined with a caret*

193.24 well] *interlined with a caret*

193.31 fire!"] *quotes inserted*

194.3.1 III] TMs *line of four asterisks inserted in ink*

194.8 'something'] *first quote mark and italicization added in ink*

194.8 wrong!] *exclamation point*

deletes closing single quote, both ink additions

194.11 planned] *altered from* 'planed'

194.28 And] 'A' *typed over typed double quotes*

194.28 Jack, . . . ¹ill,] *commas inserted*

194.33.1 [space]] TMs *line of four asterisks inserted in ink*

195.4 ²into] *typed* 'i' *over typed* 'o'

195.5 with] *interlined with a caret following deleted* 'in'

195.5 air] *preceded by deleted* 'manner'

195.12 everyone,] *comma inserted*

195.16 "Ah] *in italics and preceded by inserted ink dash in TMs*

195.22 madam] TMs 'madame' *altered from* 'madam|'

195.22 to . . . courteously.] 'to Mrs Linton,' *typed after* 'bowing courteously.' *and lines drawn to indicate present reading*

195.28–29 painted in] *hyphen between the words deleted*

196.1 ¹Linton] *interlined with a caret*

196.5 "be] *quotes inserted*

196.9 say] *preceded by type* x'd-out 'tell'

196.9 sir] *preceded by ink deleted* 'sir'

196.13–14 WIFE . . . MAD.] *lower case in TMs, then underlined twice*

196.14 MAD AS A HATTER!"] *added in ink in TMs with* 'M' *deleting original closing double quotes; then the phrase (lower case save for the* 'M') *underlined twice in ink*

No. 48. FOUR MEN IN A CAVE

[The copy-text is N¹: *New York Tribune*, July 3, 1892, p. 14. The other texts collated are TMs: typescript in the UVa.–Barrett Collection; E1: *Last Words*, Digby, Long, London, 1902, pp. 217–224. TMs and E1 are derived texts without authority.]

225.22   in] on E1
225.25   oration] orations TMs,E1
225.30–31   pine-knots] pine-knot
    TMs,E1
226.13   upon] on E1
226.32   stones] stone TMs,E1 (*at*
    end of TMs *typing line*)
226.32   in] on E1
226.33   a] *omit* E1 (*in* TMs *the*

impression is barely visible)
226.33   half] half-way TMs,E1
227.8   him] *omit* TMs,E1
227.24   a corner] the corner E1
227.29   ³man] *omit* TMs,E1
228.22   inscrutable's] inscrutable
    E1
229.36   onct] once E1

No. 49. THE OCTOPUSH

[The copy-text is N¹: *New York Tribune*, July 10, 1892, p. 17. The other text collated is TMs: typescript of "The Fishermen" in the UVa.–Barrett Collection. All differences between N¹ and TMs are recorded here except those which have constituted emendations to N¹.]

230.13   went] came TMs
230.15   sheets of water] ponds
    TMs
230.17   to] of TMs
230.17   wandered] wandered aim-
    lessly TMs
230.19   forest] dense forest TMs
230.19   In consequence] Conse-
    quently TMs
230.19   sheet] smooth sheet TMs
230.21   stumps,] ~ ∧ TMs
230.21   stretched long,] idly
    stretched∧ TMs
230.22–23   Floating . . . dam.]
    omit TMs (*see* 230.25)
230.23   manner] manners TMs
230.25   edge.] edge. Floating logs
    and   sticks   bumped   gently
    against the careening dam.
    TMs (*see* 230.22–23)
230.27   from] as from TMs
230.28   graveyard] sepulchral
    TMs
230.29   agreed.] agreed to accept
    his services. TMs
230.30   a recess] an inner recess
    TMs
230.30   he] he then TMs
230.31   with   yellow   finishings]
    omit TMs
230.32   Sullivan] Sullivan County
    TMs
230.32   boards] boards, with a
    jack knife, TMs
230.33   sides] side N¹

230.34   In (*no* ¶)] ¶ TMs
231.1   knowledge,] certain knowl-
    edge∧ TMs
231.2   was] we TMs
231.2   'skidder'] ∧kidder∧ N¹
231.3   stumps."] ~ ". TMs
231.3   The] So the TMs
231.3   clambered] climbed TMs
231.3   beautiful] beautifully blue
    TMs
231.4   craft] craft over the waters
    TMs
231.5   to four . . . fishers.] four
    large   low-spreading   stumps to
    the   four   men,   with   fishing
    tackle. TMs
231.5   thereupon] then TMs
231.6   where] to which TMs
231.6   boat. Perching] boat, and
    perching TMs
231.7   he] *omit* TMs
231.7   grasped a] attacked a worn
    and TMs
231.8   between his teeth] *omit*
    TMs
231.8   , eloquent] *omit* TMs
231.8–9   tobacco. At . . . men.]
    tobacco which smote the chests
    of the four men, all within
    hailing distance. TMs
231.10   gleamed] gleaned N¹;
    beamed TMs
231.10   waters]   riffled   waters
    TMs
231.11   -trunks∧] ~ , TMs

231.11–12 stumps . . . clouds.] low-lying stumps. TMs

231.12–13 darningneedles danced] needles darted TMs

231.13 surface.] surface of the pond. TMs

231.13–15 Bees . . . air.] *omit* TMs

231.15 water] waters TMs

231.15 fern] moss TMs

231.15 quavered] waved gently TMs

231.16 still] *omit* TMs

231.16 'skiddered.'] ∧~.∧ N[1]; '~'. TMs

231.17 tremendously.] tremendously at his pipe. TMs

231.18 madly. His] dreadfully; and his TMs

231.19 either find him] find him either TMs

231.19 holding] holding in joyous fingers TMs

231.20 nervously] *omit* TMs

231.21 vindictive . . . bottom.] grasping weeds, sticks, and stumps, at the bottom of the pond. They fished until the sun slunk down behind some tree-tops and peered at them like the face of an angry man over a hedge. TMs

231.22 fortune] good fortune TMs

231.22–23 fish. His . . . are] fish, his . . . being TMs

231.24 bit] bits TMs

231.24 glitter∧] ~ , TMs

231.25 it.] it. Each one of the four had mighty strings of fish. TMs

231.26 At noon, the individual] The individual sat enthroned cross-legged on his stump all day, pipe in mouth. From time to time in hollow tones he would venture suggestions, relate anecdotes, ask questions or volunteer information about his domestic life with great abruptness as the inspiration

struck him. About noontime he TMs

231.26 upon a] on one huge TMs

231.27–28 lunched . . . anecdote.] lunched. TMs

231.28 Afterward . . . them,] Later he distributed them about, TMs

231.30 observations] occasional observations TMs

231.30 water . . . men∧] waters to them, TMs

231.31 Toward (*no* ¶)] ¶ Towards TMs

231.31–36 evidently . . . stump.] silent and, evidently, thoughtful. When the sun had slid down until it only threw a red flare among the trees, one of the four men stood up and shouted to the individual: TMs

231.37 The (*no* ¶)] ¶ TMs

231.38 come] *omit* TMs

231.38 ashore.] ashore now. TMs

231.39–232.2 Whereupon . . . roar.] The individual raised himself on his stump suddenly and waving a black bottle around his head, roared: TMs

232.3 ¶ "You] (*no* ¶) ∧You TMs

232.3 blazersh] blazerish TMs

232.4–6 The sun . . . men.] There were a few moments of intense silence. Then the man who had sttod up, drew a long, deep breath and sat down heavily. The rest were frozen in silence. TMs

232.7–9 Dusk . . . waters.] The night came creeping over the tree-tops. The stillness of evening rested upon the waters. TMs

232.10 ¶ The] *no* ¶ TMs

232.12 the little] a little TMs

232.13 groaned.] groaned in reply. TMs

232.13 They] They all TMs

232.14 mighty] gigantic TMs

232.14–15 Occasionally (*no* ¶)]
¶ TMs

232.15 took a] would take another TMs

232.15 bottle] inexhaustable bottle TMs

232.16 bellowed] would cry TMs

232.17 pondered.] had been
deeply thoughtful for a few
moments. TMs

232.17–18 got up finally] now
got up TMs

232.19 which∧ he alleged∧] ∼ ,
∼ ∼ , TMs

232.20 Next∧] Then, TMs

232.20 woe] utter woe TMs

232.21 Then∧] Later, TMs

232.22 them,] ∼ ; TMs

232.22 appeal] plea TMs

232.23 , alleging . . . virtues]
omit TMs

232.24 object . . . address] individual TMs

232.24 feet,] ∼ ∧ TMs

232.24–25 in a . . . g'home."]
cried: [¶] "G'home, dern fool."
TMs

232.25 The (*no* ¶)] ¶ TMs

232.26 oaths.] oaths. Then, in
chorus they entreated, threatened, cursed and berated. All
to no purpose. He called them
names and told them to
"g'home". He drank deeply.
TMs

232.27 roar] moan TMs

232.28 heavens . . . position.]
lofty heavens. TMs

232.29–31 Suddenly . . . gulfs.]
omit TMs

232.32 flopped] splashed TMs

232.33–35 weeds . . . alive.] debris on the water. Crooked,
slimy sticks seemed to squirm
like snakes. The four men began to feel that they were sitting on live things. TMs

232.36–37 in the grass . . .
chanted.] and tree-toads
chanted a solemn dirge on the
pond's edge. TMs

232.38 inside] crawling about inside TMs

232.38–39 Then . . . objects]
Each felt himself alone and at
the mercy of unseen horrors
which TMs

233.1 The (*no* ¶)] ¶ TMs

233.1 drinking] still drinking
TMs

233.2–3 "G' . . . fools."] *omit*
TMs

233.3 Among themselves∧] To
each other, TMs

233.4–5 escape . . . wriggled.]
escape but they gazed down
into the black waters and
thought that it teemed with
slimy life. TMs

233.6 ghost-like] ghost TMs

233.6 upon the waters.] above
the water TMs

233.6–7 The pond . . . -yard.
The] In the shadows, the pond
began to look like a vast graveyard, the TMs

233.7–8 -trunks . . . crypts.]
-trunks turning to aged marble
pillars and monuments. TMs

233.8 were] began to look like
TMs

233.9 graves] the graves TMs

233.10 brass] the brass TMs

233.11 appals] apalls TMs

233.11–12 It . . . genie.] *omit*
TMs

233.13 two remaining] remaining
two TMs

233.15 yell] dreadful yell TMs

233.16 heads] head's N[1]

233.17 waters] surface of the
water TMs

233.17 Chattering,] Chattering
frenziedly∧ TMs

233.18–19 tumbled] jumped
TMs

233.19–20 feet, . . . unknown.]
feet. TMs

233.22 howled] said TMs

233.24 move] wriggle'n twine
'round me TMs

233.24 octopush!] ∼ , TMs

233.26 But others (*no* ¶)] ¶ The others TMs
233.26 him,] the little man; TMs
233.27–28 so . . . proceeded] so he desisted and, climbing into the boat, aculled about and collected his companions. They proceeded then back TMs
233.29 "octopush."] across the water at his octopus. TMs

233.31 "How (*no* ¶)] ¶ TMs
233.32 him.] the individual. TMs
233.32 "Four (*no* ¶)] ¶ TMs
233.32 of] made of TMs
233.32–33 The four men (*no* ¶)] ¶ They TMs
233.33 him] at him TMs
233.34–35 individual∧ . . . edge∧] ~ , . . . ~ , TMs
233.36 octopush."] ~ ". TMs

No. 49a. EARLY DRAFT (THE FISHERMEN)

[The copy-text is TMs: typescript in the UVa.–Barrett Collection.]

Alterations in the Typescript

234.3 County] 'r' *before* 'y' *struck through on typewriter*
234.15 to] *typed over* 'in'
234.16 his] *typed above* x'd-out 'their'
234.34 darted] 't' *over obscured and possibly altered typed letter, probably* 'n'
234.37 ecstatically] *originally* 'estatically' *but* 'c' *typed over initial* 'e' *and* 'e' *then typed in, running the word together with preceding* 'cry'; *later the two were separated by an ink slash*

235.17 close] 'clo' *typed over* 'end'
236.12 they] 'y' *typed over* 'i'
236.19 them nought] 'the' *typed over* 'nou'
237.9 built] 'uilt' *typed over* 'made' *and initial* 'b' *typed in, running the word together with preceding* 'and'; *later the two words were separated by an ink slash*
237.9 great] *typed as an interline with ink caret*

No. 52. THE BLACK DOG

[The copy-text is N[1]: *New York Tribune*, July 24, 1892, p. 19. The other texts collated are TMs[1]: ribbon typescript in the Special Collections of Columbia University Libraries; TMs[2]: carbon of a later typescript, also in the Special Collections at Columbia. TMs[1-2] are derived texts without authority.]

242.24 drooping] droping TMs[1-2]
242.29 a porridge] porridge TMs[2]
243.3 road] a road TMs[1-2]
243.5 wind-waved] the wind-waved TMs[1-2]
243.9 skirled] skirted TMs[1-2]
243.11 rapped] wrapped TMs[1](u)
243.24 The latter's] His TMs[1-2]
243.34 on] upon TMs[1](c),TMs[2]
244.3 dorg] dog TMs[2]
244.10 ter] to N[1]
244.11 an' . . . an'] and . . . and N[1]

244.13 saw] at TMs[2]
244.17 Wot] What TMs[1](u)
244.18 and ghosts] an' ghosts TMs[1-2]
244.22 curved] was curved TMs[2]
244.37 The] A TMs[2]
244.39 quavering] quivering N[1]+
245.7 [2]the] teh N[1]
245.9 Mutterings] Muttering TMs[2]
245.10 were] was TMs[2]
245.11 stumbled] tumbled TMs[1-2]

245.17   become] became TMs[2]
245.27   groaned] sighed TMs[1](c),
         TMs[2](c)
246.1   drooped] dropped TMs[1-2]
246.5   replied] said TMs[1-2]

246.15   than] then TMs[1-2]
246.20,39 on] upon TMs[1-2]
247.11   companions] companion
         TMs[1-2]
247.17   its] his TMs[1-2]

No. 57. THE HOLLER TREE

[The copy-text is MS: manuscript in the UVa.–Barrett Collection.]

Alterations in the Manuscript

259.13   a] *interlined above deleted*
         'the'
259.27   espied] *preceded by de-*
         leted 'discover'
259.30   an] 'n' *added*
259.32   got] *interlined with a*
         caret
260.1   asserted] 'a' *made from* 'd'
260.2   four] *preceded by deleted*
         'put'
260.12   it?] *question mark over*
         period
260.14   up.] *interlined above de-*
         leted 'it.'
260.24   The little man] *interlined*
         above independently deleted
         'The' *and* 'His comrade'
260.30   began] *preceded by de-*
         leted 'looked'
261.5   Well?] *question mark over*
         comma
261.5   man.] 'man' *followed by de-*
         leted 'loo'; *period inserted*
261.7   [2]a] *interlined above deleted*
         'one'
261.7-8 [2]a . . . and] *written up-*
         side down beneath this is the
         deleted phrase ' "Certainly I
         do" '
261.8   two] *interlined above de-*
         leted 'some'
261.13   there."] *period over a*
         comma and following 'he said.'
         deleted
261.17   Certainly] 'n' *over up-*
         stroke of 'l'
261.25   little   man] *interlined*
         above deleted 'other'
261.32   tree. . . . dark.] *periods*

altered   from   exclamation
points
261.37   you] *preceded by deleted*
         'yeh'
261.37   bet.] *period altered from*
         exclamation point
262.12   th'] *altered from* 'the'
262.13   th'] *inserted in line after*
         deleted 'th' ' *which had been*
         altered from 'the'
262.13   you know] *upstroke of* 'k'
         over a comma with intent to
         delete
262.17   Oh . . . surprised.] *pre-*
         ceded by deleted 'I'm sur-
         prised." '
262.22   In] *preceded by deleted*
         'They'
262.27   a] *interlined above de-*
         leted 'some'
262.31   tree?] *question mark over*
         period
263.7   he ceased] *squeezed in at*
         end of line; just possibly sen-
         tence beginning 'Presently' *is*
         an addition
263.12   hours?] *question   mark*
         over period
263.13   instead] *originally* 'in-|
         stead' *preceded by deleted* 'in-
         side of', *then* 'in-|' *deleted and*
         'in' *joined in left margin to*
         'stead'
263.13-14 much? . . . anyway?]
         question marks over periods
263.17   quiet] *preceded by deleted*
         'quite'
263.19   pudgy] *preceded by de-*
         leted 'pud'

263.30 furious] *preceded by deleted* 'lou'

263.31 The] *preceded by deleted* 'In'

263.33 Suddenly] *preceded by interlined paragraph sign*

263.36 wrathful] *preceded by deleted* 'little man'

264.1 a thicket,] *preceded by deleted* 'some bushes.'

264.7 him.] *preceded by deleted* 'it.'

264.9 After] *preceded by deleted* 'Finally'

264.10 stagger] *followed by deleted* 'about.'

264.13 moaning] *first* 'n' *over possible* 'a'

264.13–14 by 'bout] 'by' *interlined;* 'a' *deleted from* 'about' *and apostrophe inserted*

264.16 corner] *final* 's' *deleted*

No. 58. AN EXPLOSION OF SEVEN BABIES

[The copy-text is MS: manuscript in the UVa.–Barrett Collection. The other texts collated are TMs¹: typescript in Comdr. Melvin Schoberlin's private collection; TMs²: typescript in the Special Collections of Columbia University Libraries; HM: *Home Magazine of New York*, XVI (Jan., 1901), 75–80. HM and TMs¹⁻² are derived texts without authority.]

265.9 had] *omit* HM

265.10 a] an MS

265.22 toward] towards TMs²

265.24 you,] you? TMs¹

265.25 here] her HM

265.28 little] *omit* HM

265.29 She (*no* ¶)] ¶ TMs¹+

265.34 The (*no* ¶)] ¶ TMs¹⁻²

265.37 bone] bones HM

265.38 bended] bent HM

266.5 wriggling] wraggling HM

266.10,18 its] it's MS

266.19 It] It is MS

266.26; 267.8 The (*no* ¶)] ¶ TMs¹+

266.31 strided] strode TMs¹(u), TMs²

266.31 ferocious] a ferocious HM

267.5 brown] *omit* TMs¹+

267.5 wheeled] wheeled round TMs¹(u),TMs²

267.7 half] top TMs¹+

267.15 wished] wish MS

267.22 tore] fell TMs¹(u),HM

267.31 dusty] dust-covered HM

267.36 Heaven's] heaven's HM, TMs²

268.6 nor] or TMs²

268.6 bloomin'] blooming TMs²

268.7 day-gloom] dry-gloom HM

268.19 comrades] companions TMs²

Alterations in the Manuscript

264.26 indignantly] *interlined with a caret*

264.34 stomachs] 's' *added*

265.2 stood] *preceded by deleted* 'climbed'

265.6 bowed,] *comma squeezed in before deleted period*

265.8 Scott!"] *added in pencil after pencil-deleted* 'God!"'

265.9 seven] *interlined with a caret*

265.10 giantess] *inserted*

265.10 the glare] *preceded by deleted* 'gl'

265.10 a tigress] MS 'an enraged tigress' *with* 'enraged' *deleted in pencil*

265.13 glowing] *interlined in pencil above pencil-deleted* 'lurid'

265.13 fury] *followed by inserted period and deleted* 'and'

265.13 the] *over 'a', followed by* 'lithe,' *deleted in pencil*

265.14 motion] *followed by penciled 'as' interlined with a caret, deleted in ink*

265.14 about] *preceded by 'which is' deleted in pencil, and then ink*

265.20–21 hips; her lips] 'her lips' *interlined with a caret and semicolon squeezed in after* 'hips'

265.21 curled] *followed by* 'back' *deleted in pencil*

265.23 staring in] *interlined above deleted* 'wild with astonishment.'; *then* 'bewilderment' *added*

265.28 man,] *comma added after deleted period*

265.30 to] *interlined with a caret*

265.33 Beast] 'a' *over* 's'

265.33 made'm] *apostrophe* 'm' *added*

265.34 That] 'a' *over* 'e'

265.38 dragon] 'a' *over beginning of* 'g' *and word preceded by deleted* 'fire' *and possible hyphen*

266.1 "Gawd,"] *inserted in pencil after pencil-deleted* ' "Gad," '

266.1 moaned.] *followed by pencil-deleted* 'hoarsely.' *with a penciled period then inserted between the words*

266.2 of] *inserted in line later*

266.9 a] *interlined in pencil above pencil-deleted* 'the'

266.10 man,] *comma mended, perhaps from a period*

266.16 kaleidoscope] 'eidoscope' *filled in later in space left for purpose*

266.17 bellowing] *preceded by pencil-deleted* 'terrible,'

266.20 He] 'e' *over* 'i' *and beginning of* 's'

266.21 talons] *preceded by pencil-deleted* 'frightful'

266.25 life] *preceded by deleted* 'wal'

266.36 pudgy man] *preceded by deleted* 'little man'

266.37 babies] *following period deleted*

266.38 ²the] *interlined*

267.8 over] *interlined above deleted* 'at'

267.8 of it.] *added later;* 'of' *over a period*

267.8 The giantess] *interlined above deleted* 'She'

267.25 as, perhaps, they] *interlined with a caret above deleted* 'as'

267.26 returning] *interlined above deleted* 'returned' *of which the 'ed' appears to have been added*

267.26 to . . . house.] 'to the' *interlined above a deleted period and* 'worn-out house.' *squeezed between lines below it with a line drawn in to separate it from the line following*

267.27 As . . . woods,] *interlined below deleted* 'As the little man turned again toward the woods, he' *followed by* 'went on into' *interlined above* 'turned again'

267.27 he] *inserted at same time as 267.27 above*

267.28 figure] 'g' *altered from* 'q'

267.33 broke] 'b' *over* 'a'

267.34 Devilish] *first* 'i' *over* 'e'

267.34 pudgy] 'p' *over* 'li'

267.36 Heaven's] *interlined in pencil above pencil-deleted* 'God's'

267.39 What?"] *double quotes added in pencil before pencil-deleted* 'Nothing?" '

268.2 kids] *apostrophe over the* 's' *deleted*

268.16 notice.] *period altered from an* 's'

268.18 at] 't' *over beginning of* 'n'

No. 59. THE MESMERIC MOUNTAIN

[The copy-text is TMs: typescript in the UVa.–Barrett Collection. The other text collated is E1: *Last Words*, Digby, Long, London, 1902, pp. 225–230.]

268.32   the opening] an opening E1
269.14   Damned] Dammed TMs
269.14–15   anymore] any more E1
269.36   unstirred] untired TMs(c)

270.19,32   Jones's] Joneses TMs
270.36   foot] feet TMs(c)
270.36   its] it's TMs
271.15   foot] feet TMs
271.19   ¹to] omit TMs(u),E1

Alterations in the Typescript

268.30   stomach] *a final typed* 's' *deleted in ink*
269.1–2   he said] *preceded by type* x'd-out 'said' *then ink deleted*
269.6   can't] *apostrophe inserted in ink*
269.10   waved] TMs 'waived' *with* 'i' *type struck*
269.13   am——"] TMs 'am—' *with typed double quotes over first hyphen*
269.16   wonderin'] 'i' *typed over an apostrophe*
269.22   Lumberland] *ink* 'L' *over typed* 'S'
269.23   Ho!] *ink exclamation point altered from typed comma*
269.23   believe] TMs 'beleive' *corrected in pencil with a caret after* 'i' *and a line connecting the caret with circled* 'e'
269.24   then?"] *quotes added in ink*
269.32   "He's] *quotes added in ink*
269.36   unstirred] TMs 'unstired' *with* 's' *deleted in pencil*
270.20   crow] *a final* 's' *type struck*
270.24   swamp,] TMs 'swamp;'

with semicolon inserted in ink
270.28   . . .] TMs *has six spaced* 'x's' *made into asterisks by the superposition of ink crosses*
270.29   am] *preceded by x'd-out, ink-deleted* 'am'
270.34   mouth] *preceded by x'd-out, ink-deleted* 'mouthmouth'
270.36   the foot] TMs 'the feet' *with ink* 'ee' *over possible typed* 'oo'
270.38   the pines] *preceded by seven typed* 'x's', *also ink deleted, under which only a* 'the' *is discernible*
271.4   himself] *typed* 's' *over typed* 'm'
271.16   God!] *ink exclamation point altered from a comma*
271.18   moaned] *preceded by* 'wail' *which was type x'd-out and then deleted in ink*
271.19   ¹to] *interlined with a caret in pencil*
271.21   "Damn you!" he] *quotes inserted in ink; exclamation point altered from a comma*
271.26   smite] *typed* 'i' *over typed* 'o'
271.32   Ho!] *exclamation point altered from a comma*

No. 62. AN EXPERIMENT IN MISERY

[The copy-text for 283.14–284.24 is E1: *The Open Boat*, Heinemann, London, 1898, pp. 211–226. The copy-text for 284.25–293.24 is N¹: *New York Press*, April 22, 1894, part III, p. 2. Accidental as well as substantive differences are recorded for N¹ where E1 is copy-text.]

283.14–22 It . . . sleep.] Two men stood regarding a tramp. [¶] "I wonder how he feels," said one, reflectively. "I suppose he is homeless, friendless, and has, at the most, only a few cents in his pocket. And if this is so, I wonder how he feels." [¶] The other being the elder, spoke with an air of authoritative wisdom. "You can tell nothing of it unless you are in that condition yourself. It is idle to speculate about it from this distance." [¶] "I suppose so." said the younger man, and then he added as from an inspiration: "I think I'll try it. Rags and tatters, you know, a couple of dimes, and hungry, too, if possible. Perhaps I could discover his point of view or something near it." [¶] "Well, you might," said the other, and from those words begins this veracious narrative of an experiment in misery. [¶] The youth went to the studio of an artist friend, who, from his store, rigged him out in an aged suit and a brown derby hat that had been made long years before. And then the youth went forth to try to eat as the tramp may eat, and sleep as the wanderers sleep. It was late at night, and a fine rain was swirling softly down, covering the pavements with a bluish luster. He began a weary trudge toward the downtown places, where beds can be hired for coppers. N^1

283.18 trousers'] trouser's E1

283.18; 284.1 toward] towards E1

283.25 intervals,] $\sim_\wedge N^1$

283.26 the most] omit N^1

283.26–29 dejection. The . . . searching] dejection, and looked searchingly N^1

283.30 highest] high N^1

283.30 the two] they too E1

283.34 freights] freights of sorry humanity N^1

284.1 well-dressed] $\sim_\wedge | \sim N^1$

284.3 time$_\wedge$] $\sim$, N^1

284.4 Row] row N^1

284.5–6 , and . . . country] omit N^1

284.6 tatters that] others whose tatters N^1

284.7 Square] square N^1

284.8–9 , standing . . . storm] omit N^1

284.11 flowing . . . great] pageantry of the N^1

284.12 Through the] The N^1

284.12 storming] damp N^1

284.12–16 , the cable . . . gong.] made an intensely blue haze, through which the gaslights in the windows of stores and saloons shone with a golden radiance. The street cars rumbled softly, as if going upon carpet stretched in the aisle made by the pillars of the elevated road. N^1

284.16 rivers] interminable processions N^1

284.16–17 swarmed . . . sidewalks] went . . . wet pavements N^1

284.17 mud,] $\sim_\wedge N^1$

284.17 which] that N^1

284.18 scar-like] $\sim_\wedge \sim N^1$

284.18–22 Overhead . . . heard.] The high buildings lurked a-back, shrouded in shadows. N^1

284.22 an alley] a side street N^1

284.22 sombre] mystic N^1

284.23 street] omit N^1

284.28 as] as if N^1

284.28 gorged] were gorging N^1

284.29–31 , eating . . . superstition] omit N^1

285.14 t'] to E1

285.16 ¹up] omit E1

285.17; 286.24 th'] the E1

286.5 obstacles] cobwebs N^1

286.9 "Let's (no ¶)] ¶ E1
286.23 feller] fellow E1
287.2 the] a E1
287.6 man] omit N1
287.21 released] omit E1
288.1 his] omit N1; an E1
288.2 handled] handed E1
288.3 leather covered] covered with leather E1
288.3 cold] as cold E1
289.2 man's] mans N1
289.10 these] the E1
289.12 biographies] the biographies E1
289.24 shadows] mystic shadows N1
289.31 their] ther N1
289.33 shoes and hat] clothes N1

290.12 went] and went E1
290.35 d——] d—d E1
290.38 "Yes (no ¶)] ¶ E1
290.39 time] moment E1
291.2 "Yessir (no ¶)] ¶ E1
291.4 Nosir] No, sir E1
291.21 weak] charitable E1
291.28 fer] for E1
292.19 O-o-o-oh] O-o-oh E1
292.24 hell of a] fine N1
293.24.1 omit] * * * * * * * [¶] "Well," said the friend, "did you discover his point of view?" [¶] "I don't know that I did," replied the young man; "but at any rate I think mine own has undergone a considerable alteration. N1

Subheadings

(N1)

284.2.1 He Finds His Field.
284.36.1 He Finds His Supper.
285.21.1 Enter the Assassin.
286.14.1 He Finds His Bed.
287.5.1 A Place of Smells.

287.29.1 To the Polite, Horrors.
288.24.1 Men Lay Like the Dead.
289.14.1 Then Morning Came.
291.13.1 Breakfast.
291.36.1 A Retrospect.
292.31.1 The Life of a King.

No. 63. AN EXPERIMENT IN LUXURY

[The copy-text is N1: *New York Press*, April 29, 1894, part III, p. 2.]

Subheadings

295.11.1 At the Portals of Luxury.
296.33.1 "The World of Chance."
297.21.1 The Glory of Gold.
298.4.1 Parental Portraits.

298.29.1 The Joys of a Millionaire.
299.16.1 The Gold Woman.
300.20.1 The Business of Being Beautiful.
301.16.1 Croesus Dines.

No. 66. THE ART STUDENTS' LEAGUE BUILDING

[The copy-text is MS: the untitled manuscript to be found in Crane's Notebook in the UVa.–Barrett Collection.]

Alterations in the Manuscript

313.18.2 omit] *deleted first line read* 'There was a ball in'
313.18.3 omit] *second line begins with deleted illegible first letter followed by* 'ew'
313.19 the fine] *preceded by deleted* 'their fine'

313.22–23 common-place] *followed by deleted* 'commercial'
313.24 of] *followed by deleted* 'one'
313.27 public] *preceded by deleted* 'building'
313.29 The] *preceded by deleted*

'In th' *and the beginning of another letter*

313.32   slumberous] *followed by deleted* 'ram-'

313.33   curves.] *period squeezed in at end of line; followed by deleted* 'thro'

313.33   studios] *followed by deleted* 'once the abode' *and* 'are now occupied by quiet'

313.33   rafters] *followed by deleted* 'toward'

314.2   captured] *preceded by deleted* 'crep'

314.2   creeping] *followed by deleted* 'up'

314.3   the] *followed by deleted* 'artists give'

314.4   struggle] *followed by deleted period*

314.4   time] *preceded by deleted* 'con'

314.5   plumbers] 'lu' *mended*

314.9   student] *a final* 's' *deleted*

314.13   austere] *followed by deleted* 'q'

314.18   another.] *period squeezed in at end of line; followed by deleted* 'upon the'

314.20   hopes] *interlined above deleted* 'class' *and* 'future'

314.26   new] *preceded by deleted* 'bran'

314.27   function] 'i' *added later*

314.28   christened] *preceded by deleted* 'created'

314.28   with] *beginning stroke of* 'w' *over comma with intent to delete*

314.32   followed] *followed by deleted* 'those are'

314.33   gorgeous] *followed by deleted* 'pl'

314.33   The] *preceded by deleted* 'Ther'

314.33   custom,] *followed by deleted* 'in'

314.34–35   member] *followed by deleted* 'to make'

314.38   After] 'A' *over* 'W'

314.39   school] 'c' *added later*

315.2   spirit.] *original period deleted and followed by* 'but' *which was then deleted, period not restored in error*

315.2   After] *followed by deleted* 'that'

315.3   down] *followed by deleted* 'again to their'

315.5   hear] *followed by deleted* 'one v'

315.5–6   accompaniment] *second* 'm' *over* 'e'

315.8   plumbers.] *followed by the beginning of an* 'I'

No. 67. THE MEN IN THE STORM

[The copy-text is Ar: *Arena*, x (Oct., 1894), 662–667. The other texts collated are Ph: *Philistine*, IV (Jan., 1897), 37–48; E1: *The Open Boat*, Heinemann, London, 1898, pp. 227–238. Ph and E1 are derived texts without authority.]

315.14   At . . . afternoon,] *omit* Ph,E1

315.22   positions] position E1

315.25   erect and] erect, Ph,E1

315.26   the trains] trains Ph,E1

315.29   it] *omit* Ph,E1

316.7   accented] accentuated E1

316.16   calculations] calculation E1

316.30   doorways] the doorways Ph,E1

317.10   become] became Ph,E1

317.35   lodging-house] *omit* Ph, E1

318.17   ears] ear Ph,E1

318.22   toward] towards Ph,E1

318.26   lite] light Ph,E1

318.36   doors] door E1

318.36   ag'in] agin Ph,E1

319.2   to] into Ph,E1

319.7   Give] G've E1

319.7,9   chanct] chance Ph,E1

319.9   damned] dam Ph,E1
319.11   frantic] *omit* Ph,E1
319.18   yeh ——" and] ~ "— ~ Ar+
319.22   seen;] ~ ‸ Ph,E1
319.27   opportunity] opportunities Ph,E1
319.28   are] were Ph,E1
319.34   an] *omit* Ph,E1
320.4   whiskers were] beard was E1
320.5   those] that E1

320.11   environment . . . relatively.] delightful environment. Ph,E1
320.12   perceive] perceived Ph,E1
320.25   all] *omit* Ph,E1
320.27   me] my E1
321.23   on] of Ph,E1
321.24   who] that E1
321.28   thus stood] stood thus Ph, E1
321.29   content] contented E1

No. 68. coney island's failing days

[The copy-text is N[1]: *New York Press*, Oct. 14, 1894, part v, p. 2.]

Subheadings

323.26.1   Crabs   That   Seemed Fresh.
324.39.1   Dreariness in the Music Halls.

326.11.1   The   Philosophy   of Frankfurters
327.2.1   The End of It All.

No. 69. in a park row restaurant

[The copy-text is N[1]: *New York Press*, Oct. 28, 1894, part v, p. 3. The other texts collated are MS: manuscript draft in the Crane Notebook in the UVa.–Barrett Collection; TMs: typescript made from the manuscript draft, also in the UVa.–Barrett Collection.]

328.13   Battle] battle N[1]
328.13   remarked] said MS,TMs
328.13–14   To . . . for] *omit* MS, TMs
328.15–16   noon-hour rush.] noon-hour. MS,TMs
328.16–17   that . . . place]   if Pickett and his men charged in here MS,TMs
328.18–21   They . . . ignorant.] *omit* MS,TMs
328.22   ¶ "I] (*no* ¶) ‸I MS,TMs
328.22–34   You . . . days."] I feel a thrill and exhilaration during the noon hour in here such as I might have felt if I had stood upon the summit of Little Round Top and overlooked the battle in some safe manner. It is a frightful struggle. [TMs: struggle,] I have often wished to induce Detaille to come to this country and get a subject for a melee that would make his frenzied Franco-Prussian battle-scenes look innocent! [TMs: innocent.]" MS, TMs
329.1   I was] We were MS,TMs
329.1   my . . . forward,]   our heads close together‸ MS,TMs
329.1–2   [2]I . . . heard] *omit* MS, TMs
329.2   stranger's remarks.] strangers remarks would have never been known. MS,TMs
329.2–7   Crowds . . . those] Even as he spoke more men were thronging in from the streets, clapping their hats upon pegs and sitting down with more or less violence. The men MS,TMs
329.8   impatient or tempestuous] stormy MS,TMs

329.9 at the waiters. [¶] Meanwhile] after the waiters. [¶] "Hey! [TMs: waiters,[¶] "Hey.] Did you forget those chops?" [¶] "Waiter! Here! A napkin, please!" [TMs: please.] [¶] "Hurry up that pie, will you, [TMs: you∧] old man!" [TMs: *no exclamation*] [¶] "Got that mutton-stew yet?" [¶] "Buttercakes and coffee! Certainly! About ten minutes ago!" [TMs: *lacks all 3 exclamations*] [¶] "You needn't mind the pie! I cant wait!" [TMs: *lacks both exclamations*] [¶] "Bring me a ham-omelet, a cup of coffee, and some corn muffins! [TMs: *no exclamation*] What? Well, send the right waiter here then! [TMs: *no exclamation*] I can't wait all day." [¶] Meanwhile MS,TMs

329.10–11 a monster pursued] something threatened MS,TMs

329.11 sought escape wildly] were trying to escape MS,TMs

329.12–14 It was . . . Withal,] *omit* MS,TMs

329.15–24 Perspiration . . . horses.] *omit* MS,TMs

329.20 two] too N[1]

329.24 From] And always from MS,TMs

329.25 places of communication] cummunications MS,TMs

329.25 there] *omit* MS,TMs

329.26–27 the sound . . . vehement,] hoarse roars and screams in a long chorus, vehement and excited, MS,TMs

329.27–28 regiment under attack.] ship in a squall. MS,TMs

329.28–330.19 A mist . . . plain] "You will percieve," [TMs: precive] said the stranger, MS,TMs

329.33; 330.27 latter] later N[1]

330.19 here] *omit* MS,TMs

330.20 provided] armed MS,TMs

330.20–21 that would shoot] loaded with MS,TMs

330.21–23 stews . . . As] stew or whatever was in particular demand, the public would be saved this dreadful strife each day and as MS,TMs

330.23 competent] fairly competent MS,TMs

330.24 the meals here] each man could cease his worry for the affair MS,TMs

330.25 difficulty] great difficulty MS,TMs

330.26 made] would make MS, TMs

330.27 The] This MS,TMs

330.27 difficulty] trouble MS, TMs

330.28 one. Of] one. Everybody, I think, would grow dexterous in catching their meals in these derby hats which you wear so much in the east. Of MS,TMs

330.28 the system] look [TMs: like] all innovations, it MS,TMs

330.29 important] important-looking MS,TMs

330.31 an] the MS,TMs

330.32 door. The] door. You see of course that the MS,TMs

330.33 that] which MS,TMs

330.34–37 possession . . . Of] possession and this would entail a certain loss to the house. And then undoubtedly there would develope [TMs: *no final 'e'*] a certain class of unscrupulous persons, clever at catching liners right off the bat so to speak, who would stand up in the front rank and appropriate a good many orders that were meant for quiet citizens in the rear. [¶] But after a time the laws would arise that always come to control these new inventions and the system would settle into something neat and swift. At these places where butter cakes are at a premium, batteries of rapid-fire ordnance could be erected to cammand

[TMs: errected to comiand] every inch of floor-space and at a given signal, [TMs: *no comma*] a destructive fire could sweep the entire establishment. I estimate that forty-two thousand people could be feed [TMs: fed] by this method in establishments which can now accomadate but from one of [TMs: to] three hundred during the noon rush. Of MS,TMs

330.39 gentleman] gentlemen MS(c),TMs

330.39–331.2 consider . . . assault.] resent what would look to them like an assault and retort with western fervor [TMs: fevor]. MS,TMs

331.3 ex-sheriff] sheriff MS,TMs

331.4 very] *omit* MS,TMs

331.4 wandered] strolled MS,TMs

331.5 that] *omit* MS,TMs

Subheadings

(N¹)

329.9.1 Like Distracted Water Bugs.

330.3.1 The Habit of Great Speed.

330.34.1 To Save Time.

No. 69a. NOTEBOOK DRAFT

[The copy-text is MS: manuscript draft in the Crane Notebook in the UVa.–Barrett Collection.]

Alterations in the Manuscript

331.10 ¹the] *interlined*

331.13 and] *the page is torn at this point and the 'a' is missing*

331.13 during] 'd' *over* 'i'

331.14 have] *interlined with a caret*

331.14 had] *interlined with a caret*

331.14 Little Round Top] *preceded by deleted* 'Cemetery Ridge'

331.17 make] *interlined above deleted* 'put'

331.18 battle-scenes] *preceded by deleted* 'scenes to scorn'

331.27 old] *interlined*

331.31 and] 'a' *over illegible letter*

332.1 skill] *interlined above deleted* 'speed'

332.2 screams] *final* 's' *over* 'in'

332.2 long] *followed by deleted* 'and exciting'

332.9 marksmen] *apostrophe after* 'k' *deleted*

332.11–12 for instance] *interlined*

332.16 innovations,] *followed by deleted* 'there'

332.17 time] *interlined above deleted* 'while' *of which* 'w' *is over* 'b'

332.18 up] *over* 'to'

332.20 bound for] *preceded by deleted* 'bound f' *on line above*

332.22 possession] *interlined with a caret above deleted* 'position'

332.25 would] *interlined*

332.28 into] 'to' *added*

332.31 ²a] *preceded by deleted* 'the'

332.34 hundred] *followed by deleted* 'people'

332.36 gentlemen] *third* 'e' *over* 'a'

332.36 resent] *followed by deleted* 'the ass'

332.37 what] *followed by deleted* 'loo'

332.38 remember] *followed by deleted* 'once'

332.40 alley] *followed by a deleted period*

No. 70. HEARD ON THE STREET ELECTION NIGHT

[The copy-text is N^c: newspaper clipping, probably from the *New York Press*, in the Crane scrapbook in the Special Collections of Columbia University Libraries. The other text collated is MS: manuscript draft in the Crane Notebook in the UVa.–Barrett Collection.]

333.1 chee!] gee! MS

333.1 Everything's] Everyting's MS

333.2 g'l'men] gen'l'm'n MS

333.2 fer‸bein'] fer-bein' MS

333.2 s'] so MS

333.2 , fact is,] *omit* MS

333.2–3 Republican! What?] Republican! See? I'm Republican! What? MS

333.4–5 I'm . . . am."] *omit* MS

333.6 if] do MS

333.6 that] wether MS

333.8 like a race-horse] away ahead everywhere MS

333.10–11 That's . . . him.] Not by a blame sight he didn't! MS

333.12 with] *omit* MS

333.15–16 The . . . goned.] *omit* MS

333.17 them this trip.] that crowd, you bet. MS

333.19–21 "Say . . . yeh?"] *omit* MS

333.22 "Strong] Say, Strong MS

333.23 Hughie] Hughey MS

333.26–29 "Down . . . ground."] *omit* MS (*placed at* 334.3 *after* with.")

334.1 to Camden] live in Jersey MS

334.2 of] *omit* MS

334.2 we're only fit] we ought to be used MS

334.3.1 *omit*] "Down . . . ground." MS (*see* 333.26–29)

334.3 'Goff.'] for Goff! MS

334.3 I guess yes."] Well I should say! MS

334.4–7 "He . . . myself."] Oh, what a roast. (*placed at* 337.1)

|| Hully chee! | Who are we? | The men who did up Tammanee! (*see* 334.16–18) || "He . . . myself." MS

334.4 hey] hay MS

334.8–9 "¹Goff! . . .-W-Goff!"] *omit* MS

334.10 "Voorhis . . . rest——"] *omit* MS (*see* 334.26)

334.11–13 "Well . . . neck."] *omit* MS (*see* 334.23–24 'Well . . . people.')

334.11 monkeyin'] monkeying MS

334.14–15 "Oh . . . walk-over."] *omit* MS

334.16–18 "Hully . . . Tammanee!"] *omit* MS (*see* 334.4–7)

334.19 seen] see MS

334.19 Tammany] *omit* MS

334.20 another] another one MS

334.20–21 three. . . . . "Oh] three. || I'd . . . eye-sight." (*placed at* 334.27–29) ||| "Oh MS

334.21 Bennett] Bennet MS

334.22 going . . . -feet." |] looking at himself with operaglasses to see if ||| MS

334.23–24 "Who . . . Grady."] Well, . . . people. MS (*placed at* 334.11–13)

334.26 it."] it!" | Now . . . earth. *in* MS (*placed at* 335.10–13) *followed by* "Voorhis . . . rest——" (*see* 334.10) *and* Who . . . Grady! (*see* 334.23–24)

335.1–9 "Don't . . . aye."] *omit* MS

335.11 a man has] you MS

335.11–12 level . . . Why,] level, why MS

335.13–337.2 The . . . dumped!"] *omit* MS

No. 70a. NOTEBOOK DRAFT

[The copy-text is MS: manuscript draft in the Crane Notebook in the UVa.–Barrett Collection.]

Alterations in the Manuscript

337.4 me,] *interlined*
337.11 Not by] *preceded by deleted* 'Say, how'
337.17 but] *followed by deleted* 'a'
338.1 Oh] *preceded by* 'X' *and, on line above, by deleted* 'Not on'
338.2–4 Hully . . . Tammanee] 'X' *appears to left of these three lines*

338.8 I've] *preceded by* 'X'
338.8 Democrats] 'D' *over* 'T'
338.10 I'd] *preceded on line above by* 'X'
338.10 see] *interlined*
338.18 Now] *preceded by* 'X'
338.18 politicians] 'i' *after* 'c' *is possibly deleted by a stroke*
338.20 face] *immediately preceded by deleted* 'sur'

No. 71. THE FIRE

[The copy-text is N¹: *New York Press*, Nov. 25, 1894, part IV, p. 6. The other text collated is TMs: typescript in the Special Collections of Columbia University Libraries. TMs is a derived text without authority.]

338.25 streets] streets of New York TMs (*interlined*)
339.15 timbre] timber N¹+
340.5 that] the TMs
340.7 spaces] space TMs
341.20 in] it N¹
342.27 were] *omit* TMs
342.28 lights] light TMs
343.2 and brass] brass TMs
343.18 noises] noise TMs

343.21 the pealings] pealings TMs
343.21 ²the] a TMs
343.32 street] the street TMs
344.1 a window] the window TMs
344.17 sprung] sprang N¹+
344.30 blasé] blaise N¹; blazé TMs

No. 72. WHEN MAN FALLS, A CROWD GATHERS

[The copy-text is N¹: *New York Press*, Dec. 2, 1894, part III, p. 5. The other texts collated are MS: manuscript draft in the Crane Notebook in the UVa.–Barrett Collection; TMs: Cora's typescript derived from MS (one carbon in the Special Collections of Columbia University Libraries and one in the UVa.–Barrett Collection); WG: *Westminster Gazette*, Oct. 9, 1900, pp. 1–2; E1: *Last Words*, Digby, Long, London, 1902, pp. 148–154. TMs, WG, and E1 are derived texts without authority.]

345.1–5 A . . . a-glare.] *omit* TMs+
345.4 shop‸men] ~ - ~ MS
345.4 dinners.] dinners, made more eager by the recollections

of their toil and by the shop-windows, glaring with light, suggesting those MS
345.5 The . . . a-glare.] *omit* MS+

345.7–9 They . . . street.] *omit*
MS+

345.9 at] a N[1]

345.10 ¶ Suddenly_∧] (*no* ¶) ~,
MS+

345.10 wavered . . . glared]
glared, and wavered on his
limbs for a moment MS+

345.10–11 bewildered and help-
less] *omit* MS+

345.13 companion's] *omit* MS+

345.13 frantically] convulsively
MS+

345.14 him] his companion MS+

345.14 limp form] body MS+

345.15 as a body sinks] like a
corpse sinking MS+

345.15 in] into MS(Cora)+

345.17 from] in MS(*deleted by*
Cora)

345.17 Instantly, from . . . peo-
ple] Instantly, in all directions
MS(u); Instantly people from
all directions MS(c[Cora *inserted* 'people from' *and deleted* ' , in'])+

345.18 the prone figure.] that figure prone upon the side-walk.
MS+

345.18–19 pushing, peering
group] peering, pushing crowd
MS+

345.20 above] among MS+

345.23 Nit;] Aw, MS+

345.24 ¹matter?] ~ ! MS

345.26 crowd] great crowd MS+

345.28 throng] mass of people
MS+

345.29 the man] a man E1

345.31 the foremost] foremost
MS

345.31 down,] ~ _∧ MS+

345.31–32 shouldering each
other,] *omit* MS+

345.32 eager, anxious] eagerly_∧
anxious MS+ (TMs+ : ~ , ~)

345.33 for a place] *omit* MS+

345.35 ²the] th' MS+

346.1 can't] cant MS,TMs

346.1 can't yeh] can't yer WG

346.2 d'] do MS+

346.3 A man . . . crowd] Somebody back in the throng MS+

346.4 you're . . . me!"] cheese
dat pushin'! I aint no peach!"
MS+ (TMs+ : cheese that;
WG+ : ain't)

346.6 walking . . . fell_∧] with
the Italian, MS+

346.7 terrified] frightened MS+

346.7 eyes. He held] eyes and
holding MS+

346.8–11 Sometimes . . . fingers.] *omit* MS+

346.12 Occasionally] Sometimes
MS+

346.12–13 with . . . might]
dumbly, with indefinite hope,
as if he expected sudden assistance to MS+

346.14 near] about MS+

346.14–16 questioned. . . .
They] *omit* MS+

346.19 ¶ Those] *no* ¶ MS+

346.19 that were] *omit* MS+

346.19 to] *omit* MS+

346.22 slowly,] ~ _∧ MS,TMs

346.22 relentlessly] pitilessly
MS+

346.23–24 hands clenched] hand
clinched N[1]

346.24–25 A . . . chin.] *omit*
MS+

346.25–26 could be seen] one
could see MS+

346.26 -colored_∧] ~ , MS

346.26 gleam] assassin-like
gleam MS+

346.26 eyes] eye MS+

346.26–28 were . . . shining]
shone MS+

346.27 in the] in this N[1]

346.29 light,] ~ _∧ MS+

346.31 ¶ As] *no* ¶ TMs+

346.32 to] might MS+

346.32 clutch at] grab MS+

346.33–34 seemed scarcely]
scarce seemed MS+

346.34; 348.20 breathe] breath
TMs

346.36 or] and WG

347.1 Less . . . persons] More self-contained men MS+

347.1 men] persons MS+

347.2 trod] tred MS; tread TMs(u),E1; trod TMs(c) (Cora's *alteration only appears on the* UVa. *carbon*)

347.3 loaded] *omit* MS+

347.4 from] down MS+

347.4 railroad] road MS+

347.5 there . . . roar] one could hear some|times a thunder MS+ (TMs,E1: sometimes; WG *omits* some times)

347.7 cents."] cents." [¶] The body on the pave seemed like a bit of debris sunk in this human ocean. MS+ (WG : pavement)

347.8 After] But after MS+

347.9 consider ways] bethink themselves of some way MS+

347.10 called] called out MS+

347.10 some one] a man MS+

347.11 man] body MS+

347.11 ¹his] the MS+

347.11–13 slap . . . stick.] slap the palms of the man. MS+ (WG : man's hand.)

347.15 continually repeated] repeated continually MS+

347.15 as] while MS+

347.15 pushed] pushed at MS+

347.16 had . . . they] seemed to have authority; the crowd MS+

347.17 another] another man MS+

347.17 knelt] knelt down MS+

347.21 throng] crowd MS+

347.22 battle] riot MS+

347.24–25 with . . . were] had been MS+

347.26 name?" "Where] ~ ?ʌ ʌ ~ MS+

347.27 of the] of this TMs+

347.27 play] drama MS+

347.28 came‸ swiftly] came, striding swiftly MS+ (MS, TMs[u]: strideing; *the* UVa. *carbon has been corrected*)

347.29 above . . . derbys] over the crowd MS+

347.30 confident, self-reliant] impenetrable MS+

347.32 He] Occasionally he MS+

347.33 there! Make way!] there. Come now! MS+

347.34 the inhabitants . . . city] people MS+

347.35 sufficiently] sufficently MS,TMs

347.35 as] *omit* WG

347.35 being] walking MS+

347.36–38 His . . . clouds.] He felt the rage toward them that a placid cow feels toward the flies that hover in clouds and disturb their repose. MS+ (WG: towards . . . towards; TMs[u] *at* UVa., WG: her repose; E1: its repose)

348.1 ¶ When] *no* ¶ MS+

348.1–2 demanded] said MS+

348.2 Well,] *omit* MS+

348.2 here?] ~ . MS,TMs(u) (Cora *altered the* UVa. *carbon to a question mark*)

348.4 outa] out E1

348.8 Can't] cant MS,TMs

348.10 "He's sick!"] *omit* MS+

348.11 th' ell] *omit* N¹

348.11 'm] 'im MS+

348.11 be!] ~ . MS

348.13 interior] precincts MS+

348.15 upreared] reared up MS+

348.16 away] way N¹

348.16 threats, his admonitions] admonitions, his threats MS+

348.20–21 with . . . machinery,] strainedly‸ MS+

348.22 tongue] way MS+

348.22–23 a babyish] like a baby's MS+

348.23 like] *omit* MS+

348.23 sad] sade MS; side TMs+

348.24–25 jostling and crowding‸] jostling, crowding, MS+ (WG,E1: crowding‸)

348.25 recommenced] recommenced again furiously MS+

348.26 an] the MS+

348.28   When] Then TMs(c)+
348.28 *et seq.*   its] it's MS,TMs
348.29   one] man carefully MS+
348.30   or fracture] *omit* MS+
348.30–31   side-walk, the] ~ - ~. The E1
348.32–33   anticipated . . . positions.] expected to see blood by the light of the match and the desire made them appear almost insane. MS+ (WG: almost mad.)
348.34–35   frequently] occasionally MS+
348.35   at . . . space.] and demand room. MS+
348.36   golden . . . lamps] faint haze of light MS+
348.37   beaten] beating E1
348.37–38   impatiently] *omit* TMs+
348.38   barrels∧] ~ , MS+
349.1   ambulance] wagon MS+
349.1–2   its red . . . gong] it's gleam of gold lettering and bright brass gong MS+ (WG, E1: its)
349.2   view.] view, the horse galloping. MS+
349.3   imperturbable] *deleted in* MS

349.3   always] almost E1
349.3   going] *omit* TMs+
349.3   to] on MS,TMs(u); at TMs(c)+
349.4   thoughtfully] *omit* TMs+
349.5   ¶ When] *no* ¶ TMs
349.6–8   mob, a silent . . . some] mob. When the ambulance started on it's banging and clanging return, they stood and gazed until it was quite out of sight. Some MS+ (WG,E1: its)
349.8   ways] way E1
349.8–9   , as if . . . recovered] *omit* MS+
349.10–14   at   the . . . drama. And] after the vanished ambulance and it's burden as if they had been cheated, as if the curtain had been rung down on a tragedy that was but half completed and MS+ (WG,E1: its)
349.14   fabric] blanket MS+
349.14   suddenly] *omit* MS+
349.15   suffering creature] sufferer MS+
349.16   appear . . . as]   make them feel MS+

No. 72a. NOTEBOOK DRAFT

[The copy-text is MS: manuscript draft in the Crane Notebook in the UVa.– Barrett Collection.]

Alterations in the Manuscript

349.18   evening] *followed by deleted* 'in the'
349.19   ferries] 'f' *over* 'F'
349.19   men] 'm' *over* 'w'
349.21   shop-] *preceded by deleted* 'glo'
349.22   suggesting] *followed by deleted* 'those Engl'
349.28   made] *preceded by deleted* 'made him'
349.29   in] Cora *added* 'to' *in pencil*
349.31   , in] *deleted by* Cora *and*

'people from' *interlined in pencil with a caret*
349.34   all] *interlined with a caret*
350.16   dat] 'd' *over* 'th'
350.21   The] 'T' *over* 'S'
350.23   maintain] *interlined above deleted* 'keep fro'
350.23   Those] 'ose' *squeezed in over* 'e' *and following* 'man' *deleted*
350.28   upward] 'u' *over period*
350.29   steel-] *followed by deleted* 'like feve' *and* 'wi'

350.30   a corpse] *interlined above deleted* 'the dead'

350.32   back] *followed by deleted* 'afraid'

350.33   spring] *preceded by deleted* 'jump'

350.37   way] *interlined with a caret*

350.41   street-] *preceded by deleted* 'ho'

350.41   in] *preceded by deleted* 'in a'

351.2   canvas] 'nv' *over* 'rv'

351.4   body] 'd' *over* 'l'; *preceded by deleted* 'man'

351.6   But] *followed by deleted* 'it'

351.10   and] *followed by deleted* 'shouted out excit'

351.13   ²man] *interlined above deleted* 'body'

351.16   match's] *apostrophe over an* 'e'

351.21   he] 'e' *over* 'is'

351.26   people] *followed by deleted* 'were'

351.32   "What's] 'W' *over* 'w' *and preceded by deleted* 'Come'

351.40   doin'?] *question mark over exclamation point*

352.2   create] *final* 'd' *deleted*

352.8   sad wail] *originally* 'side moan' *with* 'a' *over* 'i' *and* 'e' *undeleted in error;* 'wail' *interlined above deleted* 'moan'

352.10   doctor] *second* 'o' *over* 'e'

352.18   almost] 'a' *over* 'i'

352.21   sound] *preceded by deleted* 'rapid impatient'

352.23   And] 'A' *over* 'T'

352.24   view,] *comma preceded by deleted period*

352.25   imperturbable] *deleted in* MS

352.26   seat.] *preceded by deleted* 'side-walk.'

352.30   quite] 'qu' *over* 'al'

352.33   tragedy] *preceded by deleted* 'journey'

Alterations in the Two Typescripts

[All alterations are Cora's in ink (some in pencil in the UVa.–Barrett typescript) unless otherwise specified. Although derived, alterations for these typescripts may be of special interest.]

349.31   , in all directions people] TMs ', people from all directions' *preceded by x'd-out and then ink-deleted* 'in all' *following the comma*

350.8   anxious] *final* 'ly' *deleted*

350.14   anyhow?] *period in* UVa. TMs *altered to question mark in* Columbia TMs

350.18   helplessly] *final* 'ly' *added*

350.40   trod] Columbia 'tread' *altered in* UVa. *to* 'trod'

351.16   match's] Columbia 'mathe's' *corrected in* UVa.

351.31   repose] *preceding* Columbia 'their' *altered to* 'her' *in* UVa.

351.33   here.] *period altered to question mark in* UVa.

352.13   When] 'T' *over typed* 'W'

352.25   man] *followed by typed* 'whose face might have been wooden, so little change of expression was there upon it' *deleted in ink*

352.25   on a picnic] TMs 'at' *interlined above deleted* 'or'

No. 73. THE DUEL THAT WAS NOT FOUGHT

[The copy-text is N¹: *New York Press*, Dec. 9, 1894, part III, p. 2. The other texts collated are MS: manuscript draft in the Crane Notebook in the UVa.–Barrett Collection; E1: *The Open Boat*, Heinemann, London, 1898, pp. 241–250.]

353.1   Patsey] Patsy N[1],E[1]
353.1–11   Patsey . . . there]
Mike Tulligan and two friends
went into a corner-saloon to
get drinks. There MS
353.4 *et seq.*   Patsey] Patsy E[1]
353.12   lamp glare and] *omit* MS
353.13–14   outside, . . . wood.]
outside and everything
gleamed in the mellow rays
of the lights. MS
353.15   in . . . seeing,] used to
over in their own East Side
MS
353.16   They] They entered and
MS
353.17   bar and] bar. They MS
353.17   beer. They blinked] beer
and then sat blinking MS
353.21   place] saloon MS
353.21–24   At . . . occupied]
When it became midnight there
happened to be but three men
besides themselves and the bar-
tender in the place. Two of
these were well-dressed New
Yorkers who smoked cigars
rapidly and swung back in
their chairs occupying MS
353.25   manner, never] manner
and never MS
353.26   that other folk] anybody-
else MS
353.26–28   At . . . slim] The
third man was a lithe MS
353.29   a youthful] the faintest
MS
353.29   his lip] his youthful upper lip MS
353.30   2time] time to his lips,
MS
353.30   was bended] crooked MS
353.31–32   there . . . light.] one
could see the flashes of light in
an emerald. MS
353.32–357.3   The . . . fight] He
sat | [10 *leaves torn out of*
Notebook] MS
354.35–36   s-s-satisfact-shone]
s-s-satisfac-shone N[1],E[1]

354.38   s-s-satisfact-shone]
s-s-satisfac-shone E[1]
355.2   curved] curve N[1],E[1]
355.4   toward] towards E[1]
355.5   yer] per N[1]; fer E[1]
355.10   elegant] eloquent E[1]
355.36   2and] [*blank*] N[1] (*possibly mutilated*)
357.3   'bout] about MS
357.4   "Well] But never an inch
did Patsey give way. "Well MS
357.4,5,21   giv'] give MS
357.4–5   said . . . resolute.] he
said, stoutly. MS
357.6   'im long] 'im as long MS
357.8–11   face radiant . . . expression.] face was radiant was
joy and his eyes shot a murderous gloating gleam upon Patsey
MS
357.12   posture of a] attitude of a
practised, skilful MS
357.12–13   He . . . swordsman]
omit MS
357.14(*twice*)   b-r-r-rute] brrute
MS
357.14   a pig!"] pig." MS
357.15   peacemakers] well-dressed
men MS
357.15   still] *omit* MS
357.18   commit suicide] die MS
357.20   Patsey . . . granite.]
Patsey made one persistent
retort. MS
357.20,29   t'] to MS
357.21   wid] with MS
357.21   he'll get it.] *omit* MS
357.25   d—d] *omit* N[1],E[1]
357.26   understand it] understand
that it MS
357.27   sure . . . duel] pure suicide for you to fight with
swords MS
357.28   See? . . . business.]
omit MS
357.29   one . . . understan'?"]
with swords, he'll git it! Dat's
all!" MS
357.30–34   "Have . . . serious]
omit MS
357.35   out:] out excitedly: MS

357.35   on, sirs; come] on! Come MS

357.36   cab.] cab! MS

357.36   cow] calf MS

357.36–37   you, . . . you.] you very pretty! MS

357.38   on, sirs. We] on, we MS

357.38   hotel—] *omit* MS

357.38   I . . . weapons.''] I have weapons there!'' MS

357.39   yeh? Yeh] yeh, yeh MS

358.1   hoarse and maddened] enraged MS

358.2   forward.] forward fiercely. MS

358.2   d—n] d—d MS

358.2–3   swords,'' . . . quick!] swords! Get 'em! MS

358.3–4   wi'che! I'll] wi'che! Go ahn. Git 'em! I'll MS

358.4   , too] *omit* MS

358.5   so!] so, MS

358.5   ²yeh] yer N¹

358.5–6   I'll fight yeh in h—l, see?] *omit* N¹,E1

358.6–7   Patsey . . . gestures,] This intense oration Patsey delivered with sweeping gestures, MS

358.8   eloquently, . . . glaring.] eloquently, his body leaning forward, his jaw thrust out. MS

358.9–359.18   ''Ah . . . cathedral.] The wrath in the little Cuban's [*end of* MS] MS

358.20   fer] for E1

359.15   a-givin'] a-given E1

Subheadings

(N¹)

354.4.1   A Declaration of War.
355.16.1   Desperation.
356.8.1   A Duel to the Death.

357.0.1   The Challenge Accepted.
358.13.1   The Trouble Grows.

No. 73a. NOTEBOOK DRAFT

[The copy-text is MS: manuscript draft in the Crane Notebook in the UVa.–Barrett Collection.]

Alterations in the Manuscript

359.19   a] *interlined above deleted* 'the'

359.27   ¹it] *interlined*

359.32   with] 'w' *over illegible letters, possibly* 'in'

359.34   a] *preceded by deleted* 'an'

359.34   with] *followed by deleted* 'a'

360.2   crooked] *followed by deleted* 'out'

360.2   one] *interlined with a caret*

360.5   inch] *followed by deleted* 'to'

360.8   Cuban] *preceded by deleted* 'little'

360.8   quivering] *preceded by deleted* 'fairly'

360.11   unconsciously] 'i' *deleted in* MS

360.17   Patsey] *followed by deleted* 'was as honest and serious as dai' *with first* 'as' *interlined over deleted* 'a'

360.21   honestly,] *comma preceded by deleted period*

360.24   fellow?] *question mark altered from a period*

360.25   Dat's] 'D' *over* 'Th'

360.27   excitedly] 't' *over* 'd'

360.31   ''Yeh] 'eh' *over* 'ou'

360.33   yer] 'e' *over* 'ou'

360.34   anyting] *an* 'h' *after* 't' *deleted*

360.36   yeh] *interlined*

360.36   delivered] *interlined*

360.37 eloquently] *preceded by deleted 'in'; 'tly' over 'ce'*

360.38 leaning] 'in' *over* 'e' *and beginning of* 'd'

No. 75. OPIUM'S VARIED DREAMS

[The copy-text is N¹: *Detroit Free Press*, May 17, 1896, p. 20. The other texts collated are N²: *Portland Oregonian*, May 17, p. 17; N³: *New York Sun*, May 17, part III, p. 3; N⁴: *Kansas City Star*, May 17, p. 16; N⁵: *Buffalo Express*, May 17, sec. II, p. 3; N⁶: *Philadelphia Inquirer*, May 17, p. 28; N⁷: *Denver Republican*, May 17, p. 21. Since all texts are of equal authority, an agreement of two or more newspapers in an accidental is recorded here.]

365.1 this country] the United States N¹

365.3 men and white] *omit* N⁷

365.4 lamp∧] ∼ , N²⁻³

365.6 afterward] *omit* N³

365.10 Tenderloin,] Tenderloin, and N²

365.16–17 race track] ∼ - ∼ N²,⁵

365.24 there have] have there N³

365.25 ivory,] ivory, and N³,⁷

365.26 crowded∧] ∼ , N³⁻⁶

365.28 newspapers∧] ∼ , N³,⁵

365.29 opens] opened N²

365.29 anxious] *omit* N³

365.32 reigns] reins N¹,⁴,⁷

365.32 reigns∧] ∼ , N³,⁵

365.32 undoubtedly be] be undoubtedly N³

365.34 whisky] whiskey N³,⁶

365.37 These] The N³

365.37 lay and] lie and N¹; lay down and N²; *omit* N³

366.1–2 The . . . shafts.] *omit* N³

366.2 dumb-waiter] ∼ ∧ ∼ N⁶⁻⁷

366.3–4 *et seq.* opium-smokers] ∼ ∧ ∼ N³,⁷

366.4 street] streets N¹

366.4 are usually] usually are N³

366.5 deacon may] deacon N⁵

366.6 One . . . other.] *omit* N³

366.7 can] *omit* N³

366.8 cravats] cravat N²

366.8 coat-tails] ∼ ∧ ∼ N³,⁷

366.15 gracefully] *omit* N³

366.16 cents] cents' N³⁻⁴

366.17 smoke] smoked N⁵,⁷

366.17 $1] a dollar's N⁴

366.19 smokers . . . indulge] smoker . . . indulges N¹,⁵⁻⁶

366.21 about] of about N³

366.23 Habit-smokers] ∼ ∧ ∼ N²⁻⁷

366.23,27 sensation-smoker] ∼ ∧ ∼ N³,⁷

366.24 This latter is a person] *omit* N³

366.24 glamour] glamor N⁴⁻⁵,⁷

366.25 vice∧] ∼ , N²⁻³

366.25 who] *omit* N³

366.28–34 It . . . use.] *omit* N⁴

366.29–30 As . . . that] but probably N³

366.31 only smoked] smoked only N³,⁵

366.32 pipe∧] ∼ , N³,⁷

366.32 they "talk] a man ∧talks N³

366.33 upon them] *omit* N³

366.34 at any rate they] he is N³

366.34 to easily . . . use.] to stop its use easily. N³; easily to stop its use. N⁵

366.35 ¶ When] *no* ¶ N³

366.37 casino] cassino N³

366.38 chimney-sweep] ∼ ∧ ∼ N³,⁷

367.1 appears] comes N³

367.3 it] *omit* N¹⁻²,⁴,⁷

367.3–5 The . . . coffee.] *omit* N²

367.6 him∧] ∼ , N³⁻⁷

367.13 takes] it takes N³

367.25 hop-fiend] fiend N³

367.28–38 A . . . am."] *omit* N⁴

367.28 A "hop-fiend"] The fiend N³

367.32 "Opium (*no* ¶)] ¶ N³

367.33 does!] ∼ . N³,⁶

367.35 whisky] whiskey N³,⁶

367.38 me‸] ~ , N^{2-3}
368.1 at the present time] now N^{3}
368.2 one] a den N^{3}
368.8 li-shi] li-shu N^{4}
368.9–10 cap-boxes] ~ ‸ ~ $N^{3-4,7}$
368.12 is of] is N^{6}
368.12–13 the . . . ivory] *omit* N^{7}
368.17 darning-needle] ~ ‸ ~ $N^{3-4,7}$
368.17 the opium] opium N^{7}
368.25 pipe‸] ~ , $N^{2-3,5-6}$
368.25 where] when N^{7}
368.28 two] both N^{1}
368.28 He (*no* ¶)] ¶ N^{7}
368.30 smoke‸] ~ , $N^{2-3,6}$
368.30 this latter] the smoker N^{3}
368.32 Whereupon,] ~ ‸ N^{2-3}
368.33 splutters] sputters N^{3}
368.34–35 agreeable‸] ~ , $N^{3,6}$
368.36 powers] power N^{6}
369.6 camp-fire] ~ ‸ ~ N^{2-3}; campfire $N^{4,7}$
369.7 the] a N^{6}
369.9 half‸ perhaps‸] ~ , ~ , N^{3-4}
369.9 height‸] ~ , N^{2-4}
369.11 But (*no* ¶)] ¶ N^{7}
369.12 wealth of] *omit* N^{4}
369.12 faces‸] ~ , N^{2-3}
369.14 brotherhood] resemblance N^{3}
369.15 camp-fire] ~ ‸ ~ N^{2-3}; campfire N^{4}
369.16 logs‸] ~ , N^{2-4}
369.17 yellow] *omit* N^{3}
369.18–33 There . . . dinner.] *omit* N^{6}
369.19 arm-chairs] armchairs $N^{3-4,7}$
369.22 Den‸] ~ , $N^{2,7}$
369.25 arm-chair] armchair $N^{3,4}$; arm chair N^{7}
369.30–33 It . . . dinner.] *omit* N^{4}
369.32 baby] a baby N^{3}
369.35 a sky] sky N^{2}
369.35–36 , from all accounts,] *omit* N^{3}
370.2 re-adjusted] readjusted $N^{2-3,7}$
370.3 a soothing] soothing N^{2}; *omit* N^{3}
370.5–14 And . . . thought.] *omit* N^{6}
370.11 definition] consummation N^{3}

Subheadings

(N^{5})

365.7.1 Opium in the Tenderloin.
366.11.1 What Constitutes a "Habit."
367.5.1 A "Yen-Yen."
369.33.1 Under the Spell of Opium.

(N^{6})

366.11.1 What Constitutes a "Habit."
367.5.1 A "Yen-Yen."
368.6.1 Inside a "Joint."
369.33.1 Under the Spell of Opium.

(N^{7})

365.19.1 New York Joints.
366.34.1 When Opium Gets a Hold.
368.6.1 Inside a "Joint."
369.11 (undisturbed.|) The Real and the Ideal.

No. 76. NEW YORK'S BICYCLE SPEEDWAY

[The copy-text is N(p): *McClure's* proof. The other texts collated are N^{1}: *New York Sun*, July 5, 1896, part III, p. 5; N^{2}: *Boston Globe*, July 5, p. 30; N^{3}: *Pittsburgh Leader*, July 5, p. 22.]

370.15 has] omit N³
370.17 city's] city N³
370.19 It . . . position.] omit N¹
370.22–23 vaulted . . . bicycle.] attracted more interested sight-seers than any other ten streets of this great city. This is because of the bicycles. N¹
370.26–27 Also . . . hotels.] omit N¹
370.29 these gorgeous spring] fine N¹
371.7 still] omit N¹
371.17 note] notice N¹

371.18 will] omit N¹
371.29 then] men N²
371.31 concerned] omit N¹
371.35 a sombre] sombre N¹
372.1 new] omit N¹
372.8 wheelmen] wheelman N¹
372.11 in the] omit N¹
372.14 as good] so good N¹
372.26 most] omit N¹
373.6 simply and industriously] omit N¹
373.8 farthest] most friendly N¹
373.13 We are] It seems N¹
373.15 is] and is N¹
373.17 policemen] policeman N³

No. 77. IN THE BROADWAY CABLE CARS

[The copy-text is N¹: *Pittsburgh Leader*, July 26, 1896, p. 22. The other texts collated are N²: *Denver Republican*, July 26, p. 24; N³: *New York Sun*, July 26, section 2, p. 3; E1: *Last Words*, Digby, Long, London, 1902, pp. 173–180. E1 is a derived text, without authority. Since all the newspapers are of equal authority, an N²⁻³ agreement in an accidental is recorded here.]

373.19 Lodore] Ladore N¹⁻²
373.19 Some] omit N³+
373.19–20 would have] omit N³+
373.20 if anyone had] when it was N³+
373.21 they] the cars N³+
373.22 color] column N³+
373.32 neighbor's] neighbors' N²
373.32 to New York] omit N³+
374.7 feminine . . . give him] omit N²
374.7 two-dollar] $2 N²⁻³
374.12 be] is E1
374.13 ¹road∧] ~ , N²⁻³
374.15 chariot∧] ~ , N²⁻³
374.18 man] men E1
374.23 $3.98] three dollars and ninety-eight cents E1
374.28 mud] any mud E1
374.29 "Do (*no* ¶)] ¶ N³
374.31 Sometimes] Some time E1
374.32–33 moves forward] goes N³+
374.35 Tenderloin∧] ~ , N²⁻³
374.36 10,000,000] 1,000,000 N¹
374.37 Barrett] Barret E1

375.2 uncontrolled] omit N³+
375.2 crossing] crossings N²
375.3 two old] two gold N²
375.6 beards] boards N²
375.12 and] an E1
375.14 car] cars N¹
375.16 action] actions E1
375.19 jungles] jungle E1
375.19 cañons] canons $N
375.22 a lone] the N³+
375.28 Of course] omit N³+
375.28 troop] troup E1
375.29–30 complication] complexion N²
375.33 acute] route N²; omit N³
375.36 from] omit N²
376.10–11 neck . . . quit your] omit N¹
376.10 it] omit E1
376.12 rears] roars on N²; roars N³+
376.13 dude] due N¹
376.19 in] into N³+
376.25 Towards] Toward N³
376.28 trip] trips N²
376.29,30,33 park] Park N²⁻³
376.31 uptown] up town N²⁻³

376.32   signs] sign N[1]

376.35–36   to good purpose] *omit* N[3]+

376.37–38   restaurants] restaurant E[1]

377.1   [2]one] *omit* E[1]

377.3   up] *omit* N[1]

377.4   and] and and N[1]

377.5   lamp] lamps N[2]

377.7   just] *omit* N[1]

377.7–8   sideways] sidewise N[3]+

377.8   as] *omit* N[1]

377.9   the] *omit* N[1]; all N[3]+

377.9   said] says N[3]+

377.9–10   Aw, go ahn] Ah, gwan N[3]+

377.10   but] But N[2–3]

377.10   was] is N[3]+

377.11   Here he] That N[3]+

377.14–15   Perhaps . . . car.] *omit* N[1]

377.19   gold] and gold N[3]+

377.35   replies] reply E[1] (*following marked clipping*)

377.38   abandon] *abandon* E[1]

377.39   does] do N[3]+

378.1–2   [1]less . . . number] fewer and fewer N[3]+

378.3   car] cars E[1]

378.5   the few] a few N[2]

Subheadings

(N[2])

374.34.1   Down Through the Tenderloin.

375.34.1   The   Buzz-Saw   Hat Brim.

376.36.1   In the Evening.

No. 78. THE ROOF GARDENS AND GARDENERS OF NEW YORK

[The copy-text is N(p): *McClure's* proof. The other texts collated are N[1]: *Cincinnati Commercial Tribune*, Aug. 9, 1896, p. 18; N[2]: *Washington Post*, Aug. 9, p. 20; N[3]: *Portland Oregonian*, Aug. 9, p. 16; N[4]: *Pittsburgh Leader*, Aug. 9, p. 20; N[5]: *Denver Republican*, Aug. 9, p. 21; WG: *Westminster Gazette*, Oct. 17, 1900, pp. 1–2; E[1]: *Last Words*, Digby, Long, London, 1902, pp. 166–172.]

378.9   Chicago] Cincinnati N[1]

378.12   These] There N[4]

378.21   circular] the circular N[1]

378.24   suggestion] a suggestion N[3],WG

378.25   a roof-] the roof- WG,E[1] (~ ∧)

378.28   seventy- . . . finger] *omit* N[5]

378.28   little] *omit* WG,E[1]

378.30   a] *omit* N[1]

379.3   Yorkers] Yorker's N[2]

379.3–4   He . . . change.] *omit* WG,E[1]

379.6   roof-garden prices] roof gardens N[1]

379.7   ordinarily] cordially N[1]

379.10   the] *omit* N[1]

379.11   oblivious] obvious

N(p[c]),N[2,4],E[1]; abvious N(p[u])

379.18   numbers] the numbers N[3]

379.18   on] of N[3]

379.24   has] had N[5]

379.33–35   flashing . . . should] *these two lines of* N[1] *are transposed*

379.35   should] would N[3]

380.4   This] One N(p[c]),WG,E[1]

380.4   have opened] opened WG

380.5   Grand] the Grand N[3]

380.13   is] was N(p[c]),WG,E[1]

380.20 $22,000∧] twenty-two thousand dollars' WG,E[1]

380.25   yet] *omit* N[5]

381.3   decorative] the decorative N[3]

381.9   say] stay N⁵
381.9   he] that he E1
381.15–37   The bicycle . . . pines.] omit N¹
381.17   as soon as] soon— E1
381.19   long-gone] long-ago N⁴

Subheadings

(N²)

378.30   (miracle. |) Forgetful of His Proportions.
379.29.1   Gaining Glimpses by Strategy.

(N⁵)

378.24.1   Roof Garden Waiters.
379.17.1   The Beer Overture.

381.25   stifle] stifled WG
381.25   more air] omit WG,E1
381.32   problems] the problems N⁵
381.33   roofs] roof N⁵

380.14.1   Oscar's Multitude of Injunctions.
381.8   (none. |) A Gaudy and Dazzling Scene.

380.3.1   Two Roof Gardens.

No. 79. AN ELOQUENCE OF GRIEF

[The copy-text is E1: *The Open Boat*, Heinemann, London, 1898, pp. 267–270. The other text collated is MS: manuscript fragment in the UVa.–Barrett Collection present at 382.27–383.8 'constantly . . . exhibits'.]

382.28–29   in . . . court-room] , rearward, MS
382.30   upon] to MS
382.30   tears] tears however MS
382.31–32   Occasionally (*no* ¶)] ¶ MS
382.32   the girl] this girl MS
382.35   a jail] jails MS
383.1   officer] policeman MS
383.1   contingent] party MS

383.2   preliminary] prelimary MS
383.3   fire-wheels] rockets and fire-wheels MS
383.4   dollars'] dollar's MS
383.5   clothing] underwear MS
383.5   women] woman MS
383.7   an accuser] a plaintiff MS
383.8   exhibits‿] shows, MS

No. 80. IN THE TENDERLOIN: A DUEL

[The copy-text is TT: *Town Topics*, xxxvi (Oct. 1, 1896), 14. The other text collated is TTT: *Tales from Town Topics*, No. 33 (Sept., 1899), pp. 119–123. TTT is a derived text without authority.]

385.8   paused] paused in TTT
385.8   a] omit TT
385.15   glared out suddenly] suddenly glared out TTT

385.39   still] omit TTT
385.39   to] into TTT
386.15   juke] duke TTT
387.30   softly] omit TTT

No. 84. STEPHEN CRANE IN MINETTA LANE

[The copy-text is N¹: *Nebraska State Journal*, Dec. 21, 1896, p. 3. The other texts collated are N²: *Galveston Daily News*, Dec. 20, p. 24; N³: *Philadelphia Press*, Dec. 20, p. 34; N⁴: *San Francisco Chronicle*, Jan. 10, 1897, p. 2; N⁵: *New York Herald*, Dec. 20, 1896, sec. v, p. 5; N⁶: *Minneapolis Tribune*, Dec. 20, p. 21; TMs: typescript in the UVa.–Barrett Collection; E1: *Last Words*, Digby, Long, London, 1902, pp. 154–166. Since all newspaper texts are of equal authority, agreement of accidentals in two or more texts is recorded here. TMs and E1 are derived texts without authority.]

399.4   of] and N⁶,TMs(u),E1

399.6   conversant] conversing N⁵

399.6   negroes‿] ∼ , N²,⁴⁻⁵

399.7   a] *omit* N²

399.7   growler] " ∼ " N⁵

399.8   identity‿] ∼ , N⁵⁻⁶

399.8   unless‿ indeed‿] ∼ , ∼ , N²,⁴⁻⁵

399.9   policeman] patrolman N⁵

399.9   post] his post TMs; his coast E1

399.10; 400.3,5   Lane] lane N²⁻³

399.10   Lane‿] ∼ , N⁴⁻⁵

399.11 *et seq.*   MacDougal] M'Dougall E1

399.13   absurdly] assuredly TMs(c),E1; ansuredly TMs(u)

399.14   Lane,] ∼ ‿ N²,⁵

399.14   from it] it from N²

399.15   Bleecker] Bleecher N¹

399.16   in New York] in the city N⁵

399.18   unmistakably] unmistakeable TMs

399.18–19   but . . . out] *omit* N⁶,TMs,E1

399.20   days,] ∼ ‿ N⁵⁻⁶

399.23   negroes‿] ∼ , N⁴⁻⁵

399.24   elements] element TMs

399.29   any] every N²

399.30   "‿Big Jim‿] ' 'Big Jim' N⁵

399.30   Jim] Joe N²

399.31   "‿No-Toe's‿]   " 'No‿Toes' N⁵

400.7   any] many N³

400.8   them,] ∼ ‿ N²,⁴⁻⁵

400.9   Lane] lane N²,⁴⁻⁵

400.9   departure,] ∼ ‿ N⁴⁻⁵

400.12   plain‿] ∼ , N²,⁵

400.12   knock-out] knockout N³,⁴; ∼ - | ∼ N⁵

400.14   of] on E1

400.15   of] on TMs(c)

400.16   town] city N⁵

400.17 *et seq.*   Bloodthirsty] " ∼ " N⁵

400.20   Lane] lane N⁴⁻⁵

400.26   habituated] habitated N⁶, TMs,E1

400.26   old‿timers] ∼ - ∼ N²,⁴

400.29   wide‿] ∼ , N²,⁵

400.31   City] the City N²,⁴

400.32   single-minded] simple-minded N²; ∼ ‿ ∼ N³,⁵⁻⁶

400.32   ingenuous] ingenious N¹⁻²

400.34   Bloodthirsty,] ∼ ‿ N⁴⁻⁵

400.34   importance,] ∼ ‿ N⁴⁻⁵

400.34 *et seq.*   No-Toe] ∼ ‿ ∼ N³,⁶

400.35   enough,] ∼ ‿ N⁴⁻⁵

400.35   solely] Charley TMs,E1

400.36   to] on N⁶,TMs,E1

400.37–38   was . . . As] *omit* N⁶,TMs,E1

400.38   way] ways N²

400.39   round-about] ∼ - | ∼ N²; roundabout N³; ∼ ‿ ∼ N⁵

401.1   corkscrew,] ∼ ‿ N⁵⁻⁶

401.3   gentlemen] gentleman N²,⁵

401.4   river.] river—Sing Sing TMs,E1

401.5   Lane] land TMs,E1

401.6   It . . . that] *omit* TMs,E1

401.10–11   Guinea . . . figure.] *omit* N²

401.12–13   Sometimes . . . crooks] *omit* N²

401.12   the other] other N⁵

401.13   make] made N²

401.15   in] is E1

401.18   head-light] headlight N²⁻⁵

401.19   the reporter] I N⁵

401.20 *et seq.*   Mammy] " ∼ " N⁵

401.24   sailor's] sailors' N⁵,E1

401.24   boarding house] ∼ - ∼ N²,⁴

401.24   prison] Prison N³⁻⁵

401.27   pedestrians] the pedestrians N³

401.29   to] of N⁴
401.29   is pasted] are pasted N⁴,
    TMs,Eɪ
401.31   throat∧] ~ , N³⁻⁵
401.33   old∧] ~ , N³,⁵
401.33   ²very] ve'y N⁵
401.36   a reporter's] my N⁵
401.36   visit,] ~ ∧ N³⁻⁵
401.36   old] od N²
401.38   great . . . clicked] *omit*
    N²
401.39 respirations] respiration N¹
402.2   of a] of N¹
402.11   and presently] presently
    N¹
402.18–19   what she . . . said;]
    omit N⁶,TMs,Eɪ
402.19   said.] said; what Mag
    said; what she said. N²
402.20   in] and in N²
402.26   says:] ~ , N⁴⁻⁵
402.27–28   You   des . . . o'ny]
    omit N³ (*and repeats* 402.26
    'You . . . Gal-|')
402.31   'im] 'm N³,⁶
402.31   lan'] lan's N⁴; law Eɪ
402.33   noting] no 'ting N⁵
402.36   applies] applied N⁵
402.37   back-handed] black-
    handed N⁶,TMs,Eɪ
402.37   and,] ~ ∧ N²,⁵
403.3   Lane] lane N²⁻⁵
403.4   restaurant∧] ~ , N³,⁵
403.5   one] *omit* N²
403.6   that] *omit* N⁶,TMs,Eɪ
403.8   in,] ~ ∧ N²,⁵⁻⁶
403.9   small∧] ~ , N²⁻³,⁶
403.9   shelf] dusty shelf N⁶,TMs,
    Eɪ
403.9   This] If N²
403.10   mind,] ~ ∧ N²,⁵
403.16   Pop's] Pops's N¹
403.19–20   the   door . . . keep]
    omit N²
403.28   condition] conditions N¹
403.29   Lane] lane N²⁻⁶
403.29   Lo'd] Lord N⁵
403.29   ain't!] ~ ? N⁴⁻⁵
403.31   disher'] dis her' N⁵,Eɪ(er')
403.32   indeed] 'deed N⁵
403.33   ain't] haint N⁶,TMs

403.33   des] *omit* N¹,Eɪ
403.34   was] wos N⁶,TMs,Eɪ
403.35   diff'rent] dif'frent N¹,⁴;
    dif-|frent N³; diff'ent N⁵;
    different N⁶,TMs,Eɪ
403.35   dar] der N⁶,TMs, Eɪ
403.36   Cou't] cou't N⁴,⁶
403.36   yer] yere N⁵
403.38   a-roamin'] a-roarin' N²;
    a-romin' N⁶,TMs; a-comin' Eɪ
403.38   round] roun' N²
403.38–404.1(*twice*)   a-slashin']
    slashin' N²
403.38   a-cuttin'] cuttin' N²
404.2   gave] gave the N¹
404.4   on] of N⁶,TMs,Eɪ
404.5   wouldn't] would N⁶,TMs,
    Eɪ
404.7   many's] man's N⁴
404.7   agin] again N⁶,TMs
404.7   Yes, sir!] *omit* N⁶,TMs,Eɪ
404.8   time∧] ~ , N⁵⁻⁶
404.9   the two] two N⁶,TMs,Eɪ
404.11   man] *omit* TMs,Eɪ
404.12   edged] edge N²
404.12   Lane] lane N⁴⁻⁵
404.13   Hank∧ . . . course∧] ~ ,
    . . . ~ , N³⁻⁵
404.13   shadow] shadows TMs,Eɪ
404.15   gives] gave Eɪ
404.15   in each] a N²
404.16,18   street] Street N³
404.18   each] every N²
404.19   again] *omit* N²
404.20   barge∧] ~ , N²,⁵
404.20   occasion] excursion N⁶,
    TMs,Eɪ
404.26   Boss] " ~ " N⁵
404.27–28   anyone] ~ ∧ ~ N⁴⁻⁵
404.28   Bill] " ~ " N⁵
404.30,36   Hank] " ~ " N⁵
404.33   Dignities] Dignitaries N⁴
404.34   organization] organiza-
    tions N²,Eɪ
404.36; 405.2,19,24   Lane] lane
    N²,⁴⁻⁵
405.1   strange . . . good] strange
    and good tales N⁵
405.2   Lane∧] ~ , N²,³,⁵
405.2   in the] in TMs
405.3   steal] steel N⁶

405.4 Joel] " ~ " N⁵
405.5 mixed-ale] ~ ∧ ~ N³,⁵
405.5 mixed-] middle- N²
405.8 Kenny] Kenney TMs
405.9 Carey] Carrey TMs
405.9 a hundred] 100 N²
405.11 New York] the city N⁵
405.14 longer,] ~ ∧ N³,⁵
405.18 the present] a TMs,E1
405.19,24 has] *omit* TMs,E1
405.20 peace,] ~ ∧ N³,⁵
405.24 old] *omit* N⁶,TMs,E1
405.26 as∧] ~ , N³,⁵
405.28 in] of N⁶,TMs,E1
405.28 Paradise.] Paradise. [¶] Hector Worden, one of the plain clothes men of the precinct, who has devoted a great deal of attention to the lane, told me that the property owners, strangely enough, placed about as many obstacles in the way of the destruction of dives as do the thugs themselves. The rent to a keeper of some kind of a den is naturally higher than it would be to a laboring man, and the house owner sometimes prefers the dive keeper as a tenant. It is a perilous chance, but some of them take it, and, moreover, they occasionally resort to curious subterfuges to protect their tenants from police interference. Others keep their proprietorship a secret, if possible, never coming near the lane, but leaving their houses in the hands of agents and winking the other eye from a safe distance. It is an interesting fact that in a great city like New York we never know how much money from the shame of women and from the pockets of robbed men ends in the form of wine and truffles upon the tables of our proudest. When Minetta lane and streets like it pursue the elusive rent money, Fifth avenue has educated itself to look another way, to steadfastly regard the frescoes over the altar. N⁵

405.29 meantime,] ~ ∧ N²⁻³,⁵
405.29–30 possession] the possession N⁴,⁶,TMs,E1
405.31 MacDougal] MacDugal N⁶,TMs
405.33 seems] seem N²,E1
405.33 overfond] ~ - | ~ N¹; ~ ∧ ~ N⁵⁻⁶
405.33 fashions] fashion N³,⁶, TMs,E1
405.36 there] there | there TMs
405.37 are these people] *omit* N¹
406.2 child∧] ~ , N²,⁵

Subheadings

(N³)

399.32.1 Not Then a Thoroughfare.
400.33.1 No Toe Charley.
401.35.1 A Picture of Suffering.
402.33.1 Memories of the Past.
403.27.1 "Pop's" View of It.
404.35.1 Keeping in Touch.

(N⁵)

399.32.1 "No Thoroughfare."
401.19.1 One of the Relics.
403.2.1 The "Restaurant."
405.10.1 No More a Bloody Lane.

No. 85. NEBRASKA'S BITTER FIGHT FOR LIFE

[The copy-text is N¹(p): proof for the *Nebraska State Journal*, Feb. 24, 1895, p. 14, in the Special Collections of Columbia University Libraries. The other texts collated are N¹: *Nebraska State Journal* (it should be noted that the designation N¹ applies to both the proof and the final published version and only where they differ will the symbol N¹[p] appear); N²: *Salt Lake City Tribune*, Feb. 24, p. 14; N³: *Buffalo Morning News*, Feb. 24, p. 5; N⁴: *New Orleans Times-Democrat*, Feb. 23, p. 9; N⁵: *Galveston Daily News*, Feb. 24, p. 10; N⁶: *Cincinnati Commercial Gazette*, Feb. 24, p. 17; N⁷: *Philadelphia Press*, Feb. 24, p. 25; N⁸: *New York Press*, Feb. 24, sec. v, p. 2; N⁹: *Rochester Democrat and Chronicle*, Feb. 24, p. 7.]

409.3–7   Some . . . sufficient.] *omit* N³

409.7.1   sufficient. [¶] The] sufficient. | east . . . sufficient. [*lines* 409.4–7 *repeated*] | [¶] The N¹(p)

409.10   then] *omit* N³

409.10   when] *omit* N²

409.11   a hundred] 100 N³,⁸

409.11   wide] in width N²

409.12   this] the N²

409.13   there] *omit* N⁵

409.17   prolific] omit N³

409.19   corn] corn standing waist high N³

409.20   that were congregated] *omit* N³

409.21   and brave] *omit* N³

409.21   healthy and] health and N²; *omit* N³

409.22   with the] with N²

409.22–28   of an . . . stalks] *omit* N³

409.27   waist-] water- N²

409.29   Then,] *omit* N³

409.31   these] those N⁶

410.9   hot] as hot N⁶

410.10   disc appeared] dis-|appeared N³

410.11   mass] was N⁹

410.15   this] the N⁶

410.17–20   ²their . . . deity] *omit* N³

410.21   In . . . wind,] *omit* N³

410.24–27   shivering . . . breath,] *omit* N³

410.26   pulled] pulled and N²

410.27   and sometime beautiful] *omit* N³

410.31   straws] straws and N⁶

410.33   swirling] whirling N⁴

411.2–5   The . . . men.] *omit* N³

411.7   And yet] *omit* N³

411.7–8   no absence] *omit* N³

411.9   few] *omit* N⁹

411.9   despaired] departed N²

411.11   district] desert N⁶

411.12   their neighborhoods] their neighborhood N⁶; the neighborhood N⁷

411.12–13   their farms . . . counties] *omit* N³

411.13   in] to N²

411.13–17   which . . . lands] *omit* N³

411.17   toward] towards N⁶

411.17   And] *omit* N³

411.20–21   Their . . . tables.] *omit* N³

411.20   sitting] setting N⁷

411.21   tables] plates N⁵

411.23   crop of] crop in N⁸

411.25–29   It . . . distances.] *omit* N³

411.27   peoples] people N⁶

411.31   morally] mortally N³

411.35–37   where . . . earn] in search of N³

411.39–412.3   Then . . . teeth.] *omit* N³

412.4   Men] Those who stayed N³

412.7   they] he N⁸

412.13   wind] winter N⁵

412.14–15   And . . . despair.] *omit* N³

412.16   cattle in] cattle N²

412.19   fuel . . . and where] *omit* N²

412.19   as scarce . . . was] *omit* N⁹

412.22   in . . . and] *omit* N³

412.23   Holcomb] Halcombe N¹,³,⁵,⁷,⁹; Holcombe N²,⁴,⁶,⁸

412.33   and corresponds] *omit* N⁴⁻⁶

412.37   car] cars N⁷

412.37   contain] contains N²

412.38   all] for N²

412.39 facetious] faceteous N^1(p); *omit* N^1

413.1 food] good N^9

413.2 after the] after N^8

413.3 and re-explanations] *omit* N^8

413.6 in order] *omit* N^3

413.7 they] the N^9

413.7 Also various] *omit* N^3

413.10 of] *omit* N^{5,8}

413.12 the price of] *omit* N^3

413.17 practice] prey N^3

413.18–19 As . . . nevertheless,] *omit* N^8

413.20 drought] drouth N$^{2,4-5}$

413.21 vociferously shouting] asking N^3

413.22–23 one . . . dollars] $150,000 N$^{2-8}$

413.25 ingenuously] ingeniously N^5

414.8 the suffering] suffering N^6

414.8 do] *omit* N^9

414.13 awake] asleep N^8

414.17 He] He had N^5

414.21–22 He . . . ability.] *omit* N^8

414.23 virtuous] various N^5

414.25 received] receive N^6

414.31 uncompromising] uncomprising N$^{1,6-8}$

414.34 rural] rival N^2

415.2 the abuse] abuse N^5

415.2 of] *omit* N^4

415.7 this] the N^7

415.11 degrees] deg. N^6

415.13 one and a half] 1½ N$^{2-6}$

415.13 degrees] degree N^4; deg. N^6

415.15 shriek] shrieks N^2

415.18 The . . . day.] *omit* N^3

415.20 traversing] traveling N^6

415.22–23 high upon] upon high N^{2,5}

415.24 houses] house N^7

415.25 -fire] ₐfires N^2

415.27; 416.7 drought] drouth N$^{2,4-6}$

415.29 stores] stories N^5

415.32 prairie] prairies N^2

415.37 rears] rear N^{4,9}

415.38 farms] farmers N^4

416.2 scudding] scuddling N^6

416.7 -pestered] -stricken N^3

416.10 might] he might N^2

416.16 neighbor was] neighbors were N^4

416.23 here, a] here, and a N^9

416.25 huddle] huddled N$^{5-6}$

416.27 eye] eyes N^2

416.28 crusts] encrusted N^5

416.32 out] out out N^1

416.32 theirselves] themselves N^7

416.36 round] around N^{2,4}

416.37 ploughin'] plowin' N$^{3-4,6,8}$; ploughing N^9

416.38 upon] up on N^2

416.39 th'] the N^{2,7}

416.39 comes] come N^7

416.39 all] *omit* N^2

417.5 if] of N^7

417.6 warm] good N^2

417.7 to think now] now to think N^6

417.12 little] *omit* N^7

417.15 an] the N^7

417.18 were] *omit* N^5

417.19 the corn] corn N^3

417.20 had] *omit* N^2

417.22 of the misfortunes] *omit* N^3

417.23–25 It . . . it.] *omit* N^3

417.24 tempest] temperature N^2

417.30 ²the] their N^3

417.31 bended] bent N^2

417.33 subtle] subtile N^7

418.1 I hadter] A hadter N^2

418.3–4 I'd . . . an'] I . . . and N^3

418.5 did] do N^{2,6}; *see* 418.6–7 *for line repeated with correction in* N^1(p)

418.6–7 Who . . . along] Who the | "How do you get along?" N^1(p); Who the h—— tol' you I got along?" N^2; *omit* N$^{3-8}$; Who the —— can get along?" N^9

418.8 meantime] meanwhile N^7

418.15 babes] babies N^9

418.18 Holcomb] Holcombe N$^{1,3-4,6-9}$; Halcombe N^5

418.19	²is] it N²
418.27	at present] *omit* N²
418.29	cause] course N²
418.29	districts of] districts in N³
418.34	observed] described N²
418.36	homes] their homes N⁶
418.37	unwise] universal N²
418.40	the people] people N⁵
419.1	other] the N²
419.3	causes] cause N²
419.4–13	It . . . droughts.] *omit* N³

419.12–13	in a degree] *omit* N²
419.13	droughts] drought N⁷
419.17	23.85] 28.85 N⁹
419.22	portion] part N⁶
419.23	They] To N³
419.27–33	Almost . . . people.] *omit* N³
419.30	in] with N⁴
419.34–35	But . . . country.] *omit* N⁸
420.4–6	In . . . courage.] *omit* N³

Subheadings

(N⁷)

409.28.1	Menace of the Sun.
410.28.1	Despair in the Desert.
411.29.1	Facing the Struggle.
412.30.1	Relief in Pawn.
413.17.1	A Fradulent Cry.
414.10.1	The Over-Worked Secretary.

415.6.1	Heart of the Storm.
416.7.1	A Pitiable Story.
418.7.1	Business Feels It.
419.3.1	Hope in Irrigation.
419.33.1	Waiting with Faith.

(N⁸)

409.28.1	A Menace from the South.
410.28.1	Soil Turned to Powder.
411.29.1	Farmers Were in Debt.
412.30.1	Relief Cars in Pawn.
413.17.1	Thieving Counties.

414.10.1	An Unhappy Commissioner.
415.6.1	The Real Sufferers.
415.32.1	Cruel Suffering.
417.2.1	Extraordinary Features.
417.25.1	Honest Pride.
419.20.1	The Farmers' Faith.

No. 86. SEEN AT HOT SPRINGS

[The copy-text is N¹(p): proof for the *Nebraska State Journal*, March 3, 1895, p. 10, in the Special Collections of Columbia University Libraries. The other texts collated are N¹: *Nebraska State Journal*; N²: *Galveston Daily News*, March 3, p. 11; N³: *Cincinnati Commercial Gazette*, March 3, p. 17; N⁴: *Buffalo News*, March 3, p. 8; N⁵: *Philadelphia Press*, March 3, p. 29; N⁶: *Rochester Democrat and Chronicle*, March 3, p. 7. It should be noted that the designation N¹ applies to both the proof and the final published version and only where they differ will the symbol N¹(p) appear.]

420.13	¹that] the N⁵
420.30	And] *omit* N³
420.31	badgers] badges N¹⁻²,⁵⁻⁶
421.4	air of] air N¹⁻²,⁵⁻⁶
421.8	a man] the man N⁵
421.28	nor] or N³,⁵
421.34	An . . . that] *omit* N⁴

421.36–422.19	If . . . stars.] *omit* N⁴
421.39	Broadway] Fourth Street N³
422.3	and . . . Turks;] *omit* N³
422.3	why there] why they N⁵
422.8	This] The N³

422.9–10 a wide] wide N[2,5–6]

422.11–19 It . . . stars.] *omit* N[1] (*present in* N[1][p])

422.18–19 the . . . stars] *omit* N[5]

422.31–423.3 Crowds . . . air.] *omit* N[1] (*present in* N[1][p])

423.17–32 The . . . discovered.] *omit* N[1] (*present in* N[1][p])

423.20–26 They have . . . jig-trot.] *omit* N[4]

423.27–425.7 And . . . whiskers.] *omit* N[2]

423.40 the hat] that hat N[4]

424.2 Arlington] hotel N[5]

424.10–11 "All . . . even."] *omit* N[4]

424.13 I] I'll N[5]

424.14 your] you N[6]

424.15 The . . . bones."] *omit* N[5]

424.15–16 "I'll . . . won.] *omit* N[4]

424.17–18 man.[¶] "No] man. [¶] "I'll shake you for four bones." [¶] The traveller won. [¶] "No N[4] (*see* 424.15–16)

424.35–425.2 "But . . . friend.] *omit* N[1] (*present in* N[1][p])

424.35 for] from N[6]

425.1 kickin'] kicking N[4]

Subheadings

(N[5])

420.29.1 The Station Crowd.
421.28.1 Cosmopolitan Visitors.

423.16.1 The Colored Servants.
424.7.1 The Young Bird Is Wary.

No. 87. GRAND OPERA IN NEW ORLEANS

[The copy-text is N[1](p): proof for the *Nebraska State Journal*, March 24, 1895, p. 11, in the Special Collections of Columbia University Libraries. The other texts collated are N[1]: *Nebraska State Journal*; N[2]: *Philadelphia Press*, March 24, p. 25; N[3]: *Galveston Daily News*, March 24, p. 4; N[4]: *Minneapolis Tribune*, March 24, p. 17; N[5]: *Rochester Democrat and Chronicle*, March 24, p. 10; PO: *Public Opinion*, XVIII (July 4, 1895), 770. It should be noted that the designation N[1] applies to both the proof and the final published version and only where they differ will the symbol N[1](p) appear.]

425.8–426.33 In . . . room.] *omit* PO

425.9 uprears] appears N[3–4]

425.12 prime donne] prima donnas N[3]

425.14 scarred] scared N[1,4]

425.31 his] the N[4]

426.5 Luc] Lac N[5]

426.7 vast] *omit* N[3]

426.9–33 This . . . room.] *omit* N[2]

426.12 this] the N[3]

426.20 the wealthy] wealthy N[3]

426.27 opera] open N[1,5]

426.36 as mentioned] as mentioned of grand opera N[4]; *omit* PO

427.11–428.2 This . . . performances.] *omit* PO

427.12 thorns] thrones N[1]

427.21 weightier] weight N[4]

427.24 Chavaroche] Chavaroach N[1–2,4–5]

428.1–2 performances] artistic earnest, engrossed in the opera N[1–2,5]; artistic interest, engrossed in the opera N[3]; artistic earnestness and are engrossed in the opera N[4]

428.3–7 The . . . versatile.] *omit* N[1] (*present in* N[1][p])

428.3 varies] varies in N[4]

428.5 for musical] musical N[4]

428.5 stars] four stars N[4]

428.8–27 In . . . world.] *omit*
PO
428.8 Amours] Armours N[1,3,5]
428.8 Dragons de Villars] Dragon
de Villar $N
428.22–32 At . . . classes.] *omit*
N[2]

428.25 yet] *omit* N[3]
428.29 toward] towards N[4]
428.31 see] be N[1,3],PO
428.31 grand opera given] given
grand opera N[3,6]

No. 88. THE CITY OF MEXICO

[The copy-text is MS: the untitled manuscript in the Special Collections of Columbia University Libraries.]

Alterations in the Manuscript

429.3 hour] *interlined with a caret*
429.10 coachmen] 'e' *over* 'a'
429.10 proud] *preceded by deleted* 'clatterin'
429.10 horses. A] *period inserted, followed by deleted* 'and' *and* 'A' *altered from* 'a'
429.17 rain] *preceded by deleted* 'shower'
429.18 atmospheric] *interlined with a caret*
429.18 coolness,] *followed by deleted* 'of the'
429.19 rumbling] *preceded by deleted* 'rumbling'
429.19 a] *interlined*
429.21 vivid] *followed by deleted* 'and'
429.22 dark] *final* 'e' *and the start of an* 'r' *deleted*
429.28 calm.] *period inserted before deleted* 'for the most part.'
430.1 associate] *preceded by deleted* 'always'
430.3 but] *written over* 'but' *partially obscured by an ink stain, or a blot on the paper*
430.4 the] *written over* 'the' (*see* 430.3 *above*)
430.5 contemplative] 'con' *written over* 'con' (*see* 430.3 *above*)
430.13 interested] 'ed' *over* 'in'
430.16 erect.] *preceded by deleted* 'build.'
430.18 senoritas] *final* 's' *and part of* 'a' *beneath ink-blot*

430.18 can] *preceded by deleted doubtful* 'on', *only the* 'n' *being certain*
430.20 shaded] *preceded by deleted* 'shadows'
430.22 nothing] *preceded by deleted* 'lit'
430.25 distance.] *followed by deleted* 'And what is part'
430.26 the] *interlined with a caret*
430.27–28 structures] *followed by a deleted period*
430.31 to] 't' *partially obscured by ink-blot*
430.33 massive] *preceded by deleted* 'bro'
430.37 is] *preceded by deleted* 'was on'
431.1 has] *followed by deleted* 'one of'
431.7 American.] *period inserted before deleted* 'and'
431.8 than] 't' *over doubtful* 'a'
431.11 which] *preceded by deleted* 'which make'
431.18 [1]a] *inserted later*
431.19 But] *followed by independently deleted* 'it is co' *and* 'he ha'
431.22 States,] MS 'states' *with a horizontal ink mark over the final* 's' ; *period deleted before the comma*
431.26 populace] *interlined above deleted* 'people'
431.27 are a most] 'are' *followed*

by deleted 'perhaps the most interestin' ; *then* 'a most' *interlined with carets*

431.27 type] *final 's' deleted*

431.36 you . . . you] *interlined*

above deleted 'one . . . **one**'

432.1 the countenances] 'the' *interlined after deleted* 'the bull-fighters'

No. 89. THE VIGA CANAL

[The copy-text is MS: manuscript in the Special Collections of Columbia University Libraries.]

Alterations in the Manuscript

432.4 not] *followed by deleted* 'at'

432.5 We took] *interlined above deleted* 'You take'

432.5 rattled] 'd' *added later*

432.5 our] 'y' *of* 'your' *deleted*

432.7 thronged] 'ed' *added later*

432.7 were] *interlined above deleted* 'are'

432.8 trotted] 'ted' *added later*

432.10 glanced] 'd' *added later*

432.11 were] *first* 'e' *over* 'a'

432.14 arose] *interlined above deleted* 'arises' *in which the* 'i' *had been altered to an* 'o'

432.14 squawling] MS 'squaling' *with* 'w' *interlined*

432.16,17 was] 'w' *squeezed in and* 'a' *over* 'i'

432.17 them,] *interlined with a caret*

432.18 crowded] 'ed' *added later*

432.18 lay] *interlined above deleted* 'lies'

432.19 blades] *preceded by deleted* 'grass'

432.20 bended] 'ed' *added later*

432.20 swooning] *preceded by deleted* 'lazy'

432.21 paused] 'd' *over* 's'

432.22 ¶ The] *preceded by deleted beginning of a paragraph:* 'The boatman beseech, pray, appeal. It is enough to confuse an expert linguist and' *of which* 'confuse' *is preceded by deleted* 'con[*and beginning of an* 'f']'

432.23 clamor] *interlined with a caret*

432.24 an] *interlined with a caret*

432.24 ecstasy] *second* 's' *over* 'c'

432.34 on] 'o' *over* 'i'

433.1 the] *interlined*

433.1 foliage] *followed by deleted comma*

433.1-2 boatmen] 'e' *over* 'a'

433.10-11 contemplative.] *no period in MS; followed by deleted comma and* 'upon his horse.'

433.12 canoe] *preceded by deleted* 'wooden boa[*and the beginning of an upstroke*]'

433.14 in] *preceded by deleted* 'in' *and the beginning of a new word starting with a stroke including a descender*

433.17 Frequently] *preceded by deleted* 'O'

433.17 Reposing] 'i' *over* 'e' ; *preceded by deleted* 'Lay'

433.20 laconic] *interlined above deleted* 'swift'

433.21 these] *preceded by deleted* 'this'

433.26 boats] *interlined above deleted* 'boats'

433.33 ¶ At] *preceded by the deleted beginning of a new paragraph:* 'Behind the blue formidable hills of the west there was a faint show'

433.35 effect] *preceded by deleted* 'scene.'

433.37 more] *interlined*

433.38 their horses] *preceded by deleted* 'their horses'
434.2 into] 'to' *added*
434.3 strutted] 'ed' *over* 'in'
434.16 appeared] 'ed' *over* 'in'
434.17 fence] *interlined above deleted* 'wall'
434.20 youths] 's' *added later*
434.21 seated] *interlined*
434.22 man] 'a' *over* 'e'
434.24 crowd.] *interlined above deleted* 'ground.'
434.25 "Niña! Niña!] 'N' *over* 'M'
434.26 dark] *preceded by deleted* 'formidable'
434.26 ²the] *interlined*
434.30 an] *interlined with a caret*
434.32 two] 'w' *over* 'o'
434.33 us] *interlined with a caret*
434.33 The] *preceded by independently deleted* 'As' *and* 'On further'
434.34 grew] *preceded by deleted* 'began to'
434.35 peaks] *preceded by deleted* 'volcani'
434.35 heavens.] *interlined above deleted* 'sky.'
434.37 ¹the] 'th' *over* 'a'
434.37 it] *interlined*

434.38 musicians] *preceded by deleted* 'two'
435.1 resemble] *final* 's' *deleted*
435.3 there] *interlined*
435.3 faded] *followed by deleted* 'from there'
435.3 outlines] *preceded by an upstroke*
435.5 reminiscent of] *interlined above deleted* 'as delicious as'
435.9 We] *interlined above deleted* 'One'
435.10 lie] *interlined above deleted* 'lay'
435.11 from] *a final* 's' *deleted; preceded by deleted* 'of' ; *followed by deleted* 'one'
435.12 an] *preceded by two deleted* 'a's
435.13 part] *interlined above deleted* 'emotion'
435.13 of] *preceded by deleted* 'of'
435.14 times] *interlined above deleted* 'nights'
435.14 wanderer] 'a' *possibly altered from* 'o'
435.16 boatman's] *second* 'a' *over* 'e'
435.18 had] *interlined*

No. 90. THE MEXICAN LOWER CLASSES

[The copy-text is MS: manuscript in the Special Collections of Columbia University Libraries.]

Alterations in the Manuscript

435.26 visitor] *final* 's' *deleted*
435.28 futile] *preceded by deleted* 'stu'
435.32 Yet] *preceded by paragraph symbol*
435.34 baby] 'a' *over* 'o' *before second* 'b' *written*
435.34 his] 'h' *over* 'a'
436.1 it] *interlined after deleted* 'yet'
436.1 wisdom] *interlined with a caret*
436.2 yet] *interlined with a caret*

436.7 written] *followed by deleted* 'hurriedly'
436.13 there] *possibly altered from* 'their'
436.13 but] *followed by deleted* 'on'
436.16 The] *final* 'y' *deleted*
436.16 strangers] *interlined*
436.23 death] *preceded by deleted* 'their'
436.23 would] *preceded by deleted* 'seemed'
436.27 it] *interlined with a caret after deleted* 'that'

436.28 afraid.] *interlined above deleted* 'feel awe.'

436.29 moment] *preceded by deleted* 'terrible'

436.34 They] *preceded by deleted* 'He'

436.36 those] *interlined above deleted* 'that'

436.36 lines] 's' *added later*

436.36 extend] *final* 's' *deleted*

436.39 ¶ I am] *on the line above is the deleted start of a paragraph:* 'I am going to observe'

437.2 last] *preceded by deleted* 're[*and the beginning of another letter, possibly an* 's']'

437.4 part] *followed by a deleted period*

437.5 so] *interlined with a caret*

437.10 an] *altered from* 'in'

437.18 belong] *followed by deleted* 'in part'

437.18 him?] *question mark altered from a period*

437.20 after all] *interlined with a caret*

437.23 A] *preceded by a paragraph symbol*

437.28 Indeed] *preceded by deleted* 'I' *at end of line*

437.29 devout,] *followed by deleted* 'and faithful,'

437.29 worshipping] 'ing' *over* 'er'

437.30 a blind faith] *interlined above deleted* 'a blind faith' *of which* 'faith' *has been deleted and* 'belief' *interlined above and then deleted*

437.32 measure] *preceded by deleted* 'way'

437.32 their] 'i' *over* 'r'

437.33 detect] *preceded by deleted* 'see'

437.34 a fair] *interlined with a caret above deleted* 'an'

437.36 the] 't' *over* 'a'

438.2 I] *followed by deleted* 'myself'

438.3 religion.] *followed by deleted* 'I h'

438.8 example] *preceded by deleted* 'insta'

438.11 instance] *preceded by deleted* 'exampl'

No. 91. STEPHEN CRANE IN MEXICO (I)

[The copy-text is N[1]: *Nebraska State Journal*, May 19, 1895, p. 13. The other texts collated are N[2]: *Galveston Daily News*, May 19, p. 13; N[3]: *Buffalo Morning News*, May 19, p. 11; N[4]: *Louisville Courier-Journal*, May 19, part II, p. 7; N[5]: *Philadelphia Press*, May 19, p. 33; N[6]: *Chicago Daily News*, June 6, p. 10; N[7]: *Rochester Democrat and Chronicle*, May 19, p. 9; N[8]: *Savannah Morning News*, May 16, p. 9.]

438.29 were standing] *omit* N[3]

438.30–31 at the paintings] *omit* N[2]

438.31 paintings] painting N[8]

439.6 thing] thong N[8]

439.20 at it] *omit* N[7]

439.26 his] is N[8]

439.31 its] his N[2]

439.36 daylights] daylight N[5]

439.37 in] *omit* N[4]

439.38 purposes] purpose N[3]

440.3 quiver] driver N[8]

440.6 Well . . . [2]load] *omit* N[8]

440.28 it] is N[3]; its N[5]

441.2 considerable] considerably N[6]

441.6 then] them N[1]

441.10 much] *omit* N[7]

441.11 unballasted] unbalanced N[7]

441.17 long distances] a long distance N[5]

441.17 most] almost N[6]

441.20 beside] besides N[3,5–6]

441.22 del] de $N

441.25 houses] the houses N[8]

441.33 in] of N[3]

441.35 canes,] *omit* N[7]

441.39–442.22 Those . . . flood.]
  omit N⁵
442.2 has] had N⁸
442.2 deduct] deduce N⁴
442.6 from] of N⁷
442.12 then] when N³
442.13 and] *omit* N³
442.36 hated] acted N⁷
443.13 your] you N⁸

443.14–29 The . . . on.] *omit*
  N⁵
443.14 sell] sells N⁸
443.17 and] *omit* N²
443.31 almost] *omit* N⁶
443.33 gives] *omit* N⁸
443.36 States] states N²,⁶⁻⁸
443.37 is] it N²

Subheadings

(N¹⁻³,⁶)

441.19.1 Street Venders of Mexico.

(N⁵)

439.28.1 Aztec Ingenuity.
440.16.1 Like an Arab Steed.

441.19.1 Street Venders of Mexico.

No. 92. FREE SILVER DOWN IN MEXICO

[The copy-text is N¹(p): proof for the *Nebraska State Journal*, June 30,
1895, p. 13, in the Special Collections of Columbia University Libraries.
The other texts collated are N¹: *Nebraska State Journal*; N²: *Cincinnati
Commercial Gazette*, June 30, p. 9; N³: *Chicago Daily News*, July 23, p. 2;
N⁴: *Minneapolis Tribune*, June 30, p. 4; N⁵: *Galveston Daily News*, July 1,
p. 4; N⁶: *Philadelphia Press*, June 30, p. 31. No differences have been
observed between N¹ and its proof.]

444.2 at] *omit* N⁵
444.13 hoard] horde $N(−N³)
444.24 and . . . ²money] *omit*
  N⁵
444.28 very] pretty N³
444.30 per] a N³
445.5 the men] men N⁵
445.9 the hats] hats N²
445.12 buy] get N⁴

445.29 quite a number] many N³
445.35 the rates] rates N²
445.37 but] but but N⁶
445.37 plays] pays N⁶
446.6 in] of N⁶
446.20 luxury] luxuries N³
446.21 little] *omit* N²
446.23 cents] cents in N⁶

Subheadings

(N⁶)

444.21.1 How the Money Goes.

446.4 (Mexicans.|) A Cheap
  Jag.

No. 93. STEPHEN CRANE IN MEXICO (II)

[The copy-text to 451.2 is N¹(p): proof for the *Nebraska State Journal*,
July 21, 1895, p. 13; after 451.2 the copy-text is N¹: *Nebraska State
Journal* (no differences between N¹ and its proof have been observed). The

other texts collated are N[2]: *Galveston Daily News*, July 21, p. 10; N[3]: *Cincinnati Commercial Gazette*, July 21, p. 18; N[4]: *Philadelphia Press*, July 21, p. 32; N[5]: *New Orleans Times-Democrat*, July 23, p. 8; N[6]: *Rochester Democrat and Chronicle*, July 21, p. 16.]

447.8 our] the N[6]

447.19 uh] eh N[2]

447.20 F-i-n-n-e] F-i-n-e N[2]

447.26 conversational] conversation N[2]

447.31 jiminy] jimmy N[2]

447.31 you're] you've N[1,6]

448.4 leaned] leaning N[2]; leaned forward N[3]

448.5 and] *omit* N[5]

448.9 speckless] speechless N[2]

448.15 some typical] typical N[2]

448.29 Presently . . . station.] *omit* N[3]

448.37–449.8 There . . . money!"] *omit* N[5]

448.38 to] into N[2]

449.1 passengers] passenger N[1]

449.2–3 interest] great interest N[2]

449.22 records] record N[2]

449.37–38 while . . . blankets] *omit* N[3]

450.2 each] each one N[2]

450.6 somehow] somewhere N[6]

450.21 paused] passed $N(−N[3])

451.2 prairie] prairies N[3]

451.15 portentously] portentiously N[1,4,6]

451.16 train] trains $N(−N[6])

451.17–18 In . . . forth.] *omit* N[2]

451.19–30 The . . . asparagus.] *omit* N[3]

452.4–17 As . . . volcanic.] *omit* N[3]

452.4 toward] towards N[1,5-6]

452.12 was] as N[4]

452.18 pattered] patted N[4]

452.23–453.5 From . . . gleaming.] *omit* N[3]

452.28 expressed] express N[2]

452.30 monotonous] mountainous N[4]

452.34 in] by N[2]

452.36 of] a N[4]

453.6 roared] roaded N[4]

453.16 bases] base N[5]

453.24–25 tender . . . biscuit] *omit* N[4]

453.26–27 and a] had a N[4]

453.35 red-tiled] reddish N[5]

454.8 inexplainable] in explainable N[3]

454.22 streets] the streets N[5]

454.26 [1]and] in N[3,5]

454.35 arose] rose N[2]

454.36 Nevado] Nevada $N (−N[5]); the Nevada N[5]

455.5 around] round N[2]

455.14 harangued] haranged N[1,6]; harranged N[5]

455.20 grey] *omit* N[2]

455.20 ladened] laden N[2]

456.8 maguey] mague N[1-2,4,6]; bague N[5]

456.12 mountains] mountain N[3]

456.16 Ixtaccihuatl] Iztaccihuatl N[2]; Ixtaccihautl N[3]

456.24 a uniform] uniform N[6]

Subheadings

(N[4])

447.22.1 Comrades.

448.26.1 For the Promised Land.

449.22.1 Crossing the Portals.

450.20.1 The First Glimpse.

451.18.1 Traversing the Land.

452.17.1 The Siren's Song.

453.13.1 The Native Flora.

454.11.1 The Archaeologist's Opportunity.

455.5.1 Culinary Item.

456.3.1 The Snow-Clad Sentinels.

No. 94. A JAG OF PULQUE IS HEAVY

[The copy-text is N[1]: *Nebraska State Journal*, Aug. 12, 1895, p. 5. The other texts collated are N[2]: *Salt Lake City Tribune*, Aug. 11, p. 15; N[3]: *Cincinnati Commercial Gazette*, Aug. 11, p. 17; N[4]: *Philadelphia Press*, Aug. 11, p. 26; N[5]: *Galveston Daily News*, Aug. 10, p. 9; N[6]: *Rochester Democrat and Chronicle*, Aug. 11, p. 10.]

456.33	This] The N[3]	458.6	rustle] hustle N[6]
457.27	delirium] dream N[5]	458.33	in] to N[2]
457.31	thirsty] thirty N[2]	458.36	of] to N[5]
457.37	earthern] earthen N[2,4]	459.5	do] does $N
458.2	thirsts] thirst N[2-3]	459.11	necks] neck N[3]
458.4	the] an N[3]	459.16	combinations₋] ~ , N[2,5-6]
458.5	Americans] American N[5]		

Subheadings

(N[4])

457.18.1	An Educated Taste.	459.4.1	Eternal Friendship.
458.15.1	Made from Century Plants.		

No. 95. THE FETE OF MARDI GRAS

[The copy-text is N[1](p): proof for the *Nebraska State Journal*, Feb. 16, 1896, p. 11, in the Special Collections of Columbia University Libraries. The other texts collated are N[1]: *Nebraska State Journal* (it should be noted that no differences have been observed between N[1] and its proof, and that the designation N[1] in this instance refers to both the proof and the final published form); N[2]: *Philadelphia Press*, Feb. 16, p. 30; N[3]: *Cincinnati Commercial Gazette*, Feb. 23, p. 19; N[4]: *New Orleans Times-Democrat*, Feb. 17, p. 9; N[5]: *Rochester Democrat and Chronicle*, Feb. 16, p. 9.]

459.25–460.24	It . . . avenue.] It could not rain on Mardi Gras. It never did, and it did not this week. N[3]	463.14	chanct] chance N[4]
		463.34–35	The . . . over] *omit* N[3]
460.31	represented as] representing N[3]	463.36	wood and] wood, N[3]
460.31	rambled] rambling N[2]	464.19–21	Further . . . estate.] *omit* N[3]
461.24	Too] Then N[3]	464.33	sputtered] spurted N[4]; spluttered N[5]
461.26	great] *omit* N[5]	465.6	had] has N[5]
461.36	outa] out a N[5]	465.9–23	Down . . . darkness.] *omit* N[3]
462.12	wide] *omit* N[3]	465.20	Comus'] their N[1-2,5]
463.3	crowd] the crowd N[4-5]		
463.11	policemen] police N[5]		

Subheadings
(N[2])

460.24.1	Gypsy Hues of Maskers.	463.17.1	The Pageant Comes.
461.19.1	The Crowd Stares.	464.18.1	Incidents of the Parade.
462.17.1	Around the Throne.		

No. 96. HATS, SHIRTS, AND SPURS IN MEXICO

[The copy-text is N[1]: *Detroit Free Press*, Oct. 18, 1896, p. 20. The other texts collated are N[2]: *Louisville Courier-Journal*, Oct. 18, sec. III, p. 2; N[3]: *Buffalo Evening News*, Oct. 18, p. 9; N[4]: *San Francisco Chronicle*, Oct. 18, p. 12; N[5]: *Galveston Daily News*, Oct. 18, p. 10; N[6]: *Nebraska State Journal*, Oct. 18, p. 9; N[7]: *Philadelphia Press*, Oct. 18, p. 34; N[8]: *Chicago Daily News*, Oct. 29, p. 5; N[9]: *St. Louis Globe-Democrat*, Oct. 18, p. 33; N[10]: *Rochester Democrat and Chronicle*, Oct. 18, p. 9. Since all the newspapers are of equal authority, an agreement in an accidental of two or more texts is listed here.]

465.24   true] *omit* N[2,8]

465.25   gentleman]   gentlemen N[5,7]

465.26   fifty dollars] $50 N[2-9]

465.26   spends] spend N[5]

465.26   a hundred dollars] $100 N[2-5,8-9]; a $100 N[7]

465.31   and as] and N[2]

465.33   sombreros,] ~ ∧ N[5,8]

466.1   This] The N[1]

466.1   good] great N[8]

466.4   rhinoceros]   rhinocerous N[2,6]

466.5   may,] ~ ∧ N[8-9]

466.7   extend] extends N[3,5,8]

466.8   trousers∧] ~ , N[2,7,9]

466.9   this,] ~ ∧ N[7-9]

466.10   sultan] Sultan N[2-3,7,9]

466.11   use] to use N[2,4]

466.11   foot-stool] footstool N[4-5,8-9]

466.12   mincing] a mincing N[10]

466.12   crowded] covered N[9]

466.13–14   mustache] moustache N[3,6,10]

466.14   eye,] ~ ∧ N[8,10]

466.17   combated] combatted N[3-4]

466.20   capital,] ~ ∧ N[2,4,8-9]

466.22   younger] members of the younger N[8]

466.25   holy] *omit* N[1]

466.26   vivid] *omit* N[1]

466.27   clash∧] ~ , N[3-4,9]

466.27   for] of N[10]

466.30   at] as N[6]

466.30   enumeration.] ~ : N[2-5,10]

466.31 *et seq.*   I.] I. N[1,5,9]; First N[2,4]

466.31   A] *omit* N[10]

466.33   lace∧] ~ , N[4-5]

466.36   10:30] 10 N[2]

466.36   a.m.] A.M. N[3-4,7,10]

467.9   crimson,] ~ ∧ N[8,10]

467.11   people,] ~ ∧ N[6,8]

467.12   years,] ~ ∧ N[2-4,8-10]

467.13   blood∧red] ~ - ~ N[2,8-10]

467.14   lanterns] lantern N[1]

467.19   here] in the city of Mexico N[1]

467.19   sun-light] ~ - | ~ N[2]; sunlight N[4-5,8,10]

467.21   upon] on N[10]

467.23   to] in N[3]

467.24   thought] have thought N[5]

467.25   They (*no* ¶)] ¶ N[6]

467.27   street] streets N[10]

467.27–28   Mexico City] the City of Mexico N[10]

467.28   dress] is dressed N[8]

467.28   they do] *omit* N[8]

467.29   perhaps,] ~ ∧ N[3-4,6,8]

467.29   and∧ of course∧] ~ , ~ ~ , N[2,8]

467.30   Indians,] ~ ∧ N[8-9]

467.30–31   But . . . similarity.] *omit* N[1]

467.32   wish] wish to N[6]

467.32   side] the side N[1]

467.33–35   The caballero . . . -heavy.] *omit* N[6]

467.34   trousers∧] ~ , N[3-5,7]

467.37   eyes∧] ~ , N[4,8]

468.1   his] this N[6]

468.1   or not] *omit* N[1,8]; or red, N[4]; or not, N[9]

468.1   or of] or N[1,10]

468.1   dull] other N[10]

468.2   the green] green N[6]

468.2   sky∧] ~ , N[4-5,8-9]

468.4   compose] complete N[8]

468.5   crouches] couches N[10]
468.6   by] with N[1]
468.8   him,] ∼ ∧ N[6-7,9-10]

468.8   mystic] majestic N[1]
468.11   the melted] melted N[1]
468.13   of] *omit* N[1]

No. 97. STEPHEN CRANE IN TEXAS

[The copy-text is N[1]: *Pittsburgh Leader*, Jan. 8, 1899, p. 23. The other texts collated are N[2]: *Savannah Morning News*, Jan. 8, p. 10; N[3]: *Omaha Daily Bee*, Jan. 8, p. 15; N[4]: *Louisville Courier-Journal*, Jan. 8, sec. III, p. 4; N[5]: *St. Louis Globe-Democrat*, Jan. 8, sec. III, p. 6. Since all texts are of equal authority, agreement of accidentals in two or more texts is listed here.]

468.15   6, 1899.] 6.— $N(−N[1])
468.16   Anton] Antonio N[4]
468.18-19   of a] of N[2]
469.2   the holy] holy N[5]
469.8   of the] of N[3]
469.12   Here,] ∼ ∧ N[3,5]
469.14   have] has N[3]
469.15   importance,] ∼ ∧ N[3,5]
469.15   whirl] will N[2]
469.16   quarter] quarters N[4]
469.23   look] too N[3]
469.25   not] *omit* N[1]
469.28   Texan] Texas N[2]
469.36   interval] the interval N[3]
470.2   in] *omit* N[3]
470.3   plains,] ∼ ∧ N[3,5]
470.3   churches∧] ∼ , N[4-5]
470.26   Tradition] tradition N[5]
470.26   her] his N[5]
470.27   guide-book] ∼ ∧ ∼ N[2-3] (N[2]: guid)
470.27   published] publisher N[2]
470.28   these] the N[2]
470.28   friend] friends N[5]
470.33   portentous] portentious N[1-2]; pretentous N[3]
470.34   fathers,] ∼ ∧ N[2-5]
471.5,30   state] State N[4-5]
471.5-6   [1]of . . . Texas] *omit* N[3]
471.10   populous] populous N[1,3]
471.10   city∧] ∼ , N[4-5]
471.11,38   Crockett] Crocket N[2]
471.11   comrades,] ∼ ∧ N[3-4]

471.15   pauses] pause N[1]
471.16-17   silence,] ∼ ∧ N[2-5]
471.19   was] was in N[4]
471.20; 472.1-2   one . . . fifty] 150 N[1-3,5]
471.21   those] these N[2]
471.22   decides] decide N[4]
471.24   of them] *omit* N[4]
471.27   Santa Anna] Santa Ana N[3]
471.29   republic] Republic N[4-5]
471.29   Mexico,] ∼ ∧ N[2-3]
471.32   sergeant] Sergeant N[4-5]
471.36   wide,] ∼ ∧ N[2-3]
471.37   southeast] southwest N[4]
471.37   *et seq.* Colonel] Col. N[2,4-5] (*except at* 472.19)
471.39-472.1   enclosure] inclosure N[4-5]
472.17   and] *omit* N[4]
472.19   with] of N[4]
472.19   colonel] Colonel N[4-5]
472.22-23   There is] There's N[1]
472.27   at] upon N[4]
472.34   quarter] quarters N[4]
473.3   images,] ∼ ∧ N[2-3]
473.7-22   Upon . . . mesquite.] *omit* N[5]
473.7   plazas] piazzas N[2]
473.28-38   Upon . . . proud.] *omit* N[5]
473.30   squadrons] squadron N[2]
473.35   besides] beside N[1-4]

Subheadings

(N[1])

470.14.1   Ravages of Time and the Relic Hunter.

471.33.1   How Bowie and Crockett Met Santa Anna.

(N²)

469.2.1 Reared on the Ashes of Ambitions.	471.33.1 How Bowie and Crockett Met Santa Anna.
469.35.1 When the Priests Ran Short of Indians.	472.12.1 Three Ways of Being Killed.
470.14.1 Ravages of Time and the Relic Hunter.	473.6.1 Food That Is Hot When It Is Cold.

(N³)

469.2.1 Ashes of Ambitions.	471.33.1 A Famous Meeting.
469.35.1 Ran Short of Indians.	473.13.1 Around the Town.
470.38.1 Literary Aspirants.	

(N⁴)

469.2.1 The Ashes of Ambition.	Santa Anna.
469.35.1 Priests Ran Short of Indians.	472.12.1 Three Ways of Being Killed.
470.14.1 Ravages of Time.	473.6.1 Food Hot When It Is Cold.
470.38.1 Literary Aspirants.	
471.33.1 Bowie, Crockett and	

No. 99. QUEENSTOWN

[The copy-text is N¹: *New York Journal*, Oct. 18, 1897, p. 6. The other texts collated are WG: *Westminster Gazette*, Oct. 19, pp. 1–2; N²: *Kansas City Star*, Oct. 24, p. 5. N² is a derived text without authority. Since N¹ and WG are of equal authority, all variants between the two texts are recorded here.]

483.1 one,] ~ ₍ WG	484.24 a hotel] an hotel WG
483.3 west₍] ~ , WG	484.26 porters₍] ~ , WG
483.6 government] Government WG	484.26 guards₍] ~ , WG
483.6 Afterward₍] ~ , WG	484.27 poem₍] ~ , WG
483.8 H.M.S.] her Majesty's ship WG	484.28 conformation₍] ~ , WG
483.10 buoy₍] ~ , WG	484.29 et seq. color] colour WG
483.10 steeples₍] ~ , WG	484.35 Western] western WG
483.12 ¶ Queenstown] no ¶ WG	484.35 world₍] ~ , WG
483.14 man₍] ~ , WG	484.37 vision,] ~ ₍ WG
483.14 cuffs₍] ~ , WG	484.39 Irish₍] ~ , WG
483.15–16 violence,] ~ ₍ WG	484.39 position₍] ~ , WG
483.22 Cork₍] ~ , WG	485.11–24 For . . . Jerry?] omit N¹⁻²
483.22 band₍] ~ , WG	485.29–30 cup₍ and] ~, ~ WG
483.23 steamer₍] ~ , WG	485.32 -out₍] ~ , WG
483.29 dock₍] ~ , WG	485.35 said] said that WG
484.7 comparison,] ~ ₍ WG	485.36 the others] others N²
484.7 the ambitious] this WG	486.4 his] this WG
484.8–9 Nevertheless,] ~ ₍ WG	486.6 there₍] ~ , WG
484.18 splendor] splendour WG	486.8 mug₍] ~ , WG
484.24 thence] from thence WG	486.8 a half crown] half-a-crown WG

486.11   time₁] ~ , WG   486.15   waters] water WG
486.15   -colored] -coloured WG

No. 100. BALLYDEHOB

[The copy-text is WG: *Westminster Gazette*, Oct. 22, 1897, pp. 1–2. The other texts collated are WB: *Westminster Budget*, Nov. 5, p. 15; TMs: typescript in the UVa.–Barrett Collection; E1: *Last Words*, Digby, Long, London, 1902, pp. 198–203. The two latter texts are completely derived and without authority.]

487.7   valuable] *omit* TMs
487.11   seduction] seductions TMs
487.12–13 a cow] cow WG,TMs, E1
487.13   live] lives TMs
487.20   a brook] the brook TMs
487.23   quite] quiet TMs
487.33   Irishman] Irish TMs(u)
487.33   retains] retain TMs(c)

488.10   who] which TMs(u)
488.12   sometimes] sometime TMs
488.12   shop] shops TMs
488.13   of] *omit* TMs
488.35   from] from from TMs
489.1   unkempt] unkept TMs
489.8–10 And . . . eel.] *omit* WB

No. 101. THE ROYAL IRISH CONSTABULARY

[The copy-text is WG: *Westminster Gazette*, Nov. 5, 1897, pp. 1–2. The other texts collated are TMs: typescript in the UVa.–Barrett Collection; E1: *Last Words*, Digby, Long, London, 1902, pp. 203–207. Both TMs and E1 are derived texts without authority.]

490.16   constables] constable TMs
490.17–18 stranger and friend] strangers and freinds TMs
490.18   the road] road TMs
490.19   human] humane TMs
490.25   policing] police E1

490.26   its] it's TMs(c)
490.27   a hand] hand TMs
491.8   crises] crisis E1
491.21   haunted] hunted E1
491.22   streams] stream TMs
491.28   the county] county E1

No. 102. A FISHING VILLAGE

[The copy-text is WG: *Westminster Gazette*, Nov. 12, 1897, pp. 1–2. The other texts collated are WB: *Westminster Budget*, Nov. 19, p. 13; Ph: *Philistine*, IX (Aug., 1899), 71–77; E1: *Last Words*, Digby, Long, London, 1902, pp. 207–213.]

492.1   The brook . . . white,] Innocent and white, the brook curved down over the rocks, WB,Ph
492.12   cleaned] the cleaned Ph
492.23   tackle] the tackle E1
493.4   Aw] Ah E1
493.7   along] long Ph
493.8   a] *omit* E1
493.10   in] 'n Ph
493.19   baskets] basket E1

493.20   little] *omit* Ph
493.31   microscopic] microscope E1
493.33   last] *omit* E1
493.36   and] *omit* Ph
494.3   the market] market E1
494.9–10 the gorse] gorse E1
494.18   too many] many Ph
494.19   the] *omit* E1
494.25   spot was] spot were Ph
494.29   men's] *omit* E1

495.3   a high] high EI
495.5   the potato] potato EI
495.9   strained] stained Ph
495.11   tip] top EI

495.21   toward] towards WG,WB, EI
495.21–22 toward the intense] and was lost in the Ph

No. 103. AN OLD MAN GOES WOOING

[The copy-text is WG: *Westminster Gazette*, Nov. 23, 1897, pp. 1–2. The other texts collated are Ph: *Philistine*, IX (July, 1899), 44–50; EI: *Last Words*, Digby, Long, London, 1902, pp. 193–198.]

495.29   these] the EI
496.5   This] The EI
496.7   fowls] fowl EI
496.9   darker] dark EI
496.20   From] For EI
496.25   the crash] crash EI
496.33   emerging] emerged Ph
497.6   toimes] toime Ph
497.8   thim. . . .] ~ . EI
497.16   wringing] weeping Ph
497.26   a] *omit* EI
497.29   o'] 'o WG
497.30,35 toward] towards WG+

497.32–36 she said. . . . Mickey?"] *omit* EI
498.2   pockets] pocket WG,Ph
498.5   "There (*no* ¶)] ¶ EI
498.6   the] *omit* Ph
498.7   it] it out EI
498.9   movements] moments WG+
498.19   old] *omit* EI
498.21   loike thim buyers] the loikes of thim Ph
498.25   generation. He] ~ , and then EI
498.35   into] out into Ph

No. 149. A FOREIGN POLICY, IN THREE GLIMPSES

[The copy-text is MS: manuscript in the UVa.–Barrett Collection.]

Alterations in the Manuscript

574.14   huts] 'h' *over* 'co'
574.15   young] *preceded by deleted inserted* 'are'
574.15   laugh] *final* 'ing' *deleted*
574.16   -crested] 'c' *preceded by deleted* 'b'
574.20   ²the] *inserted later*
574.22   outside] 't' *over* 's'
574.23   bumps] 's' *added later*
574.24   men] 'e' *over* 'a'; *preceded by deleted* 'a'
574.24   white faces] *final* 's' *added; preceded by deleted* 'a'
575.2   island.] *preceded by deleted* 'natives.'; *then followed by* 'Lonelyisle.' *but this deleted*
575.5   voice.] *followed by deleted* 'but the'
575.5   hand] *preceded by deleted* 'white'; 's' *of* 'hands' *deleted; followed by deleted* 'an'

575.6   mouth] *preceded by deleted* 'thro'
575.10   'is] *preceded by deleted* 'his'
575.12   gaze] *preceded by deleted* 'frown and ga'
575.15   retreat] *first* 'r' *over what may be the start of* 'w'
575.16   sand] *preceded by deleted* 'white'
575.19   A] *over* 'T'
575.19   crowd] *followed by deleted* 'upon'
575.19   from] *preceded by deleted* 'upon'
575.23   the island.] *interlined above deleted* 'Lonelyisle.'
575.24–25 men-of-war] *preceded by deleted* 'gun-boats'
575.26   bayonet.] *final* 's' *deleted after period written*

575.27 thus] 't' over 'e'; *preceded by deleted* 'those'

575.32 seizes] *preceded by deleted* 'seizin'

575.34 says] *interlined above deleted* 'said'

575.36 indignity] *preceded by deleted* 'in'

576.4 won't] 'w' *over* 'c'

576.6 victim] *interlined above deleted* 'native'

576.7 had] 'd' *over* 's'

576.9 commanding] 'o' *over* 'a'

576.11 our] *preceded by deleted* 'your'

576.14 -pin,] *followed by deleted quote marks*

576.16 exasperated] *preceded by deleted* 'expas'

576.17 I'd] 'I' *over doubtful* 'a'

576.19 name] *inserted*

576.20 a] *preceded by deleted* 'an'

576.20 bloody-] 'y' *altered from tail of* 'd'

576.21–22 And . . . out?] *squeezed in between two regular lines*

576.22 See?] *squeezed in below line preceding deleted* 'Hear?' , *above which it had originally been placed, then deleted, as it interfered with squeezed-in line* 'And . . . out?'

576.22 Get] *preceded by deleted* 'D'

576.22 that's] ' 's' *added*

576.23 Hear] 'H' *over* 'S'

576.25 it] *interlined*

576.34 powerful] *preceded by deleted* 'adequate'

577.3 improve] *followed by deleted comma and* 'they'

577.3 rescue] 's' *over* 'c'

577.4 ²him] *interlined*

577.4 dicker] *followed by deleted* 'him'

577.5 ³him] *upstroke of* 'h' *over a comma with intent to delete*

577.7 ²his] *preceded by deleted* 'his'

577.8 uproariously] 'i' *inserted*

577.8 the worst] *preceded by deleted* 'a nickel'

577.10 that] *preceded by deleted* 'thats ['s' *deleted*] it's all right.'

577.18 we] *interlined with a caret*

577.18–19 our interests] *preceded by deleted* 'Lonelyisle without'

577.19 it?] *interlined before deleted* 'the country?' *of which the question mark is below an interlined deleted period*

577.19–20 done! Of] *exclamation point over comma;* 'O' *over* 'o'

577.21 British] 'B' *over* 'p'

577.21 annex] *preceded by deleted* 'ad'; *followed by deleted* 'the'

577.21 Lonelyisle] *preceded by deleted* 'islan'

577.31 The] *preceded by deleted* 'Britis'

577.31 "Oh] 'O' *over beginning of* 'I'

577.31 now] *originally* 'know' *with* 'k' *deleted*

578.1 big] 'b' *altered from* 'l'

578.1 peaceable] *first* 'e' *over* 'i'

578.4 once] *interlined above deleted* 'time'

578.7 history] *preceded by deleted* 'the' *and followed by deleted* 'of the world' *interlined with a caret*

578.12 but] *interlined*

578.12 ²and] *interlined*

578.13 virtuous] *followed by deleted* 'and god-like'

No. 150. GREAT BUGS IN ONONDAGA

[The copy-text is N¹: *Syracuse Daily Standard*, June 1, 1891, p. 6. The other text collated is N²: *New York Tribune*, June 1, p. 1.]

578.17–23 A . . . fact:] *omit* N²
578.24 here] this place N²
578.25 Delaware . . . Western] Lackawanna N²
578.29–30 accommodation] hauling N²
579.2 at] of N²
579.4 Last night] To-night N²
579.6 cut] put N²
579.10 immense proportions] great size N²
579.10–11 huddled] *omit* N²
579.12 over . . . backs.] game. N²
579.13 the tracks] the the tracks N¹
579.15 began] begun N¹

579.16 scudded] scud N¹; ran N²
579.18 which] that N²
579.20 adoption.] adoption in cities. N²
579.20 The (*no* ¶)] ¶ N²
579.22 things . . . ghost] insects died N²
579.24 iron monster] engine N¹
579.27 an] a N²
579.28 multitudinous] *omit* N²
579.30 crushed vitals of the] crushed and N²
579.30–580.14 An examination . . . bugs."] *omit* N¹
580.15–20 The . . . nature.] *omit* N²

No. 151. THE WRECK OF THE "NEW ERA"

[The copy-text is MS: manuscript in the UVa.–Barrett Collection.]

Alterations in the Manuscript

580.27–28 from . . . marked] *interlined above deleted* 'from'
580.30 few] *interlined above deleted* 'few'
580.31 alive] *preceded by deleted* 'living'
580.32 covered] *followed by deleted* 'by'
580.34 scene of the] *interlined with a caret*
580.34 at] *followed by deleted* 'quite'
581.1 and] *preceded by deleted* 'and'
581.2 *Eras*] 's' *added*
581.5 reputation] 'r' *over* 'a'
581.17 not] *interlined above deleted* 'pa'
581.20 A] *preceded by deleted* 'Th'
581.21 but] *followed by deleted* 'th'
581.22 He] 'H' *over* 'h' ; *preceded by deleted* 'But'
581.25 an] 'n' *added later*
581.27 desolate] *followed by deleted* 'and'
581.29 ²of] *squeezed in*

581.31 eloquently] 'ly' *added*
581.32 justly-] 'j' *over* 'c'
581.33 ²a] *interlined with a caret*
581.35 have been] *preceded by deleted* 'be very ba'
581.35–36 indeed. But] 'indeed.' *originally intended as the end of the paragraph with beginning of new paragraph on next line deleted:* 'Immediately the ship struck, a scene of the wildnest [deleted] wildest confusion' ; *after the deletion, the sentence beginning* 'But' *continues the original paragraph*
581.36(*twice*) from] *interlined with a caret*
581.37 hastened] *preceded by deleted* 'all'
582.8 ¹the] *interlined*
582.9 waves of the] *interlined with a caret*
582.10 struggling] 's' *over a doubtful* 'c' ; *preceded by independently deleted* 'the doo['m' *nearly completed]*' *and* 'unlu'
582.11 Suddenly] *preceded by de-*

leted 'The'

582.14 persons] 's' *added later*

582.16 drowning] *corrected from* 'drownding'

582.17 in them.] *squeezed in at end of line; followed on next line by deleted* 'there.'

582.20 thus] 'u' *over doubtful* 'o'

582.21 there. Then] 'there.' *originally intended as the end of paragraph, with beginning of new paragraph on next line deleted:* 'On shore, the few' ; *the sentence beginning* 'Then' *continues the original paragraph*

582.22 seek to] *interlined with a caret*

582.23 ship,] *comma over period*

582.24 of] *interlined above deleted* 'from'

582.29 assistance] *interlined with a caret*

582.29 the] *interlined*

582.32 ²the] *interlined with a caret*

582.37 The] *preceded by deleted* 'The'

583.1 toward] *followed by* 'the shore' *to end the page but deleted and* 'the shore was stopped' *added*

583.3 could] *preceded by deleted* 'was t'

583.7 eagerly] *preceded by deleted* 'to'

583.7 that] *inserted after deleted* 'who'

583.8 by each wave] *interlined with a caret*

583.8 attempted] 'ed' *interlined above deleted* 'ing'

583.8 any] *followed by deleted* 'ap'

583.9 of life] *interlined with a caret*

583.11–12 and at] 'at' *squeezed in;* 'and' *preceded by deleted* 'and at'

583.16 smaller] *followed by deleted* 'until it would seem as if'

583.16 their] 'ir' *added later; fol-*

lowed by deleted 'men's'

583.16 gave out] *interlined with a caret*

583.17 fell] 'e' *over* 'a'; *preceded by deleted* 'would' *interlined with a caret*

583.19 night.] *followed by deleted* 'One after another'

583.21 dead-houses] *preceded by deleted* 'mor[*and the beginning of a* 'g']'

583.23 ¹were] *interlined above deleted* 'had'

583.23 ²were] *interlined with a caret*

583.24 When] 'W' *over* 'w'; *preceded by deleted* 'Then'

583.24 cleared] *followed by deleted* 'away'

583.26 white-] *preceded by deleted* 'grey'

583.27 Out] 'O' *over* 'o'; *preceded by deleted* 'And'

583.28 and] 'a' *over* 'w'

583.29 like] 'l' *over* 'w'

583.29 sorely] *interlined above deleted* 'to death'

583.30 and] *squeezed in*

583.36 spray] *preceded by deleted* 'the'

583.37 of those alive] *interlined with a caret*

583.39 boats] 's' *added*

583.39 could] *preceded by deleted* 'was'

584.2 search] *preceded by deleted* 'p'

584.3 of] *interlined above deleted* 'over'

584.5 saved] *preceded by deleted* 'dea'

584.12 huge] *preceded by deleted* 'great'

584.14–15 Monument Association] 'M' *over* 'm'; 'A' *over* 'a'

584.17 All] *preceded by deleted* 'Being'

584.18–19 contributions] *preceded by deleted* 'subscriptions'

584.20 liberally.] *followed by deleted* 'Few Germa'

No. 152. ACROSS THE COVERED PIT

[The copy-text is MS: manuscript in the UVa.–Barrett Collection.]

Alterations in the Manuscript

584.21 Rev. . . . Conn] *deleted in pencil*

584.26 caverns] *interlined above deleted* 'caves'

584.26 visited] *interlined above deleted* 'throughly explored'

584.27 him.] *preceded by deleted* 'the doctor.'

584.29 unknown] *preceded by deleted* 'do'

584.31 any] *interlined above deleted* 'no'

585.1 As] *preceded by deleted* 'The'

585.2 place,] *following period and* 'The' *deleted; comma inserted and following* 'it's' *inserted in the left margin*

585.5 depth.] *period inserted before deleted* 'of the pit.'

585.8 been] *interlined with a caret*

585.12 he . . . wonder] 'he' *inserted in the left margin and* 'ed' *deleted from* 'wondered'

585.13 caverns] *preceded by deleted* 'the'

585.19 one] *followed by deleted comma*

585.20 him.] *at the foot of the page a following paragraph symbol deleted*

585.23 darkey] *final* 's' *deleted*

585.26 made] *preceded by deleted* 'stole'

585.29 As . . . it,] *preceded by an asterisk and written at the foot of the page; the corresponding asterisk appears after* 'once.' *with the notation* '(Insert here)' *interlined above*

585.30 ¹their] 'ir' *added later*

585.30 knowledge] *preceded by deleted* 'the' *and followed by deleted* 'of the authorities'

585.31 would be] *interlined above deleted* 'was'

585.32 Dr. Hovey] *deleted in pencil*

586.2 to] *inserted*

586.3 grave,] *following period deleted and comma inserted*

586.7 might] *interlined above deleted* 'made'

586.8 also] 'so' *interlined above deleted* 'ways' *of original* 'always'

586.13 It] 'I' *over* 'H'

586.15 plainly] *inserted in the left margin*

586.19 William's] *apostrophe and* 's' *added*

586.23 a] *an upward loop, possibly the beginning of an* 'f' *appears above*

586.25 doctor's] *apostrophe and* 's' *added*

586.26 of] *written over* 'in'

586.28 connection] 'ion' *interlined above deleted* 'ion' *over* 'ed'

586.29 one] 'o' *over* 'a'

586.30 slab] *following period deleted*

586.32 communicated] 'o' *mended from* 'u'

586.33 slab] *preceded by deleted* 'stone'

586.33 thought . . . gone.] *interlined above deleted* 'gave himself up for lost.'

586.35 was] *inserted in the left margin*

586.37 on] *preceded by deleted* 'one' *in which there is the beginning of an upstroke following the* 'o'

586.37 spirits] *final* 's' *added later; followed by deleted* 'at'

586.38 earth] *followed by unde-*

leted comma and deleted 'the'

587.1 he] *preceded by deleted* 'the'

587.3 bridge was] *final 's' of* 'bridges' *deleted and* 'was' *interlined above deleted* 'were'

587.5 chattered] *followed by deleted* 'like'

587.12 on] 'o' *over upstroke of probable* 't'

587.13 two] 't' *over possible* 'n'

587.14 adventures] *final 's' added later*

587.14 returned] *interlined above deleted* 'passed'

587.15 the] *final 'y' deleted*

587.18 needed] 'ed' *in pencil over deleted* 'n't'

587.19.1 [*At the foot of the sketch is a pencil deleted* 'S.C.']

No. 153. THE GRATITUDE OF A NATION

[The copy-text is MS: manuscript in the Special Collections of Columbia University Libraries.]

Alterations in the Manuscript

588.5 the] *interlined with a caret*

588.12 Gratitude] 'r' *over* 'a'

588.36 that] *interlined*

589.1 ¹and] *interlined with a caret which deletes a comma*

589.12 benefactions] *followed by deleted* 'here'

589.13 we] *followed by deleted* 'do mourn; it'

589.23 while] *interlined above deleted* 'will'

589.28 we] *interlined with a caret*

589.33 graves] 's' *added*

589.36 we] *interlined with a caret*

589.37 rush] *preceded on the line above by deleted* 'rush' *written over* 'cro'

590.2 time] *final 's' deleted*

590.2 ²of] *interlined above deleted* 'and'

590.4 ¹their] *interlined*

590.8 which] *interlined above deleted* 'that'

590.13 It] 'I' *altered from* 'i' *and preceded by deleted* 'And of those who still remain'

590.16 places] 'pl' *over* 'f'

590.21 the] *preceded by deleted* 'the'

No. 154. IN THE DEPTHS OF A COAL MINE

[The copy-text is McC: *McClure's Magazine*, III (Aug., 1894), 195–209. The other texts collated are MS: manuscript draft version in the UVa.– Barrett Collection; N¹: *Detroit Free Press*, July 22, 1894, p. 2; N²: *St. Paul Pioneer Press*, July 22, p. 13; N³: *Buffalo Express*, July 22, p. 17; N⁴: *Philadelphia Inquirer*, July 22, p. 21; N⁵: *St. Louis Republic*, July 22, part III, p. 17. In order to enable a reader to reconstruct the three authorities, all variants whether substantive or accidental in MS, McC, and N are recorded here save for unique accidental readings in only one N text and for all accidental readings noted in the List of Emendations. In some cases $N means only the agreement of all newspapers that print the part of the text in question, owing to variable cutting in all N texts except N⁵.]

590.24–591.11 The . . . earth.] *omit* $N

590.26 smoke] smoke and dust MS

590.27 ravaged . . . fragrance.] devastated the atmosphere. MS

590.28   the vegetation] vegetation McC

590.31   far away] faraway MS

590.32   the colliery] our first colliery MS

590.33   The] A McC

590.34   frame] building MS

590.34   wood.] It quaintly resembled some extravagant Swiss chalet. MS

591.1 *et seq.*   its] it's MS

591.1   sides] side MS

591.3   Through‸] ~ , MS

591.4–5   and garments] *omit* MS

591.5   came] sometimes came MS

591.9   our new eyes] the new eye MS

591.10   a] this MS

591.10   war . . . waged] life MS

591.11   earth.] earth. They came like black, industrious beetles from a hole. A little girl was waiting to meet her father. She went away holding to his hand. MS

591.12   the] a McC,$N

591.13   engine-houses] ~‸~ $N(−N⁵)

591.13   machine-shops] ~‸~ MS,$N

591.13   Railroad] The MS

591.14   files] the rows of countless MS; piles N⁵

591.15   begrimed] begrimmed N²،⁵

591.15   Other (*no* ¶)] ¶ MS

591.15   similar to] counterparts of MS

591.18   from] *omit* $N

591.18–19   mines, mules] miners, mules N¹⁻²،⁴; miners' mules N³،⁵

591.20   railroads] railroad tracks N³

591.20   painfully] *omit* MS

591.21   low-hanging] low MS

591.22   indicated a town.] denoted the presence of a true town of the coal districts. MS

591.23–24   Car . . . dragged] We saw car after car of coal come from where the mouth of the shaft was hidden in a shed. They went MS

591.25   breaker.] breaker. They suggested to us then the mystery of toil in the earth's heart. After certain experiences, they expressed the net-work of tunnels far below where the dim orange light gleams on the visages of the men laboring where roofs are as a menace and the sound of trickling water may send a chill to the untried blood. MS

591.26   ³the] *omit* $N

591.29   on revolving cylinders] *omit* MS

591.31   bid] bade N³

591.31   go] to go MS

591.31   chute.] chute. A mighty banging and clattering filled the ears. MS

591.33   violent] mad and violent MS

591.33   mighty] huge N¹

591.33–36   A . . . uproar.] *omit* MS

591.37   slate-pickers] ~‸~ $N(−N³)

591.38   forty-five] 45 $N(−N⁴)

591.39   great teeth] teeth of the huge revolving cylinders MS

592.2   slowly,] ~‸ N²،⁴⁻⁵

592.2   slowly,] slowly passt them, MS

592.3   therein] *omit* MS

592.3   were] was N³⁻⁵

592.3–4   , one above another,] ‸ seated in a row‸ MS

592.4   fairly] reasonably MS

592.5   final] last MS

592.5–7   The . . . clouds.] *omit* MS

592.5–593.6   The . . . creature.] *omit* N²

592.6   up,] ~‸ N³⁻⁴

592.8   These little men] They MS

592.8   band.] band, and scoundrels every one of them. After I had come to know them better, I discovered that they took a higher pride in their villiany than any urchins I had yet experienced. They are a class unto themselves. MS

592.8–9 resembled] resemble MS

592.9 gamins] ragamuffin MS

592.9–10 laughed . . . laughed_∧] laugh . . . laugh, MS

592.10 were] are MS

592.11 terror.] delight and a terror. MS

592.11–13 They had . . . skill.] [¶] They swagger with consummate valor. They are obviously independent of everything under the skies, excepting perhaps their own boss and he must be in a habitual state of surprise that he continues to exist. They swear long ponderous oaths with magnificent ease. They remind one of babes armed with great swords. And there is a considerable portion of them named: "Redny." MS

592.14 ¶ Through] no ¶ N³

592.15 shoulders_∧] little bare shoulders_∧ MS; ~ , N¹,³,⁵

592.16 scrambled] scrambled about MS

592.16–17 us. Work . . . ascertain] us and to ascertain if possible MS

592.18–19 The man . . . air.] *omit* MS

592.20 slate-pickers] ~ _∧ ~ N¹,⁴⁻⁵

592.21 One . . . wonders] One wonders continually MS

592.21 continually] occasionally N³

592.22 school-houses] school-|houses McC; schoolhouses N¹,⁵; ~ _∧ ~ N⁴

592.22 them,] ~ _∧ N¹,³⁻⁴

592.23 off,] ~ _∧ $N

592.23 go] can go N¹

592.24 culm-heap] dump-heap MS

592.24 base-ball,] ~ _∧ $N

592.24 with] with the N¹

592.26 And . . . getting] Perhaps, too, they can get MS

592.27 door-boys] ~ _∧ ~ N¹,⁴⁻⁵

592.27 down] *omit* N¹

592.27 mule-boys] ~ _∧ ~ N¹,⁴⁻⁵

592.27–28 yet later] after that MS

592.28 Finally] And finally MS

592.28 have grown] grow MS

592.29 may] can MS

592.30 down] down into the mines MS

592.30 squeezed,] ~ _∧ N¹,⁴(N³ *doubtful*)

592.30–31 to a . . . estate] *omit* MS,N³

592.31 mere] mere attack of MS

592.31–32 They . . . ambitious.] *omit* MS

592.33 ¶ Meanwhile] MS *probably no ¶ but indention not clear*

592.33–593.6 Meanwhile . . . creature.] *omit* N⁴

592.33 dins] noises MS

592.35 The room . . . bellows.] *omit* N³

592.37 a-tremble] a-trembling N³

592.37 sweep] sweep and dash MS

592.38 Down] And down MS

592.39 tiny] tiny black MS

592.39–593.1 urchins, . . . breathe] urchins, breatheing MS

592.39 fifty-five] 55 N³,⁵

592.39 cents a day each] cents each day N¹,⁵; cents a day N³

593.1–6 They . . . creature.] *omit* N¹

593.1–6 heavy . . . creature.] heavy and having this clamor in their ears until they grow deaf as bats. Poor little ambitious lads, it is no wonder that to become miners, is the height of their desires. MS

593.8 said,] said, in reply to our letter, MS

593.8 if] ef N⁴

593.9 little] the little N[1]

593.9 shaft] mouth MS

593.10 fan-wheel] ~ ∧ ~ $N(−N[3]); ~ - | ~ N[3]

593.10 twirling] whirling N[1,3]

593.12 some] *omit* MS

593.12 eleven] seven MS

593.12 eleven . . . fifty] 1,150 $N (N[4]: 1150)

593.13–17 As . . . crime.] *omit* N[1]

593.14 opportunity] an opportunity MS

593.15 slimy] slimey MS

593.15 moss-grown] ~ ∧ ~ N[2,4-5]; ~ - | ~ N[3]

593.15 dripping] and dripping MS

593.16 ink-like] ~ ∧ ~ N[2,4]

593.16 blackness] darkness MS

593.17 tales] the tales $N

593.17 crime] crimes McC

593.20–22 It was . . . roof.] *omit* MS

593.22 , as . . . view,] *omit* MS

593.24 ¶ A] *no* ¶ MS

593.24–25 marched . . . daylight.] stood upon it, a little group armed with flickering lights. MS

593.24 little] the little N[4]

593.26 the] that MS

593.27 door-posts] ~ ∧ ~ N[2,4-5]; doorposts N[1]

593.29 was] was like MS

593.29–32 The . . . tumult.] *omit* N[1]

593.29 fall.] fall. The noise of the machinery was an imposing thunder. MS

593.30 the little] our little MS

593.30 tied] *omit* MS

593.31 bawled] roared MS

593.33–594.2 The . . . revelation.] *omit* N[2]

593.33 slid] slipped MS

593.34 dark] black $N

593.34 mind] eye MS

593.36 to the iron bars] *omit* MS

593.37–594.2 When . . . revelation.] *omit* MS,N[1]

593.37 lost,] ~ ∧ N[3-5]

594.3 ¶ It] *no* ¶ MS,N[1]

594.3 It . . . endlessness.] *omit* N[3]

594.5 At last] Presently MS

594.7–9 Into . . . respirations.] We were in the mines. MS

594.8 powder-smoke] ~ ∧ ~ $N

594.9 The . . . respirations.] *omit* N[1]

594.9 began] begun N[5]

594.10 the] this MS

594.11–12 a tunnel . . . shaft.] the tunnel. MS

594.12–13 Little . . . diamonds.] *omit* N[1]

594.12 caught] caught in $N

594.14 an] *omit* $N

594.15 coal-dust] ~ ∧ ~ $N

594.15 of the] on the N[1]

594.16–22 The sense . . . mass.] *omit* MS

594.18–22 It was . . . mass.] *omit* N[1]

594.18 us. It was] us, as if the roof were McC

594.19 [1]the] the the N[3]

594.23 ahead,] ~ ∧ | MS

594.24 tiny] little MS

594.24–25 wisp-light] ~ ∧ ~ $N

594.27 dance] danced MS(u),$N

594.28 time] little time N[5]

594.29–32 If . . . thing.] *omit* N[1]

594.31 summer-time] ~ ∧ ~ N[2,4-5]

594.32–33 The . . . men] Their garments MS

594.35 shone] shown N[3]

594.36 grinning] grins MS

594.36 two] *omit* N[3]

594.36 there] *omit* MS

594.36 shadows] shadow N[3]

594.36–39 The . . . spectres.] *omit* N[1]

594.37 on] in McC,$N

594.37 trembling] trembling and weird MS

594.38 weirdly shrouded] shrouded in mystery MS

594.39 spectres] specters N²⁻³

595.2 smiles—] ~ , MS

595.4 our] the MS

595.4 lamps,] ~ ∧ $N

595.4 we could see] it could be seen MS

595.5 busily] busy N¹

595.5 long∧ thin] ~, ~ N²,⁵

595.6 roof ominously] ominous roof MS

595.6 bended] bent McC,$N

595.7 behind] beside N³

595.9–25 He . . . wolves.] omit N¹

595.9–15 He . . . yellow.] omit N²

595.9 drill∧] doubtful comma in MS

595.11 poke] joke $N

595.13 up] omit MS

595.13 on'y] only MS; o'ny N³⁻⁴; o'ly N⁵

595.15 "Well . . . hurry] "Well, yeh wanta hurry MS

595.19 an] omit N³,⁵

595.19–23 altercation . . . Yet one] altercation. One MS

595.23 understand] discern MS

595.24 not . . . throats.] smiling at each other. MS

595.25 effect] effects $N

595.25 the snarling . . . wolves.] snarls of hate. MS

595.26 We came] Presently, we left them to their drear and lonely task. All along this passage we came MS

595.27 his] a MS

595.29–31 And . . . lamps.] omit N¹

595.30 satanic] Satanic $N

595.30 wild and] omit MS

595.32–33 in . . . infernal.] were absolutely infernal in their weird strength. MS

595.34 mine,] ~ ∧ $N

595.34 place] space N⁵

595.35 some] the MS

595.36 us,] ~ ∧ N¹,⁵

595.36 resembled] was like MS

595.36 resurrection] great resurrection N¹

595.36–37 uprose . . . movements] arose like ghouls MS

595.38 swift] swift menacing MS

596.1–15 At . . . yellow.] omit N⁴

596.1 time∧] ~ , $N

596.2 difficulties] great difficulties MS

596.2–3 "Molly Maguire,"] "China", MS

596.4,10 "Molly,"] "China", MS

596.5 her] his MS

596.9 all] omit N¹

596.9 cold blue flame] threats MS

596.10 the men] they MS

596.10–14 Five . . . him.] omit MS

596.13 feller] fellar N³; fellow N⁵

596.15 dancing] omit MS

596.16 tunnel . . . mine] tunnel, MS

596.18 passage] tunnel MS; passages N²

596.18 a mine] the mine MS

596.18 ∧main gangway.∧] " ~ ~ ." MS

596.19 avenues] avenue N²

596.19 noise—] ~ , MS

596.19 clatter] clatter and clang MS

596.20–21 elevator speeds . . . drops] elevators speed . . . drop MS

596.21 thunderingly] crashingly MS

596.22 of] of the N²

596.23 of] omit N⁴

596.23 coal-cars] cars MS

596.25 slow∧] ~ , N²⁻⁴

596.25 throb] throbs N²

596.26 which] that MS

596.26 in] at N²

596.27 banging and crashing] blasting and crashing and banging MS

596.30 flickering and flashing] flashing and flickering MS

596.30   stride] stride along, MS
596.31   sombre] somber $N(−N⁴)
596.32   rattle] ominous rattle MS
596.32–599.3   It is war . . . distances.] MS *missing*
596.37   ten . . . thirty] 10, 20, 30 N³,⁵
597.3–22   In . . . mines.] *omit* N¹
597.7   roofs that] roofs, and N³
597.8   twenty] 20 N³,⁵
597.8   wide,] ~ ∧ N²⁻³,⁵
597.10   three hundred] 300 N³,⁵
597.15   distances] distance N²
597.16   our] of our N²
597.17   yeh] you McC,N²,⁴⁻⁵
597.18   rolling-mill] ~ ∧ ~ $N
597.18   yeh] you N²,⁴
597.19   th'] the N²,⁴⁻⁵
597.21   miles,] ~ ∧ N²,⁴
597.23–599.12   Over . . . sunlight.] *omit* N⁴
597.23–24   mule-stables] ~ ∧ ~ $N
597.27; 598.2,7   "China"] ∧ ~ ∧ N¹,³
597.33–39   About . . . legs.] *omit* N¹⁻²
597.34   it] *omit* $N
598.4   the seasons] seasons N¹
598.11   surface,] ~ ∧ N¹⁻²
598.11   these animals] the mules McC
598.12   Later,] ~ ∧ N¹⁻²
598.13   splendor] splendors N¹
598.14   breezes∧] ~ , McC
598.14   breaks] break N¹
598.15   Once a] A McC
598.18   to be] *omit* N⁵
598.18–19   into the . . . hillside.] *omit* McC
598.18   into] to N²
598.19   the hillside] a hillside N¹⁻²
598.21–22   He . . . famous.] *omit* McC
598.23   conventions] conversations N⁵
598.27–599.12   After . . . sunlight.] *omit* N²

598.29–30   the dead] dead N³
598.30   They . . . children.] *omit* McC
598.31   once] *omit* McC
598.32   resolute] *omit* McC
598.33–35   trot . . . place.] follow. McC
598.36–599.12   To . . . sunlight.] *omit* N¹
598.36–599.3   To . . . distances.] *omit* N³
598.37   the] a N⁵
598.37   dream.] dream of a lost paradise. McC
598.37   when] as McC
598.38–599.1   in rows . . . paradise.] flapping their ears. McC
599.1   bloom] bloomland McC
599.4–7   We . . . mass.] *omit* McC
599.4   at] in our visits to the mines by MS
599.4–5   we encountered] through which we were obliged to wade MS
599.5   some of] *omit* MS
599.7   In (*no* ¶)] ¶ N³,⁵
599.7–8   In . . . gruesome] In wet mines, gruesome McC
599.9   dank] dark $N
599.10   Upon] And upon MS
599.10   ∧ too∧ there] , too, McC; , too, there $N
599.10   a] *omit* MS
599.10   fungus] fungi MS
599.11   druid's] Druid's $N
599.11   thrives] thrive MS
599.12   shrivels and dies] shrivels and die MS(c)
599.13   Great] When I had studied mines and the miner's life underground and above ground, I wondered at many things but I could not induce myself to wonder why the miners strike and otherwise object to their lot. Great MS
599.13   mine's] mines MS
599.16   final] dying MS
599.17   ²that] where N³
599.17   Heaven] heaven $N

599.18   There (*no* ¶)] ¶ MS
599.18   silent] *omit* N[5]
599.19   the top] top MS,N[1]
599.20   period,] ~ ‸ $N(−N[5])
599.20–22   death‸ and . . .
    rock.] death. McC; death in
    the mines. A panic wilder than
    any where the sun shines is
    the scene that ensues MS
599.20   death‸] ~ , N[3,5]
599.21   shone] shown N[3]
599.22   may] *omit* McC
599.22   rock] rocks N[1]
599.22–24   If . . . tunnels,] To
    him that escapes the gas,
    "squeezes," the trundling cars,
    MS
599.23   shooting] shooting down
    N[1]
599.23   little] the little N[1,5]
599.24–27   perils, . . . quarter.]
    dangers, to his bent and
    gnarled form there comes an
    inevitable disease, the "mine
    asthma." He has the joy of
    looking back upon a life spent
    principally for other men's
    benefit until the disease racks
    and wheezes him into the
    grave. MS
599.25   "miner's asthma"]
    ‸ ~ ~ ‸ $N(N[2,4]: miners')
599.25   that] and $N(−N[3]);
    which N[3]
599.26–27   three dollars] $3 $N
599.27   per] a N[3]
599.27   one . . . quarter] $1.25
    $N (N[1]: $1‸25)
599.28–31   In   the . . . them.]
    MS *different text, for which
    see the* MS *version* (606.9–
    607.16)
599.29   the men] men N[2]
599.32   lights] flame, MS
599.33   We (*no* ¶)] ¶ MS

Subheadings

(N[3])

599.33–600.8   Far . . . engineer.]
    Gradually the pungent odor of
    the mines, an odor of powder-
    smoke, kerosene, wet earth,
    went from out our nostrils.
    The cables slid rapidly and
    the platform swayed in a usual
    fashion. MS
599.34   engine-room] ~ ‸ ~
    $N(−N[5])
599.37–600.7   In fact . . . eleva-
    tor] *omit* McC
599.37–600.8   In fact . . . engi-
    neer.] *omit* N[2]
599.37   give] gave N[1]
599.38–600.8   I   had . . . engi-
    neer.] *omit* N[1]
600.9   ¶ Of] *no* ¶ MS
600.9   became] become $N
600.10–13   a downpour . . .
    wine.] streams. Then before
    our eyes burst the radiance of
    the day. We closed our lids
    before the high splendor of
    the sun afloat in a sea of spot-
    less blue. It was a new scene
    to us, and wondrous. MS
600.13   near-by] nearby $N(−N[5])
600.13   fresh] *omit* N[2]
600.13   air] breeze N[3]
600.14–19   Of that . . . labor.]
    omit N[2]
600.14   that] the MS
600.15   loaded] heavily loaded
    MS
600.16   in . . . procession] with
    terrific monotony MS
600.16   were sent] went MS(u),
    McC
600.16–19   the   incline . . . la-
    bor.] to feed the insatiate
    breaker. MS
600.18   black] *omit* N[1]
600.19   greed,] ~ ‸ N[3-5]
600.19   of] *omit* N[4]

nues.

597.22.1 Mule Life Under-
ground.

599.12.1 The Earth from a
Mine's Depth.

(N⁴)

591.36.1 The Slate Pickers
593.6.1 Down the Shaft.
594.9.1 A Curtain of Impenetrable Night.
595.8.1 A Bit of Miner's Fun.

596.15.1 Wonders of the Subterranean Avenues.
599.12.1 The Earth from a
Mine's Depth.

(N⁵)

591.36.1 The Slate Pickers.
593.6.1 Down the Shaft.
594.9.1 A Curtain of Impenetrable Night.
595.8.1 A Bit of Miner's Fun.

596.15.1 Subterranean Wonders.
597.22.1 Mule Life Under-
ground.
599.12.1 The Earth From a
Mine's Depth.

No. 154a. FIRST DRAFT

[The copy-text is MS: manuscript first draft in the UVa.–Barrett Collection.]

Alterations in the Manuscript

600.20 breakers] *double quote
marks deleted in pencil*
600.23 vegetation] *preceded by
deleted* 'grass' *and the beginning of an* 'l'
600.28 switches.] *period over a
comma and following* 'around
and' *deleted*
600.28 above] *preceded by deleted* 'high'
600.32 Through] *followed by
doubtful comma, probably an
inadvertent stroke*
600.35 went] *interlined with a
caret*
601.3 symbols] 's' *over* 'a'
601.5 was waiting] *interlined
above deleted* 'had come'
601.11 structures,] *preceded by
deleted* 'buildings,'
601.14 mines] 's' *added*
601.15 long] *preceded by deleted*
'he'
601.18 of coal] *interlined with a
caret*
601.25 blood.] *interlined above
deleted* 'heart.'
601.27 chutes] 'c' *over* 's' *in ink,*

reinforced in pencil
601.28 were] *interlined above
deleted* 'are'
601.29 chewed] *preceded by deleted* 'g'
601.29 At] 'A' *over* 'I'
601.30 its] MS 'it's' *preceded by
deleted* 'his'
601.36 cylinders] *preceded by deleted* 'st' *and followed by deleted* 'streamed'
601.38 past] MS 'passt' *with* 't'
in pencil over 'ed' *of original*
'passed'
601.39 seated] *interlined with a
caret*
601.40 The] *preceded by deleted*
'What'
601.40 reasonably] *preceded by
deleted* 'compar'
601.42 terrifically] 'a' *and second* 'l' *inserted in pencil*
602.1 had] *interlined with a
caret*
602.1 come] 'o' *altered from* 'a'
602.4 more] *followed by deleted*
'and when they laugh more'
602.6 consummate] *second* 'm'

interlined with a caret in pencil, not necessarily in Crane's hand

602.8   boss] *following* 'es' *deleted*

602.8   ¹he] *interlined above deleted* 'they'

602.16   slate-] *interlined in pencil above deleted* 'coal-'

602.18   When] 'W' *over* 'w' *and preceding* 'When' *deleted*

602.19   get] *inserted in the left margin*

602.19   go] *preceded by deleted* 'get'

602.20   from] 'fr' *over* 'wi'

602.21   too,] *interlined above deleted* 'soon'; *preceding comma inserted*

602.26   asthma."] *followed by deleted* 'Poor little ambitious lads.' *in which* 'lads.' *is interlined above deleted* 'men.'

602.26   live] *interlined above deleted* 'exist'

602.26   infernal] 'e' *over* 'o'

602.28   room] *interlined above deleted* 'air'

602.32   until] *written over interlined* 'into' *above deleted* 'until'

602.32–33   grow heavy] *inserted in the left margin with close-up symbol*

602.33   they] *interlined*

602.34   miners] *preceded by deleted* 'a' ; 's' *added*

602.38   shed] *preceded by deleted* 'ho'

602.39   was] *interlined with a caret*

602.40   who] *preceded by deleted* 'four'

602.41   seven] *interlined above deleted* 'four'

602.42   had] *interlined above deleted* 'gained'

602.42   gaze] *interlined above deleted* 'stare'

603.1   walls] *preceded by deleted* 'top-'

603.3   -like] *preceded by* '-l[*and*

the remainder of the word obscured by an ink-blot]'

603.3–4   an . . . crime.] *squeezed in at the end of a line after deleted* 'dank as an old well.'

603.5   We] *first minim over beginning of an* 'H'

603.6   appeared] *followed by deleted comma and* 'like an apparition from the cen'

603.7   it] *interlined with a caret*

603.8   stood] *preceded by deleted* 'mar'

603.9   flickering] *preceded by deleted* 'little'

603.11   flash. We] *period inserted before deleted* 'and' ; 'W' *over* 'w'

603.14   The flames] *preceded by deleted* 'Our flick'

603.17   ¶ The] *preceded by a horizontal stroke to left margin, possibly made by* Linson

603.18   eye] *inserted in the left margin*

603.23   descend] *followed by deleted* 'with'

603.23   slowly and with] 'slowly' *altered from* 'slow-|'; 'and with' *interlined above deleted* 'ness and'

603.23   crash and a jar,] *interlined above deleted* 'crunching sound,' ; 'crashi' *with* 'i' *deleted, and* 'jarr' *with last* 'r' *deleted*

603.24   an] *altered from* 'a'

603.25   loneliness] *first* 'e' *inserted in pencil*

603.26   lamp] *interlined above deleted* 'light'

603.31   All] *preceded by deleted* 'Then suddenl'

603.32   We] *first minim over beginning of an* 'H'

603.34   move to] *interlined above deleted* 'move to'; *the* 'to' *being partially obscured by an inkblot*

603.34   dance] *final* 'd' *deleted*

603.34 us.] *followed by deleted* 'Pres'

603.36 could] 'c' *over* 'o' *and the beginning of an upstroke, perhaps the beginning of a* 'p'

603.38 contrast] *preceded by deleted* 'glory'

604.1 trembling] *interlined above deleted* 'dim'

604.1 left] *interlined with a caret*

604.4 said] *following comma deleted*

604.8 drilling] *followed by deleted* 'bu'

604.21 a] *followed by deleted* 'friendly altercation.'

604.21 look] 'l' *over* 'd'

604.22 they] *interlined in pencil with a caret*

604.25 upon] *preceded by deleted* 'other'

604.29 glittering] *followed by deleted* 'with a wild light from'

604.29 glow] *interlined above deleted* 'light'

604.32 the] *interlined above deleted* 'a' *and the start of a* 'g'

604.33 lying] MS 'lieing' *with descender of* 'y' *added in pencil utilizing* 'ie' *as the upper part of the* 'y'

604.34 slowly] *interlined with a caret*

604.36 were] 'ere' *in pencil over* 'as'

604.38 China] 'C' *over* 'c'

604.41 one.] *interlined in pencil above deleted* 'position.'

605.2 were] *preceded by deleted* 'was'

605.2 eyes,] *preceded by independently deleted* 'vu glitter'; *followed by deleted* 'thre'

605.2 with] *following is erased caret and erased interlined pencil* 'cold blue flame'

605.3 roof] *preceded by deleted* 'I'

605.5 tunnel] *preceded by deleted* 'sil'

605.5 foot] *preceded by deleted* 'mouth'

605.5 main] *interlined with a caret*

605.6 Here] *followed by deleted* 'stretched the m'

605.6 were] *followed by deleted* 'we'

605.7 The] *preceded by deleted* 'A'

605.9 loaded] *interlined above deleted* 'empty'

605.13 water] *interlined above deleted* 'water' *of which the* 'r' *is obscured by an ink-blot*

605.17 flashing] 'i' *over* 'e'

605.18 But] *preceded by deleted* 'Dow'

605.19 is] *interlined above deleted* 'was'

605.21 We] 'W' *over* 'In'; *preceded by leaf 15 containing only the false start* 'We were occasi'

605.21 appalled] *first* 'p' *inserted*

605.24 churned] *followed by deleted* 'in' *and the beginning of an upstroke for a* 't'

605.24 a] *interlined with a caret*

605.26 uncertain-] *preceded by deleted* 'me'

605.27 grows] *followed by deleted* 'a white'

605.28 thrive] *final* 's' *deleted*

605.28 deep] *interlined above deleted* 'damp'

605.29 die] *final* 's' *deleted in pencil*

605.30 When I had] *interlined above deleted* 'If you'

605.30 studied] *altered from* 'study'

605.31 ¹I] *interlined above deleted* 'you'

605.31 wondered] 'ed' *added*

605.31 but] *followed by deleted* 'you are not'

605.34 Great] *preceded by deleted* 'Vas'; *a horizontal line sets this off and seems to indicate a new paragraph*

605.35 is] *followed by deleted* 'the'

605.38 lies, . . . Heaven,] *commas added in pencil*

605.38 his] *interlined in pencil with a caret that deleted a hyphen*

605.39 If] *interlined above deleted* 'Even'

606.2 in] *preceded by deleted* 'to'

606.2 panic] 'p' *over* 's'

606.2–3 sun shines] *originally* 'sunshine' *with a caret inserted after* 'sun' *and the final* 's' *added*

606.3 escapes] *preceded by deleted* 'grows ex'

606.5 to] *preceded by deleted* 'ther'

606.5 and gnarled] *interlined with a caret above deleted* 'old'

606.5 inevitable] *first* 'i' *and first* 'e' *over illegible letters, the first perhaps an* 'e'

606.7 other] *apostrophe and final* 's' *deleted in pencil*

606.7 benefit] *interlined above deleted* 'profit,'

606.13 glints] 's' *added later; preceded by deleted* 'a'

606.13 eyes,] 's' *added later; followed by deleted* 'a'

606.13–14 aspects . . . heads] *each final* 's' *added later*

606.15 buildings] *interlined above deleted* 'huts'

606.17 of never] *preceded by deleted* 'of their'

606.18 to be] *inserted in the left margin*

606.21 strength.] *altered from* 'strong' *with* 'e' *over* 'o' *and* 'th' *squeezed in before period*

606.21 They] *preceded by deleted* 'Sometimes,'

606.23 hard] *interlined with a caret*

606.24 not] *followed by a deleted period*

606.30 at a] *interlined above deleted* 'in the'

606.32 make] 'e' *interlined above deleted* 'ing'

606.33 elevator] *final* 's' *deleted*

606.36 fainted] *followed by deleted* 'from the horror it'

606.37 They] *preceded by deleted* 'The papers'

606.39 brokers.] *interlined above deleted* 'mar[and the beginning of a* 'k']'

606.41 brokers] *preceded by deleted* 'breakers'

606.41 was] 'as' *over* 'ere'

607.2 hardship] *followed by deleted* 'with the'

607.3 pangs] *following comma deleted*

607.5 they] *interlined*

607.6 -brokers] 's' *squeezed in before period*

607.9 period] *preceded by deleted* 'mo'

607.13 wage] *preceded by deleted* 'profit'

607.13 part.] *period inserted; following* 'and not' *deleted*

607.14 is] *preceded by deleted* 'lives'

607.14 man] 'a' *over* 'e'

607.14 ²miner] *followed by deleted* 'he will'

607.15 that] *first* 't' *over probable* 'o'

607.17 vanished.] *followed by deleted* 'We were on'

607.19 kerosene] 'o' *over* 's' *over original* 'e'

607.21 Of] 'O' *over* 'o'; *preceded by deleted* 'Then' *of which* 'T' *is over* 'O'

607.23 lids] *interlined above deleted* 'eyes'

607.27 emerged] *preceded by deleted* 'came'

607.28 terrific] *interlined above deleted* 'terrible'

607.28 were sent] 'were' *interlined;* 's' *over* 'w'

No. 156. HOWELLS FEARS THE REALISTS MUST WAIT

[The copy-text is N(p): *McClure's* galley proof. The other texts collated are N[1]: *New York Times*, Oct. 28, 1894, p. 20; N[2]: *Philadelphia Inquirer*, Oct. 28, p. 9; N[3]: *Louisville Courier-Journal*, Oct. 28, p. 20; N[4]: *Boston Globe*, Nov. 4, p. 32; N[5]: *St. Paul Pioneer Press*, Nov. 6, p. 4.]

636.2   She] Yet she N[2]
636.11   that] this N[1,4]
636.11   ways] way N[1]
636.13   towards] toward N[1,3]
636.16   misapprehension] appre-hension N[4]
636.21   and art] and act N(p[u]), $N
636.28   street] streets N[3]
637.15–16   "You . . . man.] *omit* N[5]

637.18   their] the N[3]
637.28   end] ended N[1]
637.28   further] farther N[3]
638.1   novelists] novelist N[4]
638.1   in] of N[1]
638.3   these] those N[1]
638.6   somewheres] somewhere $N(−N[5])
638.15   his] a N[5]
638.20   almost] *omit* N[1]

No. 157. GHOSTS ON THE JERSEY COAST

[The copy-text is N[1]: *New York Press*, Nov. 11, 1894, part IV, p. 2.]

Subheadings

639.38.1   A Reprehensible Old Spook.

640.26.1   The Tale of the Black Dog.
641.29.1   Enter the Hound.

No. 158. MISS LOUISE GERARD—SOPRANO

[The copy-text is MC: *Musical Courier*, XIX, No. 26 (Dec. 26, 1894), 30. The other text collated is MN: *Musical News*, I, No. 3 (Dec., 1894), 3.]

642.29   Gerard] Gerard, whose picture is printed on the first page of this issue of THE MUSICAL COURIER, MC
642.33   this] the MC
643.2–4   The . . . her.] *omit* MC
643.24   James's] James' MC; James MN

643.39   *Galignani's*] "Galignani's MC; Galignana's MN
644.10   quite] *omit* MC
644.11   Her] A MC
644.11–12   in . . . *Journal*] from her pen MC
644.29–33   The . . . personality."] *omit* MN

No. 159. THE GHOSTLY SPHINX OF METEDECONK

[The copy-text is N[1](p): proof for *New York Press*, Jan. 13, 1895, part V, p. 1, in the Crane scrapbook in the Special Collections of Columbia University Libraries.]

Subheadings

645.33.1   The Fisherman's Fright.

646.33.1   Source of the Mystery.
647.27.1   The Storm's Finale.

No. 160. SIX YEARS AFLOAT

[The copy-text is MS: manuscript in the Berg Collection of the New York Public Library. The other texts collated are N(p): galley proof in the Special Collections of Columbia University Libraries; N[1]: *Pittsburgh Leader*, Aug. 2, 1896, p. 20; N[2]: *Portland Oregonian*, Aug. 2, p. 18. N[1-2] are derived texts without authority.]

648.28,29; 649.3   *Tillie*] Lillie N(p),N[1]

649.2   1st] first N[1]

649.23   and] and and N(p)

649.25   later] *omit* N[1]

649.25   the] his N[1]

649.28   helltopay] hell to pay $N

649.35   NOT] not $N

649.38   *U.S.S.*] United States steamship N[2]

650.4   headed] handled N(p[u])

650.5   way] headway N[2]

650.6   customer] costumer MS

650.7   sea-] *omit* N[1]

650.22   largest] longest MS

650.25   weighed] weighs N(p),N[2]

651.5   feet] foot N[1]

651.5 *et seq.*   its] it's MS

651.12   beech] beach MS+

651.18   dollars.] dollars. | dollars. N[2]

651.39   Kilbreth] Kilbreath N[2]

652.1   tabs] tab N[1]

652.5   It is] It's N[2]

652.6   ever] *omit* N[2]

652.15   the] this $N

Alterations in the Manuscript

648.29   both] *preceded by deleted* 't[*and the beginning of* 'h']'

648.29   [2]the] *interlined with a caret*

648.30   just] *interlined with a caret*

648.30   a] *interlined with a caret*

648.31   questioned,] *comma added after doubtful* 'surprisingly' *erased, including an interlineation of the same word or* 'suddenly'

648.31   a] *interlined with a caret*

648.33   reputation] *preceding* 'a' *deleted*

649.1   could] *interlined above deleted* 'can'

649.1   they] *over probable* 'they'

649.1   saw] *followed by deleted* 'o'

649.2   day] *over erased* 'of'

649.2   July] *interlined above deleted* 'May'

649.4   before] *preceded by deleted* 'und'

649.4   forward] *over erased* 'at the bow'

649.14   land!] MS 'land.' *interlined above deleted* 'a ship' *and undeleted exclamation point*

649.18   sailing] *interlined above deleted* 'going'

649.18   [1]nearer] *followed by deleted* 'to'

649.24   seized] MS 'siezed' *preceded by deleted* 'wildly'

649.25   later] *preceded by deleted* 'latte'

649.28   -serpent!] *exclamation point squeezed in before deleted period*

649.29   Immediately] *preceded by deleted* 'All was'

649.29   board] 'o' *over* 'a'

649.33–34   the captain] *interlined with a caret*

649.35   sea-] 'a' *over* 'r'

649.35   I] *interlined with a caret*

649.39   useless] 'u' *over* 's'

650.1   bark] MS 'Bark' *preceded by deleted* 'Bark' *with* 'k' *not completed*

650.4   but] *preceded by deleted* 'and'

650.5   a] *interlined with a caret*
650.6   it] *preceded by deleted* 'while'
650.8   navigation] *preceded by deleted* 'the'
650.18   largest] *followed by deleted* 'ever shipped by sea'
650.20   now] 'w' *over* 't'
650.21   1890] *followed by deleted period*
650.22   The] 'T' *over* 't' *and preceded by deleted* 'While'
650.22   rafts] *interlined with a caret*
650.25   longer] *interlined above deleted* 'larger'
650.26   constructing] 'ing' *over* 'ion'
650.29   we] *interlined with a caret*
650.38   placed] *preceded by deleted* 'are'
650.39   ¹the] 'e' *over* 'is'
651.4   six] *preceded by deleted* 'side'
651.5   ¹feet] 'ee' *over* 'oo'
651.5   ²feet] *first* 'e' *over* 'o'

651.5   beam] 'a' *over* 'e'
651.6   It] *preceded by undeleted probable* 'a'
651.12–13   maple,] *following period deleted and comma added*
651.13   ¹of] *squeezed in between* 'total' *and circled* '4500000'
651.14   diameters] 's' *added*
651.20   ways] 'w' *over probable* 'w'
651.22   until] *followed by deleted probable* 'h'
651.32   expensive.] *followed by deleted closing double quote marks*
651.33   full] 'f' *over* 's'
651.39   Kilbreth] *preceded by deleted* 'Kibr'
652.4   boy] *preceded by deleted* 'body'
652.5   Listen] 's' *inserted*
652.8   that] *interlined with a caret*
652.10   land?] *question mark over period*
652.15   the] 'e' *over* 'is'

No. 161. ASBURY PARK AS SEEN BY STEPHEN CRANE

[The copy-text is N¹: *New York Journal*, Aug. 16, 1896, p. 33. The other text collated is N²: *Kansas City Star*, Aug. 22, p. 2.]

652.34   rapacity] capacity N²
653.5   baggagemen] baggageman N²
653.33   Ode] ode N²

653.38   canon] cannon N²
655.28   roar] the roar N²
655.28   gives] give N²

No. 164. HARVARD UNIVERSITY AGAINST THE CARLISLE INDIANS

[The copy-text is N¹: *New York Journal*, Nov. 1, 1896, p. 5.]

Subheadings

669.25.1   The Indians' Point of View.
670.26.1   Red Men on the Field. (*city edition only*)

671.21.1   Harvard Scores a Touchdown.
672.15.1   Indians' Last Desperate Play.

No. 165. HOW PRINCETON MET HARVARD AT CAMBRIDGE

[The copy-text is N¹: *New York Journal*, Nov. 8, 1896, pp. 1–2.]

Subheadings

673.16.1 Here Come the Teams. 675.7 Princeton Scores.
674.14.1 Fate with Harvard. 675.36 Harvard in the Shadow.

No. 168. NEW INVASION OF BRITAIN

[The copy-text is N¹: *Omaha Daily Bee*, May 9, 1897, p. 20. The other texts collated are N²: *Pittsburgh Leader*, May 9, p. 22; N³: *Chicago Record*, May 8, p. 4. Since all the newspapers are of equal authority, all accidental agreements of N²⁻³ against N¹ are recorded here excepting those which have been accepted as emendations.]

678.22–23 this metropolis] London N¹
678.28 element‸] ~ , N²⁻³
679.1 Inquiry] Inquiries N²
679.4 to . . . forth] then to shine forth suddenly N³
679.6 definition . . . volition] definition, appear of its volition N¹; definition, appearance of its volution N²
679.29 "Why . . . wasn't——"] *omit* N²
679.31 bounder, . . . bounder."]

bounder." N¹; bounder, he is a bounder." N²
680.4 Still‸] ~ , N²⁻³
680.4 go,] ago‸ N¹
680.4 an entirely] entirely a N²
680.12 axe] ax N²⁻³
680.13 Damascus] Damascus blade N²
680.19 ¹usually] *omit* N¹
680.28 roués] roues N¹·³; rogues N²
680.36 afterward] afterwards N¹
680.36 the man] that man N²

Subheadings

(N¹)

679.16.1 A Qualified Definition. 680.3.1 The Meaning of It.

No. 169. LONDON IMPRESSIONS

[The copy-text is SR: *Saturday Review*, LXXXIV (July 31, Aug. 7, Aug. 14, 1897), 105–106, 132–133, 158–159. The other texts collated are TMs: typescript in the UVa.–Barrett Collection; E1: *Last Words*, Digby, Long, London, 1902, pp. 110–130. TMs and E1 are derived texts without authority.]

681.0.1 I] *omit* TMs; CHAPTER I. E1
681.22 an] a E1
681.27 have I] I have E1
682.26.1 II] [*space*] SR; CHAPTER II. TMs,E1
683.5 paving] pavings TMs
683.10 ingenious] ingenuous SR+
683.16 very] a very TMs
683.21 a] *omit* TMs,E1
683.25 I found] found TMs,E1
684.2.1 *et seq.* III] CHAPTER III. TMs,E1
684.7 such] such a E1
684.19 precaution] percaution TMs

684.28 were] was TMs
684.31 from] *omit* TMs,E1
685.1 a] *omit* TMs
685.11,23 cawn't] can't E1
685.29 phase] phrase TMs,E1
686.3 thing] things TMs,E1
686.13 cautions] caution E1
686.16 ¹a] *omit* TMs,E1
686.21 America] American TMs
686.28 into] in TMs,E1
686.32 citizens] citizen TMs,E1
687.20 Still‸] ~ , E1
687.26 afterward] afterwards TMs,E1
687.29 somewheres] somewhere E1
687.33 purposed] purpose| TMs

688.21   this] the TMs,E1
688.28   its] his TMs
688.36   altar] alter TMs
689.2   alleys] valleys E1
689.27   a view of] view TMs,E1
689.35   a hall] the hall TMs,E1
690.6   that] omit TMs,E1
690.10   toward] towards TMs,E1
690.16   principal] principle SR,
TMs(c)
690.26   street] streets TMs,E1
690.31   enabled] able E1
690.34   street] streets TMs

691.1   the sound] sound TMs,E1
691.4   I] omit TMs,E1
691.13   off-hand] off-handed
TMs,E1
691.19   the vehicles] vehicles
TMs,E1
691.30   736] 756 E1
691.31   Rights] Right TMs,E1
691.31   require] requires E1
691.38   a] omit TMs,E1
692.7   who] that TMs(c),E1
692.14   cigarettes] cigarette E1
693.1   this] the TMs,E1

No. 170. THE EUROPEAN LETTERS

[No. 2: the copy-text for 693.5–29 is MS: manuscript in Cora's hand; copy-text for 694.1–695.3 is Stephen's manuscript; copy-text for 695.4–697.27 is Cora's manuscript; 697.28–32 is completed by Stephen. All manuscripts are in the Special Collections of Columbia University Libraries. The other text collated is N[1]: *New York Press*, Aug. 15, 1897, p. 23. In numbering, all section initials and material in brackets have been ignored.]

693.8   about] omit N[1]
693.9–10   The language . . . public.] omit N[1]
693.14   He] The King N[1]
693.25   was] has MS
693.28   more than] omit N[1]
694.1   very] omit N[1]
694.17   railway] railroad N[1]
694.23–24   properly apply] apply properly N[1]
694.24   its] it's MS
694.26   exuberantly extra] extravagant N[1]
694.27   watch] a watch N[1]
694.33   wooden-pated inebriates] intelligent functionaries N[1]
695.1   in] MS *mutilated*
695.1   practically] omit N[1]
695.2   just] omit N[1]
695.3   in] just in N[1]

695.4–22   The . . . method.] omit N[1]
695.25   -looking] omit N[1]
695.26   them] it N[1]
696.7   a . . . figure] omit N[1]
696.12–35   The . . . Queen.] omit N[1]
696.29   nurse's] nurses' MS
696.30–35   The . . . Queen.] deleted in MS
697.2   gentleman] man N[1]
697.3   "Can (no ¶)] ¶ N[1]
697.4   is it] it is N[1]
697.6,7   mairred] married N[1]
697.6,7   waddin'] weddin' N[1]
697.9–32   The . . . often.] omit N[1]
697.12   Madame] Madam MS
697.17   The] The The MS

Alterations in the Manuscript

[Cora's *hand*]

693.15   ornaments] 'a' *over* 'i' *by* Crane
693.16   altogether] 'a' *deleted after first* 'e'

693.20   interest] *first* 'e' *inserted by* Crane
693.20   created] *preceded by deleted* 'was'

693.22 with] 'i' *inserted*

693.23 thoroughly] *preceded by deleted* 'through|'

693.24 conventional] *a final* 'l' *deleted*

[Stephen's *hand*]

694.2 Put] *interlined with a caret above deleted* 'Let'

694.4 Europe] *followed by a deleted period*

694.7 should] *interlined above deleted* 'can inform'

694.7 porter] *followed by deleted* 'and t' *and an almost formed* 'h'

694.8 kind.] *followed by independently deleted* 'This last has been' *and* 'In the third place'

694.11 in time] *interlined above deleted* 'at a particular'

694.16 a free] 'a' *interlined*

[Cora's *hand*]

695.6 use] *preceded by deleted* 'want to'

695.9 gently] *interlined by* Crane *above deleted* 'gentlely'

695.16 cleaning] *preceded by deleted* 'w'

695.17 It] *preceded by deleted* 'The'

695.17 can] *interlined by* Crane *above deleted* 'and'

695.18 a] *interlined with a caret by* Crane

695.18 it.] *interlined by* Crane *with a caret deleting original period*

695.19 gives] 's' *added by* Crane

695.21–22 This . . . method.] *added by* Crane

695.23 who] *preceded by deleted* 'yo'

695.25 grimy] MS 'grimey' *interlined by* Crane *above deleted* 'grimmy'

695.25 great] *followed by deleted* 'and old'

695.26 public] 'c' *over* 'ce'

693.27 Crown] 'C' *over* 'c'

693.29 English] *preceded by deleted* 'other' *and followed by* 'boys' *interlined by* Crane *above deleted* 'lads'

694.17 because] *interlined above deleted* 'through'

694.23 could] *preceded by deleted* 'was'

694.24 apply] *preceded by deleted* 'reply'

694.30 was] *over* 'were'

694.33 these] *first* 'e' *over* 'i'; *second* 'e' *added later*

695.1 was practically] *interlined above deleted* 'appeared to be'

695.2 technical] *interlined*

695.2 appeared] *followed by deleted period*

695.2 him] *interlined*

695.27 They] *interlined with a caret, perhaps by* Crane, *above deleted* 'Those' *preceded by deleted* 'H'

695.29 behind.] *interlined by* Crane *above deleted* 'outside.'

695.29 hum] *interlined above deleted* 'rum'

695.30 London.] *period added before deleted* 'town.'

696.1 interrupted] MS 'inte-rupted' *preceded by deleted* 'nt'

696.5 Then] *followed by deleted doubtful* 'these' *or possibly* 'the'

696.6 watermen,] *first* 'e' *over repeated* 't'; *followed by deleted* 'with'

696.8 this lake] 'this' *over* 'lake'

696.9 mound,] *followed by deleted* 'up wh'

696.12 out] *preceded by false-start* 'ot'

696.15 also] *interlined with a caret by* Crane

696.17 jewels.] *period over comma or semicolon*

696.20–21 dressed in black and white silk,] *interlined with a caret above deleted* ', looking the charming old lady she is'

696.21 drinking] 'ing' *added by* Crane

696.22 chatting] *followed by deleted* 'brightly'

696.22 those] 'ose' *over* 'em'

696.23 Much] *preceded by deleted* 'Grea'

696.25 on] *preceded by deleted* 'of'

696.28 little] *interlined with a caret*

696.28 looked] 'ed' *added by* Crane

696.30–35 The . . . Queen.] *deleted in MS*

696.31 board] 'r' *over* 'd'

696.34–35 with soda water] *interlined with a caret*

697.2 says] *preceded by deleted* 'said'

697.3 two] 'w' *over* 'o'

697.4 wumman] *preceded by deleted* 'wum< >|'

697.5 "Weel] *preceded by paragraph sign*

697.6,7 mairred] *altered from* 'married'

697.9 of Paris] *interlined with a caret by* Crane

697.12 , Madame Virot,] *interlined with a caret*

697.14 newspapers] 's' *added by* Crane

697.14 heralding] 'r' *over* 'a'

697.16 are] *interlined with a caret by* Crane

697.16 to] *interlined with a caret by* Crane *above deleted* 'the'

697.17 ¹The] 'T' *over* 't' *preceded by undeleted* 'The' *and deleted* 'Right Honerable'

697.18 been] *followed by deleted* 'over'

697.19 was] *interlined with a caret above deleted* 'is'

697.21 at] 't' *over* 's'

697.21 The] 'T' *over* 't' *by* Crane *and preceding period over comma*

697.23 models] *interlined by* Crane, *with its following period deleted and comma added, above deleted* 'moddles.'

697.25 models] *interlined by* Crane *above deleted* 'moddles'

697.25 fabulous] *interlined by* Crane *above deleted* 'fabolous'

697.25 women] *interlined by* Crane *above deleted* 'ladies'

697.28–32 Nevertheless . . . often.] *added by* Crane

[No. 3: the copy-text is MS: manuscript in Cora's hand in the Special Collections of Columbia University Libraries. The other text collated is N¹: *New York Press*, Aug. 22, 1897, p. 23.]

698.5 the] *omit* N¹

698.5–7 I have . . . that that] it is understood that the N¹

698.7 donated] gave N¹

698.9 traditionary gift] tradition N¹

698.11 tradition] legend N¹

698.12 holy spot] racing holy of holies N¹

698.14 this] the N¹

698.25 perceive] see N¹

698.27 around] about N¹

698.29 it.] it accordingly. N¹

698.30 where] were MS

699.5–7 crowd . . . The] *omit* N¹

699.9 racegoer] goer MS

699.12 cry] cries N¹

699.13–26 It . . . world.] *omit* N¹

699.30 host's] hosts MS

699.32–700.2 It . . . family.] *omit* N¹

700.3–4 called . . . fact] been muttering N¹

700.10–14 This . . . that] *omit* N¹

700.22 very] *omit* N¹

700.27   who] *omit* N[1]
701.6–15   The . . . people.]
  omit N[1]

Alterations in the Manuscript

[Cora's *hand with her alterations*]

698.2   slopes] *interlined above deleted* 'levels'
698.3   on] *interlined above deleted* 'among'
698.4   He] *preceded by deleted* 'I have an impression that when the Richmond family'
698.8   present] *interlined with a caret*
698.9   a] *interlined with a caret*
698.12   ²to] *written over doubtful* 'as'
698.13–14   pilgrimages] 'es' *over doubtful* 's'
698.23   This] *altered from* 'The'
698.33   other . . . from] *interlined with a caret*
698.36   The] *originally* 'This' *with* 's' *and dot of* 'i' *deleted*
699.4   distance] *followed by deleted* 'to London is'
699.11   bettor's] MS 'bettors' *with* 'r' *over doubtful* 'u' *preceded by deleted* 'reason'
699.12   beseeching] 's' *over* 'c' *and upstroke of* 'h'
699.21   other] *final* 's' *deleted*
699.21–22   wonders] 's' *added later*
699.23   spends] *interlined above deleted* 'loses'
699.29   was served] *interlined with a caret above deleted* 'at'
699.33   House] 'H' *over* 'h'
699.36   for] *preceded by deleted* 'of one'
700.1   This] 'T' *altered from* 't'

702.2   very] *omit* N[1]
702.5–8   It . . . judgement.]
  omit N[1]

700.29   The] 'T' *altered from* 't'
700.29   "Aye] 'A' *over* 'I'
700.30   makes] 's' *added later*
700.30   them?] *question mark altered from exclamation point*
701.4–5   Yachting] 'a' *over* 'c'
701.7   in] *crowded in later*
701.10   particular] *interlined with a caret above deleted* 'any'
701.12   the second] *preceded by deleted* 'after that'; 'second' *interlined with a caret above deleted* 'other'
701.13   Of] 'O' *over* 'o'; *preceding period altered from a comma*
701.16   Goelet's] *first* 'e' *over* 'l'
701.19   causes] 'a' *over* 'r' *and* 's' *over* 'd'
701.20   manufacture] *second* 'u' *over* 'o'
701.23   amazes] 'z' *over* 's'
701.26   all. They] *period added and* 'T' *over* 't'
701.28   Zoological] 'Z' *over* 'z'
701.30   prize] 'i' *inserted*
701.30   an altogether] 'an' *interlined with a caret*; 'a' *after first* 'e' *deleted*
702.9   Augusta] MS 'Auguste' *preceded by deleted* 'Agust Auggu'
702.12   simply] *interlined above deleted* 'had only to'
702.14   ogre] 're' *over* 'er'
702.17   if] *added later*
702.18   And] 'A' *over* 'a'

[No. 4: the copy-text is MS: manuscript in Cora's hand in the Special Collections of Columbia University Libraries. The other text collated is N[1]: *New York Press*, Aug. 29, 1897, p. 21.]

702.23   trampling] tramping N[1]
702.27   phenomenon] phenomena MS

702.32   occupants] occupant MS
702.35   now] *omit* N[1]
703.11   quite] *omit* N[1]

703.11 The (*no ¶*)] ¶ N[1]
703.12 idiotic] *omit* N[1]
703.12 describe always] always describe N[1]
703.13 supposed] *omit* N[1]
703.19–21 This . . . But] *omit* N[1]
703.19 if] *omit* MS
703.22 least] last MS
703.26–29 Now . . . Americans.] *omit* N[1]
704.8 that] *omit* N[1]
704.18 stock] poetical stock N[1]

704.18 of . . . poets] *omit* N[1]
704.24 Parisiennes] Parisians MS
704.26–709.19 It . . . difficulty.] *omit* N[1]
705.11 ruler's] rulers MS
707.34 weeks] week MS
709.4 ever] every MS
709.4 God's] God MS
709.5 and] as MS
709.8 wear] were MS
709.9 belles] bells MS

Alterations in the Manuscript

[Cora's *hand with her own and* Stephen's *alterations*]

702.23 subtraction] *preceded by deleted* 'dim'
702.24 meant] *interlined by* Crane *over deleted* 'ment'
702.25 gone away from] *interlined with a caret by* Crane *above deleted* 'left'
702.25 While] 'W' *over* 'w'
702.28 observable] *preceded by deleted* 'pe'
702.28 New] 'N' *over* 'n'
702.29 does not] *interlined with a caret by* Crane *above deleted* 'dont'
702.33–34 performance] 'per' *over* 'pro'
703.2 at this] 'this' *interlined above deleted* 'durin' *and then preceded by* Crane's 'at'
703.2 conscience] *interlined by* Crane *above deleted* 'conscious'
703.3 elite.] *added by* Crane *after deleted* 'ellete' *in space left by* Cora *before start of next sentence*
703.7 reputation] *followed by deleted* 'of how dull'
703.11 grows] 'r' *over doubtful* 'o'
703.12 idiotic] *second* 'i' *over doubtful* 'e'
703.12 describe] *first* 'e' *over* 'i'
703.15 convey] *preceded by deleted* 'are' *and followed by* 'an' *with* 'n' *deleted*

703.16 unconsciously] *interlined with a caret by* Crane *over deleted doubtful* 'unceously'
703.17 semi] 'i' *and a deleting stroke correcting* 'semmi'
703.17 -instinctive] *no hyphen in* MS *and* 'c' *squeezed in later*
703.19 this] *interlined by* Crane *above deleted* 'they are a'
703.20 had] *added by* Crane *after deleted* 'and if they'
703.23 English] *interlined by* Crane *with a caret*
703.23 any] 'an' *over* 'con'
703.26 Now] *preceded by deleted* 'At this'
703.28 trail] *interlined above deleted* 'and'
703.28 this] *altered from* 'the'
703.33–704.1 public] *interlined with a caret*
704.1 food] *preceded by deleted* 'their'; 'fo' *over* 'r' *and start of another letter*
704.4 one] *preceded by deleted* '£'
704.20 English] *interlined with a caret*
704.21 Englishman] 'a' *over* 'e'
704.21 to] *followed by deleted doubtful* 'a'
704.26 remains] 's' *over* 'es'
704.28 apoplexy] MS 'appolexy' *with* 'y' *over* 'ity'

704.29 change.] *followed by deleted* 'Meanwhile'

704.34 in] *interlined by* Crane *above deleted* 'about'

704.34 here] *interlined by* Crane *above deleted* 'in Europe'

705.1 Sick Man] 'S' *over* 's'; 'M' *over* 'm'

705.10 fez] 'z' *over* 's'

705.15 it.] *interlined by* Crane *above deleted* 'the Harem'

705.16 . It] 'I' *over* 's'; *period inserted*

705.20 his] 'h' *over* 't'

705.26 Speaking] 'S' *over* 's'

705.27 were] *interlined above deleted* 'was'

705.30 under-handed] *interlined by* Crane *with a caret*

705.31 the women] 'the' *interlined with a caret above deleted* 'his'

705.32 change] *preceded by deleted* 'other'

705.34 also] *interlined by* Crane *with a caret above deleted* 'at all events'

705.35 of the other sex] *interlined by* Crane *with a caret*

705.37 Harem] 'm' *over* 'ms'

705.37 a] *interlined by* Crane *with a caret above deleted* 'some two'

705.39 wives] *interlined with a caret above deleted* 'wifes'

706.2 six] *followed by deleted* 'women'

706.2 members.] *period inserted and following* 'of the Harem.' *deleted*

706.6 Western] *preceded by deleted* 'towering'

706.7 one after another of the] *interlined by* Crane *above deleted* 'one'

706.7 -dresses] 'es' *added*

706.8 pearls] *followed by deleted* 'after another'

706.9 modern] *preceded by deleted* 'wra'

706.11 silk. The] 'T' *over* 't' *and*

period altered from comma

706.13 pompoms] *interlined by* Crane *above deleted* 'a ponpon'

706.13 them.] *follows deleted* 'it.'

706.14 house] *interlined with a caret*

706.19 muslin] *preceded by deleted* 'white'

706.26 Hers] *interlined with a caret above deleted* 'This'

706.27 gorgeous] MS 'goreous' *with first* 'o' *over* 'eo'

706.28 The] *preceded by paragraph symbol*

706.29 latticed] 'i' *over* 'e'

706.30 Persian and Turkish] 'P' *over* 'p'; 'T' *over* 't'

706.32 cushions] 'h' *over* 's'

706.33 At] 'A' *over* 'a'; *preceded by deleted* 'at'

706.33 ebony] *preceded by deleted* 'in'

706.35 Swiss] 'S' *over* 's'

706.37 incessantly.] *period above deleted period and followed by deleted* 'and of attar of roses.' *in which* 'of' *was interlined with a caret*

706.38 priceless] *preceded by deleted* 'tiny' *which is interlined with a caret*

706.38 rested] 'ed' *over* 'in'

707.1 served] 'd' *over* 'r'

707.5 tourist.] *a final* 's' *deleted*

707.5–6 nuisances] *followed by deleted* 'which'

707.9 Their] 'ir' *over* 're'

707.10 veiled] *first* 'e' *over* 'a'

707.10 visits] 's' *over doubtful* 'in'

707.10 Bazaar] 'z' *over doubtful* 'as'

707.12 some] *preceded by deleted* 'Sund'

707.13 excursions] *interlined above deleted* 'visits'

707.16 ¹a] *interlined with a caret*

707.17 existence] *second* 'e' *over* 'a'

707.17   seem to] *interlined with a caret*

707.21   gets . . . few] *interlined above deleted* 'lets his'

707.21   cousins] *preceding* 'his' *deleted*

707.22   aunts] *preceding* 'his' *deleted; followed by deleted* 'nor their own com'

707.22   Heaven] 'H' *over* 'h'

707.24   It is the] 'It is' *crowded in; 't' of* 'the' *over* 'T'

707.26   by] *preceded by deleted* 'by'

707.27   discovered] *preceded by deleted* 'is of'

707.31   pitch] *preceded by deleted* 'boiling'

707.35   recognized] 'z' *over* 's'

708.3   succumbed] MS 'seccumbed' *with first* 'c' *inserted*

708.7   which] *interlined above deleted* 'whom'

708.8   ²he] *preceded by deleted* 'the'

708.10   northern] *preceded by deleted* 'north of Ireland towns'

708.14   turbulent] *first* 't' *over* 's'; *preceded by deleted* 'turburlen'

708.15   is] *interlined with a caret*

708.19   Americans] *final* 's' *added; followed by deleted* 'wo'

708.24   Bruges] *preceded by paragraph symbol*

708.24   Flanders] 'F' *over* 'f'

708.25   as] MS 'as is as' *with* 's' *over* 't' *of second* 'as'

708.25   one] *interlined with a caret*

708.28   one meets] *interlined*

709.2   ambition, do] ', do' *inserted with* 'do' *over an original comma*

709.3   despot] 's' *inserted*

709.3   ²the] 'e' *over* 'is'

709.7   Theatre] MS 'theatre' *with second* 't' *over* 'r'

709.8   costumes] 's' *added*

709.9   dress] *followed by deleted* 'ball'

709.10   a] *interlined above deleted* 'some'

709.12   on] *preceded by deleted* 'of'

709.15   a wholesale] *final* 'n' *of* 'an' *deleted;* 'wholesale' *interlined with a caret*

709.18   obtained] *preceded by deleted* 'arrang'

[No. 8: the copy-text is MS: manuscript in Cora's hand in the Special Collections of Columbia University Libraries. The other text collated is N¹: *New York Press*, Sept. 26, 1897, p. 23.]

710.7,23   season's] seasons MS

710.10   fifty guineas or] *omit* N¹

710.18   affect] effect MS,N¹

710.18   both] heather N¹

710.19   Scotchman] Scotchmen MS

710.19   doesn't] does not MS

710.24   The (*no* ¶)] ¶ N¹

710.24   very] *omit* N¹

710.29–32   But . . . Scotland.] *omit* N¹

710.33–711.8   The . . . Paris.] Mr. Harold . . . title. N¹ (*see* 711.9–19)

710.34   15] 13 N¹

710.35   and] an MS

710.35   unkempt] unkept MS

711.9–19   Mr. Harold . . . title.] The . . . Paris. N¹ (*see* 710.33–711.8)

711.20–28   Queen . . . candies.] *omit* N¹

712.1–13   A . . . generally.] N¹ *prints after* 714.32 *to end the article*

712.6   ¶ He] *no* ¶ N¹

712.18   researches] researchers MS

712.20   those of] *omit* MS

712.24   Geiza] Geiga N¹

712.25   Zapolya] Gapolya N¹

712.26   Each (*no* ¶)] ¶ N¹

712.34 Bishop's] Bishops MS

713.2 Stephen's] Stephens MS

713.11 *et seq.* Oberammergau] Ammergau MS,N[1]

713.16 Oberammergauans] Ammergauns MS; Ammergauans N[1]

713.16 to] of MS(u),N[1]

713.23 visitors'] visitor's MS

713.23 has] only has N[1]

713.24–25 and . . . quiet] *omit* N[1]

713.28–30 Also . . . beautiful.]
omit N[1]

714.1 Ludwig (*no* ¶)] ¶ N[1]

714.5 too] to MS

714.6 landscaper's] landscape gardener's N[1]

714.8 At (*no* ¶)] ¶ N[1]

714.13 exquisite] the exquisite MS(u),N[1]

714.23 be] *omit* N[1]

714.33–715.20 The . . . presence] *omit* N[1]

715.5 centimes] centime MS

715.19 is] *omit* MS

Alterations in the Manuscript

[Cora's *hand with her own and* Stephen's *alterations*]

709.22 always] *preceded by deleted* 'd'

709.25 invariably] *preceded by deleted* 'also'

709.27 water] *a second* 't' *deleted*

709.27 witnessing] *preceded by deleted* 'witt'

709.27 hunt] *interlined by* Crane *above deleted* 'hunt'

709.28 Pennsylvania] 'sylvania' *inserted by* Crane *after* MS 'Penn.' *deleting the period*

709.30 maybe] MS 'may-be' *with* 'y' *over* 'b'

710.6 frightful] 'ful' *by* Crane *over* 'ing'

710.7 ten] *preceded by deleted* 'three'

710.9 Scottish] *preceded by deleted* 'Scotchi'

710.9 Laird] 'r' *interlined with a caret by* Crane

710.9 An] *written by* Crane *over* 'The'

710.9 income] *final* 's' *deleted by* Crane

710.9 one] *interlined by* Crane *above deleted* 'some'

710.9 amounts] 's' *mended by* Crane

710.10 guineas] 'ea' *over* 'ae'

710.10 day] *following period deleted*

710.12 the season] *independently interlined with carets above deleted* 'a winter'; 't' *of* 'the' *over* 'h'

710.13 his] *preceded by deleted* 'this'

710.14 Scotland] *interlined by* Crane *above deleted* 'London'

710.17 rods and gun cases] *altered from* 'rod—gun case'

710.19 wily Scotchman] *preceded by deleted* 'w'; MS 'Scotchmen' *with* 'S' *over* 's'

710.21 seven] *preceded by deleted* '7'

710.22 his] *altered from* 'this'

710.23 season's] MS 'seasons' *interlined with a caret*

710.25 and] 'd' *over* 'f'

710.32 forests] MS 'forrests' *with* 't' *inserted*

710.33 [1]francs] 's' *added*

710.35 or] *preceded by deleted* 'for'

711.6 proprietor] *preceded by deleted* 'lat'

711.8 with] *interlined with a caret above deleted* 'which'

711.10 prefer] Crane *added an* 'r' *to make clear an imperfectly formed* 'er' *in* Cora's 'prefer'

711.11 new] *preceded by deleted* 'b' *or possibly* 'l'

711.12 departed] *followed by de-*

leted 'entirely'

711.15 England] *followed by deleted period*

711.17 other] *interlined with a caret*

711.17 in] 'n' *altered from* 's'

711.22 purchase] *final* 'e' *added by* Crane

711.24 candies] *followed by a deleted period*

711.27 many] *interlined with a caret*

711.28 brother] *preceded by deleted* 'brother'

712.1 to the] *interlined above deleted* 'an order'

712.3–4 the conduct of] *interlined with a caret*

712.6 riotous] 'io' *over* 'oi'

712.10 where] 'h' *interlined with a caret; preceded by deleted period and* 'He brawls'

712.11 nightly] *interlined above deleted* 'frequent'

712.11 conduct hardly befits] *interlined separately over separately deleted* 'is scarcely befitting'

712.12 are] *interlined above deleted* 'and'

712.13 ¹in] 'n' *altered from* 's'

712.13 ²in] *inserted later*

712.14 as] *interlined with a caret*

712.16 plundered] *preceded by deleted* 'robe'

712.18 Turks] *followed by deleted* 'in 1869'

712.26 Pasha.] *period over semicolon*

712.28 stone] *preceded by deleted* 'a'

712.31 loft] *preceded by deleted* 'lof'

712.34 sure] *interlined by* Crane *above deleted* 'suree'

712.35 garden, the] MS 'garden. The' *with period altered from a comma*

713.3 with] *preceded by deleted* 'acco'

713.6 was also] *interlined with a caret*

713.7 the] *over* 'a'

713.9 and] 'nd' *over* 'n'

713.10 Royal] *preceded by deleted* 'skulls'

713.11 petitioned] *first* 'e' *over* 'i'

713.15 portrayal] *interlined by* Crane *above* 'portrayal' *altered from* 'portraial'

713.16 altogether] 'a' *deleted after first* 'e'

713.16 to] *interlined by* Crane *above deleted* 'of'

713.17 tourist's] *interlined by* Crane *above deleted* 'turists'

713.19 elusive] 'l' *deleted before* 'l'

713.20 petition] 'e' *over* 'i'

713.26 Pilate] *interlined by* Crane *above deleted* 'Pillate'

714.4 Lindenhof] *final* 'f' *deleted*

714.13 make] *followed by deleted* 'the'

714.16 dodges] *second* 'd' *inserted by* Crane

714.16 Lohengrin] 'h' *over doubtful* 'u'

714.16–17 navigate] 'i' *inserted*

714.18 triumphantly] 'u' *altered from* 'h'; 'ly' *over* 'y'

714.19 attendants] *second* 'a' *over* 'e'

714.19 in] *over* 'as'

714.21 enthusiasm] MS 'enthusism' *with second* 's' *over possible* 'is'

714.22 is] *inserted*

714.23 for instance] *interlined with a caret*

714.24 -a-] 'a' *over* 'e'

714.24 with] *interlined by* Crane *above deleted* 'which'

714.25 Napoleon] *second* 'o' *over* 'a'

714.26 gorgeous] *first* 'o' *over* 'eo'

714.26 suicide] *preceded by deleted possible* 'suicide'

714.26 left] *preceded by deleted* 'at least'

714.29 spectacle of his] MS 'specticle' *or* 'spectecle' *with* 'le' *over* 'al'; 'his' *altered from* 'this'

714.33   ²in] *crowded in after deleted* 'at'

714.34   There] *preceded by deleted* 'It'

714.34   in] 'n' *altered from* 's'

714.34   it] 't' *over* 'n'; *followed by deleted* 'which it'

714.35   serving] *preceded by deleted* 'f'

715.2   The investment of] *interlined with a caret*

715.2   franc] *followed by deleted* 'in the slot' *which had been interlined with a caret*

715.3   sight] *preceded by deleted* 'ap'

715.3   pint] *preceded by deleted* 'hal'

715.3   Half] 'H' *over* 'h'

715.4   ten] *preceded by deleted* 'a nickle of'

715.6   ten] *interlined above deleted* 'nickle'

715.7   centimes] 's' *added*

715.7   a] *interlined above deleted* 'an excellent'

715.8   vessels] MS 'Vessels' *preceded by deleted* 'Vessel' *and a high upstroke*

715.9   automatic] *preceded by deleted* 'method'

715.12   almost] *interlined with a caret*

715.15   a] *final* 'n' *deleted*

715.20   presence] *followed by deleted* 'and a perfect gown'

[No. 9: the copy-text is MS: manuscript in Cora's hand in the Special Collections of Columbia University Libraries.]

Alterations in the Manuscript

[*Alterations in both* Cora's *and* Stephen's *hands*]

715.21   a stranger] 'a' *interlined with a caret; final* 's' *of* 'stranger' *deleted*

715.22   professional] *preceded by deleted* 'nurse'

715.23   and] *interlined above deleted* 'with the'

715.23   trimmed] *followed by deleted* 'only'

715.24   and] *interlined above deleted* 'the'

715.24   which tie] *interlined above deleted* 'tieing'

715.28   rather] *interlined with a caret and written over illegible word*

715.29   profession] 'f' *deleted before* 'f'

716.1   of] 'o' *over* 't'

716.5   becomes] 's' *added*

716.13,17   Cross] MS 'cross' *interlined above deleted cross sign*

716.17   attribute] *preceded by deleted* 'attrib'

716.19   wounded] *second* 'd' *over possible* 's'

716.20   In] *preceded by deleted* 'It'

716.23   fro] *an illegible final letter deleted from* 'fro'; *word followed by deleted* 'wh'

716.24   combatants] MS 'combatance' *with second* 'c' *over* 's'

716.24   would] *preceded by deleted* 'who'

716.25   absurd] *preceded by deleted* 'abs' *in which* 'b' *over* 's'

716.35   extraordinary] MS 'exterordinary' *with* 'inary' *over* 'enry'

716.36   divisions] MS 'devisions' *with* 's' *added*

717.4   wish] *preceded by deleted* 'attempt'

717.13   but] 'u' *over* 'y'

717.16   it] *final* 's' *deleted*

717.18   also] *preceded by deleted* 'the'

717.20   The] *division marks and word count in line above have been deleted*

717.23   cycling] *interlined above deleted* 'bycicling'

717.26 dress] *followed by a deleted period*

717.26–27 wheelwomen] *preceded by deleted* 'b'

717.32 as] *preceded by deleted* 'that'

717.32 with] *preceded by deleted* 'wh'

718.1 at] 'a' *over* 'o'

718.4 anything] *followed by deleted* 'astounding'

718.6 aimed] 'e' *over* 's'

718.7 dress] 'd' *over* 'r'

718.8 supreme.] *a final* 'e' *deleted before period written*

718.10 House] 'H' *over* 'h'

718.10 Denmark] *preceded by deleted* 'Copenhagen'

718.13 Court] 'C' *over* 'c'

718.13 ²in] *interlined above deleted* 'in'

718.13 Europe.] *followed by deleted* 'It'

718.16 Consequently] *interlined above deleted* 'an'; 't' *of following* 'the' *over* 'T'

718.20 in Danish] *interlined with a caret*

718.21 Amalienborg] 'a' *over* 'e'

718.22 on] *over* 'ov'

718.28 his] 't' *deleted before* 'h'

718.30 Princes] MS 'Prices' *with* 'P' *over* 'p'; 'e' *over doubtful* 'i'

718.30 much] *interlined above deleted* 'more'

718.30 from] *deleted and* 'in' *interlined with a caret but then deleted and* 'from' *interlined*

718.30 Palace] 'P' *over* 'p'

718.31 King] *preceded by deleted* 'King |' *with* 'K' *over* 'k'

719.4 young] *interlined above deleted* 'little'

719.5 often] *preceded by deleted* 'in'

719.9 now] *interlined with a caret*

719.9 enjoys] MS 'enjoyes' *with* 'es' *added*

719.11,16 Wood] *final* 's' *deleted*

719.16 House] 'H' *over* 'h'

719.17 that] *interlined with a caret*

719.17 vertu] *preceded by deleted* 'vertu' *in which* 'r' *is inserted*

719.18 of] *preceded by deleted* 'to have a whack'

719.19 Japan] *preceded by deleted* 'the'

719.21 palaces] *preceded by deleted* 'imperial'

719.22 Mikado] *preceded by deleted* 'Mik' *of which* 'i' *over* 'a'

719.31 a] *preceded by deleted double quotes*

720.2 woman] *followed by deleted* 'first'

720.6 as] *preceded by deleted* 'in'

720.6 in the Bois] MS 'in the bois' *interlined*

720.7 who] *followed by deleted* 'and'

720.9 Chicago] MS 'Chiacago' *with* 'ca' *over illegible letters*

720.9 her] *preceded by deleted* 'the'

720.16 Egypt] *preceded by deleted* 'Ed'; *followed by deleted* 'of'

720.16 And] 'A' *over* 'a'

720.18 have] *interlined above deleted* 'share'

720.20 ¹the] *interlined above deleted* 'his'

720.20 which] *preceded by deleted* 'on'

720.20 his] 's' *over* 'm'

720.21 statues] *first* 't' *inserted*

720.21 representing] *interlined with a caret after deleted* 'of'

720.22 and which] 'and' *interlined with a caret*

720.24 have] *followed by deleted* 'had'

720.24 Was] *preceded by deleted doubtful* 'w'

720.26 Barnato's] MS 'Barnotos' *with first* 'o' *over* 'a'

720.26 for] *followed by deleted* 'it'

720.30 custom] MS 'costom' *al-*

tered from 'costume'

720.32 throw] *preceded by deleted* 'blind a' *with the start of an upstroke after* 'a'

720.33 tax] *preceded by deleted* 'rev'

720.34 stated] *followed by deleted* 'that'

720.35 when] *preceded by deleted* 'th'

721.1 Barnato] MS 'Barnoto' *with first* 'o' *over* 'a'

721.2 wishes] 'hes' *over possible* 'es'

721.3 therefore] *second* 'e' *inserted*

721.4 £16300. in] *interlined with a guideline above deleted* 'the following'

721.4 £250.] '£' *inserted later*

721.4 £3000] *interlined above deleted* '£5000', *the* '5' *perhaps over an illegible number*

721.6 they] *interlined above deleted* 'it'

721.6 have] 've' *over* 's'

721.7 the facts] *preceded by deleted* 'a are but a' *the first* 'a' *independently deleted*

721.8 story] 'y' *over* 'ie'

721.10 starting for] *interlined*

above deleted 'on her way'

721.10 ²the] 'he' *over* 'o'

721.11 stops] *preceded by deleted* 'is solemnly'

721.14 always] *interlined with a caret*

721.17 unused] *interlined above deleted* 'untouched'

721.18 kerchief] *preceded by deleted* 'han'

721.22 so] *inserted later*

721.24 she could use the] *interlined above deleted* 'there was a'

721.24 piano] *followed by deleted* 'in'

721.25 by] *followed by deleted* 'the'

721.26 that] 'at' *over* 'ey'

721.26 of] *inserted later*

721.29 music] *followed by deleted* 'can be heard'

721.33 light] 'g' *over* 't'

722.2 pairs] 's' *added later*

722.2 bicycles] *preceded by deleted* 'a'; 's' *added*

722.4 sombre] *preceded by deleted* 'black'

722.4 nuns] *interlined above deleted* 'women'

722.4 black] 'b' *over* 'v'

[No. 10: the copy-text is MS: manuscript in Cora's hand in the Special Collections of Columbia University Libraries. The other text collated is N¹: *New York Press*, Oct. 10, 1897, p. 18.]

722.9 in] and N¹
722.12 It (*no* ¶)] ¶ N¹
722.17 estate] estates MS
722.19 One (*no* ¶)] ¶ N¹
722.21 of the family] *omit* MS
723.3 Victoria's] Victorias MS
723.14 However (*no* ¶)] ¶ N¹
724.4 phrases] phrase N¹
724.5–31 If . . . it.] *omit* N¹
724.6,7 Ladies'] Ladies‸ MS
724.29 Beresford's] Beresford'

MS

724.33 are] were N¹
725.9 list] host N¹
725.15 recently] when MS; once N¹
725.24 It is said that his] His MS
725.24 woman] women MS
726.9 In (*no* ¶)] ¶ N¹
726.16 one's] ones MS
726.18 father's] fathers MS
726.18 pence] penny N¹

Alterations in the Manuscript

[Cora's *hand with her own and* Stephen's *alterations*]

722.7 Duchess] MS 'Dutchess' *with final* 's' *added*

722.12 about] *interlined with a caret*

722.20 back] *final 's' deleted*
722.25 Kenmare] *interlined with a caret*
722.25–26 it looks] *'it' followed by deleted 'does not'; 's' of 'looks' added later*
722.28 Peerage] *'P' over 'p'*
722.28 dated] *second 'd' over 's'*
722.30 became] *'c' over 'g'*
723.21 and] *interlined above deleted 'but'*
723.25 no] *final 't' deleted*
723.31 has] *'s' over 'v'*
723.31 Shakespeare's] MS *'Shakespears' with 'S' over 's'*
723.32 heroines] *altered from doubtful 'heroins'*
724.1 referred] *preceded by deleted 'sp'*
724.4 phrases] *'hr' over 'ra'*
724.9 Ghost] *following double quotes deleted*
724.10 deeply.] *following double quotes deleted*
724.12 Seraph] *'S' over 's'*
724.17 almost] *preceded by deleted 'f'*
724.17 unborn] *interlined by Crane above deleted 'unborne'*
724.18,21 She] *'S' over 's'*
724.21 kits] *preceded by deleted 'handsome'*

724.24 quite] *'q' over 'g'*
724.26 birth] *preceded by deleted 'brith' of which 'i' is inserted*
724.27 kind:] *colon over comma*
724.29 Julu] *'J' over 'j'*
725.9 Rosebery] *first 'e' inserted*
725.11 with] *followed by deleted 'ab'*
725.11 a large] *preceded by deleted 'al'*
725.13 ²and] *interlined with a caret which deletes an ampersand*
725.15 Egmont] *preceded by deleted 'Edgm'*
725.18 solemn] MS 'soloemn' *altered from 'solomen'*
725.21 witch] *'i' inserted*
725.22 water"] *preceded by deleted 'watter" '*
725.25 South] *'S' over 's'*
725.27 Britain] MS 'Brittian' *with second 't' deleted*
725.30 Great] *'G' over 'g'*
726.5 ladies] *'s' added*
726.10 press] *preceded by deleted 'Press' of which 'P' over 'p'*
726.11 entirely] *preceded by deleted 'thr'*
726.14 this] *preceded by deleted 'she'*
726.18 at] *interlined with a caret*

[Unplaced: the copy-text is MS: manuscript in Stephen's hand in the Special Collections of Columbia University Libraries.]

726.21 in] *followed by deleted 'driving'*
726.23 members] *preceded by deleted 'a'*

726.24 left] *interlined with a caret above deleted 'right'*
726.27 is] *interlined with a caret*
726.28 A] *interlined with a caret above deleted 'The'*

No. 171. HOW THE AFRIDIS MADE A ZIARAT

[The copy-text is N¹: *New York Press*, Sept. 19, 1897, p. 23.]

Subheadings

727.16.1 Their Greatest Weakness.

727.28.1 How to Get a Saint.
728.6.1 How They Were Muzzled.

No. 175. THE SCOTCH EXPRESS

[The copy-text is MS: the untitled manuscript in the Special Collections of Columbia University Libraries. The other texts collated are Cs: *Cassell's*

Magazine, n.s., XVIII (Jan., 1899), 163–171; McC: *McClure's Magazine*, XII (Jan., 1899), 273–283. McC is a derived text without authority.]

739.23   This] The Cs,McC
739.25   ¶ In] *no* ¶ Cs,McC
739.30–740.9   The . . . mountains.] *omit* Cs
739.32   baggage] luggage McC
740.1   an important] a MS
740.6   in] within McC
740.11   bowl] bowled MS
740.19 *et seq.*   its] it's MS (*except at* 741.29)
740.34   Napoleon's] Napoleon MS
740.35   bins] "bins" Cs
740.39   monster] "flier" Cs,McC
741.8   ¶ In] *no* ¶ Cs,McC
741.8   meantime] interval Cs, McC
741.9–10   signal house] house Cs, McC
741.13   than] that MS
741.25–26   North Western] Northwestern MS,McC
741.27   sweep] swept Cs
741.33   long] *omit* Cs,McC
741.39   into] in Cs,McC
742.2   gait of turtles] pace of mice MS
742.4   respectfully] respectful McC
742.11   the grouse,] *interlined in pencil by* Cora *in* MS
742.12   the romantic] a romantic Cs,McC
742.30   doubtlessly] doubtless Cs,McC
743.19   bolt] boat MS
743.24   was] were Cs,McC
744.3   that] who Cs,McC
744.10   tens upon] ten upon MS
744.12   owns] traverses Cs
744.25   that] by which McC
744.27–745.2   Of . . . conscience.] *omit* Cs
744.29   vale] vane MS (*preceded by* Cora's *pencil cross*)
744.35   ²an] *omit* McC
744.39   later] latter MS
744.39   becomes] became MS
745.4   is] are Cs

745.18   the station] a station Cs, McC
745.23   was] were Cs,McC
746.10   toward] towards MS
746.21   speculated] wondered MS (*marked by* Cora's *pencil cross*)
746.28   do] *omit* MS
746.34   this] the Cs,McC
746.39   principal] principle MS
747.7   This] The Cs,McC
747.8   ²is] are McC
747.9   An] A MS
747.9   an hour,] *omit* MS
747.10   drag] bring MS
747.14   the train] train MS
747.16   dove] drove Cs
747.17   habitant with] inhabited by Cs,McC
747.19   a vast] vast MS
747.30   It was] *omit* Cs
747.31   ¹that] *omit* Cs
747.31   his] one's Cs
748.19   an] *omit* Cs
748.23   longest] long Cs,McC
748.28   swung] *omit* MS
748.28   ²at] on Cs,McC
748.30   the moment] moment MS
748.30–31   to particularly] particularly to Cs,McC
748.34   regulation] regulations MS
748.39   larder] the larder Cs,McC
749.3,8   menu] *menu* Cs
749.6   by] *omit* MS
749.6   London] a London MS
749.12   populace] public Cs,McC
749.13   as] *omit* Cs,McC
749.16   define] mean MS
749.18   the little] little Cs,McC
749.22–23   in this case carry] attract Cs,McC
749.23   are] is Cs
749.27   this] the Cs,McC
749.29   as] is MS
749.31   also rang] rang also rang MS
750.1   baggage] luggage- Cs,McC
750.10   be] are Cs,McC

750.21 then] then|then MS
750.23 one could see] could be seen Cs,McC
751.1 reaching] retching Cs

751.9 forty- . . . -third] 49⅓ MS
751.19–22 As . . . heard.] *omit* McC

Alterations in the Manuscript

739.18 form] *followed by deleted* 'no doubt of'
739.18 imitation] *second 'i' over* 'a'
739.18 the front of the] *interlined with a caret above deleted* 'the'
739.23 Pelagic] *interlined above deleted* 'wide avenue'
739.33 beat] *'b' over an illegible letter, possibly a 'w'*
740.2 cities] *second 'i' inserted later*
740.5 concealed] *'a' over 'e'*
740.8 shore or] *final 's' deleted and 'or' interlined above deleted* 'and'
740.17 the] *interlined with a caret*
740.23 in] *preceded by deleted* 'on'
740.25 diligently] *interlined with a caret above deleted* 'properly'
740.36 no] *interlined with a caret*
740.37 first-class.] *original period after 'first' deleted*
740.39 down] *followed by start of 't'*
741.1 platform] *preceded by deleted* 'f'
741.3 braid] *'br' over 'lea'*
741.7 looking at his] *interlined with a caret above deleted* 'with his'
741.7 watch.] *period inserted before deleted* 'in his hand.'
741.10 many] *preceded by deleted* 'rows of'
741.10 thick] *'t' over 'r'*
741.11–12 it were not that these] *interlined with a caret*
741.12 handles] *followed by deleted* 'if it were r'
741.12 typify] *'y' over 'ie' and 'd' deleted*

741.14 the] *interlined above deleted* 'their'
741.23 those proper] *interlined above deleted* 'that combination of'
741.25 London] *'L' over 'N'*
741.26 Railway,] *followed by deleted* 'Company'; *comma inserted later*
741.26 had] *interlined with a caret*
741.33–34 along the platform] *interlined with a caret*
741.35 probably] *interlined above deleted* 'as eas' *and the beginning of a 'y'*
742.3 way] *interlined above deleted* 'manner'
742.6 passing] *preceded by deleted* 'swing'
742.11 the grouse,] *interlined with a caret in pencil in* Cora's *hand*
742.13 house] *followed by a deleted period*
742.14 this] *interlined above deleted* 'a'
742.14–15 string of coaches] *interlined above deleted* 'train of this kind'
742.16 and bellowed;] *interlined with a caret*
742.18 cut] *followed by deleted* 'of London'
742.19 coolness] *preceded by deleted* 'the'
742.21 travellers] *'s' added later*
742.26 greatly] *interlined with a caret*
742.28 to be heard] *interlined with a caret*
742.30 track] *preceded by deleted* 'cab'
742.31 ear] *'e' over illegible letter, perhaps an 'a'*

742.34 a] *preceded by deleted* 'th'

742.36 curious] *followed by deleted comma and* 'if science'

742.36 can] *squeezed in at end of line*

742.37 breathes] *second* 'e' *added later*

743.2 an] *interlined with a caret above deleted* 'the'

743.5 man] *preceded by deleted* 'comfort of the'

743.7 has no] *preceded by deleted* 'is not'

743.7 at] *altered from* 'in'

743.11 railway] *preceded by deleted* 'L'

743.14 he] *preceded by deleted* 'it'

743.15 -hole] *followed by a deleted period*

743.16 fireman] 'i' *over* 'o'

743.16 had] *interlined above deleted* 'was much'

743.17 would have had] *interlined with a caret above deleted* 'had'

743.18 there] *preceded by deleted* 'he'

743.19 also] *interlined above deleted* 'alwa'

743.21 kept] *preceded by* 'st' *with* 's' *deleted and* 't' *altered to form a* 'k'

743.28–29 had been] *interlined above deleted* 'was now well'

743.32 endures] *preceded by deleted* 'la'

743.34 in which] *interlined above deleted* 'when'

743.39 Those] 'o' *altered from* 'e'

744.3 somebody] *altered from* 'some o'

744.5 one,] 'one' *followed by deleted period; comma added later*

744.9 railway] 'way' *interlined above deleted* 'road'

744.14 term] *final* 's' *deleted*

744.15 constructed] *preceded by deleted* 'built'

744.15 creators] *interlined above deleted* 'inventors'

744.17–18 encounter—] *dash over comma*

744.20 country—] *interlined above deleted* 'contin'; *dash over a comma*

744.21 respectable portion] *preceded by deleted* 'tithe'

744.25 pattern] *interlined with a caret above deleted* 'way'

744.25 ²the] *interlined*

744.25 built] *interlined with a caret above deleted* 'made'

744.29 vale] MS 'vane' *preceded by* Cora's *pencil cross*

744.29 and] *followed by deleted* 'posterity'

744.29 the] *followed by deleted* 'w'

744.30 men] *preceded by deleted* 'to'

744.32 laborers] *followed by deleted* 'in Cornwall'

744.35 an eight foot] *interlined above deleted* 'a fourteen inch' *in which* 'fourteen inch' *has been deleted and* 'four foot' *interlined and then* 'four' *deleted in favor of* 'an eight'

744.35–36 an impossible] *interlined with a caret*

744.36 rivulet] 'u' *over* 'a'

745.1 consider] *final* 'ed' *deleted*

745.7 caution] *interlined above deleted* 'conditions'

745.9 a] *preceded by deleted* 'th[*and beginning of an* 'e']'

745.14 toward] *interlined above deleted* 'through'

745.15 had] *interlined with a caret*

745.16 plenty of room.] *preceded by deleted* 'passage.'

745.19 procession] *followed by deleted period*

745.21 the] *preceded by deleted* 'a'

745.21 a] *interlined with a caret*

745.21–22 that was close to the track,] *interlined with a caret after* '-box' *before a comma* which was not deleted in error

745.23   ¹a] *preceded by deleted* 'th'

745.27   winds] *preceded by deleted* 'th'

745.30   with] *interlined with a caret*

745.32   at] *interlined above deleted* 'of'

745.33   ²the] *written over* 'a'

745.33   intersects] 's' *interlined above deleted* 'ed'

745.35   was] *interlined with a caret*

745.36   quite] *interlined above deleted* 'quiet'

745.37   windy;] *semicolon altered from comma*

745.39   ¹from] *interlined with a caret above deleted* 'off'

746.2   fingers] *preceded by deleted* 'fin' *mended*

746.2   been] 'b' *over* 's'

746.3   in] 'n' *over* 's'

746.5   lying] 'y' *altered from* 'ie'

746.7   worth] *final* 'y' *deleted*

746.11   from time to time] *interlined with a caret*

746.12   levers.] *period inserted before deleted* 'testing this and changing.' *of which* 'ch' *is over* 'th'

746.15   inarticulate] *followed by deleted period or comma*

746.17   displayed] *preceded by deleted doubtful* 's'

746.20   lost] *interlined with a caret above deleted* 'buried'

746.21   one speculated] 'one' *interlined;* MS 'wondered' *has* Cora's *pencil cross above it*

746.30   man] *interlined with a caret*

746.31   station] *followed by deleted* 'guarding the whizzing'

746.39   popular idea] *interlined above deleted* 'sort of an'

747.2   always] *interlined above deleted* 'constantly at'

747.4   door—] *dash over comma*

747.6   diabolic] *final* 'al' *deleted*

747.7   it appears] *preceded by deleted* 'it becomes the'

747.8   ¹is] *interlined above deleted* 'was'

747.11   task] *preceded by deleted* 'labor'

747.12   View of the] 'View of' *squeezed in at beginning of paragraph and* 'T' *of* 'The' *altered to* 't'

747.12   often] *interlined above deleted* 'enough'

747.16   engine] *preceded by deleted* 'dove'

747.17   place] *followed by deleted* 'people'

747.18   had] *interlined above deleted* 'was'

747.21   proclaimed] *preceded by deleted* 'knew had'

747.24   ²the] *interlined above deleted* 'one'

747.25–26   a man] *interlined with a caret above deleted* 'one'

747.27   coloring] *interlined above deleted* 'amid'

747.27   bottom] *followed by deleted* 'he can sometime'

747.30   was] *followed by deleted* 'fine'

747.31   his] *interlined*

747.34   bursting] *interlined above deleted* 'shooting'

747.35   everything] *preceded by deleted* 'the'

747.36   passing.] *followed by deleted* 'A giant shadow roared and banged' *then* 'rumbled throu' *written but deleted*

747.37–39   when . . . fires.] *interlined* [*in which* 'was bathed' *preceded by deleted* 'stood'] *above deleted* 'that requires for expression* ['expression' *deleted and* 'description' *interlined*] a particular out pour of adjectives.* ['adjectives.' *deleted and followed by* 'delirious adjectives.']'

748.1   ¹a] *preceded by deleted* 'these'

748.2 One] *preceded by deleted* 'One'

748.2 whirling] *preceded by deleted* 'th[*and the beginning of* 'e']'

748.7 the] *interlined*

748.8 England] *followed by a deleted period*

748.10 nothing] *preceded by deleted* 'ease'

748.12 immature] 'i' *altered from* 'e' *but undotted*

748.17 engine] *followed by deleted* 'which had seemed'

748.20 railway] *preceded by deleted* 'statio'

748.21 noisily] *preceded by deleted* 'pus'

748.22 a] *preceded by deleted* 'the'

748.24 rumble] *interlined above deleted* 'nois'

748.27 ²the] *interlined*

748.28 into] 'i' *over* 'o'

748.28 ¹at] *followed by deleted* 'a'

748.28 Crewe] 'C' *over* 'c'

748.31 engine] *interlined with a caret*

748.36 one] *interlined above deleted* 'first'

748.37 other] *interlined above deleted* 'second'

748.39 by] *followed by deleted* 'that part of the'

748.39 engine] *preceded by deleted* 'roaring'

749.1–2 of passengers] *interlined with a caret*

749.2 tranquility] *interlined with a caret above deleted* 'peace'

749.3 domestic] *followed by deleted period*

749.3 potatoes,] *followed by deleted* 'ch'

749.4 watched] *preceded by deleted* 'marke'

749.7 supported] *preceded by deleted* 'att'

749.11 when . . . railway.] *interlined above deleted* 'on a

railway train.' ; *with* 'one is' *interlined with a caret*

749.12 named] *interlined above deleted* 'called'

749.13 Train] *followed by a deleted period*

749.13 corridor] *followed by deleted* 'ent' *or* 'ext'

749.16 it] *preceded by deleted illegible letter, perhaps the start of a* 't'

749.22–23 in this case] *interlined above deleted* 'carry' *which is followed after a space, by another* 'carry' *also deleted*

749.24 third-class] *followed by a deleted period*

749.24 Europe] *preceded by deleted* 'En'

749.24 Many] *preceded by deleted* 'Ver'

749.30 assistance] *followed by a deleted period*

749.33 custom. No] *period altered from comma;* 'N' *over* 'n'

749.36 then] *preceded by deleted* 'that'

749.36 rings] *preceded by deleted* 'is'

749.38 guard] *followed by deleted* 'from his comf'

750.1 of] *followed by deleted* 'by'

750.5 town] *preceded by deleted* 'train'

750.6 the] *interlined with a caret*

750.11 without] 'out' *interlined with a caret*

750.13 from] *interlined above deleted* 'out of'

750.16 could] 'c' *over* 'w'

750.17 blocks] 's' *added later*

750.21 to] *preceded by deleted* 'up'

750.26 shapes.] *followed by deleted* 'The cold wind circled ['circled' *deleted and* 'circling' *interlined*] swiftly around the cab the cab. and Forests the'

750.27 evening] *interlined above deleted* 'avenue'

750.28 bade] *preceded by deleted*

'told them'

750.29 station] *followed by deleted* 'became a broad yellow ba'

750.29 lamps] *interlined above deleted* 'lights'

750.30 a deficient] *interlined with a caret above deleted* 'one'

750.31 [1]a] *preceded by deleted* 'an'

750.32 made] *preceded by independently deleted* 'went' *and* 'moved'

750.33 vanished] *preceded by deleted* 'van'

750.34 was] 'w' *squeezed in and* 'a' *over* 'i'

750.36 strange] *interlined with a caret*

750.37 track] *preceded by deleted* 'clean'

751.1 factories] *preceded by deleted* 'chimn'

751.2 emit] *followed by deleted* 'from'

751.3 it,] *interlined with a caret*

751.5 [1]resembling] *interlined above deleted* 'like'

751.5 in one way resembling] *interlined with a caret above deleted* 'something like'

751.6 appeared] *second* 'e' *over* 's' *and* 'd' *squeezed in*

751.8 come to the edge.] *preceded by deleted* 'all but run.'

751.16 dignity] *followed by deleted* 'which marks'

751.16 had] *followed by deleted* 'm'

751.17 London] *preceded by deleted* 'the' *and followed by deleted period and* 'It was the entrance'

751.18 It] *preceded by deleted* 'A'

751.20 jet] *interlined above deleted* 'stream flow burst' *and preceded above the line by deleted* 'torrent'

751.21 feathered] *interlined with a caret above deleted* 'curled' *and preceded above the line by deleted* 'whirled'

No. 176. FRANCE'S WOULD-BE HERO

[The copy-text is N[1]: *New York Journal*, Oct. 15, 1899, p. 25. The other text collated is N[2]: *San Francisco Examiner*, Oct. 15, p. 15.]

751.27 national] natural N[2]

751.33 *et seq.* Chabrol] Chambrol N[2]

752.1 ¶ It] *no* ¶ N[2]

752.9 in] of N[2]

752.15 chieftains] chieftain's N[2]

752.36 that] the N[1]

753.3 But (*no* ¶)] ¶ N[2]

753.22 to] in N[2]

753.25 be sooner or later] sooner or later be N[2]

753.26–27 resolved] reasoned N[2]

753.27 to that] that N[2]

753.38 trouble] the bill N[2]

754.18 ¶ The] *no* ¶ N[2]

754.22–24 , and naturally . . . lion] *omit* N[1]

754.25–26 misfortunes] misfortune N[2]

754.30 Déroulède] Deroulode N[2]

755.3–8 Of course . . . for Coxey.] *omit* N[1]

755.26 ¶ But] *no* ¶ N[2]

755.27 too silly] silly N[2]

No. 177. "IF THE CUP ONCE GETS OVER HERE . . ."

[The copy-text is MS: untitled manuscript in Edith Richie's hand in the Special Collections of Columbia University Libraries.]

Alterations in the Manuscript

756.6 screen] 'en' *over* 'an'

756.38 candidate] *second* 'd' *over* 't'

756.38 try to] *interlined with a caret*

757.11 sloops] *second 'o' over possible start of 'p'*

757.13 back] *followed by deleted* 'again'

757.18 much] *'m' over 'd'*

757.19 have] *interlined with a caret*

757.32 raid] *preceded by deleted* 'Raid'

No. 179. LONDON'S FIREMEN FALL FROM GRACE

[The copy-text is N¹: *New York Press*, Nov. 28, 1897, p. 15.]

Subheadings

764.24.1 Flaws in the Service.

No. 180. ENGLAND A LAND OF ANXIOUS MOTHERS

[The copy-text is N¹: *New York Press*, Dec. 5, 1897, p. 13.]

Subheadings

766.10.1 Tommy in a High Place.

767.4.1 Makes Room at the Top.

767.30.1 How the Mothers Take It.

Index of Assigned and Variant Titles

INDEX OF ASSIGNED AND VARIANT
TITLES

[The first figures represent the text, and the second group, the "The Text: History and Analysis".]